Ralph Ellison

Three Days Before the Shooting . . .

*Edited by John F. Callahan
and Adam Bradley*

THE MODERN LIBRARY

NEW YORK

Ralph Ellison

Ralph Waldo Ellison was born in Oklahoma City, Oklahoma, on March 1, 1913. His father, a construction foreman and later the owner of a small ice-and-coal business, died when his son was three. Ellison and his younger brother, Herbert, were raised by their mother, who worked as a nursemaid, janitor, and domestic, and was active in politics. As a child he was drawn to music, playing trumpet from an early age and studying classical composition at Tuskegee Institute under the instruction of William L. Dawson. Of his musical influences he later said: "The great emphasis in my school was upon classical music, but such great jazz musicians as Hot Lips Page, Jimmy Rushing, and Lester Young were living in Oklahoma City. . . . As it turned out, the perfection, the artistic dedication which helped me as a writer, was not so much in the classical emphasis as in the jazz itself."

In July 1936, after his junior year at Tuskegee, Ellison went to New York to earn money for his senior year and to study sculpture, and stayed. In June 1937 his friendship with Richard Wright began and led him toward becoming a writer. Ellison also made the acquaintance of Langston Hughes and the painter Romare Bearden, among others. From 1938 until World War II he worked on the New York Federal Writers Project of the WPA. Starting in the late 1930s, he contributed reviews, essays, and short fiction to *New Masses, Tomorrow, The Negro Quarterly* (of which he was for a time managing editor), *The New Republic, Saturday Review, The Antioch Review, Reporter,* and other periodicals. During the war he served in the merchant marine, and afterward he worked at a variety of jobs, including freelance photography and the building and installation of audio systems.

Over a period of seven years Ellison wrote *Invisible Man,* which was recognized upon its publication in 1952 as one of the most important works of fiction of its time. It was on the bestseller list for sixteen weeks and won the National Book Award. Its critical reputation and popularity have only grown in the more than five decades since its publication. Although an excerpt from a second novel was published in the magazine *Noble Savage* in 1960, and seven other selections in various literary magazines between then and 1977, no other work of fiction appeared under Ellison's name during his lifetime. *Shadow and Act* (1964) and *Going to the Territory* (1986) collect essays and interviews written over more than forty years.

From 1955 to 1957 Ellison was a fellow of the American Academy in Rome. Returning to the United States, he taught and lectured at a wide range of institutions including Bard College, the State University of New York at Stony Brook, the University of Chicago, Rutgers, Harvard, Brown, and Yale. He was awarded the Presidential Medal of Freedom in 1969; was named a Chevalier de l'Ordre des Arts et Lettres in 1970 by the French minister of culture, André Malraux; and was given the National Medal of Arts in 1985. He was a charter member of the National Council on the Arts and Humanities, and from 1970 to 1979 was Albert Schweitzer Professor in the Humanities at New York University.

After a brief first marriage Ellison married Fanny McConnell in 1946; for more than forty years, until his passing on April 16, 1994, they lived on Riverside Drive in Harlem.

Posthumous editions of Ellison's work, edited and with an introduction by John F. Callahan, include *The Collected Essays of Ralph Ellison* (1995); *Flying Home and Other Stories* (1996); *Juneteenth* (1999), the central narrative in the unfinished second novel; and *Trading Twelves: The Selected Letters of Ralph Ellison and Albert Murray* (2000), each published by Random House, Inc.

CONTENTS

PART III

CHRONOLOGY OF COMPOSITION

1951

MAY 14

Ellison writes to the essayist and novelist Albert Murray that he is "trying to get started on my next novel (I probably have enough stuff left from the other if I can find the form)."*

1953

APRIL 9

Writes Murray of his intention "to drive out to Oklahoma this spring . . . and I plan to scout the southwest. I've got to get real mad again, *and* talk with the old folks a bit. I've got *one* Okla. book in me I do believe."

1954

FEBRUARY 14

Writes to Murray, "As for me I'm in my old agony trying to write a novel. I've got some ideas that excite me and a few scenes and some characters, but the rest is coming like my first pair of long pants—slow as hell. Never mind, I'll get it out, it just takes time to do *anything* worth while."

MAY 19

Writes to Morteza Sprague, an English professor at Tuskegee, that "the whole road [of post-segregationist America] stretched out and it got all mixed up with this book I'm trying to write and it left me twisted with joy and a sense of inadequacy." He says he is "writing about the evasion of identity which is another characteristically American problem which must be about to change. I hope so, it's giving me enough trouble." [Written two days after Supreme Court handed down *Brown v. Board of Education* decision.]

* *Trading Twelves: The Selected Letters of Ralph Ellison and Albert Murray,* ed. Albert Murray and John F. Callahan (2000), is the single best source on Ellison's progress and perspective on the second novel from 1951 to 1960.

1955

APRIL
Sends to Murray "a few riffs from Cliofus," an early draft excerpt from his work-in-progress.

SEPTEMBER
Arrives in Rome to take up residence as a fellow at the American Academy of Arts and Letters (until September 1957).

NOVEMBER 22
Writes to his editor, Albert Erskine, "Dear Albert: I received your message about spending eight hours in my study and I'm glad to inform you that while I don't quite manage eight hours, I do spend the major part of the day here—and working."

DECEMBER 14
Writes to Erskine, "As for me the cold and my upset over the misunderstanding [over *Invisible Man* printings and stocking] threw me off schedule for a few days but I'm back at it, with the first section still giving me hell. I'd like to junk it but without it I wouldn't have a story. But thank the gods that I haven't reached the point where you have to be worried with that!"

1956

MARCH 20
Murray writes to Ellison, "Dear Ralph, You writin' good, boy, realgood, blowing good, cutting good, keen & deep. If you gettin' any of this stuff working in there with old Cleofus & em you still swinging that switchblade and you aint got nothing to worry about. For my money you're in there with that shit, man."

JUNE 22
Writes to the literary critic Stanley Edgar Hyman, "As for me, most of my writing is on the book, which is much more difficult than I had imagined. Still it's rolling along and I've become quite fond of the Old preacher and his six year old revivalist whose great act is an antiphonal rendering of the seven last words of Christ with the little boy sitting in a small coffin. Wild things arise from this, but I'm still having trouble giving the book the dramatic drive I feel it needs. Will do, though; will do. Just learned that the kid preacher's name, Bliss, means rapture, a yielding to experience. Very American because of the overtones of progress and this guy really becomes Dick Lewis' 'in space.' Having fun, as you can see. Today the old preacher is talking Aristotle (though unaware) as he tells kid just why coffin has to be a certain size. So I guess if I don't succeed in making book

dramatic I can at least reveal the principles as they operate in life. Trick of course it [*sic*] to do both. Read Radin's TRICKSTER, give it a look if you haven't . . ."

1957

April 4
Writes to Murray, "I've been up to my ass in typescript and have only just climbed out of one level of the mess after another back to my novel."

September
Returns to United States from American Academy in Rome.

1958

February 6
Writes to Murray, "As for me I'm working hard now both with the novel and a piece which Hyman feinted me into doing . . ."

February 26
Writes to Saul Bellow, "Things aint coming worth a damn."

June/July
Writes to Murray, "I've been working frantically on the book, trying to complete a section while the emotion was still strong within me. . . . Bellow has read book two and is to publish about fifty pages in a new mag which he is editing."

September 21
Writes to Bellow from Bellow's house in Tivoli, New York, where Ellison is living while he teaches at Bard College, that he has brought up his electric typewriter in hopes that it will expedite his work on the novel.

1959

June 27
Writes to Murray, "It has been a most interesting year, full of irritations and discoveries; progress on the novel and a definite deepening of my perception of the themes which I so blindly latched on to. I guess old Hickman is trying to make a man out of me—at this late date."

1960

January 19
Writes to Bellow, "I haven't been able to work for two weeks and I feel that I'm falling apart. I find myself in strange places in my dreams and during the days Hickman and Bliss and Severen seem like people out of some faded dream of nobility. They need desperately to be affirmed while I seem inca-

pable of bringing them fully to life. I hope seeing some of the book in print will improve my morale and this shouldn't be long now . . ."

Publishes "And Hickman Arrives" in Saul Bellow's *Noble Savage,* first excerpt from novel-in-progress.

Publishes "The Roof, the Steeple and the People," *Quarterly Review of Literature* 10, No. 3.

1963
Publishes "It Always Breaks Out," *Partisan Review* 30, No. 1.

1965
Publishes "Juneteenth," *Quarterly Review of Literature* 13, Nos. 3–4.

"Bliss's Birth" draft, hand-dated by Ellison.

1967
Fire at Plainfield, Massachusetts, home destroys what Ellison calls "a summer's worth of revisions on my novel."

1968
"Hickman and Wilhite at Mister Jessie's."

1969
Publishes "Night-Talk," *Quarterly Review of Literature.*

1970
Publishes "A Song of Innocence," *Iowa Review* 1, No. 2.

Becomes Albert Schweitzer Professor of the Humanities at New York University (to 1979).
1971
Draft of "Mother Strothers."

Draft of "Through the Lilt and Tear," long variant of opening for Book II.

1972
June/July
Completes revisions of Book I and II typescripts.

Draft of Lonnie Barnes speech from Rockmore's.

1973

FEBRUARY
Publishes "Cadillac Flambé," *American Review* 16.

1974

NOVEMBER 14
Random House writes to extend delivery date of second novel from August 17, 1965, to September 30, 1975.

1977

Publishes "Backwacking, a Plea to the Senator," *Massachusetts Review* 18.

1978

JUNE 5
Random House writes to extend delivery date for second novel from August 17, 1965, to May 1, 1980.

Revises "A Song of Innocence."

Revises "Through the Lilt and Tear."

1981

NOVEMBER
Forty-page hand-edited draft entitled "Bliss" typed and filed under "Bliss-Hickman (Final)." (Additional drafts dated 1959.)

1982

JANUARY 8
Purchases Osborne 1 computer.

1983

JUNE 20
Writes to literary critic and philosopher Kenneth Burke in computer-printed letter, "You're probably right about a sequel to I.M. being impossible, but even if it weren't I'd have no desire to undertake it. I'm having enough trouble just making a meaningful form out of my yarn concerning a little boy preacher who rises to *high estate* and comes asunder. There are all kinds of interesting incidents in it, but if they don't add up it'll fall as rain into the ocean of meaningless words. I guess what's bothering me right now is working out a form for that NEXT PHASE of which you write. // Anyway, I'm still writing—or will be at it again as soon as we can get out of the city and end up in the Berkshire hills. . . ."

OCTOBER 11
Purchases Osborne Executive computer.

1985

JANUARY 9 (POSTMARK DATE ON ENVELOPE)
Writes note of frustration about his computer: "Osborne // I'm writing this on an EXECUTIVE computer and an IBM Quiet printer that am so ignorant of the how to patch the damn thing that I'm wasting a good part of my investment."

1988

JANUARY 7
Purchases IBM computer.

OCTOBER
Hires friend David Sarser to transfer files from old computer to new computer. Transfer erases all file dates prior to 1988.

1992

MAY–SEPTEMBER
Revises all but three "Hickman in Oklahoma" files from "Hickman in Georgia and Oklahoma" section.

1993

JULY
Revises all of "Hickman in Washington, D.C." section on computer.

DECEMBER 30
Saves last known file, "Rockmore."

1994

APRIL 16
Dies at his home on Manhattan's Riverside Drive.

General Introduction to
Three Days Before the Shooting . . .

I

WHEN RALPH ELLISON DIED, on April 16, 1994, he left behind no explicit instructions for what should be done with the multiple drafts of his unfinished, untitled second novel. What he left instead was an expansive archive of handwritten notes, typewritten pages, and computer files that he had been at work on since the early 1950s. In an interview just two months before his death, Ellison affirmed that "the novel has got my attention now. I work every day, so there will be something very soon." This undoubtedly came as welcome news for readers of Ellison's fiction, who had been waiting some forty years since the publication of Ellison's 1952 classic, *Invisible Man,* for the promised second novel. For them, "soon" was not nearly soon enough.

Taking Ellison at his word, one might reasonably have expected to find among his papers a single manuscript very near to completion, bearing evidence of the difficult choices he had made during the protracted period of the novel's composition. One might have expected, perhaps, that Ellison's manuscript-in-progress might resemble F. Scott Fitzgerald's *The Last Tycoon,* a fragment with a clearly drafted, clearly delineated beginning and middle, whose author's notes and drafts pointed toward two or three endings, each of which followed and resolved the projected novel as a whole. Or, to cite a more contemporary example, it might have resembled Roberto Bolaño's unfinished novel *2666;* upon its posthumous publication in 2008, Bolaño's editor remarked that, had the author lived to see it through to publication, "its dimensions, its general content would by no means have been very different from what they are now." In the extreme, one might have expected something like James Joyce's *Finnegans Wake,* a glorious mess of a novel that defies the very generic constraints of the form.

Ellison left behind something else entirely: a series of related narrative fragments, several of which extend to over three hundred manuscript pages in length, that appear to cohere without truly completing one another. In fact, the thousands of handwritten notes, typewritten drafts, mimeographed pages and holographs, dot-matrix and laser printouts, testify to the massive and sustained effort Ellison exerted upon his fiction, but also to his ultimate failure to complete his manuscript so long in progress. In Ellison's second novel we have a work whose very incomprehensibility nonetheless perhaps extends the boundaries of the novel form, as Ellison suggested, in his 1956 essay "Society, Morality, and the Novel," every serious novel ought to do.

As the facts about Ellison's second novel come into focus, it becomes more and more difficult to imagine him completing the book even if he had enjoyed a run of good years beyond 1994. This is not to say that he would have stopped writing. Far from it. Ellison once said by way of describing himself as a novelist, "I'm a fast writer, but a slow worker." This may help explain the seeming paradox of his writing thousands of pages over the second half of the twentieth century, yet never mastering many of the basic textual challenges presented by his material, not the least of which was the "very stern discipline" of bringing his narrative to some kind of resolution. Instead, he drafted multiple versions of the same handful of scenes, sometimes with subtle, sometimes with striking differences, while seeming never to have composed the necessary connective episodes that could have made his fiction whole.

With all the mystery that has surrounded the second novel over the years, it seems only natural that public discussion has centered almost exclusively upon why Ellison never published the book. Speculation was generated by a handful of published excerpts and the increasing secrecy with which Ellison guarded the novel from his closest friends and even from his editor. Nonetheless, in the face of so much evidence of literary activity, a new question looms: What is it about this material—either in its focus, form, or theme—that kept Ellison writing so much for so long?

Over the decades Ellison's various iterations of his characters, plot, and themes testify to an artist in the process of stylistic evolution. Uncoiled, the serpentine fragments of the surviving, unfinished work show a writer responding to an America evolving from Jim Crow to Civil Rights to Vietnam to the Digital Age during the span of the novel's composition. The basic plot of Ellison's novel as it emerges in these manuscripts centers upon the connection, estrangement, and reconciliation of two characters. The one is a black jazzman-turned-preacher named Alonzo Hickman, the other a racist "white" New England Senator named Adam Sunraider, formerly known as Bliss—a child of indeterminate race whom Hickman had raised from infancy to adolescence. The action of the novel concerns Hickman's efforts to stave off Sunraider's assassination at the hands of the Senator's own estranged son, a young man named Severen. We follow Hickman from his home in Georgia to the Oklahoma City of his jazz-playing youth to the nation's capital, in search of clues that will not only save the Senator but also perhaps unlock the mystery of the child Bliss's disappearance decades before and his reemergence as the race-baiting Sunraider, a political archenemy of the very people who raised him and continue to love him.

Along the way Hickman reconnects with his old flame, Janey Glover; meets Love New, a half-black, half-Cherokee medicine man who weaves a mysterious fable for Hickman of fathers and sons; and encounters Cliofus, a "teller of tall tales" with the gift of gab who regales a crowd of onlookers at a bar called the Cave of the Winds. Those familiar with the excerpts from the novel published in Ellison's lifetime will celebrate the return of familiar characters like LeeWillie Minifees, the black jazzman who burns his own Cadillac on Senator Sunraider's lawn in an act of defiance and protest, and Welborn McIntyre, the white newspaper reporter in whose voice Ellison wrote the only first-person narration in the entire novel. These are only some of the voices and perspectives that emerge in the parts of the manuscripts that have never been in print before. Ellison was writing a novel concerning betrayal and redemption, love and loss, black and white, fathers and sons. It is a novel that takes as its theme the very nature of America's democratic promise to make the nation's practice live up to its principles in the lives of its citizens, regardless of race, place, or circumstance.

Juneteenth, published posthumously in 1999, may offer clues about Ellison's difficulty in striking a balance between the centripetal and centrifugal tendencies of his second novel. The proposition driving *Juneteenth* is that the center of Ellison's saga consists of the story of Reverend Hickman and Senator Sunraider from the Senator's birth as Bliss to his death. Accordingly, Book II, with its central focus on the Senator in the present of the assassination and the past of his boyhood ministry as Reverend Hickman's messenger, is the chief source of *Juneteenth*. A long separate manuscript, titled "Bliss's Birth," also uses the occasion of the boy's coming into the world, literally midwifed by Hickman, to fill in much of Hickman's past as triggered by the then jazzman's reflections on his and his family's situation in the Jim Crow South of the early twentieth century.

Even a casual comparison between *Juneteenth* and the present volume illustrates the centripetal/centrifugal tugs challenging Ellison's sense of form, subject, and focus to the uttermost. Book I belongs to the white reporter, Welborn McIntyre. He is witness to the shooting, to Reverend Hickman's presence, and to the subplots of LeeWillie Minifees burning his Cadillac and Jessie Rockmore's death or murder. Narrator McIntyre also puts his own identity and story front and center for long passages of his narrative. His crucial brief encounters with Hickman are dramatized in Book I, and re-

ferred to later in Book II. Then there is the long Oklahoma section, originally also narrated by McIntyre, who goes West to unravel the mysteries of
the Senator's assassination and his assassin's identity. Later, revising on the
computer, Ellison sends Hickman, not McIntyre, to Oklahoma and recounts
his adventures in the third person, not the first.

Each of these narrative excursions flies off from the central platform of
the Hickman–Bliss/Sunraider story and relationship, which is more central
to Book II and to *Juneteenth* than to the entirety of the unfinished second
novel Ralph Ellison left behind. Thus, readers of this volume are now able to
select for themselves what they judge to be the true center of this projected
work, or whether, as its form stands, there is such a center at all.

Because Ralph Ellison and his wife, Fanny, kept meticulous track of all
the paper and documents pertaining to Ralph's writing and writer's life, it is
possible to follow the trajectory of his work on the second novel. Almost as
important, it is also possible to place the periods of hiatus in Ellison's concentration on the novel between *Invisible Man*'s publication and the last
changes he makes to his computer files just months before his death.

II

AN IMPORTANT EARLY REFERENCE to the second novel comes in a letter to
Ellison's friend and fellow writer Albert Murray on June 6, 1951. As he goes
over proofs of *Invisible Man,* Ellison writes the following to Murray: "So I'm
trying to get going on my next book before this one is finished, then if it's
[*Invisible Man*] a dud I'll be too busy to worry about it" (*Trading Twelves,* 21).
This comment, however, reveals more about the anxiety Ellison harbored
about *Invisible Man* than it does about an actual second novel. In April of
1953, still busy touring for *Invisible Man,* he writes to Murray again of his
"plan to scout the southwest. I've got to get real mad again, *and* talk with the
old folks a bit. I've got *one* Okla. book in me I do believe" (*Trading Twelves,*
44). By 1954 he has begun drafting in earnest, and in April of 1955 he sends
Murray a "working draft" of an Oklahoma episode from that Oklahoma
book referred to two years before. Interestingly, Ellison's own riff on these
pages sheds light on his compositional habits during the next forty years of
labor on the novel he apparently never finished even in his mind. "Here are
a few riffs from old Cliofus," Ellison writes. "This chok-drinking Charlie
character appeared just as I was typing up this copy to send you, I don't see
where the hell Cliofus got him but here he is anyway. As you see, the stuff is
still crude—which means it's still building" (*Trading Twelves,* 83–84).

Several things stand out about the early draft and Ellison's comments on
its composition. First, the Cliofus–Choc Charlie material turns up again in
Ellison's last revised computer sequence of what is published here as "Hick-

man in Georgia & Oklahoma." Second, the riff is still a riff; Ellison's multiple revisions are fine-tunings, not changes that alter or deepen the implications of the original 1955 draft. The episode, along with many others in the computer-generated material, pays homage to Ellison's memories of Oklahoma and his attachment to the picaresque. Finally, Ellison's conviction that the stuff is "still building" kept him writing offshoots of old episodes and revisions of the same scenes many times, all the while knowing, as he told John Hersey in 1982, that he "was never satisfied with how the parts connected" (*CE,* 819).

As a fellow at the American Academy in Rome from 1955 to 1957, Ellison began plotting out the novel in earnest. From this point in the process, his comments to Hersey in "A Completion of Personality," interviews begun in 1974 and completed after an eight-year break, in 1982 (published in *The Collected Essays of Ralph Ellison*), are among the fullest that exist about the sequence of his composition on the unfinished novel. In these remarks one sees the vividness of the "parts" in Ellison's mind without that sense of connection and connective narrative tissue missing from the totality of what he left behind. As James Alan McPherson put the matter in a 1970 article in the *Atlantic* called "Indivisible Man," after Ellison showed him the manuscripts and discussed the novel-in-progress then read from its pages: "He has enough manuscripts to publish three novels, but is worried over how the work will hold up as a total structure. He does not want to publish three separate books, but then he does not want to compromise on anything essential. 'If I find that it is better to make it a three-section book, to issue it in three volumes, I would do it *as long as I thought that each volume had a compelling interest in itself*'" (*CE,* 391, italics added).

The evidence points in the direction of Ellison aiming for the above-mentioned "three separate books"—Books I and II and the Oklahoma material—corresponding in this Modern Library volume to the drafts Ellison composed on the computer starting in 1982 but existent in 1969 and 1970 in typescript.

It is difficult to date Ellison's composition of Books I and II and the early drafts of the Oklahoma episodes precisely. Nevertheless it is clear that much of the Oklahoma material was first drafted in the 1950s along with some of Book I (the prologue, certainly) and much of Book II (Saul Bellow describes reading some two hundred pages of Book II in 1959), and that work on Books I and II went on through the 1960s and beyond. (The last manuscript of "Bliss's Birth," which Ellison intended to place somewhere in Book II, and which became the penultimate chapter in the posthumous *Juneteenth,* is dated 1965 in the writer's hand.)

Of the eight excerpts that Ellison published during his lifetime, "And Hickman Arrives" is probably most important in terms of establishing a reliable trajectory of composition. It begins with the prologue to Book I, follows up with a manuscript not in Book I or Book II (included in *Juneteenth* as

Chapter 3), and carries on with excerpts from the almost two hundred pages of Ellison's unfinished draft of Book II climaxing with Bliss being violently claimed by a deranged white woman during a Juneteenth night celebration. Ellison wrote Murray in 1959 that he was working hard stitching this excerpt together from what he had written of Book II. He knew it would be the lead piece in the inaugural issue of Saul Bellow's magazine, *Noble Savage.* Ellison's attempt to showcase the new novel and whet readers' appetites for more was a huge success. In 1960 the literary world had a long and impressive excerpt to tide it over as it awaited the published novel.

No novel ensued. Instead, Ellison reversed the usual order of things. He published *Shadow and Act,* his influential, brilliantly sequenced collection of essays, in 1964, *before* rather than after the second novel. Moreover, this decision involved switching gears drastically; it committed him to slow work on the novel in favor of editing the essays, reviews, and interviews done over the previous twenty-five years. After publication he shouldered a taxing schedule of appearances to promote *Shadow and Act,* and for several years kept up a steady round of lectures on college campuses less than friendly to his integrationist position.

Then, not six months after the Ellisons took up residence at their summer place in Plainfield, Massachusetts, a fire swept through the house, and some of his manuscript was lost. The evidence suggests that the fire took less of a toll on the actual manuscript than it may have taken upon Ellison's morale and confidence as the years went by. In any case, the myth that slowly magnified the extent of the loss is belied by the evidence of Ellison's letters and remarks at the time. Ten days after the fire, he wrote Charles Valentine, "The loss was particularly severe for me, as a section of my work-in-progress was destroyed with it." Later in the letter Ellison outlined the task he saw before him. "Fortunately, much of my summer's work on the new novel is still in my mind and if my imagination can feed it I'll be all right, but I must work quickly." Five weeks after the event he wrote his friend Jack Ludwig, coeditor of *Noble Savage:* "I lost part of my manuscript—the revisions over which I had labored [in] the summer and valuable notebooks. But since returning to N. Y. I've been hard at work and am gradually reconstructing." Moreover, in March Fanny Ellison assured an acquaintance that Ralph would deliver the manuscript to Random House "early next year."

It is difficult to imagine Ellison not having substantial recall over the direction he had set for the novel in the several months before the fire. There is no reason to doubt his claim that he set to work "reconstructing" immediately, as his first priority. In this connection the most finished surviving manuscript of Book II suggests that Ellison was unsure which narrative fork to take at the turning point where Book II intersects with an episode in Book I. The scene in question takes place at Jessie Rockmore's townhouse, where Reverend Hickman and Deacon Wilhite pass the reporter McIntyre, shortly after Rockmore dies, possibly from shock over his visitation from Senator Sunraider. In any case, although Ellison continued to revise what he had drafted of Book II, it is not at all clear that he took the action further, let alone resolved on an ending. Still, as a way of boosting his own confidence and reassuring his readership that the long-delayed, long-promised novel was moving toward completion, he published "Night-Talk" in 1969 along with a prefatory note, which illuminates the personal and narrative relationship between Reverend Hickman and Bliss/Sunraider.

Like "And Hickman Arrives" nine years earlier, "Night-Talk" sets the table for the novel as a whole. Ellison's abiding American themes of "our orphan's loneliness" and the consequences of "the evasion of identity" are stated in the note and sounded dramatically in the memories coursing through the minds of Bliss/Sunraider and Hickman. Nonetheless, if publication held off the dogs without, it's doubtful Ellison's demons of self-doubt were long assuaged, though he tried to do so by crafting brilliant essays, pieces that mined the same themes of American complexity and restlessness so strongly present in what he had done so far with the second novel.

By the late 1970s Ellison's novel seems to have taken on the aspect of myth in his mind. In a striking note written on the back of an envelope postmarked March 24, 1977, Ellison scrawled the following words by way of summing up his work.

> Looking back it seems that three people were involved. A woman, a politician and a preacher. And yet that leaves out many others, and especially the young man who brought down the intricate structure of time and emotion, the joker, the wild card. The unexpected emotional agent of chaos. But even so, this leaves out another woman, long dead, and by her own hand, and the earlier metamorphosis of the man who was responsible and who later paid for his willfulness with his life and who thus was exposed for what he was and for who and what he had been.

Ellison's language is insular, almost cryptic, testifying to an author who has lived with his characters for years and was "looking back" as if on a distant memory rather than on a novel-in-progress. The woman, one assumes, is Janey; the politician, Sunraider; and the preacher, Hickman. The young man, the "unexpected emotional agent of chaos," is Severen, Bliss/Sunraider's son and would-be assassin. The other woman, "long dead," is Severen's mother and Sunraider's lover, Lavatrice, a young Oklahoma woman of mixed race who commits suicide soon after giving birth to his child, and leaving the infant in Janey's care. The "earlier metamorphosis of the man who was responsible" is Sunraider himself, then known simply as "Mister Movie-man," an itinerant flimflam man posing as a filmmaker who descends upon the small Oklahoma town with his partners to take what he can from the community. This is Ellison's fiction, the product of his imagination, and yet the years have conspired to create a veil of distance that has him looking upon his own creations with a mixture of reverence and remove.

Just a few years later, in June of 1983, Ellison wrote to his old friend Kenneth Burke, the source of Ellison's favored theory of narratology—Burke's tragic progression from purpose to passion to perception. "You're probably right about a sequel to I.M. being impossible, but even if it weren't I'd have no desire to undertake it. I'm having enough trouble just making a meaningful form out of my yarn concerning a little boy preacher who rises to *high estate* and comes asunder. There are all kinds of interesting incidents in it, but if they don't add up it'll fall as rain into the ocean of meaningless words."

The longer one puzzles over what Ellison left behind, the more maddening it seems that he did not simply will himself to bring the book to a close, that he didn't find his way to that "meaningful form" he sought. Is it surprising that he did not take stock of what he had of Book I, Book II, and the latest of the Oklahoma drafts? Yes and no. In its earlier drafts, *Invisible Man* was picaresque in the extreme. As Ellison wrote in his 1961 note explaining why he was bringing to publication the Mary Rambo chapter he sacrificed from an earlier draft, ". . . I have the feeling that it stands on its own if only as one of those pieces of writing which consists *mainly* of one damned thing after another sheerly happening" (Rampersad, 393, 607). The note ends with a curious statement for a writer whose creed was "a very stern discipline": "For me, of course, the narrative is the meaning."

It would be easy to brush off such a statement if made by Ellison at the beginning or midpoint in the composition of *Invisible Man*. Made by the novelist whose revisions tightened and telescoped his first novel into a classic, the words suggest something going on deep down "on the lower frequencies" of form and composition. In "Society, Morality and the Novel," written in Rome when Ellison was hatching the plot of the second novel, he declared critics "more 'adult' types" than novelists, whom he associated with playfulness and play. Here Ellison is embracing with a touch of defiance the improvisatory quality of African American culture. Whatever the tendrils, at the root Ellison seems to have resisted bringing order to bear on a reality he saw as "mainly one damned thing after another sheerly happening." Yet it should be noted that *Invisible Man,* in narration and story, was perfectly positioned to allow Ellison to enact both form and chaos. Whenever he found the going uncertain or far-fetched, he could retreat to his protagonist-narrator's voice and let him tell his story, write his memoir. In the second novel the form is mixed. It begins with a prologue told in a biblically accented third person, very much the voice of a chronicle. From there, Ellison turns over all fifteen chapters of Book I to the first-person voice of Welborn McIntyre, the Kentucky-born and -bred reporter, whose former ambition to be a novelist shows in his self-conscious style and urge to make stories out of anecdotes.

For all that, McIntyre's sign-off at the end of Book I prepares the way for the eclectic narration Ellison had in mind. It seems one of the sharpest transitions in all of what Ellison left behind. "But at least the Senator was still alive" is both definitive and mysterious, ominous and optimistic. After the break signaled by ellipses, the first words of Book II take off from the last of Book I: "Suddenly, through the sonorous lilt and tear of his projecting voice, the Senator was distracted." From McIntyre's first-person voice, Ellison deftly shifts into the third person, which allows him to move by turns in and out of the voice and consciousness of Reverend Hickman and Bliss/Sunraider. He is able to render Bliss the little boy; the young man ("Mister Movie-man") in the interstices between boy and man; and the grown-up, now grievously wounded Senator. It would seem, then, that Books I and II could have worked together well formally, technically, and stylistically had Ellison comes to grips with his plot.

However, the issue of plot was not an inconsiderable matter, as Ellison came to know and tried to address in the long computer-generated segment "Hickman in Washington, D.C." There he begins to fill in the gaps about Hickman and the brothers and sisters of his congregation between the time they are turned away by Senator Sunraider's secretary until two days later, when they witness the assassination from the Senate gallery. Yet in another instance of his commitment to "one damned thing after another sheerly happening," the more than three hundred pages of computer printouts do not really drive the plot. Rather, the narrative meanders along, with seventy-year-old Alonzo Hickman sometimes the aging jazzman, sometimes the minister, sometimes the essayist, orchestrating in a tone and style uncomfortably close to Ellison's. And not the vernacular Ellison of bold, risky, brilliant works like "Tell It Like It Is, Baby" or "The World and the Jug" or "The Little Man at Chehaw Station." Instead, some of Hickman's ruminations remind one of Ellison's later, seemingly carefully studied and revised, sometimes ponderous pronouncements. It is as if Ellison uses Hickman as the mouthpiece for all of what he came to know and think and feel about being African American in America. Indeed, this succession of episodes contains an essayistic, less dramatic repeat of the scene at the Lincoln Memorial formerly told in a gripping interior monologue of Reverend Hickman's late in the unfinished manuscript of Book II (Chapter 14 of *Juneteenth*).

III

ALTHOUGH IT IS POSSIBLE to trace the trajectory of the novel's composition through Ellison's correspondence, it is much more difficult to reconstruct that same compositional history in the manuscripts themselves. Ellison composed by episode and filed his drafts episodically as well, an organizational method continued by the Library of Congress's archivists when organizing the Ralph Ellison Papers in the years after his death. A given file may include a host of drafts, both fragmentary and complete, of a particular scene, filed together irrespective of date. Some are dozens of pages in length, others, a single page or even a single paragraph. Many of the drafts are unnumbered, or if numbered, done so with no clear relation to what comes before or after the scene. What results is a certain leveling effect, one that often renders it difficult to discern with even relative certainty the date of a given draft.

However, at least a rough estimation of compositional chronology can be gleaned from simple physical observation of Ellison's materials. One can make reasoned conjectures as to provenance based upon physical details like typeface and font (he uses different point sizes and sometimes employs italics or boldface print); paper stock (he writes on blue, aqua, and green pages in addition to white, and he writes on every thickness of paper from onionskin to cardboard); reused paper (sometimes he prints or types on letterhead from various organizations, or even on dated drafts of letters printed from his computer); and quality of preservation. Comparing a draft composed on onionskin paper in fading pica typeface and a dot-matrix printout on paper with circular guideholes running up and down both sides suggests their respective eras without specifying a precise date. These details are instructive to a point, but they do little to clarify the larger question of how—and whether—Ellison was revising his manuscript toward completion.

In addition to the numerous undated and fragmentary drafts, Ellison's archive includes sequential fragments that bear evidence of an author mastering his material. Two in particular resulted in long continuous sequences of episodes: the Book I and II typescripts dating from the 1960s and 1970s and the computer files dating from the 1980s and early 1990s. These two large narratives constitute the bulk of what is included in *Three Days Before the Shooting* . . . This volume presents the latest continuous sequences of these drafts in their entirety. When read together, they reveal both striking similarities and marked differences in how Ellison was conceiving his novel across the decades. Many of the characters and many of the key scenes remain the same. To cite one example, the last material Ellison seems to have worked on in the months before his death was a revision of a scene narrated by McIntyre from Chapter 12 of Book I—a raucous episode in which McIntyre investigates an apparent homicide at the Washington, D.C., townhouse of Jessie Rockmore, an old black man, a dealer in antiques, found dead sitting upright, dressed in his Sunday best in a termite-ridden coffin.

More striking, however, is the difference in style and form of narration between the typescripts and the computer drafts. Book I, and more especially Book II, reveal the influence William Faulkner had on Ellison in the texture of his prose and his preoccupation with the interiority of his subjects. This mode of psychological fiction marked a decided shift from *Invisible Man,* which had employed with great success a mode of narration bracketed by a prologue and an epilogue. More surprisingly, the later work on Books I and II differed substantially from early drafts of the second novel in which Ellison places much more emphasis on action. Indeed, the drafts composed in the years immediately after the publication of *Invisible Man* show a striking affinity with his classic novel, even down to the continuation of characters. (Ellison's notes suggest that Bliss/Sunraider emerged directly out of *Invisible Man*'s Bliss Proteus Rinehart.) As Ellison continued to compose, he found himself compelled to explore the psychological valences of his material. "Remember," he admonishes himself in a note, "that 'the essence of the story is what goes into the minds of the characters on a given occasion.' The mind becomes the real scene of the action. And in the mind scene and motive are joined." Although the Book I and II typescripts retain several vividly drawn episodes—most notably the car-burning scene that Ellison published in 1973 as "Cadillac Flambé" and the aforementioned episode at Jessie Rockmore's—they are dominated by Ellison's forays into the minds, both waking and dreaming, of his characters.

Given the form of narration that accounted for so much of the success of his first novel and seems to have initially shaped his second, what happens in the 1980s is entirely unexpected, even inexplicable. Seeming to put aside much of the work he had done in the preceding decades, especially the sometimes brilliant if also uneven material from Books I and II, Ellison shifts the mode of narration back to the episodic style in which it began. In the computer files, action moves decidedly outward. The dramatic consequences of this can be summed up in a single transformation: the seven pages that comprise the prologue from the typescripts, in which Hickman and his parishioners arrive in D.C. and attempt to see the Senator, only to be rebuffed, expand to *over three hundred pages* of narrative in the computer files. Hickman and his group land in D.C., walk through the airport, go to the taxi stand, drive to the Senator's offices, speak with his secretary, get searched by Capitol security, check into a hotel, go sightseeing, and eat barbecue.

Stranger still, very little of this episodic material is wholly new to the computer files. In a striking move that only adds to the mystery of the second novel's composition, Ellison appears to have returned in the 1980s and 1990s to the very earliest episodic fragments he ever composed, likely dating from the 1950s and perhaps the early 1960s. Scenes of Hickman in Oklahoma City visiting the shaman Love New, Hickman walking the streets of Washington, D.C., and being accosted by a "red, white, and blue-black" man named Leroy who mistakes him for "Chief Sam the Fucking Liberator," all xxvi · *General Introduction to* Three Days Before the Shooting . . .

of these episodes exist both in undated versions from the early period of the novel's composition and in computer files from its final period.

This is not to suggest that Ellison's episodic drafts from the early years and his computer files from the later years are identical. Quite the contrary. Ellison was doing new things with this old material as he revised it over the last decade of his life. He was attempting to draw the fragments together into narrative wholes, stitching together scenes with transitions, the very facet of composition that most dogged him throughout his career. Some of these transitions are seamless, others are still very much unfixed. But what is clearly discernible from the dates upon which he saved the latest versions of his files is that he was gradually putting the pieces together. The three long fragments included in this volume—which we've labeled "Hickman in Washington, D.C.," "Hickman in Georgia & Oklahoma," and "McIntyre at Jessie Rockmore's"—represent Ellison's last efforts to finish his novel. Even finished, however, these important narratives would cry out for transitions, connective verbal tissue that would have made them definitively part of the novel's whole and, therefore, clarified the whole.

Another significant difference between the episodes as conceived in the early years of the novel's composition and as revised in the later years is in their respective tones. Some of the early drafts read almost like extensions of *Invisible Man,* and perhaps to some extent they were in Ellison's mind. They embody his blues-toned sensibility of the tragicomic, the play-it-by-eye-and-by-ear sense of improvisation. Even in their often unpolished state, they crackle with narrative tension. By contrast, when revisited on the computer in the 1980s and 1990s, the scenes take on a ruminative quality, a kind of narrative repose that forestalls action—at least necessary action—in the name of contemplation. Interspersed with the sequence of dramatic incidents, Ellison has woven a thread of near-essayistic reflection upon his favored themes of American complexity and the black vernacular tradition.

At times, Hickman becomes less a character than a mouthpiece for Ellison as he endeavors to get it all down, to achieve what he refers to in his 1974 interview with John Hersey as that "aura of summing up" by which he could describe America to itself and the world. In one passage, for instance, a weary Hickman has retired to the lounge at the Hotel Longview to engage in a moment of reflection only to have his attention captivated by a large tapestry displayed on the wall before him. As Hickman describes it in minute detail, it becomes clear to the reader (though never to Hickman) that it is a rendering of Brueghel's *Landscape with the Fall of Icarus.* Through this act of ekphrasis, Ellison seeks to extend his core themes of fathers and sons, of the mystery that hides before us in plain sight, of falls from grace—both literal and metaphorical. While the episode itself seems to have been conceived decades before, Ellison has turned it into an occasion for an essayistic reflection that, although bearing an intrinsic interest, comes at the cost of his fiction's momentum.

When one considers Ellison's fundamental shifts in the narrative conception of his novel—from the episodic to the psychological back to the episodic, often inflected with certain essayistic qualities—it is possible to describe at least in general terms three phases of composition: the first phase comprising the undated, unsequenced drafts of episodes composed during the first years of the novel's composition; the second phase comprising the Book I and II typescripts from late 1950s and 1960s, which Ellison revised throughout the 1970s; and the third phase comprising his work on the computer from 1982 until the last dated file, on December 30, 1993. The first of these phases is the most difficult to pin down, both because the vast majority of the material is undated and because Ellison does not seem to have gathered the fragments together into continuous narratives of sustained length. The other two phases culminate in what appear to be Ellison's two most advanced efforts to bring his manuscript to completion, with Books I and II in the 1960s and 1970s and the three computer sequences in the 1990s.

Because so much of the material from the earliest phase of Ellison's composition found its way into the drafts he revised in the two periods that followed—the Book I and II typescripts, followed much later by the three computer fragments—we have elected not to include these drafts. It would be impracticable to publish such fragmented drafts in a volume such as this, though they will surely be of interest to those scholars of Ellison's fiction concerned with his habits of composition.

IV

THREE DAYS BEFORE THE SHOOTING . . . is not the novel readers were waiting for at the time of Ralph Ellison's passing. It is at once much less, and perhaps something more. It is less in that it offers no clear resolution to the story it tells; it doesn't end so much as stop. It bears the marks of its incompletion in a variety of ways, from the unpolished nature of some of the prose to Ellison's failure to settle certain basic matters of craft. An author of Ellison's exacting standards would likely not have published much of this material in its present state. Yet it is precisely the incompletion of the manuscripts that makes them such a compelling and fascinating contribution to American literature. In Ellison's numerous drafts we see a literary master at work as he confronts the challenges presented by his novelistic form as well as those presented by the nation whose abiding and shifting identity he was so intent upon rendering in fiction.

This volume draws its title from the opening line of the novel: "Three days before the shooting, a chartered planeload of Southern Negroes swooped down upon the District of Columbia and attempted to see the Senator." Among the things Ellison left unfinished was the task of settling on a title for the book. In a way, ours is not a title at all but a means of calling the reader's attention to the fact of these manuscripts' incompletion. We believe that *Three Days Before the Shooting* . . . is fitting, not only because it gestures toward the central incident of the novel—the shooting of Senator Adam Sunraider—but also because the numerous changes Ellison would make to the opening sentence over the years reflect the novel's dogged incompletion. As Ellison revised the manuscript, the three days became two—a small change, but one that suggests a significant adjustment of the architecture of the plot, telescoping action and underscoring the narrative tension that charges this central incident. We have kept "three days" in the title as a gesture to the many other small changes across the manuscripts that, in their sum, embody so much of what Ellison's second novel is—and is not.

The present edition has been in the works since 1999, when *Juneteenth* was published. In the judgment of its editor, *Juneteenth* represented "the most ambitious and latest, freestanding, compelling, extended fiction in the saga." He promised then an edition would be published that would "enable scholars and readers alike to follow Ellison's some forty years of work on his novel-in-progress." This edition makes good on that promise, reproducing Ellison's words precisely as he wrote them, save for the occasional silent correction to typographical or spelling errors. We have made a special effort to preserve rather than obscure the provisional character of some of Ellison's writing—including tics and quirks that might well have been edited out of the manuscript had Ellison been alive to oversee its publication. These are important to the intrinsic value of these drafts for what they reveal about Ellison as a stylist and his idiosyncratic process of composition and revision.

In every case, the text selected represents the latest continuous sequence of narrative from the particular period of Ellison's composition. For the Book I and II typescripts, we've reproduced the manuscripts clearly marked with the latest date in Fanny Ellison's hand. With the computer drafts, we have reproduced those files marked with the most recent dates. (This process is described in detail in the essay that introduces the computer sequences.) We carefully reviewed all earlier variants with an eye toward noting textual differences and understanding Ellison's compositional process and have included a sample of these variants in Part III. All of these materials will now be made available to scholars in the Ralph Ellison Papers at the Library of Congress.

The Library of Congress holdings include twenty-seven boxes (115 to 141) containing files related to the second novel, compared with only eleven boxes related to *Invisible Man*. Two boxes (132 and 133) include the typescripts for Books I and II that Ellison composed in 1972 and continued revising until at least 1986. Another four boxes (138 to 141) include Ellison's notes relating to the novel during the entire span of its composition. Four others (134 to 137 and a single file in 138) comprise sequential fragments Ellison printed out from his computer and often amended by hand. The remainder of the collection includes episodic drafts filed by scene or character containing material from throughout the novel's composition, much of it with ample revisions.

To say that Ellison did not come close to completing his second novel is not to say that he failed to produce a work of fiction with scenes as fully rendered and realized as anything he had ever written. One forgets that *Invisible Man* was a first novel and, even in its brilliance, displayed some of the signs of an initial work. The second novel sometimes reveals Ellison working at the height of his writerly powers, in command of voice, in command of the rudiments of his prose style, in ways not seen in *Invisible Man.* Other times, it sees him at his lowest points—unfocused, and finally unable to master his own creation.

For all their disconnections, Ellison's manuscripts reward the active reader. For those willing to confront the challenges of the work's fragmentary form, for those capable of simultaneously grasping multiple versions of the same scene, *Three Days Before the Shooting . . .* offers unparalleled access to the craft of Ellison's fiction and an unprecedented glimpse into the writer's mind. Whether one reads this edition from start to finish or jumps from section to section, the experience involves a kind of collaboration with Ellison in the creation of the novel he left forever in progress.

PART I

Editors' Note to Book I

THE FULL PROVENANCE OF Book I is uncertain. The best information we have is a note in Fanny Ellison's hand indicating that the most recent surviving draft was typed in 1972 and that Ellison's editor, Albert Erskine, had read it. Drafts of individual episodes written, in all probability, during the mid- to late 1950s exist on both blue and yellow paper in the Ellison Papers.

Readers will quickly see that, unlike the thoroughly revised, apparent last typescripts of Book II and "Bliss's Birth," the text of Book I drifts between truly polished and rough work. Nevertheless, however rough the composition of several passages in the typescript, the prologue and fourteen chapters answer in the affirmative for Book I the question Mrs. Ellison posed for the entire novel. ("Does it have a beginning, middle, and end?" she asked in Ralph's teeming study a few days after his death in 1994.) For, unlike Book II, and unlike the sequences of computer printouts published in Part II of this volume, Book I, even in its current form, somewhat uneven and full of small inconsistencies, unquestionably has "a beginning, middle, and end."

In contrast to Book II, which though highly polished for the most part and put through multiple revisions over at least two decades, seems to break off in midair without any true hint of what is to come, Book I ends with a perfectly modulated sentence. The words both recapitulate the action and point toward what follows in Book II. "But at least the Senator was still alive," McIntyre observes, recovering his reporter's equilibrium after he watches Hickman and Hickman alone disappear through the closing door of Sunraider's hospital room. At once we know that the Senator has conferred special status on Reverend Hickman in the present moment and that he likely is doomed to die of his wounds. Like a crafty veteran major league pitcher, the novelist can throw any number of pitches from this delivery, and he does so by opening Book II with Sunraider speaking extemporaneously, floridly, provocatively on the Senate floor just before an assassin's bullets silence him.

Clearly the trajectory of Book I is true to the central narrative Ellison refers to over and over again in his notes. After the prologue's biblically toned chronicle of Reverend Hickman and his congregation's arrival in Washington, D.C., Book I unfolds in first-person voice from the point of view of Welborn McIntyre, a Kentucky-born and -bred white reporter who witnesses Senator Sunraider's assassination, and sets out to unravel the identity, mystery, and motive of the "pale young Negro" who leaps to his death after shooting the Senator. Throughout Book I McIntyre and Ellison tantalize the reader with cryptic hints of the assassin's tie to the Senator and Sunraider's former life as Bliss, the boy of indeterminate race raised by Reverend Hickman and the women in his black congregation.

McIntyre roots his narrative in both the present and the past. The present episodes bring to life the fascination Sunraider inspires in McIntyre's journalists' fraternity and in others, most notably the antic, tragicomic figure of jazzman LeeWillie Minifees, whose burning of his Cadillac on the Senator's lawn lands him in the psychiatric ward of the same hospital where Sunraider rests uneasily in critical condition. But McIntyre is also a failed novelist. And although his narrative begins focused keenly on the assassination, it is soon apparent that Ellison intends him to be an important character in his own right as well as a witness to and commentator on the life and times of the Senator and the nation. For example, McIntyre interrupts his account of the assassination and its aftermath with excursions and reveries into his own life, including his affair in the 1930s with a Negro girl, whose mother unleashes her fury on him when he comes to tell her he wants to marry her pregnant daughter and be a true father to their child. Book I also puts Hickman squarely into McIntyre's path as a presence in his own right and as a black preacher who explodes the white reporter's assumptions about racial boundaries and the Senator's history.

This volume presents Book I in its totality as a draft much less polished and revised than the more finished drafts that survive of Book II and "Bliss's Birth." Chapters 4 and 5 of the version published here are Ellison's drafts of "Cadillac Flambé" and "It Always Breaks Out," episodes he published separately during his lifetime and which are included in Part III as they appeared in print, in the case of "It Always Breaks Out" considerably revised from the version in Book I.

PROLOGUE

THREE DAYS BEFORE THE shooting, a chartered planeload of Southern Negroes swooped down upon the District of Columbia and attempted to see the Senator. They were quite elderly: old ladies dressed in little white caps and white uniforms made of surplus nylon parachute material, the men dressed in neat but old-fashioned black suits and wearing wide-brimmed, deep-crowned panama hats which, in the Senator's walnut-paneled reception room now, they held with a grave ceremonial air. Solemn, uncommunicative, and quietly insistent, they were led by a huge, distinguished-looking old fellow who on the day of the chaotic event was to prove himself, his age notwithstanding, an extraordinarily powerful man. Tall and broad and of an easy dignity, this was the Reverend A. Z. Hickman—"better known," as one of the old ladies proudly informed the Senator's secretary, "as God's Trombone."

This, however, was about all they were willing to explain. Forty-four in number, the women with their fans and satchels and picnic baskets, and the men carrying new blue airline take-on bags, they listened intently while Reverend Hickman did their talking.

"Ma'am," Hickman said, his voice deep and resonant as he nodded toward the door of the Senator's private office, "you just tell the Senator that Hickman has arrived. When he hears who's out here he'll know that it's important and want to see us."

"But I've told you that the Senator isn't available," the secretary said. "Just what is your business? Who are you, anyway? Are you his constituents?"

"Constituents?" Suddenly the old man smiled. "No, miss," he said, "the Senator doesn't even have anybody like us in *his* state. We're from down where we're among the counted but not among the heard."

"Then why are you coming here?" she said. "What is your business?"

"He'll tell you, ma'am," Hickman said. "He'll know who we are; all you have to do is tell him that we have arrived...."

The secretary, a young Mississippian, sighed. Obviously, these were Southern Negroes of a type she had heard of all her life—and old ones; yet, instead of being already in the herdlike movement toward the door, which she expected, they were calmly waiting, as though she hadn't said a word. And now she had a suspicion that, for all their staring eyes, she actually didn't exist to them. They just stood there, now looking oddly like a delegation of Asians who had lost their interpreter along the way, and who were trying to tell her something, which she had no interest in hearing, through this old man who himself did not know the language. Suddenly they no longer seemed familiar, and a feeling of dream-like incongruity came over her. They were so many that she could no longer see the large abstract paintings which hung along the paneled wall. Nor the framed facsimiles of State Documents which hung above a bust of Vice President Calhoun. Some of the old women were calmly plying their palm-leaf fans, as though in serene defiance of the droning air conditioner. Yet, she could see no trace of impertinence in their eyes, nor any of the anger which the Senator usually aroused in members of their group. Instead, they seemed resigned, like people embarked upon a difficult journey who were already far beyond the point of no return. Her uneasiness grew, then she blotted out the others by focusing her eyes narrowly upon their leader. And when she spoke again her voice took on a nervous edge.

"I've told you that the Senator isn't here," she said, "and you must realize that he is a busy man who can only see people by appointment."

"We know, ma'am," Hickman said, "but—"

"You don't just walk in here and expect to see him on a minute's notice."

"We understand that, ma'am," Hickman said, looking mildly into her eyes, his close-cut white head tilted to one side, "but this is something that developed of a sudden. Couldn't you reach him by long distance? We'd pay the charges. And I don't even have to talk, miss; you can do the talking. All you have to say is that we have arrived."

"I'm afraid this is impossible," she said.

The very evenness of the old man's voice made her feel uncomfortably young, and now, deciding that she had exhausted all the tried-and-true techniques which her region had worked out (short of violence) for getting quickly rid of Negroes, the secretary lost her patience and telephoned for a guard.

They left as quietly as they had appeared, the old minister waiting behind until the last had stepped into the hall. Then he turned, and she saw his full height, framed by the doorway, as the others arranged themselves beyond him in the hall. "You're really making a mistake, miss," he said. "The Senator knows us and—"

"*Knows* you," she said indignantly. "I've heard Senator Sunraider state that the only colored he knows is the boy who shines shoes at his golf club."

"Oh?" Hickman shook his head as the others exchanged knowing glances. "Very well, ma'am," Hickman said. "We're sorry to have caused you this trouble. It's just that it's very important that the Senator know that we're on the scene. So I hope you won't forget to tell him that we have arrived, because soon it might be too late."

There was no threat in it; indeed, his voice echoed the odd sadness which she thought she detected in the faces of the others just before the door blotted them from view.

In the hall they exchanged no words, moving silently behind the guard, who accompanied them down to the lobby. They were about to move into the street, when the security-minded chief guard, observing their number, stepped up and ordered them searched.

They submitted patiently, amused that anyone should consider them capable of harm, and for the first time an emotion broke the immobility of their faces. They chuckled and winked and smiled, fully aware of the comic aspect of the situation. Here they were, quiet, old, and obviously religious black folk who, because they had attempted to see the man who was considered the most vehement enemy of their people in either house of Congress, were being energetically searched by uniformed security police, and they knew what the absurd outcome would be. They were found to be armed with nothing more dangerous than pieces of fried chicken and ham sandwiches, chocolate cake and sweet-potato fried pies. Some obeyed the guards' commands with exaggerated sprightliness, the old ladies giving their skirts a whirl as they turned in their flat-heeled shoes. When ordered to remove his wide-brimmed hat, one old man held it for the guard to look inside; then, flipping out the sweatband, he gave the crown a tap, causing something to fall to the floor, then waited with a callused palm extended as the guard bent to retrieve it. Straightening and unfolding the object, the guard saw a worn but neatly creased fifty-dollar bill which he dropped upon the outstretched palm as though it were hot. They watched silently as he looked at the old man and gave a dry, harsh laugh; then as he continued laughing the humor slowly receded behind their eyes. Not until they were allowed to file into the street did they give further voice to their amusement.

"These here folks don't understand nothing," one of the old ladies said. "If we had been the kind to depend on the sword instead of on the Lord, we'd been in our graves long ago—ain't that right, Sis Arter?"

"You said it," Sister Arter said. "In the grave and done long finished molding!"

"Let them worry, our conscience is clear on that...."

"Amen!"

On the sidewalk now, they stood around Reverend Hickman, holding a hushed conference, then in a few minutes they had disappeared in a string of taxis and the incident was thought closed.

Shortly afterwards, however, they appeared mysteriously at a hotel where the Senator leased a private suite, and tried to see him. How they knew of this secret suite they would not explain.

Next, they appeared at the editorial office of the newspaper which had been most critical of the Senator's methods, but here, too, they were turned away. They were taken for a protest group, just one more lot of disgruntled Negroes crying for justice as though theirs were the only grievances in the world. Indeed, they received less of a hearing here than elsewhere. They weren't even questioned as to why they wished to see the Senator—which was poor newspaper work, to say the least; a failure of technical alertness, and, as events were soon to prove, a gross violation of press responsibility.

So once more they moved away.

Although the Senator returned to Washington the following day, his secretary failed to report his strange visitors. There were important interviews scheduled, and she had understandably classified the old people as just another annoyance. Once the reception room was cleared of their disquieting presence, they seemed no more significant than the heavy mail received from white liberals and Negroes, liberal and reactionary alike, whenever the Senator made one of his taunting remarks. She forgot them. Then at about eleven A.M. Reverend Hickman reappeared without the others and started into the building. This time, however, he was not to reach the secretary. One of the guards, the same who had picked up the fifty-dollar bill, recognized him and pushed him bodily from the building.

Indeed, the old man was handled quite roughly, his sheer weight and bulk and the slow rhythm of his normal movements infuriating the guard to that quick, heated fury which springs up in one when dealing with the unexpected recalcitrance of some inanimate object. Say, the huge stone that resists the bulldozer's power or the chest of drawers that refuses to budge from its spot on the floor. Nor did the old man's composure help matters. Nor did his passive resistance hide his distaste at having strange hands placed upon his person. As he was being pushed about, old Hickman looked at the guard with a kind of tolerance, an understanding which seemed to remove his personal emotions to some far, cool place where the guard's strength could never reach them. He even managed to pick up his hat from the sidewalk, where it had been thrown after him, with no great show of breath or hurry, and arose to regard the guard with a serene dignity.

"Son," he said, flicking a spot of dirt from the soft old panama with a white handkerchief, "I'm sorry that this had to happen to you. Here you've worked up a sweat on this hot morning, and not a thing has been changed—except that you've interfered with something that doesn't concern you. After all, you're only a guard, you're not a mind reader. Because if you were, you'd be trying to get me in there as fast as you could instead of trying to keep me out. You're probably not even a good guard, and I wonder what on earth you'd do if I came here prepared to make some trouble. You think of trouble as coming from numbers, but you're wrong. It comes in all sizes."

Fortunately, there were too many spectators present for the guard to risk giving the old fellow a demonstration, and he was compelled to stand silent, his thumbs hooked over his cartridge belt, while old Hickman strolled—or, more accurately, *floated*—up the walk and disappeared around the corner.

Except for two attempts by telephone, once to the Senator's office and later to his home, the group made no further effort until that afternoon, when Hickman sent a telegram asking Senator Sunraider to phone him at a T Street hotel. A message, which, thanks again to the secretary, the Senator did not see. Following this attempt there was silence.

During the late afternoon the group of closemouthed old folk were seen praying quietly within the Lincoln Memorial. An amateur photographer, a high-school boy from the Bronx, was there at the time, and it was his chance photograph of the group, standing with bowed heads beneath old Hickman's outspread arms while facing the great sculpture, that was flashed over the wires following the shooting. Asked why he had photographed that particular group, the boy replied that he had seen them as a "good composition.... I thought their faces would make a fine scale of grays between the whiteness of the marble and the blackness of the shadows." And for the rest of the day the group appears to have faded into those same peaceful shadows, to remain there until the next morning—when they materialized shortly before chaos erupted.

BOOK I

CHAPTER 1

UNDERSTAND ME, I WAS there; sitting in the press section at the start of the shooting. I had been rereading M. Vannec's most unexpected letter when suddenly it was as though a certain long-forgotten night of violence to which he referred had flared from the page and accelerated into chaotic life.

First, the popping sound had drawn my attention down to the orating Senator; then, far across in the visitors' gallery, there came a flash of movement—and then it was as though the letter had caught flame in my hands. Then, for some reason the photographic image of the elegant magnesium-bodied sports car which ignited and burned during the recent running of the Le Mans Grand Prix—that awe-inspiring sabre of flame and destruction—flashed through my mind just as I was looking out past the great chandelier of the chamber to see an elegantly dressed man lean over the visitors'-gallery rail and point down to where, gripping the sides of the lectern and tossing his head, Senator Sunraider was speaking. Then things seemed to reel out of phase.

Directly below me, on the floor of the chamber, the Senator's colleagues sat calmly engrossed in his argument, while along the curving rail to either side of the pointing man I could see visitors leaping to their feet and away, scattering. Then something thudded against the lectern, and somewhere above me I could hear a gay, erratic ringing, like the musical jangling of a huge bunch of keys.

Then, as the sound and the rising of the man's arm flew together in my mind, my nerves snapped like a window shade: He was firing a pistol at the Senator. *Oh, no*, I thought, *OH, NO! We were only betting, it was all in fun. This can't be happening!*

Yet, with the swiftness of glass ornaments sent bursting from a Christmas tree by the fire of a circus sharpshooter, arrows of prismatic light were flying from the swaying chandelier. And above the furious action below me there sounded a ringing as of a thousand crystal bells, the hysterical cries of women. From somewhere in the distance came the angry shrilling of a whistle, the harsh staccato of commands.

On the floor directly below me I now could see the Senator staggering backwards, and around in a narrow circle, a spot of blood blooming on his face. Then he seemed to look up to where the gunman, crouching now, his elbows resting on the railing, gripped the pistol with both hands and got off a final shot.

This time the Senator was sent lurching sideways, turning to his left, and I could hear him calling out in a strangely transformed voice and going over to land on his back. Then, "My God! My God!" some man was calling, and it was bedlam.

Behind Senator Sunraider, members of the Senate were scattering and dodging, hitting the floor and yelling, making for the exits. A pair of eyeglasses glittered near the leg of an overturned chair, while across the vast space of the chamber, past the swaying chandelier, I could see three guards fighting their way through the milling spectators—several of them Negro women—trying to get to the gunman who, standing erect now, turned to look behind him, his movements oddly like those of one intentionally deaf to all sounds of external confusion. He seemed absolutely calm, as now, immediately behind him, I could see, looming up like a bear suddenly cresting a hill, a huge old whiteheaded Negro. This man yells something which I can't grasp as he rushed toward the gunman, stepping over a bench and down like a bear hurdling a stone fence, his arms outstretched as he calls out once more.

The effect is electric. Suddenly the gunman throws down his weapon and seems to freeze, waiting. Then, as the old Negro comes on down the aisle, the gunman swivels suddenly and throws his leg over the railing, resting there a moment, his arms rigid as he grips the railing with both hands, calmly contemplating the approaching man.

"Wait, boy! Wait!" I hear. Then above the turbulent heads I see a pistol waving, and a uniformed guard bursts into view behind the old Negro who turns, suddenly enfolding the helpless guard in his great arms, yells out once more, "Wait!"

Seizing the incongruous images of the man on the rail, the old Negro, and the struggling guard, my mind leaps ahead on a wave of heat and nausea, lifting me from my chair. For a moment the gunman stares straight at the old Negro, then, violently shaking his head, he was gone, plunged calmly over the railing.

The nausea shook me then, and I went over—carefully avoiding the railing and the floor below—even as the sound of a crunching impact, the splintering of wood, filled the great room.

There followed a shattering silence which whimpered and gasped, sideslipping and quavering, welling up thunderously in a reverberation that struck the chamber in great tremulous waves. These seemed to last for endless minutes, for vast suspensions of breath. And then, as though what was still in anguished progress wasn't frightening enough, outrageous enough, *terrible* enough, the old Negro, who is now grasping the gallery rail and looking down at the fallen Senator, suddenly calls out in a voice like a roughly amplified horn and begins to relieve himself of an inarticulate combination of prayer, sermon, prophesy, and song!

It was absolutely confounding! A projection so resonant with anguish, bitterness, yes, and with *indictment*—that for a brief moment that entire frenzied, stampeding body broke its flight to whirl around and stand looking up to where he holds forth, white head thrown back, arms outstretched—caught up in the confounding and full-throated anguish of his cry.

And in that place what an awe-inspiring sound! Yes, and what confounding conduct. A terrible calamity strikes the nation and this character out of nowhere—Hickman is his name—*he* converts it with a blast of his own voice into an occasion for condemning the entire United States Senate! What a state of affairs—one break in the wall of decorum, one fissure in this pattern of orderly events, and a Negro, a *Negro,* is crying in the gap like blackest chaos! And it was as though he had been waiting for years, prepared and ready. It was, there's no other word, absolutely scandalous!

What's more, for some time afterwards I had the unshakable impression that even his big *whah-whah* Negro voice, sounding with its wildly misdirected note of doom, was still reverberating there beneath the dome, beating like the wings of some dark bird trapped in a steeple. Yes, and it would continue to do so until the mystery of the occurrence is explained, for even now there is much mystery. One thinks of ghosts crying in clear summer sunlight, of obscene guests at a wedding, of lewd behavior at a funeral, of a crowd of drunken lunatics howling and tearing up the room beyond where, lonely and sleepless, I lay long ago on a hot night in Paris.

And all of this over Senator Sunraider! I was convinced that it all began as an act to confuse us. And more likely than not this man Hickman is a charlatan, a flunky hired by Sunraider himself in one of his endless tricks of political showmanship which, through some unfortunate miscalculation, blew up in his face.

Otherwise, it's as though the High Chief Rabbi of Minsk were to have stood in front of the Pentagon and broken into loud lamentations over the death of Adolf Hitler—completely illogical, a scandalous affront to our sense of order. A slap in the face! Indeed, for me this man Hickman's conduct is more upsetting than the shooting. Sunraider is not, after all, the first politician to get himself shot.

Nevertheless, I was almost out of my mind over having failed to observe the tragedy from its beginning. For just at the split second when a simple outcry might have alerted the Senator and frustrated the gunman's aim, I was flagrantly inattentive. I failed, I soiled the morality of my craft. Instead of working, instead of being objectively observant of fact and process, I had been reading (and enjoying) M. Vannec's letter. And the fact that it was an unexpected relief from a series of dull speeches gives me no comfort whatsoever. For I painfully perceive that the source of my failure was not boredom but vanity. A vanity springing from the simple fact, I must confess, that I'm so far from the top of my profession that I possess not one solitary autographed photograph—those emblems of a certain journalistic success— from a president, cabinet member, or leader of Congress. True, I often come near these great figures, but I've never reached the proximity which conveys status. Nor have I complained, for I have long cherished the uses of relative anonymity. Hence my secret pride in having received a piece of correspondence from such a distinguished figure as M. Vannec. I've long admired M. Vannec (though from a great distance), who counts in my estimation of the scheme of things for far more than does the Senator. Thus the very unexpectedness of his letter gave me a sense of plunging suddenly into more important areas of life, of being in contact with one possessing a higher consciousness of the complexity of culture. Yes, and I felt somehow in touch with the darker, mysterious areas of events. The questions he asked had left me with the notion that I understood many grave and complex matters. But more about his letter later.

Then, as I say, completely without warning, while I had been enjoying this most tenuous contact with one considered a leading figure of our time, the Earth seemed to slip its orbit; the Senator was being fired upon, the Senate was in panic. And with all hell erupting around us, this Negro Hickman was *singing*!

CHAPTER 2

THEN IT WAS ABSOLUTE chaos. When I left the elevator and tried to get onto the main floor of the chamber, guards and security people were all over the place, blocking the exits and challenging reporters and legislators indiscriminately. Looking past the clustered heads of a group guarding the door through which I had tried to enter, I could see the gunman's form, sprawled near a shattered bench; a whiff of gunpowder lingered in the air. The shot-up chandelier hung in sad, damaged glitter above, while three Secret Service agents with pistols exposed at the hip stood underneath, looking up to the gradually emptying visitors' gallery with alert eyes. It was hot, and an air of shocked depression hung over all.

Backing away, I moved along the hall, elbowing a path through the crowd as I listened to rapid, hysteria-edged discussions of the shooting. I learned that during the brief interval when I was blocked on the stairs leading from the press gallery, the Senator had been rushed off to the hospital, that the Negro Hickman, and his followers, had been rounded up and placed under arrest, and that now the visitors' gallery was being searched for a possible second gunman, and, some said, for bombs—news which heightened our tension.

I was kept moving by the crowd, which milled slowly about in its frustrations for explanations and its desire to get a closer look at the assassin. And now, with my eyes watering from the cigarette of some inconsiderate smoker, I found myself pressing against the wall near another entrance to the chamber where a group was speculating as to the nature of the Negroes' involvement in the shooting. One man was quite certain that he had the picture.

"I tell you they're part of the plot," he said.

"I agree," another man said.

"I don't," a calm voice behind me said. "They were simply hysterical. When the shooting started everybody was hysterical—"

"Hysterical, hell," the first man said, "I saw them attacking the guards—"

"Oh, no, you merely saw some old ladies waving their arms around."

"Say," the hysterical man said, "are you a reporter?"

"No, I'm a member of the Congress."

"Well, excuse me, sir, but I'm a reporter and trained to observe, and I saw them attack the guards. I was upstairs, looking across. You were below, and evidently you couldn't see what was happening."

"That's right, those of us above saw it all," another reporter said.

"You're damn right, and they were acting with *discipline*," the hysterical man said.

"Look, they were simply acting like a bunch of frightened Negroes," the Congressman said. "Let's not add to the confusion."

"I tell you they were part of a plot."

"What plot?"

"The plot to get Sunraider," the hysterical man said. "They were under orders, and what's worse, I believe that the gunman was under orders."

"Now I don't know about that, although things did seem to happen all at once."

"You're right there, the plot moved like clockwork!"

"But under whose orders?" someone said.

"That old burly Negro's," the hysterical man said. "Didn't you see the assassin throw down his gun when the old man yelled at him?"

"Did anyone catch what the Negro said?"

"No, not exactly, but I saw the assassin throw down his gun."

"But then why did he jump?"

"Because," the hysterical man said with emphasis, "that old nigger *ordered* him to!"

"Nuts! Are you out of your mind?"

"No, I'm not. He jumped, didn't he?"

"Yes, but how do you know that he even heard the Negro?"

"I tell you he was ordered to jump. We all *saw* him jump. That old nigger barked and he went over the rail like a trained seal."

"But why would you think that he'd take orders like that?"

"Wait a second," someone said. "Was the assassin a white or a nonwhite?"

"White," the hysterical man said. "Everyone saw him. You can look in there and see for yourself."

"White or nonwhite, what I want to know is, why do you think the assassin would take an order like that?"

"Because there's more to this thing than meets the eye. Those niggers had something on that fellow. Most likely they're all under Communist discipline."

"Look, my friend," the Congressman said, "you're getting hysterical."

"That's right," I said. "I can't imagine anyone taking an order like that from anyone, let alone a Negro."

"But these are revolutionary times," the hysterical man said. "There're a lot of misguided people around who'll take orders from anyone to do anything."

"You've got something there," someone else said.

"You're damn right I have! They're fanatics! Terrorists! They'll do whatever they're told! And you have to remember that we're dealing here with a background of slavery. For years back those people have been trained to take orders, and now the Communists have moved in. Didn't they run one for vice president? That's why I say that old bastard was probably under orders to have that fellow shoot Senator Sunraider and then kill himself."

"Of course this is nonsense," someone said.

"I agree," the Congressman said, "and you should remember that the government isn't exactly uninformed as to the activities of the Communists and other such subversive groups. Don't let yourself be carried away, at least not before we have more information."

"I trust my own information," the hysterical man said.

"Was that what the old man yelled?" the Congressman asked.

"What?"

"Dive in the name of the Party?"

"Sir, this is no kidding matter. You should study the history of terrorism, of brainwashing, the uprising in Santo Domingo, the Nat Turner rebellion!"

"But did anyone hear the old Negro's words?"

"Hear? Who had to *hear* it?" the hysterical man said. "We all saw that nigger grapple with the guard, we saw him yell something to the gunman, and we saw the gunman leap. He was like somebody hopped up or hypnotized, wasn't he? What more do we have to know?"

"There's a hell of a lot we have to know," another man said.

"Yes, we're leaping to conclusions. We don't know the gunman's race, nationality, name, or age—"

"Listen," the hysterical man said, "if that nigger *wasn't* giving orders, why didn't the gunman shoot him?"

"Maybe he was out of bullets."

"I doubt if that's the explanation," someone said. "A terrorist on a mission like that would carry extra clips. Even an extra weapon."

"That's possible," the Congressman said, turning again to the hysterical man, "but now I'll ask you this: Why, instead of throwing himself over the railing, didn't he try to escape through the crowd?"

"Because that big nigger was in the way, that's why! If he hadn't jumped, that nigger would have blown his head off and thrown him over. Didn't you see how the burly bastard handled that guard?"

"But the old man was empty-handed."

"I tell you that fellow would have been shot!" the hysterical man said.

"By whom, the guard?"

"Hell, no, by that big nigger! Or by one of those nigger women. I'll bet you every one of them was armed."

"But I heard the old man yell, 'Don't shoot that boy,'" a man who had been silent said.

"I'll be damn if I heard him say anything like that."

"Well, I did, and that's when he overpowered the guard."

"Did anyone actually see whether the Negro was armed or not?"

"All I know is that when he started that damned singing and praying he threw out his arms and his hands were empty."

"Look," the hysterical man said, "that nigger probably passed his own gun to one of those other niggers."

"That's raw speculation," the Congressman said. "We don't know anything for sure. I wish they'd find that bomb and let us out of here so that we can gather the facts."

"Hey, McIntyre!" a voice called, and I snapped around to see McGowan, his face red with excitement, pushing his beefy way toward me.

"It's unbelievable," he said. "I just got through a call to my editor, and it's unbelievable!"

"What are you talking about?"

"Do you know what they've done with that nigra Hickman?"

"Hickman?"

"The big one who did the singing."

"So that's his name," I said. "What happened, did someone kill him?"

"Hell, no. That nigra's got more guards around him than Fort Knox."

"Then what happened?"

"Man, instead of taking that nigra to the Justice Department with those other nigras, they have taken him to the *hospital*—along with the *Senator!*"

"*With* him, my God," I said. "What do you mean?"

"I mean in the same ambulance," McGowan said. "Did you ever hear of such a thing?"

"But why? Did the old man have a heart attack?"

McGowan shook his head. "Heart attack, hell! Dammit, ma-yan, what I'm trying to tell you is, they took that nigra along because the Senator *demanded* that they take him!"

Suddenly I felt cold. Only yesterday morning the Senator had been insulting Negroes before television cameras, and during the afternoon he'd castigated them from the floor of the Senate, and now this round-about-face. It was unbelievable.

"I don't get it," I said. "You must be leaving something out. It just isn't logical—"

"Like hell, I am," McGowan said. "That's the point, McIntyre. What I mean is, this thing has gone stark, raving *crazy!* When they took him out of here the Senator was damn near dead—some say in a coma—but still he comes to long enough to demand that that old nigra be taken to the hospital along with him, and he ordered them to keep the bastard on hand while he's undergoing surgery. What's more, he ordered them to make a place for the nigra in his own private room! Now, I could understand it if this had taken place before the War and the Senator was a Southerner. Because then that nigra would've been a body servant or some kind of old family retainer. But not this, because that there nigra that the Senator's got with him, he ain't *no*-body's servant. His attitude is wrong, I can tell from the way he made all that fuss up there in the visitors' gallery. I'm telling you, it's enough to make a man go homesteading in Bolivia!"

It was indeed, and as McGowan puffed off to spread the news, I forced a path to the wall, backing against it and fending off the crush as I tried to make sense of this latest development.

In spite of the shock, the emotional drain, the sickening incredibility of the assassination attempt, I was flabbergasted. Why would the Senator, of all people, demand to have a *Negro* with him in this crucial moment? The old man's conduct had been confounding enough, but if McGowan's news was correct, the Senator had outreached even this extreme of unreason. Suddenly things had ricocheted from the potentially tragic to the blatantly bizarre, and the image formed in my mind by the incongruous juxtaposition of the Senator and old Hickman in an ambulance—the one shot and bleeding, and the other weeping and praying, speeding along together through frozen lines of traffic with the screaming of sirens and the roaring of an outriding escort of policemen on motorcycles—shook me in ways I couldn't analyze, resounded with overtones of possibility that I was reluctant to hear....

How could I ever describe to someone like M. Vannec the element of free-floating threat introduced into the scene by this simple yet incongruous fact? He'd think me mad. And perhaps he'd be right, I told myself. Perhaps the shooting has unhinged you just as it has old Hickman. Then the distasteful idea which I mentioned earlier struck me full force, that it was not only a plot, like the hysterical man insisted, but a piece of conmanship, with Sunraider performing as actor-dramatist, and old Hickman as supporting player in yet another Sunraider plot to confound the public.

But what of the gunman? His bullets were real, his leap no piece of playacting, his crushed body was no mere piece of stage property. In fact, it was rapidly becoming the only "normal" detail in the entire chaotic scene. Even so, now that the idea had gripped me, I couldn't rule out the possibility that the Senator had indeed seized upon his own shooting as a final opportunity to arouse widespread consternation, a means of making what might well be his parting assault on the public's credulity.

Because from what I knew and had heard about the Senator, it wasn't at all beyond him to have conceived of such a ploy, even while going down under a hail of lead. Was it possible that he had planted the Negroes there to interrupt his speech, and then had had the plot explode in his face with the deadly and unscheduled appearance of the gunman? Had Fate stepped in to give a sinister twist to his cynical scheme? It all seemed possible. And where I had begun to think that we had been the unwitting witnesses to a single outrageous plot, it now seemed quite possible that there were two, separate and unconnected: one to deprive us of an important politician, the other to sever us from our sanity. What on earth had happened to this nation?

CHAPTER 3

AROUND ME NOW, LEGISLATORS, reporters, and lobbyists were going over the Senator's career, much of it in whispers, recalling his combination of geniality and viciousness, his technique of delivering jabs below the belt in the guise of humor, the manner in which his obsession with racial matters had recently led to sharp discontinuities of argument, non sequiturs, gaffes—all erupting during moments when he seemed most seriously concerned with major legislation. Some noted his excellence in debate and his great skill in mimicry (a gift which provided his opponents with much discomfort), his frequent violations of private confidences in public debate, during which he was apt to say almost *anything.* And from a position of apparent logic, and in the interest of the highest principles.

Others were rehearsing how the Senator, a Northerner, flaunted his association with the Southern bloc to the embarrassment of his party, and how he boldly asserted the realism of his actions. Several of the discussants held that the Senator was more honest and responsible to the public than those who pretended that such collaborations across party and sectional lines were both unnecessary and immoral. To pretend that such wheeling and dealing isn't necessary, the Senator has insisted, is to misguide and miseducate the public as to the real difficulties of governing a diversified nation, and to obscure from the electorate the true nature of its conflicting interests. Certain party leaders have regarded the Senator's position as an attack upon the very foundation of their power.

The talk then returned to the news concerning the Senator and Hickman, and this sparked an intense discussion of the malicious attacks which Senator Sunraider had made against Negroes and Jews, whose working alliance he seems bent upon destroying by dividing their leaders over issues usually assumed to reflect their common interests as political minorities. On several occasions he has remarked that such collaboration not only presented possible violation of the principle demanding separation of church and state, but were to be distrusted by both sides because of the basic religious differences of the parties involved. For Jews, he claims, are Jews, while Negroes are "black white Anglo-Saxon Protestants," and that such alliances were unnatural. This caused quite an outcry and presented the occasion for McGowan to create a most unlikely—and inaccurate—acronym. "Well, I'll just be damn," he said, "here I been thinking all along that ole Brer Rabbit and ole Uncle Remus and Sam the waiter were just nigras, but now ole Senator Sunraider swears they aren't nigras at all, they're goddamn *burrwasps!*"

That others have made such statements is bad enough, but the Senator's attacks against Negroes have become so gratuitous and in such extremely bad taste as to cause resentment far beyond the Negro community. Recently even reporters have found his provocations revolting.

Listening as they furiously re-created the Sunraider legend, I felt that, despite the heated blending of fact and fiction, real incident and rumor, cold observation and wild opinion, no one, not even those who "knew" the Senator, seemed to know exactly who he was, nor what to make of him. It was difficult to decide whether he was actually as reactionary or as radical as some of the men were insisting. For in matters like his support of scientific research, his efforts to preserve our national resources, our parks and shorelines, he seemed forward-looking. In other matters he seemed like a figure out of some past which had never existed—at least not in *our* history.

But what was clear is that there is something basically willful, quirky, exasperatingly capricious, and downright questionable about him. And there was no question but that even while lying shot, with his voice silenced and with no cloak of charm and eloquence to shield or project himself, he had, through the simple expedient of having a Negro present during his hour of mortal crisis, rendered himself even more confusing in the public mind.

And yet, as one man was pointing out, in spite of the confusion which he created, for many people the Senator possesses a mysterious charm, a *charisma.*

"You know," the man was saying, "the reason why I say this is that I've felt it myself. I went to see him about a certain matter, and a most interesting thing occurred. . . ."

"You mean that he hit you for a contribution?"

"Oh, no, nothing like that. We were talking over a proposition, and all of a sudden I could actually feel the magnetism surging from the man. It was almost physical, a vibration. Unfortunately he was unable to do anything about my immediate problem, but I left his office feeling that everything would work out okay. And so it did, by the way. Up to then I'd been pessimistic."

"Yes, I experienced something similar," another man said. "I never talked about it before because it's pretty strange. Still, I discovered that he has the ability to make you feel somehow relieved."

"What do you mean by 'relieved'?"

"Relieved of my uncertainties, of some of my deepest fears...."

"Maybe so, but I don't get you."

"I don't either," I said. "Develop it a bit."

"It's hard to explain. But the way he goes over the details of a problem and relates them to other things, to other moves in government, to the economic cycles, you come away feeling that you're ten times more perceptive than you usually are."

"But perceptive of *what?*"

The man reddened, gave a quick shake of his head.

"Hell, of life, events; of the patterns underlying the processes of public affairs. What am I, a philosopher? What I'm trying to convey is something he makes you feel—or makes *me* feel."

A faraway look came into his eyes as he broke off, shaking his head again.

Suddenly I felt uneasy, as though we had approached an unknown, dangerous, and somehow unclean territory dominated by one near death. The image of a grimacing halitosis ad flashed through my mind.

"You know," another man said, "I believe that one of the main sources of the Senator's power lies in his ability to make so many people feel that he justifies their *weaknesses*. He makes them feel that they have a human right to be weak, and he even justifies their unfairness to others weaker than themselves."

"Oh, bull!" a man wearing a hairbrush moustache said. "You make him sound like some kind of saint of negative permissiveness!"

"No," the man said, completely undaunted by the rococo definition, "I don't mean to do anything like that. But whether we like it or not, many people seek comfort from their political leaders, and the Senator is one who delivers. And in spite of what his many critics say, he has insight. He has a subtle understanding of people. And when he wishes, he can be like a wise priest who sees their secret failings and understands them. Besides, he hands out excellent advice on many things having nothing to do with politics per se...."

"Sweeney," the man with the moustache said, "you sound like Sunraider's done you a few favors."

"He has and I'm not hiding it. But in my opinion he's done the whole country a lot of good, and I'm proud to have him for a friend."

"Well, at least you admit it," the man with the moustache said. "But you really don't have to go mystical about it, just because he's allowed you to get close to the pork barrel. As far as I'm concerned, Sunraider is such a crook that all he has to do is to look at a man in a certain way and he feels that he's automatically involved himself in a conspiracy."

"Tell me, Larson," Sweeney said, "why is it that you always have to get personal whenever you present your bigoted and lamebrained political opinions?"

"Lamebrained!" the moustached man said. "Who are you calling lamebrained?"

"You," Sweeney said, "and in spades!"

"Why, you sentimental sycophant, you self-serving creature of Sunraider's guile. You bumptious blatherskite from Boston!"

Larson reached out, and I saw a short fat man pushing his way between them.

"Now wait, fellows," the fat man said. "Remember where we are—let's not get upset."

Someone cleared his throat. Sweeney and Larson glared.

"I'll tell you something else that's interesting about the Senator," the fat man said. "That fellow has the damndest way of making a man want to laugh!"

Larson and Sweeney glared silently down upon him and then across at one another.

"You mean when he mimics his colleagues?" someone said.

"Oh, no." The fat man shook his head. "He's a riot when he does that, but I'm speaking of what goes on in private. You can be in his office talking about something as serious as all hell, you can be worried near to death and damn near in tears, and he'll be looking at you with a perfectly straight face while he goes on talking seriously, explaining something—and the next thing you know, you're breaking up. Laughing your head off. Everything appears in a funny light. I can't explain it, but it's happened to me a couple of times."

"Oh, come off it, Pat," a voice said, "you live for laughs. Your mind wandered and you thought of some of Sunraider's tricks and you broke up. There's nothing mysterious about your laughing at anybody."

"But that isn't it," the fat man said. "Now, I admit that I live for good food, strong liquor, and laughs, but this is something else. He makes you feel that there's a joke lying at the bottom of everything."

"So now we have the testimony of a philosopher," Larson said with a grimace.

The fat man smiled. "What makes a philosopher," he said, "a bad temper, a bad case of boils? But it's not just me. Why, coming from a funeral one time, I rode in the same car with old Judge McCaslin and some friends, and that dignified old gentleman, who had been standing beside the Senator at the graveside—and it was a very sad funeral—the old gentleman almost embarrassed himself. Had to jam a handkerchief into his mouth to keep from exploding right there in the funeral car. He was crying like a baby, and when he finally got himself under control and we asked him what had happened, all he could do was shake his head and say, 'Oh, that Sunraider! That damnable Sunraider!' And then he had to jam that handkerchief right back into his mouth!"

There were smiles, then Larson said, "Listen, Sweeney, getting back to this name-calling—you have your opinion about Sunraider and I have mine, and I think it's too early to start turning a character like him into some kind of saint or even into a perfect politician. Anyway, not before he's cold!"

For a moment this produced silence, which was broken by a policeman who approached through the crowd calling for "Congressman Brock," and the calm man excused himself and left. Then the fat man chuckled. "Saint?" he said. "Who the hell said he was a saint? Why, I could tell you things about Sunraider that..."

And now it was as though he'd given a signal to release a veritable deluge of the lies and rumors that had collected about the figure of the Senator. Drawing together, they pressed me even closer to the wall as they let themselves go. First they rehashed the rumor that for a time during his youth the Senator had been the leader of an organization which wore black hoods and practiced obscene ceremonials with the ugliest and most worn-out prostitutes they could find. Like certain motorcycle gangs of today they also engaged in acts of violence and hooliganism and were accused of torturing people—derilicts and such. They were also said to have distributed Christmas baskets and comic books to the poor.

I was familiar with this rumor and had found no substantiation for it, except for the hardly related fact that the Senator *was* famous for wearing a spectacular black cashmere overcoat of balmoral cut that was lined full length with sable.

Next came the rumor that the Senator, a wealthy bachelor, had kept for a time a beautiful Jewish mistress whom he showered with expensive jewelry, furs, works of art (he was alleged to have given her one of the finest Picassos), but I dismissed this as untrue when the narrator, a columnist known as a notorious liar, claimed that this fair lady was kept locked in a luxurious establishment in Georgetown which was staffed with mute Oriental servants and guarded by three vicious dogs—a Doberman pinscher, a German shepherd, and a Weimaraner.

"Sonsabitches would let you enter," the columnist said, "but God help anyone who tried to leave without the Senator's permission."

"What happened to the mistress?"

"Damn if I know," the columnist said. "But I understand that one night she got the dogs to turn on Sunraider, and he got rid of the whole shooting gallery. He was jealous as hell of that woman."

Then came the hair-raising and eye-stretching story that cast the Senator as villain in the destruction of a highly skilled diplomat's career. For rea-

sons of his own—about which the gossipmonger relating it was unclear—
Sunraider was said to have persuaded a pious Pullman porter to accuse the
diplomat of having approached him, the porter, with some odd deviationary
sexual proposition while returning in his Pullman car via San Francisco
from Casablanca. The porter, said to be an extraordinarily homely black
man, was described as a high deacon of his church, a Shriner, a Prince Hall
Mason, an Elk of the I.B.P.O.E. species, an Alpha Phi Alpha, a lifetime member in good standing of the United Sons of Georgia—all highly respected
Negro fraternal organizations. Thus, with these charges coming from such
quarters, the diplomat's goose was cooked. The executive branch simply
could not withstand the anticipated outcry.

Which makes us once again aware that anyone can do just about anything
in this country—throw it off track, strip its gears—if only he knows where
to throw a fistful of mud or where to stand to speak out of turn. In this
democracy, of course, all things are possible. But why on earth should a Pullman porter, at that time privy by the very nature of his employment to all
manner of peccadilloes of the great, be allowed to affect the destiny of a
diplomat? Even so, I don't believe that the Senator could be that malicious or
irresponsible. And besides, the official records show that the diplomat in
question left the service simply because he wished to retire. Objectively, the
dwindling of his family fortune, one of the official reasons given, not to mention the increasing complexity of the world situation, what with so many of
the old orders changing, was reason enough for his voluntary departure.

We had begun to sweat now, both from the press of bodies and the frenzy
of gossip. It had become a lying contest. When, I wondered, would the security people be done and allow us to go and seek out the facts behind the
shooting? I wanted to consult a policeman, but there was no space in which
to move, and I wanted especially to move now that a rumor was being repeated which I consider of such unique nastiness that I was distressed to hear
it again. It has to do with an incident in which the Senator is said to have
gone to an ultra-extreme of unconventional conduct, and although it distressed me and I deliberately refused to listen, the details came alive in my
mind with the vividness of a disturbing dream.

Besides the Senator, two other people were involved, a highly respected
Justice of the Supreme Court (now deceased) and a young man of twenty or
so, all of whom moved like phantoms through my mind.

The scene was an elevator in a government building, and I could see it all
with startling clarity: the small automatic metal cage, garlanded with abstract laurel wreaths of antiqued bronze, with the Senator the first to enter,
wearing a superbly tailored suit and broad-brimmed planter's panama. He
presses the button for the lobby. It moves, drops a floor, stops. The distinguished old Justice steps slowly in, lost in some profound judicial abstraction, his eyes looking straight through the Senator. The car falls, stops again.

The young man enters with noncommittal countenance; then, looking up, he recognizes—doubtlessly with delight—the two important figures of Congress and Court. He moves uneasily aside, his eyes alight; it's as though he has encountered two kings at a crossroad. The car moves again, seeming now to glide on frictionless air.

The young man steals a glance at his fellow-passengers. There's a clean smell of oil, metal, topped by a whiff of wintergreen. The Justice stands stiffly, he's lost in thought, his eyes pale behind his glasses.

The Senator smiles.

The young man looks swiftly from face to face, and then away. The great men stand remote. He feels an obvious glow—perhaps like that which a toddler who has just reached the delightful, goose-stepping stage of walking displays when he struts about swinging his little arms in the familiar manner which a highly emphatic friend of mine calls "feeling good in his growing shoes"—he's delighted heel and toe, head and sole. Great vistas of possibility spring wide before him. Bodiless voices whisper down encouragement from the clouds, the laurel leaves. He stands in a deep, dark gorge, looking up at two distant mountain peaks, one shining white in the sun, the other brooding blue in the icy shadow. Strands of patriotic music murmur in his ears. And before his inner eyes a marvelous eagle plummets screaming into the gorge to brush his face with the tips of wide, majestic wings; then up and away it swiftly climbs to cleave the high rare air. His heart pounds, he trembles, for he has been caressed by history and mystery. And then the elevator seems to do a barrel roll!

He sees the Senator, still smiling, leaning forward as though to greet the Justice—then *zzzzzzspat!* and his heart and mind would deny the evidence of his own dear eyes. But there it is, the lenses of the old jurist's pince-nez are flooded blind, the eyes obscured! And now the boy's ears ache of anguished decibels unboomed, of shrieks unshrieked. His shoes inflate, his trousers sag, he's in a spin, and a stench of doom has shrunk the intimate air. And through it all not a word is spoken. Floors flash past, flickering breathlessly as in a dream. His mind reels backwards in desperate reversal of the scene, but he can't cast out his ravaged eye. The Senator looms, still smiling in calm unrufflement. And yet there, too, the startled Justice, the man of lofty vision also stands, dripping as with two suddenly acquired cataracts!

The car revolves, the air expires, the young man's mind is now a snarl of strings, a ruptured kite in turbulent air, a rampaging stagecoach with the driver shot dead from the seat and there the random-flying, slapping of the reins in nerveless hands and the shotgun rider dead drunk back in Deadwood; a stampede of walleyed stallions; a panicked regiment in headlong flight dragging its tattered flag, stone-deaf to the rallying cry of shrilling bugles. His brain pops, swirls, becomes a pot of boiling spaghettini!

Now the elevator seems itself disinclined to plunge to its Chthonian

Nadir in such outrage. The boy's mind boils, but still the pause, the smile, the blotted eyes, both burning like a branding iron. He looks from giant to giant but still the frozen silence. He waits for the action to complete itself, for his head to clear, but only the dropping of the car.

It's awful. I ache even to think of it, and how they survived I'll never know. Doubtless the old jurist was saved from a stroke or heart attack only by his intense dedicated concentration on the law. As for the Senator, I would have imagined that the mere impulse toward such an act would have brought on general paralysis. Even now the very idea leaves my mouth a desert. In other words, I'm left quite spitless. So that here, let's face it, I'm one with the young man. For both the Senator and the Justice were men of enormous capacity. They lived with fire and with ice, with sun and with lightning, with huge worlds of power, guilt, and aspiration. No wonder that the terrible impact of the gratuitous insult was sustained not by them, but by the young man, that eager innocent caught unaware between titans.

The rumor holds that the boy was simply unhinged. He was running even before the elevator reached the lobby, running frenziedly in that tight place, and hammering the unyielding doors with his fists. And when the doors slid open upon the stately, high gold-leafed and becolumned lobby, he plunged through the crowd assembled there to ascend, knocking them about like ninepins, as he dashed for the street, jabbering like a madman.

One man, annoyed by being so rudely pushed about, rushed out after the boy and saw him start into the stream of passing cars, screaming now, then whirling suddenly as though aware of the danger and running back onto the sidewalk, where he bumped into a blind man who happened, as fate would have it, to be tapping his way along. This seemed to enrage, to further unhinge the boy—those sightless eyes, that halting, three-legged locomotion—because, seizing the blind man's lapels, he pushed him away at arm's length, staring for a moment into that bewildered face, the two leaning there, poised in silent interrogation, the blind man with one foot upraised. And it was as though something in the man's unseeing eyes threw the boy into a higher pitch of madness.

Suddenly he screamed, "No, No, NO!" in a rising pitch of despair and cryptic denial. Whereupon he released the man, turned, and started off— only to whirl back and, running forward, seize the man's white cane and struck him repeatedly, beating him to the walk, and when the blind man tried to escape on all fours, he was knocked flat and stomped upon. It was a swift, outrageous, savagely unrestrained assault, which ended only when three men leaped from a passing car, tackled the youth, and held him until the police arrived.

It was just too shocking, and all the more so because this boy was no hoodlum. He was from a good family and far above the average in intellect and ambition. He is said to have won several highly coveted scholarships and prizes and, when only ten, was the undefeated winner of a nationwide contest in which a series of especially difficult puzzles designed by a group of metaphysicists were presented for solution. And yet, these accomplishments notwithstanding, he would have killed a blind man, no doubt about it. Now the youth is vegetating in an institution and of no aid whatsoever in reconstructing exactly what happened in the elevator. His hair fell out long ago, and now he sits for hours staring blankly at the ceiling, where he managed somehow to draw one blankly staring eye.

Compounding the mystery, the police were said to have located Senator Sunraider at his office shortly after the disturbance, but he was cold sober and denied any knowledge of the incident. As for the Justice, clothed in the austere dignity of his high office and regarding any direct linkage between the Court and politicians distasteful as a matter of principle, he refused to discuss the matter. So the incident, which haunts my mind with threatening significance, has retained its dream-like mystery. What awful terrors rage in the young man's shattered mind? What chaos actually erupted there? What deep depths of forbearance lie within the Justice's dark ceremonial robes? What secret tensions boil beneath that crusty dignity? And who, as I say, knows the Senator? One thing only is certain: Truth is extremely difficult to come by, here in the Capitol.

When I allowed myself to listen again, Morris Moskowitz, a book reviewer, was explaining that it was later determined that, while unquestionably brilliant, the young man had had a long history of personality instability, and that a week before the incident, on a night of the full moon, his mother had been startled into wakefulness by a presence in her bedroom and, springing up in terror, had found him standing beside her bed, weeping, in a state of stark nakedness.

"Gentlemen," Moskowitz said, "I don't know what happened on that elevator, but if I know my Freud at all, this indicates beyond question that there was a screw loose there somewhere!"

"Maybe the young fellow simply couldn't stand being in a tight place with such powerful men," Sweeney said. "Maybe he was suffering from claustrophobia."

"It's possible," Moskowitz said. "But we don't want to overlook the powerful side effects which such accidental encounters can have. They can be pretty mysterious, pretty fateful. For instance, I recall hearing that years ago the late J. P. Morgan saw a woman bearing a babe in arms during the opening of an exhibition at the Metropolitan Museum and was moved to present her, right there on the spot, with a life membership for the child. But what happens? Before the child was old enough to make use of the membership he went stone-blind! I tell you, these things are mysterious! Fate gets into the act, various obscure lines of causation come together. Private destinies brew public awe!"

"Yes," the fat man said. "But now since you've mentioned accidents and mysteries, how about those other crazy things that the Senator has done? Like the thing at the National Gallery?"

And this led to one of the wildest rumors of all.

The occasion was all white tie and evening gown, all high style in a setting of great, transcendent art. With the ladies beautiful in their silks and satins, their diamonds and pearls, their mink and sable, with countless tiaras sparkling away like the stars. A scene of culture and power, an elegant scene of elegance; with the gentlemen handsome in their tails, their sashes, their beribboned medals, their diverse emblems of rank and status. It was, in a sense, a gathering of eagles and cooing doves. The rumor goes that, in such an august setting, mind you, the Senator noticed the courtly and quite prickly chairman of an important senatorial committee (a tiny old man and a Southerner, by the way), doddering past, his shirtfront gleaming. His wife, a famous Charleston belle still quite beautiful despite the frost of age, leaned gracefully on his arm, while in his free left hand he held a glass of bourbon. It was then, it was said, that the Senator broke off a conversation with the curator of a famous Boston museum and a certain political commentator and, moving abruptly forward as in a trance, seized this very severe, irascible old man—this living symbol of a gracious and formal way of life—and spilled his bourbon as he pinned his arms to his sides in a kind of genial bear hug, then, raising him up like some outraged puppet, some demented Punch, clear off the floor, began whirling him so swiftly that their coattails were set flying, creating a whirling totem pole.

Talk of consternation—but wait! While this was going on, the Senator is said to have shouted, with that marvelous vocal projection for which he's famous, these outrageously provocative words:

"Now that he's communed with great art, it's time to swing my little nigger!"

One can imagine the effect of this in the mere telling. The gathering gasped, the old man went apoplectic, his wife turns deathly pale. A waiter drops a tray of champagne glasses; the protocol officer of a foreign embassy, entering the room just as the whirling stops, stands with his eyes popped and his mouth agape, pointing frantically to the scene—as though everyone else in the room has had his head stuck in the pages of the *Philadelphia Bulletin*!

Finally, the wife broke the spell by stammering, "Unhand my husband, you beast! Unhand him now, I say! Put him down this very instant!"

To which the Senator answers quite gaily, "Of course, ma'am, yo'ah lawd and mahster and mah little jigaboo!"

Then, as the gathering watches, he slowly lowers the old man to the floor, saying, "Come on down now, J.P. Come on down off your cross," laughing in the friendliest manner. Then, taking the hand of the outraged wife, he kisses it three times quite gravely, and turning swiftly on his heel moves away and out. All of this very quickly, and his face was described as "suddenly mask-like and grave, his eyes bright with a quick welling of tears."

"Now what the hell did he mean?" a reporter said. "What kind of a connection was he making between *art* and communication?"

And now, shifting about and sweating, they discussed the Senator's man-handling of the old gentleman and his use of the naughty, naughty epithet, and how our attitude toward personal insult and matters of honor had changed. Years ago, it was said, the old man would have sought out the Senator with a set of dueling pistols, a bowie knife, a Colt Navy Special, a commemorative shillelagh—and have done with him. He would have caned the Senator, "thrashed" him. But then they went into the fact that the great repercussion that had been expected to take place in the Senate the following day failed to come off. For this some blamed the telephone, others the District's gossips and servants, through whose eager, swift, and countless retellings the cruelty of the act became quickly submerged and the malicious comedy implicit in the scene accentuated.

It had soon become obvious that although the Senator refused to explain his action there was no real danger of retaliation against him in the situation. Because for all the high respect in which he was held, there was something quite pompous about the older man. His flinty and most bigoted principles, sharpened by his wit, had over the years drawn too much blood and had too long defied change and historical and political realities. During his endless tenure he made countless enemies by frustrating the ambitions of many of his colleagues, businessmen, minority groups, and labor leaders indiscriminately. So that far from being censured for his cruel act, the Senator emerged as something of an underground hero, a dragon slayer, a holy fool manqué.

But as always, there was a sinister undertone throbbing beneath the Senator's maneuver. Far from giving way to impulse, one of the men insisted, the Senator had acted with careful calculation; he'd stacked the deck. A few years ago, it was said, he had provided, quietly and without publicity and from his own pocket, a dozen generous scholarships for graduate students in American history. They were required to do nothing in return, simply to follow their own researches. However, it was gotten across to them that the Senator would be most pleased that if in the course of their work they would look into the court records of several cities of the old South and jot down any information concerning the blood relationship between the old families and their slaves and between contemporary members of these families and the descendants of the slaves who share their esteemed names.

Our informant went on to say that the result of these researches was quite startling, even though he could not name anyone who had seen the actual documents. Nor is there knowledge that the Senator has ever discussed the material. Indeed, the scholars themselves have denied that it exists. Nevertheless, all who were said to have received the Senator's assistance are now tenured members of the faculties of important Southern universities. Perhaps the information doesn't exist. Perhaps they became innocently involved in a situation which many people find threatening, but there is no question but that the very rumor that such information exists, carefully arranged and codified by certified scholars, and in the hands of the Senator, makes some bloodstreams approach the freezing point. Nor is it unthinkable, as the gossip insists, that upon hearing of its existence, a number of people left for parts unknown. And whatever the truth of the rumor, there has been, without doubt, an aura of impending revelation emanating from the Senator. It was as though he walked over in a suit of blackmail which not only rendered him invulnerable to would-be attackers, but intimidated their ability to act by threatening to turn some secret but forgotten weakness against them. Very few have been willing to take such chances.

CHAPTER 4

AROUND ME NOW A thousand questions were echoing through the hall, each concerning some contradiction of character, some trope, some scandal, some audacious Sunraider caper.

"Did you know? Did you see? Did you hear?"

They swirled about my head like a swarm of flies.

Why? Why? But why?

And it came to me that only yesterday I had overheard a most innocuous question which, although addressed to another, resulted in my witnessing not only one of the oddest incidents involving the Senator, but one of the few from which he could be said to have emerged less than triumphant.

It had been a fine spring day made even pleasanter by the lingering of the cherry blossoms, and I had gone out before dawn with some married friends and their children on a bird-watching expedition. Afterwards we had sharpened our appetites for brunch with rounds of Bloody Marys and bullshots. And after the beef boullion ran out our host, an ingenious man, had improvised a drink from chicken broth and vodka which he proclaimed the "chicken-shot." This was all very pleasant, and after a few drinks my spirits were soaring. I was pleased with my friends, the brunch was excellent and varied—chili, cornbread, and oysters Rockefeller, etc.—and I was pleased with my tally of birds. I had seen a bluebird, five rose-breasted grosbeaks, three painted buntings, seven goldfinches, and a rousing consort of mockingbirds. In fact, I had hated to leave.

Thus, it was well into the afternoon when I found myself walking past the Senator's estate. I still had my binoculars around my neck, and my tape recorder—which I had along to record birdsongs—was slung over my shoulder. As I approached, the boulevard below the Senator's estate was heavy with cars, with promenading lovers, dogs on leash, old men on canes, and laughing children, all enjoying the fine weather. I had paused to notice how the Senator's lawn rises from the street level with a gradual and imperceptible elevation that makes the mansion, set far at the top, seem to float like a dream castle; an illusion intensified by the chicken-shots, but which the art editor of my paper informs me is the result of a trick copied from the landscape architects who designed the gardens of the Belvedere Palace in Vienna. I was about to pass on when a young couple blocked my path, and when I saw the young fellow point up the hill and say to his young blonde of a girl, "I bet you don't know who that is up there," I brought my binoculars into play, and there, on the right-hand terrace of the mansion, I saw the Senator.

Dressed in a chef's cap, apron, and huge asbestos gloves, he was armed with a long-tined fork which he flourished broadly as he entertained the notables for whom he was preparing a barbecue. These gentlemen and ladies were lounging in their chairs or standing about in groups sipping the tall iced drinks which two white-jacketed Filipino boys were serving. The Senator was dividing his attention between the spareribs, cooking in a large chrome grill cart, and displaying his great talent for mimicking his colleagues with such huge success that the party was totally unaware of what was swiftly approaching. Nor, in fact, was I.

I was about to pass on when a gleaming white Cadillac convertible, which had been moving slowly in the heavy traffic from the east, rolled abreast of me and suddenly blocked the path by climbing the curb, then rolling across the walk and onto the Senator's lawn. The top was back and the driver, smiling as though in a parade, was a well-dressed Negro man of about thirty-five, who sported the gleaming hair affected by their jazz musicians and prizefighters, and who sat behind the wheel with that engrossed yet relaxed, almost ceremonial attention to form that was once to be observed only among the finest horsemen. So closely did the car brush past that I could have reached out with no effort and touched the rich leather upholstery. A bull fiddle rested in the back and I watched the man drive smoothly up the lawn until he was some seventy-five yards below the mansion, where he braked the machine and stepped out to stand waving toward the terrace, a gallant salutation grandly given.

At first, in my innocence, I placed the man as a musician, for there was, after all, the bull fiddle; then in swift succession I thought him a chauffeur for one of the guests, a driver for a news or fashion magazine or an advertising agency or television network. For I quickly realized that a musician wouldn't have been asked to perform at the spot where the car was stopped, and that since he was alone, it was unlikely that anyone, not even the Senator, would have hired a musician to play serenades on a bull fiddle. So next I decided that the man had either been sent with equipment to be used in covering the festivities taking place on the terrace, or that he had driven the car over to be photographed against the luxurious background. The waving I interpreted as the expression of simpleminded high spirits aroused by the driver's pleasure in piloting such a luxurious automobile, the simple exuberance of a Negro allowed a role in what he considered an important public spectacle. A small crowd had gathered, which watched bemusedly.

Since it was widely known that the Senator is a master of the new political technology, who ignores no medium and wastes no opportunity for keeping his image ever in the public's eye, I wasn't disturbed when I saw the driver walk to the trunk and begin to remove several red objects and place them on the grass. I wasn't using my binoculars now, and thought these were small equipment cases. Unfortunately, I was mistaken.

For now, having finished unpacking, the driver stepped back behind the wheel and suddenly I could see the top rising from its place of concealment to soar into place like the wing of some great, slow, graceful bird. Stepping out again, he picked up one of the cases—now suddenly transformed into the type of can which during the war was something used to transport high-octane gasoline in Liberty ships (a highly dangerous cargo for those round bottoms and the men who sailed them) and, leaning carefully forward, began emptying its contents upon the shining chariot.

And thus, I thought, *is gilded an eight-valved, three-hundred-and-fifty-horse-powered lily!*

For so accustomed have we Americans become to the tricks, the shenanigans and frauds of advertising, so adjusted to the contrived fantasies of commerce—indeed, to pseudo-events of all kinds—that I thought that the car was being drenched with a special liquid which would make it more alluring for a series of commercial photographs.

Indeed, I looked up the crowded boulevard behind me, listening for the horn of a second car or station wagon which would bring the familiar load of pretty models, harassed editors, nervous wardrobe mistresses, and elegant fashion photographers who would convert the car, the clothes, and the Senator's elegant home into a photographic rite of spring.

And with the driver there to remind me, I even expected a few ragged colored street urchins to be brought along to form a poignant but realistic contrast to the luxurious costumes and high-fashion surroundings: an echo of the somber iconography in which the crucified Christ is flanked by a repentant and an unrepentant thief, or the three Wise Eastern Kings bearing their rich gifts before the humble stable of Bethlehem.

But now reality was moving too fast for the completion of this fantasy. Using my binoculars for a closer view, I could see the driver take a small spherical object from the trunk of the car, and a fuzzy tennis ball popped into focus against the dark smoothness of his fingers. This was joined by a long wooden object which he held like a conductor's baton and began forcing against the ball until it was pierced. This gave the ball a slender handle which he tested delicately for balance, drenched with liquid, and placed carefully behind the left fin of the car.

Reaching into the backseat now, he came up with a bass-fiddle bow upon which he accidentally spilled the liquid, and I could see drops of fluid roping from the horsehairs and falling with an iridescent spray into the sunlight. Facing us now, he proceeded to tighten the horsehairs, working methodically, very slowly, with his head gleaming in the sunlight and beads of sweat standing over his brow.

As I watched, I became aware of the swift gathering of a crowd around me, people asking puzzled questions, and a certain tension, as during the start of a concert, was building. And I had just thought, *And now he'll bring out the fiddle,* when he opened the door and hauled it out, carrying it, with the dripping bow swinging from his right hand, up the hill some thirty feet above the car, and placed it lovingly on the grass. A gentle wind started to blow now, and I swept my glasses past his gleaming head to the mansion, and as I screwed the focus to infinity, I could see several figures spring suddenly from the shadows on the shaded and shrub-lined terrace of the mansion's far wing. They were looking on like the spectators of a minor disturbance at a dull baseball game, then a large woman grasped that something was out of order and I could see her mouth come open and her eyes blaze as she called out soundlessly, "Hey, you down there!" Then the driver's head cut into the field of vision and I took down the glasses and watched him moving, broad-shouldered and jaunty, up the hill to where he'd left the fiddle. For a moment he stood with his head back, his white jacket taut across his shoulders, looking toward the terrace. He waved then, and shouted something which escaped me, then, facing the machine, he took something from his pocket, and I saw him touch the flame of a cigarette lighter to the tennis ball and begin blowing gently upon it, then, waving it about like a child twirling a Fourth of July sparkler, he watched it sputter into a blue ball of flame.

I tried to anticipate what was coming next but simply couldn't accept it. The Negro was twirling the ball on that long, black-tipped wooden needle—the kind used to knit heavy sweaters—holding it between his thumb and fingers in the manner of a fire-eater at a circus, and I couldn't have been more surprised if he had thrown back his head and plunged the flame down his throat than by what came next. Through the glasses now I could see sweat beading out beneath his scalp line and on the flesh above the stiff hairs of his moustache as he grinned broadly and took up the fiddle bow, and before I could move he had shot his improvised, flame-tipped arrow into the cloth top of the convertible.

"That black son of the devil!" someone shouted, and I had the impression of a wall of heat springing up from the grass before me. Then the flames erupted with a stunning blue roar that sent the spectators scattering. People were shouting now, and through the blue flames before me I could see the Senator and his guests running from the terrace to halt at the top of the lawn, looking down, while behind me there were screams, the grinding of brakes, the thunder of footfalls as the promenaders broke in a great spontaneous wave up the grassy slope, then, sensing the danger of exploding gasoline, receding hurriedly to a safer distance below, their screams and curses ringing above the roar of the flames.

How, oh, how I wished for a cinema camera to synchronize with my recorder!—which I brought automatically into play as heavy fumes of alcohol and gasoline, those defining spirits of our age, filled the air. There before me unfolding in *tableau vivant* was surely the most unexpected picture of the year: in the foreground at the bottom of the slope, a rough semicircle of outraged faces; in the midforeground, up the gentle rise of the lawn, the white convertible shooting into the springtime air a radiance of intense blue flame, like that of a welder's torch or a huge fowl being flambéed in choice cognac; then on the rise above, distorted by heat and flame, the dark-skinned, white-suited driver: standing with his gleaming face expressive of high excitement as he watched the effect of his deed. Then, rising high in the background atop the grassy hill, the white-capped Senator surrounded by his notable guests—all caught in postures eloquent of surprise, shock, and indignation.

The air was filled with an overpowering smell of wood alcohol, which, as the leaping red and blue flames took firm hold, mingled with the odor of burning paint, and leather. I became aware of the fact that the screaming had suddenly faded now, and I could hear the swoosh-pop-crackle and hiss of the fire. And with the gaily dressed crowd having become silent, it was as though I were alone, isolated, observing a conflagration produced by a stroke of lightning flashed out of a clear springtime sky. We watched with that sense of awe similar to that which medieval crowds must have observed during the burning of a great cathedral. We were stunned by the sacrificial act, and indeed, it was as though we had become the unwilling participants in a primitive ceremony requiring the sacrifice of a beautiful object in appeasement of some terrifying and long-dormant spirit, which the black man in the white suit was summoning from a long, black sleep. And as we watched, our faces strained as though in anticipation of the spirit's materialization from the fiery metamorphosis of the white machine, a spirit which I was afraid, whatever the form in which it appeared, would be powerfully good or powerfully evil and absolutely out of place here and now in Washington; it was uncanny. The whole afternoon seemed to float, and when I looked again to the top of the hill the people there appeared to move in slow motion through watery waves of heat. Then I saw the Senator, with chef cap awry, raising his asbestos gloves above his head and beginning to shout. And it was then that the driver, the firebrand, went into action.

'Til now, looking like the chief celebrant of an outlandish rite, he had

held firmly to his middle ground; too dangerously near the flaming convertible for anyone not protected by asbestos suiting to risk laying hands upon
him, yet far enough away to highlight his human vulnerability to fire. But
now as I watched him move to the left of the flames to a point allowing him
an uncluttered view of the crowd, his white suit reflecting the flames, he was
briefly obscured by a sudden swirl of smoke, and it was during this brief interval that I heard the voice.

Strong and hoarse and typically Negro in quality, it seemed to issue with
eerie clarity from the fire itself. Then I was struggling within myself for
the reporter's dedicated objectivity and holding my microphone forward as
he raised both arms above his head, his long, limber fingers widespread as he
waved toward us.

"Ladies and gentlemen," he said, "please don't be disturbed! I don't mean
you any harm, and if you'll just stay quiet a minute I'll tell you what this is
all about. . . ."

He paused and the Senator's voice could be heard angrily in the background.

"Never mind him up there on top of the hill," the driver said. "You can listen to him when I get through. He's had too much free speech anyway. Now
it's *my* turn."

And at this a man at the other end of the crowd shouted angrily and tried
to break up the hill. He was grabbed by two men, and a hysterical, dark-
haired woman wearing a well-filled chemise-style dress slipped to the
ground holding a leg, shouting, "No, Fleetwood, no! That crazy nigger will
kill you!"

The arsonist watched with blank-faced calm as the man was dragged
protesting back into the crowd. Then a shift in the breeze whipped smoke
down upon us and gave rise to a flurry of coughing.

"Now believe me," the arsonist continued, "I know that it's very, very
hard for you folks to look at what I'm doing and not be disturbed, because for
you it's a crime and a sin."

He laughed, swinging his fiddle bow in a shining arch as the crowd
watched him fixedly.

"That's because you know that most folks can't afford to own one of these
Caddies. Not even good, hardworking folks, no matter what the pictures in
the papers say. So deep down it makes you feel some larceny. You feel that
it's unfair that everybody who's willing to work hard can't have one for himself. That's right! And you feel that in order to get one it's okay for a man to
lie and cheat and steal—yeah, even swindle his own mother *if* she's got the
cash. That's the difference between what you *say* you believe and the way
you *act* if you get the chance. Oh, yes, because words is words, but life is hard
and earnest, and these here Caddies is way, way out of this world!"

Pausing, he loosened the knot in his blue-and-white tie so that it hung down the front of his jacket in a large loop, then wiped his brow with a blue silk handkerchief.

"I don't mean to insult you," he said, bending toward us now, the fiddle bow resting across his knee, "I'm just reminding you of the facts. Because I can see in your eyes that it's going to cost me more to get *rid* of this Caddie the way I have to do it than it cost me to get it. I don't rightly know what the price will be, but I know that when you people get scaird and shook up, you get violent. —No, wait a minute." He shook his head. "That's not how I meant to say it. I'm sorry. I apologize.

"Listen, here it is: This *morning*," he shouted now, stabbing his bow toward the mansion with angry emphasis. "This morning that fellow Senator *Sunraider* up there started it when he shot off his mouth over the *radio*. That's what this is all about! I realized that things had gotten out of *control*. I realized all of a sudden that the man was *messing*...with...my *Cadillac,* and that's serious as all *hell*....

"Listen to me, y'all: A little while ago I was romping past *Richmond*, feeling fine. I had played myself three hundred and seventy-five dollars and thirty-three cents' worth of gigs down in Chattanooga, and I was headed home to *Harlem* as straight as I could go. I wasn't bothering any*body*. I didn't even mean to stop by here, because this town has a way of making a man feel like he's living in a fool's *paradise*. When I'm *here*, I never stop thinking about the difference between what it *is* and what it's *supposed* to be. In fact, I have the feeling that somebody put the *Indian* sign on this town a long, long time ago, and I don't want to be around when it takes effect. So, like I say, I wasn't even thinking about this town. I was rolling past Richmond and those white-walls were slapping those concrete slabs and I was rolling and the wind was feeling fine on my face—and that's when I made my sad mistake. Ladies and gentlemen, I turned on the radio. I had nothing against anybody. I was just hoping to hear some Dinah, or Duke, or Hawk so that I could study their phrasing and improve my style and enjoy myself. —But what do I get? I'll tell you what I got—"

He dropped his shoulders with a sudden violent twist, and his index finger jabbed toward the terrace behind him, bellowing, "I GOT THAT NO GOOD, NOWHERE SENATOR SUNRAIDER! THAT'S WHAT I GOT! AND WHAT WAS HE DOING? HE WAS TRYING TO GET THE UNITED STATES GOVERNMENT TO MESS WITH MY CADILLAC! AND WHAT'S MORE, HE WAS CALLING MY CADDY A 'COON CAGE'!

"Ladies and gentlemen, I couldn't believe my *ears*. I don't know that Senator, and I know he doesn't know me from old *Bodiddily*. But just the same, there he is, talking straight to me, and there was no use of my trying to dodge. Because I do live in Harlem and I lo-mo-sho drive a Cadillac. So I had to sit there and take it like a little man. There he was, a United States SENATOR, coming through my own radio telling me what I ought to be driving, and recommending to the United States Senate and the whole country that the name of my car be changed simply because *I*, me, LeeWillie Minifees, was driving it!

"It made me feel faint. It upset my mind like a midnight telegram!

"I said to myself, 'LeeWillie, what on earth is this man *talking* about? Here you been thinking you had it *made*. You been thinking you were as free as a bird—even though a black bird. That good-rolling Jersey Turnpike is up ahead to get you home. —And now here comes this Senator putting you in a cage! What in the world is going on?

"I got so nervous that all at once my foot weighed ninety-nine pounds, and before I knew it I was doing *seventy-five*. I was breaking the law! I guess I was really trying to get away from that voice and what the man had said. But I was rolling and I was listening. I couldn't *help* myself. What I was hearing was going against my whole heart and soul, but I was listening *anyway*. And what I heard was beginning to make me see things in a new light. Yes, and that new light was making my eyeballs ache. And all the time Senator Sunraider up in the Senate was calling my car a 'coon cage.'

"So I looked around and I saw all that fine red leather there. I looked at the steel and at the chrome. I looked through the windshield and saw the road unfolding and the houses and the trees was flashing by. I looked up at the top, and I touched the button and let it go back to see if that awful feeling would leave me. But it wouldn't leave. The *air* was hitting my face and the *sun* was on my head and I was feeling that good old familiar feeling of *flying*—but ladies and gentlemen, it was no longer the same! Oh, no; because I could still hear that Senator playing the *dozens* with my Cadillac!

"And just then, ladies and gentlemen, I found myself rolling toward an old man who reminded me of my granddaddy by the way he was walking beside the highway behind a plow hitched to an old, white-muzzled Missouri mule. And when that old man looked up and saw me, he waved. And I looked back through the mirror as I shot past him, and I could see him open his mouth and say something like, 'Go on, fool!' Then him and that mule was gone even from the mirror, and I was rolling on.

"And then, ladies and gentlemen, in a twinkling of an eye it struck me. A voice said to me, *'LeeWillie, that old man is right: You are a fool. And that doggone Senator Sunraider is right; LeeWillie, you are a fool in a coon cage!'*

"I tell you, ladies and gentlemen, that old man and his mule both were talking to me. I said, *'What do you mean about his being right?'* And they said, *'LeeWillie, look who he is,'* and I said, *'I know who he is,'* and they said, *'Well, LeeWillie, if a man like that, in the position he's in, can think the way he does, then LeeWillie, you have GOT to be wrong!'*

"So I said, '*Thinking like that is why you've still got that mule in your lap.*' I said, '*I worked* hard *to get the money to buy this Caddie*,' and he said, '*Money? LeeWillie, can't you see that it ain't no longer a matter of money? Can't you see it's done gone way past the question of money? Now it's a question of whether you can afford it in terms other than money.*'

"And I said, '*Man, what are you talking about, "terms other than money"?*' and he said, '*LeeWillie, even this damn mule knows that if a man like that feels the way he's talking and can say it right out over the radio and the TV, and from the place where he's saying it—there's got to be something drastically wrong with you for even wanting one. Son, the man's done made it mean something different. All you wanted was to have a pretty automobile, but, fool, he done changed the Rules on you!*'

"So against myself, ladies and gentlemen, I was forced to *agree* with the old man and the mule. That Senator up there wasn't simply degrading my Caddy. That wasn't the *point*. It's that he would low-rate a thing so truly fine as a *Cadillac* just in order to degrade *me* and my *people*. He was accusing *me* of lowering the value of the auto, when all I ever wanted was the very best!

"Oh, it hurt me to the quick, and right then and there I had me a rolling revelation. The *scales* dropped from my eyes. I had been BLIND, but the Senator up there on that hill was making me SEE. He was making me see some things I didn't *want* to see! I'd thought I was dressed real FINE, but I was as naked as a jaybird sitting on a limb in the drifting snow. I THOUGHT I was rolling past *Richmond*, but I was really trapped in a COON cage, running on one of those little TREADMILLS like a SQUIRREL or a HAMSTER. So now my EYEBALLS were aching. My head was in such a whirl that I shot the car up to ninety, and all I could see up ahead was the road getting NARROW. It was getting as narrow as the eye of a NEEDLE, and that needle looked like the Washington MONUMENT lying down. Yes, and I was trying to thread that Caddy straight through that eye, and I didn't care if I made it or not. But while I managed to get that Caddy through, I just couldn't thread that COON CAGE because it was like a two-ton knot tied in a piece of fine silk thread. The sweat was pouring off me now, ladies and gentlemen, and my brain was on fire, so I pulled off the highway and asked myself some questions, and I got myself some answers. It went this way:

" 'LeeWillie, who put you in this cage?'

" 'You put yourself in there,' the answer came.

" 'But I paid for it, it's mine. I own it…,' I said.

" 'Oh, no, LeeWillie,' the answer came, 'what you mean is that it owns *you*, that's why you're *in* the cage. *Admit* it, daddy; you have been NAMED. Senator Sunraider has put the badmouth, the NASTY mouth, on you, and now your Cadillac ain't no Caddy anymore! Let's face it, LeeWillie; from now on, every time you sit behind this wheel you're going to feel those RINGS shooting round and round your TAIL and one of those little COON'S masks is going to settle down over your FACE, and folks standing on the streets and hanging out the windows will sing out, "HEY! THERE GOES MISTER COON IN HIS COON CAGE!" That's right, LeeWillie! And the little husky-voiced colored CHILDREN playing in the gutters will point at you and say, "THERE GOES MISTAH GOON AND HIS GOON GAGE"— and that will be right in Harlem!'

"And that did it, ladies and gentlemen; that was the capper, and THAT'S why I'm here!

"Right then and there, beside the *highway,* I made my decision. I rolled that Caddy; I made a U-turn, and I stopped only long enough to get me some of that good white wood *alcohol* and good *white* gasoline, and then I headed straight here. So while some of you are upset, you can see that you don't have to be afraid, because LeeWillie means nobody any harm.

"I am here, ladies and gentlemen, to make the Senator a present. Yes, and it's Sunday and I'm told that *confession* is good for the *soul.* So Mister Senator," he said, turning toward the terrace above, "this is my public testimony of my coming over to your way of thinking. This is my surrender of the Coon Cage Eight! You have unconverted me from the convertible. In fact, I'm giving it to you, Senator Sunraider, and it is truly mine to give. I hope all my people will do likewise. Because after your speech they ought to run whenever they even *look* at one of these. They ought to make for the bomb shelters whenever one comes close to the curb. So I, LeeWillie Minifees, am setting an example and here it is. You can HAVE it. I don't WANT it. Thank you KINDLY and MUCH obliged...."

At this point I saw a great burst of flame which sent the crowd scurrying backwards down the hill, and the white-suited firebrand went into an ecstatic chant, waving his violin bow, shaking his gleaming head and stamping his alligator-shod foot:

"Listen to me, Senator: I don't want no JET! (stamp!) But thank you kindly.

"I don't want no FORD! (stamp!)

"Neither do I want a RAMBLER! (stamp!)

"I don't want no NINETY-EIGHT! (stamp!)

"Ditto the THUNDERBIRD! (stamp-stamp!)

"Yes, and keep those CHEVYS and CHRYSLERS away from me—do you (stamp!) *hear* me, Senator?

"YOU HAVE TAKEN THE BEST," he boomed, "SO, DAMMIT, TAKE ALL THE REST! Take ALL the rest!

"In fact, now I don't want anything you think is too good for me and my people. Because, just as that old man and the mule said, if a man in your position is against our having them, then there must be something WRONG in our wanting them. So to keep you happy, I, me, LeeWillie Minifees, am prepared to WALK. I'm ordering me some clubfooted, pigeon-toed SPACE SHOES. I'd rather crawl or FLY. I'd rather save my money and wait until the

A-RABS make a car. The Zulus even. Even the ESKIMOS! Oh, I'll walk and wait. I'll grab me a GREYHOUND or a FREIGHT! So you can have my coon cage, fare thee well!

"Take the TAIL FINS and the WHITEWALLS. Help yourself to the poor raped RADIO. ENJOY the automatic dimmer and the power brakes. ROLL, Mister Senator, with the fluid DRIVE. Breathe that air-conditioned AIR. There's never been a Caddy like this one, and I want you to HAVE IT. Take my scientific dreamboat and enjoy GRACIOUS LIVING! The key's in the ignition, and the REGISTRATION'S in the GLOVE compartment! And thank you KINDLY for freeing me from the coon cage. Because before I'd be in a CAGE, I'll be buried in my GRAVE— Oh! Oh!"

He broke off, listening; and I became aware of the shrilling of approaching sirens. Then he was addressing the crowd again.

"I knew," he called down with a grin, "that THOSE would be coming soon. Because they ALWAYS come when you don't NEED them. Therefore, I only hope that the Senator will beat it on down here and accept his gift before they arrive. And in the meantime, I want ALL you ladies and gentlemen to join LeeWillie in singing 'God Bless America' so that all this won't be in vain.

"I want you to understand that that was a damned GOOD Caddy and I loved her DEARLY. That's why you don't have to worry about me. I'm doing fine. Everything is copacetic. Because, remember, nothing makes a man feel better than giving AWAY something, than SACRIFICING something that he dearly LOVES!"

And he threw back his head and actually sang a few bars before the noise of the short-circuited horn set the flaming car to wailing like some great prehistoric animal heard in the throes of its dying.

Behind him now, high on the terrace, the Senator and his guests were shouting, but on the arsonist sang, and the effect on the crowd was maddening. Perhaps because from the pleasurable anticipation of watching the beginning of a clever advertising stunt, they had been thrown into a panic by the deliberate burning, the bizarre immolation of the automobile. And now with a dawning of awareness they perceived that they had been forced to witness (and who could turn away?) a crude and most portentous gesture.

So now they broke past me to dash up the hill in moblike fury, and it was most fortunate for Minifees that his duet with the expiring Cadillac was interrupted by members of the police and fire departments, who, arriving at this moment, threw a flying wedge between the flaming machine and the mob. Through the noisy action I could see him there, looming prominently in his white suit, a mocking smile flickering on his sweaty face, as the action whirled toward where he imperturbably stood his ground, still singing against the doleful wailing of the car.

He was still singing, his wrists coolly extended now, in anticipation of handcuffs—when struck by a veritable football squad of asbestos-garbed policemen and swept, tumbling in a wild tangle of arms and legs, down the slope to where I stood. I noted then that he wore expensive black alligator shoes.

And now, while the crowd roared its approval, I watched as LeeWillie Minifees was pinned down, lashed into a straitjacket, and led toward a police car. Up the hill two policemen were running laboredly for where the Senator stood, silently observing. About me there was much shouting and shoving as some of the crowd attempted to follow the trussed-up and still-grinning arsonist but were beaten back by the police.

It was unbelievably wild. Some continued to shout threats in their outrage and frustration, while others, both men and women, filled the air with a strangely brokenhearted and forlorn sound of weeping, and the officers found it difficult to disperse them. In fact, they continued to mill angrily about even as firemen in asbestos suits broke through, dragging hoses from a roaring pumper truck and spraying the flaming car with a foamy chemical, which left it looking like the offspring of some strange animal brought so traumatically and precipitantly to life that it wailed and sputtered in protest, both against the circumstance of its debut into the world and the foaming presence of its still-clinging afterbirth....

And what had triggered it? How had the Senator sparked this weird conflagration? Why, with a joke! The day before, while demanding larger appropriations for certain scientific research projects that would be of great benefit to our electronic and communication industries, and of great benefit to the nation, the Senator had aroused the opposition of a liberal Senator from New York who had complained, in passing, of what he termed the extreme vapidness of our recent automobile designs, their lack of adequate safety devices and of the slackness of our quality-control standards and procedures. Well, it was in defending the automobile industry that the remark was passed which triggered LeeWillie Minifees' reply.

In his rebuttal—the committee session was televised, and aired over radio networks—the Senator insisted that not only were our cars the best in the world, the most beautiful and efficiently designed, but that, in fact, his opponent's remarks were a gratuitous slander. Because, he asserted, the only ground which he could see for complaint lay in the circumstance that a certain make of luxury automobile had become so outrageously popular in the nation's Harlems—the archetype of which is included in his opponent's district—that he found it embarrassing to own one. And then with a face most serious in its composure he went on to state:

"We have reached a sad state of affairs, gentlemen, for this fine product of American skill and initiative has become so common in Harlem that much of its initial value has been sorely compromised. Indeed, I am led to suggest, and quite seriously, that legislation be drawn up to rename it the 'Coon Cage Eight.' And not at all because of its eight superefficient cylinders, nor because of the lean, springing strength and beauty of its general outlines. Not at all, but because it has now become such a common sight to see eight or more of our darker brethren crowded together enjoying its power, its beauty, its neopagan comfort, while weaving recklessly through the streets of our great cities and along our superhighways. In fact, gentlemen, I was run off the road, forced into a ditch by such a power-drunk group just the other day. It is enough to make a citizen feel alienated from his own times, from the abiding values and recent developments within his own beloved nation.

"And yet, we continue to hear complaints to the effect that these constituents of our worthy colleague are ill-housed, ill-clothed, ill-equipped, and under-tread! But, gentlemen, I say to you in all sincerity: Look into the streets! Look at the statistics for automobile sales! And I don't mean the economy cars, but our most expensive luxury machines. Look and see who is purchasing them! Give your attention to who is creating a scarcity and removing these machines from the reach of those for whom they were intended! With so many of these good things, what, pray, do these people desire—is it a jet plane on every Harlem rooftop?"

Now, for Senator Sunraider this had been mild and far short of his usual maliciousness. And while it aroused some slight amusement and brought replies of false indignation from some of his opponents, it was edited out when the speech appeared in the *Congressional Record* and the press. But who could have predicted that he would have brought on LeeWillie Minifees' wild gesture? Perhaps he had been putting on an act, creating a happening, as they say, though I doubted it. There was something more personal behind it. Without question, the Senator's remarks were in extremely bad taste, but to cap the joke by burning an expensive car seemed so extreme a reply as to be almost metaphysical.

And yet, I reminded myself, it might simply be a case of overreacting expressed in true Negro abandon, an extreme gesture springing from the frustration of having no adequate means of replying, or making himself heard above the majestic roar of a senator. There was of course the recent incident involving a man suffering from an impacted wisdom tooth who had been so maddened by the blaring of a moisture-shorted automobile horn, which had blasted his sleep about three o'clock of an icy morning, that he ran into the street clothed only in an old-fashioned nightshirt and blasted the hood of the offending automobile with both barrels of a .12-gauge over-and-under shotgun.

But while toothaches often lead to such extreme acts—and once in a while even to suicide—LeeWillie Minifees had apparently been in no pain—or at least not in *physical* pain. Certainly his speech had been projected clearly enough (allowing for the necessity to shout), and he had been smiling when they led him away. What would be his fate, I wondered; and where had they taken him? I would have to find him and question him, for there in the jammed hallway his action began to sound in my mind with disturbing overtones which last night had hardly been meaningful. Rather they had been like the brief interruption one sometimes hears while listening to an FM broadcast of the musical *Oklahoma!,* say, with original cast, when the signal fades and a program of quite different mood from a different wavelength breaks through. It had happened, but then a blast of laughter had restored us automatically to our chosen frequency.

CHAPTER 5

THAT EVENING I HAD joined a group of reporters for our weekly gathering at the club, where it is our custom to eat and drink and chat. Often we exchange information and discuss aspects of the news which, for one reason or another, is considered untimely or unfit to print. Here we enjoy our private jokes at the expense of some public figure or some incident which in our stories we find expedient to treat with formal seriousness and propriety. From the moment of gathering, our mood had been gay, for we were delighted that at last one of the Senator's victims had succeeded in answering him, even at such outrageous expense. Looking back, it is possible that each of us felt a slight uneasiness beneath our banter; if so, the wild bravura character of LeeWillie Minifees' response allowed us to ignore it. Nor was there reason to dwell upon our inner doubts, not there in the quietly lit room with its spark of silver and crystal, its tinkle of iced glasses, its buzz of friendly talk. It was a familiar setting for a comfortable ritual occasion, and even Sam, our inscrutable but familiar Negro waiter, was an unobtrusive part of it. Now I don't by any means imply that the club is a *great* place, but it is, nevertheless, a good place; and its food and drink are excellent, its atmosphere relaxing, and it provides a welcome hideaway from the stresses and strains of the profession.

It was this release, this feeling of relaxation which we sought in our gatherings, and if there was something working deep within each of us, some nagging unease, the direction of the conversation diverted our attention. Sam's dark hands had just swept up the empty glasses of our first round of drinks and replaced them when Virgil Wiggins, the economics expert, introduced the incident which determined the drift of talk.

"What," he said, "do you think of the new style of conspicuous consumption?"

And there it was, right out in the open, wearing a comic mask. We laughed explosively, LeeWillie Minifees' car sprang aflame in our imaginations, and I could see him vividly, orating on the startled Senator's hillside.

"It was a doozy," Thompson said, "a first-class doozy!"

"No," I said, "not a Duesenberg, a Caddy, a Cadillac."

"Of course," Thompson said. "You mean the car, I'm referring to this act—*that* was a doozy!"

"Well, whatever the brand, he burned it with malice and forethought!"

"Where on earth did that fellow come from?" Wiggins said.

"Hell, from Chattanooga," Stiles Larkin said. "He rose like a wave of heat from the Jeff Davis Highway. McIntyre was there and heard him admit it."

"Actually he was from Harlem," I said. "He'd been working in Chattanooga."

"I would have given a week's salary to have seen it," Wiggins said. "When I heard about it I thought, 'Thorstein Veblen, sir, today your theory has been demonstrated to the tenth power!'"

"And in horsepower. . . ."

We laughed.

"How the hell did Veblen get into it?"

"Veblen? Why, he was in it all the time," Wiggins said.

"You mean that colored fellow had been reading *Veblen?*"

"Oh, no, man," Wiggins said. "I mean that at bottom Veblen was an ironist, a humorist among the economists. The essence of his concept of 'conspicuous consumption' is comic."

"That fellow played hell with classical economic theory. Maybe the publisher should have that black boy illustrate Veblen's books."

Larkin swirled his glass. "Did you ever hear of anything like it," he said, "a man burning his own automobile before an audience?"

"No," Thompson said, "but during the twenties and thirties there were those rich Oklahoma Indians who traveled around in hook-and-ladder fire trucks and in brand-new red custom-built hearses."

"You're right," Wiggins said. "That is a near precedent but not quite. This fellow went far beyond the Indians. Because while one could say that the Indians did such things because they were outside our culture, or from a different culture, this colored fellow was born to our own values and knew exactly what he was doing. —Or else he was mad. He had to be."

Wiggins shook his head. "Just leave it to Sunraider; if there's something outrageous to be ignited in people, he's the man to do it."

"It took more than the Senator to set that fellow off," Thompson said. "All Sunraider did was to tip his balance."

"Well, it'll be interesting to see what that car-burning will bring out of the insurance people," Larkin said.

"They'll be wild," McGowan said, looking at us each in turn. "They'll be ass-kicking wild!"

"They won't be as wild as the Senator is."

"He's wild all right," Wiggins said, "but can you blame him? That boy tried to tie a knot in his tail."

I could see McGowan's eyes light up. "Yeah, gentlemen, like we say down South, ole Senator Sunraider is as hot as Little Sister—and as you know, there ain't a thing anybody can do about that!"

I shook my head, "No, I wouldn't be too sure about that. The Senator's a strange one, and I wouldn't be surprised if he isn't sitting in his study right this minute laughing his head off. Do you forget what he did at the National Gallery that time? He's such a professional at provoking people that nothing appears to get to his emotions."

"True," Wiggins said. "He's something of an actor, but I suspect that this got to him. You said yourself that he was shaking his fist and raving while the car was burning."

"That colored fellow really had the capper," Thompson said. "He turned that joke by an angle of one hundred and eighty degrees."

"He switched it all right," Larkin said, "but in a hell of a masochistic way. Can you imagine the frame of mind a man has to be in to commit such an extreme act?"

"The act speaks for itself," I said, "but what it says is as confusing as hell to me, and I was there when it happened. The car was burning, and that takes a bit of doing, and yet and still he *was* laughing and going on while he harangued us."

"The point that interests me," Wilson said, "is that a fellow like that was willing to pay for it. People like that don't come by Cadillacs so easily. He probably decided to do anything he could think of to get back at the Senator, and this was the damndest way he could find to do it. Reminds me of the one last year who tried to hold up a bank with a zip gun. When they caught him his teeth were chattering, his eyes were rolling in his black face, and his knees were knocking, and all he could say was, 'White folks, please don't shoot! Please don't shoot!' Bastard almost got away with fifty thousand dollars!"

"Hell," Larkin said, "if I'd done all that with a zip gun, I would have been scared too—not for taking the money, you understand, but for having the nerve to attempt it with something like that."

"I hadn't thought about it that way," Wilson said. "You're right, too. It reminds me of the two out in California who robbed a bank which had signs all over it stating that it was protected by motion-picture cameras. They had cased the bank for days and carried off the robbery like clockwork and got away for three weeks. Then one of them happened to recognize his own picture in a magazine, and when he had a friend read it for him he got so disgusted that he turned himself in. Pleaded guilty and told the judge that he belonged in jail so he'd have time to learn how to read!"

"I read it, I read it," Larkin said. "He said he was too ignorant to be robbing banks."

"He wasn't too ignorant to rob a bank," Wilson said, "he was just too ignorant not to leave his calling card. But when I consider such exploits, I'd be a bit worried if *I* were the Senator."

"What do you mean?" I said.

"That someone else might call his joke in a more personal fashion. In fact, I'm surprised that he hasn't provoked someone long before now."

Then, as the barely formed thought took shape in my mind, Wilson looked up, frowning.

"Say," he asked, "have we ever had a colored assassin?"

I looked at him, my mouth agape. It was as though the words had leaped from my mind to his, or his to mine. Across the room, past his shoulder, I could see Sam, our waiter, standing against the blue wall with folded arms. Several pitchers of iced water and a large white bowl piled high with iced squares of butter stood on the low serving table beside him as he looked down the long sweep of the room to where a girl, whose red hair flowed to the shoulders of her white suit in gorgeous waves, was moving through the door. Then I heard Thompson asking indignantly, "Do you mean in the *United States?*"

"That's right. Have we?"

"Now, why on earth would you think of *that?*"

"It just struck me," Wilson said, "after this car-burning thing, maybe it's time we started thinking of such possibilities."

"Gentlemen, what Wilson means," McGowan said, "is that a nigra who'd burn a Cadillac would do just about anything. Ain't that right, Wilson? A nigra like that'll burn good United States money!"

We laughed. McGowan could be quite amusing on the Negroes and was constantly sounding off over affronts, real or imagined, which he felt that Negroes in the District committed against his idea of a well-ordered society. My problem with him was that I had difficulty in determining when he was serious and when simply joking. For him, colored people were either objects for amused contempt or the greatest danger to the nation. Now I could feel him working up to one of his endless tirades on the nature and foibles of the Negro, and I was relieved that Sam the waiter was far across the room.

"Now that was quite a nigra," McGowan said, "but, gentlemen, y'all don't have to go into any brainstorm in order to analyze what that nigra was doing, because I'm here to tell you. What that nigra was doing was simply running amok! His brain snapped! And far as he was concerned he was back up a tree throwing coconuts!"

Across the table Wilson was frowning, looking like a man remembering a bad dream. McGowan's humor hadn't fired me either, although the others were laughing.

"But I'm serious," Wilson said. "Can anyone think of one?"

"I'm thinking about it," Larkin said. "Let's see, there was McKinley, Roosevelt—I mean Cermak—Huey Long...but none of the assassins were colored."

McGowan thumped down his glass. "A nigra *assassin,*" he said, "are y'all getting drunk already?"

"There might have been a few local killings with a political motive," Thompson said. "Here and there over the years some small-town politician might have been shot or knifed—like that fellow down in Louisiana who made the mistake of getting into a colored man's bed and allowed himself to get caught in the act. But you wouldn't call that *political;* that was sheer bad judgment. I'd have shot the bastard myself."

"I say," McGowan said, "are y'all getting drunk?"

"Come to think of it, though," Wiggins said, "how can you tell when those people are doing something politically significant? Until recently not enough of them voted in the South, and here in the North so few take roles in civic affairs or express themselves on matters beyond civil rights even within the major political parties, so how can you tell what they're up to? We just don't know enough about them. We don't have enough social forms through which we can see them. I'll have to do a think piece on this problem. We need to have a few more participating in our major institutions if for no other reason than to provide social perspectives through which we can keep in touch with what's happening among them—"

"Forms!" McGowan said. "*What forms?* Hell, we don't need any cotton-pickin' forms! Don't you Yankees recognize that everything the nigra *does* is political? Thompson, you amaze me, you really do; because you're Southern-born. Down South even the little-bitty children know *that* much about the nigra. Because unlike you Yankees, there are three things we Southerners are brought up knowing all about, and that's history, politics, and nigras. And especially do we know about the political significance of the nigra!"

"Oh, drop it, Mac," Wiggins said. "I'm being serious."

"No, suh, I beg to differ," McGowan said. "I'm being serious; you're being Yankee frivolous. Now I'm going to tell you one more time: *Almost everything the nigra does is political!*"

"Literally everything?"

"I mean everything, starting with things you Yankees would pass off as insignificant. Will you give me a few minutes?"

"Give you?" Thompson said. "Hell, you can't talk without making a filibuster. So go on, get it over with."

McGowan rested his forearms on the table, gripping a dead cigar between his caged fingers, his head to one side.

"Listen," he said, clearing his throat, "if you catch a nigra in the wrong section of town after dark, he's being political, and that's basic because he knows he's out of his place. If he brushes against a white person on the street or on a stairway, *that's* political. Because, you have to understand, every once in a while the nigras get together and organize these bumping campaigns. They'll try to knock you off the sidewalk and break your ribs, and then they'll beg your pardon, pretending it was an accident. But down South we know it's nigra politics. So you want to watch the nigra's face, because that way you can catch his mood and intention.

"If a nigra rolls his eyes and pokes out his mouth at you, that's not only politics, but downright subversion. If he puts on airs, watch him! If he talks about moving up North, he's being political again. Because we know for a fact that the nigras are moving up North in keeping with a long-range plan to seize control of the American Government. So watch his conduct. If he talks too loud on the street or talks about sending his kids north to college, or if he buys a tractor—all this is of political significance. Be especially wary of the nigra who tries to buy himself a bulldozer, because that is one of the most dangerous political acts of all. A nigra like that is out to knock down Southern tradition and bury it lock, stock, barrel, and gatepost! He's worse than a whole herd of carpetbaggers or seven lean years of boll weevils— Waiter," he called, "bring us another drink!" And then to us, "There's absolutely nothing to dry a man out like trying to educate a bunch of Yankees."

I watched Sam the waiter approach, with uneasiness, fearing that McGowan would offend him. After all, during the thirties I had learned to regard the sensibilities of his people and to avoid all anti-minority stereotypes and clichés. One simply didn't laugh at victims of minority persecution. But if Sam was aware of our conversation, he revealed nothing in his face.

"H'ya Sam," McGowan said.

"Fine, Mr. McGowan, sir," Sam said. Then he silently filled our glasses, smiled remotely and, as silently, slipped away. Then McGowan went on.

"Let me tell y'all something else. If you catch a nigra buying his food and clothing from the wrong dealer—or worse, if he goes to another town to trade, that's nigra politics *pretending* to be nigra economics. That's something for you to think about, Wiggins. And if a nigra owns more than one shotgun, rifle, or pistol, it's political. If he forgets to say 'sir' to a white man or tries to talk Yankee talk, if he drives too doggone fast or too doggone slow, or if he comes up with one of these little bug-eyed foreign cars—all these things are political, and don't y'all forget it!"

McGowan paused, drank, and looked around the table.

"Come on, educate us some more," Thompson said. "Then we can talk seriously."

McGowan's eyes twinkled. "I'd be glad to," he said. "If a nigra buys his woman a washing machine—watch him, he's dangerous! And if he gets her a clothes dryer and a dishwasher—put that nigra under the jail, he's trying to undercut our American way of life. Y'all can smile all you want, but things like that are most political. And in point of fact, there are few things in this world as political as a black nigra woman owning her own washing machine! Now don't laugh. You Yankees must remember that the Industrial Revolution was *revolutionary*, because if y'all don't know it, the nigra does, and he never stops scheming to make it more so. So verily, verily I say unto you Yankees: Watch the nigra who owns more than one TV set because he's getting too ambitious and too well-informed, and that's bound to *end up* being political.

"Because if you let the nigra see Indians killing white folks week after week—which is another Yankee mistake—he's apt to go bad, and the next thing you know he's learning about Nehru, Nasser, and the Mau Maus, and that's politically unwise. It doesn't matter that the Indians are always defeated, because the nigra feels that *he* can win. After all, nigras are *Southerners* too. That's something else you Yankees had better remember, nigras are *Southern* too!

"And I'll tell you something else: If his woman or his gal chillen come up wearing blond wigs, or if they dye their kinky nigra hair red, they're being defiantly political. On the other hand, if they stop straightening their hair in the old Southern darky tradition and start wearing it short and natural like those African nigras—right there you have a bunch of homegrown nigras who are on the way to being hopelessly contaminated. Those nigras are sweating and breathing politics—call Edgar Hoover!

"Watch the papers the nigra reads, especially if you see him subscribing to *The Wall Street Journal* or *The New York Times*. Watch him closely if he gets interested in the stock market. Such a nigra is power-hungry, and the next thing you know he'll want to vote and run for public office—"

"There," Wiggins said, "that's what really worries you, isn't it?"

McGowan shook his head.

"I wouldn't say that. Although I'll admit that between a nigra making big money and getting the vote, money is the lesser evil. A nigra millionaire, once you can stomach the idea, is a pretty safe nigra. Because if there's anything to the old saying that there's nothing more timid than a million bucks, then a million nigra bucks is bound to be ten times as afraid. So don't worry about the nigra millionaire; he's just a nigra with more money than he knows what to do with. Y'all ever heard of one endowing?"

"I'm glad to learn that there's at least *something* about the Negro which isn't political," Thompson said.

"There is, but not too much," McGowan said. "Because the nigra is a *political* animal. He came out of Africa that way. He makes politics as naturally as a dirt dauber makes mud houses or a beaver builds dams. Watch his environment. If you see his woman putting pictures other than snapshots up on the wall, regard her with suspicion; she's likely to break out in a rash of politics.

"If a nigra joins the Book-of-the-Month Club or the Great Books Program, investigate him, because when nigras get hold of such deals they become more political than *Das Kapital* and the Communist Manifesto put together. Now, there was a time when the Bible was considered the only book that a nigra should be allowed to read, but now I'll be damned if he hasn't made even the Good Book political. So I counsel you to watch your educated nigra.

"If he reads Bill Shakespeare, that's all right, because no nigra who ever *lived* would know how to apply the Bard—not even that big stupid buck nigra, Othello; who was so dumb that when his poor, dear, sweet little wife, Desdemona, dropped her Kotex in the wrong place and he heard about it, right away he thinks in his ignorant nigra fashion that she's been allowing somebody to tamper with her, and he lets that nasty Italian bastard, what's-his-name—Iago, that's him—confuse him and agitate him into taking her poor, sweet life. Poor little ole thing. No sir, no nigra born has ever been up to dealing with Bill Shakespeare: but if you catch you a nigra reading that low-down, traitorous, nigra-loving Bill Faulkner and *liking* him, there you have a politically dangerous integrationist nigra!"

"Why do you specify *liking* him?"

"Because a proper nigra is supposed to get scared as hell when he sees that kind of treachery going on.

"And now let's look into another area. You want to watch what the nigra eats, because it has been established that some diets are political while others are not. And it's a proven fact that the moment the nigra changes his diet he gets dissatisfied and restless. So watch what he eats. Fat meat, corn bread, lima beans, ham hocks, chitterlings, watermelon, black-eyed peas, molasses, collard greens, buttermilk and clabber, neckbones and red beans and rice, hominy—both grit and lye hominy—these are traditional foods and healthy for the nigra and are *usually* not political—"

"You left out chicken," Larkin said.

"Chicken?" McGowan said. "That there is a good question. Chicken is also traditional and harmless in the political sense—unless, of course, a wrongheaded, political nigra is caught stealing one. And even so, there's really nothing *political* about a nigra stealing a chicken. In fact, down South we agree that a nigra is *supposed* to steal him a chicken ever now and then, and the only *crime* involved is in his getting himself caught.

"But"—McGowan held up his hand then and allowed it to slap the table POW!—"*lobster* is out!"

Wiggins sputtered over his drink. "Oh, Lord," he said. "Oh, Lord, protect us. Give me some black coffee!"

"Gentlemen, I tell you truly, lobster on a nigra's table is political as hell! Lobster gives a nigra false courage. It puts rocks in his nigra jaws and wild ideas in his nigra brain. In short, lobster—any *kind* of lobster—whether broiled, boiled, fried, fra diavoloed, or thermidored—serve it any damn way you please—lobster simply messes up a nigra! If the price of lobster ever goes down in this country, we'll have trouble on our hands.

"And watch the rascal if he develops a taste for T-bone steak, Cornish hens, sweetbreads, calf's liver (although pig liver is traditional and okay), parsnips, artichokes, venison, or quiche lorraine—he's been under bad influences and getting political again.

"And it's a good idea to watch what he does with traditional foods. For instance, if he starts *baking* his pig's feet in cheesecloth instead of boiling them in the Southern nigra fashion—right there you have a bad nigra on your hands.

"And don't overlook the political implications of a nigra eating too much Chinese or Japanese or Jewish food. Call the FBI if you catch him buying French wines, German beer, or drinks like Aquavit or Pernod. In New Orleans one time a nigra drank a glass of Pernod and went down to the courthouse and cussed out the judge in pure Parisian French! Nigras who drink such liqueurs have jumped the reservation and are out to ruin the nation.

"And Scotch whiskey is just as bad. Just as bad...." He shook his head grimly. "A nigra doesn't even have to have heard about Bonny Prince Charlie, but let him start drinking Scotch and right away he swears he's George Washington's great-grandson and the rightful head of the United States Government. And not only that, a nigra who switches to Scotch after being brought up on good corn and bourbon is putting on airs, has forgotten his place, and is in implicit rebellion! Besides, have y'all ever considered what would happen to our liquor industry if all the nigras switched to drinking Scotch? A calamity!"

I watched him bend forward, his eyes intense.

"Now I want to get on to other matters, but before I do, let me say that one of the meanest, low-downest forms of nigra politics I know of, and one which I don't like to bring up among a bunch of gentlemen, and that's when a sneaking, ornery, smart-alecky nigra stands up in a crowd of peaceful, well-meaning white folks who've gathered together in a public place to see justice done and that nigra ups and breaks wind! Wait a minute now! Wait one minute. This ain't funny a'tall! I was at a murder trial once, and just as the judge was charging the jury, some politically subversive nigra standing back in the rear let loose in there, and the next thing you know the judge has cleared the courtroom! Things are in an uproar, and the poor jury gets so confused that the case has to be thrown out, and the guilty nigra who was standing trial got away scot-free!

"It's sad, gentlemen, but it's true," McGowan said, shaking his head as we gasped for breath. "You simply have to be alert and vigilant against nigra politics at all times. For instance, when you find a nigra looking at those girlie magazines that display naked white womanhood—which is something else you Yankees are responsible for—or irresponsible for—*whip his head*! Because when you see a nigra boy looking at that type of magazine, he's long gone on the road of those Japs who broke the white man's power in Asia by ordering their soldiers to sleep with every white-trash whore gal—mostly European, understand—they could lay their yalla hands on. In the hands of a nigra boy all such photographs and cartoons become insidiously political."

"Oh, come now," someone said.

"You wonder why? Because they expose the white woman's mystery and undermine the white man's mastery, that's why. They show the buck nigra everything we've been working three hundred years to keep concealed. Because with the nigra even poontang is political. That's right! Those Renaissance fellows don't have a thing on the nigra except power! Think about it.

"Now Thompson, here, was talking about our not having any *forms* through which we can see what the nigra is up to politically, and I've been demonstrating that he's mistaken—but he's right to the extent that the nigra hasn't developed any forms of his own. He's just copied the white man and twisted what he's copied to fit the nigra taste. But he does have his own nigra church, and his own nigra religion, and the point I want to make is that he gets political according to his religion. Did y'all know that?"

"No," I said, "I never even dreamed it was possible."

"I know you didn't," McGowan said, "so I'd better tell you. Baptist nigras and Methodist nigras and Holy Roller nigras are okay. Even Seventh Day Adventist nigras are okay—even though they're a bit strange even to other nigras. I've heard them sound off about it. So all these nigra religions are okay. But you have got to watch the nigra who changes *from* Baptist *to* Episcopalian or Catholic, because that is a nigra who is gone ambitious and has turned his back on the South. That nigra's not searching for God; he's looking for a political scantling to head-whip you with.

"And watch the young nigra who joins up with Father Divine. It's not the same when up North a poor ole-fashioned nigra grows homesick for the South and joins up; the young one is out to undermine society and is probably staying up nights scheming and trying to get God on the nigra side. Same thing if a nigra becomes a Jew—who the hell ever heard of one of our *good* nigras joining up with the Jews? When a nigra does that, he's political, subversive, unruly, and probably oversexed—even for a nigra!

"Now, what are some of the political aspects of the nigra here in D.C.?

Well, around here things are so out of hand, mongrelized, and confused that I don't know where to begin, but here are a few manifestations: nigras visiting white folks, walking or riding along the streets with white women; visiting the Congress, hanging around Abe Lincoln's monument; visiting white churches; carrying picket signs; sending delegations to see the President; carrying briefcases with real papers in them; nigras wearing homburg hats and chesterfield overcoats; hiring uniformed chauffeurs, especially if the chauffeur is white—all these things are political because the nigra who does them is dying to be a diplomat so that he can get assigned abroad from where he aims to monkey with our sovereign states' rights. To these add those nigras from Georgia and Mississippi who turn up wearing those African robes and turbans in an effort to break into white society and get closer to white folks. Because there's nothing worse than a nigra who denies his country 'cause that is a nigra who not only denies his mammy and his pappy but the South as well!

"Here are some other nigra political forms, Thompson: These young buck nigras who go around wearing berets, beards, and tennis shoes in the wintertime and those britches that are so doggone tight they look like they're about to burst out of them—they're not the same as the white boys who dress that way; they're politically dangerous, and it's worse, in the long run, than letting a bunch of nigras run around the capital carrying loaded automatics. Somebody ought to pass a law against it right away.

"And be on watch for your quiet nigra. Be very careful of the nigra who is too quiet when other loudmouthed nigras—who are really safe nigras—are sassing white folks on the street corners and in the Yankee press and over the Yankee radio and TV. Never mind the loudmouthed nigras, they're like those little fice dogs that bark at you when you approach the big gate and then, when you come into the yard, they run to lick your hand—throw them a bone now and then. But keep your eye on the quiet nigra who watches every move the white man makes and studies it, because he's probably trying to think up a theory and some strategy and tactics to subvert something."

"But go back to the automobile," Wiggins said. "My father-in-law is a dealer, and I think he should be warned."

"I'm glad you reminded me," McGowan said. "Now I've told you about those little foreign cars, but there's more to the political significance of nigras and autos. Cadillacs used to be okay, but after the mess that nigra made today on Senator Sunraider's lawn, I'm not so sure. Gentlemen, that nigra was trying to *politicalize* the Cadillac—which proves again what I say about everything the nigra does being potentially political. But one thing I do know is, you have to watch the nigra who doesn't *want* a Cadillac, *he* can stand a *heap*—I say a *heap*—of political analysis. And pay close attention to the nigra who has the money to buy a Cadillac but who picks an Imperial instead. Likewise, the nigras who love those English and French cars. Also watch all nigras who pick Lincolns and brag about the nigra vote electing the President of the United States; these nigras are playing politics even though they might not be able to vote themselves. And watch the nigra who comes telling a white man about the nigras' 'gross yearly income' or the nigras' stake in the 'gross national product,' because there you have an arrogant, biggety nigra who is right up in your face talking open politics and thinks you don't know it. —Unless, of course, you're convinced that the nigra is really trying to tell you that he knows how you and him can make some money. In this case the nigra is just trying to make a little hustle for himself, so make a deal with him and don't worry about him because that nigra doesn't give a damn about anybody or anything except himself, while the other type is trying to intimidate you.

"Finally, but by no means the least important, there's the nigra who reads the Constitution and the law books and *broods* over them. And like unto him is the nigra who instead of scratching his head from time to time (which is the traditional Southern nigra manner when talking to a white man), *he* reaches back and scratches his *behind;* or else he scratches both his head *and* his behind at the same time and lets you see him doing it. Watch this type especially close because, gentlemen, even where the nigra *scratches* is political!

"But, gentlemen, after this very brief and inadequate catalog of nigra political deviousness, I must say once more that, to my knowledge, no nigra has ever even thought about assassinating anybody, because we bred that possibility out of him years ago!"

Even as I laughed I watched the conflicting expressions moving back and forth across McGowan's broad face. It looked as though he wanted desperately to grin, but his grin, like a postage stamp which had become too moist, kept sliding in and out of position. And I in turn became suddenly agitated. There was pain in my laughter, and it seemed to me that McGowan was obsessed by history to the point of nightmare. He had confined the dark man in a mental package which he carried with him as constantly as the old-fashioned watch which he wore on a chain, and I imagined him consulting the one for time and the other for social and historical orientation. *What time is it, ole watch? Hey, black man, what place, what year, what social milieu is this?* Or perhaps he even had the dark man confined in the watch itself....

But as I laughed I realized that I envied McGowan, and I admitted to myself, with a twinge of embarrassment, that many of the things he said were not only amusing but contained an element of truth: And perhaps that truth lay precisely in Negroes being the source of his exasperated humor. For McGowan said things openly about Negroes, and with absolute conviction, that I dared not even think lest I undo my delicate balance of tolerance, justice, and sense of fair play. And I wondered if it could be that he was actually more honest than I, that his open expression of his feelings, his prejudices, made him freer than I. And could it be, I wondered, that his freedom to say what he felt about all that Sam the waiter symbolized actually made him more honest than I. I was unsure of the answer, but suddenly I loathed his ability to make me feel buried fears and undesirable possibilities, his power to define so much of the social reality in which I lived and about which for a long time now I had ceased to think. And I asked myself if it were possible that the main object of McGowan's passion was really not such as Sam but really a notion of history; a notion concerning a nonexistent past rather than a living people.

"Yes, gentlemen," McGowan was saying, "the only way to protect yourself from the nigra is to master politics, and that you Yankees have never done because y'all have never really *studied* the nigra."

Across the room I had watched Sam, his hands behind his back, smiling as he chatted pleasantly with a white-haired old gentleman. Were there Negroes like McGowan? I wondered. And, if so, what would they say about the likes of me? How completely did I, a liberal, ex-radical Northerner, dominate Sam's sense of life, his idea of politics? Absolutely, or not at all? Was he, Sam, prevented by some social piety or psychological intimidation from confronting me in a humorous manner, as my habit of mind, formed during the radical thirties, prevented me from confronting him? Or did he, as some of my friends suspected, regard all whites through the streaming eyes and aching muscles of one continuous, though imperceptible and inaudible, belly laugh? *What the hell,* I wondered, *is Sam's last name?*

All this, imagine, while laughing with the others, but now I was growing more and more disturbed as such ideas flickered through my mind. I realized that McGowan was playing an important social and political role for me, and I didn't like it. Out of his own needs he simultaneously described the Negro as a threat and then disarmed him with comedy; projected him as boogeyman-clown and presented him as an ever-present danger, in the presentation clothed him in a straitjacket of humor which made it possible for me to approach him more closely than I had done in more years than I was willing to think about.

Deep down, I suspected that I despised McGowan. I despised his freedom to make me feel buried motives and memories. I despised his taking over the power to define so much of the reality in which I lived. And most of all I despised him for making me realize that he in his very injustice was quite possibly more *just* than I, and that hurt because I regarded my sense of justice with a tender feeling of pride. Across from me Wilson was looking at McGowan with a tight face.

"Well," he said, "Sunraider had better make allowance for unexpected mutations. Otherwise, he might be surprised by more serious, more *political*

political incidents than today's. Some black boy without a car to burn might go after him more directly."

I was excited by the idea. "Wilson might have something there," I said. "And I'll even bet that we can come pretty close to describing the type most likely to do it. . . ."

"Do what?"

"Assassinate the Senator."

"Hell, you're nuts," Larkin said. "Negroes don't have the stomach for that kind of thing."

"You agree with McGowan, then?"

"No, when I listen to Mac I don't know whether to laugh or to be afraid of Negroes, but they just don't . . ."

"Go ahead, McIntyre," Wiggins said. "Let's see what you come up with; project the bastard!"

And I tried desperately to rise to the occasion, to keep up with McGowan, though on a different level.

"He'll probably be," I said, "a disgruntled, half-crazed ex-serviceman who will have won some decoration for bravery and who returned home full of great expectations. He'll have expected the world to have changed simply because he faced death for the nation. . . ."

"You mean a sorehead," Larkin said.

"If you will," I said. "Perhaps he'll have saved the life of his commanding officer, who, let us say, was a Southerner. . . ."

"*Our* nigras are loyal," McGowan said. "You Yankees have never been able to change that."

"Go on," Wilson said.

"Maybe he'll have been an athlete," Thompson said, "a basketball player, or a football scatback. . . ."

"Why not?" I said. "It's a good possibility."

"Like hell it is," McGowan said. "Nigras like that have it made. They make a lot of money—more than the average white man—and they get special treatment. Too *much* special treatment. You think one of them is going to mess up, you don't know nigras."

"But I specified that he'd be crazed, psychotic even. He'd have to be of the psychological type which turns its hostilities inward and represses them."

"He's still too much of an abstraction for me," Wiggins said. "Spell him out a bit."

"Well, he won't be a woman chaser," I said, "nor a drunk. Neither will he be the type who ordinarily expresses himself through violence—which would be an effective way of blowing off steam. Instead, he'll be the introspective type whose repressed emotions would slowly transform him into a walking bomb."

"Now you're talking about these Northern nigras," McGowan said, "the kind who've been too close to white folks in a social way. Nigras like that get awful restless."

"You mean too close to white women, don't you, Mac?" Thompson said.

"You can kid all you like," McGowan said, "but down South we know the political implications of such things, and we simply don't let it happen without the most drastic consequences."

"Perhaps," I said, "but that would be a problem for the man I'm describing, because he'd be too bitter and introspective."

"You mean too damn sullen and sulky," McGowan said. "Only your dream nigra has nothing to do with real live nigras because they never get introspective like you're saying. By the way, what kind of nigra are you trying to describe?"

"A rebel against authority out of frustration," I said. "Violence will be eating at his nerves and at his muscles. And given his experience with danger and death, his need to do violence to someone of importance will be a *physical* as well as psychological need."

"That kind of negra never existed," McGowan said. "Why not attack a cop?"

"That would be meaningless to him," I said. "It would have to be someone of national stature. This fellow will be on edge to destroy some figure of stature, someone whose importance is commensurate with his own capacity for anger. He'll select someone to attack through whom he can express his profound sense of humiliation...."

"Just listen to the man," McGowan said. "He's heading straight for cloud ninety-nine. McIntyre, this is nonsense. Let me tell you something about nigras. There's no such nigra as you're trying to describe. When a nigra gets all filled up, he grabs himself a woman, or he gets drunk and sleeps it off, or he goes after another nigra with a razor, a rusty pistol, or a half a brick. Nigras are outrageous brick fighters, by the way, and not bad with an iron top on the end of a broomstick. But checks and balances, man. You have to remember the good old American system of balances because they work on the nigra too. And when they don't, you have to step in and check him and balance him yourself."

"But what about the fellow who burned his Cadillac?" Wilson said. "He was going after Sunraider in a strange way, but he was going after him just the same."

McGowan laughed and shook his head. "I guess you got me there. That was a *new* kind of political nigra. That kind of nigra would steal a Barnum and Bailey elephant and ride it down through Mississippi just to prove he's voting Republican back up North."

"Quit kidding, and let's keep to McIntyre's idea for a moment," Wilson said. "Weren't those fellows who took a shot at Harry Truman Negroes?"

"No, sir, they were not," McGowan said. "Those nigras weren't real nigras. Those were Puerto Ricans—by which I mean nigras who don't know they're nigras."

"I recall that their leader was deranged, remember?" Larkin said.

"Look," I said, "I'm willing to bet. I'm not enough of a psychologist to describe him, but I'll lay a bet that he'll materialize."

"Are you serious?"

"To the extent of fifty dollars: Is that serious enough?"

"I'll take that," McGowan said. "Anybody else want to give away some money?"

"What on earth is happening?" Wiggins said. "We started out talking about that crazy fellow who burned his car and the next thing I know we're discussing an attempt made on the life of one of our most colorful Senators. That boy has spooked everybody. —Sam"—he beckoned—"bring us another round of drinks. Make them doubles; this is becoming a bloody congress of bloody sociologists!"

"Never mind knocking sociology," I said. "Make a bet and you can reduce it to mathematics, simple mathematics."

"Wiggins is right," McGowan said. "The nigras have taken hold of sociology and politicalized the hell out of it, and you Yankees are out to ruin the best country in the world."

"You mean you prefer your own brand of sociology to McIntyre's," Larkin said.

"Hell," McGowan said, "I ain't no sociologist, I just know nigras."

"McIntyre's not going to start something like this and get away with it so easily," Wilson said. "I'm betting fifty dollars. Sunraider needs shooting, but I'm betting no one will do it. Especially not a Negro. He'll be around as long as Uncle Joe Cannon...."

Suddenly, back in the jam of the crowded hall, I felt the pressure around me ease. The men near the entrance had begun to move, and word was passed swiftly along that we were at last being allowed to leave. There was a rush forward, and as I passed the entrance to the chamber I could see the gunman's body still lying where he had crushed out his life, covered by a sheet now, but the guards would neither allow me to enter nor give any information as to his identity, and I joined a group of reporters who were rushing to the hospital, seeking news of the Senator and to verify McGowan's news of old Hickman. I intended to interview Hickman, but at the hospital, despite the antiseptic change of scene, things continued to unfold outrageously.

CHAPTER 6

SENATOR SUNRAIDER WAS STILL in surgery, but we found old Hickman on the seventh floor. He sat in a dimly lit section of the corridor, grasping the arms of a white metal chair that had been placed to the left of the door leading to the room assigned to the Senator, his huge body showing in silhouetted profile against the brightness flooding from the turn in the corridor some fifty yards beyond. Two security men were facing him, bending slightly forward with folded arms, their bemused faces illuminated by a fixture located on the wall behind his head. They were listening to Hickman as we hurried along the corridor.

"...No, like I tell you, they had nothing to do with it," Hickman said. "They were just there looking on like the rest of the visitors, and they should be allowed to go free and unharmed."

He was not pleading but speaking matter-of-factly, looking up gravely at the security men as we came up and jockeyed for places before him.

"So why'd they attack the guards?" one of the security men said.

"They didn't," Hickman said. "Like I told you, they were trying to protect me...."

"Protect you from what, from whom?"

Hickman sighed. "You have to understand that we're from down South, and in all that excitement, when they saw those pistols flashing around, they naturally thought they were meant for me. In their minds they were back down in Georgia, and so, figuring that the tallest tree usually draws the lightning, they were trying to save me."

The security men looked at one another and smiled.

"That's pretty much a military reaction for a group of church people, isn't it?" one of them said.

Hickman frowned. "Military? Well, there's a lot of military action in the Bible, remember; but, like I say, they were simply trying to protect their minister."

"Well," the security man said, "they might have gotten you shot—not to mention themselves. You were lucky. But at any rate, we have nothing to do with releasing anyone. And if it weren't for Senator Sunraider, you'd be in jail with the rest. Frankly, though, I wouldn't release you even if I could."

"I can understand that," Hickman said. "Of course you wouldn't. That's why I'm asking you to please get me Deacon Wilhite. Just let me have a few words with him."

"Who is this Will Hiate?"

"He's my deacon," Hickman said, "my second in command. . . ."

"There goes that military terminology again," one of the security men said.

"I hear it," the other said.

Hickman looked at him quizzically. "Mister," he said, "what's your religion?"

"Catholic."

"Mine too," the other said.

"Then you ought to have heard church folks talk this way before, with Saint Ignatius and all those other soldiers of the Lord."

The security man frowned. "It's not the same thing," he said.

"You're right," Hickman said. "We're Protestants."

"This isn't getting us anywhere," the other security man said. "Revern, just what do you wish to speak to this Will Hiate about?"

"About my people you're holding," Hickman said. "They're old folks who have to be looked after. You can understand that. Most of them haven't even been north before."

"And what do you want the deacon to do?"

"Look," Hickman said, "can't you let me speak with him? You can listen to every word I say."

"I'm afraid we can't," the security man said. "We have to follow orders."

Hickman slapped the arms of his chair. "Then get me J. Edgar Hoover—whosoever's in charge. I want Deacon Wilhite to get a lawyer—not for me, tell him; I'm *willing* to be here. It's my *duty* to be here. But I want a lawyer for those old folks. They have to have bail; maybe a doctor—"

"What do you mean that it's your 'duty' to be here?" one of the reporters broke in, thus setting off a bombardment of questions:

"Why did you prevent the guard from performing his duty?"

"Who was that gunman?"

"Where did you people come from?"

"From Georgia," Hickman said.

"What is the name of your county sheriff?"

"Oh, DeCarter," Hickman said, shaking his head, "Carter G. DeCarter. I was raised with him. If you don't believe me, call him."

"Mr. Hickman," another voice broke in, "what is your connection with Senator Sunraider?"

He looked at his hands.

"Would you care to explain why you were crying?" I said.

Suddenly I heard McGowan's Deep South accent, "Doctor, now you just rest back there comfortable in your chair and take your own good time, and tell us in your own words who—"

I saw his huge head shift slightly at the voice, but McGowan's insinuating "Doctor" earned him nothing more than a quizzical roll of old Hickman's bloodshot eyes.

"Can you tell us the gunman's name?" someone said.

He shook his head.

"Can you identify the assassin in any way?"

He shook his head.

"Then perhaps you can tell us when it was you realized that the gunman was firing at the Senator."

"When he hit him the second time and nobody else seemed to be shot," Hickman said.

"Reverend," a sharp-faced man from the *Post* said, "are you and your group members of a political-action group?"

He was silent.

"Communist, then?"

"Civil-rights agitators?"

"Where are you stopping in Washington?"

"What on earth is going on here?" a feminine voice broke in.

We swung around. It was a small, stiff-backed, gray-haired nurse, her eyes glittering. She said, "This is outrageous. Don't you men realize that you're in a *hospital?* It's highly irregular, your being here, and if you don't keep the corridor clear and keep your voices down, I shall see that you're evicted! I don't care who you are!"

"We're sorry, ma'am," McGowan said. "We'll keep it down."

"Well, see that you do," she snapped, leaving with a snap-and-crackle of tinlike linen.

For a moment Hickman watched remotely as we jostled one another around his chair, then he held up his enormous hands.

"Gentlemen, that nurse is right; we're making too much noise, and it isn't getting anybody anywhere. Now, I've been long-trained both in keeping the peace and in holding my peace, so while I'm sorry, you will have to wait just like I'm having to wait."

"Now see here, Doctor," McGowan began, "we have our duty—"

"Yes," Hickman said, "and I have mine, so there's no point in asking me anything more because *he's* the one to do the telling."

Suddenly, but for the scratching of a single pen, the corridor was hushed. I stared into his face, uncertain as to whether he was referring to Deacon Wilhite, to J. Edgar Hoover, or to some more transcendent "he"—even God.

"Doctor," McGowan said, "did I hear you say that *he* would have to tell us?"

"That's right," Hickman said.

"Then why didn't you tell us that in the first place?"

Suddenly I was swept along in a hushed stampede for the elevators. Then in the crush going down, it came to me that Hickman's "he" was not Deacon Wilhite, but the Senator, and when the others rushed off to the Justice Department I phoned Scoggins, my editor, to say that I was sticking with Hickman.

Scoggins was harassed, his voice intensely irritated. "Who is this?"

"It's me, McIntyre," I said.

"McIntyre! Where in hell are you?"

"At the hospital."

"What goddamned hospital?"

I named the hospital where they had taken Senator Sunraider.

"Well, why are you still there?"

"*Why,* what do you mean?"

"Why, don't you know that the Senator's dead?"

"Dead? No, he *isn't* dead!"

"Are you sure?"

"Yes!"

"How do you know?"

"Because he's still in surgery."

"Did you see him?"

"No, but I know that he's still alive. A nurse just passed through the hall."

"Alive, hell, we've had one report that he was DOA and another that he's in a coma; now you tell me he's still in surgery. What are the facts?"

"I don't know yet. He might be in a coma, but they're still trying to save him. That's the latest word around here."

"It had better be, McIntyre. And you stay there and get the latest facts. You stay there, you hear?"

"I'm sticking here," I said. I hurried back upstairs with a growing sense of alarm. Suppose the Senator *was* dead? Something sinister seemed to have taken over the District. In the elevator I was taken with a fit of nervous shaking.

CHAPTER 7

I FOUND HIM STILL there in the hushed, clinical atmosphere of the corridor, kneeling with his elbows resting on the seat of the chair, his face in semi-shadow. I could see his lips moving above his clasped hands, and with the security men having taken position down at the turn of the corridor, he seemed utterly alone. I was puzzled, then drawing closer I saw that his eyes were closed, and upon reaching him I realized that he was praying what was possibly one of the most improbable prayers ever addressed to God, his voice a passionate but almost inaudible whisper which reached my ear in hoarse bursts and soaring flights of supplication.

"Lord, have mercy," he prayed, "have mercy, Lord, on this unhappy land. . . .

"Yea, Lord, this land that's left its substance to burn bone-dry in Thy blameless sun, unstrung from Thy ever-redeeming voice . . .

"This new, most heathenish land, Lord. This land that's soiled itself before the ancient flight of doves, the screams of eagles, the fall and rise of wheat, corn, cotton, and red roses, Thy Son upon his cross . . .

"Please, Mahster, I ask your help for this most woeful, mammy-made, and wilful of nations, this nation born in blood and redeemed by sacrifice and sorrow—yea!—but that's left its God-earned path in doggish devotion to Caesar's own green bile!

"Yea, Lord—Amen!—its Bible forgot, its own laws bleeding from the raw self-laceration and desecration of its ancient dream . . .

"Yes, Lord, I know it's true. Its honor compromised and sullied, its sacred, sea-crossing, years-in-the-wilderness memory mocked in talking tubes, in bottles, in hypodermic needles, and in booze . . .

"Oh, yes, Lord, but knowing all this, I, your poor, guilty, defaulting steward who failed his sacred charge must still ask Thy grace for him who lies beyond these hospital walls in pain.

"Spare him, Lord, and keep him for later days of retribution.

"Give him, Lord, a Jonah's chance. Just one further opportunity to make the shore and do Thy holy bidding.

"Oh, because both land and child are still *your* land, still *your* child, Lord. And Thine the mystery we suffer and behold.

"So please, Mahster, visit not the father's sins upon Thy errant children.

"Oh, just one more smile, Lord, upon him and us whose life now lies twisting and turning in the palm of Thy most delicate and powerful, most wrathful and merciful, *all*-creature-creating holy hand....

> "Oh, do not close Thy hand,
>   "Lord!
> "Please,
>   "do not clinch
> "Thy fist,
>   "Lord!"

It was utterly uncanny and unintelligible, and my mind was revolted by that which my ears and eyes recorded: Old Hickman really was *praying* for Sunraider! I simply couldn't bear it. Suddenly I was crouching beside him, one knee on the floor, shaking my head as I tried to bring matters back to the plane of reason.

"Mr. Hickman," I said, "won't you please answer a few questions?"

He stiffened, seemed not to breathe, then, slowly lowering his hands, he turned his head, facing me with closed eyes, waiting.

"I believe that you owe it to the public," I went on. "Already this shooting has created a panic which will soon be tearing through the streets unless you cooperate."

His eyelids flickered, and I paused before the force of his moist old eyes.

"Yes, and I suppose with a cloudburst of brickbats and switchblade knives," he said hoarsely. "Young man, can't you see the *position* I'm in?"

"Yes, I do, but the news has gone out over the wire services and the world—"

Suddenly I broke off, hearing his question echoing through my head.

"No," I said hurriedly, "I mean, yes—that's why I'm asking you to cooperate."

His voice came sadly, almost pleading in rising inflection, "Young man," he said, "I'm on my *knees*!"

I felt perspiration break from my forehead, a flush of heat. "But listen, but, sir," I said, "I won't quote you, sir. I'll keep it off the record. But why on earth would you weep for a man who is known, who is *notorious* for hating your people?" *It's masochism,* I thought, *masochism and anarchy.*

He spoke as to the seat of the chair, his voice echoing—*spink-spink*—against the corridor walls as from the depths of a well.

"Hate? So that's it. Why should I— Listen, you ask me why, but would you understand it if I told you? Son, who do you think I am?"

"Who?" I said. "I don't know, that's why I'm seeking answers."

"*What* do you think I am?"

"A minister, I suppose. I don't know."

"That's right, you won't take my word that I'm a man of God, so you don't know *who* and you don't know *what.* —But still you think you can just break into this thing and get answers simply by asking a question. Is that how you people who work for newspapers think?"

Suddenly he dropped his arms to his sides. "Boy, I'm on my *bended knees*! Don't that mean anything to you?"

I nodded. "But there are questions that—"

"What on earth has your life taught you?" Hickman said. "What has it prepared you to understand, or to respect? You really think that all you have to do is to come at me like I was a book in the public library—when you don't know the right questions to ask or how to go about asking them? Man, if you don't have manners, at least use some *intelligence*!"

"But it's not for me," I said. "I'm neutral—"

"Like the devil, you are," he said.

"I would argue that," I said, "but the nation must have answers."

He got to his feet, towering above me now, his head working slowly up and down. "They're the same old answers, son: Cain and Abel, the prodigal son and his father, backsliders and blind believers, worshippers of the things of this world and those who thirst and hunger for the things of the spirit. Those who remember and those who forget."

He studied me from far away.

"Now," he said, "you're a Northern boy, and you look intelligent, but here you're acting as squareheaded as that clown who was up here a few minutes ago calling me 'Doctor'!"

I watched him sit, bending toward me, his arms hanging floorward as he thrust out his legs. "You people," he said, "oh, you confounded people!"

And suddenly he sat up, his eyes holding me in a red blaze of fire; then, heaving himself around in the chair, he said, "Boy, get out of my face!" and moved, rolled in the other direction.

As I crouched there, a scene flashed through my mind of a witness trapped in perjurious testimony before a hostile Senate investigating committee, the network microphones with identifying call letters arrayed before him, the audience bending forward listening intensely. Then I pulled erect, looking at Hickman's broad back and thinking, *Boy, he called me* boy! as he turned facing me with a sad expression.

"No," he said, "I'm sorry. You don't understand. You're like a youngster who has grabbed his instrument and jumped on a bandstand full of strange musicians right in the middle of a complicated number and insists on trying to play without even knowing the riffs, the chords, and barely the melody. That's the way it is. You don't mean any harm. No, you're just young; uninitiated. I should have seen that. But you have to understand that at a time like this it's awfully hard for a man like me to put up with some of the conditions and attitudes that I've had to live with. But things like this shooting change the rules. It's like a cyclone or hurricane, a break on the levee, or the time the Mississippi River ran backwards in its bed for miles and miles. So I apologize. I beg your pardon. But the fact is, you'll still have to wait. Now I oughtn't have to tell you that, but it's not in my hands, son. I'm an outsider here and I'm waiting too. Besides, everybody waits when the Mahster is deciding. So in the meantime, if you believe in prayer—pray."

He reached out then, touching me lightly on the shoulder, "This is an awful event, but don't forget," he said, "we'll all be reborn someday," and I arose and backed up the corridor. I could see him watching me kindly from the shadows as I rested my back against the cool white wall. Farther along, the security men, prominent in the light at the turn of the corridor, regarded us with remote curiosity.

I felt embarrassed. He had rebuked me and, worse, he had allowed me to see a force more withering than raw violence looking out at me from behind the dark face of his ludicrous and inexplicable grief. I had been allowed to hear the voice of a mysterious authority, the existence of which I was completely unaware; an authority that rested on no form of power that I understood or respected and which, in all probability, had been limited until now to such as his followers.

And suddenly the growing sense of threat which I'd felt since the shooting became intensified. For the fact that the old man now dared assert this force over me seemed to imply a disorder in the society that was far more extensive, and potentially more destructive, than was indicated even by the shooting of the Senator.

Not only had he called me "boy," he had dismissed me as though all I represented—the press, the public, everything—were no more than an invasion of his privacy and were superfluous before his mysterious grief. Yes, the rules had been changed all right, but how? At what point and by whom, I didn't know. I only knew that I felt stripped and disoriented. For with but the slightest change of expression, the barest inflection of phrase and modulation of voice, Hickman had allowed me the most fleeting revelation of the commanding arrogance that laced a humility which McGowan considered traditional, and girdled my shoulders with a treacherous and invisible yoke. And now, despite the sad expression which shaped his shadowed features, I felt that he was laughing at me.

Who does the old clown think he is? I asked myself. I was accustomed to having my questions ignored; Americans are expert at that, but there he sits defying the entire intricate structure of the nation's power, blocking its right to essential information affecting its destiny. It was unbelievable. With such a crime having been committed in the U.S. Senate, how could one old white-headed Negro who certainly knew some of the facts be allowed to frustrate millions of anxious citizens? Why were the FBI agents taking so much time? Why weren't *they* interrogating the old buzzard? And when I considered that Senator *Sunraider* was responsible for his being in the hospital, I wanted to scream.

Looking across at Hickman, I felt that my wires had been hopelessly snarled, that twenty years of hard-earned but relatively tranquil "adjustment to life" had been shattered into a million jangling pieces. Now this old Negro could speak to me of rebirth! Who the hell was Hickman, anyway? Watching him, I decided by way of relieving my mind to retrace the action of the day, but I didn't know where to begin. Events from the day before, stories to which I had been assigned joined with the incident into which I had stumbled that morning and clanged in my mind with hints of covert connections which would never have occurred to me before the shooting.

I knew, for instance, that there was no *rational* link between at least three of the incidents which now assaulted my mind: the arrival of M. Vannec's letter, my inattention during the shooting, and the bet which I had made the night before with McGowan and a few friends at our club.

The letter had arrived as the result of an incident that had occurred in France more than a decade before....

The betting had come about in a spirit of fun released by our reaction to LeeWillie Minifees' outrageous reply to a joke which the Senator had made shortly before. And while it was true that our betting expressed our annoyance over certain of the Senator's attitudes, it was not malicious, and it certainly had done nothing to bring about the shooting....

And as for my reading the letter at the time the shooting began, it was my way of avoiding a boring speech. Therefore, if the various events had chosen to collide at that particular moment, it was, rationally, a matter of accident—like the unforeseen combustibility of the sports car at Le Mans, which, leapfrogging another machine, struck a wall, ignited its magnesium body and, rocketing its heavier parts through the crowd, killed some eighty people. This accident, by the way, still fills me with an unfathomable pity and terror—for who could have anticipated that magnesium would burn? Similarly, the shooting couldn't have occurred in the Senate as the result of a sudden whim. It had either to have been plotted or emerged as the end product of some miscalculation, an oversight, a failure of somebody's vision occurring long ago—or the result of some malice-breeding act of arrogance suddenly come to fruition in a boil-burst of bullets and blood. I wasn't sure how old Hickman fitted into it, but if his presence meant anything it was probably that the shooting had been preceded by vicious events hidden in darkness.

But here I was blocked, for while many diverse things may be joined under a cloak of blackness, the slightest ray of light reveals their separateness. Thus, my every effort toward insight succeeded only in highlighting a mare's-nest, jumble-riot of loose ends. I was growing weary and increasingly nervous, and my need to discover links between all the things which had occurred struck me as evidence of a hopeless subjectivity. I recognized danger here, but it was as though I had been shackled to the bench, manacled to old Hickman: I couldn't let go. Indeed, I was so roiled and shaken that it was as though a younger, more uncertain, idealistic, and guilty self which I had discarded following the war was being painfully resuscitated. It was like having a long-knitted bone broken afresh at the old point of fracture—blood vessels, marrow, nerves, and memory were all a-scream.

Let's be calm about this, McIntyre, I told myself. *Try to be objective, which has been your training. Despite your inattention during the moments leading up to the shooting, perhaps your guilt, your upset, is neither strange, unique, or even personal. What if it's merely the foreshadowing of a general mood which is already seizing millions of citizens as the news that a senator has been shot spreads throughout the nation? Perhaps identical symptoms would have appeared (and in epidemic proportions) had someone been rash enough to have given the works to the late and most unlamented Theodore Bilbo. So don't allow the impertinence of an old, upset Negro to get to you; he's probably mad, but you have the responsibility of remaining calm.*

But this didn't help, because I knew that old Hickman *wasn't* mad; he was arrogant, devious, and something else at the moment undefinable, but definitely not mad. And so my mind surged on.

Couldn't it be, McIntyre, that everyone in this country harbors a deeply repressed compulsion to shoot senators—no, wait—because wouldn't this be the simplest explanation of the gunman's unaccountable action? And if not, isn't it at least possible that everyone wishes, in his most secret heart, that someone else, some proxy, some utterly detached, resigned, and self-alienated individualist with nothing to lose, would perform the job in his stead?

It's a horrible idea, McIntyre, but hasn't it been said that at some point each and every son wills his father's death? And isn't a nation a larger, more intricate form of the family, and thus, like most families, thronged with dark, mysterious yearnings? Taunted by envious second sons, even Smerdyakovs full of dark passion? What would Freud say about this? And who, by the way, was the mother of our country? Yes, and how does old Hickman fit into this family pattern?

Oh, yes, my mind was leading me into dark and treacherous territory! I realized it, but I was powerless to resist.

Suddenly I was tired of standing, and the hospital odors and heat were becoming depressing. Slowly I moved farther up the corridor to a bench beside the elevator shaft from where I could keep an eye on Hickman. He sat bent over now, his head resting wearily on his crossed arms and knees; while far beyond him, at the point around which the Senator would appear—if he survived to appear—I could see the security man at his post. Dressed in a blue tropical worsted suit, he seemed tuned to a fine alertness and prepared to deal with any familiar form of disorder. But against my growing sense of the enormity of what had happened, his presence only accelerated my mind in its subversive gropings. It ran and stumbled, grasping desperately at the dark objects of my thoughts.

I asked myself again: *Could there be within the mind of each and every citizen an undiscussed but widely recognized urge toward assassination which functions to lend a certain depth, density, and ambiguity to our political life? An urge which provides the lonely citizen in his weakness a psychic linkage to such powerful figures as Sprott, Fullbore, Joplin, and Sunraider? An urge closely related to the widely noted phenomenon that almost everyone in a democracy seems compelled to make speeches? Perhaps herein lies the meaning of old Hickman's outburst in the Senate: Observing a powerful figure tumbled into the dust, he simply couldn't resist the compulsion to have his say. This by no means explains his presence in the hospital or the Senator's motive in having him there, but it must have had something to do with his strange conduct.*

Yes, perhaps that was it; at the sound of the shots a powerful underground urge burst forth, and with the normal barriers down he was compelled to give voice, to let out a howl—although he didn't know whether to sing or pray, celebrate or mourn. Yes, it was possible. His outburst anticipated and gave expression to a nationwide recoil to the chaos which spills forth from the side of the body politic, as it were, whenever there is an attack on the life of a sacrosanct personage. Think of our dead so slain, of President Lincoln.

No, don't *think of him. Sunraider couldn't light a torch to Abe Lincoln, even during the darkest night of the nation's soul. And anyway,* I told myself, *these notions are unsound, the results of excitement, frustration, and loss of sleep during recent nights and days.* Yet my mind lunged wearily on, challenged by my traumatic awareness of the heavy cloak of mystery surrounding these great figures, our senators.

We love them, yes. And we hate them—I hadn't thought about this contradiction before. We admire them and we envy them. This at least is sound. It's true; they determine our fate and that of our children for generations to come, and yet most of us live out our entire lives without ever being in the presence of a single one of them. Think about it, McIntyre. We speak of them in the possessive mode, but we know very well that it is they who possess us. All we possess is the right to confer power upon them. Which is very much like the right of one-hundred-and-seventy-five-pounders like myself to donate blood to heavyweight wrestling champions. Once transfused, our blood becomes part of a power system which could easily crush us should we become so foolish as to press some special claim. For aren't our senators really, when we think calmly of actualities, the "kings" of this sprawling, many-regioned, diversified land? Masked kings, if you will, who wear democratic felt and straw on their powerful heads, but kings neverthe-less. And far more powerful than any ancient king or Renaissance prince. What would Lorenzo the Magnificent be to Sunraider the Ruthless; the Duke of Urbino to Fitzger-ald of the Graceful Flair; or Machiavelli to Fullbore the Baleful? Think about that, McIntyre, and think of those who've parlayed one six-year term into a rule of countless decades. These are kingly reigns, McIntyre, this is quite plain; it's a matter of terminol-ogy.

Thus, doesn't it follow that our senators are the natural targets of all manner of in-tense and ambivalent emotions?

And shouldn't it be expected that, figuratively, lions and tigers, chimpanzees and jackals—chimeras even—should prowl the atmosphere around them, very much as pimps and gamblers, thugs and confidence men swagger in the train of prizefight cham-pions and successful jockeys? No doubt about it, and no product of overheated fancy, ei-ther. Men like Fullbore, Joplin, Plummer, Towbitt, and Sunraider move in an electric atmosphere, breathe a different air than that we breathe. And it doesn't matter that we create that atmosphere of our mixed attitudes, because once they breathe power they are truly free of us. There's nothing we can do about it, either, even though we put them in their positions. They can be amused by us and even contemptuous, as Fullbore and Sun-raider are contemptuous (each in his respective way) of most everyone. We put them on their thrones, as it were, but once there they follow their own desires, not ours—even to the point of causing immeasurable confusion by standing most of the national values on their heads. Only their fellow senators can unseat them, really, and it's been years since a single one has been caned or had a carload of constituents descend upon him to ex-press their wills, dissents, or what have you, with horsewhips, clubs, or loaded handbags. Times have changed, McIntyre. We've descended like worms in winter, far below the grass roots of the land, while they have taken off into the most rarified air.

Yes, but just the same, I thought, *each and every one of them, even the most charm-ing, statesmanlike, and endearing—even that lovable Senator Barkley, everybody's uncle, is probably somebody's secret candidate for a blasting.*

There came a sound of opening doors, and a slender young nurse, graceful in her white uniform, stepped from the elevator carrying a tray covered with a towel and went past me with averted eyes. She moved with a lilting walk of clicking heels, her white-capped golden head erect, and I could hear the gentle swishing of her garments fade as she went past old Hickman, who was nodding. I watched her until she reached the security man and moved on into the light beyond. Then, I saw vividly in my mind's eye the runner that flawed the right silk hose of her shapely calf. *Sweet angel of mercy, thou art fair,* I thought. *Thou art gentle, too, I hope.* Then my mind resumed its musings:

Blasting? You mean that symbolically, don't you?

Perhaps, but I'm not too sure....

Well, while it's true that we are terribly excitable, we are nevertheless a very peaceful people. Perhaps this is the true form of our national courage, since we have more than most to irritate us.

Yes, that's true. And though dedicated to the democratic dream of our fathers, we know pragmatically that some must possess more democracy than others. For instance, that old Negro down there punishing that chair has certain built-in disadvantages.

Yes, there's no denying it. I faced that fact twenty years ago—or at least I tried for a while.

And you realize too, and without bearing a grudge, that our forefathers' accomplishment was not so much a break with the power that went with kingship as the achievement of a multiplication of the number of possible kinds, and a transformation and multiplication of kingly styles.

Do you mean that you consider Sunraider the possessor of a "kingly" style?

Hell, no!

Fullbore?

He would like to think so, but with him it's a matter of having been corrupted by reading Sir Walter Scott during his senior year in college...a year in England...his realization that he'll never be President.

Don't kid. What was that about our peaceful nature?

I'm not—who could kid at a time like this? Perhaps we're so peaceful because deep down we are bound by an agreement, by an unspoken but nevertheless sacred pact, based on an instinctive knowledge which the shooting and our reaction to it is already verifying.

What kind of knowledge?

Well, intuition. The intuition that we are held together by a delicate system of alliances and agreements as to the nature of reality, based on the recognition that whenever someone becomes rash enough or desperate enough to shoot one of these powerful figures, strange, furious forces will break free from behind their restraining walls and take us over.

It's quite possible....

Possible? Isn't that why you're sitting here full of strange doubts, feeling that you've participated in the downfall of someone sacred—if not your father, then a rowdy, rascally, buffoon of an uncle?

What? Sunraider? That's outrageous! That...that...

I looked up to see a tall physician moving swiftly up the corridor, bouncing along on white, ripple-soled shoes. He had just reached old Hickman when I heard the big voice again.

"Doctor, how's he doing?"

The physician paused briefly, shaking his head.

"Well, you tell him for me that I'm waiting," Hickman said. "And, Doctor, tell him also that I'm praying and that I'll keep on praying until he pulls through. And if he needs blood you can call on me. I'm strong and healthy, and I have never had the yellow jaundice or been sick a day in my life."

What on earth is this all about? I asked myself. And suddenly I began to shake again. My hands trembled, and I felt as though the floor had dropped away, leaving me suspended there in white space. And yet I could still see old Hickman hulking before me, and down the corridor the security man standing his post. I felt light-headed. I tried to shake it away by concentrating on old Hickman's clothing: his soft pongee shirt with maroon bow tie, his straw-colored suit, his white suede shoes. He sat in tranquil stillness, like a huge stone, his legs crossed and his white socks revealing a clock of dark design. A white panama hat rested brim-down on the floor beside him, and it came to me that he was dressed as no minister that I'd ever seen. Yet, his clothing reminded me of the costume of someone I'd seen quite recently—but who? Actually, he looked like a wealthy man attired for a summer party at Newport which had taken place some thirty years ago. No, Hickman's clothing didn't tell me a thing; instead, it increased my sense of confusion.

How long would the Senator be in surgery? I wondered. What was the state of his health? Then my mind leaped back to M. Vannec's letter, but now, with the Senator shot and my nerves in an uproar, I wondered how I could have been flattered by its contents, its shower of questions. Yes, and with Hickman not only praying for Senator Sunraider's life but offering to donate blood, it was as though M. Vannec had been playing a joke on me. I took out the letter and looked at it, and the longer I looked, the more the conviction grew that the letter was indeed linked to what had happened. It was part of a whole, tied not to the shooting itself—for that would have been either sheer insanity, or inescapable evidence of an international incident pregnant with war—but nevertheless connected to it in some way I couldn't understand. This was wild, but who was to say that Vannec hadn't plotted his moves so that I would be reading his letter during the very moment when the string was pulled or the button was pushed that released the towering monkey house of outrage which exploded with the shooting?

No, I thought, *it isn't the shooting itself which has me shaking, but something far more insidious. Something which accounts for that old Negro sitting there beside the door.* For after all, events may be shattering, shocking, violent, comic, tragic even, all in themselves. Or all of these at one and the same time, it depends mainly upon the observer's point of view, his prior conditioning. I knew, because I had seen enough of violence and general human foolishness to be immune from simple shock. That's what one gained from dealing with facts unemotionally, and I had learned as early as 1939 that human beings are capable of anything and everything—especially betrayal in the name of honor. I knew all this, but here Vannec's letter got into it with its questions.

The questions which arise immediately after a traumatic event—*these*

cause the maximum confusion. They envelop us like the smoke of a horrify-
ing fire and remain active and torturous long after the event which gave
them birth has become formalized history or been forgotten—which
amounts, perhaps, to the same thing.

Now, who knows this better than Monsieur Vannec? In his own country he
is famous for raising those profound questions of a political-philosophical
nature which upset wise men and ordinary citizens alike. He is forever explaining the meaning of everything—events, art, politics, stray blasts of tor-
pid air. He informs the world with brain-rattling, spine-chilling eloquence
just what is implied by historical developments, cultural fads, styles, costumes, slang, manners—all matters which usually leave me baffled. This is
one reason I have admired him for so long. He gives me an assurance that
logic is still a dominant force in human affairs, even though he frequently
confuses me. As when he questions the existence of Europe and then expands the concept of Europe to include New York, Chicago, and Hollywood. As when he views the United States as European and then insists that
the only really *united* states are those of Europe. As when he denies that
Hitler left any effect on the political life of the postwar continent and yet
wears a silver plate in his skull from a wound suffered fighting in the Resistance, *and* drives a Volkswagen.

Yet the fault was mine. M. Vannec is possessed by a fury to have everyone
live with that extreme consciousness and ultrasensitivity to events which
marked his own sensibility. And for a time I had tried to follow him, but I
simply wasn't gifted enough. I had to settle for reading his articles now and
then. Still, I had lost none of my admiration. But now the juxtaposition of the
shooting, the Senator and Hickman, and Vannec's letter, his ability to make
meaningful patterns of apparently unrelated events suddenly seemed sinister. It threatened me from afar. Could it be that he had kept an eye on me
during all the years since the war—when I had first laid eyes upon him—and
had plotted and waited to post his letter at the precise moment when it
would do me the greatest damage? Could it be that he waited until the
shooting was set to occur before firing his questions?

Oh, I knew that this was less than rational, but with the old Negro having
called me "boy," sitting there in his pongee shirt, questions of mere rationality were no longer binding.... I was swept along. In my mind I could see
M. Vannec, impressive and grave (he was up to his neck in the Algerian trouble), turning from his affairs of State to divert himself with his plot against
me. I tried to shake it, but a stream of images now pursued me like the scene
from a movie which I had seen as a child, a scene of hell into which the lost
souls, stripped to their loincloths, girdles, can-can panties, and brassieres,
were made to enter by standing on their heads upon a large manhole cover
which flipped over and plopped them screaming into a huge pit of fire,

smoke, and sleek black pitchfork-wielding devils. I had dashed bawling from
the theater then, but now there was no escape. I was struck by a fantasy in
which I could see a great room cluttered with exquisite paintings and sculptures, objets d'art and fetishes, tapestries and leather-bound volumes—a virtual pirate's treasure of the world's art and literature—in which M. Vannec
sat at his desk day after day, winter and summer, spring and fall, consulting
his calendar from time to time and thinking of me. Finally, the fateful moment having arrived, he smiles knowingly and I could hear him say to himself, "*Alors,* McIntyre, you chose to forget me for all these years but I willed
to *remember* you, and now, since you've devoted your best energies to reporting facts and describing appearances, let us have a little testing. Agreed,
McIntyre? Yes? No? Very well, within a few hours I shall put to you a few
questions—then let us see what you make of the facts!" He then calls a servant, a small evil-looking man with thin hair and thick glasses, who whines
and sniffles like Peter Lorre, a villain out of Dickens, and the Karamazovs'
bastard brother, all in one, and has him post the letter. . . .

Oh, it was wild, like the world of dreams; yet, there was a certain reality
underneath, in that the circumstances which led to my initial encounter
with M. Vannec were decidedly mysterious.

It was during the Battle of the Bulge, when the ship on which I served as
purser was anchored in the Seine below Rouen. I had gone ashore for a stroll
in the town when, moving along the blacked-out quay, I had come upon
three American infantrymen attacking one of my shipmates. It was a fierce,
wordless struggle in which bottles flashed, glinted, and flew, and I had joined
in. Then, when the fight broke up at the approach of a group of white-
helmeted MPs, I had half-carried my shipmate as we escaped into the dark.
A blow to the head had left him quite groggy, but when, standing close to a
wrecked building in the dark, I had suggested that we stop at the military-
base hospital to have a doctor look after his wound, he declined, explaining
that he had to keep an urgent appointment up in the town.

He was still quite rocky, but when I offered to go along until his head
cleared, he insisted that he could make it alone. Then, moving away, he had
gone a few yards when I saw him plunge to his knees, a dark shape in the
dark, starting to crawl, and I had run up and helped him to his feet. Then,
despite his protests, I had insisted on going along. He was angry, and as we
started off he charged me with meddling—which wasn't, I admit, entirely
untrue.

All during the journey across the Atlantic, I had sensed some mystery
about the man, some undefined aura of wealth and comfortable living. Actually, he seemed more the type who'd have sought a commission as a cadet officer, as other wealthy young men had done. Instead, he'd signed on as an
able-bodied seaman. On a small vessel a purser gets to know all of the crew,

but before that night I had never gotten more than a few words out of him. There was something profoundly detached about him. Nothing on board seemed to interest him except books. He did his work and that was it. No argument among the crew seemed to arouse him, no union matter, no scuttlebutt. No talk of music or sports, no comparison of adventures with women in strange ports, nothing aroused his slightest participation.

"Where are we headed?" I said.

"To the cathedral," he said. "And I can get there by myself."

"Not the way you're stumbling," I said. "You're apt to get hit by a truck."

He still protested, but now my curiosity was aroused. Why the cathedral? Surely he didn't plan to meet a girl there; the waterfront cafés were the place for that. Nor did he appear to be the type who dealt in the black market. Certainly he wasn't bent upon a pilgrimage—unless for aesthetic motives, and even so the night was so dark that most of the time we couldn't see our hands before us. But whatever his motive, I sensed that his need was urgent.

We were going uphill now, and as his head cleared he pulled away from my assisting arm, and as we went staggering up the hill past the old Hall of Justice in the dark, I had to hurry to keep abreast. It was hot and the going was rough. Broken masonry and shattered glass lay over the road, and twice I had to help him to his feet. Then we were moving through the old marketplace and on beneath the great medieval clock (knocked awry by bombs and shell fire), and heading toward the square.

Sometimes in the cold, breathless middle of the night I relive our approach to the cathedral, our emergence into the deserted square, where it looms like a mountain which was felt rather than seen in the predawn darkness, its roof smashed in, its stained glass removed, and its lower walls and buttresses protected by sandbags. I can still see my shipmate heading straight into the dark interior as though he had been there many times before. Perhaps he had during times of peace. I didn't ask, I was too busy trying to keep up to speculate too much about it. But there we were, and I had no time even to try to penetrate the darkness about me, for now two maquis stepped out of the shadows with burp guns trained straight at us. This was a bad moment for me. The night before, the Germans had made a parachute drop of troops dressed in civilian clothing into the hills overlooking the town, and being sure that the maquis were searching for these, I thought us triply doomed: by our dress, by our semi-civilian status, and by the fortunes of war. I fully expected that we would be killed, swiftly and without interrogation.

It was then I heard my companion's excited whispering—he had the odd name of Severen—and we were being swiftly searched for weapons, then hurried along a path cleared through the broken masonry which cluttered the vast enclosure. As we moved along, I could feel the great walls of the edifice sweeping up, up, in great shattered curves to the dark dome of the sky, where the stars, there so far above us, showed like tiny lights stuck in the ceiling. I was awed by the sweep of it, and the very damage, the smashed incompleteness, made me realize as never before the grandeur of its inspiration. It was like watching two great arms reaching up to encompass all of heaven. And indeed, in that moment I could believe in heaven, no questions asked.

Then came the sound of a voice which seemed, there in the shadows and vast space, utterly sourceless. It seemed, in my excited state, to rise from the walls or from beneath the broken masonry. And all the more because it was hardly more than a whisper. Afterwards, I learned that acoustical perfection was frequently a property of such buildings, but then I realized that my nerves had been rendered supersensitive by danger and by darkness, and I almost bolted. In that instant a scent of tobacco came to me, and I was aware that the voice had spoken in English. Then close by I saw the glow of a cigarette, and the sharply defined face of a man appeared, whom my shipmate recognized with a low greeting. And somehow the sharp, amused eyes which looked out of the fatigued face were as reassuring to me as to Severen. It was only for the briefest instant, then the two of them moved off into the shadows and I, still wondering what I had pushed myself into, found myself being marched by the two maquis through a labyrinthine darkness, and suddenly I was standing outside the towering walls.

They showed me the path down to the dock area below and left me there, and I made my way, puzzling over the true identity of my shipmate, down to a Red Cross club near the Seine. There I found a gear-laden group of soldiers just back from the front lines standing in quiet, worshipful repose before an oil portrait of the singer Lena Horne. They uttered no word; they simply stood there gazing upward as at a brown goddess in an apple-green dress. It was, to say the least, quite odd. Leaving them at their communion, I started back to the ship. It was necessary to avoid two groups of brawling soldiers along the way, and to avoid a third up ahead, I stopped in a café for a drink. There were a few Frenchmen at the tables, and three GIs who stood at the bar looked up when I came in, studied me briefly, then resumed their conversation.

"No, that's not him," one of them said as I waited for the bartender. He sported a moused eye.

I ordered a calvados and as I drank I listened, hoping to learn if these were the men who had attacked Severen.

"So how'd it happen, Cyril?" one of them said.

"Oh, hell," the one with the moused eye said, "Rooster and Ringo and me were up the street drinking in a bar when this seaman came in looking all nice and clean and one of the fellows called him Joady."

"Who did? You?"

"Hell, no, one of the other guys. It was Rooster Mills. I don't have a girl to worry about."

"So what happened?"

"Oh, hell, we were just kidding, but the mother got mad. He said something about, 'Soldier, did you call me Joady? If so, you must have received some pretty jazzy letters from home.' Then he turned back and took a drink."

"Yes? So?"

"Then Rooster said, 'Aw, listen, Joady, don't try to kid us, we know your type.' So then the fellow looks at Rooster and says, 'Fellow, you really must be cockeyed.' And Rooster says, 'Who's cockeyed?'

" 'You,' the fellow says. 'You're cockeyed; coming over, we lost five ships to the subs, and they'll probably sink others before we get back. So if you can stand here in Rouen and call me 'Joady,' then, hell yes, you must be cockeyed.' "

"So then what did Rooster do?"

"Rooster told him, 'Aw, you're still a Joady, Joady.' And the guy pushes his drink back on the bar and stands up. He says, 'Yeah, and I'm sitting in a fine hotel room wearing silk pajamas and waiting with a bottle of cold champagne for your best girl to arrive.' "

They laughed and slapped the bar.

"Old Joady had him a pretty sharp tongue, didn't he?" one of them said.

"All of these Joadies have a sharp tongue," Cyril said. "Too sharp."

"Was that when he hit you, Cyril?"

"Naw, it was later."

"I bet he went on to tell you about the great contribution the merchant marine is making to the war effort and all that bull," one of the others said.

"No," Cyril said. "But then Rooster turned to us and said, 'What do you think, man, is he or ain't he a Joady?' and Tom said, 'Well, he *looks* like a Joady,' and I said, 'Yeah, and he sure *talks* like a Joady,' and then Rooster said, 'Then, hell, I was right, so he *must be a Joady.*' "

"Was that when he hit you, Cyril?"

"Not yet! That's when he picked up his bottle and started out. He said, 'Man, I be damn if I'll ever understand the military mind, if it's got a mind. But since you all think everybody who rides ships is a Joady, I hope somebody back stateside is performing a few Joady-grinding favors for all three of you.' "

They laughed.

"What happened then, Cyril?"

"The mother left then, and we took a drink and laughed about it. But then old Rooster got to thinking about his broad back stateside, and in two minutes flat he's all red in the face and says, 'Come on, I'm going to get that Joady sonofabitch,' and we went out and saw the mother going up the road and caught up with him and the mother struck at Rooster and missed—and that's when he knocked the living hell out of me! Man, that Joady sonof-abitch could rumble like gangbusters! But if you think my eye is bad, you wait 'til you see Rooster's!"

No, I thought with relief, *it doesn't sound like Severen's style.*

They were still laughing when I went out and returned to the ship.

I kept a lookout for my shipmate throughout the night, but he failed to appear, and when I saw him at mess the following morning, he appeared tired and excited but offered me no explanation of our adventure. By now, however, being both resentful and respectful of his privacy, I had decided not to question him.

In another two days the ship was unloaded, and we made our way down the Seine past Le Havre, where we joined our convoy, then moved on to Milford Haven from whence our flotilla of merchant ships, baby flattops, and cruisers set sail for the U.S. But I had no further opportunity to question Severen. He avoided me, and I, having decided that he was probably connected with some government agency, the OSS or the like, thought it best to leave him with his secrets. In fact, acting on the premise that some knowledge might be quite inconvenient to one of my background—if not highly dangerous—I quit the ship in New York. Two trips later I was drafted and assigned to the ETO, and I quickly allowed the strange young man and the night's incident to slip from my mind.

The war went on until the fall of that year, and upon its conclusion I returned to the States and became so busy picking up some of the threads of my life (while avoiding others) that I thought little of the war except in terms of the interruption it had caused me. I forgot both Severen and the mysterious figure in the cathedral until some time later, when I thought of writing a novel about the war. At the time, books about the recent conflict were quite popular, and I thought to do something more romantic than the works then being offered by the contenders in the field, but I found it more than a notion. I discovered that I possessed little talent for invention, and my experience gave me so little to go on, so little to feed my rather limited imagination, and, although I was taking courses in sociology on the GI Bill at the time, the prospect of serving up yet another set of case histories as fiction repelled me. So I began with a street fight among Americans along the bank of the Seine during a night of war, followed by a trip which the hero made as the barely tolerated companion of a mysterious American student turned merchant seaman to contact a group of armed members of the French Underground in a bomb- and fire-gutted cathedral. But I got no further. I couldn't plot it, couldn't extend these bare details into a significant action. I knew none of the related facts, and my discipline, such as it was, had been geared to the searching out and weighing of facts, not to imaginative speculation. So I forgot it—we Americans are great forgetters. Yes, we are as competent at forgetting things which confuse us as we are at begetting confusion (and often it is our attempt to forget which causes the confusion in the first place). Whatever. I next made an attempt at writing a philosophical novel of wartime adventure—with political overtones—and discovered that I was as ill-equipped for this as for the first project, so reluctantly I put it aside. I told myself that the idea wasn't in the American mode anyway and convinced myself that I, at least, possessed few ideas worth troubling the reader's mind.

So Severen and the mysterious maquis were not to cross my mind again until sometime later when, through my work in Washington, I became interested in Europe again. This was probably a holdover from the thirties of my eager youth, but I now wished to see what Europe was like during the tumult of the postwar years. I wanted to retrace my steps, as it were. For now I was sharply aware that much of my youth had been left there, and that the war had been no mere incident, no mere interruption but involved the only living I had done during those violent years. It was, except for my concern over Spain, the one great fact of my youth and my youth's true end. I was by now too wise to think that I could recapture those lost years and certainly not so isolationist in my thinking as to believe that I had been robbed of them by Europe in the interest of goals that were not my own, or at least not *our* own. Nowadays, few Americans cling to that illusion and most have made peace with the fact that the world is of a sad, complex whole.

So I wished to see the place again, to regard once more the people and the old ancestral earth. I wished to see some of what had been so telescoped and explosive and accelerated and youth-consuming with my older, more sober—and conservative—eyes. For all my suspicions and discouragements, I wished to understand, to glean just what had actually happened during that time when my sense of the ideal, my yearning for perfect political solutions for all human problems, rejected that which my sense of patriotic duty had made an act of irrational faith—for I believed in our allies and had gone to sea long before I had been called up by the draft. So now, as I say, I wanted to view the land as one returns to view an old movie years after it no longer possesses such immediate power to guide one's actions and perceptions, when its spell can no longer deaccelerate one's breathing or expand one's sense of wonder. It was with this in mind that I took a quick trip to London, Paris, Salzburg, and Rome, and on my return put great energy into trying to obtain an extended assignment in Europe. It was during this effort that I saw the Frenchman for a second time. I was assigned to cover a press interview at the French Embassy which he had granted, and it was then that the incident in the cathedral returned once more to mind.

For it was only when I confronted M. Vannec from my place in the ring of photographers and reporters that I realized that the legendary artist, activist, and French dignitary before me and the mysterious man in the dark cathedral were one and the same. I was both startled and relieved, for there had been many times during the latter days of the war when I had wondered if I might not have aided the contact between two enemy agents, and now at last I felt reassured. M. Vannec appeared not to have noticed my shock of recognition, and as I observed him handle questions I congratulated myself that I'd had enough self-control not to make myself known to him. Observing his answering my colleagues' questions, I even congratulated myself that I possessed a certain advantage, since I recognized him while he was unaware that I had participated in what might have been for him a significant historical encounter. I felt proud that I had dropped into that underground—if only briefly—out of which M. Vannec was to emerge after the war to take his place of importance in the world's affairs; that I had touched, even this slightly, the fluid center wherein postwar Europe was being reorganized— a matter which brought me then and there, and most ironically, the most meaningful sense of what had happened to my war-spent youth.

I say "ironically" because I recognized my pride as a reflection of that helpless, American, most democratic yearning which seeks ever to effect some sense of personal connection between the self and historical events, our need to write, as did so many GIs on the backsides of statues of Italian saints "Kilroy Was Here" if only on the backside of history. Involved here, I knew, was the driving desire to be "in the know," to step behind the scene, which arises, perhaps, out of the fluid, shifting center of power and the absence of ancient hierarchical structure which is native to our form of government.

So, standing before him, I was filled with a kind of joy, as though watching a skillful act of impersonation. For my work in Washington had made me aware that behind the political parties and the public gestures of public figures there is usually in progress a game of hide-and-seek. Ofttimes relatively obscure men write the political speeches which affect our destiny, and much too often disreputable machine politicians, a holdover from more rambunctious days, formulate policies (and ofttimes wise policies) that are proclaimed publicly by respectable public servants who are themselves little more than masks, the true mouthpieces and figureheads of the nation. Not always, fortunately, for some public figures are indeed what they profess to be. They do their own thinking, their own speaking, and their own dirty work—much as our prewar gang leaders were wont to do. They make no pretense that politics can ever be pure and unambiguous, and they recognize that no politician is ever free of the murky mysteries handed down to them from tribal chieftains through medicine men, publicity experts to ministers of state. Yet, even this makes for more mystery and speculation rather than less. It is still difficult to distinguish real man from mask, true voice from recording, real leader from actor.

I had left the interview without putting a single question; it wasn't necessary. M. Vannec was highly competent, and he led the line of questioning with such skill that each of us was satisfied with the information received and the analysis of events presented. I was pleased to know that for once, unexpectedly, I had left my boring work on shipboard to glimpse behind the European scene. I had peeped into chaos and encountered a hero, and now I could see some of the results. It pleased me that for all the relative stability attributed to prewar European class lines, M. Vannec, who comes from the upper class, and who had an established identity as an artist before the Spanish outbreak, exhibited some of that same mobility of identity and shifting of purpose which my work in Washington led me to believe was so common to our own society. I had known of his legend as reported in our press, but the brief personal identification made during the war rendered it all the more meaningful to me. I speculated as to the transformations, or, to use a favorite term of one of the more intriguing French writers, the *metamorphosis*, the process, by which he had transformed himself. Certainly transformations of identity were necessary under the Nazi occupation, but, on the whole, the concrete conditions in France were too much for me. I had to settle for the small, silent satisfaction of having recognized him in an earlier role, while he had been completely unaware.

Then, when his letter arrived on the morning of the shooting, I realized that the laugh had been on me. M. Vannec had indeed picked me out of the crowd and had been no less poker-faced than I. When I first read his letter, this had delighted me, but now, sitting in the hospital corridor in my shaken state, my response was vastly more questioning. I felt that he had subjected me to an insidious inquisition. Insanity, I am told, is a coincidental state. Correspondences flutter ever before the victim's eyes. Faces appear in rocks, clouds, streams, and fireplaces. Everything and anything becomes imbued with personal significance, and in Auden's words "Time remembered becomes one with time required." Dreams cling, gongs make waves of deep silence, ten-ton trucks glide past like trout plying the sandy, pebble-strewn bottom of a stream; artificial flies come alive and curve around to attack the artful fisherman. It happens to each of us at some point, I'm sure. And what is the recommended cure? A "plunge into reality," that is the recommended cure. A plunge into life's "well of facts." So with old Hickman and the FBI man before me to mark my boundaries of speculation, the one a symbol of authority and the other of some nameless chaos, I tried to reread the letter carefully and coolly—and only succeeded in increasing my agitation.

CHAPTER 8

AFTER BLANDLY INTRODUCING HIMSELF and recalling our encounter in Rouen and at the press conference, M. Vannec's letter was one question after another.

> Prior to my visit of last year, I hadn't seen your country since 1937, during the crisis of the Spanish Civil War.... I see American journals and newspapers, of course, but so much has happened since my first visit that I now find myself confused whenever I compare the "factual data" of the United States with the ideas which I've formed at this distance. Thus, if you would be so kind, I should like to have the private unofficial opinions of one so well informed as yourself. In other words, the opinions of an informed citizen who sees his country from the inside, one who sees, shall we say, with the warm mystique and intuition of the heart as well as with the intellect.... I am confused, for instance, when I read the statement of one of your leading men of letters who says that he no longer recognizes as his own the country which is presented photographically by one of our leading journals. What do you make of this statement?

Looking down the corridor at old Hickman I thought, *How blinding is flattery!* Why on earth had I kept reading the first time? And why on earth didn't M. Vannec write to our so-called leading man of letters, who, perhaps, would have been overjoyed to convey his national and most unoriginal disgust to one so distinguished. And why did M. Vannec consider me privy to our superior leading man of letters' opinions, perceptions, insights, outsights, hindsights, around-sights, or lack of such? Me, a mere reporter and taxpayer. And what did that bored old party expect from his complaints, when he should know very well that in this country a man is exceptionally lucky if he is able to recognize the child he rears as his own. Hadn't he noticed, I thought, that besides the normal factors that have always made family life a cuckoo's delight—the culture, environment, whatever it is—is in such a constant and cyclonic whirl that our children not only grow like weeds, but they grab such strange nourishment out of the air that their mothers might well chuck the traditional concern with getting their brats to wash their hands and faces, and see to it that whenever they come in off the street they washed their brains? Our leading man of letters should consider a Boston child of proper background whom I know, who spoke with a South Carolina Geechee lilt after brief contact with the Negro maid who worked next door on Williamsburg Square. Within two weeks he was referring to his father, a Harvard professor of distinguished attainments, as "de buckra."

> *Oh de burrhead and de buckra*
> *Dey de same in de dark, ainty?*

I heard him sing. What would Vannec's leading man of letters, that matinee idol of the word, that latter-day Francis X. Bushman of prose, make of this? How does this child fit into *his* America? His America indeed! Where does he keep it, in what safe-deposit box? And is his America old Hickman's America or that of the FBI man?

And when did this country ever slow down long enough for him to stake out his claim? Perhaps the deed his grandfather filed expired long ago, or perhaps his father, armed with Civil War plunder, was too busy pushing to establish himself with his betters to keep up with the changes. Why on earth should Vannec think that I should give my attention to such a haughty gentleman? My job is reporting the facts, and change is implicit in the fact—or isn't it?

M. Vannec, I thought angrily, is like many Europeans whom I've met; he expects us to be familiar with all of *their* proprieties but fails absolutely to recognize the few we have of our own. The first shot out of the bottle and he's revealed himself as the type of European who delights in telling you endless stories illustrating American materialism, vulgarity, uncouthness, pushiness, ignorance, etc., while observing your reaction with eager and calculating eyes. But why should he ask a favor of me—if it *was* a favor—and then go on to inquire: "This Senator Sunraider of yours, how is he able to function in your section of the country?"

Vannec really got to me now. This question had aroused no reaction when I first read the letter, but now with the Senator shot and in surgery it brought a chill. Here was the shadow no bigger than a man's hand which announced the storm, and I had ignored it. Once, Europeans slapped us in the face with Joseph McCarthy, and now that McCarthy has had it, they are beginning to express their superiority by hitting us over the head with Sunraider. But it was what came in the very next line that made my hair stand on end.

"What, by the way, has happened to our young friend Severen?" he wrote—a question which had appeared innocent enough on first reading. But now I realized that the very circumstances of my first contact with Vannec should have made it plain that I was no friend of Severen's, and had no idea of what he and Vannec had been up to. Hadn't they sent me packing the moment they exchanged passwords? And what frightened and infuriated me now was having such a question put to me at a time when the whole country seemed on the verge of collapsing under the weight of a fantastic practical joke. It struck me, in other words, that M. Vannec's questions were not only exceedingly malicious and calculating, but the product of some special, inside knowledge of our national affairs.

> When I was a child, . . . I thought as a child:
> but when I became a man,
> I put away childish things.

So saith the Scriptures, and so 'til now I had thought of myself. And so, too, my sober mind told me, I should think of M. Vannec. For not only did charity require it, but my desperate sense of hope—which is a *will* to sanity if nothing more—demanded it. But with the shooting and with old Hickman waiting, I no longer knew where one drew the line between the childish and the mature matters of this world. What is play and what sheer desperate thrashing to keep a foothold on the whirling sphere? What are the uses of sober reflection, and what the role of "infantile regression and passionate irrationality"?

I asked myself quite seriously: *Is Vannec playing with you, McIntyre? Plotting against you out of some godlike sense of humor? Or has he involved you in some deadly serious political game? Has he fed you into some rare and elaborate machinery of historical spite, a machine geared to his European desire for revenge against the brash and self-assured upstarts living across the seas?*

And suddenly, just as the nurse left the elevator and hurried down the corridor, it occurred to me that it was even possible that old Hickman might very well know M. Vannec, even as he appeared to know the Senator. It was highly unlikely, I knew, but now anything seemed possible. Hickman appeared to be nodding, and when I hurried down to him I could hear the slight buzz of his breathing.

"Mr. Hickman, sir," I said, "excuse me, but I'm burning with curiosity. . . ."

He looked up suddenly, saying, "What?" and I could see a thin blue circle rimming each brown eye. He sat up, looking toward the sound of the retreating nurse.

"Oh, *burning*," he said, clearing his throat. "Well, you'll get over it, son. Saint Paul's got something to say about that. But you take old Jack Johnson's advice and take cold showers, eat pickled walnuts, and think distant thoughts. Besides, son, nurses are dedicated to the Lord—at least when they're on duty."

And before I could reply or explain, he was snoring again. I shook my head and went back and sat down. He appeared in calm sleep now, his chin against his chest, but he'd succeeded in making my thoughts even more turbulent.

And now, for all my desire to deny it, I sensed a plot, scaled to huge democratic proportions, having as its driving and malicious essence the feat of selecting for its victim, not some American dignitary or captain of industry or hero of the intellect—i.e., someone of Vannec's own stature—but some unimportant, near-anonymous common man such as I. I realized that this resounded with delusions of grandeur; indeed, it was as though a squadron of bombers were dispatched to pinpoint Joe Doe with the latest in bombsights for the express purpose of blasting him with ten megatons of Silly Putty, that defining substance of our own stoned age and of which it is both product and symbol. But the feeling not only persisted, it grew.

And why aim at Joe Doe? I asked myself. *Ah, but here,* I thought, *is where Vannec is most clever. It is because Joe Doe is the nut who holds the entire complex of highly unstable political machinery together. Hit him* hard enough, *give him a sudden lefthanded wrenching, and the whole business gets the jitters, falls apart! He shakes, the next man shakes, you and I shake, those around us do a shake-shake, and the tremors move swiftly out across the countryside. Joe Doe shakes and yells, and the next thing you know everyone is shaking and yelling. Soon it becomes a contest with everyone trying to outdo the other. Then the politicians get into the act and promote the shaking. Then the magazine writers move in along with the village intellectuals, the provincials, exradicals, pseudo-avant-gardists, the parochial savants, and the radical hipsters, and hysteria itself becomes ashamed before all of the extremes committed.*

For instance, in Salzburg once, while on my first trip to peacetime Europe, I was dining at a restaurant near the Festung where it was the custom for the host to place upon the tables miniature versions of the guests' national flags. It was a pleasant custom, usually evocative of national pride and quite productive of friendly inter-table conversation—truly a civilizing custom. Now this evening, since there were French, English, Australian, Belgian, Swiss, Italian, and American nationals present, their flags shone brightly throughout the room, and while the four-piece orchestra played waltzes by the elder Strauss, the guests smiled and bowed to one another in an atmosphere of gustatory goodwill, national affirmation, and international good fellowship. I had been enjoying myself with a meal of wild pig, stuffed with wild rice and wild mushrooms, when I looked up to see a large group of Americans entering with their European friends. They were seated at a nearby table and were laughing and talking pleasantly when a minia-

ture version of Old Glory was placed on their table. Then one of them, a poet of some rep-
utation—which accounts, perhaps, for his charismatic effect upon his fellow countrymen—
this gifted and highly volatile man suddenly grabbed the flag and—with a grand
gesture—threw it beneath the table! I dropped my forkful of pork, the others fell back in
slack-jawed shock, and I looked on with frozen disbelief as the poet leaped to his feet, yelling:

"*Chau–*
    vin–
        ism!

            Con–
                form–
                    ity!

                        Self–
                          de–
                            termi–
                              *na*tion!
                                Freeeeeeeeee–*dom!*"

    He then threw himself into so impassioned a speech that the waiters were brought
skidding to a tray-banging, dish-crashing halt, the guests shot to their feet in neck-
stretching confusion, and a table of hot-eyed Frenchmen leaped up yelling, "Down with
the Plan Marshall!"
    Four little words, and all hell broke loose! And with the Mozart Festival in progress,
there were many Americans present (including a knock-kneed American Negro wear-
ing lederhosen, a Tyrolean hat, and smoking a meerschaum pipe), and I watched the
hysteria hit them en masse. Some, following the poet's lead, cast their flags under the
table, while others—whether in agreement or simply out of embarrassment is a ques-
tion—hastily thrust Old Glory under their coats or into their pockets, and still others
ran from the premises. It was disgraceful. Even some of the Europeans were outraged
and utterly bewildered. But others, sensing a show, cheered and waved their countries'
flags as the poet's wild speech sputtered and raged with references to his highly distin-
guished forefathers, the Battle of Bunker Hill, the War of 1812, the feats and character-
istics respectively of the Maccabees and the Radical Abolitionists, the tail fins of the
Cadillac Coupe deVille, Søren Kierkegaard and Saint John of the Cross. And while the
orchestra struck up a desperate version of "The Ride of the Valkyries," the poet called
for a march on the nearby American Consulate.
    The place was going like a teeter-totter, a roller-coaster gone berserk, when from out
of nowhere there appeared a little black bowlegged GI whose nickname escapes me—
Poppa Stoppah or Fathah Stophidt—down from Darmstadt in his immaculately pol-
ished jump boots, who pushed his way to the poet, trembling with emotion, and yelled:

"Listen, you wild-eyed, Joady-looking sonofabitch, put that pappy-grabbing flag back on that table, or I'mah kick your butt 'til your nose bleeds."

Oh, but his language was most foul—and sobering. At this, the poet fell back into his chair as though someone had struck him from behind with a club, his mouth agape and his eyes wildly rolling. But instead of waiting for him to comply, the little soldier snatched up the flag and, ducking down again, dumped the table, water glasses, silver, beer, and all, upon him. And then, waving the dishonored pennant aloft, he roundly denounced the dripping poet and all Americans present—including yours truly.

Nor could I reply when he turned, looking straight at me, and asked, "Goddamit, what's wrong with y'all? How come you're looking at me? Even I never did anything like that, so what makes y'all think I'mah stand by and let a nowhere sonofabitch like him get away with it?"—a most perplexing question indeed, which, fortunately, no one tried to answer. I stood there trying to guess how much damage had been done to our national image, and I'm sure that the incident escaped a violent climax only because the poet suddenly came alive and agreed to hold the flag and repeat the Oath of Allegiance as administered by the indignant little paratrooper in a thick Mississippi accent.

But, as though this were not enough of a spectacle for the round-eyed and by now utterly delighted Europeans, a madness of patriotic redemption swiftly caught fire. Whereupon each and every American present felt compelled to repeat the Oath, and had to administer it one to the other on a Gideon Bible, which some thief in the crowd just "happened" to've had with him. I joined in, there was simply no escape. It was enough to make a man shed tears.

Sitting there in the hospital, the very memory made me all the angrier and more certain that M. Vannec had chosen me as his point of attack. Worse, his questions seemed to imply a low opinion, both of my intelligence and stability—and his aim was most accurate. Sitting there with my eyes focusing on his letter and with my mind throwing up wild scenes from the past, I suddenly, and for no rational reason, saw the image of a horse, a huge Percheron such as I'd seen during the war in the fields of Normandy. Rising some twenty hands in the hindquarters, she was moving along a frost-white cobblestone road in the dawn, stepping with that haughty, heavy-hipped, iron-shod yet delicate, matronly movement—

Shift, hip, clop, clip, shift, strike-sparks, cloppity-clip—of such great beasts moving; over cobbles, ringing the stones, rocking so gently from side to side—a ship in a swell, a kite on a breeze—that her old dour-faced dozing farmer, resting high there on her rump, needs grasp only his pipe while the brass-studded harness gently jangles from her collar far ahead with the flowing of her mane. On they come, *clip-clop*, ignoring the din in the dawn's early light that precedes our advance to the small village square—

Clop, shift, hips, shift, hooves, scrape-sparks, cloppity-clip—and now great vaporous apples are falling, steadily as she goes, to steam in her wake as she takes her time, switching the flies, tossing her wide prehistoric head—a great, broad fawn; fat, indolent matron of the fields, a creature of peace suddenly blocking the road to bring machines and men to a brake-slamming, spine-jolting, helmet-banging halt! And the old farmer yelling, "Eh? Eh?" as the air rings loud with curses....

Now where in the hell did she *come from?* I wondered. It was insane, I know. Nevertheless, I felt as though M. Vannec had thrown such a mare from outer space and, with old Hickman astride, to hit me squarely on the head while I sat in the press gallery of the United States Senate. I knew this was preposterous. I even found myself laughing, but deep within myself, lest old Hickman think I'd lost my grip. Still, I couldn't break my train of speculation. I was sure that Vannec was bent upon a policy of *épater les* Américains. I asked myself: Didn't Comrade Fu Manchu force us to fight for perfectly worthless military objectives in Korea simply because they were worthless and thus of inestimable value to him, because no matter how many lives they themselves lost, they knew that we Americans would be rattled, as though fighting a dragon with an endless capability for sprouting heads? And didn't Comrade Fu take advantage of the circumstance that we cling so tenaciously to the rational, to the "plan," to the slippery surface appearance of reality, that we go to pieces when we confront the unexpected, the illogical? And especially in strange countries? Upset our frame of values, and you have us dead and gone. Ditto when reversed English, Russian, Chinese, Spanish—you name it—is used against us. We go into a spin, fall out of stance. *No, McIntyre,* I thought, *you mustn't keep to the national pattern. Calmly does it. Vannec's timing could only have been coincidental, his letter has nothing to do with what's happened, and he couldn't have been aware that it would arrive when it did. Relinquish the last hero of your youth if you must, but don't make him a scapegoat. You'll have to take action, start talking, and reveal your state of mind to others. Wait until all of the results are in. Look to yourself! What has happened is but a coming together of disparate incidents. Vannec merely helped to jar you with questions, so don't hold it against him. This is no time to kill the bearer of bad news or for shooting those who raise embarrassing questions.*

But immediately I asked myself if this was actually true and the argument started all over again. *Such thinking is out of place in the U.S.,* I told myself. *Science is against it. The times are against such primitive reactions, McIntyre. And even most of the primitive countries are becoming active in the U.N. The witch doctors are patronizing Brooks Brothers, the shamans are taking the M.D. degree and lining up with Sartre, Freud, Jung, Horney, Sullivan, and Norman O. Brown. They're dabbling in the market, doing analyses for B. B. D. & O. They're advising government. Even Negro ministers like old Hickman there have underground connections with U.S. senators. Former medicine men are shooting around the great capitals of the West in Jaguars, Rolls-Royces, and Mercedes SL 300s. Americans have lived the unexpected, unstructured life longer than any other people. Therefore they simply do not do certain things.*

Yes, but who, I asked myself, *really knows what Americans will or will not do? How can you be sure?* And I recalled an incident which had occurred in Rome where I had gone to visit friends on my way home from Salzburg. It concerned a dispute which developed among the members of a colony of Americans living in that ancient city of Christendom, cat cults, the evil eye, and *la dolce vita,* and took place in an old palazzo where the group was experimenting in communal living.

It began either with some mild argument over a menu or the attitude which the American wives and women should hold toward the Italian servants—nothing of real consequence. But soon they were squared off in two passionate camps—which reminds me, wasn't it another of our leading men of letters who said years ago that disruptions of class lines are productive of a type of social insanity? Which, I suppose, is a polite and scholarly way of saying that most Americans are nuts. For, logically, if there are no stable class lines in this country—as we so endlessly repeat—how can there be any norm of rationality? Is that a fair question, or am I merely projecting my own upset condition? Perhaps this explains our tendency to go off half-cocked at the slightest opportunity. Or, to put it in a whiter light, this is why we do as well as we do in all the sound and fury of this reeling world. Perhaps it's when we come up against strange circumstances, when the world starts whirling to a different asymmetrical rhythm (or to no definable rhythm at all) that we really blow our tops. Strange personality types come out of the sunlight and do dark deeds. Anonymous figures appear and attack the illustrious. This is perhaps what happened with the opposing members of the colony. Soon, as I say, they were lined up on opposing fronts. One was led by an acquaintance of mine, a specialist in Greek tragedy, and the other by a small maiden lady who possessed, as my friends informed me, "bluest blood, blue stockings, and a nose downright indigo from having it stuck in places where it had absolutely no business."

A lean, thyroid type of stubborn will, great energy, and scornful eloquence, she was said to have measured personally every stone along the Via Appia Antica. With her blue-dyed hair and, at sixty-five years of age, weighing eighty-five pounds in her stocking feet and measuring seventeen inches in the tongue, she was capable, my friend said, of swarming over any opponent or group of opponents like a flock of crows attacking an owl—even if it were the Owl of Minerva. I was never able to learn the true cause of the dispute. Some said that it was over the servants and the state of the cooking, then someone hinted confidentially that although it *started* with these matters, it really became nasty when someone introduced the issue of the Civil War, General Sherman's march, and the contrasting attitudes toward ritual and ceremony held respectively by Generals Grant and Lee.

Whatever, in the ensuing argument this woman so infuriated the others that the next evening, when her name was mentioned at a cocktail party, the participants became so worked up that soon the place was an emotional shambles. We had been having a perfectly good time, drinking, reciting limericks, playing charades, and improvising verses—which, being the play of those highly cultivated and clever people, were quite ingenious and a witty delight to hear.

But during the lull, when a thin, boyish-looking little composer, wearing thick glasses and a heavy forelock of black hair, pounded on the seat of a chair for order and uttered the fateful name, the colonists became so incensed that soon they were yelling at the tops of their voices, stamping the floor, smashing wine carafes, and before anyone realized what was under way they were chin-deep in a raving rite of primitive magic. Which, giving way to alcohol, frustration, yes, and to the heady sense of unrestraint which Americans seem to feel when they collect together in strange lands, they improvised right there on the spot.

I watched a prominent sculptor (who the moment before had been improvising amusing verses) seize a piece of stove wood and a knife and in a flash he had whittled an effigy, protruding eyes and all, which he slammed angrily upon the cocktail table, shouting, "Here, damn her, is the image of the bug-eyed bitch who bugged us!"

This brought a volley of angry cheers. Then I heard a tipsy, raven-haired Latinist, a lovely girl visiting Europe for the first time, yell, "Yes, yes, YES!" and saw her grab a pair of scissors and stumble off into a corner where she went through a swift and occult operation and returned to the center of the room waving a fistful of bright orange hair.

"And here, dears," she said, waving the tuft above her head with a grand gesture, "is royal red hair for the wooden head of the bug-eyed bitch who bugged us!"

There were gasps of delight, both at the surprising contrast and the bravura offering and several of the colonists were seized with an image-making fervor.

Quickly with lipstick, chewing gum, and pecan hulls, they assembled an ingenious mana-exuding, eye-fixing fetish, complete with orange coiffure, enormous breasts, delicate legs—although the original of the image was quite flat of chest and knocked of knee—carpet-tack teeth, and a gay red rag of a dress. I downed my drink in a gulp as they drove nails into it, scarified it with pocketknives and nail files, burned it with cigarettes, and spat upon it, all to the accompaniment of a great uttering of curses.

A visiting Fulbright singer broke into a soaring and quite florid rendition of "I'll Be Glad When You're Dead" which spurred the colonists to further extremes. The participants were jumping up and down now, and I watched a group lock hands and swing in a reeling square-dance circle around the modeling table on which the doll had been propped against a glass brick.

Others knocked them aside by ducking under the chain of arms to squirt the fetish with fountain pens, to jab it with needles, hairpins—anything with a point or cutting edge. I pushed one man away as he tried to smash it with a small hand axe, only to have him swing at me, miss, and go shooting head-long into a corner where he crashed against the bottom of an upright piano. He lay yelling, "Praise the Lord and pass the goddamn ammunition," then, "Somebody give me a fucking drink...."

Now people were rushing into the room from other parts of the palace. Small, white-jacketed servants with bright eyes and gleaming hair, elderly scholars in bathrobes, fat ladies in wrappers and with hair done up in curlers. Someone slung a howling black cat into the room, and I saw it land atop the piano, where it stood arched-back and wild-eyed, spitting and striking the air with a wide-spread claw.

The tortured doll was now doused with brandy and set afire, raising a stench of burning hair, cloth, and Strega. And in a flash the fetish took on the look of an insane gollywog, and this raised the pressure all the more.

"That's the ticket!" someone cried.

"That'll fix the black-hearted bitch!"

"It's just what she deserves!"

"I'll be glad when you're dead, you dirty slut," the soprano sang:

> *"We'll be glad when you're dead, you dawg!*
> *We'll all yell, 'Hooray!' in Rome*
> *When they ship your dead bones home*
> *We'll be stoned when you're gone*
> *You black bitch, you!"*

"Wait! Hold it right there," a voice commanded. It was a jolly-faced brown-skinned fellow, holding up his hand. "I want to remind you fellow members that that bitch ain't black, she's blue!"

"Come on, men," someone yelled behind me, and suddenly four male members of the party plunged in, grabbing the doll, then whirled and crashed through the crowd and into the hall. I followed as they reeled down the long corridor and up a marble staircase as one man sang, *"On away awake, beelooooved,"* all the way to the offending woman's door. Where, stumbling and cursing, they hung the doll to the knocker with a necktie. By now the party was reduced to a drunken and incoherent shouting, and in spite of my own drinking I was profoundly disturbed. What had begun as highly civilized and sophisticated play, a conscious sublimation of hostile emotions, had become a force which had swiftly swept the annoyed colonists into regions where I was sure they had never ventured before, regions where they would have been outraged had anyone suggested they might ever arrive—except, perhaps, a psychoanalyst in slow, private sessions. And now I feared that should the woman show herself she would be attacked most brutally.

I watched as they hammered on the door, demanding that she appear, and when she failed to materialize they stood in a drunken row and, as by pre-arranged signal, relieved themselves thunderously against the oaken panels of her door.

I reminded myself that these were all refined, scholarly Americans, people with whom I was proud to be identified. Doubtless their opponent was vastly provocative, and there was the added circumstance that they were living far from home and the scenes of their childhood, apart from the land-scapes of their dreams, the countries of their minds. Indeed, all were dangling out of the familiar ridges and grooves which would have guided them at home. There they would have found quite adequate forms for dealing with both their emotions and their trying stone measurer. At home they would have ignored her, snubbed her. So, I thought, perhaps M. Vannec's leading man of letters is correct: Lose your supports, and go into a spin. Fall out of your well-worn groove, and you skate in chaos. Perhaps our little colony was pushed by irrepressible forces like those which I felt myself.

We're all being subjected to strange forces these days, I thought. Not only from abroad but right here at home. Only yesterday, a man of fifty, an early pioneer in the sexual revolution, a master of ideas, ancient and modern, a Ph.D. in anthropology, sociology, and English literature, was convicted of seducing an eleven-year-old babysitter while occupying a stool in an Orgone Box—which is, I understand, a scientific device designed to capture from the air an elusive element which is said to be the source of the life force. In fact, the man's defense was that there was such a concentration of life force within the box that he was *compelled* to his sad action. He insisted that the force was ir-resistible; he had been bombarded to supersaturation with *orgone,* that sub-stance of which the best and most metaphysical orgasms are made, to the point where, he insisted, he was no longer responsible for his actions. His in-discretion, he argued, was thus no more than the discharge of a natural force, like a flash of lightning.

Unfortunately, it was brought out by the prosecutor that he had given in to this irrepressible force on other occasions and with other babysitters, frumpy cooks and rump-sprung matrons in suburbia. When I read of this case, I had dismissed it as a special instance, but now I wasn't so sure. Perhaps the uncommon is far more real than we like to suspect. And perhaps, I thought, this *is* a country for shooting the bearer of bad news after all. Per-haps Sunraider had become for too many people the bearer of bad news. . . .

CHAPTER 9

THEY SWEPT AROUND THE far corner of the corridor in double-quick time, four dark-suited men hurrying toward me with submachine guns at the ready, followed by two men in white pulling and pushing a sheet-covered form on a smoothly rolling table. Two tense nurses, flanking the table, steadied a blood-plasma apparatus, their quick-thudding heels the dominant sound as they came on, followed by the two familiar security men, Tolliver and McKnight, armed with pistols. They moved on so swiftly that I could see old Hickman's head snap around at their approach, and then he was pulling quickly to his feet. I plunged the letter into my jacket pocket then and started forward—only to be motioned back by the hard-faced advance guards. They were swinging the table in a wide arc before the Senator's room now, opening the door and starting inside, and I got a glimpse of old Hickman's anxious eyes as they swept over the Senator's prone, white-faced form; then the door snapped shut, the security men were taking positions to either side, and old Hickman was asking,

"How is he?"

"Just stand aside," Tolliver said.

"I asked you how is he doing?" Hickman said.

"Just sit down and wait!" Tolliver said.

Hickman gave him a long, slow look, then turned abruptly back to his chair, his face a mask.

My attempt to question the security men bringing no better results, I hurried downstairs and telephoned Scoggins my information. Then, after making a vain attempt to locate the operating surgeon for a statement, I hurried back to the seventh floor. Where, I wondered, are the members of the Senator's staff?

I was relieved to see that old Hickman hadn't been called into the Senator's room while I was downstairs, but sat as before, huge in his chair. The corridor was hot and silent and I nodded to the security men, Tolliver and Bates, and threw myself back onto the bench, thinking to study Vannec's letter while I waited. I must have dozed off immediately, for suddenly the red image of plasma which I had seen sloshing in the blood-transfusion apparatus when the Senator was rolled past, burned in my mind. I could see the operating table with the Senator's chest cavity laid open, the flesh rolled back, clamps, lights; an atmosphere of tense concentration, the perspiring precision of nurse and surgeon, the labored diastole and systole of the struggling heart as they balanced his life on the tip of needle and suture, scalpel and sheer professional skill. The click and slap of instruments sounded in my mind, the rasp and pause of anesthetized breathing— I came to with a start, hearing the interrupted gasp which came with my own snoring.

I looked around. Hickman was still there. How was the Senator faring? Surely the very best surgeons had been called in, but what of his luck? What if he were on the fading edge of life? What if he possessed some rare blood type and old Hickman should actually have to be called in to supply it? Though aware that I was in the grip of an irrational force, a superstition, I shuddered at the thought but was unable to throw it off even while realizing that the main thing was to save the Senator's life.

Damn Hickman anyway; if he wasn't an accomplice, why was he here in the first place? Could the Senator be laughing at the confusion which his presence was causing—even while deep in anesthetic slumber? Hickman was under arrest, of course, but why had he been so obscenely *willing* to come here? Was it that he'd gladly surrender his pride in order to be near an important man? But what did he expect would come from his standing by an archenemy of his people? A headline? He called himself a minister; was he opting for some sort of sainthood? Did he think that he'd be considered the spokesman for a higher morality? The embodiment of some higher Christianity, some black fundamentalist agape? Was something like this behind his confounding conundrum of a forgiveness and charity surpassing earthly understanding? If so, he was politically naive, for no one in his right mind would accept the intrusion of such a kooky religious motive into the world of Sunraider politics, certainly not from anyone like Hickman.

I closed my eyes, seeing once more the Senator reeling under the impact of the bullets, the stain blooming through his shirt, Hickman crying out with upraised arms. Politics and blood, blood and religion, I thought, what a confusion has been released. And now, remembering that during the war I had written one of the first articles on blood-bank techniques, my irritation intensified. I realized that my upset over Hickman's offer of a transfusion was concealing something else, something painful and vile which I feared to face. But even as I snatched out Vannec's letter to try to switch my train of thought, I looked up to see old Hickman staring at me and shaking his head mysteriously. *What does he mean?* I thought. *Is he reading my mind?* It was something in his expression which started it, something abstractly accusatory and evocative of a buried time and a repressed defeat, all there on the broad dark face. Then I could hear McGowan's voice as it had sounded last night at the club, and something seemed to crash in my head and I was on my feet, propelled by a surge of pain which, like a long-suppressed sob, tore through me accompanied by an excruciating sense of shame.

I could see Hickman there as though illuminated by a spotlight, his face seeming to draw out that which I knew and did not know to lie behind my pain, and I could hear the sound, the rumble of an elevated train, could see the blue of sparks shooting from its wheels onto a dark day of slanting snow illumined by flashing lights, and I sensed where the speeding phantom train would stop, and to prevent its doing so, to block it, wreck it, I felt a compulsion to swift physical action, any relieving action, and Hickman was its target. I could feel my face flaming, and I wanted to tear him apart, but even as I willed myself to move forward I was overwhelmed and stood there, before my bench, staring through him in a paralysis of pain and lucid memory, pleasant now but then, oh, the pain.

Shortly before the war, back when I still thought of myself as a champion of "social significance"—*Oh, sing ah-me/ ah-song/ ah-so/ ah-glad*—I met while attending a dance held in a famous Harlem hall now destroyed, a young girl, a Negro (she taught me to capitalize the *N* and to never say "Negress") with whom I had an affair. It was intense, it was passionate, it was brief. But during the first blush of what we both regarded as love, I considered it as the most wonderful thing that had ever happened to me. For beyond the normal explosion of youthful emotion, there was a daring about it, a thrill arising from the socially forbidden made acceptable by the approbation of our friends, and rendered titillating by the hostility of those who automatically disapproved. Personally, I lived in a state of high delight. I felt that Laura endowed me with a special potency, thus I considered myself the possessor of a mysterious knowledge which gave me a touch of swagger whenever we strolled the easily challenged streets arm in arm, eye to eye, mentally hypnotized by our daring. And all this was given further sanction by our group zeal to improve, redeem, and, if need be, revolutionize society. But basically we were in love, and in our circles it was agreed that Laura and I represented, if not the future, at least a good *earnest* of that time when the old conflicts left unresolved by the great war between the states (and we were nothing if not historical-minded) and the wounds, outrages, and inequities which haunted contemporary society would be resolved by transcendent love. I spent hours in Harlem. I visited clubs, attended dances, absorbed the slang, the music, the turns of phrase, made great efforts to identify with all of Laura.

"Democracy is love, love is democracy," we often said, and our friends agreed. And this became, for a time, my personal slogan. Laura was lovely, eager, and brave, and there was much about the world which she didn't know, and I was delighted and proud to teach her of the many things which lay beyond the arbitrary boundaries placed around her freedom, and mine. We were dedicated to love and society, thus we looked to the future but, as it turned out, not quite far enough ahead.

Our affair went on for a year of glory that began in the spring and reached wild heights of passion, discovery, and delight during the holidays which ended the fall. Then during the winter, nature caught up with us, and what with our dream of a socially ideal alliance become a matter of parturition, we were suddenly faced with the hostile realities of both society and state, and I with my own astonished self.

I say "astonished" because of what I discovered about myself when facing the ordeal of confronting Laura's mother. I delayed for days, rushing about like a man searching for a hidden time bomb. It was a sore, nerve-racking trial; for as the implications of our situation began to come home to me, I found myself torn between my love, my sense of honor, and the fierce new aspect which the future revealed, now that I would have a dark wife and child perhaps as dark. Frankly, I was frightened. The rose-tinted bloom of Laura's brown complexion which had been until now an intriguing veil hiding a lovely human mystery, had suddenly become the very skin of terror itself. In my passion and joy I had never allowed the practical problems of our relationship to give me real concern; now the questions of where we would live and how my parents and employers would react to our marriage confronted me—and suddenly I was no longer courageous, nor avant-garde, nor even sure of my own mind and heart.

I told myself that I loved Laura just as much, perhaps even more, now, with the confluence of our bloods. And for herself alone, for she was a unique and lovely individual, a rare person. But now the questions of who I was, and who and what my parents and relatives were and had been, tore me apart. History, both past and future, haunted my mind. It was no longer merely an Hegelian abstraction, for I had been plunged into its bewildering interior. Now, for the first time since childhood, I felt need for the security symbolized by that thin chain of being personified by my parents, that lifeline of kinship which extended through time and space, from England and France to America, that I hoped would sustain me in my adventure into the dark interior of society. I visited the genealogical room of the Forty-second Street Library and brooded over the charts. I became obsessed with coats-of-arms, the signs and symbols of heraldry, the sounds and overtones of the name "McIntyre." I burned to know by what chain of genes Laura was sustained, and knowing my own pressing need and being alerted to the existence of gaps and mysteries, I surmised that Laura probably knew very little of whence she came, and this filled me with panic. Where, out of what past had she actually come to so dazzle me? Who and what stood back there in the dark behind her? How would they assume form, become repersonalized, now that they were linked with my future destiny? And what, I wondered— and here was the most embarrassing question of all—just what color would the baby's bottom be?

I became so upset that I couldn't eat. Nevertheless, I was determined to do the manly thing, although I couldn't imagine that any pressure of outrage or revenge would be brought against me as might have been true had ours been a more orthodox relationship. Instead, I reassured myself that when the initial shock and unpleasantness were past, Laura's parents might even find our marriage highly desirable. Given the shape and values of society, I saw no reason why they shouldn't. After all, my prospects were, relatively, unlimited.

Nevertheless, I realized my inexperience in these matters; I knew that mothers were formidable—at least, my own could be—and thus I found myself numb before the prospect of meeting my girl's parents. We'd never met because her father was always away on his job, her mother was never a participant in our activities, and because Laura had been shy about inviting me to her home (a circumstance that I had interpreted generously in my own direction—which was, I believed, the direction of the smooth and unhampered future). Since my own parents lived in another state, there had been no problem of introducing Laura to them. And this aside, I was on my own and, I thought, in absolute rebellion against the past, all ties of family. I would cross that bridge when and if I came to it.

But now, since I had the responsibility of informing a mother of her daughter's unwed condition, it was necessary that I meet Mrs. Johnson. She would become aware sooner or later, since Laura was attending City College and living at home, and I hoped that, by informing her now, things would be made easier for all concerned. There would soon be doctor bills and special care for which, naturally, I would pay, and the time would soon arrive when she'd walk heavy with my love and then, by mid-July, be introduced to motherhood. So after a night of terror and a morning of indecision, I braced myself and took the elevated train up Columbus Avenue to Harlem....

Standing there numb in my pain and watching old Hickman squirm in his chair, it was as though he were sitting beside me on the heavy-hearted ride, high there above the street. Then in my mind's eye I was looking out at the Cathedral of St. John the Divine, which loomed to our left, a flock of pigeons kiting lazily above its unfinished dome as the train climbed high above 110th Street, curving eastward. Then we were rumbling down to the dark of

Eighth Avenue and curving northward again with a noisy grinding of wheels and rails.

It was a chill, slate-gray wintry day when I climbed down to the street. Dirty snow lay over the ground and, though now late afternoon, cans spilling over with snow-drifted ashes and garbage still lined the walks. I moved beneath the thundering El for a few blocks, past small restaurants, barbershops with idle, slickheaded barbers, pink-and-blue-fronted beauty parlors and cheap law offices with windows prominently displaying red public notary seals, then turned into Laura's windy side street, where a funeral cortege of black limousines with dark people in mourning dress, the women in crepe-covered hats, the men grim-faced and still, began creeping eastward behind a dark maroon hearse. Behind the ornately framed glass a gray coffin with a large military flag lay exposed beneath a wreath and a few sprays of white carnations. In the family car a light-skinned woman in widow's weeds sat silently weeping. *A soldier,* I thought. I had forgotten that some were career army men. Then, keeping carefully to the deeper ruts of the ice-caked street, it was past, and a gang of ragged, snotty-nosed black children swept by, brushing my legs and jeering like a catastrophe of starlings. A short distance ahead I saw them sliding, arms and legs spread wide, over the icy walk to stop before a basement candy store, then, shouting like a band of Comanches taking a fort, they plunged inside. There was not a single mulatto among them. . . .

At Laura's building I began to feel like a man condemned to death row. My girl's mother was an immigrant from the South. A short, large-breasted, matronly dark woman whom I'd seen only in photographs, she was quite religious and outspokenly hostile to many of the more interesting forms of Harlem life as well as to the world of social action in which Laura moved. Until now, I had thought of her as an amusing, old-fashioned, and probably superstitious Southern figure whose relation to most of Laura's life was conveniently shadowy. But now, as I moved to meet her, it was as though to confront for the first time all of the darker complications of life, society, and history.

There were seven Johnson families living in the building, and the bell system was faulty, requiring that I try five doors before receiving the proper instruction. It was on the seventh floor, and I climbed the narrow stairs heavy with the odor of food and living. *It's fish,* I thought, half humorously, *old fish. The ghosts of a school of dead fish swimming forever in the air of the stairs.* Then I was pressing the bell with shaking hand and hearing its watery ringing within. *Fish,* I thought, *the entire building must live on cabbage and fish.* Then the door was cracked and I saw her; a large woman with graying hair drawn back from a smooth brown high-cheekboned face. Her coloring was dark, with a blush of red showing through like that of certain Indians. Her eyes seemed to look into me from behind a mask or a thicket of smooth leaves. She wore a shapeless black-and-white-checked dress.

"Yes, sir?" she said.

"If possible, I'd like to see Mrs. Johnson," I said.

"You have the correct one," she said. "I'm Mrs. Johnson."

"Oh, good," I said. I stared; the resemblance was unmistakable; she was a darker, older Laura, gone to plumpness, humility, and suspicion.

"Yes, sir, I'm Mrs. Johnson," she said. "I'm Mrs. Ernestine Johnson, and Thomas Jonathan Johnson, he's my husband. Just what is it you want to see me about?"

My stomach tightened and my mind took off, and I thought, *Would one have to call her "Mother," this big black woman, and be part of her most likely classic matri-archy, and my boy baby grandson to a dining-car waiter always on the railroad destiny while Laura flew out of nest but still in net with fish and turnip greens Southern-style always, and my baby son her grandson and me her son-in-law to be . . . to be . . . ?*

She had begun to frown. "Mister," she said, "are you all right?"

"Oh, yes, Mrs. Johnson; forgive me," I said. "I have to talk with you. It's urgent. May I come in?"

She looked at my hands, her eyes narrowing.

"Why can't you just say it right here?" she said.

"I'd rather speak to you inside, if I may. It's about Laura and our plans—"

"What! Laura Jean?" Her eyes widened as she took a step backwards, the door swinging wide. "Step right in here," she said.

I hesitated, her face suddenly glistened with beads of perspiration. A sharp, sultry fog of deodorant pressed around me. Then I was brushing past the huge softness of her into a dark vestibule. The odor of spiced apples coming to me from somewhere down the hall was a breath of relief.

"Go on into the living room on your right," she said behind me. "We can talk in there."

I found myself in a medium-sized, high-ceilinged room, furnished with three modest upholstered chairs, a coffee table, and a sofa set on a blue rug. Against the opposite wall an upright piano stood with a row of framed photographs arranged on top, one of them of Laura in white cap and gown, flanked by her smiling parents. Across the room to my left there stood a small bookcase containing a few books and a group of childlike porcelain shepherds and shepherdesses in eighteenth-century dress and genteel postures. Two potted poinsettias, one of them with a natural bract of scarlet and the other a pale green, almost albino, sat on the window ledge. It was all quite neat and surprisingly clean.

"Take that comfortable chair over there," Mrs. Johnson said. And I sat, facing the blue-draped window as she took a chair with her back to it, watching me nervously from the back-lighted shadow.

"Mrs. Johnson, my name is Welborn McIntyre," I began.

"Oh!" she gasped, becoming quickly silent. I counted to ten in my mind, then, "I'm pleased to make your acquaintance, Mr. McIntyre—though I must say that Laura didn't tell me that you were white...."

"She didn't?"

She shook her head. "That's right, she didn't."

I tried to smile. "That was probably because between us it isn't significant."

"Well, it is to me, Mr. McIntyre...." Her voice was throaty with sudden emotion.

She sat back, folding her broad arms across her breasts, regarding me.

"And I'll tell you something else, Mr. McIntyre: Something warns me that I'm not going to like whatever it is you come up here to tell me. So unless you're sure that you just have to say it, maybe you better go back and think about it awhile...."

A smile fluttered up then died stillborn somewhere behind the stiff surface of my face. I wished urgently to take her advice and leave, but I could only sit there, looking with silent fascination into her eyes. She looked like many of the black women whom I had seen so often, moving about the streets of downtown residential areas, and now, although I had never been in a room alone with one before, I was bound to her through Laura. Then I was seized with a sense of the unreality of it all. And suddenly I was no longer simply looking into her own eyes but through a window onto a long-forgotten scene in which my mother was calling to me in her own sweet, coaxing voice....

And I was four and playing in the backyard with friends while mother's club was meeting, and hearing her calling from the porch, "Welborn, darling, come here a minute."

"But gee, Mother, I'm playing."

"I know, darling, and I won't keep you long. You just tell the children to wait."

"But do I have to? We're playing."

"Now, Welborn, just tell them to hold the game. You won't be long."

"Oh, all right."

"Hurry back, Wel," Jimmy called, and I was running to where Mother waited, holding open the screen door.

"This won't take long, Welborn, darling," she said. "There's just something I want you to do for Mother. You'll do it, won't you, darling?"

"I guess so," I said, and I was thinking, She wants me to recite "Invictus" for those ladies but I'm tired of "Invictus." "If" is better. *Then we were in the hall and she was looking me over, saying, "Wel, dear, you'd better run and wash your hands and face—especially your hands, they're filthy—then you come into the parlor and we'll only keep you a minute," and I was running up the stairs to splash and hurry down again....*

They were sitting about in their summer dresses, drinking from cups of tea and all talking at the same time, and there was a coconut cake on the coffee table and I hoped there'd be some left for me and the gang, then Mother was saying, "Oh, there he is, ladies," and some of them said, "Hello, Welborn," and I said hello and was running "Invictus" through my mind so as to remember the order of the words—black pit pole pole unconquerable soul head bloody head unbowed—*and they were smiling and waiting and I said, "Mother, where do you want me to stand?" and she said "Come-over-darling. Come over where the ladies can see you better. And ladies, perhaps it would be better if you all gathered around...." And I thought,* Gather around for what? *"He's a fine-looking boy, isn't he?" one of them said. "He looks just like his mother." "Yes, and that's a sure sign of good luck," and Mother got up and took me by the hand. "Welborn, darling," Mother said, "the ladies have been listening to a very interesting and important and serious discussion but some of them are unfamiliar with the problem, so I told them that you wouldn't mind giving them a hand. And I looked at my hands, and said, "But don't you want me to recite 'Invictus'?" and she smiled and said, " 'Invictus,' darling? Oh, that's not it at all." "But what is it, then," I said. "I don't remember another one." "Oh, it isn't to recite, dear, it's something much easier," and she was smiling and they were watching and I said, "What is it, then?" And she said, "And now won't you be surprised— Wel, dear, I only wanted you to be nice and show the ladies your recent operation." And I was looking at her and shaking my head and feeling her grip tightening on my hand and my face burning. "Oh, no," I said, thinking she was teasing. "Now, Welborn," she said, "be nice, darling, all you have to do is allow the ladies to see what a nice neat operation the doctor performed." "But I can't do that." "But why, Wel?" "Because Daddy wouldn't like it and you told me never to—" "Oh, no, Wel, Daddy would be proud. So now be nice." "But why?" "Because some of the ladies don't have little boys of their own. So now you just show them and then you can go play." And I tried to fall down but she held me up. "Aren't men the darndest?" a large lady with a drawl said. "Always modest before our curiosity and spirit of inquiry, but you just let the wind blow and then watch them break their necks." "Please darling," Mother said, "or I won't allow you to go outside; you'll have to go up to your room instead...." "Oh, leave him alone, Agnes," Mrs. Waters said. "He's bashful and not at all the little man we thought he was...." "Is that true, Welborn?" Mother said, "Aren't you my little man?" "Of course I am, but I don't think men do what you want me to do. Daddy wouldn't—"*

Then they were laughing, and someone said, "He'd be surprised. Oh, but wouldn't he be surprised...." "Hush, Doris," someone said, and Mother said, "Then if you're manly, really manly as I know you are, darling, go ahead and show these ladies your little man— Here, I'll help you," and she left me no time to think it through and I felt her hand go away and stood looking through the window past the honeysuckle vine above the porch and on past the yellow light into the blue of the sky. She was working with my buttons and then I felt the air and she said, "There now, there, it's done so now you can show the ladies." And they came forward, gathering around with a closeness of perfume and powder and rouge and eyes. Then I was looking into the sky and it was between my finger and thumb; hearing, "That's fine, darling; Oh, that's lovely. I knew you'd oblige.

Now wait, don't go, just a moment longer. See what happens here, ladies? Now, darling, turn him over. There, so the ladies can see the beautiful stitches. Isn't that marvelous, ladies?" And they were looking at him silently and I could hear them breathing and the large lady was fanning herself with a pink handkerchief. "It's hygienic and absolutely beautiful," Mother said. "And did it hurt much, Welborn?" Mrs. Mayfield said, and my neck was stiff. "Go on, Gladys," Mother said, "Touch him; I'm sure Wel wouldn't mind." "Oh, thank you, no," Mrs. Mayfield said. "But didn't it hurt even the tiniest bit?" "No," Mother said. "But he's so young," Mrs. Mayfield said. "Absolutely not," Mother said. "I discussed it with Mr. McIntyre, and he says that it's done absolutely without pain and that Welborn will be thankful and very happy later on when he assumes the pleasures and responsibilities of the, er, marital state, ladies; you understand, marriage and all that," and I was thinking, Marriage, I will never get married, never, never, never, and through the shimmer I could see their faces go away, smiling as they talked on as though I was no longer there. "Thank you, darling," Mother said. "You can go now." And I was gone. "What took you so long?" Jimmy said. "Hey, you're crying." "No, I'm not crying," I said. "Yes, you are." "Oh, no, I ain't," I said. "Then what took you so long?" "Oh, I had to do something for Mother. Let's go play." But I could see their eyes, and then I was looking into that strange, dark, yet familiar, face again, hearing my voice blurting, "Mrs. Johnson, I've come to tell you that Laura and I have to get married," and seeing her shoot up in her chair.

"You have got to do *what*! With *my* daughter—boy, who do you think you're talking to?"

"But, Mrs. Johnson—" I began, but already she was up and leaning through the doorway, calling into the hall.

"Laura Jean, git up here this very minute!"

"What is it, Mother?" I heard Laura's distant voice reply. Thinking her at the college, I was surprised.

"Gal, don't stand back there asking me what is it; git up here!"

Laura's hair was in curlers and she wore a blue bathrobe.

When she saw me she stopped short.

"Oh, my God," she cried.

"Gal, who is this—this *white* man? Is he telling me the truth?"

"Oh, Mother, this is awful. You shouldn't use such a tone! That's Welborn. I love him!"

"*Love* him," Mrs. Johnson said. "What you mean is you been laying around with this white boy after I brought you all the way up here in order to get away from that kind of stuff down South! Who is he, anyway? Where'd you find him?" Her voice was a plea, a cry of despair, a scream emitting beneath a tumbling structure.

"Oh, I know he's a poor one. He looks poor! He *smells* poor! In fact, he looks poor and acts trashy! Coming in here without any warning, talking about marrying my daughter! You been sleeping around with him and his people are probably some of those old foreigners who think they're better than us because the first words they learned when they hopped off the boat were 'dirty nigger'— Answer me, you slut; I say, who is this peckerwood?"

Laura broke into tears, and I wanted to sink through the floor.

"Mama, please don't do this to me," she cried. "This is Welborn McIntyre. I've told you about him. He's no foreigner. He's none of those things you say."

"Far as I'm concerned, they're *all* foreigners," Mrs. Johnson shouted. "Is what he says true?"

"Yes, Mama, but not like you make it sound."

Mrs. Johnson's hands flew to her hips. "I say, is it true that you have to git married?"

"But Mother, it's all right, I love him—"

"Love?" Mrs. Johnson whirled completely around, her eyes blazing. "You mean to stand there and talk to me about loving this peckerwood—you, my own daughter? Loving him when even if he ain't a foreigner, he's probably the kind who sucks a black woman's tit from the minute he's born and lets her change his didies and feeds him and teaches him his manners and protects him, and then, when he's fourteen and feeling himself, he calls her a 'nigger bitch' and proceeds to hop on top of the first young black gal he can get to catch his devilment. You been knowing this ever since you were thirteen years old and still you can talk to me about loving a peckerwood—*any* peckerwood?"

Laura was suddenly calm. "Yes, Mother," she said, "I can, and do. I love him very much and what he says is true. But he's not a peckerwood and I'm not forcing him. It was as much my fault as his. I didn't even know that he was coming up here because I meant to tell you myself. He came on his own accord and wasn't forced—"

"Forced?" Mrs. Johnson said. "You're mighty right, you're not forcing him. And long as I have something to say about it, there ain't going to *be* any forcing. You just wait until your daddy comes in off the road, he'll be fit to be tied. After all our hopes and scheming and sacrifices, and you think that we're going to let you get tied up with the first poor-white-trash peckerwood that comes along, then I have raised a fool!"

"No, Mother," Laura said quietly. "Let's talk this out—"

Mrs. Johnson swung around, filling the door. "Talk," she said, "that's a good idea, because my mama taught me a long time ago the right way for a black woman to talk to a peckerwood about her daughter."

Then she was gone and I was looking at Laura, who pleaded with me with her eyes. Then Mrs. Johnson filled the doorway again, holding a shotgun.

"Now I'm ready to talk," she said. "Mr. McIntyre, you've done had your little talk, and you've told me what it is you *want* to do. All right, so now I'm

telling you what you're *going* to do: You are going to git out of this apartment, and you're going to git on back downtown, and you're going to forgit that you ever knew my daughter along with whatever it is she's been fool enough to let you git her with. That's right! Because if I ever see or hear of you two being together again, *I'm* going to kill you both and go to hell and pay for it— Now you git!"

I stood, moving forward like one in a trance. She was blocking the doorway.

"Mrs. Johnson," I said, "I'm not Southern, I came here to ask your permission to marry—"

"Oh, no, you didn't! You came up here to brag and try to impress Laura Jean. You don't want to do good, you just want to *look* good. Well, I'm telling you now that you can forgit it— Now ain't you glad? I just told you what you want to hear: All your troubles with your black woman are over!"

"But that's not it at all, Mrs. Johnson."

"Oh, yes, it is, and don't think I'm going to change my mind. And neither will Stone, except he's liable to kill you. We can take care of our own, Mr. McIntyre, and don't think I don't know what I'm saying! It'll be *ours,* black or white, red or green. You hear? It'll be *ours,* not y'all's, and it'll have to live *our* life, so it might as well get started from the beginning. You have broke your own rules, and you have shamed us, Mr. McIntyre, but one thing you haven't near 'bout done is beatin' us. Oh, no! Laura Jean is going to go South to her grandmother, and we'll all pull together and make the best of this mess. So now you go, and thank the Lord that you came on a day when Stone, Laura Jean's father, is out on the road."

My legs flowed toward the woman with the shotgun and stopped, seeing her turn aside, her face grim as I pressed myself past.

"Please, Welborn, don't leave," Laura called. "Not this way. Don't let her do this to us. Don't go in this way that'll leave you, oh, so ashamed later on. Welborn, please, Wel—born!"

I left, trying to shut out the sound of her tears. I was unable to look back to Laura even to make an affirmation with my eyes as I went out and down through the fishy air and out into the cold blast of the street. I felt wet and limp, a sharp odor issued from within the upturned collar of my overcoat.

I started for the subway, walking blindly, but found that I couldn't return downtown. How strange it all was. On my way uptown I would have felt lucky with the prospect of such an easy solution to my problem—even though I believed that I would have rejected it, but now, trudging along in the falling snow, there was no satisfaction within me. No satisfaction and no sorrow, only a deep emptiness, a feeling of defeat and rejection. I felt suddenly older and that I had learned a harsh wisdom not only as to the cost of love but of some precious but untenable vision of life. *And, yes,* I thought, as

I considered the poor people hurrying past me through the streaking snow, *I've suffered a defeat of hope. Our love had meant to help them, and now it was broken.*

But more confounding, I had been defeated not by my own family ties, or by the codes of my own social background, as I'd feared, but by an outraged, ignorant black woman who wanted no one like me, no one who even *looked* like me, in her family. And what I couldn't have allowed myself to believe but which she insisted that I secretly hoped: She preferred to have her daughter bear the burden of white bastardy rather than accept me as a son-in-law.

CHAPTER 10

I STUMBLED THROUGH THE snow-curtained streets like a man carving a snowbank with a white-hot iron attached to his brow. Everything I thought I had known melted into a hot, scalding contradiction that froze immediately into a chiller form. I walked blindly and so found myself back in her block, approaching her building again, but there I stopped. I hadn't the heart to face Mrs. Johnson again. Nor was it the shotgun which stopped me but the dread of an ever more final rejection. For a while I stood on the stoop, hoping that Laura would appear, but in vain.

Soon I began to attract attention. Dark faces appeared at the windows, peering out at me. I walked to the corner and southward, then moved east to find myself on Lenox Avenue. People hurried past bundled in their overcoats. Far ahead the streetcars clanged along on 125th Street, rocking slowly across the avenue, a mask of yellow swiftly disappearing from view. The snow fell wetly. There was a strong smell of barbecue in the air, then as I passed an apartment building a gust of wind blew a cloud of sulfurous smoke into the street, and I stood there in the slanting snow, shaken with a fit of coughing that brought tears to my eyes. I cried and cried. Finally it passed and I walked on.

(It's all still so vivid, after all the years of repression.) Near a corner, standing before a storefront window painted with a garish red-and-green scene of the Crucifixion, a blind man wearing a drab olive-green stocking cap, a frayed soldier's overcoat, and knitted gloves with missing fingertips, sang sadly as he strummed a battered twelve-string guitar. Flakes of snow sparkled in his moustache as he sang with uplifted head, and I could see the harsh scene of snow, grinding cars, and hurrying people reduced and vividly reflected in the dark lenses of his steel-rimmed glasses. *Damn it all*, I thought. *Damn it all!* Then, walking close, I dropped a quarter into the dented tin cup attached to the neck of his guitar.

He paused. "Thank you, brother," he said. "For a while there, I thought I was singing to an empty-hearted world."

I was silent.

"You still there, aren't you, brother?"

"Still here," I said with anguished tongue, "and thanks for the song."

"The pleasure is all mine, brother."

"It's getting much colder," I said. "Don't you think you should get out of it?"

"Not yet awhile," he said. "Got to get my cornmeal made."

"How is it going?"

"Bad, brother. It's going bad—for the time being, that is. I been working along here for about two hours, and I made all of forty cents, including what you just paid me. And two cents of the rest come from some little kids. Still, the way I see it, a man has to stay on the job and take his chances."

"Sure, but it's getting much colder," I said, "too cold for me, so I must leave. But before I go here's an advance for the next time we meet." Listening to the thump of the coin falling into the cup, I walked away.

"Hey there, brother," he called. "Come back a second. I got something to tell you. . . ."

"Take care," I called, moving on. What could he have to say?

As I passed a bar the door opened and I could hear voices raised in argument and thought of Laura and Mrs. Johnson, and the image of the bright red and pale green poinsettias glowed in my eyes like a suddenly illuminated neon sign. Back up the street behind me I could hear the blind man's voice rising once more in strong, clear song:

> *Every shut eye ain't sleeping, baby,*
> *And every goodby don't mean gone,*
> *So you're bound to think about me, baby,*
> *When those hard, hard times come 'long. . . .*

How strange, I thought, that the song could sound so sad, yet when he'd talked his voice had seemed somehow quite gay.

I went into a bar and ordered a bourbon. Down at the other end of the counter three men were telling tales of Dutch Schultz and someone named "Pompey." A stuffed owl and the head of a twelve-point buck were fixed to the wall above the back bar. A photograph collection of black prizefighters in pugilistic poses showed in the mirror frame, along with a sign in red letters asking, "WHERE HAVE ALL THE WHITE HOPES GONE?" I drank up, paid, and went out into the cold.

It was still snowing. I walked along, looking into the faces of the people and into shop windows displaying cheap goods. Statuettes of Malvina Hoffman, African warriors, Jesus Christ, and straightening combs; Kewpie dolls stood in a Gethsemane of   . At the corner I saw people boarding a streetcar headed west and followed them on. It didn't matter where it would take me, only that it wasn't downtown. Perhaps it would turn up Amsterdam Avenue and rumble north to Fort Tryon and then I could walk up to the Cloisters. I would watch the broad vista of the Hudson. As it rumbled westward my mind floated; passengers got off and on; a woman carrying a kerosene stove came on; then the motorman was calling back to me, "Hey, fellow— you going cross on the ferry?"

"Ferry?" I said, "Why, no, I thought you were going north."

"No," he said, "That's the next car. We go back and forth, just back and forth. From here you cross the river."

For a moment I hesitated, thinking, *Why not cross the ferry?* But then I got off and walked east again, slowly against the wind. I had lost track of time. At a fork in the wide street a car traveling furiously east skidded on the ice, cutting a broad figure eight and came to a rattling stop beside me. And as I waited, a black man wearing a derby stuck his head out of the window, laughing uproariously. (Hickman was looking at me curiously now, but I still couldn't move.)

"Wheeee, goddamn!" the man yelled. "Man, man, as you are my witness, I'm driving the *hell* out of this sonofabitch this evening!" Then he was shifting gears and roaring away, gone. I hadn't noticed the dark, but the streetlights were coming on and yellowish lights were blooming in apartment windows. The cold had begun to numb me. I continued east, still unable to go down into the subway.

Noticing a brightly lit movie entrance, I bought a ticket and went in, but dropped off to sleep before the film came on. I dreamed fitfully of my mother, of a wild ride down a snowy hill on a red sled, of a cloud of stinging bees. Then someone was shaking my shoulder and I looked into a blaze of lights, out of which the face of a man wearing a porter's cap suddenly appeared.

"Hey, buddy," he said, "it's time to go unless you aim to find you a home in here."

"What? Oh, I guess I fell asleep," I said.

"Oh, you been sleeping all right. You been doing some of the damndest sleeping I ever seen. You been trucking and pecking in your sleep, and that's no lie. What's more, I've had to chase two hard-hustling chippies, a couple of kids with rubber bands and bent pins, and a lousy amateur pickpocket with a razor blade—all off of you, and you ain't even blinked an eye. You a detective or something?"

"Why, no, why do you ask?"

"Because I figure that only a detective that's trying to catch him somebody special would play it as cool as you have."

"Well, I'm not a detective," I said.

"You were really asleep?"

"Yes."

He shook his head. "Well, you better take care of yourself, because sleeping the way you been doing in a place like this is just begging for trouble."

I stood up. "Thanks for protecting me," I said, feeling for my wallet. It was still there. I offered him a dollar bill.

He shook his head. "Oh, no, man; that's okay. I was just doing my damn job. You just keep your eyes glued back."

"Thanks again," I said.

When I went out a crew of men were changing the signs on the marquee to one announcing "The Lost World Returns" and the street was almost empty.

Again I walked westward toward the subway, and now, although I had been consciously aware that I was refusing to think about Laura, the anguish overtook me. I ached to see her and my mind kept anticipating the outcome of our affair, screaming to me of the paradox that although ended, cut off, severed, it could never end. What would happen to her and to the child, or that which was swiftly becoming a child? What would become of that part of me that would be taken south to grow up in a lowly and alien section of the land? Would any trace of me remain to find existence there; my voice, my face? And what lay ahead? Would I encounter in some future time and place, perhaps along such a street as this, a dark youth bearing my father's features, moving with reflections of my mother's grace—a black boy with a brown face in a black crowd reminding me of my grandfather's patrician presence, his cast of features, his flair of phrase? I felt utterly heartbroken, walking desperately through a slum of heartbreak which seemed, like the blind man's song, to have evaded ultimate defeat. And yet I was myself defeated.

I was walking westward slowly, and sweating in spite of the cold. If only I had been more careful! More thoughtful! I could feel the guilty consequences (was it guilt? guilty so soon!) growing in secret darkness, nourished and warm yet bomblike, a fertile seed in metamorphic change extending itself into the distant future, completely out of control; toiling beyond my capacity for action, responsibility, or understanding. I wanted desperately to stop it, to cast it out before it could further extend its physical dimension and my guilt. How was it done? *It's dishonorable and a crime,* I thought. Then hurriedly, abstractly: *But man is obligated to exercise control over nature, to make his own destiny. Change the course of rivers, protect his heritage, perform appendectomies, hysterectomies, lobotomies. This is no abstract matter unfolding within a rigid frame; flexibility is demanded; yes, and the assertion of will against chaos.... There are physicians expert in such matters. But who? Where do I find them? Surely there are black ones for that black art. Yes....*

But I knew even as my mind turned to such desperate measures that Laura would never accept such a solution. Nor would her mother. They would rather punish me. *Of course, that's what they're doing*, I thought. *The mother's vicious, uncivilized. Civilization is the acceptance of the implicit violence necessary to social stability with the maximum consciousness and grace*, I formalized. *Man has to say no, he even has to kill. Life is death, capital punishment. Live with his acts.* But something was wrong with this, I didn't like it. I left it like a breath of fog in the cold air.

I walked along, my mind in a fever as I cursed the state of things. I thought of lying in wait for Laura, in a hired car, to take her away to a nearby state to marry her. I would hire a private detective to find her. But then a part of my mind argued passionately, even there in the icy air, that this would mean to give in to the harrassments and intimidations of society and to the tyranny of the future, and to use force—when Laura and I had agreed that the only proper motive for marriage was love. Why had it come to this? Why had it turned out like this, when I had meant so well, when I had come up to—

Suddenly I was startled by a shrill whirring sound. From an optometrist's window on my right, a clock in the shape of a huge glowing eye stared at me from a darkness of black velvet. Slanted black Roman numerals stood out around the dingy and bloodshot white like a heavy fringe of lashes or thickly applied mascara, and the hands were attached to the dilated pupil of the blue-black iris of the eye. And now I realized that the sound, high-pitched and irritating even through the thick glass, was coming from its quivering red second hand.

Racing with a frantic circling—a sign of time out of synch with time—it was spinning as though some electronic instrument had been released and then taken over by an energy more powerful than its cogs and gears, its condensers and resistors, its rectifiers and negative feedback systems, could ever contain. A sound of nerve-scraping anguish, it caused a feeling of the uncanny to sweep swiftly over me and evoked a scene which I had observed on an empty winter street of a night long ago: *The walks were glassy beneath my feet, snow drifted in the gutters, and the trees of crystal snapped and swayed in a wind that howled, raw and searching. I had been returning from a party, and, in passing a lighted department-store window, my eye had been caught by a tableau of the Nativity, a crèche, in which all of the familiar figures of that Bethlehem stable scene were charmingly displayed—with the Babe in the manger and the Holy Family, sad and sweet in their ancient clothes, looking down with rapt adoration upon the Babe, and all surrounded in a gentle light by sloe-eyed cattle and the patient donkey; with the kneeling shepherds' worn, worshipful faces transformed by the living miracle of the spirit incarnate in the infant boy, their god and promise of a new dispensation. And above the stable, the hovering, long-pointing star beneath which on a long and winding road, the Three Wise Men, the Magi, magnificently dressed with their regal gifts on camelback, seeking out the Babe, with sad hopes for future joy and willingly suspending their ancient beliefs for a world announced in the Infant's cry, the future certified and showing forth in a radiant Boy in a filthy stable. . . . And I had been carried away then as I had now been carried away by memory before the anguished eye in the darkness. . . .*

But then, in the whirl of artificial snow which surrounded the remote and transcendent scene in the stable, I saw a tiny mouse racing hysterically about as though in a blizzard, a true storm of whiteness. Around and around and around it darted and probed in that swirl of snow, blown by a hidden electric fan, trying in vain to find an escape into its own quiet hole of darkness. And I had stood transfixed, there in the cold before the scene, hoping for its success—until a policeman had come up and ordered me along home. . . .

Now all this recurred in the split second it took that screaming hand to negotiate its ambiguous eye, and then a wave of anguish had racked me and, "Ah, Laura, forgive me," I cried—and the man stepped out of the darkness of the optometrist's deep doorway.

He stood pale and brutalized in the light of a passing car as he brushed at his clothes and stretched and yawned, and I could see a red scar which started at the corner of his left eye and moved in a livid welt down his cheek to disappear beneath his chin. Wearing, incongruously, a filthy maroon turban and no overcoat, he stared at me from beneath heavily drooping lids.

"Look a-here, buddy," he said, with a wave of his hand, and in my shock I blurted out that which was on my mind.

"Look," I said, "I came up here to do the proper thing, the manly thing. Her mother was the one who stopped me. It was her fault."

He looked at me, wavering, chuckling, shaking his head. "I dig you, man. Uh-huh, I dig you; I *know*. These here bitches is out to get us all. You don't believe it, you just take a good look at me. Nine months ago, man, I had me five thousand dollars and a baby grand, fifteen suits of clothes, and an Oldsmobile Ninety-Eight with brand-new rubber, then I met a bitch who dropped me smack-dab in the middle of trouble like a yolk, man; I can tell you all about these whores. But look here now, can you spare a nickel for a cup of coffee? I ain't et since way this morning, and out here it's cold as a bitch's cast-iron heart."

I took out some coins and watched him take them with trembling hands, flinching inwardly at the touch of his filthy long-nailed fingers.

"Thanks, man. You're a friend in need—I mean a friend indeed."

"It's nothing," I said.

He looked at me, wavering languidly in the wind.

"What did you say was the name of that bitch who done you in? It wasn't Agnes, was it? Agnes Jenny Jenkins? 'Cause if it was, you lucky you got away in such good condition. That's a *bad* bitch, man, with zippers on everything, including her funky drawers. It wasn't Agnes Jenny Jenkins, was it?"

I shook my head, breathing the foulness of him despite the cold.

"Well, don't let her get you down, man, whoever she was. Go get you another one as quick as you can, and forget it. Go to another town and git you a young one that ain't been broke in yet. Yeah, that's what you got to do." He wiped his mouth with the back of his hand, then scratched his arm, shivered. "Damn, but this is a cold night. I better go git that coffee. I be seeing you now."

I watched him move away, his arms stiff to his sides, walking back on his heels and staggering slightly, then bending forward; a thin figure in a summer suit, he headed into the wind.

Reaching the entrance of the subway again, I remembered an after-hours nightclub located a few blocks north where I'd once gone with Laura and some friends, and was suddenly taken with the hot certainty that if I went there I would see her. She would be trying to forget. Perhaps she hoped I'd remember and go there too. . . .

It was crowded. Even the bar near the entrance was packed with drinkers, and the tables along both walls and the narrow space in between were crowded with dark people drinking and listening to a group of musicians playing on the bandstand set against the rear wall. A jam session, for which the place was famous, was taking place, and I checked my coat at the door and took a seat at a side table near the rear.

The room was warm, reeking with perfume, smoke, and alcohol and quickly made me so drowsy that I found it difficult to focus as I looked around for Laura in the dim, smoke-filled light. There were many women in the room, but I couldn't tell who were alone, who with escorts. A waiter came, and I ordered a double bourbon, drank it quickly, and ordered another as he rushed past on his way to the bar. Although no one paid me the slightest attention, I felt strange and out of place. Then a big dark man, wearing a tuxedo which threatened to burst across the shoulders and a very white shirt with a black bow tucked beneath the collar, came over and spoke as though he knew me.

"And how are you this evening?" he said.

"Fine," I said. "I'm fine."

"That's fine," he said with a smile. "That makes me feel good, just to hear it. We want you to make yourself at home, enjoy yourself. We'll be having a real battle of music in a little while. You know, when the top musicians start coming up from their jobs downtown. Big DeWitt is coming in soon, and he'll get it started. You want anything you just ask the waiter; anybody get out of line with you, call me. I'm the owner *and* the bouncer." He chuckled.

"Thanks," I said. "I'm waiting for a friend who should be here by now."

He leaned over the back of a chair.

"A gentleman friend or a lady friend?"

"A girl," I said.

"Uh-huh," he said pointedly, waiting. "Did you look around?"

"Yes, but it's so crowded and dim and ..." My voice trailed off.

He laughed again. "And it's so awfully hard to see us in this light and everything," he said.

"Oh, no, I didn't mean that," I said.

"I know," he said, "but there's no point in being embarrassed by the facts, is it now? In fact, some of us are proud of it. Not me, necessarily, but some are. What kind of looking chick is she?"

"She's ... she's beautiful," I said.

He studied me a second, his face suddenly blank.

"I bet she is too." He shook his head, smiling. "It's the damndest thing, they *all* beautiful. Yes, it's the damndest thing, you just mix 'em up a bit and give 'em some contrast and they *beautiful!*"

"But she *is*," I said, "very beautiful...."

"I don't doubt it one single bit; didn't I just say it? But what I mean is, what *shade* is she?"

"Shade?"

"Color," he said.

"I don't know, really, but maybe brown. Her name is Laura Johnson. Do you know her?"

He was no longer smiling.

"Is her daddy named *Stone* Johnson?" he said.

"That's right, her father is called 'Stone.' Have you seen her?"

He straightened up.

"No, I haven't seen her, and if I were you I wouldn't ask anybody about her. I'd just sit here and enjoy myself until she comes in. Stone's a friend of mine, and a fool. He's one way on those dining cars—smiling and laughing for tips and all that. But on the streets of Harlem he's a different man. Stay away from him. He's rough. He quotes the Bible like a goddamn preacher, and he whips heads—anybody's head—in the name of the Lord. Have fun now," he said, and was gone.

And I was more uneasy than ever now, even though he hadn't been unfriendly. As I drank I continued to look about at the women's faces, but guardedly, so as not to give offense. Why had he laughed at me? I wondered. What did he know?

A large yellow man, looking shaggy in a loosely fitting tux, squeezed past the table now, carrying a saxophone, and he was smoking a cigar and smiling, and I saw a girl jump up from one of the center tables and embrace him.

"It's Big D," she cried, and I thought it was Laura. "He's here like they said he'd be," she cried delightedly, then she turned to wave toward the bouncer, and I saw my mistake.

"Thanks, Barrelhouse," she called to him. "Now we'll have some action. Daddy D, I mean the great *Big* D, is going to blow and blow!"

She knew whereof she spoke, for though I returned to my drink and thoughts of Laura, the atmosphere seemed to change. Spurred by the big man with the saxophone, the music soon reached a hysterical pitch of surprise-producing unrestraint, creating a mood which reached inside and grabbed me. They played now with a controlled wildness, a dazzling burst of improvisational pyrotechnics which left me even more out of phase than before. Around me the rapidly drinking audience had begun shouting exhortations to first one and then the other of the drum-, guitar-, and bass fiddle–driven soloists. The room shrank and expanded before my eyes. The trumpet player drew himself into a knotted, squat position as the drummer rolled away with a set, remote expression, and blasted my ears with what sounded like screams of mocking laughter. There was something cruel about the sound, something unforgiving intensified by his posture, which was neither one of standing nor of sitting but of some strained torturous position in between. My eardrums throbbed. I wanted a drink, but the waiters kept rushing past me with their trays held high, literally dancing back and forth between the tightly grouped tables. Finally one stopped and took my order, and it was then, as my eyes followed him back to the bar, that I saw a short dark figure, dressed in the black habit and head cloth of a nun, coming forward carrying with ceremonial gravity a Bible which rested on a small tambourine.

Moving with strange, crablike steps she seemed headed straight for me, when a passing waiter yelled, "Lawd, lawd, here comes Mother Smathers!" And I saw her bow piously to him, then, pausing for a long moment to look me straight in the eye, she moved on to the table next to mine and extended her tambourine.

"Darlings," she said in a hoarse voice, "give a little something for the poor widow womens and the hongery little orphans."

I looked around for the bouncer. It seemed hardly the place or time for such a figure, but evidently she bore special privilege. For despite looks of annoyance, most of the guests paused long enough to toss coins into the tambourine, then, ignoring her "God bless you, baby," they returned to the roaring contest of sound. *To what order does she belong?* I wondered. *Who is her bishop, her mother superior?* She had the full-cheeked, full-lipped expression of a petulant baby and seemed to regard my presence with silent disapproval as she continued from table to table. I looked away.

The big saxophonist was improvising now, seeming to talk, to speak in a hoarse, reedy stylization of human speech; pleading, crooning, coaxing, then rising to great heights of abstract eloquence which evoked for me, in my disturbed state, those movies in which great Indian chieftains bespeak in the native tongue their tribe's vision of the world to representatives of the white man's church, his army, and the executive branch of his government. I could see mountains and canyons, forests and plains, a row of horsemen bearing feathered lances, their warbonneted heads outlined against the sky along the curve of a noble hill. Then he was laughing maliciously through the melody of a popular love song, lacing it with raucous catcalls, hoots, howls, bear growls, and belches which ridiculed its sentiments, mocked its pretensions. Then the sound subsided into a serene, delicately phrased song. And it was the same song but now transformed by a mood which belied the man's appearance, the people, the place, the very banality of the song itself. Tears flooded my eyes as I watched his big bulk swaying gently back and forth, thinking as applause roared up, *You nasty bastard, you're playing with me. You're playing on me, and all the rest, but you're laughing at me, and I have to stay here for Laura....*

Then, "Go, man, go!" a voice yelled behind me, and looking toward the bar, I wiped my eyes to see a slender solitary drunk, wearing a tuxedo and a red cummerbund, who had cleared a spot and was improvising dance steps to the music. Past the toiling waiters I could see him clearly now, shaking his shoulders, bending his knees, gyrating his hips, and snapping his fingers, backwards and forwards with his head loosely bobbing—all in a wild but what seemed to me beautiful relationship to the music. The bartender and nearby customers were urging him on in his struggle to outdo in the extravagance of his movements the intricate patterns created in sound. It was then I saw the nun moving crabwise around a perspiring waiter and coming toward him with her tambourine extended.

"Hey, watch it there," the bartender called. "This ain't no time for no damn preaching; can't you see this man is riffing him a dance!"

Preacher? I thought. *So that's* her role—just as the circle of wood, taut skin, and metal disks came into contact with the dancer's arm, causing his eyes and mouth to snap open like one jolted out of a trance.

"Hell-yeah," he yelled, "that's *just* what I need to blow that tenor player to hell and gone!" And without missing a step in his dance, he snatched the tambourine and sent bills and coins flying—as the lady preacher fell backwards, surprised—and began striking himself on head, elbow, palm, and backside; twisting and turning, sliding and weaving, shaking and skidding, now in spasmodic competition with the big-bellied saxophonist who, as my head came round, stood with widespread legs and backward tilt to his body, sounding as though bent upon blasting himself—hands, feet, and bucket-sized head—through the reed and bell of his own outthrust and rampaging horn. The sound rang the room like hammers, causing it to rise, fall, and reel beneath his blasts and spurring the dancer to ever more frenzied twists and turns.

Then, through the smoke and roar of sound, I could hear the rapid *ching-chingle-jing, chingle-jangle, ching ching ching!* of the tambourine as he shook and whirled himself about; moving now like a proud Spanish dancer, stamping his heels and flinging his head; to become with a twist and a flash of leather a prancing horse, a fish on its tail, a circus bear, an aristocrat on roller skates holding his crotch with one hand while the other pointed toward the ceiling; then he became a trailer truck in a crowded street, a knock-kneed camel with a limber neck, a pecking rooster, a mating stallion, a transported suppli-cant in a frenzied rite, a twisted cripple with two dancing legs—and through these flying formations the watchers were joining in with clapping hands en-thusiastically.

Until now the lady preacher had stood by with arms akimbo, staring like one in a daze at the coins scattered beneath his flashing feet, and it was now that he began to try high kicks, sending a coin rolling across the floor to strike her shoe, that she went into action.

Bending in what I thought was an effort to retrieve her scattered harvest, Mother Smathers came up flashing a vicious, high-heeled, black patent-leather shoe and charged the oblivious drunk like a pantheress. A blow to his head brought a spurt of blood flashing red beneath the low ceiling light, and as she grunted and struck again, I tried to stand but stumbled and fell back, watching openmouthed as now, her broad backside working as though two furious midgets were fighting beneath her wide black robes, she rushed the drunk like an experienced street fighter, tilting tables and knocking cus-tomers aside as she drove him down the polished floor toward the bandstand.

Now women were screaming, chairs were clattering, musicians with in-struments held above their heads were trying to escape. I grabbed a quick drink and got to my feet, sensing danger but too fascinated by what I saw, feeling too intensely alive, to leave.

Strolling with Laura, I had often encountered such black nuns and women preachers on the streets of Harlem, had listened to the preachers' apocalyptic sermons, but never had I seen anything like this. With images of a hatchet-wielding Carrie Nation wrecking saloons springing to mind, I took another drink and stepped upon the bench for a better view.

Looking across the swirling heads, it was as though the drunk was danc-ing again, only now with the irate preacher. For, with his arms held high, he weaved and bobbed, dodging rhythmically from side to side, back and forth, as Mother Smathers struck at his head with her shoe.

"Somebody better grab this woman," he yelled. "They better grab her!" Then, trapped by the bandstand to his rear, with customers milling on either flank and with Mother Smathers before him, he suddenly bent forward and

lunged, driving into her middle with his bleeding head. It was his first blow
in self-defense, bringing a loud explosion of breath as it bent her double.
And I could see him reach out and grab, snatching her forward and sharply
down to snap her erect and back with the full jacking force of his knee.

"Goddamn, save me from Arkansaw and Mississippi," a man's voice
shouted, and as in an act of magic I could see a black cloth billow up to
tremble, momentarily airborne, then turning in upon itself like a child's
parachute and collapsing. I almost lost my balance then, striking my head
against the wall in recovering, and it was like watching a motion picture
from which, in a television version, an important phase of encrossing action
had been cut and spliced together with outrageous disregard for my sense
of credibility.

Below me the faces suddenly flowed, liquid and loose and with a sudden
slackening of feature, to freeze into masks of wide-eyed disbelief. I could
hear the clanging and lazily shimmering sound of an object striking against
the strings of an amplified guitar, producing an idiotic degenerating, slackmouthed musical chord. And in the sudden hush, Mother Smathers swung
around, her back to me now and directly beneath a light, and I was looking
down upon a closely cropped Negro head in which a part had been expertly
cut with a barber's razor. An X-shaped scar marked the dead center of her
scalp, and I could see the luxurious flowing of a row of wrinkles rippling in
stylized and orderly procession down the rear of her skull, disappearing beneath the high neck of her habit.

She flounced to her left then, and a woman screamed, "Oh, no, it can't *be!*"
And I could see the lethal shoe flash up and away as Mother Smathers
whirled about, throwing her hands to her head as the drunk shot past, making for the door. She backed against the bandstand now, glaring and at bay, as
a man yelled, "Hey! Ain't this *heah* a bitch!" and grabbed for her robe. And
suddenly the faces flowed again, breaking up and coming apart in the hic-
cuping beginning of a wild surge of laughter.

"Don't a motherfucker move," Mother Smathers cried, trying frantically
to snatch up her gown; and I could see the drummer now, his face agleam
with angry concentration, leaning over the bandstand and aiming a nasty
blow with the sharp edge of his high-hat cymbal at the squat and exposed
head.

A sharp odor of incense seemed to pervade, arising on the high-pitched,
gonglike sound which tore through the room, as Mother Smathers went
reeling sideways and back into the waiting hands of Barrelhouse, who, applying a headlock, rushed her, bucking and cursing and striking out, up the
stairs into the street.

There was silence, broken by the sound of shifting feet and creaking
chairs, then the room erupted in a laughing uproar. A waiter, short-armed

and long-waisted like a dwarf, was scooping up the tambourine and running with rolling, short-legged steps, up the stairs to the entrance where outlined in the brightness of the doorway, white jacket against the dark, he sailed it vigorously into the street, whereafter a madness seemed to take over the room. People were bending double and falling across tables as I climbed down. Someone knocked over the snare drum, a woman shrieked. And by the time I could push my way forward to join the line forming before the checkroom, there came a blast of cold air and Barrelhouse started down the stairs, rubbing his knuckles in his palm. His face was grim, but I could see small insurrections of laughter threatening to break out around the corners of his mouth.

"Hey, Barrelhouse," a man laughed at the bar, "that was the lick that did it!"

"Yeah," Barrelhouse said, "but that lick was way damn late. My ace had been hunching me all along that something wasn't right about that fool, but those Jesus clothes fooled me."

He stood on the bottom step looking indignantly around. "Who the hell *ordained* her, that's what I want to know!"

"You mean who ordained *him*," the man said.

" 'Him' or 'her,' I don't give a damn, from now on I'm barring 'em all. It makes for too much confusion, bringing religion into a jazz joint— Hey, where you people think you're going? The session ain't over, the musicians are still charged up, some others are coming soon, *and* I'm fixing to serve everybody breakfast on the house. Eggs to order and everything. Come on back and sit down!"

He came quickly down the steps, then, noticing me, he stopped, his face suddenly blank. "Hey," he said in a gruff, deadpan voice, "that was a bitch, wasn't it? A lo-mo funky row, huh?" He watched me shrewdly.

"It was too much for me," I said.

He threw back his head and roared. "Yeah, it was for ole Heapachange Hudson too," he said. "I never seen such action in a tux in all my born days. When I got to the street he was cold sober and long gone. He was probably in the hospital before I could get that flimflamming phoney bastard up to the street. By the way, did you see your girl?"

"No," I said, "she didn't come."

"Well, you never know about a woman. Maybe if you come back tonight she'll be here. Done mixed up the date, you know. But hell, stay anyway and enjoy the music; have some food. The musicians are bound to come on strong, because there's nothing like a little extra excitement to get them really jumping."

I thanked him but declined. When the check girl brought my coat she was as excited as the others. I tipped her and smiled, but I didn't share her high-pitched laughter. As I moved away, the musicians had returned to their places, and now deep, rumbling piano chords were sounding beneath the roar. I moved up to the street, feeling a deepening sense of isolation, a growing emptiness.

It was the weird mixture of sacred and profane which provoked the laughter and gave it its character that got me. There was a note sounding through it that was more upsetting than the violent and androgynous figure who had aroused it. It was too inclusive, it hinted at too many unnameable, chaotic, and unpleasant things, of   that were beyond my capacity of confrontation, and I was relieved to put them behind me with the closing of the door. But even so, it wasn't ended, only muted. For I could still hear it behind me, buoyed now by searching minor chords.

Outside it was cold, silent along the avenue. I looked around for the exposed preacher, but no one was in sight. Pellets of ice whistled past in the brisk wind, peppered my face. Drops of blood were splattered at intervals along the walk past the silent buildings. In front, signs of struggle and the trampled tambourine showed in the snow piled along the curb before the club. Looking directly across the avenue through the slowly lifting light, I faced a high sheer wall of gray-hued rock which swept northward on a gradual rise to become, two blocks away, a slanting, tree-strewn park showing white with crystal shrubs and drifted branches, and then arose, silently exalting the drifted snow, to emerge again, metamorphosed—gray rock again, but chiseled now and mortar-bound into a line of college buildings set like battlements, crenelled and merloned, embrasured and bartizaned, yet looming serene and decorous in the first light, high on the hill.

There soon the flags would fly, rippling briskly in the wind, and students clad in winter wool would gather from throughout the city, and girls with snowflaked breath would slowly trudge fresh paths upon the drifted whiteness. And would Laura, with our hidden secret, climb that hill today, rise to the invincible battlements? I turned. How could I have hoped to see her here? The laughter beneath the walk would continue into the middle morning, the horns contending through the day. They were wild there below, laughing at chimeras; locked out of time....

I shook my head, baffled by what I'd seen and by what I couldn't face. Vague currents of thought swirled up and away as I tried vainly to bind basement and battlement into a skein of meaning, while far up the curving avenue below the colleged hill, the traffic lights were turning green, green.

I turned, preparing to start south for the subway, then high above the street two black cats with crooks in their tails streaked past along the snowy ridge of the rock—just as the basement behind me exploded with an uproarious version of an old spiritual tune, "Ain't Gon' Study War No More," through which wild accents of laughter sounded.

Going to lay down
    my sword and shield
      Down
        by
          the riverside
      Down
        by
          the riverside
      Down
        by
          the riverside
Going to lay down
    my
      sword and shield
      Down
        by
        the
          riverside . . .
Stud-day-eh
   War
   No
   More!

It was a rowdy farewell fanfare, I later realized, announcing both the end to my relation with Laura and to my efforts at social action. I turned up my collar and hurried away, feeling myself the victim of an impossible and impractical love.

CHAPTER 11

MY LOSS, HOWEVER, HAD not been easy to accept. Emotionally I did not so soon surrender. I fell into a depression which led to several fruitless consultations with an analyst (who told me little that I was prepared to understand, things about my psyche which seemed ridiculous). Then, as suddenly as one's hair is said to turn white overnight, I forgot it. Both my concern with the social future and my shame and sorrow were buried beneath a burst of activity brought on by the war. And all that had defeated me had become, it seemed, part of a time out of mind, a life lived and lost. But now as I stood there in the hospital corridor, it was all back and ripping me apart.

A wave of humiliation swept over me, shaking me, and I thought, *So it was that and then that has me now. Two dark women and a piece of lost time bound to a section of a city left long ago which I haven't seen in years.... Here and now dark things and dark people lost in the dark places of my mind are with me, and no search for peace nor pining for the past released them here, but him, sitting there!* And I looked at Hickman, feeling as though my chest, my throat, were splitting apart.

Then an amused voice like that of McGowan drawled to me sotto voce but with the penetrating clarity of a mosquito's drone: *"Now take it easy, McIntyre; don't go letting a thing like* that *get you down. Not with that Hickman watching you. Sit down, man, or he'll see you. And don't forget, we've all got something to hide; we wouldn't be men if we hadn't. Besides, whoever heard of a bastard born out of a plasma bottle, or a nigra bred of a transfusion of blood through a hollow needle!"*

As the outrageous joke exploded in my head I heard a wild burst of laughter rip from my lips and quickly stifled it, looking behind me for McGowan.

Emptiness!

The elevator droned, dropping past with a blur of slitted light. Things seemed suddenly darker. Then completely without warning I was bounding down the corridor through a hot thickness of light and shadow, heading toward Hickman and shouting within myself, *How dare you force your way into my secret mind, intrude on memories!*

I was standing over him then, with the eerie sounds of collapsing structures, the blaring of an automobile horn, echoing through my head. I stared at him, still sitting with closed eyes, unaware and yet seeming to judge me. And still unaware as my arm moved. Then I could feel the fierce swing of it, starting from my right thigh and scything upward. And even as my hand snaked out palmwise, I was listening with savage expectation for the sound, the impact against the smooth dark face. *Now we'll test that moral superiority of yours,* I thought. *Now—*

But there was no sound, only a dream-like floating moment, during which it was as though my frenzied anticipation had short-circuited my hearing, destroying time and sequence. I seemed to see the start of my hand's flight again, yet even as it streaked toward its target I was aware of a flash of movement beneath me, felt a crunch of pain—"Oh!"—and, looking down, found my wrist clamped in old Hickman's huge fingers.

I winced, seeing a ripple pass over his features as I spun sideways and tilted toward him—finding myself held by the eruptive throbbing of a single vein in the middle of his forehead, then staring into his questioning eyes.

Someone called my name from far away now, and I turned to see Tolliver moving across the corridor through a pink mist. He yelled, "McIntyre!" clearly now, coming on.

"What the hell's happening here?" I heard, trying vainly to free my wrist.

I looked at Hickman silently. The pressure in my wrist was building rapidly, pounding. I could hear quick footsteps hurrying up the corridor as Tolliver moved around me, facing Hickman.

"What're you doing?" he said. "What's going on?"

Hickman shook his head, and I could feel his grip suddenly tighten.

"Mister, you're asking the wrong man."

The footsteps had ceased. It was Bates, his face looming close to mine, his eyes bright.

"Damn it, don't we have enough trouble without this?"

"We certainly have," Tolliver said, "and I intend to get to the bottom of it."

I watched Hickman, waiting tensely. Then his eyes met mine and I returned his gaze with mixed feelings of anger and defiance, expecting him to denounce me as his great chest rose and fell. Then—*hazzzzzzz*—he sighed softly, a slow emission of breath, pursed his lips, and his eyes were on Tolliver.

All right, I thought, *why're you holding back? Get on with it*—wondering what my next move would be.

From somewhere in the building a rapid thudding, like that of a dental chair being elevated, began—ceased. Outside, an approaching siren sounded surprisingly near, whirred lazily to a dying fall, quickly revived, rising to a hysterical screaming as it sped away, fading.

"I'm talking to you and I want an answer," Tolliver said. "Who started this ruckus?"

Hickman's head tilted alertly, his face a brown pattern of dark highlights above a grotesque shadow which Tolliver cast across his chest. I felt a pain knife through my wrist as he watched Tolliver, then I was free and he shifted his position, grasping the arms of the chair as I took a step backwards. *Now,* I thought, *now he'll spill it.*

"Take it easy, Marv," Bates said. "I saw part of it. McIntyre swung on the old guy. That much I saw. Didn't you see him?"

"Yes," Tolliver said, "but can't you see there's more to it than that? I want to know what caused him to do it!"

Hickman's voice seemed to resonate the floor. "Maybe," he said, "he wanted to see if I believed in turning the other cheek."

I flushed, searching his face for signs of mockery. *He knows,* I thought with growing conviction. *Somehow he knows more than I know he knows.... But why is he waiting? To tease?*

"Now you listen to me," Tolliver said. "If you think this is a kidding matter you're mistaken. Answer the question!"

The pressure of Hickman's grip seemed to have passed from my wrist to my eyes, demanding that I speak, and I opened my mouth, inhaled sharply, feeling a furious pounding in my throat, closed it immediately. An urge to confess was upon me, a compulsion to explain myself and to—Hickman. But I was embarrassed and afraid that, once begun, I'd lose all control and speak not only of Laura but of other forgotten and perhaps compromising things. I dropped my eyes.

"You'll still have to ask him," Hickman said, "because I actually don't know. Now, you saw me sitting here, and if you still want to know what I was doing, I was thinking. I've got a heap on my mind, and I don't mean Mister McIntyre. I've got that shot-up boy in there to worry about. I've got those old folks to worry about. I've got tomorrow to worry about. I've got enough on my mind without thinking about Mister McIntyre.... Though now that I've come to think about it, he could go and find out what happened to my people and get me a lawyer for them. That is, if he had the charity of heart—"

His voice broke off as though he were awaiting a reply. *"Charity of heart!"* I thought. *What kind of talk is that* here?

"Is that what you asked him to do?" Tolliver said.

"No, sir, I didn't, although I wish I'd thought of it."

"What did you ask him?"

"Not a thing."

"Then did you make some gesture toward him?"

"Gesture?" Hickman frowned, studying Tolliver. "You mean did I beckon him?"

"You know what I mean!"

"No, sir, I don't."

"I mean did you insult him, challenge him, or make some kind of provoking gesture toward him?"

"You mean like thumbing my nose?"

"Yes, anything of that order."

Hickman smiled, "Mister, you'd better take a good look at my gray head of hair. I told you I have things on my mind. So no, I didn't gesture toward him. In fact, I didn't even raise my hand—neither to beckon nor to bless him, nor make the sign of the cross. In fact, until I felt him come up on me, my eyes were closed."

"Then why were you holding him?"

"Oh, be reasonable, man," Hickman said. "He tried to strike me!"

"But why? That's my question."

Hickman shook his head. "Mister," he said, "I've seen fairer judges hanging around courthouse squares in Mississippi." Then pointing to me, "Why don't you ask him? You see him down here standing over me. I'm not up there where he was sitting, am I? Are you interested in the truth, or are you trying to blot out your God-given vision?"

Tolliver reddened, leaning toward him. "Never mind my eyes, you're not answering the question!"

"Well, it's the best I can do," Hickman said. "Mister McIntyre can talk, and he's standing right here. Besides, you were close enough to have seen or heard me if I'd said or done anything. I can't figure what you're trying to do. Is there a rule which says that you can't ask him about what happened? Maybe I need a lawyer for myself! You must know that it takes at least two to tell the truth about a thing like this, so even if I could tell you something you'd still have to let Mister McIntyre speak."

Tolliver shook his head disgustedly, turning to me.

"All right, McIntyre, maybe you can help us get somewhere. What'd he do?"

I could feel perspiration coursing down the small of my back, my mouth dry with embarrassment. I was unable to speak, shook my head.

Tolliver cursed beneath his breath.

"Are you two playing some kind of game? What the hell's going on? I look up and see two men about to fight, and now neither of them wants to talk!"

"But Marv," Bates said, "maybe the reverend here doesn't know anything. He was just sitting there when McIntyre shot down here like someone had give him a hotfoot."

"Well, it wasn't me," Hickman said. "Maybe he was dreaming or something...."

Now it'll come, I thought. *He's going to pretend to read my mind.* But could he know—even about Laura? Could she have gone to live in his town? How long ago? Or could one of the old folks he's worried about be her grandmother?

"No," Bates was saying, "he wasn't dreaming, not the way he was swinging."

"Then maybe he just came to understand something he's been puzzled about, or overlooking for a long time," Hickman said.

"Like what?" Tolliver said.

"I wouldn't know," Hickman said. "Why don't you ask him?"

"Why can't you answer a simple question?" Tolliver said. "Just say what you mean."

"I'll try, but it won't be simple. What I meant was that sometimes a man will have such a sudden revelation that the shock will make him act before he knows what he's doing. Like sometimes in church, when the Spirit strikes right past a man's brain and hits his heart and limbs and gets him going. One minute he's just sitting there in the heat of the service, looking and listening and maybe thinking that the preaching and the singing has nothing to do with him. But then—hallelujah!—and next thing he knows he's already on his feet and heading to the mourners' bench. Way deep inside he's on fire and thirsty for that old healing water. But even though his legs are moving, he's confused in his mind, because he's in the midst of a transformation. He's both lost and found. He's passing among strangers who are friends and friends who are strangers. His mind is confused but he's already saved and celebrating in his transformed heart. Understand?"

Tolliver stepped back, staring at him. "Is that supposed to explain something?" he said.

Hickman returned his gaze. "Well, I tried," he said.

"What has all that to do with what he asked you?" Bates said.

"I was trying to discuss what happened in the blanks between seeing and not-seeing," Hickman said. "Between acting and understanding the act; between the tick and the tock, the now and the then...."

The voice trailed off, and Tolliver stared at the old man with great distaste. I shivered.

Hickman sighed, his eyes turned inward, and I could hear the silence of the corridor, the click and slide of distant elevator doors. What on earth was the old Negro talking about? Is he kidding the three of us, I wondered, or is he simply poor at similes; with his status outside the complexities of society making for a hazy sense of correspondences? Where was he taking me?

His eyes fluttered then and he was looking up at Tolliver.

"I was only speculating on what happens in the still moment between the now and the then," he said. "All I know for certain is that today the depths have been stirred up. The grave has yawned and the house has rocked and the mighty laid low. So that anybody is likely to act strange. Maybe something happened in Mr. McIntyre's head, some kind of unusual connection was made that caused him to act before he knew what he was doing. On the other hand, he might just have gotten impatient with sitting around here waiting and decided to see how I'd take it if he was to hit me one. But whatever it was, it isn't important."

"I'll decide what's important," Tolliver said. "Anything that happens around this case is important."

"Of course, and you're right," Hickman said. "All I meant, as the prize-fighters say, is that he didn't lay a glove on me. I've been struck at before, so I was prepared."

Suddenly his face changed, his voice becoming briskly matter-of-fact as he looked at me. "Son, will you tell this man what it was you thought you were doing?"

And with his "son" my voice was back again. "You know what happened," I shouted, almost convinced by the words. "And don't pretend to defend me!"

He watched me calmly. "No, son," he said, "you might think that I do, but I really don't know what happened. But you might look at it this way: I have to defend *you* so that I can defend myself. This officer thinks I did something to bring you down here, but you know that I didn't and I think you should tell him so."

The old sound of authority was back in his voice and his eyes calmly demanding. I felt trapped, held by the presence of some dark and insidious force. Tolliver was growing visibly annoyed with both of us. And puzzled. "You must have done something to provoke this incident," he said, "and if McIntyre didn't have such a misplaced sense of honor he'd tell us what it was. He's a reasonable man, a liberal man, and I intend to get to the bottom of this before you leave here."

He turned. "And you, McIntyre, you must be as upset as hell to think you can get away with hitting a man in my custody. You shouldn't be here, you know. Another move like that and I'll throw you the hell out; I don't care what he did to provoke you. And it doesn't matter to me whether you get a story or not. In fact, it might be better for everyone if you didn't. So now get back there and sit down!"

"Before it's all over, the truth will show its face," Hickman said. "So go in peace, Mister McIntyre."

"Oh, shut up!" Tolliver said.

I moved away, still feeling the imprint of Hickman's fingers cutting into my wrist, his eyes pressing against the back of my skull. Recalling the strength which he'd displayed in the visitors' gallery, I wondered how I had been so overwhelmed as to attack him. He'd picked off my blow like an outfielder snagging a long, slow fly....

"Say, McIntyre!"

It was Tolliver again, coming toward me. And looking back past his rolling shoulders, I could see Bates and Hickman watching me, and tensed, wondering if Hickman had sent him to question me further. Then he had reached me, saying, "Listen, McIntyre, I don't want you to misunderstand me; that old darky gets on my nerves as much as he gets on yours. Sitting there with his eyes closed, praying and mumbling to himself. But hell, I can't let you attack him; he's in custody."

He frowned, staring. "Man, you look all done in. Why don't you take a breather and back off of this thing a bit? Go stretch your legs."

"I'm tired as hell," I said, "but I can't risk it, because the moment I leave, something new is sure to erupt."

"I doubt if anything will happen," he said. "At least not for a couple of hours."

"What are you telling me?"

"I mean that the Senator won't come out of sedation before that."

"How do you know?"

"I heard one of the surgeons instructing the nurses."

"That's good to know," I said. "Still, I'd better stick here. But thanks for the information, and I'm sincerely sorry I caused the trouble. I don't know what came over me."

"Oh, forget it, that old bastard provoked you. He got out of line somehow."

"I don't know," I lied. "I was thinking about something else, something unrelated—then bang!—and I was standing over him."

"Well," Tolliver said, "I have no doubt who triggered it. He said something or did something extreme. In fact, the whole bunch of those people seem to have turned extremist all of a sudden. You'd be surprised at the reports coming into the Bureau. Like the one who set that fire on the Senator's lawn..."

I looked away, holding on tight to myself. *Here comes that burning Cadillac again!*

"What is it, fellow?" Tolliver said. "Are you ill?"

I shook my head, closing my eyes to find flashes of flame streaked behind my lids. For a split second the name whirled up and away from me, then struck fire in my mind.

"You mean Minifees," I said, "LeeWillie Minifees."

"Right," Tolliver said, "that's the boy. That's him! Could you've imagined such a thing? It's gotten so that every time one of these spades moves within shouting distance of Sunraider everything goes to hell!"

Down the corridor Bates had returned to his post, and I could see Hickman, resting like a bear stuffed into the white iron chair, his hands clasped peacefully over his stomach. A tremor swept over my body.

"Burning a Cadillac!" Tolliver said with strong feeling. "It's an atrocity!"

"Yes," I said. "In the excitement I'd almost forgotten the incident. Has Minifees been released?"

"Released! Are you kidding? After what *he* did? And now this shooting?"

"Are you saying that he's implicated?"

"That's just the point, we don't know, we're investigating him. But anyone who'd do what he did is capable of doing anything. So we've got him right here, in the psycho ward."

"Here?" I said. "My God, I'd like to see him. What are the charges?"

"He's under observation, he hasn't been charged. But when he is, if you ask me, it can be any number of charges: arson, felonious assault, resisting arrest, the wilful destruction of private property, endangering the public safety, inciting to riot, making incendiary speeches—*er,* if it turns out he's connected with this shooting, it could even be treason."

"He's in bad trouble," I said. "If there's any way possible, I'd like to have a talk with him. I had no idea he was here."

"I'll look into it," Tolliver said. "It'll depend on others. But you shouldn't be surprised that he's being held here. A number of suspects and criminal psychopaths, rapists, and the like are held here. Clyde Sterling the poet is here; a Negro janitor—what's-his-name—who's suspected of murdering his rich buddy and stealing his life's savings, is here—killed him at a birthday party."

Suddenly I came down hard on the bench, my legs giving way beneath me. "But that man was drunk," I said.

"Who?"

"McMillen, Aubrey McMillen."

Tolliver leaned close. "What do you know about it, McIntyre?"

"I covered the story. The dead man's name was Jessie Rockmore."

"That's right, it was. And as you say, McMillen was drunk, but it's our guess that he's also a murderer and a psychopathic liar. That's why he's under observation. There's a three-ringed circus of psychos here, but if you ask me, that fellow Minifees takes the cake!"

"He was pretty wild," I said, "but it hadn't occurred to me that he might be implicated in the shooting."

"Listen," Tolliver said, "in an event like this *anyone* could be involved. You have to look for motives everywhere and in everybody. Maybe this fellow has nothing to do with it, but on the other hand that car-burning might have been an act, a diversionary tactic intended to prepare for an attack that misfired until this morning. During that Minifees confusion anything could have happened to Senator Sunraider. In fact, if we're able to place some character on the scene with a pistol or grenade or rifle, we'll have him nailed. I understand that there were important details to what went on out there which didn't get into the news accounts. Even your paper ran an odd little story that played the incident for laughs. Did you have anything to do with it?"

"No." I shook my head. "No, I didn't."

"I wish you had, maybe you'd have supplied us with more to work on, some significant detail instead of that lame attempt to make a joke out of it."

"We do our best," I said.

"*Some*times you do. But I'm not criticizing you, McIntyre; I'm speaking of the press in general. For instance, I heard that that clown was wearing alligator shoes which cost fifty bucks apiece! Now if you ask me, that's some kind of crime in itself!" He grinned. "Anyway, you take it easy. Take a nap if you like, and don't worry about Hickman, he's not going anywhere. And when the Senator comes out of it we'll alert you."

He moved away and I was relieved that he hadn't questioned me further. I felt completely turned around, what with his having thrown Minifees into juxtaposition with the gunman and having revealed McMillen's presence in the hospital. Watching Tolliver disappear into the Senator's room, I began to shake and tremble. Then I was looking at Hickman nodding in his chair, and suddenly I was laughing within myself.

I wanted to roar, to scream, but held it inside. I turned back. I bent forward, head upon knees. I held my breath. I shut my eyes and bit my lips. But as it continued, I saw that I couldn't contain it and got up and hurried past the elevator to the other end of the corridor and turned the corner. And there, under a dim light and facing a wall, I stuffed a handkerchief into my mouth and let go.

It was a painful laughter, tearing at the lining of my empty stomach, a laughter springing from my sudden awareness that each second I had waited for the outcome of the Senator's wounding and had searched my mind for the motives behind it, I was being forced steadily back upon *myself*. It was as though Sunraider, McGowan, Minifees, McMillen, the fellows at the club, Vannec, and countless forgotten or unknown others had combined to force me into retracing my movements, not only over the last several hours, but over a period which I'd long ago forced from my mind.

Even Laura had come back to haunt me. How had I ever managed to forget her? How had I exorcised that painful period so completely from my mind after having been so intensely involved? Loving her, I'd lost myself in

Harlem for a highly intense time, had surrendered to its fascination as to some great foreign city. And willingly, as one gives one's heart and mind to Paris. I had spent every free moment of my time there. I had wandered for hours among its street scenes, I had haunted its bars and nightclubs, spent hours in its dance halls and burlesque houses. And Laura had taught me to see the life there as not exotic but as extensions of her own life (a life quite different from that of which McGowan ranted) in the South. And through my fascination with language—languages are best learned in bed, it is said—I had come to see its speech idioms and its slang as extensions of Southern speech modified and amplified by the exciting contrasts of the Harlem melting pot. Ever concerned with children, Laura had even taught me to understand the games played and danced by kids in the streets as versions of games and jingles which she had played and sung in Georgia. I'd been so spellbound, so enthralled, so captured by the black magic of the area that for a time I had come to see the crime and squalor which I found there as part of the poetry of the place; and the street characters, the eccentrics, the pimps, the drunks, the criminals (I had known no preachers, not even one like Hickman, and only a few teachers, a labor organizer, and two physicians)—all as part of a vital and somehow hopeful scene. Then I had approached the people then through my love for Laura, had seen them, in effect, through her own eyes. And then when it had reached its end in the basement nightclub, and I went there no longer, I had resolved my pain and my inability to deal with the problem of marriage and her mother's rejection by substituting instead the theories and definitions of sociologists and politicians. I had, in effect, accepted their formulas as a means of ordering that sense of chaos which had been released in me by my loss of love.

But what else could I have done after the shock and disappointment I sustained? I was not given to lost causes, I had to establish myself in life, and with Harlem no longer a place of adventure, Laura out of sight was Laura out of mind—until at this great distance in time and place, the depths, as old Hickman had put it, had been stirred.

Now everything had been stewed together, the mighty, the lowly, the past and the present, the seen and the unseen. And I was in trouble because, in putting Laura behind me, I had developed a different quality of attention, a different sense of direction. Events had come to possess a more limited extension of significance, and I no longer thought of the world in which she moved—wherever she now moved—as relevant. I lived in a quite different sphere, bound by different values, and events drew their meaning from within a different frame of reference. All else was beyond the pale, lost in the abyss of the past or in the mist of the future. All tock and tick with nothing in between. And there was nothing I could do about it.

Actually, I could hardly remember the sensation of love, the thrill of being with Laura, or the sense of release and power-over-life which she had afforded me. I did realize that the sense of daring which I had felt had come not so much from the unabashed gratification of forbidden emotions, but from the fact that the atmosphere in which we moved had then seemed to condone and encourage broad freedom of expression. For there life had seemed generally more openly expressive. Thoughts were uttered, actions were taken—even violent actions, erotic actions—with a facility and openness that was unknown to my own background. But now, even as these thoughts came painfully to me in an agony of laughter, I realized that I had seen and experienced only a part of the truth, for I knew now that Aubrey McMillen was here in the hospital, and Jessie Rockmore had died his strange death for his own strange motives, and Miss Duval had been present to create a situation which would have made McGowan's wildest fantasies seem tame by comparison. I'd touched another world.

Suddenly two images flashed through my mind. I could see a fat black woman with a face rouged almost lavender standing on a spotlighted stage, dressed in a white satin suit of tails which gave her a full, pear-shaped, Henry-the-Eighth aspect, as she sang a song of double entendre with a refrain of "Sweet Violets" as a diamond flashed from a tooth in her wide, darkly painted mouth; and that of myself chasing myself desperately around the rim of a depthless crater. It was quite vivid, *but what,* I wondered, *does it all mean?...* I felt faint. I threw it off.

Across the corridor I noticed a window and went over to stand looking out. It was dark. The streetlights silhouetted the tender new leaves of a tree. Down the walk from the hospital a tulip tree showed pink in the light of a street lamp. A white ambulance with lighted interior and roof beacon lazily revolving flashed a rhythmic message of red and white as it cruised silently along the curving drive, moved out into the avenue. There was little traffic and no pedestrians but the world out there in the dark seemed enormously normal and I, the lone disorganized and agitated witness to the scene. I didn't trust it—I didn't trust my vision. How could I after such a day? I went back and sat down, expecting anything to erupt and trying to prepare myself. For whatever it would cost me there was a story here, and I meant to get it, come hell, come high water, come fire, come smoke, come laughing gas. And now I had no doubt but that anything and everything could come. And not only once but, I suspected, several times and in several forms and in widely scattered places.

Like the car-burning, which appeared first as a farce only to turn up now as a foreshadowing of something close to tragedy.

All great, world-historical facts and personages occur twice..., I suddenly recalled from the thirties, *the first as tragedy, the second as farce,* but here this analysis of history offered no security. For who involved, other than the Senator, could be called "historical"? Could LeeWillie Minifees? Could Laura? Could Hickman? Could Aubrey McMillen? I doubted it. Nevertheless, they each kept popping up in wild reversals. And under the most devious circumstances.

But who, you ask, was McMillen?

CHAPTER 12

IT WAS LIKE THIS: Last night, during the drinking and joking at the club, I had completely forgotten that earlier in the day I had agreed to cover for a young colleague who had decided, rather impulsively, I thought, to slip away to Boston to marry a Radcliffe girl. The night editor had left me alone during the evening (he knew where to locate me), but then around four A.M. I found myself rushing in a still-drunken and dream-thronged state with notebook and tape recorder to the scene of a killing which had been reported in the vicinity of the Capitol. It was the location which disturbed Scoggins, the night editor, and caused him to awaken me.

The cabbie let me out in front of an old three-storied Georgian house, and I hurried up the steps to find two beefy policemen being directed in a thunderous attack against a door set to the right of a dimly lit vestibule by a sergeant of detectives. He acknowledged my press card with a nod, but when I tried to get a line on what had happened his hands flew to his ears and he gestured toward the two officers who threw themselves forward—*hungh!*—and bounced off the door as though they were made of rubber.

"Hit 'em again!" a deep voice growled behind me, and I became aware of other faces emerging from the darkness.

Back in the shadow of the vestibule a half dozen or so black folk in night dress stood on the steps of the stairs leading up to the second floor, quietly looking on. Two of the women held their hands over their mouths and eyes, as though suppressing tears or the sound of weeping. I thought, *Grieving servants.* Then a man's hostile gaze caused me to turn away, thinking, *But you can trust me to tell the truth.* Then came a crash, the door flew open, and I hurried behind the policemen into a blaze of light and brilliant color.

We didn't get far. A few steps inside, a wave of alcohol fumes swept to meet us, and I discovered that I had entered a ragtag museum that had been thrown together according to no easily discernable plan. In the first blinding glare of light, vague objects and artifacts appeared to have been wrenched from their place, time, and function and thrown together in such volatile and insane juxtaposition that I feared that one false move, one stumble or jog or careless pitch of voice might trigger a debacle. Dust and signs of disuse and decay were everywhere. Crystal flashed from obscure corners, a policeman sneezed from the dust. And yet, it was not the disorder of a junkyard nor attic nor cellar; I sensed a design underneath it all. But whose and to what end, *that* was the perplexing question. It was the last place I would have imagined.

I was familiar with the fashionable notion that the American home has been steadily becoming a combination art gallery and technological museum, but here the process had gotten quite, and most deviously, out of hand. Tables and chairs, divans and chaise longues, cabinets and chests, scale models and sculptures—all of miscellaneous styles and periods, and many in various stages of disrepair—confronted me on every hand, and some of the furniture was loaded with books, musical instruments, objets d'art.

"What the hell kind of joint *is* this?" someone said.

"I was about to ask myself," I said.

"Yeah, and where the hell is it? Who put it together, that's what I'd like to know."

"Hell, men, this is our own, our native land. And I'll bet you two for one that we'll find some booze. Isn't that right, McIntyre?"

I shook my head. "I'm as puzzled as the next man. Besides, I can hardly see."

"Better put on your shades, McIntyre," the first man said.

"No luck, I left them at home."

"Then squint, my friend, and you'll find your way."

My trouble was caused by a collection of converted oil lamps and vases, some of which blazed away innocent of shades. Across the room two panels of the long wall were loaded from wainscoting to picture molding with sconces and bracket lamps which threw such a glare that the intention appeared to be deliberate concealment rather than revelation. And while the others moved about, I closed my eyes and puzzled over what made the place so personally disturbing.

Perhaps, I thought, *it's simply the fact of finding such a place so close to the Capitol, so near the center of our national source of order. There are slums nearby, of course, but slums are different. They emerged from history and are unhappy marks on the road of progress. What's more, we were doing something about the slums. But this place—my God, the fact that it exists means that something has been going on that has completely escaped me and everyone else. . . .*

Suddenly, to my left, a violent rocking began, and my eyes sprang open to see one of the policemen reaching out to catch at a pile of heavy books that were falling from a small colonial table. He missed several, which thudded to the floor, causing the sergeant to swear beneath his breath.

"Now clean it up," he said. "And from now on watch your step!"

Bending, I helped the officer pick up the books, partially to be helpful, partially out of curiosity. But when I tried to read their titles, there was such a clashing of reds, yellows, and blues lingering in my eyes that I couldn't read. And the whiskey fumes were heavier now, seeming to roll from beneath the door to the other room, and as I stood and looked around, it came to me that anything could happen in such a place. For it seemed that in an atmosphere so heavily saturated with alcohol the very clutter and the clashing of objects of such divergent styles and intention would lead inevitably to some form of violence, to some excess of emotion or assertion of will, and thus to grave physical conflict and, as the presence of the police indicated, to murder. *The miracle,* I thought, *is that it hasn't happened before.*

The officers were making their way carefully to the door now, and I felt an urgent need to have the victim's body found so that I could get my story and leave. It was as though a human agent, who could be definitely identified with all the apparently calculated chaos, was called for to remove what I felt as a mounting threat to us all. Nor did it matter that that agent was dead; what was important was the establishment, once and for all, of the fact that the chaos was his and not ours. Especially not *mine.* And in fact, it might be that his being dead would guarantee that whatever the nature of the force that seemed so threatening, it had been appeased and would strike no more. It was my duty to stay but I felt an urgent need to leave. Because, hell, it was *their* chaos, the Negroes and the police, not mine. . . .

"Say," one of the officers said, inhaling noisily, "there must be a still hidden around here somewhere. There's enough booze in the air to get a man tight."

"You'd like that, wouldn't you?" the sergeant said. "Well, you can forget it; if we find something you're not to touch it. Now let's find this stiff."

"But Sarge, stills are more interesting than stiffs," the policeman said.

"Don't you worry, the stiff will be still," the sergeant said. He grinned, pleased with himself. "Come on, let's have a look. The report said he'd be in the back room."

Then, as we reached the door, I could hear the sound of a man's moaning voice issuing from somewhere in the depths of the room beyond.

"Hell, Sergeant, there's somebody alive in there," one of the officers said.

"Don't you think I hear it?" The sergeant tried the door. "Open up in there!" he said.

The moaning ceased. We waited.

Silence.

The sergeant pounded the panels. "Open in the name of the law!"

Again silence. The officers looked at one another. The moaning resumed, "Aaaaaaaaaah. . . ."

"Sergeant, that stiff ain't so stiff after all."

He rattled the doorknob. "Mr. Rockmore," the sergeant called, "open up, we're the police."

The moaning continued, a droning monotone. We waited.

"See if you can get it open," the sergeant said. "Hop to it. I'd hoped it would be simple."

"Break it in?"

"Hell, no, pick it. Use your set of keys. Since he's alive, we don't want to scare him to death."

The officer opened a small black case, and I could hear the rattle of metal.

"Sergeant," I said, "did anyone see the attack?"

"Not now, McIntyre. Not now."

"Did they see who the attacker was?"

"Later, McIntyre..."

"But what information do you have? How did the question of murder come up?"

"Please, McIntyre, step aside and let the men get this door open. And you, Lawson, go around to the back and see if any windows are open."

I stepped aside, listening as one of the policemen left. As they began to pick the lock the moaning continued. It was slow, tedious work, and while they labored I grew nervous with waiting. Finally, I moved away and tried to make sense of the chaos around me.

My eyes become partially adjusted to the blaze of light, and the wall before me seems to flicker like an early silent movie, its brightly colored lithographs creating a feeling of vertigo in which I fall back into a swirl of images of earlier times athrob somehow with the pain of neglected memory.

A vague sense of humiliation came over me now, as though here in this obscure and unexpected part of one of our most historical cities someone had calculated to exhume much of what I knew about our past along with much which I either didn't know or admitted only to partial recognition as a means of confounding me. Something told me to turn away, to return and watch the policemen pick the lock, but I couldn't. I was looking straight ahead with squinted eyes when suddenly President Lincoln's funeral cortege sprang from the glaring wall before me. Flag-draped and crepe-shrouded, it floated past with a creaking of camion and leather, the clink of chains. The lithographs had come sharply alive. General Robert E. Lee galloped past on Traveller, resplendid in broad hat and riding crop.

John Brown marched past on his way to the gallows at Harpers Ferry, guarded by soldiers, while a slave mother held her baby above the crowd for Brown's blessing. Brown's face is sad, his eyes resigned, his bearded chin thrust forward as though baring his throat for the noose.

A horse race thunders past, a contending of thoroughbreds and black jockeys in vivid silks, who ride with lengthened stirrups, their legs down-thrust in the style of earlier times when such as they rode in races. I read:

THE FAMOUS PROCTOR KNOTT
Pick Barnes Up
Winning the first Futurity, 1888

Dust stings my nostrils as the horses pound; I hear the spectators cheering from the stands, see the dark riders thrashing left and right with their riding crops as their splendid mounts carry them past me, rising and falling as in a dream.

Now comes a line of gaudily dressed couples strutting a cakewalk, a flurry of plumed hats, feather boas, whirling ebony canes. White teeth flash in dark faces as the women high-kick in their gleaming shoes, touching ag-ilely the silken top hats which the black beaus flourish above their heads with regal gestures. Wild melodies sound in my ears, evoking scenes of min-strel days:

If you lak a-me
Lak I lak a-you . . .
Under the bam-
boo-
tree . . .

They dance on with backwards slant, fading into a scene of two Missis-sippi riverboats, the *Natchez* and the *Robert E. Lee,* plowing past a levee—their smokestacks billowing, side wheels churning, the river white with spume—to the shouts of a crowd of black folk cheering along the levee. . . .

I turned away, stumbling over an old Edison phonograph with a large morning-glory horn encrusted with dust. A telegraph key, a Leyden jar, a tintype camera, a stereopticon viewer with a stack of early American views—Niagara Falls, Old Faithful, Jamestown, Virginia—lay on the floor. A small drum table held a stack of phonograph records topped by a badly scratched disk of the "Bearmash Blues" . . .

Behind me one of the policemen said, "Look, Sarge, can't we give it the old shoulder treatment?"

"No, just keep working, you'll solve it in a minute."

"Yes, but whoever's in there could climb out the window by then."

"Don't worry about it, the place is surrounded," the sergeant said. "Now snap it up!"

I moved around. The place was a pack rat's burrow, an oddball treasure house, and as I inched my way through the narrow passages I was growing dizzier every second. Here was a Franklin stove supporting a huge framed portrait of Teddy Roosevelt attired in Rough Rider's uniform. A full-length portrait of Senator Stephen A. Douglas looked out from the wall surrounded by a series of escaped-slave notices. A playbill for April 14, 1865, announcing the last performance of OUR AMERICAN COUSIN with Laura Keene at Ford's Theatre, hung beside it. The attraction for the following day was Miss Jennie Gourlay, and for the evening of April 15, a presentation of Boucicault's "Great Sensation Drama, THE OCTOROON."

I moved on, only to be brought to a shuddering halt by a particularly repulsive example of a traditional cast-iron hitching-post figure in the form of a small blackamoor with dull black face, bright red lips, and popped thyroid eyes. An inverted chamber pot had been placed upon its head at a rakish angle, the handle resting just above one ear, and for a moment the popped eyes held me in what seemed to be a derisive interrogatory gaze; then I broke the spell by taking up the utensil and trying to translate the legends which had been painted upon it in a florid Italianate hand:

> *Mange Bene*
> *Cacca Forte*
> *Vida Longo!*
> UNA FURTIVA LANGRIMA

which someone had translated in red grease pencil as, "Down her soft cheek here a pearly tear."

I returned the vessel to the iron-napped head, wondering if I were still a bit high, or actually seeing what I thought I saw. If not, where were all the fumes coming from—the fireplace? Could all this be as the policeman had suggested, a front for a bootleg operation? Could all this junk, these forgotten and discarded images, be the façade behind which some illegal operation has gone unnoticed, only now to run its opaque path to murder? How did one begin to think about such a place with its collection of *things*? Why didn't they hurry and open the door! The fumes annoyed me. Perhaps, I thought, there is a still here with copper coil winding its tedious way between the walls and down to the basement, where drops of illegal distillant were collected—perhaps in a fireplace. Hidden spirits fuming to make a fire. But now, turning to inspect the fireplace behind me, I found an old iron safe bearing the incongruously placed advice: REMEMBER THY FATHER IN THE DAYS OF THY YOUTH in black-and-red-bordered letters of gold.

The policemen had changed their tactics now and were thudding against the door with little effect as I moved past a series of lithographs and fading photographs of famous American Indians. Black Hawk and Tecumseh, Sitting Bull and Stumickosucks, Chief Joseph and Oceola, Crazy Horse and

Little Hand. Here was a ceremonial scene of white men and Indians making the Treaty of Dancing Rabbit; a group of Plains Indians in full regalia posing with impassive dignity for some daguerreotypist of long ago, perhaps even Brady.

Then came photographs of President Warren Gamaliel Harding and a group of friends—probably holding, as Harding might have alliterated, a "palaver on progress without pretense or prejudice or accent upon personal pronouns and without regard to perennial pronouncement and unperturbed by a people passion-wrought over the loss of promises proposed"—Albert Falls and Harry Daugherty were among them—taken at the time Teapot Dome was about to explode. It was Harding! Harding! Harding!

Harding in white flannels, silk shirt, bow tie, and panama hat, playing croquet on the South Lawn of the White House; Harding on a balcony with ladies displaying wide hats and generous bosoms, waving to Easter-egg rollers on the lawn below; Harding taking the oath of office, his hand upraised, his face somber beneath neatly parted white hair. And earlier still, Harding in top hat and fur-collared coat smiling suavely as he waved grandly from a limousine to a crowd gathered along Fifth Avenue.

I had begun to feel a poignant sadness over these reminders of the nation's palmier days with their doctrine of *normalcy,* but then I was face to face with Jack Johnson, the notorious heavyweight boxing champion, whom certain sportswriters, and Sam, the waiter at my club, regard as an underground hero. Now he came toward me, broad-shouldered and tall, wearing a suit of giant houndstooth check, white turtleneck sweater, and round, flattopped cap of lion skin, gripping a clublike blackthorn walking stick midway its length, as he jogged along with majestic mien; Johnson stretched on the canvas at Havana, nonchalantly shading his eyes from the sun while the referee counts him out and Jess Willard, the triumphant white hope, moves heavily toward a neutral corner.

The policemen were cursing loudly now as one of them backed into a pile of junk and set a huge music box to glangling a nostalgic nineteenth-century tune as I inspected a photo of Johnson dressed in a bullfighter's costume, a "suit of lights," as he posed with arms around the shoulders of Belmonte and Joselito, the great masters of the Spanish bullring, somewhere in Spain. And now Johnson tall and sinisterly graceful in fighting togs, his shaven, high-domed head bobbing and weaving as he taunts and punishes Jim Jeffries in defense of the championship— And then it was as though Johnson's fist had burst from the wall and struck me full-face. Before me the hand of God was displayed reaching down in a glowing light from beyond the picture frame and the Holy Family showed forth with the dark skins and features of Negroes.

The words "It's heresy," broke from my lips with the shock of it—but fortunately my voice was lost in the crash of splintering wood. Whirling, I made my way behind the policemen into a scene of such dissonant, brilliant, rowdy, and dream-like disorder as I'd never encountered even in a nightmare.

Objects in the room seemed to flow, turning in a slow, tumbling motion of time as, behind me, the sound of splintering wood degenerated noisily and my eyes came to focus on a point near the rear of the high-ceilinged and brightly lit room from where, sitting upright in an ornate mahogany coffin which, in turn, rested high on a stout library table, an ancient Negro sat looking down in my direction. I seemed to fly out of my shoes then, rushing back past the lithographs and piles of junk in the room behind us and out through the dark vestibule into the rational dark of the street—but I was still there, staring.

The front of the coffin pointed toward me at an angle from which I could see the old man's prominent Adam's apple exposed by the imperious thrust of his bearded chin. Then my eyes seemed to become detached and floating downward, like two flat wafer-thin rocks falling lazily in limpid water; dropping past the gleaming tips of a winged collar with purple ascot tie displaying the pearl of a stickpin in its folds, then slanting off to brush past the rough texture of an old-fashioned morning coat edged with braid, lingering lightly on a white feathered boutonniere in the shape of a Japanese rose, then falling past a pince-nez with thin-lensed and winglike disks of crystal glass which dangled on a delicate golden chain, to sideslip suddenly and fall like lead upon his ancient hands.

Bony and long, these rested on the closed section of the coffin lid, which hid the lower part of his body, and held in death one half-empty bottle of Jack Daniel's whiskey and a water glass in which four fingers of amber spirit showed. I was aware of labored breathing behind me as my eyes flew back to the face. And it was as though he had just thundered out against our intrusion in a voice so loud and indignant that I was forced to grasp his meaning from the eloquence of his expression alone. And it was in straining to understand that I suddenly realized that his wide, staring eyes were not focused at me, but *through* me, past me, and now I became aware of the other man.

Wearing overalls and sprawling in a high-backed, slipcovered chair which faced the coffin on the left, he was pointing with a wavering arm toward the man sitting above us, his mouth working meaninglessly above a guttural moan.

I moved then, stepping around to see his face, when one of the policemen gave explosive voice to my own amazement:

"What the hell," he yelled. "What's going on here?" And something frightening and dangerous in his voice spun me around, sending the microphone from my tape recorder slapping sharply into my crotch as it fell from its case, and I grabbed it, flicking it on just as I looked past his shoulder and saw the woman.

Back across the polished floor and behind the door—which explains how we missed her upon entering—she knelt with her golden hair fanned out across the upholstered seat of an early American Chippendale chair. Her backside greeted us like some reluctantly rising moon—completely bare except for a crude and inadequate skirt, which had been threaded together from, of all things, a series of old twenty-dollar gold certificates. These were of the type withdrawn from circulation many years ago, and must have amounted to a small fortune. But there they were, greeting us like a badly wilted sunburst. And our shock and embarrassment held us rigid, as though we were, indeed, watching the death of the sun.

Suddenly the sergeant whirled around to a cluster of dark faces which were now peering in at the doorway, his face flaming.

"Tillman," he yelled, "get these people out of here and hold every one of them, you hear me! Every single damned one of them!"

Tillman moved off and he turned to the woman then, and with a look of profound distaste and much effort, got her giggling and squirming ticklishly into the chair and covered with his jacket. Whereupon she gave a drunken smile which exploded into a moist hiccup, breaking my enchantment, and I returned my attention to the man in the coffin.

Approaching him now I saw that the coffin was in an advanced stage of decay; and here, according to the moaning man, lay the beginning of the whole fantastic development. Jessie Rockmore, the man in the coffin, had undergone the loss of his lifelong religious conviction, had fallen into profound disillusionment, because *time, life, and termites had reduced his coffin to a hollow shell!* Yes! this was the start of a chain of events which had dragged me from my bed. A man lives long enough to outlast the usefulness of his coffin, but instead of rejoicing and taking pride in his longevity, he loses his lifelong faith. Our Negroes are indeed a strange people!

Nor was the moaning man an exception. When the sergeant began questioning him he had to be reassured that yet another man, a white man (whom no one else had seen), was no longer present in the building. Only then did he try to pull himself together, helped by sips of whiskey which the sergeant sloshed generously into his glass. Then, as we stood in a semicircle between him and the man in the coffin, he looked at each of us with wavering eyes and nodded his head.

"Okay," he said, "I'll try to tell you all I know."

"That's fine," the sergeant said. "You can start by giving Officer Tillman here your name."

"Yes, sir. My name's Aubrey McMillen."

"And his?" The sergeant nodded toward the man in the coffin.

"That's Mister Jessie...."

"What's his first name?"

"That *is* his first name; his last name's Rockmore, just like you called it outside the door. Mister Jessie Rockmore's his full name."

"You get it, Tillman?" the sergeant said.

"Yes, sir. Got it!"

"All right, Aubrey," the sergeant said, bending forward. "Now tell us what you do."

"I'm a super."

"For whom?"

"For Mister Jessie. I work right here."

"Do you have other jobs?"

"Not anymore. I been working for Mister Jessie for close to ten years. Before that I worked for—"

"Hold it," the sergeant said. "We'll come back to that later. Now just tell us what happened here."

"Well, suh, it was thisaway," McMillen began. "A few days ago Mister Jessie told me to bring the coffin up from the celler, so I got holt of Leroy— that's the boy what helps me—and we brought it up, and at first we sat it on a couple of chairs like he told us."

"Why did he want the coffin up here?"

"That's just it, I don't rightly know. Me and Mister Jessie have been friends since I can remember, and he liked to talk to me a lot. In fact, he talked to me more than he did to anyone else."

"Did he have any relatives?"

"Yes, suh, he does. But he can't stand them, so he lives here by hisself."

"What about his wife?"

"She's dead."

"Did his family visit him?"

"Sometimes, but not very often. Because, you see, he's so strict and strait-laced that they can't get along with him, so they just let him alone. And he liked it that way fine. Mister Jessie used to sit here day after day reading his Bible and *The Washington Post* and that *Congressional Record*, fussing about the things he read in them, and trying to get me interested so I could argue with him about them. Now I argue with him about the Bible, although I don't have much religion, but that Congress paper, it just makes me mad. It made Mister Jessie mad too...."

"Why?"

"Because he didn't agree with what it said. He was all the time arguing back with it and talking about the law and stuff which I don't have the education to know much about—not that Mister Jessie had been to school either, but he taught hisself a lot of things."

"So he was self-educated," the sergeant said. "Now tell us what happened."

"Well, like I started to tell you, when me and Leroy got the coffin up here and resting on some chairs, Mister Jessie looked at it a long time, and right away he seemed to forget about us. He started to mumble to hisself and walk around it, then he began to knock on it with his fist and making a hollow sound. Then all at once he tapped it like a man thumping a watermelon, and you could see a cloud of brown dust rising up out of there.... Mister Jessie bucked his eyes, then turned and looked at me, and he looked like he'd done see a ghost. He shook his head and went to mumbling something I didn't get, then he balled up his fist and came down real hard and stood back and watched the dust rising up and settling down. Me and Leroy started to sneezing then, and I watched Mister Jessie bend down and unbolt the lid and run his hand inside. And when he straightened up he brought out some ole rotten suit cloth and a pair of those ole sharp-toed, button shoes with gray tops, like they used to wear years ago, and held them up, inspecting them. And all the time he's looking at them he's shaking his head and mumbling, and his face was working and that loose skin under his chin was shaking like a mad turkey gobbler's. Then he got to sneezing and leaned way over and really started to pulling things out of there...."

"Like what?"

"Well, the first thing was a plate and a bowl and a pitcher and some knives and forks. Then out came the statue of a horse, and one of those bottles with a ship in it, and a box of grits, the kind with the colored man on it—"

"Grits? What the hell are you telling us?" the sergeant said.

"That's right, grits," McMillen said. "You can see for yourself right over there on the table."

"What else did he take out of there?"

"He took out a Bible and a little ole wrinkled up U.S. flag and an ole owl-head pistol. A forty-four on a thirty-eight frame—you can see it, it's right over there—and some old life-insurance policies. Yes, suh, and some no-good oil shares. And then he reached in again and when he straightened up he's got an old tin box in his hand...."

"Said, 'It's been so doggone long that I'd almost forgot about this.' Then he turned to me and said, 'McMillen, give that there little nappy-bearded boy a dollar and let him go.' So I give Leroy a dollar and he went on off."

"Why did *you* pay the boy?"

"Well, you see, Mister Jessie used to borrow money from me all the time. Borrow it one day and give it back the next. He just like to see if I had it, or if I'd let him have it. Not that he needed it, 'cause he has plenty money in the bank and hardly spent nothing at all except for something to eat and a few shirts now and then. Well, yes, and his newspapers and magazines. He didn't even smoke or chew."

"But he drank a hell of a lot."

McMillen's head snapped up. He looked indignant. "No, suh, he didn't, and I tell you about the whiskey in a minute."

"Go on."

"No, suh, he didn't drink and he didn't chew, so he didn't need much money. Besides, a man from that big New York museum was always down here trying to get him to sell those plates and things over there in those cases. Offered him all kinds of money for that stuff—way up in the thousands—but he wouldn't sell.... And another man from a place here in D.C. wanted those pictures of Indians and other folks, but Mister Jessie wouldn't hear him either. Told me one time he would give them to those folks over there at the university for nothing if they would have the sense to appreciate them, but he said they weren't interested because they didn't understand that they had something to do with them. They ought to raise some hell in the Indians' name once in a while, he said. And he told me once that he tried to give them those Indian pictures—he's got some really fine ones—but they didn't want them, and Mister Jessie got mad as a bitch, as he told it. Said, 'Those fools are supposed to be educated, and they don't even realize that for better or worse they have taken the place of the Red Man, even to getting scalped and swindled every time they turn around.' This was too complicated for me, but Mister Jessie used to say some pretty low-rating things about those folks over there. Course, as far as I'm concerned they seem to be doing a pretty fair job."

"Stick to the point," the sergeant said.

"Yes, suh," McMillen said, taking a drink. "Anyway, so Leroy took his money and left and I went and locked the door after him, and when I got back in the room Mister Jessie was counting out that money that that lady over there is wearing, and spreading it out on the coffin lid.

"He said, 'McMillen, this stuff has been in there so long it's against the law to even own it.' And all at once he turned around and looked at me with a bunch of those big goldbacks fanned out in his hand, and right then he did something I never heard him do before in all the years I been knowing him—he cussed. He said, 'Goddamn it, it had to slip up on me at a time when by rights I ought to be dead and gone. But now I'm glad, because at least I can say that for once in my life I broke the goddamn law!'

"I was so surprised I didn't know what to say. Because Mister Jessie was as straight as a die and as hard as steel, and as clean-cut a man, black *or* white, as I've ever seen. He was what you call a good, upright Christian man...."

"All right, all right, get on with your story," the sergeant said.

"Yes, suh," McMillen said, and I watched him sip the whiskey, then lean forward shaking his head.

"Well, suh, it looked like using that cussword caused something to snap in

Mister Jessie's head. At the time he was dressed in his bathrobe and with his scrawny neck coming up out of his shirt neckband with the button in but no collar. So he stood there mumbling and counting out the money, then he looked at it a minute and all at once he took his hand and swept it to the floor, disgusted-like.

"I said, 'What in the world are you doing there, Mister Jessie, treating that money thataway? That's still good money. You ain't no criminal or nothing like that,' I said. 'You can turn that money in and the bank will give you full value.'

"Well, suh, why did I say that! Mister Jessie looked like he was going to pick up that coffin and throw it at me.

" 'Full value!' he said. 'Full value, my foot! There ain't enough gold in Fort Knox to give me the value of what that money cost me. Back there in the nineties, denying myself and my family, pulling dollars and pennies out of my black hide, helping that white man take heirlooms—all that Spode and Chelsea and Sandwich and Sterling—from ignorant folks. McMillen, wars and thievery in high places and bad monetary policies have put more lead in our silver and more brass in our gold than was in all the bullets shot up during the Civil War. And now time has cut the value of whatever's left. McMillen,' he said, 'let me tell you one goddamn thing: When a man gets as old as I am, money is nothing but the cold excrement of all his life's labor. Even sweat has more value, because in this hell of a Washington, sweat will at least cool him once in a while. I wore out fifteen of those little ole straight-life, nickel-today-nickel-when-you-git-it insurance policies before I learned I was being drained of my just interest and started saving my money in the banks. Then the Depression started eating on me, and twice, once before they set up the Federal Reserve Board, and again in '29, I was the victim of embezzlers. And all this time the value of the money going down and down like that elevator in the Washington Monument. Don't talk to me about getting my value out of that stuff!'

"And then he really went to preaching. Said, 'I tried to live by a devalued standard. I've denied myself whiskey, women, and warfare, and I've seen my labor go to hell and my life turn into a P. T. Barnum sideshow, and all the time I've been patient and law-abiding. I've prayed and believed and kept the faith. When I was young I never went to a dance or visited a whore. I never knowingly cheated or lied, even when I had to suffer because I didn't. And I always believed even when times was at their very worse that things would get better. McMillen,' he said, 'this was my philosophy. I believed in two things: I believed in the perfectibility of man—including Negroes like you and me—and in the progressive improvement of the American form of government and the American way of life. These two beliefs have been the rock upon which I based my life and my faith. God has seen fit to free me from slavery when I was still a young boy, and I determined to live according to His rules and according to His time and win as much human perfectibility as I could. Mr. Lincoln tried to make a way for us in this society and had the Constitution amended to help us over the rough places and then got the back of his head blown off for his pains, but still I was determined not to be impatient and to learn citizenship and practice manliness so that at least his spirit would never be embarrassed by me.' "

McMillen said, "Mister Jessie looked at me then, gentlemen, and all at once he got to laughing. He laughed until he cried, and he got me to laughing at *his* laughing, then he stopped for a second and leaned back against that coffin, and you could hear something give way inside it, and he started to laughing some more.

" 'McMillen,' he said, 'for years you have respected me as an intelligent man, but I want to confess right now that you've been wrong, 'cause I'm nothing but a ninety-five-year-old goddamn fool!'

"I told him, 'Take it easy, Mister Jessie; you oughtn't to play yourself cheap like that.' And he said, 'No, you listen to me. I had everything all figured out logically. I had been a slave, you see, so it would take me quite a while to catch up with the liberty that Jesus Christ and Mr. Lincoln provided for me; and since the nation had men at the bottom, where I started both in terms of place and in terms of time, and men at the top like Mr. Lincoln and Ralph Waldo Emerson' (he always talked about those two), 'and Jay Gould,' and somebody he called the Right Reverend Henry Ward Beecher, 'there was order in the nation and in the world,' he said. 'And since the Bible teaches me that there is a heaven above and a hell below, with Satan the master of hell and God the Father and Christ Jesus sharing the throne of heaven above, then everything was in universal metaphysical order and in orderly process. A man was born and he had his chance to help himself by the manner in which he lived his life, and when he died he was buried and in time he was judged and he went either to heaven or to hell. Everything fitted the scheme, and if God could send His son down here as a man, that was a good enough guarantee that I could at least be a full citizen.

" 'So you see, McMillen,' Mister Jessie said, 'I lived the best way I knew how, and I was determined to take care of all those earthly things I could control. I refused the notion of rebellion. I didn't drink whiskey, chase women, or sing the blues. I would play the game. Therefore, I bought that damned casket there while in the full strength of my manhood. I bought it so that when my time came I could be put away in the proper fashion and with no debts outstanding to man or government. I figured that time is but so long, and flesh is surely frail and unpredictable. So I lived in fear of God and in respect of law. I kept the faith in the orderly processes of justice and in the checks and balances of good government. But now just look at me and look around me! Things have gone to hell right here in Washington. Here I've had to live these ninety-five years until I'm so old that I'm no good to myself or to anybody else. I've got as many gadgets on me as a five-and-dime store. My teeth are false, I have to hold my gut in with a truss, I can't see worth a damn without my glasses, I have to hook up my ears to a doggone radio in order to hear, and I walk with a cane. I'm no good to myself or to anybody else. My children don't want me and I'm even in my own way. And *still* I don't see any prospect of passing on to my reward.

" 'McMillen, I was in this town when they killed Mr. Lincoln, and I watched with these eyes when they took FDR to his last resting place. And I've seen all kinds of crooks and thieves come up to Washington and do their nastiness in the name of country, liberty, freedom, and economy, and pass on. Different names but the same nastiness. With but a few exceptions, it's been a matter of highbinders, clipsters, phonies, and confidence men in high places since I can remember. And they don't get any better, they get worse.' "

McMillen interrupted himself now. "Gentlemen," he said, "I want y'all to understand that this was Mister Jessie talking, not me. I don't know nothing about politics."

"We're listening," the sergeant said.

"Then he got going again. Said, 'I fought in the Spanish-American War and left some of my blood down there on San Juan Hill, with Teddy Roosevelt getting so much credit that you'd have thought he fought the Spanish single-handed, while our people got none of the recognition and the crooks in the War Department even found a way to swindle me out of my pension. I've been a fool, McMillen, I've been a goddamn fool! Here I've been worrying all these years about dying well and not being a burden to anyone, and I've neglected to *live* well. In fact, I haven't been living, I've been dying. Forty years ago I took my savings and bought me a decent suit of clothes and a pair of fine Johnston & Murphy shoes of the kind I'd denied myself the pleasure of wearing here on earth—and I bought me some decent linen. And now look at it, all worn out with waiting. The suit's crumbling into dust, the shoe leather is hard and dry as Adam's first fig leaf, and worst of all, the damned coffin is full of bugs and worms raising hell and stamping their feet even before I have a chance to get in there and serve them up their long-expected meal. Even *they* knew I was dead. This is the last straw, McMillen. I got nothing to live for or to look forward to. No *now* and no *hereafter*. No justice from my government and no hope for heaven or escape from hell. It's shit hawks flying and shit hooks grabbing. Because both God and government have just been taking me for granted. Talking about God and the Devil making a pawn out of Job! Hell, I've been ignored and held in such contempt that even my coffin has fallen to dust, and that took away the only guarantee I have left in this world, so it's time I started living for *me!*' "

Suddenly McMillen paused and looked at each of us. "And to the best of my recollection, gentlemens," he said, lowering his eyes to his empty glass, "that's how it happened...."

"That's how *what* happened?" the sergeant said. "Listen, McMillen, are you trying to snow us? You haven't said a word about what he's doing propped up in that coffin—or about what that...that...woman over there—what's she doing in here? What else was going on in here besides a lot of drinking and a lot of subversive ranting? Did you two rob him and put him in that coffin?"

McMillen became visibly upset at this particular question. I had noticed him avoiding looking in the direction of the woman, who sprawled in her chair, and now he shook his head in violent denial.

"No, suh, it wasn't nothing like that. No, suh!"

"Then get on with your story. What the hell went on in here?"

"Yes, suh," McMillen said. "But first, can I ask you gentlemen a question?"

"What is it?"

"I'd like to ask you all if you all are Northern gentlemen or Southern gentlemen?"

"Quit stalling," the sergeant said. "What's that got to do with it?"

"Well, Officer, it's like this," McMillen said, "Southern gentlemen is kinda touchy about some things, and I don't want what I have to tell you now to be misunderstood."

But before McMillen could continue, there was a whoop of laughter behind us, and I turned to see the woman in the corner, who I had thought was asleep, looking at us with unsteady head.

"Gen'lmen," she said, "gen'lmen, what the man wants to know is, are you John Law gen'lmen in *back* of Mister Mason or in *front* of Mr. Dixon...."

The sergeant banged his fist on the table, sending up a cloud of dust which settled on the corpse in a fine brown veil. "That's enough out of you," he shouted. "Just one more word—"

"Sure, sure," the woman said, "but just answer Uncle Tom's question. 'N I want you to answer *me* one lil ole thing, 'n that's how could that poor bastard confuse you buncha faggots with gen'lmen? Far's *I* can see, he's the only dam' gen'lman in the crowd. Thass right, 'cause who but a gent would pay me to do my number in this kinda costume?" and she flung Officer Tillman's jacket aside, trying vainly to stand, and fell back, laughing.

The pitch of McMillen's voice leaped an octave. "Officer, Officer!" he said, "I want it strictly understood that that woman's being here wasn't no idea of mine!"

"Then how'd she get here?" the sergeant said.

"Oh, I'm going to tell you," McMillen said. "You can bet your life I'm going to tell you. And this is what happened. After Mister Jessie raved awhile about his coffin rottening out on him, he just stood there in the middle of the floor with his eyes shining. He must have been thinking up a storm too, because all at once he started to yelling, 'Hell and damnation!' He said, 'McMillen, when I was a young fellow I worked for a while as a porter in a house of ill-fame'—he meant a whorehouse—'and I never even tried to sample the goods!' And I started to say, 'Now is that a fact' when he called my name like someone had stuck him with a pitchfork.

" 'McMILLEN,' he said, 'here's what I want you to do. I want you to take this money—he carries his money in one of those ole long ole-fashioned leather pocketbooks with a snap on the top. You can see when you search him.... He said, 'You take this money and go get us a case of the best bourbon whiskey you can find, and then I want you to get—'

"And I broke in then and said, 'Now wait, Mister Jessie, you don't want no *case* of whiskey....'

"And he said, 'Boy, don't tell me what I want! I say get me a *case* of whiskey like I told you. And when you get the whiskey, I want you to get me a sporting woman. Get me a raving blonde!'

"Gen'lmen, that's when I really got disturbed. Now I knew Mister Jessie was disgusted, but I didn't see any reason for him to be *that* disgusted; so I said, 'Mister Jessie, I know you're upset, but you don't have to get all *that* upset. First you call for whiskey, and you don't drink, and now you're calling for a woman and you know,' I said, 'you know you too old for that kind of foolishness. And now on top of all that you asking for a blond pink-toe strumpet!'

" 'That's right,' Mister Jessie said, 'that's what I called for and that's what I want. Here, take this damn money. I want you to get me one about forty-five, if you can find one who hasn't hung up her bloomers and retired, as those Jezebels and Magdalenes I worked around used to say.'

"So this time I asked him real quiet, 'Mister Jessie, have you been drinking?' And he said, 'No, but I plan to be as quick as you stop hanging around here asking questions and get back here with some whiskey. No, dammit, I'm not drunk; I'm just full of ninety years of disgust. You just get me the liquor and the gal.'

"So you see, gen'lmen, I really tried to argue him out of it, but I couldn't get nowhere. He always was a stubborn ole man, still, he was my friend. So I found a taxi and went and picked up a case of Jack Daniel's, and when I went to pay for it, I found out that Mister Jessie had give me an ole mildewed five-hundred-dollar bill. The man in the liquor store didn't even want to change it. In fact, he sent a clerk to the bank to see if it was good or if it had been stolen. So then I took the same taxi and went and looked up a fellow I knew who used to work at one of these what they call 'hit 'em and skip 'em motels,' and he laughed at me like I was crazy and called me a fool, but he give me that lady over there's telephone number."

"How much did you pay her?" the sergeant said.

"I offered her seventy-five dollars and a tip if she satisfied Mister Jessie.

But she said that there was a big convention in town so that she'd have to have the union scale—a hundred dollars."

"A hundred dollars—her?" one of the officers said. "I'll be damn!"

"Yes, suh. She sounded like she was juiced already, and I started to tell her to forget it—"

"Juiced?"

"I mean she sounded like she had been drinking, about three sheets in the wind—high. But much as I wanted to help Mister Jessie, I didn't want to go around looking for another woman for him. So I told her okey and dropped by her place, and though she didn't look like she was worth any hundred dollars to me, I paid her most of the money right then and there; so that if she came out here and found that Mister Jessie had changed his mind, or if she didn't like the deal, she wouldn't start no black-and-white—I mean she wouldn't cause no trouble. And to tell the truth, the fellow who give me the address also give me a drink, and I had started to get awful curious to see what Mister Jessie was going to do."

"So what did he do?" the sergeant said.

"I'm gon' tell you, Officer. So then I told the lady the address, and she said she'd be here in about thirty minutes. And then I got in a taxi and came back here with the case of whiskey. I was pretty worried, because not only was Mister Jessie acting like he'd been drinking billiards or something, but I was afraid that the lady had taken his money and wouldn't show up.

"Well, gen'lmen, when I got back here Mister Jessie had shaved and got dressed up in that suit he used to wear when he served on the ushers' board of his church. He was a trustee too, and always a very neat and dignified-looking man. And now although he wasn't no calmer than when I left, he looked really sharp.

"I said, 'Mister Jessie, here's all this whiskey you ordered,' and right away he wanted to know if it was the best, and I told him it was the best I knew about. So then he said, 'I told you to bring me some whiskey *and* a woman, McMillen—where's the gal?'

"So I said, 'Now don't get excited, Mister Jessie. She'll be along in about twenty minutes.'

" 'She'd better be,' he said. 'McMillen, she'd sure better be. Because if she ain't, I'll go out and find another one. I'll find me a half dozen! How much money did you spend?'

" 'About two hundred dollars,' I told him, and I starts to give him his change.

"Well, he looks at me like I'd stepped on his corn then and said, 'Two hundred dollars! And you talking to me about *value?* Why, when I was a boy you could buy a whole barrel of whiskey for fifteen dollars!'

"And I said, 'Yes, suh, Mister Jessie, I reckon that's when you should've been buying it. Times have changed. I told you you didn't want no whole case of whiskey. You can't even buy a gallon of jump-steady bootleg for no fifteen dollars. Not today!'

"He said, 'McMillen, I know what I want and I don't want it for free. I got the money to pay for it and I'll pay. How much did it cost?'

"Almost a hundred dollars—ninety-three dollars and seventy-three cents.'

"Well, then Mister Jessie looked at me kind of hard and said, 'McMillen, what kind of damn woman did you get me?'

" 'I don't know what kind she is, Mister Jessie,' I said, ''cepting that she's supposed to be a blonde.' And just as I said that, that lady over there in the corner, she knocked on the door and Mister Jessie told me to let her in.

"And that's when he did something else that was strange. When I walked back in here with the lady, Mister Jessie was nowhere to be seen. So I told the lady, 'I guess he's in the kitchen or the bedroom. You just take a seat while I go see.'

"But before I could move I heard Mister Jessie's voice say, 'McMillen, I'm not in the bedroom, I'm right here.'

"Both me and the lady gave a jump at this, and that's when I realized that Mister Jessie had climbed into that coffin and was propped up on his elbow, looking down over the edge at us. And when I saw that, I made up my mind that I had business in the basement.

"So I turned to the lady and told her, 'There he is, ma'am. He's the one who sent for you,' and then I headed straight for the door. I figured that since *she* was juiced and Mister Jessie was headed straight for St. Elizabeth's, they didn't need me to introduce 'em. I almost made it to the door too, but Mister Jessie wouldn't let me leave. He sat up then and said, 'McMillen, where you think you're going? You're invited to this party too.'

"And that was when the lady spoke up for the first time. She said, 'That'll cost you double, Dad'— That's right," McMillen said indignantly, "never seen Mister Jessie before in her life, and right away she's calling him 'Dad'! I expected Mister Jessie to take her head off because getting sassy with him is like getting out of line with the high Chief Justice of the Supreme Cote. I was even about to straighten her out myself, but before I could open my mouth she said, 'That's right, Dad; the fee will be double. And while you're thinking about it, what do you think you're doing receiving me in that box?'

"Then Mister Jessie said, 'Miss, you have been paid once and for all. If my terms are unsatisfactory, just return my money and leave us and there'll be no hard feelings. I intend for this to be a party and I want no contention. How about it, now?'

"That calmed the—well, gen'lmen, that cooled her down a bit. She said, 'Okey, Dad. But tell me something, *what* do you think you're doing up there in that thing?'

" 'Miss, I'm resting,' Mister Jessie said.

"And she said, 'Dad, you sure must be awful tired.'

"So she looked at him all juiced-eyed then and shook her head like she was woozy, and she said, 'Dad, you must be beat to your righteous socks. But why make it so easy for the body snatchers? All they'd have to do is shoot you full of formaldehyde, and you're on your righteous way. You picked a strange place to entertain, Dad.' And Mister Jessie said, 'Are you objecting, miss?' And she said, 'Oh, no, Dad. But from where you're sitting maybe you can tell me just why it is that every time I do business with one of you spooks it turns out mad? I have never known it to fail. Either the joint gets raided or the john's ambitious to start him a family, or he thinks he's a stud; or somebody shoots out the lights and throws a cat and a bulldog into the room. It's always mad, Dad. Like in Baltimore the time that lady preacher who turned tricks herself until she went over the hill and had to hang up her drawers—*she* crashes into the joint like Carrie Nation—only she's got a forty-five instead of a hatchet—and she stands everybody against the wall and tries to convert us to her religion. And now I pick one who wants to be entertained in a coffin!' "

McMillen shook his head, his voice coming dolefully.

"So that's when I knew for sure that Mister Jessie wasn't hisself; that he had gone *see*nile. 'Cause all he did was look at that female snake real stern. But to tell the truth, I was really irritated. . . . That kind of woman coming into Mister Jessie's house and starting right off calling us spooks. She didn't even know our names. At first I was hoping deep down that when she saw him she'd speak up and tell him he was acting a fool and that he ought to be ashamed. 'Cause anybody could see that Mister Jessie was upset in his mind. But instead of doing that, she started talking all that old jive talk and calling us spooks. I tried again to leave, but before I could get out of the room Mister Jessie stopped me.

"Said, 'Wait a minute there, McMillen,' and he asked the lady, 'Miss, what's your name?'

"And she said, 'Cordelia Duval, doll. What's yours?'

"And he said, 'I'm Mister Jessie Rockmore, Miss Duval. And that's Mister Aubrey McMillen. We're pleased to make your acquaintance. But before you take your things off, let me ask if you—' And before he could finish she said, 'Take them off? Dad, are you kidding? These are the McCoy!'

"Mister Jessie looked at her and kinda frowned and said, 'No, ma'am, you misunderstood me, Miss Duval. I don't question that at all. I just wanted to ask if you danced?'

" 'Dance?' she said, and that's when she threw back her head and started to acting real grand, talking about, 'Why I was in the Follies, doll.'

" 'Is that so?' Mister Jessie said. 'I would have thought you would have been too young, Miss Duval.'

"And she said, 'You don't believe me, doll? Well, I was. I knew Mr. Ziegfeld and Mr. George White too.'

"So Mister Jessie just looked at her awhile. Then he said, 'And have you been practicing your present profession long?'

"And the lady said, 'Long enough to know all the tricks, Dad. You know any new ones? I think you're trying to insult me, Dad. I was in the Follies and I knew Flo Ziegfeld and Will Rogers and I knew that spook boy Bert Williams too. He was a great performer and real cute when he took off his greasepaint. And wasn't he a riot when he walked around pecking in his rooster costume! "Ah ain't evah done nothing to *no*body," he used to sing, and "Take Away Those Pearly Gates" was another. We were all friends together and they were all sweet to me!'

"Then Mister Jessie said, 'That's all very interesting, Miss Duval.' And she said, 'It was, doll; you have no idea. It was the height of my career and, doll, it seemed all clear, bluebird weather. Then I was betrayed by a playboy out of the Social Register and became disillusioned. Do you still think I'm lying, Dad?'

"And Mister Jessie said, 'No, Miss Duval.'

"But that's when I had to speak up myself. I said, 'Mister Jessie, you know this strumpet's lying. You know this whore ain't been in no Follies. She's just trying to insult your intelligence.'

"But all he said was, 'Watch your language, boy.'

"Then he said, 'That's too bad, miss, I'm sorry to hear it. I guess we've all had our disappointments.' And she said something about, 'Yes, doll, but we're still in there pitching, ain't we? Why did you ask me if I could dance, doll?'

" 'Because it would be my pleasure to watch some nice dancing, Miss Duval. Would you be willing?'

" 'You mean that's all you had me come out here for, Dad? Don't I appeal to you? What's wrong with me? I'm a professional, you know, and you have to have pride in what you do.'

" 'Yes, we do,' Mister Jessie said, looking down at us like a preacher. 'Mankind has to have pride as well as humility,' he said, 'and that's why we're having this party because I forgot just that. I never had a party before, but every party needs women and whiskey, and music and dancing. It took me a long time to learn it but I know it now. So would you care to dance, ma'am, or shall we break our contract?'

"She was laughing then, gen'lmen, and she changed her tune. I had been watching her hard, and I saw her when all that money that Mister Jessie had knocked on the floor jumped up and liked to've popped her eyes outta her head. Gen'lmen, those bills bugged her eyes out like a weak spot in a rubber inner tube. And she said, 'Oh, sure, Dad, sure. If it's dancing you want, I guarantee to satisfy. Where do I put my wraps?'

"So Mister Jessie told me to take her things and bring a bottle of whiskey and some ginger ale and stuff which he'd ordered while I was out getting the whiskey. And so I left them talking while I went to get the glasses and things. I was still worried about Mister Jessie, sitting in the coffin and wanting a woman like that in his house, but he was sounding pretty sensible again."

"There's not a damn thing sensible about anything you've told us," the sergeant said. "Snap it up, will you?"

"Yes, suh," McMillen said. "I'm trying to remember how it went after that point."

"Why after that point? What happened?"

"Well, suh, while I was out in the kitchen I had me a drink of that good whiskey. In fact, I had me a good *strong* one so that woman wouldn't bug me too much. 'Cause I figured it was Mister Jessie's party, and if he wanted her here it was his business. So I had me a strong drink of that good whiskey, and when I got back, things had got to going pretty fast and confusing.

"Mister Jessie was leaning with his elbow propped up on the side of the coffin. Him and the woman is talking like old friends, and she wasn't trying to act so grand now—though ever' now and then when she thought nobody was paying any attention I could see her eyes cutting down to those bills. She had larceny in her heart all right, and I decided right then and there I was going to stay right here and look after Mister Jessie and his interests...."

"You mean you meant to get the money before she did," the sergeant said.

"Oh, no, suh. I could've kept some of that five hundred he gave me to get the whiskey with. No, suh, I drink my whiskey but I work hard and I got too much self-respect to steal. You might think different but that's the truth."

"Go on."

"Well, so then I decided to lay right there in the bend and watch out for Mister Jessie. I figured that, after all, I'd been drinking since I was a boy and he was just starting, so it wouldn't be long before he'd be needing the benefit of my experience. So I kept my eye on him real close when he was taking his first drink, but I couldn't tell much about how it was hittin' him because his eyes were hid behind his glasses. He was busy asking the lady if she liked her work and she was saying something about having her a 'rich full life' on account of she got a lot of the Capitol trade...."

"She said that?" the sergeant said.

"Yes, suh, she shorely did...."

"Be sure you take all of this down," the sergeant said to Tillman. "I want to check on this woman, check the FBI. Go on, boy."

McMillen stared silently into his glass.

"I said, get on with your story," the sergeant said.

"Oh," McMillen said, "I didn't know you were talking to me...." His eyes were far away. "Now, let's see. Well, pretty soon, Mister Jessie was drinking that whiskey like he was drinking water, but I couldn't see no change in him. He just sat up there in that coffin, leaning on his elbow like a judge and taking him a sip of whiskey now and then.

"Once he said, 'McMillen, what kind of damn whiskey is this?' And I told him. And he said, 'Then why ain't I getting any action?'

"And the lady said, 'You just wait, Dad. This is fine whiskey.'

"Then she got up and threw up her arms and whirled around and said, 'Dad, you have a nice little pad here.' She was looking at that money on the floor; I was watching her. She said, 'It's very nice, Dad, only kind of overfurnished. What do you do for a living?' And Mister Jessie told her he was retired, and she said, 'You wouldn't kid me, would you, doll? You might be retired but you were in the rackets; I can tell, Dad; you were a slick spook. You were probably peddling horse, or maybe you were a fence.'

"But instead of telling her to get the hell out of here, Mister Jessie said, 'McMillen, pour this little lady some whiskey and then pour me some and help yourself.'

"She was leaning against the table while I poured, and Mister Jessie looked her in the eye. Then he told her, 'Miss Duval, the only way I ever come close to breaking the law was by not telling my customers that the man on the other end of the telephone wire was a black man, or that the post-office box they wrote to was rented by a black man, or that the man who paid for the ads I used to run in the newspapers and magazines was black.' Then he started telling her all about his business—which *I* never would've done. Not me.

"You see, Mister Jessie used to sell that glass and stuff over there in them cases. He used to go down in Alabama and Georgia and Mississippi and South Carolina and buy it and bring it up here and sell it through the newspapers and magazines. He only let a few white folks know who he was, and he let even fewer come here to his house. And even then he'd play like he was just looking after things for a white man. He never had any arguments that way, and if they wanted to change the price he'd say he was sorry but he had to sell it for what he had been told.

"And not only did he sell glass and stuff, he used to watch for whenever they was tearing down those old houses, and he'd turn up dressed in overalls and driving an old horse and wagon he used to have, and he'd buy the marble off those old beat-up fireplaces, and he'd buy the old wood the walls was lined with. And sometimes he'd even buy up old staircases and picture molding and all that old stuff. Sometimes it didn't even cost him anything, the builders was so glad to have it hauled away for nothing. Then, you see, Mister Jessie would take it to his storehouse and clean it up and take a picture of it and send it off to folks that he said were in the business of decorating houses in the old style and things like-a that. Sometimes he sold to people who put on plays. Once he even had him one of those old-time electric automobiles that steered with a handle. He was kinda nuts 'bout the china and glass, though.

"He said, 'Miss Duval, you see those cases of fine porcelain? Well, I know the children of some of the white folk who owned many of those pieces, and I know more about the value of it than they do. They didn't even know enough to keep it and prize it; still, they think they're better than me because they don't, and they thought I was a damn fool because I wanted it. I've bought whole crates of it along with fine old shotguns and beautiful old candelabra from them for little or nothing. Not just because I simply wanted to make money out of it, Miss Duval, but because I felt the meaning of fine things ought to be kept alive. In fact, this is the kind of thing they should have worried about passing along, not their blood, most of which was mixed up anyway. All saturated with the germs of the world, leaping with consumption and cancer. They try to preserve the wrong things, things that can't be preserved anyway, instead of the good things that will be here after they're all passed away. So you see, Miss Duval, I tried to preserve some of it to the best of my ability. Therefore, I had to learn something about it, about what it meant and why it was considered better than other things of the same order, and about why it came into existence. My mind expanded, Miss Duval. I grew to love good things, fine workmanship, beautiful objects. Oh, yes, I came to love fine quality as I loved God's plan for man and the order of the universe. It seemed to fit in its wonderful way like the silkworm's cocoon and the butterfly's wings. Sunrise and sunset, the seasons wheeling through space to bring forth their flowers and fruits at their appointed time.'

"He took off then, gen'lmen. He said, 'Miss Duval, did it ever occur to you that snowflakes are the flowers of winter just as violets are the flowers of spring? The Chinese knew it years ago. Nighttime and daytime; cool and balmy; hot and cold; sweet and sour; tart and bland; sugar lumps and pepper pods; wood grain and stone grain; rubber tires and steel rails; rabbit tracks in the snow; bird's-eye maple and flame-grained mahogany; water and fire; milk and wine; rotation and propagation—'

"And then the woman started to laugh and interrupted him. She said, 'Don't forget ham and eggs, doll. We couldn't do without them either. And boy and girl, Dad, that's a good little ole deal.'

"And Mister Jessie shook his head and looked up at the ceiling and said something about, 'Yes, that's true, Miss Duval. The orders of mankind and the animal kingdom, the vegetable kingdom too; and the arts of the husbandman and the arts of the wifewoman, the schoolwoman, the nursewoman—'

" 'And the professional woman, like me, doll,' Miss Duval said.

"They was getting pretty wild. And I said, 'Y'all better eat something along with your whiskey, otherwise y'all going to get looped too soon.'

"And Mister Jessie said, 'That's right, McMillen, go out there and bring us some of those sandwiches and cheese and crackers and pickles and things. Open a can of smoked oysters.'

"So I took a good look at the way that money was scattered on the floor and went on out and got the sandwiches while they kep' up their talking."

Suddenly the sergeant held up his hand, frowning, "Wait a minute, McMillen, goddammit," he said, "What kind of work do you do?"

McMillen looked up, surprised. "Like I said, I'm the caretaker, the janitor," he said.

"And what did you do before that?"

"Oh," he said proudly, "I used to work at the racetrack. I was a clocker, and I used to identify horses for a man who sold tips. I was a tout's tout, I guess you would call me. I used to know all the bloodlines of the big stables and could keep it in my head. I could even remember the colors of most of the big owners."

"How could you remember all that?"

"I had to have a good memory because in those days I couldn't read and write too good, so I had to remember. I could tell time though. I used to know those horses and their sires and dams like a preacher knows the begats in the Bible."

"Begats?"

"The family trees, the bloodlines."

The sergeant shook his head, looking at McMillen with an expression of disbelief. "Take that down, Tillman," the sergeant said. "Go on, and hurry it up!"

"Well," McMillen said, "so Mister Jessie got to raving again. He said, 'Look at me, Miss Duval, just look at me. I'm just an old fool and this is what I've come to. This is my promised land! I had to have this birthday years after I have any right to be alive before I could see the truth, and it had to get to me through this damn rotten coffin. Now I've got nothing; they tricked me on the there-then and on the here-now, and I tricked my own damned self on the here-after because I wanted to believe I had lived long enough even thirty years ago to know better. So when I went to examine my guarantee of safe conveyance to the hereafter, what happens?'

"And the woman broke in, 'That's right, Dad, what *did* happen to make you take that seat?'

"And Mister Jessie looked down at her and said, 'I'll tell you what happened. This damn coffin and the bugs and worms inside it liked to cracked their sides laughing at me. Here, I'll show you one.'

"And that's when he reached down inside and brought out a little ole moth worm and layed him on top there where that bottle of whiskey is standing and he said, 'Miss Duval, you come over here and listen close and you can *hear* this little bastard laughing.'

"So she said, 'How does he sound, doll?'

"And Mister Jessie said, 'He sounds like my last rotten tooth did when it gave way under the dentist's forceps. Others sound like a knife scratching on glass, others like the hinges of an old gate swinging in the wind or a blind banging against the window of an empty house.'

"And the woman laughed and told Mister Jessie he was better than a sideshow at a circus, and he told her not to laugh because those bugs were laughing the truth about his life.

"He said, 'No wonder I couldn't find where those silverfish that were making a hash out of my history books were coming from. They were right in here!'

"I poured them another drink then, and the woman said, 'Dad, what would you do if you could have your birthday wish?'

"And Mister Jessie thought a bit and ran his eyeglasses up and down on that golden chain that he wears and he said, 'Miss Duval, I'd like to get dressed in my best suit, with my best shoes and glasses and take my gold-headed walking cane and gray fedora hat and my best gloves and be standing at the White House gate when the President takes his morning ride, and I'd like to be standing right there at the driveway when the chauffeur stops to see if the way is clear of cars and I'd like to step up to his limousine and I'd say, "Good Morning, Mister President, this is Mister Jessie Rockmore, and I'm my own man!" Then I'd say, "I'm one of the nation's oldest citizens, sir. I was here when Mr. Lincoln held your position, and though just a baby, I was here when he used to pass back and forth through those gates, and I've been living right here while all the other presidents, including General Grant, Warren Gamaliel Harding, and FDR were occupying the White House. I don't stand for much in the scheme of things, as you can clearly see, but if there are to be men in *your* position then there have to be men in *my* position. And men in my position *have a need to be heard*. So I want you to know that I have a long memory, and I want you to know that I've been watching you out of over threescore and ten years of living and hoping. And I want you to know, too, that I have prayed for you to be given the strength to live up to your Office like Mister Lincoln did and that the cares of the Republic would not be too wearing on your shoulders. . . .

" ' "But now, Mister President, I think you should know that things have changed. And my way of thinking has changed. I was ninety-five years old at about three forty-five this morning, and I want you to know that after all these years I no longer believe in prayer or have any hope for the fulfillment of this nation's promises. I want you to know that as of now, you have been relieved of the burden of my hopeful watching and waiting. Think about what that means, sir, when you're guiding the deliberations of your cabinet." '

"And Miss Duval looked down at those goldbacks and said, 'Take another drink, doll. You are truly wonderful. Then what else would you do?'

" 'Well, Miss Duval,' Mister Jessie said, 'then I'd say, "Good day, sir—Mister President, gentlemen" because he'd have all his bodyguards and maybe a cabinet member or two with him, and maybe there'd be reporters present. And then I would bow as men used to have the grace to do in the old days, and I'd tip my fedora and swing on down the avenue.

" 'That's what I'd like to do, Miss Duval,' Mister Jessie said. 'But as big a fool as this laughing coffin and its bugs and worms have shown me up to be, I'm still not so big a fool as to think I could get away with it. Because harmless as I am, they'd probably shoot me down. They'd think I was trying to get close to the money or trying to get into the newspaper headlines. And they'd laugh at me, which would be worse, even though I'd probably deserve it for speaking to him.'

"Then Mister Jessie looked up at the ceiling a while, and when he spoke up again, gen'lmen, he sounded just like a little child. He said, 'People used to write Mister Lincoln letters and he'd answer them.'

"Didn't anybody say anything for a while after that, then the woman said, 'Well, Dad, today you know we *do* have television. Today the President can get to us much quicker than Old Abe could.'

" 'Yes,' Mister Jessie said, 'but Mister Lincoln could touch you to the quick and make you feel that you counted in the scheme. Today they stand there on television drinking water and talk flimflam to everybody. And they don't really speak to anybody. I bought a television set to see why everybody was excited about the damned thing, and what did I get? I got that Senator Sunraider coming right into my living room, mouthing insults to me and my people in the name of the government and the rights of man. He's the devil who's always preaching about science and working for government ownership of the television networks. Next thing you know, the rascal will be presenting a measure for the building of government-owned gas ovens.' He hit the coffin then and sent up another cloud of dust, and he looked so mad and down in the dumps that this time *I* spoke up.

"I said, 'Mister Jessie, don't you go getting yourself worked up on your birthday; this here is a party, you know.' And he looked down at me and shook his head, and he took him a sip of whiskey and adjusted his glasses and looked at me. He said, 'Yes, McMillen, you're right. What can folks like us do about the gimmicks and gadgets, the highbinders and clipsters? And what good would it do if we could? Folks nowadays don't remember a death in the family any longer than it takes to slam the body in the ground and cover it up. Back in his time Mister Lincoln could begin a speech with "Fourscore and seven years ago," and it meant something to everybody because he made it real; they remembered. But today he could begin with "Four minutes and seven seconds ago," and folks wouldn't remember who the hell he was talking about. So let's be like other folks and forget our condition—the liquor is getting good, and we three are getting along just fine. Miss Duval, would you care to dance?'

"So then the woman grinned and cut her eyes down at all that money on the floor again, and I could've kicked myself for switching Mister Jessie away from talking about politics. Gen'lmen, I could see the electric lights start to blinking and the wheels start whirling in her head like the lemons and cherries in a slot machine when the jackpot's about to fall. She gave Mister Jessie a great big, juiced-up smile and she said, 'Why of course, Dad. I'd love to dance, but I . . . er . . . I've got a problem, Dad.' And Mister Jessie said, 'What's the problem, Miss Duval?' And she said, 'McMillen didn't tell me you wanted me to dance, so I didn't bring a costume.' And she gave him another juiced-up grin then, and I wanted to kill her for trying to hook me in her devilment. But before I could tell her off, Mister Jessie pointed to that chest over there beside the wall and told me to open it so she could see if there was anything in it she could wear. So after I filled her glass again, she staggered over there and started pulling all those old clothes out and looking at them, and I knew she wasn't going to be satisfied with anything she found.

"And sure 'nough, she staggered round and said something about, 'This is all very nice stuff, doll, but it's too old-fashioned to do the kind of number mine is. Maybe I can improvise something, though.' So she stood there picking up pieces of cloth and feather fans and neck pieces and things and trying them around her, trying to pose and wobbling around on those high heels. Once, she picked up a pair of those old spike-heeled, hightop button shoes, and she wiggled and said, 'Dad, these make me feel real Frenchy! They're almost the thing I need to do my number but a little stiff.' Then she picked up that old feather neck piece over there and wrapped it around her behind and said, 'This is almost the thing, doll, but it would be a crime to cut up such a lovely old piece.'

"And that's when Mister Jessie cleared his throat and said, 'McMillen, call a taxi and escort Miss Duval home to get her costume and anything else she needs, and hurry back, as I want to see her dance.'

"But then she said, 'No, doll, wait! If Josephine Baker could do her number wearing bananas, I ought to be able to do mine in newspapers, headlines and all. McMillen can just bring me a needle and some thread and a pair of scissors.'

"So Mister Jessie told me to get them for her, and though I knew she was outthinking me, I didn't know how. So then, gen'lmen, I said, 'First let me get Miss Duval a fresh drink.' And I got a big water glass this time and filled it with that good whiskey, knowing that I was wasting it, but there wasn't nothing else I could think to do. I brought her the paper and scissors and needle and thread and then, gen'lmen, she tipped her ballbusting hand! You see, she started cutting the paper in pieces about the size of those goldbacks and laying them out in a wide circle.

"So I said, 'Mister Jessie, while she's getting ready I think I'll straighten up the floor a bit,' but he was looking down and watching her, kinda brooding-like, and said, 'McMillen, leave the damn floor alone!'

"So, gen'lmen, I was blocked, stalled at the starting gate. I had to sit there and watch her do everything I knew she was going to do. When she got through cutting up those pieces of newspaper, she started running a length of thread through one end of them. And when she had about a dozen threaded she held it up and frowned, and said, 'Dammit, doll, this cheesy newspaper keeps tearing. I'll never make a costume out of it. Have you got some wrapping paper?'

"Then Mister Jessie said, 'McMillen, go in the library and get Miss Duval some of my stationery.' And gen'lmens, that's when she leaped in and scored.

"She said, 'Oh, don't go to that trouble, doll; I see just the thing I need, right there on the floor.'

"So there it was. Juiced as she was, she knew what she was after all the time, and in a few minutes she'd done grabbed up some of those goldbacks and strung them on a piece of thread and held it up for Mister Jessie to see. She asked him how he liked it, and he said, 'Miss Duval, I'll leave the details to you. If you like it then I'm happy that some use has been found for the stinking stuff. All I'm waiting for is to see you dance.'

"She told him, 'Doll, you just wait until I change. The number I do is a killer. I guarantee you won't be disappointed. Once when I was in the Follies, doll, I was put into a big pie covered with meringue and all done up with cellophane and a big pink ribbon and a bow. And don't you think those Wall Street aristocrats weren't surprised when the host cut the crust—he was in the Stock Exchange, doll—and I came stepping out. You should've seen me then, doll. I broke out and struck a pose, and every man at that banquet table drank champagne out of my boot. And I must admit, I was lovely, doll. You may ask how do I know I was lovely, but every *lovely* woman *knows* that she's lovely. It's all part of *being* lovely. Besides, the men won't let you forget it. It gives them the glad eyes and the feelie-feelies! The pie was really a Baked Alaska, doll, and I stepped out wearing an ermine chubby and white leather boots with fur tops and an ermine muff. I was a queen, doll, and all those millionaires knew it. I danced slowly down the center of the table, letting them take me all in, and there was a row of waiters dressed in red uniforms with braid and white gloves, like in England, standing back of each of the chairs, popping corks of big magnums of champagne and serving it like water. It sounded like the Fourth of July, doll, and it wasn't only corks that were popping out either, there were a few eyes popping along with them. I did the shimmy, like this, doll, smiling down, and I tell you I won them all—only I played no favorites, doll, I was there for *all* to enjoy....'

"Mister Jessie raised his hand then, looking all straight-faced and solemn, and said, 'Miss Duval, I'd really appreciate seeing you dance,' and she said, 'Sure,' and struggled out into the other room.

"She was in there a while while me and Mister Jessie sat here drinking, not saying anything, him up there and me right where I am. I tried to warn him about his money but he wouldn't let me talk, and then she came back wearing nothing but those goldbacks.

"Gen'lmens, you'll have to pardon me for having to say it, but when she came twisting through that door on those high-heeled shoes, she had spread out so much behind and was so hung down up front that I dropped my eyes and they swung right back up again just like the needle in a compass when you turn it fast from south to north. And Mister Jessie—he sat up in that coffin and took off his glasses and rubbed his eyes, and I coughed and almost strangled on a sip of whiskey.

"Said: 'Miss Duval, is that *you?*' And she said, 'Yes, doll, the one and only, in the very flesh. Don't you think my costume's a darling?' And Mister Jessie looked at her awhile and shook his head, and then he said real loud, 'Dance, Miss Duval, dance!'

"And I could see him break out in a sweat, and I broke out too, because man and boy, up in the country and down in the town, down home and up north, I'd never expected to see anything like that in my whole life.

"So she started trying to dance and, gen'lmens, it was like what they call a 'ca'astrofee.' Juiced as she was and with all those goldbacks hanging around her belly, she was like somebody made out of soft rubber and no bones. She held out her arms and tried to do a waltz step, but she couldn't make it. Those high heels kinda scrounched on the floor and she skidded, and with that, every pound of her started swinging. Then she held up one arm while she put her other hand on her hip and tried to strut like she was something grand to look at, but she was too juiced to do even that good. Then she started to walk a few steps, and throwing her head back over her shoulder and posing like Miss Theda Bara used to do—only she's too juiced to hold any of them poses for long, and Mister Jessie was looking down at her all absorbed like a judge listening to a murder trial. And the next thing I know, she's trying to do a split—and that's when it happened...."

McMillen paused then, taking a gulp of whiskey.

"Will you quit stalling and tell us what happened before the coroner gets here?" the sergeant said.

"Yes, suh!" McMillen said. "I'm going to tell you. She'd just started to stick out her legs and was sliding down heel and toe when the doorbell rang, and she stopped and tried to come out of it but she was too far down to make it and she plopped on her side, cussing a blue streak and started to turn with her legs in the air, and I heard Mister Jessie yell, 'McMillen, answer the door.' And at that, I pulled myself together and wiped my face and went past her out through the other room to see who it was. Then just as I reached the door, it came open and this white man comes in...."

"*What* white man?" the sergeant asked.

"The same one I asked you if he was still here," McMillen said.

"And how did he get in?"

"He *walked* in. I guess I must have left the door unlocked, or I got up and buzzed, but I swear I don't recall doing it. But anyway, this white man is here, and late as it is he wants to see Mister Jessie about something he heard that Mister Jessie had bought from some old house down South. I tried to tell him that Mister Jessie was busy and wouldn't do no business at that time of night, but he pushed past me like he was somebody important, and when he saw that lady over there with her heels in the air and all those goldbacks flapping, it was like somebody had cool-cracked him with an axe handle. He hadn't seen Mister Jessie yet because he was sitting so high, nor had Mister Jessie seen *him,* because he was so busy watching Miss Duval. But when he did see him he let out a yell and said, 'You, sir! What are you doing in my house?'

"And the man, he said kind of agitated-like, 'I'm here to make a purchase.' And Mister Jessie said, 'Purchase, hell; this is a party, and I don't want no goddamn yellow Negroes in my house!' And the man stopped short and turned red, and he said, 'But I'm not colored.' And then Mister Jessie reared back in his coffin, and said, 'So I don't want no goddamn *white* folks in my goddamn house— What do you think of that? Now get the hell out!'

"Then the man saw what Mister Jessie was sitting in, and his eyes got big and he started to sputter, and all at once he said a mighty strange thing...."

We waited now while McMillen shook his head bemusedly.

"You all will have to remember that I was pretty juiced by now, but I swear that the man said something like, 'What are you doing in my coffin!' "

"He said WHAT?"

"I know it's hard to believe," McMillen said, "but that's what it sounded like to me. And when he said that, Mister Jessie liked to blowed his top. He was looking at the man and his mouth was working and all at once he yelled something about, 'Now I recognize you—you're that throat-cutting' so-and-so, and he called a name; but Mister Jessie was so mad that he just messed it plumb up. He blew a hole straight through it like when you let out a yell with a mouthful of soda crackers. But the man got it just the same, and when Mister Jessie called it I could see that white man step back and turn pale, then he whirled around like he'd been hit by a forty-five and he started for the door.

"Mister Jessie was cussing and yelling for me to grab the man—which I wasn't even thinking about doing—when the lady over there, *she* grabbed the man's ankle from where she was splitting on the floor, and he dragged her along for a couple of yards like she was on a sled. I don't think that she was

trying to stop the man for Mister Jessie, though; she was just juiced and acting a fool. She said something about, 'Wait there, good-looking, and watch
me do my number,' and the man was cutting out and Mister Jessie was trying to get out of that coffin like it was on fire.

"He was yelling, 'Let's discuss the issues, you jacklegged highbinder! Let's
consult the record!' and his face was red and those tendons in his neck were
all roped out like they were about to bust. Then the man kicked Miss Duval
off his ankle and got the door open, and Mister Jessie gave a lunge, trying his
level best to get out of the coffin and just then he fell back, still yelling at the
man like he had blowed his top. I guess that's when the stroke hit him, and
that was that."

"What do you mean, 'That was that'?"

"I mean that's about all I know about what happened."

"What did he call the man? Can't you recall the name?"

"No, suh, I can't. I had been holding on to my liquor for so long and trying to protect Mister Jessie's interests that, by then, with all that hell done
broke loose, and with that important-looking white man probably gone to
call y'all, I figured I might as well let go my holt. I do remember that later
somebody come in and opened the door and let out a scream while I was trying to phone the doctor. And when he didn't answer, I closed the door to the
room and locked it. Then I come back and tried to bring Mister Jessie to,
poor fellow, but he was long gone. So I just got myself another drink and sat
back down and passed out. I don't know what you want to do to me now, but
I don't *know* no more and I can't *tell* you any more. And that's that."

The sergeant gave McMillen a long, flabbergasted look, then turned
toward the man in the coffin and shook his head, cursing softly under his
breath.

"Aubrey," he said, "I want you to think back and consider this carefully:
What kind of name did your friend call the white man?"

"He called him a jacklegged highbinder—"

"No, I mean his surname."

McMillen moved his head slowly from left to right, emphatically. "I don't
remember what he called him. He was so mad, he just sputtered like a
preacher shouting a sermon. All I know is that it didn't sound like any ordinary name."

"Did it sound foreign? Russian or Chinese?"

"No, suh, at least I don't think so."

"How do you know? Had you heard it before?"

"Now that's what has me puzzled, I have a feeling that I have— Yes, suh,
I'm pretty sure that I've heard it before, but I figured that I must've been
hearing through my whiskey, and that's why I can't recall it. Because what
would a man with an important name be doing coming here to this house at

that time of night? Don't nobody set out to buy anything that Mister Jessie sells at that time of night. And we ain't got no whores or dope pushers or anybody like that living here. So naturally I figured that I was either drunk or dreaming."

Suddenly the door to the outer room came open, and I looked back to see the frowning face of Officer Tillman.

"Sergeant," he called, "could you step out here a moment?"

"Not now," the sergeant said, "I'm busy."

"I understand, but I've got a fellow out here who says he's got a message for someone named McMillen. He claims he's a minister, but I've got a notion that he's here to buy some booze. I thought you might want to question him—"

"Who's that out there looking for me?" McMillen interrupted.

"I'll ask the questions!" the sergeant said.

"Yeah, but that man's signifying that I'm selling whiskey, and I want to know who it is."

"What shall I do with him?" Tillman called.

"Hold him along with the others, and I'll have a look at him as soon as I'm finished here. Now close the door!"

"Booze," McMillen mumbled. "Somebody is lying on me, and I want to know who it is."

He looked at me as the door was closed. I could hear voices but caught no glimpse of the new arrival. Then the sergeant resumed his questioning, and while I listened I found myself staring at Miss Duval.

Sprawled in the chair with Tillman's jacket across her lap, she appeared asleep, but I was prepared to see her open her eyes at any moment and say something to send the sergeant into a sputtering rage. How on earth had she come to this state? I wondered. And in what Harlem had she learned to speak that semi-underworld Negro idiom? Had it been through an act of rebellion? Of love? And now, despite a certain fastidiousness of taste, I found myself drawn to Miss Duval, lifted out of myself as it were, fascinated by certain challenges and possibilities of actuality which she seemed by her presence and rowdy disorder to suggest. I felt in the presence of unacceptable mysteries. My face was ablaze, and my imagination plunged into a vortex of vague, unformed emotions and fleeting images: my mother dressed in a white pique dress and floppy hat, cutting long-stemmed roses in the garden on a summer afternoon long ago; Sara Delano Roosevelt wearing a choker of pearls and a great fur piece which rippled luxuriantly in the wind along Pennsylvania Avenue as she passed in a chauffeur-driven car with top back; three bridesmaids in pastel dresses, holding bouquets in a Gilbert and Sullivan "Three little maids from school are we" attitude as they posed for a photographer whose head was far hidden beneath the folds of a black camera cloth; Mae West in a Lillian Russell hat, walking her famous Westian walk....

I wondered how it would be to know such an experienced woman who had, apparently, abandoned the known and accepted paths of society and come to explore the forbidden places that existed within those realms of chaos which seemed, to all appearances, there in Jessie Rockmore's strange house, to be boiling and steaming within everything which we regard as solid, stable, and respectable. *Under our blaze of lights, perhaps these darknesses steadily explore us,* I thought. *The deep, the dark, the forbidden seek out our uncertainties when our guards are down....*

And what would McGowan make of Miss Cordelia Duval, and who was the real woman behind that unlikely name? Did McGowan know of the existence of such women, or did his strongly held views prevent him from seeking them, from even recognizing their existence? He held that girlie magazines lead to social disorder because they unmask woman's mystery, but Miss Duval, sprawled in her goldbacked frill of a skirt, seemed far more mysterious to me than had she been fully clothed. Indeed, she was covered by a texture of mysteries. There was a mystery behind the language she used and behind the account of her past as reported to McMillen. Yes, she was a tangle of fleshy mystery even if McMillen's story turned out to be a lie. She repelled and attracted, attracted and repelled, and I wondered if the mystery of murder lay somewhere behind her rowdy conduct, her presence here. What if she and McMillen had actually done the old man in and then placed him in the coffin?

I was in a sweat now, realizing that it was almost morning and that I would have to file my story for the early edition, but drawn to her and finding myself edging over to where she slouched, even as the sergeant's interrogation resumed behind me.

She must have felt my presence, for now she looked up.

"Why in hell don't you two-bit gumshoes leave Uncle Tom alone?" she said, regarding me through slitted eyes. "The poor bastard's told you everything there is to know. Why don't you go and find that stuffed shirt who got Dad over there excited? Everything was going fine. He ruined my number and everything else when it was all going fine. I never knew it to fail, jus' let me come near a spook and everything comes unraveled...."

"Miss Duval," I said, "did you recognize the man?"

"Hell, no, but it was probably some prowling drunk looking for a spade broad to change his luck, or trying to find his mama masquerading as a coal-shuttle blonde."

"What?"

"That's right. What's so strange about that? Luck is luck, and you no-good men all believe in magic."

"I don't understand," I said.

She sat up, smiling. "Oh, doll, don't be so square— Say, did I tell you about the spook I had one time?"

"No," I said, "but do you think that you could recognize the man who was here?"

"*Recognize* him? I want to forget that bastard. Come here," she said, beckoning coquettishly. "Jus' a lil closer, doll..."

I approached her, feeling a mounting confusion.

"Doll," she said, "would you believe it, I had a private spook for a while, and I swear, he was the damndest man who ever kicked off a pair of shoes and punished a bed. That spook was simply awful. Not that he didn't know his business, he did. He spook-handled everything—the cops, the johns, the bellhops, madams, and everything. And he took care of me fine. But that's not what I mean. My point, Dad, is that the spook didn't have any rules or laws. That's what the problem was, doll. Damned spook would do anything just because people *said* a spook will do anything. 'N when I say anything, I mean anything! He jived a society broad into setting him up in a penthouse, then he went for her seventy-year-old sister and messed it up. The sister's husband didn't like the idea, you see. That spook was a true phenomenon, doll.

"Why, one day I came home and discovered that he had killed my pet canaries and parakeets because they wouldn't let him sleep—which although brutal was understandable, doll; but then the spook went on to bake them in a pie with pigtails, sweetbreads, and bell peppers. Doll, that spook was an ee-nig-ma!"

She yawned, then studied me with a mocking expression. "Know what else he did, doll?"

"No, Miss Duval."

"Well, I'll tell you; just bend down, doll; with those clowns over there listening, I have to whisper what that crazy spook did."

I leaned toward her now, seeing Tillman's jacket slip as she raised herself and as her face wavered up to mine. I hesitated.

"Doll, are you a damned faggot or something? You want me to tell you or not? Hell, you act like you've never been close to a real woman before."

And then, as I bent closer, reaching out to grasp the chair arm, Miss Duval threw her arms around my neck and pulled me toward her. Whereupon a quite unbelievable thing occurred: She kissed me. First my lips and then my eyes, and as I turned my head and tried to get away, she giggled and ran her tongue into my left ear, and I felt the hot, moist shock of it as she released me and fell back into the chair, laughing.

"*That's* what that crazy spook of mine used to do, doll. What do you think of that?"

I backed away, repelled for reasons that I couldn't admit, even to myself. I was speechless, her action causing a sudden disarray of my senses. Someone else seemed to look out from behind the face of Miss Duval, and now I was aware of sounds coming from elsewhere in the building—music, voices. And as I backed away from the laughing woman, the articles in the room became extremely vivid, each creating in some strange way its own visual space, offset by a throbbing glow.

"Listen, you!" a voice shouted, and I whirled seeing the sergeant pointing his finger in McMillen's face, while high on the table old Jessie Rockmore seemed about to hurl some stern and outraged judgment down upon us all.

I had passed through the door then, closing it upon Miss Duval's bubbling laughter. As I moved through the cluttered room I noticed a large dark man standing with his face turned toward the blazing wall, gazing through the stereopticon. Then I was past the policeman and the Negroes huddled in the vestibule and upon the stairs, into the hot darkness of the street.

Sometimes, as I say, this American scene tries to outdo itself in the extremes which it throws up to us. And it usually selects precisely those moments when we are least prepared to confront or even make sense of them. And, in fact, when we are least prepared to be attentive. Perhaps when such events occur we're too relieved to get away, to make tracks for a more tranquil territory of place or mind, that we fail even to consider the possibility that these events might be far more than simple occurrences in themselves but tame forecasts of more tortuous puzzles, of more drastic revelations. Even of disasters of tragic proportions. Of one thing I am certain, I was so relieved to be out of Jessie Rockmore's house and into the sultry rationality of the nighttime street that I felt a certain sense of innocence, thankful that I had been born to a stable level of society in which such chaos had been eliminated, tamed, filtered out. It had difficulties, true, but at least there was ORDER. Oh, yes, I was relieved, but how was I to know that after those confounding moments of night I was yet to face a more terrible day?

CHAPTER 13

LOOKING DOWN THE CORRIDOR toward Bates, I wondered what would have happened had I tried to describe what I'd seen and observed in Jessie Rockmore's house to Tolliver. He probably would have rushed me upstairs to join McMillen—whom I can't believe to be a murderer—and Lee Willie Minifees. And now I asked myself if it was not one more cryptic foreshadowing of more chaos to come, with the old Negro in his coffin chair–judgment bench but one more arrow pointing to the bringing low of a powerful senator.

But there was no time for further speculation, for now the elevator opened and a young nurse hurried past me and entered the Senator's room. Then, hardly had the door closed than one of the men carrying a machine gun came out and hurried down the corridor to speak with Bates and then disappeared around the corner. All this occurred swiftly, without a stir from old Hickman. But now, as the nurse came out again, she spoke to him and he seemed immediately alert. I could see him smile and nod his head and the nurse hurrying down the corridor where the guard had disappeared. My nerves tightened as I watched him, his eyes closed again, and I fought down an impulse to ask if she'd given him some word of the Senator's condition. And where was Tolliver, I wondered, and would he remember his promise to alert me to any new development? I got up and walked back and forth before the bench, waiting. I thought of Miss Duval, my mother, Laura, of the Holy Family as sepia-tinted Negroes. What a mishmash of images! What a nutty blend of values! The world had become a Mr. Badbar of nutty contradictions.... I was starving, my gut growling.

I was about to sit down when the nurse returned with a tray and handed Hickman a glass.

"Thank you, ma'am," he said, clearing his throat, then nodded to me and I watched her smile, come toward me.

"That gentleman thought you might be thirsty," she said.

"Thank you," I said. "As a matter of fact, I am."

I took the glass and drank, returning it to her slender fingers.

"How is the Senator?" I said.

She shook her head. "Still critical, I'm afraid. Would you care for more water?"

"That'll be enough, thank you."

She left and I watched her return to the Senator's room. I sat then, determined to control my impatience. I would rest until Tolliver came and alerted me, or until I saw old Hickman called into the room. I thought of Minifees. Where were they holding him? And what was his role, if any, in this rotten fudge of a day? It was growing hotter. I rested my head upon the hard back of the bench, closed my eyes. I thought of my tally of birds, the sound of mating and nesting songs, the flicker of swift wings. *I came out of the woods into a strange street which looked as though it had been recently bombed. There was a hushed air of mystery over all. The houses seemed mere façades. Bricks, broken glass, and charred timbers were scattered about. Train rails were twisted like cables around the trunks of charred and splintered trees. And to one side I saw a billboard from which a huge Bull Durham Tobacco sign on which the once-proud bull, now ripped partially from its frame, swayed gently back and forth in the sunlight. Rust and blistered paint powdered his sides, his torn right horn revealing rusted tin behind. Then above, on the sun-shrunk frame, I saw a small conclave of buzzards engaged in furious argument. I was halted in the full rush of a running stride, my senses whirling as the question WHEN WILL YOU EVER LEARN MODERATION? sounded in my head as a voice cried:*

"Modernize! Sophisticate the techniques! Pollute the controls!"

"No, no, I insist," one of the buzzards said. "The best way is the traditional way. First you wait until he's properly ripened, and then hit him in the eyeball, and, after making sure that the coast is clear, after making certain that there are no intruders lurking around the edges to interrupt, you proceed just as the buzzards have always done. The first blow to the eye, however, is most important. Only then, after delivering the stroke with precision, should one proceed."

"Ah, tradish, tradish!" one of the younger buzzards said, "I'm sick to the stomach of all this tradish!"

"I agree, I quite agree," another small buzzard said, thrusting out his beak to the first speaker. "But how have the honorable old-timers gone about it, Altercocker?"

"Sneer if you like, you little unsanitary son-of-a-cuckoo-clock," the old buzzard said, "but my method is tried and true. Just as I've said, first you hit him in the eyeball, and then, taking your time so as to preserve your strength and steady your aim, you march around to the backdoor and there, with the proper dignity and decorum attuned to the delicacy of our dedicated task, you march straight up through his vast passage. That is the way! Proceed in this manner; taking your time and working him

thoroughly, you'll come out refreshed and reinvigorated. And, you'll be strengthened in heart and mind, sharpened in insight and lifted aloft in your morale down to the last frolic and—"

"Yes," another old fellow said, "and with your appetite absolutely satisfied."

"That's absolutely correct," the first buzzard said. "You'll preen with satisfaction, gleam with the sheen of a job well done. And that's the only proper manner in which it should be done. So don't bore me with your modern methods with their utter disregard for ceremony and good taste. I don't even wish to contemplate them. They are a virtual rape of proper procedure. An assault upon our past and repast! I've had too much vivid experience to think otherwise. Indeed, my boy, if one could arrange all the horses that I've worked my way through and place them in a straight line, one could march three times around the world without encountering the necessity of touching the earth! That's right: I know. I have done the state some service. Indeed, quite a bit of service. And all with this tried-and-true method!"

And suddenly his bald head came around, his ruff rippling greasily in the sunlight as he looked straight at me, "Isn't that true, friend?" he said. And without a word I turned and ran, hearing the buzzard laughter arising behind me as they sang:

> *See Mac run!*
> *See Mac run!*
> *He's a running son-of-a-gun!*
> *He's a running son-of-a-gun!*
> *He'll outrun the sun—yeah!*
> *And then right out of gas, oh, yas!*
> *He'll run right out of gas!*
>
> *Oh, see Mac run!*
> *Oh, see Mac run!*
> *Can anyone tell us why he fled?*
> *Y'all heard what the man just said*
> *Oh, I'll tell you just what Papa said*
> *He's running for where the living don't*
> *Bury the living dead, my son,*
> *Don't bury the living dead!*
>
> *See Mac run!*
> *See Mac run!*
> *He's a running son-of-a-gun!*
> *He's a running son-of-a-gun!*
> *Man, he'll outrun the sun—yeah!*
> *And then right out of gas, oh, yas!*

Lawd, see Mac run! Ah say,
See Mac run!
Can anyone tell us why he fled?
Ah said, who knows just why he fled?
Now y'all heard what the man just said
Yas, I can tell y'all what old Pappy said
He's running for where the living don't
Don't bury the living dead!

I ran now in earnest, sailing past broken houses and scenes of great devastation.
And yet, off to my right, I could see a thriving field in which an odd-shaped machine
rested like some strange and satiated Moloch, while beyond the field the roofs and smok-
ing chimneys of a thriving city showed.

God, *I thought,* I must be as drunk as a coot!

Then, just as I was passing a burning automobile, I saw McGowan leaning wearily
against a lamppost. Obviously, he was waiting for me, and I thought, Oh, hell, here
comes another lecture on the fourth dimension, *and tried to hurry past as*
though I hadn't seen him—only to have him reach out and grab my sleeve.

And when I looked at him, I immediately felt guilty; he looked strangely transformed
and extremely weak.

"Look, McIntyre," he said, "I'm having terrible trouble with a nigra, and I don't
know what to do about him. Man, I need some HELP!"

"You?" I said. "What's he doing to you? Where is he?"

"Why, the bastard's blocking my doorway, McIntyre, and I can't get him to leave."

I watched him warily, expecting a trick. "That's rather odd, isn't it?" I said. "What's
the matter with him? Who is he?"

"I don't know," McGowan said. "McIntyre, I really don't know."

"But this is impossible."

"Like hell, it is. This is some new *kind of nigra."*

"A new kind?"

"That's right; I wouldn't lie about a thing like this."

"So why don't you simply push him aside?"

McGowan recoiled. "Hell, man, I don't want to touch him," he said, staggering a bit
as he rubbed his wrists. Great beads of sweat stood out over his hands, and there was a
genuine expression of revulsion on his face. "This ain't the kind of nigra you touch," he
said, "not even for luck!"

"Then call the police," I said. "That's what they're paid for. Why not make use of the
law for once in your life?"

"Hell, no, McIntyre; I can't do that. It would be against my honor."

"Your honor!" I said. "What has honor to do with it? A man should have free access
to his own house. His home is his castle, so defend it!"

"But you haven't seen him yet," he said. "He's too little to head-whip, and it's against

my tradition and my principles both to call the police to handle a nigra. It just ain't Southern. Besides, I think he's crazy, and today I simply don't feel up to dealing with a crazy nigra."

There was real anguish in his face, and I felt an uneasiness growing within me. It simply wasn't like McGowan to be fazed by a Negro. . . .

"What did you do to make this fellow block your doorway?"

"I be damned if I know, McIntyre; but I've already told you that the nigra is loco. This is some kind of metaphysical nigra bastard!"

"He's what?"

"I just told you, he's metaphysical."

"But that isn't logical."

"Does he have to be logical for you to help me get him out of my door?"

"No, I guess not, but—"

"Then why don't you help a man instead of standing here arguing with me like a damn Yankee lawyer!"

He was quite exasperated and so weak that he hardly seemed his old blustering self. All of the old rebel verve and bluster were gone.

"Okey," I said, "so I'll help, but first tell me, did you say something outrageous to him? Insult him in some way?"

"Oh, hell, no, that was the Senator, not me. Didn't I just tell you that I didn't bother that nigra?"

"But you must have done something to him. Now I'm going to help you, but it's only because I believe that the rights of property must be respected. Nevertheless, I don't think you're telling me the whole story."

He looked away, shrugging impatiently.

"Oh, I know that the nigras are getting awful touchy these days, McIntyre, but I swear that I didn't do a thing to this one. All I tried to do was to enter my own house. But like I told you, this is some new kind of little nigra. He talks Yankee talk, McIntyre. Why, you never heard anything like it. This nigra talks what the hack editors call Mandarin prose! That's right, man; and he's got a tongue that's as hot as the south end of a yellow jacket. I tell you, somebody must have done something awful to that little bastard for him to be acting like he is, but it sure wasn't me. I swear it wasn't."

"I can't understand it," I said.

"I'm not asking you to explain him, McIntyre. All I want you to do is to tell him to let me into my own house. I'm tired as hell, and I need to get some sleep. Be a good fellow and go tell him."

"Okey," I said, "where do I find your house?"

"It's just down the street a piece. It's the one with the white pillars. Number sixty-eight. You just pass through the gate and go along the path, and you'll see the bastard on the porch."

It's probably Sam or one of the bellmen at the club, *I thought. Moving along the street, I felt a sudden gratification for the opportunity of undoing some of the effects of McGowan's constant provocation, his humiliating attitudes. I would persuade the ob-stinate Negro with logic and kindliness. When, I wondered, would McGowan learn that politeness was always more effective than insults? Anyway, it was flattering to have him admit that someone else might be able to deal with these people more effectively than him-self. God, I thought, old Mac must be pretty sick. Too much burb, too little branch. Yes. I smiled, thinking,* Spare the branch and roil the Bible. . . .

I hurried now, but at the address he'd given me I found not a mansion but a pathet-ically mean, badly designed little bungalow which, instead of occupying the spacious grounds and gardens that I'd expected, sat rather close to the public sidewalk behind a barren yard. And then I received the real shock. Instead of the stubborn, angry Negro of the stature of Jack Johnson or Joe Louis whom I'd expected, I saw, standing smack in the middle of the doorway, a small cast-iron hitching-post figure in the form of a diminutive Negro.

What the hell goes on here? *I thought. It was the figure of a little jockey or groom, such as were once to be seen mainly in the South, but which in recent years have mushroomed throughout the North and are now all over the place—especially before the meanest, least aristocratic of dwellings—where they stand in strident pos-tures. It was a cheap, crudely made symbol of easily acquired tradition; the favorite statuary of the lazy seeker for facile symbolic status. I was sweating profusely now, for I had approached the house with the growing certainty that I'd find Sam the waiter—* what the hell is Sam's last name?—*standing at the door with a tray of iced drinks; now I was staring down at this iron manikin the size of a small child, its face gleaming black with white teeth showing through parted bloodred lips, its peaked head reminiscent of a famous boogie-woogie pianist whom I'd admired during the thirties, and its thyroid eyes, jaded and froglike, reminded me of certain examples of primitive African sculpture which appear to have grown satiated on the blood of endless human sacrifices.*

But hell, *I thought,* it's only a hitching-post boy, a little iron groom. What the hell's wrong with McGowan? Is he that drunk?

Then I stopped short, for instead of the traditional blouse, short-visored beanie, and flapping trousers of such figures, this one wore a tiny blue suit which, oddly, was cut in the fashionable short-jacketed style known as "Italian Continental." Its sharp-toed shoes, with large brass buckles, were also Continental. Four closely set mother-of-pearl buttons adorned its single-breasted jacket, which, cut loose and capelike in the shoulders, gave the eerie effect of bat wings at rest. And with its white shirt, which was rather grubby about the cuffs and collar, it gave me the uncanny feeling that he could run straight up a vertical wall and walk across a ceiling with no show of exertion whatso-ever. One of the tiny hands rested delicately on a tiny hip, and the other, outstretched in the classical manner designed to receive the reins of a horse—but now I saw that the traditional metal ring had been replaced by a glass of dark oily liquid.

Is this some crazy joke McGowan is playing on me? *I thought. But when I turned to look down the street, I couldn't see him, he'd disappeared.*

He's probably too drunk to handle the weight of this thing—or too weak. If so, why does he try to hide it? We're all weak in some fashion. In any case, I'd better move it, or the poor bastard might stumble over it and break his neck....

All of this passed through my mind so logically that I could hear the words echoing in my head as I bent and lifted the figure, the iron boy, straining with the unexpected weight, and I had hardly taken three steps when the voice spoke in my ear:

"Watch it, baby, you mustn't squeeze!"

The heavy weight barely missed my foot as it plunged to the floor of the porch. I stepped back, staring as it rocked with a dull rumbling, back and forth on its feet. I looked quickly around. Except for the roar of a distant truck, it was silent. Hell, I'm hearing things, *I thought. I bent, lifting the figure again.*

"What are you staring at, McGowan, baby?"

Still stooping, I looked around. There was no one in sight. The door to the house was closed, the street empty. There was no doubt about it; the sound had come from the hitching-post boy. He had spoken. And now the eyes appeared to have come alive with malicious fire.

"Why are you staring, McGowan?" the voice said.

"Sir? McGowan? Hell, my name is McIntyre*!"*

"Really now," it said, regarding me with the fixed intensity of a hypnotist. "Well, baby, you're McGowan to me. All of you ofays are McGowan to me—McGowan."

McGowan! I shook my head and closed my eyes, then opened them rapidly. He was still there, blazing back at me.

Are you drunk? *I thought.* You must be. True, it is said that on rare occasions animals and birds have been known to talk to human beings who are in tune with nature, and I know too that this is the age of the semiconductor, the transistor, space probes—But hell, this is obviously a piece of old iron, a hitching-post groom. There's even rust on his pants leg....

"Hitching post?" he said. "It's been a hell of a time since I had anything to do with a horse, so why are you staring? Answer me, baby!"

"This," I said aloud, "is insanity!"

Whereupon I gave a mighty heave, determined to lift it out of the way, and discovered that it had suddenly become so heavy that I staggered with the weight.

This time the voice was imperious: "I demand *an answer, baby!"*

This was too much. I banged it upon the white floor of the porch and stepped back, looking down. What trick was this? Who wired this thing for sound?, *I thought, seeing the eyes widen and stare up at me indignantly.*

"Well, McGowan, I'm waiting!"

What on earth? My mind flew up and around. Overhead, three black-and-yellow wasps flew in circles, intersecting my field of vision. It's all rationally explainable, I told myself. And remember, this is a nation of practical jokers, so play along with the gag. Don't be taken in....

I stopped and set it on its feet again, carefully.

"*Forgive me,*" I said, *forcing a pleasant tone.* "*And just how did you come to be here? I mean, who left you here?*"

The eyes narrowed. "*Take it easy, baby; I'm asking the question. Where are your manners? And take your drink before you answer!*"

"*Drink?*" I said. "*An iron tonic, I suppose. But thank you, no. A drink's the last thing I want just now.*"

"*Oh, but you do, baby. You really do, you know you do. And of course if* I *say you do, you doooo!*"

I didn't know what to make of it. The voice was getting to me, irritating me. The speech was precise, even cultured, with a certain archness and theatrical stridency. It was the very last type of speech I'd have associated with a hitching-post figure—even taking into account the absurd clothing. Indeed, that voice and diction would have been incredible even if I'd encountered him in the window of a women's shop, dressed in ballooning pantaloons and silken turban and holding the train of a high-fashion mannequin bride. Clearly, things were quite mixed up. How are they getting this stuff into his head? Because obviously Mac and some of his friends are behind it all, having fun with a Yankee. Very well, we'll see.

"*Listen,*" I said, *touching its shoulder with my index finger,* "*it's all a mistake. I didn't order a drink because I had quite enough hours ago, and I didn't even ring for you. . . .*"

"*Oh, but you didn't have to ring, McGowan. I have the ring in my pocket. So why be rude simply because you sent for me yesterday and and I've arrived today?*"

"*But I'm not being rude,*" I said, *feeling suddenly hot and, despite myself, on the defensive.*

"*Variety,*" he said, "*after all, and no matter how intensely one would deny it, is the very froth of existence, baby. So now drink your medicine and when you've finished I've got your bathwater on.*"

"*Bathwater!*" I cried, "*BATHWATER! Now you listen: My name is Mc-In-Tyre! Get that into your iron head! What's more, I don't want a bath, and I don't want a drink!*"

"*McGowan, dear—*" he began.

"*Mc-IN-TYRE!*"

He grinned. "*So solly please, not interested in fetal position. Most blad. Bathwasser so necessary for be born one more in time fugit. WE splesiall, if you wish to follow me. Please, no speak now. Because, baby, you'll bathe! Because you see,*" he said, *rocking his head delicately on his slender neck,* "*there'll be no funky blues here tonight. Mister Crump forbids it, Miss Vanderbilt rejects it, Miss Otis regrets, and* I *abhor it. So, McGohard, you'll bathe . . .*"

I studied him silently, thinking: If I ignore him he'll simply talk on. Perhaps if I move him and remain silent, I can be done with him. And besides, this is sheer foolishness, a delusion. . . .

This time I managed to take a few steps before it spoke again, in a coy, ingratiating tone.

"McGow-wand, baby, tell me true—do you fine me repulsive?"

I was silent, aware now of an odor like that of old tennis shoes.

"You'd better answer, McGowan; repression is bad for the bowels, and we won't mention the soul."

I gave a brisk shove, trying to push him out of the doorway as he laughed maliciously. It was oppressively warm and he moved barely an inch.

"Take it easy, baby. Even if it hurts you to do so. And by the way, McGowan, everything seems to hurt you. That's because you think only of yourself. That's why you're no damn good. You find me repulsive, and you have absolutely no feeling for my suffering, simply because I don't choose to reveal it to every passerby. You refuse to recognize my humanity, you really do, so admit it!"

Wow, *I thought,* I am drunk. Imagine imagining a piece of iron speaking of its humanity! Sam the waiter must have Finned the drinks. Wake up, McIntyre.

"Did you say iron, baby?" the voice said. "If so, you're wrong. Mine is a human figure. Keep holding me and you'll find out. This indicates clearly enough that you find me repulsive. Well, I'll admit that I'm repulsive—but so are you, baby. We both are. As repulsive and as noxious as crows. That's how it is: black crows and white crows. But you love it, baby; or you will *love it, just as soon as you admit it. Face up to reality, baby. Because that's the way it is. It's a simple equation. Repeat after me, and it'll do you worlds of good. Indeed, it'll allow you to achieve humanity:*

> *I am contemptible*
> *You are contemptible*
> *They are contemptible*
> *She is contemptible*
> *We are contemptible*
> *He-she-it is contemptible.*

The black face smiled mockingly as it spoke and despite myself, I found my lips silently forming the words. I felt unclean.

"See," he said, "that's the way it is, only you won't admit it. And because you refuse to admit it, you're the most contemptible of all!"

Whereupon, at the sound of wild laughter, the hot fumes of old tennis shoes or Limburger cheese filled the air, and I released my hold, watching him land on the floor with a deafening thud.

"McIntyre?" McGowan's voice arose once more behind me, plaintive and tired.

"Did you get him to go away, McIntyre? Did you get rid of that little nigra?"

Suddenly furious, I yelled, "Shut up, you indecent bastard," looking around for him. The street was empty, without shade.

"I'll get rid of this thing if it's the last thing I do," I said. Then, squatting in the recommended manner for lifting heavy objects with the least danger of ruptures, strains, or

slipped disks, I lifted him chest-high and began taking short shuffling steps toward the right side of the doorway.

As I did so, the groom cleared his throat in my ear. "Oh, so you've returned," the voice said blandly. "Are you becoming used to my repulsiveness, baby? No? Well, just keep holding me and you will. You have my permission to squeeze me if you like. And don't be upset if I speak to you; eloquence is eloquence, no matter how we attain it, and I am nothing if not eloquent. Nor should you confuse irony with iron, baby."

"Listen," I exploded, "I've had enough—"

"No, you listen, McGowan; or I'll step on your toes. I'll bump you! Do you know, McOldcowhand, that I'm really very beautiful? You refuse to see it because you are not. You aren't and neither are most hitching-post boys. In fact, they're quite ugly. What's more, they act *ugly. You made them act ugly, McGowan, even to me. And before I learned to defend myself, they used to chase me and treat me something awful. Through vacant lots and under stairways and through empty hallways, all foul and filthy, McGowan. And they did awful things to me, baby. Terrible things. Things so terrible that I had to accept them. They were, I grew to believe,* preordained *for me. And I tell you, baby, they did happen to me. Now of course I know that they happen to everyone. It's* la condition humaine, *baby—nez pas? Everyone is thrown into the alley like choice pieces of airmail garbage. So why should I complain?*

"And I'll tell you something else. Do you know that now, after having lived this long and having seen and done so much, I'm willing to concede you any and everything you might think about me? That's because I've put you down, baby. You don't really matter to me anymore. And now you'll learn that little wisdom which has escaped you for so long: You never miss your water until your well runs dry, you'll never miss your wise man 'til your fool gets shy. And if you doubt me, look at the details. I never entered your head before, did I? Yet, here I am in all the factual details you pretend you love so much. 'Significant details,' I believe you call them. But what's significant, baby? Am I? Is the cloud on the horizon, the pimple on the nose, the missed tick in the tock, the Snicker in the chocolate box?"

I shook my head, trying to rid myself of the spell and feeling the weight bearing me down as I moved again.

"Oh, no, none of that," he said. "None of that! Obviously, you wish to convince yourself that I'm not here. You'd rather pretend that I'm simply a 'figment of the imagination,' a trace of the 'irrational' which has seeped in with your liquor. You'd rather plead insanity than deal with me honestly, such is your McGowan pride. But don't cliché me, baby. I'm real and there's nothing simple about me. I'm here and very much myself. Do you still doubt me?"

A stream of sweat was running into my right eye now, and I wished to wipe it away but kept inching silently toward the door frame.

"Very well, baby, since you wish to act rude, I shall commune with myself—in ironic, as it were; and now you'll consider me a 'hard case.' Very well, I am indeed a hard case. You might even say that I'm a rough case, but what I tell you about yourself is nonethe-

less true. You're no good, McGowan! You suffer from the puritan chill; that is, pure tan chills you—which is worse, to my mind, than a compounded case of VD—or déjà vu. You drug yourself with easy answers, and you probably think that I'm taking horse. Well, allow me to suggest this, baby: I ride horses, they don't ride me. I'm in the saddle and I've sharpened my spurs. It's you who's on the needle, baby, on the very point. So coo-coo cock-a-doodle-do to you, McGowan. Now shall we talk crow?"

Straining, inching sideways again, I held my peace. For some reason I seemed to make little progress. My arms ached. I felt breathless.

"You have no feeling for my suffering, McGoldinhand, and you deliberately refuse to understand. And that's why you have so little insight into yourself. You fail to grasp your own nature. You insist upon a stance of innocence and . . ."

Where, *I thought*, does one's human obligation end? Here an iron monster is demanding—

"Iron? IRON?" he shouted. "Why, mine is a human figure, McFoldedhand! Ask your mother, she'd know. Women have fine perceptions in these matters. Yes, and a capacity for telling the truth—if only those like you would let them! Now put me down!"

And despite my determination to hold on, he fell, landing squarely in the doorway.

Thank God that we're alone, *I thought, looking wildly around me. Down near the corner of the block a flag fluttered high from a pole, its colors translucent in the sunlight. Then a burst of yellow butterflies swirled up and around the little porch. How-when-where had I learned that they were once regarded as symbols of the soul?*

"Look down this lonesome road a moment, baby," the voice said, as he gestured floorward with his head. "And don't go dreaming off, you might miss your cue, your train, your 'flang,' as the old-fashioned colored say. Remember the famous cartoon of the old man and his grandson watching Indians dancing in the smoke from a pile of burning leaves? You should, it was fall in the spring and all you know is what you read in the newspapers. But now ask yourself seriously what it was you saw. Under the bare trees beyond the fence and the fading bush beyond, the old man and the boy saw 'Indians'— so you saw Indians. But did you see them truly? Think now on those Indians, baby. And on that smoke. Oh, you had a ball!

"War bonnets!

"Smoke signals!

"Bare bucks buck-dancing with tomahawks!

"Braided scalp locks!

"War paint!

"Battle chants!

"Ghost Dancers going, 'Woo-woo-whoo-whooo-whoo, whah-whah, whah-ha!' Are you recalling? Are you with it? Because now comes the question, baby: Was the smoke from an Indian tribe? Really?

"Mohican?

"Seneca?

"An Algonquin round-robin?

"*Rubber-tired moccasins burning on a Pontiac?*

"*Was that it, baby? Or were those 'Indians' a tribe of smokes slow-dragging a juba-jumping, boondoggling, tea-dumping hoedown in the land of rum, four masters, and molasses? Don't blink, just tell me what you saw. Was the grandfather the son of the son? Did he raise up the smokes Lazarus-like, or put out the fire when he saw them burning for the shore? When your heart's on fire there are smokes in it, baby. And even when he smoked tea in the bay? Yes, and was Finny more of a cooper than he knew? Killdeers no kill deer, so what did dearslayer slay? And when you've answered, baby, then tell me where are the smokes of yesteryear. Think on it, baby. Think on it hard!*"

Suddenly he was silent, his face frozen once more into its fixed, ingratiating smile.

I stepped over his body, circling him slowly, as one does a sculpture displayed in a museum, noting the Italianate suit, the thyroid eyes. He lay rigid, silent. I shook my head, laughing quietly at myself. Obviously, I was drunk. Yes, and just as obviously, McGowan and the others were playing a clever joke on me. They'd had the boy wired for sound, that was it. That explained it. Somehow they'd gotten a transmitter-receiver inside the peaked iron head, or into the chest, and somewhere along the citizen's broadcast band there were some jokers giving it taunting voice, bugging me. Very well, to hell with them. I'd play along and bide my time. Let them keep fighting the war if they chose, my time would come to retaliate. Besides, it was possible that they were actually after McGowan rather than me. Perhaps that's why he's made me the goat. They'd simply scared hell out of him. . . .

Yes, but what if the groom was actually speaking to me, actually knew that my name was McIntyre, and his insistence on calling me "McGowan" was deliberate? Or was it that I had in fact *become* McGowan? Whatever the case, there he was, lying in the doorway and as clear and present a danger to anyone trying to enter the house as I could imagine. So it was still my obligation to remove him, for I was still under the conditioning of my Boy Scout days not to leave such items as carpet tacks, broken glass, banana peels, roller skates, and the like in the path of the myopic and/or drunken citizenry—so why not this voluble piece of iron? In such situations one has to be true to something, so what is more suitable than to be constant to the ideals of one's early youth? Therefore, there's nothing to do but pick up McGowan's burden and walk. . . .

And for a moment it seemed to work. I handled him gently and managed to take four short steps before I heard him yawn lazily and address me again.

"Well, baby, so here you go waltzing me around again—and so roughly!"

This time I kept silent, looking out into the empty vista of the street as I inched him along. The sun was high, the shadows near nonexistent. High on the pole the flag still fluttered beneath a cloudless sky in which a faded three-quarters of a pale moon still showed. Then, when I lowered my eyes, the porch seemed to have narrowed.

I'll have to set him in the yard, *I thought*—whereupon his voice shrilled up in protest.

"Not out there, dammit! There's a dog around here who likes to take liberties with my leg—the canine sonofabitch!"

I paused, holding my breath.

He laughed. "Shocked you, didn't I, McGowan? So now you don't know what to do. It's always the little things that matter with you, McGowan. All I did was call a dog his bitch's son, and your teeth are on edge. Such facile identifications make for confusion, baby; learn to call a spade a spade! I'm sorry for you, baby. I am indeed. I speak of a bitch and the cat gets your tongue. Very well, be quiet for a while, it'll be good for you. Don't talk. Make like Pete the rabbit, who had the habit of eating turnip tops and Welsh rarebit—the gummy kind. You make too much noise anyway, filling the air with static and double-talk. In fact, you live a life of noisy desperation, McCoolhand; with your tintin-timbulating anti-dialogue way of speaking. You sound the brass and tinkle the symbols all over the place, but in the clinches you're as silent as the proverbial mouse taking advantage of the mythical cotton. Only the nose knows you're there. You're a fraud, McGowan. You went over the cliff with the swine a long, long time ago, but you pretend to yourself and to the world that you're as white as the driven snow. But I'll tell you something, baby: You're driven but you've only had a snow job. Imagine giving oneself a snow job! And what's more amazing, baby, is that you're insensitive to those who can never be snowed. You believe it to be a natural phenomenon. Yes, that's the way it is with you, McGobback. And you feel definitely superior to me because I will not be, cannot be, snowed! Isn't it true? Why don't you confess, McGee? Why don't you try for once in your life to be a man!"

Suddenly, standing there holding all that cumbersome weight, I felt awful. It was as though it was three o'clock in the morning, and all the anxieties of the day, freed now of the qualifications of the light, had taken me over in the dark. And yet the street showed with the brightest of suns.

"Listen," I said quietly, "my name is McIntyre. I am a newspaper man. I was born in Massachusetts. My Social Security number is 15-100-369. My dogtag number is 1234567983, and according to the Geneva Convention this is all I have to say. Besides, what have we here, an immoral equivalent for warfare?"

"Very good, McGoahead," he said. "Very good, indeed. Watch it, though, you almost slipped that time. But you can't get out of it so easily. I know you too well, baby. You're one of those who love humanity real good, like a proper Christian should. You help the poor and the needy and you contribute to the care and feeding of the unknown heathen hordes abroad. You love everybody and anybody until you see their faces, or hear their voices raised in passionate description of the truth of their own condition. But then, baby, your love goes limp. Your sterling 'integration of personality' tarnishes and cankers, and then Uncle Sugar grabs the scatological imperative and hides himself like foxes in holes. At the first sound you tell yourself, 'Oh, oh, they're suffering so hugely that they must hate *me! Why can't they be more* considerate? *That's what you do.*

"One could be suffering all of the anguish of the world, baby—and suffering for you; quietly, *sans* self-pity, *sans* self-indulgence *and with an admirably heroic silence which, if you merely* heard *about would move you to tears. You'd be so moved that you'd even add up your bank account immediately, looking for possible charity deductions. And*

you'd consult the welfare associations and the philanthropic foundations to aid him. You'd become a whirlwind of emotional action. Yes! But just let the silent sufferer show his true face, or speak what is truly on his mind—then my-oh-my, how you'd put him down. Oh, but you would! What right has he to complain? you'd scream. Who the hell does he think he is, you'd say. Why is he crying out for snow when ever so many Americans must suffer the slings and arrows of too much good fortune? Does he think he's better than anyone else? That he has more claims upon humanity? Let him freeze his instincts as we've frozen ours! Let him prepare himself to face his face. Let him discipline himself and forget his extremist behavior on both sides, front and rear, top and bottom, and then, other things being equal, perhaps, in time, when the circumstances are propitious, the frost on the old banana, the lily without dew, he shall be truly as purely driven and snowed as we. But not with all of this against him! History was against him in the beginning and so was Jehovah—look at his birthrate, his crimerate, his heartrate, his deathrate, raperate, sweatrate, B.O.-rate, his you-name-it-and-I-reject-it-rate. . . ."

I shook my head, filled with a heavy sadness. So much bitterness.

"Oh, don't give me that, baby! Don't try to pretend it isn't so. Oh, yes and quite right, you're a man of high principles. Your ideals soar up to the stars, and you hear the tragic music of the spheres with a wan smile as you go forth each day to do your duty in the public press. And what a duty you do!

"Oh, I know you, baby. I remember two years ago when they found that head floating in a jar of alcohol sitting in the middle of the road out there. The sheriff brought it and sat it alongside of me, and the photographers took pictures and the sightseers came and gawked. Imagine, they propped it beside me! I wanted to die right then and there. Cast out my sight, take a vow of silence. But when I read how you reported it, baby, I wanted to . . ."

Oh, no! *I thought, moving again.* Oh, no! Could this be true? Had I written about such an incident? How could I be sure, with all the news that flowed over my desk during any given day? . . .

"You told the world that a lab specimen had been placed there in the street by medical students who were playing a joke! Well, you knew better and I certainly knew better. Because there isn't a medical college within three hundred miles. Not even a clinic. And what's more, everyone in town knew whose head it was. Yes, and I knew that beautiful boy because he had struck me with a ripe tomato only a few days before. Everyone knew him because he was so free and full of lovely fire. He made everyone nervous with his joyful laughter. So he paid, you might say, for his freedom with his head. Which is rare enough these days, for his head to merit being placed in a museum along with Bishop Berkley's and Injun Jody's. The problem, though, is that we've failed to put such acts behind us.

"But did you tell the truth, McGowan? Did anyone tell the truth? Don't sputter, McGowan—because I might just ask if you were intimidated the first time you saw your father in the bath, lying there like a raw, becalmed whale, soapsuds glistening him over, and his nasty mast flying an amorphous flag of foam. . . ."

"What the hell are you saying?" I yelled, "You . . . you—"

And suddenly he lay on the porch staring up at me like a ventriloquist's dummy.

"McIntyre!" It was McGowan calling from a distance. "Help me, McIntyre! Help me get him off my back!"

I didn't look around. "To hell with you," I called. "And damn both of you and the jokers who produced you!"

And yet, still feeling a compulsion to complete the job, I bent once again and struggled with the heavy, unhandy weight of McGowan's burden.

This time the jeering began immediately.

"Easy there, baby, ahm most sore and weary, I'se most worn with care. Did it ever occur to you, McGowan, that I might be fatigued and sorely driven? Pained in body, perplexed of mind?"

I eased him along, thinking, A sad case of metal fatigue.

"None of that!" he said. "If I were you, baby, I wouldn't try to make jokes. You haven't the temperament, nor the necessary psychic distance. Your experience has been too protected, insulated, and bland. You don't associate the disassociated quickly enough. So, of course you have no idea of my troubles, so why should I waste my time asking? Well, I suffer nevertheless. In fact, I'm in worse shape than that cartoon of the poor heavy-laden cow that has stepped on her own teat, the one which so amused you and your vulgar friends. Yes, indeed, baby. I tell you no lies, I suffer immeasurably and unceasingly. And do you know why? I'll be pleased to inform you, baby; I carry the weight of society on my shoulders. You just think about that, baby; and you'll see that it's true. It's not you, not the President, not the political gang, and not the preachers, but yours truly. I carry the stinking weight.

"And do you know why? It's because there are certain little necessities which must be taken care of, certain small costs of civilization—and I am nothing if not civilized! So someone has to pay the fee, there are many fees, baby, and I have picked up the tab for far too long. I've suffered long and patiently, but now I've become tired of trying to teach you by example to be honorable and manly. I have now lost faith in my appointed role, so that you must understand that the check—my check—is long overdue and the balance is upset and the hockey's piled high as an elephant's eye. . . ."

I inched along, thinking: It's no more than a buzzing in the head, an aural hallucination. Remember the mask of coconut husks that frightened you when you were a boy with its nighttime judgments on your daytime conduct? It must be something of that order—but what could have shaken you up, McIntyre?

"I'm speaking to you, baby!" the groom yelled, sending a blast of hot air past my ear. "I said! What would you do if your daughter brought home a chocolate—no, a gingerbread—boy? Throw him in the oven? Answer immediately!"

I tensed, lowering him to look into the face with the mocking grin.

"My question frightens you, baby? Or is it the answer which is bounding around in your head this very instant? Be so kind as to reply, and don't leap to conclusions—I might not like it."

I strained along once more, suddenly taken with an idea I dared not utter. Since he thinks I'm McGowan, I'd have loved for him to marry "my" daughter, because it would surely get him silenced. Melted down, rolled into ingots, made into the small screws and bolts of some vast anonymous machine....

"Oh, don't be ridiculous, baby; I'm already part of the machine and a more important part than you recognize. Now what about the gingerbread boy? You don't intend to answer? Well, what am I to expect, when there has been such a general decay of manners in this country? Haven't you noticed the smell? So forget it, your answer wouldn't matter because nothing would be changed. I refer, of course, to the gingerbread boy, who is, after all, substantially cake. A true cookie, McGowan; thus it's all a matter of taste. So why not sweets to the sweet? Let your daughter take her choice, vanilla or chocolate. Be at least as liberal as the good Marie, the maiden who lost her head. And so allow me, then, another approach. Agreed?"

He stared into my eyes, waiting. I didn't answer.

"Answer me this: Is it preferable for a queen to marry her brother as against surrendering herself to the butcher boy? Surely you can answer that one, McGoback; aren't you constantly referring to your English background? Of course. Purity is all, after all, isn't it? So keep the good stuff in the family. Isn't that it? Well enough, but remember this, baby, even chastity belts were made of iron. *As too are prison bars, barriers, bridges, chains, cannon, and cannonballs...."*

Suddenly I realized that I was no longer on the porch but was inching him along a walk leading to the porch. It was odd, and in my surprise I relaxed my grip.

"No, none of that!" he cried. "And don't go getting peevish. I remind you of these matters simply because you'd like to view me as no more than a natural resource. Isn't that true? Isn't such a view consoling? Convenient? Oh, you needn't speak, baby; I'll take a simple nod of the head to mean 'Amen' as the darktown strutters say on Wednesday nights. Yes, but it might be even more convenient to consider me as Mister Andy Jackson's ace in the hole.... A novel idea, that, don't you think? Well, he put me down like an old pawtater. Planted me deep but now is later. Now Ii yam a coymantater."

I struggled silently along, sweat pouring down my face, my biceps aching.

"Giving me the silent treatment, eh? Very well, be *stiff-necked if you like. I must confess that I find some truth in your view. For I am quite resourceful. You've hit upon a basic truth, only you miss the fact that there are gradations and hierarchies and contradictions in these matters. Nor must one forget to consider process. Oh, yes, baby, process is ever so important. It isn't always where you start or where you arrive, but how you get there, and all too often the process of arriving is more satisfactory than the arrival itself. Here you have the arousal, the tension, the friction, and satisfaction of most expectations. You take it easy, baby—that's good policy in many things—but take it! And that too is process.*

"Oh, yes, process is ever so important, baby. It makes for change. In truth, it's the swing and flow of change. And I should know, because I've been through many changes. I've undergone, in other words, many, many metamorphoses...."

What is this thing called? *I thought, making slow progress, moving an inch at a time.* What is his name, and who put the curse of speech on him or the plague of voices upon me?

"It's true, baby. Don't you recall the time long ago when I was the boy serving on your mother's boat? You should; you envied me my cozy position so much, you were almost wild—and especially when you guessed my importance. It was a tea party when she made you go Minsky. You were quite young, but afterwards you guessed quite correctly. Jack was in the pulpit and I was in the boat. In fact, I was the captain of that fine craft. I had no credentials, of course; but even so, you couldn't understand why you *couldn't have the job. Imagine, and you a mere babe! With no powers of control! Not to mention the social, the technical, or climatic considerations which you couldn't possibly have mastered. Nor the danger. For although you wouldn't believe it, baby, it was a* highly *dangerous pre— I mean work, occupation—with working conditions that were far from the best. Ask Joe Curran! Ask Captain Bradley—not that I would have cared for a union shop! But consult Sugarhips, the seaman. Or Johnny Velasco. They both knew, they trod the deck!*

"What's more, little recognition went with the job. Not even a uniform. In fact, I worked in the damp, exposed to the elements during all those stormy voyages and without shoes or overcoat. And let's not mention the heat and all the roar. No, nor the stench when her bilge was stirred up! I manned the pump! I swabbed the deck! I was the lookout in times of storm!

"Yes, baby; but these were minor problems beside the aggravation your father caused us. Understand me? Try, it isn't too difficult. Besides it's time you faced up frankly to the ABC's of it. And, oh, what a butchery blunderer he was! Coming in drunk, staggering limber-legged and cockeyed all over the place. Boasting like a clown. And then collapsing at the very moment when he should have had his best sea legs. It was just as well that you weren't ever allowed along, baby. You would have died of shame. And what a bad example he set you. There were the times, too, when the moon was full and he'd get frantic and come barging in wearing rough-weather gear and sou'wester, playing Captains Bly and Ahab rolled up in a single slicker. The crud! And then instead of navigating as a proper captain should, he'd brush me out of the way—I'd have to run for my very life, I tell you. Oh, yes, and after knocking me out of the way he'd try to push a hole straight through her bottom! What he did to that poor dear craft! And such lousy craftsmanship! And him having the nerve to boast of being the captain of his fate!

"I tell you, your mother was ofttimes disgusted with his conduct. Often disgusted! *And what would you have done, baby, on those occasions when, after he'd molested some poor woman in the town and been frustrated for his pains, he'd come plunging in trying to make his getaway with those two irate, uncouth, redheaded, evil-tempered Irish bulls on his drunken heels? With him screaming 'police brutality' and those red-faced clowns sweating and puffing as they chased him up and down and below decks and all? Funk out? Scream for outside help? Choke up? You'd have yelled for old black Joe playing his banjo in the basement! Yes, you would've, baby, and ole Joe would've.*

"You would have simply flipped over the side. You'd never have thought to call on me, and I was right there, trying to keep neutral in such a family ruckus. Well, I knew how to turn the brute around. Yes, indeed. And not with soft answers or turning the cheeks, but with the utmost firmness. Eye to eye! Chin to chin! He'd knock on the door but he wouldn't get in. Not even on deck. Oh, don't be misled by my size, baby; it's character that counts. Besides, I've always been quite manly—as your mother well knew. Shall I show you my muscle? No? Perhaps later, when you've been properly instructed. . . . Besides, I'm all muscle.

"So, as I say, I kept him from becoming a complete beast—ha-haaa! And what an ugly animal he was! You knew it too. No conscience what-so-ever! And did he ever thank me for keeping the family together? Did it make him more considerate, more human? Do fruit flies practice continence? And such complaining to your poor mother to get rid of me, to de-captain me! And him going to Dr. Reich and all that nursery mumbo jumbo of sitting in a canless can to change his luck! Imagine! I tell you, baby, I had a rough time of it. Yes, and with you wanting to kill me from sheer ignorant envy.

"Fortunately, though, your mother wouldn't hear of it. And why should she, since I did, after all, serve an admirable purpose? And I must admit that I served her rather well whenever it was my opportunity and pleasure to do so. In truth, and if it wasn't a bit immodest, I might say, entre nous, that during all those trying years it was I who kept the family intact. Nor should you misunderstand me, baby; for in spite of all the unpleasantness involved in leaving the old man behind, we had some most delightful sails together. We most certainly did. Just your mother and I. With me in my proper place, of course, in the little Amour Propre *as she called the little craft, and delightful times were had by all.*

"It was up the lazy river in the moonlight while your old man lay drunk and sleeping on the shore. And in the summer when the heat was gone and the gentle breeze came with the cool of the night on the lake, and with your old boy boozing in his cups—that was the very best time of all. I'd be in command then, like the boy who stood on the burning deck from whence all else had fled—Hot peanuts! Hot peanuts!—braced against her gunnels, and she relaxed and powdered from her bath, resting in the stern and trailing her gentle fingers in, shall we say, the limpid lapping of the lake? For with me she could man the craft alone. No messy roll calls. No fruitless inspections. No blanging bells, no pip-squeak bos'un's pipe, only me, baby, rowing her merrily on and on; through the singing shadows beneath the slender trees, and so gently down the stream that she would swoon!

"It was really a delightful duty, mon enfant. *And such delightful sighing sounds she made as bye and bye we reached that farther shore. You know? It was always the same; the row, the sail, the sighing sound, and then such sweet exhaustion!*

"And here's something else you didn't know, baby: She called me her 'little man,' and I was proud. And sometimes her 'darling darky darling.' And again her 'handsome African commodòro' *and 'Otello mio'—how do you like the swing of that? And in especially pensive moods it was in quick succession 'Oh, my jigging Joy Boy, Master of my Solitude,*

Dark Secret Delight, Gypsy Lover, Cellmate, Joy Rocker, and Dirty Richard.' And once in a moment of classical exuberance she called me her Jockey Boy of Artemesion!

"How I thrived, how I expanded! How gently she touched me with her compassion! I tell you, baby, there's absolutely nothing like good treatment. Why, under her encouragement, and with three more inches added to my height—and how I do wish I'd known of those lovely elevator shoes at the time—I do believe that I'd have taken her exploring. And now, as a matter of fact, we did, but why go into that here? It was in another country, and besides, she went quite out of her head in the brush and tangle of that wild terrain, poor thing."

Suddenly feeling a release of strength, I raised him above my head, trembling as I prepared to slam him to the earth, hearing him say, "Easy, baby! Ease—sy!"

"Why the hell is he calling me 'baby'?" I said aloud.

"Why? WHY? Because you are a follower while I am a leader, that's why. And why am I a leader? It's because I have been there, baby. I've been to all those places that you only think about and fear to investigate. And while you were yearning for the boat, I was the pilot. And there's the other painful fact that when your old man started forcing me into the seams and cracks of things I was compelled to grow up in the ways of the wise. One swing things another, you see? Rocks in mother's arms puts babe up the tree. So you see, it's simple; and as a result I've undergone many metamorphoses. Don't you believe me? You do and you don't? You don't trust me? Is that it? Well, you're quite right to be suspicious. I do have this gap between my upper central incisors—which is called a 'liar's gap,' and so I suppose that I'm sometimes compelled to tell lies. But not always, baby—as your dear mother could very well affirm. Au contraire, *I sometimes tell incisive truths, as she could also affirm. . . . But as I say, I've undergone many, many changes. . . ."*

This time I didn't hesitate. It was as though a powerful spring had torn free within me, and I raised him above my head, striding forward with a burst of unexpected strength as I yelled, "Speak up, you—you Joady. Get on with your confession!" and sent him against the ground with a resounding WHUMP!

"Speak up!" I yelled, becoming aware that now, no longer loquacious, he lay staring fixedly at the sky.

"Go on, tell me about your metamorphoses," I shouted, running forward to continue my attack—only to stop short at a sudden movement in his face. For a flash his expression seemed to waver and flow, accompanied by a high, grating sound. Then I was watching the black orbicular cheeks give way and my own face, pale and ghastly, eyes closed and dank-haired, was emerging as from the cracked shell of a black iron egg. I thought, Something horrible is about to happen, *as a movement underneath me hurled me backwards and away to land on a hard surface. Whereupon, looking straight ahead I faced a dim white rectangle of a wall cut by a threatening grid of cagelike shadows which popped in and out of focus in time with a throbbing which had set up in my ears.* Where did I throw him? *I thought, for now the groom was nowhere to be seen.* Where did he land?

Then a grating sound from somewhere above and beyond caused me to roll swiftly to my left, and I could feel my chin brush the hardness as I came over, flush on my stomach now, from where, looking a distance along the slight incline, I could see the soles of a large pair of men's shoes. He's growing, *flashed through my mind,* expanding like a balloon— What the hell?

Fighting to focus my eyes, I could see them, toes up and tilted slightly forward, resting back on their heels, as though a body had been suspended four-fifths of the way down in the sudden interrupting of a slow, nerve-chilled fall. As heavy as he was, what could be delaying him, holding him up, I wondered as I watched them warily for signs of continued expansion. Then my eyes snapped into sharp focus, and I came out of it.

The shoes were Hickman's, and I lay on the corridor floor watching with disgust as he slept with his huge legs stretched full-length before him, his head resting against the back of his chair. I could see the fleshy darkness of his chin, the broad curve of his chest, his arms hanging limply to either side so that the backs of his fingers gently touched the floor. And as I watched the rise and fall of his breathing, there came a peaceful sigh which erupted in a grating gasp which sent him snapping erect to look blankly around.

"Bones! We need Elisha," he said. "Get us Elisha!" Then, falling back as though stoned, he snored again; so swiftly asleep that I wondered if I were awake or still dreaming. Why was he calling for Bones and Elisha? And who was Elisha—Deacon Wilhite? What was going on with him?

I lay watching him out of a depth of disorientation. From the floor, vibrations arising deep within the building reached me through elbow and knee, stirring like the low, barely audible tone of a pipe organ. Yet the quiet of the corridor was broken only by the rattling gasps of surprise which continued to punctuate Hickman's snoring. Echoes of the iron groom's precise and tauntingly loquacious ventriloquist's voice sounded in my head as I watched him.

What in my waking life could have conjured *him* up? I wondered. What taking place in the depths of my mind would bring on his malicious insinuations? Surely it wasn't Hickman, because as annoying as I found him, I could see nothing about the old man that should inspire me to dream of the iron monster. And yet, as I watched him fold his hands across his lap in sleep, I couldn't be sure. Perhaps if I looked at him for a moment longer he'd become aware of me and I'd see the smaller, iron-cast face again, grinning at me through the features of a living man.

I got to my feet now, thinking, *To hell with this story. It's costing me too much. I'll have to take care of myself, or soon I'll do something to get myself thrown into a cell such as Tolliver said LeeWillie Minifees is occupying.*

Besides, I was hungry. I needed fresh air and a bath. And where was Tolliver? I'd seen him last entering the Senator's room—what if he'd left while I slept? How long had it been?

As I looked down the corridor past the sleeping Hickman even Bates was no longer to be seen. Perhaps he was standing just around the corner, but I wouldn't trust myself to investigate; I might be tempted to stay and forgo my need for food and air. Hurrying, I left by the stairs, hoping that nothing would develop before I returned.

CHAPTER 14

OUTSIDE IT WAS BREATHLESS, the stars hanging high and the street-quiet broken only by the ringing clang of a distant piece of metal, struck by a passing car. At the corner I hailed a cruising taxi and climbed inside.

"Where to?" the driver said.

"Just drive until I tell you to stop," I said. "I'm bushed."

Through his mirror his eyes met mine.

"It's okey," I said, taking out my press card. "I'm a reporter. I've been inside too long, working on my story. I need the air. And food."

Then, as he pulled away, I told him on impulse to drive west. A voice from the nighttime radio sang languidly,

> *Oh, darlin', squeeze me*
> *And squeeze me*
> *Ag'in*
> *Oh, mama, don't stop 'til I*
> *Tell you when . . .*

as the driver made a U-turn, slamming down the flag as we rolled.

I watched the darkened buildings, spotlighted national monuments, park spaces. The Capitol glowed pristine upon the hill. An old lady carrying a clublike cane walked a large black dog. Planes blinking their landing lights wheeled above, vibrating the night as they circled the field. And in my mind the events of the day rolled in a whirlpool of anxiety as we rolled wordlessly to the sound of the radio's *You must remember this / A kiss is just a kiss, a sigh is just a sigh . . . / As time goes by.* Then as we stopped for a traffic light, I noticed a lunchroom, paid the driver, and hurried inside.

The place was a bright, cool flash of monel metal and white enamel, a parade of empty stools. A noisily droning air conditioner muffled the sound of my entrance, and I felt dreamy and remote, as the chef-capped counterman who occupied the last stool failed to look up from his engrossment with a newspaper. I watched him remove a pencil from his cap and begin to print upon the page and realized that he was working a crossword puzzle. My stomach growled impatiently with the lingering aroma of fried onions as I watched him with silent self-containment, expecting him to look up. Finally I called out, "What word are you looking for?" and saw his head swing up and around.

"Oh," he said, "sorry, I didn't hear you come in. I've had a request in about that air conditioner for over a week, and nothing has been done about it— I was looking for a twelve-letter word meaning 'peace.' "

His was a Southern accent, though not so aggressively Southern as McGowan's, and I thought *Virginian* as I suggested "tranquillity."

"Tranquillity," he said.

"That's right."

His lips moved, spelling. "But that's only eleven."

"No," I shook my head, "twelve. Two '1's."

His lips moved again as he counted the spaces with his pencil. "Hey, you're right," he said, printing it in the squares with slow deliberation.

He stood now and went around the counter. "Thanks," he said. "All I could think of was 'death'—which didn't even begin to be long enough. I knew it was a 't' word, though, because the vertical called for 'taxes.' "

He shook his head. "Tranquillity *and* taxes, who would have thought of that!"

"Some congressman," I said. "He promises us tranquillity and taxes us for it. Anyway, I'd like two double hamburgers and a chocolate malted. I'll have coffee later."

"Coming up," he said, and while he prepared the order I sat on a stool thinking of tranquillity and death, the disturbing illogic of dreams, the dream-like illogic of my recent hours....

The counterman hummed an indistinct tune as he worked, but the food was nothing special. Nevertheless, I left feeling much better physically but no calmer in my thoughts.

Out in the quiet of the street, strands of the dream still teased me. If a hitching-post boy could really speak, what would he say? What would he really tell us about ourselves, society, the world? What if all the little black cast-iron bastards on all the lawns throughout the country started talking? What a horrible, obscene chorus of accusations, insinuations, and provocations *that* would be! I could still hear the voice so vividly as I strolled along that I wondered whether I'd left the hospital so much for food and air as to offset its possible return. But where was I headed now? I asked myself, since there were still the facts to be gathered, a report to be written. Where was I heading, when anything could be happening in my absence!

A glance at the street markers supplied an answer. I was only a few blocks from the morgue, and I hurried there under the pressure of a growing sense of urgency, feeling that by seeing the gunman's body I would be able to reestablish the boundaries between dream and reality. Nor was I unaware that our discovery of Jessie Rockmore sitting erect in his coffin had led us not into logic and tranquillity, but into a more intense confusion. Indeed, it had foreshadowed the shooting which I in all innocence was to witness only a few hours later.

My God, I thought. McMillen's story had led me to think that Jessie Rockmore's indignant eyes had dulled while looking through the empty space where the mysterious stranger had disappeared—when in fact he might have been looking straight through time and space into the Senate chamber where the shots were soon to send the Senator reeling, the gunman crashing bodily to the chamber floor, and shatter the nation's peace. And instead of dying of a stroke or heart attack upon seeing an uninvited visitor in his house, it was this vision which had killed Jessie Rockmore.

I hurried on, trembling, incoherent, and distrustful of my thoughts, but determined to have a look at the man who had brought all the random chaos which seemed to be bursting steadily from the springtime air into such confounding bloom.

Standing in the cool of the morgue, I watched the attendant roll out the sheet-covered form on a smooth, soundless swivelling of wheels, positioning it beneath a low-hanging metal-shaded light. He gave me a quizzical glance as he swept the cover aside—and I was looking down upon a fully clothed human form.

"You've been through this enough to know not to touch anything," he said. "Just call when you've finished. I'm expecting a call."

He started away before I could ask why the clothing was still intact, and I could hear the closing of the door as I studied the gunman's intriguing face.

In the stillness of death it bore an expression eloquent of an eerie peacefulness combined with an inner violence externalized now and spent. It appeared quite young, but for all its unlined youthfulness there was something prematurely aged about it; a face which seemed either to have seen and felt more than most people or to have lived through more in its self-terminated span than most managed to live. I asked myself if this was the effect of what he had done, or whether he had looked essentially like this before the murder, assassination, had ever crossed his mind. What cross had he borne to have pushed him across the boundary he had crossed? And the ambiguous look of aging—could it be that what he had done, his action, had blasted him into his present appearance within the split instant when intention had blossomed into act? How old could he have been? Twenty-nine? Thirty-nine? Looking down, I really couldn't determine.

And what was his motive? How long had he nurtured his will to kill? And why the Senator? Who was he? Where was he from? What had the authorities learned? Was there actually a plot?

With such questions flashing through my mind, I noted the light brown hair waved back from its high forehead, the recently barbered cheeks with a small razor nick showing at the corner of the full-lipped mouth; the left cheek displaying a violence of red and blue flesh which marked, I suspected, a crushed misalignment of the bone. A trickle of blood had flown from the right ear onto his collar, leaving a dry, flaky line.

But despite all evidence of the impact of his fall, I couldn't shake off the impression that I was watching a young man napping after having participated in a wild party which, unfortunately, had ended in a brawl. *If only this were true,* I thought, *if only he had!*

Jotting down notes for my story now, I observed that he had dressed himself carefully, even gravely, for the shattering occasion, and an air of an expensive and refined taste clung to his rumpled clothing—as though he had worn his best in order to do his worst. Or had he in fact considered this last act his best, his most meaningful assertion of self? But if so, why had he sought to render himself anonymous—or was this posture of anonymity a challenge by which he sought to more thoroughly establish an identity?

A fine silk handkerchief blossomed sadly in the breast pocket of his jacket, a black tie with an almost imperceptible pattern of red was knotted Duke of Windsor style beneath the widespread collar of his light blue shirt, and beneath the French cuff held by square gold links a thin platinum watch was strapped to the inner side of his right wrist. The crystal of this had been shattered, making it impossible to read the exact time of impact, and I was fighting off an impulse to lift the wrist to inspect it when I became aware of a lush, cloying scent, incongruous in such a place, pressing upon me as my eyes were drawn to the crumpled gardenia in his lapel. There, thin rustlike lines were spreading in the places where the fleshy ivory-toned petals had been broken, a sign of organic life still lingering while the human life had fled. Yes, but soon a timeless shadow of beard would bloom up on the dead, still-dying, no-longer-human face, and I was held by the feeling of a mystery deeper than that of his personal identity.

Such things shouldn't happen, my mind went on. *Society should be so ordered. But how, by lighting the shadows? This one struck, stepped out of sunlight....*

Who am I? the face before me seemed to ask, and I had no answers. It might have been the face of one of our Air Force generals, who for all the responsibilities undertaken at such an early age manage to appear eternally boyish, eternally romantic; striding ever to the air of some devil-may-care Mexican military marching song beneath pennants that snap ever in a breeze stirred by the soaring of golden eagles' wings. *Pancho Villa's men marched to death singing of a cockroach,* my mind went on. *What songs sang within this man's reckless head?*

I could feel the strain of weariness in the calves of my legs as I was taken by a fantasy in which I watched him posing before a full-length mirror of a fashionable apartment or hotel suite, girding himself for his twin acts of destruction. A soundless, dream-like scene. With sunlight streaming through a tall window and with the gunman gazing at his own image with remote and critical eye. A part of the wavy hair, a precise two inches of cuff showing below his expensive jacket sleeve. While in the background near an arched doorway a dark valet waited with hat, gloves, and fresh gardenia for his finely wrought lapel.... Did he wear a hat, I wondered, and when had he armed himself? It must have been in private, for surely he had the weapon with him when he left for the Hill. Yes, but what had he told himself as he made his way to the visitors' gallery to stand so calmly firing down? What could have kept him so cool, icy in all the confusion; calm even with Hickman's voice booming out beneath the dome?...

Hickman, I thought, *HICKMAN!* bending forward and seeing my shadow sweep across the face, sliding away as I bent forward, suddenly taken by the disturbing feeling that I had seen the face somewhere before. Yes, and at a much more intimate distance than when, immediately after the shooting, I had looked through the doorway to see it lying like a broken puppet upon the Senate floor. But where? Where? It was eerie. I wanted to leave, but the face was speaking to me now, and in some disturbing accent which prickled the hair on the back of my neck. I peered at the texture of the bruised skin with its mass of red and blue ruptured blood vessels, the dim highlights and transparent shadows thrown against the skin of the forehead by the high-hanging incandescent bulbs, asking myself what secret knowledge was frozen there.

For even in death he seemed utterly aware of himself. Perhaps he had trained his face to keep itself under scrutiny; like a famous movie star once observed walking along a crowded street with his eyes riveted maniacally to his own moving image as it came and went in shop windows, stopping to stare, grinning, frowning, looking sinister, joyful, sad, in swift succession—utterly oblivious to the attention of fascinated pedestrians, himself his own best rubberneck. Yes, but here was a face long-trained to guard and direct its expression at all times. A face without spontaneity on a mission of no return. Could it be? It was like those faces once seen in the experimental silent-movie close-ups which owe their expressiveness not so much to the actor's skill as to hard work performed in the editing room; images wherein each lift of eyelids, each movement of mouth, are calculated in advance and in which each of the complex movements necessary to achieve even the most casual expression of humanity are the results of the splicing together in skillful montage a series of carefully selected isolated exposures that are then projected and accelerated, controlled shadows against conspiratorial screen, into a flickering semblance of life.

All this, I realized, was quite far-fetched, a product of my imagination beginning to run away with itself. Yet it held me even though I realized that I was undergoing a kind of slow, snowballing panic in which I was projecting upon the dead man my own ideas of the kind of person *I* would have had to have been in order to do what he had done. For certainly I would have had to die myself even before the deed, and even from the moment it was conceived. For I would have been so frightened by the idea that the expressiveness of my face would have reduced to slow motion or frozen of itself. Otherwise, I couldn't have brought it off. I fought away this drift of thought, for beneath it I sensed the stirring of some even more unpleasant idea, some knowledge too threatening to be willingly brought to the surface. But in vain; I had to know who he was. It was my duty.

I became so worked up that now it was as though the dead man was questioning me as to my own identity. If he was an assassin, what, then, was I who had witnessed his action?

I suppose it was then that I became committed to learning who he was and what he was—even though I had to throw myself bodily into every bit of the wild confusion which had exploded around me. If only I had known what this would entail, where it would lead!

As I turned away, the face continued to speak to me mutely, trying to tell me something which I could not, or would not, comprehend, even though the feeling that I had seen it somewhere before was growing even stronger. It was then, in reaching for my notebook, that I touched Vannec's letter and had a sense of bad luck, an illogical feeling that by reading it, it had helped bring on the disaster. What would Vannec with his hero-of-the-intellect mind, his search for the significant gesture, make of the gunman? And the very suggestion that he might see implications and foreshadowings which I had neither the will nor the imagination to see made me suddenly nauseous. Turning abruptly, I hurried out of the building into the hot night street as though I'd heard the ticking of a time bomb.

I moved so fast that I was several yards away before it caught up with me, before I realized what it was that had put me to flight. And now as one caught in a sudden fog while fishing in a skiff looks up to see a ship bearing noiselessly down, I realized that the haunting face lying there in the cool behind me might well be that of the young man whom I'd accompanied to his rendezvous with Vannec during that dark night of war so long ago.

Then I was running, at first away, past the line of parked cars, then back toward the morgue. It was as though something was drawing me back against my will. I told myself that I was overwrought from the excitement and fatigue. So much had happened in so short a time, so many things had clashed together that I was losing my objectivity. But then I was there, and despite the annoyance of the attendant I went back once more to stare down at the face.

It lay as before, the eyes closed, the bruised flesh appearing colder, bluer, more translucent, but despite a strong sense of familiarity, I was tortuously unsure. It might be him, I thought, but that was so long ago. And even the fact that I thought of Severen was a coincidence. If I hadn't touched the letter, I wouldn't have thought of Vannec. And if I hadn't thought of Vannec, I wouldn't have thought of Severen. But I *had*! Out of all the many names, people, who might have arisen, it was his name which my mind wanted to fit to the face. It was a mystery. Yes, but what if my suspicions were correct? If so, then I had the responsibility of telling the police. I looked at the dark roll of the eyelashes, the sweep of the hairline and asked myself, *What if you're wrong? If so, you'd never live it down. And after the fool you made of yourself by striking Hickman, you can't even risk telling Tolliver of your suspicions. Yes, but what if you're right? What if you managed even to question Hickman about Severen?* Dammit, why didn't the authorities make the old Negro explain his relations to the whole affair! Why, by what tortuous connection was the wounded Senator allowed to give him sanctuary?

I moved now, noticing my shadow falling across the silent face. *What will you do now?* it seemed to say. I hurried out, thanking the attendant as I made for the street.

The hospital was still quiet when I returned, and in approaching the admissions desk I had the presence of mind to inquire if LeeWillie Minifees was still being detained. He was, but the nurse refused to give me any further information. She had her orders, and I couldn't persuade her to break them. If I was to see him, it would be through other, less responsible channels. But what and how? Hospitals such as this are so efficient and strict in their procedures, so   in their structure of security and responsibility.*

When I reached the corridor Hickman was still sleeping in his chair. It was disgusting. Where had he acquired his self-composure? I wondered. How was it that under all the tension, with the security authorities suspecting him of complicity in a plot, could he sleep so soundly? Was it through his religion or through a racial habit of escaping turmoil? Perhaps here was proof of McGowan's assertion that Hickman's people rested between every fifth tick of the clock—even when involved in the most intense and grueling activity.

"They aren't on our time, McIntyre," he had said. "They have their own *nigra* time. You watch those athletic-type nigras, the way they move around all loose-jointed and falling apart. Hell, one minute they running like they been caught stealing chickens and the Man's after them with a shotgun, and the next thing you know, they're creeping along like molasses on a cold morning in January and flopping around like they got no bones. That's because they're resting in between, man. Time is money and nigras are *expert*

---

* Word(s) missing after "so" in the typescript.

at stealing time, *and* they're the most expert boondogglers in the civilized world!"

I had my doubts, but there was no question but that Hickman wasn't wasting his energy. I started impulsively toward him, thinking to put the question of the gunman's identity to him at the moment of awakening so as to observe his reaction, but restrained myself. He was certain to be on guard for such a maneuver, and especially from me.

Sitting back on the bench, I thought to follow his example and conserve my energy. It didn't work; my mind kept returning to the man in the morgue. I searched my memory for details, images, echoes—anything that would help me establish an identification. But things were too confused. An image came to mind of LeeWillie Minifees standing in confounding triumph on the Senator's lawn as he watched his Cadillac burn. And I asked myself if this had been, as Tolliver had suggested, actually a political gesture, a "diversionary tactic" and part of an earlier attempt to shoot the Senator. A few hours ago it had seemed impossible, but now anything and everything seemed possible, and this being so, I would have to have a talk with Minifees. But how? Where was he being held, and who, under the circumstances, would give me permission to see him?

Whatever the answer, it seemed obvious that I'd have to wait until morning, and perhaps by then I'd know the Senator's fate if not the agent of that fate. So once more I rested my head against the back of the bench, thinking to nap awhile; but immediately the image of the hitching-post groom loomed behind my eyelids, and I got up and stretched my legs, taking a quick turn before the bench before I sat down again. I simply couldn't bear another such encounter, and for the time being my only defense against that horrible nightmare's attendant was wakefulness.

I was looking over my notes, trying to make an outline of all that had occurred from the burning of the Cadillac to the present moment, when the elevator droned slowly up the shaft and stopped to discharge a nurse, who hurried past to the Senator's room. I could hear the elevator drop below as I watched Hickman, who slept on, unaware. In the spreading silence I watched for further activity and was about to return to my notes when another nurse came out carrying a tray. She looked at Hickman a moment, then drifted down and around the curve in the corridor, disappearing.

CHAPTER 15

I INSPECTED MY AILING watch. What was the time? An odor of iodoform drifted to me, bringing an image of a lonely seashore in high summer, the blue mutability of foam-fringed waves. Away. Far off a buzzer sounded, faded, leaving an interval of silence from which slowly emerged the faint clink and tinkle of glass striking against metal, and my eyes were drawn down to the end of the corridor where there now appeared a white-suited attendant pushing a metal steam cart.

Taking his time, pushing at a forward slant with his red head low over the handlebar, he approached until abreast the sleeping Hickman, pausing to gaze at the old man for a moment, then roll the cart to the other side of the Senator's door. And now, seeing him about to knock, I got to my feet, hoping that I might have a word with one of the nurses, but as the door came slightly ajar I saw one of the security men looking through and stayed where I was, watching them. He said something to the attendant and disappeared. Then immediately a nurse took his place, carefully blocking the view as she began passing the attendant several napkin-covered trays which, squatting and rising rhythmically, he placed on a rack underneath the cart, then proceeded to hand her trays of food covered with silver serving bells. He worked swiftly, negotiating the narrow passage with professional skill, but someone inside the room must have become nervous, for he had barely handed over the last tray when the door snapped to, almost catching his hand, and a look of high indignation flashed over his freckled face and he pronounced a silent obscenity with such graphic expressiveness that I was forced to stifle a laugh. His lips continued to work angrily as he knelt beside the cart and came up with two heavy silver coffeepots and went to stand close to the door, waiting until the door swung inward and then, moving with the abrupt precision of a marine presenting a rifle for inspection, he plunged the gleaming vessels into the crack with a resounding *clank!*

There was a splash of liquid, accompanied by protesting voices, to which, standing with back rigidly arched, he replied vehemently until the pots were removed from his hands and the door swung shut. He continued to curse at the blank white panel for a moment, then aimed a mock backhanded blow at Hickman's chin, watching the old man sleep, then wheeled the cart around and, passing me as though I didn't exist, headed for the elevator. He rang impatiently, leaning against the button, his head resting upon his folded arm. The car came slowly and I was about to sit down when I heard a low sound like that of a bass viol being played pizzicato. He had begun to hum a tune of eccentric rhythm oddly skipping intervals:

> *Ah-zoom-zee-zoom-zoom*
> *A-bach-ditty beep broom,*
> *Ah-zoom, ah-zoom-ah-zoom-zoom*
> *A-bach-rock, ah-mop-mop . . .*

The name *Minifees* flashed in my mind, and I found myself following him into the now-opening door of the elevator. *I'm probably so tired that I'm as nutty as the nonsense he's humming,* I thought. *But on the other hand, he may very well lead me to the car-burning fiddler. . . . What, by the way, are a "beep broom" and a "baccarat mop"?*

With the car beginning its sluggish ascension, he turned his attention to a narrow lip of paper, leaning on the handlebar and muttering a mysterious series of numbers: "Four-eleven-forty-four, two-eleven-twenty-two, three-six, nine." As he wrote them down, all traces of annoyance had left his freckled face; now, as he paused, looking off into space, I made my approach.

"Pardon me," I said, "but I wonder . . ."

He shook his head, frowning as he stared at the paper.

"Hold it, man," he said, "I'm trying to remember the figures for blood on the floor. . . ."

I apologized, watching him as he continued to write; then, folding the slip, he placed it in the breast pocket of his jacket, and I saw a pair of yellow-green eyes.

"Now," he said, "what was that you were saying?"

"Sorry for interrupting," I said. "I was about to ask if you could do me a favor?"

"A favor?"

"Yes."

He sighed. "Doc, don't you think it's kind of early in the morning to start that?"

"Pardon?"

"I mean I just got started on my rounds. . . ."

"Of course," I said, "I understand that, but I only wanted—"

He shook his head, looking down at the cart, and I could hear the slow exhale of breath as he straightened and leaned against the wall.

"I'm sure glad you understand what I mean, Doc, because I have a hell of a lot to do."

"It's okay," I said. "Forget it."

"Yeah, Doc," he said, looking me in the eye, "I have my responsibilities too, you know?"

"Sure, I know, but I didn't mean to interfere with your work."

"Now that's just fine. If it was later in the day, it would be different."

"Sure, and I wouldn't have bothered you if I knew my way around. But I'm a newspaper reporter assigned to keep an eye on the condition of Senator Sunraider and—"

It was as though I'd stuck him with a pin. Suddenly he struck the cart, *"Sunrainder,"* he said. "Did you say *Sun*rainder?"

"Yes, Senator Sunraider."

"Well, I'll be damn! If I hadn't been half asleep I would've known that that was who it was. That's where I just came from; I was right outside his door!"

"Of course, I saw you there."

"I'll be damn! No wonder they didn't want me to get a look inside the room. I thought they thought I was trying to meddle."

"Of course," I said. "I assumed you knew."

"Naw, man; *hell* naw!" He shook his head in violent denial. "I just came on the job and *wham!*—they sent me up there without a word. They ought to warn a man."

"You can understand their problem," I said. "The Senator's under heavy security, so I suppose the authorities are allowing as few people to know his whereabouts as possible."

"Yeah, but they could've warned *me*. That was like sending a man into a lion's mouth in the dark." He pointed toward the floor of the elevator, his eyes afire. "Those people down there are acting trigger-happy as hell. I bring them some food, and they try to take my arm off with the goddamn door!"

"You were lucky you weren't injured," I said, "but I don't think it was intentional. Having such a grave responsibility has probably put them under a strain."

"Strain, hell! This is *me*, man. What do they think I was going to do?"

"I doubt it was you so much as the fact that they've been ordered to treat anyone they don't know as suspicious."

"But I *work* here, that nurse down there *knows* me."

"Then it was probably one of the security men who closed the door. By now their nerves must be on edge. Having to guard the Senator makes them jumpy."

"Yeah, but why the hell should we *all* start jumping? Before I went up there, *my* nerves were fine. What are they so jumpy about, anyway? Didn't the cat who did the shooting kill himself?"

"There's no doubt about that."

"So what's worrying them?"

"Accomplices," I said. "They're afraid that he might have had accomplices."

"Is that right?" He gave me a questioning look. "So that's all the more reason for that damn dietician to have warned a man. Those cops could've blasted me, and I wouldn't have known what it was all about. That woman let me come on like a square. When I saw that big fellow sleeping next to the door and you sitting up the hall there, I knew right away that somebody was going through a crisis, but it didn't occur to me that it was *Sun*rainder. Damn!"

Suddenly the car jerked to a stop, and he pushed the cart into the corridor, still shaking his head as I followed. It was quiet, the corridor was empty, a red light glowed above a door.

"Listen," he said quietly, "have they learned why he got blasted?"

"Not yet," I said, "but it's hoped that when the Senator comes to he'll be able to make a statement."

"And ain't *that* a hell of a deal," he said, "because if he runs true to form he's liable to say something that don't *nobody* want to hear."

"Like it or not," I said, "they'll have to listen and do something about it. The whole country's upset over this affair."

He rolled the cart and I followed, wondering how to make my approach, then saw him stopping, staring down at the polished top of the cart; then, looking at me with the utmost seriousness, he said, "Man, just thinking about it cold sober, that shooting was a mother— Hell, what I mean is, it was *something!*"

"Unless I'm overstating the case," I said, "it was a disaster."

"You're damn right—and I'll tell you something else: Sunrainder might get better, but he won't *ever* be the same. No, sir! He'll never be the same. That cat who did it was playing for keeps. It was like he had told Sunrainder, 'Sunrainder, man, you have messed with me and hurt my feelings, so now I'm going to blast your butt and go to hell...and pay for it!' And he did it, man. He kept his word and dealt himself a natural mess!"

He shook his head, marveling at the enormity of it all. His white skin had reddened beneath the freckles of his now-animated face, and something in his voice made me wonder if he were about to laugh, cry, or say a prayer: reminding me of Hickman's reaction at the time of the shooting.

"Yes, sir," he said, moving off, "that man turned out that Senate like a stud who has taken his gal to a public dance and got mad over somebody eyeballing her too hard and he decides to clear out the joint—commencing by *head-whipping* the poor, innocent piano player! The only thing about it is, this cat probably blasted the right man."

He chuckled. "I can't figure him out, though, pulling a stunt like that up there on the Hill. He must have been trying to make himself some history."

"He did," I said, "terrible history, there's no predicting the aftereffects it will have on the country."

He stopped the cart, giving me a searching glance, the humor fading from his eyes.

"You're probably right," he said. "That kind of mess can rub off on every-body—*and* could already have got me shot. How is old Sunrainder making out?"

"I can't say; I've been here all night, and as far as I've been able to learn, he's still in a coma."

He moved again. "You know," he said, "it must be hell to have something like that happen when you're not even thinking about it."

"But that's the way such things happen, they're meant to be unsuspected."

"Yeah, and quick and nervy. According to the paper that cat stood up in front of all those people, whipped out his piece way up there in the visitors' gallery, and before Sunrainder knew anything—" he stopped suddenly, lean-ing across the handlebar to make the gesture of firing a pistol—"before he could catch the shuffle, that cat had leveled down—*bam! bam!*—and *wasted* him!" He pulled erect, grimacing and shaking his head. "Oh, he garbaged him, man! *Ruined* him—*sieved* him! It was awful. The paper said he hit him everywhere, including the bottom of his *feet*! So you *know* he meant to kill him. Hell, yes! It said he dotted Sunrainder's *i*'s and crossed his *t*'s. Said he . . ."

He was becoming quite carried away, and I reached out, touching his arm. "Wait," I said, "just a second—what paper did you read?"

He froze, his green eyes regarding me as though I were suddenly insane. "What?"

"I said, where did you read all that?"

"Oh, hell, man, are you kidding? I didn't *read* it that way, I'm just translat-ing it into my own way of speaking so I can get the feel of what was put down. You know no newspaper writes like that."

I shook my head, feeling a flash of unreality, the fuzziness of fatigue.

"You have to change that stuff so it will move, man. You see the headline said the man 'fired' at Sunrainder and so on, but if it had said something like 'Mad Cat Blasts Sunrainder, In God We Trust,' you'd know right away that he blasted him in the Senate standing up on top of all that power and—"

"But wait," I said. "*Wait*— Why 'In God We Trust'?"

"Because that cat's proved that his intention to kill Sunrainder was as strong as the Government's faith in money, battleships, bombs, and God, that's why. Because just like we back our cash with everything we have, he backed up his intention to kill that bastard with his life—and did! Understand what I mean?"

"I'm beginning to," I said. "It's your way of coloring the news...."

He looked up quickly, giving me a searching glance.

"Yeah," he said drily. "Maybe. I guess so."

I smiled. "It was the style that puzzled me. It was unfamiliar."

"You damn right," he said drily, "It's unfamiliar because that was me. That was Charleston."

For a moment he looked at me blank-faced, then suddenly he was smiling. "Man, for a moment there I thought you were trying to pull some of that Sunraider shit. But pay me no mind. What was that favor you wanted to ask me? If it's about Sunrainder, you can see already that you know more about him than me. I didn't even know he was here."

"No," I said, "it wasn't about the Senator, but I do need information concerning another patient here. A man named Minifees."

And suddenly he was wary. "Do you mean *LeeWillie* Minifees?"

"Yes," I said. "Do you know him?"

He frowned. "But didn't you just say you were here on account of Sunrainder?"

"Yes, I did, but that's an official assignment: I'm interested in Minifees on my own."

"You mean you dig LeeWillie?"

"Dig?"

"I mean do you understand him, like his music?"

"Oh, sure, I admire him very much. Do you know him?"

"Hell, yes I know him. But I said do you really dig him."

"Well, I think I do. Shouldn't I?"

He gave me a slight smile. "Well, man, to tell the truth, just by looking at you, I wouldn't have believed that you ever even *heard* about LeeWillie—at least until he burned his rubber...."

"But do his admirers have to look a certain way?"

He looked me up and down, amused. "No, man, but likely as not they're a certain kind of cat. As you know, LeeWillie is way out. He's gone. So don't get me wrong and think I'm trying to put you down, because in fact, I'm glad to know that you have such good taste."

He smiled his freckle-faced smile. "If you dig LeeWillie, though, you're all right with me."

"Thanks," I said. "Now can you tell me whether Mr. Minifees is still here in the hospital?"

"Sure he's here. I wish he wasn't but he is."

"And is he very ill?"

"You mean is he nuts?"

"That's a way of putting it, but I was told that he was being held for observation."

"Observation, my butt!" he said explosively. "They know LeeWillie's not sick! He just hit them where it hurts, so now they want to keep him here and forget him. They're just upset over seeing all that loot go up in smoke."

"But it couldn't be simply a matter of money," I said. "People don't burn such cars every day, and besides, it couldn't have involved more than seven thousand dollars at the most."

"Yeah, but when they're turned into a Cadillac every one of those dollars has a rainbow around its shoulders. Hell, yes, every one of those caddidollars has some glamour added. *That's* why they're upset. LeeWillie blasted him some *dreams!*"

Perhaps he's right, I thought. It wasn't merely the money involved that had upset me as I watched Minifees sacrifice his car, but something of a more metaphysical significance. Something having to do with the defiance, the mockery, the aggressive and insidious self-sacrificial ambiguity of his gesture....

"This here is a country that rolls on rubber, man. We eat rubber and we drink rubber and we dream about rubber sleeping on rubber mattresses. You let Detroit shut down, and everybody gets hurt. So when LeeWillie lit that fire, he singed him some behinds. But just the same, no matter how you look at it, all he did was destroy his own property."

"Perhaps," I said, "but you'll have to admit that he did a few other things along the way...."

"Like what?"

"Like damaging a beautiful lawn and turning it into a junkyard, like disturbing a gathering of peaceful citizens and polluting the atmosphere for miles around, and like creating panic in a public thoroughfare."

He laughed, holding on to the cart and staggering helplessly backwards and forwards. "Yeah, and old LeeWillie pitched himself a thoroughbred bitch, didn't he? He bugged the whole damn town!" He laughed again, then his face was suddenly serious. "So all right," he said, "if all that's his crime, why don't they give him a trial and fine him? They don't have to *observe* him in order to do that."

"I don't have the answer to that," I said. "Maybe they're afraid that Mr. Minifees might do it again. Burn somebody else's car. But one thing that I do know is that a true and accurate account of *why* he burned his own would make a very interesting story."

He snorted. "Let me tell you something, man: Everything LeeWillie *does* is interesting—but who the hell's going to print the facts about how he really feels?"

"Get me to him," I said, "and I'll see to that. I'll report his story in his own words and my paper will publish it: I'll guarantee it."

"Yeah, that's what *you* say, but a hell of a lot of things happen that don't get into the papers."

"I won't dispute that," I said, "but I'd like to give it a try. Could you arrange for me to speak with him?"

He studied my face for a moment, then began pushing the cart again. "I'm hungry as hell," he said. "They rushed me up here even before I could have my breakfast. Could you drink some coffee?"

"Yes, as a matter of fact I could."

"Then come on. Talking with you has already put me behind, so we might as well make it a little longer."

Stopping the cart, he handed me two hot cups and a pot of coffee. "Over here," he said, opening the door to an empty room and stepping aside. "We can drink in here."

"You know," he said, as he filled the cups, "what you're asking me to do is against the rules, don't you, man?"

"But I wouldn't want to compromise you," I said. "You get me to Minifees, and I'll take full responsibility for anything that happens."

He sat on the bed, pointing to a chair. I sat, taking a sip of the coffee.

"Hell, man," he said, "let's be realistic. In this place you can't guarantee me a damn thing. Anyway, LeeWillie's my friend, and I'm bound to help him, so what is it you're so anxious to talk to him about?"

"Well, for one thing I'd like a clearer explanation of why he burned his automobile."

"But that's no mystery: He burned it because he *felt* like burning it."

"But my readers wouldn't accept that: It doesn't explain anything."

"But it's the truth. What more do you want? What you probably mean is that it upset you too."

"That's true, but it upset a great number of people: That's why it's important to get the facts."

"Yeah, it upset them all right: more than if LeeWillie had barbecued a man."

"Oh, I doubt that," I said.

"Doubt it if you want to, but many a man has been burned without causing all that much excitement—*and* nobody got arrested, much less thrown into a *nut* ward. Here," he said, gesturing with the pot, "have some more."

"Thanks," I said, extending the cup away, wishing I'd thought to tell him that I liked sugar.

"I'm not denying that such things have happened in the past," I said, "but that doesn't explain why Minifees did what he did, and my readers require an explanation in the context of today."

"Hell, don't they read the papers? Didn't LeeWillie say that he was burning it because that fellow Sunrainder—who's lying right downstairs this very minute—was *bugging* him? God damn! What more of an explanation do they want?"

"Now, don't get excited," I said. "I'm merely trying to get the facts. Is that what Minifees told you?"

"Yes, and he'll tell you the same thing."

"Good, that's exactly what I need: If I could present his point of view to the public, in his own words, it would be excellent. By the way, how's he being treated?"

He swallowed a sip of coffee, shaking his head. "Man, it's *got* to be bad! With all those psychiatrists and sociologists up there bugging the man all the time, it's *got* to be bad. They're treating LeeWillie like he blowed his top and scattered the pieces. And I can tell you this: When the news hits the street, a lot of folks who dig LeeWillie are going to be mad as hell."

"Are you saying that he's being abused?"

"Yeah," he said pugnaciously, "he's being abused; hell, yeah!"

"How?"

"*How?* Hell, they *abused* him when they put him up there with all those far-out nuts, with heavy screens on the door and everything. No visitors and all. They abusing him by having some sonofabitch with a doctor to his name looking up his nosehole every time he turns around, peering around trying to find out what he's thinking. Just why the NAACP don't do something about it, I simply can't understand. It's a crying shame to let them treat a great man like that and get away with it."

"Do you feel that a question of civil rights is involved?"

"Hell, yes! They haven't let him have a lawyer, have they? They haven't charged him with anything, have they? And where's the goddamn judge? Those people ought to be on the job, man; if LeeWillie was a Jew, five minutes after he hit the door other Jews would've had him out of here! Those folks don't fool around; they're *always* ready for crap like this. They're yelling even *before* one of them gets busted. All somebody has to do is to point his finger and say, 'Hey, you!' and they goin' finish it for him by yelling 'dirty Jew' and start raising hell. Then they start to yelling to all the other Jews, 'Hey, y'all, here's a cat who's against us; let's get the sonofabitch!' And that's the way the NAACP ought to be. If they were, LeeWillie would've been out of here making some music. We don't have but so much civil rights anyway, so at least they could keep the musicians free."

I watched him staring silently into his cup now; there was no doubt that Minifees was an important figure in his personal scheme of things. Nor was there any doubt that he had found some kind of affirmation in what the musician had done to his automobile. I looked at the stilled hands of my watch, wondering how things were going below.... What would the Senator think of this kickback from his joke?

"Don't worry about the time," he said. "Enjoy your coffee because no-body'll come in here."

"Thanks," I said. "I was just wondering in what part of the hospital Minifees is being held."

He swirled his cup, grimacing painfully. "Right here, man. Up in the nut ward. He's up there with guys like the one who claims he's George Washington. Sonofabitch hides it in his dresser and under the bed—phew!"

I lowered my cup. "What is it he hides?"

The green eyes flashed. "*It*, man! Shee-it! Hockey! Doo-doo! Which *he* claims is the secret weapon. That cat is *gone!*"

He threw back his head, laughing at my expression. "Maybe he's right at that. Fool makes all kinds of trouble up there. When they take it away he pitches a *bitch!*"

"I don't envy the attendants."

"But wait, man, I haven't begun to tell you what kind of hole LeeWillie's in. There's another one who they say is a poet who would like to forget it; he's an old fellow who's hung up on things like the gold standard, birth control and foreign policy and Chinese cooking. He talks about a dozen foreign languages, and when he gets going on one of those subjects *nobody* has any peace."

"Is he violent?"

He shook his head. "Only with his mouth. I understand that some of the other poets are trying to get him out, and I wish the hell they would. He bugs the hell out of the patients by talking about those things all the time. And singing. The other day I was up there and he was trying to sing the front page of the *New York Times!* You should have heard the bastard."

"What's his ... er ... nationality, do you know?"

He grinned. "You mean his *race*, don't you? If not, he's American but white. *We*," he said pointedly, "don't have *that* kind of nut; he's one of y'all. And from up North at that. He's all right with LeeWillie, though. In fact, he's the only one who's keeping LeeWillie from *really* blowing his top. They get to riffing back and forth through the bars about how messed up the country is, and they have a low-ratin' ball. Besides, this poet cat knows a lot about music, and he's been trying to get LeeWillie to study some kind of jive they used to play way back in Shakespeare's time. He says that poets and musicians are more important than cats like Sunrainder and all those millionaires."

"He sounds mad but very interesting," I said. "Do you recall his name?"

"His name's Sterling, Clyde Sterling. I've talked with him a few times, and although he's wild he didn't have a bit of trouble in understanding why LeeWillie burned his rubber. They get along fine together, and the way I see it is that while they both are radical as bears with their habits on, neither one has any business being up there with those other nuts. If anything, they might just be too sane for most folks to deal with—except LeeWillie's music makes it a little easier to understand him—*if* you dig his kind of jazz."

I said, "I'll have to look up his poetry, it might be interesting."

"You do that; they say it's great. But man, they have another nut up there who's supposed to have committed treason or something."

At the word "treason" I almost dropped my cup, feeling the hot coffee through the cloth covering my thigh.

"Treason," I said, "when? What did he do?"

"That's what I'm trying to find out," Charleston said. "It was some time ago, but all I can learn that he did was to call the President's wife on the telephone and try to talk trash."

I stared into his face, thinking I had misunderstood. *"Trash?"* I said, "What did he do, threaten her? Attempt to blackmail her?"

For a moment he gave me a silent stare, then cut his eyes, looking away. "Forget it, man," he said wearily. "Are you *sure* you dig LeeWillie?"

The green eyes were boring into me now, and I sensed that I'd made a serious mistake.

"Yes," I lied, "I collect his records."

"Look, man, that don't mean a thing. A lot of folks collect him who don't *dig* him. They just follow the damn crowd, who follow the dog-butted critics, who say whatever those record companies *tell* them to say. They talk more shit than the radio! I don't mean to put you down, but you really don't seem to understand the language that goes with LeeWillie's music."

He sounded quite earnest, and because I didn't understand much of what he said and had been thoroughly baffled by his talk of treason, trash, and the First Lady, I allowed myself to become annoyed.

"Look," I said, "let's not argue about it; you want to get Minifees out of here and I'd like to get a story, so if you intend to help, we'd better get on with it."

Studying my face, he stood, moving toward the door.

"Okay, buddy," he said. "You're right. You don't have to *dig* a man in order to want to help him. What's your name? Mine's Charleston, like in South Carolina."

"I remember," I said, following him into the hall. "Mine is McIntyre."

"Okay, Doctor McIntyre," he said, placing the cups and pot in the cart, "I'll see if I can help you."

"Thanks," I said, "I'd certainly appreciate it. But I'm not a doctor, remember, I'm a reporter."

His face went blank again. "Now ain't *that* a damn shame!"

"What's wrong?"

"Hell, man, that means I can't help you."

"But you just said you would."

"Yeah, but the only ones I can help are doctors. You dig?"

"No, I'm afraid I don't."

"No, I didn't think you would. Look, man, they told me that I was to give the *doctors* any assistance they asked for; they didn't say a damn thing about any reporters. Now you dig?"

"I'm beginning to, I think."

"So now, after giving it your undivided attention, are you a doctor?"

I nodded. "Yes, I'm a doctor."

"Good. You really make it hard for a man, McIntyre. But now you're beginning to riff. I knew damn well that you had *some* kind of degree—don't you now?"

"Yes," I said, "as a matter of fact, I have."

For a moment he watched me silently and I saw his green eyes pale and his features becoming subtly more Anglo-Saxon, more refined, and when he spoke again his speech was precise, Northern, as though he were doing a mocking imitation of a white man.

"Doctor," he said, "I take it that what you mean to say is that as a matter of *tact* you have . . ."

"Perhaps, since it's necessary," I said, "yes. . . ."

He grinned, his face relaxing. "Skip it, man. Pay me no mind. Just tell me how by dint of hard work and study and the burning of midnight oil what *kind* of degree do you have?"

"A Ph.D.," I said.

"I knew it! Didn't I know it? What in?"

"Sociology."

He struck his thigh. "There you go! Didn't I know it? Man, you're lucky because I'm always happy to help a scientist—especially one who digs good jazz. But, Doctor," he said, leaning close and bringing the smell of coffee and fresh bread, "let me tell you something . . ."

"Yes?"

"Once I get you to LeeWillie, I don't know anything about you, you dig?"

"Yes, I follow you."

"I've only *seen* you, and you've seen *me* but that's all."

"Agreed."

"You better, because if you get caught, as far as I'm concerned you're like the bear—you're nowhere. Because while this job ain't nothing but a slave it's the only one I got. So if you get caught, as far as I'm concerned you're just another one of those psychiatrists or some other kind of bullshitter that I try to have nothing to do with. You dig me?"

"Don't worry," I said, "I'll protect your confidence. Reporters do that all the time. It's part of our tradition."

"Man, never mind your tradition, just don't put me in no swindle."

"I won't," I said, "you can count on that."

"Okay, Doctor McIntyre. So now I'll tell you what I want you to do. While I'm working this floor and the next, I want you to walk down to the end of this hall and turn left. When you turn left you'll see some stairs. So now I want you to go up those stairs and turn left again, and go on up two more flights, and when you get there I want you to stand there on the landing. Understand?"

I nodded.

"What I mean is, I want you to stand there on the landing but *don't* open the door and go in. You just stand there and wait until *I* open the door. Get me?"

"I understand."

"Good," he said, and pushed off down the corridor.

I watched him go, thinking, *Perhaps my luck has changed,* then saw him stop suddenly and turn, frowning.

"Well, go 'head on!"

I hurried past him and headed for the stairs, still wondering at my luck. Perhaps this was the wedge to break through the system of mysteries.

I had begun to ask myself whether I shouldn't forget the whole project and return to the Senator's floor when the door opened and Charleston stood before me holding a mop in a bucket. Without a word he beckoned, and I followed him down a dimly lit corridor, hearing the gentle sloshing of the mop water as we passed a series of rooms with heavy screening and bars on the doors. Stopping before one of these, he put down the bucket and knocked.

"Hey, LeeWillie, you awake?"

Silence. I looked down the corridor from whence we'd come, noticing a thin trail of water sparkling in the dim light. Then from inside the room a muffled voice said, "Who is it?"

"This is Charleston, LeeWillie; you 'sleep?"

"Hey, there, Charleston, my man," the voice said with a yawn. "How're you doing?"

"Fine, man. I say, are you 'sleep?"

"Naw, I wish I were; but after all these years of gigging I guess I'm a night creature. What's happening, man?"

"I brought a doctor to see you."

"Another one? Man, you know I'm sick of doctors! I thought you were bringing me that portable radio."

Charleston winked at me. "Hush, man," he said. "Keep it down in there! You'll get the damn radio just as soon as I can sneak it up here."

"Did you get some earphones?"

"Yeah, it's got earphones so you can listen without everybody knowing that you're tuned in. Now look: I'm going to open the door so Doctor McIntyre can talk with you; he wants to ask you some questions."

"But I don't want any more questions, man!"

"Yeah, but these will be different," Charleston said. Then, glancing furtively down the shadowed corridor, he produced a set of keys and went to work on the lock.

"Yeah, but I've answered all those damn questions a hundred times," the voice said in garrulous complaint, growing stronger as it metamorphosed into a mock dialogue of interrogation:

" '[*Archly*] Mister Minifees, do you...er...get a *bang* out of watching fires?'

" 'No! [*a gruff, heavily Negro accent*]'

" 'Mister Minifees [*high and effeminate*], was your father...often absent from the home?'

" '[*Matter-of-factly*] Yes, sir, he was.'

" 'And did he [*eagerly*] abandon your mother?'

" 'Hell, no.'

(*Pause.*)

" 'Would you [*coyly*] explain that, Mister Mini-fees?'

"Yeah [*blandly*], he had to be on his job.'

" 'Oh, yes, I see [*disappointedly*]. And how did you *feel* about your father, Mister Minifees?'

" 'Feel? Hell, I love him—[*very aggressively*] although plenty of times I used to want to kick his behind!'

" 'Yes, yes? And why was that? [*eagerly*] Go on, Mister Minifees....'

" 'Because *he* used to kick mine—Go-odd-damn!'

(*Muffled laughter.*)

" 'Oh, I see. Yes. And now [*with dry professionalism*], Mister Minifees, do...you...er...*piss* straight?'

" 'Oh, sure, Doc, sure [*broadly stage Negro now*] except for once in a while....'

" 'Once in a while, Mister Minifees? And when [*eagerly*] is that?'

" 'When I'm cutting those figure eights.'

" '[*Silence, followed by heavy intake of breath, then doggedly*] Yes, I understand. And what do you think about when you're doing this?'

" 'Oh, come on, Doc [*reluctantly*], you don't want me to tell you *that*....'

" 'Yes, yes, I do [*objectively*]. What is the problem?'

" 'But look, Doc [*awefully*], have you ever considered the *shape* of a figure eight?'

" 'The shape? [*warily, suddenly on guard*] Why no, Mister Minifees, but that's an interesting question....'

" 'Yeah, Doc [*broad Southern accent*], and if you put a head with long hair on top and two big legs on the bottom, and two loving arms on the side—it's even more interesting. In fact, Doc, it's a bitch! I call 'em "golden girls"!'

" 'Er... interesting, Mister Mini-fees, very interesting. However, I think we can drop that. But now [*cagily*], tell me, were you ever a member of a subversive group?'

" 'Not that I know of.'

" 'Do you belong to *any* organizations?'

" 'Sure.'

" 'What are they?'

" 'The Rhythm Club, Elks, Odd Fellows, and the United Sons of Georgia— And, man, if those are not subversive enough for *you,* they damn sure are for me. After one of those conventions I feel like I've been Triple-A plowed under and turned wrong side out!'

" 'And [*bewilderedly*] are these groups, Mister Minifees, *foreign?*'

" 'You might say that; they're colored.'

" 'Why, yes, of course. But now, tell me [*ingratiatingly*], do you think that the colored man has a harder time than others?'

" 'Doc, are you kidding? Hell, yes! You goddamn right!'

" 'Why?'

" 'Because everybody thinks he's black, that's why.'

" '[*Agitatedly*] Now don't become excited, Mister Minifees. But tell me, which baseball team do you prefer, the New York *Yankees* or the Brooklyn *Dodgers?*'

" 'Neither goddamn one.'

" 'But *why* [*dismayed*], Mister Minifees, *why?*'

" 'Because I'm a *football* fan—Go-odd-damn!'

"No, Charleston," the voice sang, in character again, "those guys can go on for hours asking questions, and I've answered them until they're coming out of my goddamn ears. You get that man the hell away from here."

I listened to Charleston struggling with laughter as he worked on the lock. I had great misgivings about Minifees.

"But wait, man," Charleston said, "you know I wouldn't be bringing up any *ordinary* doctor this early in the morning. This one is special, I trained him myself...."

"You what?"

"That's right, man: I gave him his M.D. Before he met me he was just a reporter...."

"Oh, Lord!" the voice said, then the lock clicked and Charleston was looking quickly down the corridor and pushing the door in upon a dark interior. A light flashed on immediately, and back in the rear of the narrow room I saw Minifees. He lay full-length on a small bed, holding the switch of a small

bedside lamp in his long fingers. He wore white blue-striped hospital pajamas, and above the calm curiosity of his eyes a dully gleaming scarf of black
silk protected his hair.

"Hey, man," Charleston whispered, "put out that damn light. You're going
to have to talk to this one in the dark!"

For a moment Minifees stared at the two of us, then a flash of cold fire
broke from his finger, and we were in the dark again.

"Charleston," he said, "what the hell are you up to now? And what kind of
snake oil is this he's bringing me that has to be sold in the dark?"

Listening to Charleston's joking explanation, I began to doubt once more
that there was anything but the most far-fetched connection between
Minifees and the gunman, and their playful approach to my presence
seemed to reinforce this view. Yet even as I listened I could not completely
dismiss the possibility that Minifees had sacrificed his car as a diversion during an earlier attempt to assassinate the Senator. Until the firing of the gun
in the Senate, Minifees had seemed far removed from the world of politics,
but with the sound of gunfire the world had become dream-like, and I could
no longer be certain. I'd have to follow through and seek out a different logic
of events. Certainly Charleston and Minifees were more than they appeared
to be; their speech contained depths and traps which I had not suspected,
and for all I knew they were listening even now to detect any nuance of suspicion in my voice and conduct. It was frightening, considering the possibility that Minifees might in fact be insane, might turn violent. Still, I was here
now and would have to learn whatever I could. For even in itself the car-
burning was such a threat to the normalcy of existence that its meaning required urgent exploration. The very fact that they could laugh at such a time
and in such a place could be in itself evidence of some underground connection and thus of the possibility of even greater violence and chaos to come.

Across the room bed clothing rustled as Minifees stirred on the cot.
"Charleston," he mused, "I swear that I think you ought to be behind these
bars instead of me. You know you're liable to get bounced off your job for
bringing a newspaperman up here."

"Hell, it's all right, man, and I can take care of myself. This man swears he
digs your music and he wants to help you, and I want you outta here, so it's
worth taking a chance."

I heard the mop splash into the bucket and felt a nudge.

"Step in, Doctor," Charleston said. "I'm going to cover you with this
mop," and I moved in, standing just inside the door and trying to see
Minifees by the dim light from the hall.

"What's your name?" Minifees said.

"It's McIntyre, Welborn McIntyre," I said, naming my paper.

"Pleased to meet you," Minifees said. "So what is it you want from me?"

"Mr. Minifees," I began, "I'd like to do a story about your situation. As you know, your burning your car caused quite a sensation, and I think it's important that the public understand your motives and point of view. And all the more so, now that Senator Sunraider has been shot...."

"Shot!" His voice rang with surprise as the bed groaned and his feet slapped the floor.

"Yes, shot," I said. "Didn't you know?"

"Hell, no! My God, is he dead?"

"No, he was critically wounded but as late as a few minutes ago he was still holding on."

"God! This is awful! Who shot him?"

"The gunman hasn't been identified—but the authorities are working on it. He was a young fellow, about thirty. Rather well-dressed and handsome."

"Do you mean that he got *away?*"

Charleston stuck his head in the doorway. "No, man. The cat shot Sunrainder and then *killed* himself. He leaped from that gallery and tried to turn himself into hamburger meat!"

"Good God-a-mighty! What gallery?"

"The goddamn Senate visitors' gallery, man."

"What! So why didn't you tell me about it?"

"Because it just happened a few hours ago. I was off duty. You know I meant to tell you...."

For a moment it was silent, and I could hear the dripping mop water striking the floor.

"Lord, Lord," Minifees said, "that cat must have been out of his mind. This is crazy! Me, I meant to terrify the bastard and teach him something, but I wouldn't have wasted the *time* it takes to *kill* him!"

"Obviously this man had a different attitude," I said. "Could you have noticed such a man at the time you burned your car?"

"Hell, no, not that I recall."

"Perhaps he was there when you drove across the sidewalk. Did you see anyone acting suspiciously?"

"I don't recall. No."

"Perhaps you noticed him standing in the crowd when you made your speech?"

"Man, *no!* NO! Too many people were out there! All I saw were faces, people. I was too mad to be looking at anyone in particular."

"What about Senator Sunraider. Did you see him?"

"Sure, I saw *him.* I spoke to him, but what has that got to do with it?"

"I was wondering if this man might have been present when you were on the Senator's lawn."

"He might have been, but if he was *I* didn't know it."

"Did anyone besides yourself know what you were planning to do?"

"How could they, when I didn't even know it myself?"

"What about the man who sold you the gas?"

"Folks who sell gas don't ask you what you're going to do with it, man."

And suddenly to my bewilderment the Dorothy Parker line *Men seldom make passes/ At girls who wear glasses* flashed through my mind as I said, "That's usually true, but you bought quite a lot of gas."

"Yeah," Minifees said, "and he was damn glad to take my money—but he didn't ask me any questions."

"And this is actually the first time you've heard of the shooting?"

"Yes, and I ought to whip Charleston's head!"

"None of the doctors or nurses mentioned it?"

"Man, *no!* I wouldn't jive you about anything like that."

"What if you'd have found the Senator in the Senate instead of at home, would you have shot him instead of burning your car?"

I could hear him stand. "*Me?* Are you kidding? I don't even own a gun. And besides, I didn't even *know* he was at home."

"Then why did you go there?"

"Because I hoped he'd be there, man, and it was the best place I could think of to make my point. If I'd made a speech in the Senate gallery they'd have only thrown me out. You know that!"

"But would you have burned your *car* if he hadn't been at home?"

"Sure, I would have. That's why I went there. But I still wouldn't have shot the bastard."

I heard the mop smack the floor behind me and Charleston saying, "Yeah, man, but you didn't have to shoot him; you hit him with that Cadillac and that was enough to break his dickstring," and Minifees' laughter coughed and sputtered in the dark.

"Charleston," he said, "this is serious, don't start me to laughing, or we might as well turn on the light and call the guard. Damn, it looks like I hit a riff and now all hell has broke loose."

"Man, and you can say that again, I bet old Sunrainder thought it was you standing up there blasting him; instead it was some white cat."

"WHITE? What the hell do you mean, white? Why didn't somebody tell me that?"

"I meant to," I said. "I thought I had; he was blond."

"Yeah, and wouldn't you know that that's how it would be? That granny-dodging sonofabitch!"

"That's right, they'll do it every time," Charleston said.

"But I don't understand," I said.

"The hell you don't; ain't it usually some white cat who moves in on a man like that?"

"I don't know, but does the gunman's color make such a difference to you?"

"You're damn right it does!"

"But why? I doubt if the Senator considers it important."

"Well *I* do!"

"But you said that you wouldn't have shot him…."

"No, but that's not it. What I'm talking about is how some white cats feel that they have the right to move in on anything you do. You take your time and you work out a riff from way deep inside yourself, and just as sure as you're born, some white cat is bound to come up and grab it and *distort* it!"

"Oh, but he's telling it like it is," Charleston sang out behind me.

"That's a fact, man," Minifees said. "The cat's going to grab it and then he's going to distort the hell out of it. No matter what you come up with, if he sees that it works and stirs folks up a bit, he's out to grab it and try to outdo you with it—even if he has to blow it all out of shape."

"You're goddamn right," Charleston said, wringing the mop noisily into the bucket. "Like they grabbed 'Tuxedo Junction' from Erskine Hawkins and ain't even smelled the funk of Birmingham! Like they grabbed credit for Don Redman's 'Marie,' and never even rubbed a chick at a breakfast dance!"

"That's very interesting," I said, trying to get them back on the shooting, "but I'd like to ask you this…"

"Yeah," Minifees said, "it happens every damn time. You work 'til your brain sweats and try to come up with something nice and beautiful and sincere, you think it up and shape it and polish it until it swings, and then you blow it in public and it works and then—*bam!*—some white cat has stole it from you faster than a catfish can grab a turd. And what's worse, he tries to hide the fact that he's stealing by playing it on a hundred goddamn fiddles and a sonofabitching pipe organ!"

I was at a loss—where were the shooting and car-burning leading me?

"Perhaps you should have a lawyer to handle your copyrights," I said.

"Hell, man, you can't copyright a riff. Besides, the guys who do that kind of thing can hire better lawyers than I can because they can steal my stuff and make more money off of it than I can. But this is going too far! I thought I'd been served up all kinds of larceny, but now here comes a cat who's done grabbed my Sunraider riff and blowed it through a goddamn *shot*gun!"

"Not a shotgun, man," Charleston said, "it was a pistol."

"Hell," Minifees said wearily, "it's all the same: A gun's a gun, and besides, that bastard was trying to blast both me *and* the Senator. It's enough to make a man take off and go live in Paris. I bet if I had shot the man with a BB gun that bastard would have raced up behind me and blasted him with a bazooka—just to pretend that shooting him was *his* idea. Yeah, and to prove that the white folks are still in the lead!"

He struck the bed and was silent, and I could hear the music of Charleston's mop dripping into his bucket.

"Tell me, Mr. Minifees," I said, "if you had been present in the Senate would you have tried to *prevent* the shooting?"

"Prevent it? I don't know. It's hard to tell what a man will do on the spur of a moment. But I doubt if I'd have stepped in front of any bullets to save him...."

"He's asking you that because some goddamn jackleg Boot preacher was up there trying to grab the cat with the gun when he should've been trying to steady his aim."

"He did? Well, Charleston, a preacher is supposed to be against murder. They find out who he is?"

"His name is Hickman," I said. "Do you know him?"

"Hickman? Hickman what?"

"Doctor Alonzo Hickman...."

"Alonzo Hickman...no, I don't think so."

I was waiting for Charleston to reveal that Hickman was below, but instead he said, "Look, y'all, I have to get back downstairs. So get on with your talk, and break it up before the nurses start making their rounds. I'll check you later."

And before I could protest, the door closed and I found myself alone with Minifees in the dark. I hadn't expected this development and didn't like it. Before now the questions of Minifees' sanity and involvement in a plot had been abstract, now it might well be a matter of life or death. I turned, feeling for the door when he spoke behind me.

"All right, Doctor," he said calmly, "what do you want to ask me?"

I hesitated and then, feeling assured by his calmness, I said, "Let's start with your reason for burning your car."

"Okay, man; she was a beauty."

Through the dark his voice sounded with nostalgia, puzzling me.

"But surely that isn't why you burned it?"

"Oh, no. I burned it because I had to. I had to answer that half-assed senator."

"But why did you decide that you had to answer him, and why in that fashion?"

"Because he *messed* with me, man."

"But it seems such an extreme thing to do."

"Extreme, hell! Did you ever have a bastard signifying at you the way he did? Making fun of you?"

"No, at least not anyone so high in the Government. But he wasn't referring to you personally...."

"Yeah, but I took it personally. Somebody had to, so I decided to hit the bastard, and I had to hit him in such a way that everybody would know that I'd hit him. . . ."

"And burning your Cadillac was the only way?"

"That's it. You got it. It was the best way."

"But why go to such expense?"

"Man, you can't worry about money when you're in that kind of fight. Any way you proceed you know you're going to have to make a sacrifice just to get in a position where you can draw some blood. I wanted people to know how I felt about that bastard, because *somebody* had to tell him off."

"I'm beginning to understand, but did you consider that the results might be different?"

"What do you mean?"

"I'm referring to the possibility that you might have done more harm to yourself than to the Senator. Many people were so shocked that they failed to appreciate what you were attempting to do. They were terrified."

"Are you telling me? Hell, I knew it and I thought about it and I'm glad it upset them. Many of them didn't want me to have a Caddy in the first place, and when I realized that that Senator thought that by owning one I was trying to imitate him, I decided to change the rules of the game. I don't have to drive a Caddy, but he didn't think about that because he has to drive one in order to feel he's got it made. Me, I'm free."

Free, I thought. *Perhaps he's insane after all. How can he speak of freedom while locked up without access to lawyer or judge?*

"But let me ask you this," I said. "Why didn't you burn the Senator's automobile instead?"

"Because I hurt him more by burning my own, that's why. If I had burned his I'd just be another outlaw, but this way he and everybody else has to know that I don't have to take their crap. I realized that I didn't have to *hit* him to hurt him; all I had to do was hit myself and he'd hurt more than I did. Him and a lot of others. I'm tired of people thinking that they can intimidate me just because I drove a Caddy."

"Do other people feel as the Senator does?"

"Hell, yes."

"How do you know this?"

"Hell, man, it's impossible to miss it. Almost every time I pull up to a stoplight, I can see it in their eyes."

"See what, Mr. Minifees?"

"I could see their eyes saying, 'Hey, that Caddy's too good for that Boot!' And not only that, sometimes they put it into words. Take the other day when I'm in New York driving through Greenwich Village on my way to work a gig. I'm coming to a corner with the traffic light on the green, and I see a little old lady and a little freckle-faced girl about to cross the street from the other side, and I put on the brakes and let them cross.

"Now understand me, I'm not asking for any special credit for letting them pass; many a driver gives pedestrians the right of way and tries to be polite. Besides, my mama taught me manners. In fact, she beat them into me in order to save me from you people and in order to save you from me. So that's not the point. The point I'm making is that when that little old lady and the little girl reached the curb, what do you think happens?"

"Was this recently?"

"Yeah, it was recent and it was still on my mind when Sunraider made his goddamn speech!"

"I see," I said, "and what happened?"

"So when that little old lady gets the little girl over the curb, she looks around, and I could see a smile start to bloom on her face and then, man, she sees *me* behind the wheel—and after that, buddy, the weather took a sudden turn for the worst! The sun dropped down into a bottomless hole! Ice a foot thick frosted over the street! And all of a sudden that little old lady wrinkled up her face and something went SPLAT!"

"What?"

"Yeah, that's right," his voice dropped dolefully in the dark, "you got the message. Instead of thanking me, that...little...old...lady...*spits*...on... the...hood...of...my...nice...clean Cadillac!"

"That's outrageous."

"Yeah, and you can play that in brass. That hood of mine looked like sixteen seagulls suffering from the Georgia trots had got my range at the same time and the captain gull had yelled, 'ATTACK!' And after that, man, came the deluge! I was dumbfounded. I'd never witnessed such conduct in all my born days, man or boy, North or South. I just sat there with my mouth open, watching while she gives that little girl a jerk that lifts her clean off the walk and shoots her draw's leg down around her little ankles and starts her to bawling like she's got the blues long before her time. Man, in this country there's truly no rest for the weary, no peace for the soul!"

In the quiet I could hear him swallow, the sound of a glass striking a table-top, then his voice resumed, swollen with emotion.

"Mr. McIntyre, I just sat there and shook my head, too outdone to move. And then, when she's a few steps away, the light turned red so that I couldn't pull off, she turns and shakes her bony fist at me and screams so that all the people on the street could hear, 'We'll get you, Mister black Bogy-wah-zee! We'll get you! Comes the revolution and we God-fearing, genuine Americans are going to put you back in your place. Just you wait and see! We'll make the streets safe for democracy, and we'll put you back in the cotton patch where you belong, and then we'll raise the tariff to see that you stay there!'

"Did you ever hear anything like that, Mr. McIntyre?"

"No," I said, "I haven't."

"Then you're lucky, because that's how far this Cadillac confusion had gone before Sunraider shot off his mouth. That little old lady—and she was *old*—she's going to start a bloody revolution! She's going to kill up a lot of people and take away their hard-earned property just so she can get *my* Cadillac! Never seen me before in her life, and she's going to do all that, and all I did was to try to protect her while she's breaking the traffic laws and risking that little girl's life!

"Man, you should have seen her. She was holding on to that child's arm with her eyes popping out and her face working, looking like she could've knocked out my teeth one by one with a ball-peen hammer! Hell, no wonder the kids are running wild. No wonder they're smoking pot in the fourth grade and burning down houses! That old lady was broadcasting murder in front of that little child, and I haven't even opened my mouth, much less raised my hand: All *I* did was to own a Cadillac. But now that little girl is well on the road to hating anybody who looks like me and drives an automobile...."

"She must have been cracked," I said as his voice became silent. "There are bigots of all ages."

"Yeah, that's right," he said, and I could hear the bed give as he lay down. "But don't go putting that woman down for a crackpot, that would be a mistake, because there are plenty like her, and when I heard that Sunraider playing up to them, I knew I had to do something."

"I think I'm beginning to understand you now," I said, "but why, precisely, were you so angered by his remarks? After all, what he said seems tame after what you've told me about the reactions of other people."

His feet scraped the floor. "Not tame, man; because being what he is made it much worse. I can take things like cops always coming up to me talking about, 'Boy, what white man's car is this you all being so reckless with?' That's right, and I'm parked at the goddamn curb. Or they see you on the highway and make you pull over to the side so they can examine your license, talking about, 'Boy, you be more careful with that white man's car, y'all hear?' Sure, I've had to put up with a lot of that kind of bullshit, but I expect a senator to *act* like a *senator*, not like a clown. Something must be wrong with that cat, seriously wrong. Because he sounds frantic to me. No wonder somebody tried to kill him."

"What do you mean by 'frantic,' Mr. Minifees?"

"I mean he sounds touched. Off his rocker, like what comes out isn't what it started out to be. He reminds me of a barbershop quartet of nigger-hating crackers singing 'Shortenin' Bread'—which is one of the most frantic exhibitions a man could see. Those cats work themselves up into such a state singing about 'Mammy's li'l baby' and the rest of that jive that by the time they reach the last chorus somebody has to run out on the stage with a bucket and mop to clean up the mess. That's what I mean by frantic. Sunraider gets to talking and his mouth runs away with him, especially when he gets to talking about us. No wonder somebody shot him."

"Speaking of the shooting, Mr. Minifees, have you any idea of just who might have shot him?"

"No, I don't, but a cat like that is liable to have folks coming out of the woodwork to get him."

"Have you ever heard anyone *discussing* the possibility of shooting him?"
"No."

"Have you ever discussed doing so yourself?"

"No, but I've thought about all the possible ways of kicking his butt."

"Was that recently? I mean, was it after his speech or before?"

"Before. When I heard him coming through my radio talking that mess about Cadillacs, I didn't take time to talk about it; I came after him."

"And you decided to burn your own property instead of attacking him personally?"

"That's right, because it was the logical thing to do. If I'd have shot him, or knocked a hole in his head, it would have been like getting mad when you're playing the dozens. I would've lost the game."

"I don't get the point."

"Well, in the dozens each player tries to say the worst things he can say about the other's mother and father, their families, and the one who gets mad loses the game. So it was like Sunraider was playing the dozens with me, and I wasn't going to lose by getting mad and blasting him. But while I had no trouble restraining myself from doing that, I also knew that he couldn't afford to have folks like me giving up all the things Cadillacs have come to stand for. And, man, if enough of us give them up, it will hurt Sunraider a hell of a lot worse than a bullet. The point is to make him live with it, not to kill him. In fact, I'm sorry that the bastard got shot...."

Listening to his voice fade in the dark, I didn't know whether to laugh or to throw up my hands before the incongruity between his act and his intention, between the Senator's reckless joke and the old woman's bigotry and Minifees' extreme reaction to them. That such as they could produce such a sense of outrage and revolt as the car-burning expressed was too much for me. It had appeared that Minifees had allowed himself to become so provoked that he'd destroyed something that had meant far more to him than a simple—though expensive—apparatus of locomotion, and his answer to my next question gave indication of this.

"Mr. Minifees," I said, "I get the impression that your automobile meant far more to you than cars do to most people."

"Yeah? Well, I wouldn't know about that," he said, "but since I've been here, I've been thinking about what mine really meant, and now that I've thought about it, the difference between what cars mean to most folks and what mine meant to me is the difference between knowing only the melody of a song and knowing the melody and the chords *and* the lyrics. Now I know what it meant to me from top to bottom."

"Would you explain that?"

"Sure. I mean that now I dig the romance of owning something fine that costs a lot of cash. You know: A big car means a big man. Own a convertible and be hell with the women. Own a limousine and be a man of distinction. Hell, I know all of that bullshit which they put in the ads. And I also know about the engine and the suspension and all of the technical features—but after what I did, and since I've had time to think about it a bit, I realize that for me that Caddy wasn't simply a car."

I felt myself take an involuntary step forward.

"That's what I'd like to understand," I said. "Would you please spell it out? That's precisely the kind of detail that my readers need to understand."

"Well, for one thing, she was my boon companion...."

"Yes?"

"She was like a guaranteed freedom to move—*when* I wanted to and *where* I wanted to—you dig?"

"Yes, I think I do."

"And she was my rolling hideaway and my thinking room."

"In other words," I said, "it was a mode of escape and a place of contemplation, is that it?"

"Right! All of that. And what's more, she eased my nerves when the strain mounted up, and she gave me a lift when I was feeling low. Because that Cadillac got me further when I wanted to clear the territory, and she told me that good times were somewhere up the road. There's many a cat who was saved from a busted jaw through my being able to climb into that Caddy and take off!"

Obviously, I thought, *he used it as a means of controlling aggression: perhaps a device of sublimation. A mechanical compensation for powerlessness of a kind....*

"Yes, sir," he said, "if Sunraider hadn't driven me into a corner, I'd still be rolling away from things that drag me."

I said, "Mr. Minifees, in his speech the Senator referred to the design of American automobiles. He felt they were excellent; would you have anything to say along that line?"

"Well, there are some I wouldn't use to haul hogs in, but that Cadillac was different. You have to give it to those people, when they say they make a fine automobile, then by God they make a *fine* automobile. Anyway, that Caddy of mine gave me pleasure whenever I looked at her because I knew that she was something that had been put together, as fine music written by a fine composer for fine musicians. Looking at her could work on me the same way as watching a speckled puppy playing with an India-rubber ball, or a young colt racing across a field of Kentucky bluegrass."

"Very interestingly put," I said. "Anything else?"

"Yes, to me that Cadillac was to other cars what good jazz is to noise. And to my own music she was what a curly-haired brown-skinned woman wearing gold earrings, red patent-leather sandals, and a blue gingham apron with a big bow tied behind is to the groovy blues. You know, they kind of naturally go together...."

"It was really quite important to you," I said, "an aesthetic as well as a utilitarian value...."

"Yes, you're right," Minifees said. "It was all of that, but now it's gone and I'm free."

Free, I thought, *free! What would M. Vannec think of that?* Minifees was too much for me. He'd allowed himself to destroy something precious in reaction to a deranged old woman and an irreverent and reckless senator, and now, sitting in a cell, he could speak in this darkness of freedom! I yearned to see his expression, wished that he'd turn on the light. Somehow he had rearranged reality in his mind in such a way that he could believe that Sunraider's insult had set him free, and he was not complaining of the cost. I didn't know how to continue the interview, for standing there, I felt in the presence of one taken over by the lucidity of madness. One who by a strange dislocation of values had come to see things, events, with an unreal clarity of vision. What would he do now? Where could he go, and what would happen to his music—or did his "far-out" jazz, as Charleston called it, actually foreshadow his present state of mind? I couldn't stand it. I wasn't prepared for it and wouldn't have been even if I hadn't been exhausted by all of the wild events which had exploded since he burned his Cadillac.

Nor was I helped when, now from across the room, I heard him sit up and say quite loudly, "Oh, Lord, there goes my boy Clyde again!"

I heard it then and turned, staring toward the door. From somewhere beyond the corridor a high, piercing tenor voice had begun to quaver of all things, the ballad of John Henry:

> *Oh, the hammer that John Hen-nery swung*
> *It weighed over nine cold pound'*
> *John Hen-nery broke a rib in his left-hand side*
> *And his guts fell on the ground, Lord, Lord!*
>
> *So they took John Hen-nery to the White House,*
> *And they buried him in the sand*
> *And every locomotive that comes roaring by,*
> *Says there lays that steel-driving man,*
> > *Lord, Lord!*
> *Says there lays that steel-driving man!*

It was a mocking, hallucinated voice which made the hair stand up on the back of my neck, and I knew that in a matter of minutes it would bring nurses and attendants to the floor and I'd be caught in Minifees' cell.

"Man, you'd better cut out of here," Minifees said, moving forward. Then the door was opening, and I was relieved to see the silhouette of Charleston standing before me.

"Goddamn, McIntyre," he said, "I thought you'd be through in here and gone! Are you and LeeWillie trying to lose me my job?"

"No, I was just leaving," I said, brushing past and hearing the voice clearly now as it sang,

> *Oh, I'll tell you the story of Chickenshack Ernie*
> *He painted a rooster on his Cadillac car*
> *Was a grand entrepreneur, this Chickenshack Ernie,*
> *Whose chicken fried, was praised near and far. . . .*

"Git, man," Charleston said behind me. "And you'd better hit those stairs before that singing fool does it for you! Besides, things have begun to happen downstairs. Sunrainder has come to and is trying to make them bring that big fellow who was sleeping into his room. Who is that sonofabitch, anyway?"

"That," I called over my shoulder as I ran down the corridor, "is Alonzo Hickman."

"Hickman? HICKMAN!" he said. "Well, I'll be damn!"

I ran for the stairs and plunged down three steps at a time, passing a startled nurse as I reached the floor below, and moving as fast as I could go, I made for the next floor, only to fall, knocking myself senseless for a moment, then, getting to my feet, hurtled down the next—only to arrive just in time to see Hickman's broad shoulders disappearing inside the Senator's room.

Cursing myself, Charleston, Minifees, and fat, I watched the door come to, then slumped on the bench again, exhausted. For all I'd learned, I might have spent the time trying to interview the gunman's body in the morgue. Now I'd simply have to wait. But at least the Senator was still alive. . . .

BOOK II

Editors' Note to Book II

Book II is the most thoroughly worked over and revised section of Ellison's unfinished second novel. A partial draft of 185 pages survives in which the manuscript breaks off halfway down the last page in the middle of an episode—indeed, in mid-paragraph, with a line hastily scribbled in the writer's hand: "trying to make the blackness go all away." This typescript is quite likely the same manuscript from which Ellison edited all but the first two scenes of "And Hickman Arrives" in 1959 for the first issue of Saul Bellow's *The Noble Savage* (1960), the first selection he published from the then novel-in-progress.

That partial typescript tracks and anticipates much of what Ellison went on to accomplish with Book II. In its four-page version of the book's beginning, the long speech Senator Sunraider gives on the Senate floor in subsequent drafts is merely alluded to as Ellison cuts quickly to the assassination. In later versions Ellison includes the Senator's speech, expanding the opening scene first to eleven pages and then, in the most recent surviving typescript, which was much revised, to some twenty-four pages. (Both the four- and eleven-page versions are included in Part III of *Three Days*.) Published here, the longest version is evidence of Ellison's revision and expansion of Book II from the early sixties until at least 1986, when, according to Mrs. Ellison's handwritten note, her husband took the latest, most complete typescript to their rebuilt summer home in Plainfield, Massachusetts.

Published in the present volume, this 355-page typescript is the longest version of Book II as well as the most recent. That being said, pages 319 to 352 (pages 422 to 455 in this volume) appear considerably less revised and polished—less settled on—than pages 1 to 319; also, the text on pages 352 to 355 has handwritten pagination and a handwritten notation by Ellison ("follows Book II") in the top right corner of page 352. Interestingly, Ellison filled out this episode from Book II in the computer-generated narrative "Hickman in Washington, D.C." There are also other partial surviving typescripts of certain episodes from Book II, in particular the visit to the Lincoln Memorial by Reverend Hickman and his congregation before the assassination of Senator Sunraider.

Publication of Book II, both in *Juneteenth* and in this volume, was informed by the fact that Ellison made extensive revisions in pencil on his carbon copy of pages 1 through 284 of the latest, most complete typescript as well as some—fewer, but still some—revisions on the original manuscript. In *some* cases there is reworking of the same passage. In these instances our editorial judgment has had to do due diligence for a definitive reading of Ellison's intention since neither the original typescript nor its carbon are dated, and since there is no clear evidence of the order in which Ellison penciled in his changes or even whether he revised either manuscript completely before turning to the other. Finally, we would note that no *original* manuscript survives of pages 285 through 355; on these pages Ellison's revisions were made to the carbon. Like the two excerpts from Book I published in Ellison's lifetime, we have published the four selections he published from Book II in an appendix, presenting those episodes in the present volume as they appear in his last surviving typescript of Book II.

With respect to Book II and *Juneteenth,* it should be noted that the chapter breaks of *Juneteenth* are space breaks in Book II, that pages 422–455 of Book II, as published here, are not included in the *Juneteenth* narrative, and that the narrative sequence of Book II was shifted at several points during the editing of *Juneteenth.*

Book II shows Ellison working with the voices and perspectives of Reverend Hickman and Bliss/Sunraider in an antiphonal call-and-response form common to the black church. He also renders each man's inner life in silent interior monologues reminiscent of Faulkner, Joyce, and other high modernists. More than Book I or any of the computer sequences, Book II tells the story of the two protagonists in what becomes a call-and-response between action and brooding interiority. The two men often keep in silent touch with each other "on the lower frequencies" of memories triggered by connections in the present, connections one man pursues and the other tries unsuccessfully to evade. Finally, though, even with the end seemingly in sight, Ellison does not bring the story told in Book II to closure any more than he did those stories he began so bravely in the other sequences of the second novel.

...SUDDENLY, THROUGH THE SONOROUS lilt and tear of his projecting voice, the Senator was distracted. Grasping the dimly lit lectern and concentrating on the faces of colleagues seated below him behind circular, history-stained desks, his eyes had been attracted by a turbulence centering around the rich emblazonry of the Great Seal. High across the chamber and affixed midpoint the curving sweep of the distant visitors' gallery, the national coat of arms had ripped from its moorings and was hurtling down toward him with the transparent unsubstantiality of a cinematic image that had somehow gone out of control.

Increasing alarmingly in size while maintaining the martial posture of tradition, the heraldic eagle with which the Great Seal was charged seemed to fly free of its base, zooming forward and flaring luminously as it halted, oscillating a few arm's lengths before the Senator's confounded head. There, pulsating with the hallucinatory vividness of an eidetic image, the rampant eagle aroused swift olfactory memories of dried blood and dusty feathers and stirred within him, as by the motion of swift silent wings, fragmentary images of warfare tinged with conflicting details of heroism and betrayal....

Stepping instinctively backwards and fighting down an impulse to duck, the Senator managed by benefit of long practice to continue the smoothly resonant flow of his address, but before what appeared to be the product of an insidious practical joke contrived to test his equanimity a cascading weakening of muscular control. For now, armed of beak and claw, the barred inescutcheon shielding its breast and the golden ribbon bearing the mystic motto of national purpose violently aflutter, the emblematic bird quivered above him on widely erected wings—while the symbolic constellation of thirteen cloud-encircled stars whirled furiously against a spot of intense blue which flashed like cold lightning above its snow-white head.

Shutting his eyes in a desperate effort to exorcise the vision, the Senator projected his voice with increased vigor and was aware of distorting the shape of what he had conceived as a perfect rhetorical period. But when he looked again the eagle was not only still there, but become more alarming.

For at first, clutching in its talons the ambiguous arms of olive branch and sheaf of arrows, the eagle's exposed eye had looked in profile toward the traditional right, but now it shuddered with mysterious purpose, turning its head with sinister smoothness leftward—until with a barely perceptible flick of feathers two sphinx-like eyes bored in upon him with piercing frontal gaze. For a breathless interval they held him savagely in mute interrogation, causing the Senator to squint and toss his head; then, with the stroke of a scimitar the curved beak carved the air. And with its wingspread thrusting upward and the feathers of its white-tipped tail flexed fanlike between feathery, wide-spread thighs, the eagle was no longer scrutinizing his face but staring blandly in the direction indicated by its taloned clutch of sharp-pointed arrows.

Alarmed by the image's stubborn persistence, the Senator felt imprisoned in an airless space from which he viewed the placid scene of the chamber as through the semi-transparent scrim of a theatrical stage. A scrim against which the heraldic symbols in whose name he served flashed and flickered in wild enigmatic disarray. And even as he forced himself to continue his address, he was aware that his voice was no longer reaching him through the venerable chamber's acoustics but now, sounding muted, metallic, and stridently strange, through the taut vibrations of his laboring throat. Leaning forward and controlling himself by grasping the lectern, he recalled the famous cartoon which presented a man struggling desperately to prevent a huge octopus from dragging him into a manhole while a crowd thronged past unnoticing. For despite the disorder within his vision, the chamber appeared quite normal. Listening attentively, his audience was apparently unaware of his distress.

In whose name and under what stress do they think I'm speaking? the Senator thought. *For whose hidden interests and by what manipulation of experience and principle would they hang the bird on me?*... But now upon a flash of movement from above the eagle appeared to leap aloft, reducing the rich emblazonment of the Seal to an exploding chaos of red, white, blue, and gold, through which the Senator's attention flashed to the distant gallery—where with the amplified roar of his echoing voice he became aware of a collectivity of obscure faces, staring down....

Anonymous, orderly, and grave, they loomed high across the chamber, receding upward and away in serried tiers, their heads protruding slightly forward in the tense attitude of viewers bemused by some puzzling action unfolding on a distant screen which they were observing from the tortured angle provided by a segregated theater's peanut gallery. And as his words sped out across the chamber's solemn air the faces appeared to shimmer in rapt and disembodied suspension, as though in expectation of some crucial and long-awaited revelation which, by affording them physical completion, would make them whole. A revelation apparently even now unfolding through the accelerating rhythms, the bounce and boom of images sent flighting across the domed and lucid space from the flex and play of his own tongue, throat, and diaphragm....

The effect upon the Senator was electric. Reassured and pleasurably challenged by their anonymous engrossment, he experienced a surge of that gaiety, anguished yet wildly free, which frequently seized him during an oration, and now, as with a smooth shifting of emotional gears, he felt himself carried swiftly beyond either a concern with the meaning of the mysterious vision or the rhetorical fitness of his words onto that plane of verbal exhilaration for which he was notorious. And thereupon, in the gay and reckless capriciousness of his virtuosity, he found himself attempting to match that feat, long glorified in senatorial legend, whereby through a single flourish of his projected voice the orator raises his audience to fever pitch and shatters the chamber's windowpanes.

Do that, the Senator thought, *and without a single dissenting Heh-ell-naw! the gentleman from Little Rock will call for changing the outlandish name—of Arkansaw!*

Stifling an upsurge of laughter, the Senator plunged ahead, tensing his diaphragm to release the full resonance of his voice. But as he did so it was as though his hearing had been thrown out of phase. Resounding through the acoustics of the chamber it was as though it was being controlled by the stop-and-go fluctuations of a hypersensitive time-delay switch, forcing him to monitor his words seconds after they were uttered and feeding them back to him with a hollow, decaying echo. More puzzling, he became aware that between the physical sensation of statement and the delayed return, his voice was giving expression to ideas the like of which he had never articulated, not even in the most ambiguous of rhetorical situations. Words, ideas, phrases, were jetting from some chaotic region deep within him, and as he strived to regain control it was as though he had been taken over by some mocking ventriloquistic orator of opposing views, a trickster of corny philosophical ambition.

"But...but...but...now...now...now...," he heard, "let let us consider consider consider, the broader broader implication...cations of of our our current state. In this land it is our fate to be interrogated not by our allies or enemies but by our conduct and by our lives. Our...ours...ours is the arduous burden burden...den privilege of *self*-regulation and *self*-limitation. We are of a nation born in blood, fire, and sacrifice, thus we are judged, questioned, weighed—by the revolutionary ideals and events which marked the founding of our great country. It is these transcendent ideals which interrogate us, judge us, pursue us, in terms of that which we do or do *not* do. They accuse us ceaselessly and their interrogation is ruthless, scathing, seldom charitable. For the demands they make of us are limitless. Under the relentless pressure of their accusation we seek to escape the intricate game-work of our enterprises. We make for the territory. We plunge into the Edenic landscape of our natural resources. We seek out the warm seacoasts of leisure, the quiet cool caverns of forgetfulness—all made possible by the very success of our mind-jolting revolution and the undeniable accomplishments of our labor and dedication. In our beginning our forefathers summoned up the will to break with the past. They questioned the past and condemned it and severed themselves from its entangling tentacles. They plunged into the future accepting its dangers and its glories. Thus with us it is instinctive to evaluate ourselves against the examples of those, humble and illustrious alike, who preceded us upon this glorious stage and passed on. We are a people of joy and anguish. Our joy made poignant by our anguish. Of us is demanded great daring, great courage, great insight, prudence, and even greater self-discipline.

"For we are like those great birds which, moved by an inborn need to test themselves against the mystery and promise of the universe, take off on powerful wings to be carried by fierce winds and gentle currents to great heights and far places. Like them we are given to maneuvering miraculously through treacherous passages and above marvelous plateaus and fertile valleys. It is our nature to soar, and by following the courses mapped through the adventurous efforts of our fathers we affirm and revitalize their awesome vision. We are reapers and sowers, destroyers and creators, wheelers and dealers, finders and keepers—and why not? Since we are also generous sharers of that which we discover through our dedication and daring.

"Time flows past beneath us as we soar. History erupts and boils with its age-old contentions. But ours is the freedom and decision of the New, the Uncluttered, and we embrace the anguish of our predicament, we accept the penalties of our hopefulness. So on we soar, following our dream. Time flows past beneath us, history erupts and boils with its age-old contentions. But ours is the freedom and decision of the New, the Uncluttered, even though basically ours has remained the eternal human condition. Sometimes our clouds are fleecy and translucent, veiling thinly the sun; sometimes dark and stormy, lashing us with the wickedness of winter. We toss and swirl, pivot and swoop. We scrape the peaks or go kiting strutless toward the void. Ofttimes, as it appears to be true of us today, we plunge down and down, we go round and round faltering and accusing ourselves remorselessly until, reminded of who we are and what we are about and the cost, we pull ourselves together. We lift up our eyes to the hills and we arise.

"God enclosed our land between two mighty oceans and setting us down on the edge of this mighty continent, he threw us on our own. Our forefathers then set our course ever westward, not, I think, by way of turning us against the past and its lessons, although they accused it vehemently—for we are a product of those lessons—but that we should approach our human lot from a fresher direction, from uncluttered perspectives. Therefore it is not our way, as some would have it, to reject the past; rather it is to overcome its blighting effects upon our will to organize and conduct a more human future. We are called a consumer society and much is made of what is termed the 'built-in obsolescence' of our products. But those who do so miss the point: Yes, we are a consumer society, but the main substance of our consumption consists of *ideals.* Our way is to render ideals obsolescent by transforming them into their opposites through achieving and rejecting their promises. Thus do our ideals die and give way to the new. Thus are they redeemed, made manifest. Our sense of reality is too keen to be violated by moribund ideals, too forward-looking to be too long satisfied with the comforting arrangements of the present, and thus we move ever from the known into the unknown, for there lies the more human future, for there lies the idealistic core.

"My friends, and fellow citizens, I would remind you that in this our noble land, memory is all; touchstone, threat, and guiding star. Where we shall go is where we have been; where we have been is where we shall go— but with a difference. For as we proceed toward our destination it is ever changed by the transformations wrought by our democratic procedures and by the life-affirming effects of our spirit. Here we move ever toward past-future, by moonlight and by starlight, soaring by dead reckoning along courses mapped by our visionary fathers!

"Where we have been is where we shall go. We move from the realm of dreams through the valley of the practical and back to the realm of rectified dreams. Yes, but how we arrive there is *our* decision, *our* challenge, and *our* anguish. And in the going and in the arriving our task is to tirelessly transform the past and create and re-create the future. In this grand enterprise we dance to our inner music, we negotiate the unknown and untamed terrain by the soundings of our own inner ear. By the capacity of our inner eye for detecting subtleties of contour, landmark, and underground treasure, we shape the land. Indeed, we *shall* reshape the universe—to the forms of our own inner vision. Let no scoffers demand of us, 'How high the moon?' for not only can we supply the answer, in time we shall indeed fly them there! We shall demonstrate once again that in this great, inventive land man's idlest dreams are but the blueprints and mockups of emerging realities, technologies, and poems. Here in the fashion of our pioneer forefathers, who confronted the mysteries of wilderness, mountain, and prairie with crude tools and a self-generating imagination, we are committed to facing with courage the enormous task of imposing an ever more humane order upon this bewilderingly diversified and constantly changing society. Committed we are to maintaining its creative momentum.

"Committed we are to maintaining its involved and complex equilibrium.

"Committed to keeping it soaring ever forward in the materialization of our sublime and cornucopian dream. We rush ever onward, and often violently, yes, but on the adventurous journey toward the fulfillment of that dream, no one . . . no . . . one . . . not one, I say, shall . . . shall . . . be . . . bee . . . bee . . . denied . . . denied . . . !"

Thinking, *Am I drunk, going insane,* the Senator paused, sweeping the curve of anonymous faces above him with his eyes.

"No," he continued, "no one shall be denied. An enormous task, some might say, a rash dream. Yet ours is no facile vision. Each day we suffer its anguish and its cost. It requires effort of an order to which only a great and unified nation, a nation conditioned to riding out the chaos of history as the eagle rides out the whirlwind, can arise. Therefore it is our duty to confront it with subtle understanding. Confront it with democratic passion. Confront it with tragic insight, with love and with endless good humor. We must confront it with faith and in the awareness of that age-old knowledge which holds that it is in the nature of the human enterprise that great nations shall not, *must* not, *dare* not evade their own mysteries but must grapple with them and live them out. They must solve their innermost dilemmas through the expenditure of great physical and spiritual effort. Yes, for great nations evolve and grow ever young in the conscious acceptance and penetration of their own most intimate secrets.

"Thus it is that we must will to remember our defeats and divisions as we remember our triumphs and unities so that we may transcend and forget them. Thus we must forget the past. Indeed, our history records an undying, unyielding quest for youthful sages, for a newfound wisdom fired by a vibrant physicality. Thus again we must forget the past by way of freeing ourselves so that we can reassemble its untidy remnants in the interest of a more human order.

"Oh, yes; I understand: To some this goal appears too difficult. To others too optimistic, too unworldly—even though they would agree that we are indeed a futuristic people. Ah, but in the face of this bright and inescapable intuition dark doubts afflict them. Dark realities inhibit their powers of decision. They succumb to the shallow, somber materiality of our bountiful power and pursue it blindly, selfishly, for itself. They yearn for a debilitating and self-defeating tranquillity. They falter before the harsher necessities of action, whether that action calls for the exercise of force or charity, charity or force. And before those ever-present dilemmas requiring the exercise of charity supported by force they oscillate pathetically between olive branch and arrows. They lose their way and in their stumbling indecision they reward aggression and justify indolence. In their hands charity becomes a force of cancerous malignancy, and power a self-destructive agency that destroys themselves, their children, and their neighbors.

"Nevertheless, we must accept forthrightly that arduous wisdom which holds that those who reject the lessons of history, or who allow themselves to be intimidated by its rigors, are doomed to repeat its disasters. Therefore I call upon them to remember that societies are artifacts of *human* design and that they are *man* determined. Human societies float like great spaceships between earth and sky, dependent upon both but enjoying the anguish of human will and initiative. Man is born to act, to make mistakes, and to die. This all men know. But in the graceful acceptance of his fate, and in his protracted and creative dying, man builds his monument, he structures and makes manifest his accusation of the universe. He secures his earthly gains, sets the course of the ever-receding future and makes art of his yearning.

"So again, my friends, we become victims of history only if we fail to evolve ways of life that are more free, more youthful, more human. We are defeated only if we fail in the task of creating a total way of life which will allow each and every one of us to rise high above the site of his origins, to soar released and ever reinvigorated in human space!"

The Senator smiled.

"I need not remind you that I am neither seer nor prophet," he went on, "but history has put to us three fatal questions, has written them across our sky in accents of accusation. They are: How can the many be as one? How can the future deny the past? And how can the light deny the dark? The answer to the first is: through a balanced consciousness of unity in diversity and diversity in unity, through a willed and *conscious* balance—that is the key phrase, so easy to say yet so difficult to maintain.

"For the second the answer lies in remembering that, given the nature of our vision, of our covenant, to remember is to forget and to forget is to remember selectively, creatively! Yes, and let us remember that in this land to create is to destroy, and to destroy—if we will it so and make it so, if we pay our proper respect to remembered but rejected things—is to make manifest our lovely dream of progressive idealism.

"And how can the light deny the dark? Why, by seeking ever the darkness in lightness and the lightness in darkness. As we incorporate and humanize nature we filter and blend the spectrum, we exalt and we anguish, we order the world.

The land was ours before we were the land's

So sayeth the poet. And so it is as it was in Eden. In darkness and in lightness it is ours to name and ours to shape and ours to love and die for. Therefore let us not falter before its complexity, its riddles. Nor become confused. So let us not falter before our complexity. Nor become confused by the mighty, reciprocal, engine-like stroking of our national ambiguities. We are by no means a perfect people—nor do we desire to be so. For great nations reach perfection, that final static state, only when they pass their peak-promise and exhaust their grandest potentialities. We seek not perfection, but coordination. Not sterile stability but creative momentum. Ours is a youthful nation, the perfection we seek is futuristic and to be made manifest in creative action. A marvel of purposeful political action, it was designed to solve those vast problems before which all other nations have been proved wanting. Born in diversity and fired by determination, our society was endowed with a flexibility designed to contain the most fracticious contentions of an ambitious, individualistic, and adventurous breed. Therefore, as we go about confronting our national ambiguities let us remember the purposes of our built-in checks and balances, those constitutional provisions which serve like subtle hormones to regulate the ingenious metabolism of our body politic. Yes, and as we check our checks and balance our balances, let us in all good humor balance our checks and check our balances, keeping each in proper order, issuing credit to the creditable, minus to plus and plus to minus.

"E Pluribus Unum," the Senator shouted, pointing toward the Great Seal attached to the wall of the gallery. "Observe there the message borne in the beak of the noble bird under whose aegis our nation thrives! Note the olive branch and arrows! Contemplate its prayer and promise—E PLURIBUS UNUM—Regard the barred shield that protects us, the stars of state leaping high in the sunburst of national promise. Mark the olive branch extending peace and prosperity to all. Consider the historically established fact that its ready arrows are no mere boast of martial preparedness, they are symbolic of our aggressive determination to fulfill our obligations to humankind in whatever form they take or wherever they might arise. So let us take wing with our emblem. Let us flesh out its ideals. Let us unite like the flexing feathers that lift it aloft. Let us forge ahead in faith and in confidence— E PLURIBUS UNUM!"

In the hushed silence the Senator stared out across the chamber as though taken with a sudden insight. Then leaning forward with a look of amazement he stroked his chin and waved his hands in a gesture of impatience.

"Recently," he continued in a quietly confidential tone, "our national self-confidence has come under attack from within. It is said that too many of our national projects have gone astray; that problems of long existence are proving to be unresolvable; that our processes of governance have broken down, and that we are become a distraught and weary people. And I would agree that something of a darkness, an overcast has come upon us. There are seasons in the affairs of nations and this is to be expected. But I disagree that the momentary disruptions which wrack our society are anything new or sufficient reason for despair.

"My friends, in such a nation as ours, in a nation blessed with so much good fortune, with so much brightness, it is sometimes instructive, when we are so compelled, to look on the *dark* side. It is a corrective to the bedazzlement fostered by the brightness of our ideals and our history. The gentlemen from Pennsylvania will recall that the dark and viscous substance which once fouled the water of their fair state gave way under scientific scrutiny and soon gave radiance to their gloom. It made bright their homes and cities, became a new source of wealth. The gentlemen from Alabama and Georgia will recall the life-giving resuscitation of the old legend of sailing-ship days in which sailors dying of thirst took what appeared to be black-humored advice from a passing ship's captain and, plunging their buckets into what appeared to be pure brine, drew sweet spring water from the depths of the sea. They'll recall too that during a dark time in a dark section of the South a miracle was discovered beneath the hull of the humble peanut which proved similar to that of the loaves and the fishes. Yes, and this to the well-being of their state and nation.

"So in dark days look steadily on the darker side, for there is where brightness sometimes hides itself.

"Therefore let us have faith, hope, and daring. And who can doubt our future when even the wildest black man behind the wheel of a Cadillac knows— Please, please!" the Senator pleaded, his face a mask before the rising ripple of laughter, the clatter of applause, "Hear me out— I say that even the wildest black man rampaging the streets of our cities in a Fleetwood knows that it is not our fate to be mere victims of history but to be courageous and insightful before its assaults and riddles. Let us keep an eye on the outrages committed by the citizens whom I've just described, for perhaps therein lies a secret brightness, a clue. Perhaps the essence of his untamed and assertive wilfulness, his crass and jazzy defiance of good taste and the harsh, immutable laws of economics, lies his faith in the flexible soundness of the nation.

"Yes," the Senator smiled, nodding his head with mock Elizabethan swagger, "methinks there is much mystery here— But one mystery at a time, I say. In the meantime, let us seek brightness in darkness and hope in despair. Let us remind ourselves that we were not designated the supine role of passive slave to the past. Ours is the freedom and obligation to be ever the fearless creators of ourselves, the reconstructors of the world. We were created to be Adamic definers, namers and shapers of yet undiscovered secrets of the universe!

"Therefore, let the doubters doubt, let the faint of heart turn pale. We

244 · *Three Days Before the Shooting...*

move toward the fulfillment of our nation's demand for citizen-individualists possessing the courage to forge a multiplicity of creative selves and styles. We shall supply its need for individuals, men and women who possess the highest quality of stamina, daring, and grace—Ho,

> *Build thee more stately mansions,*
> *Oh, my soul—Yes!*

"For we," the Senator paused, his arms reaching out with palms turned upward in all-embracing gesture, "by the grace of Almighty God are A-MERI-CANS!"

And it was now, listening to his voice becoming lost in an explosion of applause, accented here and there by enthusiastic rebel yells, that the Senator became aware of the rising man.

Up in the front row center of the visitors' gallery the man was pointing out across the guardrail as though about to hurl down a vehement denunciation. *For Christ's sake,* the Senator thought, *Why don't you sit down or simply leave? Only spare us futile theatrical gestures. I always lose a few—the old, the short-of-attention-span; the mama's boys answering mother nature's call—but use your ears. Most I'm holding hard, so what can you hope to do?* But just as he lowered his eyes to the faces of his colleagues applauding on the floor below, the Senator became aware of the abrupt rise and fall of the man's still pointing arm. Then a sound of ringing, erupting above, seemed to trigger a prismatic turbulence of the light—through which, now, fragments of crystal, fine and fleeting as the first cool-touching flakes of a fall of snow, had begun to shower down upon him, striking sleet-sharp upon the still upturned palms of his gesturing hands.

My God, the Senator thought, *it's the chandelier! Could it be I've shattered the chandelier?* Whereupon something smashed into the lectern, driving it against him; and now, hearing a dry popping sounding above, he felt a vicious stinging in his right shoulder and as he stared through the chaotic refraction of the light toward the gallery he could see the sharp kick of the man's gesturing arm and felt a second flare of pain, in his left thigh this time, and was thrown into a state of dream-like lucidity.

Realizing quite clearly that the man was firing toward the podium, he tried desperately to move out of range, asking himself as he attempted to keep the lectern before him, *Is it me? Am I his target?* Then something struck his hip with the force of a well-aimed club and he felt the lectern toppling forward and he was spun forcefully around to face the gallery. Coughing and staggering backwards now, he felt himself striking against a chair and lurching forward as he marked the sinister *pzap! pzap! pzap!* of the weapon.

I'm going.... I'm going... he told himself, knowing lucidly that it was most

important to fall backwards if possible, out of the line of fire; but as he struggled to go down it was as though he were being held erect by an invisible
cable attached somehow to the gallery from where the man, raising and lowering his arm in measured calm, continued to fire.

The effort to fall brought a burst of moisture streaming from his pores
but even now his legs refused to obey, would not collapse. And yet, through
the muffled sound of the weapon and the strange ringing of bells, his eyes
were recording details of the wildly tossing scene with the impassive and
precise inclusiveness of a motion-picture camera that was toppling slowly
from its tripod and falling through an unfolding action with the lazy motion
of a feather loosed from a bird in soaring flight; panning from the image of
the remote gunman in the gallery down to those moving dream-like on the
floor before him, then back to those shooting up behind the man above; all
caught in attitudes of surprise, disbelief, horror; some turning slowly with
puppet gestures, some still seated, some rising, some looking wildly at their
neighbors, some losing control of their flailing arms, their erupting faces,
some falling floorward.... And up in the balcony now, an erupting of
women's frantic forms.

Things had accelerated but, oddly, even now no one was moving toward
the gunman—who seemed as detached from the swiftly accelerating action
as a marksman popping clay birds on a remote shooting range.

Then it was as though someone had dragged a poker at white heat straight
down the center of his scalp and followed it with a hammering blow; and at
last he felt himself going over backwards, crashing against a chair now and
hearing it skitter away, as, thinking mechanically, *Down, down...* he felt the
jolt of his head and elbows striking the floor. Something seared through the
sole of his right foot then, and sharply aware of losing control he struggled
to contain himself even as his throat gave cry to words which he knew, whatever the cost of containment, should not be uttered in this place.

"Lord, LAWD," he heard, "WHY HAST THOU..." smelling the hot
presence of blood as the question took off with the hysterical timbre of a
Negro preacher who in his disciplined fervor sounded somehow like an accomplished actor shouting his lines. *"Forsaken"...forsaken...forsaken,* the
words went forth, becoming lost in the shattering of glass, the ringing of
bells.

Writhing on the floor as he struggled to move out of range, the Senator
was taken by a profound sense of self-betrayal, as though he had stripped
himself naked in the Senate. And now, with the full piercing force of a suddenly activated sprinkler, streams of moisture seemed to burst from his face
*and somehow he was no longer in that place, but kneeling on the earth by a familiar
clearing within a grove of pines, trying desperately to enfold a huge white circus tent
into a packet. Here the light was wan and eerie, and as he struggled, trying to force the*

cloth beneath chest and knee, a damp wind blew down from the tops of the trees, causing the canvas to toss and billow like a live thing beneath him. The wind blew strong and damp through the clearing, causing the tent to flap and billow, and now he felt himself being dragged on his belly steadily toward the edge of the clearing where the light filtered with an unnatural brilliance through the high-flung branches of the pines. And as he struggled to break the forward motion of the tent a cloud of birds took flight, spinning on the wind and into the trees, revealing the low shapes of a group of weed-grown burial mounds arranged beneath the pines. Clusters of tinted bottles had been hung from wooden stakes to mark the row of crude country graves, and as the tent dragged him steadily closer he could see the glint and sparkle of the glass as the bottles, tossing in the wind, began to ring like a series of crystal bells. He did not like this place and he knew, struggling to brake the tent's forward motion by digging his toes into the earth, that somewhere beyond the graves and the wall of trees his voice was struggling to return to him.

But now through the amber and deep-blue ringing of the glass it was another voice he feared, a voice which threatened to speak from beneath the tent and which it was most important to enfold, to muffle beneath the billowing canvas . . .

Then he was back on the floor again and the forbidden words, now hoarsely transformed, were floating calmly down to him from gallery and dome, then coming on with a rush.

"For Thou hast forsaken . . . me," they came—but they were no longer his own words, nor was it his own echoing voice. And now, hearing what sounded like a man's voice hoarsely singing, he struggled to bring himself erect, thinking, *No! No! Hickman? But how here? Not here! No time, no place for HICKMAN!*

Then the very idea that Hickman was there somewhere above him raised him up, and he was clutching onto a chair, pulling himself into a sitting position, trying to get his head up so as to see clearly above as now there came a final shot which he heard but did not feel. . . .

He lay on his back, looking up through the turbulent space to where the bullet-smashed chandelier, swinging gently under the impact of its shattering, created a watery distortion of crystal light, a light which seemed to descend and settle him within a ring of liquid fire. Then beyond the pulsing blaze where a roiling darkness grew he was once more aware of a burst of action.

Now he could hear someone shouting far off. Then a voice was shouting quite close to his ear, but he was unable to bring his mind to it. There were many faces and he was trying to ask them *Why the hell'd he do it and who else was it?*

I can't understand, can't understand. My rule was graciousness, was politeness in all private contacts, but hell, anything goes in public. What? What?

Harry said if it gets too hot hop out of the pot. I say, if the tit's tough no one asks for milk when the steaks are high.

Lord, Lord, but it's hot. HOT! It hurts here and here and there and there, a hell of a clipping. How many rounds?

Lawd... Say Lord! Why? Ha! No time to go West but no time to stay East either, so blow the wind westerly, there's grease for the East.

I said, Donelson, crank it, man! Who broke the rhythm of the crowd? Old fat, nasty Poujaque! Don't accuse me; if I could pay them I could teach them! If they could catch me I could raise them up. That's their god-given historical, wood-pile role! Where was Moses, I mean to say?... No, let the deal go down. And if the cock crows three, I'm me, ME!—in the dark.

Roll the mammy-scratching camera, Karp! On with the lights! Hump it, now! Get them over to the right side. It hurts, it was worth something in the right body for the right hand...

Then I said, Politics is an art of maneuvering, and to move them you must change home base. Now you tell 'em because Ah stutter, Donelson said. But minds like that will never learn.... Hell, I've out-galloped gallup—New Mexico, wasn't it? What happened to Body? Well, so long old buddy, I missed touch, lost right hand but didn't forget. How the hell explain stony-going over stony ground?

Karp, you high-minded S.O.B., will you please *get some light over here! And keep the action going!...*

Yes, Yes, Yes! I'm all cud, bud; all chewed up like a dog! Like a dog. It was like shooting fish in a barbell. Fall! Fall! Take a dive! Green persimmons...

She said "mother" and screamed and I said "mother" and it shot out of my throat and something ran like hell up the tent and I doubled back and when I lifted the flap— dark again!

Roll the cameras!

What? What?

Perhaps you're right, but who would have thought what I knew on the back of my neck and ignored was ripening? A bird balled! That was the way it was. Oh, I rose up and she said "mother," and I doubled back and he looked down upon the babe and said, "Look, boy, you're a son of God! Isn't that enough for you?"

But still I said "mother" and something ran up the tent like a flash and then they came on, grim-faced and glassy-eyed, like the wrath of God in the shape of a leaping, many-headed cat... a stewardess's cap.... What dreams... what dread...

Don't ask me, please. Please don't ask me. I simply can't do it. There are lines and shadows we can't stand to cross or recross. Like walking through the sharp edge of a mirror. All will be well, Daddy. Tell them what I said.

ROLL THE CAMERA!

What? What?

Who was? Who did that against me? Who untuned Daddy's fork when he could have preached his bone in all positions and places? I might have been left out of all that—Ask Tricky Sam Nanton, there's a preacher hidden in all the old troms—Bam! Same tune in juke or church, only Daddy's had a different brand of anguish.

Lawd, Lawd, Why?

What terrible luck! What a sad kind of duck! Daddy strutted with some barbecue and the hot sauce on the bread was red and good—good—good. Yes, but in Austin they chillied the beans.

"Mother," she said.

"But weren't the greens nice in Birmingham," Sister Lacey said.

And she said "mother" and I came up out of the box and he said "Let there be light"—but he didn't really mean it. And she said "cud" and that should have been worth the revival. But he wouldn't tell.

Oh, Maggie, Jiggs and Aunt Jemima! Jadda-dadda—jing-jing! I miss those times sometimes. . . .

This game of politics is fraught with fraud, Ferd said—And a kiyi yippi and a happy nappy! So Pappy now praise the Lord, and pass the biscuits! Oh, yes, the A.G. said, Give ole Razorback Bill a guitar and the room to holler nigger and he'll forget about trying to pass for an intellectual. . . . A slow train through East Razorback on a Captain Billy's Whizbang more pious than the Pharisees. . . . Hell, it was easy, easy. I was working as the old gentlemen's chauffeur and he caught me in bed with his madam. He was amazed but calm. Who are you, anyway, he said. And I thought fast and said, I'm a nigger; so you can forget it, it don't count. I'm outside the game. What? he said. Yes, I said, I am—or at least I was raised for one. So what are you going to do about it? And he said, Do? Hell, first I'm going to think about it. And then I'll decide. Was she satisfied? I don't know, I said, but I've had no complaints. Well, he said, taking that into consideration you might as well continue until she does. I'm a busy man and no old fool. Meanwhile I'll think about making you a politician. That should teach you to obey the Commandment. . . . So because she was years younger than the old gentleman I made a classical entry into the house. Bull-rushed the bully raggers. . . . Yes, but you just wait, he said. The spades'll learn to play the game and use their power and the old war will be ended. . . .

Oh, no! We'll legislate the hell against them. Sure, they must learn to play the game but power is as power does. Let's not forget what the hell this is all about. They'll have to come in as I did—through the living gate and sometimes it's bloody. But they ought to know from back in seventy-four.

Mister Movie-man . . . she said.

God is love, I said, but art's the possibility of forms, and shadows are the source of identity. And Donelson said, You tell 'em, buddy, while I go take a physic. . . .

Hold the scene, don't fade, don't fade. . . . Seven's the number, Senator, I said. Fiscal problems come up seven, remember? Even for Joseph. . . . So she said, "mother" and I said me and she said cud was worth all that pain. But he still wouldn't tell.

Back away from me! Cat . . . cat . . . what's the rest?

I simply refused, that was all. Chicken in a casket was a no good-a union like-a da cloak. Too dark in there. Chick in this town, chick in that town and in the country. Always having to break out of that pink-lined shell.

No, not afraid after a while, but still against it. I was pretty little—little though not pretty, understand? Saw first snow in Kansas. The wind blows cold, but I can't tuck it.

Look, I have to climb out of here immediately, or the wires will flash Cudworth moos for Ma—a hell of a note from now on. And on the other side there's the dark. Daddy? Hic, hic, what day?

To hell with it, I've stood up too long to lie down.

Lawd, Lawd, why?

Inevitable? Well, I suppose so. So focus in the scene. There, there. The right Honorable Daddy—where?

Karp! Karp, pan with the action—See! See! He's riding right out from under his old Cordoba. But watch him, Stack wore a magic hat—Listen for a bulldog!

Beliss?

No! What do you know about that? I can't hear him bark . . .

Bliss be-eeee thee ti-ee that binds . . .

For an instant the Senator was aware of being lifted up and then he heard a voice speaking to him out of blackness. Straining to hear through the clamor of voices sounding in his head, he felt himself entering a region of blacks and grays which seemed now to revolve slowly around him like a cloud of smoke. And yet he felt in the presence of an unyielding center of darkness which seemed to speak to him words that were weighted with meanings he dreaded to grasp.

It hurts here, shadowless, his mind went on. *If only the throbbing would stop. . . . Who-what-why—Lord? Why, why, the smithereening heart . . .*

Then from far away someone was calling to him, "Senator, do you hear? Senator?"

And yes, the Senator did; very clearly now. Yes. . . . But when he tried to answer he seemed to fall into a dream, to recall to himself a dream. . . .

It was a bright day and he said, Come on out here, Bliss. I've got something to show you. And I went with him through the garden past the apple trees and on beneath the grape arbor to the barn. The bees were around us and yellow butterflies. And there it was, sitting outside the barn on two sawhorses.

Look at that, he said.

It was some kind of long narrow box. I didn't like it.

I said, What is it?

It's for the services, Bliss. For the revivals. Remember me and Deacon Wilhite talking about it?

No, sir.

Sure, you remember. It's for you to come up out of. You're going to be resurrected so that the sinners can find life everlasting. Bliss, a preacher is a man who carries God's load; and that's the whole earth, Bliss boy. The whole earth and all the people thereupon. And he smiled.

Oh, I said, I remember. But before it hadn't meant too much. Since then Juney had died and I had seen one. Juney's was pine, painted black, and without scrolls; this one was fancy, covered with white cloth. I felt cold. He held his belly in his hands, thumbs stuck in trousers top, his great shoes creaking as he rocked back and forth on his heels.

So how you like it? he said.

He was examining the lid, swinging it up and down with his hand. I couldn't see how it was put together. It seemed to be all white cloth bleeding into pink and pink into white again.

I said, Is it for *me?*

Sho, didn't I just tell you? We get it all worked out the way we want it, and then, sinners, watch out!

I could feel my fingers turn cold at the tips. But why is it so big? I said. I'm not that tall. In fact, I'm pretty little for my age.

Yeah, but this one has got to last, Bliss. Can't be always buying you one of these like I do when you scuff out your shoes or bust out the seat of your britches....

But my feet won't touch the end, I said. I hadn't looked all the way inside.

Yeah, but in a few years or two they will. By time your voice starts to change your feet will be pushing out one end and your head out the other. I don't want even to have to think about another one before then.

But couldn't you get a smaller one?

That's *just* what we don't want, Bliss. If it's too *small* they won't notice it, or think of it as applying to themselves; if it's too big they'll laugh when they see you come rising up.

No, Bliss, it's got to be *this* size. They have to see it and feel it for what it is, not take it for a toy like one of those little tin wagons or autos. Down there in Mexico one time I saw them selling these here in the form of sugar candy along with skulls and skeletons made out of sugar candy, but ain't no use trying to sugarcoat it. No, sir, Bliss. They've got to see it and know that what they're seeing is where they've all got to end up. Bliss, that thing sitting on these saw hosses there is *everybody's* last clean shirt, as the old song goes; and they've got to realize that when that sickle starts to cut its swath it don't play no favorites. *Every*body goes when *that* wagon comes, Bliss. Babies and grandmaws too, 'cause there simply ain't no exceptions. Death *is* like Justice is *supposed* to be. So you see, Bliss, it's got to be of a certain size.... Hop in there and let's see how it fits....

Lord, Lord, Why Hast...

Then he was being lifted up and struggling, trying desperately to make himself heard:

No, please, please, Daddy Hickman. PLEASE!

Oh, it's just for a little while, Bliss. You won't be in the dark for long, and you'll be wearing your white dress suit with the satin lapels and the long pants with the satin stripes down the sides. You'll like that, won't you, Bliss? Sure you will. In that pretty suit? Of course!

Now you see, you breathe through this here tube we done fixed here in the lid. See? It comes through right here, only the opening is hidden by this scroll. You hear what I'm saying, Bliss? All right, pay attention. Look here at this tube! All you have to do is lay there and breathe through it. Just breathe in and out like you always do, only through the tube. And when you hear me say, "Suffer the little children..." you push it up inside the lid, so's they can't see it when me and Deacon Wilhite open up the lid.

But then I won't have air.

Don't worry about that, Bliss; there'll be air enough left inside and Deacon Wilhite will open it right away.

But I'm scaird. In all that darkness and all that silk cloth around my mouth and eyes....

Silk, he said, Silk? He looked down at me steadily. What else you want it lined with, Bliss? Cotton? Would you feel any better about it if it was something most folks have to work all their lives for and wear every day, weekdays and Sunday too? Something that most folks never get away from? You don't want that, do you?

I shook my head, shamed. Oh, the tyranny of King Cotton....

And it won't be but a few minutes, Bliss. You can even take your teddy with you—no, I guess you better take your toy Easter bunny. With your Easter bunny you won't be afraid, will you? Course not. And like I tell you, it will last no longer than it takes the big boys to march you down the aisle— I'll have you some good strong, big fellows, big ones, so you don't have to worry about them dropping you.

Now, Bliss, you'll hear the music and the boys will march in and set it down right in front of the pulpit. Then I'll say, "Suffer the little children," and you sit up, see? I say do you see, Bliss?

Yessuh.

Say *Sir.*

Sir.

Good. Don't talk like I talk, Bliss; talk like I *say* talk. And use your ears. Words are your business, boy! not just *the* Word. Words are everything and don't you forget it, ever.

Yes, sir.

Now, when you rise up you come up slow—don't go bolting up like a jack-in-the-box, understand? Because you don't want to scair the living daylights out of everybody. You just want to come up slow and easy. And be sure you don't mess up your hair. I want that part to be still in it, neat. So don't forget when we close you in. And don't be chewing on no gum or sucking on no wine balls! You hear me? Hear me now, boy!

Yes, sir, I said. I was watching it. I couldn't turn my eyes away.

Can you hear me?

Hear, the Senator thought, *Here it must have been a forty-five, no thirty-thirties in here. . . . It hearts here, four cross. Here and hear and there and air. Light-throbs. . . . Chandelier. . . . How high the night? How far? Far . . .*

It all depends on the size of the church, Bliss. You listening to what I'm saying?

Yes, sir.

Well, when you hear me say, "Suffer the little children," you sit up slow, and like I tell you, things are going to get as quiet as the grave. Yes, and I better have the ladies get us some flowers. Roses would be good. Red ones. Nobody in this town would have any lilies. Least not anyone *we* know. So now, we'll have it sitting near the pulpit so when you rise up you'll be facing forward and every living soul will see you. It'll be something, Bliss. It'll be astounding!

Yes, sir.

So now I don't want you to open your eyes right off. Yes, and you better have your Bible in your hands—and leave that rabbit down in there.

Yes, sir.

So what are you suppose to say when you rise up?

I ask the Lord how come he has forsaken me.

That's right, that's correct, Bliss. You ask him, *Why hath Thou forsaken me?* But say it with the true feeling, hear? And in good English. That's right, Bliss, in Good Book English. I guess it's about time I started reading you some Shakespeare and some Emerson. Yeah, it's just about time. . . . Who's Emerson? Why, he was a preacher, Bliss, and a philosopher too. He knew that every tub has to sit on its own bottom—which is a fact that a lot of folks would like to forget. He wrote a lot of good stuff. Poetry and all. Have you remembered the rest of the sermon I taught you?

Yes, sir, but in the dark I don't think I . . .

Never mind the dark, Bliss. When you come to *Why hast Thou forsaken me,* on the "me" I want you to open your eyes and let your head go back, slow. And you want to spread out your arms wide—like this, see? Lemme see you try it. . . .

Like this?

That's right. That's pretty good. Only you better look a bit sadder, more solemn. Things have gotten to you, remember—those Roman soldiers and all, you see?—and you're sad and bewildered by what's happened. And although you know it had to happen because the prophets had predicted it, you just can't help but ask the question. That's the human in you. So you want to look like you feel it, Bliss. So I want you to spread your arms out slow, like this. Then you start with *I am the resurrection and the life.* Say it after me:

I am the resurrection . . .

I am the resurrection.

And—

An' the life...

Good, but not too fast, now. I am the Lily of the valley...

I am the Lily of the valley...

Uh huh, pretty good.... I am the bright and morning star...

The bright and morning star...

Thy rod...

Thy rod and Thy staff...

Good, Bliss, I couldn't trap you in the rhythm. All right, that's enough. You remember all those *I's* have got to be in it. Don't leave out those *I's,* Bliss, because it takes a heap of *I's* before the folks can see the true vision or hear the true Word.

They pain here and here and there and there. How far the sight? The Scene?... In Tulsa, after the tent meeting, they gave me a Black Cow, sweet teat of root beer and cool glob of ice cream.... He taught me to ha and ah deep in my throat like a blues singer. Horehound, honey, and lemon drops. Cool against the heat of all that fire.... It hurts here and here and there and there. Long nails.

"Senator, can you see me?"

Ha! The merry-go-round broke down!

Up there on Brickyard Hill the octagonal tents shimmered white in the sunlight. Below, My God, sweet Jesus, lay the devastation of the green wood! Ha! And in the blackened streets the entrails of men, women, and baby grand pianos, their songs sunk to an empty twang struck by the aimless whirling of violent winds. Behold! Behold the charred foundations of the House of God! Oh, but then, in those sad days came Bliss, the preacher.... Came Bliss, the preacher.... No more came Bliss.

Daddy Hickman, I said, can I take Teddy too?

Teddy? Just why you have to have that confounded bear with you *all* the time, Bliss? Ain't the Easter bunny enough? And your little white leather Bible, your kid-bound Word of God? Ain't that enough for you, Bliss?

But it's dark in there and I feel much braver with Teddy, because Teddy's a bear and bears aren't afraid of the dark....

Never mind all that, Bliss. And don't you start preaching me no sermon—especially none of them you make up yourself. You just preach what I been teaching you and there'll be enough folks out there tonight who'll be willing to listen to you, and some will even be saved. I tell you, Bliss, you're going to make a fine preacher and you're starting at just the right age. You're just a little over six and even Jesus Christ didn't get started until he was twelve. But you have *got* to leave that bear alone! Why, I even heard you *preaching* to that bear the other day. Bears don't give a doggone about the Word, Bliss. Did you ever hear of a *bear* of God? Of course not. Now there was the Lamb of God, and the Holy Dove, and one of the saints, Jerome, he had him a lion, and another had him some kind of bull with wings—a flying bull, that is—it was probably some kind of early airplane; and Peter had the keys to the Rock. But, Bliss, no *bears*! So you think about that, you hear? You find yourself another mascot.

He looked at me with that gentle, joking look then, smiling with his eyes, and I felt better.

You think you could eat some ice cream?

Oh, yes, sir.

You do? Well, here; take this four bits and go get us each a pint. You look kinda hot. Just look at you, Bliss, I can see the steam rising right out of your collar. In fact, I suspect you're already on fire. You better hurry and get that ice cream fast. Make mine strawberry. Ice cream is good for a man's belly and if he has to sing and preach a lot like we do it's good for his throat too. Wait a second, where'd I put that money? Here it is. Ice cream is good if you don't overdo it—but I don't guess I have to recommend it to you though, do I, Bliss? 'Cause you're already sunk deep in the ice-cream habit, aren't you? In fact, Bliss, if eating ice cream was a sin you'd sail to hell in a freezer.... Ha! Ha! Now, now, don't look at me like that, Bliss. I was only kidding. Don't look at me that way, old boy. Here, take this dime and bring us some of those chocolate marshmallow cookies you love so well. Hurry on now, and watch out for the wagons and those autos....

Hickman? How here? Long past. From far off he could hear the tinkle of ice in a glass. When he laughed his belly shook like Santa Claus. Huge, tall, slow-moving, like a carriage of state in ceremonial parade, until on the platform, then a man of words. Black Garrick, Alonzo Zuber, "Daddy" Hickman. Reverend Doctor Mixeddiction, Dialectical Donne, Shookup Shakespeare....

GOD'S GOLDEN-VOICED HICKMAN

BETTER KNOWN

AS GOD'S TROMBONE

they billed him. Brother A.Z., to Deacon Wilhite, when they were alone. Drank elderberry wine beneath the trees together discussing the Word, and me with a mug of milk and a buttered slice of homemade bread.

It was Waycross.

I came down the plank walk past the Bull Durham sign where a white, black-spotted dog raised his leg against the weeds and saw them. They were squatting in the dust along the curb, pushing trucks made of wood blocks with snuff-box tops for wheels. Garrets and Tube Rose but all the same size. Then I was there and one turned, fingering for a booger in his nose, saying:

Look here, y'all, here's Bliss. Says he's a preacher.

They stood, looking with disbelieving eyes, dust on their knees, making me like Jesus among the Philistines.

Who, him? One of them pointed. A *preacher?*

Yeah, man.

Hi, I, Bliss, said.

He looked at me, one eyebrow raised, his lips protruding. A dark, half-moon-shaped scar showed beneath his left cheekbone. The others were ganging up on me in their faces, closing in.

What he doing all dressed up like Sunday for? he said.

Who?

Him.

'Cause he's a preacher, fool.

Heck, he don't look like no preacher to me. Just looks like another lil ole high-yaller. What you say's his name?

Bliss. They swear he's a preacher.

Sho do, the bowlegged one said. My mama heard him preach. Grown folks talking 'bout him all over town. He real notoriety, man.

Shucks! Y'all know grown folks is crazy. What can this here lil ole jaybird preach? A.B.C.? Hell, I can preach that just like ole Rev-um McDuffie does and he's the best.

I watched his hands go behind his back, his chin drawing down and his eyes looking up, as though peering over the rims of spectacles as he frowned.

Brothers and sisters, ladies and what comes with you, my text this mawning is A.B.C. Y'all don't like to think about such stuff as that, but you better lissen to me. I said *A*—Whew, Lord! I says A! Just listen, just think about it. A! A! *Assay!* In the beginnin' there was A.B. and C. The Father, the son, and the son-of-a-gun! I want you to think about it. Git in it and git out of it. I said A.B.C., Lawd....

He shook his head grimly, his mouth turning down at the corners, his tone becoming soft then rising as he hammered his palm with his fist. A.B.C.D.E.F.—double-down D! Think about the righteous Word. Where would we be without A? Nowhere 'cause it's the start. Turn b around and what you got? I'll tell you what you got, you got a doggone nowhere d! Y'all better mind! I say you sinners better mind y'all's A.B.C.s and zees!

He grinned. I had me a Bible and a pulpit I could really lay that stuff, he said. Is that the kind of preachin' he does?

And one in a blue suit and tettered head defended me on heard words.

You crazy, man. 'Cause he *really* preaches.... Any of us can do what you doing.

That's what *you* say. So what do he preach?

Salvation. What all the grown preachers preach.

Sali*vation?* Hey, that's when your mouth gits sore and your teeth fall out, ain't it? Don't he want folks to have no teeth?

I said sal-*va*tion. You heard me.

Oh! Well tell a poor fool!

Don't you min' him, Bliss. He's just acting a clown.

He grinned and picked up a pebble with his toes.

No I ain't neither, I just ain't never seen no half-pint preacher before. Hey, Bliss, say "when."

"When" what?

Just *when.*

Why?

Just 'cause. Go on, do like I tole you; say "when."

So maybe I wouldn't have to fight him—and blessed are the peacemakers—"When," I said.

Aw come on; if you a preacher say it strong.

WHEN!

WHEN THE HEN BREAKS WIND—See, I got you!

They laughed. I tried to grin. My lip wouldn't hold.

I sho got you that time, Bliss. Hell, you can't be no preacher, 'cause a preacher'd know better than to git caught that easy. You all right, though. You want to shoot some marbles? Man, dressed up the way you is, you ought to be a *real* gambler.

Not now, I have to go to the store. Maybe I can tomorrow.

Say, Rev, if you so smart, what's the name of that dog who licked those sores poor Lazarus had?

He didn't have a name, I said.

Yes he did too. He name Mo' Rover! Dam', Rev, we got you agin!

I said, You mean *more*-over.

He said, Shucks, how can you have *Mo'* Rover when he ain't got *no* Rover?

They laughed.

He a nasty dog, licking blood, someone said.

Sho. There's a heap of nasty things in the Bible, man.

Hey y'all, he said, even for a yella he's a good fella. Let's teach him a church song before he goes. They crowded around.

Sing this with me, Rev, he said, beginning like Daddy Hickman lining out a hymn:

> *Well, ah-mazing grace*
> *How sweet*
> *The sound. . . . .*
> *A bullfrog slapped*
> *His grand-mammy*
> *Down. . . . .*

He watched me, grinning like an egg-sucking dog. I looked back, feeling my temper rise.

Hey, whatsamatter, Rev, he said. Don't you like my song?

Man, Bowlegs said, you know don't no preacher go for none of that mess. Bliss here is a real preacher and that stuff you singing is sinful.

Oh, it is, he said. Then how come nobody never tole me? I guess I better hurry up and sing him a *real* church song so he'll forgive me. What's more come Sunday I'm going to his church and do my righteous duty. Here's a real righteous one, Rev!

> *Well, I'm going to the church house*
> *And gon' climb up to the steeple*
> *Said I'm going to Rev's little ole church house*
> *Gon' climb up on the steeple*
> *Gon' take down my britches, baby,*
> *And doo-doo—whew, Lawd!—*
> *Straight down on the people!*

I looked at him and gritted my teeth. My face felt swollen. No bigger'n me and trying to be a great big sinner. I thought: Saint Peter bit off an ear but still got the keys. Amen! I looked on the ground, searching for a rock.

Boy, I said, before you were just pranking with me; now you're messing with the Lord. And just for that He's going to turn you into a crow.

Shoots, he said. *Who?* You can't scair me. Less see you.

I said *He* will do it, not me. You just wait and see.

Hell, I can't wait that long. Goin' on a cotton-pick next month. Goin' hear all those big guys tell all those good ole lies. See, he said, bending over and patting his bottom. I ain't no crow. Can't see no feathers shooting outta my behind....

They laughed, watching me. I reproached him with all the four horses galloping in my eyes.

Suddenly Bowlegs stepped close and looked him up and down, frowning.

Yeah, man, you might be right about your behind, he said. But while I don't see no feathers, your *mouth* is getting awful long and sharp. And while you always been black now I be dam' if you ain't begun to turn *blue* black!

Man, he said, taking a swing at Bowlegs, you better watch that stuff 'cause I don't play with no chillen.

Hey, Rev, he said, here's a church song my big brother taught me. He up in Chicago and this one's *really* religious:

> *Well, the tom cat jumped the she-cat*
> *By the bank of a stream*

> *Started howling and begging for that*
> *Natural cream.*
> *Soon the she-cat was spitting and*
> *A-scratching and a-kicking up sand*
> *Then the he-cat up and farted*
> *Like a natural man.*
> *The she-cat she jumped salty, looked around*
> *And screamed,*
> *Said, Hold it right there, daddy,*
> *Until your mama's been redeemed.*

As they laughed he joined in with his juicy mouth, rearing back with his thumbs thrust in his suspenders.

Hell, he said, I'm a poet and didn't know it.

He did a rooster strut, flapping his arms and scuffing up the dust.

Hey, y'all, he said, listen to this:

> *Bliss, Bliss*
> *Cat piss miss!*

He flicked his fingers at me like a magician, taking my name in vain.

Man, you sho got a fine kinda name to put down a conjur with. If a man was to say your name at two dogs gitting they ashes hauled the he-dog'll git a dog-knot in his peter as big as a baseball! They be hung up for ninety-nine days. That's right y'all. You say Rev's name to a guy throwing rocks at you and he couldn't hit the side of a barn with a wiffle tree! Heck, Bliss, you say your name and hook fingers with another guy when a dog's taking him a hockey and you lock up his bowels like a smokehouse! Yeah, man, the First National Bank! Constipate that fool for life!

They laughed at me. I saw a good egg rock now and looked at him, mad. I was going to sin. Saint Peter, he got the keys.

Since you think you're so smart, now here's one for you, I said. *Meat Whistle.* That's for you.

What?

He puzzled up his face.

You heard me, I said. *Meat Whistle.*

He bucked his eyes like I had hit him. It was quiet. I bent and picked up the rock. Someone snickered.

What you mean? he said, I never heard of no *meat* whistle. . . .

They looked at us, changing sides now. Ha, he got you! one of them said. Ain't but one kind of meat whistle and us all got one, ain't we, y'all?

Yeah, yeah, that's right, they said.

The whites of his eyes were turning red. I backed away.

What kinda dam' whistle is that, he said. It bet' not be what I think it is.

He doubled up his fists.

I watched his eyes.

It blows some real bad-smelling tunes, don't it, Bliss? one of the others said.

I watched his eyes, red. You ain't the only one who knows stuff like that, I said. Just because I'm a preacher, don't think you can run over me.

They were laughing at him now.

Tell him 'bout it, Rev!

Ole Bliss is awright!

Watch out now, ole Rev's colored blood is rising....

Indian, man! Look at him!

Ole Bliss is awright! Look at him, y'all. He probably got him some mean cracker blood too, man!

He looked angry, his lips pouting. Maybe you know this one, I said.

Clank, clank, clank, I said and waited, watching his eyes.

What you mean, "clank, clank, clank," little ole yella som'bitch?

Clank, clank, clank, I said, that's your mama walking in her cast-iron drawers.

Seeing his face looming close, I moved.

He came on at me but too late, I wasn't there. Always switch the rhythm—

Watch out, Bliss! they called, but I missed him not. I struck hard, seeing his surprise as the blood burst from his forehead like juice from a crushed blackberry. His face went gray as his hand flew to his forehead. I looked, then I ran backwards with sin running with me in my eyes. I held the rock cupped in my hand like an egg, feeling his blood on my fingers. On this rock I will build my ... Kept it with Teddy, my leather-bound Bible.

You shoulda used some catpiss, man, their shouts sounded behind me. 'Cause he ain't missed *nothing*. Look at ole Rev run! Boooom! Barney-O-Bliss, man! Barney-O-Blissomobile.

Put some salt on his tail. You aim to catch him you got to turn on the gas, man.

Man, he may be a reverend but he runs like hell!

Taking it on the lamb chop, man.

Aches, breaks. Wine and crackers, you're out, Bliss. Out!

No, I'll be there when he arrives. We agreed.... I'll ...

They relaxed in their chairs, the whiskey between them. Only the air-conditioning unit hummed below their voices. O'Brien was intense.

Listen, he said. Dam' it, we're losing your state and my state and even

New York seems doubtful. You'll have to lay off the nigger issue because the niggers and the New York Jews are out to get us. This year they don't have to take it and they won't. Here, try one of these. No, smoke it. There's plenty where that comes from.... But you restrain yourself, you hear? We want you to curb that mouth of yours or else.... *Make me whole, patch my sole... It hurts here and here and there and there.*

We made every church in the circuit. Lights! Camera!

Suffer the little children to come suffer the little children to come sufferthelittlechildrentocome Sufferthelittlechildrentohospodepomeli—

Why don't they hurry and open the light? Please, Please, Please, Daddy!

And I rose up slow, the white Bible between my palms, my panicky head thrusting up into frenzied shouting and the hushed silence, up, up, up, up—into the certainty of his mellow voice now soaring isolated and calm like a note of spring water burbling in a glade haunted by the counter-rhythm of tumbling, nectar-drunk bumblebees....

Teddy, Teddy! Where's my bear? Daddy!

You bear as you've sown. A growl.

Then, he appeared out of the brilliant darkness, dark and handsome.

You must not be startled at this blessed boy-chile, sisters and brothers, he intoned. Not by this little jewel. For it has been said that a little child shall lead them. Oh, yes! Where He leads me, I shall *follow*. Amen! And our God said, "Go ye into the wilderness and preach the Word," and this child has answered the sacred call. And he obeys. Suffer the little children. Yes! And it is said that the child is father to the man. So why be surprised over the size, shape, color of the vessel? Why not listen to his small sweet voice and drink in the life-giving water of the Word?...

Listen to the lamb, he said. But I heard the bear a-growling. Teddy! Teddy! Where? Gone on the lamb's chop.

I used to lie within the box, trembling. Breathing through the tube, the hot air heavy with muted hypnotic music, hear the steady moaning beneath the rhythmic clapping of hands. And boxed they marched me down a thousand aisles on a thousand nights and days. In the dark! Trembling in the dark. Lying in the dark while the words seemed to fall like drops of rain upon the resonant lid. Until each time, just at the moment the black shapes seemed to close in upon me, smothering me, Deacon Wilhite would calmly raise the lid and I'd rise up slowly, slowly, creating a scene. Frightened, I arose, slowly, stiffly, as melodramatic as della Francesca's bombastic ham actor flaunting his shroud. With my white Bible between my palms, carefully lest the pink lining disturb my parted hair. Trembling now, with the true hysteria of my voice giving cry: LORD, LORD, WHY....

Mankind? What? Correct. Lights in. Camera!

Donelson, the makeup is too pasty. The dark skin shines through like green ghosts.

Yeah, but you tell me how to make up a flock of crows to look like swans.

Donelson, you can do anything that you really try. In the beginning is the image. Use your imagination, man. Imagine a nation. New. Look into the camera's omniscent eye, there's a magic in it. And the crows shall be...

Whiter than swans? Balls! Let's change the script and make them Chinamen or Indians.... What do you say, Karp?

And in the confusion birthed by women that world rolled on like rushes on a Moviola. There'd be shouting and singing and that big woman in Jacksonville came running down front, looking like a fullback in a nurse's helper's uniform, crying, He's the Lamb of God, he is! And trying to lift me out and Teddy coming up with my legs and my cap pistol catching in the lining and Daddy Hickman grabbing her just in time to prevent the congregation from seeing, saying sotto voce, Deacon Wilhite, *git* this confounded woman away from here even if you have to put a headlock on the fool! She's about to upset *everything!*

He took Teddy and refused to buy me a soda and the next night I refused to rise up. I refused the call, just lay there in the throbbing death-like stillness with the top up and my eyes closed against the brilliant light and him looming with outstretched arms above me, until he got them singing strong and came down and promised me I could have Teddy back.... When? *Beary me not in lone Calv'ry....* Then standing there above me the shadow leaving and the light bright to my opened eyes, saying, This boy chile, brothers and sisters, lies here in a holy coma. No doubt he's seeing visions beyond this wicked world. Ah, but he shall rise up as all the saved shall rise up—on that morning....

But I didn't budge, demanding an ice-cream cone with silence. Vanilla I wanted.

Suffer the little children to come....

Flora was in the alley picking sunflowers. We were alone. I'll show you mine if you'll show me yours, I said.

What! Button up your britches, lil ole boy, she said. You ain't even old enough to dog-water.

But I just want to *see.*

You goin' see stars, that's what you gonna see, 'cause I'm goin' to tell my mama if you don't go 'way.

Nine stitches saved Choc Charlie, or so they say.

One morning shining his shoes in Georgia I heard him singing,

> *I'm going to the Nation, baby,*
> *Going to the Territory.*
> *Says I'm going to the Nation...*
> *Going to the Territory...*

like any lonesome sinner but making it sound like "Beulah Land," puzzling me.

It haunts here and there; in and out.

Why don't Revern' Hickman open. . . . They were all hicks; I told me then, that's why I renounced them beyond all recovery. What a hickery-docket was Hick hock—the camera, Donelson; we've got to keep moving west. Hail to the great hickrocracy. It hurts there. The waters of life. Thirst. Texas hots. Ladies and gentlemen, I swear, it was a strange adventure.

I met Mr. Rabbit
Down by the pea vine
And I asked him where he's gwine
Well, he said, Just kiss my b'hin'
And skipped on down the pea vine

Mr. Speaker, Mr. Speaker! I should like to call to the attention of this great body the insidious activities of those alien-minded groups who refuse the sacred obligations of becoming true Americans. . . . *How here I reject them and out of my rejection rule them. They create their own darkness and in their embarrassment left all to chance my changed opportunity. It haunts hard in this moment.* . . . Oh, they sweep around us with their foreign ways. Yes, and in the second and third generations they reject even these foreign but respectable traditional modes of their parents and become barbarians, maimed men; moral terrorists, winos, full of self-pity. Men filled only with the defeatist spirit of rejection. They become whiners and complainers, demanding the deification of their sloth. The soft touch. Nothing here in our fine, hard-won American tradition is good enough for them. Always it is some other way of life which wins them. It is the false promises of our enemies for which they thirst and hunger. Yes, and sabotage! Mr. Speaker, in their arrogance they would destroy our tender vines. And in their fury they would weaken the firm foundation of our way of life. In their malicious frenzy to evade responsibility they would destroy that which has given them shelter and substance, and the right to create themselves. Oh yes! Yes! These rootless ones would uproot us all! Consider the time-scene: When they watch our glorious flag passing on parade they greet it with an inward sneer. When we honor our fallen dead, they secretly applaud the marksmanship of our enemies. When we set forth to preserve our honor and the sanctity of our homes and the health of our customs they would cast into the smooth machinery of our national life their intractable and treacherous wooden shoes. Abuse, abuse! In the name of lawful dissent they seek our destruction. They would poison the spring of our unity. They would destroy the horses of our power. They would reduce our sacred diversity and dominate us! They would send the zapper of their hate to mine the defenses of our belief. They would pull down the protective walls of our fortress. But leave us to the peaceful glories of this great land they will not!

Ah Bliss, Bliss, so you've come to this. And I believed . . .

Nay! Nay! They would sweep over us with their foreign ways. They would undermine us with their un-Christian doubt. They are a thorn in our flesh, a dagger in our back; a putrid offense in the nostrils of every true red-blooded American. And it is time that we defend ourselves. We have been asleep, Mr. Speaker, my fellow citizens; asleep in our dream of security! Asleep in our well-meaning, sportsmanlike way of wishing the other fellow well. Asleep in the false security of accepting all men of goodwill who would be free as men of honor. And, I'm sorry to say, we have not been vigilant enough in administering our heritage. Our stewardship has been indeed faulty, so the fault is our own. For while we've looked the other way these internal enemies have become in the words of that great Irish poet, kinsman no doubt to many of our colleagues here, in the words of Yeats—these enemies have become all too full of passionate intensity! Though fluent and often multilingual, they have not learned to speak in the true spirit of our glorious tongue—and yet, they strive to destroy it! They have not earned the right to harbor such malice, for this country has been kind to them. It has demanded little of them, and yet, they declare us decadent, deceptive, immoral, and arrogant. Nor has our social life given them justification for such cynical disillusionment; such loss of confidence. Indeed, the country has strengthened them. It has freed them of the past and its terror. Yes, we have given them the strength which they would use against us. They have not the right even when most sincere to criticize us in the name of other so-called democracies. For they believe in *no* democracy! For there are those among us who yearn for the tyrant's foot upon their necks! They long for authority, brutal and unyielding. It is their nature to lick the boots of the strong and to spit in the faces of those weaker than themselves. This is their conception of the good life. This is their idea of security! This is their way, the way they would substitute for our principle of individual freedom, the way in which man faces nature, society, and the universe with confidence. Moving from triumph to triumph, ever increasing the well-being of all. . . . Each and every true American is the captain of his fate, the master of his own conscience.

Ah, yes! But somewhere we failed. We let down the gates and failed to draw the line, forgetting in our democratic pride that there were men in this world who *fear* our freedom; who, as they walk along our streets, cry out for the straitjacket of tyranny. They do not wish to think for themselves and they hate those of us who do. They do not desire to make—they tremble with dread at the very idea of making—their own decisions; who feel comfortable only with the whip poised ever above their heads. They hunger to be hated, persecuted, spat upon, and mocked so that they can justify their overwhelming and destructive pride and contempt for all who are different, for they are incapable of being American. They are false Americans, for being an American is truly to accept the hero's task as a condition of our everyday living and to bring it off with conscious ease! It is to take the risk of loneliness with open eyes; to face the forest with empty hands but with stout heart. To face the universal chaos in the name of human freedom and to win! To win even though we die but win and win again each day! To win and take the suffering that goes with winning along with the joy. To look any man in the face, unhindered by Europe's deadweight of vicious traditions. It is to take a stand, a man alone. . . . Going West.

Ah, it holds hard. Camera! Lights! Lights! Never cut call—now action.

Bliss, he said, there's but one thing keeping you from being a great preacher—you just won't learn to sing! A preacher just has *got* to sing, Bliss. But I guess from whoever it was gave you that straight hair and white skin took away your singing voice. Of course you're still pretty young. I just don't know, Bliss. I guess I have to do a lot of praying over you, 'cause you're definitely a preacher. . . .

Preach, cried the King and forty thousand strained out the words.

Mr. Speaker. . . . How far the heights?

Yes, preach! But how could I sing the Lord's song, a stranger man?

Mr. Speaker, I will be recognized. . . .

I took her for a walk under the cottonwood trees. The sticky buds lay on the ground. Spring warned me but I was young and foolish and how could I not go on and then go on? How make progress with her along? I had nothing, I was a bird in flight. And it was as though I mounted her in midair, and we were like a falcon plummeting with its prey. Pray for me—now. No, I was gentle then. She melted me. She poised me in time tenderly. Pray, for it was so. A gentle bird, but I was high and flying faster, faster, faster. I traveled light, Donelson said, so I could roll up the moss. To make the most of circumstance, I flew. What was possible was possible in one way only, in a spiralling flight. Who could release more than vague hopes for heaven on a movie screen. . . . Lights!

Now the Senator could hear a voice quietly calling, *Bliss? You hear me, Bliss?* but was too weary to respond. His lips refused to answer, his throat throbbed with unstated things, the words starting up from deep within his mind and lodging there. He could not make them sound, and he thought, The circuit is out; I'm working with cables like those of Donelson's lights, scenes go dark and there's only a sputtering along the wire.

Yet his mind flowed dreamily and deep behind the purple shadows, welling from depths of time he had forgot, one short-lived self mysteriously surviving all the years and turns of face. Once I broke the string I whirled, I scudded the high places, bruised against treetops and building spires, snagged here and there for a time but always sailing. But once spring turned me turtle, I tried to sing—that's a part he doesn't know. The old bliss still clung to me, childlike beneath my restlessness, stubborn. Liked the flight of birds then; cardinals streaking red across the fields, red wings on blackbirds and whistling quail at eveningtide. And metal-blue dragonflies and ladybirds in the dust, and catleaps in the sun. Black cat poised on hind feet like a boxer, paws poised, waiting to receive a squirt of milk from a cow's teat, the milk white on the whiskers and the flash of small pink tongue.

Inwardly he smiled. Where—Kansas? Bonner Springs, Kansas City, buildings black from the riots. No one would believe it me, not even for that flash of time and pleasure which I have denied on platform and in Senate a million times by word, gesture, and legislation. Now it's like a remembered dream or screen sequence that—listen to the mockingbird up in his apple tree—that time-slain moment breathed in and cried out and felt ago. This Bliss that passeth understanding you never know, you Reverend H, but still a turn in the dance.... Where am I?

Bliss? I say, can you hear me, Bliss? You want the nurse? Just move your fingers if you do and I'll get the girl.

Girl? There was a girl in it, yes. What else? There and then. Out there where they thought the new state a second chance for Eden.... Tell it to the Cherokees!

What are you trying to say, Bliss? Take it slow, boy. I'm still with you. I'll never leave now, so...

...We were under the trees, away from the town, away from Donelson, Karp, and the camera. There, how glorious to have been there. Below the park-space showed; shade here, sun there, in a dreamy, dappled mid-afternoon haze. We were there. High up the trees flurried with birdsong, and one clear note sang above the rest, a lucid, soaring strand of sound; while in the grass cicadas dreamed. For a moment we stood there looking down the gentle rising-falling of the land, while far away a cowbell tinkled, small across some hidden field beyond the woods. Milkweed ran across the ground. Imagine to remember—was it ever? Still. Thistle purple-blue, flowers blue, wisteria loud against an old rock wall—was this the season or another time? Certainly there were the early violets among the fallen pine needles—ago too, but that was Alabama and lonesome. Here she was close beside me and as we moved down the grassy slope the touch of her cool sweat-dampened arm came soft against me and went and came coolly again and then again as we went down the hill into the sun. Oh keep coming coming— Then through the sun into the dappled shade. How long ago, this comes comes a fall? Aches here, aches in spring like a lost limb refusing to recognize its dismemberment, no need to deny. Then too, but sweet. Coming just above my shoulder her glossy head her hair in two heavy braids, and I seeing the small gold ring sunk snug in the pink brown berry of her ear. A smile dreaming on her serenely profiled face. And I remembered the Bliss years. He, Bliss, returned. (Laly was like 'lasses candy, with charm of little red socks in little girls' black patent-leather shoes on slim brown legs, her gingham panties playing peeka-boo beneath a skirt flip as a bird's tail, and her hair done up in tight little braids. *Bliss loves Laly,* I wrote in the sand where the ladybirds lived but the me preacher wiped it out. Then I wrote, *Bliss loves you know who,* and the preacher me wiped that away. So only *'Bliss'* and *'loves'* remained in the sand.) But she coming now was no Laly and I no preacher for a long time now and Bliss no more, though blissful beside her moving there. Saying inside my head, Touch me, touch me, touch me, you...And remembered the one phrase, "teasing brown," and used it, feeling her cool bare flesh so thinly veiled with fragrant sweat against my short-sleeved arm and said aloud,

Are you one?

One what? she answered me, turning her face with her eyes dreaming a smile. What're you talking about, Mister Man?

You, I said. Are you a teasing brown?

She laughed and I could feel her coming to me in waves, heavy around me, soft like hands pressing gently along the small of my back, sounding the column of my spine. I breathed her in, all the ripeness, all the sweetness, all the musky mysterious charm and the green afternoon approving. She smiled, her eyes turned up to mine, her irises soft as scuppernongs in their gentle, bluewhite orbs.

It must have been some ole blues singer you learned that from, she said.

Maybe so, you're probably right, but are you?

I'm brown, and that's a plain fact for anybody to see, she said. And the full black eyes were on me, now, softly laughing. But I'm not teasing anybody. I'm the country one, Mister Big-city Man. Mister Moving-picture Man. You teasing me. Don't you like brown-skinned folks?

Now just what do you think, I said.

I think a lot of things, she said, but—

She smiled again and the whole afternoon seemed to swing around her glossy head. I breathed deeply the blossoms and sunlight and there was a sigh in it. I thought, Here is the place to stay, grow up with the state, take root.... Yes, here. Come, come. She pointed:

You want to go down yonder under those trees? It looks to me like a fine place to lay the spread.

Yes, I said, swinging the basket in my hand. Yes, I want to go anywhere you say, Miss Teasing Brown, yes I do. He was trying to break out of my chest. Bliss, fighting me hard. But you're looking at *me,* she said. Look down yonder where I mean, she pointed. See, under that tree with the blossoms.

A fine peach fuzz of hair showed on her leveled arm, almost golden in the sunlight.

It's fine, I said. Just the place for a time like this.

A bee danced by as on a thread. I felt a suspension of time. Standing still, my eyes in the tree of blossoms, I let it move through me. Eden, I thought, Eden is a lie that never was. And Adam, his name was "snake" And Eve's? An aphrodisiac best served with new fresh oysters on the half shell with a good white wine. The spirit's there.... She arose she rose she rose up from the waves.

Mister Man, she said, you sure have a lot of sleep in your voice.

And her laughter was gay in the afternoon stillness. There, of itself shaping and making the quiet alive. And suddenly I wanted to say, Hey, I'm Bliss! I'm Bliss again, but there's hell in me. There was no alienation ringing in that laugh, so I joined her, startling the quiet. We laughed and laughed. I picked up a smooth stone and sent it sailing, a blossom bursting as it was kissed by a bee. Dreamer, I said, I'm full of dream—

And we came through the park-like space, into shade and out again, her cool skin touching mine. Touching and leaving and coming again unselfconsciously, skin-teasing skin in gentle friction. Damn Bliss! And she was a fragrance mixed with the spicy odors of the park-like space broken by light and shadow. My purpose too. And I thought, Turn back now. Now is the time, leave her and go West. You've lingered long enough, so leave before complications. So I thought. But Bliss said *Come. Come.* And I turned turtle and tried to sing. Suddenly she said,

Look!

And there beneath a bush I saw a white rabbit, its pink nose testing the air before its alerted, pink-veined ears. It watched us moving by, frozen beneath a flowering shrub.

That's somebody's Easter bunny lost out here in the woods, she said. I hope nothing gets him 'cause he don't look like he knows how to take care of himself. There's foxes and hawks out here. Even evil ole wildcats. Poor little ole thing.

And I was disturbed with memory. Sister Wilhite had nicknamed Bliss "Bunting," a bird. But some of the kids had changed it to "Bunny," a rabbit, and this had led to fights. I had been lost too, in Atlanta—but later. I thought, He'll be all right, innocence is its own protection—or would be in the snows. Hey, Rev Hickman, gospel truth or pious lie?

We went on, in the shade now, the light softly filtering the high-branched trees, her shoulder touching my arm and that wave of her enfolding me as cool mist clings to a hot hollow at twilight; my mind saying, No, this is enough; leave now. Leave the moment unbroken in its becoming. Fly before you fall, flee before you fail.... And then I stumbled over the buried stone and heard her saying,

Watch out there, Mister Movie-man.

And I felt her hand upon my arm and I could not breathe. Then we moved on and I fought Bliss for my arm to keep in its place against my side, denying that sweet fugitive fulfillment. And somehow there were three of us now, although only two were actually within the trees, Bliss inside me but still I felt the stranger following. Twice I turned but couldn't see him. I should have run.

Pink blossoms were thick in the tree, the petals scattered broadside upon the grass, and as I breathed them in the fragrance mixed wildly with her own and that cool touching and going of her peach-brown arm sang in me like passionate words whispered in a dark place. Who spread the petals along our path? my mind asked, who arched this afternoon above our heads? And looking down at her feet twinkling in and out below her long, ankle-length skirt, I said, How beautiful are your feet in shoes, Miss Teasing Brown.

She stopped and looked at me full face, a question in her dark eyes.

You're the tease, she said. I think you're laughing at me, Movie Man. Though he *was* part Cherokee my papa wasn't no prince and you know it. You see, I know where those words come from.

I looked at her, suddenly cold, and from far back I could hear a voice saying, Reveren' Bliss, do you preach Job? And I thought, *Give Job back his boils, he deserved them* as I saw the sparks in her eyes' black depths. I said,

No, no, I'm not laughing at all. To me they are beautiful, princess or no princess. And it doesn't take a Solomon to say how beautiful are thy feet in sandals.

I don't know about you, she said, I swear I don't know about you, Mister Movie-man.

There's nothing to know, I said. I come like water and like wind I go— only faster. I laughed, remembering:

> *Said a rabbit to a rabbit*
> *Love ain't nothing but a habit*
> *Hello there, Mister Rabbit.*

You're fast, all right, she said, kneeling and looking up past my head to the sky.

There's not a cloud to be seen, she sighed.

That's how it was, no clouds, only tall trees filtering the sunlight back across the clear space and the blossoms above. Standing there I watched her remove the cloth from the basket and begin spreading it upon the grass.

Why don't you sit down and stay awhile, she said, patting a place for me.

I sat, watching with my chin resting upon my knees as her hands came and went, removing sandwiches wrapped in waxed paper from the basket, placing them on the cloth.

These here are chicken, she said, and these ham, and *these* are Texas hots.

And there were boiled eggs wrapped in twists of paper like favors for a children's party; and tomatoes, and a chocolate cake and a thermos of iced tea with mint leaves and lemon slices floating in it. She served with a gentle feminine flair I would have denied her capable of. I was on dangerous ground.

Do you like a drumstick, she said. Men usually like the drumstick, though we also have the breast.

I prefer the drumstick, I said. Do you know many men?

More than we have drumsticks. More than we have breasts too. She broke off. What you mean, do I know many men?

Thanks, I said. It was crisp and flaky, a nice weight in the fingers. I mean *beaux,* I said.

Boy beaux but no men beaux. They all been boy beaux, Mister Movie-man, and they don't really count. Lord, I almost forgot the cole slaw. Here it is in this mayonnaise jar. Let me help your plate to some.

I watched her, thinking wildly, What would happen to this natural grace under coaching? With a formal veil placed between it and the sharp world and all the lessons learned and carried out with this native graciousness to warm the social skills? Not a light against a screen but for keeps, Newport in July, Antibes with the proper costumes. Saratoga. Could she fly right? With a sari, say, enfolding her girlish charm? What if I taught her to speak and not to speak, to parry in polished tone the innuendoes dropped over cocktail crystal? To master the smile in time that saves lines? With a diamond of a certain size on that slender hand. Or an emerald, its watery green in platinum against that peach-brown skin. Who blushed this peach?... Did the blight I brought begin in fantasy? There was a part in her black hair, her scalp showed clearly through.

I said, The chicken is wonderful. How'd you get it so flaky?

I cooked it 'til it was done, she said. She made a face at me. How'd you learn to make moving pictures?

Oh, that's a secret, I said.

Frying chicken is a secret too, she said.

I laughed. You baked the bread too, is that a secret?

Uh huh, sure I did. Most folks do their own baking in this town—only that's not a secret.

It's almost as good as the chicken, I said.

Thank you, Mister Movie-man. It's right nice for you to say so. But I won't believe you unless you eat a lot. There's plenty and I expect a man to eat like a man.

And suddenly I had dressed her in a pink sari, swathing her girlish form in Indian silk, a scarlet mark of caste on her forehead, and me in tails and turban of immaculate white observing her with pride as now her head goes back with gay burst of laughter, her throat clean and curved and as alive as a robin's, following some polished shaft of wit. No, the turban a mistake for me but the sari for her, yes. Gold brings out the blue of blue eyes. A gold turban for me. Walking her along Fifth Avenue with all the eyes reacting and she no flapper but something more formed, more realized, more magically achieved, and the crowds' imagination whirling like these blossoms tossed in a whirlwind and blown in the million directions of their hopes, hates, fancies, dreams, and we, she and I, become all things to all minds, drawing out their very souls, their potentialities set athrob by the passage of our forms through their atmosphere, sending them ever seeking for some finer thing. Angels and swine and bearers of divers flags and banners becoming more and less than themselves in the vortex of our ambiguity.... Thoughts like these while before me she nibbled a chicken wing undreaming of my wildness. Ah, my fair warrior, my cooing dove, we'll create possibility out of rags and bones and hanks of hair; out of silks and satins and bits of fur, out of gestures and inflections of voice and scents orchestrated funky sweet; with emphatic nods and elusive sympathies and affirmations and every move to all of them a danced proclamation of "I believe you can, I know you can; we can in faith achieve the purest dream of our most real realities—look upon us two and be your finest possibilities."

Why are you looking at me like that, she said.

And there she was again, before me with her warm, high-cheeked face tilted to one side in question, the fine throat rising out of the white blouse, brown, be-peached, as alive and expressive as any singing bird's. She wore a small gold watch pinned to her waist and her napkin was tucked there and I said, I was dreaming. Did you realize that you make men dream?

Her mouth became a firm straight line beneath her smiling eyes.

You sitting here eating my fried chicken and can tell me you're dreaming? And her head went back in a girlish pout. You give me back my something-to-eat this very minute!

But it's all part of the dream, I said. You and the blossoms and the lunch and the weather. All we need is some cold watermelon or perhaps some peach ice cream.

She arched her eyebrows and shook her head. Now just listen to him. Sounds like he wants everything. I can't figure you out, Mister Movie-man, she said.

What do you mean?

The way you talk sometimes. Once in a while you sound just like one of us and I can't tell whether you mean it or just do it to make fun of me.

But you know I wouldn't make fun of you. You know I wouldn't....

I hope not, she said, but you do sound like us once in a while, especially when you get that dreamy look on your face....

I haven't noticed, I said. I just talk as I feel.

Well, I guess you feel like us—every once in a while, I mean. Can I ask you a question?

Anything at all, Miss Teasing Brown, I said.

She smiled and lowered her sandwich. Where'd you come from to here, Mister Movie-man?

From different places back East, I said.

Oh, she said, I kinda thought so.... You not from Chicago?

Never been there, I said. And looking at her nibbling the sandwich, her soft eyes on my face, I thought of some of them. We had had a rough time, coming through all of that cloudburst of rain, having to avoid the towns where I might have been recognized and the unfriendly towns where the oil rigs pounded night and day, making the trip longer and our money shorter and shorter. Getting stuck in the mud here and having engine trouble there, the tires going twice and the top being split by hailstones the size of base-balls and almost losing all of the equipment off a shaky ferry when we crossed a creek in Missouri. Still, there was some luck with us—my luck or maybe Karp's—I have always honored my luck—and we managed to keep the film and the equipment dry and the patches and the boots held on the tires until we reached her town. But on our way, moving through the Ozarks and the roads steep and rocky and having to push the car out of ruts and Karp complaining of ever having left the East and complaining, as we strained and sweated in the mud, against all the goy world and all our troubles were goy and our journey goy and goy our schemes; complaining all the way of what we did and now several times a millionaire with air immaculate and still complaining only now more pious. But then along the way Donelson goaded him on: *Why the hell, Sweet Jesus, did you ever leave Egypt and all those spades? Why didn't you stay and lay Pharoah's second best daughter and make another Moses? Put your back into it, Jew boy. Act like a white man for once.*

And having to step between them.... What would she have made of it, the glamour she longed for locked in such grubby circumstance? Driving them as I was driven and some towns suspicious and others without the proper places to work and the people uninterested or the days without sun and the long hot stretches of green green green with no thoughts beyond continuing and little shade—Amen! Then back there in the town where Hickman had taken me long ago, a stop on the endless circuit and Donelson trying to get permission from the warden to shoot scenes (We cain't use them we'll sell them to Griffith or Zukor, he said) but getting nowhere. We were lucky they didn't keep us there, what with that cross-eyed bass drummer recognizing Donelson and dropping his cymbal and yelling Hey Rube! from the band-stand and how were Lefty Louie and Nick the Greek? How do you know them, I said. Lester Donelson said, Places where I've been there's always a Lefty Louie and a Nick the Greek. And in the hotel the whores were all so ladylike, with high style airs and comic bitchery and the bellhops black. . . . Except for the fat, baldheaded, full-lipped captain whose pale, milky skin was so dense with freckles that he looked like a white man who'd rusted in the rain three days after drowning. He had our number when we first walked in, though how much of it I couldn't tell, but when I looked at him the spots seemed to detach themselves before my eyes and move to a tango rhythm across his broad expanse of face—Da de dum dum—and back again. His eyes casing me as though to say, I know and you know that I know, so what are you going to do about it? I slipped him a five we couldn't afford and I swear those spots returned each to its alloted place—*muy pronto.*

Thank you suh! he said. It's awfully white of you.

He knew all right, and he knew someone important too, selling white women and bootleg whiskey to the leading white citizens and the drummer trade and to a few not-so-leading black ones who slipped in unctuously wearing starched waiters' jackets with the buttons missing. Yes, suh! and donating good sums of money to the Afro-American Episcopal Missionary Society and to a finishing school for young black upper-class ladies in Baltimore. He had it made all right, with certain complications of adjustment it's true, but made. He could have taught us all. Should find the bastard, make him a career diplomat. Chief of Protocol. He trained them all to Southern manners. Smarter than most men in the House—any house. I kept away from him while we waited for sun and opportunity in that town in which he appeared to be the only one with a capacity for fantasy. Dominated by those high gray walls and the freedom of both those inside and out seemed to be measured in days marked off on the calendar. I'm number so-and-so and I know my time and knowing my time I know the who-what-why-wherefore of me. No dreams, please. Well, so much the worse for you. . . . We tried everyone from the Chamber of Commerce to the bootleggers and no one interested in backing us in bringing a little poetry to the town. We almost starved. Broke and cooking beans in our room, patching and pressing with a secret iron borrowed from one of the girls until her pimp threatened Donelson and I was forced to do once more that which I said I'd never do again. But we were hungry and the memory of Eatmore came to the rescue. That was long ago. Grant and forgive us our agos. Amen. We left before dawn, half drunk and unwashed and our bills unpaid, slipping into the damp streets by the baggage entrance, past seven stacks of pulp magazines abandoned by the drummers—*Argosy, Blue Book, Ace,* and *Golden Book* being saved by the baggage man for the kids in his neighborhood—agent of cultural baggage, doing what he could to keep them reading, stopping on the outskirts of the town as the light grew and buying cheese and crackers in a lamplit general store where the men on the road gang bought their lunch. That smell of hogshead cheese, that greasy counter, that glass case with trays of dull penny candy. John Deere plows set in neat bull-tongued rows on a side of the porch and the boxes for benches the barrels the drums the baby crib, well used from its yellow pad, a string of pecans strung end to end for a teething toy was dangling; that great crock of lye hominy setting on the counter looking white and sinister and garnished by a single blue-tailed fly yet making me twinge for home—*Hickman?* There were shelves of prison-made shoes and peg after peg hung with prison-made harness—Donelson, I said, shoot those horse collars hung round the walls, they're frames for por-traits of future Presidents. Yeah, he said, I know a few bastards who'd look pretty natural with their heads stuck through one of those; the mayor, the mine owners, the Chamber-pots-of-Commerce gang. And near Holdenville getting those shots of the motorcycle circling the overflow embankment around the storage tank in the refinery yard, leaning toward the parallel and his eyes like set points of madness behind his goggles, led low close over the handlebars, roaring as though intent upon circling there forever.... MOVIE TYCOONS VISIT CITY was the headline, and there we were looking out from page one, my arms across their shoulders and all three looking dashing, and devil-may-care, each with goggles on forehead and each with an air of po-tency, mystery. The camera in the foreground. It made it easy and I kept things simple, a pageant dedicated to the founding of the town with all the old-timers parading past the camera on horseback, or in buckboards, then sitting before the courthouse in funeral-parlor chairs and an Indian or two in the background. Shot everything from low angles to make them tall and im-posing, and the fire engines I made half a block long. Holdenville, yes, the weather was fine and Holdenville couldn't hold us. No, but what we made there was lost in Ponca City. Roustabouts, Indians, 1,001 ranch hands, and Wild Bill Tillman in the flesh in a white suit and white Stetson and astride a white horse every hour of every day in the streets. Yes, but in the middle of a roaring circus who has time for silent scenes? Donelson went wild in the town, getting hot on the dice and winning a thousand then losing our stake before they cooled him off. Then when he asked to see the dice they threw him into the street. There was hardly enough money for gas, then Karp to the rescue, found a cousin who helped us on our way. And what a cousin, walking around in a blanket, a bullet-smashed derby, and a necklace of rat-tlesnake buttons, selling snake oil and mustard plasters. Morris, the Osage Indian Jew, of whom Karp disapproved. Listen, Morris said, here there's no minyan in fifty miles, so what if I temporarily joined another tribe? And let me tell you something, wise guy: I been scalped like the best of them!

I wanted him to join us but Karp was against it. But what a town, every-thing in our grasp; gunplay and Indians, dance-hall girls, cowboys and gam-blers, gunmen, bandits, rustlers and law officers, the real frontier atmosphere and Wild Bill acting himself right off a circus poster. But it was all too real and when we set up the camera on the street they gathered around, looking as everywhere. Then understanding, they knocked us down and fifteen forty-fives were looking us dead in the eye.

What's the big idea, I said.

What's your name, the one-eyed one said.

We told him and what we were about.

Pictures, he said. We don't need any damn pictures around here.

Maybe *you* don't, but other folks do, Donelson said. We'll put this town on the map.

Map? the one-eyed one said. We don't want it on any goddamn map. You want to ruin everything?

We're trying to help, Karp said. We can help it grow.

We don't need any help. We don't want no growing. Get up on your knees. He pointed the pistol.

We looked into their miscellaneous faces and did what he said.

All right, One-eye said, from now on you three cockies are going to be known as the three monkeys . . .

Why you— Donelson began, starting up.

One-eye moved without bending. There was a flashing arc of movement and at the smackcrunch of impact Donelson sprawled in the dirt, his cheek flaming with the red imprint of a forty-five's long barrel.

Now shut up, Rebel, One-eye said, and you'll keep healthy.

Goddamn you, Donelson said, scrambling to his knees. But this time I grabbed him, holding on.

Shut up, I said, we're outnumbered. Can't you see that?

Now you're talking, One-eye said, glaring down. And don't you forget it! Out-numbered, out-gunned, and out-manned!

He grinned, shaking the whiskey to an oily foam, his thumb over the bottle mouth. And you, he said, dowsing whiskey on Donelson's head, are now baptised Mister Speak-No-Evil. So from now on keep your big cotton-pickin' mouth shut tight as your daddy's smokehouse!

Then, pouring whiskey on Karp's bowed head he said, And your buddy here is named forthwith, like the lawyers say, Hear-No-Evil.

Out of the corner of his swelling mouth Donelson's voice came harsh and violent. All right, Israelite, he said, Where's your goddamned cunning now? Why don't you blow your fucking horn!

Karp looked straight ahead, his face calm, his eyes tragic and resentful yet resigned. As though kneeling there in the dust the world was affirmed in the pattern of his forefathers' prediction. So he was prepared to die resigned before even this random fulfillment of prophesy. A stranger in a strange land, the goyim were repeating once more their transgression against him. . . .

I shook my head feeling the hot splash of whiskey soaking my skull. My eyes stung as it coursed down my face and I suppressed a scream, holding my breath. And I seemed to be walking under water and I no longer saw them there above me. For I was in the kingdom of the dead, tight and enclosed. Back in the box....

Don't appear to like it much, someone said and laughed.

And you, One-eye said, I name See-No-Evil.

I could see him then, his collar band held with a brass button, his rotten teeth, his drooped lid, stepping back and the others no longer threatening but laughing. My knees were aching but I could see very sharply now. The hair that showed on his knuckles, sprouted from his ear, his flared nostrils.

All right, boys, One-eye said, let 'em up.

We got up and I picked up the camera and folded the tripod. A drop of whiskey had splashed the lens and I polished it away with the end of my tie. I looked—Donelson's face was bright red and twitching as he watched One-eye take a drink and pass the bottle around. One-eye stuck the pistol in his waistband and rocked back and forth on his heels, smiling now, and his missing eye giving his face the look of a battle-scarred shell-shocked tomcat. Then the bottle came to Donelson, paused before him, and before he could open his mouth I said,

Drink up. Go ahead.... Then Karp took it, even though he didn't drink.

Now you got the right idea, One-eye said. You're getting the hang of how to live in this town. This here's a good town, you monkeys; the best town in the West. All you have to know is how to live in it. So I says: Go drink yourself some whiskey. Go diddle yourself some *broads*—we got all kinds from all kinds of places. Fact we got Frenchies, we got Poles, we got Irishers, Limeys, Eskimos, Yids, and even a few coal-shuttle blondes. That's right, and the price of poontang ain't high. So go shack up with a few and change your luck. We know the kind old Rebel here cottons after, don't we, boys? Let him sleep with Charleston Mary and he'll start to winning with the dice. What I mean is *enjoy* yourself. Why, there's money laying around on the streets in this town. You can do most anything here as long as you can outdraw and outshoot the ones who don't like it. So like I say, you can do anything only don't let us see you poking that goddam piece of machinery at us. You understand?

We get it, Donelson said. But tell me something....

What's that?

What time would you say it was?

Time? One-eye said. How the hell would I know, in this town we make our own fucking time....

Mister Movie-man, she said, You dreaming again?

Not now, I said. *Time is a juxtaposing of pains and pain hurts even after the object is gone, faded.*

You better not be while you're eating. But you were gone somewhere, flew right away from me. Or maybe you were thinking about the picture?

No, I said. Only about you. You make a very nice picture.

She looked a question, her head to one side. I sure hope I can act like you want me to, she said. I really never thought of being in a picture before but now I sure want to be able to do it. Will there be any fighting in it?

Some, I said.

And horses?

I'm not sure about that, I said. But there'll be love scenes....

You mean I'll have to kiss somebody?

Sure, that's part of the love scene.

But in front of all those folks...and with his girl looking? She's angry with me already—

There'll be many more folks to see the picture, I said.

But that's different, she said. I won't be there....

Don't worry about it, I said. I'll teach you how it's done. Now was the time to begin and I put down my sandwich and moved. I saw her large eyes and suddenly I ceased to dream.

You just work in the contest and win, I said. I'll take care of the rest. I was disturbed.

Oh, I will, she said. I'll raise more money than all the other girls put together. You'll have to give me the best part....

Yes, I said, the best is yet to be, but you girls will have to work hard. Stir up the interest of everyone. Karp insists that we have the full cooperation of the community....

Which one is Mr. Karp, the one with the camera?

No, that's Donelson. Right now Donelson is doing the shooting. Later on I'll take over. Karp is the other one.

Well, he won't have to worry because everybody is interested already. Two clubs are planning dances and another one—well, they're going to give a barbecue. Is Mr. Karp the boss?

Boss? No, he's just a partner like the rest of us. We're the three partners. What other plans do you have?

We're still thinking up things to do. We plan to give a combination hayride and trip-around-the-world.

What's a trip-around-the-world?

That's when you ride to different parts of town and go to different houses and in each house they have the food of some country—like Mexico for instance, and it's all decorated like a Mexican house and the boys and girls who give that part of the party will be dressed in Mexican costumes. And when you get there you buy the food and they give you some drinks and you can dance and have a good time. Then after a while everybody piles into the hay and the wagon goes to another house and there they'll find another country and another party. It keeps going on just like that.

That's interesting, I said, but you want to work hard on the popularity contest.

I mean to, she said, I really have to have that part. I like plays and things, they kind of take you out of yourself.

They do, I thought, and you have no idea how far.

Some English people were here last year and they put on some wonderful shows. With nice scenery and music and everything. You couldn't always understand what they were saying but it sounded so fine. Like listening to folks sing some of that opera music in a different language.

Did many folks go to see them?

Quite a few, she said. I went every night. A lot of folks did.

That's very good, but where'd they give the plays?

They gave them in the school auditorium. There's a stage there and they brought their own scenery for one of the plays. But you know something, Mister Movie-man?

No, what?

When you listened to them real close you could see scenery that wasn't on the stage. They *said* the scenery and you could see it just as clear. You really could.

That's right, I said. Sometimes you can. But that's with a certain kind of play, movies are different. Everything has to be seen or scene. You've got good ears, though. I touched where the gold wire entered the soft lobe of her ear. She watched silently. Watched my hand.

Thank you, Mister Movie-man, she said, and have another drumstick....

I thought about the contest and all their plans. A thousand would get us to the coast and help us get a start.... Going to what nation in what territory? And this time I'd let Karp hold the cash, he was practical and more dependable than Donelson. He was down in the business district picking up a few dollars at his jeweler's trade. He could make a watch from the start, give him the tools, the metal, and the lathe....

What will the story be about? she said.

I haven't decided yet, I said, but I'm working on it.

Well, I'm sure glad to hear that.

Why?

Because I saw your friends taking pictures all over the place. What were they doing that for?

Oh that, I said, they're just chasing shadows, shooting scenes for background. Later on when we start working we'll use them, splice them in. Pictures aren't made in a straight line. We take a little bit of this and a little of that and then it's all looked at and selected and made into a whole....

You mean you piece it together?

That's the idea, I said.

Well tell me something! she said. Isn't that just marvelous? Just like making a scrap quilt, I guess; one of those with all the colors of the rainbow in it—only more complicated. Is that it?

Just about, I said. There has to be a pattern though, and we only have black and white.

Well, she said, there's Indians, and some of the black is almost white and brown like me.

I looked up the hill, hearing the distant cowbell. Far above us the black-and-white coats of the herd lay like nomadic blankets against the close green hill, and higher still on the edge of the shade, two young bulls let fly at one another, head-on into the sun. They must have jarred the hill like thunder.

Hosan Johnny! Hosan Johnny!

Where'd I hear?

> He shake his tail, he jar the mountain
> He shake his tail, he jar the river

A long time ago. I could see them back off and paw the earth preparing to let fly again. What was I doing here when there was so much to be done? Movement was everything. I had to move on, westward. How would I plot the scenario with these people? What line would engage them, tie them up in an image that would fascinate them to the maximum? Put money in thy purse, the master said. I needed it.

What time is it? I said.

She looked into the trees. A pink petal clung to her hair. About two-thirty, she said.

Two-thirty, I said. How can you tell without looking at your watch?

By the way the shadows slant against the trees, Mister Movie-man.

By the shadows? Why don't you use your watch? Doesn't it run?

Sure, it runs, listen. . . .

I lowered my head to her blouse, hearing it ticking away. It was a little past two-thirty but she was close enough. She wore some faint scent—a trace of powder. I looked at her. There was no denying the charm of her.

You're right, I said. I wish I could do that. . . .

You could if you would stay in one town long enough, she said. Don't you have a watch?

I had it stolen back East, I said. I had pawned it in Newark.

Look, Donelson said, What's the plot of this thing?

We won't plot it, I said, we'll make it up as we go along. It depends upon how much dough they can raise. I'll think of something. Just shoot anything interesting you see.

Play it by ear, you mean? Karp said, with this little film we have?

That's right. By ear and by nose, by cheek and by jowl, by the foresight and the hindsight, by the foreskin and the rear skin, by the hair of my chinny chin chin and my happy nappy!

We stood in the street beneath a huge cottonwood tree, the camera resting on a tripod near the curb. For once there was no crowd. Sunlight, clear and unhazed, flooded the asphalt and the odor of apple blossoms drifted to us from a pair of trees in a yard across the street. I could hear the bounce-rattle-scrape as a pair of little girls tossed jacks on the porch of a small house that sat behind a shallow lawn in which a bed of red poppies made bright red blobs in the sun. Beside me Donelson was rolling a Bull Durham cigarette and I fought my irritation under control. He was arrogant and impatient and he had no discipline. If I didn't guide him every minute he'd waste the film and antagonize the people. I'd look at the day's shooting and there would be nothing more than a jumble of scenes, as though the rambling impressions of an idiot's day had been photographed. With Donelson it was gelly, gelly, gelatine—all day long and all images ran to chaos, as though Sherman's Army had traumatized his sense of order forever. Once there was a sequence of a man whitewashing the walls of the slaughterhouse which stood at the edge of the town near the river, and this followed by a flock of birds strung out skimming over a stretch of field; then came shots of the courthouse clock at those moments when the enormous hands leaped across the gaps of time to take new positions but ever the same on the bird-fouled face, then a reversed flight of birds, and this followed by the clock hands whirling in swift reversal. Donelson ached to reverse time, I yearned to master it, or so I told myself. I edited a series of shots, killing time. The darkness between the frames longer than what was projected. Once there was a series consisting of a man and a boy and a boar hog, a cat and a great hairy spider—all shot in flight as they sought to escape, to run away from some unseen pursuer. And as I sat in the darkened hotel room watching the rushes, the day's takes, on the portable screen, the man seemed to change into the boy and the boy, changing his form as he ran, becoming swiftly boar and cat and tarantula, moving ever desperately away, until at the end he seemed, this boar-boy-spider-cat, to change into an old man riding serenely on an old white mule as he puffed a corncob pipe. I watched it several times and each time I broke into a sweat, shaking as with a fever. Why these images, and what was their power?

And Donelson had sung, "Oh, while I sit on my ass on the ass of my ass a curious paradox comes to my mind, While three-fourths of my ass is in front of my ass the whole of my ass is behind." Oh, Donelson, that impossible

Donelson. That bad boy with his toy. Sometimes I wondered if any of it had meaning for him beyond the joy of denying the reality of all that which he turned his lenses upon. . . .

From the walk I was listening to the dry, rhythmical, bounce-scrape-scrape-bounce of the knucklebone jacks and ball of the two little girls continuing—when suddenly from behind us a dark old fellow wearing a black Cordoba hat, blue denim jacket, and a scarf of fuchsia silk wrapped around his throat moved stiffly past on a fine black seven-gaited mare. Small and dry, he sat her with the stylized and monumental dignity of an equestrian statue and in the sun-slant the street became quite dream-like. His leathery hands held the gathered reins upon the polished horn of a gleaming cowboy saddle and his black, high-heeled boots, topped by the neat, deep cuff of short tan cowhide riding chaps, rested easy and spurless in the stirrups as he moved slowly past in meditation, his narrowed eyes bright glints in the shadow of his hard-brimmed hat. Donelson started to speak but I silenced him as I watched with whirling mind, filled with the sight and listening now to the mare's hooves beating with measured gait through the bright suspense of the afternoon—when suddenly a little boy in blue overalls exploded from between two small houses across the street and ran after the horseman, propelled by an explosion of joy.

Hi, there, Mister Love, he yelled. Make her dance, Mister Love, I'll sing the music. Will you, Mister Love? Won't you please, Mister Love? Please, *please,* Mister Love? Clapping his hands as he ran pleading beside the mare's flank.

Dance her, Mister Love, he called, and I'll call the others and we'll all sing for you, Mister Love.

Well, I'll be goddam, Donelson said beside me. What does the little bastard mean, he'll sing the music?

He means what he says, I guess, I said.

And who the hell is that, the Pied Piper on a gaited mare?

The children were singing now, following alongside the arch-necked mare as she moved, the old fellow holding his seat as though he were off somewhere in an elder's chair on a church platform—or on the air itself—watching the kids impassively as he stroked the horse's mane in time to its circus-horse waltzing.

There, I said, Now *there's* something we can use. We could use that man, I said.

Donelson looked at me. So write a part for the nag and the kids, he said. You decided all of a sudden to make it a horse opera? He laughed. Now, by God, I've seen everything, he said.

No, I said, I was looking at the children move, some were waltzing in a whirl along the sidewalk, their arms outstretched, shouting and singing.

They went past the houses, whirling in circles as they followed the dancing mare. A dog barked along a fence and I could hear through it all the first little boy's pure treble sounding high above the rest.

Suddenly I looked at Donelson. Why the hell aren't you shooting, I said, and saw his mouth drop open in surprise.

No film in the camera, he said. You told me to shoot exteriors of that mansion up in the north section of town. I forgot to reload. Besides, you know we're short of film.

And all this happening right before our eyes, I said.

Maybe we could get them to run it through some other time, Donelson said. With a few chocolate bars and cones of ice cream you could buy all the pickaninnies in town. Though God knows what the horse and rider would cost. That old bastard looks like weathered iron. D'ya ever see anyone like him?

No, I said, and it'll never happen like this again. How often do I have to tell you that you have to have film in the camera at all times? We don't have the dough to make up everything, we have to snatch everything that passes and in places like this anything can happen and *does*.

I cursed our luck.

A woman came out to stand on the porch of one of the houses shaking her head and hugging her body as though she were cold.

That Love, that ole hoss and those chillen, she said. They ought to put them all out in the meadow somewhere.

What is his name? I called.

That's ole Love, she said. That's ole Love New.

Then another voice spoke up and I became aware of an old woman sitting in a rocking chair on a porch two houses away down the street.

That's him all right. He's just the devil hisself and he's going to take those chillen off to Torment one of these days. You just mark my words.

She spat into the yard. Calling hisself an Indian and hound-dogging around. The old black tomcat. She spat again and I saw the snuff flash brown through the sunlight, then snake across the bare yard to roll into a ball, like quicksilver across the face of a mirror.

Find out where the old fellow lives, I told Donelson. I watched them dancing on past the big cottonwood tree, the glossy horse moving with ceremonial dignity, its neck beautifully arched, and hearing the children's bright voices carrying the melody pure and sweet along the air. They were coming to the corner now and suddenly I saw the old man rear the horse, the black Cordoba hat suddenly rising in a brisk salute above his white old head, freezing there for a moment as the mare danced a two-step on her well-shod hooves. Then, as he put her down I could hear the hooves ringing out on the road as he took the corner at a gallop, the children stringing after, cheering.

Damn, Donelson said, where do you think he comes from? Is there a circus in town?

Only you, I said. Only us out here without film.

We found Karp with one of his faith who ran a grocery store. They were discussing politics. We drank a soda and went back to the hotel to discuss the film. So how do we start? Donelson said. With a covered wagon? There must be enough of them rotting away in barns around this town.

Or how about an Indian attack? Karp said. Enough of them look like Indians to make things go fairly well. . . .

I was watching a little boy in blue overalls who had been left by the others. He had suddenly become a centaur, his foreleg arched as he waltzed horse-style to his own *Taaa ta ta ta taaa ta ta*, back between the houses. At that age I preached Job, boils and all, but I didn't dance, and all his losses my loss of mother. . . .

What about doing the Boston Tea Party, Donelson said, with these coons acting both the British and the Beantowners? That would be a riot. Make some up as Indians, take the rest and Harvard-up their talk. Even the camera would laugh. Too bad we can't film sound. We could outdo the minstrels, 'Lasses White and all. I understand enough of them around here are named Washington and Jefferson and Franklin—put them in powdered wigs, give them red coats, muskets, carpetbags. . . .

Some are named Donelson too, I said, watching the smile die out on his face.

So why not, he said. I'd feel awful bad if my folks didn't get their share.

No, I said, it'll be a modern romance. They'll have dignity and they'll play simple Americans. Good, hardworking, kindly ambitious people with a little larceny here and there. . . . Let's not expect to take their money and make fools of them while doing it.

What! And how the hell are we going to make these tar babies look like God's fair chosen creatures?

That's your problem, Donelson, I said.

God's going to turn you into a crow for that. . . . Who? You, that's who.

You must think you're a magician, Donelson said. Sometimes I have the feeling that you think you can do anything with a camera. So what's the romance all about? What'll we call it?

The Taming of the West, I said, or The Naming of the Baby, or Who's Who in Tamarac. . . .

That's enough, Donelson said, I'll get it by-and-by.

Donelson, I said, we can shoot the scene right here. See, the lights should shine from above there, at an angle, cutting the shadow. And the leading lady will move through just as the hero comes into the door. . . .

Okay, okay, but who's going to play the part?

Never mind, there's bound to be some good-looking young gal in this town who'll be anxious to play it. There's bound to be plenty of talent here. I have a hunch.

Donelson looked at his glass. Say, he said, what you say they call this drink?

Black Cow.

You sure it isn't white mule? From the way you're talking I'd think so.

You just wait, you'll see.

I'll have to wait but we'd better get something going quick, because the dough is going fast. Go West, young man, where the pickings are easy.... That's still the best idea for us.

We'll go West, but for the while we'll linger here.

So we'll stay, but what about a script?

She smiled, her head back, and I could see the sweet throbbing of her throat. Thinking, *Time—time is all I need to take the mountain.* But now her mind was on the sheerest shadow she hoped to be upon the wall. I looked into the trees, the shadows there. Blossoms fall.

He had called me to him on a bright day....

Bliss, Daddy Hickman said, you keep asking me to take you even though I keep telling you that folks don't like to see preachers spending too much time around a place they think of as one of the Devil's hangouts. All right, so now I'm going to take you so you can see for yourself, and you'll see that it's just like the world—full of sinners and a few believers, a few good folks and a heap of mixed-up and bad ones. Yes, and beyond the fun of sitting there looking at the marvelous happenings in the dark, there's all the same old snares and delusions we have to sidestep every day right out here in the bright sunlight. Because you see, Bliss, it's not so much a matter of where you *are* as what you *see....*

Yes, sir, I said.

He shook his head. No, don't go agreeing too quick, Bliss; wait until you understand. Now like old Saint Luke says, "The light of the body is the eye," so you want to be careful that the light that your eye lets into you isn't the light of darkness and confusion.

I nodded my head, watching his eyes. I could see him studying the Word as he talked, the way his eyes seemed to look inside in order to look out. He was looking through and beyond me.

Yes, sir, I said.

That's right, he said, many times you will have to preach goodness out of badness, little boy. Yes, and hope out of hopelessness. God made the world and gave it a chance, and when it's bad we have to remember that it's still his plan for it to be redeemed through the striving of a few good women and men. So come on, we're going to walk down there and take us a good look. We're going to do it in style too, with some popcorn and peanuts and some Cracker Jacks and candy bars. You might as well get some idea of what you will have to fight against, because I don't believe you can really lead folks if you never have to face up to any of the temptations they face. Christ had to put on the flesh, Bliss; you understand? And I was a sinner man too.

Yes, sir.

But wait here a second, Bliss—

He looked deep into me and I felt a tremor. Sir? I said.

He hesitated, his eyes becoming sad. Then:

Now don't think this is going to become a habit, Bliss. I know you're going to like being there looking in the dark, even though you have to climb those filthy, piss-soaked stairs to get there. Oh, yes, you're going to enjoy looking at the pictures just about like I used to enjoy being up there on the bandstand playing music for folks to enjoy themselves to, back there in the olden days before I was called. Yes, you're going to like looking at the pictures, most likely you're going to be bug-eyed with the excitement; but I'm telling you right now that it's one of those pleasures we preachers have to leave to other folks. And I'll tell you why, little preacher: Too much looking at those pictures is going to have a lot of folks raising a crop of confusion. The picture show hasn't been here but a short while but I can see it coming already. Because folks are getting themselves mixed up with those shadows spread out against the wall, with things that are no more than some smoke drifting up from hell or dreams pouring out of a bottle. So they lose touch with who they're supposed to be, Bliss. They forget to be what the Book tells them they were meant to be—and that's in God's *own* image. One of the preacher's jobs, his main job, Bliss, is to help folks find themselves and to keep reminding them to remember who they are. So you see, those pictures can go against our purpose. If they look at those shows too often they'll get all mixed up with so many of those shadows that they'll lose their way. They won't know who they *are*, is what I mean. So you see, if we start going to the picture show all the time, folks will think we're going to the Devil and backsliding from what we preach. We have to set them an example, Bliss; so we're going in there for the first and last time—

Now don't look at me like that; I know it seems like every time a preacher turns around there's something else he has to give up. But, Bliss, there's a benefit in it too, because pretty soon he develops control over himself. *Self-control*'s the word, Bliss. That's right, you develop discipline, and you live so you can feel the grain of things and you learn to taste the sweet that's in the bitter and the bitter in the sweet too and you live more deeply and earnestly. A man doesn't live just one life, Bliss, he lives more lives than a cat—only he doesn't like to face it because the bitter is there nine-times-nine, right along with the sweet that he wants all the time. So he forgets.

You too, Daddy Hickman? I said. Do you have more than one life?

He smiled down at me.

Me too, Bliss, he said. Me too.

But how? How can they have nine lives and not know it?

They forget and wander on, Bliss. But let's us leave this now and go face up to those shadows. Maybe the Master meant for them to show us some of the many sides of the old good-bad. I know, Bliss, you don't understand that, but you will, boy. You will. . . .

Ah, but by then Body had brought the news:

We were sitting on the porch-edge eating peanuts, goober peas, as Deacon Wilhite called them. Discarded hulls littered the ground below the contented dangling of our feet. We were barefoot—I was allowed to be that day—and in overalls. A flock of sparrows rested on the strands of electric wire across the unpaved road, darting down from time to time and sending up little clouds of dust. Body was humming as he chewed. Except in church we were always together, he was my right hand.

Body said.

Bliss, you see that thing they all talking about?

Who, I said.

All the kids. You seen it yet?

Seen what, Body? Why do you always start preaching before you state your text?

You the preacher, ain't you? Look like to me a preacher'd *know* what a man is talking about.

I looked at him hard and he grinned, trying to keep his face straight.

You ought to know where all the words come from, even before anybody starts to talk. Preachers is supposed to see visions and things, ain't they?

Now don't start playing around with God's work, I warned him. Like Daddy Hickman says, everybody has to die and pay their bills. . . . Have I seen what?

That thing Sammy Leatherman's got to play with. It makes pictures.

No, I haven't. You mean a kodak? I've seen one of those. Daddy Hickman has him a big one. Made like a box with little pearly glass windows in it and one round one, like an eye.

He shook his head. I put down the peanuts and fitted my fingers together. I said,

> *Here's the roof*
> *Here's the steeple,*
> *Open it up and see*
> *the people.*

Body sneered. That steeple's got dirt under those fingernail shingles, why don't you wash your hands? Besides, you think I'm a baby? Lots of folks have those kodaks, this here is something different.

Well, what is it then?

I don't rightly know, he said. I just heard some guys talking about it down at the liberty stable. But they was white and I didn't want to ask them any questions. I rather be ignorant than ask them anything.

So why didn't you ask Sammy, he ain't white.

Naw, he a Jew; but he looks white, and sometimes he acts white too. Specially when he's with some of those white guys who think they so fine.

He always talks to me, I said. Calls me *rabbi.*

The doubt came into Body's eyes like a think cloud. He frowned. He was my right hand and I could feel his doubt.

You look white too, Rev, he said. Why you let him call you "rabbit"?

I looked away, toward the dusting birds. They were ruffled out and fluttering.

Body, cain't you hear? I said he calls me *rabbi.*

Oh, it sounds like my little brother trying to spell rabbit. Re-abbi-tee, *rabbit,* he say. He a fool, man.

He sure is, he's your brother, ain't he?

Don't start that now, you a preacher, remember? How come you let Sammy play the dozens with you, you want to be white?

NO! And Sammy ain't white and that's not playing the dozens, it means "preacher" in Jew talk. Quit acting a fool. What kind of box is this you heard them talking about?

His lids came down low and his eyes hid when I tried to look for the truth in them.

All I know is that it makes pictures, Body said.

It makes pictures and not a kodak?

That's right, Rev.

I chewed awhile and thought of all the things I had heard about but hadn't seen; airplanes and angels and Stutz Bearcats and Stanley Steamers. Then I thought I had it:

It makes pictures but not a kodak? So maybe he's got hold to one of those big ones like they use to take your picture at the carnival. You know, the kind they take you out of wet and you have to wait around until you dry....

Body shook his head. No, Rev, this here is something different. This is something they say you have to be in the dark to see. These folks come out already dry.

You mean a nickelodeon? I heard them talking about one of those when we were out there preaching in Denver.

I don't think so, Rev, but maybe that's what they meant. But, man, how's

Sammy doing to get something like that just to play with? A thing like that must cost about a zillion dollars.

I don't know, I said. But remember, his papa has that grocery store. Besides, Sammy's so smart he might've made him one, man.

That's right, he a Jew, ain't he? He talk much of that Jew talk to you, Bliss?

No, how could he when I can't talk back? I wish you would remember some more about that box. It's probably like the magic lantern I seen one time—except in those the pictures don't move.

I hulled seven peanuts and chewed them. I could smell the fresh roasted smell and I tried to imagine what Body had heard while his voice flowed on about the Jews. Somehow I seemed to remember Daddy Hickman describing something similar but it kept sliding away from me, like when you bob for apples floating in a tub.

Say, Rev, Body said.

What?

Can't you hear? I said do you remember in the Bible where it tells about Samson and it says he had him a boy to lead him up to the wall so he could shake that building down?

That's right, I said.

Well, answer me this, you think that little boy got killed?

Killed, I said, who killed him?

What I mean is, do you think that maybe old Samson forgot to tell that boy what he was fixing to do?

I cut my eyes over at Body. I didn't like the idea. Once Daddy Hickman had said: *Bliss, you must be a hero just like that little lad who led blind Samson to the wall, because a great many grown folks are blind and have to be led toward the light....* The question worried me and I could hear Body popping peanut hulls. I was looking up at the ceiling of the porch where dirt daubers were building a nest.

Look, Body, I said, I truly don't feel like working today. Because, you see, while you're out playing cowboy and acting the fool and going on cotton picks and chunking rocks at trains and things like that, *I* have to always be preaching and praying and studying my Bible....

What's all that got to do with what I asked you? You want somebody to cry for you?

No, I said, but right now it looks to you like we just eating these here good goobers and talking together and watching those sparrows out there beating up dust in the road—but I'm really resting from my pastoral duties, just like Daddy Hickman does; understand? So now I just want to think some more about this box that Sammy Leatherman's supposed to have. How did those white boys say it looked?

Man, Body said, you just like a bulldog with a bone when you start to thinking about something. I done told you, they say Sammy got him a machine that has people in it . . .

People in it? Watch out there, Body. . . .

He rolled over, looking at me now.

Sho, Rev—folks. They say he point it at the wall and stands back in the dark cranking on a handle and they come out and move around. Just like a gang of ghosts, man.

Like ghosts?

Yeah, Body said. That's how he can keep so many of 'em in that machine. Ghosts don't wear no shoes so you can jam a heap of 'em in a tight place.

Body, you expect me to believe that?

He frowned. Now listen here, Bliss, I had done left that box because I wanted to talk about Samson and you didn't want to. So don't come trying to call me no lie. . . .

Forget about Samson, man. Where does he have this thing?

In his daddy's basement under the grocery store. You got a nickel?

I looked far down the street, past the chinaberry trees. Some little kids were pushing a big one on a racer made out of a board and some baby-buggy wheels. He was guiding it with a rope like a team of horses, with them drawn all up in a knot, pushing.

I said: Man, we ought to go somewhere and roast these goober peas some more. That would make them even better. Maybe Sister Judson would do it for us. She makes some fine fried pies too, and she just might be baking today; I have to remember to pray for her tonight, she's a nice lady. What's a nickel got to do with it?

'Cause Sammy charges you two cents to see them come out and move.

I looked at him. Body had a round face with laughing eyes and a smooth black skin. He was a head taller than me and very strong. He saw me doubting and grinned. He was going to tease.

They *move,* man, he said. I swear on my grandmother that they come out of that machine and *move.* And that ain't all: They walk and talk—only you can't hear what they say—and they dance and fist-fight and shoot and stab one another; and sometimes they even kiss, but not too much. And they drink liquor, man, and go staggering all around and they hit one another in the face with pies.

They sound like folks, all right. I said.

They folks all right, Body said. And they ride hosses and fight some Indians and all stuff like that. They say it's real nice, Bliss. It's really keen.

Who says?

Those white guys, man.

I willed to believe him. I said, And they all come out of this box?

That's right, Rev.

How big are the people he has in there, they midgets?

Well, it's a box about this size.

I looked at his hands, his thumbs back like the hammer on a pistol. Now I *know* you're lying, I said.... Body?

What?

You know lying is a sin, don't you? You surely ought to by now because I've told you enough times.

He looked at me then cut his eyes away, scowling. Listen, Bliss, a little while ago you wouldn't tell me whether that boy who was leading Samson got killed or not, so now don't come preaching me no sermon about lying. 'Cause you know I can kick your butt. I don't have to take no stuff off you. This here ain't no Sunday, nohow. Can't nobody make me go to church on no Friday, neither on Monday, Tuesday, Wednesday, or Thursday. In fact, on Friday I'm subject to boot a preacher's behind 'til his nose bleeds. I'm liable to kick him straight up a tree and throw rocks at his butt! *And* won't let him come down 'til Sunday!

I rebuked him with my face, but now he was out to tease me.

That's the truth, Rev, and you know the truth is what the Lord loves. On a Friday I'll give a doggone preacher *hell*. Let him catch me on Sunday if he wants to, that's all right providing he ain't too long-winded. And even on Wednesday ain't so bad, but please, *please,* don't let him fool with me on no Friday.

I flipped a goober at his boasting head.

That's right, he said, on Friday I'll boot a preacher's butt 'til it ropes like okra.

I flipped another goober but he wouldn't dodge, trying to stare me down. Then we dueled with our faces, our eyes, but I won when his lips quivered and he had to laugh.

Rev, he said, shaking his head, I swear you're my ace buddy, preacher or no—but why do preachers *always* have to be so serious? Look at that face of yourn! Let's see how you look when you see one of those outrageous sinners, one of those midnight rambling, whiskey-drinking gamblers come p.i.-limping by....

I've told you now, Body....

He stopped teasing and lay back with head upon his arms, his knees crossed. Man, you too serious. But I'm not lying about that box though, honest. It's suppose to be about this size, but when they come out on the wall they git as big as grown folks—hecks, bigger. It's magic, man.

It must be, I said. What kind of folks has he got in that box? You might as well tell a really big lie.

White folks, man. What you think? Well, he *has* got a few Indians in there. That is if any of them are left after they're supposed to have been killed.

No colored?

Naw, just white. You know they gon' keep all the new things for they-selves. They put us in there about time it's fixing to wear out.

We giggled, holding one hand across our mouths and slapping our thighs with the other as grown men did when a joke was outrageously simple-minded and yet somehow true.

Then that's got to be magic, I said. Because that's the only way they can get rid of the colored. But really, Body, don't you ever tell the truth?

Sure I do, all the time. I know you think I'm lying, Rev, but I'm telling you the Lord's truth. Sammy's got them folks in that machine like when you put lightning bugs in a jug.

And about how many you think he's got in there?

He held his head to one side and squinted.

About two hundred, man; maybe more.

And you think I'm going to believe that too?

It's true, man. He got them jugged in there and for four cents me and you can go see him let 'em come out and move. You can see for yourself. You got four cents?

Sure, I said, but I'm saving them. You have to tell a better lie than that to get my money. A preacher's money comes hard.

Shucks, that's what you say. All y'all do is hoop and holler a while, then you pass the plate. But that's all right, you can keep your old money if you want to be so stingy, because I seen it a coupla times already.

You saw it? I felt betrayed. Body was of my right hand. I saw him skeet through the liar's gap in his front teeth and roll his eyes, pouting.

So why're you just now telling me?

Shoots, you don't believe nothing I say nohow. I get tired of you 'sputing my word. But just the same, I'm telling the truth; they come out and move, and they move *fast*. Not like ordinary folks. And last time I was down there Sammy made them folks come out real big, man. They was twice as big as grown folks, and they had a whole train with 'em. . . .

A whole train?

Sho, a real train running over a trestle just like the "Southern" does. And some cowboys was chasing it on they hosses.

Body, I said, I'm going to pray for you, you hear? Fact is, I'm going to ask Daddy Hickman and the whole church to pray for you.

He stood up, brushing the hulls from his overalls.

Don't you think you're so good, Bliss, he said. You better ask them to pray for you while they doing it, 'cause you don't believe nothing nobody says. Shucks, I'm going home.

Now don't get mad—hey, wait a minute, Body. Come back here! Where're you going? Come on back. *Please,* Body. Can't you hear me say *Please?*

But now I could see the dust spurting behind his feet as he ran toward home. I was sad, he was of my right hand.

Mister Movie-man, she said. I smiled. High up the hill the cattle tinkled their bells. So now I wanted to say, No, Daddy Hickman; if that's the way it has to be, let's not go. Because it was one more thing I'd have to deny myself because of being Appointed and Set Aside, and I didn't want the added yearning. Better to listen to the others telling the stories, as I had for some time now, since Body had brought the news and the movies had come to town. Better to listen while sitting on the curbstones in the evening, or watching the boys acting out the parts during recess and lunch time on the school grounds. Any noontime I could watch them reliving the stories and making the magic gestures and see the flickery scenes unreeling inside my eye just as Daddy Hickman could make people relive the action of the Word. And seeing them, I could feel myself drawn into the world they shared so intensely that I felt that I had actually taken part not only in the seeing, but in the very actions unfolding in the depths of the wall I'd never seen; in a darkness I'd never known, experiencing with the excruciating intensity of a camel being drawn through the eye of a needle a whole world issuing through an eye of glass.

So Daddy Hickman was too late, already the wild landscape of my mind had been trampled by great droves of galloping horses and charging redskins and the yelling counterattacks of cowboys and cavalrymen, and I had reeled before exploding actions that imprinted themselves upon one's inner eyes with the impact of a water-soaked snowball bursting against the tender membrane of the outer eye to leave a felt-image of blue-white pain throbbing with every pulse of blood propelled by the eager, excited heartbeat toward heightened vision. And I sat on the hard clay behind the white clapboard schoolhouse dizzy before the vastness of the action and the scale of the characters and the dimensions of the emotions and responses that whirled in my mind; had seen laughs so large and villainous with such rotting, tombstone teeth in mouths so broad and cavernous that they seemed to yawn well-hole wide and threaten to gulp the whole audience into their traps of hilarious maliciousness. And meanness transcendent, yawning in one overwhelming face and heroic goodness expressed in actions as cleanly violent as a cyclone seen from a distance, rising ever above the devilish tricks of the bad guys, and the women's eyes looking ever wider with horror or welling ever limpid with love, shocked with surprise over some bashful movement of the hero's lips, his ocean waves of hair, his heaving chest, his eyes anguished with love, despair, or the sheer impossibility of communicating feeling through words. Or now determined with womanly virtue to foil the bad guy and escaping in the panting finish with the good guy's shy assistance; escaping even the Indian chief's dark dark clutches even as I cowered—sharing my friends' fear now, in my imagined seat underneath the Indians' galloping ponies' flying hooves, yet surviving to see her looking with wall-wide head and yard-wide smile of mouth melting with the hero's to fade into the darkness sibilant with women's and young girls' swooning sighs.

Had seen already the trains in my imagination, running wild, threatening to jump the track and crash into the white section below our high enthronement, with smoke and steam threatening to scald the air and bring hellfire to those trapped in their favored seats—screaming as fireman and engineer battled to the death with the Devil now become a Dalton boy or a James or a Younger, and whose horses of devil flesh outran again and again the iron horses of the rails, up-grade and down, and with their bullets flying to burst ever against the sacred sanctuary of Uncle Sam's mail cars, where the gold was stored and the hero ever waited; killing multitudes of clerks and passengers, armed and unarmed alike, in joy and in anger, in fear and in fun. And bushwhacking the sheriff and his deputies again and again, dropping them over cliffs and into cascading waterfalls, until like the sun the Hero loomed and doomed the arch-villain to join his victims, tossed from cliffs, shot in the heart with the blood flowing darkly or hung blackhooded with his men, three in a row, to plunge from a common scaffold to swing like sawdust-filled dolls or blackbirds hung from electric wires by pieces of thread, moving slowly—down in the valley, valley so low—in lonely winds.

All whirled through my mind as filtering through Body's and the others' eyes and all made concrete in their shouting pantomime of conflict, their deadly aimed pistol and rifle blasts, their dying falls with faces fixed in death's most dramatic agony, struck down as by the wrath of God, their imaginary six-shooters blazing one last poetic bullet of banging justice to bring their murderers down down down to hell, now heaving heaven high in wonder evoked in a far white wall of mystery. . . .

So now I wanted to leave the place unentered, even if it had a steeple higher than any church in the world, leave it, pass it ever by, rather than see it once then never enter it again—with all the countless unseen episodes to remain a mystery and like my mother flown forever. But I could not say it, nor could I refuse to enter; for no such language existed between child and man. So I, Bliss, the preacher, ascended, climbed, holding reluctantly Daddy Hickman's huge dark hand. Climbed up the steep, narrow stairs crackling with peanut shells and discarded candy wrappers through the stench of urine—up into the hot, breathing darkness; up, until the slanting roof seemed to rest upon the crowns of our retracted heads.

And as we come into the pink-tinted light of the gallery with its tiered, inverted hierarchical order of seats, white at bottom, black at top, I pull back upon his hand, frightened by what, I did not know. And he says, Come along, Bliss boy—deep and comforting in the dark. It's all right, he says. I'm with you. You just hold my hand.

And I ascended, holding on. . . .

Mister Movie-man, she said . . . and I touched her dark hair, smiling, dreaming. Yes, I said . . . still remembering.

The pink light faded as we moved like blind men. All was darkness now and vague shapes, the crackling of bags and candy wrappers, the dry popping of peanut hulls being opened and dropped to the floor. Voices sounded in the mellow idiom back and forth behind us as we found seats and waited for the magic to begin. Daddy Hickman sighed, resting back, overflowing his seat so that I could feel his side pressing against me beneath the iron armrest. I settled back.

Why don't they hurry and get this shoot-em-up started, someone behind us said. It was a sinner.

Git *started*? a deep voice said. Fool, don't you know that it was already started before we even sat down? Have you done gone stone blind?

It was another sinner. I could tell by the don't give a damn tease in his gravelly voice!

No, the first sinner said. I don't see nothing and you don't neither. Because when it comes to looking at shoot-em-ups I'm the best that ever did it. What's more, I can see you, my man, and that ain't so easy to do in the dark.

Well, the deep voice said, it's starting and I'm already looking and you don't even know it. So maybe you see me but you sho in hell don't see what I see.

Yeah, I know, but that because you drunk or else you been smoking those Mexican cubebs agin.

Listening, I looked to see how Daddy Hickman was reacting. Silently eating popcorn, he seemed to ignore them, feeding the white kernels into his mouth from his great fist like a huge boy.

See there, the second sinner said, because you black you're trying to low-rate me. All right, call me drunk if you want to but any fool knows that a shoot-em-up don't have no end or beginning; but go on playing all the time. They keep on running even when the lights is on. Hell, it's just like the moon in the daytime, you don't see it but it's dam' sho up there.

Now I *know* you been drinking, the first sinner said. Man, you high.

No, but I been studying this mess. Now when the man turns off the lights and tells everybody to take off you think these folks in the shoot-em-ups go away . . .

You dam' right . . .

Yeah, and you think they just wait around somewhere until the nighttime comes and then they come out again.

That's right.

I know, but that's because you're a fool. You ignorant. But in fact, it's just like the moon, and folks who got sense know that the moon is hanging up there all day long. . . .

Oh come on, man. Everybody knows about the moon.

Yeah, but you don't understand that the same thing happens with these shoot-em-up guys. All those guys, even the houses and things, they don't go nowhere when the lights come on. Hell naw! They just stay right here with shooting and fighting and hoss riding and eating and drinking and jiving them gals and having a ball after the man puts us out and locks the door downstairs and goes on home to inspect his jelly-roll. That's how it really is.

Bull, the first sinner said. Bull!

No bull, nothing! Folks like us get tired and have to get some sleep and maybe eat some grits and greens, but hell, those people in the shoot-em-ups they lay right there in the bend. They don't need no rest....

Dam' if you don't make it sound like they in slavery, cousin, another sinner said.

Now you got it, the deep-voiced one said. Ace, take it from me, they in slavery. And man, just like the old folks say, slavery is a war and war is hell!

They laughed.

I was disturbed. Could this be true? Could the people in the pictures always be there working even in the dark, even while they were crowded back into the machine? Forever and forever and forever?

I turned to look at the laughing men. They slouched in their seats, their heads back. One had a gold tooth that flashed in the dim light. Maybe they were just making up a lie for fun, like the boys did at school.

Bliss, Daddy Hickman said.

He touched my arm. Bliss, it's coming on, he said.

I tensed and it was as though he knew before it happened, as though it switched on at his word. For there came a spill of light from behind us, flooding past our heads and down to become a wide world of earth and sky in springtime. And there was a white house with a wide park of lawn with flowers and trees in mellow morning haze.... *Far shot to medium, to close: poiema, pathema, mathema—who'd ever dream I'd know? Me, hidden in their very eyes....* Then it happened, I went out of me, up and around like a butterfly in a curve of flight and there was moss in the trees and a single bird flipped its tail and flew up and away, and just as when watching the boys in the schoolyard I was drawn through the wall and into the action. Over there, graceful trees along a cobblestone drive now occupied by a carriage with a smooth black coachman in livery sitting high and hinkty proud holding the reins above the gleaming backs and arched necks and shining harness of the horses, sitting like a king, wearing a shiny flat-topped hat with a little brush in its band. I am above them as it moves to stop before the big house and a man opens the coach door and descends, hurrying along the walk to the porch, and I descend and go along behind him. He wears a uniform with sabre and sash, boots to his knees. *Ep-aul-ets* (that's the way to say it) show as his cape swings aside and hangs behind him like a trail as he takes long strides, handsome and tall. A black man in black suit with white ruffles at the neck meets him at the columns of the porch and in answer to a question, points to a great doorway, then moves ahead to open the door and then steps aside with a little bow, like Body's when he has to recite a verse on an Easter program at church. *Jesus Wept, Body says and bows, looking warily at his mother across the pews. She had taught him a longer verse but either he's forgot it, or refuses to recite it on a bet. It's the shortest verse in the Bible and the other boys snicker. He'd got away with it again.... Body bowed and hurried back to his seat....* The servant's bow is lower and he holds it until the man sweeps past and I go in behind the man and now I can see past him, over his shoulder, into a large room bright with sunlight and vases of flowers. Near a big window a pretty lady with hair parted in the middle and drawn down to her ears in little curls sits at a piano and as she looks up, surprised, and then with pleasure, I think suddenly, *What is the color of her hair?* And I wish to get past the man to see if she has freckles on her nose, but he keeps coming toward me and I strain to get behind him. I press on as in a dream. It's very hard to do but I made it happen—only now she doesn't see me as she looks up at the man who is still ahead of me. And then as I strain to draw closer something happens—and I feel myself falling out....

Disturbed, I fly back to my seat, hearing in my mind Body saying *Man, them ghosts don't wear no shoes* as I sat back beside Daddy Hickman watching her loom shy and strange, smiling out into the dark not even seeing me in the cool sweet flooding of light. I feel high and lonely. My eyes tickled with tears, until she grew soft and hazy, still looking outward, dreamy-eyed into the darkness and then I knew.

Look, I said, Daddy Hickman, it's her....

Un-huh, he said. He shifted contentedly beside me. Un-huh.

But he doesn't hear me, I thought, *because he's still in the room. He's still back in the wall there.* I couldn't see him there because he was also here, his body pressing forward in the seat. And as she moved toward the man in the elegant room, I searched his face for a sign of recognition. I touched his arm twice, then saw him looking down at me with a smile. Then his hand came up, holding the bag of popcorn toward me.

Excuse me, Bliss boy, he said. Take some.

No thank you, sir, I said. It's her, the same one. You see?

Huh?

It's *her,* I said.

He glanced at me and back again to the screen. Oh sure, he said. She's the lead, Bliss, the heroine. She'll be all through the picture. Because, you see, everything turns around her. Have some. He pushed the bag toward me and I took some, thinking, *He doesn't want to hear me. He doesn't want to tell me....*

Looking back to the wall, I watched them talking earnestly in the room below, then suddenly Daddy Hickman turned, listening to something behind us and I felt myself slip in again and then the man was outside the house and I was above it a ways, watching some men on horses come cantering along the curving drive, moving past the hedges and the tulip trees. They wore uniforms and flowing capes and were proud. And some had whiskers and wore swords. Then I went over their heads and was looking behind the house where some of our own people were watching them coming on. I could tell that they were excited but trying not to show it, leaning forward with hands on hips or holding the handles of their rakes and hoes, looking. Some of the women wore headcloths and had no shoes. I saw a big lazy dog come out of the hedge and bark at the horses. One of the horses, a white one, shied. Then I moved along behind the horses again. I couldn't smell, only see. Couldn't hear clearly either, but some. Where has she gone? I wondered.

Above the house now, I could see a road curving through rolling country-side and on it another body of horsemen, riding hard, in close formation, the dust rising from the horses' hooves. Their buckles and buttons sparkled along the lines. They were coming on. The banner streaming, riders slanting forward in the wind.

And now they were passing some croppers' cabins and some of our people wearing old clothes, headrags, bonnets, and floppy straw hats came out and stood and some others who were dragging cotton sacks raised up in the fields and looked at the men up high and all our people waved.... Then a sinner behind me said something and I fell out again, hard. I was mad.

Here they go again, y'all, the sinner said. Dad blame it! In a second them peckerwoods will be fighting over us again. I sho be glad when they git it over with and done.

Me too, the second sinner said. You'd think they'd git taird of the same thing over and over again.

They already taird, but they have to keep on fighting 'til they can tell it straight. Oh yeah, they taird all right.

Hell, Ace, they ain't never going to get it straight. That's why they keep on messing with it, so that they won't *have* to get it straight.

Listen, you granny dodgers, a voice behind them commanded, I want you to *hush up!*

Hey, granny dodger, who you calling a granny dodger?

You! Granny dodger, so shut up before I kick yo' granny-dodger butt.

They were quiet. I moved behind my eyes as when I tried to fall asleep, then I slipped in again, looking for her.

I was back in the big house now and she was coming out of the door and I thought, *It's her all right,* and I started in close to see her when her face swelled up—then something snapped and I fell out. My face felt slapped.

High up behind me I could hear a flapping sound, very fast—like a window shade when the spring is too tight—then slowing down to a whirr.

From my seat now I could see only a series of black numbers flashing before me in a harsh white light that danced with specks and squiggles. I was breathing hard and my eyes tickled like tears. I was straining to keep it, thinking *Please don't say anything. Please don't say...* I closed my eyes tightly and throbbed my eardrums but I heard anyway.

That was the end of the reel, Bliss, Daddy Hickman said. Just sit tight a second and it'll take up where it left off....

Yes, sir, I said. I wanted to ask him again but was afraid that now he'd understand and say no....

I chewed some popcorn. My throat was dry, thick. The sinners were laughing behind us.

They call this doo-doo *history*, one of them said.

Yeah, but it's got the trots, it don't stack worth a dam and smells like hell.

I closed my eyes. *Why doesn't Daddy Hickman shut them up*, I thought. Then the sound of flapping began again and for a second the light came back again very bright, then faded to become soft and full of wiggles, and there was Daddy Hickman's face smiling in the dim light.

You see, Bliss? he said.

Yes, sir. I was looking hard.

You like it, Bliss?

Oh, yes, sir.

Does it come up to what you expected?

It's better, I, Bliss, said; it's pretty keen.

Yes it is, Daddy Hickman said. It's marvelous and at the same time it's terrible, but that's the way the world is, Bliss. But *shhh* now, it's started again.

She was back, sitting down at a distance in the room looking at a book and I strained to be there and went in. She wore pointed white shoes, with buckles. I was glad.... But then the house... *the house was not there and that old fool high coffin and that strumpet doing splits on the floor without her drawers what the—* Then I was with a soldier galloping on a white horse through a tree-lined lane. Fast, this time, his long cape streaming in the wind. Things tossed. The road ran wobbling up and down before us, the trees tearing at my face, as the hot horse went tearing along with a smell of oak and leather. Too fast now to see all but suddenly I could hear the leather and the brass creaking and straining and it was like sitting in the barber chair and hearing Mr. Ivey say, *Gentlemen, I swear, when that ole hoss went into that backstretch he was running so fas' you could hear him sucking air straight up through his ass!* I held on tight, ducking the branches. Then someone was rushing behind us but I couldn't see. We were stretched out now and suddenly we turn and fire a pistol and now I can see the man on the black horse coming on. Then we're through the trees and approaching a big house with cabins behind it. It's her house and we leap off while the horse is still in motion, tossing its head as we yank on the bit and throw the reins to a servant who looks like he knows us. But his face isn't happy. Then we're inside the house and coming into the room where she stands wearing a long white cape and as she comes forward and sees us, she stops short, then throws out her arms and runs forward and her face painful with eyes closed, flies toward me, filling the room and I screamed....

Daddy Hickman whirled in his chair. What's the matter, Bliss?

It's her, the lady ... I was crying.

What lady, Bliss. Where? This is a moving picture we're watching.

I pointed toward the light.

She's the one. She tried to take me out. The one who said she was my mother.... Goodehugh ...

He sighed. Oh no, Bliss, he said, and talk low. We can't be disturbing the other folks like this.... This is a *moving picture* we're watching, Bliss.

But it's her, I whispered.

No, Bliss. That's not that woman at all. She only looks a bit like her, a bit, but she's not the one. So now you sit back and enjoy yourself. And don't be afraid, she cain't hurt you, Bliss boy; she's only a shadow ...

No, I thought, *it's her. He doesn't want me to know, but just the same, it's her....* And I tried to understand the play of light upon the dark whiteness, the rectangle of cloth that would round out the mystery of my mother's going and her coming.

They're only shadows, Bliss, Daddy Hickman whispered. They're fun if you keep that in mind, they're only dangerous if you try to believe in them the way you believe in the sunlight or the Word.

Yes, sir, I, Bliss, said.

But for me now the three had become hopelessly blended in mystery: My mother gone before memory began, then she who called me Goodehugh Cudworth, and now she I saw as once more I entered the shadows.

Say there, Mister Dreamer Man, she beside me said.

Goodehugh-cudworth, she called me Goodehugh. If not my mother, who moves in the shadows? And again as I look through the beam of pulsing light into the close-up looming wide across the distant yet intimate screen I'm enthralled and sweetly disintegrated like motes in sunlight and I listened as when in the box, straining to hear some sound from her moving lips, holding my breath to catch some faint intonation of her voice above the printed word which Daddy Hickman reads softly to me, explaining the action. And I knew anguish. Yes. There was the wavery beam of light. There was the smoke-like weaving of the light now more real than flesh or stone or pain pouring at a slant down to the living screen. And there behind me now I hear a whirring, a grinding, a hum, broken by the clicking of cogs and rapid wheels. But from her no sound...

I would like to have seen you when you were a little boy, she said.

That was a long time ago, I said.

Did you have a happy childhood?

I looked into her serious eyes. She was smiling.

It was blissful, I said.

I'm happy. I'm very happy because now there's something sad about you, she said. Something lonesome-like.

Like what?

She turned to rest on her elbow, looking into my eyes.

I don't rightly know, she said. It's something moody, and in the way you look at me sometimes. Do you feel sad?

No, I said, I just have a lot on my mind these days.

Yes, I guess you do, she said. Must be a lot on your hands too, judging from the way it's wandering.

I removed my hand. I'm sorry.

And is your hand sorry?

Yes.

Then give it here.

I gave it and she looked at me softly, taking my hand and holding it against her breast.

I didn't mean to be mean, she said.

I came close now, breathing the fever, the allure playing about her lips, her quick breath.

Please, I said, *Please....*

You'll be good to me? *Really* good? Her eyes were frightened, the whites pale blue.

Oh yes, I said, Oh yes!

Come back, Body!... How it hurts, here and here and there and there. His soles flashed in the dust as he ran. I stirred the hulls at my feet, disconsolate below....

Ho, all that the seed, for all that became the seed of all this, the Senator thought— hearing, *Bliss? What are you trying to tell me, boy? Want me to get you the nurse?*

Tell? Ah yes, tell.... How she looked when I took her there in the shade, beneath the flowering tree, that warm brown face looking past my head to the sky, her long-lashed eyelids dreamily accepting me, the stranger, and lifelove the sky—What? Who? Fate? All creation, the rejected terms I fled?

Mister Man, she said, you're making me a problem I never had before.

What kind of a problem?

She teased me with an elfish smile, then for a while she seemed to dream.

What is the problem?

Well, I'll tell you the truth, Mister Movie-man—I'm so country I don't know where the long nose you have is suppose to go. . . .

She laughed then, placing the tip of her fingers there, tweaking my nose. Her own was barely flatter than mine and I was provoked, sweetly. My face suspended in her breath, the moisture came and I went through, upon the sweet soft lips I rested mine. . . .

Bliss?

. . . And I could tell you how I drew her close then and how her surrender was no surrender but something more, a materialization of the heart, the deeper heart that lives in dreams—or once it did—that roams out in the hills among the trees, that sails calm seas in the sunlight; that sings in the stillness of star-cast night. . . . The heart's own that rejoins its excited mate once in a lifetime—like Adam's rib returned transformed and glorious. I can tell you of her black hair waved out upon the grass with leaves in it; the demands of her hand, soft and soothing, with the back of my neck in it; her breath's sweet fever inflaming my face. Even after all these years I can tell you of passion so fierce that it danced with gentleness, and how the whole hill throbbed with silence, the day gathering down, ordered and moving radiant beneath the firm pumping of our enraptured thighs, I can tell you, tell you how I became she and she me with no questions asked and no battle fought. We grasped the secret of that moment and it was and it was enough. I can tell you as though it were only an hour past, of her feel within my arms, a girl-woman soft and yielding. Innocent, unashamed, yet possessing the necessary knowledge. How I was at rest then, enclosed in peace, obsessionless and accepting a def-inition for once and for once happy. How I kissed her eyes, pushed back the hair from her smooth forehead, held that face between my palms as I tried to read the mystery of myself within her eyes. Spoke words into her ear of which only then I was capable—how the likes of me could say, I love, I love. . . . And having loved moved on.

Bliss, boy?

Leaning forward, mountainous in the dwarfed easy chair, the old man watched the Senator's face now, observing the expressions flickering swiftly over the restless features of the man tossing beneath the sheet. He called again, softly, *Bliss?* Then heaved with a great sigh. I guess he's gone again, he thought.

Hickman searched his lower vest pockets with a long finger, extracting a roll of Life Savers and placing one of the hard circles of minty whiteness upon his tongue as he rested back again. Before him the Senator breathed more quietly now, the face still fluid with potential expressions, like a rubber mask washed by swift water. He looks like he's trying to smile, Hickman thought. Every now and then he really looks as though he would, if he had a little help. Maybe that's the way. When he wakes up I'll see what I can do. Anyway, he looks a little better. If only I could do something besides talk. Those doctors are the best, though; the government and his party saw to that. He'll have the best of everything, so there's nothing to do but wait and hope. The fact that they let *me* in here when he asked them is proof of something—I hope that they mean to save him.... There's such a lot I have to ask him. Why didn't I hop a plane and go and find out just what Janey Mason was telling me in her letter? I *knew* she didn't know how to say very much in a letter. Why? And who was that young fellow who did the shooting? Was it really that boy Severn? It'll all come out, they'll find it out even if they have to bring him back from the dead—Ha! Bliss lost all sense of reason; he should have known that he couldn't do what he did to us without making somebody else angry or afraid. This here is a crazy country in which politicians have been known to be shot; even presidents. Pride. Let it balloon up and some sharpshooter's going to try to bring you down. What did Janey mean? Who? I remember back about twenty-five years ago when Janey sent word that a preacher showed up out there. That may have been Bliss. That's when he started whatever she was trying to tell me. One thing is sure, I heard that young fellow speak to the guard, he wasn't from Oklahoma and he wasn't one of us. A Northern boy, sounded like to me....

Suddenly he was leaning forward staring intently into the Senator's face. The eyes, blue beneath the purplish lids, were open, regarding him as from a deep cave.

"Are you still here?" the Senator whispered.

"Yes, Bliss, I'm still here. How do you feel?"

"Let's not waste the time. I can see it on your face, so go ahead and ask me. What is it?"

Hickman smiled, moving the Life Saver to the side of his mouth with his tongue. "You feel better," he said.

"I still feel," the Senator said. "Why don't you leave? Go back where you came from, you don't owe me anything and there's nothing I can do to help your people...."

"My people?" Hickman said. "That's interesting; so now it's *my* people. But don't you realize we came to help *you*, Bliss? Remember? You should've seen us when we first arrived; things might have been different. But never mind all that. Bliss, was it you who went out there to McAlister and fainted on the steps of Greater Calvary one Sunday morning? That would be about twenty-five years ago. Was that you, Bliss?"

"Calvary?" The Senator's weak voice was wary. "How can I remember? I was flying above all that by then. I was working my way to where I could work my way to...." He sank to a safer depth. It was hot there but he could still hear Daddy Hickman.

"Think about it now, Bliss. Didn't you light there for a while and didn't you land on the Bible? In fact, Bliss, haven't you landed on a church each and every time you had to come down?"

Twenty-five years? He thought, maybe he's right. "Perhaps the necessities, as they say, of bread brought me to earth. But remember, they always found me and took me in. It was in their minds. They saw what they wanted to see. It was their own desire. . . . It takes two as with the con game and the tango—Ha!"

"Maybe so, Bliss," Hickman said, "but you allowed them to find you. Nobody went to get you and put you up there in the pulpit. Look here, can you see me? This is Daddy Hickman, I raised you from a little fellow. Was it you? Don't play with me."

"So much has happened since then. I was at McAlister, yes; but they were white. Or were they? Was it Me? Are you still here?"

"You mean you preached in a white church? That early?"

"I think it's all mixed up." He closed his eyes, his voice receding. Is it my voice?

"Yes, High Style," the Senator said. "Huge granite columns and red carpets. Great space. Everyone rich and looking hungry; full of self-denial for Sunday. Ladies in white with lacy folding fans. Full bosoms, sailor straws. White shoes and long drawers in July. Men in shiny black alpaca, white ties. Stern puritan faces, dry concentrate of pious Calvinist dilution distilled and displayed for Sunday. Yes, I was there. Why not? They sang and I preached. The singing was all nasal, as though God was evoked only by and through the nose, as though He lived, was made manifest, in that long pinched vessel narrowly. That was a long time ago. . . ."

"So what happened?"

"I've told you, I preached."

"So what did you preach them, Bliss? Can you remember?"

Where can I hide? Nowhere to run here. It's a joke.

Yes, but what kind of joke?

"I preached them one of the famous sermons of the Right Reverend John P. Eatmore. In my, *our*, condition, what else?"

"Ha, Bliss, so you remembered Eatmore, Old Poor John. Now that there was a great preacher. We did our circuit back there. Revivals and all. Don't laugh at fools. Some are His. Holy, Holy, Holy, Lord God Almighty. Which of Eatmore's did you preach 'em, Bliss? Which text?"

Dreamily the Senator smiled. "They needed special food for special spirits, I preached them one of the most subtle and spirit-filling—one in which the Right Reverend Poor John Eatmore was most full of his ministerial eloquence: *Give a Man Wood and He Will Learn to Make Fire. . . .* Eatmore's most Promethian vision. . . ." Hot here.

No, Reverend Hickman seemed to say, his eyes twinkling, that's one that I've forgotten. I reckon I'm getting old. But Eatmore was the kind of man who was *always* true to his name and reputation. He put himself into everything he did. Preach me a little of it, Bliss; I'll lean close so you won't have to use up your voice. Let's hear you, it'll probably do us both some good. Go on, son.

But how? the Senator thought. *Where are the old ones to inspire me? Where is the Amen Corner and the old exhorters, the enviable shouting sister with the nervous foot tapping out the agitation on which my voice could ride?*

I don't think I can, he said. But his throat was silent and yet Hickman seemed to get it, to understand.

I taught you how, Bliss. You start it, you draw your strength and inspiration out of the folks. If they're cold you heat them up; when they get hot, you guide the flame. It's still the same. You did it in the Senate when you told them about those Nazi fellows and swung the vote....

What, the Senator said. You knew even then?

Eatmore, Bliss. Never mind the rest; let's talk about you preaching Eatmore in a white church. Do I have to start you off like I used to do when you were a baby? Didn't Eatmore begin something like this: He'd be walking back and forth with his head looking up at the ceiling and his hands touching prayer-like together? Then stop suddenly and face them, still looking out over their heads, saying:

Brothers and sisters, I want to take you on a trip this morning. I want to take you back to the dawn of time. I want to let you move at God's rate of speed. Yes, let's go way back to the time of that twilight that had settled down upon the earth after Eden. Ah, yes! I want you to see those times because Time is like a merry-go-round within a merry-go-round, it moves but it is somehow the same even if you're riding on an iron tiger. Eden's fruit had done gone bad with worms and flies. Yes! The flowers that had been the dazzling glory of Eden had run wild and lost their God-given bloom. Everything was in shambles. It was a mess. Things were hardly better than jimson and stink weeds. The water was all muddy and full of sulfur. The air back there stunk *skunk*-sharp with evil. And the beasts, the beasts of the jungle had turned against Man who had named them and no longer recognized him as the head of the animal kingdom. In fact, they considered him the lesser of the animals instead. Oh, Man had come down so low that he was eating snakes. Brothers and sisters, it was an unhappy time. Yes, but even then, even in his uncouth condition, Man somehow remembered that he was conceived in the image of Almighty God. He had forgotten how to take a bath and John the Baptist was yet unborn, but still he was conceived in the image of the Almighty and even though he had sinned and strayed, he still knew he was Man. He was like that old crazy king I once heard about, who had messed up his own life and that of everyone else because he demanded more of every-body than they were able to give him and was living off of roots and berries in the woods but who knew deep down in his crazy mind that he was still a king, and knew it even though the idea made him sick at the stomach. King-ship was so *hard* and manship was so disgusting! He wanted to have it both ways. He wanted folks to love him like he wasn't a king when he was carry-ing around all that power. Yes, Man had sinned and he had strayed; he was just doing the best he could, and that wasn't much.

Now, that's enough for me, Bliss; you take it from there. Let's hear the old Eatmore, boy.

It's been a long time.

Bliss, all time is the same. Preach. Time is just like Eatmore used to say, a merry-go-round within a merry-go-round; only people fall off or out of time. Men forget or go blind like I'm going. But time turns, Bliss, and re-membering helps us to save ourselves. Somewhere through all the falseness and the forgetting there is something solid and good. So preach me some Eatmore....

You won't like it, the Senator said, closing his eyes.

I'll be the judge, Hickman said.

Amen. Yes, Man had sinned, brothers and sisters, and he had strayed. But he was still the handiwork of a merciful God. He carried within him two fatal weaknesses—he was of little faith and he had been contaminated by the great gust of stardust that swept over the earth when Proud Lucifer fell like a blazing comet from the skies. For Man had breathed the dust of pride, and it wheezed in his lungs like a hellish asthma. Thus even though he mingled with the beasts of the forest and Eden had become a forgotten condition rankling with weeds and tares, a lost continent, a time out of his brutish mind, still he retained his pride and his knowledge that he was conceived in the image of God. Two legs God gave him to walk around, two hands to build up God's world, and his two eyes had seen the glory of the Lord. His voice and tongue had praised the firmament and named the things of the earth.

Thus it was, brothers and sisters, that remembering his past grace Man called upon the Lord to give him fire. Fire now! Just think about it. In *those* times—fire! Even God in his total omniscience must have been surprised. Man crying for *fire* when he couldn't even deal with water. Remember, Old Noah was *long* since forgot. Man drank dregs standing unpurified in the muddy tracks of tigers and rhinoceroses! Fire! Why my Lord, what did he want with *fire?*

He ate raw roots and the raw, still-quick flesh of the beasts.

He drank the living blood jetting from the severed jugglar veins of cattle—and yet he cried for fire. Ah yes, today, long past we now know it: give a man wood and he will *learn* to make fire. But back there in those days man knew *nothing* about wood. Oh yes, Oh sure—he slept in trees, he swung from vines. He dug in the earth for tender roots—but wood? What in the world was wood? He used clubs of hickory and oak and even ebony.... But wood— what was wood? Did old Nero know about stainless steel? Man knew no more about wood than a hill of butter beans!

Ha! Now that was a true Eatmore line, Bliss. Preach it.

Suddenly Hickman turned. The door had opened and he saw a severe-looking, well-scrubbed young nurse, her blond hair drawn back severely beneath her starched cap, looking in.

"Don't you think you should leave and get some rest?" she said.

The Senator opened his eyes. "Leave us, nurse. I'll ring when I want you." She hesitated.

"It's all right, daughter," Hickman said. "You go on like he said."

She studied the two men silently, then reluctantly closed the door.

Don't lose it, Bliss, Hickman said. Where did Eatmore go from there?

...Knew no more about wood than a hill of butter beans.... And still, this ignorant beast, this dusty-butted clown, this cabbage-head without a kindergarten baby's knowledge of God's world—brothers and sisters, this lowest creature of creatures was asking God for fire! I imagine that the Holy Creator didn't know whether to roar with anger or blast Man from the face of the earth with holy laughter. Fire! Man cried, *Give me fire!* I tell you it was unbelievable. But then time and circumstance caught up with him. *Give me fire!* he cried. *Give me fire!* Man became so demanding that finally God did rage in righteous outrage at Man's mannish pride. Oh, yes!

For man was beseeching the Lord for warmth when it was the *sun* itself he coveted. And God knew it. For he knoweth all things. Not fire, oh no, that wasn't what Man was yelling about, he wanted the sun!

Oh, give a man *wood* and he will *learn*—to make fire!

Amen!

So God erupted hell in answer to Man's cries of pride. For Man had told himself he no longer wished to wear the skins of beasts for warmth. He wanted to rise up on his two hind legs and *be* somebody. That's what he did! He had seen the sun and now coveted the warmth of the blue vault of heaven!

Ah Man, ah Man, thou art ever a child. One named Hadrian, a Roman heathen, he built him a tomb as big as a town. Well, brothers and sisters, it's a jailhouse now!

One named Morgan built the great *Titantic* and tried to out-fathom one of God's own icebergs. Even though they should have known God's icebergs were still God's and not to be played with. Where are they now, Lord?

Full fathom five, thy father lies, that's where. Down in the deep six with eyes frozen 'til judgment day. There they lie, encased in ice beneath the seas like statues of stone awaiting the day of judgment to blast them free.

Ho, ho, they forgot to sing as the poet was yet to sing:

> *Lo, Lord, Thou ridest!*
> *Lord, Lord, Thy swifting heart*
>
> *Naught stayeth, naught now bideth*
> *But's smithereened apart!*
>
> *Ay! Scripture flee'th stone!*
> *Milk-bright, Thy chisel wind*
>
> *Recindeth flesh from bone*
> *To quivering whittlings thinned—*
>
> *Swept—whistling straw! Battered,*
> *Lord, e'en boulders now out-leap*
>
> *Rock sockets, levin-lathered!*
> *Nor, Lord, may worm out-deep*
>
> *Thy drum's gambade, its plunge abscond!*
> *Lord God, while summits crashing*
>
> *Whip sea-kelp screaming on blond*
> *Sky-seethe, high heaven dashing—*
>
> *Thou ridest to the door, Lord!*
> *Thou bidest wall nor floor, Lord!*

Bliss, that's not Eatmore but it's glorious.

No, it's Crane, but Eatmore would have liked it, he would have sung it, lined it out for the congregation and they would have all joined in.

Yes, he would. Go on, boy. . . .

Thus when God did send the lava streaming and scorching, searing and destroying, floating warmth and goodness within the concentric circles of evil which Man had evoked through his thunderous fall, his embrace of pride, though he had his chance. And now was time for God to laugh, because you see, sisters and brothers, just as today, Man was blind to the mysterious ways of God, and thus Man ran screaming among the mastadons and dinosaurs. Ran footraces with the flying dragons, the hairy birds and saber-toothed tigers—tigers, Ha! Imagine it, with tusks as sharp, as long, as cruel as the swords of the Saracens who did attempt by bloodshed and fire to keep the Lord's message from the Promised Land, the land of Bathsheba's bright morning, of Solomon's enraptured song....

Preach it, Bliss. Now you're preaching Genesis out of Eatmore....

Yes, ran screaming among the hellish beasts and his beastly fellow-men, all wrapped in the furs of beasts, with his hair streaming and his voice screaming. Running empty-handed, his crude tools and weapons, his stone axes and bows and arrows and knives of bone abandoned in his beastly flight before the fire of God! Ho, he stampeded in a beastly panic. Ha! He scrambled in terror under his own locomotion—for Ezekiel was not yet and Man knew not the wheel. Ho yes!

> Yes!
> Yes!
> Yes!
> Do you love?
> Ah,
> Ah,
> Ah, do

you *love?*

Man ran crying, Fire! And running as fast as Man can away from the true gift of God, crying Fire! and flinging himself in wild-eyed and beastly terror away from the fire that was his salvation had he but the eyes of faith to see. Running! Leaping!—Slipping and sliding!—Leaving in his wake even those lesser gifts, those side products of God's Holy Mercy and His righteous chastisement of Man's misguided pride. Man missed, brothers and sisters, missed in this flight the lesser good things: the huge wild boars, those great, great, *great* granddaddys of our greatest pigs, that in the fury of the eruption were now succulent and toasted to a turn by the unleashed volcanic fire. Ran past these most recent wonders, yes; and past whole sizzling carcasses of roasted beeves, and great birds covered with hair instead of feathers, for in those days *nothing* could look like angels' wings. Yes, and moose that stood some forty hands high, with noble countenance, a true and nobly cooked creature of God. But on Man ran, past rare cooked bears; those truly rare bears that made their lesser descendants of the far north, the grizzlies, the great Kodiaks, the great brown bears—yes, and the white polar bears, even the cinnamon bears, made all them bears seem like the pygmies of darkest Africa.... Ah yes! Yes, yes-es-yes! Do-you-love? Doyoulove!

(Preach, Bliss. That's the true Eatmore now. Go get it!)

I say that Man ran! Ran in his headlong plunge, in hectic heathen flight, stumbling over acres of roasted swans and barbecued turkeys and great geese—yes, Lawd!—great geese that fed on wild butternuts and barley grain—imagine, ignored and lost for centuries now but then there they were, cooked in that uncurbed fire. Yes, and God laughing at the godly joke of prideful, ignorant, limited Man.

For, Dearly Beloved, Man in his ignorant pride had called for that for which in his Godlike ambition he was unwilling to suffer. So, having asked and received that for which he asked, he fled with ears that heard not and eyes that saw not, ran screaming away from this second Eden of fire, head-long to the highest hill he fled. He leaped out of there like popcorn roasting on a red-hot stove and with his nose dead to all that scrumptious feast God had spread for his enjoyment.

Now what should he have done? What was Man's mistake?

HE *SHOULD* have asked for *WOOD*! That's what he should have asked! Because give a man wood, and he will *learn* to make his own fire! But man-like he asked for a gift too hot to handle. Yes indeed! So he bolted. He ran. He fled headlong to the highest hill. Yelling, *Fire! Fire! Fire,* Lawd! Then gradually he realized what had happened and Man yelled Ho! This hot stuff that's nipping me on my heels, this is fire!

This wind that's scorching my shoulder, is *fire*!

This heat that's singeing my head bald is *fire*!

Yes! He yelled it so strong that God remembered in His infinite and mysterious mercy that now was not His time to destroy the world by fire and sent down the water from the rocks.

Yes, brothers and sisters, He sent down the cooling water. He unleashed the soothing spring within the heart of stones that lay where the wild red roses grew. Up there, up *yonder,* where the bees labored to bright humming music as they stored their golden grub. And He, God the Father, did give Man another chance. Ah, yes.

For although in his pride Man had sacrificed whole generations of forests and beasts and birds, and though in the terror of his pride he had raised himself up a few inches higher than the animals, he was moved, *despite* himself he was moved a bit closer, I say, to the image of what God intended him to be. Yes. And though no savior in heathen form had yet come to redeem him, God in His infinite mercy looked down upon His handiwork, looked down at the clouds of smoke, looked down upon the charred vegetation, looked down at the fire-shrunk seas with all that broiled fish, looked down at the bleached bones piled past where Man had fled, looked down upon all that sizzling meat and natural gravy, parched barley, boiled roasting-ears and mustard greens.... Yes, He looked down and said, Even so, My work is good; Man knows now that he can't handle unleashed hell without suffering self-destruction! The time will come to pass when he shall forget it, but now I will give him a few billion years to grow, to shape his hand with toil and to discover a use of his marvelous thumb for other than pushing out the eyes of his fellow-man. After all, I put a heap of work into that thumb of Man. And he'll learn that the index and second fingers are meant for something other than playing the game of stink finger and pulling his bow. I'll give him *time*, time to surrender the ways of the beasts to the beasts, time to raise himself upright and arch his back and swing his legs. I shall give him *time* to learn to look straight forward and unblinking out of his eyes and to study the movement of the constellations without disrespecting My essential mystery, My prerogatives, My decisions. Yes, it will take him a few billion years before he'll discover pork chops and perhaps two more for fried chicken. It will take him time and much effort to learn the taste of roast beef and baked yams and those apples he shall name Mack and Tosh.

Until then he will only know charred flesh and a little accidental beer. And if he ever learns to take the stings along with the sweets, I'll let him have some of that honey those bees he's busy slapping at down there are storing up right beside him. He'll come to love it even as much as the burly bears and long before he learns about bear steaks and kidneys, and he'll take it from the hollow trees and learn to take his stings and like it. Yes, and I'll give him a little maize and breadfruit and maybe a squash or two. And it won't be long before he'll live in caves and then he'll start to worshipping me in magic and conjuration and a lot of other ignorant foolishness and confusion. But in time Man will learn to eat like a man and he'll rule his herds and he'll move slowly toward the birth of Time.

Oh Yes, but now Man is but a babe, hardly more than a cub like the children of the bear or the wolf. And like these he soils himself. It will take him a few million years of a few seconds of My time. I shall watch and suffer with him as he goes his arduous way, and meanwhile I shall give him wood and I shall send him down a ray of light, send him a bright prismatic refraction of a drop of crystal dew and then onto a piece of dry wood and Man will in time see the divine spark and have his fire.

Give a man wood, and he will learn—to make fire. Give him a new land and he will learn to live My way.

Yes, and it took all that time, brothers and sisters. Man went on starving amid plenty; thirsting in the midst of all that knowledge being spelled out for him by the birds, the beasts, the lilies of the field. But in time the smoke cleared away and it all came to pass....

The Senator's voice was silent now, his eyes closed.

Hickman shook his head and smiled. Amen, Bliss. You haven't forgot your Eatmore and you haven't forgot the holy laughter. I like that about the gift of roast pork, though I think Eatmo' used to throw in some pigs' feet and lamb chops. Yes, and those luscious chitterlings. And when he did he could make them cry over the sad fact of Man's missing such good grub out of his proud ignorance. He was a joke to some but a smart wordman just the same. He knew the fundamental fact, that you must speak to the gut as well as to the heart and brain. Then they've *got* to hear you one way or the other. Eatmore did all that, sure, but it's been a long time and you smoothed up his style a bit. Ole Eatmore had mush in his mouth too, 'til he worked up to the hollering stage, then it didn't really matter what he said because by then he was shaking them like the Southern Pacific doing a highball. By the way, you were signifying about that new state, weren't you?

Yes, but they were so surprised by the sermon that they forgot they were in a new state.

Bliss, the old man laughed, that was a pretty mean thing you did, springing Eatmore on those folks. But the last part was true. Even here in this aggravating land God gave Man a new chance. In fact, He gave him forty-eight new chances. And He's even left enough land for a few more—though I think by now the Lord's disgusted.... Well, don't let me get started on that; but how about Greater Calvary, Bliss, was that you too?

Ay, it was I, the Senator said. Yes, I was doing what I had to do at that time in that place. I stood there grown tall, but they didn't recognize me. My elbows rested where my hand couldn't reach in the old days, and I looked above their heads and into their hopes. They'd managed a stained-glass window divided into four equal parts and the strawberry light caressed their heads. They'd sweated and saved themselves an organ too, and it rose with its pipes behind me. In the floor at my feet, showing between the circular cut in the red carpet, I could see the zinc edge of the baptismal pool. Looking out at them from behind my face I had the sensation of standing on a hangman's trap, with only the rope missing. And later, I thought of it as the head of a drum because it throbbed beneath me. I made them make it throb.... So yes, it was me, do I have to go on?

I know what you mean by the throbbing, Reverend Hickman said, because I've been there myself. I've made that whole church throb. The Word is a powerful force. Go on, Bliss, tell me.

So I knelt down like I'd seen you do when you were about to take over another man's pulpit, and when he came close to touch me with his hands he was chewing cinnamon to cover the fragrance of his morning's glass of corn...

Suddenly the Senator struggled upward, his eyes wild as Hickman rose quickly to restrain him. "Bliss, Bliss!"

"Corn! Corn whiskey and the collection and the pick of the women! And you wouldn't even allow me ice cream.... In all that darkness, undergoing those countless deaths and resurrections and not even ice cream at the end...."

Hickman restrained him gently, a look of compassionate surprise shaping his dark face as the Senator repeated as from the depths of a forgotten dream, "Not even ice cream," then settled back.

"Steady, Bliss, boy," Hickman said, studying the face before him. The little boy is still under there, he thought. He never ran way from *him*. "I guess that must have been my first mistake with you. It wasn't my teaching you the art of saving souls before you were able to see that it wasn't just a bag of tricks, or even failing to make you understand that I wasn't simply teaching you to be another trickster or jackleg conman. No, it was that I refused to let you have a *payment*. You wanted to be paid. That was probably the first mistake I made. You coulda saved more souls than Peter, but you got it in your mind that you had a right to be paid—which was exactly what you weren't supposed to have. Even if you were going down into the whale's belly like Jonah every night. It wasn't that I begrudged you the ice cream, Bliss. It was just that you wanted it as payment. But that was my first mistake and yours too. Now you take that preacher, he probably took that drink of corn to help him reach up to the glory of the Word, but he took it *before* he preached, Bliss. And that made it a tool, an aid. It was like the box, or my trombone. But you now, you wanted the ice cream *afterwards*. Every time you preached you wanted some. If you said 'Amen,' you wanted a pint. Which meant that you were trying to go into business with the Lord...

"I should have explained it to you better, and I sure tried. But, Bliss, you were stubborn. Stubborn as a rusted iron tap, boy. Well, I'm a man and like a man I made my mistakes. I guess you looked at the collection plates and got confused. But, Bliss, that money wasn't ours. After all these years I'm a poor man. That money went to the church; for the widows and orphans. It went to help support a school down there in Georgia; and for other things. So you went off for ice cream? Is that it? Is that why you left us? Come on now, we might as well talk this out right here because it's important. Anything you hold in your heart after so long a time is important and this is not time for shame."

The Senator was silent for a moment, then he sighed.

"Meaning grows with the mind, but the shape and form of the act remains. Yes, in those days it was the ice cream, but there was something else...."

"It had to be, but what?"

"Maybe it was the weight of the darkness, the tomb in such close juxtaposition with the womb. I was so small that after preaching the sermons you taught me and feeling the yawning of that internal and mysterious power which I could release with my treble pantomime...Oh, you were a wonder, if only in quantitative terms. All the thousands that you touched. Truly a wonder, yes. I guess it was just too much for me. I could set off all that wild exaltation, the rending of veils, the grown women thrown into trances; screaming, tearing their clothing. All that great inarticulate moaning and struggle against what they called the flesh as they walked the floor; up and down those aisles of straining bodies; flinging themselves upon the mourners' bench, or rolling on the floor calling to their God. . . . Didn't you realize that afterwards when they surrounded and lifted me up, the heat was still in them? That I could smell the sweat of male and female mystery?"

"But Bliss—all small children and animals do that. . . ."

"Yes, but I had produced it. At least I thought I had. Didn't you think of what might be happening to me? I was bewitched and repelled by my own effects. I couldn't understand my creation. Didn't you realize that you'd trapped me in the dead center between flesh and spirit, and that at my age they were both ridiculous?"

"You were born in that trap, Bliss, just like everyone was born in it. We all breathe the air at the level that we find it, Bliss."

"Yes, but I couldn't put the two things together. Not even when you explained about the Word. What could I do with such power? I could bring a big man to tears. I could topple him to his knees, make him shout, crack him up with the ease with which shrill whistles split icebergs. Then when they gathered shouting around me, filling the air with the odor of their passion and exertion the other mystery began. . . ."

"What was it, Bliss? Was it that you wanted the spirit without the sweat of the flesh? The spirit *is* the flesh, Bliss; just as the flesh is the spirit under the right conditions. They are bound together. At least nobody has yet been able to get at one without the other. Eatmore was right. . . ."

"Yes, but back there between my sense of power and the puzzling of my nose there were all those unripe years. I was too young to contain it all."

"Not *your* power, Bliss; it was the Master's. All you had to do was live right and go along with your God-given gift. Besides, it was in the folks as well as in you."

"Well, I was in the middle and I was bringing forth results which I couldn't understand. And those women, their sweet . . ."

Hickman was silent, his gaze suddenly turned inward, musing.

"Bliss, come to think about it, it just dawned on me where you might be heading. Didn't you misbehave once on the road somewhere?"

Suddenly the Senator's expression was that of a small boy caught in some mischief.

"So you knew all along? Did she tell you?"

"She told me some, but now I'm asking you."

"So she did after all. How old was she, Daddy Hickman?"

"Well sir, Bliss, I thought you'd forgot you used to call me 'daddy.' " Hickman's eyes were suddenly moist.

"Everyone did," the Senator said.

"Yes, but *you* gave me the pleasure, Bliss. You made me feel I wasn't a fraud. Let's see, she must've been thirty or so. But maybe only twenty. One thing is sure, she was a full-grown woman, Bliss. As grown as she'd ever get to be. She was ripe-young, as they used to say."

"So. I've always wondered. Or at least I did whenever I let myself remember. It was one of your swings around the circuit and she'd taken me to her house afterwards. A tent meeting on that old meeting ground in Alabama."

"That's right."

"... That they had been using since slavery days. Thinking about it now, I wonder why they hadn't taken it away from them and planted it in cotton. I remember it as rich black land."

"It wasn't taken because it was ours, Bliss. It used to be a swamp. The Chocktaws had it before that but the swamp took it back. So then we filled it in and packed it down with our bare feet—at least our folks did—long before we had any shoes. Sure, back in slavery times we buried our dead out around there, and the white folks recognized it as a sacred place. Or maybe just an unpleasant place because of the black dead that was in it. You been on the outside, Bliss, so you ought to know better'n me that they respect *some* things of ours. Or at least they leave them alone. Maybe not our women or our right to good food and education, but they respect our burying grounds."

"Maybe," the Senator said. "It's a game of power."

"Yes, and maybe they're scared of black ghosts. But you ought to know after all this time, Bliss, and I hope you'ee tell me sometimes.... Anyway, boy, it was out there. You remember what it was, don't you?"

"The occasion? It was another revival, wasn't it?"

"Course, it was a revival, Bliss—but it was Juneteenth too. We were celebrating Emancipation and thanking God. Remember, it went on for seven days."

"*Juneteenth,*" the Senator said, "I had forgotten the word."

"You've forgotten lots of important things from those days, Bliss."

"I suppose so, but to learn some of the things I've learned I had to forget some others. Do you still call it 'Juneteenth,' Revern' Hickman? Is it still celebrated?"

Hickman looked at him with widened eyes, leaning forward as he grasped the arms of the chair.

"Do we still? Why I should say we do. You don't think that because you left.... Both, Bliss. Because we haven't forgot what it means. Even if sometimes folks try to make us believe it never happened or that it was a mistake that it ever did...."

"Juneteenth," the Senator said, closing his eyes, his bandaged head resting beneath his hands. "Words of emancipation didn't arrive until the middle of

June so they called it Juneteenth." *So that was it, the night of Juneteenth celebration,* his mind went on. *The celebration of a gaudy illusion.*

No, the wounded man thought, Oh no! Get back to that: back to a bunch of old-fashioned Negroes celebrating an illusion of emancipation, and getting it mixed up with the Resurrection, minstrel shows, and vaudeville routines? Back to that tent in the clearing surrounded by trees, that bowl-shaped impression in the earth beneath the pines?...Lord, it hurts. Lordless and without loyalty, it hurts. Wordless, it hurts. Here and especially here. Still I see it after all the roving years and flickering scenes: Twin lecterns on opposite ends of the rostrum, behind one of which I stood on a wide box, leaning forward to grasp the lectern's edge. Back. Daddy Hickman at the other. Back to the first day of that week of celebration. Juneteenth. Hot, dusty. Hot with faces shining with sweat and the hair of the young dudes metallic with grease and straightening irons. Back to that? He was not so heavy then, but big with the quick energy of a fighting bull and still kept the battered silver trombone on top of the piano, where at the climax of a sermon he could reach for it and stand blowing tones that sounded like his own voice amplified: persuading, denouncing, rejoicing—moving beyond words back to the undifferentiated cry. In strange towns and cities the jazz musicians were always around him. Jazz. What was jazz and what religion back there? Ah yes, yes; I loved him. Everyone did, deep down. Like a great, kindly, daddy bear along the streets, my hand lost in his huge paw. Carrying me on his shoulder so that I could touch the leaves of the trees as we passed. The true father, but black, black. Was he a charlatan—am I—or simply as resourceful in my fashion. Did he know himself, or care? Back to the problem of all that. Must I go back to the beginning when only he knows the start?

Juneteenth and him leaning across the lectern, resting there looking into their faces with a great smile, and then looking over to me to make sure that I had not forgotten my part, winking his big red-rimmed eye at me. And the women looking back and forth from him to me with that bright, bird-like adoration in their faces: their heads cocked to one side. And him beginning:

On this God-given day, brothers and sisters, when we have come together to praise God and celebrate our oneness, our slipping off the chains, let's us begin this week of worship by taking a look at the ledger. Let us, on this day of deliverance, take a look at the figures writ on our bodies and on the living tablet of our heart. The Hebrew children have their Passover so that they can keep their history alive in their memories—so let us take one more page from their book and, on this great day of deliverance, on this day of emancipation let's us tell ourselves our story....

Pausing, grinning down.... Nobody else is interested in it anyway, so let us enjoy ourselves, yes, and learn from it.

And thank God for it. Now let's not be too solemn about it either, because this here's a happy occasion. Rev. Bliss over there is going to take the part of the younger generation, and I'll try to tell it as it's been told to me. Just look at him over there, he's ready and raring to go—because he knows that a true preacher is a kind of educator, and that we have got to know our story before we can truly understand God's blessings and how far we have still got to go. Now, you've heard him, so you know that he can preach.

Amen! They all responded and I looked preacher-faced into their shining eyes, preparing my piccolo voice to support his baritone sound.

Amen is right, he said. So here we are, five thousand strong, come together on this day of celebration. Why? We just didn't happen. We're here and that is an undeniable fact—but how come we're here? How and why here in these woods that used to be such a long way from town? What about it, Rev. Bliss, is that a suitable question on which to start?

God bless you, Rev. Hickman, I think that's just the place we have to start. We of the younger generation are still ignorant about these things. So please, sir, tell us just how we came to be here in our present condition and in this land....

Not back to that me, not to that six-seven-year-old ventriloquist's dummy dressed in a white evening suit. Not to that charlatan born—must I have no charity for me?... Not to that puppet with a memory like a piece of flypaper.

Was it an act of God, Rev. Hickman, or an act of man?

We came, amen, Rev. Bliss, sisters and brothers, as an act of God, but through—I said through, an act of cruel, ungodly man.

An act of almighty God, my treble echo sounded, but through the hands of cruel man.

Amen, Rev. Bliss, that's how it happened. It was, as I understand it, a cruel calamity laced up with a blessing—or maybe a blessing laced up with a calamity....

Laced up with a blessing, Rev. Hickman? We understand you partially because you have taught us that God's sword is a two-edged sword. But would you please tell us of the younger generation just why it was a blessing?

It was a blessing, brothers and sisters, because out of all the pain and the suffering, out of the night of storm, we found the Word of God.

So here we found the Word. Amen, so now we are here. But where did we come from, Daddy Hickman?

We come here out of Africa, son: out of Africa.

Africa? Way over across the ocean? The black land? Where the elephants and monkeys and the lions and tigers are?

Yes, Rev. Bliss, the jungle land. Some of us have fair skins like you, but out of Africa too.

Out of Africa truly, sir?

Out of the ravaged mama of the black man, son.

Lord, thou hast taken us out of Africa...

Amen, out of our familiar darkness. Africa. They brought us here from all over Africa, Rev. Bliss. And some were the sons and daughters of heathen kings....

Some were kings, Daddy Hickman? Have we of the younger generation heard you correctly? Some were kin to kings? Real kings?

Amen! I'm told that some were the sons and the daughters of kings....

...Of Kings!...

And some were the sons and the daughters of warriors....

...Of warriors...

Of fierce warriors. And some were the sons and the daughters of farmers....

Of African farmers...

...And some of musicians...

...Musicians...

And some were the sons and the daughters of weapon-makers and smelters of brass and iron....

But didn't they have judges, Rev. Hickman? And weren't there any preachers of the Word of God?

Some were judges but none were preachers of the Word of God, Rev. Bliss. For we come out of heathen Africa....

Heathen Africa?

Out of heathen Africa. Let's tell this thing true: because the truth is the light.

And they brought us here in chains....

In chains, son: in iron chains....

From half a world away, they brought us....

In chains and in boats that the history tells us weren't fit for pigs—because pigs cost too much money to be allowed to waste and die as we did. But they stole us and brought us in boats which I'm told could move like the swiftest birds of prey, and which filled the great trade winds with the stench of our dying and their crime....

What a crime! Tell us why, Rev. Hickman....

It was a crime, Rev. Bliss, brothers and sisters, like the fall of proud Lucifer from Paradise.

But why, Daddy Hickman? You have taught us of the progressive younger generation to ask why. So we want to know how come it was a crime?

Because, Rev. Bliss, this was a country dedicated to the principles of Almighty God. That *Mayflower* boat that you hear so much about Thanksgiving Day was a *Christian* ship—Amen! Yes, and those many-named floating coffins we came here in were Christian too. They had turned traitor to the God who set them free from Europe's tyrant kings. Because, God have mercy on them, no sooner than they got free enough to breathe themselves, they set out to bow us down....

They made our Lord shed tears!

Amen! Rev. Bliss, amen. God must have wept like Jesus. Poor Jonah went down into the belly of the whale, but compared to our journey his was like a trip to Paradise on a silvery cloud.

Worse than old Jonah, Rev. Hickman?

Worse than Jonah slicked all over with whale puke and gasping on the shore. We went down into hell on those floating coffins and don't you youngsters forget it! Mothers and babies, men and women, the living and the dead and the dying—all chained together. And yet, praise God, most of us arrived here in this land. The strongest came through. Thank God, and we arrived and that's why we're here today. Does that answer the question, Rev. Bliss?

Amen, Daddy Hickman, amen. But now the younger generation would like to know what they did to us when they got us here. What happened then?

They brought us up onto this land in chains....

... In chains ...

... And they marched us into the swamps....

... Into the fever swamps, they marched us....

And they set us to work draining the swampland and toiling in the sun....

... They set us to toiling....

They took the white fleece of the cotton and the sweetness of the sugarcane and made them bitter and bloody with our toil.... And they treated us like one great inhuman animal without any face....

Without a *face*, Rev. Hickman?

Without personality, without names, Rev. Bliss, we were made into nobody and not even *mister* nobody either, just nobody. They left us without names. Without choice. Without the right to do or not to do, to be or not to be....

You mean without faces and without eyes? We were eyeless like Samson in Gaza? Is that the way, Rev. Hickman?

Amen, Rev. Bliss, like baldheaded Samson before that nameless little lad like you came as the Good Book tells us and led him to the pillars whereupon the big house stood. Oh, you little black boys, and oh, you little brown girls, you're going to shake the building down! And then, oh, how you will build in the name of the Lord!

Yes, Reverend Bliss, we were eyeless like unhappy Samson among the Philistines—and worse....

And WORSE?

Worse, Rev. Bliss, because they chopped us up into little-bitty pieces like a farmer when he cuts up a potato. And they scattered us around the land.

All the way from Kentucky to Florida: from Louisiana to Texas: from Missouri all the way down the great Mississippi to the Gulf. They scattered us around this land.

How now, Daddy Hickman? You speak in parables which we of the younger generation don't clearly understand. How do you mean, they scattered us?

Like seed, Rev. Bliss: They scattered us just like a dope-fiend farmer planting a field with dragon teeth!

Tell us about it, Daddy Hickman.

They cut out our tongues....

...They left us speechless....

...They cut out our tongues....

...Lord, they left us without words....

...Amen! They scattered our tongues in this land like seed....

...And left us without language....

...They took away our talking drums....

...Drums that talked, Daddy Hickman? Tell us about those talking drums....

Drums that talked like a telegraph. Drums that could reach across the country like a church bell sound. Drums that told the news almost before it happened! Drums that spoke with big voices like big men! Drums like a conscience and a deep heartbeat that knew right from wrong. Drums that told glad tidings! Drums that sent the news of trouble speeding home! Drums that told us *our* time and told us where we were....

Those were some drums, Rev. Hickman....

...Yes, and they took those drums away....

Away, amen! Away! And they took away our heathen dances....

...They left us drumless and they left us danceless....

Ah yes, they burnt up our talking drums and our dancing drums....

...Drums...

...And they scattered the ashes....

Ah, Aaaaaah! Eyeless, tongueless, drumless, danceless, ashes...

And a worse devastation was yet to come, Lord God!

Tell us, Reveren' Hickman. Blow on your righteous horn!

Ah, but Rev. Bliss, in those days we didn't have any horns....

No *horns?* Hear him!

And we had no songs....

...No songs...

...And we had no...

...Count it on your fingers, see what cruel man has done....

Amen, Rev. Bliss, lead them....

We were eyeless, tongueless, drumless, danceless, hornless, songless!

All true, Rev. Bliss. No eyes to see. No tongue to speak or taste. No drums to raise the spirits and wake up our memories. No dance to stir the rhythm that makes life move. No songs to give praise and prayers to God!

We were truly in the dark, my young brothern and sistern. Eyeless, earless, tongueless, drumless, danceless, songless, hornless, soundless.

...And worse to come...

Tell us, Rev. Hickman. But not too fast so that we of the younger generation can gather up our strength to face it. So that we may listen and not become discouraged!

I said, Rev. Bliss, brothers and sisters, that they snatched us out of the loins of Africa. I said that they took us from our mammys and pappys and from our sisters and brothers. I said that they scattered us around this land....

...And we, let's count it again, brothers and sisters: Let's add it up. Eyeless, tongueless, drumless, danceless, songless, hornless, soundless, sightless, dayless, nightless, wrongless, rightless, motherless, fatherless—scattered.

Yes, Rev. Bliss, they scattered us around like seed....

...Like seed...

...Like seed, that's been flung broadcast on unplowed ground.... Ho, chant it with me, my young brothers and sisters! Eyeless, tongueless, drumless, danceless, songless, hornless, soundless, sightless, wrongless, rightless, motherless, fatherless, brotherless, sisterless, powerless...

Amen! But though they took us like a great black giant that had been chopped up into little pieces and the pieces buried; though they deprived us of our heritage among strange scenes in strange weather; divided and divided and divided us again like a gambler shuffling and cutting a deck of cards; although we were ground down, smashed into little pieces, spat upon, stamped upon, cursed and buried, and our memory of Africa ground down into powder and blown on the winds of foggy forgetfulness...

...Amen, Daddy Hickman! Abused and without shoes, pounded down and ground like grains of sand on the shores of the sea...

...Amen! And God— Count it, Rev. Bliss...

...Left eyeless, earless, noseless, throatless, teethless, tongueless, handless, feetless, armless, wrongless, rightless, harmless, drumless, danceless, songless, hornless, soundless, sightless, wrongless, rightless, motherless, fatherless, sisterless, brotherless, powerless, muleless, foodless, mindless—and godless, Rev. Hickman, did you say godless?

...At first, Rev. Bliss, he said, his trombone entering his voice, broad, somber, and noble. At first. Ah, but though divided and scattered, ground down and battered into the earth like a spike being pounded by a ten-pound sledge, we were on the ground and in the earth and the earth was red and black like the earth of Africa. And as we moldered underground we were mixed with this land. We liked it. It fitted us fine. It was in us and we were in it. And then—praise God—deep in the ground, deep in the womb of this land, we began to stir!

Praise God!

At last, Lord, at last.

Amen!

Oh the truth, Lord, it tastes so sweet!

What was it like then, Rev. Bliss? You read the scriptures, so tell us. Give us a word.

WE WERE LIKE THE VALLEY OF DRY BONES!

Amen. Like the Valley of Dry Bones in Ezekiel's dream. Hoooh! We lay scattered in the ground for a long dry season. And the winds blew and the sun blazed down and the rains came and went and we were dead. Lord, we were dead! Except...except...

...Except what, Rev. Hickman?

Except for one nerve left from our ear...

Listen to him!

And one nerve in the soles of our feet...

...Just watch me point it out, brothers and sisters...

Amen, Bliss, you point it out...and one nerve left from the throat...

...From our throat—right *here*!

...Teeth...

...From our teeth, one from all thirty-two of them...

...Tongue...

...Tongueless...

...And another nerve left from our heart...

...Yes, from our heart...

...And another left from our eyes and one from our hands and arms and legs and another from our stones...

Amen, hold it right there, Rev. Bliss...

...All stirring in the ground...

...Amen, stirring, and right there in the midst of all our death and buriedness, the voice of God spoke down the Word....

...Crying Do! I said Do! Crying Doooo—

These dry bones live?

He said, Son of Man...under the ground, Ha! Heatless beneath the roots of plants and trees.... Son of man, do...

I said, Do...

...I said Do, Son of Man, Doooooo!—

These dry bones live?

Amen! And we heard and rose up. Because in all their blasting they could not blast away one solitary vibration of God's true Word.... We heard it down among the roots and among the rocks. We heard it in the sand and in the clay. We heard it in the falling rain and in the rising sun. On the high ground and in the gullies. We heard it lying moldering and corrupted in the earth. We heard it sounding like a bugle call to wake up the dead. Crying, Doooooo! Ay, do these dry bones live!

And did our dry bones live, Daddy Hickman?

Ah, we sprang together and walked around. All clacking together and clicking into place. All moving in time! Do! I said, Dooooo— these dry bones live!

And now strutting in my white tails, across the platform, filled with the power almost to dancing.

Shouting, Amen, Daddy Hickman, is this the way we walked?

Oh, we walked through Jerusalem, just like John— That's it, Rev. Bliss, walk! Show them how we walked!

Was this the way?

That's the way. Now walk on back. Lift your knees! Swing your arms! Make your coattails fly! Walk! And him strutting me three times around the pulpit across the platform and back. Ah, yes! And then his voice deep and exultant: And if they ask you in the city why we praise the Lord with bass drums and brass trombones tell them we were rebirthed dancing, we were rebirthed crying affirmation of the Word quickening our transcended flesh!

Amen!

Oh, Rev. Bliss, we stamped our feet at the trumpet's sound and we clapped our hands, ah, in joy! And we moved, yes, together in a dance, amen! Because we had received a new song in a new land and been resurrected by the Word and Will of God!

Amen!

... We were rebirthed from the earth of this land and revivified by the Word. So now we had a new language and a brand-new song to put flesh on our bones....

New teeth, new tongue, new word, new song!

We had a new name and a new blood, and we had a new task....

Tell us about it, Reveren' Hickman....

We had to take the Word for bread and meat. We had to take the Word for food and shelter. We had to use the Word as a rock to build up a whole new nation, 'cause to tell it true, we were born again in chains of steel. Yes, and chains of ignorance. And all we knew was the spirit of the Word. We had no schools. We owned no tools, no cabins, no churches, not even our own bodies. We were chained, young brothers, in steel. We were chained, young sisters, in ignorance. We were school-less, tool-less, cabinless—owned....

Amen, Reveren' Bliss. We were owned and faced with the awe-inspiring labor of transforming God's Word into a lantern so that in the darkness we'd know where we were. Oh, God hasn't been easy with us because He always plans for the loooong haul. He's looking far ahead and this time He wants a well-tested people to work his will. He wants some sharp-eyed, quick-minded, generous-hearted people to give names to the things of this world and to its values. He's tired of untempered tools and half-blind masons! Therefore, He's going to keep on testing us against the rocks and in the fires. He's going to heat us 'til we almost melt and then He's going to plunge us into the ice-cold water. And each time we come out we'll be blue and as tough as cold-blue steel! Ah yes! He means for us to be a new kind of human. Maybe we won't be that people but we'll be a part of that people, we'll be an element in them, amen! He wants us limber as willow switches and he wants us tough as whit leather, so that when we have to bend, we can bend and snap back into place. He's going to throw bolts of lightning to blast us so that we'll have good footwork and lightning-fast minds. He'll drive us hither and yon around this land and make us run the gauntlet of hard times and tribulations, misunderstanding and abuse. And some will pity you and some will despise you. And some will try to use you and change you. And some will deny you and try to deal you out of the game. And sometimes you'll feel so bad that you'll wish you could die. But it's all the pressure of God. He's giving you a will and He wants you to use it. He's giving you brains and He wants you to train them lean and hard so that you can overcome all the obstacles. Educate your minds! Make do with what you have so as to get what you need! Learn to look at what *you* see and not what somebody tells you is true. Pay lip service to Caesar if you have to, but put your trust in God. Because nobody has a patent on truth or a copyright on the best way to live and serve Almighty God. Learn from what we've lived. Remember that when the labor's back-breaking and the boss man's mean our singing can lift us up. That it can strengthen us and make his meanness but the flyspeck of irritation of any empty man. Roll with the blow like ole Jack Johnson. Dance on out of his way like Williams and Walker. Keep to the rhythm and you'll keep to life. God's time is long: And all short-haul horses shall be like horses on a merry-go-round. Keep, keep, keep to the rhythm and you won't get weary. Keep to the rhythm and you won't get lost. We're handicapped, amen! Because the Lord wants us strong! We started out with nothing but the Word—just like the others but they've forgot it. . . . We worked and stood up under hard times and tribulations. We learned patience and to understand Job. Of all the animals, man's the only one not born knowing almost everything he'll ever know. It takes him longer than an elephant to grow up because God didn't mean him to leap to any conclusions, for God Himself is in the very process of things. We learned that all blessings come mixed with sorrow and all hardships have a streak of laughter. Life is a streak-a-lean—a streak-a-fat. Ha, yes! We learned to bounce back and to disregard the prizes of fools. And we must keep on learning. Let them have their fun. Even let them eat hummingbirds' wings and tell you it's too good for you. Grits and greens don't turn to ashes in anybody's mouth.... How about it, Rev. Eatmore? Amen?

Amen!

Let everybody say amen. Grits and greens are humble but they make you strong and when the right folks get together to share them they can taste like ambrosia. So draw, so let us draw on our own wells of strength.

Ah yes, so we were reborn, Rev. Bliss. They still had us harnessed, we were still laboring in the fields, but we had a secret and we had a new rhythm....

So tell us about this rhythm, Reveren' Hickman.

They had us bound but we had our kind of time, Rev. Bliss. They were on a merry-go-round that they couldn't control but we learned to beat time from the seasons. We learned to make this land and this light and darkness and this weather and their labor fit us like a suit of new underwear. With our new rhythm, amen, but we weren't free and they still kept dividing us. There's many a thousand gone down the river. Mama sold from papa and chillen sold from both. Beaten and abused and without shoes. But we had the Word, now, Rev. Bliss, along with the rhythm. They couldn't divide us now. Because anywhere they dragged us we throbbed in time together. If we got a chance to sing, we sang the same song. If we got a chance to dance, we beat back hard times and tribulations with a clap of our hands and the beat of our feet, and it was the same dance. Oh, they come out here sometimes to laugh at our way of praising God. They can laugh but they can't deny us. They can curse and kill us but they can't destroy us all. This land is ours because we come out of it, we bled in it, our tears watered it, we fertilized it with our dead. So the more of us they destroy the more it becomes filled with the spirit of our redemption. They laugh but we know who we are and where we are, but they keep on coming in their millions and they don't know and can't get together.

But tell us, how do we know who we are, Daddy Hickman?

We know where we are by the way we walk. We know where we are by the way we talk. We know where we are by the way we sing. We know where we are by the way we dance. We know where we are by the way we praise the Lord on high. We know where we are because we hear a different tune in our minds and in our hearts. We know who we are because when we make the beat of our rhythm to shape our day the whole land says amen! It smiles, Rev. Bliss, and it moves to our time! Don't be ashamed, my brothers! Don't be cowed. Don't throw what you have away! Continue! Remember! Believe! Trust the inner beat that tells us who we are. Trust God and trust life and trust this land that is you! Never mind the laughers, the scoffers, they come around because they can't help themselves. They can deny you but not your sense of life. They hate you because whenever they look into a mirror they fill up with bitter gall. So forget them and most of all don't deny yourselves. They're tied by the short hair to a runaway merry-go-round. They make life a business of struggle and fret, fret and struggle. See who you can hate: See what you can get. But you just keep on inching along like an old inchworm. If you put one and one and one together soon they'll make a million too. There's been a heap of Juneteenths before this one and I tell you there'll be a heap more before we're truly free! Yes! But keep to the rhythm, just keep to the rhythm and keep to the way. Man's plans are but a joke to God. Let those who will despise you, but remember deep down inside yourself that the life we have to lead is but a preparation for other things, it's a discipline, Reveren' Bliss, sisters and brothers; a discipline through which we may see that which the others are too self-blinded to see. Time will come round when we'll have to be their eyes; time will swing and turn back around. I tell you, time shall swing and spiral back around....

No, the Senator thought, *No more of it! NO!*

"Yes, Bliss; Juneteenth," he could hear Hickman saying. "And it was a great occasion. There had been a good cotton crop and a little money was circulating among us. Folks from all over were in the mood for prayer and celebration. There must've been five thousand folks out there that week—not counting the real young chillen and the babies. Folks came all the way from Atlanta, Montgomery, Columbus, Charleston, and Birmingham, just to be there and hear the Word. Horse teams and mule teams and spans of oxen were standing under the grove of trees around the clearing, and the wagon beds were loaded down with hay and feed for the animals and with quilts for the folks who had come in from the far sections, so they could sleep right there. All those wagons made it look as though everybody in the whole section was waiting for the Word to move on over across Jordan. Or maybe migrate West, as some later did. The feel of those days has gone out of the air now, Bliss. And the shape of our minds is different from then, because time has moved on. Then we were closer to the faceless days, but we had faith. Yes, and ignorant as we knew we were, we had more self-respect. We didn't have much but we squeezed life harder and there was a warm glow all around. No, and we hadn't started imitating white folks who in turn were imitating their distorted and low-rated ideas of us. I'm talking now about how it felt when we were together and looking up the mountain where we had to climb....

"But you remember how it was, Bliss: In the daytime hot under the tent with the rows of benches and folding chairs; and the ladies in their summer dresses and their fans whipping up a breeze in time to the preaching and the singing. And the choirs and the old tried and tested workers in the vineyard dressed in their white uniforms. That's right. All the solid substance of *our* way of doing things, of *our* sense of life. Everything ordered and in its place and everything and everybody a part of the ceremony and the evocation. Barrels of ice water and cold lemonade with the cakes of ice in them sitting out under the cool of the trees, and all those yellow cases of soda pop stacked off to one side. Yeah, and at night those coal-oil flares and the lanterns lighting things up like one of those county fairs.

"And the feasting part, you must remember that, Bliss. There was all those ladies turning out fried fish and fried chicken and Mr. Double-Jointed Jackson, the barbecue king, who had come out from Atlanta and was sweating like a Georgia politician on Election Day—excuse me, Bliss—supervising sixteen cooks and presiding over the barbecue pits all by hisself. Think about it for a second, Bliss; it'll come back to you, because even if you look at it simply from the point of eating it was truly a great occasion."

Hickman laughed, shaking his white head, then pushing back in his chair he held up his great left hand, the fingers spread and bending supple as he counted with his right index finger.

"Lord, we et up fifteen hundred loaves of sandwich bread; five hundred pounds of catfish and snapper; fifteen gallons of hot sauce, Mr. Double-Jointed Jackson's formula; nine hundred pounds of barbecue ribs; eighty-five hams, direct from Virginia; fifty pounds of potato salad; and a whole big cabbage patch of cole slaw. Yes, and enough frying-size chicken to feed the multitude! And let's not mention the butter beans—naw! And don't talk about the fresh young roasting ears and the watermelons. Neither the fried pies, chocolate cakes, and homemade ice cream. Lord, but that was a great occasion. A *great* occasion. Bliss, how after knowing such times as those you could take off for where you went is too much for me to truly understand. At least not to go there and *stay*. And don't go taking me simpleminded either. I'm not just talking about the eating. I mean the *communion*, the coming together—of which the eating was only a part; an outward manifestation of which it was only a symbol, like the Blood is signified by the wine, and the Flesh by the bread.... Ah yes, boy, we filled their bellies, but we were really there to fill their souls and give them reassurance—and we *filled* them.

"We *moved*'em!

"We preached Jesus on the cross and in the ground. We preached Him in Jerusalem and walking around Atlanta, Georgia. We preached Him, Bliss, to open up heaven and raise up hell. We preached Him 'til the Word worked in the crowd like a flash of lightning and a dose of salts. Amen! Bliss, we preached and you were with us through it all. You were there, boy. You...."

The Senator lay listening, feeling the pain rise to him again as he tried to surrender himself to the mellow evocation of the voice become so resonant now with pleasure and affirmation. For the moment his powers to resist were weak, as though the word *daddy* in his mouth had opened a fresh flood of memory. Perhaps if he entered into the spell he could escape, could scramble the images that now were rising in his mind, could melt them down. . . .

"Think back, Bliss," Hickman was saying, "Seven preachers in black broadcloth suits and Stacy Adams shoes working full-time to bring them the Word of God. Starting with sunrise services, all kneeling in the dark down on the black earth, bending there on our knees and praying the sun right up out of the ground and into the sky there in the green dawn. Then preaching the clock around; sun up and sun down—from kin to cant. What I mean is seven *powerful* men; men who had the true feeling and the power to drive it home. Men who had the know-how of the human heart!

"What? *Who?* Seven grade-A-number-one, first-class preachers. *Big* men. Sitting up there on the platform, big-souled and big-voiced; all worked up by the occasion and inspiring one another as well as the congregation. Seven great preachers, not to mention Eatmore and you, Bliss.

"And lots of unbelievers were there too; there just to hear those big Negroes preach. Ha! Some of them thought they came out there to hear a preaching contest—which was all right because when the good ones at anything get together there is just naturally going to be a battle. Men who love the Word are concerned with the way they preach it, that's how the glory comes shining through. . . . Oh, but we caught our share of those who thought we were nothing but entertainers. Reveren' Eubanks got aroused there one evening and started to preaching up under some sinner women's clothes and brought 'em in like fish in a net. One got so filled up with the Spirit she started testifying to some things so outrageous that I had to grab my trombone and drown her out. HA! HA! HA! Why, she'd have taught them more sin in trying to be saved than they'd have blundered into in a whole year of hot Novembers. Don't smile, Bliss; it's not really funny and you have to save your strength. Sho, I myself preached fifteen into the fold—big gold earrings, blood-red stockings, short skirts, patent-leather shoes and all. Preached them right out of the back of the crowd and down front to the mourners' bench. Fifteen Magdalenes, Bliss. 'Fancy who's in fancy clothes.' Yes, indeed. Brought them down humbled with hanging heads and streaming eyes and the paint on their faces running all red and pink with tears. . . .

"But what could they do, Bliss? We were playing for *keeps;* we had seven of the most powerful preachers you could find *any*where; we had the best individual singers in the nation; we had the best choirs from all over the southeastern division—and look who else we had: Singing Williams was there, remember him? And Laura Minnie Smith, who could battle Bessie note for note and tone for tone, and on top of that was singing the Word of God. Fess Mackaway was there playing the piano most of the time and conducting the assembled choirs like the master he was. Young Tom Dorsey had come down all the way from Chicago to sit in—even then flirting around with God. Whitby's Heavenly Harmonizers were there, singing the Word in a way that made everything from animals to birds and the flowers of the fields to L & N railroad trains sing in the sound and give thanks to God. There, Bliss, were four Negroes who could make everything of this earth burst into song. They played on Jew's harps, hair combs, zu-zus, washtubs—anything. They blowed Joshua on sorghum jugs. And harmony? Shucks, it ain't never been writ down!

"So what could the poor sinners do? In fact, what could anybody do? Bliss, let me tell you: Ole Eatmore, God bless his memory, Ole Rev Eatmore un-limbered some homiletic there one evening that had the hair standing up on *my* head—and I was already a seasoned preacher! Why, I sat there listening to that Negro making pictures rise up out of the Word and he lifted me plumb up out of my chair! Bliss, I've heard you cutting some fancy didoes on the radio, but son, Eatmore was romping and rampaging and walking through Jerusalem just like John! Oh, but wasn't he romping! Maybe you were too young to get it all, but that night that mister was ten thousand mis-ters and his voice was pure gold. And it wasn't exactly what he was saying, but how he was saying. That Negro was always a master, but that evening he was an *inspired* master. Bliss, he was a super-master!"

Hickman chuckled, studying the Senator's face; thinking, *This won't hurt him, not this part and the smile in it might catch him and help him....*

"And did he set *me* a hard row to hoe, Bliss, when it came my turn I was so moved I could hardly make words. He had us up so high, Bliss, that it called for pure song. I just took off and led them in *Let Us Break Bread Together* 'til I could get myself under control and relieve the strain a bit. I taught you that song, Bliss. It was the very first. It's a song of fellowship, so simple and yet so deep and powerful because in it the lion and the lamb lie down together. Out there in Oklahoma, where they sometimes had the nerve and weren't ashamed to be helped, I brought many a poor white sinner to God with that song.... Well, as I stood there singing I looked out there into all those faces shining there in the dark and in the light, and I asked the Lord, 'Master, what does it all mean beyond a glad noise for Juneteenth Day? What does free-dom, what does emancipation mean?' And the Lord said to me through all that sound, 'Hickman, the Word has found its flesh and there's salvation in the Word.' 'But, Master,' I said, 'back there in the night there's those mean little towns, and on beyond the towns there's the city, with police power and big buildings and factories and the courts and the National Guard; and newspapers and telephones and telegraphs and all those folks who act like they've never heard of your Word. All that while we here are so small and weak....' And the Master said, 'Still here the Word has found flesh and the complex has been confounded by the simple, and here is the better part. Hickman,' He said, 'Rise up on the Word and ride. All time is mine.' Then

He spoke to me low, in the idiom: He said, 'You just be ready when the deal goes down. And have your people ready. Just be prepared. Now get up there and ride!' And Bliss, I threw back my head and rode! It was like a riddle or a joke, but if so, it was the Lord's joke and I was playing it straight. And maybe that's what a preacher really is, he's the Lord's own straight man.

"Anyway, Bliss, that night, coming after Eatmore and Pompey and Revern' Brazelton—yes, and that little Negro Murray, who had been to a seminary up North and could preach the pure Greek and the original Hebrew and could still make all our uneducated folks swing along with him; who could make them understand and follow him—and not showing off, just needing all those languages to give him room to move around in. Besides, he knew that ofttimes the meaning of the Word is in the way you make it sound. No, now don't interrupt me, save yourself. I know that you know these secrets; you have hurt us enough with them. . . . But as I was saying, what's more important, Revern' Murray's education didn't get him separated from the folks. Yeah, and who used to sit there in his chair bent forward like a boxer waiting for the bell, with his fists doubled up and his arms on his knees. Then when it came his turn to preach, he'd shoot forward like he was going to leap right out there into the congregation and start giving the Devil some uppercuts. Lord, what a little rough mister! One night he grabbed a disbelieving bully who had come out to break up the meeting, and threw him bodily out into the dark; tossed him fifteen feet or more into the mule-pissed mud. Then he came on back to the pulpit and preached like Peter. . . ."

"Yes," the Senator said, "I remember him. And there was the tongue-tied one. . . ."

"Yes, yes, I'm not forgetting Reverend Eubanks. He's the one who folks couldn't understand any more than they could Demosthenes before he put those rocks in his jaws—but when he got into the pulpit and raised his hands to heaven—then whoooo, Lord! didn't the words come down like rain!

"Well, Bliss, coming after all them and having to start up there in the clouds where Eatmore left those five thousand or more folks a-straining, I found myself knowing that I had to preach them down into silence. I knew too that only a little child could really lead them, and I looked around at you and gave you the nod and I saw you get up wearing that little white dress suit—you were a fine-looking little chap, Bliss; a miniature man of God . . . and I saw you leave the platform to go get ready while I tried to make manifest the Word. . . ."

Suddenly the Senator twisted violently upon the bed.

"Words, words," he said wearily. "What you needed was a stage with a group of actors. You might have been a playwright."

"Rest back, Bliss," Hickman said. "I preached them down into silence that night. True, there was preacher pride in it, there always is. Because Eatmore had set such a pace that I had to accept his challenge, but there was more to it too. We had mourned and rejoiced and rejoiced and moaned and he had released the pure agony and raised it to the skies. So I had to give them transcendence. Wasn't anything left to do but shift to a higher gear. I had to go beyond the singing and the shouting and reach into the territory of the pure unblemished Word. I had to climb up there where fire is so hot it's ice, and ice so cold it burns like fire. Where the Word was so loud that it was silent, and so silent that it rang like a timeless gong. I had to reach the Word within the Word that was both song and scream and whisper. The Word that was beyond sense but leaping like a tree of flittering birds with its *own* dictionary of light and meaning.

"I don't really know how I got up there, Bliss, there's no elevator for such things. First it was Eatmore and then I was leading them in *Let Us Break Bread Together,* on our knees—and it happened. Instead of sliding off into silence I started preaching up off the top of that song and they were still singing under me, holding me up there as I started to climb. Bliss, I was *up* there, boy. I was talking like I always talk, in the same old down-home voice, that is, in the beloved idiom, but I was no loud horn that night, I was blowing low— and we didn't have microphones either, not in those days. But they heard me. I preached those five thousand folks into silence, five thousand *Negroes,* and you know that's the next thing to a miracle. But I did it. I did it and it was hot summertime, and the corn whiskey was flowing out back of the edge of the crowd. Sure, there was always whiskey—and fornicating too. Always. But inside there was the Word and the Communion in the Word, and just as Christ Jesus had to die between two criminals, just so did we have to put up with the whiskey and the fornication. Even the church has to have its outhouse, just as it has to have a back door as well as a front door, a basement as well as a steeple. Because Man is always going to be Man and there's no true road without sides to it, and gulleys too, no true cross without arms that point away in two directions from the true way. But that Juneteenth night they all came quiet. And, Bliss, when I faded out they were still quiet. That's when ole Fess took over and got them singing again and I came down out of it and gave the nod to the boys and they started marching you down the aisle...."

Wait. Wait! the Senator's mind cried beneath the melodic line of Hickman's reminiscing voice, feeling himself being dragged irresistibly along. And now he could see himself, Bliss again, dropping down from the back of the platform with the seven black-suited preachers in their high-backed chairs onto the soft earth covered with sawdust, hearing the surge of fervored song rising above him in the hot night and Daddy Hickman's voice sustaining a note without apparent need for breath, rising above the tent as he moved carefully out into the dark to avoid the rope and tent stakes, walking soft over the sawdust earth and heading across the clearing for the trees where Deacon Wilhite and the big boys were waiting. He moved reluctantly as always, yet hurrying, thinking, *He still hasn't breathed, he's still up there,* hearing Daddy Hickman soaring above the rest like a great dark bird of light, a sweet yet anguished mellow cry edged with a painful sob. Still hearing it hovering there as he began to run to where he could see the figures standing around where the box lay supported by a table set under the pines. Leaning huge against a tree was the special-built theatrical trunk they shipped it in. Then he was climbing onto the table side, hearing one of the boys giggling and saying, "What you saying, Deadman?" Then looking back without answering he saw with longing the bright warmth of the light beneath the tent with the worshippers and caught the surging movement as they rocked in their chairs to the song which now seemed to rise up to the still sustained note of Daddy Hickman's soaring cry. Then Deacon Wilhite said: "Come on, little preacher; in you go," lifting him, his great hands around his ribs, then his feet going inside and the rest of him slipping past Teddy and his Bible, lying and beginning to shiver as the tufted top brought the blackness down.

And not even ice cream, nothing to sustain me in my own terms. Nothing to make it seem worthwhile in Bliss terms.

I seemed to float in the blackness, the jolting of their measured footsteps guided by Deacon Wilhite's precise tones, across the contoured ground, all coming to me muted through the pink insulation of the padding which lined the bottom, reaching me at blunt points along my shoulders, buttocks, heels, thighs. A beast with twelve disjointed legs coursing along, and I its inner ear, its anxiety, its anxious heart; straining to hear if the voice that sustained its line and me still soared, because I believed that if he breathed while I was trapped inside I'd never emerge, and hearing the creaking of a handle near my ear, the thump of Cylee's knuckles against the side to let me know he was there squinch-eyed and probably giggling. And through the thick satin cloak of the lining the remote singing seemed miles away and the rhythmical clapping of hands coming to me like sharp, bright flashes of lightning, promising rain. Moving along on the tips of their measured strides like a boat in a slow current as I breathed through the tube in the lid the hot ejaculatory air, hushed now by the entry and passage among them of the ritual coat of satin, my stiff dark costume in their absurd, eternal play of life and death.... Back to that? No!

"Bliss, I watched them bringing you slowly down the aisle on those strong young shoulders and putting you there among the pots of flowers, the red and white roses and the bleeding hearts—and I stood above you on the platform and began describing the beginning and the end, the birth and the agony, and ..."

Screaming, mute, the Senator thought, not me but another. Bliss. Resting on his lids, black inside, yet he knew that it was pink, a soft silky pink blackness around his face, covering his nose. He was fitted in the satin closing round him like the lining of the knife case which he'd seen in a jewelry store window, only the box was closed and the pinkness was turned to blackness. Always the blackness. Inside everything became blackness, even the white Bible and Teddy, even his white suit. It was black even around his ears, deadening the sound except for Reverend Hickman's soaring song, which now, noodling up there high above, had taken on the softness of that piece of soft black velvet cloth which Grandma Wilhite had used to make him a nice fulldress overcoat like Daddy Hickman's, only better because it had a wide cape for a collar.... He listened intently, one hand gripping the white Bible, the other gripping Teddy's paw. Teddy was down there where the top didn't open at all, unafraid, a bold, bad bear. He listened to the voice sustaining itself, the words rising out of the Word like Ezekiel's wheels, without breath, straining desperately to keep its throbbing waves coming to him, thinking, *If he stops to breathe, I'll die, my breath will stop too. Just like Adam's clay if God had coughed or sneezed.* And yet, he knew too that he was breathing through the tube set in the lid. *Hurry, Daddy Hickman,* he thought, *Hurry and say the word. Please, let me rise up. Let me come up and out into the air....*

The big boys were walking him slowly over the smooth ground and he could feel the slight rocking movement as the box shifted on their shoulders. That means that we're out in the clearing. Trees back there, voices that-a-way, life and light up there. Hurry! They're moving slow, like an old boat drifting down the big river in the night and me inside looking up into the black sky, no moon or stars and all the folks gone far beyond the levees. He could feel the shivering creep up his legs now and squeezed Teddy's paw to force it down, thinking, *Hurry, please hurry.* Then the rising rhythms of the clapping hands coming up to him like storming waves heard from a distance; waves that struck the boat and flew off into the black sky like silver sparks from the shaking of the shimmering tambourines, showering at the end like the tails of skyrockets. *If I could only open my eyes. It hangs heavy-heavy over my lids. Please hurry! Restore my sight.* This black night is dark and I am far... far... He came from the dark inside of a red-and-white-striped egg....

> *They took my Lord away*
> *They took my Lord*
> > *Away,*
> *Please, tell me where*
> > *To find Him....*

Then they were letting him down, down, down and he could feel the jar as someone went too fast, as now a woman's shout came to him, seeming to strike the side near his ear like a flash of lightning streaking jaggedly across a dark night sky:

Jeeeeeeeeeeeeeee-sus! Have mercy, Jeeeeeeeeee-sus!

and a quivering flashed up his legs.

Everybody's got to die, sisters and brothers, Daddy Hickman was saying remotely through the dark. That is why each and every one must be re-deemed. YOU HAVE GOT TO BE RE-DEEMED. Even He who was the Son of God and the Voice of God to man—even *He* had to die. And what I mean is die as a *man*! So what do you, the lowest of the low, expect you're going to have to do? He had to die in all of man's loneliness and pain because that's the price *He* had to pay for coming down here and putting on the piti-ful, unstable form of Man. Have mercy! Even with His godly splendor which could transform the built-in wickedness of Man's animal form into an organ-ism that could stretch and strain toward sublime righteousness—Amen! That could show Man the highway to progress toward a more noble way of living—even with all that, even He had to die! Listen to me tell it to you: Even He who said, Suffer the little ones to come unto *Me*! had to die as a Man. And like a Man crying from His cross in all of Man's pitiful puzzle-ment at the will of Almighty God!

It was not yet time. He could hear the waves of Daddy Hickman's voice rolling up against the sides, then down and back, now to boom suddenly in his ears as he felt the weight of darkness leave his eyes, his face bursting with sweat as he felt the rush of bright air bringing the breath of flowers as he lay blinking up at the lights, the satin corrugations of the slanting lid, and the vague outlines of Deacon Wilhite, who now was moving aside. And it was as though Deacon Wilhite had himself been the blackness. He lay breathing through his nose now, deeply inhaling the flowers as he released Teddy's paw and grasped the white Bible with both hands, feeling the chattering and the real terror beginning, aching his bladder. For always it was as though it waited for the moment when he was ready to answer Daddy Hickman's sig-nal to rise up that it seemed to slide like heavy mud from his face to his thighs to hold him like quicksand. Always at the sound of Daddy Hickman's voice he came floating up like a corpse shaken loose from the bottom of the river and the terror came with him.

We are the children of Him who said, Suffer.... And in his mind he could see Deacon Wilhite, moving up to stand beside Daddy Hickman at the lectern, holding on to the big Bible and looking intently at the page as he re-peated:

SUFFER....

And the two men standing side by side, the one large and the other small;

and behind them the other reverends rowed behind them, their faces staring serious with engrossed attention to the reading of the Word; like judges in their carved, high-backed chairs, as Daddy Hickman's voice began spelling out the text which Deacon Wilhite was reading just as he did with his trombone when he really felt like signifying on a tune the choir was singing:

Suffer, meaning in this workaday instance to surrender, Daddy Hickman said.

Amen, Deacon Wilhite said, repeating, Surrender.

Yes, meaning to surrender with tears and to feel the anguished sense of human loss. Ho, our hearts bowed down!

Suffer the little ones, Deacon Wilhite said.

The little ones—ah yes! *Our* little ones, Daddy Hickman said. Our little loved ones. Flesh of our flesh, soul of *our* soul. Our hope for heaven and our charges in this world. Yes! The little lambs. The promise of our fulfillment, the guarantee of our immortal continuity! The little wases-to-bes—Amen! The little used-to-bes that we all were to our mammys and pappys and with whom we are but one with God....

Amen! Deacon Wilhite sang out. Now the Scripture next says, To Come....

Oh my Lord, just look how the word leaps! Daddy Hickman said. First the babe, then the preacher. The babe father to the man, the man father to us all. A kind father calling for the babes in the morning of their earthly day. Then in the twinkling of an eye Time slams down and He calls us to come....

... To come, Brother Alonzo!

Ah yes, to come, meaning to *approach.* To come up and be counted; to go along with Him, Lord Jesus. To move through the narrow gate bristling with spears, up the hill of Calvary, to climb onto the unyielding cross on which even lil babies are transformed into men. Yes, to come upon the proving ground of the human condition. Vanity dropped like soiled underwear. Pride stripped off like a pair of duckings that've been working in all week in the mud. Feet dragging with the gravity of the moment; legs limp as a pair of worn-out galluses; with eyes dim as a flickering lamp wick! Read to me, Deacon; read to me!

He said, Come unto me, Deacon Wilhite cried.

Come to me—Yes! Meaning to take up His burden. At first the little baby-sized load that with the first steps we take weighs less than a butterball; no more than a sugar-tit. Then, Lord help us, it grows heavier with each step we take along life's way, until in that moment it weighs upon us like the headstone of the world. Meaning to come bringing it! Come hauling it! Come dragging it! Come on, even if you have to crawl. Come with your abuses! And come with no excuses! Amen! Let me have it again, Reveren' Wilhite....

Come unto Me, the Master said.

Meaning to help the weak and the downhearted. To stand up to the oppressors. To suffer and hang from the cross for standing up for who you are and for what you believe. Meaning to undergo His initiation into the life everlasting. Oh Yes, and to cry...cry....cry......eyeeee!

Bliss could hear the word rise and spread to become the great soaring trombone note of Daddy Hickman's singing voice. It seemed somehow to arise there in the box along with him, shaking him fiercely as it rose to float with throbbing pain up to Daddy Hickman again, who now seemed to stand high above the tent. And trembling now, he tensed himself and rose slowly upright in the controlled way Daddy Hickman had taught him, feeling the terror gripping like quicksand. He could feel the opening of his mouth and the spastic flexing of his diaphragm as the words rushed from his throat to join the resounding voice.

Lord, Lord!

Why...

...Hast Thou...

...Forsaken me?

And now Daddy Hickman was opening up and bearing down,

More man than men and yet in that world-destroying-world-creating moment just a little chile calling his father.... Then pausing before his next cue:

HEAR THE LAMB A-CRYING ON THE TREE!

LORD, LORD, Bliss cried, WHY HAST THOU FORSAKEN ME?

Amen, Daddy Hickman answered, Amen!

Then his voice came fast, explosive, with gut-toned preacher's authority, awe-inspiring:

The Father of no man who yet was the Father of all men; the human-son-side of God—Great God A-mighty! Calling out from the agony of the cross! Ho, open up your downcast eyes and see the beauty of the living Word.... All babe, and yet in that mysterious moment, ALL MAN. Him who had taken up the burden of all the little children crying, LORD....

LORD, Bliss cried.

Crying plaintive as a baby sheep...

...Baaaaaaaa!

The little lamb crying with the tongue of Man...

...Lord...

...Crying to the Father...

...Lord, LORD...

...Calling to his pappy...

Lord, Lord, why hast...

...Amen! Lord, Why...

...Hast Thou...

…Forsaken me.…

Aaaaaaaah!

WHY HAST THOU FORSAKEN ME, LORD?

Bliss screamed the words in answer and now he wished to cry, but the sound of Daddy Hickman's voice told him that this was not the time, that the words were taking Daddy Hickman where they wanted him to go. Now he could hear him beginning to walk up and down the platform behind him, pacing in his great black shoes, his voice rising with his heavy tread, his great chest heaving:

Crying—Amen! Crying, Lord, Lord—Amen! On a cross on a hill, His arms spread out like my grandmammy told me it was the custom to stretch a runaway slave when they gave him the water cure. When they forced water into his mouth until it filled up his bowels and he lay swollen and drowning on the dry land. Drinking water, breathing water, water overflowing his earth-bound lungs. Nailed! NAILED! Riveted to the cross-arm like a coonskin fixed to the door of the House of God, but with the live coon still inside the furry garment! Still in possession of his body and his mind, with all nine points of the Roman Law a fiery pain to consume the earthly house. Yes, and every point of law a spearhead of injustice.

Look! See with me! His head is lollying! Green gall is drooling from his lips! Drooling, yes! down his chin like pap from his mammy's breast as it had drooled in those long, sweet, baby days long gone.

AH YES! BUT NO TIT SO TOUGH NOR PAP SO BITTER AS TOUCHED THE LIPS OF THE DYING LAMB!

Oh, no! Oh, Grandmother Death was suckling the son of MAN! Yes, and the son of God was beginning to shine in all His beauty.

There He is, hanging on; hanging on in spite of knowing the way it would have to be. Yes! Because the body of Man does not wish to die! It matters not who's inside the ribs, the heart, the lungs. Because the body of Man does not sanction death! Suicide is but a sulking in the face of hope! Ah, Man is *tough*. Man is *human*! By definition Man is *proud*. Even when heaven and hell come slamming together like a twelve-pound sledge on a piece of heavy-gauged railroad steel, Man is tough and Man is *mannish*—and Ish means *like*. There *He* was, stretching from hell-pain to benediction; head in heaven and body in hell.… Tell me, who said He was weak? Who said He was frail? Because if He was, then we need a new word for *strength*. We need a new word for *courage*! We need a whole new dictionary!

Ah, but there He was, with the others laughing up at Him, their mouths busted open like rotten melons—laughing! You know how it was, you've been up there; you've heard that contemptuous sound: "IF YOU BE THE KING OF THE JEWS AND THE SON OF GOD, JUMP DOWN." Jump down, black bastard, dirty Jew, Jump down!

Scorn burning the wind. Enough halitosis alone to burn up old Moloch!

The many ganged up against the few!... He's bleeding from his side. Hounds baying the weary stag.... And yet there is the power and the glory locked in the weakness of His human manifestation; bound by His human limitation, His sacrificial humanhood! Ah, yes; for He willed to save Man by dying and dying as *Man* died. And He was a heap of man in that moment, let me tell you. I say, let me tell you, that mister was much *man* in that awful moment. He was Man raised to his most magnificent image, shining like a prism with all the shapes and colors of man, and dazzling all who had the vision to see. Man moved beyond mere pain to tragic joy.... There He is, with the spikes in his tender flesh. Nailed to the cross—first with it lying flat on the ground, and then being raised in a slow, flesh-tearing, bone-scraping arc, one hundred and eighty degrees—Up, up, UP! Aaaaaaaaah! Up until He's upright like the ridge-pole of the House of God.

Lord, Lord, Why?

See Him! Watch Him! Feel Him! His eyes rolling as white as our eyes, looking to His, Our Father, the tendons of his neck roped out, straining like the steel cables of a heavenly curving bridge in a storm. Help me! Help me now! His jaw muscles bursting out like kernels of corn on a hot stove lid. Yes! And His mouth trying to refuse the miserable human questioning of the words....

Lord, Lord...

...Oh yes, Reveren' Bliss, crying above the laughing ones for whom He left His Father to come down here to save, crying.

...Lord, Lord, Why?

Amen! Crying as no man since, thank you, Jesus, has ever had to cry.

Ah Man, Ah human flesh! This side we all know well, on His weaker, human side we were all up there on the cross, just swarming over Him like ants. Yes, but look at Him with me now. Look at Him freshly, with the eyes of your most understanding heart. There He is now, hanging on in man-flesh, His face twitching and changing like a field of grain struck by a high wind, hanging puzzled, bemused and confused, mystified and teary-eyed—wracked by the realization dawning in the gray matter of His cramped human brain; knowing in the sinews, in the marrow of his human bones, in the living tissue of his most human veins—realizing that Man was born to suffer and to die for other men! There He is, look at Him. Suspended between heaven and hell, hanging already nineteen centuries of time to one split second of His torment and realizing in that second of His anguished cry that life in this world is but a zoom between the warm womb and the lonely tomb. Proving for all time, casting the pattern of history forth for all to see in the undeniable concreteness of blood, bone, and human grace before that which has to be borne by every man.... Proving—proving that in this lonely, lightning-bug flash of time we call our life on earth we all begin with a slap of a hand across our tender baby bottoms that starts us to crying the puzzled question with our first drawn breath—Why was I born.... Aaaaaaaah!... And hardly before we can get it out of our mouths, hardly before we can exhale the first lungful of life's anguished air...even before we can think to ask, Lord, what's my true name? Who, Lord, am I?—here comes the bone-crunching slap of a cold iron spade across our puzzled countenance and it's time to cry, WHY, LORD, WHY WAS I BORN TO DIE?

Yes, why? Reveren' Hickman, tell us why?

Why, Reveren' Bliss? Because we're men, that's why! The initiation into the lodge is hard! The dues are outrageous, and nobody can refuse to join. Oh, we can wear the uniforms and the feathered hats, the tasseled fez and the red-and-purple caps and capes a while, and we can enjoy the feasting and the marching and strutting fellowship—then Dong, Dong! and we're caught between two suspensions of our God-given breath: one to begin and the other to end, a whoop of joy and a sigh of sadness, the pinch of pain and the tickle of gladness; learning charity if we're lucky, faith if we endure, and hope in sheer downright desperation!

And now, thank God, because He passed his test like any mannish man—not like a god, but like a pale, frail, weak man who dared to be his Father's son...amen! Oh, we must dare to be, brothers and sisters.... We must Dare, my little children.... We must dare in our own troubled times to be our Father's own. Yes, and now we have the comfort and the example to help us through from darkness to lightness, a torchlight along the way. Ah, but in that flash of light in which we flower, we must find Him so that we can find *us,* ourselves. For it is only a quivering moment—then the complicated tongs of life's old good-bad come clamping down, grabbing us in our tender places, locking like bear's teeth beneath our short hair—Lord, He taught us how to live, yes! And in the sun-drowning awfulness of that moment, He taught us how to die. There He was on the cross, leading His sheep, showing us how to achieve the heritage of our godliness which HE in that most pitiful human moment—with spikes in His hands and through His feet, with the thorny crown of scorn studding His tender brow, with the cruel points of Roman steel—not Jewish, *Roman*—with those points of Roman steel piercing His side....

Crying, Lord...

...Lord!

LORD! Amen. Crying from the castrated Roman tree unto His Father like an unjustly punished child. And yet, Reveren' Bliss, Glory to God.... And yet, He was guaranteeing with the final expiration of His human breath our everlasting life....

Bliss could feel the words working in the crowd now, boiling in the heat of the Word and the weather. Women were shouting and far back in the dark he could see someone dressed in white leaping into the air with outflung arms, going up, then down, over backwards and up and down again, in a swooning motion which made her seem to float for a moment in the air which was being stirred by the agitated motion of the women's palm-leaf fans.

It was past the time for him to preach Saint Mark, but each time he cried "Lord, Lord," he couldn't hear his own voice as they shouted and screamed even louder. He tried to see to the back of the tent, back where the seams in the ribbed white cloth curved down and were tied in a roll; past where the congregation strained forward or sat in rigid fixation, seeing here and there the hard, bright disks of eyeglasses glittering in the hot yellow light of lanterns and flares. The faces were rapt and owl-like, gleaming with perspiration in the heat of Daddy Hickman's interpretation of the Word.

Then suddenly, right down there in front he could see an old white-headed man beginning to leap in holy exaltation, bounding high into the air and sailing down; then up again higher than his own head, moving like a jumping-jack, with bits of sawdust dropping from the bottom of his white tennis shoes. A brown old man, whose face was a blank mask, set and mysterious, his lips tight, his eyes starry like those of a china doll, soaring without effort through the hot shadows of the tent; sailing as you did in dreams just before you fell out of bed and woke up. A holy jumper, Brother Pegue....

Bliss turned to look at Daddy Hickman, seeing the curved flash of his upper teeth and the swell of his great chest as with arms outspread he began to sing.... When suddenly, from the left of the tent he heard a scream. It was a different note, and when he turned he could see the swirling movement of a woman's form, but strangely, no one was reaching out to keep her from hurting herself, or from jumping out of her underclothes and showing her womanness as some of the ladies sometimes did. Then he could see her coming on, a tall, redheaded woman in a purple-red dress, coming on screaming through the soprano section of the big choir where the members, wearing their square, flat-topped caps, were standing and knocking over chairs, letting her through as she dashed among them striking out with her arms as she moved forward toward the front.

She's a sinner coming to testify, he thought.... *A white—? Is she white...?* hearing,

He's mine, mine! That's Cudworth, my child. My baby. You gypsy niggers stole him, my baby. You robbed him of his birthright!

Yes, she is white, he thought, seeing the wild eyes and the hair streaming like a field of wheat coming toward him now at a pace which seemed suddenly dream-like. *What's she doing here, a white sinner?* Moving toward him like the devil in a nightmare, as now a man's voice boomed from far away, Madam, Lady, please—this here's the House of God! But even then not realizing that she was clawing and pushing her way toward him; thinking, *Cudworth? Who's Cudworth?* Until suddenly there she was, her hot voice screaming in his ear, her pale face shooting down toward him like an image springing out of a toppling mirror, her green eyes wide, her nostrils flaring. Then he felt her arms lock around him and his head was crushed against the hardness of her breast, hard into the sharp, sweet woman-smell of her. *Me, she means me,* he thought, as something strange and painful stirred within him. Then, as she crushed him closer, he could no longer breathe, squeezing and shaking him and he felt his Bible slipping from his fingers and tried to hold on, but she screamed again with a sudden movement, her voice bursting hot and shrill into the sudden hush. And he felt his Bible fall away in the well-like echo now punctuated by the heavy rasping of her breathing. It was then he realized that she was trying to lift him from the coffin. Tearing at it to get him out.

I'm taking him home to his heritage, he heard. He's mine. You understand. I'm his mother.

It was strangely far away, like a scene unfolding under water. *Who is she?* flashed through his mind. *Where's she taking me? She's strong. But my mother went away. Paradise, up high. . . . A ghost . . .*

Then he was looking at the familiar faces, seeing their bodies frozen in odd postures like Body and the others when they played a game of statue. He thought: *They're scared. She's scaring them all. . . .* Then his head jerked around and he could see Daddy Hickman leaning over the platform just above them, bracing his hands against his thighs, his arms rigid, with a look of amazement on his great laughing-happy face as he violently shook his head.

Then he was twisted again and as his head came around, his teeth clicking, it was as though a stick had stirred quiet water. He could see the people all standing looking on, one woman still rapidly fanning herself, while some were standing on chairs, holding on to the shoulders of those in front of them, their eyes and mouths wide with disbelief—until the scene crumpled like a funny paper burning in a fireplace and he saw their mouths open to utter the same words so loud and insistently that he heard only a blur of loud silence. Yet her breathing came hard and clear. His head came round to her now, close up, so that he could see the light fringe of freckles shooting across the ridge of the straight, thin nose like a covey of quail flushing across a field of snow, the wide-glowing green of her eyes. Stiff copper hair was bursting from the white temple like the wire of Daddy Hickman's red rubber "electric" hairbrush. Then the scene swirled again and he heard a calm new sound bursting in.

JUST DIG MY GRAVE, he heard, JUST DIG MY GRAVE AND READY MY SHROUD, 'CAUSE THIS HERE AIN'T HAPPENING! OH NO, IT AIN'T GOING TO HAPPEN. SO JUST DIG MY GRAVE!

It was a short, stooped black woman, hardly larger than a little girl, whose shoulders slanted straight down from her neck and into the white collar of her oversized black dress, from which her deep and vibrant alto voice seemed to issue as from some source other than her mouth. He could see her coming through the crowd, shaking her head and pointing toward the earth, crying, I SAID DIG IT! I SAID GO GET THE DIGGERS! the words so intense with negation that they sounded serene, the voice rolling with eerie meaning as now she seemed to float in among the white-uniformed deaconesses. And he could see the women turning to stare wonderingly at one another, then back to the little woman who moved between them, grimly shaking her head. Then suddenly he could feel the arms tighten around his body and he was being lifted up out of the coffin and the redheaded woman screamed past his ear, Don't you blue gums touch me! Don't you dare!

And again it was far away, beneath the water in a dimly lit place where nothing responded as it should. For at her scream he seemed to see the little woman and the deaconesses pause as they should have paused in the House of God as well as in the world outside the House of God—then she was lifting him higher and he felt his body come up until only one foot remained caught in the pink lining and he looked down just as she swung him in her arms and he felt the coffin hard against his foot. Then it was going over, slowly like a turtle sliding off a log. It seemed to rise up of its own will, lazily; then one of the sawhorses moved and it seemed to explode.

He felt that he was going to be sick; for, glancing downward from the woman's tightening arms, he could see the coffin still in motion. It seemed to rise up of its own will, lazily, sleepily, like Daddy Hickman turning slowly in a pleasant sleep—only it seemed to be laughing at him with its pink frog-mouth. Then as she moved him again, one of the sawhorses shifted violently and he could see the coffin tilt up at an angle and heave.

It seemed to vomit now, spilling Teddy and Easter Bunny and his glass pistol with its colored-candy BB bullets, like prizes from a paper horn-of-plenty. And now even his white leather Bible was spilling out, its pages fluttering open for everyone to see. He thought, *He'll be mad about my Bible and my bear*—and he felt a scream start up from where the woman was squeezing his stomach, as now she swung him swiftly around, causing the church tent, the flares and the people, to spin before his eyes like a great tin humming top. Then his head snapped forward and back, rattling his teeth, and in the pause he could see the deaconesses spring forward even as the spilled images from the toppling coffin lingered vividly before his eyes—gone like a splash in the sunlight, as a tall woman with short, gleaming hair and steel-rimmed eyeglasses shot from among the deaconesses, her lenses glittering harshly, and he could see her mouth come open and the other women freezing in their places, making a great silence beneath the upward curve of his own screaming voice and her head went back with an angry toss, and he could feel the high shrill slap hard against him.

What! Y'all mean to tell *me?* the woman shouted, Here in the HOUSE OF GOD? She's going to come in *here?* Who? *WHO!* JUST TELL ME! WHO BORN OF MAN'S HOT CONJUNCTION WITH A WOMAN'S SIN-FUL BOWELS?

And like an echo now, the larger voice of the smaller woman, seeming to float up from the floor,

JUST DIG MY GRAVE, JUS' READY MY SHROUD! I SAY JUST . . . the voices now booming and echoing beneath the tent.

And it was as though something heavy had plunged from a great height into the water, throwing the images into furious motion. His face was pressed hard against the red hair as now the women moved. They came like shadows flying before a torch tossed into a darkened room, their weight seeming to strike him and the strange woman who held him out of a single slow, long-floating, space-defying leap, sending the woman staggering backwards and causing her tightening arms to squash the air from his lungs so that his chest ached as it did whenever he held his breath too long between sobs. Their faces, hallowed with wrath, loomed before him, seeming to enter where his breath had been, their widespread hands beginning to tear at his body like the claws of great cats with human heads, lifting him clear of earth and coffin, and he felt himself suspended there between the redheaded woman, who now held his head, and the sisters who had seized his legs, arms, and body. And again he felt, but could not hear, his own throat's painful *Aaaaaaaaaaaaaah!*

The Senator's eyes rolled, the taste of fever filled his mouth. It was as though the stream of memories had reopened his wounds. His fingers found the button with which he could ring for the nurse but he hesitated. The large, kindly face was still looking across at him, the hoarse voice moving mellow, still evocative and compelling around him. He would wait, this time he wouldn't run. Not now . . .

"Well sir, Bliss," Hickman was saying, "here comes this white woman pushing over everybody and up to the box, and it's like hell done erupted at a sideshow. She rushed up to the box. . . ."

"Box?" the Senator said wearily, "You mean *coffin,* don't you?"

Hickman looked quickly down, slightly frowning. "No, Bliss, I mean 'box.' It's not a coffin 'til it holds a dead man. . . . So as I was saying, she rushed up and grabs you in the box and the deaconesses leaped out of their chairs and folks started screaming, and I looked out there for some white folks to come get her, but couldn't see none, so there it was. I could have cried like a baby, because I knew that one miserable woman could bring the whole state down on us. And there she is, out of nowhere like a puff of poison gas, right smack in the middle of our Emancipation exaltation. Bliss, it was like God had started playing practical jokes.

"Next thing I know she's got you by the head and Sister Suzie Trumball's got one leg and another sister's got the other and some others are snatching you by the arms. Talking about King Solomon, he didn't have but two women to deal with—I had seven, and one convinced that she was a different breed of cat from the rest. Yes, and the others were chock full of disagreement and dead set to probe it. I tell you, Bliss, when it comes to chillen, women just ain't gentlemen, and the fight between her kind of woman and ours goes way back to the beginning. Back, I guess, to when women found that the only way they could turn over the responsibility of raising a child to another woman was to turn over some of the child's love and affection along with it. They been battling ever since. One trying to figure out how to get out of the work without dividing up the affection, and the other trying to hold on to all that weight of care and those cords of emotion and love for which they figure no wages can ever pay. Because while some women work and others don't, to a woman a baby is a baby. She ain't rational about it, way down deep she ain't. All it's got to be is little and warm and helpless and cute and she wants to take it over, just like a she-cat will raise a litter of rabbits, or a she-bitch dog will mama a Maltese kitten. I guess most of those deaconesses had been nursing white folks' chillen from the time they could first take a job and each and every one of them had helped raise somebody's baby and loved it. Yes, and had fought battles with the white women every step of the way. It's a wonder those babies ever grow up to have good sense with all that vicious, mute-unspoken female fighting going on over them from the day they was passed from the midwife's or doctor's hands into his mother's arms and then from the minute it needed its first change of swaddling clothes, into some black woman's waiting hands. Talking about God and the Devil fighting over a man's soul, that situation must make a child's heart a battleground. 'Cause, Bliss, as you must know by now, women don't recognize no rules except their own—men make the public rules—and they knew all about this so-called psychological warfare long before men finally recognized it and named it and took credit for inventing something new.

"So there this poor woman comes moving out of her territory and bursting into theirs. Mad, Bliss, mad! That night all those years of aggravation was multiplied against her seven times seven. Because down there her kind always wins the contest in the end—for the child, I mean—with ours being doomed to lose from the beginning and knowing it. They have got to be weaned—our women, I mean, the nursemaids. And yet, it just seems to make their love all the deeper and the tenderer. They know that when the child hits his teens they can't hold it or help it any longer, even if she gets to be wise as Solomon. She can help with the first steps of babyhood and teach it its first good manners and love it and all like that, but she can't do nothing about helping it take the first steps into manhood and womanhood. Ha, no!

Whoever heard of one of us knowing anything about dealing with life, or knowing a better way of facing up to the harsh times along the road? So the whole system's turned against her then from foundation to roof; the whole beehive of what their folks consider good—'quality,' we used to say—is moved out of her domain. They just don't recognize no continuance of anything after that: not love, not remembrance, not understanding, sacrifice, compassion—nothing. Comes the teen time, what we used to call the 'smellyourself' time, when the sweat gets musty and you start to throb, they cast out the past and start out new—baptised into Caesar's way, Bliss. Which is the price the grown ones exact for the privilege of their being called 'miss' and 'mister.' So self-castrated of their love they pass us by, boy, they pass us by. Then as far as we're concerned it's 'Put your heart on ice, put your conscience in pawn.' Even their beloved black tit becomes an empty bag to laugh at and they grow deaf to their mammy's lullabyes. What's wrong with those folks, Bliss, is they can't stand continuity, not the true kind that binds man to man and to Jesus and to God. My great-great-granddaddy was probably a savage eating human flesh, and bastardy, denied joy and shame, and humanity had to be mixed with my name a thousand times in the turmoil of slavery, and out of all that I'm a preacher. It's a mystery but it's based on fact, it happened body to body, belly to belly over the long years. But then? They're all born yesterday at twelve years of age. They can't stand continuity because if they could everything would have to be changed; there'd be more love among us, boy. But the first step in their growing up is to learn how to *spurn* love. *They have to deny it by law,* boy. Then begins the season of hate AND SHAMEFACEDNESS. Confusion leaps like fire in the bowels and false faces bloom like jimsonweed. They put on a mask, boy, and life's turned plumb upside down.

"'Cause what can be right if the first, the *baby love,* was wrong, Bliss? Tell me then, where's the foundation of the world? The tie that binds? You tell me, if with a boy's first buzz and a gal's first flow 'warm' has to become 'cold' and 'tenderness' calls forth 'harshness' and 'forthrightness' calls forth 'deviousness,' and innocence standing on the shady side of the street is automatically to be judged guilt? Hasn't joy then got to become flawed, just another name for sadness, like a golden trumpet with a crack in the valves and then with a pushed-in bell? Yes, and gratitude and charity and patience, endurance and hope and all the virtues Christ died to teach us become nothing but a burden and a luxury for black, knotty-headed fools? Speak to me, Bliss. You took their way, so speak to me and let me see by the light of their truth. I have arrived in ignorance and questioning. I'm old, my white head's almost forgot its blacker times and my sight's so poor I can almost look God's blazing sun straight in the face without batting my fading eyes. And I'm a simple man and nothing can change that. But I'm talking about simple things. For me, Bliss, the frame of life is round and looking through I see the spirit does not die and neither does love when she smells of she and he smells of he, and the skirts git short and the voice cracks and deepens to mannish tones. No, but the way they've worked it out, tears become specialized, boy; and Jesus looked at the lot of Man and wept for everybody. But those people put a weatherman in control of the sky. They cut the ties between the child and the foundation of his love. Laughter cracks down like thunder when tears ought to fall. And would have too, the year before. But standing in the doorway of manhood and womanhood you have to question yourself how to feel in the simplest things. You fall out of rhythm with your earliest cries, your movements. Little signs have to be stuck up and consulted in the heart: How must I feel, Mister Weatherman? His face over there is dark, though I used to know it, can I say 'howdy'? She stretches forth the same old hand for charity that used to cook the fudge and plait my braids, can I acknowledge it? She cries for understanding and a recognition of that old cut nerve that twitches in my heart—can I afford to hear the voice of this bowed-down heart? How much money will it cost me, Mister Weatherman? He wrestles over there in pain, ain't this the time to laugh; with misery monkeying up his wrinkled face? Or he speaks polite and steps aside, isn't this the way of fear and a sign that God has spit on him? Bow down, bow down! Step aside and out of my exalted human sight.

"Then a little later, Bliss, when he's found a mate, that old severed nerve throbs again; they're laughing like fools out in the quarters—is it to mock my dignity? Is it zippered up? Listen to them praying, is it for my abject destruction? I built my house on King Mountain stone, will it crumble before their envying eyes? In the dark in the alley, in the summer night some mister man is making a woman howl and spit like a rapturous cat—could that black tomcat have prowled in my bed? *Could* he? *Could* he? How now! He's a buck stallion full of stinking sweat, I'm an eagle, bright with the light of God's own smile. His woman's a bitch and mine a doe. . . . Ah, but think about it with the blue serge hanging on the rack: Has a black stallion ever mounted a snow-white doe at her frisky invitation when the sun was down? What goes on in that darkness I create when I refuse to see? What links up with what? Who reaches out to whom within that gulley, under that lid of life denied? You want me to hush and go away, Bliss?

"Not now, it's been too long and some things just won't stand not being said. Oh, all I've been talking about is human, Bliss. All human weakness and human pride and will—didn't Peter deny Christ? But you had a choice, Bliss. You had a chance to join up to be a witness for either side and you let yourself be fouled up. You tried to go with those who raise the failure of love above their heads like a flag and say, 'See here, I am now a man.' You wanted to be with those who turn coward before their strongest human need and then say, 'Look here, I'm brave.' It makes me laugh because few are brave enough to be for right and truth above all their other foolishness. There wasn't a single man in that jail that night they beat me who didn't know I was innocent, and there wasn't a single person in that town who didn't know that woman was crazy, but not a single one was brave enough and free enough simply not to beat me. I don't mean defend me. I don't mean take up the cause of Justice. 'Listen, this man is innocent. He was preaching before a tent full of people and so couldn't have touched that woman with a ten-foot pole.' No, Bliss, I didn't expect that because I knew the score. But even knowing it I found I still had something to learn. I had to lay there while they beat me and what I learned was that there wasn't a mother's son among them who, knowing my innocence, had the manhood and decency to refuse to whip my head. I guess if there'd been a preacher among them he'd've got in his licks with the rest. I lay there and laughed, Bliss. Sure, I laughed. I laughed because there is some knowledge that's just too hopeless for tears. That was a long time ago and a few years before you were to make your choice, Bliss, but the devilment I'm describing has been going on for years and it's a process for blinding and all the hell unleashed in the church that night sprang from it. The eye that was trained by two women's love to love and respond to life now must be blind to the spirit that shines from all but a special few human eyes, and now you can't look beneath the surface of a window-pane and see fire and the mirrors are rigged so you can't see what you would deny in those whom you would deny. Oh, sure, Bliss; you can cut that cord and zoom off like a balloon and rise high—I mean that cord woven of love, of touching, ministering love; that's tied to a babe with its first swaddling clothes—but the cord don't shrivel and die like a navel cord beneath the first party dress or the first long suit of clothes. Oh no, it parts with a cry like a rabbit torn by a hawk in the winter snows and it numbs quick and glazes like the eyes of a sledgehammered ox and the blood don't show, it's like a wound that's cauterized. It snaps with the heart's denial back into the skull like a worm chased by a razor-beaked bird, and once inside it snarls, Bliss; it snarls up the mind. It won't die and there's no sun inside to set so it can stop its snakish wiggling. It bores reckless excursions between the brain and the heart and kills and kills again unkillable continuity. Bliss, when Eve deviled and Adam spawned we were *all* in the dark, and that's a fact."

Suddenly the old man shook his head. "Oh, Bliss; *Bliss*, boy. I get carried away with words. Forgive me. Maybe a black man, even one as old as me, just can't understand the mystery of a white man's pain. But one thing I do know: God, Bliss boy, is Love."

The Senator looked up at the fading voice, gripped by the fear that with its cessation his own breath would go. But there was Hickman still beside him, looking down as with the wonder of his Word for God.

"Perhaps," the Senator said, "but it makes the laces too tight. Tell me what happened while there's still time."

"Lord, Bliss," Hickman said, "Here I've gone off and left you suspended in those women's hands and you crying to beat the band. Well, for a minute there it looked like they was going to snatch you limb from limb, tear you apart and dart in seven different directions. *And* the folks were getting outraged a mile a minute, because nothing makes our people madder and will bring them to make a killing-floor stand than to have white folks come bringing their craziness into the church. We just can't stand to have our one place of peace broken up, and nothing upsets us worse than that—unless it's messing with one of our babies.

"You could see it and hear it, Bliss. I turned and yelled at them to regard the House of God—when here comes another woman, one of the deaconesses, she's a big six-foot city woman from Birmingham, wearing eyeglasses and who was usually the kindest woman you'd want to see. Sister Beaumasher, she had a French name. But like now she was soft-spoken and easygoing the way some big women get to be because most of the attention goes to the little cute ones. Well, Bliss, she broke things up. I saw her tearing down the aisle from the rear of the tent and reaching over the heads of the others and before I could move, she's in that woman's head of long red hair like a wildcat in a weaving mill. I couldn't figure what she was up to in all that pushing and tugging, but they kind of rumbled around the floor until somebody's shoe came sailing out of there like a big comet and then they ducked down in a squat like they were trying to grab for better holts and when they come up she's got all four feet or so of that woman's red hair wrapped around her arm like an ell of copper-colored cloth. And, Bliss, she's talking calm and slapping the others away with her other hand like they were babies. Saying, 'Y'all just leave her to *me* now, sisters. Everything's going to be all right. She ain't no trouble, darlings. Not now. Get on away now, Sis Trumball, and let her go. You got rheumatism in your shoulder anyway. You all just let her loose now. Coming here into the House of God talking about this is *her* child. Since when? I want to know, since *when?* HOLD STILL, DARLING,' she tells the white woman, 'NOBODY WANTS TO HURT YOU, BUT YOU MUST UNDERSTAND THAT YOU HAVE GONE TOO FAR....'

"And the white woman is holding on to you for dear life, Bliss; with her head going back, back, like a net full of red snappers and flounders being wound up on a ship's winch. And this big Amazon of a woman who could've easily set horses with a Missouri mule starts to preaching her own sermon, saying, 'If this Revern' Bliss the preacher is her child, all the little yeller bastards in the nation has got to be her child. So when's she going to testify to all *that?* You, sister, just let her go now. Just let me have her and y'all take that chile. Take that chile, I say! I love that chile 'cause he's God's chile and y'all love that chile, so I say take that chile. Remove that chile out of this foolish woman's sacrilegious hands. TAKE HIM, I SAY! And if this is the time, then this is the TIME. If it's the time to die, then I'm dead. But take that chile. 'Cause this is one kind of foolishness that's got to be stopped before it goes any further.'

"Well sir, there you were, Bliss, with that white woman still got holt of you but with her head snubbed back now and her eyes bucking like a frightened mare's, screaming, 'He's mine, he's mine!' *Claiming you,* boy, claiming you right out of our hands. Least out of those women's hands. 'Cause us men were petrified, all thrown out of action by the white woman's awful nerve, and that big strong bear-mashing woman threatening to snatch her scalp clean from her head.

"And all the time Sister Bear Masher—what was her name?—she's talking 'bout, 'If he was just learning his A.B.C.'s like the average chile instead of being a true, full-fledged preacher of the gospel you wouldn't want him and you'd yell down destruction on anybody who even signified he was yours— WHERE'S HIS DADDY! JUST TELL US WHO'S HIS DADDY! YOU AIN'T THE VIRGIN MARY SO YOU SHO MUSTA PICKED OUT HIS DADDY. WHO'S THE BLACK MAN YOU WANT TO DIE?'

"And women all over the place started taking it up, Bliss. 'Yes, that's right, who's the man? AMEN!' and all like that. You could almost see the tent start to flapping.

"Bliss, I'm a man with a great puzzlement about life and I enjoy the wonderment of how things can happen and how folks can act. In this land the unexpected always pops out, there's no straight lines once you get a few feet off the ground, and I must have just been standing there with my mouth open taking it in. But when those women started making a chorus and working themselves up to do something drastic, I broke loose. I reached down and grabbed my trombone and started to blow but instead of blowing something calming, I broke into 'The St. Louis Blues' like we used to do when I was a young hellion and a fight would break out at a dance. Just automatically, and I caught myself on about the seventh note and smeared into 'Listen to the Lambs,' but my lip was set wrong and I was half laughing at how my sinful days had tripped me up anyway so it came out 'LET US BREAK BREAD TOGETHER,' and by that time Deacon Wilhite had come to life and started singing and some of the men joined in. . . . In fact, it was a men's chorus, 'cause those women was still all up in arms. I blew a few bars and put down that horn and climbed down to the floor to see if I could untangle that mess.

"I didn't want to touch that woman, so I yelled for somebody who knew her to come forward and get her out of there. Because even after I had calmed them a bit she kept her death grip on you and was screaming and Sister Beaumasher still had that red hair wound round her arm and didn't want to let go. Finally, a woman named Lula Strother came through the crowd and started talking to her like you'd talk to a baby and she gave you up. I'm expecting the police or some of her folks by now but luckily none of them had come out to laugh at us that night. So Bliss, I got you into some of the women's hands and me and Sister Beaumasher got into the woman's rubber-tired buggy and rode off into town.

"She had two snow-white horses hitched to it and luckily I had handled horses as a boy because they were almost wild. She was screaming and they reared and pitched until I could switch them around. They hit that midnight road for a fare-thee-well. The woman's yelling at 'em to make them smash us up, screaming and cursing like a trooper and calling for you, though by the name of Cudworth, and Sister Beaumasher's still got her bound up by her hair. It was dark of the moon and a country road. We took every curve on two wheels and when we crossed those lil wooden bridges it sounded like a fusillade of rifle fire. It was like those horses was rushing me to trouble so that I'd already be there before I could think of what I was going to say. How on earth was I going to explain what happened, with that woman there to tell 'em something different? With her just being with us more important than truth. I thought about Sister Beaumasher's question about who the man was that had been picked to die and I tell you, Bliss, I thought that man was me. There I was, hunched over holding to those reins for dear life and those mad animals frothing and foaming in the dark and the spray from their bits flying back and hitting me in the face. I could have taken a turn away from town, but that would make it worse, with the whole church in danger. So I was bound to go ahead as the minister responsible for their souls. Sister Beaumasher was the only calm one in the carriage. She's talking to the woman as polite as if she was waiting on table or rubbing her feet or something, and all the time she's still wound up in that woman's hair.

" 'Now, now, we're taking you where your folks is. You'll be all right. You sure will.'

"But the woman wouldn't stop screaming, Bliss. And she's cussing—speaking out some of the worse oaths that ever fell from the lips of Man. We're flying through the dark and I can see the eyes of wild things shining all along, at first ahead of us glowing up and then disappearing. And the sound of galloping that those horses made! They were hitting a lick on that road like they were in a battle charge.

" 'Reveren' Hickman,' Sister Beaumasher yelled over to me.

" 'Yes, Sister?' I called back over to her.

" 'I say, are you praying?'

" 'Praying?' I yelled, 'Praying! Sister, my whole body and soul is crying to God, but it's 'bout as much as I can do t'hold on to these devilish reins. You just keep that woman's hands from scratching my face.'

"Well, about that time, Bliss, we hit a straightaway, past some fields, and way off to one side I looked and saw somebody's barn on fire. It was like a dream, Bliss. There we were making better time than the Hamiltonian with foam flying from those white horses' bits, the woman screeching, leather straining, hooves pounding, and Sister Beaumasher no longer talking to the woman but moaning a prayer like she's bent over a washtub somewhere on a peaceful sunny morning and managing to sound so through all that rushing air; and then, then there it was; way off yonder across the dark fields, that big barn filling the night with silent flames. It was too far to see if anyone was there to know about it, and it was too big for nobody except us not to see it; and as we raced on there seemed no way NOT to see it burning across the night. We seemed to wheel around it, the earth was so flat and the road so long. Lonesome, Bliss, that sight was lonesome. Way yonder, isolated and lighting up the sky and the dark around it. And then as we swung and swayed around a curve where the road swept into a tree-lined lane I looked through the flickering of the trees and saw it give way and collapse. The flames spread sparks and swept up toward the sky. Poor man, I thought; poor man, God help him, just as the buggy hit a rough stretch of road. And I was praying then, boy; I was really praying. I prayed,

" 'Lord, bless these axles and these singletrees,

" 'Lord, bless these bits, these bridles, and the reins,

" 'Keep, Lord, these wheels and rubber tires hugging solid to Thy solid earth,

" 'And bless, Lord, these hames, these cruppers, and this carriage tongue.

" 'Yea, bless, Lord, these breast-straps and these leather bellybands,

" 'Yea, Lord, and whatever you may choose to do with me,

" 'Bless, Master, please this straining whiffletree!'

"And listening to those pounding hooves and feeling those horses trying to snatch my arms right out of their sockets I said, 'And Lord, even bless this wild redheaded woman sitting here between us who, in her outrageous pride, interrupted our praise to Thee. And bless, too, that man back there with his burning barn. And since, Lord, you know all about Sister Beaumasher and me being caught out here on this rocky, night-shrouded road, all I ask is that you keep us focused in Thy merciful all-seeing eye until we reach the living end....'

"Those horses moved, Bliss. Zip, and we're through the lane and passing through a damp place like a swamp, then up a hill through a burst of heat. And all the time, Bliss, I should have been praying for you. Because after all I suppose a lot of prayer and sweat and dedication, as well as money-greed and show-off pride and general wickedness had gone into making that buggy because it held together through all that rough ride and with its wheels humming like guitar strings took me and Sister Beaumasher and a pretty hot time before they let us go. So there between a baby, a buggy, and a burning barn, I prayed the wrong prayer. I left you out, Bliss, and right there and then you started to wander. But you, I left you in some of the sisters' hands and you misbehaved. Bliss, you was the one who needed praying for and I neglected you. . . ."

He, Bliss, sat at the kitchen table drinking the ice-cold lemonade and listening to the tinkle the chunk of ice made when he stirred it with his finger. The others were sitting quietly in the room with Daddy Hickman and he could see Sister Wilhite nodding in her chair over near the window. Sister Wilhite's tired, he thought. She's been up all night and Deacon has too. He looked at the cooking stove, dull black with shining nickel parts around the bottom made in the shape of scrolls. They're the same shape as the scrolls on the lid of my coffin, he thought. Why do they put scrolls on everything? Sister Wilhite's sewing machine has scrolls made into the iron part where her feet go to pedal and it has scrolls painted in gold in the long shining block that holds the shiny wheel and the needle. Scrolls on everything. People don't have scrolls, though. But maybe you just can't see them. Sister Georgia . . . Scroll, Scroll Jellyroll . . . That's a good rhyme—but sinful . . . Jellyroll.

The stovepipe rose straight up and then curved and went out through a hole up near the ceiling. The wallpaper up there was black where the smoke had leaked through. The stove was cold. No fire is showing through the airholes in the door where the wood and coal went, and he thought, It's sleeping too. It's resting, taking a summer vacation. It works hard in the winter though, it goes all day long eating up wood and coal and making ashes. From early in the morning 'til late at night and sometimes they stoke it and it burns all night too. It's just coasting then though, but it's working. Summertime is easy except for Sunday, when a lot of folks have to eat string beans, turnip greens, cabbage and salt pork, sweet-potato pie, ham hocks and collards, egg-cornbread and dandelion greens is good for you. Make you big and strong. Summer is easy except for those good things so the stove can take a rest. It wakes up for oatmeal for breakfast and eggs and grits and coffee but then it goes out. Not a stick of wood in the corner or bucket of coal. No heat for lemonade but it's good. In the fall is the busy time. In the fall they'll be killing the hogs and taking the chitterlings and the members will be bringing a whole pig to Daddy Hickman all scalded and scrubbed clean, then he'll give it to Deacon Wilhite and Deacon'll give it to Sister Wilhite and that's when the stove will really have to work. The door where the fire goes'll be cherry red and the stovepipe too. That big pot on the back there will be puffing like a steam engine Meshack, Shadrach, and Abednego, and I like black-eyed peas and curly pig tails and collards, hogs head hopping John—Pa don't raise no cotton or corn and neither no potatoes, but Lord God the tomatoes. I like candied yams, spare ribs, and Sister Wilhite's apple brown Betty with that good hard sauce. Sister Lucy, Daddy Hickman said that time, Don't let the you-know-whos learn how good you can cook, because they're liable to chain you to a kitchen stove for ninety-nine years and a day. Chained? she said. I already been chained for fifteen years. I wouldn't want to be chained to any stove, but Sister Lucy just laughed about it and looked at Deacon. He looked at Sister Wilhite sleeping in the chair. She's really getting it, that sleep, he thought. She's making up for lost time. . . .

Then he must have dreamed, because Sister Georgia was there in the kitchen and she was leading him over to the red-hot stove and asking him about Meshack, Shadrach, and old bigheaded Abernathy and shaking him—

But it wasn't Sister Georgia, it was Sister Wilhite.

"Wake up, Revern' Bliss," she said, "Revern' is calling you." And he got up sleepily and yawned and she guided him into the bedroom.

The others were still there, sitting around and talking quietly. Then he was at the bed looking once more at the bandaged face. Daddy Hickman's eye was closed, hidden beneath the bandages and he thought, *He's asleep,* when Sister Wilhite spoke up.

"Here's Revern' Bliss, Brother A.Z." And there was Daddy Hickman's eye, looking into his own.

"Well, there you are, Bliss," Daddy Hickman said. "Did you have enough lemonade?"

"Yes, sir."

"That's fine. That's very good. So what have you been doing?"

"I had a nap and I've been wondering. . . ."

"Wondering, Bliss? What about?"

He hesitated, looking at Deacon Wilhite, who sat with his legs crossed, smoking. He was sorry he had said it, but it had come out.

"About that lady," he said.

"No, Revern' Bliss," Sister Wilhite said from behind him. "Let's forget about that. Now let Revern' rest. . . ."

"It's all right," Daddy Hickman said. Then the eye bored into his face. "She frightened you, didn't she, boy?"

He bowed his head. "Yes, sir, she sure did."

Then he tried to stop the rest from coming out, but it was too late. "She said she was my mama. . ."

Daddy Hickman lifted his hands quickly and lowered them back to the sheet. "Poor Bliss, poor baby boy," he said, "you really had yourself a time. . . ."

"Revern'," Sister Wilhite said, "don't you think you should rest?"

Daddy Hickman waved his hand toward Sister Wilhite.

"Is she, Daddy Hickman?" he said.

"Is she what, Bliss?"

"My mother?"

"That crazy woman? Oh, no, Bliss," Daddy Hickman said. "You took her seriously, didn't you? Well, I guess I might as well tell you the story, Bliss. Sit here on the bed."

He sat, aware that the others were listening as he watched Daddy Hickman's eye. Daddy Hickman was making a cage of his big long fingers.

"No, Bliss," he said. "The first thing you have to understand is that this is a strange country. There's no logic to it or to its ways. In fact, it's been half-crazy from the beginning and it's got so many crazy crooks and turns and blind alleys in it, that half the time a man can't tell where he is or who he is. To tell the truth, Bliss, he can't tell reason from *un*reason, and it's so mixed up and confused that if we tried to straighten it out right this minute, half the folks out there running around would have to be locked up. You following me, Bliss?"

"You mean everybody is *crazy?*"

"In a way of speaking, Bliss. Because the only logic and sanity is the logic and sanity of God, and down here it's been turned wrongside out and upside down. You have to watch yourself, Bliss, in a situation like this. Otherwise you won't know what's sense and what's foolishness. Or what's to be laughed at and what's to be cried over. Or if you're yourself or what somebody else says you are. Now you take that woman, she yelled some wild words during our services and got everybody upset and now you don't know what to think about her, and when you see me all wrapped up like the mummy of old King Tut or somebody like that, you think that what she said has to have some truth in it. So that's where the confusion and the craziness comes in, Bliss. We have to feel pity for her, Bliss, that's what we have to feel. No anger or fear—even though she upset the meeting and got a few lumps knocked on my head. And we can't afford to believe in what she says, not that woman. Nor in what she does, either. She's a sad woman, Bliss, and she's dangerous too; but when you step away and look at her calmly you have to admit that whatever she did or does or whoever she is, the poor woman's crazy as a coot."

"She's crazy all right," Sister Lucy said. "Now you said something *I* can understand."

"Oh, you can understand all right, Sister Lucy," Daddy Hickman said, "but you don't want to let yourself understand. You want something you can be angry about; something you can hold on to with ease and no need to trouble yourself with the nature of the true situation. You don't want to worry your humanity."

"Maybe so," Sister Lucy said, "but I see that frightened child and I see you all wrapped in bandages and I can still see that woman dressed in red interrupting in the House of God, claiming that child—and I'm supposed to feel sorry for..."

"Yes," Daddy Hickman said. "Yes, you are. Job's God didn't promise him any easy time, remember."

"No, he didn't." Sister Lucy said. "But I never been rich or had all the blessings Job had, neither."

"We'll talk about that some other time," Daddy Hickman said. "You have your own riches. You just have to recognize what they are. So Bliss, not only is that woman sad, she's crazy as a coot. That woman has wilder dreams than a hop fiend."

"What's 'hop,' Daddy Hickman?"

"It's dope, Bliss, drugs, and worse than gin and whiskey...."

"Oh! Has she been taking some?"

"I don't know, Bliss; it's just a way of speaking. The point is that the woman has wild ideas and does wild things. But because she's from a rich family she can go around acting out any notion that comes into her mind."

"Now that's something I can understand," Sister Lucy said.

"They taught that they own the world," Sister Wilhite said.

"Just like they got it in a jug, Revern' Bliss," another sister said.

"Here," Sister Lucy said, and she held out a licorice cigar.

"Thank you, Sister Lucy."

"So listen," Daddy Hickman said. "Let me tell Revern' Bliss a bit about that woman. A few years back she was supposed to get married. She was going to have a big wedding and everything, but then the fellow who she was supposed to marry was killed when his buggy was struck by the Southern at the crossroads and the poor woman seemed to strip her gears...."

"So *that's* what started it," Sister Wilhite said.

"That's the story anyway," Daddy Hickman said. "For a while the poor woman couldn't leave her room, just lay in the bed eating ambrosia and chocolate éclairs day and night."

A new tone had come into Daddy Hickman's voice now. He looked at the eye set in the cloth, searching for a joke. "Eating what?" he said, removing his cigar.

"That's right, Revern' Bliss. Ambrosia and chocolate éclairs."

"Day and night?"

"That's what they say."

"But didn't it make her sick?"

"Oh, she was already sick," Daddy Hickman said. "Anyway, when she finally could leave her room she came up with some strange notions...."

"What kind of notions?"

"Well, she thought she was some kind of queen."

"Did she have a crown?"

"Come to think about it, she did, Reveren' Bliss, and she had a great big Hamilton watch set right in the middle of it and she used to walk around the streets wearing a long white robe and stopping everybody and asking them if they knew what time it was. It wasn't a bad idea either, Bliss—except for the fact that her watch was always slow. Folks who didn't want to set their watches according to her time was in for some trouble. She'd start to screaming right there in the street and charging them with all sorts of crimes. You have no idea how relieved folks were when she misplaced that watch and crown and went off to Europe with her aunty on her father's side."

Daddy Hickman's voice stopped and Bliss could see the eye looking from deep within the cloth.

"Then what happened?" he said.

"Oh, she stayed over there about a year, taking the baths and drinking that sulfur water and mineral water and consorting with the crowned heads of Europe. And I heard she was at a place called Wiesbaden where she enjoyed herself losing a lot of money. Then I went up north to Detroit and worked in the Ford plant for a while and I didn't hear any more about her. Then I came back and I heard she had come home again and how she had a new mind and a new notion. . . ."

"What kind of new mind and notion?"

"Well, now she not only insisted she was a queen but she had the notion that all the young children belonged to her. She had the notion she was the Mary Madonna. Bliss, pretty soon she was making off with other folks' children like a pack rat preparing for hard times. The story is that she grabbed a little *Chinee* baby and took him off to New Orleans and named him Uncle Yen Sen, or something like that. . . ."

"She really stole him?"

"Yes she did, Bliss. And she rented a room and opened up what *she* called a Chinee laundry in one of those old houses with the iron lace around the front. It was on a street where a bunch of first-class washerwomen lived too, and she had that poor little baby lying up there on the counter in a big clothes basket wearing a diaper made out of the United States flag. . . ."

"Oh, oh!" someone behind him said.

"Now, how patriotic can you get," Sister Wilhite said.

"Didn't anyone come looking for the baby, Daddy Hickman?"

"Oh, sure they did, Bliss. But she had covered her tracks like an Indian. She was supposed to be up in Saratoga, that's in New York, you see, but instead she went up to Washington, D.C., with the baby dressed up in a Turkish turban and little gold shoes that turned up at the toe and they spent two days up there riding up and down the Washington Monument and after that they doubled back. That's how that was. You see?"

"Yes, sir," he said. "They probably had them a good time."

"I don't know, Bliss. They just might have got awfully dizzy."

"So what happened then, Revern'?" one of the women said.

"Well, things went along for a while. She wasn't doing much business but things were quiet and nobody bothered them and they ate a lot of buttered carrots and shoofly pie, but mostly carrots . . . and—"

"Why they eat all those carrots?"

"Because she thought they would improve the baby's vision, Bliss."

"He means she was trying to straighten out his eyes, Revern' Bliss," Deacon Wilhite said and suppressed a laugh.

"I hear that carrots make you beautiful," Sister Lucy said.

"And did they ever find the baby?"

"That's right, after a while they did, Bliss. And it happened like this. They was down there waiting for the Mardi Gras to come. One day an old Yankee veteran from the Civil War walked in there to get some shirts washed and ironed and when he looked in that basket and saw Old Glory pinned around that Chinee baby he like to bust a gut. Excuse me, ladies. He saw that, Bliss, and he wanted to start the war all over again. He called the police and the fire department and wired the President up in Washington and raised so much Cain that they ran him out of town for a carpetbagger—while she was treated like she'd done the most normal thing in the world. The poor Chinee lady had a world of trouble getting her little boy back again, because folks tend to take what rich women like that say as the truth. *And*, on top of that, the child had come to like her, didn't think he was a Chinese at all. . . ."

"What'd he think he was?"

"A confederate named Wong E. Lee."

"So what happened to them then?"

"Well, Bliss, the news got around and her folks heard about it and came and took her home and they gave the Chinee lady some money for all her trouble and grief and they turned over the laundry to them and they stayed there and made a fortune and now the little boy is glad he's a Chinese."

"Wong E. Lee," Bliss said.

"They should've put that woman under lock and key right then and there," Sister Wilhite said. "If they had we would've been saved all this trouble."

"That's right, Bliss," Daddy Hickman said. "That's one of the points. Down here a woman like that can get away with anything because not only is her family rich, it's old and has standing position. They're quality—of some kind. But no sooner did she get out of that mess than she ups and grabs a little Mexican boy. This was down in Houston, wasn't it, Deacon?"

"Dallas," Deacon Wilhite said, his head back, his eyes gazing at the ceiling. "Dallas is where it happened."

"That's right, Bliss; Dallas, Texas. She kidnaps this little boy and names him Pancho Villa Van Buren Starr and rushes him up to the Kentucky Derby—which was being held at the time. That was Louisville. Sports and hustlers from all over were there making bets and drinking mint juleps, having a little sport—innocent and *un*-innocent. Well, up there after she had lost five thousand dollars, a piebald gelding, and all the jewelry she had taken along, she tried to use the baby to place a bet with, like he was cash on the line."

"Now Revern'," Sister Lucy said, "she didn't do a thing like that!"

"Oh yes, she did. And it was logical from her point of view. To her way of thinking property like that is negotiable and she swore that little Mexican boy was a family heirloom that had been in the family for years. . . . So, knowing who she was and how solid her background was and all, they took Pancho for the bet and called the president of the Jockey Club about it, but the horse she picked came in last."

"And did they get the baby?"

"They did, Bliss, but it was a long time afterwards. The boy took off and got lost. He had a hard time, Bliss, because she hadn't let him eat anything but chop suey, and although he found a Chinese restaurant he couldn't eat because he only spoke Mexican and the restaurant folks couldn't understand him. So I guess you were lucky because she only *tried* to steal you. The sisters took care of that. So I want you to forget that woman, you hear?"

"Yes, sir."

"You forget all about her, Bliss; I'm talking to you seriously now. Forget her and the foolishness she was saying because she'd never seen you before and I hope she never sees you again. All right now, I better rest so I can help you preach next week. Meantime, I want you to do like I say and forget the woman and if you do I'll take you— Here, come close so I can whisper. . . ."

He bent close, smelling the medicine and then Daddy Hickman was whispering, "I'll take you to see one of those moving pictures you've been hearing about. Now that's a secret. You'll keep it, won't you?"

"Yes, sir. The secret."

He looked but suddenly the eye was gone—as though someone had turned down the wick on a lamp.

"Daddy Hickman—" he began, but now Sister Lucy had him by the arm.

"Shhh," she said, "he's sleeping now," and he was being led quietly away.

It's like trying to reconstruct your own birth as *cherchez la femme* and find the man. Sin, Hickman'd call it, but all men are of larceny to the fourth power of the newborn heart, then it's run not walk to avoid escape, ignore the recognition. Hairs bursting isolated and red out of the white temple and her strange voice screaming *Cudworth, Cudworth*, and I followed I went I fled up and out of the darkness and she lived behind a wall so strong it had no need for altitude. No foot transgressed no alien bird's song aggrieved her privacy. Was this my home, my rightful place?—Cudworth, she called—I heard dragonflies, I saw the great house resting in the gentle shade of her cottonwood mimosa wisteria, the tulip trees. *No Mister Movie-man,* she said, locking her legs before the rise of magnolias, smiling, no peach blossoms no not that.... She's my mother *she* said and I answered she is my mother she Get out the vote Senator, vote. Senator promise them anything but wheel and deal. She said, Baby, baby, always insisting upon appellation the fruit Eve conned Adam with I'll call you by your true name, Baby she—said after the snake Cudworth from the cow's belly a round ball of hair regurgitated. Call me Hank, no Bone. Important not to get lost—I followed Cudworth, Cudworth he's my— Yes sir by following the line of Body's mother and Mrs. Proctor discussing my aborted emancipation from the dark down labyrinthine ways of gossip being hung on lines in the sun the hot air. Body's mother was there before me, broadbacked and turning great curved hips with intent face and mouth spiked with wooden clothespins we used for soldiers in our games, her hair hidden beneath a purple cloth. I yearned for her love of Body as my own. Mrs. Proctor, short and fat rocking from side to side, gently as she slow-dragged from left to right, her man's shoes shuffling over the earth leaving ridges of dust in the soil—her hips tossing languidly, a gentle, mysterious tide of gingham beneath the line hanging the underskirts, slips, bloomers, as they talked up under her wet clothes. Red-white-blue democracy for you bleached and clean making transparent shadows upon the red clay ground the sun filtering pastel through the cloth and the air clean to the smell with me crouching underneath, the first well-hung line, my finger tracing upon the hard earth, wondering how did I get out and get lost, did I come down from under these thin petticoats out of these in order to ascend—clank-clank-clank your mother.

She's got to be a fool, from Body's mother. Coming into our meeting like that. Either that or she was drunk or something, her voice rising in invitation to a re-creation of my soul's agony. And Mrs. Proctor accepting,

Ain't it the truth? And there we was just wanting to be left alone in peace to serve God for a few days and to praise Him—but can we do it? Oh no. She so high and mighty she gon take that chile without the hardship and pain, without even gitting struck good and hard on the maidenhead—and not only take him from us but from the Lord as well.... Looking around

Then, seeing me, Shhhhh....

What is it, girl?—Oh, Revern' Bliss, Body's mother said. She looked down at me, her hands on ample hips.

Mam? I, Bliss, said, my face feeling tight, wan.

Honey, will you go send Body to me, please?

I looked for judgment in her broad face. She held the clothespins fanned out between her fingers like a marksman holding shotgun shells during a trap shoot.

Yes, mam.

Thank you, Revern' Bliss.

And I arose and moved down the line of clothes and then under a line of stockings and pink and blue underthings and back three lines 'til I was behind drying sheets, hearing her softly saying. These children, I swear they all alike, even Revern' Bliss. They never stop trying to listen to grown folks talking, and they always rambling in trunks and drawers. Lord knows what they 'spect to find. Him and Revern' Bliss was playing with some toy autos one day and I looked out and Body has done found one of my old breast pumps somewhere and is making out it's a auto horn!

I went past bloomers billowing gently in the breeze *Clank-clank-clank, that's your ma's with a fleet of them big Mack trucks and nineteen elephants. A whole team of mules could walk through there.* I went toward the back door where the washtubs glinted dully on the low bench, trailing my finger and thumb as I went past and around to the front of the house, calling, Body! Hey Body! Your mother wants you, Body. Knowing all the while that he had gone to dig crawdads. He was my right hand but I had been told not to go there. Calling: Body? Hey! Body! lying in word and deed while my mind hung back upon their voices like a feather upon a gentle breeze. Behind me, over the top of the house I could hear their voices rising clear with soft hoarseness, like alto horns in mellow duet across the morning air. I looked down the street. Except for a cat rubbing itself against a hedge down near the corner nothing was moving. I was alone and lonely, the porch was high and I crawled beneath and lay still in the cool shadows thinking about the crawdad hole over where the cotton press had burned down across from the railroad tracks, the tall weeds and muddy water. Body could swim, I wasn't allowed. Along the slippery bank the crawdads raised up their pale brown castles of mudballs. We fried their tails in cornmeal and bacon grease, ate them with half-fried Irish potatoes. In the gloom I lay, beside the discarded wheel of a baby buggy. Body's mother saved his baby shoes. They hung by a blue ribbon from the mirror of the washstand. Where were mine? Near my arm a line of frantic ants crawled down the piling, carrying specks of white, sugar or crumbs. Piss ants, sugar ants, all in a row, coming and a-going like my breath their feelers touch and go. Patty cake. Then I could hear their sighful voices approaching full of heat and sounds of rest, and through the cracks between the steps I could see their broad bottoms coming down upon the giving boards and saw their washday dresses collapsing stretching taut between their knees as they rested back, their elbows upon the floor of the porch as slowly they fanned themselves with blue bandannas.

So she keeps on asking me what I do to get her washing so white, Mrs. Proctor said, and I keep telling her I didn't do nothing but soak 'em and boil 'em and rub 'em and blue 'em and rinse 'em and starch 'em and iron 'em, but she never believed me. Said, Julia, *nobody* does clothes like you do. The others don't get them so clean and white, so you have got to have some secret. Oh, yes, Julia, you have a trick, I just know you have. So finally, girl, I gets tired and the next time she asked me I said, Well, Miz Simmons, you keep on asking me so I guess I have to tell you, but first you have ta promise me that you won't tell nobody. And she said, Oh I promise, you just tell me what you do. Ho Ho! So I said, well, Miz Simmons, it's like this, after I done washed the clothes and everything I adds a few drops of coal oil in the last rinse water.

Girl, she slapped her hands and almost turned a flip. Talking about, I knew it! And she said, Is that all? And I said, Yessum, that's it and please don't forget that you promised you wouldn't tell anybody. Oh no, I won't tell, she said. But I just knew that you had a secret, because no one could do the clothes the way you do with just plain soap and water. So girl, I thought maybe now she'd let me alone and be satisfied, because you see, I knew that if I didn't tell her *something* pretty soon she was going to fire me.

So how'd it work out? Body's mother said.

Wait, Mrs. Proctor said. The next week I picked up her laundry and she was still talking about it. Said: Julia, you sure are a sly one. But you didn't fool me, because I knew you had some special secret for getting my clothes so clean. And I said yessum, I don't do it for everybody but I know how particular you all are and all like that. And she said, Yes, that's right, and it just proves that if you insist on getting the best you'll get it. And I said, Yessum, that sure is the truth.

Body's mother laughed. Girl, you oughtn't to told that woman that stuff.

Don't I know it? Mrs. Proctor said. It was wrong. Because as I was luggin' those clothes of hers home something way back in the rear of my mind hunched me. It said: Girl, maybe you wasn't so smart in telling that woman that lie 'cause you know she's a fool—but I forgot about it. Well suh, I did her laundry just like I always done it and when I went to deliver it there she was, waiting for me—and I could tell from the way her face was all screwed up like she was taking a dose of Black Draught that I was in trouble. Said, Julia, I want you to be a little more careful when you do the wash this time. And I said, What's wrong, Miz Simmons, wasn't the clothes clean? She said, Oh yes, they was clean all right. But you didn't rinse them enough and you put in a bit too much of that coal oil. Last night when he got home Mr. Simmons complained that he could smell it in his shirts.

Oh, oh, Body's mother said.

Mrs. Proctor said: Well, girl, I liked to bust. I said, I knew it, I knew it! You been snooping around for something to criticize about my work. Well, now you have gone and done it and I'm here to tell you that you just been telling a big ole coal-oil lie because I never put a thing in those clothes but plenty soap and water and elbow grease. Just like that.

And what'd she say then?

Say? What could she say? She stomped out of there and slammed the door. Stayed awhile and then, girl, she come back with her eyes all red and *fired* me! The ole sour fool!

Their voices ripped out and rose high above me as they laughed and I closed my eyes, seeing the purple shadows dancing behind my lids as I held my mouth to keep my laughter in. I could hear it wheezing and burbling in my stomach. It was hard to hold and then it stopped, their voices were low and confidential....

... You'd think that with all her money and everything a woman like that wouldn't even know we was in the world, wouldn't you, girl, Body's mother said.

Sho would, Mrs. Proctor said, but that ain't the way it seems to work. Seems like they can't be happy unless they know we're having a hard time. Some folks just wants it all, the prizes of this world and God's own anointed. It's outrageous when you think about it. Imagine, coming into the meeting and trying to snatch Revern' Bliss out of the Lord's own design. She's going to interrupt the *Resurrection of the spirit from the flesh!* Next thing you know she be out there in her petticoat telling the Mississippi River to stand still. I tell you that woman is what they call *arragant*, girl. She so proud she's like a person who done drunk so much he's got the blind staggers....

You telling me! But she's always cutting up in some fashion so I guess that sooner or later she had to get around to us. But to interfere with the Lord's...

Girl, Mrs. Proctor said, I saw her one morning just last week. She was riding one of those fine horses they have out there and she's acting like she was a Kentucky woman, or maybe a Virginian. One of those F.F.V.'s as they call them. Up on that hoss's back wearing black clothes with a long skirt and one of those fancy sidesaddles but riding a-straddle that hoss like a man in full, and with a derby hat with a white feather in it on her head. Early in the morning too, Lord. I was on my way to deliver some clothes and here she come galloping past me so fast I swear it liked to sucked all the air from 'round me. Had me suspended there like a yolk in the middle of an egg. It went SWOSH just like a freight train passing a tramp and that hoss was steaming and lathering like he been racing five miles at top speed. And in this weather too. You should a seen it, girl. I whirled around to look and there she went with that red hair streaming back from under that derby. Done almost knocked me down now but when she went past with that wild look on her face it's like she ain't seen me.

It's a sin and a shame, Body's mother said. You'd think that she'd at least respect how much labor and pain goes into keeping her garments clean. Washerwomen have rheumatism like a horse has galls.

Yes, and this is one who knows it, Mrs. Proctor said. But, girl, that woman's a fool, that's the most Christian thing you can say about her. It ain't as if she was the mean kind who'd run a person down just for fun or to see you jump and get scaird, *she just naturally don't see nobody.*

That might be true, Body's mother said, but she saw Revern' Bliss, all right. Now just why would she decide to come out there and break up our meeting?

Crazy, girl! That's all there is to it, the woman's crazy, and while we sitting here talking between ourselfs we might as well go ahead and admit it. You and me don't have to deny the truth when we talking between ourselfs. Rich and white though she be, the po' thing's nuts.

No, No, No, she's my mother my mind said, and I lay rigid, listening.

I don't know, Body's mother said. Maybe she is and maybe she ain't. Maybe she just knew she could get away with it and went on and did it.

You mean she started to do it but she didn't count on us women.... Neither on the outrage of the Lord.

That's right, she didn't take the chile but she busted up the meeting. She still got no regard for other folks, but this time *she went too far.* She's strong willed even for a high-tone white woman, girl. Let me tell you something! One day I was out there to see Irene and just as I got around in the back I heard all this shooting and yelling and what do I see? Over there down where the grass runs down to the lake she's got a half dozen or so little black boys and has them pitching up those round things rich white folks shoot at all the time when they ain't shooting partridges or doves and girl, I tell you, it was something to see. Girl, she's got them standing in a big half circle and she's yelling at first one and then the other to sail those things up in the air and bang! She's shooting them down just...

WHO? NOT THOSE CHILDREN?

No, *noo*, girl, those clay birds.

Thank goodness, that's what I thought, but with her you can't be too sure.

I know, Body's mother said. But girl, you never saw such a sight. She's yelling and those little boys are raring back and flinging those round black things into the air with all their might, and her dancing from side to side with that shotgun and busting them to dust, and as fast as she empties one gun here comes another little boy running up with a fresh one all loaded and *bang! bang! bang!* she's busting 'em again. I stood there with my mouth open trying to take it all in and looking to see if Body was amongst those boys— thank God he wasn't, because the way she looked, with her red hair all wild and wearing pants and some kind of coat with leather patches on the shoulder she's liable to...

Girl, Mrs. Proctor said, that was a shooting jacket.

A *shooting* jacket?

Mrs. Proctor laughed a high falsetto ripple. Why sho, girl. You know these rich folks have a different set of clothes for everything they do. They have tea gowns for drinking tea, cocktail dresses for drinking their gin and whiskey, *ball* gowns for doing what they call dancing, Yes! And riding habits when they got their riding habits on—that's what she was wearing when she almost run me down. Then they even have dressing gowns for wearing when they're putting on their other clothes.

Oh yes? Body's mother said. Well, I guess they have to have *something* to do to take up all the time they have on they hands. But tell me something—

What's that?

What was that red thing she was wearing when she tried to take our little preacher?

Well, Mrs. Proctor said, without making a joke about something religious I'd say maybe it was a maternity dress. . . .

If it was, Body's mother said, she was dressed for the wrong occasion. She surely was. Anyway, girl, she was really shooting that day. Jesse James couldn't have done no better. She ain't hardly missed a one. And if one of those children didn't pitch in time to suit her she'd cuss him for a little gingersnap bastard and the rest of them would just laugh. Oh, but it made me mad, hearing her abuse those children like that. Not that it seemed to bother those little boys, though. In fact, when she cussed one of 'em he just laughed and sassed her right back. Said, Miss Lor, don't come blaming me 'cause you caint shoot a shotgun. You missed that bird a country mile. . . .

And what happened then? Mrs. Proctor said.

Something crazy just like always with her. She started to laughing like a panther and gave out one of those rebel yells. Said, Enloe, you *are* a sassy little blue-gummed bastard, but if I miss the next twenty birds I'll have Alberta freeze you a gallon of ice cream!

Now you see what I mean: That woman is dangerous! You take that boy Enloe, she oughtn't to treat him that way, because he's liable to pull that with some *other* white woman and git hisself kilt.

You're right, and somebody had better speak to his mama about him. And that's the truth. Only when children reach the size of those boys they usually know when they dealing with a fool. But it's her I'm worried about, anybody who plays around with the Lord's work that way is heading for trouble. In fact, that po' woman is *already* in trouble and I been thinking a heap about what she did. But did it occur to you that she might really *be* Revern' Bliss' mother?

Who, a child like that girl? No!

She *said* he was hers, didn't she?

She surely did, wasn't I listening like everybody else? But how is a woman like that going to be *his* mama? It would've made more sense if she'd a-claimed Jack Johnson and all those white wives of his and his uncles and cousins too. How she going to be that child's mama even in a dream *I* simply can't see.

How! Are you asking me? Man is born of woman, and skinny as she is she still appears to have all the equipment. Besides, does anybody know who his mama is?

No, they don't; less'n it's Revern' and he ain't said. But remember now, Revern' *brought* that child here with him, so he can't be from around here anywhere....

And how do you know that? Half the devilment in this country caint be located on account of it's somewhere in between black and white and covered up with bed clothes in the dark.

That's the truth—but, girl, Revern' ain't no fool! He wouldn't bring that baby back here if that was the case. Not even if he'd found him in a grocery basket with a note saying the child was a present from Pharoah's favorite daughter. Besides, that woman would have to either be drunk or out of her mind to claim him anyway. And you know that while a white man might recognize his black bastards once in a while, if they turn out *white* enough, and if he's stuck tight enough to the mother, might even send them up north to go to school—but who in this lowdown South ever heard of a white *woman* claiming anything a black man had something to do with?

Yes, that's true, Mrs. Proctor said, 'cept he don't show no sign in his skin or hair or features, only in his talking. But this here ain't no ordinary chile and everything has its first time to happen. Besides, there's quite a few of them who have turned their heads and made their sweet-talking motions as if to say, "Come on, Mister Nigger, here's my peaches you can shake my tree if you man enough or crazy enough to take the consequences." And as you well know, some of ours is both man enough and crazy enough and prideless enough to take hold to the branch and swing the dickens out of it—even knowing that if they git caught she gon' scream and swear he stole her.

Yes, I know all that. And as mama told me long ago, all those who cries denied in darkness ain't black, and a woman's lot is a woman's lot from the commencing of her flow on. It sure does make you wonder. Still, a woman like that is apt to do what she did just for the notoriety and the scandal for the rest of her own folks. But what can you expect from somebody who got started out wrong like she done?

What you mean? Mrs. Proctor said. Who?

Their voices fell and I strained to hear, finally rolling over softly and over again, until I was directly beneath them, hearing:

...And Irene told me her ownself that whenever Miss Lorelli comes around, which ain't too regular, she screams like a cat in heat. Says she has such pain they almost have to tie her to the bedposts and keep the ice packs on her belly all the time. Irene said it's worse than somebody birthing triplets.

Talking about the curse, she's got a real curse, Mrs. Proctor said. That woman is damned!

Ain't it the truth; Irene said it's really something to witness. Said that the first time it come down on her the poor chile was tomboying around up on top of the grape arbor. . . .

Well, I hope she was prepared, Mrs. Proctor said.

Prepared my foot! Is a sow prepared? Is a blue tick bitch? Irene said that it was at a time when her mama was entertaining some ladies on the lawn too, but instead of being there learning how to entertain like any other young girl would've been, this Miss Lorelli is so uncontrollable she's up there on that grape arbor climbing around! Well suh, Irene said it was like a dam bursting or something. The po' thing come tumbling off of that tree like a scalded cat and come running across the lawn, straight to where Irene was serving those ladies. She almost knocked over the tea cart and with it all over her hands and all. Irene said when she realized what was happening she got so mad at the child's mama that she dropped a whole tray of fine china. Said she'd wanted to prepare the chile for what all the signs—her birthday, the calendar, and the sign of the moon—all of them, said she was fixing to happen soon, but no, the mama was so jealous and so vain about her age that she wouldn't let Irene tell the chile a thing. She was going to do it herself when *she* got ready.

As though nature was going to wait on *her,* Mrs. Proctor said.

Well, girl, it didn't. Irene said it come right on schedule, right up on that grape arbor.

Girl, that's enough to make anybody act peculiar.

Are you telling me? So there it was, Irene has to stop serving and teach the chile right then and there, and she said she didn't bite her tongue in telling her, either. Told her in plain language right there in front of all those fine ladies.

Oh wow, girl! You must be yeasting this mess!

She sho did, told her all about her womanhood and about boys while she snatched off her apron and wrapped it around the chile and carried her upstairs and went to work on her. Poor thing, she thought she was bleeding to death and giving birth, all at the same time. She had it all mixed up, poor thing. Irene said she asked her where her baby was and everything and Irene had some time calming her. Can you imagine that, having to fall out of a tree in order to pick up your woman's burden?

That woman shoulda been whupped for doing that to that chile, Mrs. Proctor said. One woman acts a fool out of her vanity and pride and ignorance. So now everybody has to suffer for it. That woman was just plain ignorant! Yes, that's what it is. Whenever I think about it I remember what the monkey said when the man cut off his tail with the lawn mower. Poor monkey just looked at his tail laying there in the grass and tears came to his eyes and he shook his head and said: My people, my people.

The voice had ceased. Then the Senator heard, "Bliss, are you there?"

"Still here," the Senator said from far away. "Don't stop, I hear."

Then through his blurring eyes he saw the dark shape come closer and now the voice sounded small and distant, as though Hickman stood on a hill somewhere inside his head.

"Bliss, I say that all the time I should have been praying for you, back there all torn up inside by those women's hands. Because, after all, a lot of prayer and sweat and dedication had gone into that buggy, not simply the money-greed and show-off pride. It held together through all that rough ride, even though the wheels were humming like guitar strings. Yes, and it took me and Sister Beaumasher to jail and a pretty rough time before they let us go. So there between a baby, a buggy, and a burning barn I prayed the wrong prayer. I left you out, Bliss, and I guess right then and there you started to wander...."

Aaaaaaaayeeeeee...! it ripped his ears in a rising curve, choked and bubbling like the shout of a convert who had started screaming while Daddy Hickman was still raising his head from beneath the baptismal waters... *Aaaaaaaaayeeeeee!* and he could feel it coming in sharp, shrill bursts, but the redheaded woman was holding him so fiercely that he could not tell if they came from her heaving body or his own. Arms and hands were flying and he was plunging toward the coffin, catching sight of Teddy sprawled in the sawdust—only to be snatched up again, feeling a pain burning its way straight up his back as she screamed *He's mine! He's*— her head snapping back and the scream becoming the sound of Daddy Hickman's trombone and saw the white sleeve of a tall sister's arm flash red, hearing, "Y'all leave her to me now," and thinking *Blood* as they whirled him around and her arms tightening and thinking that's flying *bloody blare of horn she's bleeding*—feeling himself being ripped completely away from her now, the sisters with faces hard and mask-like coming on and twisting him from her arms like a lamb bone popped out of its socket, holding him kicking high and passing him between them as he looked wildly for the flowing blood....

Catch him, someone shouted, and he then felt himself hanging by his heels and they were grabbing and slapping him across his burning back, lifting, and his head came up into a confusion of voices, hearing, *Here, let me take him. Let's get the poor child out of here,* seeing Sister Wilhite and another sister was saying, *Better give him to Sister Mary,* holding her broad hand against his stomach, *Sister Mary's home, she's got kids of her own,* and another voice saying, *No, she's too crowded and lives too close to here....* and *Then who?* Sister Wilhite was saying and long smooth fingers were reaching for him saying, *Me, Sister Wilhite, let me have him,* and Sister Wilhite looking intensely at the young woman, her eyes sparkling, *You?* and the smooth Elberta peach brown face with curly hair covering her ears saying, *Let me, Sister Wilhite, I live far and I got no husband and I know my way through these woods like a rabbit. . . .* And Sister Wilhite turning her head, saying, *What you all think?* and he tried to open his mouth but she shook him, *Hush, Revern' Bliss,* and someone said, *She's right. Give him to Sister Georgia, only get him out of here.* And he was leaning forward, hearing Sister Wilhite's *Here, sister, take him,* and he began again, *I want Daddy Hickman* and Sister Wilhite saying, *And you hurry.* He was being handed over once more and he said, *I want Daddy Hickman,* hearing, *Hush Revern' Bliss, honey,* in the hot blast of Sister Georgia's breath against his cheek. *You're going with me 'cause this ain't no place for you to be—not right now it ain't.* Then she turned and he caught sight of Daddy Hickman climbing down from the platform. Then he recognized the little slant-shouldered sister's deep voice, *Will y'all sisters get out of the woman's way?* she said, and the others were pushing and shoving and Sister Georgia was pushing him against them and the little sister said with her head on Sister Georgia's shoulder, *Go with the speed of angels, love. Madame Herod done come, Mister Herod be coming soon; the snake! So take that child and let 'em dig a my grave. . . .*

And already Sister Georgia was rushing him along with her quick, swinging-from-side-to-side walk, away from the screaming white woman and the angry deaconesses in their ruffled baby caps, going straight through the strangely silent members, stepping over fallen folding chairs, lunch baskets, and scattered hymnbooks, past the slanting tent ropes and a smoking flare, into the open. Beginning to run now as though someone was chasing them, on out across the sawdust-covered earth of the clearing, through the big trees into the bushes in the dark. She was saying baby words to him as she ran and he twisted around to see behind them, hearing, "Hold still now, honey," as he looked back to the moiling within the yellow light of the tent. The woman was screaming again and a team of mules was pitching in their harness rising up and breaking toward the light, then plunging off into the shadow. Then Deacon Wilhite's voice was leading some of the members to singing and the sound rose up strong, causing the woman's screams to sound like red sparks shooting through a cloud of thick black smoke. Sister Georgia stumbled, sending them jolting forward and he could hear her grunt and her breath coming hard and fast as she balanced herself, causing him to sway back and forth in her arms and his back to burn like fire.

"It's all right now, Revern' Bliss," she said as he began to cry.

"I want Daddy Hickman," he cried. "I want to go back."

"Not now, Revern' Bliss, darling. Right now he's got his hands full with that awful woman."

"But I hurt," he cried. "I hurt bad."

"Hurt? What's hurting you, Revern' Bliss?"

"I hurt all over. They scratched me. Please take me back."

"But the meeting's all over for tonight," she said. "That woman broke it up. Lord help us, but she *really* wrecked it. I hope the Lord makes her suffer for it too. Doing such an awful thing, and we supposed to act Christian toward them. Knocking over your coffin and everything...."

He thought, *I want Teddy and my Bible.* Then, remembering the look on the woman's face when she picked him up, he was silent. It was like a dream. He had been in the coffin, ready to rise up and all of a sudden there she was, screaming. Now it was like a picture he was looking at in a book or in a dream—even as he watched the tear-sparkling tent falling rapidly away. And in the up and down swaying of the sister's movement he could no longer tell one member from another; he couldn't even see Daddy Hickman. *She was really one of them,* passed through his mind, then the road was dipping swiftly down a hill in the dark and he was being taken where he could no longer see the peak shape of the tent rising white above the yellow light. Only the sound of singing came to him now and fading.

They were moving through low-branched trees where he could smell the sticky little blossoms which the honey bees and fireflies loved so well, then the branches grew higher up on the trunks of the trees and the trees were taller and they were dropping down a slope. "Hold tight, Revern' Bliss," she said. "We have to cross over somewhere along here."

"Over water?" he said.

"That's right."

"Deep water?"

"Not very. You don't have to be afraid. Hush now, we be there in a minute."

"I'm not afraid of any water," he said.

She was moving carefully and he looked down, hearing the quiet swirl of the stream somewhere ahead before he could see its smoothly glinting flow. And she said, "Hold tight, honey, hold real tight, we got to cross this log," and was balancing and carrying him rapidly along a narrow tree trunk that lay across the stream, then breathing hard up the steep slope of a hill into the bushes. He could hear twigs snapping and plucking at her dress and raised his arm to keep the limbs from his face as she climbed. She was breathing hard and he could feel her softness sweating through the cloth of his full dress jacket and the heat of her body rising to him. And he could hear himself thinking just as Body would have said, *She's starting to smell kinda funky,* and was ashamed. Body said that ladies could smell a *good* funky and a *bad* funky but men just smelled like funky bears. But this was a good smell although it wasn't supposed to be and the sister was good to be carrying him so gently and she was nice and soft. Her pace slowed again now and suddenly they were out of the dusty bushes and he sneezed. They were moving along a sandy road.

"Wheew!" she said, "That was *some* thicket, Revern' Bliss, and you went through it like a natural man. You all right now?"

"Yes, mam," he said. "But I want to go back to Daddy Hickman."

"Oh, he'll be coming to get you soon, Revern' Bliss. He knows where you'll be. You're not afraid of me are you?"

"No, mam, but I have to go back and help him."

"I guess we can rest now," she said, bending, and he felt the sand give beneath his feet. She was breathing hard. Her white dress made it easier to see in the dark, just as his white suit did. She was younger than Sister Wilhite and the others. And he thought, *We are like ghosts on this road.*

"Of course you want to help, Revern'," she said, "and as much as I'd like to have a little boy as smart as you, I know you're a minister and not meant to be mine or anybody else's. So don't worry, Revern' Bliss, because as soon as Revern' gets through he'll be coming after you. That woman needs a good beating for doing this to you...."

She was breathing easier now and looking up and down the dark road.

"She called me a funny name," he said.

"I could hear her yelling something when she broke in. What'd she call you?"

"Cudworth..."

"*Cudworth*—Revern' Bliss, are you sure?"

"I think so," he said.

"Well, I wouldn't be surprised. Doing what she done it's a wonder she didn't call you Lazarus...or Peter Wheatstraw.... Even Shorty George," and she laughed. "The old heifer. They always slapping us with some name that don't have nothing to do with us. The freckle-faced cow! You think you can walk now, Revern' Bliss? My house is just up the road behind those trees up yonder. See, up there."

"Yes, mam, I can walk," he said. But he couldn't see her house, only a dark line of bushes and trees. *This is a deep black night,* he thought. *She's got eyes like a cat.*

"Walk over here on the side," she said, "It's firmer."

"She made the members afraid," he heard himself saying.

"Afraid? Now where'd you get that idea, Revern' Bliss? As outraged as those sisters was and you talking about them being *afraid*? Were *you* afraid?"

"Yes, mam," he said, "but the sisters were hurting me. They were afraid too. I could smell them..."

"*Smell* them? Well, did I ever!" She stopped, her hands on her hips, looking down into his face. "Revern' Bliss, what are you talking about? You must be tired and near-half asleep, talking about *smelling* folks. Give me your hand so I can get you to bed."

She was annoyed now and he could feel the tug on his shoulder as she pulled him rapidly along. *She doesn't want me to know it,* he thought, *but they were afraid.*

"Revern' Bliss, you are *something*," she said.

They went along a path through the trees, then they were climbing and suddenly there was the house on a hill in the dark. He could smell orange blossoms as she led him up to it, then they were going across the porch up to a doorway.

"Stand right here a minute while I light the lamp," she said. Then the room was lighted and she said, "Welcome to my house, Revern' Bliss," and he went in. She was fanning herself with a handkerchief and sighing. "Lord, what a hot evening and it had been going so good too—Revern' Bliss, would you like a piece of cold watermelon before you go to bed?"

"Yes, mam, thank you, mam," he said. And he was glad that she wasn't angry anymore.

"You don't think it'll make you have to get up in the night, do you?"

"Oh no, mam. Daddy Hickman lets me have watermelon at night all the time."

"Are you sure?"

"Yes, mam. He gives me melon and ice cream too. You wouldn't have any ice cream, would you, mam?"

"No I don't, Revern' Bliss, bless your heart. But if you come back on Sunday I'll make you a whole freezer full and bake you a cake, all for yourself. Would you like that, Revern' Bliss?"

"Yes, mam, I sure would," he said. And she bent down and hugged him then and the woman smell came to him sharp and intriguing. Then her face left and she was smiling in the lamplight and beyond her head two tinted pictures of old folks frozen in attitudes of dreamy and remote dignity looked down from where they hung high on the wall in oval frames, seeming to float behind curved glass. They had the feel of the statues of the saints he'd seen in that white church in New Orleans. It was strange. And he could see the reflection of his shadowed face showing above her bending shoulders and against the side of her darkened head. He felt her about to lift him then and suddenly he hugged her. And in the warm surge that flowed over him, he kissed her cheek, then pulled quickly away.

"Why, Revern' Bliss, that was right sweet of you. I don't remember ever being kissed by a minister before." She smiled down at him. "Let's us go get that melon," she said.

He felt the warmth of her hand as she led him out through a dark kitchen that sprang into shadow-shrouded light before them, placing the lamp on the blue oilcloth that covered the table, saying, "Come on, Revern' Bliss."

And they went out into the dark, into the warm blast of the orange-blossom night and across the porch into the dark of the moon. Fireflies flickered before them as they moved across the yard.

"It's down in the well, Revern' Bliss; it's been down there cooling since yesterday."

She went up and leaned against the post that held the crosspiece, looking down into the wide dark mouth of the well, and he followed to stand beside her, looking at the rope curving up through the big iron pulley that hung above. And she said, "Look down there, Revern' Bliss; look down at the water before I touch the rope and disturb it. You see those stars down there? You see them floating down there in the water?"

And he boosted himself up the side, balancing on his elbows, as he looked down into the cool darkness. It was a wide well and there were the high stars, mirrored below in the watery sky, and he felt himself carried down and yet up. He seemed to fall down into the sky and to hang there, as though his darkened image floated among the stars. It was frightening and yet peaceful and close beside him he could hear her breathing.

Then suddenly he heard himself saying, "I am the bright and morning star," and peered below, hearing her give a low laugh and her voice above him saying serenely, "You are too, at that," and she was touching his head.

Then her hand left and she touched the rope and he could see the sky toss below, shuddering and breaking and splashing liquidly with a dark silver tossing. And he wanted to please her.

"Look at them now," he said. "See there, the morning stars are singing together."

And she said, "Why, I know where that's from, it's from the *Book of Job,* my daddy's favorite book of the Bible. Do you preach Job too, Revern' Bliss?"

"Yes, mam. I preaches Job *and* Jeremiah too. Just listen to this: *The word of the Lord came up to me, saying, 'Before I formed thee in the belly I knew thee, and before thou camest forth out of the womb I sanctified thee, and I ordained thee a prophet unto the nations . . .'"*

"Amen, Revern' Bliss," she said.

". . . Ah, Lord, God!" he said, making his voice strong and full, *" 'How can I speak, when I am just a child,' "* and it seemed to echo in the well, surprising him.

"Now ain't that wonderful?" she said. "Revern' Bliss, do you understand all of that you just said?"

"Not *all* of it, mam. Even grown preachers don't understand *all* of it, and Daddy Hickman says we can only see as through a glass darkly."

"Ah yes," she sighed. "There's a heap of mystery about us people."

She was pulling the rope now and he could hear the low song of the pulley and the water dripping a little uneven musical scale a *ping pong pitty-pat ping ping pong—pat* back into the well, and he said,

"Sure, I preaches Job," and started to quote more of the scripture but he couldn't remember how it started. *It's the thirty-eighth chapter, seventh verse,* he thought, *that's where it tells about the stars singing together....*

"Revern' Bliss, this melon's heavy," she said. "Help me draw it up."

"Yes, mam," he said, taking hold of the rope. And as he helped her he remembered some of it and said, *"Gird up your loins like a man for I will demand of thee, and answer thou me...."* He heard the pulley singing a different tune now and as the melon came up the water from the rope was running cool over his hands and his throat remembered some more of the lines and they came out hand over fist as the melon came up from the well:

> *"Where wast thou when I laid the foundations of the earth?*
> *Declare, if thou hast understanding.*
> *Who hath laid the measures thereof, if thou knoweth?*
> *Or who hath stretched the line upon it?*
> *Whereupon are the foundations thereof fastened?*
> *Or who laid the cornerstone thereof?*
> *When the morning stars sang together, and all the sons*
> *Of God rejoiced?*
> *Or who shut up the sea with doors when it brake forth,*
> *As if it had issued out of the womb...?"*

Then she said, "There!" and he saw the melon come gleaming from the well and she reached out and pulled it over to the side, setting the bucket on the rim. He could hear it dripping a quiet wet little tune far below as she removed it from the bucket.

"It's a mystery to me how you manage to remember so much, Revern' Bliss— Lord, but this sure is a heavy one we got us tonight! Come on over here where we can sit down."

So he followed her over the bare ground and sat on the floor of the porch beside the wet, cold melon, his feet dangling while she went into the kitchen. Behind him he could hear the opening of a drawer and the rattling of knives and forks, then she was back holding a butcher knife, the screen slamming sharply behind her.

She said, "Would you like to cut the melon, Revern' Bliss?"

"Yes, mam, thank you, mam."

"I thought you would," she said. "The men always want to do the cutting. So here it is, let's see how you do it."

"Shall I plug it, mam?" he said, taking the knife.

"*Plug* it? Plug this melon that I *know* is ripe? Listen to that," she said, thumping it with her fingers.

"Daddy Hickman always plugs *his* melons," he said.

"All right, Revern' Bliss, if that's the way it has to be, go ahead. I guess Revern' has plugged him quite a few."

And he took the knife and felt the point go in hard and deep to the width of the blade; then again, and again, and again, making a square in the rind. He felt the blade go deep and deep and then deep and deep again. Then he removed the blade, just like Daddy Hickman did and stuck the point in the middle of the square and lifted out the wedge-shaped plug, offering it to her.

"Thank you, Revern' Bliss," she said with a smile in her voice, and he could hear the sound of the juice as she tasted it.

"See there, I knew it was ripe," she said. "You try it."

It was cold and very sweet and the taste of it made him hurry. He cut two lengthwise pieces then, saying, "There you are, mam," and watched her lift them out, giving him one and taking the other.

And they sat there in the dark with the orange blossoms heavy around them, eating the cold melon. He tried spitting the seeds at the fireflies, hearing them striking the hard earth around the porch and the fireflies still blinking. Then Sister Georgia stopped eating.

"Revern' Bliss," she said, "I don't think we want to raise us any crop of melons this close to the porch, do you? 'Cause after all, they'd just be under our feet and getting squashed all the time and everything."

"No'm, I don't guess we do and I'm sorry, mam."

"Oh, that's all right, Revern' Bliss. You care for some salt?"

"No'm, I like it just like it is."

"You really like it?"

"Oh yes, mam! It's 'bout the sweetest, juiciest melon I ever et."

"Thank you, Revern' Bliss. I told you it was a ripe one and I'm glad you like it."

"You sure told the truth, mam."

So they sat eating the melon and he watched the fireflies but held the slippery seeds in his fist. Then suddenly from far away he could hear boys' voices floating to them. "Abernathy!" they called. "Hey, you, Abernathy!" and waited. There was no answer. Then it came again. "Where you at, ole big-headed, box-ankled Abernathy?" And she laughed, saying, "That Abernathy'll be looking to fight them tomorrow, 'cause he's got a real big head and don't like to be teased about it."

"Who's Abernathy?" he said.

"Oh, he's a little ole mannish boy that lives down the road over yonder. You'll see him tomorrow," she said. "You'll hear him too, 'cause his head is big and he's got a big deep voice just like a grown man."

He could hear the boys still calling as she talked on—until a grown woman's voice came clear as a note through a horn, "Abernathy's in bed, just where y'all ought to be. So clear on 'way from here."

"And who is you?" a voice then called.

"Who you think *you* is?" the woman's voice said.

"Don't know and don't care!"

"Well, I'm his mother, and you heard what I just said."

"Well 'scuse us, I thought you was his cousin," the voice yelled, mocking her, and he could hear some of them laughing and running off into the night, calling "Hey, Abernathy—How's your ma, Abernathy? Hey you, Abernathy's ma, how's old big-headed Abernathy?"

"That part about being in bed goes for you too, Revern' Bliss," she said, "considering all you been through with that terrible woman and all. You sleepy?"

"Yes, mam," he said. He'd had enough of the melon and his stomach was tight. "Where must I put this melon rind, mam?" he said.

"I'll take care of it," she said. "Don't you think you better pee-pee before you go to bed? The privy's right out there at the back of the lot."

"But I don't have to now," he said, thinking, *She must think I'm a baby.... Body says the first thing a man has to learn is to hold his water.*

"Well, you will by the time you get your clothes off, so you go on and do it now."

"No," he said, "because I don't have it."

"Then you do it for me, Revern' Bliss," she said. "Because while you might know all about the Bible, *I* know all about little boys from having to take care of a couple on my job and even they ain't the first. So now don't be ashame and go make pee-pee. After all, I only have but one sofa and us don't want to ruin it, do us now?"

"No'm," he said.

So he walked back through the dark and came to grass and growing things and stopped, looking around. But then she called through the dark,

"You can do it right there if you scaird to go clear to the back, Revern' Bliss; just don't do it on my lettus."

He didn't answer, hearing her low laughter as he walked back until he could smell the hot dryness of lime and sun-shrunken wood. He paused before it but didn't go in, standing looking down the hill where he could see a street light glowing near a house with a picket fence and a flowering tree. The blossoms were white and thick and motionless in the breathless dark and he stood looking at it and making a dull thudding upon the hard earth, his mind aware of the hush around him. Then he looked back toward the house and there was Sister Georgia, a black shadow in the door with the light behind her.

"I told you so," she said, her voice low but carrying to him sharp and clear. "I can hear you way up here. Sounded like a full-grown man."

And he could hear her laughing mysteriously, like the big girls when they teased him. He didn't answer, there were no words to say when a lady teased you like that. He could feel the pulsing of his blood between his fingers and the orange blossoms came to him mixed with the sharp smell of the lime. He turned and looked past the yard with the fence and the tree, to a row of houses where a single light showed. Then the confusion in the tent seemed to break through the surface of his mind, bringing a surge of fear and loneliness....

"Come on in, Revern' Bliss," she called. "You can sleep on the sofa without my having to worry now. We'll leave the door open so the breeze can cool you."

So he went back across the yard into the house and sat up on the sofa, looking around the room as she stood near the doorway, smiling. There was an old upright piano across the room and he went to it and struck a yellowed key, hearing the dull shimmer of its tone echoing sadly out of tune.

"Don't tell me you play on the piano too, Revern' Bliss," she said.

"No, mam, but Daddy Hickman does."

"Oh, him," she said, "Revern' can do just about anything, and I suspect he has, too."

"He sure can do a heap of things," he said, yawning.

"Oh, Oh! Somebody's sleepy; I better make down the bed."

He watched her go into a dark room and light a lamp, then he took off his shoes and socks, then his soiled white dress trousers. Then she came back with a sheet and pillow in her arms and he stood up, watching her spread the sofa and fluffing up the pillow and putting it in place. She left then and he could hear her humming softly and the sound of a bed cover being shaken as he removed his tie and shirt. In his undersuit now, he sat looking up at the people in the frames on the wall and at a paper fan with the picture of a colored angel pinned below them to the wallpaper. *Wonder are they her mother and father,* he thought. *Daddy Hickman has some little pictures of his mother and father in his trunk.... He had a brother too.*

She came through the door with a glass of milk in her hand and gave it to him.

"You tired, Revern' Bliss?" she said.

"Not very much, mam," he said.

"You lonesome?"

"No, mam."

She shook her head. "Well, you sure ought to be tired. After all that preaching you did this week. And all those women pulling on you. Anyway, I bet you're sleepy, so I'm going to say nighty-night now. That is, unless you want me to hear you say your prayers...."

"No thank you, mam," he said, taking a sip of the milk. "A preacher like me has to pray to the Lord strictly by hisself."

He could see the question in her eyes as she looked down into his face. "I guess you right, Revern' Bliss," she said, "but I still just can't get it out of my head that you needs your mama...."

"I don't have a mama," he said firmly. "I just have Daddy Hickman and my Jesus." He set the milk on the table and pushed it away.

"Yes, I know," she said. "And no papa either, have you?"

"No mam. But Daddy Hickman teaches us that the father of all the orphans is God."

"Poor lil lamb," she said. And he could see her moving toward him with tears welling in her eyes and stuck out his hand to halt it there. She hesitated, staring down at his extended hand in puzzlement with that sudden suspension of movement just as the deaconesses had done when the woman had taken hold of him. For a long moment her eyes swam with tears, then she moved past and turned back the sheet, and waited silently for him to lie down. He could see the hurt still there in her eyes but was afraid to feel sorry. She smiled sadly as he moved past and got in and he lay looking straight up at the dim ceiling. She turned to the table and blew out the light. Now she moved to the doorway of her room, her face half in shadow.

"Nighty-night," she said. "Night-night, Revern' Bliss."

"Good night, mam," he said. He felt sad, lying down now and watching her standing there watching him. She seemed to be there a long time, and then suddenly someone was calling *Cudworth, Cudworth,* and he looked toward her and she was still standing there and he could hear someone shaking a tambourine and he began to preach and call for converts, looking lonely and yearning as the others responded to the Word, and still there watching as a woman wearing a black veil came down the aisle past the rows of members wearing a thick veil over her face, and he thought, *This is my mother,* without surprise but a surge of peace, and he took her hand with deep joy and pointed to the bench and watched her going over to take her place upon it. And he was filled with pride that with his voice he had brought her forward at last, had brought her forth from the darkness, and he turned now to exhort the others to witness the power and the glory and the living Word.... But when he looked again she had disappeared. The congregation was gone and a great body of water swirled up where it had been, shooting toward him to wash him from the pulpit. And he was screaming and trying to run, as now the waterspout became a spray of phosphorescent fish shooting at him, sweeping him off his feet now and pulling him across the floor with a loud thump. And now he could hear screaming. And through the dream into the dark he saw Sister Georgia still there bending over him, saying, "Lord, Revern' Bliss, I *thought* you was eating too much of that melon for so late at night. Hush now, you'll be all right. You really are having yourself a time. All scratched and bruised purple like a grape and now this here bad dream. And all you was trying to do was convert a few sinners...."

"No! I wasn't dreaming," he said. "It wasn't a dream. I don't want it to be a dream...."

"Wasn't a dream? Well, you might be a preacher but I know all about lil boy dreams and nightmares." She lit the lamp, looking down upon him with a puzzled frown.

"You was having a nightmare, all right, and judging from that slobber drying on your mouth you was sucking the old sow too. So don't try to tell me, Revern' Bliss, 'cause once in a while the lil boys where I work have trouble just like you been having."

She came over and helped him back onto the sofa. "Let me see your back, Revern' Bliss," she said. "That's it, take off your undershirt. Now turn round here so's I can see."

He saw her bend and could feel the tips of her fingers on his skin. "Lord, look what she did to you! All those scratches. I better get the salve."

He saw her take the light into the kitchen, then she returned with a small jar in her hand.

"Will it burn?" he said.

"Burn? Not this salve, Revern' Bliss. It'll soothe and heal you, though. Hold still now."

"Yes, mam." He could feel the cool spreading over his back beneath the soft circular motion of her hand. Then she was doing the scratches on his arms and legs. His eyes were growing heavy again and she said, "There, that ought to do it. This is a wonderful salve, Revern' Bliss, and it don't burn or make grease spots either. You'll feel good by morning."

"Thank you, mam," he said.

"You welcome, Revern' Bliss; and I'll tell you what we'll do about that nightmare—you just come and get in bed with me a while and it'll be sure not to come back."

She lifted him gently then and he could feel the heat of the lamp come close as she bent to blow out the flame, then they were moving carefully through the dark and he was being lowered to her bed.

"Go to sleep now," she said. "You'll be all right here."

He lay feeling the night and the strangeness of the room and the bed. He could not remember ever being in bed with a woman before and it seemed like another dream. And he thought, *So this is the way it is. This is what Body and the others have.* Then far off in the dark a train whistle blew and he could feel a slight breeze sweeping gently across the bed, bringing the orange blossoms into the room to fade away in the heat as it died, and he could see the stars in the well again and there came again the rising feeling of falling well-ward into the watery sky, falling freely, well and sky, uply downly skyly, starly brightly well-ly wishing her mother No finish go to sleep No this out there She well-ly she was she very nice to let me see them there she was very nice as sugar and spice nicely well-ly nice are made of are you a lady or a girl Sister Elberta—I sleep? Shake the tree run hide and seek No are you no are you not one like Georgia peaches no shake not the tree was very nice. Will there be any seeds in the well? Asleep? Awake. No stars in my crown. And now he moved close I curl beside, she sighing sleeping soft. Not she close Awake how here? It's her—

"Thank you for being so nice to me, Sister Georgia," he said very quietly and waited. But she didn't stir. Zoom! Slide down the hill. *She a-snoring? She sleep pretending?* I rise up, her face flowed my eyes rock heavy my head wandering in here out there stars *She there she gone she dreaming? She see she sigh she saw the morning stars she singing she well she ward her father who our awake....* There she is. I see like watching real quiet while a mouse came out of its hole and ran around the floor. A feeling of tingling delight came over him. He stared hard, trying to see her clearly in the dark, nodding, thinking, *She there.* Then before he was aware he had thrust himself forward and was kissing her softly on the cheek. Mother, he said, Mother... you are my mother. And something unfolded within him and he kissed her again. She was what he'd never allowed himself to yearn for. She was what Body's mother meant to him when he hurt himself or felt so sad. She's what she said I need. *Mother,* he thought, *Mother,* and suddenly he could feel his eyelids stinging and tried to hold it back, but it came on anyway. He stuffed the corner of the sheet into his mouth, rolling to the edge of the bed, crying silently.

Before him the window opened onto the porch and he lay looking through his tears into the shimmering night now lighted with a lately risen moon. Brightness lay beyond the shadows and on the tops of trees and the tears were coming now, steadily, as though they flowed straight from the moon. *Mother, mother...* He could feel the bed giving as she stirred in sleep and held his breath, thinking *Mother, I wish—Mother* until it was as though he had yearned to the end of the world, to the point where the night became day and the day night and on until he seemed to float.... Then he was back in the hands of the angry woman, seeing the members freezing and the redheaded woman taking hold of him and her hands white against his own and his own white, not yellow as Body said and he thought We are the same— Cudworth am I she called and the others were afraid beneath Daddy Hickman's sliding horn Cudworth she called me out of darkness for a mother, not you not you not you just one of the sisters.... Then Body was there and they were walking through the thick weeds beside a road and Looka yonder, man, Body said, pointing to something half-concealed in the dirt, saying *Peeeeew!* And he could see Body hold his nose and spit. Ain't on my mama's table, Body said. And he looked again wondering what it was and saying Mine neither. You better spit then, Body said. But when he tried his mouth was too dry to spit and he looked around and the women had him again and his hands had turned white as the belly of a summer flounder....

Suddenly the sound of fighting cats streaked across the night with a swirl of flashing claws and he was sitting up in the bed, looking wildly around him.

She was still there, sleeping quietly. The room was breathless and her odor, warm and secret, came to him, and just then she turned to rest on her back, her breathing becoming a quiet, catchy snore. Somehow all had changed. He shook his head, "No, I can't sleep with you," he said to her sleeping face. "I don't want you for my mother. I'm going back to the sofa."

Then it was as though a hand had reached down and held him, forcing him to look at her once more, and before he realized it he was looking at the hem of her gown resting high across her round, wide-spread thighs. *I've got to get out of here,* he thought. *I got to move.* But suddenly he was caught between the movement of his body and the new idea welling swiftly in his mind, feeling his foot dangling over the side of the bed while in the dream-like, underwater dimness of the light, he seemed to be looking across a narrow passage into a strange room where another, bolder Bliss was about to perform some frightful deed. *No,* he thought, *No no!* seeing his own hand reaching out like a small white paw to where the hem of her nightgown lay rumpled upon the sheet, and lifting it slowly back, stealthily, cunningly, as though he had done so many times before, lifting it up and back. He watched from far back in a corner of his mind, disbelieving even as he saw the gauze-like cloth lifted like a mosquito net above a baby's crib—then he had crossed the passage and was there with the other Bliss, peering down at what he had uncovered, peering into the shadow of the mystery. Peering past the small white paw to where the smooth flesh curved in the dim light, into the thing itself, the dark impression in the dark. *But what,* he almost said.... He saw yet he didn't see what he saw. There was nothing at all, a little hill where Body'd said he'd find a lake, a bushy slope where he thought he'd find a cave.... It was as though he had opened a box and found another box inside in which he was sure he'd find another and in that, still another—and by then she'd wake up. Yet he couldn't leave. Fragments of stories about digging for buried treasure whirled through his mind and suddenly he was standing in a great hole reaching for an iron-bound chest which he had uncovered, but just as he took hold of it a flock of white geese thundered up and around him, becoming as he watched with arms upraised a troop of moldy Confederate cavalry galloping off into the sky with silent rebel yells bursting from their distorted faces. He wanted desperately to move away but the cloth seemed to hold him, and now she gave a slight movement and his eyes were drawn to her face, seeing faint lights where before there had been dark shadows.... He jumped, hearing himself say "Oh!" and feeling the film of cloth rolling like a grain of sand between his fingers.

"Revern' Bliss, is that you?" she said from far away.

"I didn't mean to do it, mam...."

She sighed sleepily. "Do? What'd you do, honey?"

He held his breath, hearing *dodododododododododododo!*

And again, "Revern' Bliss?"... *dododo....*

She stirred and he saw her arm go over as she started to turn only to halt with a deep intake of breath which suddenly stopped and he realized that he had trapped himself. *It's happening and it will be like Daddy Hickman says Torment is, forever and forever and ever...* Then as though the other Bliss had spoken in an undertone, he thought, *You're It this time for sure but you must never be caught again. Not like this again—move. When they come toward you, move. Be somewhere else, move. Move!*

But he couldn't move. He was watching her hand reaching out searchingly, patting the spot where he had lain. And he thought, *She thinks I wet the bed and I didn't and now her fingers are telling her that it's dry and if I only had, like the Jaybirds spying on you and telling the ants and telling the Devil, and she's raising up and her eyes growing wide and I shall be punished for what I can't even see. Please Lady God Sister Mother.*

"Oh!" Sister Georgia said, sitting up with a creaking of the bedsprings, and he felt the sheet swing across his leg and up around her body so swiftly that it was as though she or I'd never been exposed. He could see his upraised thumb and finger making an "O" of the darkness and she was saying, "Oh, oh, oh," very fast and the night seemed to rush backwards like a worm sliding back into its hole. And he told himself, *It was only a dream I am in the other room lying on the sofa where I went to bed and that woman with the veil is coming toward me and I know who she is and I'm overjoyed to see her save her and now dodging waterspout of fish and falling and screaming and now this one will come in a second and lift me from the floor—save me from...*

"NO!" she said, "OH NO! Revern' Bliss, Revern' Bliss! YOU WERE LOOKING AT MY NAKEDNESS! YOU WERE EXPOSING MY NAKEDNESS!"

He was mute, shrinking within himself, his head turning from side to side as he thought, *If I could fall off the bed it would go away. If I had wings I could—*

But her words were calling up dreadful shapes in his mind. A black horse with buzzards tearing at its dripping entrails went galloping across a burning field, making no sound.... A naked, roaring-drunk Noah stumbled up waving a jug of corn whiskey and cursing in vehement silence while two younger men fought with another trying to cover his head with a quilt-of-many-colored cloth and he could feel her words still sounding. All the darkness seemed to leave the room. Nearby the cats which had hurtled across the night like a swirling wheel of knives had cornered now, filling the air with an agony of howling.

"You were, weren't you, Revern' Bliss?" she said. "Tell me, what was you doing?" And the minor note of doubt in her voice warned him that there was still time to lie, to erase it all with words and he seemed to be running, trying to catch up but he wasn't fast enough and felt the chance slipping through his hand like a silver minnow. He seemed to hear his voice sounding unreal even before he spoke.

"I didn't mean to do it, mam, honestly, I didn't...."

"But you *did*!" she said in a fierce whisper. "You ought to be ashamed of yourself, peeping at my nakedness and me asleep. Sneaking up on me like a thief in the night, trying to steal me in my sleep! You, who's *supposed* to be Revern' Bliss, the young preacher!"

"Please, mam, *Please* mam. I really didn't mean to do it. Forgive me. Please, forgive me...."

She shook her head sadly, sitting higher and clutching the sheet around her.

"Oh, you really ought to be ashamed," she said. "That's the least you can do. Acting like that, like an old rounder or something that's had no training or anything. What I want to know is ain't there *any* of you men a God-fearing woman can trust! I thought you was a real genuine preacher of the gospel and I was proud to have you staying in my house. You never would've had to sleep in any hay around here. But now just look what you done. I guess I been offering my hospitality to an old jackleg. A midnight creeper. I guess you just another one of these old no-good jacklegs. You're not good and sanctified like Revern' Hickman at all and it'll probably break his heart to hear what you done."

He cried soundlessly now, wanting to go to her, his whole body, even his guilty fingers crying Mother me, forgive me. He felt cast into the blackest darkness, the world being transformed swiftly into iron.

"Please," he cried, touching her arm, but she pulled away, refusing to touch him as he reached out to her.

"No," she said, "Oh no. You get out of my bed. Get on out!"

"Please, Sister Georgia."

"I said, get!"

"Yes, mam," he said. He dragged himself from the bed now and found his way back to the sofa and lay sobbing in the dark.

"Sister Georgia," he called to the other room. "Sister Georgia..."

"What is it, ole jackleg?"

"Sister Georgia, please don't call me that. Pleeease..."

"Then you oughtn't to act like one. What is it you want?"

"Sister Georgia," he said, "are you a lady or a girl?"

"Am I *what*?"

"Are you a lady or a girl?" he said.

She was silent, then, "After what you done you shouldn't have to ask."

"But I have to know," he said.

"I'm a woman," she said. "What difference does it make, ole jackleg preacher?"

"Because...maybe if you're a girl what I did isn't really so bad...."

She was silent and he lay straining to hear. Finally, she said, "You go to sleep. It won't be long before day and I have to have my sleep."

She won't tell me, he thought, *she won't say.*

His tears were gone now and he lay face downward, thinking, *I don't care, the other one is the one for a mother....*

It was a bigger tent than ours. The seats went up and around the sides and we had to sit up high at the end over near where the animals were coming through. I was looking down at the pumping and swaying of their backs and at the tops of the heads of the men in red coats walking beside them as they came through. I said, "What kind of elephants are those?"

"Those are African, Bliss," Daddy Hickman said. "There's African elephants and Indian elephants."

"But how do you tell them apart?"

"By their ears, Bliss. The African ones have big ears," Daddy Hickman said.

"What about the noses?"

"You mean *trunks.* They're about the same."

They were strung out like fat boys moving around the ring holding trunk to tail.

"How about those lions?" I said. The man in the white-and-gold coat and the shiny boots was shooting a pistol in the air and waving an ice-cream-parlor chair at the lions.

"What do you mean, Bliss?"

"I mean, where do they come from?"

"They're from Africa too, little boy."

I looked at the lions, sitting up on some stools with their lips rolled back, snarling. One struck at the air with his paw, like Body trying to shadowbox. The man snapped the whip and he stopped. I said,

"Why don't they catch him?"

Daddy Hickman was bent forward, looking hard.

"Why don't they catch him?" I said.

"They're mastered, Bliss. He's scared them. They could destroy him like a cat with a mouse if they weren't scared. But that's the test of his act. He can outthink them from the start because he's a man, but in order to get in there with those animals and master them he has to master his nerves." He laughed. "Bliss, you can't tell it from up here, but he's probably popping his whip and shooting off that pistol at his own legs about as much as he's doing it at the lions. Because sometimes the trainer makes a mistake and that's it, the lions take over. But we don't want that to happen, do we? It's enough to know it's a possibility. Is that right, Bliss?"

"Yes, sir."

Now the man was popping the whip and making the lions gallop around in a circle, while he stood in the same spot, making them gallop around and around him. I said,

"Could you do that, Daddy Hickman?"

He laughed and looked down at me.

"What's that, Bliss?"

"I say could you make those lions do like he's doing?"

"No, Bliss, I'm only a man tamer. Lions are not in my line." He laughed again.

"Daniel could," I, Bliss, said.

"Yes, but Daniel wasn't a lion tamer either, Bliss. It was the Lord who controlled those lions. What Daniel had to do was to have faith."

"But don't you have faith?"

"Sure. But if the Lord ever wants to test me with a lion, He'll do it, Bliss. And He'll put the lion in my path. I won't have to go looking for him. I don't think he intends for me to go bothering with these lions. Would you want to get in there with them?"

"Uh-uh—No, sir. I'm too little."

"What if you were big, Bliss?"

"Maybe. If I was as big as you I might."

"What if they were little lions?"

"That would be better. I'm not afraid of little ones. How long do you think it took that man to learn to scare them?"

"I don't know, Bliss. He probably started when he was your age. Maybe he started with dogs, little puppies or little kittens.... Look yonder, Bliss, here come the clowns. My, my! Now watch this, you'll like the clowns."

He was smiling.

They came through the tent flap in a burst beneath us, all dressed up in funny clothes. I could see down on top of their heads. Seven clowns, one of them short and black, another tall and skinny in underwear and a fat one wearing a barrel, running to the center of the tent, and they were hitting one another over the head with clubs that exploded and sent flowers and birdcages shooting out of their hats and heads, while the black one runs in and out, holding on to his britches with one hand and hitting at them with the other like a girl, a washerwoman, in and out between their legs. Then the others were turning and hitting him on the head and each time they hit he dropped his britches, showing his short bowed legs and his flour sack drawers with printing on them and a big red star in the center and one of them hits him there with a big paddle and he sounds like a hoarse jackass, hoarse and disrespectful early in the morning, while he skips around trying to pull up his britches and falls and turns a flip and gets up and rolls and skips and runs real fast, still holding on. Then the one with the big red nose pulls out a big mallet and hits him on his head and he squashes down to his knees and a big red rooster flies out and runs squawking around in the ring with the others chasing him over the sawdust and he hits him again and again, real fast, and hams and sides of bacon and cabbage and spurts of flour and eggs start falling out of his clothes and he starts running out of his bloomers and a clown dog drops out and starts barking and chasing him along with the others and him skipping and running and turning double flips and more chickens squashing out and a little pink clown pig with a black ring around one eye and the whole tent is laughing while the big clowns are hitting one another with the eggs and hams and sides of bacon and it sounds like the Fourth of July. He was just my size.

"Why does he just run, Daddy Hickman?"

He was laughing. I pulled his sleeve.

"What's that, Bliss?" Tears were running down his cheeks from laughing.

"Why does he always run?"

"Because that's his part in the act, Bliss."

"But why can't he hit and see what he can knock out of them?"

"That would be good, too, Bliss. But he's acting his part. Don't you like him? Listen to how all the folks are laughing. These are real fine clowns, Bliss."

"I don't like him," I said.

"Why?"

"Because I don't like him to be hit all the time. It would be better if *he* hit *them*. They're hitting him because he's the littlest. Are they real people?"

"Of course, Bliss. What's wrong with you? I bring you to see the circus and to have a good time so you can see the clowns and you asking if they're people."

"What kind of people are they?"

"*People*. Humans."

"Like us?"

"Sure, Bliss. Look at that little dog do his act."

He was walking on his front legs.

"Colored?" I said.

"Oh—" He gave me a quick look. "No, Bliss, they're white folks—at least as far as I know. Look at the little dog, Bliss." He was doing a backflip now.

"Back there some were Germans," he said. "Billy Kersands is colored but you haven't seen him. But they're supposed to be funny, Bliss. That's the point. This is all for fun. So when we laugh at them we can laugh at ourselves."

I looked at the little one. "Him too?" I said.

"Sure, he's just short, a dwarf."

"I mean is he white?"

"Sure, Bliss. Don't you feel good? You think you want to go to the toilet?"

"No, sir, not now. Is that little one really white?"

"Sure, Bliss. Of course that's not the point. He's a clown. He's there to make us laugh just like the rest. That's burnt cork he's wearing on his face. Underneath it he's white."

"Is he a grown man like the others?"

"Of course. Look a-there, he's turning flips. See, there he goes. Now there's what you wanted to see. He's hitting the great big fellow. See, Bliss, he's hitting him on his feet and the big one is hopping around. Look, look, there's a stalk of corn growing out of the shoe where he hit him. Oh, oh, the others are chasing him again, look at him go! Right under that elephant!"

I watched. He, the little one, was running around the circle now, with the little clown pig under his arm, feeding it from a baby bottle.

The little pig was still after the bottle as they chased him out of the tent and everybody was laughing. Then the band started playing and two horses galloped in with women standing on their backs in very short flip-up skirts and shiny things in their hair, and down at the center of the tent the music was going and I could see the band master swaying in time as he played a short little horn. They were pretty ladies on horseback and they bowed up and down and turned flips in the air and came down still on the backs of the cantering horses, all in time with the music and their little skirts flipped up and down like a bird's tail or a branch of peach blossoms swaying in the wind. I wanted some ice cream, and started to ask when a man in tights came running in and the music speeded up the horse to a gallop that was like a fast merry-go-round and the man was running beside him and jumping on top along with the lady and they were galloping galloping and then she was standing on top of his shoulders and the horse still galloping along.

"Daddy Hickman," I said, "I'm hungry."

"What do you want now, Bliss, some popcorn?"

"No, sir."

"What?"

"Some ice cream."

"Do you know how to go to get it and come back without getting lost?"

"Yes, sir. I can do it. I'm kinda hungry."

"Here," he said, "go get yourself a cone of cream. And hurry right back, you hear?"

I got a mix, vanilla and strawberry. I didn't like chocolate. Body did. *I'm dark brown, chocolate to the bone,* Body liked to brag about everything but I couldn't, not about that. As I started back, I licked the cone slow to make it last.

Some ladies were dancing on a platform in front of a tent. Behind them and up high was a picture of a gorilla taking a white lady into the jungle. He had big red eyes and sharp teeth and she was screaming and her clothes were torn and her bubbies were showing. I went on. The next tent had pink lemonade and watermelon on ice. I watched a man throwing baseballs at some wooden milk bottles. He knocked them over the second time and won a Dolly Dimples Kewpie doll. He had three already. Out in front of another tent a man was saying something real fast through a megaphone and pointing to a picture of a two-headed man, and a lot of folks were listening to him. One of the heads was laughing but the other head was crying. I watched the man a while. He waved his arm in a circle in the air like he was doing magic and some of the people were going inside. Then two big white guys came up and pinched me and I said "Oh!" and they laughed and called me Rastus. They knew me. I didn't cry. I backed away and went behind the tent. It was quiet, the crowd was all out front. I saw the wagons and the ropes and cages for the animals. Some wet clothes were hanging on a line stretched between two of the wagons and I could hear the music coming up from the big tent and I could smell the hamburgers frying. My ice cream was running out so I ate it very slow, but it didn't last. It was all down in the little end and I bit it off and let the cream run down in my mouth. Then I thought of some fine little-end barbecue ribs and wanted some but nobody was selling any. Pig feet neither. I went on past the back of the tent where the fat lady lived. She looked like a Dolly Dimples too, and I went around and took a look at her. She was holding a handkerchief in her two fingers and her pinkie was crooked like Sister Wilhite's when she drinks her coffee and her hair was cut short in a bob with a pink ribbon around it. A man said, Hi there, to her and she said, Hello dear, and smiled and winked her eye. She looked just like a big fat Dolly Dimples doll and I wondered if she was made like Body said all the littler women were. She winked at me and smiled.

I went on. I was still hungry for ice cream but I saw those two big guys again and went behind the tent and over the staked ropes and sawdust. That's when I saw him. He was sitting on a little barrel looking down at a black and orange felt beanie with a little flowerpot and a paper flower attached to the top and I didn't know what I was going to do but when I went up to him I could see that we were the same height, then he looked up and said, Hi, kid, and I hit him. I hit him real quick and it glanced off his cheek and I could see the blackness smear away and the white coming through and then I hit him again, hard and solid this time and he yelled, Git outta here, y'little bastard! What's the matter with you, kid? You nuts? trying to push me away and I hit and hit, trying to make all the blackness go away. He was surprised and his arms were too short to push me far and I was hitting fast with both fists, going as fast as I could go and he was cursing. Then something snatched me up into the air and I was trying to hit and kicking at him until Daddy Hickman shook me hard, saying, Boy, what's come over you? Don't you know that that's a grown man you're trying to fight? You trying to start a riot? And saying to the little clown, I'm sorry, I'm very sorry; I sent him to get an ice-cream cone and here I find him trying to fight. Who are you, the little one said. You work for his folks? No, Daddy Hickman said, but I know him; he's with me. Then you better get him the hell out of here before I forget he's just a kid. In fact, I should get you instead. What the hell do you mean letting a wild kid like that run around loose? Don't worry, Daddy Hickman said, we're leaving and I mean to take care of him. He won't do it again.... And then he was running with me under his arm, puffing around the tent and across the lot into an alley and someone behind us screaming, "Hey, Rube! Hey, Rube!" and the blackness was all over the back of my hands....

"...Oh, yes," Hickman said, fanning the Senator's perspiring face, "you were giving us a natural fit! All of a sudden you were playing hooky from the services and hiding from everybody—including me. Why, one time you took off and we had about three hundred folks out looking for you. We searched the streets and the alleys and the playgrounds, the candy stores and the parks and we questioned all the children in the neighborhood—but no Bliss. We even searched the steeple of the church where the revival was being held but that only upset the pigeons and caused even more confusion when somebody knocked against the bell and set it ringing as though there had been a fire or the river was flooding.

"So then we spread out and really started hunting. I had begun to think about going to the police—which we hated to do, considering that they'd probably have made things worse—because, you see, I thought that she, that is, I thought that you might have been kidnapped. In fact, we were already headed along a downtown street when, lo and behold, we look up and see you coming out of a picture house where it was against the law for us to go! Yes, sir, there you were, coming out of there with all those people, blinking your eyes and with your face all screwed up with crying. But, thank God, you were all right. I was so relieved that I couldn't say a word, and while we stood at the curb watching to see what you would do, Deacon Wilhite turned to me and said, 'Well, 'Lonzo—A.Z.—it looks like Reverend Bliss has gone and made himself an outlaw, but at least we can be thankful that he wasn't stolen into Egypt.'... And that's when you looked up and saw us and tried to run again. I tell you, Bliss, you were giving us quite a time. *Quite* a time..."

Suddenly Hickman's head fell forward, his voice breaking off; and as he slumped in his chair the Senator stirred behind his eyelids, saying, "What? What?" But except for the soft burr of Hickman's breathing it was as though a line had gone dead in the course of an important call.

"What? What?" the Senator said, his face straining toward the huge, shadowy form in the bedside chair. Then came a sudden gasp and Hickman's voice was back again, soft but moving as though there had been no interruption.

"And so," Hickman was saying, "when you started asking me that, I said, 'Bliss, thy likeness is in the likeness of God, the Father, because, Reverend Bliss, God's likeness is that of *all* babes. Now for some folks this fact is like a dose of castor oil as bitter as the world, but it's the truth. It's hard and bitter and a compound cathartic to man's pride—which is as big and violent as the whole wide world. Still, it gives the faint of heart a pattern and a faith to grow by....'

"And when they ask me, 'Where shall man look for God, the Father?' I say, let him who seeks look into his own *bed*. I say let him look into his own *heart*. I say, let him search his own *loins*. And I say that each man's bedmate is likely to be a Mary—No, don't ask me that—is most likely a Mary even though she be a Magdalene. That's another form of the mystery, Bliss, and it challenges our ability to think. There's always the mystery of the one in the many and the many in one, the you in them and the them in you—Ha! And it mocks your pride, mocks it to the billionth, trillionth power. Yes, Bliss, but it's always present and it's a rebuke to the universe of man's terrible pride and it's the shape and substance of all human truth...."

... Listen, listen! Go back, the Senator tried desperately to say. It was Atlanta! On the side of a passing streetcar, in which smiling, sharp-nosed women in summer dresses talked sedately behind the open grillwork and looked out on the passing scene I saw her picture moving past, all serene and soulful in the sunlight, and I was swept along beside the moving car until she got away. Soon I was out of breath, but then I followed the gleaming rails, hurrying through crowded streets, past ice-cream and melon vendors crying their wares above the back of ambling horses and past kids on lawns selling lemonade two cents a glass from frosted pitchers, and on until the lawns and houses gave way to buildings in which fancy dicty dummies dressed in fine new clothes showed behind wide panes of shopwindow glass. Then I was in a crowded Saturday afternoon street sweet with the smell of freshly cooked candy and the odor of perfume drifting from the revolving doors of department stores and fruit stands with piles of yellow delicious apples, bananas, coconuts, and sweet white seedless grapes—and there, in the middle of a block, I saw her once again. The place was all white and pink and gold, trimmed with rows of blinking lights red, white, and blue in the shade; and colored photographs in great metal frames were arranged to either side of a ticket booth with thin square golden bars and all set beneath a canopy encrusted with other glowing lights. The fare was a quarter and I felt in my pocket for a dollar bill, moist to my touch as I pulled it out, but I was too afraid to try. Instead I simply looked on a while as boys and girls arrived and reached up to buy their tickets then disappeared inside. I yearned to enter but was afraid. I wasn't ready. I hadn't the nerve. So I moved on past in the crowd. For a while I walked beside a strolling white couple pretending that I was their little boy and that they were taking me to have ice cream before they took me in to see the pictures. They sounded happy and I was enjoying their talk when they turned off and went into a restaurant. It was a large restaurant and through the glass I could see a jolly fat black man cutting slices from a juicy ham. He wore a white chef's cap and jacket with a cloth

around his neck and when he saw me he winked as though he knew me and I turned and ran, dodging through the sauntering crowd, then slowed to a walk, going back to where she smiled from her metal frame. This time I followed behind a big boy pushing a red-and-white-striped bicycle. A small Confederate flag fluttered from each end of the handlebars on which two rearview mirrors showed reflecting my face in the crowd, and two shining horns with red rubber bulbs and a row of red glass reflectors ridged along the curve of the rear fender, throwing a dazzled red diamond light, and the racing seat was hung with dangling coon tails. It was keen and I ran around in front and walked backwards a while, watching him roll it. He looked at me and I looked at him but mainly at his bike. A shiny bull with lowered horns gleamed from the end of the front fender, followed by a screaming eagle with outstretched wings and a toy policeman with big flat hands which turned and whirled its arms in the breeze as he guided it by holding one hand on the handlebar and the other on the seat. And on the fork which held the front wheel there was a siren which let out a low howl whenever he pulled the chain to warn the people he was coming. And as it moved the spokes sparkled bright and handsome in the sun. It was keen. I followed him back up the street until we reached the picture show where I stopped and watched him go on. Then I understood why he didn't ride: His rear tire had a flat in it. But I was still afraid so I walked up to the drugstore on the corner and listened a while to some Eskimo Pie men in white pants and shoes telling lies about us and the Yankees as they leaned on the handlebars of their carts, before going back to give it another try. This time I made myself go up to the booth and looked up through the golden bars where the blue eyes looked mildly down at me from beneath white cotton candy bangs. I . . .

"Bliss?"

Was it Mary? No, here to forget is best. They criticize me, me a senator now, especially Karp who's still out there beating hollow wood to hully rhythms all smug and still making ranks of dead men flee the reality of the shadow upon them, then Who? What cast it? stepping with the fetch to the bank and Geneva with tithes for Israel while ole man Muggin has to keep on bugging his eyes and rolling those bales so tired of living but they refuse to let him die Who's Karp kidding? Who's kidding Karp? making a fortune in bleaching cream, hair straightener, and elevator shoes, buying futures in soy beans, corn, and porkers and praising his God but still making step fetch it for the glory of getting but keeping his hands clean, he says. And how do they feel, still detroiting my mother who called me Goodrich Hugh Cuddyear in the light of tent flares then running away and them making black bucks into millejungs and fraud pieces in spectacularmythics on assembly lines? Who'll speak the complicated truth? With them going from pondering to pandering the nation's secret to pandering their pondering? So cast the stone if you must and if you see a ghost rise up, make him bleed. Hell, yes, primitives were right—mirrors do steal souls. So Odysseus plunged that matchstick into Polyphemus' crystal! Here in this country it's change the reel and change the man. Don't look! Don't listen! Don't say and the living is easy! O.K., so they can go fighting the war but soon the down will rise up and break the niggonography and those ghosts who created themselves in the old image won't know why they are what they are and then comes a screaming black babel and white connednation! Who, who, who, boo, are we? Daddy, I say where in the dead place between the shadow where does mothermatermammy—mover so moving on? Where in all the world-pile hides?

"Bliss?"

... but instead of chasing me away this kindly blue-eyed, cotton-headed Georgia-grinder smiled down and said, What is it, little boy? Would you like a ticket? We have some fine features today.

And trembling I hid my face, hoping desperately that the epiderm would hide the corium and corium rind the natural man. Stood there wishing for a red neck and linty head, a certain expression of the eyes. Then she smiled, saying, Why of course you do. And you're lucky today because it's only a quarter and some very very *fine* pictures *and cartoons....*

I watched her eyes, large and lucid behind their lenses, then tiptoed and reached, placing my dollar bill through the golden bars of the ticket booth.

My, My! but we're rich today. Aren't we now, she said.

No, mam, I said, 'cause it's only a dollar.

And she said, That's true, and a dollar doesn't go very far these days. But I'm sure you'll get plenty more because you're learning about such things so early. So live while you may, I say, and let the rosebuds bloom tomorrow—ha! ha!

She pushed the pink ticket through the bars so I could reach it.

Now wait for your change, she said. Two whole quarters, two dimes, and a nickel—which still leaves you pretty rich for a man of your years, I'd say.

Yes, mam. Thank you, mam, I said.

She shook her blond head and smiled. We have some nice fresh buttered popcorn just inside, she said, you might want to try some. It's very good.

Yes, mam, thank you, mam, I said, knotting the change in the corner of my handkerchief and hurrying behind the red velvet barrier rope. Then I was stepping over two blue naked men with widespread wings who were flying on the tiled lobby floor, only the smaller one was falling into the white tile water, and approached the tall man who took the tickets. He wore a jaunty, square-visored cap and a blue uniform with white spats and I saw him look down at me and look away disgusted, making me afraid. He stood stiff like a soldier and something was wrong with his eyes. I crossed my fingers. I didn't have a hat to spit in. Then suddenly he looked down again and smirked and though afraid I read him true. You're not a man, I thought, only a big boy. You're just a big ole freckly face....

> *Peckerwood, peckerwood,*
> *You can't see me!*
> *You're just a redhead gingerbread*
> *Five cents a cabbage head—*

All right, kid, he said, where's your maw?

Sir?

You heard me, Ezra. I'm not supposed to let you little snots in here without your folks. So come on now, Clyde, where's ya' maw?

Watching his face, I pointed into the dark, thinking, I ain't your Clyde and I ain't your Ezra, I'm Bliss. . . . She's in there, I said. She's waiting for me.

She's in dere, he mimicked me, his eyes crossing upon my face and then quickly away. You wouldn't kid me would you, Ezra, he said.

Oh no, sir, I said, she's really and truly in there, like I said.

Then in the dark I could hear the soaring of horns and laughter.

Oh, yeah— he began and broke off, holding down his white gloved hand for silence. Out on the walk some girls in white silk stockings and pastel dresses came to a giggling halt before the billboards, looking at the faces and going "Oooh! Aaaah!"

Well, did Ah evuh wet dream of Jeannie and her cawn sulk hair, he said, snapping his black bow tie hard against his stiff white collar. He stood back in his knees, like Dea-con Wilhite then, and drummed his fingers on the edge of the ticket hopper and grinned.

Inside the music surged and flared.

Hold it a minit, Clyde, he said, Hold it!, looking out at the giggling girls.

Sir? I said, Sir?

Hush, son, he said, and pray you'll understand it better by-'n-by. 'Cause right now I got me some other fish to fry. Y'all come on in gals, he said in a low, signifying voice. Come on in, you sweet miss-treaters, you fluffy teasers. I got me a special show for evuh one of you lily-white dewy-delled mama's gals. Yes, suh! You chickens come to papa, 'cause I got the cawn right here on the evuh-lovin' cob!

Here mister, I said. . . .

He rubbed his white gloves together, watching the girls. What's that you say, kid?

I say my mama's in there waiting for me, I said.

He waved his hand at me. Quiet, son, quiet! he said.

Then the girls moved again. Oh, hell, he said, watching them as they turned on their toes, their skirts swirling as they flounced away, laughing and tossing their hair.

Then he was looking down again.

Clyde, he said, what's your mama's name?

Her name's "Mama"—I mean Miz Pickford, I said.

Suddenly his mouth came open and I could see the freckles bunch together across his nose.

Lissen, kid—you trying to kid me?

Oh, no sir, I said. That's the honest truth.

Well, I'll be dam!

He shook his head.

Honest, mister. She's waiting in there just like I said. . . . I held out my ticket.

He pulled hard on the top of his glove, watching me.

Honest, I said.

Dammit, Clyde, he said, if that's the truth your daddy shore must have his hands full, considering all the folks who are just dying to help him out. I guess you better hurry on in there and hold on to her tight. Protect his interest, Ezra. Because with a name like that somebody big and black might get holt to her first. Yas, suh! An' mah mammy calls me Tee-bone!

Smirking, he took the ticket, tearing it in half and holding out the stub. Here, Mister Bones, Mister Tambo, he said, take this and don't lose it. And you be quiet, you hear? I ain't here for long but don't let me come in there and find y'all down front making noise along with those other snotty-shitty little bastards. You hear?

Yes, sir, I said, starting away.

Hey, wait a minit! Hold it right there, Clyde!

Sir?

Lissen here, you lying little peckerwood—why aren't you in school today?

I looked at him hard. Because it's Saturday, *mister, I said, and because my mamma is in there* waiting *for me.*

He grinned down at me. Okay, Ezra, he said, you can scoot—and watch the hay. But mamma or no mamma, you be quiet, you hear? This is way down South and de lan' uv cotton, as the nigger boys say, but y'all be quiet, y'all heah-uh? An' Rastus, Ah mean it!

I hesitated, watching him and wondering whether he had found me out.

Well, go on! he barked.

And I obeyed.

Then I was moving through the sloping darkness and finding my way by the dim lights which marked the narrow seat rows, going slowly until the lights came up and then there were red velvet drapes emerging and eager faces making a murmuring of voices, and golden cherubim, trumpets, and Irish harps flowing out in space above the high proscenium arch, while in the hidden pit the orchestra played sweet, soothing airs. Then in the dimming of the lights I found a seat, and horses and wagons flowed into horses and wagons surrounded by cowboys and Indians and Keystone Kops and bathing beauties and flying pies and collapsing flivvers and running hoboes and did ever so many see themselves comfortably, humorously in quite so few? And ads on the backdrop asking Will the Ladies Please Remove Their Masks and Reveal Their True . . . and everyone and everything moving too swiftly, vertigoing past, so that I couldn't go in, couldn't enter even when they came close and their faces were not her face. So in the dark I squirmed and waited for her to come to me but there were only the others, big-eyed and pretty in their headbands and bathing suits and beaded gowns but bland with soft-looking breasts like Sister Georgia's only unsanctified and with no red fire in green eyes. She called me Goodhugh Gudworthy and I couldn't go in to search and see. . . .

On the hill the cattle tinkled their bells and she said, Mister Movie-man, I have to live here, you know. Will you be nice to me and the blossoms were falling where the hill hung below the afternoon and we sprawled embraced and out of time that never entered into future time except as one nerve cell tooth hair and tongue and drop of heart's blood into the bucket. Oh, if only I could have controlled me my she I and the search and have accepted you as the dark daddy of flesh and Word—Hickman? Hickman, you after all. Later I thought many times that I should have faced them down—faced me down and said, Look, this is where I'll make my standing place and with her in all her grace and sweet wonder. But how make a rhyme of a mystery? If I had only known then what I came to know about the shape of honor and the smell of pride—I say, HOW THE HELL DO YOU GET LOVE INTO POLITICS OR COMPASSION INTO HISTORY? And if you can't get here from there, that too is truth. If he can't drag the hill on his shoulders must a man wither beneath the stone? Yes, the whole hill moved, the cattle lowed, birds sang and blossoms fell, fell gently but I was . . . I was going in but couldn't go in and then it ended and the lights came on. But still I waited, hoping she'd appear in the next run, so I sat low in my seat, hiding from the ticket man as they moved in and out around me. Then it was dark again and I knew I should leave but was afraid lest she appear larger than life and I would go in. . . . Why couldn't you say, Daddy Hickman: Man is born of woman but then there's history and towns and states and between the passion and the act there are mysteries. Always. Appointive and elective mysteries so I told myself: Man and woman are a baby's device for achieving governments—ergo-ego and I'm a politician. Or again, shadows that move on screens and words that dance on pages are a stud's device for mounting the nightmare that gallops by day. And I told myself years ago, Let Hickman wear black, I, Bliss, will wear a suit of sable. Being born under a circus tent in the womb of wild women's arms I reject circumstance, live illusion. Then I told myself, speed up the process, make them dance. Extend their vision until they disgust themselves, until they gag. Stretch out their nerves, amplify their voices, extend their grasp until history is rolled into a pall. The past is in your skins, I cried. Face fortune and be filled. No, there's never a gesture I've made since I've been here that hasn't tried to say, Look, this is me, me; can't you hear? Change the rules! Strike back hard in angry collaboration and you're free—but I couldn't go in I have to live here, Mister Movie-man, she said, and I found a resistance of buttons and bows. Imagine, there and in those times, a flurry of fluffy things, an intricacy of Lord knows what garment styles, there beneath the hill. . . .

"Bliss, are you there?"

So I waited, hoping I could get into it during the next show and she would be there and I waited yearning for one more sight word goodhugh even if seventy outraged deaconesses tore through the screen to tear down the house around us. But couldn't go in and sat wet and lonely and ashamed and wet down my leg and outside all that racing life swirling before me but once more the scenes came and tore past, sweeping me deeper into anguish yet when I came out of all that intensified time into the sun the world had grown larger for my having entered that forbidden place and yet smaller for now I knew that I could enter in if I entered there alone. . . . I ran—Bliss ran.

. . . Where are we? Open the damper, Daddy; it heats hard. So I told myself that I shall think sometime about time. It was all a matter of time; just a little time. I shall think too of the camera and the swath it cut through the country of my travels, and how after the agony I had merely stepped into a different dimension of time. Between the frames in blackness I left and in time discovered that it was no mere matter of place which made the difference, but time. And not chronology either, only time. Because I was no older and

although I discovered early that in different places I became a different me. What did it all mean? Was time only space? How did she who called Cud forth become shadow and then turn flesh? She broke the structure of ritual and the world erupted. A blast of time flooded in upon me, knocking me out of the coffin into a different time.... My grandpap said the colored don't need rights, Donelson said; they only need rites. You get it? Just give niggers a baptism or a parade or a dance and they're happy. And that, Karp said, is pappy crap.... And I was stunned.

So now when I changed places I changed me, and when I entered a place that place changed imperceptibly. The mystery went with me, entered with me, realigning time and place and personality. When I entered all was changed, as by an odorless gas. So the mystery pursued me, shifting and changing faces. Understand?

And later whenever instead of taking in a scene the camera seemed to focus forth my own point of view I felt murderous, felt that justifiable murder was being committed and my images a blasting of the world. I felt sometimes that a duplicity was being commissioned, an ambuscado trained upon those who thought they knew themselves and me. And yet I felt that I was myself a dupe because there was always the question aroused by my ability to see into events and the awareness of the joke implicit in my being me. Who? So I said, What is the meaning of this arrangement of time place and circumstance that flames and dampens murder in my heart? And what is this desire to identify with others, this need to extend myself and test my most far-fetched possibilities with only the agency of shadows? Merely shadows. All shadowy they promised me my mother and denied me solid life. Oh, yes, mirrors do steal souls. So indeed Narcissus was weird....

"Rev. Bliss," Hickman was saying, "in the dark of night, alone in the desert of my own loneliness I have thought long upon this. I have thought upon you and me and all the old scriptural stories of Isaac and Joseph and upon our slave forefathers who killed their babes rather than have them lost in bondage, and upon my life here and the trials and tribulations and the jokes and laughter and all the endless turns-about that mark man's life in this world. And each time I return, each time my mind returns and makes its painful way back to the mystery of you and the mystery of birth and resurrection and hope which now seems endless in its complication. Yes, and I think upon the mystery of my involvement in it. Me, a black preacher's wilful son, a gambler-musician who rejoiced in the sounds of our little hidden triumph in this world of deceitful triumphs. Me, given you and your gifts, your possibilities in this whirlwind of circumstance. How and why did it happen? Why was I, the weakest of vessels, chosen to give so much and to have to try to understand so much which hardly seems understandable? Why did He give me this mysterious burden and then seem to mock me and challenge me and let men revile and despise me and wipe my heart upon the floor of this world after I had suffered and offered it up in sacrifice because in the coming together of hate and love and life and death, that marked the beginning, I looked upon those I love and upon them who caused their deaths and was unable to accept it except as I'd already accepted the blues, the clap, the loss of love, the fate of man.... I bared my breast, I lowered my head into the ashes where they had burned my own, my loved ones, and accepted Thy will. Why didst Thou choose me, single me out for further humiliation who had been designated for humiliation by men unworthy, by men most unworthy, Lord? Why? Why me? Me who had accepted my blackness as my fate, in the dark and shadowy complication of Thy will? And yet, down there in the craziness of the southland, in the madhouse of downhome, the old motherland where I in all my ignorance and desperation was taught to deal with the complications of Thy plan, yes, and at a time when I was learning to live and to glean some sense of how Thy voice could sing through the blues and even speak through the dirty dozens if only the players were rich-spirited and resourceful enough, comical enough, vital enough and enough aware of the disciplines of life. In the zest and richness Thou were there, yes! But still, still, still, my question, Lord! Though I say, Quiet, quiet, my tongue. So teach me, Lord, to move on and yet be still; to question and not cry out, Lord, Lord, WHY?... WHY?"

And Hickman slept.

The air was stirring gently across his face now and the Senator could hear dimly the "Son, are you there?" of Hickman's voice softly murmuring—but when he tried to respond Bliss had moved on....

... Stirring beneath the sterile grain of the sheet the Senator felt a binding pressure on heel and toe, and now alone in the hot world beyond the puckered seal of his lids he found himself wading through a sandy landscape bathed in an eerie twilight. In the low-hung sky before him, vaguely familiar images of threatening shapes appeared, flickering and fading as though to taunt him, and he found himself lunging desperately across the sandy terrain in a compulsive effort to grasp their meaning. But the closer he approached the more rapidly the images changed their shape, tearing apart in smoke-like strands only to reappear in ever more ambiguous forms further, further ahead.

The Senator struggled on, his right foot flaming, and now as he paused for breath the sudden rhythmical gusting of a slight breeze irritated the feverish surface of his skin and he could hear Hickman's voice again; at first muted and low, then becoming a booming roar. Hickman was somewhere above him but suddenly as he strained toward the sound he was swept up and carried through the air with such force that his body slanted headfirst into the wind and he kept his balance only by rotating his arms in the manner of a skier soaring in exhilarating flight above the earth. Then came a burst of light followed by a shrilling of whistles and the clanging of bells and the Senator realized that he was standing atop a speeding freight train, his feet dancing unsteadily upon the narrow boards of a catwalk that ran the length of the car. It was a long freight and far up the tracks he could see the engine, pouring a billowing plume of smoke against the sunny landscape as with a nervous, toy-like shuttling of driving-rods it curved the rails to the west....

Wondering at the sudden change of scene, the Senator fought desperately to keep his feet, holding on by flexing at ankle and knee in a bending, straightening, balancing, swaying, dance-like motion which moved his body with and against the erratic rhythms of the bounding car. In the blazing sun the train was hurtling downgrade now and the engineer seemed determined to send him flying into space, for he had the impression that every car in the train was being forced to knock the car just ahead into a capricious, off-beat, bucking increase of speed which nothing on top could withstand. For a while it caused him to bounce about like a manic tap dancer, rattling his teeth and fragmenting the landscape into a whirl of chattering images; then the grade was leveling off and with the going smoother the Senator looked about.

Beyond the rows of cross ties and gleaming rails to his left wheat fields, turned tawny and dry by the sun, wheeled away at a slant accented by flashing telegraph poles, and below he could see his own thin shadow atop that of the car flickering swiftly along the grading. Flocks of blackbirds were whirling up from the strands of wire which fenced off the field and swinging in broad circles over the tilting land.

Sweeping ahead the train screamed shrilly as it gathered highball speed, its whistle sending snatches of vapor into the blaze of sun. Then to his right, past a sparse wind-break of trees, three dark dogs raced over a harvested field, the agitated music of their trailing cry reaching him faintly through the roar. The dogs ran with nose to earth and far beyond, where the land rolled down to a sparkling stream, he could see the white, semaphore-flashing of a rabbit's tail as it coursed in curving flight away from the hounds.

Hurry, hurry, little friend, the Senator thought, hearing the engines whirling again, the sound distraught and lonely as he heard a woman's voice speaking to him in an intimate, teasing drawl, "So, honey, I tell you like the rabbit tole the rabbit, 'Darling, love ain't nothing but a habit'*—Hello, there, Mister Babbitt Rabbit—Now, now, honey, don't go getting mad on me. All I mean is that you can come see me again sometimes; 'cause short-winded and frantic as you is I still think you kinda cute. You kinda fly too, and I like that. So whenever you feel like coming down to earth, why, drop in on a poor soul and thank you kindly...."*

And in the cool shade of the back-alley porch he could see Choc Charlie pausing to drink from his frosty bottle of Chock beer then look out bemusedly across the yard ablaze with a center bed of red canna flowers, shaking his head. Beyond the yard, the rutted roadbed of the alley was covered with broken glass of many colors and beyond its sparkling surface he could see a black cat yawning pinkly in the shade of the high, whitewashed fence which enclosed the yard beyond. Then Choc Charlie belched and turned, winking at Donelson, and he could see tiny wrinkles forming at the corners of Choc Charlie's eyes as his querulous voice resumed.

"So now," Choc Charlie said, "the damn hound was so hot on Brer Rabbit's trail that

he had to do something real quick because that hound was chasing him come hell for breakfast. So 'bout that time Brer Rabbit sees him a hole in some rocks—and, blip! he shoots into it like a streak of greased lightning. . . . And too bad for him!"

"Looks like he made a mistake of judgment," Donelson said. "How come, how come?"

"How come? Man, do you know who was holed up in that hole?"

"Not yet," Donelson said. "You didn't say. . . ."

"Well, it was ole Brer Bear! That's *how come. Man, Brer Rabbit liked to shit his britches then, because didn't nobody in his right mind mess with Brer Bear—and Brer Bear had done already looked up and seen him!"*

"Dramatic as hell, isn't it," Donelson said. "A turn in the plot; a 'reversal.' David and Goliath . . . Daniel in the goddamned lion's den! Ole J.C. couldn't do better."

"Drink some beer, man," Choc Charlie said, "I'm telling this lie and my initials ain't J.C., they're C.C. *You see, Brer Bear had been sleeping and when he sits up and rubs his eyes he's flabbergasted! He's hornswoggled! He's hyped! He's shucked! But he don't know who dropped it! He's looking right at him too but he can't believe his own God-given eyes! Here's Brer Rabbit in his very own bedroom! Somebody go get the chief of police, 'cause now Brer Bear is 'bout to move!"*

"Ulysses alone in Polly-what's-his-name's cave," Donelson said. "And without companions. . . ."

"Man, what are you talking about?" Choc Charlie said. "How the hell did she *get in there?"*

"She?" Donelson said, "I didn't say anything about 'she,' I said 'he'—but forget it. What happened then?"

"Man," Choc Charlie said, "you drinking too fast. And sit back out of that sun. Anyway, don't nobody name of Polly mess with Brer Bear, male or *female. Not when he's trying to get his rest. . . ."*

"That's his name," Donelson said, "Polly-fee-mess."

Choc Charlie took a drink and looked wearily at the Senator. "Make him quit messing with this lie, will you please? I appreciate your buying me this Choc and those ribs last night and all but it ain't really that good—know what I mean? Anyway, Brer Rabbit was there and he thought real hard and came up with what he hoped would be a solution. Because with Brer Bear in front of him and with that hound right on his heels Brer Rabbit had to come up with something quicker than the day before yestiddy . . . and that's no bull."

"We're with you, hanging on," Donelson said. "He's reached a moment of grave decision . . ."

"Now you're talkin'," Choc Charlie said, "grave is right. He better do something quick or he's in his grave, and that's when Brer Rabbit made his move. Gentlemen," Choc Charlie said, "git this: He spins in front of Brer Bear like a wheel of fortune, he spits on the floor like a man among men, he spins back around and makes his white tail flash like the nickel-plated barrel of a .45 pistol, then he wheels around agin and jumps way back and slaps his hips like he's wearing two low-slung, tied-down holsters and a

bushel of bullets, then he basses out at Brer Bear like he's all of a sudden ten feet tall and weighing a ton. Said, 'Let a motherfucker move and I'll mow him down!' "

Donelson let out a howl, "Oh no, man, I must protest! You can't do that, not add incest and insult to trickery...."

"Man, hush," Choc Charlie said. "Now don't forget, while this was happening the hound is streaking in like a cannonball, but when he hears all that evil talk coming out of the hole that hound throws on brakes and makes a turn so fast that not only is he running along the wall but his own tail is whipping his head like a blackjack in the expert hands of Rock Island Shorty, the railroad bull—and man, he highballs it the hell out of there yelling bloody murder.

"Gentlemen, by now Brer Bear is sitting there in a flim-flam fog and before he can git hisself together, Brer Rabbit reaches up and snatched off his cap in order to cut down on the wind resistance and bookety-bookety-bookety, he lit up out of there and is long gone!"

"Act five, scene one coming up," Donelson said. "What did they do then?"

"They? Hell, man, other than Brer Bear wasn't no one left in there—unless'n it was that Polly fellow you brought up, and if so I guess he musta been under the bed. But Brer Bear, poor fellow, he was in a hell of a fix. He's just sitting there rubbing his eyes, sweating gallons and shaking all over like he's got the palsy. Gentlemen, it was pathetic..."

"Tragic," Donelson said.

"Whatever it was," Choc Charlie said, "it was a bitch and it gave Brer Bear the bad-man blues. Said, 'What on earth is this here country coming to, with these bad-acting bab-bub-bub-bad-talking bad-men breaking into folks' homes talking 'bout their mamas and threatening them with these outrageous, dum-dum-bullet-shooting pearl-handled .45s? Poor Brer Bear thought Brer Rabbit's tail was a pearl-handled pistol grip and he felt so bad he started to cry like a baby. Said, 'What did I ever do to have a fellow like that come imposing on me? What this here dam country needs is more law and order—and that's a fact! Where the hell did I put my Gatling gun...?'

"But, gentlemen, Brer Bear was already too late, because by the time he located his shooting-iron Brer Rabbit was already going slam—bam—thank you, mam, through all those fine young lady rabbits back in the briar patch."

"And there," Donelson said, "you have a scenario with conflict of will, high skulduggery, gunplay, escape, and rampant sex!"

Smiling into the sun, the Senator had begun to enjoy the familiar sensation of flying, the rush of wind against his face, but as he looked back along the tops of the swaying cars a cloud of black dust had begun to rise from where, several cars to the rear, three hulking figures were slipping and sliding through a gondola loaded with soft coal. The figures were shouting and gesturing in his direction and for a moment the Senator hesitated, but now, seeing a flash of metal burst from a gesturing hand he turned, and bending low, pushed hurriedly through the heavy pressure of the wind to the metal ladder attached to the forward end of the boxcar. Reaching it, he looked back, and seeing the *figures crawling in a line along the top of the boxcar, he clambered down the ladder and held on. Looking along the top where the figures came slowly forward he looked quickly ahead, seeing a cindered path running beside the tracks and to the right of the path the roadbed was falling steeply down into a narrow field. Sunflowers grew tall in the field and at its edge a wall of closely planted trees arose. The trees were tall with sunlight filtering through the high-flung branches and flickering gloomily upon the slender trunks, and as the train swept him past, the Senator looked some dozen cars ahead to where a sunny clearing was suddenly breaking and growing wider and as now the car came abreast he braced himself and let go, feeling his body flying away from the car and trying to run only to see the cindered path slamming up to meet him as with a palm-searing, knee-burning explosion of breath he landed hard upon the shuddering roadbed.*

Fighting for breath against the heaving path, he lay as though paralyzed, watching the wheels and under-carriages churning the light just beyond his head. Dust and bits of trash were whirling furiously about and he could see the rhythmical rise and fall of the sleepers as they took the pound and click of wheel on rail. Then, his breath returning, he was sitting up and watching the tail end of the train whipping swiftly up the track. The red lenses of lanterns glinted like enormous jewels from either side of the caboose and a flag was snapping briskly from the handrail as the three figures ran back along its top, continuing doggedly to advance toward him even as the train bore them smoothly away.

Sweeping on, with smoke and flame pouring from its stack, the engine screamed again as it plunged toward a rise of rocky country that lay to the west. And suddenly it was as though he were watching a scene from a silent movie—with the train hurtling toward a point in the rocks where, as it approached, a spot grew like that which blossoms in a paper napkin at the touch of a lighted cigarette. Widening mysteriously around its periphery, the hole was turning rapidly inward upon itself and in a flash the three figures, the train, and the sunlit surrounding scene had vanished, leaving behind only the cindered grade, the cross ties, and gleaming rails, now running in steely convergence into the darkness of a void.

For a moment the Senator had the impression of gazing toward a rumpled sheet which hung against the landscape with a mysterious hole burned in its center, but still hearing the muffled, clicking sound of the receding train he got to his feet and plunged in jolting, stiff-legged bounds down the grade and into the trees.

The Senator was moving through deep country now, the sound of the train a faint rumble in the distance. Here in the shade of the trees the air was clear and cool and he walked beneath stands of towering walnuts, oaks, and cottonwoods that grew in clumps broken by park-like spaces of grass accented by bushes and trailing vines. His leg and palms smarted from his fall but now he moved ahead with a sense of relief, breathing the spicy air and trying to recall when he had passed through such woods before.

Off to his right an abandoned apple orchard stood with gnarled limbs in surreal disarray and farther beyond he could see a stand of elders displaying clusters of dark red berries in the sunlight. He was moving in silence, brushing embedded cinders from his palms and stepping carefully to protect his injured leg—when, suddenly, a covey of quail flushed at his feet, breaking the cathedral quiet with a roar that caused his heart to pound and his nerves to hum as he watched the rocketing birds reel off and sail with set wings into a nearby thicket. A dampness broke over his skin, chilling him as he watched where the birds had blended magically into the background, and for a moment he stood silent, searching in vain for the slightest telltale motion from the quail.

Now the afternoon was motionless, the brown and green foliage where the birds had gone inscrutable. But for the distant cry of a single bird the only sound was that of his own breathing, and the Senator's mind stirred with excitement, thinking: Surprise, speed, and camouflage are the faith, hope, and charity of escape, and the essence of strategy. Yes, and scenes dictate masks and masks scenes. Therefore the destructive element offers its own protective sanctuary. Hunting codes are a concern of human hunters or otherwise. To imaginate is to integrate negatives and positives into a viable program supporting one's own sense of value. Flown before the unseeing hand the bird crouches safe in the bush. Therefore freedom is a wilful blending of opposites, a conscious mixing of ungreen, unbrown things and thoughts into a brown-green shade.... Where's the light? What's the tune? What's the time?

For a moment he mused, his eyes playing along the quiet hedge. There was something missing from the formula but he would work it out later, for now he must move ahead.

But hardly had he approached a mossy clearing in the trees than the Senator froze again. Before him two foxes were moving past at a leisurely trot, their elegant brushes floating weightlessly upon the quiet air. One fox carried a limp rabbit retriever-wise in its jaws and he could see the lazy flopping of the rabbit's leaf-veined ears, observed its white powder puff of a tail. And now, reaching the center of the clearing the animals paused, delicately sniffing the air as they regarded him quietly out of the amber remoteness of vulpine eyes. One of the animals was gravid and the forgotten image of plump fox puppies playing upon the hard bare bone-and-feather-strewn earth before a rocky burrow flashed through his mind and a fragment from the Scriptures sang in his head:

> *Oh, the foxes have holes in the ground . . .*
> *But son of man . . . son of man . . .*

And before the quiet confrontation of their eyes the Senator stood breathless, feeling a breeze passing over the dampness of his arms and watching a lazy rippling begin to play through the fur of the foxes. And he felt the hairs stirring lightly along his own forearms as the breeze blew slowly past pointed muzzles and alerted ears to part with a gentle, silk-like ruffling the long fine fur of the high-held tails.

> *Oh, the foxes have holes in the ground . . .*
> *But son of man, son of man . . .*

Then imperceptibly the foxes moved, becoming with no impression of speed twin streaks of red moving past the thicket of green, and he watched their brushes floating dream-like into the undergrowth.

All this I've known, the Senator thought, but had forgotten. . . . Then in the sudden hush, accented by a pheasant's cry he felt as though no trains nor towns nor sermons existed. He was at peace. Here was no need to escape nor search for Eden, nor need to solve his mystery. But again he moved, somehow compelled to go ahead. . . .

Soon the Senator was beyond the woods, his throat throbbing with nameless emotion stirred by the foxes, and he moved with inward-turning eyes—until, high above, where it flashed like a minnow in an inverted bowl of a clear blue lake, a small plane caught his eye and he moved beneath the boughs of a pine tree, watching the plane bank languidly into the sun to write in smoke across the sky:

Niggers

Stay

Away

From

The Polls

And watching the words expand and drift in ghostlike shapes he shook his fist at the sky and ran again, cursing the taut constriction of the sand.

Following the upward slant of the terrain the Senator found himself approaching a crowd gathered below the terrace of a clubhouse resting on the broad, level surface of a cliff which overlooked a winding river. Below the cliff and atop the river's farther bank, a flock of grazing sheep were strung out along a rolling meadow, making dark foreshortened shadows against the green, and far below, past the brown-and-gray outcroppings of the meadow's rocky edge, he could see the dark swirl and sparkle of the river as it flowed past a pile of boulders which protruded white and brilliant in the sun.

There was a feeling of holiday in the air now, and on the terrace he could see uniformed waiters serving pale yellow melon, frosted drinks, and ices to smiling couples who lounged at tables set in the pastel shades of brightly colored parasols.

Moving painfully through the fashionable crowd the Senator squeezed past handsome women clad in sports clothing and tweedy, heavily tanned men sporting alpine hats decorated with the feathers of a game bird, silver-mounted brushes of badger fur, or tiny medals celebrating the hunt, and was suddenly aware of the fresh scents the women wore, the fine, smooth texture of their complexions. Then he had pressed to the front of the crowd and found himself leaning against a low barrier that fenced off the broad semicircle of a grassy shooting ring.

To his right, just inside the barrier, a group of men with guns cradled in the crooks of their arms were looking out to the center of the ring where three workmen knelt in the grass working over a device attached to a length of rubber hosing. The hosing ran back to a truck parked at the rear where it was attached to the storage tank of a mobile air compressor. Other workmen, wearing black berets and blue coveralls, were standing in groups of three at four stations arranged at equal distances across the ring, all marked, like that where the men were working, by stacks of bright yellow dovecotes. They too were looking toward the kneeling, frantically busy men, and back near the compressor truck the Senator could see dozens of dovecotes stacked high on a wagon before which a small, bony horse with docked tail wearing a farmer's straw hat in which holes had been cut for its twitching ears, dozed wearily between the shafts. Then, as though someone had pulled a switch, the Senator was aware of the throbbing sound made by the cooing of many birds. The dovecotes were crammed with pigeons and he could see the nervous motion of their beaked heads thrusting back and forth between the bars. The air throbbed with the sound of their cooing, reminding him of a crowd of summer passengers looking out of the grill of a trolley car as they commented upon something out in the passing scene.

And now as the annoyed voices of the spectators began drowning out the noise of the birds, he saw the men drawing erect and heard one of them call out to the men with guns.

"Okay, gentlemen, it's now in working order."

"And it's damn well time," a spectator called; then a bell sounded and the Senator could see a uniformed official wearing a green sun visor stepping across the springing turf and signaling to a marksman who took the firing line and the action was resumed.

Suddenly, at the cry of "MARK!" the Senator heard a fierce sound like that of air bursting from a punctured tire and saw a surprised pigeon bouncing some twenty feet into the air above the trap, hanging there for an instant of flurried indecision, then taking off on a swift, rising course to the right; and he could see the marksman now, taking his time, his feet precisely placed, swinging smoothly onto and past the rising bird, and at the sound of the shot the bird abruptly folding on its course and as a second shot exploded bursting apart in the air.

"Onesie, twosie, It's a doosie," a supercilious voice called behind him, but before he could turn to see who it was, the cry of "MARK!" came again and he was watching a pigeon taking off to the left and halting suddenly as though struck by a baseball bat, its feathers flying, as yet another bird shot aloft on a screeching jet of air.

Having dropped his final bird, the smiling marksman stepped back with lowered gun and waved as applause and shouts of "Bravo!" erupted from the spectators; and now, as another gunman took the firing line, the action accelerated, moving so swiftly that the Senator had an uneasy feeling that things were getting out of hand. A fateful accuracy marked the match, disturbing him profoundly, as the gunners, coming and going in swift rotation, took continued advantage of second shots and made great slaughter on the grass.

Suddenly, as a huge marksman wearing baggy seersucker pants took the line, a small, stooped, stiff-necked man appeared, smoking a long cigar. As he came prancing along just inside the ring and waving a sheaf of banknotes about, he yelled, "Heads, gentlemen! I'm taking bets on heads alone!"

Heads, the Senator thought, what does he mean . . . ?

"What! Are you kidding?" another man called.

"Not kidding, sir," the little man said. "I'm betting a thousand that he leads the next bird so precisely that the pattern alone will take off the head and leave the body untouched."

"*You're nuts and you're covered,*" *the second man called, and now, as the next pigeon sprang free the Senator watched the huge marksman wave his gun about like a weighted pool cue and, waiting until the bird had leveled, he cut loose shooting from the hip. And now he could see something fly away from the bird to sail across the ring as its body continued a few feet in headless flight and then collapsed.*

There was wild applause and the Senator watched the little man laughing and dancing a jig step as he waved a fist full of money and yelled,

"*Heads today and tails tomorrow! Heads! Heads! Heads! Who'll bet three grand that he touched nary a tail feather, a breast feather, nor nary a feather in either wing? Speak up!*"

"*What's the bet?*" *someone called from the rear.*

"*No breast! No tail! No wing! And ding-a-ding ding at three thousand bucks a number seven shot,*" *the little man called.*

"*Covered!*" *the voice called, and as the Senator watched the little man scampering around the ring to where an attendant was picking up the headless bird the betting became furious.*

Returning with the bird now plucked of its feathers, the little man displayed it proudly, pointing to the unblemished state of its skin and collecting his bets with an air of fierce satisfaction.

"*How about you, sir,*" *he said to the Senator, his teeth clamped fiercely upon his long cigar. "You look like a man of quality, a betting man. Clarence has one bird left in the set and I'll bet you ten thousand that he'll turn him over easy, or turn him over slow. He'll hit him high, he'll hit him low—tip, tail, wing, or duster—as you please, sir. Just say the word.*"

"*No,*" *the Senator said, "not today or ever.*"

The little man laughed, revealing a set of wolfish teeth. "Smoked you out, didn't I," *he said, "Four little children and a very nowhere wife, is that it?*"

But when the Senator started to answer he moved quickly back into the crowd—which was stirring about and roaring so loudly that the Senator quickly lost sight of him.

Out in the ring the traps were being sprung in no discernable order and the firing becoming so rapid that windrows of ejected cartridge hulls were piling up near the firing line. Rings of sweat showed at the armpits of the gunners' jackets and the Senator could see waves of heat dancing along the vented gunbarrels. Things were getting so much out of hand that he felt that the officials should do something to restore order, or at least slow the pace, but none were to be seen. And as fast as one stack of dovecotes was emptied of birds the handlers rushed replacements to the traps.

The Senator's head felt light now, his nose stinging from the acrid gunsmoke, and he looked skyward with a feeling that the sun had halted just above his head. I must get out of here, he thought, but when he tried to leave the howling spectators pressed in upon him so tightly that he was unable to move.

Turning his back to the ring, he tried to break free to the rear, to make for the shade of the terrace. But now a woman whose luxuriant auburn hair showed beneath a white leghorn hat with aqua ribbon pressed so closely against him that he could see beads of moisture standing out on the flesh beneath her deep blue eyes. The woman was smiling mysteriously into his face and he could see deep wrinkles breaking through her mask-like makeup, revealing a far darker complexion underneath. Then the woman was saying something which he could not understand and as he bent closer to hear he was struck by a blast of disinfectant which was so repulsive that he turned quickly around and backed against the barrier. It's Lysol, he thought, It's Lysol!

Far to the rear of the crowd now he could hear a husky voice keeping score of the kills while a woman's voice repeated the count in a shrill Spanish accent, lisping her words and shouting, "Olé! Olé!" as the firing accelerated in pace.

Closing his eyes against the blazing scene, the Senator plunged the tips of his fingers into his ears, trying to escape the noise. His leg had begun to pain again and he remembered the refreshment that he'd seen the waiters serving back on the terrace. He longed for a cold slice of melon, an iced drink, a bit of quiet. But now an explosion of shouting caused him to open his eyes to a crowd that was leaning over the barrier and shaking its fists in anger. Things had come to a halt, the guns were silent and no birds flying. At first he thought the object of the spectators' disapproval was an official's ruling, or some act of unsportsmanlike conduct by a contestant, and discovered instead that the anger was caused by a single slate-gray pigeon.

Out near the rear of the ring the bird was moving over the grass with the grave, pigeon-toed dignity of a miniature bishop, its head bobbing from side to side as it ignored the shouting crowd.

Close by, a man cupped his hands to his mouth, screaming, "Flush, you fink! Use your wings!"

"You're wasting your time with that one," another man called. "Where's the official? Get him over here! Does he consider that a sporting bird? Who the hell bred the charac-terless fowl? I say Who?"

"Now wait," the sun-visored official called from within the ring. "These birds are the very best. Bred for the ring, for hand-launching and for the trap!"

"Then make him fly, dammit; make him fly!"

"It's sportsman's luck," the man in the visor called. "Some fly, some fail. We put enough air under these birds to launch a rocket, so if one doesn't fly it's just too bad. The gunner simply calls for another bird."

"But I want this one," the gunner called. "He owes me a chance!"

"He's right," a small blond woman called. "Make the buzzard fly! Up in the air . . . you . . . you pretentious pouter. We didn't come here to see you strut or take a dive. Play the game, you're stalling the match!"

But the pigeon continued walking.

Behind the Senator the auburn-haired woman was in tears.

"It's a crime," she called past his ear. "It's a disgrace. It's impotence, it's perversity, a politics of evasion and calculated defiance. . . ."

Bewildered by her analysis, the Senator watched a soft-drink bottle land and scud across the grass, just missing, and the pigeon turning aside but still refusing to fly. And now a man with leather patches on the elbows of his fawn-colored jacket aimed an empty cartridge hull at the bird and began cursing when it fell far short of the mark.

"Up, sir," he called, "into the air!"

A tall man with the blue eyes and blond hair of a Viking stepped over the barrier and snatched off his yachtsman's cap, rumpling it in his hands as he addressed the crowd in a cavernous voice:

"It's against the rules," he cried passionately. "The bird should fly! Damn his wings, it's his profession, his identifying characteristic. The other two birds in the set took off, so why should he be a dirty third? If he continues this outrageous conduct I say let the officials give the gunner permission to lower his sights and blast the craven-souled varmint off the face of the earth!"

And before the Viking could continue a short-armed fat man whose eyes burned angrily behind yellow shooting lenses bounced into the ring carrying a gun with an exceptional length of barrel, and with cheek pressed tightly against the stock, got off a shot.

The report was like that of a small cannon and the Senator could see grass and bits of earth fly into the air as the blast lifted the pigeon a foot above the ring. But instead of taking wing, the bird landed on its feet and continued forward, limping now and with a small spot of blood showing on its breast.

For a moment the crowd was silent, gazing out across the ring in amazement, then the Senator's ears were blasted by a howl of rage.

Out in the ring the fat man was in tears.

"Now I get it!" he cried. "Listen to me. We've been betrayed! *Some anarchist has slipped a cynical, gutter rat of a New York pigeon into our dovecotes. That's what has happened. A gutter snipe!"*

"A New York pigeon?" someone called. "What do you mean? Tell us!"

"Hell, it's sabotage," the fat man said. "New York pigeons are simply awful! They walk along the subway tracks, hitchhiking on freight trains! They fornicate on the hoods of moving cars and in the air. It's treason!"

Whereupon he snatched off a shoe and sent it arching over the ring where it missed the pigeon and struck a blue-clad handler, who now stood glaring at the crowd.

"Now, you watch it, Mac," the handler called. "Respect the working man!"

"Respect?" the fat man called, "you don't need respect, you get paid. And if you were earning your pay you'd give that stupid bird a goose so the match could continue. Instead, you make us speeches about the rights of labor!"

The fat man was speechless, his face red with anger, but as he started out toward the handler a tall, distinguished-looking man in a white deerstalker's hat grabbed him and pushed him back. Then, raising his arms for quiet the tall man called out, "My advice is to have the handlers wring the bird's neck and end this impasse! Any way we look at it, a bird such as that is a disgrace. It's a disgrace to the breed and to the sport. It's a bloody spoilsport, a cringing dog-in-the-manger! A malicious nigger in the woodpile! A vengeful ghost at the wedding! In other words, it makes everything go bad. So I say, let's wring its neck and immediately after the shoot I shall call a meeting of the governing board to see to it that in the future all such birds are black-balled. . . ."

"There's no need to wait," the fat man said, slamming a shell into his weapon. "I'm taking no more crap from this walking. . ." But just as he raised his gun to fire a woman ran forward and knocked him off balance, causing the gun to discharge into the air and sending the fat man back upon the grass with a bump, where he sat cursing the woman.

Watching the pigeon's progress, the Senator felt that he was suffocating. He felt responsible for the pigeon's life but was unable to do a thing about it. Flashes of blue-green appeared above the ring now as the crowd began lobbing Coca-Cola bottles at the bird; but still the pigeon refused to flush, and its orange-ringed eyes seemed to look straight at the Senator as, skirting both the bottles and the bodies of its fallen fellows, it continued with calmly bobbing head toward the barrier. He watched the iridescent play of the light upon its gorget and the slow pulsing of blood from its breast with painful feelings of identification which were interrupted by a sudden silence: The bird had stopped its stroll and was extending its wings.

"Now! At last," the Viking called, "he's found his courage! He's about to take off, so careful, Mr. Marksman, careful!"

Thinking, Oh, no! Not after resisting this far, the Senator strained forward, seeing the pigeon's head come around and the remoteness of its orange-ringed eye as the bird plucked a single feather from its breast and released it with a sharp snap of its head. Then with a series of short, hedge-hopping spurts it covered the remaining distance to the barrier, where it paused, calmly preening itself for a moment, then, turning its back to the crowd, it dived with set wings below the cliff.

As the bird dropped from sight the Senator seemed to fall within himself, and as he struggled to keep his feet he was aware of a sudden darkening of the sun and looked up to see, at the point where the pigeon had disappeared, a huge hatch of flies boiling up from the river and swarming above the ring, where once again the birds were flighting before the guns.

Perhaps for you there's safety in darkness, the Senator thought. Perhaps a few will have a chance. . . .

But already the flies were thinning out, swarming veil-like in broader circles, and as they boiled above the ring he heard an explosion of shrill cries and watched the arrival of a virtual aerial circus of small, sharp-winged birds.

Pouring down as from a net released high in the sky, a flock of swallows began swooping and wheeling between the booming patterns of the guns as they attacked the flies, bringing the air alive with graceful motion. Plunging and climbing, banking and whirling, skimming and gliding, the hunting birds filled the air with high-pitched, derisive cries as they executed power-dives and Immelmanns, sideslips and barrel rolls and dazzled the Senator with the cool, audacious miracle of their flight. Not a single swallow was struck by the flying shot, and as they swirled above the ring it came to him that the swallows were contemptuous of both the pigeons and the guns, and there, braced between the auburn-haired woman and a man in a wide planter's hat, and feeling the dank, steaming wetness of their bodies against him, he watched the swallows swoop and soar in grace, moving invulnerable among the doomed and falling rockdoves....

Suddenly released and moving through the crowd, the Senator had started along the walk leading back to the clubhouse when suddenly something landed a sharp, stabbing blow to his right heel and he whirled to see a small, handsome child who looked up at him out of a pair of intense, black, long-lashed eyes.

Why, I'll be damned, the Senator thought, *it's a boy! A fine, grand rascal of a little boy!*

The little boy, whose hair was cut in a Buster Brown bob, was dressed incongruously in the red satin pantaloons and white satin blouse such as were worn by a child in a painting by Goya, a copy of which the Senator had seen long ago in a museum. Even his pom-pom-topped white satin slippers were from another time, and behind him, attached to a silken cord which the boy held in a chubby fist, there stood a stuffed goldfinch mounted on a small gilted platform equipped with wheels.

He's been gotten up for either a wedding or a masquerade, but in either case he'll steal the show. Dressed to kill, that's the word, the Senator thought, resisting an impulse to sweep the child into his arms as he smiled down, saying,

"Why, hello there! Don't I know you from somewhere? You look awfully familiar...."

But instead of answering, the little boy darted around him, the goldfinch clattering on the walk as the Senator turned to see the child standing in the middle of the path and confronting him with an expression of hostility which distorted his tiny face.

"My, but you're fast," the Senator said. "What's your name? Mine's Adam Sunraider...."

Silently the little boy stuck out a small blue tongue, making an angry face, then with his fingers rigidly extended he thumbed his nose.

The Senator laughed, thinking, *My, but he's aggressive. Probably a dissatisfied constituent....* And yet he had a nagging impression that he knew the child, had seen him before, even though he could think of no one with a child so young.

"Look," he said, leaning forward, "I don't know what you've got against me but I'd like to be friend with such a fine young fellow as you. Shall we shake hands?"

His head shaking violently, the boy's hands flew behind his back as he stared up at the Senator out of hot, black eyes.

"Very well," the Senator said, "people who can't talk probably can't know very much. I'll bet you can't even say your father and mother's name...."

The boy grinned, his face transformed into that of a malicious adult as he retreated a step and spat at the Senator's feet, and in a flash his tiny hands were at his head, fluttering like the wings of a hummingbird as he stuck out his tiny blue-coated tongue and thumbed his ears.

Thinking, *How on earth could he have become so ill-mannered so young,* the Senator chuckled at the incongruity between the child's size and his aggressiveness.

"Young man," the Senator began, "I have an idea you're lost. Maybe you'd better try to take me to where you last saw your mother—" and broke off, taken aback as the child went suddenly into a frenzy of action.

Turning his back and jackknifing forward, the boy was looking up from between his short legs and making a horrible face as he patted his backside and made nasty sounds with his vibrating lips. Then, straightening, he raised his leg like a dog and with a grave expression on his face he thumbed the seat of his red satin pants.

"Hey!" the Senator cried, "that's enough of that! Cut it out! What do you think you're doing?"

But instead of answering, the boy began to run in circles before him, moving like a demented toy and stopping every few feet to repeat his insulting gestures.

Profoundly disturbed and depressed, the Senator looked beyond the child into the crowd, hoping to see a frantic mother emerging to find the boy. A bird was rising above the crowd and all backs were turned, watching the marksman and the flighting target.

This is awful, the Senator thought, this one certainly needs attention. How did he ever get this way so soon? Probably doesn't even know his alphabet, yet he's already expert in the manual-of-arms of vulgar put-down!

His leg was paining again and now as he started around the boy he saw the child sneering malevolently as he leaned back and pushed out his little satin-clad stomach and began vigorously to thumb the fly of his red satin pantaloons.

It was too much for the Senator but as he reached out the boy leaped backwards, running and making a turn which caused the stuffed bird to disintegrate in an explosion of flying head and whirling feathers as it struck the walk and lay vibrating there as the boy shot silently into the crowd.

For a moment the Senator stood looking blankly at the shattered goldfinch in his path, thinking, He'll be furious, absolutely furious, and his mother will probably blame me and her with a boy running wild while she devotes herself to shooting matches.... It's a crime.... And the Senator moved away.

There was a faint odor of smoke around him now and as the Senator came out upon the steps leading from the building his senses were assaulted by the hushed humid heaviness of the late afternoon air. And then, as at a signal, a silence seemed to move before him and grow like a rolling crescendo of suddenly inverted sound. Sometime earlier a shower had left the atmosphere unbearably hot, and although the sky had begun to clear he could see drops of moisture still clinging to the leaves of the trees, and the walks glistened with the rain.

Surprisingly, the traffic had disappeared, and as far as his eyes could see the traffic signals were blobs of red, shimmering against the moist mistiness of the fading light. Then a movement down at the intersection of the street and the avenue caught his attention and he saw a bent little black-skinned woman moving toward him.

Wearing a blue bandanna headrag and a faded yellow apron over a red housedress, she made her way along in a pair of black high-topped old lady's shoes which seemed, suddenly, to expand about her ankles and begin creeping up her legs: expanding and *contracting violently as they climbed. It was as though they were intent upon engorging her within the bunion-distorted maws of their interiors. Yet she continued painfully forward and as she moved closer the Senator could hear the rhythmical beating of a clanking sound. But then she was no longer there but transported across the avenue where, standing before a building which showed dark against the eerie light of the fading sun, she called out in a senile quaver, "Hey! Heah Ah is, over heah!" and threatened him with an old-fashioned washing stick that she shook with awkward vigor.*

"Oh, Ah knows you," she called, "You old jacklegged, knock-kneed, bowlegged, box-ankled, pigeon-toed, slack-asted piece of peckerwood trash gone to doo-doo! Ah knows you, yas Ah do! Yo' mammy was yo' sister and yo' grandmaw too! Yo' uncle was yo' daddy and yo' brother's cousin! You a coward and a thief and a snake in the grass! You do the dirty bo-bo and you eats bad meat! Oh, Ah knows you, yas Ah does, and I means to git you! I means to tell everybody who you is and put yo' nasty business in these white folks' street...."

What on earth is this, the Senator thought; who is this senile old mammy-aunty and what's she doing up here on the Hill? Where did she come from?

"Ah'll tell you what you is," the old woman called. "You ain't nothing, that's what you is! You is simply nothing done gone to waste, and if somebody was to plant you in a hill with a rotten piece of fish you wouldn't even raise a measly bush of beans! You think you so high and mighty but you ain't doodly-squat! You ain't no eagle, fox, or bear! You ain't a rabbit or a skunk or a wheel-in-a-wheel! You ain't nothing—neither a moaning dove or a lily of the field! You ain't a bolt or a nut or a crupper scrap. Ah even knows pimps and creepers who're better'n you...."

Very well, the Senator thought, but you'll have to admit that if I'm not all that you say I'm at least a walking personification of the negative....

"Shet up! Shet up! You nothing!" the old woman screamed, "SHET UP! Or Ah'll tell you who you really is!"

Shaking his head, the Senator turned away, amused but filled with a strange foreboding. Never mind, he thought, I know who I am, and for the time being at least, I am a senator.

But now for some reason he recalled a church service of a summer's evening long past, during which in rapid succession a gust of wind had torn a part of the roof away and a stroke of lightning had plunged the church into darkness. The choir had faltered in its singing and women had begun screaming—when in the noisy confusion and whirling about Hickman had stamped three times upon the pulpit's hollow floor, shouting, "Sing! Sing!," startling them and triggering some of the singers into an outburst of ragged, incoherent sound. Frightened by the storm, he himself had been crying, but as the old church creaked and groaned beneath the lashing of wind and rain and the screaming continued, the foot-pounded rhythm had come again, this time accompanied by Hickman's lining-out of a snatch of a spiritual in hoarse, authoritative recitative. And suddenly the singers were calmed and the screamers were silenced and a disciplined quietness had spread beneath the howling of the storm. Then through a flash of light-

ning he had seen the singers straining toward Hickman who, with voice raised in melody was stomping out the rhythm on the floor. And as the singers followed his lead and were joined by the nervous choiring of the congregation, he had heard the blended voices rise up in firm array against the thunder. Up, up, the voices had climbed until, surrendering themselves to the old familiar words, they were giving forth so vigorously that before his astonished eyes the pitch-black interior of the church had seemed to brighten and come aglow with a joyful and unearthly radiance generated by the mighty outpouring of passionate song.

> *He 'rose . . .*
> > *Heroes!*
> *He 'rose . . .*
> > *Heroes!*
> *He 'rose . . .*
> > *Up from the dead!*
> *He 'rose . . .*
> > *Oh, yes!*
> *He 'rose . . .*
> > *Oh, yes!*
> *Heroes . . .*
> > *Up from the dead!*

A comfort, the Senator thought.

And moving down the steps and into the familiar scene of the street he felt the images of this long-forgotten incident imposing themselves upon the scene, distorting his vision with teasing fragments of memory long rejected. And now he stumbled along the stone walk with inward-searching eyes, expecting the abrupt tolling of bells, a clash of lightning, a choir of girlish voices lifted in vesperal song. . . .

Across the way the old woman continued to rail, but now he was listening for the baritone timbre and voice-like phrasing of a muted trombone which would proclaim with broadly reverent mockery the lyrics of some ancient hymn; and looking back to the building entrance, he expected to see a crowd rush forth to shout down denunciations upon him, to shower him with stones. . . . But like the street, the entrance was empty and the door now mysteriously closed upon the brooding quiet. . . .

Soon, the Senator thought, it will come. They're beginning to stir so as the old trainer said, watch their hands. And as old fighters, he warned, watch hands, feet, and *head. Yes, they're moving out into the open and things are beginning to heave and the backwash is beginning. But Hickman here? Unlikely—though who knows who it was who came? Nine owls have squawked out the rules and the hawks will talk, so soon they'll come marching out of the woodpile and the woodwork—sore-head, sore-foot, right up close, one-butt-shuffling into history but demanding praise and kind treatment for deeds undone, for lessons unlearned. But studying war once more. . . .*

Reaching the curb now, the Senator prepared to cross the boulevard when, sensing a rush of movement from his left, he spun instinctively and saw the car.

Long, black and under-slung, it seemed to straighten the curving course of the street with the force of its momentum, bearing down upon him so relentlessly that his nerves screamed with tension as his entire body prepared itself for a supreme effort. An effort which, even as his muscles responded to the danger, was already anticipating itself in his reeling mind; projecting a long, curving, backwards-leaping motion through which his eyes were now recording in vivid detail of stone-steel-asphalt-chrome, damp leaves and whirling architectural stone as he saw himself sailing backwards and yet he was watching, still on his feet, the car approaching with such deliberate speed that now its fenders appeared to rise and fall with the heavy labored motion of some great bird flying, and the heaving of its black metallic sides like that of the barrel of a great bull charging. And now two gleaming, long-belled heralds' trumpets which lay along the engine hood ripped the air with a blast of defiant sound and he saw a pair of red-tipped bullhorns appear atop the radiator, knifing toward him—while an American flag, which snapped and rippled like a regimental pinion brought to aggressive life by a headlong cavalry charge, streamed fiercely above. . . .

Only now did his body catch up with his mind, beginning its backwards-sailing fling as the car, almost upon him now, veered suddenly and stopped with a night-piercing screaming of brakes. He was on his back then, feeling the pain of the impact exploding in his elbows and spine and in the endless, heart-pounding, head-jolting instant the car seemed to leave the roadway and hover above the curb, hanging there like a giant insect; and inside its wide front seat were three men.

Dark-skinned and broad of face behind the murky window they peered down at him through dark glasses topped by the narrow brims of high-crowned, shaggy-knapped white hats, watching him with intense concentration as their mouths stretched wide in expressions of fierce, derisible gaiety. Whereupon the driver reached for a microphone and looking around his companions addressed him through the herald trumpets which lay along either side of the rakish hood.

"Next time you better swing your booty faster, boy," the voice said, "or by God we go' lo-mo kick your nasty ass!"

Watching them, the Senator was speechless.

"Don't be laying there looking at us," the voice said. "You heard me correctly; we'll blast you and do everybody some service!"

The Senator started up, trying to answer, but now there came a jet-like blast, and seeing the machine leaping into furious motion he rolled, turning completely over as he tried to escape its path. But instead of crushing him, the machine was braking and surging backwards with a blast of red and white light erupting from its rear. And then thundering with a rapid shifting and re-shifting of gears it left the street once more and hovered above him like a hovercraft, the black passengers looking down upon him with grim satisfaction, awaiting his next move. . . .

"Hey, Mister Motharider," the voice called down to him. "How's this for a goonguage?"

"Hey, Shep," the man in the middle said, "don't ask he not'ing! Let's show Charlie how de car can curb. I don't tink he believes you cawn drive dis bloody t'ing."

"No, I don't believe he does," the driver said. "Okay, Charlie boy, watch me snatch the butter from the duck!"

Staring into the grinning faces, the Senator scrambled to his knees, thinking, Who are they? as the machine shot away and shattered the quiet of the street with the flatulent blasts from its dual exhaust. He watched it lunging up the boulevard at a forward slant, seeming to flatten out and become the more unreal the farther it receded into the distance. Techniques of intimidation, that's what they're using, the Senator thought. They were waiting for me; they were watching the building for the moment I started across the street so they could intimidate me. So they'll be back and I'd better leave.... And even as he watched the car floating away he was aware that somehow it was beginning to flow backwards upon its own movement, dividing itself and becoming simultaneously both there in the distance and here before him, where now it throbbed and puttered, a mirage-like image of black metal agleam with chrome, and there up the boulevard, where it was resonating street and buildings with the thunder of its power. And it came to the Senator that he was watching no ordinary automobile. This was no Cadillac, no Lincoln, Oldsmobile, nor Buick—nor any other known make of machine; it was an arbitrary assemblage of chassis, wheels, engine, hood, horns, none of which had ever been part of a single car! It was a junkyard sculpture mechanized! An improvisation, a bastard creation of black bastards—and yet, it was no ordinary hot rod. It was an improvisation of vast arrogance and subversive and malicious defiance which they had designed to outrage and destroy everything in its path, a rolling time bomb launched in the streets....

And now the image of the machine gleamed and quivered and throbbed before him, glowing with flames of luminous red that had been painted along the sides of the threatening, shark-finned fenders which guarded its licenseless rear. Two slender antennae affixed to either side of the trunk lazily whipped the air, one flying an enormous and luxuriantly rippling coon's tail and the other displaying in miniature the stars and bars of the Confederacy while across the broad expanse of its trunk he saw the enormous image of an open switchblade knife bearing the words:

WE HAVE SECEDED FROM THE MOTHER!
HOORAY FOR US!
TO HELL WITH CHARLEY!

They have constructed it themselves, the Senator's mind went on, brought the parts together and gathered in conspiratorial secret like a group of guerrillas assembling the smuggled parts of a machine gun! And they've made the damn thing run! No single major part goes normally with the rest, yet even in their violation of the rigidities of mechanical tolerances and in their defiance of the laws of physics, property rights, patents—everything—they've forced part after part to mesh and made it run! It's a mammy-made, junkyard construction, and yet those clowns have made it work, it runs!

And now the machine roared back, braking with a violent, stiffly sprung rocking of body and a skidding of tires, and again the men were looking out of the open window.

"Listen, Sunrobber," the nearest called, "What the hell was that you just said about our little heap?"

"Hell, mahn," the middle man said, "don't ask he no'ting! I done tole you the bahstard has low-rated our little load! The mahn done low-rated our pride and joy. So don't ask the bahstard not'ing, just show he whadt de joecah kin do!

"And remembah us mah-toe, mahn:

> *Down Wid de Coon Cawdge,*
> *Up WID DE JOE CAH!*

"Then, mahn, I say, KICK HIM ASS!"

"Yeah, man; but not so fas'," one of the others said. "Not before we give his butt a little ride...."

A blast of heat struck him then, followed by the opening of the door. And as a dark hand reached down he seemed to hear the sound of Hickman's consoling voice, calling from somewhere above.

So now I suppose that the medicine is taking him over again, Hickman thought. *The needle has reached through his flesh into his mind. Those hypos into the vein then... The way he looks at me, still wanting to talk and his eyes dulling. But the hopeful thing is that he's fighting to live, to stay alive. Regardless of what it will all have to mean if he does, he still wants to live. So my task is simply to help him to keep on fighting, to keep on wanting to live. What else is there, other than what a minister always tries to do to help? Comfort and consolation—no, not just that, because there's still the mystery to be understood. Reverse the time. Lord, but I'm tired... cramped in muscle and confused in mind.... Maybe I ought to go out and stretch my legs, get a little fresh air in my lungs. No, you can't risk it because it would be just like him to come to while I'm out and if he did, what would be the next move? Forget it; you've waited all this long time so you can afford to sit still and wait a while longer—tired or no tired.... Those hypos... He's sleeping hard, quiet in his body if not in his mind. Hypos. I sure hope so, because the time has come when everything has to be understood and I mean to be here to try....*

Just look at him, Hickman, there he is: Bliss at last. Out of all the time and racked and tiered-up circumstance, out of all the pomp and power-seeking—there's ole Bliss. It makes you wonder all over again just what kind of being Man really is; makes you puzzle over the difference between who he is and what he does. But how do you separate it? Body and soul are all mixed together and yet are something different just the same. One grows in the way it's destined to grow, flesh and bone, blood and nerves, skin and hair, from the beginning, while the other twists and turns and hides and seeks and makes up itself as it grows and moves along. So there he is and for whatever the world knows him to be, somehow he's still Bliss.... It's like hearing a firecracker go off at a parade and you look up and see the great and bejeweled king of the Mardi Gras, sitting high on his throne in all his shiny majesty, and he starts to shake and tremble and there, before your eyes, a little ole boy looks out from behind his mask. Well, the child is father and some- where back there in the past, back behind little Bliss's face, this twitching, wounded man was waiting. No point of dreaming about it either. I was in the picture and a lot of other folks too, and we made a plan, or at least we dreamed a dream and worked for it but the world was simply too big for us and the dream got out of hand. So we held on to what we saw, us old ones, and finally it brought us here.

But just look at him—who would have thought that it would come to this, that our little Bliss would come to this? But why, Master? Why did this have to be? Back there in our foolish way we took him as our young hope, as our living guarantee that in our dis- mal night You still spoke to us and stood behind Your promise, even when things were most hopeless. Now look at him, all ravaged by his denials, sapped by his running, drained and twitching like a coke fiend from all the twisting and turning that brought him here. All damaged in his substance by trying to make everything appear to be the truth and nothing really truthful, playing all the old lying, obscene games of denial and rejection of the poor and beaten down. And even at the very last moment, refusing to rec- ognize us, refusing to even see us who could never forget the promise and who for years haven't asked anything except that he remember and honor the days of his youth—or at least his baby days. Honor, oh yes; honor. But not to us but honor unto Thy dying lamb. We asked nothing for ourselves, only that he remember those days and what he had been at that time. Remember the promising babe that he was and the hope we placed in him and his obligation to the babes who come after. Maybe that was our mistake, we just couldn't surrender everything, we just couldn't manage to burn out the memory and cauterize the wound and deny that it had ever happened . . . that he had ever existed. Couldn't treat all of that like a hobo walking along the tracks back of town who passes and looks up and sees your face and spits on the cinders and crunches on. Gone without a word. . . . After having been born so close to the time of whips and cold iron shackles we could fly up here in an airplane—which is like the promise of a miracle ful- filled . . . which is no longer miraculous—but still there on the bed lies the old abiding mystery in its latest form and still mysterious. Why'm I here, Master? Why? And how is it that a man like him, who was taught so much and gone so far never learned the sim- ple fact that just as it takes two to make a bargain it takes two to bury a hatchet, or even to forget words uttered in dedication and taken deep into the heart and made sanctified by suffering? Blood spilled in violence doesn't just dry and drift away in the wind, no! It cries out for restitution, redemption; and we (or at least I—because it was only me in the beginning), but we took the child and tried to seek the end of the old brutal dispen- sation in the hope that a little gifted child would speak for our condition from inside the only acceptable mask. That he would embody our spirit in the councils of our enemies. But, oh, what a foolish miscalculation! Way back there . . . I'm no wise man now, but then, Lord, how mixed-up and naive I was! There I was, riffing on Thy Word and not even sure whether I was conducting a con game or simply taking part and leading in a mys-

terious prayer—forgive me my ignorance.… Yesterday after the shooting started.… Was it yesterday? It was, wasn't it, Hickman? How long? Have you been sitting here all that time? How many hours in this hospital waiting and talking and talking and re-membering and revealing and talking and not revealing? And all because I slipped up and was sitting there in that gallery looking on like a man watching a scene unfolding in a dream instead of acting on the facts already exploding in my face. I could have stepped in front of that boy—or at least have picked him out of the crowd and stopped and tried to talk some sense into his head. But my eyes, my old eyes failed me. So now this sitting and waiting. It was awful! Truly awful! But what's a man to do, Hickman? So you try, you do your best as you see your best. Yes, but you realize that there's no guar-antee that it's going to work. The best intentions have cracks in them, man, and that'll never change. Not until somebody puts the Lord's sun into a bushel basket—Ho now! So here we come all this way and after all these years and there was no stopping even a fraction of it. Talking about sending a boy to do a man's work, this coiled spring has been stretched out so far that when it started to snap back I'd almost reached my second childhood. Talking to myself and belching in crowds and in the deep of night dreaming kindly of my wicked days and all against my duties and my soul's need. Lucky my blad-der's still what it was years ago and I still have good breath control because my strong old slave-borne body has held up pretty well as bodies go.… Still you failed. You were in the right place but not enough in it. You saw what was coming because Janey had warned you. You knew something was going to happen but not its shape or its outra-geous face. So I simply couldn't stop it. Sometimes everything mocks a man—even his own tongue, his eyes and hands. Then babes judge him and fools ignorant of his strengths leap on his weaknesses like a mosquito finding the one tender spot at the back of his knee where it knows it can draw his blood.

    Like that reporter asking me how come I was crying over a man who hates my peo-ple so. First place, I didn't realize that I was crying. At a time like that was I supposed to be thinking of how I looked? Did those senators think about how they looked when they were breaking for those doors like a crowd of crapshooters when a raid is on? Sure, I must have looked pretty foolish crying in a place like that, but tell me, who can simply look at his own reflection at such a time? I guess that reporter, that McIntyre, was look-ing at himself looking at me while all I could see was a great part of my life blowing up to a snick-snick-snick of bullets. Was I supposed to observe some kind of etiquette that has nothing to do with how I feel about things? And surely he didn't understand my say-ing that I was crying because I didn't know what else to do—me, a man of prayer. But hadn't I been praying for Bliss all these long years? One thing is sure, I couldn't bat those bullets down in midair. Oh no, too much was riding with those bullets, and when I missed that boy I missed my chance to stop the outrage. Yes, and maybe we lost all those hard, hopeful years.… "Rejoice when your enemy is struck down, why aren't you rejoic-ing?" That's what that reporter was saying; but what if it's too mixed up for that? What if there's more than appears on the surface? You live inside it for years, moving with it and feeling it grow and change and getting more complicated and making you grow more confused and complicated—except that you keep the faith; while folks outside think it's simply just a matter of "a" or "b," or else they think that it disappeared and no longer matters; while all the time it has been growing and sending out its roots until it touches everything in sight and all the streets you walk and all the deep actions of a man's mind and heart—yes. So I was deep upset, that's all. I lost control. I admit it and no apologies. Because when something hits you where you live you have got to go. Dignity, I guess that's what that white boy was talking about. I suppose to his mind I should have been worrying about those senators who have never thought a single thing about my dignity except maybe as a joke. Dred Scott's cross is mine— Anyway, I've known crowds that had sharper teeth and more searching and penetrating eyes just because they were my own and so knew something about what it really costs to keep your dignity under pressure. In the old days I kept playing even when the bullets got to flying. We all did. I shouldn't have paid that reporter any attention because when I reacted I almost let him provoke me into telling him something, which would have been a mistake arising out of pride. I almost let him know that there was a secret to be revealed. Asking me why I was crying—well, if we can't cry for Bliss, then who? If we can't cry for the Nation, then who? Because who else draws their grief and consternation from a longer knowledge or from a deeper and more desperate hope? And who've paid more in trying to achieve their better promise?

But, Hickman, you almost gave the thing away!

Well, maybe so; but what if I had, nobody would believe it. And maybe that's because everybody dreams in the night that in this land treachery is the truth of life—so they can't stand to think about it in the light of day. That reporter—McIntyre?—yes, waiting out there in the hall. He would've just thought that I was crazy the same as he does anyway. He wouldn't know how to add up the figures; couldn't get with the beat, even if I gave them to him. It would be like him walking down into a deep valley in the dark and looking up all at once to see two moons arising up over opposite hills at one and the same time. Ha! He'd either go cross-eyed and fall on his face in trying to deal with the sight. Or maybe like the fellow in the depot who was too tight to invest a nickel, he'd simply stand there twisting and turning and trying to make up his mind until he'd invented a new kind of dance and stank. No, Hickman, not his kind; he'd simply shut one eye and swear that one of those hills and one of those moons weren't there—even if the one he was trying to ignore was coming streaking toward him like a white-hot cannonball. . . .

Well, few men love the truth or even regard facts so dearly as to let either one upset their picture of the world. Poor Galileo, poor John Jasper; they persecuted one and laughed at the other, but both were witnesses for the truth they professed. Maybe it's just that some of us have had certain facts and truths slapped up against our heads so hard and so often that we have to see them and pay our respects to their reality. Maybe wise men are just those who have had the power to stay awake and struggle. And who can blame those who don't feel that they have to worry about the complicated truths we have to struggle with? In this country men can be born and live well and die without ever having to feel much of what makes their ease possible, just because so much is buried under all of this black and white mess that in their ignorance some folks accept it as a natural condition. But then again, maybe they just feel that the whole earth would blow up if even a handful of folks got to digging into it. It would even seem a shame to expose it, to have it known that so much has been built on top of such a shaky foundation.

But look Hickman—Alonzo ... this is here *and* now *and the stuff has begun to bubble. The man who fell and the man lying there on the bed is the child, Bliss. That's the mystery. How did he become the child of that babyhood ... father to the man, as it goes? And how could he have been my child, nephew and grandchild and brother in Christ as he grew? The confounding mystery of it has to be struggled with and I wish it was all a lie and we could go back home and forget it. Still there was Robert, my brother-son. He was the second, dropping out of all that confusion. Yes, and there were all those long years before I had learned not to puzzle out questions about the babe anymore and could come to accept the sheer quickening wonder of him growing up, a young life being lived without regard to the consequences of its being put there among us, and without regard to the violent circumstances of its bawling birth. There was blood on the land and blood on my hands. I made my peace with that beginning too long ago for vengeance and finally I found my way to my ministry. Yes, the Lord and Master calls a man in strange tongues and voices, yes, and among strange scenes in stranger weather. I was never one to argue Genesis, not even in my heathen days. A start is a start, and "is" is* is, *not "was." Still, there had to be a beginning. Used to hear that crab lice came from a man and woman's unwashed secreting and that was ignorant superstition—even though there's no denying the biting and the scratching, or the fact that the big crabs made the little ones.... I'm so tired and sleepy that my mind's falling into the cracks and crevices. Wonder if that young nurse would bring me a cup of coffee? No, just hold on. Wait. You'll be asleep a long time and soon. Meanwhile stay awake and watch the story unfold. By right, he should be dead and cold, but he's holding on so you couldn't let go even if you wanted to. Stay. Yea! I wait and hope for me, because ain't this the time for me, as well as for him? Here in his condition, so late in the day, asking me to tell him and me holding back the little I do know to keep him holding on and still not knowing fully how I became the man I am but merely the start. It sure changed my life around. I was never the same afterwards and it left an ache and emptiness that I've had to live with ever since. Oh, yes, you tried to cover it over with rectitude, tried to move on up above it and grow on top of it and you didn't try to sermonize from it either. Not directly. You just allowed it to teach you to feel for others.... Hickman, you ache like he aches, and he aches, they ache, everybody aches and aches. Hickman, the guards outside the door think you want to get out, to leave. And that's the truth.... Most will to forget, they drink denial like they drink whiskey. Yes, but where's the true contrast coming from? Sugar without salt. Life without death, what kind of a world? What kind of reality? Yes, but I must live by what I've seen and remember. And I have seen my people face Death and even go a piece with him and then wrestle with him and get away, thank the Lord, and return. Yes, but how many have I seen pass on and die? How many, where there are no hospitals to take them*

in, passing on in little ole stuffy rooms lit by a dim flame guttering low in sooty chim-
neys? And me sitting in some rickety rocking chair on a bumpy boarded floor looking
across the pain-wracked face to ole Death crouching like a big bird on the head of the
bed; just sitting and a-waiting like the great-granddaddy of all poker players. Just
crouching there while I tried to give myself over to some poor soul's trial, trying to ab-
sorb his agony into my own inadequate flesh. Humming a little comfort from the Scrip-
tures, sometimes from one of his favorite hymns, and sometimes praying until I grew
mute and numb with weariness, and then leaving it up to the Lord. . . . Bliss, sometimes
I've seen Death arise and leave like smoke from the chimney when dawn grayed the
room. I've seen him wait with patience and then take off in silence, like a cat hunting in
the grass that's waited until it sees the bird break his spell and fly away. And sometimes
I've seen him come down to claim the prostrate soul and heard the rattle in the dying
throat as life left the body and the soul took flight. And sometimes in the quiet of the early
morning, around the still point of three, the simmering time, when back there in the old
days the dancers would have been bear-panting and rocking to the shouting of those
horns, getting with it, while I played the blues. Then here comes the to-be-or-not-to-be
time, the crisis time, and found me sitting and a-rocking along beside some sickbed with
sleep weighing heavy on my lids and almost exhausted with the watching and the strug-
gle and there heard some wife or mother give voice in the dark to woman's old cry of
heart-loss. I have heard it rip and tear up suddenly out of sleep as though the whole night
had drawn itself together and screamed, and me looking up then and amazed as always
to see their nightgowned forms flashing past to get to the bed to confirm what their souls
had already acknowledged and accepted across sleep and distance, known it the way a
fisherman knows when his line goes slack in the water that the fish is gone. Then I've
heard them screaming again with the full realization of eternity come down. That's
something to remember and think about, here and now. Something to remember even be-
yond the question of being ready for the time when it comes. But who can stand to stare
steady into Death's blank face and all-consuming eye all the time, every day—even as the
tens of thousands fall around us? Better to lift up our eyes to the hills and prepare for
what's on the other shore. A man has to live in order to have a reason for dying as well as
for having a reason for being reborn—because if you don't, you're already dead anyway.
Now hush, because you're simply thinking words, old saws. So hush . . . all is noise.

Yes, but what a time this has been. What an awful time this has turned out to be. And
I thought we'd make it with something to spare. I still did, even after that young gal kept
turning us away. I thought we'd contact him somewhere along the line and we'd talk a
while somewhere in private and tell him what we felt and hoped and prayed, both for
him and for us and for the country, and then go on back home and wait. Just that. Just
that; that was all, even though there wasn't a thing to justify the feeling that it might
come to pass except our old habit of hoping. Maybe it just sneaked up on me, stole me
while we were out there where I took them so they could see it for the first time and prob-
ably for most of us the last, and that got my hopes up and made me reckless. Maybe I let
them down right there. Maybe the place and the image and the associations got to me.

But what a feeling can come over a man just from seeing the things he believes in and hopes for symbolized in the concrete form of a man. In something that gives a focus to all the other things he knows to be real. Something that makes unseen things manifest and allows him to come to his hopes and dreams through his outer eye and through the touch and feel of his natural hand. That's the dangerous shape, the engraven image we were warned about, the one that makes it possible for him to hear his inner hopes sound and sing and see them soar up and take wing before his half-believing eyes. Faith in the Lord and Master is easy compared to having faith in the goodness of man. There are simply too many snares and delusions, too many masks, too many forked tongues. Too much grit in the spiritual greens. But then, there that something is. There sits his hopes made manifest and a man knows that it's not simply the mixed-up hopes and yearnings within his own mind and most secret heart that grabs him and makes him stand tiptoe inside his skin and reach up through the dark for something better and finer and more durable than he knows himself to be capable of, but something felt by a lot of other folks and even achieved and died for by a precious few. . . .

So I walked them out there just so that we could ease off from the frustration and runaround that we were getting, and so that I could have time to figure out our next move. Then we had arrived and there it was . . . there.

He slowly shook his head, staring across to the sleeping face and feeling it become almost anonymous beneath his inward-turning vision, the once familiar cast of features fading like the light. He closed his eyes, his fingers clasped across his middle as the mood of the afternoon moment returned in all its awe and mystery, and he found himself once more approaching the serene, high-columned space. Once more they were starting up the broad steps and moving in a loose mass still caught up in the holiday mood evoked by seeing the sights and scenes which most had only read about or seen in photographs or in an occasional newsreel. Then he was mounting the steps and feeling a sudden release from the frame of time, feeling the old familiar restricting part of himself falling away as when, long ago, he'd found himself improvising upon some old traditional riffs of the blues, or when, as in more recent times, he'd felt the Sacred Word surging rapturously within him, taking possession of his voice and tongue.

And now his heartbeat pounded and his footsteps slowed and he was looking upward, hesitating with one foot fumbling for the step which would bring him flush into the full field of the emanating power, and he felt himself shaken by the sudden force of his emotion. Then once again he was moving, moving into the cool, shaded, and sonorous calm of the edifice, moving slowly and dream-like over the fluted shadows cast along the stony floor before him by the upward-reaching columns, and he advanced toward the great image slumped in the huge stone chair.

From far away he could hear some sister's softly tentative, "Reverend? Reverend?" and now their voices fading in a hush of awed recognition; cre-

ating but for her echoing *Reverend? Reverend?* a stillness as resonant as the profoundest note of some great distant bell; still staring, still hearing the sister's
soft voice, which sounded now through a deep and doom-toned silence reverberating through his mind with the slow, time-and-space-devouring motion of great wings silently flying....

*Then he, Hickman, was looking up through the calm and peaceful light toward the
great brooding face; he, Hickman, standing motionless before the quiet, less-and-more-
than-human eyes which seemed to gaze from beneath their shadowed lids as toward
some vista of perpetual dawn which lay beyond infinity.*

*And he thought, Now I understand: That look, that's us! It's not in the features but in
what that look, those eyes, have to say about what it means to be a man who tries to live
and struggle against all the troubles of the world with but the naked heart and mind,
and who finds them more necessary than all the power of wealth and great armies. Yes,
that look and what put it there made him one of us. It wasn't in the dirty dozens about
his family and his skin-tone that they tried to ease him into but in that look in his eyes
and in his struggle against the things which put it there and saddened his features. It's
in that, in being the kind of man he made himself to be, that he's one of us. Oh, he failed
and he knew that he could only take one step along the road that would make us free, but
in growing into that look he joined us in what we have been forced to learn about life
and about being truly human in the face of life. Because one thing we have been forced
to learn is that Man at his best, when he's set in all the muck and confusion of life and
continues to struggle for his ideals, is near sublime. So yes, he's one of us, not only because
he freed us to the extent that he could, but because he freed himself of that awful inherited pride they deny to us, and in doing so he became a man and he pointed the way for
all of us who would be free—Yes!*

*Staring upward into the great brooding eyes he felt a strong impulse to turn and seek
to share their distant vision but was held, the eyes holding him quiet and still, and he
stared upward, seeking their secret, their mysterious life, in the stone; aware of the stone
and yet feeling their more-than-stoniness as he probed the secret of the emotion which
held him with a gentle but all-compelling power. And the stone seemed to live and
breathe then, its great chest appearing to heave as though, stirred by their approach, it
had decided to sigh in silent recognition of who and what they were and had chosen to
reveal its secret life for all who cared to see and share and remember its vision. And he
was searching the stony visage, its brooding eyes, as though waiting to hear it resound
with the old familiar eloquence which he knew only from the sound of the printed
page—when a woman's voice came to him as from a distance, crying, "Oh, my Lord!
Look, y'all, it's him! It's HIM!," her voice breaking in a quavering rush of tears.*

*And he was addressing himself now, crying in upon his own spellbound ears, as her
anguished, "Ain't that him, Revern? Ain't that Father Abraham?" came to him as from
far away.*

*And too full to speak, he smiled; and in silent confirmation he was nodding his head,
thinking, Yes, with all I know about him and his contradictions, yes. And with all I*

know about men and the world, yes. And with all I know about white men and politicians of all colors and guises, yes. And with all I know about the things you had to do to be you and stay yourself—yes! She's right, she's cut through the knot and said it plain; you are and you're one of the few who ever earned the right to be called "Father." George didn't do it, though he had the chance, but you did. So yes, it's all right with me; yes. Yes, and though I'm a man who despises all foolish pomp and circumstance and all the bending of the knee that some still try to force us to do before false values, Yes, and Yes again. And though I'm against all the unearned tribute which the weak and lowly are forced to yield up based on force and false differences and false values, yes, for you "Father" is all right with me. Yes . . .

And he could feel the cloth of the sister's dress as he gently touched her arm and gazed into the great face; thinking, There you sit after all this unhappy time, just looking down out of those sad old eyes, just looking way deep out of that beautiful old ugly wind-swept, storm-struck face. Yes, she's right, it's you all right; stretching out those long old weary legs like you've just been resting a while before pulling yourself together again to go and try to bind up all these wounds that have festered and run and stunk in this land ever since they turned you back into stone. Yes, that's right, it's you, just sitting and waiting and taking your well-earned ease, getting your second wind before getting up to do all over again what has been undone throughout all the betrayed years. Yes, it's you all right, just sitting and resting while you think out the mystery of how all this could be. Just puzzling out how all this could happen to a man after he had done all one man could possibly do and then take the consequences for having done his all. Yes, it's you—Sometimes, I guess. . . . Sometimes . . .

And then he was saying it aloud, his eyes held by the air of peace and perception born of suffering which emanated from the great face, replying to the sister now in a voice so low and husky that it sounded hardly like his own:

"Sometimes, yes . . . sometimes the good Lord . . . I say sometimes the good Lord accepts His own perfection and closes His eyes and goes ahead and takes His own good time and He makes Himself *a* man. Yes, and sometimes that man gets hold of the idea of what he's supposed to do in this world and he gets an idea of what it is possible for him to do, and that man lets that idea guide him as he grows and struggles and stumbles and sorrows until finally he comes into his own God-given shape and achieves his own individual and lonely place in this world. It don't happen often, oh, no; but when it does, then even the stones will cry out in witness to his vision and the hills and towers shall echo his words and deeds and his example will live in the hearts of men forever—

"So there sits one right there. The Master doesn't make many like that because that kind of man is dangerous to the sloppy way the world moves. That kind of man loves the truth even more than he loves his life, or his wife, or his children, because he's been designated and set aside to do the hard tasks that have to be done. That kind of man will do what he sees as justice even if the earth yawns and swallows him down, and even then his deeds will persist in the land forever. So you look at him a while and be thankful that the Lord allowed such a man to touch our lives, even if it was only for a little *while, then let us bow our heads and pray. Oh, no, not for him, because he did his part a long time ago. Let us pray for ourselves and for all those whose job it is to wear those great big shoes he left to fill...."*

And there in the sonorous shadows beneath his outspread arms they prayed.

And to think, he thought, stirring suddenly in his chair, *we had hoped to raise ourselves that kind of man....*

Opening his eyes in the semi-darkness now, he looked about him. While he had dozed the nurse and security man had gone, leaving him alone with the man sleeping before him and now, still possessed by the experience at the memorial, he looked upon the sleeping face before him and felt an anguished loss of empathy. He looked at the Senator's face half in shadow, half illuminated by a dim bed lamp as from a great distance, mist-hung and beclouded, thinking, *This is crazy; weird. All of it is. A crazy happening in a crazy place and I am the craziest of all. His being here is crazy, my being here is crazy, the reasons that brought us here are crazy as any coke fiend's dream—and yet part of that craziness contains the hope that has sustained us for all these many years.... We just couldn't get around the hard fact that for a hope or an idea to become real it has to be embodied in a man, and men change and have wills and wear masks. So there he lies, wounded and brought low but still he's hiding from me, even in this condition he's still running, still hiding just as he did long ago— Only now I'll have to stay close and seek him out. For me it's Ho-ho, this a-way, woe-woe, that-a-way, and the game is lost in the winning. Besides, they wouldn't let me leave here even if I told them that I only wanted to go back down home and forget all the things I've been forced by hope and faith to remember for all these years. What's worse, they won't want to hear the truth even if somebody could tell it. They're keeping me here for the wrong reasons and probably trying to keep him alive just because it seems the thing to do after they learned that someone faceless and out of nowhere could have the nerve and determination to do what that boy did in the place that he did it. So now they're shaking in their boots and looking for someone to give them the answer they want to hear. Not the truth, but some lie that will protect them from the truth. They really don't want to know the reason why or even the part of it I think I know because knowing will mean recognizing that they slipped up in places where they'd rather die than be caught slipping. A tint of skin—ha! They'd have to recognize that in this land there's a wild truth that they didn't blunt and couldn't bring to heel. It's like a tamed river that rises suddenly in the night and washes away factories, houses, cities, and all. Why can't they face the simple fact that you simply can't give one bunch of men the license to kill another bunch without punishment, without opening themselves up to being victims? The high as well as the low? Why can't they realize that when they dull their senses to the killing of one group of men they dull themselves to the preciousness of all human life? Yes, and why can't they realize that when they allow one group of men the freedom to kill us as evidence of their own superiority they're only set-*

ting the stage so that these killers will have to widen the game, since if anyone can kill niggers the only way left to prove themselves superior is by killing some white man high in the public eye? Attack the head since the feet are too easy a target? We have suffered and trained ourselves against their provocations, have taken low and rejected their easy invitations to die, have kept to our own vision and for the most part put down the need for bloody retaliation as foolishness. But instead of being satisfied, they've sensed the life-preserving power of our humility and gone stark crazy to destroy even that! Hickman, how can you help despising these people? How can you resist praying for the day when they shall turn upon one another as they did once before and purge this land with blood? How can you resist praying for the day when the sacrificer will be sacrificed, when the many-headed beast will rend itself, tooth, nail, and fiery tail and die?

How resist, Hickman? Why not pray for that?

Why not? Don't play me for a fool— Why not? Because this American cloth, the human cloth, is woven too fine for that, that's why. Because you are one of the few who knows where the cry of pain and anguish is still echoing and sounding over all that bloodletting and killing that set you free to set yourself free, that's why again. Because you know that we were born of sacrifice, and that we have had to live by a different truth and that that truth is good and the vision of manhood it stands for is more human, more desirable, more real. So you're in it, Hickman, and have been in it and there's no turning back. Besides, there's no single living man calling the tune to this crazy dance. Talking about playing it by ear, this is one time when everybody is playing it by ear because everybody in the band and all those out on the dance floor is as blind as a mole in a hole.

But why couldn't he have seen us, if only for a minute? Why? If he had, then all of this might not have happened. Oh, but it's the little things that find us out, the little things we refuse to do in order to avoid doing the big things that can save us. Well, there's nothing to do but wait and see. He's holding on even though Death is around somewhere close by—as Death always is. I'll just have to try once more to outwait him, to outface him, even though I've seen enough even for an old preacher like me. Death has more shapes and faces than a snake has twists and turns, and I've seen more of them than the average man—but last night, now that was something. It was as though I was being warned that something was going to strike out of all the junk and disorder of overlooked and forgotten things; out of a joke and the childish foolishness of an old man who's lost his way—and me blundering into it in the middle of the night....

Leaving the memorial in one of the taxis that some of the men had assembled for the group, he had sat up front with the driver, a rough-faced man who drove as though his passengers were concealed within a soundproof box, while Wilhite and the other two men sat talking behind him. Watching the driver's profile, he could hear Deacon Wilhite discussing President Lincoln's divided attitude toward the slaves and what his father had always referred to as the Secesh. *Wilhite,* he had thought, *is talking about him as a creature of politics—which he certainly was, and no doubt about it. But I was speaking of him as a creature of God's will, as one who did the Lord's work in rebellion and in wonder. Well, there's a lot to be discussed and even with me there's too much conflict between what I feel in my heart and what I think I know. History happens and men have a hand in it, but what the heart makes of it is sometimes more complex and contradictory than history by itself could ever be. Maybe it's the confusion in the heart which makes history in the first place. Maybe Abraham Lincoln doubted that freedom would work even if there was no black and white problem to deal with, so he preferred not to think about it while he had a war to win. But he also knew that with white folks killing off one another in wholesale lots it could become such a habit that getting the black and the white to live together in peace after the war was won was almost too much to hope for. As he saw it, Union was his hope and his responsibility and how things went after the Union was secured was another proposition. Some say he didn't see a place for us in it, but one thing cannot be denied: He signed the papers which set us free, whatever that freedom turned out to be. He did it. He wrote the words and signed them and that marked a new beginning. So let the fellows talk; you just remember that he was a politician and his moves had to be at least as complicated as any other politician's. But something deep inside him that probably had nothing to do with politics made the difference. It could have even been something shameful, or something too glorious for him to even think about directly, but thank God for it. So I won't get into this discussion, not now. Not with the problem of getting to see this boy weighing so heavy on my mind.... Lord, but it's hard! I should've known it would be because in something like this all the rules and manners are against us. The folks he's got around him can frustrate us in a crude way or in a polite way but they have the advantage and whichever way they choose they can keep us from seeing him....*

Suddenly he turned, reaching across the back of the seat to touch Deacon Wilhite's knee.

"Excuse me a second, Deacon," he said, "but do you have that address Sister Beaumouth passed along to us?"

Deacon Wilhite looked surprised.

"Why yes, A.Z., I do," he said. "But do you think we ought to use it?"

"I would rather not use it," he said, "but we came here to see him and you know why, so if this is the way it has to be, then this is the way it has to be. I'm beginning to be worried, because if I've read Janey's letter correctly there isn't much time."

"I know, A.Z.," Deacon Wilhite said, "but what you're thinking of doing is kind of delicate—I mean our using this particular address as a means. It's not good manners and it might be dangerous. Maybe we ought to give ourselves a little more time. Wait until we've tried his office again?"

He looked at the others. Their faces were interested but neutral.

"You're probably right," he said, "but good manners or not, if we're going to see him, we'd better do it as quickly as possible. I want to see him before it's too late!"

"Then maybe we ought to try to get to him through somebody else. . . ."

"But at the moment we don't know anyone else. And that's why I'm going to use the number."

"But I can think of someone," Deacon Wilhite said.

"Then who?"

"The police . . ."

"No, Deacon," he said, "You know that wouldn't do. Because what could we say to them which wouldn't be telling them too much?"

"That's the problem," Deacon Wilhite said.

"So they'd simply laugh at us. We don't know who Janey meant, or when or where. We don't even know whether she knows anything definite or just had a suspicion or what they call woman's intuition. The fact is, we're in the dark and we've got to take whatever path we can—so, Deacon, give me the number."

He extended his palm, seeing Deacon Wilhite look at the others, who were silent.

"Very well, A.Z." he said. "It looks like you've made up your mind. The number is—"

Suddenly the voice broke off, and he followed the movement of Wilhite's eyes to the back of the driver's head and back, fixing upon his own.

"Just a second and I'll write it down," Deacon Wilhite said, removing a folded newspaper from his jacket and scribbling on its border. Tearing the paper neatly, Wilhite placed it in his palm.

"I still think we ought to wait," Wilhite said.

Heaving himself around, he glanced at the piece of paper and folded it, placing it in his vest pocket.

"Maybe you're right," he said. "We'll see. But I just can't sit around and wait. Besides, coming from the place we just left makes me know it all the more. Driver, stop the car, please; I'm getting out."

"Right here?"

"Yes, sir, anywhere near the curb."

As the cab pulled over he reached for his wallet, removing a ten-dollar bill and handing it over his shoulder to Deacon Wilhite, he said, "This will take care of the fare. You all go on to the hotel and get some rest and I'll see you for supper. I have to see what I can do."

"Good luck, Reveren'," someone said, and he looked into their grave faces and smiled.

"Thanks, and don't worry now," he said, "we'll see him." Then the cab had stopped and he was getting out and heading for the corner, looking for another cab.

Wilhite's probably right, he thought, *so if I'm going to go through with this I'd better get on with it before I change my mind. Because going uninvited to a man's private*

hideaway, the place where he keeps his mistress, ain't the best idea under any circum-
stances. But since we don't seem to be able to see him at his office and can't reach him at
his home, I really don't have a choice....

Heading for the corner, he had begun trying to imagine what he'd say
when at last he'd run the boy to earth, and had just reached the corner and
was looking around for a cab—when someone called his name and he turned
to see Deacon Wilhite coming toward him.

"What happened, Deacon?" he said.

"Nothing," Wilhite said, "except I changed my mind. At the last moment
I decided it might be better if *two* of us made this particular visit."

Standing in the middle of the sidewalk, he drew himself to full height, his
fists on hips as he looked down at his old friend through squinted eyes.

"Wilhite," he said, "you don't have to bother. I think I can take care of myself."

Wilhite's face was grave. "I know," he said, "but we don't know who else is
liable to be there beside the woman he's supposed to have. Maybe there'll be
some of his friends along."

"I can still take care of myself. Anyway, I'm not going out there for a fight
and I don't think he feels that way about us. Because if he did, he wouldn't
be dodging us."

"I'm not thinking about you, A.Z. I'm thinking about *him*. Don't you see:
If there's somebody with him, then the two of us can pass ourselves off as a
delegation. Folks from the NAACP or the Elks or something like that."

Hickman chuckled. "And do you think that that would make a difference
if they decided to throw us out?"

"No, but we'd both have a witness and it's apt to prevent happening to you
what happened to old Booker T. the time that white man whipped his head
with a walking stick. We don't know how that boy will act once we corner
him but I doubt if he's going to treat you like the prodigal father even though
you are going way beyond the call of duty in trying to help him. So now let's
not waste time arguing because *I'm* going with you, and when he's cornered
it's going to be with the two of us together. That's the way it was in the old
days and that's the way it's going to be today!"

Seeing the familiar look of determination in Wilhite's eyes, he shrugged.

"Wilhite, you know something," he said, "the older you get, the more *stub-*
born you get. All right then, let's quit arguing and hop us a cab."

As the cab made its way through the heavy traffic, Hickman was silent, aware
of Deacon Wilhite holding on to the passenger's strap as he looked out on
the passing streets. Wilhite's face was calm, almost oriental in its impassive-
ness and he remembered that Wilhite's maternal grandmother was part
Cherokee. *Wilhite's got a curious mind,* he thought. *He remembers all types of things*

which most folks have forgotten and brings them up and applies them when you least expect. Then the cab was stopping for a traffic light and as a chauffeur-driven sedan drew alongside he could see an elderly white man lower his newspaper to gaze across at Wilhite with mild curiosity.

That's right, mister, he thought, *look at him and think about what he might be doing circulating through these streets, because even to me, his old friend, he's two-thirds hidden behind a wall. I can tell you this, though: As stubborn as he is and as powerful as he can speak, all he needs is the notion and a place to stand and he could make this whole street tilt up on its end like a plank that's been struck by a heavy wave. When the old slaves advised it, it sounded only slavish, but it's good advice for you too: "Humble thyself." For one thing, you see more, and sometimes you understand a little of what you see. . . . You're riding in that air-conditioned car with two telephones, a TV, and a radio, got the world in a jug and probably a million in the bank—but who's got the stopper? Who's holding down the lid? That's a question to trouble your dreams. . . .*

Then with a blowing of horns the traffic was flowing again and he saw the white man return to his paper and his limousine pulling away. *It's true,* he thought, glancing at the side of Deacon Wilhite's head, *after all these years I'm still ignorant of many of his dimensions while sometimes I feel that he knows me and what I'm feeling like a book. Better than all the others put together. Even better than his wife and the other ladies. He understands how much my getting to see the boy means to me. Personally. . . . But the boy, why is he still running from us? He must realize by now that we mean him no harm. And how long does he think we'll just go on getting thrown out of places before some reporter gets the idea that there must be more to our trying to see him than meets the eye? Power, Lord! I guess it makes you forget how other people, poor people, weak people, react to bad treatment, to promises unkept, to mean acts and insults. But then, Hickman, power doesn't have to know. In place of knowing and having to feel it has a heap of unknowing, unfeeling folks on the payroll who form an unknowing wall around it. A high wall like that one around those grounds and buildings passing out there. . . . That young secretary gal of his is one such wall. Yes, and being from way down home in her attitudes, she's even got her own private wall around her. Can't see it . . . hidden. But wall just the same, and inside herself an even more stubborn wall. Lord, it's so* hard *and I'm so tired. . . .*

Ho, a wall around a wall within a wall without a wall, with all her white-walled womanhood. Holes for eyes. A cotton sack. A gal now, a maiden then and a babe awash in the water. Still the sparrow watched. Hickman, he's somewhere out there—somewhere behind walls within walls and no wall willing nor withering. . . . No seams, no runners. Just bold defiance, narrow-nosed with folded arms, trying to stare you down. Looking straight at you but with no sight, no savvy, no sympathy. Speak it! Oh, I talked to her all that time . . . all that time . . . earnestly, tenderly, near-pleadingly calling—but she never heard a word!

Deaf but not dumb with dumbness, eyes in the head but not seeing; just Caledonia headed hard within walnut walls within thicker walls of attitude! In the grain, under the bark—there's the bite! Yes, Lord!

Words within walls within words and no word able to breach the walls. But this I still have to believe:

> *Seek*
> > *Find*
> *Knock*
> > *Open*
> *Ask*
> > *Receive*

Though still no wall withering or giving as of now.

Yea, but soon, soon! Because no wall can wallout wallin, walnut the Word. For wherever the tree liveth the kernel sprouts forth leaves to tremble in the wind of life, the roots push up....

Yes, but, Hickman, do you realize you have got the Word up against the wall—How so?

Oh, boxed, boxed, boxed! Hidden within boxes without topses is our Bliss. Walled now within a walnut wall and yet stirring—God willing—though no one here hearing, no one hear heeding, our cry—not yet.

> *Oh, Cal'don—*
> > *Yah!*
> *Cal'don—Yah!*
> *What makes your white head*
> > *So hard?*

"A.Z.," he heard ...

Snapping awake, Hickman saw the driver's dark face peering back through the rearview mirror with eyes disembodied like the eyes of conscience, and after a momentary confusion he realized where he was. Wilhite was looking out of the window.

"Yes, Deacon," he said.

"I say I think we ought to forget about it...."

"Forget what?"

"The whole thing, A.Z., the entire business...."

"After coming all this way—why?"

"Because it's beginning to seem that it's not worth it. We've done what we can. We've tried to see him, we've called him and left messages—and nothing has happened. So now it looks to me like he doesn't want to see us."

"I know, but you forget one thing: A man's life might depend on our seeing him. And what about our own need?"

Wilhite turned, facing him.

"Look, A.Z.," he said, "let's be frank about this thing. It's mostly *you* who

428 · *Three Days Before the Shooting . . .*

wants to see him. I understand that, and most of the others do too and we re-spect your feelings. Still, the truth is that it's *you* who has the *pressing* need."

"Have the members been discussing this?" he said.

"No, but it's true. They're faithful to you so they're faithful to your idea. You loved that little boy, everybody knew that, so they loved him too. We all did. But that was years ago. Since then, for them, that love was replaced by curiosity, or something else. Anger, maybe, and disbelief that after being what he *was* he could become what he *is.* They have different attitudes, but in the main what was once love was replaced with something else back far-ther than they can remember. So if you had said that you had lost interest they would have been relieved and in a day or so they would have forgotten about it—except maybe when his name came up in conversation."

Wilhite paused, looking at him.

"A.Z.," he went on, "I hope you don't mind my saying this?"

He shook his head.

"No, Deacon, I don't mind. The truth hurts but it won't kill me. What you say is certainly true of some of them and I've known it for a long time. But now, how about you?"

Suddenly Wilhite's face broke into a smile.

"Oh, I'm with you, A.Z. I'm still with you. You know that."

"Good. I don't know what I'd do without you. The only thing is that I feel that I have to do as much as I can. . . ."

"A.Z.?"

"Yes?"

"You also understand that in spite of what I say the members are still with you too, don't you? What I mean is that they haven't lost hope altogether. Be-cause they feel that even though the boy has turned his *public* face against us, maybe he's doing something behind the scenes to help us. Booker T. was like that too, remember? But mainly they've kept the faith because of you, A.Z. You justify them."

"Yes," he said with a nod. "I understand and I pray for their continued un-derstanding, especially now. I justify their hope and now I must justify it in fact as well as in spirit. So you understand why I must see him?"

"Yes I do. You have to put your faith to the test. . . ."

"Yes, Deacon, I mean to try. . . ."

"I know. And you have to know whether you've been right or wrong. After all these years, you have to know."

"Yes. And even if I'm wrong, I don't want anything like what Janey's hint-ing at to happen. Because beyond the question of living or dying there's too much to be said. Too many questions to be answered. The record has to be set *straight.*"

"That's right, A.Z.," Deacon Wilhite said. "That's the way it is."

Suddenly Deacon Wilhite leaned close, lowering his voice.

"A.Z.," he said, "how did Sister Beaumouth come by this address?"

Hickman smiled. "From her son. You remember, he used to drive and but-ler for the woman's mother. She sent him there on a few errands, and know-ing the daughter wasn't married and seeing this man there a few times, he caught on."

"But he's of the younger generation, A.Z. How'd he know about the boy?"

"Well, it was like this: At first he only knew the name our boy goes by up here, but then he was on a visit down home and his mother happened to bring up the name at supper—she'd made him some homemade ice cream and got to talking about how crazy our boy used to be about ice cream. Then later he happened to overhear his mama and daddy discussing what had hap-pened to the boy and he put two and two together. Sister Beaumouth told me that he got a big kick out of the joke of the boy's being who he is...."

"It looks like our boy is living in a glass house," Deacon Wilhite said.

"Yes, but I guess he figures he's got some good curtains and shades. Any-way, he doesn't have to worry about Sister Beaumouth's boy because he ain't too smart. He sees the whole thing as just another con game. He's happy just to see somebody beat them at their own game. To see them confused by the wrapping on the package."

Deacon Wilhite laughed.

"Yes," he said, "I guess any glass is dark if you're dumb enough, or near-sighted enough."

The address was that of a modern glass-and-concrete building that was ap-proached by a drive which curved past a gracious lawn set with blossoming cherry trees and flower beds, and seeing it he realized his mistake.

There'll be a doorman, he thought, *and that's the first wall we'll have to deal with....*

When the cab pulled near the entrance two limousines were ahead of them.

"Driver," he said, handing over a bill, "let us out here; we'll walk the rest of the way."

Outside, he caught Wilhite's arm.

"Wilhite," he said, "I think this is going to be a disappointment...."

"Yes, A.Z.?"

"Well, I hoped it would be a hotel and we'd only have a desk clerk to deal with but that doorman's going to check us and call up to see if we're expected."

"Yes," Wilhite said, "that's the way they do it. But we could use the ser-vants' entrance."

"I thought of that, but where is it? And how would we find her once we got in? We don't even know anybody who works here."

Deacon Wilhite grimaced. "Yes," he said, "and the servants are probably all white at that. Immigrants. I guess we should have had Sister Beaumouth get a phone number from her son, because folks who live like this usually try to protect themselves from surprises."

Looking down the shadowed drive to where the doorman was opening the door of one of the limousines, he felt a nudge.

"A.Z.," Deacon Wilhite said, "what's this woman's name?"

He turned. "Don't you have it?"

"Why no, I don't."

He shook his head. "So that's the real wall," he said, turning abruptly and starting back along the drive.

"Wait, A.Z." Deacon Wilhite called from behind him. "What are you talking about? What wall?"

"I mean the wall of dumbness," he called over his shoulder. "The wall of forgetfulness—I didn't bring her name and I don't remember it. A bellhop would be better at this job than me."

"Well," Deacon Wilhite said drawing abreast, "don't worry about it, A.Z. Some of the ladies will remember it. You can bet on that. We'll just come back tomorrow."

Halting a cab as it came down the drive, they rode silently to the hotel and as they entered the lobby he drew Wilhite aside.

"You explain it to the others," he said. "I'm going to stretch out for a while and try to think of another plan."

Turning off the lights, he lay across the bed in his shorts but his mind was too active for sleep. He thought of his failure to get into the apartment building and rebuked himself, both for having gone to the address and for having done so without anticipating the obvious problems which he found there. *I must really be getting anxious,* he thought, *anxious and silly. Old folk's silly....*

A feeling of anguish came over him and to fight it away he turned on the light and tried to read his Bible, but as though to mock himself he opened the well-thumbed, red-edged pages at the point in the story of David and Absalom where David was watching the approach of the two runners, one bearing news of victory and the other of Absalom's death, and he put it aside with a sigh. *All they needed to do,* he thought, *was to be in the presence of one another, just to face up to one another and say howdy, but that was a task too large for either one, father or son. Pride turned the arrows against them, making for death and anguish....*

And as his mind dwelled upon the ancient story, his thoughts drifted back to the afternoon at the monument, and once again he saw the colossus brooding enigmatically in the shadowed coolness of its edifice, and heard his words uttered there returned, sounding small and hollow in his mind like words spoken in the depths of a well. *Every time a man gives tongue to what he feels as against the doubts and restraints of his mind he's taking a chance,* he thought. *He's bared his head to foolishness and he tests his faith, and when he's trying to guide and lead others he's taken on a burden of guilt, because if he's wrong he's led them astray.*

Just the same, we shall see him and I shall see him and talk with him, he thought, *and soon.*

Then, realizing that he was hungry, suddenly very hungry, he got up and dressed. He wanted ribs and leaving the room quietly he left the building and took a cab, directing the driver to a small, smoky restaurant which he had noticed earlier in the day.

"That's Moore's," the driver said. "I know the place."

"How are the ribs?" he said.

"They'll do all right—for up here."

"What do you mean, do they know how to barbecue or don't they?"

"Well, I'll tell you," the driver said, "If you don't know too much about how ribs ought to be cooked, they'll do. They have the hickory smoke—know what I mean?—and they baste them like they ought to...."

"Yes?"

"... and they serve a pretty good cole slaw and they have good greens with ham butts and bacon scraps cut up in them but not too greasy—know what I mean?"

"Yes, that's the way I like them."

"That's right, me too. And they even have a sweet-potatoe pie which ain't too heavy...."

"Do they have them fried?"

"*Fried?* The driver stepped on the brakes, lurching forward and looking back. "Man, where you come from?"

Hickman laughed. "Why, I come from Georgia...."

"You sure must be!" the driver said. "Why I haven't even *heard* of a fried pie in twenty years. Now why don't some of our people put some of them up for sale? That's some of the best eating a man ever heard about. So you know about fried pies!"

"I know and I love them," he said.

The car shot away, moving to the left lane as the driver leaned over the wheel.

"Look," he said, "I tell you what I'm going to do. I'm going to take you to a place where you can get some *real* ribs. Moore's is okay for squares and folks in a hurry, but forget it—I know a place where they have the real hick'ry log fire, cole slaw, collards, spaghetti, potato salad, *and* some of the best hot sauce you ever et. That's what Moore's doesn't have, the real honest-to-goodness down-home hot sauce. You go up there and you smell that smoke and see the meat laying out there on the rack and you say, 'Uh huh, this man knows his business,' but then you bite into some of that meat and something's missing. That's the hot sauce. Now as I see it, this here is hot weather and if a man is going to eat him some ribs then they ought to be the best he can get. And I'ma *take* you to the best you can get. I mean here in Washington. Because if you want some real barbecue you have to go to Virginia for that...."

"I'll settle for your place," he said. "I'm too hungry and it's too late to go to Virginia."

"Well, now, you just hold on! We're going to Moore's!"

Leaving the cab, he could smell hickory smoke on the nighttime air, the bite of grease. The room was narrow and dimly lit and through the window he could see a long counter at which a number of men in shirtsleeves sat with heads bowed reverently over plates of food. From the rear, the blades of a large pedestal-mounted fan caught the light, droning loudly as it blew a warm, steady breeze toward the door, and as he entered he removed his topcoat and started toward a booth located to the side of the room and was startled to hear a voice call his name:

"A.Z., what are you doing here?"

It was Deacon Wilhite.

"Me," he laughed, "that's what I should be asking you. I thought you were in bed."

"I was, but I must have gotten homesick because I woke up with barbecue on my mind, and since I was still worrying about seeing that boy I thought I'd just go somewhere and do my worrying over a plate of ribs...." He broke off, seeing a huge, dark-skinned, weary-looking waitress approaching as though on sore feet.

"That's all right, miss," he called, "there's no point in tiring yourself, just bring me the same thing my friend here has."

"Everything?"

"Everything, only you can make the servings a little heavier and see that all the ribs are little ends. And, miss, don't hold back on the ice tea. I drink it by the gallon."

"Now, at this hour you're the kind of customer I like," she said. "A man who knows what he wants."

Smiling, she propped herself against the back of a swivel stool and called back to the kitchen, reading the order from a pad, and he could hear the cook answering as she sang out in a deep contralto voice,

"A hefty breast of guinea hen..."

"Yes!"

"All from the little end...."

"Uh huh!"

"And make it nasty and sassy, 'cause it's for a *coal* heaver!"

"Right! For a boarder and a heavy loader!"

"Hit him with some swamp seed and let it come by Charleston with black eyes looking up at him . . . 'cause he's guilty."

"Guilty of what?"

"Of being peckish!"

"So he can use some swamp seed—and why not by New Orleans?"

"It's got to be from Charleston, I say, because he's big and reachy and just might be Geechi. . . ."

"Yes, mam!"

"A side of little Italy!"

"Sing on!"

"And a mound of Irish with the Bermuda to talk sweet to him! And make his collards easy 'cause he knows that pig meat's greasy!"

"You mean he's been around and had his ups and downs so now he wants his vittles," the cook called. "What else?"

"That wraps it, darling," the waitress called, "and don't forget to sauce that breast."

Hickman laughed. "Wilhite," he said, "it's a good thing I dropped in here, because if you're eating all the things she just ordered for me you're liable to hurt yourself. How're the ribs?"

"Here," Wilhite said, pushing his plate forward, "try some; they're not the best but they'll do."

Nibbling silently on the bone, he watched Wilhite enjoying his food, the gold edge of an open-faced crown catching the light as he stripped the meat delicately from a bone.

"Look, A.Z.," he said, "I'm sorry about the way things turned out today and I guess I said too much about the members too."

"No," he said, "you were right; I shouldn't have thought about using that address—even though I might have to do it as a last resort. And you told the truth about how the members feel about the boy. I know that it's been years since most of them stopped expecting him to bring up the big fish that would feed the multitude. In fact, they only want him to explain what caused him to cut bait and run."

Suddenly Wilhite's napkin flew to his mouth as he lowered his head over his plate and laughed.

"A.Z.," he sputtered, "every time I think you're down in the whale's belly I bat my eyes and, praise the Lord, there you are, laughing on the shore!

"Well, A.Z., maybe you always expected too much from that child. Maybe the best he's ever to do was done when he got your hopes and expectations aroused over the possibility that he would become a great preacher and leader. . . ."*

---

* In the typescript for Book II, there are two or three lines of indecipherable text between the above two paragraphs of dialogue spoken by Deacon Wilhite.

"No, it wasn't him alone; it was the idea, the hope, maybe even the gamble. Anyway, I couldn't have been *completely* mistaken in my hopes, because look where he is today."

"You said something there, A.Z. I don't know what he was doing all the time we lost sight of him, but he's caught his tens of thousands and what's more, they don't even seem to know that they've been hooked."

"Yes, you have to give the little devil his due," Hickman said. "He's really gone through some changes. Just the same, I've got to catch him because if I fail, it won't be enough that the members might let me off the hook and forgive me for all the waste of time and emotion, I still have to be true to myself and to my promise to the Lord."

"You will, A.Z., and when you do there's one thing I hope you'll do for me...."

"What's that?"

"I hope that after all these years you'll tell me where on earth you got that baby. I've wondered about it and kept my peace for all these years, but now that things have come this far I'd like to know...."

Hickman raised his head, seeing a wistful half smile on Wilhite's face, the serious, almost pleading expression of his eyes, and put down his fork.

"You deserve to know," he said. "You were almost as close to him as I was and you went along with me on the basis of faith and friendship. But, Wilhite, it just ain't my story to tell...."

Wilhite waved his hand. "Now, I'm not pressing you," he said, "but, A.Z., when this is settled with I want you to *think* about telling me. Just think about it, that's all I ask."

"Very well, I'll think about it, but right now we'd better come up with a plan, otherwise I'm going to be in serious trouble. Our people tend to treat us preachers with a strictness that they never would think of applying to a politician or a protest leader. It's a weakness, as far as I'm concerned; one of our worst weaknesses. We don't demand nearly as much from even those few white politicians who use us as a left-handed source of power."

"Yes, A.Z.," Wilhite said, "and maybe that's why among the original band of members no one except old Sister Caroline Prothoroe feels really bitter about the boy. The others accepted the fact that he turned politician a long time ago and let him off the hook. But after all these years that old woman still insists that he's nothing but a backsliding minister. That's why she's never forgiven him for what he's done."

"I know, and I hope I'm not being unfair, but I think that as far as Sister Caroline is concerned the boy could go to hell unredeemed; her main interest in our being up here is that it's an opportunity for me to get some word concerning her brother."

"What brother?"

"You remember her brother, Aubrey McMillen."

"You mean the one they used to call 'Race Hoss' McMillen?"

"Yes, that's what we used to call him. His real name is Aubrey."

"That's right, A.Z., that fellow hasn't been home in years! And you mean he lives here in Washington?"

"That's what she thinks. She asked me to try to persuade him to come to see her before she dies. He's been living here ever since he and a white fellow got chased out of Kentucky over something they did that had to do with fixing a horse race. I promised her to see him, but if our boy keeps giving us the runaround, I don't see how I'm going to do—"

Suddenly he stopped, staring into his plate of ribs as he slapped his thigh with his palm.

"Look, Wilhite," he said, "I just had an idea."

"I'm glad it's that," Wilhite said, "because you look like you just saw a cockroach in your greens."

Hickman stood up, reaching for his coat and calling to the waitress, "Miss, may I have our check, please?"

"Where're you going, A.Z.?"

"I've got a hunch and I'm going to play it. Now put aside those meatless bones and let's get out of here."

Paying and tipping the waitress, they went outside into the heat of the night.

"A.Z.," Deacon Wilhite said, "where are you thinking about going at this hour?"

"We're going to find Aubrey McMillen."

"But why, man? With all we have to do in the morning?"

"But that's just it, Wilhite. I have to keep my promise to Sister Caroline and it just came to me that with liars like McMillen usually being such good observers, and that since he was around when the boy was a baby and has lived up here as long as he—"

"Oh, so that's it; you think he might have seen him operating up here and recognized him?"

"That's it, and isn't it possible? I'm pretty sure a lot of our people have recognized him and have been watching him and kept quiet—so why not Aubrey? Maybe he can tell us how to reach him...."

"I can think of a few reasons," Wilhite said. "For one thing, he never paid attention to anything except women and horses—but since you've made up your mind, let's go. I don't suppose you forgot the address?"

"No, Sister Caroline saw to that."

Taking a cab, they found the address in the middle of a quiet dark block, the silent three-story building located behind a shallow yard bordered by a hedge, and thanks to a glowing fanlight they had no difficulty in seeing the number 1369 above the entrance.

"A.Z.," Deacon Wilhite said, "if I were back in my old days policy playing and hadn't been dreaming right I think I'd have some reservations about going in there."

"Yes, but now you're a deacon, so come on. I don't like to disturb a man at such an hour, but maybe when Aubrey hears why we've come he'll understand...."

Then, taking a step inside, he stopped short and caused Wilhite to stumble against him before he could thrust out his hand in warning but not in time to prevent Wilhite from stumbling against him.

He had expected an empty vestibule with a row of apartment bells. Instead, he was looking upon a hall that was filled with men and women dressed in nightclothes. Crowding the dim stairs which led to the floors above, they pressed in a neck-craning mass around the brightly lit doorway of a room located a few feet down the hall to his right. A strong odor of whiskey was in the air, and seeing the crowd so intensely preoccupied by something happening inside he froze, signaling again for Wilhite to wait. Whereupon a shout from inside the room caused the crowd to move back and he was surprised to see the backlighted form of a white man appear in the doorway.

The man wore a narrow-brimmed straw hat, and as he gestured toward the crowd Hickman saw the cloth of his gray suit of synthetic silk rippling metallically in the light and then, hearing the man asking in an exasperated voice, "Didn't I tell you people to clear this hall?" he thought, *detective!* and watched the man come forward.

"That was over fifteen minutes ago," the man said, "and here I come back and you're still hanging around. Now this time I mean it—MOVE! Get back upstairs or I'll place the lot of you under arrest!"

"A.Z.," said Wilhite, behind him, "is that a policeman?"

But as he turned, saying "yes," a shrill, feminine voice knifed down from the shadow of the stairs:

"You do it, mister! You just go ahead and do it!"

And now looking up through the dim light to the top of the stairwell he saw a tiny, dark-skinned woman who was blazing down at the white man out of a pair of extremely crossed eyes. Standing beneath a bare electric bulb, she wore a coarse haired, oversized auburn wig, an assortment of bunched curls, loops, and dangling sidepieces which sat awkwardly atop a narrow, intense face. The wig gave her the air of a mad duchess and as she stared down imperiously at the white man she screamed, "Why don't you go on and get started? We all know that you're just burning to get brutal with us. So why don't you go ahead? It's your trade, isn't it—brutalizing folks like us? So go ahead and arrest us! ARREST US! We know you won't be satisfied until you've done something violent to somebody. But, mister, before you start your head-whipping let me tell you one doggone thing: We *live* here, you hear that? This is our *home!* We pay taxes and we pay rent and we have the right to know what's been happening to our neighbors. And what's more, we don't need *you* coming in here interfering with our rights. This is a *community!*"

"Look, lady," the white man said, "if you don't want the law on your premises all you have to do is to keep them orderly. Meanwhile, there's an investigation going on inside there and I have my orders. So now get back to your rooms because I want this hall *cleared!*"

Turning now, he took a step backwards, bumping into Wilhite as he whispered, "Move out, Deacon, this is no place for us...."

But it was too late; already the white man was looking his way.

"All right, big fellow," the white man said, "that goes for you and that fellow behind you. *Nobody* is leaving here without the chief's permission."

Sighing inwardly, he stepped forward, seeing the crowd turn to stare and feeling Wilhite moving in beside him, and now, as they advanced into the light, he saw a look of surprise come over the white man's face.

"Saaaay," the white man said, "where did you come from? I didn't see you in here before...."

"That's right, Officer," he said, "We've just arrived...."

"You just arrived from *where?*" the white man said.

"From the Hotel Longworth."

Frowning, the white man looked him up and down. "The *Longworth?* What are you, one of the doormen?"

Before he could reply, the woman screamed down from the stairs, "Now there he goes again. Did you people hear that? Just because he sees a fine, big, strapping professional-looking black man he's got to make him into a *doorman!*"

Thinking, *Here's a woman with absolutely no sense of propriety,* he quickly found his voice: "No, sir, I'm not a doorman, I'm a guest..."

But before he could finish, someone called out angrily from the dark end of the crowd, and he saw the detective turn to look, shouting, "Are you people going to clear this hall?"

As he watched, the crowd gave ground, grumbling as it retreated a few steps, only to halt as the detective turned back to face him.

"All right, so you're a guest at the Longworth," the white man said. "Now explain why you men are coming home at this hour."

"But, Officer," he said, watching the white man's eyes, "we don't live here. In fact, we've never been here before."

The eyes cut back to the tenants.

"Then where *do* you live?" the detective said, watching the crowd again.

He said, "We're from Waycross, Georgia, Officer. We're only up here for a visit."

The detective's head snapped back, staring up into his eyes. "Then why are you coming *here* at this time of night?"

"We came here because we have a message for a man who lives at this address; a Mr. Aubrey McMillen...."

"Ahaaah," the white man said, "so it's McMillen, is it? I suspected he'd have something to do with it. And I suppose you expect to take back his reply inside a bottle—is that it?"

As he studied the detective's self-satisfied expression, the strong odor of whiskey suddenly took on a vague but troubling significance.

"I don't understand," he said, "Inside a *bottle*?"

"Oh, I think you do," the white man said. "We're on to McMillen, so don't waste time pretending that you fellows are not his customers."

"Customers," he said, "customers for what?"

There was no answer. The detective was looking searchingly into Wilhite's face then back to himself, his white face taking on a knowing expression as suddenly he dropped his head, and slouched his shoulders and thrust his thumbs into his belt. *What on earth does he think he's doing?* he thought. Then the white man spoke in a voice that had become a thick-throated, inept imitation of Amos and Andy doing an imitation of a black, streetwise hipster.

"Now look, man," the white man said, "don't try to snow me, understand? Because, like, man, I been *around*, you dig?"

Suddenly, the atmosphere became dream-like. Listening to the white man, he had the sensation of having been snatched bodily from the hall, plunged outside into the night, held in black silence for an indefinite interval, and then set back to find the detective replaced by a double or an identical twin of drastically different personality. A double with whom it was nevertheless his embarrassing necessity to continue the interrupted interrogation....

"But Officer," he stammered, "but *Officer*..." hearing his voice trail off; as now, out of the corner of his eye, he could see Wilhite staring at the white man with open mouth. And beyond the sullen posture of the detective's challenge he could see the shadows coming alive with the widened eyes of the tenants. They were looking at the white man with the undisguised disgust of people who had just seen him quite deliberately degrade himself in public. Several appeared physically pained, and one man's flared nose was wrinkled as by the stench of rotten fish. Then, as his eyes shifted back to the detective's unreal face it came to him that the man was caught up in the grips of an arrogant, insane illusion which had led him to believe that with no more than a clumsy change of accent and manner he could not only transform himself from white to black but could achieve in the process such a penetrating insight into the secret lives and histories of his out-maneuvered black audience that no lies or deceptions that they might contrive to protect themselves could withstand his omniscient scrutiny.

Not only does he think he's become a Negro, Hickman thought, *he thinks he's become a super Negro. . . .*

And as the man's voice echoed in his head, he felt himself beginning to tremble, shaken by the man's apparent belief that by acting out his misguided white folks' notion of Negroness not only could he strike through all of the age-old mysteries of race and age and individuality, but that he could bewilder his audience into a defenseless state of absolute fear and truthfulness.

It's mammy-made magic, he thought, *he's acting in the name of the law and trying to work magic! Black magic! Shades of Stackalee!*

"Officer," he said, struggling to maintain his calm, "I'm trying to understand you, but you seem to have something on your mind that we don't know about. Nobody told us that Mr. McMillen had a business, so maybe if you'll take a second and explain what you're talking about we could arrive at—"

The white man held up his hand.

"Oh, man," he said, "come *on*! I dig the deal, so quit *stalling*. You know damn well that the stud's a bootlegger!"

"Bootlegger," he began, only to have the cross-eyed woman snatch the words out of his mouth, leaving him gasping the air.

"Bootlegger?" she screamed with an angry snap of her head. "BOOT-LEGGER? Did you people hear *that*? Now *that's* what we're up against! They send these young whippersnapper white cops into our community and look at what happens. Never even been here before and already he's set Mr. McMillen up in the bootlegging liquor business! I'm telling you, this white man must be out of his head! Here this building is so respectable that some of the tenants don't even want a person to cook herself some *collard* greens, and he's talking about bootlegging going on in here!"

"If you have any doubts," the white man said, returning to character now, "just take a deep breath."

"But Officer," Hickman said, "maybe if you'll let us explain the reason we had to come here at this time you could see—"

"No, mister," the cross-eyed woman called, "No! You just hold your water for a second, will you please? Because I have to get something off my chest!"

He paused, his feeling of disorientation mounting rapidly as now he found himself the object of the woman's extremely crossed eyes.

"Very well, mam," he said, "you go ahead."

"Thank you, darlin'," the woman said, with a fierce intake of breath. "That's very kind of you. Now I don't mean to be impolite but, like I say, there's something that I have *got* to get off my chest and I have to do it right here and now—understand? Things are building up...."

"Yes, mam," he said.

"Thank you, darlin'. And don't go begging that white man's pardon, you hear? Let *him* do the apologizing! He's the one who's come around here signifying to you strangers about Mr. McMillen being a bootlegger, which is a lie because everybody knows that he's a good, respectable, responsible, hardworking, God-fearing super who's *known* for going out of his way to be helpful!"

"That's right," a voice broke in, "she's telling the truth!"

"I'm glad to hear that," he said, "sister..."

"And it's the truth," the woman said, "but now, just because this rookie policeman has heard that the poor man takes him a drink every now and then—and I mean that's just to lift his spirits, you understand—right away he's done set McMillen up in the bootleg liquor business."

"What she means, gentlemen, is," a stentorian voice said from the dark part of the crowd, "that he's done up and made the man *illegitimate*—which is gross hearsay and unfounded allegation!"

Staring, he tried to identify the new speaker, as the cross-eyed woman continued, "That's right, done thrown the poor man outside the law! Why, it's enough to make a person sick to her stomach! Understand what I mean?"

He nodded, staring into the crowd, then up to the woman, who had thrust her body between the shoulders of two men now and looked down at him with a fierce expression as they tried to give her room.

"Yes, ma'am," he said, just as the voice boomed again from the back of the crowd.

"Now you listen to me, Maud," it said, "don't you go getting yourself all upset over something that ain't worth it.... Watch out the way there y'all: let a man up there who's got something to say...."

As he stretched his neck to see who was speaking the crowd gave way before a short, heavyset man who wore a nightcap improvised from the top of a woman's black nylon stocking, the frayed top of which had been tied in a fat knot and its bottom pulled down around his huge head so tightly that a network of sharp indentations appeared in the flesh above his large, frog-like eyes. Thinking, *Now here's an old chitt'lin'-eater if I ever saw one,* he noted that the man wore a mangy-looking bathrobe of dark brown artificial fur which caught the light as he came aggressively forward, bellying and elbowing people out of his path—until reaching a spot just behind the tenants standing immediately in front of the white man, where he stopped and stood gravely shaking his head, regarding the detective with the air of a world-weary judge.

"Naw, Maud," said the man over his shoulder. "Naw, sir! It ain't worth a sweat and you'll see that it ain't the moment you calm down and take a look at what's going on around here. Then you'll realize that all this cop is looking for is a little…easy…" the man paused, widening his heavy-lidded eyes and rising suddenly on tiptoe as he shouted, "GRAFT!"

He stared at the man, thinking, *Where on earth did a type like this come from? That type of Negro had gone out with the horse and buggy, but instead here's one alive and well in Washington.*

As he saw the fleshy lips shoot out and clamp down in a grimace of absolute conviction, he could see the man's barrel-like body begin bouncing up and down as though set in motion by the weight of what he had said.

"That's all it is," the man said. "So now…here…way early in the mawning, he's got the unmitigated gall to be trying to hit a bunch of sophisticated D.C. folk like us with some of his ignunt…peckerwood…law-and-order… mystification!"

As the hallway popped with a firecracker flurry of angry agreement, he could see the detective's face flame into a bright red and saw him stab an angry finger at the man in the stocking cap.

"Now you listen to this, Jack," he shouted. "That'll be enough of that! You hear me?"

"You dam' right, I hear," the pop-eyed man shot back, waving his arms for quiet. "What's more, I know my rights to an opinion. Therefore, I'm holding that Miss Maud up there's got no business getting herself worked up just because *you* want to put down a simple-minded hype!"

"What's that?" the wigged woman called, squinting fiercely as she cupped a hand to her ear, repeating shrilly, "What? WHAT?"

"…Because all that's involved here," the fat man went on, "is a little *small-time*…hustling!"

"…Lonnie!" the wigged woman called.…

"…Yes, sir," the pop-eyed man said, looking directly at him now, "when you strip it down to the nitty-gritty that's all it is: a simple case of trying, as some of the boys like to say, 'to twist the *loot* outta the *Boot!*' "

"Listen, fellow," the detective said, "what's your name?"

"…*And,*" the man said, still looking him in the eye as he ignored the detective and waved his arm above his head, "I'll be glad to explain how it's done: Now the first thing you do in a hype like this is to find you a tight situation, one that you can go about naming anything you dam' please—like larceny, suspicion, exciting a riot, spitting on the public sidewalk, littering, playing a transistor radio with the volume up—any dam' thing you dam' please. Next, you find yourself a Boot who's in some kind of questionable predicament—and, as we all know, that's liable to be true of *any* Boot at *any* time—because these white folks have got the system set up and arranged in such a way that it's more normal for a Boot to be *in* trouble than out of it.

Therefore, all the Man has to do is to find the tight situation and find him a Boot, and then set about *terrorizing* him until he can make him own up to being responsible for whatever he charges him with doing. Then the *next* thing he does is to throw the Boot smack-dab in the middle of the situation and force him to confess that he's guilty—which, unfortunately, he's more liable to do than most, because when you get right down to it the average Boot figures he's *got* to be guilty of something because otherwise he has no explanation as to why his life is always as messed up as it usually is. Therefore it's just a question of the Man finding him a situation, then finding him a Boot to match up with it—and once he does that, ladies and gentlemen, he has got it *made!*"

"Now, you listen," the white man said, "I'm asking you once more, *What is your name?*"

The pop-eyed man looked surprised. "Who, me?" he said. "Why, Barnes. Everybody around here in the community knows me. Does that satisfy you? *Barnes! Lonnie* Barnes, and at your service."

"Now, you listen, Barnes," the detective repeated, "if you..."

"So now, like I said, that's all that's happening here. As your neighbor and fellow-tenant, I'm hipping you to it so you'll *all* know what this is all about. In brief, this cop is just trying to twist him a Boot from some loot! McMillen is the Boot."

"A.Z.," Wilhite whispered behind him, "I can't figure out what's going on in this place, but from the *sound* of things some of these Negroes have got to be drunk!"

"No, Wilhite," he said. "It's more than that." Then, seeing the detective looking their way, he said, "Officer, could we please get this over with? As I've explained, we don't live here and we would like to..."

"Hold it," the white man said, starting forward, and now he saw the pop-eyed man spin with the tilting motion of a barrel bobbing in swift water and dart back into the suddenly fluid crowd; wherein, as it closed quickly around him, he stood looking out at the white man defiantly.

"Yeah," he shouted, waving a fuzzy arm, "he don't want me to expose it but he's just trying to drop a shuck that he don't know how to drop, so I'm going to spell it out so that you'll *all* be forewarned: First, he comes on this present situation in the line of duty, then he names it to his own convenience.... Which has *got* to be in the area of the criminal because as a cop he *lives* on crime. Remember that. Because any way you look at him you're up against crime. That's a fact! He eats crime and he drinks crime. He pays for his suits with crime and he buys his hats and shoes with crime. As a matter of fact, he's situated in crime from the heels of his shoes up to the fillings in his teeth! So like I say, he finds him some kind of questionable, borderline situation, the kind which is neither criminal or un-criminal but can look like either one, then he pokes around until he finds somebody he can drop into it without any backfire, and somebody he can use to make it pay off. Which appears in this case to be Brother McMillen. So now what he's trying to do is to trap Brother McMillen and make him confess to some bogus, unfounded, and ill-conceived circumstantial evidence, and he means to try to make Brother McMillen, our neighbor, buy his way out of it. And sad to say, if he can just twist McMillen *hard* enough he'll make it stick—and then WHAM!—he's got it *made*! All he's got to do then," the fat man said, grimacing sadly as he slowly shook his head, "is twist the Boot and he's *got* the loot!"

"Officer," he began, but again the cross-eyed woman was speaking:

"Now you lissen to me, Lonnie," she screamed, "You stop referring to us as 'Boots,' you hear? Don't do it! Don't be giving that white man the immoral satisfaction of hearing you talking so common. You know that he's the kind who likes to twist and turn everything a colored person does and says wrong-side out! He's the kind who if he was to see one of us ladies being escorted along the streets a few times by different gentlemen friends he'd be calling us prostitutes! You *know* that. He's the kind who has the low-rating kind of mind!"

"Now you're talking!" Barnes said, nodding judiciously. "You're correct—but it ain't uncommon. And like I say, after he's done low-rated and yeasted the situation to his own satisfaction, and after he has put the badmouth on you—" he paused, stabbing the air with a fat finger, "he will be trying to twist some Boot—" he made a twisting motion with his hand, "for some loot!"

"Lonnie!" the cross-eyed woman said, "LONNIE!"

"... Then the next thing you know, instead of arresting somebody for breaking the law, he'll be breaking down the dam' door demanding some free trade! Which *I* would describe as the compounding of a criminal misnaming of situations, plus the bearing of false and malicious witness *with* an act of *de facto*—I said '*de facto*'—*bribery*! In other words—twisting the *Boot*!"

"Lonnie," the woman screamed, her eyes a-blazing crossfire as she gave her wig a violent tug, "I have told you now..."

"... But that," the pop-eyed man said, "is just another way of upending a Boot for some loot..."

"Lonnie," the woman screamed, "now don't you interrupt me any more because *I'm* going to tell these gentlemen about this white man and I don't want to hear another word out of *you*."

"Wilhite," he whispered, "that detective had better watch himself, because if I know anything about our women this sister is working herself up to a point where she'll be preaching his funeral and talking about his parents at one and the same time."

"Yes," Wilhite said, "and if I were superstitious and she was looking at me the way she's looking at *him*—I'd cross my fingers and spit in my hat. Because now that white man's going to have to pay for all that agitation that fellow with the mush-mouthed legal mind is working up. That woman is getting as hot as a Charleston pistol . . . and I don't want to be here when she explodes. Just look at her!"

"Lonnie," the woman was saying as he looked back and saw her, wagging her finger at the pop-eyed man, "if you don't hush I'm going to *read* you! I'm telling you now, I'm going to *read* you!"

Barnes drew himself up, his head turning from side to side following her wagging finger.

"You're going to do *what?*" he said, his voice vibrant with indignation. "Where do *you* get the right to threaten *me* like that? This is a free country and open to all *kinds* of opinion; therefore I have the right—"

"No! No! And you lissen to me, Lonnie Barnes! You lissen to *me!*"

Frowning, Barnes stuck out his lips, his forehead wrinkling beneath his stocking cap. "Now how come I have to do that?" he said. "Tell me how come I have to lissen to *you* when I already know all about his kind? When I've seen them operate for over fifty—"

". . . Because," the woman screamed, "you're so full of *bull* hockey and everybody knows it, that's why! I want these two gentlemen who just came in to listen because I have a real problem. . . ."

"Now you done said something," Barnes said, "you really do have a problem."

". . . which maybe they can help me with. . . ."

". . . Yeah, but for that," Barnes said, "you need to get organized. We need *organization!*"

"Oh, organize my butt!" the cross-eyed woman screamed. "Go organize your mama!"

Suddenly Barnes spun as though shot, the topknot of his greasy stocking cap catching the light as he stared in outrage toward the stairs.

"Now look here, Maud," he roared, "don't you go dragging my mama into this discussion."

"Me?" the woman screamed, "ME! You brought her into it yourself! The only reason *I'm* mentioning her is because she had the misfortune of bringing you into the world where you have got yourself in my way and made me *mad*—So now hush! And don't you roll your bloodshot eyes at me—

"Gentlemen," she said, "forgive me for talking like that. I'm sorry. But as you can plainly see, our neighbor, Lonnie Barnes there, he just has too much mouth! Now the point I'm trying to get across is that we're all out here at this time of night because we have had some serious trouble here in our building—which is our home—understand? And that does something *awful* to a woman. It upsets her! It makes her *nervous!* Now that white man there won't tell you, but I will: Mr. Rockmore, who is our landlord, and Mr. McMillen, who you came here to see, are in some kind of trouble. That's what this is all about. I don't know what kind of trouble it is, but we know that it's something serious. Because besides that rookie standing there next to you all, there's some *big*-time detective and some other folks have been in there with Mr. Rockmore and Mr. McMillen. Not that we have been meddling; I don't believe in that; but early this evening it sounded like there was a *party* going on in there, and can't nobody here ever remember Mr. Rockmore ever doing any partying...."

"That's right," a woman said, "that sure is the truth."

"Yes! and then there was some loud noises and a woman was laughing and all like that...."

"...And music," a voice said.

"Yes, and some dance music and all like that," the cross-eyed woman said. "So pretty soon the front door was slamming and folks was stumbling around out here in the hall and the next thing I know I'm wide awake and all *kinds* of rumors and questions is whirling around out here in the hall—understand? But in spite of all that nobody seems to know what the *truth* is. And that's because that white policeman there won't tell us anything, and neither will he let us go in and find out anything for ourselves.

"So now, that's why I'm asking for your help. I'm in trouble, understand? I mean, when something like this happens I get to thinking I must be going out of my mind. That's right, gentlemen. That's the truth! Everything starts to getting so *unstable*—you know? I get the hot flashes and it's like my *brain* gets to spinning so hard that I seem to be staggering on my feet. The *ground* starts to be trembling, and right now all this whiskey that's in the air isn't helping it one single bit! Understand? What I mean is, when something like this develops, a person like me doesn't any longer know who she is or where she's at!"

"All right now, lady," the detective said, "I've let you speak your piece, so now—"

"...Man, you haven't let me do nothing," the woman said. "Gentlemen, as you can smell for yourself, there's whiskey in the air, a heap of whiskey, and this ain't no hangout for no bums or winos; this is a *respectable* building. But yet and still, there's been some partying going on even though our landlord isn't the kind of man who *parties*. And...and...well, I might as well tell it all 'cause I know it's what got that white man so upset: Some say that there was a *white* woman—"

"Now there you go," Barnes exploded. "There you go! Putting all the man's business in the street. You Negroes will do it *every time!*"

"Oh, shut up, fool!" the woman snapped, waving her hand. "Gentlemen, listen to me: Like I was fixing to say, everybody knows that when it comes to *visiting*, Mr. Rockmore has even less for the whites to do than he has for the colored—which ain't too much by any standard. So I have some serious doubts about the white-woman part. Especially since there's plenty of us colored around. So now I'm asking you all: What does it mean? Our neighbors are in some kind of trouble, but we don't know its *name* and we don't know its *face*, and, if you know what I mean, we don't even know its *race*. That's why we're so upset. We want to be helpful in the way good neighbors ought to be, but we don't know how. Things have been messed up for most of the night and we have cried and we have prayed, but all we can get out of that rookie cop down there trying to play god, is some stupid talk about McMillen being some kind of bootlegger—which we *all* know to be a garbage-mouthed lie! So now, since you look like fine, intelligent gentlemen and I know you haven't been around here long enough to breathe up too much of this here whiskey-polluted air, I'm asking you to please tell me something that I personally need to know...."

"...Organization is what *we* need," Barnes broke in, "*Organization!* I've been telling black people that for years!"

The woman paused, looking down and over the banister at Barnes with a fierce expression. "Yes," she said, "but you talk so loud and wrong that by now even the *dumb* white folks take you for a natural-born clown, you old micturating rascal, you! So now you hush while I finish—"

"Now *you* listen," the detective broke in. "You've said enough, and if you continue I'm booking you for resisting an officer."

"Resisting an officer!" the woman said. "Man, can't you stand the truth? Is my telling the truth a transgression against you? Besides, how're you going to arrest me, sprout wings and fly up here over my neighbors' heads? Shucks, man!"

"Now you listen, I mean what I say," the detective said.

"And I hear you," the cross-eyed woman said, "and you still ain't saying nothing!"

"Tell it to him, Maud," a voice called from the rear.

"So now," she said, focusing on Hickman and stabbing the air for emphasis, "before I'm interrupted again, I want you two gentlemen to answer me this: What I want to know is how *long* are our colored *men* going to *stand* for these here white police to always be coming around dragging their nasty, filthy minds into the places where we colored folks are *forced* against our own free wills to live? That's what I want to know! How long are you men going to stand for it?"

"But, lady," Wilhite said, "Why are you asking us? We just walked through the door...."

"I know that, mister, and that's *exactly* why I'm asking you. Because being strangers and coming here at this time of night, and with all this trouble and all—you *must* have been sent here for a *purpose*...."

Suddenly she paused, seeming to look over Hickman's head and then at Deacon Wilhite, her eyes widening.

"Saaaay! Look here. What happened to the other one?"

"Who?" Hickman said. "Who do you mean?"

"Your friend..."

"But nobody came here with us," Wilhite said. "We're alone; just the two of us..."

"Oh, no," the woman said. "When you started out there must have been another one. There *has* to been. What happened, did he fall by the wayside to get him a beer? Did he get lost?"

"*Who?*" Wilhite said. "Miss, you must have us confused with some other fellows. Nobody came here with us...."

"That's the truth," Hickman said, seeing the woman frown and a bewildered expression pass across her face.

"Well, if you say so," she said. "But somehow it seems to me that there ought to be *three* of you. Don't you usually travel in threes?"

Hickman looked quickly at Wilhite, who was staring at the woman with an alert expression. "No, ma'am," Wilhite said, "only two. It's been a long time since we traveled with anybody else...."

"That's correct," Hickman said, "a long, long time...."

"Well," the woman said, "I guess you gentlemen ought to know.... But anyway, even if there are only two of you, being strangers you ought to be able to tell us something intelligent about our situation that we can't see for ourselves. We need some leaders and fresh thinkers, and you look like you can help us...."

"Hell, Maud," Lonnie Barnes growled, "haven't I already diagnosed the situation? So why are you bothering these strangers when we got leadership right here in the community? All we need to *do* is git...ourselves...together!"

"Fool," the woman said, trembling as she drew her folded arms close to her body, "have you ever heard of the *change?* I don't have no *time* to wait, that's why I'm asking them. Whenever a situation like this comes up I get the feeling that I must be losing my righteous mind! I want these gentlemen to tell me if what's going on around here is *normal,* and if it's the same way where *they* come from. And if it *is,* I want them to tell me what I'm supposed to be doing while I'm *waiting* for us to get ourselves together!"

"Now, now, Maud, that's enough," a woman called down from the second floor. "Like Lonnie said, you're just getting yourself all worked up for nothing. Why don't you come on up and get some rest?"

"What do you mean?" the cross-eyed woman screamed, turning and waving a skinny arm over her head, " 'for nothing'? I'm here calling on these gentlemen for help with my problem and you're telling me that ain't nothing the *matter?* That's exactly why I'm calling on somebody that's not all snarled up in this mess like we are. We been in it so long that we're blind and I want to be taught to *see*! So, darlin', I'm calling on *them* because I feel like I'm about to blow my top! Understand? You're a woman, so you ought to. I'm calling on these gentlemen because they *appear* to be *sane*. So I want them to put my mind at *ease*! The building is reeling and rocking and knocking with trouble and I believe to my soul that these two millionaire doctors of the spirit have been sent here in the nick of time to *save* us and you talking about it being *nothing*? Good God-a-mighty!"

"A.Z.," Wilhite whispered, "you hear what she just called us?"

"If you did," Hickman said, "then I guess I did too. But I wonder who on earth does she think we are?"

"Why, I knew when I woke up this morning that something terrible was going to happen," the woman said, addressing him directly now. "Oh, yes! Because, gentlemen, last night I dreamed that I had given birth to three sweet little babies. That's right! One of them was black and one was white and one was 'riney red, and they looked alike as three little green peas. And, gentlemen, it was all so real that I still can't believe that it didn't happen. In fact, I don't know whether it happened or not from the way I feel and remember it, it must have been real, it had to be. . . ."

"Oh, come on now, Maud," Lonnie Barnes said. "Dammit, woman, you better git a *holt* of yourself. You know dam' well that you ain't even married!"

"And don't I know it," the cross-eyed woman said. "Oh, but don't I know it. But I'm going to be; oh, yes, I am! My bridegroom shall cometh! Yes he will! And besides, what has that got to do with it anyway? What does it matter if he comes before or after as long as he comes? Is that too much of a riddle for you, Mister Bigshot Lonnie Barnes? I gave birth to those babies just the same, all three of them; and I was so proud, so very, very proud. They come one right after the other—one, two, three!—and without all that labor and pain you hear so much about and even without a midwife or doctor. And I got right up and fixed them up real pretty in little pink and blue dresses and everything. Yes, and I bathed them and oiled them and powdered them and I wrapped them in a nice blanket and took them in my arms and went out on the street and showed them to everybody and told them how it happened and all. Oh, but they were so beautiful! So sweet and charming; such *dear* little babies. And they recognized me as their mother right away and they cooed and gurgled and looked at me with such dear little ole Negro smiles. Oh, yes! the sweetest kind of baby smiles.

"And do you know something, gentlemen? At first folks were surprised. They were shocked to see me with my babies. But then they started laughing at me and told me that I'd better quit kidding them and take those dear little babies back to their rightful mother. That's right! And me so proud of my motherhood! And when I insisted that *I* was their mother they called me a liar. I tell you, gentlemen, there's a lot of talk about love going around but it don't stop our folks from treating one another unkindly. So to prove my motherhood I took some of the ladies into a hallway and pulled up my clothes and I *showed* them. Yes, sir, gentlemen, I showed them myself and let them see from where all the life-giving blood and water had flowed.

"What! Oh, yes! I showed them the fish in the bird nest! I wasn't ashamed.

"I showed them the O where all the A.B.C.s came out! I showed them the black eye that they were striking at and trying to ruin my good name!

"And I showed them the babies' little raw belly buttons too. Showed them *everything*! But instead of *apologizing* for calling me a liar, and instead of being thankful for the wonderful thing that had happened to me, they *scorned* me. Here I have known some of them for years and thought they were my friends, but they upped and called me an ole loose-tailed bitch! That's what they did, gentlemen. And so I want you gentlemen to know that I was hurt to the quick, to my heart and soul.... Because I had always wanted me a nice little baby and here I had been blessed with three. Not just one, but *three*—

"Sweet ones," she said, smiling triumphantly and counting on her claw-like fingers. "One little, two little, three little, pretty little, plump little, cunning little cute ones!

"But," she paused, frowning sadly as she shook her bewigged head, "but instead of being *happy* and *congratulating* me on finally coming through on my womanhood even though it was kinda late, they scorned me and called me a bitch! A *bitch*! How do you like that, gentlemen? And after I had *showed* them all my evidence, after I had gone so far as to uncover the boat in the bulrushes for them all to see, they *still* called me a bitch! You hear me? A bitch! How about that, gentlemen?"

Turning his head, Hickman caught a glimpse of Deacon Wilhite's dumbfounded face—just as Lonnie Barnes threw up a fuzzy arm and gestured violently toward where a cluster of women were looking at the cross-eyed woman with expressions of fascinated disapproval.

"Dammit," Barnes shouted, "will some of you ladies stop standing around looking like a bunch of gossip-sprouting bitches and get this dam' woman out of here? This is awful! Disgraceful! Why ... hell! that dam' cherry of hers must have dried up and blown away way back around nineteen twenty-nine! I tell you this is *awful!*"

"Yes, it was awful. Yes!" the cross-eyed woman snapped. "But what does an old micturator like you know about something wonderful like this? What do *you* know about the woman's role in life? Nothing!

"That's why," she said, appealing to Hickman in an earnest voice, "I want you two fine, intelligent-looking, leader-type gentlemen to answer me this: Was I wrong? Was I a bitch to give birth without a husband? And was it any worse than it would be if one of you gentlemen was to give a woman a baby without marrying her, without letting her be a mother?"

"What!" Barnes exploded. "Now how can anybody do that? How can a man give a woman a baby *without* making her a mother, that's what I want to know—yeah. And how can a *woman* give a man a baby without his being a father?"

"Oh, you make me sick, Lonnie Barnes; you make me sick to my stomach! It's for me to know and for you to find out, so shut up! But was it, gentlemen? Is it? Is it any worse than it would be if a woman was to give *you* a baby that you didn't know she was going to give you? Tell me, because I have to know!"

Suddenly Hickman felt a tightening of his nerves that seemed to bring a sharpening of his hearing as now with a sense of unreality he watched the woman's eyes appear to flame brighter than the lightbulb suspended from a cord above her head. Somehow her questions had taken on a note of personal significance and as his sense of unreality grew he heard a young woman's thin, anguished voice calling down from the floor above:

"But Miss Maud, you...you just told us that it was all a *dream*, Miss Maud..."

"Yes, darlin'," the cross-eyed woman said, raising her head with a wildly radiant smile, "that's right. But you forget, darlin', that sometimes dreams are *real*...."

Then he could hear Lonnie Barnes roaring, "Oh, my God! Will you listen to that? Now she's done gone to contradicting a *contradiction*! By which I mean, she's now trying to stand a dream on its head, turn the truth wrong-side out, and talking a dam' hole straight through our skulls! Dammit, Maud, you have *flipped*! You have blown your top! Scrambled your brains! No doubt about it! If that dream was real, then where the hell are the babies? That's what I want to know, WHERE ARE THE DAM' BABIES!"

"Fool," Hickman heard, "they were taken away! That's what I'm trying to tell these gentlemen. Somebody slipped into my room and *took* them! While I was out buying them some soft little booties for their little feet and little ribbons and bows and such things as Johnson's Baby Oil and talcum powder and safety pins for their little didies, and some soft little brushes and some nice little combs, somebody came in and took them away. One of the brushes and combs was white, one was pink, and the other was blue, and you can go look in my room and see for yourself. They're all up there. And when I came back and found that the babies were not in their bed I rushed out to look for them and I searched for them everywhere. Over on the Howard campus, under the statues and by the trees in Lafayette Park. Up along the Mall and around the Washington Monument and near the middle gate in the White House fence. Even in back of Mister Lincoln's knees, and all down along the riverbank where the people fishes. I asked everybody I met if they had seen my lost little babies, but nobody had seen them. And nobody would help me. I looked and I looked. I searched until I could barely walk and until I was so tired that I broke down and cried.

"Oh, I cried and *cried*! I cried so hard that I had to get off the street and come home to get some rest, and when I got here I was so brokenhearted that I cried myself to sleep. So now all this is happening to Mister Jessie...and me now babyless."

Hickman watched her wiping her eyes with the back of her hand as she shook her head and then fixed him once again in her cross-focused eyes. "So please, please, gentlemen," she pleaded; "please tell me: Am I being punished by having my three little babies kidnapped just because I wasn't married? And if so, is that *justice*?"

"OOOOOH, NO!" Barnes moaned, "*now* she's done jumped on *justice*! They'll do it every time! First they jump salty with the truth and then they start yelling about justice!"

"...I say is it justice," the woman went on, "because does the good earth have to be married before it can give birth to spring? And if *it* doesn't, then tell me why *I* have to be? Because aren't all of us genuine, nitty-gritty black women the daughters of the earth? Of the rich, black, fruitful earth, who is the mother of us all, including that little nasty white rookie cop down there? And aren't us black women supposed to be natural like the earth, our mama? So now tell me about this mixed-up mess! TELL ME!"

At the woman's shout, Hickman stiffened, watching a glistening tear break from her eyes and course slowly down her cheeks, and he was stirred by a feeling mixed of compassion and painful distrust.

Falling silent as she awaited his answer, the woman's crossed eyes were awash with tears; and as her imperious question flared and plunged through his mind on a series of swiftly repeated echoes, it was as though the taut covering of a child's toy kite, flayed by the force of a sudden squall, was being ripped from the slender wooden cross which formed its fragile skeleton. Feeling compelled to answer, yet struggling against his sense of unreality, he was suddenly aware of the distorted surfacing of a story so intimately a part of him that for years it had existed in his consciousness less as a structure of events than as an emotion, an article of faith, a feeling, a vague yet basic and unquestioned support of his sense of life's meaning, one which revealed itself in a special gentleness toward mothers and infants. So that now, as he struggled to bring it fully to consciousness it eluded him, it teased him cruelly. And all the more so because he knew, even as it evaded him, like the beating of his heart, or the rise and fall of his lungs in breathing, it had been with him constantly and for a long, long time. Still, for reasons which he suspected as being too painful for consciousness, it was reluctant to reveal itself, to announce its true name. And as he stood silently opening and closing his mouth, it whirled in his mind with the elusive, now-you-see-me, now-you-don't motions of a single moth that opened suddenly and began a frantic flickering from light to shadow and back again in a parabolic flight above the cross-eyed woman's head.

Straining forward, she addressed him again and waited, but now it was as though a wall of thick glass had descended between them, behind which, like a turbulence of smoke in a bottle, the traces of the story were reforming and becoming an even older but no less familiar one—of which, with quickening heart, he sensed it to be but a hysterically distorted shadow, a mocking mask.

His body and face were damp with sweat now, and as he stared upward across the massed heads and into the woman's tear-stained face, this deeper story struggled gently but determinedly to assert itself. And in the turmoil of his mind he could feel its dispersed elements flying languidly together, as when a motion picture recording the bursting of a beautiful rose is reversed in slow motion, causing its scattered petals to float back with dream-like precision to resume the glorious form of its shattered design. Oblivious both to his will and to the goading of the woman's shrill insistence, this older story was reassembling itself, roiling with silent swiftness out of the shadow of time and the decay of memory as it reassumed in his mind a transcendent and luminous wholeness. It was as though it contained a life of its own, and now having been summoned up, it was insisting upon making its presence known against all that opposed it—the times, the policeman, the pulsating crowd, even his own memory's resistance toward recognizing its resurrection in the grotesque and incongruous details of the cross-eyed woman's condition.

Sounding within him now with somber harmonies, it brought a strong surge of emotion, a wild beating of his heart, and as it deepened he felt himself growing into a full and lucid awareness of its long existence, its mystery and wondrous promise. Then, as his eyes welled with the poignant emotion of recognition it came to him that far from having been simply listening to the retelling of a dream or to the wild, frustrated outpouring of a deranged female fantasy, he had been listening to a confession. Yes, a confession in which the cross-eyed woman was giving voice to a confusion of despair, hope, and a forlorn prayer.

Pulling an old handkerchief of pongee silk from the breast pocket of his jacket, he mopped his face, feeling a certain relief. Over the long years he had heard many confessions, both private and public, and he recalled that frequently he had encountered in them a note of desperate, unashamed, and deeply disturbing frankness. And he thought, *But even for our people, who are accustomed to saying and hearing things said in public that other folks keep strictly to themselves, this here is strong medicine. Very strong. That's why these here in the hall are getting embarrassed; public unburdening like this can be as upsetting as news of rape or murder, because they make everybody recall their own dreams and frustrations and guilt. It makes everyone feel naked, exposed. And sometimes that goes even for me. Maybe that's why for a second there I had the feeling that she had singled me out with those crossed eyes of hers just so that she could signify at me, had selected me, a stranger, for abuse and mockery—even though she's never seen me before and knows nothing about what brought Deacon and me to this crazy house. But she's touched me and touched me hard, not because she knows anything whatsoever about our mission but because of what lies in my secret heart. No, something else is going on here, something that has nothing directly to do with us. She's desperate, man; and at her age a woman can be terribly desperate. Desperate enough to expose herself before her neighbors in order to appeal to a couple of strangers for comfort. Well, she sure made a poor choice considering what we're able to do, but, then again, she might be seeing straighter than she appears to see, because at least she senses that I'm supposed to be a minister....*

"Gentlemen," he heard, "I'm waiting. I say tell me!"

"Yeah, somebody tell her *something* so she'll shut up," Lonnie Barnes said, snapping his stocking-capped head.

Hickman looked at Barnes, then back at the woman, thinking, *But what can I tell her in all this crowd, with these sophisticated Washington Negroes? And with this white detective looking like he's watching a circus ring full of sideshow freaks? Tell her that her dream seems to be the reflection of a miracle? An old, old sacred song, played on a wheezy, out-of-tune organ? Tell her that what happened in it has occurred to others, and usually with unforeseen consequences of mixed pleasure and pain? Should I tell her that she's in the grips of a dream that was actually experienced in all its fullness and mystery only once, by one woman and by one woman only, and that long ago?... Tell her something in this crowd when I've had trouble getting it across even with my own members?*

"Mister," the woman called, "I can see you're about to tell me, so go ahead and don't mind Lonnie. *I'm* the one who's in trouble. So don't just be standing there opening and closing your mouth, and saying nothing, because I need an *answer*. My brain needs it, and my *soul* needs it. In fact, since everything has gotten so crazy you can forget about my brain and just speak to my soul. Because I have been laughed at and I have been scorned, and this fool Lonnie Barnes is trying to put me down—and that not only makes for soul-pain, it upsets the mind. Yes, and before you answer, here's something else I have to know: Was I wrong... I mean when my own folks scorned me and called me a bitch... was I wrong when I said to those women who I thought were my good friends and had them turn against me: 'All right, all right now,' I said, 'How many little saviors have y'all thrown into the garbage can or flushed down the toilet? How many of you women who're out here calling *me* a bitch have had a little savior to die because of your just wanting to live free off the Welfare? And how many of you have lost your chance to raise up a little black savior by being kicked in the belly by your evil boyfriends or no-good husbands? And how many of you have lost your little saviors because you didn't *love* them enough to cherish them and keep them?'

"Because you see, gentlemen, I believe in my heart that one of their babies might have been meant for a savior or a great leader just as one of mine must surely have been meant to be—otherwise, why did I have three . . . been given *three*, when all *they* had was one? And then they wasted him and denied him his chance to lead the people? I told them that too, gentlemen. And I told them that I loved my babies and that I intended to keep them, no matter what *they* thought about it. So now you tell me, was I wrong? Tell me, gentlemen! You, the big, fine, Joe-Louisish–looking one! You don't have to tell me anything fancy, just tell me whatever it is you have to say to a black daughter of mother earth who broke down on these hard ole Washington, D.C., streets and cried!"

Moving forward on impulse, Hickman felt the resistance of hot bodies as suddenly he was drawn toward the stairs. He could see the woman waiting with lips pressed tightly together now, and above the confusion of his emotion he heard the hoarse, restricted sound of his own voice addressing her, thinking *What am I about to say? What can I—* Then hearing, "No, mam, you're not wrong! I'm not sure that I understand what you've been telling us, but I feel in my heart that you're not wrong. You've had an experience that most folks will never understand, one that many wouldn't *want* to understand— but it's not wrong, it's only confusing. So I take off my hat to you and I pray that you'll be blessed with peace and understanding. Because . . . because I believe that in all your confusion and pain you have seen the promise and the responsibility unafraid and it seems to me that you're reminding us of some things that we can't afford to forget. . . ."

"Oh, I knew it! I *knew* it," the cross-eyed woman said. And as he struggled to grasp the meaning of what he was still trying to say he saw her throw out her arms in his direction, causing the others on the stairs to move aside.

"I just knew that you'd say that," she called, "I knew that you'd understand. . . ."

Then nearby he heard Barnes asking, "Understand *what?* Now we have another one on our hands. I don't know this ole burly Negro from Adam's off ox, but I swear that he's as nutty as Maud! Next thing you know he'll be telling us how many babies *he's* done lost!"

And now as the hallway exploded with laughter Hickman saw Barnes turn to the white man, an expression of high indignation on his blustering face.

"Officer," he said, "you ought to throw them both into St. Elizabeth's— call for some straitjackets!"

Aware both of the cause for laughter and the troubling emotion beneath it, Hickman gazed sternly into Barnes' face during a noisy interval, silently taking in the reddish tint of the popped eyes, the moist, rough, pockmarked skin, the shiny forehead topped by the black nylon stocking cap. And even as he resisted the temptation to punch the man, calmly and dispassionately in his eye he suddenly felt himself giving way to a roar of hilarious laughter.

Run a chicken bone through the knot in that cap and he'd look like a cannibal king in a comic strip, he thought. *Yet give him half a chance and he'll run for public office and be telling everybody how to serve his God and grease his greens!* Then, as suddenly as it had begun, his laughter subsided and he stood shaking his head.

"Never mind this man," he said, smiling up at the cross-eyed woman. "Never mind him, Sister Maud, because he... well, I'm not allowed to call him a fool, but I think you'll understand if I call him a *clown....*"

"Yes, darlin', yes!"

"... So you just forget him and don't worry over his or anybody else's failure to understand what you've been trying to tell us. What happened to you has a deep meaning—a profound and *marvelous* meaning! I don't say that I understand it fully myself, but I tell you that I *feel* its meaning in my heart. It speaks to me beyond speech and I accept it. It says something comforting to me and I'm a stranger and so I believe that if only other folks will listen to it with their hearts it will give them comfort too. And so you should let it be a comfort to you. Never mind the clowns and cynics, folks like us just have to have the conviction and the faith of our dreams...."

"Oh, yes, darlin'," the woman cried, "Yes! I could hug you, for speaking those words of peace to my soul!"

And now as she started forward, attempting to descend the steps, Hickman saw her kimono swing apart, hearing a woman's voice saying, "Watch it, girl!" as he turned his head to see the white man gazing in openmouthed fascination toward the stairs.

"Oh, but I need more, darlin', more," she said, and as his eyes swung away from the white man he saw her stumble, causing her robe to slip and revealing a flat, thin, pitiful little breast, then found himself fixed again by the wild intensity of her cross-focusing eyes.

"Don't stop now, darlin', tell me some more. Tell me it isn't so! Tell me that I haven't lost my three little babies! Tell me it isn't! Tell me it ain't—you hear me, darlin'? Tell me, *tell* me! Hell, gentlemen, one of you *say* something! Let the other one, the short one, say something. Tell me that stone is stone gone stone! Tell me, I don't care! I can stand bad news, only tell the *truth!* Tell me that flesh is still flesh with the bone underneath it! Tell me, I say! Tell me that I'm not awake and standing on these stairs in the middle of the night! Tell me that I'm up there in my bed waiting for my righteous *bridegroom* with my three little babies beside me...."

And now Hickman saw Barnes swing toward the stairs, his eyes bulging with disbelief as he shouted, "Bridegroom! Dam' if she ain't took off again!"

"... Tell me, darlin's, that pretty soon my righteous bridegroom is going to come tipping down the hall with the pretty blue carpet on the floor and that the little pink roses will still be up there on the *wall*paper! Aaah, tell me, tell me!"

Editors' Note to "Bliss's Birth"

ELLISON SCRAWLED "BLISS'S BIRTH" across the top of the first page of this discrete thirty-eight-page manuscript next to a circle with the date 1965 written within, also in his hand. The opening passage dovetails with (and to some extent repeats) passages preceding and following the episode toward the end of Book II in which Hickman and his congregation visit the Lincoln Memorial. (As noted in the General Introduction, Ellison wrote a more essayistic version of this episode in the Hickman in Washington, D.C., fragment composed decades later on the computer.)

In any case, the "Bliss's Birth" episode is prominently mentioned in several of Ellison's notes. Once or twice he jotted marginal notes about where these pages might go. In each case his intention was to place them somewhere in Book II, an obvious choice since the episode is so central to the Hickman-Bliss relationship at the heart of Book II. The version published here contains Ellison's last handwritten revisions and emendations, and, judging from its own state and earlier drafts, constitutes his fully realized account of the tragic circumstances of Hickman's brother Robert's lynching and his mother's death shortly after her son's murder. The mother of Bliss is a white woman known to Hickman and his family who had fingered Robert Hickman to divert suspicion from the real father of her unborn child. Intending to burn alive the pregnant woman and himself in his mother's cabin, Hickman relents and finally, out of respect for life's continuity and power, delivers Bliss into the world.

The manuscript (Chapter 15 in *Juneteenth*) sows the seeds of the mystery of Bliss's parentage and the deep roots of Hickman's spiritual paternal love for the boy. It also recounts his turn from a jazzman of the world and of the flesh to one called by God to preach. Finally, the manuscript presents powerfully, sparely, and dramatically material that Ellison much later extended into long digressive passages. For example, in "Bliss's Birth" Janey writes

Hickman a short letter full of implications for the present threat to Bliss, now Senator Sunraider. But some two decades later Ellison turns this trenchant device of character and plot into a long rambling letter (see pages 666–675), more in his voice than Janey's, that chooses digression over acts advancing the plot.

In any case, Ellison's notes indicate that he intended to place "Bliss's Birth" somewhere within Book II.

BLISS'S BIRTH

AND I NAMED HIM Bliss, Hickman thought, shaking his head. Resting back in his chair now, his hands shading his eyes from the light, he stared sadly at the man on the bed. Lord, he thought, here he is at last, stretched out on his bed of pain. Maybe his dying bed. After flying so far and climbing so high and now here. Just look at him, Lord. Why does this have to be? I know it's supposed to be this way because in spite of all our prayers it is, still, why does it have to be? I'm tired; for the first time I feel *old*-tired, and that's the truth. And this is what's become of our Bliss.

He wasn't always ours and yet he first was mine. It wasn't easy either; far from easy. My hardest trial....

Hickman, maybe she was as Christian as she thought she was, maybe she was doing just what she had to do.... Then it seemed like Wickham said the Jews used to put it out there in K.C.; like killing your mother and father and then asking the court for mercy because you're an orphan.... Maybe she was driven, like those gamblers who couldn't stand to win. But just think about it—coming there wrapped in a black shawl through the rutted alley over all that broken glass shining in the starlight...past all those outhouses, yard dogs, and chicken coops, long after dark had come down. Coming into *that* house at a time like that. Having the nerve, the ignorant, arrogant nerve to come in there after all that had happened. Hickman, do you know that that was *something*? Talking about Eliza crossing the ice! Ha! But her—having the arrogance to come there after all that had happened.

Maybe she was innocent, Hickman.

Innocent?

I can't understand what people mean when they call somebody like her innocent. A man murders sixteen people on a city street at high noon he'd never seen before in his life, and they call him innocent? Maybe she had innocence in her but she was not of it. You couldn't believe it, could you?

The first, yes; all that about Mama and Bob, I could. Because that terrible story has happened to so many that it's new only when it happens to you and to yours. You get to live with it like the springtime storms. So that it gets to be part of your sense of what life is. You learn to live with it like a man learns to live with only one arm and still get his work done. But not the Bliss part, *that* was the stinger on the whip!

There you were, sitting again in the lamplit room feeling the weight of the rifle across your knees and a shotgun and two pistols on the table beside you; sitting dressed in your working tuxedo and your last white, iron-starched shirt, there staring into the blank wall at the end of time. Yes, and with death weighing down your mind. They'd already told you to get out of town, because you reminded them of what they'd done and you'd refused to go; yes, and maybe they recognized what it would cost some one or two of them at the least to force you, so after all those months you were still there. And instead of the end it was the beginning. Maybe it would help him to know. Yes, but in his condition it might *kill* him to know; the truth can humiliate those who refuse to meet it halfway. And I couldn't believe it myself when it was happening. You'd heard the expected knock on the door and said Come in with the rifle ready, taking a glance at the shotgun and the pistols on Mama's table and at her Bible open to where you'd written the record, hers and Bob's; and with your own all written down to the month, feeling that this was to be the month, and just waiting for some unknown hand to write in the date. It's still waiting, after all these years, thank you, Master— my best-loved Bible to this day.... I never thought of it before, but maybe it all began with my writing my death in the Book of Life, who knows? Yes, and with me sitting just like I'm sitting now.... It's like I've never gotten up or recognized her presence in all these elapsed years. Ha! Sitting there in death's dry kingdom preparing myself for seven months to take a few of them along with me. Yes, ready to write your name in blood and to go to hell to pay for it. Hickman, you were too big and black for anybody to ever have called callow, but, man, you were *young*! Waiting for more liquored-up, ganged-up violence to come get you—and then seeing her standing there. There, Lord, after the double funeral and all, you thought you were seeing an evil vision, didn't you, Hickman? Yes, indeed, or at least that I had dozed. I shot bolt upright in the chair. Yes, you sure did. Standing there, looking at me out of those hollow eyes; not saying a word. I thought, *If I take a deep breath it'll go away*, then she stretched out her hand and kind of fluttered her fingers and tried to speak and I knew she was real. Shot up with a pistol in my hand, no longer surprised as Bob must have been, just dead sure her being there meant more deathblood to flow, and dead set to drown her in it along with me. A church organist, come to think of it. I never thought about that before, but, Hickman, look at the pattern it makes.... Tall and wrapped in a black shawl like those Mexican women in mourning, shaking her head at my pistol like I was some child she'd come upon in the woods about to go after a bear with an air rifle, saying:

No, no, it won't help us, Alonzo Hickman; you and I, we're beyond help; I had to come. Have you a woman here, a wife? You'd better call her because there isn't much time.

Just like that. And I felt the pistol throbbing beneath my hand like a hungry hound that's sighted game. So she wants me too, it's not simply the men who want me. She got Mama and Robert and now she wants me. I'm supposed to be next. Less than seven months to pickle me in my pain and now she wants me. All right, if that's the deal, then all right. But she goes too. This time she'll lead the way.

There's not much time, she said.

All right.

Standing there, leaning—Lord, I can see her after all this time—leaning a little to one side with her fingers just touching the back of the chair as though she knew it was Mama's, and so to her a rocking accusation, and me looking across the room at those black-smudged eyes in that chalk-white face, not even a tint of rouge to give it the color even a corpse would have nowadays.... Me, looking at her and all dedicated to one last act and trying to hold on to my life and trying to live my life fully in those few seconds I felt I had left to live.... Oh, Hickman, you'd been a rover and a rounder, but man, you were *young*. Young? Wasn't even born! No, and you couldn't see the side of a church house: There the lamp on the table was telling you to look at the facts of life staring you dead in the face and you seeing only the white paperish mask above that black lace shawl; standing there with that heavy Colt forty-five so light in your hand that it seemed to be part of your own body, then her coming toward me casting the shadow across the floor and the opposite wall and then across me, and that was the first time I noticed that she was moving like a woman pushing a basket of clothes in a wheelbarrow—that slow, heavy-laden walk, yet swift in the mind's eye tightened with my feelings. Moving the omen or sign I couldn't read. Yes, coming like a sick woman carrying a Christmas gift under her coat to hide its shape from the children's eyes; seeing it floating before her as I raised my hand toward her and still could not accept what my eyes screamed to me was there and which my brain refused to deal with because it didn't want to give up its simple-minded interpretation of the scene as through a glass darkly. Like my eyes had jumped clean out of my head and flew up there beside Papa's picture on the wall and were just sticking there watching and recording and saving 'til later what I was trying to see through my fingers or my skin. Yes, my brain refusing to accept the bold-faced evidence because knowing that Bob hadn't been anywhere around and wasn't the type. So it doubly wasn't him, and so making her big-bellied ripeness a fact as meaningless to me as a mole on her shoulder blade beneath the shawl, or an offending tonsil that had been removed and dropped in a jar of alcohol when she was twelve years old.

And then we were joined together. Me without realizing it, sailing past the table with the lamp and the Bible and jamming the pistol barrel there where I knew the pain would wind slow and live and give birth to death long after I was beyond the revenge of screams.... *Rest, Bliss— Wonder why they don't give him something to really ease him?...*

Brother Bob, the only brother I had left; the good, true, and dutiful son to Mama while I the preacher's hellion son rambled and gambled out there in the Territory; in Joplin, St. Joe, and K.C. You, Hickman, that was you. Yes indeed. I had prayed for the end of her and all like her, and for revenge, and here, I thought, was the answer. How many have shriveled with that pain? It was for me to round out the order, to bring it to a halt, dead end. But all the time saying not a word to her, just thinking in snatches and hearing breathing sounds, hers and mine. Standing there gripping her neck in my hand like it was a base fiddle's and with the sight of the barrel pressing into the curving of her belly. Still refusing to recognize what it all meant. Just trying to feel it all as I saw it, so that I could say it all, so she could suffer it all and feel it keen in one red burst like an abscessed tooth at midnight on a highballing train. No relief. No red lights. No one to flag it down. So that she'd know what it meant to let loose all that old viciousness out of the pit to strike down some innocent man in his defenselessness; so that I could throw her upon the same old disgusting sacrificial altar on all the ignored blood still screaming there for justice. Ay, so that in my anger the high and mighty young priestess would for once sprawl where her victim fell.... But those must have been the terms that came afterwards, sitting in the chair; not then. Then was more blind feeling and thinking. I was swept backwards into deeper and older depths of living, down where the life had gone out of the air and only animals could breathe— Just why I didn't slap her backhanded across the room and kick her into a corner like a bouncer or a dance-hall floor-manager would have done any overbearing whore who'd interrupted a dance just to win herself some cheap notoriety at the expense of his good nature, I'll never know. Such I had learned to watch without flinching back there in those places where the music was more important than any violation of a woman's womanliness by a man's male strength. I was sure a big heathen, back there. *You sure were, although Lord knows you were taught better.* Yes, but it's a fact that those women knew that the consequences of fooling around like that was either a black eye, a lumped head, or a bruised behind. As Rush used to sing it, *Women all screaming murder. I never raised my hand....* But that would have been too personal, I was beyond just that, I was as a thousand in my ache for vengeance. So I *must* have been changing.... Old clock used to work by weights passing one another, up and down. Maybe the shock of their death *had* to change me if I was to live even a second after I heard the news. Maybe the shock was so great that I knew even in my tongue-tied condition of wickedness that there was a moment when all heaven and hell had come together to purge men with the pill of eternal judgment, emptying us just like those old Greek folks were emptied after they committed some of their God-cursing crimes. And, in fact, the same kind of crime it was and just as holy-horrible even though we ignore it and let it happen year after year after year and no punishment or hope for justice. Thy must regulate thyselves or take the pill. Ha, yes! But one day soon now it'll come back to us from strange places, seeking us out with sword and fire in a strange sunburned hand, saying, Here, you folks without recollection or feeling for the humiliation and the wasted blood, take some of old Dr. Time's Compound Cathartic.... *Thou shalt not bear false witness*— No, but that don't even begin to describe it, not what she did ... they do. Maybe something like that went on under the old skin of my brain back there. Ah, Bliss, would knowing the story have helped you? ... *With her breathing between my hands and me recognizing that here was more than we actually saw when we sat up there on the bandstand playing while they danced, or when we passed on the street and thought: That there now is a woman who flows with the moon and who squats in the morning like other women but who by law and custom can spread herself or smile only for those she knows as her own kind. She there is a woman who wills herself to believe that she's different from my women and better than my women simply by being born and not because of anything she can do that's more womanly or wifely or motherly, but who can prove she is what she's supposed to be when the chips are down only by letting hell yell rape from the pit between her thighs and then pointing her lying finger at me.* Talking about having the power of life and death! Maybe the shock of Bob's death—poor Mama was old and sick and wore out with trouble, so I had faced up to her leaving us before long, I had only hoped to see her once more before— But Bob, Lord, their doing that to him was such a shock that even in my lost condition I understood that even if she, there in the palm of my hand and curved hard against the pistol barrel, even if she were the finest of the fine, a lady fair and gentle-wayed was now become a pus pot slopping over with man's old calcified evil and corruption. What kind of love and respect is that—raised up like a golden cow just to plunge then in the raising lower than those poor whores performing daisy-chain circuses in dope-fiend cathouses and West Coast opium dens? Lower! Those poor lost souls couldn't touch the downright obscenity of one of these. Not even the ones who perverted themselves with dogs and goats before fly-specked spotlights for money and then moved from table to table lifting their tips from dirty, liquor-ringed tabletops with the shaved, raw, puffed, dry, slackmouthed lips of their corrupted and outraged businesses. Those shameless whores with their guts fish-mouthing for filthy old limp and wrinkled dollar bills that they had to straddle the corners of the tables and grind down to in order to retrieve. No, Hickman, not even these. And back there you had seen life raw. You had seen the bottom of the bucket and the hole in the bottom of the bucket and the cruel jagged edges of the hole. Yes, and seen the bitter lees lying on the bottom, the very dregs, and under the gritty bottom level of the dregs those poor lost souls. But none so lost and bound for perdition on Perdido Street could touch those who had been armed with the power to kill with *that* lying cry....

Lord, Hickman, I wonder what you'd done if she had been a man? You know what you would've done; that's why women could do so much good if they would, they're meant to make us men put on brakes, meant to break our headlong pace. Ay! but anyone seeing us that night would have been justified in calling for the straitjackets! This here is insanity, I told myself. This here is the instant before you foam at the mouth and bite off your tongue; the split second when you see the man pull the trigger just five feet away and you realize when still without pain that you have been hit because you can't hear the gun go off and then he's turning cartwheels with the gun still pointing straight at you.... In Tulsa, that was, and lucky I threw my trombone and the bullet went through my shoulder.... Oh yes, indeed. That was me back there—wild and reckless. Who used to hit the poolroom's swinging doors yelling,

> *Fe Fi Fo Fum*
> *Who wants to shoot the devil one?*
> *My name is Peter Wheatstraw,*
> *I'm the devil's son-in-law,*
> *Lord God Stingeroy!*

Both of us must have risen up about three feet off the floor and been standing there in the air by now, because no floor in Alabama could support such goings-on. No, and no one could live through it without some modification of his deepest soul. So I was already changing, I suppose. Hearing her saying like someone in a trance:

If you've got to do it, go ahead; only hurry. But it won't help either of us, Alonzo Hickman, it wouldn't help a bit and I'm not worth what it'll cost you....

And me repeating, *He didn't do it; Robert didn't do it and you know dam' well he didn't do it....*

That's right, I lied. You don't have to say it again because I acknowledge it.

Just breathing, nervous between my hands like a scaired convert standing chest-deep in the baptismal water. Then that word "lied" started banging around in my head. Like when you put a coin in one of those jukes, yes, and it takes a while before the machinery goes into action, then all of a sudden—wham! the red and blue lights go on and the sound comes blaring out.

Woman, is all you can say is that you lied? What's that word got to do with it? If you're going to use these last minutes to talk, then say something. Say you burned up all the cotton and polluted the water works. Say that you dried up all the cows; that you spread the hoof-and-mouth disease throughout the state and gave all the doctors the bleeding piles. Even that you brought everybody down with the galloping consumption and the sugar diabetes. But don't come here telling me that you lied. Everybody, including the littlest children, know that you lied—what's all this death got to do with the truth?

What? What?

Tell me that you're responsible for the Johnstown flood.

What?

. . . That you can stir up cyclones just by waving your naked heels in the air. Tell me that you breathe fire and brimstone from your belly every time the moon comes full—but don't come talking about you lied! Don't you realize what you did?

Yes. Shaking her head. Yes, can't you see that I'm here? I'm not a loose woman. . . . I'm from a good family. . . . I'm a Christian!

You're a *what?*

Yes, a *Christian.* I lied, yes. I bore false witness and caused death. Yes, and I'm a murderess. Can't you see that I understand? How could I help but know? I'm here. Can't you see, I'm *here. . . .*

And Lord knows, she was. . . .

You couldn't deal with that about her being a Christian, could you A.Z.? Ho, Ho! No, she could just as well said she was the head Chief Rabbi of Warsaw, or the Queen of Sheba . . . or Madame Sisseretta Jones. So I ignored that one.

I said: Why Bob? You've been knowing me from when we were children, but you didn't know him from Adam's off ox. . . .

But it wasn't him. I didn't wish to hurt him. Nor anyone. Can't you understand that, Alonzo Hickman? You have to try. He just didn't exist for me. He was just a name; just a name which by saying I could protect someone more precious to me than myself or mother and father, or anything he and I might have together. But I wanted only to protect my own. Not to destroy anybody. It was fate. Please, is there a woman here? There's very little time. . . .

A woman? Won't I be enough for you this time? Do you have to have another woman as well as another man? Don't you know that what you did has killed the only woman of this house, my mother?

Yes, I heard. You don't have to remind me. I'm here. I've put myself in your hands but it's still beyond the two of us. Still I tell you, if you don't hurry and shoot you'd better hurry and get a woman because you're going to have too much on your hands for any man. . . .

And even in the hard cold center of my anger I was confounded. I simply couldn't link all that death back to life. No, I couldn't fit the links into a chain. Said:

Another woman for what? To lay out our bodies? You want a woman for that? Don't worry about it, because I'm putting a hot bullet through that oil lamp sitting right there on the table. We won't need her. Besides, we'll both be in hell watching the confusion long before she could even get here.

Oh, I was already feasting on revenge and sacrifice, telling myself: Those eyes for Bob's eyes; that skin for Bob's flayed skin; those teeth for Bob's knocked-out teeth; those fingers for his dismembered hands. And remembering what they had done with their knives I asked myself, but what can I take that can replace his wasted seed and all that's now a barbaric souvenir floating in a fruit jar of alcohol and being shown off in their barbershops and lodge halls and in the judge's chambers down at the courthouse? And then beginning to really see, my own eyes betraying my aim and my understanding growing and making me say:

Bob's, You know damned well it can't be Bob's.

I tell you I didn't know him, she said. Can't you get a woman?

I said, whose is it, then?

All I can tell you is that it wasn't your brother. It's cost too much my trying not to tell to tell it now. But not his. He had nothing to do with it. . . .

Just like that. So Hickman, maybe *that's* when you started to change. It was like seeing all of a sudden the air falling apart so that you could recognize the separate gasses and molecules that made up its substance and which you'd have to see gather quick and mix together again if you meant to continue breathing. She had been protecting her secret and her man. That's all it was for her—all of that destruction just to deny that little growing bit of truth. Gone and set fire to the whole house just to hide where she'd spilled a little grease on the rug. Talk about all those lives ground up to build the pyramids, she'd have destroyed the nation just to protect her pride and reputation in that little old town. Slop the juice and cause a flood. Fire is more like it. So naturally she couldn't go to a doctor for help and in confidence. Not after screaming Robert's name, because then everybody would have yelled Bliss's question even before he could draw his first living breath. Just as surely as Mary had a baby, King Herod had him a daughter; thousands of 'em.

Where could she go? So not to her doctor, or to her pastor, both those ministering roles were scratched from the book and denied. Neither to her mother, nor to her father; nor to her sister or to any friends or kinfolks. Neither could she go to any maidservant, to no black cook or washerwoman, nor to any of our preachers, teachers, or doctors. The blind man could stand on the corner and cry, and folks would drop money in his cup so they could ignore his pain, but she bred and spread muteness and blindness and deafness. That poor girl had cut herself loose from both sides. She must have thought about each and every grown person in the whole town, like someone turning over each and every pebble on a mile-square stretch of seashore, hoping to find just one that would give her relief from that terrible loneliness. Misery doesn't just love company, it reaches out for its own through all the man-erected walls and then claims its own.

So *I* had to be the one. Me, the least likely, the anyone-else-but and she finally sifted the grains down to me. Oh, she could be wilful and blot Bob out without ever bothering to think that there was a body attached to his name and life in that body, and she could do it and be beyond the consequences. But now her own belly said Let the disgusting, foul-aired truth come clean, and it turned her wrong side out. Or maybe right side, because she must have had to have more than simple arrogant nerve to come there that night.

But to who else could she go, Hickman? Who but to the one who had suffered deep down to the bottom of the hole, down where there's nothing to do but come floating up lifting you in his own arms into the air, or die? Oh, John the Baptist was a diver into those lonely depths, I do believe. I *do* believe.... In all that frenzied agitated searching she must have been like a man being chased west so hard and fast that he stumbles and falls into the ocean and has either got to swim or sink. Don't tell me a human don't live by instinct when he reaches bottom, because when he's just about to go to pieces his instinct tries to guide him to where he can save himself. That's when God shows you his face. That's when in a split second you're about to be nothing and you have a flash of a chance to be something. She must have been sore desperate, like backed into the corner of a red-hot oven. Hickman, that was when your heart stopped beating like a run-down clock. Oh, yes; and that's when you got your first peep through the crack in the wall of life and saw hell laughing like a gang of drunk farmers watching a dogfight on a country road. All at once you were standing there smelling her sour, feverish, white woman's breath mixed up with that sweet soap they used to use and you were hearing the hellish yelling and tearing around and about of a million or so crazy folks. Ha, yes! That's when the alphabet in your poor brain was so shaken up that the letters started to fall out and spell "hope," "faith," and "charity"—it would take time for them to fall all the way into place, so you could recognize it, but it was beginning to happen. Yes, it was happening even while you were saying:

So now you come to me. Out of all the rest you come to me. I guess you think that old lady who died doesn't mean anything to me because she was only a black man's old worn-out mother who was soon to die anyway. I guess I'm supposed to forget about her. So now here you come to me after all that to demand that I get you aid to perpetuate all that you have done without even thinking. So I'm to stand here on the spot and switch over from the animal you consider me to be to the human you've decided I could never be, so that I can be understanding and forgiving—woman, do you think I'm Jesus Christ? Do you think a man like me is even interested in the idea of trying to be Christlike? Hell, my papa was a preacher while I'm a horn-blowing gambler. Do you think that after being the son of a black preacher in this swamp of a country I'd let you put me in the position of trying to act like Christ? Make it easy for you to destroy mine and me without even the need to remember, and humiliate mine and me and, dam' you, expect me to understand and forgive you and then minister to your needs? Destroy me and mine so that you can cast me down into corruption and the grave and then dig me up next week so that I can serve you? Tell me, what kind of endless, bottomless, blind store of forgiveness and understanding am I supposed to have? Just tell me where I'm supposed to carry it. What kind of meat and bread am I supposed to eat in order to nourish it?

Hickman, you didn't know it at the time but when you started talking she had shifted out of your hands and put you into hers. She really had you then. You were talking so fast you were foaming at the mouth, but that instinct and life inside her had reached out and tagged you and you were "it." A pair of purple smears sagging shuteyed in my hands and me standing there holding her and unable to let her fall. If we ever learn to feel real revulsion of the flesh—any flesh—that's when hell will truly erupt down here and the whole unhappy history become an insane waste; if we ever learn to hate the mere rind in the same way we ignore the spirit and the heart and the hopeful possibility underneath.... And there I stood—me, cursing her for using a woman's weakness as a club to kill me there and to deny me anger and hate because I was my mother's boy child and my father's son who they had brought up on the ideas and standards that made any human beings bearable one to the other.... That woman, coming there using my very black manhood to deny me grief and to deny me love and to deny me thirst and hunger and weakness and hope and joy—denying me even denial and rejection and contempt and vindictiveness against any claim her kind had upon mine... denying me even the need for anger or life. There she'd been feeding two for all those months and now sagging in my hands like the shadow of some little ole frightened bird about to take off and fly.

And then it really started, and me still cursing but helpless before the rhythm of those pains that started pulsing from him to her to me, as though some coked-up drummer was beating his snares inside her belly and I was being forced against my will to play or dance, and dance or play, even if I had nothing left but bleeding stumps for arms and legs. Me, a full-grown man crying, "Mama, Mama," with tears running down my face, while I was getting her to bed. Me, crying helpless at a time like that, as though my body had somehow to register a protest against what I was being forced to do, and getting her into Mama's bed and starting to uncover all that that Bob had died for not even thinking about uncovering: white and blue-veined and bulging like that boa constrictor I saw back there during my days with the circus band, after it had swallowed a lamb. Yes, and went about dressing her just the same in one of Mama's gowns. Then going on to tear up Mama's sheets, and pouring the water I'd heated for my own last bath in case the men had come.... Yes, almost convinced that I was in a dream. Too mad and outraged now to be afraid that she had been followed and still determined to make small-town history in blood. Determined after letting out the life that bulged her belly to let out the life that had drained me dry of love.

Oh, ashamed too; shamed and too outraged with myself to call a woman to come do the midwife's work. Asking myself, Man, where's your dignity, where's your pride? Where, at what point is my hate spilling out between my hands and my determination? What do you *call this* situation? Who's doing this to me? Who's got me hypnotized? And all the while doing the whole thing myself in spite of myself: Holding the damp cloth to her brow and placing the pillow beneath her quivering backside to ease and aid the flesh in its quaking and quickening and holding firm to her weaving hands while she gave birth to that bawling, boiled-red and glistening baby flesh. Watching my own big black hands going in and out of those forbidden places, ha! into the rushing fluids and despising it all. No mercy in my heart, Lord, no! Only the choking strangulation of some cord of kinship stronger and deeper than blood, hate, or heartbreak. And stopped from killing the two of us only by the third that was coming screaming in all his innocent-evil bewilderment into that deathhouse.... Ho! if anyone passing in the night had heard him cry.... They had me battling against myself, but I went all the way, I suppose by then to prove to myself, even to the Lord, that I was mean enough to play the cards that life had dealt me and still stick to my will. They say a doctor is a butcher underneath; it's a wonder I didn't try to use those pistol barrels for forceps. No, but I took Papa's old straight-edged razor and boiled the blade to sterilize it and divided the fruit from the tree. Yes, and tied up his navel cord with Mama's embroidery thread, fixed his first belly band. Him, Bliss. Wiped his unseeing eyes and anointed his body with oil. You, Bliss. I wrapped you in the sheet around and placed you in the crook of her sleeping arm and saw her try after all of that to smile. Her face all beaded over with sweat and I wiped that too away; then sat way back in Mama's rocking chair, just looking at them dazed and defiant.

I was too tired to sleep or rest and my mind wouldn't stop. There she was, relieved of her burden and sleeping like a peaceful child, and him beside her with his little fists already balled up for the fight of life. I couldn't look at him too steady either. There was that one bright drop of blood on the white sheet and I watched it growing dark, thinking: Now there's two, one to accuse me and the other to hang me; one to point the finger and the other to rise up and shoot me down, or pull the rope to break my neck. Yes, and because of these there is no one of my own to come cut me down. There they are in Mama's own bed, outraged and outrageous. I started thinking about those old Hebrew soldiers who use to leave their prisoners castrated on the battlefield—but for what Jehovah could I even play Abraham to that little Isaac? Lord, my eyes must've been bloodshot with my thoughts and frustrations. And there Bliss was, puckered up and so new he looked like if you were to drop him he would bounce like a rubber ball. . . .

How long did I sit there? Nobody would come to mark the passage of time and I had long ago drawn the shades and let the clock run down and she'd made me a pariah even to my own. Pariah and midwife too, and raped me of my will and my manhood. Dehumanized my human needs. Told myself, it won't stop here. When she gets her strength she'll scream again. Yes, but now the life is out of there and she'd beat me with a little child. . . . *Hickman, you were crazy.* Yes, but I was sane too; because what I thought there was true, though it took time to learn it in. She had torn me out of my heathen freedom so she could save herself, that was the truth. And all with that baby. With just that little seven-pound rabbit. Not even a few minutes of pleasure or relief either. Which was the last thing I would have thought about. She wasn't even good-looking, with that thin nose and high forehead; with just that ugly-sounding way of talking through her lips and nostrils. I knew her before her skirts went down, gangle-legging along the street like a newborn foal, trying to walk with class. And him not even brown so that I could have made some sensible meaning out of her coming here to me; just nothing definite, just baby-mouse-red and wrinkled up like a monkey with a strawberry rash. And me such a slave to what a human is suppose to be that I couldn't refuse to help him into the world. Helped him when I should, according to the way I felt then, have left him stranded and choking with the cord wrapped around his neck when her mammy-waters burst.

Now she's sleeping, I thought. Now she's in her woman's exhaustion, resting out of time like a stranger to both good and evil—while here I am, tired and feeling with no relief or rest inside me or outside me. She, resting up so she can scream again and they'll hear it all the way to the State House. Yes, but now the life is out I'm going to put us all to sleep. I mean to clear the earth of just this one bit of corruption. Which is all one can do, just clean up his own mess or that which is dumped on top of him when he has the chance. . . . Just look at them sleeping there, fruit of all this old cancerous wrong. Why isn't he brown or black or kinky, so that I could see some logic in her coming here? At least allow me to see the logic of a mare neighing help from a groom who happened to be passing her stall during her foaling time. Oh no, but coming here to me . . . Easy, Hickman, don't fight old battles. Maybe it was the way the sacred decided to show Himself. Would you at this age still criticize God?

Lord, oh Lord, you must have been preparing me all those twenty-six years for that ordeal; giving me this great tub of guts and muscle and deep, windy lungs and this big keg-sized head and all that animal strength I used to have and which I thought was simply meant for holding all the food and drink I loved so well and to contain all the wind necessary to blow my horn and to sing all night long, sure; and for the enjoyment of women and the pleasures of sin.... Ah, but right then and there I learned that you had really given me all that simply so I could contain and survive all I was to feel sitting there through those awful hours. Just sitting there and hating. Just sitting there looking at the two generations of them in the ease of their sleeping, and thinking back three generations more of my people's tribulations and trying to solve the puzzle of that long-drawn-out continuation of abuse. That and why the three of us were thrown together in my house of shame and sorrow. It was a brain-breaker and a caustic in the naked eye all right, and the longer I sat there the stranger it seemed. I guess it couldn't have been stranger than if one of Job's boils had started addressing him, saying, "Look here now, Job; this here is your head-chief boil speaking to you. You just tell me my name and I'll jump off of your neck and take all the rest of the boils along with me." Yes, and ole Job so used to trouble and straitjacketed in misery by then to even be surprised to learn that a boil could talk—even one of *his* boils—only wondering why his skin or hair or toenails or something didn't speak up and tell the boil to be silent in the presence of the Lord. Because, Master, you must have been there with me at the time and probably with a sad smile on your face. Even after Mama and Robert it was like waking up on mornings in some Territory town like Guthrie in the old days and discovering that my trombone mouthpiece had grown to my lips and my good right arm changed into a slide, but with no bell anywhere to let out the sound...Hickman, you were in a fix. You and those two strangers in the most unlikely place in the world and you the strangest of all.

Yes, with the baby mewling and raising the dickens and me having to put him to that thin, white, blue-veined tit to suck. Yes, having to guide his red little gums to that blighted raspberry of a nipple so I wouldn't have to listen to him crying for a while. And my having to be gentle, not like a nursemaid who loves a child enough to give it a good hard pinch in the side when it vexes her too much, but just because of the murder in my heart having to be gentlest of the gentle. Just because he was a baby and me a man full of hate; and gentle with her because aside from everything else, she was a mother lying in the bed where my own mother had once lain. It was like the Lord had said, "Hickman, I'm starting you out right here—with the flesh and with Eden and Christmas squeezed together. Never mind the spirit and justice and right and wrong—or time—just now you're outside all that because this is a beginning. So, starting right here, what will you do about the *flesh?* That's what you have to wrestle with." He had called me and I had nothing in the hole and was in too far to pass and still couldn't take the trick by using the baby's life as my ace, no matter whether he were dealt in spades or in hearts.

So now I had to cook for her. Go out and get that little boy, Raymond, to go bring me milk and bread and meat from the store, pretending it was for his mama, and me picking the vegetables that Robert had planted for Mama's needs and then stand over the stove and prepare the meal and then feed it to her spoon by spoon. Yeah, and remembering, *A little bit of poison helped her along,* that old slave-time line, and coming as close to breaking out of my despair and grinning as I ever did for a long, long time. But still granting nothing to the facts. So all right, I told myself, you're just fattening her for the time she can understand what she did and pay for it. You just be patient, just count the rest until your solo comes up. This rhythm won't stop until you take your break, just keep counting the one-two-three-fours, the two-two-three-fours, the three-two-three-fours...

So I didn't eat, only took water and a few sips of whiskey, never leaving the house, knocking on the windowpane in the afternoons to get little Raymond to go to the store, or to stand out on the back porch in the dark to get some fresh air. And with all that feeding and clumsy grudging ministering to them I wouldn't let myself think a second about life and living, only about dying. About how to kill and the way our bodies would look when they found us. And the quickest way to get it over with, how the flames would announce the news in the night, whether to just let them find us or to have little Raymond take a note to Mama's pastor to tell the folks to keep off the streets....

Everything, but never whether I could save myself because that would have meant to run and I didn't believe I had anything left to run for.

Ah, but Hickman, you were caught deaf and blind. With eyes that saw not, and ears that heard nothing but the drums of revenge. And there was that baby growing more human every second nudging his way into your awareness and making his claim upon you, and her crying all the time—in fact, more than the baby did. You had fallen into the great hole and they'd dropped the shuck in on you. There was simply too much building up inside of you for clear vision. I guess if I could have played I might have found some relief, but I couldn't play, even if I hadn't left my horn in Dallas when I got the word. And I couldn't sing and if I had after all she'd done to me I'd probably sung falsetto. Then came the day...

Poor Bliss, the terrible thing is that even if I told you all this, I still couldn't tell who your daddy was, or even if you have any of our blood in your veins.... Like when I was a boy and guessed the number of all those beans in that jar they had in that grocery window and they wouldn't give me the prize because one wasn't a bean, they said, but a rock! What a bunch of rascals, Ha! Ha! So outrageous that I just grinned and they had to laugh at their own bogusness. Gave me a candy bar. . . . No, I'd still have to tell him as I told myself in the days that were to come: that who the man was was made beside the point by all that happened. Bliss started right there in that pain-filled room—or back when the fish grew lungs and left the sea. You don't reject Jesus because somebody calls Joseph a confidence man or Mary a whore; the spears and the cross and the crime were real and so was the pain. . . . So then came the day when I started in from the kitchen to find her sitting on the side of the bed, her bare boney feet on the bare boards of the floor as she sat there all heavy-breasted in Mama's flannel nightgown; her hair swinging over her shoulder in one big braid and with eyes all pale in her sallow skin; and all weak-voiced, saying:

Listen, Alonzo Hickman, the time has come for me to leave.

Leave, I said, who told you you were ever going to leave here?

Yes, I know, but he's growing to me too fast. So if I'm ever to leave I must do it now.

What makes you think . . .

No, let me tell you why I came here. . . .

Yes, I said. As though I don't know already; you tell me. Just why, other than the fact that you had no damn where else to turn?

Don't you be so sure, Alonzo Hickman. And don't quarrel with me after helping me. There's more to it than you think. . . .

So why? I'm listening.

I came to give you back your brother, do you understand?

You *what*!

Yes, it's true. I never knew your brother and I meant him no special harm. It was just that I am what I am and I was in trouble and so desperate that I couldn't feel beyond my heart. You must understand, because it's true and it's a truth that's cost us both all this. —No, let me finish. So now you must take the baby . . .

WHO?

. . . Take him and keep him and bring him up as your own.

WHO? I said, looking at her feet, that braid swinging across her breast. . . . WHO?

It's the only way, Alonzo Hickman. And don't just stand there in that doorway saying "who" like that. Who else can save us both? I mean you. It's the only way. After what I've done you'll need to have him as much as I need to give him up. Take him, let him share your Negro life and whatever it is that allowed you to help us all these days. Let him learn to share the forgiveness your life has taught you to squeeze from it. No, listen: I've learned something, you won't believe me, but I have. You'll see. And you'll need him to help prevent you from destroying yourself with bitterness. With me he'll only be the cause of more trouble and shame and later it'll hurt him. . . .

And you expect me...

Yes, and you can. You have the strength and the breadth of spirit. I didn't know it when I came here, I was just desperate. But I've seen you hold him, I've caught the look in your eyes. Yes, you can do it. Few could but you can. So I want you to have him—and don't think I don't love him already at least as much as I love my own mother, or that I don't love his father. I do, only his father doesn't know about him; he's far away, and unless I do something to undo a little of what I've done there'll never be a chance for us. I could go to him— Oh, Alonzo Hickman, nothing ever stops; it divides and multiplies, and I guess sometimes it gets ground down to superfine, but it doesn't just blow away. Certainly none of the things between us shall. So you must take him. Later there'll be money and I'll get it to you. I'll help you bring him up and pay for his education. Somewhere in the North, maybe. He'll be intelligent like his father and he deserves a chance... and I'll see that you're taken care of....

And I thought, so now I've got to be a pimp too. First animal, then nurse-maid, and now pimp, seeing her shake her head again:

No, please don't speak yet. I must do this for both of us....

And you think that that child there can do all that?

No, but he's all I have—unless you still want my life. And if you take that somebody will still have to take him. You don't just help a child to be born and then leave it alone. So very well, if you mean to kill me, all right, but could you destroy something as weak as that, as helpless as that?

I have killed snakes.

A snake? Can you even with death in your eyes call him a snake? Can you? Can you, Alonzo Hickman?

Ha! Hickman, and you couldn't. No, but if your heart had been weak I would have died right there of the sheer, downright nerve of it. Here I had been pushed even in Alabama. Well, God never fixed the dice against anybody, we have to believe that. His way may be mysterious but he's got no grudge against the infants, not even the misbegotten. It's a wonder I didn't split right down the middle and step out of my old skin right then and there; because even after all these years I don't see how I stood there in that doorway and took it all without exploding. And yet, there we were, talking calm and low like two folks who arrived late at the services and were waiting in the vestibule of the church. She sitting on the edge of the bed, kinda leaning forward, with arms spread out to the side and gripping the bedclothes to support herself. Still weak but with her crazy woman's mind all set. And me, telling myself that I was waiting to learn just how far she intended to follow the trail of talk she'd blazed before I would set the house afire, saying:

So supposing I say all right—what are you going to call him?

You mean what shall we name him?

Yes.

It's not for me to do, he's yours now. But why not Robert Hickman?

No!

Then just Robert, and you give him a last name. But I name him Robert as he should be....

Just like that. She couldn't face life with him, wanted to give him to me but wanted me to always remember all the circumstances that brought him to me. So there it was. Like a payday, when all the sweating and aching labor that went into a dirty job is reduced to some pieces of dirty paper and silver and coppers, which the hateful bossman handed to you in a little white envelope. As though that was the end of it and Monday would never come to start you out all over again. It was too much for me. I just listened to her and then backed out of the doorway and went and lay down and tried to think it clear. Ha! Hickman, you had wanted a life for a life and the relief of drowning your humiliation and grief in blood, and now this flawed-hearted woman was offering you two lives, your own, and his young life to train. Here was a chance to prove that there was something in this world stronger than all their ignorant superstition about blood and ghosts—as though half a town was a stud farm and the other half a jungle. Maybe the baby *could* redeem her and me my failure of revenge and my softness of heart, and help us all (was it here, Hickman, that you began to dream?). Either that or lead him along the trail where I had been and watch him grow into the wickedness his folks had mapped out for him. I thought, *I'll call him Bliss, because they say that's what ignorance is.* Yes, and little did I realize that it was the name of the old heathen life I had already lost.

So she got her way. She asked the impossible of a bitter man and it worked; I let her walk out of that house and disappear. Let her stay around and nurse the baby until dark, four or five hours more, and still let her leave. Let her come in crying and put him in my arms then walk out of the back door and gone. Oh, thank the Lord, I let her. Ah, but who but those who know life would believe that out of that came this? That out of that bed came this bed; that out of that sitting and a-rocking came this remembering, and this gold cross on my old watch chain?

That was the end of the old life for me, though I didn't know it at the time. But what does a man ever know about what's happening to him? She came in there heavy and when she went out I had his weight on *my* hands. What on earth was I going to do with a baby? I wasn't done with rambling, the boys were waiting for me out in Dallas. I hadn't ever met a woman I thought I'd want to marry, and later when I did she wouldn't have me because she insisted I had been laying around with a white gal because she thought I was traveling with a half-white baby. So not only had the woman placed a child on my hands, she made me a bachelor. And maybe after that night, after seeing what a woman could be, after that revelation of their boundless nerve and infinite will to turn a man's feelings into mush and rubber, I had lost the true will to join with one forever in matrimony. I was still young and full of strength but after that I could only come so close and no closer. I had been hit but I hadn't discovered how bad was the damage. Master, did you smile? Did you say, "Where's your pride now, young man?" Did you say, *"How now, Hickman, can you hear my lambs a-crying? You've got to do something, son; you can't stand on the air much longer. How now, Hickman?"*

And didn't I try to get away! I must have sat there for hours, numbed. Then when the realization struck me I got up and put him in the bed with a bottle and went to Beaulah's and ordered a pitcher of corn, broke in the door because she didn't want me in there and all the others leaving when they saw who I was. And I drank it and couldn't feel it so I left there. And walking down the railroad tracks, between the two shining rails not caring if a manifest struck me down or if I could get to Atlanta in one piece, stumbling between the gleaming rails like a man in a trance. Then finding myself at Jack's place and beginning to shoot craps with those farmhands and winning all the money and having to break that one-eyed boy's arm when he came at me with his blade after my winning with their own dice. Then stumbling out of there into another dive and then another, drinking and brawling, but always seeing that baby reaching out for me with his little hands that were growing stronger and stronger the farther I moved away from him. 'Til I could feel him snatching me back to the room as a dog leaping the length of his chain is snatched back to the stake driven in the ground.

That little ole baby, that lil' ole Bliss. So I had to go back and get him. Made up my mind. Slept all day and left the next night with him in a satchel. That was the beginning. Took him to Mobile where we stayed in a shack on the river. And him getting sick there, almost dying, and getting him a doctor and pulling him through with the help of God; still mixed up over why I was trying to save him but needing to bad enough to learn to pray. The Master must have really smiled then, but I was still trying to leap my chain. Running out of money in Dallas because the boys were afraid to play with me because they had heard about Robert and Mama and then I show up with the baby and they didn't know who would come looking for me and I wouldn't explain a thing. Pride, that's what it was, but I said that if they couldn't take me back for my way with a horn then they didn't need to know anything else about me. So I shined shoes and I swept the floors and cleaned the spittoons in that barbershop and paid for our room and his milk and my whiskey. Then Felix came and told me about Reverend McDuffie being in town and needing a musician for his tent meetings and I began playing my music for the Lord. That was Bliss then. He couldn't remember any of that even if he hadn't willed himself to forget us; now it was too far back. I lied that he was my dead sister's child and the ladies were kind and looked after him while I played and we were always traveling and that made it easier for me. Then a year old and never from my side, me still mixed up in my emotions about him but always having him with me.... Had to leave Memphis on a freight train once and just managed to grab a bottle of milk to feed him and them right behind me for kidnapping, running over those cinders with him under my arm like a bear cutting out with a squealing pig. Lord, but I could really pick 'em up and put 'em down in those days, kicking up dust for a fare-thee-well and making that last boxcar just in time. Poor little fellow, he didn't know what it was all about. Stripped the paper from the boxcar walls to make him a bed, then setting there with the car bumping under me wondering why I hadn't let them have him and be free.... But what could I have told them, when any part of the truth meant trouble? Master, did you grin? So we went rolling through the land over the rhythm of those wheels clicking along the tracks and when he started to cry, me lullabying him *"Make Me a Pallet on the Floor"* 'til we were long gone to Waycross.

Then gradually beginning to find my way, finding the path in the fog, getting my feet on the earth and my head in the sky. Yes, my heathen freedom gone, I followed the only thing I really knew about, my music. Followed it, right into the pulpit at last. Had found a sanctuary where all babies could grow without too much questioning as to where they came from. After all, I testified to my sins before a crowd and sat down at the welcome table and learned to open up my heart—and I was heard.

They took us in and they loved him. That was Bliss then. All the love we gave him. Now no trust for me; none of us, even though we kept the faith through all those watchful and gravelling years. We held steady, stood firm in face of everything; even after he ran away and we picked up his trail. I had been claimed by then and they loved him. Foolish to do but all those from the old evangelizing days felt the same need I felt to watch him travel and to hope for him and to learn. Yes, I guess we've been like a bunch of decrepit detectives trailing out of love. We didn't even have to think about it or talk it over, we all just missed him and keep talking about him and seeking for him and there. Lord, but we missed little Bliss. We missed his promise, I guess, and we were full of sorrow over his leaving us that way, just up and gone without a word. So we kept looking for him and telling all those who had heard him when he was traveling with me throughout the country to keep a lookout. Some thought he had been kidnapped and some that he was dead, and others that his people had come and taken him away—though they didn't know who his people were and were too respectful to ask me about him.

So we started looking and asking questions, all the chauffeurs and Pullman porters and waiters, anybody who traveled in their work—'til finally we picked up his trail again and I knew that it wouldn't do any good to go to him and say Come home, we miss you, Bliss; and we need you. Oh no, he was on another track by then and it was up to him to miss us in his heart and need us. So we just watched and waited.

Someone was always near him to watch him; maids and butlers, dining-car waiters, cooks—anybody who traveled, anybody who could keep him in our sights. Even a few of the younger ones were recruited; a few every year or so given hints that he was one of us, telling them just enough so that they could feel the mystery and start to watching him and reporting back. And all of it building up our amazement. Even when what he did left our hopes pretty weak. I guess we hoped for the prodigal's return. But in a country like this, where prodigal boys have so much that they can do and get that they can never waste it all and which makes it easier for them to forget where home is and that made our hoping and waiting a true test of our faith or at least our love. There he lies, worth about three million dollars, I understand, and ran away with five saved dollars and a leather-bound Bible. Lord, I could laugh at the "laugh-cry" of it and I could cry sure enough right now. I was pretty bad when that child started shooting, pretty hysterical. But Lord forgive me for violating my manliness, because it was little Bliss I saw going down. Instead of this one lying here I saw a little boy with the white Bible as in a waking vision. I'm getting old, but how is a man who's had to do with children but only had one child supposed to act when he sees such as we were witness to? Yes, and who'll be a witness for my grief, my awful burden? Who, when nobody knows the full story? Still the old-timers were with me and they prayed that he'd find his way back home! Bliss. All the old ones and some of the young and some of the old ones committed so long ago, many forgot just why, but still. We came when we sensed the circle was closing in upon him. Poor Bliss, he had wrapped up his heart in steel, stainless steel, and I guess he'd put his memory down there in Fort Knox with all that gold. He wouldn't see us and he only had to remember us as we were and as he was to know that we didn't come here to rebuke him, his own heart would do enough of that, considering the line he's been taking against our people all these years. Still, that too is the way of man, so he couldn't trust even me, even though I told him way back when he seemed bent on leaving us that I would live a long time and that I would arrive in his presence when he was in sore need. And I tried. We arrived and he didn't trust me enough to see me. So why'd we come, why'd we hold on so hard to hope? What about this, Master? Is this one more test of faith put to us in our old days, or just our own foolishness, just some knotted strings of slavery-time weakness still clinging to us?

Well, that is what the baby boy became and there's no denying. Poor fellow, poor Bliss lost. He's lying there twitching and groaning and I can only talk and sit and wait. We're with you, Bliss. We arrived just as we said we would, way back there when you put us down. I don't know, Hickman, maybe the real one, the true Bliss got lost and this is somebody else. Because during all that time we could never ask if he really were the true son even though we knew in our heart he ought to be. Maybe we've been following the wrong man all this time. Naw, Hickman, you're tired, *this* was Bliss. There's no doubt about that. It's him and there lies the nation on its groaning bed. Those Georgia politicians knew it twenty years or so ago, when they tried to make me admit our ties. Sure, and I lied and denied so he could climb higher into the hills of power hoping that he'd find security and in his security and power he'd find his memory and with memory use his power for the good of everyone. Oh yes, he's the one, Hickman, you won't get out of it that easy. You can't stop now by calling it all foolishness. Those politicians didn't threaten you for being foolish, they were playing for keeps. That's why they threatened to run you out of town. Well, I had been run out of better towns by then, sometimes with little Bliss with me, and always my sanctuary was the Word. Anyway, there was nothing to lose as there's nothing to lose now and the sheer amazement of God's way is a wonder and well worth it. Let me laugh, I see the links in the chain. Bliss had to bribe and deny and deny and bribe somebody to get in the position he's in. They know it and I know it, only they don't know all I know. Just like I know that I had nothing to lose when they threatened me and that they probably made a deal back there, because Bliss did turn into this, there. Rest, boy. Lord, I wish I could reach him. That doctor ought to be coming in to look at him pretty soon. Janey. After all those long years, Janey writing me that something was brewing:

Dear Brother Alonzo, a young man I know about is come hereabouts from far away and after a long time. You will know who I mean. So I think you ought to know that he's stirring up old ashes and turning over old stones and he is taking down true names and asking questions. I know you will want to know about this because I am too old now to put him off for much longer. I mean he's pressing me too hard. I have dreaded it but it had to come. I always knowed it would. Brother Alonzo I'm not strong like I used to be and I have trouble keeping quiet. I betrayed him once a long time past and now I think my time is closing down. So I hope everything is all right with you and I know you will do what you can. May the good Lord be with you and all our old friends. May he rest you and keep you and them in faith. Tell them that I'm still praying on my bended knees. Tell them I'm remembering them all in my prayers. Your sister in Christ, Janey Mason. . . .

I had to think about that one. I remember Janey from way back there in my heathen days, long before Bliss came. Riding out of the bottoms during that springtime flood on a dripping horse with five little children rowed behind her and holding on to her nightgown and to each other while she swam that horse out of the swift water and her bare heels against his belly barrel 'til he came on up to higher ground. Talking comfort to those children with weeds in her hair. Saved all of 'em too. Walnut Grove. That was a woman. Oh yes. She roused me then too, up there looking, standing on the bank of mud and silt. Oh yes, in that wet nightgown she roused me. It wasn't long before Bliss either, though I didn't know it. I was on the verge of change— Oh, how odd of God to choose—yet playing Cotch and Georgia Skin or Tonk every night I wasn't gigging or playing dances in that hall overlooking the railroad tracks, blowing out my strength and passion against those east- and west-bound trains. No little Bliss then, but a lot of easy living in that frontier town. This I could tell him, since he wandered there years later. A lot of half-Indian Negroes, those "Natives," they called them, and a bunch of hustlers and good-time gals. What times; what hard, young, wasteful living. Used to put a number two washtub full of corn on the table and drink your fill for a dime a dipperful. And there was Ferguson's barbecued ribs with that good hot sauce, yes; and Pulhams. "Gimme a breast of Guinea hen," I'd say, "And make the hot sauce sizzling." All that old foolishness. Ha! Me a strapping young horn-blowing fool with an appetite like a bear and trying to blow all life through the bell of a brass trombone. Belly-rubbing, dancing, and a-stomping off the numbers and everybody trying to give the music a drive like those express trains. Shaking the bandstand with my big feet, and the boys romping by midnight and jelly-jelly-jelly in the crowd until the whole house rocked. I should tell him about those times, maybe it was the self-denial that turned him away. Maybe he should have known all the wildness we had to bring to heel. Surely the Lord makes an allowance for all that, when you're in the heat of youth. He gave it to me, didn't he, and it was the new country which he gave us, the Indian Nation and the Territory then, and everything wide open and hopeful. You have to scream once maybe so you can know what it means to forbear screaming. That Choc beer, how I ex-ulted in that; rich and fruity mellow. A communion there, back there in that life. Its own communion and fellowship. That Texas white boy who was al-ways hanging around 'til he was like one of us, he knew it. *Tex, why you always out here hanging around with us all the time? You could be President, you know.*

Yeah, but what's the White House got that's better than what's right here?

Maybe Bliss could tell him. Old Tex. Heard he struck oil in his daddy's cotton patch but I hope he's still a witness for the good times we had. Forget the name of that State Negro with the Indian face . . . a schoolteacher, tall man, always smoking Granger Rough Cut in his pipe and talking politics and the Constitution? From Tennessee, walked all the way from Gallatin leading a whole party of relatives and friends and no preacher either. That scar on my skull to this day from going to the polls with axe handles and pistols, some whites and Indians with us, and battling for the right. Long back, now

Oklahoma's just a song, but they don't sing about that. Naw, and why not, since that's what they want to forget. Run up a skyscraper and forget about the foundation, just hope there's oil waiting to get into the water pipes. Yeah, but we got it all in the music. They listen but hear not, they feel its call, but they act not. Drink of the Waters of Life, He said. And I drank until He sent the child and I realized that I had to change. Then I drank again of the true water, I had to change so the sound of life, the life I felt in me and in the others could become words and it's still too complicated for definition. But like the Lord Himself, I loved those sinners and I'll not deny even one. They had the juice of deep life in them, and I learned to praise it to the transcending heat. Who knows, His ways are strange ways, Hickman. Maybe it was all His plan, you had to be what you were then in order to lead his flock. It took all of that to come to this, and little Bliss was the father to the man and the man was also me....

PART II

Introduction to Ralph Ellison's
Computer Sequences

In 1982 RALPH ELLISON shifted composition of his novel-in-progress from typewriter to computer and continued to create and save files until late December 1993. Word processing was his primary means of writing during those years, not simply for the second novel but for essays, lectures, and personal correspondence. Ellison was among the first prominent authors to recognize the computer's utility for the craft of fiction. The thousands of pages in hundreds of files constitute something unprecedented in American literature: an intricate if unfinished textual puzzle for the digital age.

During the decade, using three computers, Ellison amassed over 3,000 pages in 469 files on 83 disks.* The files range in length from a single paragraph to dozens of pages. Ellison named each by character or some other distinguishing aspect of scene, grouping some episodically on disk but leaving many dispersed in no discernible order throughout the archive. As in the earlier typescripts from the 1960s and 1970s, he left no comprehensive table of contents, though several partial ones provide incomplete but essential clues to narrative sequence. The Ralph Ellison Papers at the Library of Congress include among many holdings Ellison's own computer printouts from the novel, some with significant handwritten edits, the vast majority undated. The computers and disks themselves have been retained by the Ellison estate.

Without scholarly intervention, what Ellison wrote on the computer would remain practically inaccessible. Only the practiced eye can distinguish among many of the variants for a given episode. Numerous files, some differing from one another by a handful of words or even a single keystroke, others by substantial alterations to tone or incident, compete for prece-

---

* Ellison's financial records show that he purchased an Osborne I on January 8, 1982 (in addition to another for his wife, Fanny, on September 30 of that year); an Osborne Executive on October 11, 1983; and an IBM computer on January 7, 1988. The Osborne I, introduced in April 1981, was the first truly portable personal computer commercially available in the United States. After strong initial sales, Osborne ran into financial difficulties, filing for bankruptcy in September 1983.

dence, unmediated by clear authorial design. A given episode might have more than a dozen complete and partial variants, displaying subtle differences in phrasing and sentence structure. One is sometimes tempted to believe that Ellison simply produced a continuous stream of variations on the same material with no apparent sense of urgency to fashion them into a whole. This, however, overlooks other evidence that in the last years of his life, he was attempting to revise his novel toward completion.

Ellison appears to have put his computer material through several concentrated periods of revision, resulting in three related but distinct narrative sequences. Without the benefit of his chapter breaks or section titles, we have chosen to identify these sequences simply by character and setting: "Hickman in Washington, D.C."; "Hickman in Georgia & Oklahoma"; and "McIntyre at Jessie Rockmore's." Ellison completely revised and saved to disk the sixteen files of "Hickman in Washington, D.C." in July 1993. For the twenty-five files of "Hickman in Georgia & Oklahoma," he revised all but three of the Oklahoma files between May and September of 1992; the rest of Oklahoma and all of Georgia are dated between 1988 and 1991. He revised all but one of the five files of "McIntyre at Jessie Rockmore's" during the final months of 1993; the remaining file is dated May 1993. Although he left some suggestions both within the text itself and in notes saved to disk indicating how he might connect the three parts, Ellison does not seem to have composed the textual bridges required to achieve such unity.

In assembling the three sequences we have followed whenever available Ellison's own multiple tables of contents. On the occasions when no such tables exist, we have employed a combination of methods to discern the order: matching up, when possible, Ellison's pagination; seeking textual evidence to support connections among files; studying Ellison's numerous handwritten and computerized notes; and referring to older printed and paginated sequences (some amended in Ellison's hand) found at the Library of Congress.

Ellison's computer files are expansive, yet so incomplete that they render moot any discussion of final authorial intention. The multiplicity of variants and the ambiguity of Ellison's plans for the novel make it impossible to designate an "authoritative" text. Using a computer enabled him to make such frequent changes and save so many versions of a given file that distinguishing the *most* authoritative hardly applies without the accompanying authorial instructions, which Ellison failed to leave behind.

This edition presents full versions of Ellison's three computer sequences. Rather than providing every step and misstep in Ellison's composition, we have chosen to publish only the latest sequences. We do this not simply because they are the last files he modified, but also because they form part of a cluster of files saved during revision. The versions published here represent Ellison's last best efforts to master his fiction on the computer.

In editing this edition, we compared the latest textual sequences from Ellison's computer against the hundreds of Ellison's own edited printouts now housed in the Library of Congress. In many instances, we found that the latest files from his computer already incorporated the handwritten changes found on the documents from the archive. On a handful of occasions, however, we identified edited versions of the latest files in which Ellison had yet to add his changes to the computer files. Therefore, the three textual sequences that follow are drawn from two distinct sources: digital "text"—that is, word-processed files Ellison saved to computer disks—and printed text, or those computer files that Ellison printed out himself and amended by hand. Both "Hickman in Washington, D.C." and "McIntyre at Jessie Rockmore's" are made up entirely of digital text because the latest identifiable continuous sequences were found only on disk, not in printed form at the Library of Congress. However, "Hickman in Georgia & Oklahoma" consists of both digital and printed text. Ellison's own revisions of 14 of the 30 files were found among his papers; these almost certainly represent his latest versions of the files. We have elected to include Ellison's editorial changes to his drafts made on printouts of the latest files from the disks.

Perhaps the most remarkable fact about Ellison's computer archive is that for all the files he saved over the decade, the complete narrative action of the three sequences is contained in only 46 files. The remaining 423 files are almost entirely superannuated drafts of episodes revised in the three sequences presented here. Others, however, are notable for their differences from the files in the sequence, either for offering alternative renderings of a scene, or for introducing new details.

We are mindful of the intrinsic value of this material, particularly to scholars wishing to study Ellison's compositional method. However, presenting all the variants in a print edition would be impractical. Our goal with the present volume is to reproduce a series of manuscripts for scholars and general readers alike. For a novelist of Ellison's democratic cast of mind it is particularly important that his work be accessible to the widest possible audience. Therefore, those interested in considering the multiple variants of Ellison's computer drafts are encouraged to consult the full archive at the Library of Congress.

The computer left an indelible mark on Ellison's novel; few works of fiction have been so shaped by their means of composition. Since *Invisible Man* in the 1940s and 1950s (and also with his earlier unfinished, unpublished apprentice novel, *Slick*), Ellison had written by episode. Even with a means of composition as intractable as a typewriter, Ellison put each scene through numerous revisions. Using a computer, he could move entire passages and change individual words throughout a text with a keystroke, or otherwise manipulate his prose in ways unattainable through conventional typography. With the computer Ellison had a compositional tool that matched his episodic method and near-obsessive attention to detail.*

The second novel as it takes shape in the computer files is at once familiar yet distinct from that which came before it in the typescripts. Although many of the characters, episodes, and even entire passages remain unchanged from Books I and II and earlier typewritten drafts dating back to the 1950s, what Ellison produced on the computer nonetheless comprises a separate body of work. These computer drafts lay bare Ellison's process of composition in the last decade of his life, and his shifting vision of the novel.

For all the freedoms the computer afforded Ellison, it seems not to have facilitated the novel's completion. Rather than simply revising the typescripts of Books I and II, he instead chose to reopen previously settled matters of form and sequence. Ellison never saw any portion of his computer material to publication, so we can only speculate as to how near his last revisions came to meeting his exacting standards and intentions. What is certain is that, despite his efforts, he seems not to have resolved conclusively certain basic issues that might have unified the parts into a whole. Many of these textual issues extend as far back as the novel's conception. Ellison's notes over a forty-year period return to a handful of key questions: Should the novel begin, as Ellison long planned, with Hickman arriving in D.C., or should it commence instead with LeeWillie Minifees burning his car on Senator Sunraider's lawn, or McIntyre interviewing Love New, or Hickman receiving Janey Glover's letter, or Hickman recalling the young Bliss? Should he weave together the D.C. material with Georgia and Oklahoma through flashback or some other means? How might he fuse the first-person McIntyre narrative with the third-person Hickman narrative? Should McIntyre or Hickman visit Oklahoma? If Hickman, should he do it before or after the shooting?

Ellison's numerous notes over the decades show him laboring exhaustively with plotting and sequence. In an undated note, perhaps from the late 1960s or early 1970s, Ellison offers this potential sequence (Library of Congress, 139/4):

> Three days before the shooting
> Janey's letter

---

* Ellison used an early word-processing program called WordStar, which required its user to employ a series of keystrokes rather than a drop-down menu as in Microsoft Word to perform simple operations. For someone proficient in its method, it enabled the user to keep his or her fingers in the touch-typing position at all times, potentially facilitating the flow of expression. The program also employed a feature called "merge print," which allowed the user to string a series of files together to be printed through a typed command. There is evidence of Ellison's use (and occasional misuse) of this function.

> Trip west, Janey's tale, return to Georgia, trip to
>   Washington
> McIntyre gives something of Severen's background
> Goes west Janey, Cliofus, Love
> Logically, this would come after shooting—unless he has seen
>   Severen before. He hasn't so this is out.
> If this is so, Hickman has to convey needed information.
> Severen introduced when Hickman is still in town.

As is often the case throughout the notes, tables of contents become occasions for expansive speculation. What begins as a list of episodes quickly transforms into Ellison's conscious construction and reconstruction of intent, motive, and meaning. An even more dramatic example appears in the following undated, handwritten note found among Ellison's papers at the Library of Congress (139/5):

> Prologue
> They arrive in D.C.
> McIntyre reports
> But when does Hickman go looking for information?
> This comes with the extension of the prologue, or through chapters in which they search
> Visit to Rockmore's house where they encounter the cross-eyed woman
> The Lincoln Memorial
> The hotel where the senator has a suite
> Walk on which they come upon the end of car-burning
> Hickman goes on walk alone and encounters Leroy, glimpses Severen in window—which suggests that he will have to visit Janey <u>before</u> he leads group to Washington. And this is because he arrives in Oklahoma while Severen is still there. They see one another—or Severen sees him—in some neutral spot. But later Severen sees him in Washington, puts two and two together, and follows him in hope that he will be led to Sunraider—of whose identity he is uncertain...
> Actually, Severen might be their <u>observer</u> who is bent upon discovering their mission.

Interspersed within the outline of narrative sequence are questions, explanations, hypothetical suggestions; one can see Ellison seeking order out of possibility. These examples (and there are numerous others) demonstrate Ellison's constantly shifting vision of how he might construct his house of fiction. The tables of contents he saved to computer, fortunately, are more direct and definitive than those written by hand, consisting of ordered file names that provide a clear, if incomplete, indication of narrative sequence.

The computer files show Ellison fashioning imperfect provisional solutions to long-standing textual puzzles. For instance, he seems to have begun inserting Oklahoma flashbacks into the D.C. narrative through passing references to Janey, Millsap, and the Oklahoma hotel. He leaves open the connection between McIntyre at Rockmore's and Hickman (with Wilhite) at Rockmore's by having "a couple of colored fellows" appear near the end of the McIntyre sequence ("Dance"), and by having Hickman collide with an unidentified white man at the beginning of the Hickman at Rockmore scene ("McMillen"). These remnants are gestures of intentionality rather than fully achieved resolutions to textual problems. They demonstrate, however, that Ellison's mind was at work making connections and experimenting with possibilities up to his last days of composition.

Rather than reinventing his novel, Ellison's computer sequences tell old stories in new ways. His writing shows a striking consistency of detail across decades of composition. Ellison returns to the same core scenes and characters, and often to the same language that he used in drafts dating back as far as the 1950s. With few exceptions it appears likely that he had the typescript draft at his side as he composed; the phrases are often identical. Among Ellison's early drafts are versions of almost every scene he would produce on the computer. Rather than representing a radical new direction for the novel, the computer files mark an atavistic turn to past characters and conceptions.

Alongside the 1970s Book I and II typescripts, however, Ellison's computer files stand out. Where the typescripts render Hickman and Bliss/Sunraider's dual narrative voices, the computer files emphasize Hickman's alone (albeit Hickman's bifurcated voice of jazzman and preacher). Where the typescripts move action to the psychological realm, the computer files most often push it out into the street, to the picaresque narrative plane his earlier protagonist inhabited in *Invisible Man*. Where the typescripts approach Ellison's fully achieved voice and style, the computer files contain numerous typographical errors and elisions.

For all the incompletion and imperfection of Ellison's last literary efforts, they provide multiple instances that recall him at his best. Readers familiar with *Invisible Man* and the *Collected Essays* will be reminded again of Ellison's masterly command of the African American vernacular tradition. Through Hickman, Ellison weaves the sacred and profane strains of black expressive culture into a whole that finds Stackalee beside Brueghel's Icarus, Jesus Christ beside Peetie Wheatstraw. Palpable, too, is Ellison's abiding faith in American identity and black people's essential place in the nation's past, present, and future. His characters revere America and its founding principles in a manner that runs deeper than flag-waving pageantry. Theirs is a patriotism sometimes embraced at the price of freedom. As far as these themes are concerned, Ellison has extended what he began so many years ago in *Invisible Man.*

In July 1993 Ellison revised all sixteen "Hickman in Washington, D.C." files. He had long envisioned beginning the novel with Hickman and his parishioners arriving to warn Sunraider of an impending assassination attempt at the hands of the Senator's estranged son, Severen. "Two days before the bewildering incident a chartered plane-load of those who at that time were politely identified as Southern 'Negroes' swooped down upon Washington's National Airport and disembarked in a confusion of paper bags, suitcases, and picnic baskets." Versions of this sentence begin the excerpt called "And Hickman Arrives," the first one Ellison published from his novel-in-progress, as well as "Prologue" from the 1970s typescripts and "Arrival" from the computer sequence. In Ellison's early notes he mentions beginning with this scene. "The first seven pages," he writes in an undated note, "wherein Hickman and the old people are introduced, could be a prologue."

In the computer files, however, Hickman's arrival becomes much more than a prologue. What began as a seven-page introduction leading to Sunraider's assassination has transmogrified into more than three hundred pages unified by Hickman's governing consciousness. The essential encounters Ellison renders with such force in Book II (Hickman at Sunraider's bedside) and Book I (Hickman and McIntyre's hallway exchanges) are nowhere to be found. Instead, the computer sequence places Hickman and his roving consciousness in the foreground.

Instead of moving directly to the assassination attempt after Hickman and his parishioners arrive, as in "Prologue," the computer sequence follows the group for the entire day. After being dismissed by the Senator's secretary, Hickman and his followers are searched by security guards (the last scene that the computer sequence shares with Book II). After checking into the Hotel Longview, Hickman takes a nap, tries to intercept the Senator at his mistress's penthouse, attempts to contact the Senator through a "middle-of-the-road" newspaper, returns to the Senate offices but is turned back by a guard, looks for Walker Millsap (a "veteran white-folks-watcher") only to be confronted by a vernacular character named Leroy who mistakes Hickman for "Chief Sam," notices a mural of a black Christ, returns to the hotel where he daydreams in the lobby, talks with Deacon Wilhite, takes his parishioners sightseeing at the Lincoln Memorial, returns to the Longview to take a shower, retires to the lounge where he studies a reproduction of Brueghel's *Landscape with the Fall of Icarus,* catches a cab with Wilhite to visit Aubrey McMillen at Jessie Rockmore's townhouse, and after encountering the wild scene within, leaves to return to the Longview, no closer to finding Sunraider than when the day began.

The sequence ends abruptly with Hickman and Wilhite exiting Rockmore's house with "a quick look at the glowing 369 on the fanlight."* In his notes Ellison speculates at different times about fusing the Hickman and McIntyre sections, using the Rockmore scene as the bridge. Elsewhere, he considers cutting to flashbacks of Georgia and Oklahoma or moving ahead to the car-burning scene on the next day. He left no clear indications of how he might have executed these plans. Curiously, both "Hickman in D.C." and "Hickman in Georgia & Oklahoma" end with Hickman exiting a building—Rockmore's townhouse in D.C. and a bar called the Cave of Winds in Oklahoma. Crossing a threshold is, of course, a useful transitional device. However, it is unclear in both instances where Ellison intented Hickman, and the novel as a whole, to head next.

Unlike Book II, in which Ellison tests the themes of American identity and democracy through two equal protagonists, the computer files render these same concerns through Hickman's consciousness alone. Ellison attempts to make Hickman a richer and deeper character than in the typescripts, albeit at the cost of his antiphonal relationship with Bliss/Sunraider. Through Hickman Ellison explores the contrasts and the connections in a double voice. Hickman, Ellison writes, is of "two minds"—one doubtful, the other hopeful; one blues-toned, the other sanctified. One notable example of this duality comes during Hickman's solitary search through the streets of Washington when he encounters the mural depicting the black Christ's march to his crucifixion bearing a cross topped by a "bundle consisting of red, white, and blue cotton," partly unfurled. Hickman interprets this arresting religious and nationalist iconography in a way that a more limited character could not. Such a doubling of vision connects to a long-standing tradition in African American expression balancing the faith of the spirituals with the tragicomic sensibility of the blues. Hickman's riffs and reflections draw equally from both traditions, with references to New Testament scripture and folk tales, the life of the spirit and the desires of the flesh.

Throughout the sequence, Hickman's musings punctuate a series of otherwise perfunctory events. This external-internal schism is never reconciled. The result is a jarring dissonance between Hickman's calm, expansive, brooding tone and the putative necessity of action. Numerous times in his notes Ellison underscores the importance of action. "N.B.," he writes in a note from the computers dated 3/14/1991 ("After.hat"), "Whatever he [Hickman] does must maintain dramatic tension." Despite this tone of self-admonition, so much of what Ellison accomplished in these late revisions comes at the expense of narrative tension. Ellison would have us believe that

---

* Those who recall the 1,369 lightbulbs Invisible Man wires underground may be familiar with Ellison's playful reference, reprised here, to the dream-book symbolism of the number representing excrement to policy gamblers.

Hickman and his followers have come to the capital on urgent business—namely, to stave off Sunraider's assassination. And yet, after Hickman is rebuffed at the Senator's offices, this sense of purpose dissipates.

The computer files' most vivid encounters are at an almost unfathomable distance from Ellison's original purpose of rendering Hickman's efforts to save the Senator. Such obsolescence of action shifts the burden of meaning to Hickman's mind. As a result the narrative often takes on a quality more reminiscent of Ellison's essays than of the typescripts. Rather than reading the computer files for their absences or deficiencies, it may be most useful to consider them for what they contribute to Hickman, as potentially epic a character in Ellison's mind as Invisible Man.

"Hickman in Washington, D.C." contains relatively few textual anomalies compared to "Hickman in Georgia & Oklahoma," undoubtedly because, unlike the other two sequences, he revised the entire sequence in a single month. The biggest editorial challenge was in cleaning up the computer-file corruptions occurring during file transfer—perhaps during his lifetime (records show he had his files transferred in 1988). These corruptions consisted of random characters appearing in the text and unintended line breaks, neither of which disturbed the integrity of the text itself. We have removed these corruptions silently and standardized the format in all the sequences in this volume.

In addition to problems in formatting, the D.C. sequence includes a limited number of other anomalies, most dealing with transitions between files. "Trombone"'s transition to "Hotel" does not include nine lines of text found in several of "Trombone"'s variants. We have included these lines, marking them off with brackets, for the purposes of context and clarity. Another imperfect transition comes between "Maude Eye" and "Legend." "Legend" offers an alternative version of the last two paragraphs in "Maude Eye." Both are included for the purposes of comparison, respecting the absence of any clear preference on Ellison's part. Additionally, the sequence includes several narrative inconsistencies, most notably the aforementioned references to Georgia and Oklahoma, and also the numbering of Hickman's parishioners as forty-four and fifty in different files. We have left such inconsistencies unchanged as further evidence of the unfinished nature of Ellison's work.

Originally, Ellison imagined his second novel as an "Oklahoma book." The 1950s typewritten drafts dealing with McIntyre (and occasionally Hickman) in Oklahoma are among the earliest material Ellison composed for the second novel. After a long hiatus, he continued revising them in the 1990s. "Hickman in Georgia & Oklahoma" consists of twenty-five files, seven Georgia and eighteen Oklahoma. While it is clear that Ellison conceived of them as a unit, they are usefully discussed separately for the purposes of summary and editorial analysis.*

"Hickman in Georgia & Oklahoma" presents the most significant editorial challenge in all the computer sequences. Ellison revised all but five of the files in the 1990s—twenty in the late summer and early fall of 1992 alone—but does not seem to have revised three Georgia files ("Sister.wil," "Janey 3," and "Janey.alz," the first three of the seven Georgia files) and two Oklahoma files ("Movie" and "Costumes," the sixteenth and seventeenth of the eighteen Oklahoma files) during those periods. The last dates for these are in October and December of 1988, around the time that Ellison had all his files transferred to a new computer (thus erasing the original dates), meaning that these files may well be even older than their listed dates. Regardless of their provenance, they were certainly composed in an earlier period than the rest of the sequence, all of which was last saved in the 1990s.

The sequence is further complicated by the discovery of Ellison's edited printouts. The Library of Congress archive includes numerous drafts marked in Ellison's (and sometimes Fanny Ellison's) hand, but most of them appear to be early files later updated on the computer. However, three hard copies appear to be revisions of the latest files from the computer disks. We have chosen to include Ellison's handwritten edits to "Janey.Alz," the third file in the sequence. We have also included the changes found in a sequentially numbered printout that comprises the first six Oklahoma files: "Bustrip," "Visit," "Blurring," "Smoking," "BlurTwo," and "Lovecourt." A more challenging decision was presented by a similar paginated draft of five files from the latter part of the Oklahoma sequence: "Cave," "Egypt," "Windcave," "Words," and "Station." While the printed and edited "Egypt" and "Windcave" correspond to the latest computer files, "Cave," "Words," and "Station" do not. Some of the changes in the latter files—consisting almost entirely of spelling and punctuation corrections—are already reflected in the latest computer files, though some are not. Rather than picking and choosing the pertinent edits and ignoring the others, we have chosen to respect the editorial principle of using the latest established text. Since these three files do not correspond exactly with the latest identifiable files from the computer, we have no way of ascertaining with certainty whether they predate or postdate the files from the established sequence.

This is not the only complication presented in editing "Hickman in Georgia & Oklahoma." One of the most notable textual anomalies in the sequence concerns the transition between "Janey.Alz" and "Sippy.1."

---

* The Library of Congress has a sequential fragment that includes the last file of Georgia ("Decision") and the first of Oklahoma ("Bustrip") in a continuously paginated draft (134/5).

"Janey.Alz" consists mainly of Hickman's musings after reading Janey's letter. In the last two pages, however, Ellison makes the transition to the Millsap report: "An undated confidential report, he recalled that he had received some thirty years earlier from Walker Millsap..." Both the computer file "Janey.Alz" and the printed and amended version found in the Library of Congress include a false start where Ellison introduces the report with the above sentence, has Hickman begin reading it, only to break off and restart from the same point. The next file, "Sippy.1," begins at the same transition point with a similar sentence: "He had received the report, undated and stamped Confidential, during the early twenties from Walker Millsap...." Instead of including this needless repetition, we have chosen to cut directly to the "Sippy.1" version of the report rather than going to the end of "Janey.Alz" only to have to cut out the first pages of "Sippy.1." This report also presents a puzzling question of chronology. In the first version of the sentence, Ellison has Hickman date the report from "some thirty years earlier." In the other version, he states it is from the early 1920s. Together, these correspond to the putative setting of the early 1950s. However, in the report itself Millsap states that Hickman's "young man"—Bliss—"must be well into his fifties." Relying on these dates, Sunraider should be in his early eighties and Hickman well over a hundred. This clearly cannot be the case. So either it is simply an error of chronology on Ellison's part, or he intends the report to be more recent—which is difficult to fathom given that every indication in the text suggests that he is reading from the report's "faded typescript." These moments of imperfection remind us of just how much work still remained for Ellison to do to complete the novel.

Another transitional textual anomaly comes in the paragraph connecting "Blur.Two" and "Lovecourt." The last sentence of "Blur.Two" and the first sentence of "Lovecourt" are variants of one another. A similar example comes in the transition between "Station" and "Movie"; "Movie" includes a variant on the exchange that ends "Station."

The essential plot elements of the Georgia material are the thirty-year-old report by Walker Millsap, an associate from Hickman's jazz days, and a letter from Janey Glover, a sweetheart of Hickman's youth, warning ominously of lethal trouble facing Bliss/Sunraider. In an undated note (139/5), Ellison writes that "Hickman has Janey's letter with him [in D.C.?]." "It is the envelope of the plot, the seed of the catastrophe." The letter would take Hickman from Georgia to Oklahoma, and from Oklahoma to Washington, unwittingly leading Sunraider's assassin to his target. With so much significance resting on a single plot device, it is no wonder that Ellison puzzled over where to place it.

Ellison briefly considered opening the novel with Janey's letter. He writes the following in an undated note:

> Start with Janey's letter, but conceal the important information. Cut
> wherever possible, then to Washington. The letter should hint at
> motive for a quest, but not reveal it directly. And yet it should pro-
> vide Hickman enough propulsion to involve the reader. Later there
> can be flashbacks in which needed information can be revealed. The
> point is to build up ~~momem~~ thrust. (140/1)

The letter's most effective location may have been its earliest, in the typescript fragment known as "Bliss' Birth" in which Hickman, deep in reverie at
the Senator's bedside, recalls Janey's brief letter in the immediacy of dramatic action. In the computer files, the version of the letter reads instead like
an appendage, a transparent plot device.

By strict chronology, then, "Hickman in Georgia & Oklahoma" should
begin the novel. Not only does the action come before the D.C. sequence (in
fact, providing the impetus for Hickman to go to D.C.), the D.C. files make
reference to particulars one could only know having previously read "Hickman in Georgia & Oklahoma." This presents the most obvious of many
editorial challenges to sequencing. It was a problem Ellison had never completely resolved, though he seemed most compelled to present the Georgia
and Oklahoma files in flashback, with "Arrival" opening the novel. The
Georgia files offer nothing that might properly be considered the beginning
of a novel. To the contrary, they open quite perfunctorily with Hickman at
his desk going through mail.

The Oklahoma files comprise Hickman's return to Oklahoma City. His
purpose is to visit Janey and ask her to clarify the meaning of her letter. This
section includes, in addition to the Janey visit, a protracted exchange with
Love New, and a performance by a teller of tall tales and toasts, Cliofus. Ellison's narrative method consists of discursive summary rather than immediate creation or re-creation of action. Particularly with Love New, a story
leads to another story, circles within circles, relevant to the novel's theme of
fathers and sons and the spiritual knowledge and atonement needed for true
identity, but weighted down by sheer textual volume.

This sequence includes one of the most puzzling textual quirks in all the
computer files. One file in the sequence, "Blurring," ends mid-sentence with
"Which was." The file that follows, "Smoking," completes the sentence with
"the truth." From this point, however, the next seven pages of "Smoking"
simply recapitulate (often to the word) the last pages of "Blurring." Likely
this was an accident in formatting, a hazard of digital composition. It
nonetheless presents a challenge to an editor wishing to present Ellison in
his own words, even if those words are the likely product of accident or oversight. An earlier printed draft from the computer found among Ellison's papers, and marked in his hand, reveals the same anomaly, suggesting that at

the very least he had been aware of the replication. However, in the printout, he made no correction. This is only a particularly striking example of something that occurs several times throughout the computer files.

"McIntyre at Jessie Rockmore's" is the shortest of the three sequences, consisting of only five files. Consequently, it also has the fewest number of variants. However, it appears that it was the last portion of the novel to receive Ellison's attention. "Rockmore," the second file in the sequence, was last saved on December 30, 1993, the most recently dated file from Ellison's computer. Although it initially seems curious that Ellison would devote his final days of revision to what might appear to be a digression from the dominant Hickman narrative, it fits well within his overall conception of the novel.

The unity of the novel's two perspectives, the third-person Hickman narrative and the first-person McIntyre, is best achieved in Book I, where Ellison begins with Hickman and his parishioners' arriving at Washington's National Airport and jumps to McIntyre narrating the shooting on the Senate floor. No such unity exists in the computer files. Instead, Ellison has composed two separate but related Hickman sequences and a wholly distinct McIntyre sequence, a revision of Chapter 12 from Book I that relates an episode also rendered, as discussed above, in the Hickman computer files.

It seems likely that Ellison wrote "McIntyre at Jessie Rockmore's" with Chapter 12, and perhaps even Hickman's Rockmore scene from Book II, in front of him. Not only are the incidents nearly identical, but a number of the passages are rendered verbatim. In some cases, the differences are a matter of embellishment—for instance, the addition of a Native American lithograph and a photo of Klansmen in Rockmore's memorabilia-crammed rooms. Often a mere substitution of detail or phrase distinguishes the drafts. For example, in the computer materials Mister Jessie asks for "a redhead or some kind of blond," while in Book I he asks for "a raving blond."

Like the other two sequences, "McIntyre at Jessie Rockmore's" contains a handful of textual anomalies. The most revealing of these comes in the final file of the sequence, "Dance," where Ellison interrupts the narrative with the following note: "N.B. See later version of Bootleg." The "later version" to which he refers could be either one of two files labeled "Bootleg," both of which are versions of "Dance." All three files are substantially the same save for a small but significant addition: In "Dance" Ellison has the police sergeant mention that "two colored fellows" are waiting outside. This is undoubtedly a reference to Hickman and Wilhite, which suggests that Ellison was looking for ways to fuse the McIntyre and Hickman narratives through this scene.

The Rockmore scene is the only episode rendered in typescript as well as in both Hickman and McIntyre computer files. Yet its relation to the central plot elements is never fully developed. There is McMillen's recollection of a mysterious white man, likely Sunraider, who barges in and claims the coffin, shocking the aged Rockmore to death. And there is the fact that the scene offers a nexus between the McIntyre and Hickman narratives, a connection only provisionally utilized. In many ways this episode's multiple variants represent both the promise and the limitation of Ellison's novel-in-progress. It holds out the titillating possibility of unity, not simply for this section, but for the novel as a whole—a place where Ellison might have gathered together the disparate strands of narrative—while ultimately underscoring the dogged diversity and disconnection among Ellison's many visions of his second novel.

What Ellison composed on the computer between the early eighties and his death in 1994 reimagines yet again his long-awaited second novel. He achieves its transformation not by changing plot or character, but by reorienting point of view and episodic importance. What were once central concerns, the political assassination and the relationship between Hickman and Bliss/Sunraider, become tertiary or even nonexistent. In their place Ellison has elevated the incidental (the comings and goings of Hickman and his congregation in D.C., the visit to Oklahoma, and Hickman's excavation of the past—both his and others'—and his complex relation to the place) to a role of elemental importance.

Ellison's multiple drafts, prospective sequences, and multifarious connections might best be understood as producing a kind of living text, amoebic in its fluidity, integral in its essence. His improvisational relation to his material afforded him the freedom to compose and create synthesis later, or to experiment simultaneously with multiple narrative sequences. How did he plan to integrate the third-person Hickman narrative with the first-person McIntyre? How would he fuse the disparate fragments into a whole? The writing itself offers no clear answers. Instead, Ellison's computer sequences challenge his readers to imagine potentialities of order and expression in the manuscript he left unrealized.

Editors' Note to "Hickman in Washington, D.C."

In the summer of 1993, Ralph Ellison revised all sixteen computer files that comprise the untitled portion of the manuscript we've labeled "Hickman in Washington, D.C." As with the sequences that follow, we present the latest identifiable series of Ellison's computer files, including whenever available his own penciled revisions to printouts in the archives.

"Hickman in Washington, D.C." is essentially a long elaboration of the seven-page Prologue from Book I, including new versions of several other key scenes from the typescripts—most notably, those episodes at the Lincoln Memorial and at Jessie Rockmore's mansion. The balance of the scenes appear also to have been conceived at an earlier period in the novel's composition, perhaps decades before these computer files were composed. In other words, Ellison seems to have dedicated most of his work on the computer to revising scenes first written as early as the 1950s. These early fragments and the later computer sequences share a clear tendency toward the picaresque—moving the narrative from the psychological realm familiar from Hickman and Bliss/Sunraider's antiphonal exchanges in Book II to the physical realm of Hickman and his parishioners making their way through the capital in the days before the shooting. At times, this dissipates dramatic tension, leaving only Hickman's long essayistic asides, occasionally punctuated by events that seem at best distantly related to the novel's central conflict, the assassination. (It is revealing to compare the version of the scene at the Lincoln Memorial from the computer files [pages 574–578] with the sparer, more dramatically rendered version from Book II [pages 418–421].)

As in Book II, "Hickman in Washington, D.C." closes with Hickman and Wilhite leaving Jessie Rockmore's estate. In both cases, it is unclear how Ellison intended to proceed from this point in the narrative. Did he plan for this scene to close the novel, or did he plan to fashion a transition to the material set in Georgia and Oklahoma or some other portion of the manuscript? At no time in the novel's forty-year composition does Ellison appear to have written anything that moves the narrative beyond this point.

"Hickman in Washington, D.C." is at once integrally related to, yet distinct from, the two computer sequences that follow—"Hickman in Georgia & Oklahoma" and "McIntyre at Jessie Rockmore's." Following "Hickman in Georgia & Oklahoma" in actual chronology, it appears certain that Ellison intended "Hickman in Washington, D.C." to come first in narrative chronology. Ellison long imagined opening his novel with Hickman and his parishioners arriving at Washington's National Airport. For its part, "Hickman in Georgia & Oklahoma" offers an extended clarification of motive, providing essential background on the novel's main actors—the victim, Sunraider; the assassin, Severen; and the would-be savior, Hickman. "McIntyre at Jessie Rockmore's" offers a rendition of the final episode from "Hickman in Washington, D.C." from the first-person perspective of the white newspaper reporter who narrates Book I. Although Ellison's notes suggest that he had long considered including both versions of the episode in his novel, it is unclear how he planned to connect them.

This section is notably the only place in the computer sequences that Sunraider makes an appearance. While he is the putative motivation for much of the action, he remains a subject of discussion rather than an actual character. Even his one appearance is at a remove; it happens when Aubrey McMillen, Jessie Rockmore's assistant, recalls an unidentified white man arriving earlier in the evening and accusing Rockmore of stealing his coffin. Although McMillen cannot remember the man's name, he recalls having seen him on television. It seems more than conjecture that the man in question is Sunraider. Bliss/Sunraider's near disappearance in "Hickman in Washington, D.C." is perhaps the most striking of the many differences from Book I and Book II. It suggests Ellison's shifting conception of his fiction and evolving sense of aesthetic purpose.

Although the computer sequences mark a decided shift away from the narrative style of the typescripts from the 1960s and 1970s, they are very much in keeping with the episodic nature of the miscellaneous undated drafts Ellison most likely composed decades earlier. The difference, an important one, is that Ellison's labors in the 1990s resulted in long narrative sequences such as "Hickman in Washington, D.C.," while no such substantial narratives are apparent among the antecedent typewritten drafts. One of the most puzzling questions about Ellison's compositional practice in the last decades of his life is why he would step away from the Book I and II typescripts, much of which appears so close to completion, in favor of returning to the long-neglected and fragmentary episodes that he seems to have discarded decades earlier. The precise relations among the computer drafts, the typescripts, and these fragmentary episodes deserve careful consideration by scholars.

We have chosen to identify in brackets the sixteen files by the file name Ellison used when saving them to disk. We follow this practice in the other two computer-composed sequences as well. He seems not to have conceived chapter breaks, nor do we intend the computer file titles to function as such. Although some files contain discrete episodes, others follow directly upon the files that come before them, even picking up in mid-sentence. In "Hickman in Washington, D.C.," as throughout Ellison's computer disks, we have had to contend with occasional corruptions in the computer files themselves. Most often, the result was little more than lost formatting (quotation marks appearing where Ellison intended underscores, unintended paragraph breaks in the middle of sentences, and so forth). Whenever possible, we have silently restored these sections in keeping with Ellison's preferred habits. We have, however, let a number of Ellison's textual irregularities stand. Evidence of the preliminary nature of some parts of the computer drafts is apparent, from linguistic quirks like repeating words at the beginning of sentences ("And," "But," and "Yes" are among the most prevalent), to imperfect transitions between files, to unresolved details of plot (for example, the number of Hickman's parishioners is given as both forty-four and fifty).

Clearly, Ellison had yet to attend to a number of the issues that either he or his editor would have caught and corrected had he lived to publish his novel. As editors of a posthumous edition, we have elected to show forbearance, knowing that, without Ellison, we could never hope to bring his novel up to his exacting standards. Instead, we have chosen to pay tribute to his legacy by making available to readers this insider's look into Ellison's compositional method. Even more than in the typescripts, which underwent far more extensive revision, Ellison's computer sequences bear witness to the fact that his novel was still very much in progress.

HICKMAN IN WASHINGTON, D.C.

[ARRIVAL]

TWO DAYS BEFORE THE bewildering incident a chartered planeload of those who at that time were politely identified as Southern "Negroes" swooped down upon Washington's National Airport and disembarked in a confusion of paper bags, suitcases, and picnic baskets. Most were quite elderly: old ladies wearing white uniforms and small white lace-trimmed caps tied beneath their chins, and old men who wore rumpled ready-made suits and wide-brimmed hats. The single exception being a towering dark-brown-skinned man dressed in a blue well-tailored suit with a vest, a pongee shirt, blue pastel tie, and soft planters-style panama. Quiet and exceptionally orderly, considering their number, they swept through the crowded terminal with such an unmistakable air of agitation that busy airport attendants and travelers alike paused to stare.

They themselves paused but briefly when one of the women came to a sudden stop and looked around the crowded terminal with an indignant frown.

"Hold it a second, y'all," she said, looking high and low, "whilst I see if they have one of them up here like they have down in Atlanta...."

"One what, Sister Bea," one of the other women said. "What you talking about?"

"I'm talking about that ole prideless rascal they had sitting in a rocking chair besides that big dirty bale of cotton, and him propped up on a walking cane and holding a dinner bell!"

"Oh, forget him, Sister Bea," someone said, "we have other things to worry about."

"I might *forgive* him," the woman said, "but I won't ever forget him. Just imagine somebody in this day and age helping to insult his own people!"

"You mean to tell me that thing was *alive*," one of the men said. "I thought it was a dummy!"

"Dummy my foot," another man said, "that old grayheaded clown was probably pretending that ole rocking chair got him just after he made enough money
to buy him a cotton-picking machine and a Cad'llac! Yeah! And so now he's just
taking his ease and watching the world flow by."

"That's right!" another brother said. "And getting paid for jiving the white
folks!"

"You can laugh if you want to," the big woman said, "but it ain't funny. No, sir!
It ain't funny worth a damn—and may the Lord forgive me for saying so, because a thing like that is a terrible burden for the rest of us to bear. . . ."

Luggage in arm and hand, the group lurched ahead in short-stepping haste to
one of the many taxi stands, where with the aid of the dispatcher a small fleet of
taxis was assembled. Then, with the dispatcher stepping aside and looking on in
bemusement, the towering dark-brown-skinned Negro man saw to it that the
group arranged themselves beside the machines with a minimum of talk and
milling about. This done, the big Negro made his way to a public telephone, dialed a number, and carried on a brief conversation. Completing his call, he
started back and stopped short when he noted that the dispatcher's blue wind-
breaker had a pair of dice stenciled on its back. Then, shaking his head, he returned and began assigning the group their seats while pausing anxiously from
time to time to consult an old-fashioned gold watch attached to a thick gold
chain suspended between the widely spaced pockets of his vast expanse of vest.
Communicating mostly by slight nods and gestures, his voice seldom arose
above a hoarse whisper—until, just as he climbed in beside the driver of the lead
taxi, the dispatcher inquired, in a manner that betrayed something more than a
professional interest, their destination.

Whereupon, clearing his throat, the big man's mellow baritone sounded
through the din of the terminal's traffic: "We'd like," he said, "to be driven to the
offices of Senator Sunraider."

The effect was electric. Suddenly, with eyes widening and forehead lifting
the shiny visor of his cap skyward, the dispatcher's hands flew from the pockets
of his blue windbreaker to the roof of the taxi.

"*What*," he said, bending forward. "Did you say *Sunraider?*"

"That's right," the big man said. "Is there something wrong?"

"Why no," the dispatcher said, "but do you mean *all* of you?"

"That's right," the big Negro said, "to Senator Sunraider's office. And, sir,
we'd appreciate it if you'd tell the drivers that it's important that they get us
there as fast as possible. After circling around up there in the air for over forty-
five minutes we're fast running out of time. . . ."

Pausing, the big man snatched out a worn wallet, removed five one-dollar
bills, and thrust them out of the window. "We'd appreciate it very much," he said.

"Oh, that's not necessary," the dispatcher said as he pocketed the money.
"Your problem is a storm from somewhere out southwest. It's been fouling things

up all morning. But don't worry, now that you're down to earth we'll get you there, and fast. The building you want is only a hop and a skip away."

Then, looking across into the face of the driver, a small, wiry, light-skinned man who had been listening and looking his passengers over with an expression compounded of big-city condescension, disassociation, and incredulity, the dispatcher struck the taxi's door with his palm.

"Well," he roared, "what're you waiting for? You heard the man, so get them out of here!"

"Yeah," the driver said, his voice deliberately flat and hollow as he shifted his machine into gear. "Right on...."

Shaking his head, the dispatcher watched until the last of the line of taxis had pulled away, then hurried to his station and dialed the number of a leading newspaper, asking for a reporter with whom he had an agreement to supply information regarding any unusual incidents that might occur at the airport, and carried on a conversation that was punctuated by wheezing intervals of laughter.

"I don't know who they are," he said into the mouthpiece, "but I'm telling you that there's quite a bunch of them."

"..."

"*Why?* Now *that* you'll have to tell *me*. You're the reporter...."

"..."

"When? Hell, just now! That why I *called* you, McIntyre, they just took off...."

"..."

"Now, how would I know what for? Maybe they're taking him some Southern-fried chicken and candied yams. Anyway, they're headed for Sunraider's offices!"

"..."

"Yes! That's right, *Sunraider*! The big fellow who seems to be the HNIC just told me...."

"..."

"Oh, excuse me, I forgot that you're a Northern boy—it means the 'Head Negro in charge'; in other words, their leader."

"..."

"That's all I know, so if you're interested you'd better get over there!"

And now, shaking with laughter, the dispatcher hung up.

Arriving at the Senator's office building, the big man leaped from his seat and rushed to the next taxi in line to consult with a smaller man seated beside the driver. Nodding his head energetically, the little man got out and hurried back along the line of taxis. The big man looked on, consulting his watch and looking toward the building and then back to where now, as the smaller man moved past, each of the taxis was swiftly emptied. And now as the drivers placed luggage on the sidewalk in front of the building's entrance the owners assembled themselves silently beside their possessions. The process completed, the big man walked nimbly to the end of the line and started back, looking inside each of the vehicles to see that nothing had been overlooked. Then, after paying and tipping the drivers from his wallet, he herded the group, each with luggage in hand, into the building.

Upon their entrance, the several uniformed security men stationed in the lobby exchanged quick glances and came to attention, surprised by the sudden influx of Negroes. Then as the big man saw two of the guards detaching themselves and starting forward he raised his hand, gesturing for the group to halt where they were. They complied immediately, whispering and gazing at the tall pillars and high ceiling, while he continued forward and asked that the security men direct them to Senator Sunraider's office.

Once again his very mention of the Senator's name appeared to arouse first surprise and then puzzlement. However, the guards were polite, and after checking and recording the big man's identification, he was instructed to have the group fall in behind the guard who would escort them to the elevator.

Following in a silent mass, the group matched the guard's military pace with a bustling show of informal discipline as he led them through the broad sweep of the lobby to a bank of elevators.

"What are you people," the guard said, addressing the big Negro, "some kind of delegation?"

"Oh, no, sir," the big Negro said.

"A protest group?"

"Us?" The big Negro looked suprised. "Don't tell me that that's what we look like to you. . . ."

The guard grinned. "Well . . . not really," he said, scanning the group with a quick glance over his shoulder.

"I certainly hope not," the big Negro said.

"But what *are* you?"

The big Negro looked down and smiled. "You might say that we're just a group of friends."

"Friends? You mean you're *Quakers?*"

"Oh, no, sir, I didn't mean that kind—although I'll have to admit that we *have* been known to do a little shaking from time to time. Yes, sir! But all I meant was that we're 'well-wishers'—that type of friends. The kind that stick closer than brothers."

"To Senator Sunraider?"

"That's right," the big Negro said, looking at the guard with a blank face, "at a bit of a distance, maybe; but still friends. . . ."

"Here we are," the guard said as they had reached the bank of elevators where one of the doors was sliding open.

"So you're friends," the guard said, looking up at the big Negro with his thumbs stuck in his Sam Browne belt. "So now I can truly say that I've heard *everything.*"

"Well at least *some* of everything," the big Negro said, stepping aside as the group started into the elevator, "but as you must know, there's nothing really *new* under the sun, it's a matter of how old things fit together under different conditions. Ain't that right?"

"Yes, I guess so," the guard said. "Sure."

"All the way to the rear, folks," the big Negro said with a chuckle, "all the way...."

Thanks to the sudden illness of the regular receptionist, and the failure of the switchboard operator to warn her, the group was received by no less than the Senator's confidential secretary, a middle-aged blonde who was totally unprepared for their arrival. Thus, hearing a stir from her office, she entered the reception room and stopped short, visibly dismayed by the group who continued to enter.

Looming like phantoms out of her deep Southern past, the sudden intrusion of Negroes appeared about evenly divided between males and females. And as the group pressed in from the hall she noted that the women were dressed in severe white uniforms and wearing small ruffled caps worn tied beneath their chins with flat ribbons which she knew to be traditional to deaconesses of certain Protestant denominations—but why here? There was also a uniformity about the men that centered in their black summer suits, white shirts, and black ties, that was relieved only by the variety of their hats. Which, as the bucks stood looking somewhat ill at ease in the mellow, walnut-paneled elegance of the reception room, were held pressed against their left chests in a formal Southern gesture of respect commonly displayed at funerals or on occasions calling for grave patriotic decorum. It was a sign of deep respect, but the fact that the regular receptionist's absence made it necessary that she perform, even briefly, in a capacity beneath her official status (and this on behalf of the most unexpected and least desired of visitors that it had ever been her fate to receive) was so annoying that the men's solemn gesture aroused instant feelings of distrust and resentment.

As she stood scanning their inscrutable faces she could not recall ever having encountered any of the group before, but their sudden unannounced presence in the reception room was so dream-like that it evoked a background of emotional issues that marked them as automatically suspect—exactly of what, she had no idea. But there was no question in her mind that they had *not* arrived for a prayer meeting. And since she could not believe that such as they could ever associate anything having to do with the Senator with patriotic emotion their solemn appearance was simply illogical. For the Senator's sentiments regarding their race were widely known, if not notorious. Therefore, their very presence was enough in itself to arouse suspicion, and their acting as though they had come to pay him their respect suggested motives that were dark and devious. Indeed, she could feel it at work behind their bland nigra faces.

They can't possibly feel the way they're pretending, she thought in her native vernacular, but whatever they're up to it isn't going to work. Not with me! The nerve of their barging in here!

But here, nevertheless, they were—the last of them, an old man, now closing the door—and had to be dealt with.

By quick calculation there were about fifty, all peering silently into her face with that depressing nigra-solemn, nigra-patient yet demanding stare they always assumed when insisting—and against all logic, power, and tradition—upon having their own nigra way. They looked the same way on the breadlines back during the Depression except these didn't seem hungry. Nigras!

And what a lot! Old mammy nigras dressed in uniforms made from surplus nylon parachute material and loaded down with satchels, picnic baskets, and fans. And old nigra uncles standing in awkward military postures beside a collection of suitcases, baskets, battered briefcases, and what looked like a trombone case that stood upright in front of one of them. Then she saw that most of the group was clutching firmly in his or her gnarled hands a worn and much battered Bible!

And wouldn't you know it, she thought, forever trying to mix religion into any and everything. What on earth do they think they're up to, bringing their ignorant nigra religion into this office? The calls we've been getting from nigra leaders here in Washington are bad enough—and now these!

Then, as someone in the rear cleared his throat, she noted that the group had arrayed themselves in a neat semicircle according to sex, and it occurred to her that they might be gospel singers. Perhaps that was the answer. They were a group of old-time nigras who'd come to Washington hoping to sing for their supper. If so, they're in for a disappointment because Senator simply can't *stand* that—or any other—kind of nigra yelling. . . .

Now, as she looked around, so many nigras had crowded into the reception room that its Williamsburg funiture, its collection of early-American paintings, framed facsimiles of historical documents, and pedestal-mounted white marble bust of Vice President Calhoun were overshadowed. It was as though the nigras had brought with them an atmosphere of such incongruous dissonance that the room's usual tranquillity now resonated discord. So much so that she restrained herself from ordering them to leave only by reminding herself that the Senator's role as legislator made it imperative that even such undesirable visitors as these were to be accorded at least a formal show of politeness. Well, she thought, I *am* being polite, so why don't they speak their piece and get it over with? But of course! Being nigras they're recognizing that it is, after all, *my* prerogative to have the first word. . . .

"I," the secretary said, "am Miss Pryor, Senator Sunraider's secretary. May I help you?"

"Yes, ma'am, you can," a deep voice said—and she was aware of a big, brown-skinned nigra man who was moving away from the group and coming to stand a few feet before her.

"Miss Pryor," the big nigra said, "my name is Hickman ... Reverend Alonzo Hickman ..."

" ... Who's better known," a woman added in a voice which throbbed with pride, "as *God's* Righteous Trombone...."

"*Who*," the secretary began with a blink behind her glasses then caught herself. "Oh I see," she said, suppressing a smile as her eyes flashed to the instrument case. "And so, Reverend, what is your business with the Senator?"

"First, ma'am," the nigra Hickman said, "I'd like to introduce the gentleman on my right, who is one of our leaders, Deacon Wilhite...."

"I'm most pleased to meet you, ma'am," the short intense nigra on the nigra Hickman's right said, and bent with a courtly bow.

"And the rest of our group," the nigra Hickman continued, "are all leading members of our congregation. We arrived in Washington just a few minutes ago from Georgia, and—"

" ... Did you say from *Georgia?*" the secretary said.

"Yes, ma'am; all the way from Georgia, our home state. And we hurried here as fast as the taxis could bring us without breaking the law...."

"That's very interesting," the secretary said with a smile, "but for what purpose?"

"So that we could have a brief talk with Senator Sunraider, ma'am."

"And may I ask the subject of your proposed talk?"

"Yes, ma'am, you certainly may. It's about a development that is most important to the Senator...."

"Important? And does the Senator know about it?"

The nigra Hickman cocked his head, his eyes glancing thoughtfully at the ceiling. "Yes, ma'am, he knows *about* it, but he hasn't been informed about what has recently developed *because* of it."

"I don't understand—because of *what?*"

"Because of the matter we came up here to see him about."

"Are you saying that he's familiar with the matter in question?"

"Yes, ma'am, he is."

"Then why was it necessary ..."

" ... For us to come here?"

The secretary nodded, searching the bland nigra face through horn-rimmed glasses.

"Because, ma'am, there has been a new, very urgent development that came to our attention only a few days ago."

"And you came all the way to *Washington* to tell him about it?"

"That's right, ma'am...."

"But why didn't you simply write him; wouldn't that have been more conven-ient?"

"Well, ma'am, it might have been for *us*, but not for him; that's because it has to do with something that's so private that we felt that he should hear it directly from us."

"Private to whom, may I ask? Yourselves?"

"I meant to the Senator, ma'am."

Behind her glasses the secretary's eyes widened in a gesture of disbelief. "But for a group as large as yours such a trip must have to be terribly expensive," she said. "Are you sure that you aren't really thinking of yourselves?"

Suddenly the nigra Hickman smiled as though caught in a trick. "There was a bit of that, ma'am, but only to the extent that receiving the information the way we did, and knowing what we already knew of its background forced us to think beyond simply knowing what we knew and sitting on it and on to the point where we had to recognize that knowing it placed us under the pressing obliga-tion of getting our information to the Senator as fast, and as *directly*, as possible. So, yes, ma'am, you might say we were thinking about ourselves. But, like I say, that was only because we were thinking about *him*."

Sorting the confusing answer in her mind, the secretary reddened, shifting her feet, and decided to try a different approach.

"Doctor Hickman," she said, stressing the "doctor," "are you at all acquainted with the Senator? Have you ever met him?"

But before the nigra Hickman could answer, the short nigra Wilhite was shaken by a spell of coughing while the group looked on with an air of concern.

"Better do something about that," the nigra Hickman said. "Now, where was I? Oh, yes! The answer, ma'am, is not exactly, but we still..."

"... So you haven't met him, but in spite of that you still felt obligated to seek him out? But why?"

"Because, ma'am," the nigra Hickman said in a solemn voice, "we're *Chris-tians.*"

And suddenly the others broke their silence with a vigorous chorus of "Amens."

The secretary flushed and sighed. "And so you came here as Christians to perform a service for the Senator? Is that correct?"

"And that's the truth, ma'am. It was our Christian duty."

"But suppose he has no *need* for your services; suppose he doesn't *want* them?"

"Don't worry about that, ma'am, he needs help, and when he hears who's of-fering it I don't think that he'll turn it down. He only has to be told that we're here and he'll listen."

Stepping backwards, the secretary braced her body against the reception desk, thinking, *This is getting nowhere fast.*

"This has been quite interesting," she said with a tense smile, "but I'm afraid that I must disappoint you. Because here we have a strict rule that all appointments with the Senator must be made in advance. It is not my rule, but the Senator's, and what's more, I'm also afraid that the information you've supplied me simply doesn't justify my setting up an appointment in the future. I will *not* break the rule and interrupt the Senator's busy schedule."

"But, ma'am," the nigra Hickman said, "just as there's a time for being born and a time for dying death, there's also a time for rules, and a time for putting rules *aside*. Now is such a time. I've told you the truth: Our business is so urgent and so crucial to the Senator that we took time out to *fly* up here to see him. That's just how urgent we think it to be. So if you would just say to him that Reverend Hickman is here with some important information I'm sure that he'll forgive you for breaking the rule. What's more, we only have to see him for a few minutes. You have my word on that. We won't take up any more of his time than's needed to impart our information and answer any questions he might wish to ask us. Then we'll leave. And, ma'am..." the nigra Hickman paused, staring earnestly into her face.

"Yes?"

"Before you refuse maybe you ought to consider the possibility that our *not* seeing him might turn out to be much worse for everybody concerned than your breaking a rule."

"Doctor Hickman," the secretary said in a quivering voice, "I've noticed that while you hint around and use an awful lot of words, you actually *say* very little. Now who are you, *really*? And what is it that makes you feel that you have some special claim on the Senator's time? I'd really like to know—and please, a straightforward answer! Are you his constituents? If so, you should take up your problem with your district leader. There are, after all, procedures for such matters, whether you know about them or not—"

And realizing that the big nigra was smiling and shaking his head the secretary stared with a reddening face.

"Forgive me, ma'am," he said, "but the idea of our being the Senator's constituents got to me. We're anything but that, and what's more, I doubt that he has anyone like us in his entire district. No, ma'am, the fact is that we're *nobody's* constituents, not even down there where we come from. You might say, ma'am, that while we're sometimes among the counted we're seldom numbered among the heard. Instead, the politicians herd us around according to their *own* political interests and seldom ever listen to how *we* feel about it. And I doubt if that holds true of the Senator...."

And with the words "herd" and "heard" echoing in her ear the secretary thought, *Why, this nigra's insulting me with double-talk!*

"No," she said, "and none of that justifies your seeing the Senator. Nor has anything else you've said, as far as *I* can see. But if you're sincere you'll give your information—whatever it is—to me, and I'll pass it along to the Senator. So tell me now: *What is this all about?*"

Searching her face with a grave show of patience, the nigra Hickman paused as though weighing his answer.

"Ma'am," he said, "I'm sorry, but since it's his business rather than ours I'm afraid I'll have to leave that to the Senator to explain. All I'm free to say, and I'm truly sorry that I can't tell you more, is that it's urgent, and a matter of..."

"Now please don't tell me that it's a matter of life or death," the secretary said as she threw up her hands in mock alarm, "because it simply won't work!"

"Ma'am," the nigra Hickman said, staring down, "I wasn't about to say anything about it being a matter of life or death. I honestly wasn't. But who really knows? In this world some things appear to be but aren't, while others appear not to be—but, lo and behold, they are. The Scriptures tell us that in life we are in death, and in death there is life..."

"...Everlasting," a voice from the group added solemnly.

"Amen!"

"And that's the Lord's complicated truth!"

"You said it!"

"...But ma'am," Hickman continued, "you can rest easy in the knowledge that we didn't come all the way up here to waste anybody's time playing games...."

"...Amen!"...

"...Neither did we come here asking for political or any other type of favors," the big nigra said as he paused and gestured for silence from those behind him. "And if you have his interest at heart you'll believe me. All you have to do is step into his office and tell him that we're here to have a brief word with him.... That we— Why, yes, that's right!"

Suddenly the nigra Hickman's face brightened as though he'd stumbled on the solution to a difficult problem. And with a quick glance at the nigra on his right he smiled as though sharing a profound revelation.

"Ma'am," he said with a smile, "it just came to me that the best and quickest way of getting the importance of our presence across to the Senator is for you to say to him, 'Mister Senator, Hickman has finally *arrived*.' If you put it to him in those exact words it won't be necessary to tell him that our message is important, because he'll recognize it for himself...."

"...And, honey," a tall, fierce-looking, black-skinned woman interrupted, "that there's the truth if you ever heard it told! Yes, and while you're at it, you can tell him also that not only is Revern' out here waiting to see him, but that Deacon Wilhite and..."

Hickman turned, saying, "Sister Bea!"

"...That's right, dahling," the woman said, "tell him that Deacon Wilhite, Sister Wilhite, and all the rest of us is..."

"...Sister Bea," Hickman said, "the lady..."

"...What I mean, honey," the woman said, "is that you can tell him that we have *all* arrived!"

"Now that'll be enough, Sister Bea," Hickman said. "The lady understands that I've been speaking for all of us—you included."

"Well now, Reveren'," Sister Bea said, "I'm sorry, but I was only trying to save precious time. I apologize—and to you too, miss...."

But the damage was done. At the nigra woman's interruption the secretary went rigid with rage. These were nigras such as she had known during her childhood—and old ones at that; people whose lives in Georgia had to have disciplined them in the traditional attitudes and manners that governed relations between themselves and those of her own race and status. And yet, after having barely set foot in the District of Columbia, here they were trying to take advantage of what they doubtlessly considered to be "Northern" freedom and were deliberately violating the traditional code that had been developed—and under the most difficult of social and political conditions—to guide them in dealing with their superiors. And now, pretending to apologize, they were playing that disgusting nigra trick of looking humble while *acting* uppity! Worse, one nigra wench had so forgotten her place as to begin giving orders! They should have been thrown out the moment she saw them, but against her better judgment she had entertained the possibility that barging in unannounced they were simply from the country and ignorant. But now something in their attitude, and especially in that of the nigra Hickman, confirmed her initial suspicion. The nigra was using his double-talk to imply a relationship with the Senator which not only negated her authority, but left her without voice or substance. Indeed, they now appeared to be staring straight through her with eyes that focused upon some mysterious arrangement of human possibility which they assumed to be hidden beyond the door behind her.

These nigras are treating me as though I were a child, she thought, and was taken with a dream-like sensation of having plunged through a trapdoor and jolted to rest upon a platform which was bouncing and teetering just below the eye level of the shortest member of the group, a little black woman from whose chin white scraggly hairs protruded, while looming above her head the others were waiting with calm nigra faces. And now, trembling inwardly, she had a fleeting sensation of looking upward into the faces of a delegation of dark-skinned foreigners who had wandered in by mistake and were attempting to find their direction through a burly old whiteheaded spokesman whose command of English was so faulty that he failed to grasp the meaning of anything she had been attempting to say. Then, seeing that two of the old women were waving palm-leaf fans in a slow, undulating motion as though defying the room's air-conditioning, it came to her that behind their words and manner the nigras were stalling. Yes, they were hanging around in the hope that by keeping her occupied the Senator would notice her extended absence and step out of his office. If so, they're terribly mistaken!

"Ma'am," the nigra Hickman was saying, "I realize that our pressing you to let us see Senator Sunraider might seem impolite, so I apologize. But as you know, ma'am, things aren't always what they appear to be. Time is running out so now we're *begging* you to take us on faith and let us see him."

"Yes," she said, "you have indeed been *most* impolite. And what makes it worse is that you realize it. Not only have you taken up far too much of my time but I'm sure that it must have occurred to you by now that the Senator isn't here—not to say that it would have made a difference if he were. . . ."

And as she paused the nigra Hickman recoiled as though slapped in the face, saying, "Ma'am, did you say that the man isn't *here?*"

"Yes, I did, and you'll have to take my word for it."

"But, ma'am, I called from the airport and was told that he was talking on another phone. . . ."

"I can't help that, the fact is that he isn't here, and now I am asking you people to vacate these premises!"

"Very well, ma'am," the nigra Hickman said in a voice tense with emotion, "but you could have saved us all a lot of time and trouble by telling us that in the first place. While you've been wasting time the matter we came here to see the Senator about has gone on developing, so whether you believe it or not *he* needs to know about it. Why are you making it so hard for us?"

" . . . Because she don't know what she's doing, that's why," the tall wench said. "If ignorance was money that woman would be a multimillionaire!"

"I will not be referred to in that manner," the secretary said, "I simply will not!"

"I apologize for the sister," the nigra Hickman said, "and we accept your word that he's not here. But before we go, maybe you'll tell us how to reach him by telephone. Would you just do that? Because given the little time we have left it might even be better that way. We can give him our information, and if he doesn't want to see us it'll be up to him."

"Doctor Hickman," the secretary shrilled, "I wish you'd tell me what it is that I can say that will make you understand that I am *not* going to allow you to break into the Senator's schedule. It is *im*-possible! He is *unavailable!*"

"Brother Alonzo, are you going to just *stand* there and let that woman speak to you in that tone of voice?" Yes, it was the tall wench again, who now pushed forward as she said, "I'm getting sick and tired of her talking to us like she's that man's mama!"

And seeing the nigra Hickman turn to the impudent wench the secretary whirled and rushed to her office; where, slamming and locking the door behind her, she snatched up the telephone and called the security force for assistance. Then, still fuming with outrage, she stationed herself close to the door and stood listening until the guard arrived and then rushed out and demanded that he clear the reception room.

Rushing into the reception room the guard who accompanied them there stared into the secretary's face with his hand on his holster as he waited to be told what the Negroes (who seemed relatively calm) had done. But receiving no explanation he opened the door and pointed.

"All right, folks," he said, "let's do it the easy way."

And with a nod from the big Negro the group began moving out as quietly as they had upon entering.

And now, looking out through the doorway, the secretary watched as they filed past the waiting Hickman and headed for the elevator; then, as the last old man passed through, lugging the trombone case, she saw Hickman turn to face her and was struck by his sheer height and girth as he loomed in the doorway.

"Miss Pryor," he said, "I'm afraid that you've made a grave mistake. Because whether you believe me or not the Senator does know us, and given the circumstances he'd want—"

" … *Knows* you," the secretary said, hearing the rising of her voice, "KNOWS YOU! Why, I've heard the Senator state quite definitely that the only colored he knows is the boy who shines shoes at his country club!"

"Is that right," Hickman said with his head cocked to one side. "Well, ma'am, if that's what he says I won't dispute it. Anyway, we apologize for causing you trouble, and I want you to know that it's only been because we think that it's to the Senator's interest to know that we're here on the scene. It really is, and I hope you'll tell him that we have arrived. And soon, ma'am, because otherwise it might be too late. …"

There was no threat in his voice, only an echo of that odd, resigned sadness which she had detected in the faces of the other nigras just before the guard ordered them out of the room.

"Good day, ma'am," Hickman said, and was blotted from view by the closing door.

In the hall the group exchanged no words as they followed the guard, who, turning now to Hickman, said, "What was *that* all about? What got her so upset?"

"Maybe a case of mistaken identity," Hickman said. "Or a loss of memory. All I really know is that we asked to see the man for a few minutes but for some reason she refused us."

"Well," the guard said, "being strangers I guess you haven't heard about the Senator."

"I guess we haven't," Hickman said; "I guess we haven't."

Reaching the waiting elevator, Hickman stood aside with the guard as the group pressed in, thinking, *Wilhite warned me that it was a mistake to come directly here, and he was right. Phoning would have been better because if she hadn't seen us she might have made the connection—well, maybe not, since my voice is still my voice. But it's my fault for wanting so badly to see the man once again in the flesh. So between that and trying to save time we're losing it. … Still falling behind … as through all the long years … still falling behind. …*

Waiting until the members were all inside the car, he squeezed in behind the guard. Then, facing the door, he reached out and grasped its frame and assumed a spread-eagled stance as the car descended.

And now, reaching the lobby, the door glided open and he was surprised to find himself looking straight into a pair of watery blue eyes that stared from a sunburned face which smelled strongly of a visit to a barber shop. The man's eyes were but inches away, and as he pulled back he saw that they belonged to a heavy-set man who wore a gold badge, and beyond the man's shoulders he saw four guards who stood in a row, and realized that the man was deliberately blocking his path.

But now, raising his palm, the man stepped backward and said, "Hold it right there! And you, Nelson," he growled at the guard in the elevator, "how did so many of them get up there? What the hell's been happening?"

And feeling the guard's hand on his shoulder, Hickman lowered his arms and felt him squeeze past and out of the car.

"Captain," the guard said, "when I got there they were standing around in the reception room...."

"Doing what?"

"Just standing there and saying nothing, so all I can report is that Miss Pryor called down and said that when she told them they couldn't see the Senator they refused to leave."

"But how did they get up there in the first place?"

"On the elevator. They were with the Reverend here, and after checking his identification and finding it okay we allowed them through. I'll admit that it did seem a little odd that they would want to see the Senator, but after all they are a church group and we had no reason to stop them...."

"Now that was smart," the captain said. "You passed them and they proceeded up there and gave Miss Pryor a rough time—is that what you're telling me?"

"That's what she said; but when I got there they were quiet, barely whispering among themselves. Then she busted out of her office and when she ordered me to get rid of them they came along peacefully. Made no trouble whatsoever."

"All right," the captain said, beckoning to Hickman. "Have your people come out one at a time so I can take a look at them."

"Do as he says," Hickman said over his shoulder, and to the captain, "There was nothing more than a misunderstanding...."

"Just have them step out of there and line up over there," the captain said, pointing to a spot near the wall.

And now, stepping to the side, Hickman nodded to Deacon Wilhite and stood looking each of his group in the eye as they stepped into the lobby.

With luggage in hand the group stood waiting as the captain stood back and began looking them over.

"How many do we have?" he called to the guards behind him.

"An even fifty," a guard called back; "I just made the count."

"And exactly just what did she say they were doing?"

"Nothing in particular," the guard Nelson said. "They just refused to leave."

"So what does she want done with them?"

[TROMBONE]

"ALL SHE SAID WAS get them out of the reception room."

"And that was it?"

"Yes, sir; that's all she said."

"These secretaries are a pain in the butt," the captain said, "and especially the Senator's. Last time it was a worm in an apple, and now this!"

And as he gazed at the new source of trouble he turned abruptly to Hickman.

"Just what," he snapped, "are you folks doing with all that *luggage?*"

"Our plane was late," Hickman said, "so rather than miss our appointment we came here directly from the airport...."

"*Airport?* Did you just arrive in the city?"

"Yes, sir, we did."

"From where?"

"From Atlanta..."

"From *Atlanta!* And you came all that distance to see Senator Sunraider?"

"Yes, sir; we did."

"Now isn't *that* interesting," the captain roared as he wheeled toward the guards, "a flock of... of... A flock like this flies all that distance to bug the Senator, and *you* let them get up to his offices! I wouldn't believe it, but it sure gives this thing a different complexion!"

And turning to Hickman he roared, "Okay, mister preacher, since you-all come from Georgia I'd better have a closer look at you. So have your people line up against that wall over there."

"Good Lord, Reverend," Sister Gipson groaned, "after all that time in the air we end up getting *no-wheres!*"

"What was that?" the captain barked as he whirled to face her.

"That's right," Sister Gipson said, "because up here we're being treated no better than back in Georgia."

"You should have thought about that before you flew up here causing trouble! Now get over there with the rest of the girls and form me a line standing shoulder to shoulder!"

"And you-all," he barked as he turned toward the brothers, "get over there and join them!"

"Do as he says," Hickman said. And as the members moved toward the wall and began placing their luggage on the floor before them he kept an eye on the captain.

From his accent this fellow sounds Southern, he thought, but he's surely no gentleman. And now that he's feeling his power we'd better make use of our self-control. . . .

And as he watched the captain dramatizing his sense of superiority by approaching each of the members with a stare which was meant to intimidate he reacted with a feeling of disgust and irony—until, seeing him reach Brother Jefferson and stare down at his trombone case, he tensed with a frown.

"What have you in there?" the captain said.

"It's a slide trombone," Brother Jefferson said.

"A trom-bone? So you're a musician!"

"No, sir," Brother Jefferson said. "It belongs to our pastor."

Turning abruptly, the captain called, "Reverend, are you the owner of this instrument?"

"Yes, sir," Hickman said, "it's mine."

"But aren't you a preacher?"

"That's true, but I'm also a musician. . . ."

"And you play the trombone?"

"Yes, sir; for many years, both before and after. . . ."

" . . . Before and after—what does *that* mean?"

"I meant before and after I entered my ministry."

And seeing the captain take the hands-on-hips stance of a general, he thought, So now it's coming. . . .

"You sure you don't have something other than a trombone in there?" the captain said. "Maybe a machine gun?"

"A *machine* gun? Well now, if that's what you think, maybe you'd better have a look and see for yourself. . . . But Captain, I'm telling you in front . . ."

" . . . You're telling me *what?*"

"That you'll have to be satisfied with looking."

"Oh, yeah? And how do you figure that?"

"Because I'm not even *about* to prove to you that I know how to play that instrument. The case is unlocked, so go ahead and satisfy yourself."

And bristling with anger the captain snatched up the case.

"I'll do just that, and since you came here creating a disturbance I'm having every damned one of you searched—bags, baggage, and picnic baskets!"

Watching the captain kneel and begin opening his trombone case, Hickman surged with annoyance. Because evidently the captain was of the type who would regard his trombone as nothing more than an absurd device he used in exploiting what many whites disdained as a heathenish form of religion. But whatever the captain might think, his trombone had long been the agency through which he gave lyrical expression to his emotions, hopes, and spiritual gropings. And from his boyhood it had been the magical instrument through which he had sought to achieve a sense of himself, and in seeking to master its capacity for giving expression to moods, ideas, and inspirational moments he had come to recognize and express the spiritual dimension of his innermost being. Thus, over the years his trombone had become the instrumental extension of his God-given voice and the agency through which he had become skilled in defining and projecting his dreams, hopes, and yearnings. And this whether they took the form of the blues, the spirituals, or improvised jazz. And through the broad sweep of its range, tone, and timbre he had learned the secret of moving his listeners beyond the deceptive limitations of words and into those misty regions of existence wherein all things, whether sacred or profane, time-bound or timeless, were constantly mingled. Thus for years his trombone had served as his rod and his staff, and like Jacob's ladder an earthly vehicle of spiritual transcendence. And in watching its transcendental aura being profaned he could barely resist snatching it out of the captain's white hands.

"And what's this thing you have in here with it?" the white man said as he fingered a round rubber object.

"That's a matter of the user and how he employs it. Attached to a stick it's a tool for suction...."

"...*Suction?* Hell, this damned thing is a *toilet* plunger!"

"That's right, but not on a bandstand...."

"So what's it doing in here?"

"Now *that*," Hickman said as he seized the opportunity for striking back at the captain, "is because of a miracle...."

"A *what?*"

"That's right, a miracle which occurred long ago during a big public dance in New Orleans. And it came to pass after one of the musicians made the mistake of misplacing his mute. Which for the musician was terribly upsetting, because he was famous for the voice-like effects which his mute provided his playing. Therefore the idea of disappointing his listeners became so disturbing that it sent him speeding on a trip to the men's room. But he was still upset, and when he saw one of those you're holding standing beside the toilet a miracle took place...."

"Now wait!"

"That's right, but only after the musician underwent a fierce inner struggle. He couldn't figure why he was doing such a thing, but being desperate to maintain his fine reputation and artistic standards, he removed the rubber cup from its wooden stick and washed it. And then, still puzzled by his sudden urge to handle something so filthy, he dried it, stuck it in his pocket, and returned to the bandstand. But it wasn't until he'd pressed its flexible end to the bell of his horn that he began to understand just why his hands had moved so much faster in the men's room than his mind was able. But when his time came to improvise on one of his favorite tunes, he arose in the spotlight with his horn in one hand and the toilet plunger in the other, he started to sweat and tremble. And no wonder, because when folks on the dance floor saw him they began laughing so hard that he felt like a fool. But being a professional he bowed and signaled the drummer to accelerate the rhythm and come to his aid. And once he got blowing and muting his horn with that plunger the sound it produced was so thrilling that he brought down the house."

"Amen," one of the members shouted. "Amen!"

" 'Amen' is right," Hickman said, "because now folks were applauding with pleasure and dancing like mad. So with that an ordinary toilet plunger moved from bathroom to bandstand and became a musical instrument of spiritual dimensions. . . ."

"Now look here," the captain said, "are you trying to kid me?"

"No, sir, I'm just describing one of the many miracles that happen and go fairly unnoticed. As when a simple tin can becomes a fine vase when it's filled with beautiful flowers. By the way, you weren't always a captain, or were you?"

Looking up with his face suddenly crimson, the captain glared.

"*I'm* asking the questions," he growled, "and don't you forget it!"

And holding the trombone's slide in one clumsy hand and its bell in the other, the white man drew erect.

"What the hell," he growled. "Is this all there is to this thing?"

And seeing the captain frown as though examining a dangerous weapon, Hickman lost patience.

"Yes, sir," he said, "that's all except for the mouthpiece, the lips, the lungs, and musicianship that's needed to sound it. You'll find the mouthpiece in the little compartment at the end of the case. And don't get upset by the fluid you see in the bottle that's with it, it's only the oil I use in lubricating the slide."

Bending again, the captain took a brief look. And now, pulling erect, he thrust the ungainly trombone toward Brother Jefferson.

"Never mind," he said with a glare at Hickman. "Forget it."

"Does that mean you're letting us go?" Hickman said.

"No, not even as far as you could tilt Lincoln's monument!"

And turning to the guards behind him the captain growled, "You, Kimbrough, get on with it! Open the rest of those bags. And Macklin, you and Traver give him a hand. And you, Nelson, start searching their bodies!"

"Not the women," Nelson said with alarm. "You don't really mean that, do you, Captain?"

With a stare at Hickman the captain grinned.

"The hell I don't! In a situation like this they could be dangerous gun molls, so get on with it!"

And now, seeing the captain approach, Hickman raised his arms and remained silent lest he trigger the brothers' resistance. And with a blank expression he watched as the group began quietly submitting.

In spite of the captain's insults the sisters appeared amused that anyone should consider them dangerous, and for the first time he saw a release of tension which was usually concealed by their quiet immobility. It was as though being subjected to a familiar pattern of their lives had released their self-protective capacity for irony; which, supported by their religion, had made their lives endurable. So now they were responding to the absurdity of being searched for weapons by exchanging sly winks and looks of astonishment.

Thank the Lord, he thought, that we're still able to laugh at things intended to intimidate and insult us. It's been a harsh discipline but without it, how could we hope to face up to even the routine, everyday insanity of folks like this captain? Where any reasonably sane person would look at our age and attitude and see that we're law-abiding, he insults us by treating us like criminals. And simply because we came here to speak with a senator. And not to accuse or rebuke him, or ask for favors, but in order to help him. But hardly do we open our mouths than we're in a struggle of words with that woman who's so wrapped up in the white folks' games of Who's in Charge, and Keep the Nigger in His Place that she can't get our message for worrying about the blackness of the messengers. And it didn't help that we'd learned to deal with that kind of game so long ago that we politely ignored it, she still jumps salty and calls for the guards—so we end up down here being pawed over by a gang of flunkies loaded down with blackjacks, pistols, and billy clubs!

And yes, he thought with an inward smile, with sawed-off Gatling guns! And seeing the captain squat with a grunt and begin slapping him about his calves and his ankles he looked down at the white, recently shaved neck and saw traces of talcum.

Hickman, he thought, it seems that no matter whatever a man's brain orders his body to do out of vanity it can only obey according to its condition and structure. And sometimes the result is ridiculous. Just look at the position it's put this one in! So busy showing off his power that he can't see that he has to get down on his knees to do it!

But now with a grunt, the captain arose and moved to where his men were examining lunch boxes and baskets and finding nothing more lethal than Southern-fried chicken, hard-boiled eggs, store-cheese, soda crackers and bologna, peanut-butter and pork-chop sandwiches, and desserts consisting of chocolate cakes and fried sweet-potato pies. And warmed by the members' good humor he thought, Hickman, maybe this clown has a bit of truth going for him after all, because a bad fried pie can be deadly!

And with a blank expression he watched two of the older ladies making light of the situation by responding to one of the guards' orders with coquettish smiles and spinning on the floor in their flat-heeled shoes. A gesture which caused their ankle-length skirts to whirl flirtatiously as they giggled as gaily as green young girls. And now, a bit farther down the line, Brother Matt Smith was sharing their mockery.

With shoulders braced and head erect, Brother Matt was high-stepping in place and performing a straight-faced put-down of the guards' military manners by barking, "Yas, suh! Right, Suh! Very good, Suh!" and punctuating the guard's commands by stamping his foot on the floor.

I guess that's as good a way as any of reminding a youngster that you fought and survived a couple of wars, Hickman thought. But now, seeing a guard step close to Brother Provo, he recalled the reputation which the old man had acquired during his days on the Galveston docks and prepared for trouble.

Wearing a black felt hat and standing far back in his knees with his slanting shoulders relaxed and arms hanging loosely, Brother Provo's flat-nosed, lean-jawed head looked as though it had been squashed into the collar of his shirt by the weight of a boulder. In profile he appeared to be dozing—but now as the guard bent forward and gave a command, it was as though a warning signal had flashed in the path of a highballing train. For now in a flurry of movement, Brother Provo's outstretched arms were pumping the air as though he intended to clasp the guard to his bosom. But instead, leaping backwards, he assumed the crouch of a veteran street fighter—from which, balancing lightly on the tips of his nob-toed shoes with hands at the ready, he watched the guard out of fierce narrow eyes. And as Hickman moved to intervene he saw the guard's hand fly to his holster and froze, looking on.

"What do you think you're doing?" the guard said. "You hard of hearing or something?"

"What do you think *you're* doing," Brother Provo said, "coming up on a man like that! And never mind my hearing, my ears is as good as yourn—yeah, and a heap more experienced!"

"Then you know that I told you to remove your hat, not show me your combat moves!"

"Yeah, and that's what I thought you said."

"Then why don't you do it?"

"Because I like to think a bit before I take off my hat to *any* man, that's why. Especially when he giving me orders like I got no choice except to obey him. But in case you don't know it, a *man* can always choose when to die!"

And in the sudden hush Hickman's voice boomed as though shouted through a bullhorn, "BROTHER PROVO!"

"I'm hearing you, Reveren'," Brother Provo said. "What is it?"

"Look at me, Brother...."

With eyes still fixed on the guard, Brother Provo shook his head.

"Reveren', I *said* I'm listening, ain't that enough at a time like this?"

"Very well, I understand," Hickman said, "but listen carefully: I sympathize with how you feel, but since our business here is important, don't you think you ought to take your hat off so that we can end this foolishness?"

For a long interval Brother Provo remained silent, but just as he started to repeat his question Hickman saw the brother's narrow eyes shift to his own.

"Revern', maybe you're right," Brother Provo said, "but this fellow's coming up on a man all of a sudden and telling him to off with his hat raises some questions. This here's supposed to be Washington, D.C., ain't it?"

"Right! And if this was down home he wouldn't *tell* you to remove your hat, he'd knock it off. Otherwise everything you're signifying is true. But when you remember that this man is only following orders you can afford to indulge him...."

"All right, so I'll do it. But some day I hope you'll explain why it is that *we're* always the ones who have to do the indulging!"

Glancing away to catch sight of the captain's reaction, Hickman saw him looking over the shoulder of a sister who had stepped out of line for a better view, and looking back he saw Brother Provo removing his hat from his bald, battle-scarred head. And now slowly turning the black hat upside down Brother Provo was extending it toward the guard.

Careful now, Hickman thought, *because if I heard him right he's changed his strategy but still resisting*—and saw Brother Provo wait until the guard's fingers reached out, and reaching inside the hat and flipping out its leather sweatband he turned the crown upright and gave it a tap which sent a small green wad to the floor in a flash.

"Would you look at that," Brother Provo said with mock surprise as the guard dropped to one knee in retrieving the green object.

"You really are full of tricks," the guard said as he pulled erect. "Now, what is it this time?"

"You the one who has holt to it," Brother Provo said. "Why don't you look and see?"

Staring at Brother Provo as he fingered the object, the guard hesitated.

"Oh, man, go 'head on!" Brother Provo challenged. "I know they say it's the root of all evil, but shucks, it ain't goin' to hurt a tough fellow like you."

Shaking his head, the guard replied with a shrug. And patiently smoothing the tightly folded wad he held it toward the lights in the ceiling. And realizing that he was holding a badly creased banknote he gave Brother Provo a blank-faced stare.

"Does *all* of this belong to you?" the guard said with a grin.

"What do you want me to say," Brother Provo said as he looked at Hickman with a bland expression, "you just seen it fall outta my hat, and this not being a game of finders-keepers, what can I do but admit that it does. But hey! Take a look at who's picture is on it! Man, that's General Tee-cumseh Sherman, the very same General who told the world that war is hell and went on to *prove* it! Yes, suh! Somebody in your line of work could learn a heap from a man like that!"

Suppressing a smile, Hickman watched the guard drop the banknote into Brother Provo's outstretched palm as though it were flaming.

"Got you that time, didn't I," Brother Provo said, grinning at the guard. "So now I guess you want to look inside my shoes...."

But before the guard could answer the captain rushed forward and pushed him aside. "That'll be enough of that," he said and whirled angrily toward Hickman.

"Listen," he said, "didn't you say that these were church people?"

"Yes, sir," Hickman said, "I did, and they are. But that doesn't mean that they can't be provoked into acting devilish—and even enjoy it. After all, they're also Americans. . . ."

"Well, if that's what you preach you'd better not bring it in here again because we go strictly by the book—the *law* book!"

And stepping back, the captain swept his eyes along the line of blank watching faces, then down to the clutter of luggage at their feet.

"That'll do it," he said, "and now I want you people to shut these bags and get the hell out of here!"

As the group spilled onto the sidewalk smiling and shaking their heads, Hickman beckoned and they assembled around him.

"Folks," he said, "I can see that none of you are discouraged by what happened in there, otherwise you wouldn't be in such good humor. And I don't think I have to explain the reason I couldn't tell that secretary any more than I did, because that you already know. Neither do I have to explain that I had to do what I did. . . . Maybe she felt the same way. The point for us now is to find some other way of getting to this man, and if what we've been through is any indication it's going to be even harder than we anticipated. . . ."

". . . It sure is, Revern'," Sister Rogers said, "because these old folks around this town don't seem to understand *anything*! We come to try to help the man, and that white gal secretary starts acting like some kind of one-chick hen. And if *that* wasn't enough, those guards back there has to jump in and start *searching* us like criminals! So if these are the kind of folks that's helping to run this so-called government I tell you we're up against a powerful lot of ignorance! Why, if we was the kind to depend on the sword instead of the Lord we'd a-been too long gone to even think about it—ain't that right, Sister Arter?"

"Girl," Sister Arter said, "we'd have been in the grave and done long finished moldering!"

"Amen!"

"Sister Arter," Sister Dawkins said, "I'd like to see their faces if they was to search you after you come from performing some of your midwifing duties. And especially for some of our fancy white families."

"Me too," Sister Arter said, "because it might teach them some of the facts of life. And I mean both those guards and that snippy secretary. It would teach them something about the connectedness of folks and things."

[HOTEL]

"You're right," Hickman called through the laughter, "but for now we'd better find that hotel which a friend of Deacon Wilhite recommended and get us some rest."

"Now that I could use," Sister Bea said, "but from the way things are going it'll probably be a case of no room in the inn."

"Oh, no, Sister Bea," Hickman said, "we'll be accepted because this is the hotel where our top gospel singers stay when they're performing in Washington."

"I hope you're right, 'cause for today I've had my fill of white folks' foolishness! What's the name of this place?"

"The Hotel Longview—whatever that means—but like I say, that's where we're headed."

Arriving at the hotel, Hickman climbed from his taxi and gazed at its façade and surroundings while the members assembled on the sidewalk. So now, he thought, we'll see how these Longview folks react to us strangers from Georgia....

As expected, the lobby was crowded with whites, none of whom appeared disturbed by their entrance except one young man on his way out who paused and stared at his face with a startled expression.

"A.Z.," Wilhite said, "he reacted as though he recognized you...."

But as Hickman turned and stared he was interrupted by a squad of bellmen rushing to help his group with their luggage. And now as he moved through the crowd he was pleased by the sight of several young brown-skinned young women and a famous black athlete. And in passing a party of convivial white couples he was surprised when one of the men bowed with an eye-twinkling smile and turned out to be a famous politician from Harlem. And upon reaching the reception desk he noted that the clerk's reaction to the group was routine but friendly.

Good, he thought, good! This is how it should be: impersonal but gracious. So now, after getting some rest, we'll get on with the business at hand.

Having seen that the sisters and brothers were comfortable he inspected his room, returned to the lobby, and bought a newspaper. And making his way to an area in which a scattering of men sat lounging and talking, he found a chair and began scanning the paper for news of the Senator.

Which proved unsuccessful, and with a sigh of relief he began reviewing the strategic mistake he'd made in going to the Senator's office, and was suddenly aware that even the whites sitting nearby seemed undisturbed by his presence.

So, Hickman, he thought, *it appears that while some patterns have changed, others remain as they were in the old days. Here you're made welcome by a popular hotel and greeted by a powerful black congressman, but back at his office a prejudiced secretary prevented you from seeing a Senator.*

Which means that you've stayed away from Washington so long that you've lost some of your skills in interpreting its signs and its symbols. And maybe much too long for dealing with a booby-trapped town where you've always needed a map and a scenario for guiding your conduct. Yes, and an expert in D.C. double-talk to tell you what to do when words say one thing and mean their exact opposites.

So perhaps it was a mistake to persuade the members to come along with you, even though most of them have shared your quest from the beginning and are eager to be in on its outcome. Still, you gambled, and now they're frustrated, and it's all due to your eagerness.

And Hickman, his doubtful self added, *it's all because you made the mistake of hoping that when so many folks from the old days arrived unannounced you'd get to the Senator. But you didn't, so now the game is back where it started. And not only for you, but for the members as well. . . .*

All right! So the problem of getting to the man remains to be solved, but we'll do it. And even if he still rejects the ties from the past that brought us to Washington, all will be well.

Yeah, but that "if" is as high as the Washington Monument!

Even so, we'll find this prodigal son of ours and act as though it was he *who finally found* us. *And after telling him that his life is in danger we'll bless him and leave what happens next for him to decide.*

Sure, Hickman, that's what you planned, but the idea was much too hopeful—which you should have realized; just as you knew very well that anyone unaware of its background would consider your plan as a brainstorm conceived by an ignorant jazzman turned preacher. And in light of the man's reputation that was illogical.

Yes, but most of life adds up to an illogical blend of disorder and order. That's why we try to apply logic as a way of reducing our lives to patterns which we think we can manage. And the members accept that fact of living just as I do. Because life in this country has taught them that order and disorder are inseparable. So they knew what they were doing when they took on the risk of this mission.

What's important is that we came to this town to save the man's life, and one way or another we'll do it. So like it or not, what you're putting down as illogic contains a vein of good sense. And that's true even if it springs from our hopes of finding some trace of the child we once loved still hidden in the heart of the man who rejects us. That's the logic of our coming here, and in it the present is being influenced by the past. Yes, and all of the made-in-America color confusion that wrought it. . . .

Yes, Hickman, I know what you mean. But thinking of it here in this lobby full of prosperous white folks is like somebody in a loud, drunk-filled bar thinking he can get their attention by reciting a fable!

Maybe so, but even if nobody listens it's true, it happened. *Because in the not too distant past we old folks were warmed by a little child evangelist with white skin and white features, but whose speech and spirit were shaped by our own. . . .*

Yes, Hickman, but that was a long time ago. . . .

. . . A marvelous child of Ishmaelian origin and pariah's caste, but his blending of bloods and unusual experience endowed that child with a command of the Word which was so inspiring that we came to accept him as the living token and key to that world of togetherness for which our forefathers long hoped and prayed. And since that child landed among us during a time of great trouble we saw in him an answer to our hopes that this divided land with its diversity of people would at last be made whole. Yes, and instilled with our own stubborn vision and blues-tempered acceptance of this country's turbulent reality.

It was that child, that mysterious outcast of the race that opposed us, who won our hearts and filled us with hope. So we accepted that child as a gift sent from heaven, and in the unfolding drama of our lives we cast him as a hero and symbol on the order of Christ, our savior. And because of his power and grace with the God-given Word we envisioned him as a means of breaking the slavery-forged chains which still bind our country.

Yes, and then look what happened!

Sneer if you like, but what a wonderful experience he gave us!

And what pains for your trouble!

Yes, but while in those days boy evangelists were fairly common and a wide-open secret that many Southern "whites" were black and many "blacks" white—at least visually—we had known no youngster evangelist of any *race who possessed his traits of character or a gift of eloquence which promised that longed-for transcendence of the past which would free us. And since attaining the freedom to be our own unique selves while peacefully coexisting with those who outnumbered us would unify our goals, both religious and social, we rejoiced and gave thanks to the Lord for the sheer existence of our rare gifted child.*

Thus, with our little boy preacher as symbol and spokesman we set out to overcome the limitations imposed by our history and this country's ongoing contentions. And by embracing that child as the unique symbol of a unity to come we hoped that the combined promises of Scripture and this land's Constitution would be at last fulfilled and made manifest.

So in church house and tent, on highways and in byways, we engaged ourselves in spreading the glad tidings by Word, song, and ritual. And for a few bright years it was our hope-inspired mission, and an act of faith in the promised showing forth of the possible. It was a time of rejoicing and gladness, but then hostile forces before which we were powerless prevailed and once again things fell apart.

And then mysteriously, and to our utter dismay, the child reached his teens and seceded by losing himself in the black-denying world of skin whiteness. So once again, as in the days of our fathers, we were left puzzled by the wreck of our dreaming. For in the mysterious spell spun by our yearning our little orphan of mixed identity had become one of us. And no matter how often we were disappointed by others we had come to expect loyalty from one whom we'd made so uniquely our own. So the blow was shattering, yes! But the dream itself continued to haunt us, as it does to this day, here in the vastness of Washington.

So there you go, it's still the same story!

Yes and no. At first it came as a harsh reminder of earlier betrayals of our love and goodwill, and a chastening lesson in the undependability of all human hopes, whether in the form of mere dreams or in the promises of those documents of state that our enemies claim to hold sacred but constantly defile. And it forced us to recognize once again that while dreaming is human and most indispensable, even the most exalted *of dreams often turn into nightmares.*

Thus, in our own secret way we were reliving an experience which the Book of Revelation has so hauntingly described. Which is to say that in the process of exalting the child's promise we had tasted of that which is honey-sweet to the taste but in the bowels turns bitter. And so now, late in their lives, and in what for them is the most unlikely of places, the sis-

ters and brothers are reaffirming their faith in our child-fostered dream by trying to save the life of a man whose hand has been turned against us and all of our kind.

As you insist, it's illogical but an act of undying faith. And now in the elusive person of the man whom our lost child's become we're here hoping to recapture some of the mystery that glowed long ago from the image of hope which as a child he made manifest....

Yes, Hickman, but as you just admitted, the whole thing's illogical. And what's more, when the child shattered their hopes the members were outraged!

How can I deny it? But in time their slavery-born sense of life's ever comic and blues-like turns of phrase and waywardness muted their anger. So along with me they soon became fascinated by the mystery of how such a devout child could have become a man so devious. Why, having had a choice denied those who took him and gave him protection, did he turn against that part of himself which was a gift of those who loved him? What had we done, or not done? How could that much-beloved child become a man so attracted to the world which denied his friends and protectors that he chose it and denied our gift of unselfish love?

Well, Hickman, that's the question which sent you here still seeking an answer.

Yes, because over the years since the child ran away, I like the others have been patiently searching him out and following his adventures. And through the dark glass imposed by racial differences and distance we've caught glimpses of him here, heard words of him there, despairing over most of his actions and marveling at others—much as we rejoice at the achievements of the government in whose name he now acts and despair at its failures. And in time our lost errant son would become the source of yet another reversal through which we realized that it was precisely his devious scheming that was gradually drawing those like us closer to having an active, if behind-the-scenes, role in that selfsame government. And now, beyond all reasonable expectations, we're here. Unheralded, yes, but determined to see the past redeemed and the child's promise made manifest in the present—here in the District of Co-lumbia!

Which is indeed a confounding surprise. For before the boy's surfacing as a politician we thought of ourselves as simply outsiders who were strictly limited in the role they could play in the nation's affairs. We had been among the counted—as I said in the pun I laid on that woman—but seldom among the heard. Which was little more than a signifying playing with words, for in view of our lost son's prominence we have come to recognize ourselves as inside-outsiders and learned to laugh as we do at most outrageous jokes in which we're pro-jected as fools or as victims.

And why not? For like logic most jokes are two-sided, and we've come to realize that no matter what positions the Senator takes, or how much power he amasses, he remains the crea-ture of our own mixture of blackness and whiteness. Oh, yes! He remains our own fallen angel, our own prodigal son. An outrageous notion? Yes! But one for which there can be no earthly undoing. So no matter how hard the struggle has been, we have endured. And as the old saying goes, by simply enduring we've switched the yoke and changed the joke that keeps plaguing America.

So now, face-to-face, we'll seek out the child in the man who denies us while pondering anew the mystery of how he could have become that which he is. And while accepting the fact that what has been done can not be undone, perhaps we'll learn what went wrong when our dream of felicity collided with this country's most thorny reality.

For in our own down-home way we are basically realistic. And since our living has taught us that in most human affairs the victimized are at least partially *responsible for their condition, perhaps we'll learn more of the extent to which our own dreams and errors had a role in the agony we suffer.*

So, like you say, we erred by placing such a burden of hope on the child. Still, it was an act of faith, and we must accept the fact that such faith is not only thorny but makes us appear as childlike as our enemies would like us to be. For such faith is a testing of life's possibilities, and the virtue of our old act of faith lay in its being self-*chosen.*

It was ourselves who invested our hopes for the coming of a more peaceful and tolerant society in the person of a child. It was our own *vision of a Peaceful Kingdom in which the child was both visual sign and eloquent symbol. And the fact that he went on to become an insatiable lion in Washington turned out to be far beyond all our imagining. The amazing thing is that although with a few exceptions our own condition has remained much as it was, the child who inspired our dreams for a land of milk and honey has become, much to our despair and amazement, a hostile political power. So today if he rejects our act of good faith and turns us away, it will still be proof that here, and no matter how, an American mystery has been turned into history.*

So for us whatever happens will be no surprise. We've kept the faith, and for that alone all shall be well. Yes, all shall be well. But who knows? Perhaps there's a trace of our old bee tree's honey still concealed in the carcass of our raging political lion....

Yes, Hickman, he thought, *all will be well. For in exploiting our condition he's retaught us who loved him and all who'll listen a lesson taught our people following the Reconstruction: that in this land, and no matter their color, the weak and powerless are granted either false hopes or blind ignorant bliss. And that the trick of survival lies in keeping at the endless task of distinguishing the one from the other. Therefore, we must keep "keeping on." So we'll take our look at the man and this city and return home. And perhaps all we'll ever know for certain is that we have endured and endured the stress and hardships of our enduring. So, having chosen to hope for justice and equity in a land where so many are eager to exploit the mystery of color to our disadvantage, we'll have to keep clinging to hope and leave the Founding Fathers' dream of eternal bliss to the future—*

Bliss? he thought as he awoke with a start, *good Lord, Hickman, how could you come up with such a crude misnaming! Anyway, we'll have to go on struggling for our dream, because given the way the deck has been stacked, what more can we reasonably expect?*

Yes, Hickman, and that's why for us the mystery and inescapable agony of hoping lies in its being a form of gambling, a game in which winners take the leanest, hindmost part. So, like playing jazz in the days when it earned fellows like you little fame and even less money, it has to serve as its own compensation. Maybe that's its built-in joke and realistic function. If so, maybe it's still working behind the scenes in its own secret fashion. Because in spite of all our defeats it might well be blues-like and a transcendent triumph over all who would reduce us to hopelessness—Amen!

Yes, Hickman, but after staking so much on time, change, and a little lost boy you forgot the joker who can take the form of a woman! That's right, you ignored the fact that usually when folks like us reach out for a pot there's always some woman of theirs who's waiting to grab it. And I mean by any means possible. You, who learned years ago that their men have used them to block the gate to equality. And if it were left to them Saint Peter would turn out to be an evil, nigger-hating woman! It's a terrible idea, but the truth is the truth, and that's the nasty old black-and-white mess of it! So thank God that there's also been the other more charitable side, in which, sometimes, it's been the women who've extended us a helping hand. . . .

But not that secretary! Why couldn't she bring herself to bend a bit? If she had, we could be seeing something of the city instead of worrying about our next move. . . . Well, she didn't, so that increases the danger. Because even if she told him that we have arrived he might have decided to keep playing hide-and-seek, not realizing that this time, with a new player out to destroy him, the game is for keeps. But how do we reach him?

And now, thumbing through the old notebook in which he recorded bits of information supplied by friends whose work involved travel throughout the country and by former members and their children who now lived in the North, he came upon a red-inked entry which suggested a possible means of reaching his man.

Beneath the names of a woman and an exclusive hotel he had written the cryptic words: *Penthouse for pink-toed friend. Hollywood Blonde. Dallas. Likes mink coats and Dark Gables. Ellington fan.*

It's a nasty idea, he thought, *and risky, because it might mean coming up against even more hostility and in a scene that's even more unfamiliar. Still, considering the pressure of time and our limited choices it's worth exploring.*

Checking his watch to see if there had been ample time for the members of the steering committee to have rested, he telephoned Wilhite and asked that he have them join him for a strategy session. Then, selecting a quiet corner of the lobby where comfortable chairs were arranged around a low table, he waited until Wilhite, Sister Bea, Sister Arter, Brother Jackson, and Elder Whitby arrived.

"After our trip I know you should be resting," he said, "but given what happened at that office I thought we'd better come up with a new plan as soon as possible. I apologize, but that's why I asked you to join me. And since some of you are not going to approve what I'm about to propose I suggest that we keep our voices calm and act relaxed so as to avoid attracting the attention of anyone who might become curious.

"Most of all, let's talk without mentioning names, because after what we've just gone through he's probably been alerted and intends to keep out of sight. And unless he's changed, he might even have someone keeping an eye on us. If so, we could wear ourselves out knocking on doors and making telephone calls, but the closest we'll get will be some telephone operator or secretary. Therefore, while you were upstairs I've been trying to think of other ways of reaching him. And since he seems to be using women to cover his trail it occurred to me that due to the seriousness of the situation we might be forgiven if *we* use a woman to run him to earth. In brief, I have the name and address of one who might save us a lot of snooping around and lead us to him. I don't like the idea of using a woman to catch him, because not only is it unethical, but it could prove more embarrassing to us than to him. So while I apologize for the idea, it's the best I can come up with. What's your opinion?"

"Revern'," Sister Bea said, "which one of us are you talking about, me or Sister Arter?"

Hickman stared, swallowed, and grinned.

"Why neither, Sister Bea—and you should know I wouldn't put you ladies in such a position. I was referring to one of *his* lady friends."

"Now that's better," Sister Bea said, "but which one would that be?"

"Remember," Hickman said with a look around the lobby, "that I said that we'd use no names. Besides, her name's not important. But according to my information she's one of his favorites. Such a favorite that he maintains a penthouse suite for her in a high-class hotel. And because it's the last place in the world he'd expect us to have heard of it might be a good place to tree him."

"So what are you suggesting?" Elder Whitby said.

"That we try to reach him there, and if we don't we can at least tell his lady friend our reason for trying to reach him and hope that she'll pass on the word."

"I don't like it," Wilhite said, "not after that business in the elevator. It's too risky."

"I agree," Hickman said, "but since he insists on playing hide-and-seek it could be crucial. I think we should consider it, and not only because a life is at stake but because we don't know the man who's after him, where he is, or the time and place in which he intends to attack. Therefore we have to get to our man, and as quickly as possible."

Following a brief discussion it was agreed, and after the sisters had exchanged their white uniform for less conspicuous clothing the group left the Longworth by taxi and headed for another hotel which was reputed to compare favorably with the old Paris *Ritz*.

Upon reaching the entrance to the imposing establishment Hickman climbed out and stood looking on while his companions slowly assembled themselves with grave, Southern decorum. And sensing their intimidation as now they stood taking in the hotel's grandeur he recalled his recent experience with the Oklahoma hotel, and stepping between Sister Bea and Sister Arter, he nodded casually to the towering doorman and escorted the group through the doors of the hotel and toward its reception desk.

Astir with a quiet bustle of movement and a discreet murmur of genteel voices, the elegant lobby did indeed remind him of hotels he had known during his tours of France as a jazz musician; but now as he led his group toward the reception desk it was as though they were entering a televised drama in which the sound track was faltering to an inarticulate buzz while expressions of consternation were transforming most of the faces that were turning to stare. And now, reaching the reception desk, he was facing a desk clerk who was obviously startled, and the instant he named the suite to which he wished to be directed the young man turned pale with panic.

"B-b-but, sir," the young man stammered, "we have no such suite; it doesn't exist! You've made an unfortunate mis*take*!"

"Now, isn't that strange," Hickman said, "because we were reliably informed...."

"...Informed," the clerk gasped. "You were *informed*?"

"That's right, and it is extremely important that we contact the Senator...."

Suddenly throwing up his hands and sending petals flying from the white carnation which graced his lapel, the clerk started away.

"Wait here," he said. "This is a matter for the manager."

Watching the clerk rush to the rear of the reception area and disappear into an office, Hickman winked at the blank faces of the others and grinned.

"You were right, Sister Bea," he said in an undertone, "no room at the inn. So now we'll see what kind of face the manager puts on when he sees who's invaded his fancy lobby"—and looked around to see a small, dark-haired, foreign-looking man rushing toward them with his palms extended as though restraining an unwieldy wall of unwelcome air.

"There has been a mistake! There is no such suite," the little man exclaimed as he hurried around the desk, "no such suite! *Absolutely* no such suite!"

"But," Hickman began, "we were informed...."

"No, sir," the manager interrupted, "you were *mis*informed! It cannot be! Our guests are special and their privacy and security is our top priority, so I should know!... Which is to say that we are intimately familiar with each of our guests, therefore when I tell you that no such suite exists you must *believe* me!"

"But I wasn't about to contradict you," Hickman said, "it's just that we were told..."

"... Told? Told by *whom*?"

"I'm sorry," Hickman said, "but since it appears that there's been a mistake, I'd rather not say. But we're strangers in town, and since our informant was trying to help us reach a very busy official you'll understand our not wishing to embarrass him. Especially when it's possible that *we're* the ones who made a mistake by confusing the name of your hotel with the one he gave us...."

"*Undoubtedly*, sir," the manager said. "And that is most regrettable! For while we would be proud to include that most qualified and desirable gentleman among our guests, we are, alas, not so fortunate. Which makes it all the more distressing that you were so misinformed—for what if *otheirs* should hear the same canard and assume that after having been so honored we had lost the Senator's patronage? It would be a *disaster*! A loss of *prestige*! Therefore, sir, it is imperative that we be given the name of this irresponsible informant so that he can be *corrected*!"

"I understand your concern, sir," Hickman said, "but don't worry, because I'll see that he's informed of our mistake—

"Yes, Deacon," he said, turning quickly to Wilhite, "that's probably what happened—we picked the wrong hotel!"

Then back to the manager, "But just to be certain, sir, let me ask you if you were given the correct name of the individual whose suite we asked to see...."

"Why of *course*," the manager said, "everyone knows the Senator, he is a most esteemed official! Why, of course!"

"So that settles it," Hickman said. "He doesn't keep a suite here, but he's often *seen* here—is that it?"

Drawing himself up to his full height with his head thrown back, the manager's voice warbled like that of a bird thrilling in springtime.

"Monsieur, if I may say so, we are unquestionably the *best*! Therefore *every* somebody who is *somebody* is our guest at some time or the other! It is *de rigueur*! They must, as you say, make our scene!"

Hickman smiled and shook his head with his eyes playing over the richly paneled lobby and its curious guests.

"Yes, I would think so," he said, "it looks like that kind of place and I'm sorry that we disturbed you. But before we leave, would you be so kind as to do us a favor?"

"Oh, a *favor*! What *kind* of favor?"

"It's just that if the Senator happens by here at any time during the next four hours you'll be so kind as to tell him that Reverend Hickman and a group of his members have arrived and can be reached at the Longview. Would you be so kind as to give him that message?"

Suddenly beaming as though presented an unexpected bonus, the manager executed a slight Continental bow.

"Why, of course," he said, "even though I doubt that the Senator will honor us with his presence today. He does, after all, have several friends among our permanent guests. So of course! And if he happens to drop in I assure you that we'll be *delighted* to give him your message."

"And I'll bet a fat man that he'll be true to his word," Sister Bea said, her face a blank as she glared at Hickman and nodded. "Yes, sir!"

"Yes, madame," the manager said with a smile as suddenly he seized Sister Bea's hand, "I'll be delighted!"

"And we thank you, sir," Hickman said and broke off as now, with an elegant bow, the manager raised Sister Bea's worn brown hand to his lips and kissed it.

Then, thinking, *Good Lord,* he was watching Sister Bea staring at the manager's lowered head with eyes wide with wonder, then at himself with an expression that vacillated for a second between a ghostly smile and a threat of tears, then flamed abruptly into a seething mask of indignation—as now, fuming with outrage, she snatched her hand away, and he found himself fixed by the blazing eyes of a virtuous woman who appeared to hold him responsible for being near-dishonored by a sleek white foreigner's sensual guile.

"Madame . . . sir," the manager said with an eye-twinkling smile, "you are most . . . er . . . *welcome!*"

"And we," Hickman said with a woeful sigh, "are truly thankful!"

Why, he thought as he turned away, *didn't I simply ask to speak with the woman?*

Leaving the hotel for a downtown section by taxi, Hickman held a still-fuming Sister Bea's arm as he led the group to the editorial offices of a middle-of-the-road newspaper known for its unstinting editorial criticism of the Senator. Such hostility had led a rival paper to accuse its management of inspiring the wave of protest which Washington Negroes had begun directing at the Senator, but it had denied having either a pro-Negro or anti-Sunraider bias. Nevertheless, after hoping that he could count on its assistance, he was again disappointed. For after penetrating the barriers that protected the managing editor and asking his aid in reaching the Senator, the man not only refused but failed to question him as to his motive.

"We'll not be a party to any of your ill-advised protests," the managing editor said, "and you should realize that this is a *newspaper,* not a bureau of private information. Why don't you try getting him at his office?"

"That's the problem," Hickman said. "We did."

Leading the disappointed group to the street, Hickman drew Wilhite aside.

"Deacon," he said, "if we keep drawing blanks like this some of the members are going to become discouraged. So now I want you to get the others back to the hotel and wait there while I try going after him by another route.

"I don't know, Wilhite," he added, "but seeing so many of us at one time seems to make these Washington white folks nervous."

Wilhite laughed. "You're right, A.Z., they'd probably feel more comfortable if we were toting trays or dragging cotton sacks. But how about our straightlaced Sister Bea and that Frenchman manager?"

"Wilhite, believe me, I've never seen anything like it. She reacted as though instead of being kissed by a Frenchman she was being bitten by a rattlesnake! Yes, sir! And then she stared at me as if *I* had told him to do it! Yes, but for a second there she was tempted! I was watching her expression leap from 'yes' to 'no' faster than Scott Joplin could leap an octave!"

Minutes later, hoping that Miss Pryor might have changed her mind, Hickman was back at the Senator's office building—but this time he got no further than the elevators.

For as luck would have it, the single guard on duty was the same who had been teased by Brother Provo, and without ceremony he found himself being hustled from the building.

Irritated at being manhandled but amused by his memory of the guard's encounter with Brother Provo, he relaxed his body and left the smaller man struggling against the sudden inertia of his bulk as best he could. And while the guard strained to wrestle him toward the doors he withdrew into that mute, Tarbaby's state of remoteness with which he had long disciplined himself in abiding fools and avoiding most provocations of violent intent. Then, aware that a curious crowd was beginning to gather he relented and allowed himself to be pushed out of the building and onto the sidewalk. And not until the guard snatched his favorite panama from his head and threw it to the sidewalk did he react.

And now, with the guard silently daring him to retaliate he waited for him to complete the old ritual of insult by stomping his hat and selected the man's prominent Adam's-apple as the precise target for his counterattack.

Then, suddenly, he felt an urge to laugh. For in surveying the crowd for possible allies he was ambushed by an old minstrel song: *Who's been here since I been gone/ A great big nigger with a derby on,* and as the refrain resounded in his mind he was relieved to see that his man was standing with legs too far apart to stomp his hat. And experiencing a wild mixture of anger and laughter he bent, swooped up his panama, came erect, and stood calmly flicking the dirt from his hat with his handkerchief.

Then, gauging the crowd's reaction and replacing his hat, he looked the guard in the eye and stepped forward.

"Son," he said in a quiet tone of bemusement, "just looking at you makes a man *wonder.* Here with all this heat coming down you've worked yourself into a clothes-soaking sweat, but all you've done is let yourself interfere with matters that don't concern you. What *happened* to you, son? Did you forget that you're only a *guard*? Or is there something about a man like me that makes you think that you're a *mind* reader? If so, you're so wrong that it's a shame and a pity! Because if you could read my mind, instead of working up that sweat trying to keep me out—just look at that uniform!—you'd be trying to get me up to that office as fast as you could. And considering the fact that I'm a citizen who's only trying to see a member of his government, I'd say that you've allowed your stupidity to overstep your authority. Which suggests to me that you aren't even a first-class guard."

"... Now you listen," the guard shouted, "you..."

"You'd better *think* before you call me that," Hickman warned, "think! Because now you're making me wonder what you'd do if I actually came here intending to make trouble...."

Sweeping the crowd with his eyes, the guard braced himself with thumbs stuck in his Sam Browne belt. "You just try me and see," he said. "Go ahead, try me!"

"And you'd like that, wouldn't you," Hickman said, "but there I'll have to disappoint you, because wasting time with the likes of you is not on my schedule.

But I would advise you to get hold of yourself, you hear? Otherwise, you're liable to forget to tell the Senator that the Reverend *Hickman* was here to see him and left word that he can be reached at the Hotel Longview. Think you can remember that?"

"Man," the guard began, "you must be out of your cotton-picking mind...."

"... You see," Hickman said with a shake of his head, "there you go *again*! With all these folks looking on you're trying to cut everything down to your own limited size and missing completely the importance of what I just told you. Son, what is it with you? Do you think that simply being white makes you automatically older and wiser than a man like me? Than *any* man like me? That you were born knowing more about life, about this country and the world than me?

"I know, you think of men like me as 'boys,' but, son, I'm old enough to be your *grand*pappy! I've studied your kind for years and I've seen the coming and going of the generations out of whose passions and loins you sprang! Therefore I know just about from whence you came, what you've been, and where you'll end on your dying bed!

"It's in your talk, and in your manners, and in your ornery meanness. It's in your constant looking for someone else, and especially someone like me, to blame for your own lazy incompetence! Son, I have your number! I even know what you eat, and what you drink and dream! It shows in your bullying walk! It sounds in that flat-toned, self-inflating imitation of what you think is a high-class Southern accent! When in fact it sounds like somebody pretending to be General Robert E. Lee while chattering like a blue jay in a green persimmon tree!

"Son, I hear *you*, but you refuse to hear *me*. I see *you*, but you refuse to see *me*! That's why you tell yourself that you know all about me and try to dismiss me by telling yourself that you've got me covered, hemmed in, and without room to maneuver. But you're wrong, son; you're wrong!

"Because in this big, crazy country it's hard to keep men like me fenced in. In spite of everything folks like you do they find ways of getting over the walls and through the cracks, and they go on probing and making their way by using whatever paths that are here to be discovered. Otherwise they act like pioneers and blaze their own trails, then they cover their tracks to protect what they learn from your ignorant meddling. That's because they're Americans! Son, they're *Americans*! And in the process of exploring the land's possibilities they take risks! They observe the difference between what folks like you hold to be true and what proves to be false and shameful!

"Oh, yes, and they remember many things, both good and bad, which men like you try to erase from memory and then think they're done and ended. Yes! And they know that you want to think that the Lord stacked humanity in a pile and doomed men like me to always be at rock-bottom. But you're wrong again! Because even though folks like you try to deny the fact that this is an open society, it's still open, both top and bottom—thank God!—to those who are willing to test it! That's what all this endless, cutthroat struggling is all about! Folks move around and around, and up and down, trying to discover the true nature of its confusing freedom. Son, they're searching for the key.... They're searching for that ever sought but seldom found key to happiness! And because they do, men like me have seen many things, both high and low, that you'll never have the opportunity to share, eyes to see, the heart to remember, or the mind and will to grasp. They went to war along with Washington, and to the North Pole with Peary! They saved Teddy Roosevelt on San Juan Hill, then helped subdue the Boxer Rebellion! They've shadowed the best and seen the worst, so they have a good idea of what both are missing. What's more, it's a natural fact that you don't have to *be* high to *see* the high, or be low in mind to see the lowly. Neither can the high and mighty get so far out of sight that they can't be seen and judged from below! Because that depends on your mind, your heart and vision! But you *do* have to live with hope, unselfish hope, and identify with all the mixtures that make us human. And, most of all, you have to think about the amazing mixture of this country's life and try to grasp its meaning!

"So now you ask yourself this question: What would you do if you were a passenger in an airplane taking a nosedive and someone like me was the only passenger who might save your life? What would you do? And how would you want me to respond? Then think of how you'd feel if you had cancer and the only physician who could cure you happened to be black. What would your decision be? Would you choose life or untouchable whiteness? Think about that, and then maybe you'll be sensible enough to ask yourself what possible business could a black man like me have with a United States senator? And finally, I want you to ask yourself why on earth such a man as me would waste his good time in giving someone like you a lecture? Come up with reasonable answers and you *might* begin to learn who you really are and where you stand in the scheme of things!

"So now I'm leaving, but when you see the Senator I want you to tell him that Daddy Hickman has *arrived*. Remember to do that and you just might turn out to be the important man you'd like to be."

Pushing through the crowd, Hickman walked away until, reaching some ten paces up the walk, he looked over his shoulder to see the dumbfounded guard and the crowd still staring in his direction.

"Don't forget," he called. "I want you to tell him that Daddy *Hickman* has ... *arrived*."

[MESSENGE(R)]

YES, HICKMAN, HE THOUGHT, you've arrived, but so far that's all you've accomplished. And what would you have done if he'd reached for his pistol—preach him a sermon? So by asserting your pride you ended up acting ridiculous. And you did it in spite of knowing full well that whether he's black or white, a clown is a clown. Shame on you! But as he continued away and recalled the guard's reaction to a black man's addressing him as "son," he exploded with laughter.

I kept hitting him with "son" to make him realize that I was the older and more experienced, he thought, *but he reacted as though I were playing the dozens and insulting his mother. So maybe the shock of it made him realize that just as white men have fathered black children, [black] men have fathered white children. Yes, and gotten away with it in cases where there was no screaming of rape and no traces of blackness in their offspring's features. So maybe he was finally facing up to what's long been a wide-open secret—at least among black folks.*

But then I lost self-control over his snatching my hat. Because it stirred memories of what happened years ago to a well-dressed Negro who was seen in a white neighborhood smoking a fine Havana and wearing a derby. Which in the twenties was considered so threatening to white supremacy that a mob of white folks destroyed his hat and gave him a beating!

Hailing a taxi, he climbed in and asked to be driven back to the Longview. But once under way and thinking of the members' disappointment when told of his failure he decided to try a different approach.

What I need, he thought, *is help from someone who keeps an eye on everybody from the President to cops on the beat—which would be one of our veteran "white-folks-watchers," and that has to be Millsap. He'll probably laugh his head off when he hears what we're up to, but if so, I'll just have to grin and bear it. Because if he has even the* slightest *suggestion it'll be all to the good. . . .*

And postponing his return to the Longview, he directed the driver to drop him off in one of the neighborhoods where Millsap had often killed time.

Since his last report he'll probably have nothing new to tell me, he thought, *but since I've gotten nowhere on my own, there'll at least be the pleasure of reminiscing over the good times we shared in the old days.* And reaching the neighborhood where he hoped to find Millsap, he left the cab at a corner and began walking.

The street was crowded with pedestrians, but unlike the old days most were white folks; a detail which became incongruous as he reached the middle of the block and had his ears assaulted by a blast of the "Jelly Roll Blues."

Female, disembodied, and bawdy, the voice ricocheted off storefronts and buildings with a crackling abandon that stirred old memories and scenes from his days as a jazzman.

"Well, I ain't gon' give nobody none of my jelly-roll," the voice exulted as an innocent product of bakeries was endowed with sly undertones of innuendo which reminded him of "blues queens" who had reigned during the old days. And with the sound grating his ear he visualized a stately, plump, brown-skinned empress of the blues who wore a headband of silver, a necklace of pearls, and a gown of red satin as she stood in the curve of a grand piano while delighting her listeners with the bitter-sweet spell that had made the blues so consoling and popular.

Hickman, he thought, *since your footloose days in this town there's no question but that things have* changed*! But why should a man on a life-saving mission have to come all the way to Washington and have his ears punished by something like that? Whoever's broadcasting that stuff on this Washington air must be getting back at those ladies who refused Miss Anderson the use of their hall. If so, they're probably none the wiser, but he's giving the blues a function that's most unexpected....* Falling in step with the sidewalk's traffic, he moved along behind three young women who wore blue uniforms, and as they strutted and swayed in time with the music he wondered if they were getting the message of the Jelly Roll Blues.

Looking in vain for the source of the air-blasting sound, he thought, *Millsap once mentioned a record shop being in this neighborhood, yet this sound seems to be moving. So maybe it's coming from a sound truck. But as far as I can see through this traffic and crowd there's no such truck in the area.*

And, addressing his self from his jazz days, he thought, *Hickman, what kind of product would anyone hope to persuade folks to buy on the strength of some down-home gal yelling in the streets about her jelly-roll—no, I withdraw the question. So please don't tell me that it's Cadillacs! Anyway, a sound truck wouldn't be this skin-prickling shrill.*

And now, looking far up the street past neon signs and buildings decorated with patriotic bunting, his eyes were drawn to a huge sidewalk clock that loomed high above the heads and shoulders of passing pedestrians. Mounted on an ornamental pillar and enclosed in a round, weathered bronze case with its white dial, black hands, and Roman numbers protected by glass, the clock towered like the head of a giant above widespread arms formed by a long bronze bar which extended from the curb and over the sidewalk. And suddenly reminded of his mission, he thought, *So there stands a figure of time on a cross, and here I am at the crossroads of time—or am I simply being reminded of those stations of the cross that mark the thorny path which we know down home as "colored people's time"? Either way, time is something which mankind keeps striving to redeem and recover, even though all kinds of time—black time, white time, time-past, and time-future, and in whatever regions and zones you find yourself—keep ever flowing into timelessness. For between the mechanical ticks and the tocks of what we choose to call "time" all notions of "was," "here," "now," and "shall-be" get mixed in the mind....*

Am I the "me" I used to be, or someone or something I'm still becoming? That's the question. And if you rely only on clocks to guide you you'll find yourself in time suspended. But see the Cross—thank the Lord!—and you'll remember the Promise. Go seeking a man to find a boy who got lost in time-past like I'm doing, and right away you're tangled in newsprint, double-talk, radio jabber, and broadcast images—not to mention the man's own cussed orneriness. Therefore how in time redeem lost time when time itself has hidden the man it embodies in the blinding hot spotlights of high places?

Stop it, Hickman, he thought, *the answer is simple: You keep trying, you keep seeking and striving against the time when your own time is ended. 'Cause as the old saying goes, time's flying, souls dying, and the coming of the Lord draweth nigh....*

And now, drawing closer, he saw that one of the clock's hands pointed toward a bank whose name appeared on a plaque underneath and the other toward the avenue—where, now, a frustrated hearse followed by a string of black limousines with headlights aglow in the brightness was steering a slow solemn path through a stream of agitated cars, taxis, and trucks. And hearing the singer's tribute to her "jelly-roll" continue he thought, *Yes, madam, its promise still sounds in the music, but by now, as the boys on the block used to say, it's probably grown old and got weary....*

And reminded suddenly of Janey's account of her dream, he thought, *Time! One way or another everything seems to be yelling Time! Which I can't deny but would rather not hear—how long has it been since I heard those blues? Twenty years? Thirty?*

Then, catching a whiff of rum-flavored pipe tobacco he eyed the clock and snapped open the lid of his watch to compare their readings. But in the interval between his glance at his watch and the clock a flock of pigeons appeared; and as he watched them circling the clock in a sun-dazzling swing and setting wings in a gliding approach to its widespread arms there came a blare from the blues band and a shout from the singer. And struck by the shock wave of blues the birds were flaring and whirling in a wing-flapping cloud and the clock's face was veiled by a whirlwind of fluttering.

"Jelly-roll, Jelly-roll, from my bakery shop," the singer sang above a mocking riff from trombone and trumpet, "Get it while it's juicy, Get it while it's hot...."

And with birds swooping and diving in a wing-beating frenzy people were skittering close to the buildings or making for the curb in quick-stepping panic; and as they bumped and clung to their briefcases and packages, some were brushing past with annoyed expressions; while others, rushing in opposite directions, were looking back and shouting at something up the walk beyond them.

What's going on up there? he thought, and as he pressed past pedestrians and headed for the area where the clock's sun-flecked shadow slanted upon a mounting confusion of forms that were ducking and fleeing the music became ever more strident. Then, in looking past the heads and shoulders of two men wearing identical white suits and panama hats, he realized with a start that the source of the sound and confusion was a small Negro man.

White-haired and dressed in a black frock-tail coat, a white T-shirt, baggy striped pants, and soiled tennis shoes, the man appeared to be much older than himself as he approached with his right hand on hip and arm akimbo while shouldering a large portable radio which was pressed against the left side of his white hatless head like a cake of black ice applied to an ear that was aching! Which it should be, Hickman thought as he listened to the radio's shrill blaring of, "Jellee, Jellee!, Jelly-jelly all night long!"

Well, would you look at that, he thought, and as the little man rocked to the music's loud beat with a limp, and a pause, and a hand-on-hip strut he realized that he was advancing with his eyes closed and smiling as though so entranced by the sound of his blues-spouting burden as to be totally unaware of the panic being stirred by the inchworm's pace of his progress.

And as he watched people clearing the walk before the little man's advance, he thought, *I should have known it! Who else but one of our old-timers who'll exploit any opportunity the white folks leave open by dismissing them as crazy could cause such confusion! And with nothing more than a funky blues number, an old tinny radio, and a crabbed way of walking! No more than a frail bundle of bones but still taking on the world's most powerful city. And what's more, the little clown is getting away with it! Truly, Hickman, this thing called democracy is not only unpredictable, but far more fragile than anyone wants to admit—Sister Bea, where are you now that I need you?*

And spurred by a sudden impulse to see if the little disturber-of-the-peace was simply taking advantage of the self-flattering condescension which the white public extended to those of his color and style, or actually as hard of hearing and blind as he appeared to be, he rushed up the walk with footsteps pounding.

Okay, Mister Casey Jones, he thought, *if you're only playing games get ready to jump, otherwise us two old-timers are about to bump....*

But just as he drew closer he saw the little man pause with one foot in midair and his eyes popped open. And even as he thought, *I knew it,* he realized that the little man was sizing him up with a snaggled-toothed grin.

"Hey, now!" he heard through the radio's blaring. "They don't make 'em like that these days—am I right or wrong?"

"That's right," Hickman said, "nor your type either. And maybe it's a good thing"—and broke off, his ear suddenly arrested by the attack and modulations of a muted trombone and in recognizing the pulse and timbre of his own gutbucket style from the old days he gaped in amazement.

Well, I'll be, he thought with a mixture of pleasure and embarrassment, *it's really me—but how? Where'd they come up with such an old recording? It's me and Estella Moore, and we recorded it so long ago that I didn't even recognize her voice or her style—not to mention my own!*

"Hey!" the little man shouted as he nodded off-beat to the music's loud pulsing. "You know how good music like this makes me feel?"

"No," Hickman said, "but why don't you turn it down a bit?"

"... I feel exactly like the monkey when he ate the cat—you remember?"

"What!" Hickman shouted. And as he bristled at the little man's challenge, two well-dressed women, one white and the other mulatto, stepped out of a store behind them. Raising his palm he shouted, "Hold it, my friend!" Whereupon the women looked startled, frowned in dismay, and hurried away in opposite directions.

"Now, what was that?" Hickman said.

"Hell, cousin, you heard me," the little man said. "What'd the monkey say when he ate the cat?"

"Let me think," Hickman said as he studied the little man's face. Either way he's got me, he thought, and all the more if he knows I'm a preacher. So if I give the correct answer he'll laugh because he knows I'm an old-timer; pretend that I don't know it and he'll have the pleasure of having a minister tell him a lie. . . .

"Now, let's see," he said. "Wasn't it something about his . . . er . . . digestion?"

"Yeah!" the little man laughed. "That's *right*! Monkey said, 'I got me a belly fulla'—come on now, cousin, you take it from there. . . .'"

"I'm not sure," Hickman said with a frown, "but I seem to recall that the monkey said something about having a pleasant sensation. . . ."

" . . . Right!" the little man said with a cackle of delight. "What the monkey said when he ate the cat was, 'I got a belly fulla pussy and it's tight like that!' That's the lick, my man! You might *look* square, but you solid have *been* there! And I mean the *old* country!"

Yes, Hickman thought, *and you're an old down-home rascal.* But made nostalgic by the little man's irreverent folk humor, he grinned and thought, *If this ain't the mythical ole Uncle Bud I hope I'll never meet him!* And seizing the little man's free elbow, he tugged him gently to the curb of the sidewalk.

"Sure," he said as now the little man turned the volume down to a static-filled murmur, "I've been there, but that was long ago—before they flattened the hills and rerouted the river. Nowadays things have changed so much that they're even taking the whistles off the railroad trains. . . ."

"Yeah, man," the little man said with a frown, "but that don't really matter, 'cause you and me got all that good stuff *inside* us. Or at least behind us. All them sassy gals and crisp fried fish and chicken, sweet-potato pie, and good smoked Southern barbecue. All that good ole jive that keeps a man *alive*! The shim and the sham and the shim-sham-shimmy, the God-given glory and the way the weather was—hell, cousin, with all *that* inside him a man has got to *prevail*! You been blessed—you hear me? You been *blessed*!"

Head cocked to the side, Hickman stared; thinking, *Better watch him or this little devil will start quoting Scripture. . . .*

"You're right," he said, "and I'm truly grateful. But how about you?"

"Blessed too," the little man said. "I'm still here, ain't I?"

"Right!"

"I'm still traveling under my own steam and ain't on relief, ain't I?"

"Correct!"

"And you know something else?"

"What's that?"

"I'ma even be here when *Martin* comes, *and* I aim to be here after he done come and *gone*—oh, yes!"

With hands flying to his hips, Hickman roared with laughter as he recalled the old joke about Sam, the hungry hobo who had been promised a meal and a peaceful way out of town if he spent the night in an old haunted house; but who, after enduring a devilish series of hair-raising testings by animals that kept dropping down the chimney and talking like humans, lost his nerve—not because of the creatures' surprising conduct, but because just before disappearing each had asked the same mysterious question: "Sam, are you going to be here when Martin comes?"

Thinking, *Poor Sam, poor fellow*, Hickman shook his head and grinned. *Like me*, he thought, *he could deal with the hellishness of what was then-and-there before him, but was fazed by the threat of that which was unspelled, unknown, and unseen.*

"Why, I haven't heard either that story for years," he said. "Brother, who *are* you?"

"Me?" the little man said as he trembled with mock indignation. "You mean to say that an old hustler like you don't recognize *me?* Hell, man, I'm *Martin*!!! Sho! I'm the stationmaster, chief bottle-washer, and the nappy-headed judge of the court of last resort for this heah entire hainted house of a country! Hell, cousin, you *got* to know *me!*"

"Well, I'm beginning to—but are you sure you're really everything you say?"

"You damn right I am—and a hell of a lot more!" And stamping his foot for emphasis, the little man began spieling like a veteran sideshow barker:

"I'm the cat who'll be here looking at 'em after the roof falls in!

"I'm the invisible spook in the woodpile they always telling themselves big lies about! I'm the man on the stairs who they say ain't really there—but they gon' see, and you better believe me!

"I'm Willie-the-poor-boy, a little short on funds, that is, but *looong* on experience, and whale-shit deep in hard-to-earn knowledge!

"I'm the old man of the mountains who ole Cab used to hi-de-ho so loud about!

"I'm Wine-ball Bill, and while I ain't so sweet as I used to be, I'm still doing me some fine winding and grinding.

"I'm also Daddy Step with the mitch-matched feet, and the one who cries when the big shots laugh, and laughs like hell when they break down and weeps!

"I'm Oddball Papa—you know, the one with one hung way, *way* low, just so's I can keep my balance in all this confusion.

"And cousin, befo' I go I'll tell you one thing mo': Folks don't recognize it, but I'm the unknown soldier who keeps the bowels of all of these congressmen and Supreme Cote judges roaring up a storm. And I'll tell you confidentially that all this talk you been hearing about *Chicago* being the windy city is some pure-dee bull! This heah Washington is the *original* windy city and still undisputed champion of the whole wide world! And you can believe it, because it's *me*, also known as the natural-born Little Blister, who does the pumping that makes 'em keep howling and bellowing!"

"And there I was," Hickman said, "thinking you were none other than the Real McCoy...."

Staggering backwards as though struck by a blow, the little man let out a shout that leaped two octaves: "Him too! He's *me*! And when those folks up on the Hill is flying right I keep the machinery oiled and running smooth as fine silk. But when they messes up and start looking for somebody else to blame it on, I'm in there greasing the skids from under their butts! The next time they foul things up take a look and you'll see me in the background!

"In the meantime, why don't you come along while I deliver this message, which is my job these days, and then come on over to my pad and listen to some more of this music? I got records they don't even have at the Smithsonian."

"Thanks," Hickman said with a pang of regret, "I'd like to, I truly would, but I have an appointment."

"Too bad," the little man said, "because you're the kind of fellow I like because I don't have to spend a lot of time explaining what things really mean. Like the good in the bad and the bad in the good. You a messenger too?"

"No—or at least not a real professional. . . ."

"Well, don't lose no sleep over it, 'cause these days most folks don't get the word, no matter how fast you get it to 'em. I'll see you around. Been good talking with you."

"Same here," Hickman said, "and it's been good to meet an old-timer who remembers some of the good things that even most of *our* folks have let get away."

No, he thought as he watched the little man rock away with the blaring radio pressed again to his ear, *these days they don't make men like him or records like that, and somebody had to scrape the very bottom of the barrel to find one with me on it. Truly, a man's sins will find him out. But if that old signifying rascal managed to identify me with that music he's probably laughing his head off. And now I'll always wonder whether he did or didn't. Why, the nasty little devil! He admitted to being everybody but Jack-the-Jiver and Ding-Dong Daddy from Dumas—which would account for his strut. But then his true name is probably some thing like Junior Judkin Jones!*

Remembering his mission, he moved ahead, his eyes alert for anyone who might direct him to Millsap. The best place to look, he thought, would be a bar, but he might be embarrassed if I found him in one this early in the day.

Chuckling as he walked along, noting the effect of time on the unfolding scene, he amused himself by improvising on the tale of Sam and Martin. How did it go? How tell it in a barbershop? Oh, go on, give it a try! After a long hobo trip up North Sam dropped off a freight train in South Nowhere, Alabama, and hardly had he touched the cinders than he was grabbed by a gang of evil-looking deputies and an evil-looking sheriff who told him that he could either spend a night in an old mansion and report what was going on in it at midnight or go to jail.

"It's up to you," the sheriff said. "If you agree to spend the night out there we'll give you some bread and pork chops, otherwise it's sixty days in jail on stale bread and water."

So, being worn out from his long trip of hoboing, and made a bit uncomfortable by the attitude of the sheriff and his men, Sam agreed to spend the night in the mansion. He knew in his bones that the sheriff was up to no good, but being homesick and tired and less wary of ghosts than of rednecks, he figured he could eat, get some rest, and before daybreak he'd be waiting at the railroad tracks to grab the first freight that passed through long before the sheriff got back. So they drove Sam out to the old decaying mansion and gave him a batch of pork chops, some lard, a loaf of bread, and sent him inside with a lantern. And after hanging around a spell to make sure he stayed put, they left him alone in all the dust, mildew, and stillness.

But that didn't bother Sam, he was too tired and hungry. So after looking things over and making sure that he was alone, he built a fire in the big fireplace, and after finding a skillet put the chops on to fry. Then he lay back on the floor and waited while they were cooking. But just as he nodded off a noise from the fireplace caused him to open his eyes.

And that's when he saw a cute little Maltese kitten fall down the chimney and stroll out on the floor. And there in the firelight it proceeded to whistle a chorus of "Dixie" with trills that rivaled a mockingbird's. Then, after whistling and dancing a chorus of "Swanee," it took a bow and strolled over and rubbed its back against Sam's leg and said, "Hey, Sam, how about one of those pork chops?"

"So *that's* what you're up to," Sam said. "Well, the answer is NO! And you better git the hell outta here, 'cause hungry as I am I'm liable to eat you for dessert!"

"Then how about a piece of bread soaked in some of that good pork-chop gravy," the little kitten said.

"Not unless you recite me the Preamble to the Constitution of the U.S.A.," Sam said, "and I mean *backwards*!"

"O.K., Sam, if that's how you feel," said the kitten, "I'm leaving. But before I go, just tell me this: Do you intend to be here when *Martin* comes?"

"Scat!" Sam said, and with that the kitten disappeared up the chimney.

So then Sam turned his chops, rested back with his belly gnawing and growling as he closed his eyes. But before he can make himself comfortable, here comes more commotion. And he opens his eyes to see a black cat the size of a tiger barely missing his dinner as it lands in the fireplace and stands glowering with its hair standing on end and its rawhide whip of a tail whipping the air like a mad rattlesnake.

"What's going on in here?" Sam yells. "What the hell do *you* want?"

"What I'd like to know, Sam," says the big cat in a refined bass-baritone, "is are you going to be here when *Martin* comes?"

"Hell, yes," Sam says, "and if you don't get outta here I'ma whup your butt with this poker! What *is* this anyway, some kinda crazy, gut-busted cat-house?"

"Take it easy, Sam," the big cat says, "and good eating...."

"Scat!" Sam yells, and the cat flies back up the chimney. Then Sam turns his chops in that deep-frying fat, rests back, and closes his eyes.

And for a while everything was so quiet and peaceful that all he could hear was the sound of his pork chops bubbling in the fat. But then, just as his nose tells him that they're about done—here comes a terrible noise from the roof that sounds like a grand piano tumbling down three flights of stairs. And when he springs to his feet and grabs the poker, a striped yellow cat the size of a gorilla lands in the fireplace and brushes the soot off its body as it glares at him out of eyes that glow like opals.

Then as Sam freezes in his tracks the cat reaches a paw into the red-hot grease, grabs his pork chops and eats all seven in a single gulp. Then, belching like an alligator and farting like a bear, it arches its back until it's as tall as a camel. And proceeding counterclockwise it turns three times in a circle, and lays down a pile of a size that would have done credit to a constipated whale or an elephant. And then with its eyes fixed on Sam as though daring him to move, it reaches back daintily and wipes itself with a red-hot ember, shakes its legs, steps back, and takes a deep breath. And then through all the stink and steaming, it lets out a roar in a voice that rolls like thunder:

"HEY, SAM! IS YOU GON' BE HEAH WHEN *MARTIN* COMES?"

And, gentlemen, that's when Sam breaks down the door getting him some *air*!

"HEY, SAM!" the big cat yells from the broken-down porch of the mansion, "YOU AIN'T ANSWERED MY QUESTION!"

"And what's more," Sam yells back as he turns on the gas and heads for the tracks, "if *you* ain't Martin

> And mean to hang around,
> You can tell him that Sam
> Had some very urgent business
> In another town!"

And with a chuckle he adjusted his hat and returned to his search for Millsap.

[LEROY]

MOVING ON TO A street to the north, he continued his search. But in none of its shops, billiards parlors, or restaurants was there a sign of Millsap or anyone else who was familiar. And in eyeing faces in the crowd moving past for old-timers who might be of help, he became discouraged.

Forget it, Hickman, he advised himself, *because by now they've probably changed neighborhoods or passed from the scene. And remember how it is when you're in a strange city and encounter a friend you grew up with: In the joy of reunion time leaps backwards, but then you're back in the present and before it's over you both discover that time, space, and different experiences have rendered you strangers.... Yes, but let's hope that this time there's at least one left who can guide me to Millsap.*

And with a sigh he moved to a double-doored shop with the words: JANUS BARNES HAIR SALON displayed on its window and saw underneath a painting, the surprising subject of which was a double-headed black man whose faces were staring in opposite directions. And noting that the hair on one of the heads was straight and gleaming and that of the other bushy and dull, he smiled. So what about someone like me, he thought, whose hair is now old and gray but still just as kinky?

And glimpsing a group of young men through the window he thought, *Shall I risk joining them inside or simply keep walking? It has the same name, but the sign is new, and since Janus passed from the scene years ago things inside have to be different. Anyway, given such golliwog styles as the Natural, the Greasy Look, and the Afro, why would a man of Millsap's taste have remained one of its customers? So, since it was our favorite during the old days, rather than having my memories disturbed by its new owner's changes, I'd better keep walking....*

And now moving past he recalled the shop as it had been during the old days. Calling it a salon had been pretentious, but it had indeed been a fine barbershop, and a forum in which he had shared the experiences of its customers and taken part in discussions of politics, sports, and automobiles, and exchanged tall tales, jokes, and improbable lies. It was also famous for endless bull sessions in which the topics included anything from the ways of white folks, to the contrast between history as written in books, heard from grandparents who had lived it, or simply described in terms of the truth as they knew it, to the wiles of women and the immunity of pigs to rattlesnake bites. Yes, and during the Depression it had been a freewheeling haven for good fellowship. So now let it rest peaceful in memory—Amen!

But now, nearing the corner and hearing a crash, he turned to see a stocky black man bursting from the shop with a neck-cloth billowing from his shoulders and heading in his direction with an awkward, collapse-and-recover, side-to-side pumping of his knees, legs, and shoulders. And as he watched the dark face playing hide-and-seek with the white neck-cloth's swirling he heard a shout, "Hey, Lee-roy! Git your crazy butt back in this chair!"

So that's it, he thought, *the old rule still stands: Fall asleep in Janus's and some joker is sure to give you a hotfoot—which explains his running like an eccentric dancer imitating the walk of a hotfooted camel!* But just as he looked down expecting to see smoke from burning shoe polish curling from the walk-slapping feet the man veered and came directly at him and the neck-cloth became a cloud of billowing whiteness out of which his black-jacketed arms were flailing and flapping like a fish in a net.

Wrong, Hickman, he thought, *it's some joker from the old days who's out to needle you.* And recalling the surprise and delight he'd given a group of rope-skipping children by dancing double-dutch to their rhythmical whirling, he raised his fists waist-high and boogie-woogied left and then right, thinking to counter and discourage his weird-moving teaser—whereupon the man lunged and reached down, and he felt the shock of arms grasping his thighs—and coming erect with a weight-lifter's thrust, the stranger was raising him high in the air. And as he threw out his arms and swayed, passersby were stopping to stare with startled expressions. And suddenly overcome by the absurdity of what was happening he laughed to assure them that what they were watching was only a game.

I know, it's ridiculous for someone as big as me to let a man his size have him up in the air, he thought, *but if you knew my calling you'd realize that lifting me* up *is his way of putting me* down, *as in the jokes white folks tell about Negro preachers being notorious eaters of fried chicken and chitterlings.*

And amazed by the apparent ease with which his teaser was supporting his weight, he thought, *Maybe he's out to prove that he's in a class with Samson, the blind temple wrecker. But if this keeps up he'll soon have a hernia....*

"Okay, old buddy, okay," he laughed. "I surrender."

But as he peered down at his captor's partially hidden face, expecting the burst of laughter with which such kidding usually ended he was surprised. For he was met by a pair of bloodshot eyes that stared back with a wild, unaccountable emotion. And as he asked himself, *What is it with this bird,* he was surprised by a siren's shrill screaming and looked up to see a police squad car speeding in his direction.

Since they're seldom around when you need them, he thought, *why are they showing up for some foolishness like this?*

But now with a roar the squad car swept past, and above a blue-clad arm pointing from its window he saw a white blur of a face erupting with laughter—and with a squealing of rubber the car roared past and away with its roof lights flashing and its siren screaming.

Good riddance, he thought, *and enough of this foolishness.* And reaching down to have a good look at the stranger's face he again heard the voice shout from Janus's old barbershop:

"Dammit, Lee-roy! Stop that foolishness and git your butt back here so's I can be done with your haircut!"

And looking up the street he saw a barber who stood in the door with hands on hips while glaring disgustedly at the man who held him.

"You should listen to him, old buddy," he said with a tap on the stranger's partially barbered head, "because considering how long you've had me up in the air we could both use some rest."

But with a grunt the stranger was hoisting him higher, and as he swayed in the air he caught sight of a white man who seemed vaguely familiar staring from a third-story window. And feeling a pause in his lifter's exertion he sensed that his confusing ascension had come to an end. Yes! For now, straining and grunting, the stranger was gradually bringing him down.

Lucky for me, he thought, *that none of the members are watching this foolishness—* when suddenly the stranger stumbled and sent the scene flying in a blur in which traffic and buildings were whirling in a pungent confusion of bay rum and talcum, and a truck's bassy rumbling merging with the falsetto imitation of the squad car's siren being screeched by a straw-hatted boy riding a tricycle with bare legs flying like those of a high-tailing cat being chased by a dog as—*zip!*—he rounded the corner. And as he squirmed in the air his captor's head snapped back—and suddenly he was staring at a perspiring face, the skin of which appeared to have been been illuminated underneath by a powerful beam.

But instead he was gazing at a drastic loss of pigment which had left the man's face an incongruous battleground of conflicting colors. And as he blinked the taut face stared back with the fierce immutability of an African mask which bore grotesque scarification of mysterious design, and the white, red-ringed splotches of which appeared to dance above the blue-blackness of its surrounding flesh as though to challenge any quick assumptions as to its racial identity.

Good Lord, Hickman, he thought, *you've been grabbed by a red-white-and-blue black man* and recoiled with a shudder. For as he wavered before the enigmatic force of his captor's bloodshot gaze he was appalled that the wild exertions of a skin-sick stranger could have tricked him into violating a basic principle of his own racial pride.

But you laughed, he thought as he hung in the air, *you laughed! So if getting your goat was his intention he's done much better than he could have expected. And even though his coming at you so sudden threw you off guard, it's still disgraceful and shameful. So now a total stranger has you up in the air and you'll have to redeem what you've done by hanging around to find out why. And if your reaction shows on your face I hope he'll forgive you—if not, may the Lord make him saner than he's acting, or you'll probably end up having to fight him....*

And with eyes still probing the melancholy mystery of the stranger's face he felt the shock of his feet striking the sidewalk. And in stumbling and regaining his balance he saw the stranger's pink-splotched lips come apart with an explosion of breath, was sprayed with spittle, and had his ears blasted by an ecstatic shout of, "Good God, Chief, am I glad to see *you!*"

"I'd like to believe you," he said as he wiped his face with his handkerchief, "but after what you've just put me through I don't know. Anyway, take it easy, man; take it easy, or you'll drown me...."

"Man, oh, *Man!*" the stranger sang as with hands on hips he rocked back and gave him a gap-toothed grin, "I thought they'd *never* let you go; but here, years after I'd given up all hopes of ever seeing you again, I happen to look out the window back there and here you come, a man in the flesh!"

Puzzled, Hickman managed to smile while wondering if the man were someone he had known during the old days. Or had Ole Uncle Bud, the messenger, run around the corner and come back to test him under a different disguise?

"Is that right," he said. "Well, it does happen that way sometimes. You come back to town after a long time away and before you walk a block someone you least expect looks up and recognizes you...."

"That's right, Chief," the stranger said, "and that's what's so *wonderful* about our reunion! Man, I've been thinking about you, dreaming about you, and wanting to *talk* with you—which I thought I never would—and then I look out that barbershop window and here you are in the flesh!"

As he studied the stranger's face, Hickman smiled.

"And I bet I can guess why you wanted to see me," he said. "You're one of the fellows I left town owing a gambling debt—is that it?"

"*Gambling* debt? *What* gambling debt? Hell, Chief, you know that with me gambling was always easy-come, easy-go! Besides, you were never that kind of gambler. What I'm talking about is how I turned my *back* on you. *That's* the point, and I was wrong as hell! But I did it! Yes, sir! So I'm guilty and I been dying to ask for your forgiveness...."

"*Forgiveness,*" Hickman said. "Forgive you for what?"

"For *what,*" the stranger—Leroy—said. Then with an abrupt shifting of crippled legs his head shot forward. "Look, Chief," he said, "I understand what you're up to and I appreciate it, I really do. But if you make it easy on me I won't be able to stand it! So don't play me cheap, 'cause, man, I *need* your forgiveness. I need it for letting them confuse me about you when I should have known better! But, naw, after they caught you and throwed you in jail and all—that's when I began to give up on you. Me, a true dyed-in-the-wool *believer*! I can see you're surprised, but that's the truth! Instead of keeping the faith and sticking by you through thick and through thin, man, I gave *up* on you! So now you can see why I got to have your forgiveness!"

"All right," Hickman said, still puzzled but with a sense of relief, "if that's all you want, everything's copacetic. I forgive you. But to tell you the truth, in those days I was in so many raids that I don't even remember the trial you're referring to."

"Sure," Leroy said, "and that's because you tried to teach us to always remember the past but look and live for the future. Besides, with me coming at you so sudden it's no wonder you don't dig me. But hell, Chief, seeing you so unexpected has me all stirred *up*! Look, it's hot as hell out on this sidewalk, especially with me wearing this neck-cloth. How about stepping around the corner where we can talk in the shade? You don't mind, do you, Chief?"

"No," Hickman said, "because as you've probably heard listening to problems has become a kind of duty—I mean a *responsibility* of mine...."

"Then come on, man," Leroy said, "come *on*!"

And now, following Leroy's rocking gait around the corner and into the shade cast by the building, his mind reeled with the names of cripples, both white and black, whom he'd known in the old days. *Hickman,* he thought, *you've known gambling cripples, pimping cripples, even con-man cripples as well as cripples who were hardworking men with families. And some who were musicians and dancers—like Peg Leg Bates, Chick Webb, and Big-time Crip. Then there were all those assorted neighborhood cripples. Characters like No-toes, Crip Wilson... yes, and Tippy-Lee Morton, who transformed walking with his mismatched legs into an act of graceful elegance. And there was Sugar-foot, and Crippled Charleston, Stilts Benford, String-halted Harry, Dog-trot Johnson, and Jake-leg Mac, who had to wear leg braces after drinking poisoned Jamaica Ginger. Oh, yes, and don't forget Funky-fingers Hagerson, that thin claw-handed pickpocket who worked small fairs, circuses, and tent-meetings; Hagerson, who robbed school cafeterias, stole books from li-braries and silver sacramental vessels from churches, and swore that he couldn't be caught because he paid some voodoo woman to piss seven times in those high-topped, bulldog-toed shoes which he stole for luck from a tough New Orleans Cajun policeman—talk about hedg-ing voodoo mystery with civil authority! Seven times? Yes, seven times is what he insisted. . . . I'll never forget Hagerson, whose conked hair was always in a state of rebellion, and a bully who took bribes from pimps, whores, and small-time gamblers and got away with it by insist-ing that he was both a root doctor and an undercover man for J. Edgar Hoover; Hagerson, whose hand was maimed when that gal Sloppy Sal splashed him with lye from a Charleston pistol after she violated her code by giving him a freebie and discovered that the clown couldn't deliver—I've known enough such characters to make up a circus, but not a one who was named Leroy. And none of them had this fellow's sick skin, mechanical movements, or manners so violent. . . .*

"Now this is better," Leroy said as he threw the neck-cloth over his shoulder like a cape and reached into the pocket of his black sports jacket to remove a blue silk handkerchief.

"Much better," he said, leaning back and propping himself against the guardrail that surrounded a wide empty area of triangular space which dropped two floors to the building's basement. "Now we can talk."

"I'm with you," Hickman said with a look at his watch, "but you'll have to make it short, because I'm already late for an important appointment."

"Oh, sure," Leroy said. "So like I was saying, I been stirred up about you for over a *year*. That's the truth, a whole year! Ain't been able to sleep for thinking about you. Because like I say, after that trial—man, I lost heart and put you *down*! But then, about a month ago, things started *changing*!"

"What do you mean?"

"It was this way, Chief: First I had this warning that came in the middle of the night on the dark of the moon. I was beat to my socks and sleeping real sound when I heard this noise which woke me up. That's when I realized that some-thing strange was in the room. But while I could *feel* it I couldn't *see* it. So then I raised up, trying to see what it was but still couldn't see nothing. Then, after a while, my eyes adjusted to the blackness, and over in the darkest part of the room I see something curled up in my old leather chair. At first I think it's a dog or something, but the longer I look the better I could see, and that's when I realized that it was a little ole man—that's right! And I say to myself, Leroy, we're getting the hell *out* of here!

"So I reach over real quiet and get holt of my britches and start to easing them on—and you know what happens? Right away this little man raises up and reaches for *his* britches, and he's matching me move for move! So at that I freeze with one foot in the air, and he does the same thing and stops like he's waiting to see my next move. And Chief, I tell you, I don't waste any time. But when I stick my foot in my pants leg and start pulling them on I know right away that I'm really in trouble!

"Because when he starts to putting on *his* britches instead of doing it one leg at a time like an ordinary man *he* holds his out in front of him a bit and then goes into a deep kind of trance or something. And just when I'm beginning to wonder what's going on, all of a sudden he gives a little hop into the air, and zip!—he has *both* his legs in 'em! That's right! And before I can bat my eye he's already buckling up his belt! And I mean faster than a fireman when the whistle blows for a six-alarm fire! That's when I panic and try to get my foot into the other leg of my britches and start scrambling around for my shoes to get the hell out of there. But when I do he looks down at some big ole gaiters with zippers on the sides which I see sitting on the floor in front of him. And before I know what's happening he's into those suckers with both feet and has zipped them! And *then* he's looking straight at me like we were playing checkers and he's daring me by saying 'Move, sah! Move-move! Move!' And Chief, what's worse was the fact that when he zipped up those gaiters they were way too big for him, but then he started to *grow*! It was like he was being filled with an *air* hose, and the bigger he gets the more familiar he gets. And what more he's still watching every move I'm making.

"So with that I yells, 'Hey, man, what's going *on* in here!' But all he does is frown, and the way he does it makes me know that I'm *really* in trouble. And that's when it comes over me that from the way he put on his britches and gaiters and then rises up so big and starts looking at me so accusing he has *got* to be nobody but *you*!"

"Me?" Hickman laughed. "Oh, come on! Do you mean that you dreamed that I was a ghost?"

"Oh, no, Chief, not a ghost, but the special kind of man you've always been. And by the fact that anybody who could do what *he* was doing simply *had* to be *you*. Oh, yes, I knew it! You had made yourself small to get my attention, and now that you were big again I wanted to make sure. So I asked you, 'Brother, who the hell *are* you?'

"But remember, Chief, instead of identifying yourself you spoke up real stern and said, 'That's mistake number one. Don't question what you see, use your senses!'

"And that's when I see you whip out a little black notebook and write something in it.

"So then I start to ask you what you meant, but before I can open my mouth you say, 'That's mistake number two, so don't repeat it—use your eyes!'

" 'But be reasonable,' I said. 'It's dark as hell in here!'

" 'Mistake number three,' you said. 'Haven't I taught you that dark men shall see through dark days?'

" 'That's right,' I said. 'But...'

" '... And that those who seek the truth in darkness shall find it?'

" 'Right again,' I said, 'you did, but that was a long time ago....'

" '... And didn't I teach you that there's a brightness in blackness and whiteness in darkness?'

"So I said, 'Sure, you did, but in a situation like this I'd have to strike a match to see it....'

"And that's when you bowed your head and said, 'Now you're learning: Enlightenment requires unceasing effort and strong determination!' And I could see you writing in that notebook again.

"So then I said, 'Learning *what*'—and right away I knew I was wrong again.

" 'Mistake number four,' you said, and you sounded mean as hell.

" 'Look,' I said, 'I'm kinda ignorant, and besides it's been a long time, so why don't you give a man some *instruction*? Or is this some kind of examination?'

"And you said, 'Now you're riffing, are you prepared to listen?'

" 'Oh, yes,' I said, 'I'm tuned in sharp and have the volume turned up as high as it can go....'

"So then you said, 'Listen carefully and follow these rules: Think, reflect, and remember! Then advance by retracing your footsteps and casting down your bucket where you were. For then ye shall see that all things converge in thee as in me—*all* things! Yea! Go thee then to Constitution Avenue and peer into the many cracks that abound there, and watch out for the mirrors hidden within! Yea, and for the many images reflected therein. These will be many and of various shapes and sizes, but study them *all*, and with strict attention! For while some are true, many are false, as are those whom ye shall see revealed within them. Ye shall see strange shapes that are familiar and familiar shapes which are passing strange, therefore be not distracted by distractions—fish, fowl, or funky woman crying out lies against thee. And remember that when such as ye steps into a scene the action changes, for it has been structured to exclude thee. Therefore it cannot sustain thy black reality without drastic modification. This, then, is thy opportunity, for ye shall enter the cracks as a corrective. Thus be ye not sorrowful that ye lack a Cadillac—shanks' mare will get thee there!'

" 'Look, man,' I said, 'I hear you talking but I'm not digging much of anything. How come you hitting me with all these riddles? You been drinking?'

"And that's when you yelled, 'Mistake number five! Wisdom questioned is opportunity lost! Life has taught us that it is the nature of pig meat to be soft but greasy; therefore take my instruction and approach it with eloquence, silence, and cunning—yea! but with the finest of talcum powder on your hands!'

" 'All right, all right!' I said, 'you're talking about the blackness of truth....'

" 'That's right, and about illusion, reality, and the key to the lock....'

" 'But I'm confused because you also taught us that truth is a snare and a dee-lusion....'

" 'Mistake number six,' you yelled, 'and I will not be misquoted! I said that *their* truth is tricky, and that therefore ours must be even trickier! Look long into blackness! Whales dive four fathoms five and see in the darkest depths of the deep. Therefore ye must think deep black thoughts like the whale! Learn to impose our own truth upon the truth which oppresses, and then wail it on the high-ways, the byways, and in the barbershops!'

"And, Chief, when you said that I was so inspired that I wondered where you had been all this long, long time—but that's when I made another mistake!

"Because when I thought it you rose up and yelled, 'Mistake number seven! I am that which I *am* wherever I am, and ye shall be that which ye see in me, ver-ily! But only after ye grasp in thyself that which ye sense in me! Therefore I re-peat: Think! Reflect! Remember! And bear this in mind—yea, in mind bear thee this lest ye be deceived: If a smell ariseth which requires chemical analysis for its identification—it is not, was not, and cannot *ever* have been unnatural!'

"Chief, I swear: You came on like *gang*busters and had me so shook up and in-spired that I really began to smell something—oh, sure, I know today what it was, but then it was in the future—so I wanted to ask you, but before I could make up my mind to risk making another one of my mistakes, you began to dis-appear.

"Oh, yes! I remember, because then all of a sudden I was simply looking into the blackness and listening to your voice fading. Yeah, but before it was fully gone I could hear you saying, 'Go ye now and find a place to have thy say, and until I come again this way learn ye to say with true feeling that which ye have heard me say....' And then, Chief, you were gone, gone, GONE! Yes, sir! But I want you to know that I remembered and have been following your instructions ever since.

"Wait, Chief, don't go! Then a few days after you came to me I was looking through some old newspapers and came across this picture of you and it brought you alive again in my mind. That's right! That picture made me remember the way it used to be back there—how long ago was it? Let's see—Eva left me, and then Abel died.... Yeah, and I hit the numbers for a thousand bucks—that's right, Chief; four-eleven-forty-four, that was my lucky combination. Hell, Chief, that was over twenty-the-fucking-five dam' years ago! Would you believe it? But it didn't make no difference, 'cause when I come across your picture I just sat there and stared and asked myself how the *hell* it could have happened. What I mean is: How could it have taken me all that time to understand how much you had me fooled! But then as I read your statement to that cracker judge and jury it dawned on me for the first time how *wrong* I'd been about you...."

"Yes, and you still are," Hickman said, "even though I *did* undergo quite a change...."

"... Who you telling," Leroy said. "I *know!* Oh, but don't I know it! That's why I need to get this out of my system! So listen to me, Chief—hell, man, I was there when they *tried* you! But last month when I read in black and white how you told the court that you didn't rape those pale-face bitches for the sake of some uneducated pussy—which it stands to reason that a stone stud like you didn't have to do—I *understood!* So for the very first time I dug that you were telling the truth! You took those broads like you were somewhere across the street looking down from a ten-story window...."

"... WHAT!" Hickman yelled. "Are you saying that I ..."

"... And you did it out of revenge for all the wrongs those folks—and especially their damn women—had been doing to our people!"

"Now wait, man! Who *are* you," Hickman said. "I've *never*— Do you know what you're *saying*...."

"... But up to the time I read about it those bastards had me brainwashed—that's right! But then the *scales* fell from my goddamn eyes. That's right, man! And when that happened I understood for the first time that what you had really done was to change what the white folks call *rape* into something that they hadn't even *thought* about!

"Because, hell, Chief," Leroy said, reaching out and stabbing Hickman's chest with a discolored finger's manicured nail, "*you* [thump!] turned [thump!] their little chicken-shit game [thump-thump-thump!] into a form of *Black* [thump!] fucking [thump!] *Political* [thump-thump—thump] ACTION!"

Resisting an impulse to bash Leroy's face, Hickman whirled to see if anyone else was listening and shouted, "I DID WHAT!"

"Oh, come on, Chief," Leroy said, flashing white teeth in a smile of delight, "don't go acting surprised over my taking so damn long to dig it, 'cause after all, man, I'm not *educated* like you. But I finally dug it, and that's *exactly* what you did! I didn't dig it at the time, but you upped and turned the *tables* on those crackers! Yes, sir! You ran their own filthy game against them! And baby, what I mean is, you changed that stale crap of theirs into something black and *beautiful!*"

For a moment Hickman stared open-mouthed into the exalted discoloration of Leroy's face, torn between a feeling of repulsion and a need to learn the identity of the man—ghost, rapist, agitator—for whom he was being so outrageously mistaken.

"But, Leroy—*please*," he pleaded, "I don't know who on earth it is you think I am, but I *swear* that I've never been the kind of man you're describing.... I'm a *preacher*...."

Throwing up his palms Leroy racked his body backwards and braced himself with an admiring smile. "Sure, Chief, I *know*, and a dam' good one! You been preaching freedom from *way* back. I *dig* you, Daddy—understand? So don't be standing there trying to look so modest and all. You did a great thing and it was *beautiful.* Because not only did you tell them *what* you were going to do, you *did* it! And then you went to the pen like a man and paid your righteous dues! Yes, sir, you *did* it! And like I say, when I finally figured it out all I could do was just sit there with the *tears* running down my cheeks. And that's when I told myself— I said, 'Leroy, you were a mindless, gutless fool! That's what you were for ever doubting that good brave black man!' Yes, sir; that's what I said.

"Chief, that's the truth! And that's why it does me so much good to finally be able to admit it. Because I realized that back there when I was seeking for some direction I had found me a real man and a true leader! But then, after finding you, I was too dam' *dumb* to recognize you and give you the loyalty you deserved. Even now it dam' near breaks my heart to even *think* about it, because after I'd found me a black man who was a true, natural-born leader with the courage to git down in the mud and do battle with the bastards on their own fucking terms I messed up. So sitting there in my crummy little room I told myself that in a man like you we had found what we always needed—which was a man ready and willing to start down in the stone rock bottom of the shit pile and rise up shining with the pride and beauty of Black *BEING*! What I mean is: a man who had discovered the black dynamics of Black *leadership*! And I mean one who was ready and willing and able to pull himself up by his bootstraps and reach down and draw the rest of the race up to the top of the fucking mountain along *with* him! Yes, sir!"

Aware of sweat bursting from his pores, Hickman started away, thinking, If this wasn't happening to me, I wouldn't believe it—but before he could take a step Leroy reached out and seized him by the wrists.

"That's the way it was back then," Leroy said, "and I finally figured out that my problem with you was that you came to us as a mystery wrapped in a mystery, or a brightness shrouded in darkness...."

"Now, just hold it and listen to me carefully," Hickman began, but as he tried to free his wrists Leroy tightened his grip and stared searchingly into his eyes.

"Please, Chief, don't try to deny it," Leroy sang out with a sudden burst of fervor. "Because I *know*! I *know* that my redeemer liveth! Some folks said that you rose up out of Canada. Others said it was out of Africa, while still others claimed it was either Gulfport, Mississippi, or Boley, Oklahoma.... Some knew you as Prince Marcus, others as Swami Joe, and some by such names as Clexo, Newfoundland Ike, and Sweet-the-Monkey. And then you faded a while and turned up again as Ras the Cleanser, the Hot Wind Out of Africa; and in Detroit you were Dennis the Inspirer; and in Chicago, Black John, otherwise known as the Compound Cathartic-for-all-forms-of-white-sickness; and in L.A. you came as Matt the Revelator and the Dark Sequoia—oh, yes! You were known by different names in different places, but to me, my man, you were *always* none other than Chief SAM, the fucking *Liberator*!"

"...Hickman!" Hickman shouted, "It's HICKMAN!"

"...You were celebrated far and wide, but the main thing for me was that you came to us out of a mystery. And that was as a test to see if we were *ready* to be led. Yes, sir, that was it! Because brave leaders have to have brave followers. But like I said, I failed the test. And although it took me years and years, at last I *know* it. I was too dam' dumb to come up with the necessary, and you knew it. That was the trap you set for all like me who wasn't ready—just like you told that cracker judge, and, man, *man,* how you told him! You remember?"

"Oh, no," Hickman said, sighing, "but I'm sure you can tell me...."

"You're damn right I can! You said, 'Look, Judge, you don't have to waste your breath asking me *why* I'm protesting, all you have to do is look into this scumbag you people have been using to reenslave us after all these years of our so-called emancipation! Think about it! You did us wrong! You slapped us square in the face but we told ourselves, "Peace, for they know not what they do." And so we turned the other cheek and hoped that you would see the error of your ways. But what did you do? Hell, I'll *tell* you what you did: You ran around and kicked us in the right cheek of our high black innocent behinds!

" 'And when we stood there shaking and reeling and didn't go down, you hauled off with all your might and tried to kick all the patience and humility out of the *left* cheek of our behinds. And when we *still* held our peace and *still* tried to play by *your* so-called Golden Rules, you got mad and kicked us square in the middle of our *ass*! And that ain't all, because when at last we got upset and called out to you, "Cease! Halt! Let's *discuss* this mess like men and brothers," you rose up and came down on our heads, and on the poor bewildered heads of our innocent wives and our children!'

"And Chief, that's when you reached way down deep in our bag of sore trials and tribulations and hit him with some deep, *deep* shit from the nitty-gritty!

"You told him, 'Every time we look around you're crying *rape,* and when we look to see what you mean we discover that it means anything and *everything* that a black man can do! That's right!

" 'To live is to rape! And to work is to rape! And trying to learn to read and write in a broken-down school is to rape! And to pray bowed down on our bended knees is to rape—but the worst rape of *all* is for one of us to be innocent and have some lying woman swear on your dog-eared Bible that we raped her!'

"Oh, you really told him! Chief, you said, 'Hell, according to y'all even knocking out a two-hundred-and-fifty-pound white-assed *prizefighter* with sixteen-ounce boxing gloves in a ring under the control of a white referee and with five thousand mostly white folks looking on is rape! And what's more, just asking for what is rightfully ours, and which we have earned fair—if not square—is to rape!

" 'Oh, yes! And trying to vote in Ala-the-goddam-bama can get us charged with ninety-nine counts of rape for attacking a broken-down eighty-nine-year-old *ballot box*!'

"Then, Chief, they tried to shut you up, and you *really* laid it on 'em!

"I can see it now, just like it's still happening: Two had you by the arms, two had you by the legs, and a whole *gang* of the bastards had you by the *neck,* but they couldn't stop you—oh, no! 'Cause with all those crackers hanging on you r'ared back and roared in thunder:

" 'Rape! Rape! RAPE!' you blasted. 'Please, won't *somebody* be so kind as to get me a law book and a dictionary and *explain* to me what the hell *is* this *rape* I keep hearing so much about? I keep hearing it and I ask myself how can it *be* that it's all these things for you folks and only one for me? Haven't I got a right to the tree of life? Don't I have the need and the right to chase me some happiness? *I* think and feel it in my bones that I do! *I* believe in my heart that most of my people do too! Therefore I'm letting you know how *we* feel. . . .'

"You told them, Chief; you said, 'I'm a patient man of a patient people, but, hell, Judge, patience don't mean *forever*! Time is growing short, so listen to what I'm saying! Look at our condition and see your mistakes and clean up this raping mess you been making of anything and everything!'

"And that's when they hit you over the head and throwed you into the slammer! But then, Chief, God bless you, you served your time, and when they let you out, you went into righteous *action*! That's when you struck a match like back there in '35 and '43 and led us in that mighty chorus of 'BURN, BABY, BURN!'

"And when the buildings flamed and the windowpanes shattered and you saw that they *still* wasn't paying heed to your warning, you turned the tables on the bastards by grabbing you a whole *gang* of those bitches and turning them inside *out*—and oh, what a mighty strategy and glorious tactic it was!

" 'Out, Out!' you cried, 'Life is but a raping shadow, therefore who's to be or not to be, if we can't be free? The tide has turned, the righteous soot has streaked the snow and time still marches, so we're in time and in step with time! So what shall it be? You, or me, or us together? . . .'

"Chief, I tell you, I just sat there reading your confession—oh, no! That's not what I mean! It was a great *oration*! That's what it truly was! And there I was reading it and hearing it and laughing like crazy and crying like a baby! And my heart was breaking with pride and sadness. . . . And it was all because I understood for the first time what had happened to all our poor people who should have understood what you were trying to do. They should have learned the *lesson* you were teaching, but they let you *down*!

"I know, because when they charged you with rape I gave up all hope and didn't want to think about you anymore. I was so dumb and ashamed that I couldn't think straight enough to work out the puzzle you were laying down for our instruction! Chief, that's the truth! That's the truth as I finally came to see it—no, Chief, wait! Don't leave me now because I'm not *about* finished! There's more to it—and please, Chief, don't look at me like that! Forgiveness, Chief! I'm asking for your *forgiveness*! And after I'm through you don't have to say a mumbling word, not even a smile if you don't feel like it. . . .

"Because I've been punished; yes, sir, I've been punished. After that trial I gave up and just lived from day to day, and I told myself that instead of being my true leader you were just one more hustler who'd come down with white-fever. So I tried to put it all behind me and lived my life in a hound-dog way—God damn it! It's shameful but that's what I did! I confess it! And not until I was reading that newspaper did I finally admit to myself that I was only that way on the surface. That's right! It raised me from the dead and showed me the light! Because way deep down in my heart there was a part of what you had made happen that just wouldn't die. I know it now, yes, sir! Because whenever I wasn't thinking about anything in particular, or maybe when I was sipping me a little taste of gin, the thought would come to me like a little voice way back in the rear of my head, and then the high hopes and excitement of the old days would come alive again, and I'd find myself thinking about you and getting worked up over how it used to be—the pride and the hope, I mean. That's when your image would rise up and glow in my mind, and I could see you on the soapbox agitating, and leading those glorious marches! And I could see your gestures and hear your voice as clear as a bell! And that's when deep down I'd truly feel the lost hope you gave us.

"But it wouldn't last but a few seconds, and then I'd have to turn it off and think about something else. I simply couldn't stand it! I couldn't bear to think about those wonderful days and all we lost when they throwed you in jail. And especially when I considered that all that glorious promise was lost over some prissy pieces of poontang! Man, I tell you, that thing almost *killed* me! And in a way of speaking it did, 'cause until only a minute ago when I happened to look out and see you walking along the street I've been a living dead man...."

"Dammit, Lee-roy," Hickman heard suddenly from behind him, "you're 'bout the damndest fool in all D.C.! Here I been waiting to finish up with you and you're out here fooling with some stranger! Leave that man alone!"

And now with mixed feelings of relief and distrust Hickman whirled, wondering what to expect next, and saw a short, rotund, freckle-faced man who wore a barber's tunic with a fine-toothed comb sticking from its breast pocket.

"Oh, to hell with him, Chief," Leroy said with a scowl and wave of his hand, "That's Ivey, a cat who thinks cutting hair makes him some kind of philosopher...."

"Mister," Ivey said, "you'll have to excuse Lee-roy for hitting you with all that crap of his, because he don't mean no harm, not really. It's just that he's what they call a 'moon freak'—which means that when the moon's in the full he simply can't help but act the fool. Did he rough you up?"

"Why, no," Hickman said, "but he's certainly got me confused with someone I've never even *heard* about...."

"I know what you mean," Ivey said, " 'cause when Lee-roy's like this he's apt to grab *any* big, well-dressed black man who comes along and insist that he's some cat who goes by the name of Chief Sam. Hell, Lee-roy ain't even *seen* the man, he only heard about him from his *grand*daddy who's supposed to have run into him years ago somewhere out west. What's more, Lee-roy'll admit it when he's normal. But when he's like he is today he thinks every big, dark-complected fellow who comes along is some kind of cross between a conjur-man, a pimp, a prizefighter, a foot-racer—you name it—and some kind of chippy-chasing civil-rights leader—who *he* claims is operating somewhere underground. That's just how scrambled he gets. It's never a doctor, lawyer, educator, scientist, or judge—much less a politician, of whom we *do* have a few in Congress—hell, no! It's got to be some cat who so far as anybody has been able to find out, has never even *existed!*"

"Aaaw, man," Leroy said with an angry wave of his hand, "you are a *drag*—you know that? You're a faithless drag! You got no vision and can't even think from breathing all that hair and concentrated funk!"

"Yeah," Ivey said, "I'm a drag because I want you back in my chair so I can finish with your butt! But now you better git moving, or else I'ma drag you over to St. Elizabeth's and see to it that they give you some attention! I mean it, Lee-roy, so git moving! It's either that or the cops—and you *know* you don't want that to happen again, not after they caught you with your britches down orating and quoting the Constitution to your rusty pecker. And just look at the mess you're making of that neck-cloth! You trying to look like some kinda A-rab or something? Come on!"

"Chief, you hear that," Leroy said. "You try to bring our people a life-saving message and show 'em the way out of all their confusion and they call you crazy! What the hell do I care about what those jokers at St. Elizabeth's think! What the hell do *they* know?"

" ... Come on, Lee-roy!"

" ... Shit! Black people are the most complicated folks in the whole fucking *world,* but when those damn St. Elizabeth doctors come up against a man like me all they can do is put him down as a motherfucker! They think all the trouble in the world comes from some simpleminded crap like that! Hell, if that was the case all they'd have to do is round up all the motherfuckers and they'd have a perfect world—which they sho in hell don't want—and if they did they'd still blame us when things went wrong....

"Anyway, Chief, it's been a pleasure to see a truly great leader again and make my confession. Keep up the good work and I'll keep doing my part in spreading your message!"

And now, turning to Ivey and moving away, Leroy frowned.

"Come on, man," he growled, "and this time forget those moth-eaten Afros you been peddling and make sure you give me a true feather-edge!"

"And yeah, Chief," he said, turning back, "here's something else that needs your attention! These young dudes of ours are being messed up, down, and straight through the middle by wearing these Afros and platform shoes! They think they look proud when in fact they're getting rump-busted and stoop-shouldered from carrying all that weight on their ignorant heads! Why is it that so many of our folks keep trying to substitute *hair*styles for political action? Hell, after slavery was ended the old folks grabbed for the ballot. But today these young dudes grabbed the Afro like it was some kind of freedom. But while they swagger and strut and admire themselves the crackers just laugh and grab for more power! Hell, Chief, these young folks of ours are into *magic* and don't even know it—hey! Watch it, man!"

And suddenly thrown off balance by Ivey's yank on his arm, Leroy danced around the corner with a swaying, camel-walk wobble.

[CHRIST]

Watching the barber's neck-cloth disappear with a snap and a billow, Hickman turned, grasping the guardrail through a dream-like haze.

Hickman, he thought, *what on earth did you do to deserve all of* that? *And with hundreds of big Negroes wandering around this town, why would he pick on* you? *Man, if I weren't fully dressed and in my right I'd swear you're dreaming!*

Which was impossible, because the same brassy automobile horn was blaring as before Ivey snatched Leroy away, the street facing the building still filled with window-shopping people, and the odor of Leroy's Mum and bay rum still clinging to his jacket. Yes, and his hands were clutching the brass rail from which Leroy had relieved himself of his wild confession. Yet something seemed missing, some teasing segment of reality lost in the wild encounter.

Then in a flashback he was dangling again in the air, but now through the translucence of Leroy's tricolored skin he saw himself standing in the pulpit of a crowded church holding a Bible while conducting the funeral of a prominent minister. Then the scene fell apart, and as he stared down at the features of the corpse in the coffin the man's face twitched with a sarcastic smile and became that of a child. Whereupon he felt himself being raised even higher and the scene was taken over by two women mourners who leaped from their seats in a whirling, veil-snatching, hair-pulling brawl. And as he stared at the blur of their air-flailing arms the coffin's lid flew shut with a slow-motion fall....

Then through a crescendo of street sounds he was staring at the windowless wall of the building which towered beyond and above the guardrail. And with the disrupted funeral still vivid in his mind he recalled that the man dead had been a highly esteemed minister and the brawling women his girlfriend and wife. Then in a flash he realized that the man was not the minister. And struck by the incongruity of a dead man smiling and shrinking to a child in an adult's coffin struck home he flooded with sweat, reached for his panama to wipe his brow, and felt it slip from his fingers. And before he could move the hat teetered on the guardrail like a bird taking flight and swooped down to the area below him.

Grasping the guardrail in perspiring hands, he looked down to where his hat lay white in the shadows; and with a sigh of disgust followed the guardrail around to the steep flight of stairs that led down from the street, and with a sigh began making his descent through an updraft of cool air.

Now, reaching the bottom, he stood in the empty loading area of a courtyard that lay two full stories below the street and surprisingly larger than it had appeared from above. Against a nearby wall garbage cans humming with flies stood in the angle of nearby walls that were part of a vast open space, and to his right he could see ranks of white pillars that ended at a wall which loomed in the shadows; and to his left the open roofless space through which his hat had sailed extended to yet another wall that appeared to support the sidewalks which flanked the building's side street and frontage.

What a waste, he thought as he looked around, *what a waste!* And in stooping to retrieve his panama he looked up to find himself facing a massive bronze door.

Tarnished green from neglect, the door might have graced the entrance of a prosperous bank, but now [it was] tightly closed, with its handles missing, its bronze laurel wreath dangling off center, and its panels scarred as though battered by John Henry's hammer.

Thinking, *But what an odd place for such an elegant door,* he stared. Then, repelled by the odor of garbage and humming of flies, he jammed on his hat and turned to leave—but not yet. For, suddenly catching sight of a copper-clad structure projecting from the wall to his left, he took an impulsive step to its front and found himself facing a wide, plate-glass window of the type usually found in busy shopping areas.

But why down here below street level? he thought, and, stepping closer, saw what appeared to be a badly splashed house-painter's drop-cloth that covered the enclosure's rear wall. Then, in a flash, the confusion of brushstrokes and splashes sprang to form, becoming a large, unframed painting.

Then came a chilling shock of surprise. For here, in the last place in the world he would have expected, he was staring at a depiction of Christ marching to Calvary. And with the disappearing legs in the Longview's tapestry springing to mind it was as though he were staring into the window of a storefront church.

For now, through the clouded glass, he recognized the painting as a type of religious folk art familiar to Negro neighborhoods—an association of style and place immediately confirmed by the heavy symbolism of the scene's faded colors. For while the jeering, spear-wielding soldiers were unquestionably white, the skin of the thorn-crowned, cross-bearing Christ was unmistakably black. And with a gasp he asked himself, *But why in a Southern town like Washington, D.C., would one of our churches be down here in the basement of a white business building?* And appalled by the rush of implications released by his question he pressed his forehead to the clouded glass and was struck by a feeling of dread.

For immediately, something about the cross-bearing Christ seemed out of place—and it was not Christ's blackness, which he recognized as a traditional symbolism by which a people whose enemies had made their very skin tones a cross to bear asserted their most human yearnings and spiritual needs and allowed them to identify more intimately with the transcendent image of Christ. Nor was it the incongruity of the painting's location. For, years ago, hadn't he played for a dance in a South Carolina town in which a Negro confectioner and ice-cream-maker's store had faced the church in which John C. Calhoun's family had worshipped? Therefore, his anxiety sprang not from the painting's location but from something out of place in the depiction of Christ's fateful march... some flaw in its painter's conception which was so obvious and yet so elusive that it baffled his searching eye....

Then, drawn to the impression made in Christ's naked shoulder by the weight of the cross, he began to understand: For some two feet above the point where the rough-hewn upright of the cross knifed into the bruised flesh of Christ's straining shoulder, the artist, suddenly improvising on his theme like a jazzman on a familiar tune, had placed what on first sight had appeared to be the travel-soiled bundle of a hobo. There in the angle where the upright joined the sky-pointing arm of the cross it rested, a bundle consisting of red-white-and-blue cotton which was depicted as having become partially unrolled in the painful march and ended up trailing and distorting the footprints of Christ. And with eyes flying back to the point from which the striped cloth trailed he saw distorted white stars spring into focus and exclaimed, "Good Lord!" And the cloth showed forth as a bundled-up flag....

For a moment he gazed, totally unsettled by the painter's crude updating of the biblical scene as he thought, *What on earth is happening? First Leroy's craziness and now this!*

And exasperated by his inability to confront or deny the painter's eye-assaulting scene-within-scene, time-past-in-time-present depiction, he whirled in outrage toward the battered door, asking himself in an attempt to escape, *Why on earth would even an insane pastor try to establish a church down here in a storefront so far below the street? And how did his flock get to their place of worship? Was it through that beat-up door—past storage bins, air-conditioning ducts, and more garbage cans like these behind me?*

And with a sudden burst of outrage he rushed to the door and gave it a pounding blow from his shoulder. Then, bracing himself for a reaction from the other side, he prepared for a fight. But except for a single clank of metal sounding through the booming echo of his blow there was only an eerie, heart-thumping silence....

Still straining for the sound of footsteps, he stood immobile while hearing the swarming of flies. Then, seized by a mounting feeling of unease he stepped backwards and whirled, giving the painting a sweep of his eyes that flashed from Christ's thorn-crowned head to the dishonored flag and ended at the reflection of his own tense face staring back from the grime-stained glass. Then, sprinting for the stairs, he pounded upward, leaping two steps at a time for the street.

Where, now, breathing hard and squinting against the sudden assault of brilliant sunlight, he turned and stood looking over the guardrail with a feeling of having barely escaped an invisible inquisitor whose intent was to oppress him with insidious questions of a kind he had neither the will, wisdom, nor courage to answer.... Then he was pounding the sidewalk to the front of the building, where, now, he stood in the middle of the steady flow of curious sidewalk traffic inspecting the building's façade from sidewalk to roof.

But here, except for the absence of Leroy and the white man who had looked down from above, things appeared to be as before. And with his sense of disorientation increasing, he backed away. And adjusting his hat with a look into the questioning eyes of passersby, he headed on foot for the Longview.

[DECISION]

UPON REACHING THE LONGVIEW Hickman went immediately to his room with the intention of calling Wilhite. But after dialing the number he replaced the reciever.

If there's any news he'll call me, he thought, and, feeling tired and still shaken by his wild encounter, he stripped to his shorts and lay on the bed and stared at the ceiling.

When I tell Wilhite he'll swear I'm lying, he thought, *but when that man lifted me into the air it was like he was performing some kind of ritual.... It was like a devilish laying-on-of-hands. Then he insists that I'm some sort of a underground leader known as* Chief Sam *whose movement he confesses to betraying. And as though* that *wasn't enough, he glorifies Chief Sam for being a* rapist! *And the next thing I know I'm down in a cellar having my sanity challenged by that outrageous painting. If it had happened to Janey she'd call it a sign of warning....*

Well, he thought as he reached for a pillow, *I don't believe in signs, but maybe that's what it was. And even though my brain was fairly rattled I don't need that kind of sign to remind me that I still have the problem of reaching that boy—not after I wasted all that precious time looking for Millsap only to get myself put through a cross between a living nightmare and a wringer! So now I have nothing hopeful to tell the members, and somewhere out there that little man of Janey's is on the move and preparing to act.... Hickman, instead of wasting more time chasing after the man maybe you should try to find his stalker—but where would you start? You don't even know the name he's using, whether he's reached town or still on his way.... So why switch from chasing the man to chase his shadow? The problem is how do we find him?...*

Closing his eyes he thought, *Only three years old and already asking more questions than a crossword puzzle:*

Daddy Hickman, Who killed Cock Robin, was it really the sparrow?

Probably, Bliss; isn't that how the story goes?

Yes, sir. But did he really do it with a bow and arrow?

Watch it, Bliss! Be careful, or you'll ruin your book with that lemonade—that's how the sparrow said he killed him, didn't he?

Yes, sir; but . . .

So I guess we'll have to give him the benefit of the doubt. But then, on the other hand, it's well known that sparrows don't always tell the truth. So he could have used a slingshot—or even a double-barreled shotgun. . . .

A shotgun?

Why not? If he could handle a bow he could handle a gun. . . .

Now you funning me, and that's not fair!

No, Bliss, do I look like I'm laughing? I'm just reminding you that when a sparrow starts talking he's capable of all kinds *of amazing things. Like pulling a lion's tail and getting away with it.*

A real lion?

Oh, no, Bliss; I meant a baby *lion. Grown lions are much too dangerous for sparrows to fool with. But Cock Robin? Now that's something different. . . .*

How come?

Because in the first place he didn't know exactly from what direction ole Sparrow was coming at him, and in the second he made the mistake of being so overconfident that he thought nothing could harm him. And besides, maybe he was so busy with other matters that he didn't let it bother him. You know how it is with robins: They have to search for worms, bawl out the cats, hold choir practice—not to mention all those solos he has to sing. . . .

So why didn't his friends tell him what that mean ole sparrow was up to?

I don't know, Bliss. They probably tried, but maybe they simply couldn't get to him in time. Or maybe he was just so cocky that he wouldn't listen. . . .

But why would the sparrow want to kill him?

I don't know, Bliss. Maybe he was simply jealous of Cock Robin's musical ability. . . . And like the Bible says, pride is a sin, but envy is dangerous. . . .

Amen, Daddy Hickman, but do you really believe that the sparrow shot *Cock Robin?*

Probably, Bliss, but remember that the story you're reading is a kind of poetry. So by saying that the sparrow used an arrow the writer was making it sound more musical and heroic. You know, it was like the sparrow was outdoing a hero like Robin Hood. And besides, while "arrow" rhymes fine with "sparrow," "gun" falls flat on the ear. Would you like it if his friends had said, "Hey there, Sparrow, who killed Cock Robin," and he came up with something like, "Well now, pard'ner, I blasted him with my shotgun"?

No, sir! Because like you say, "arrow" goes much better with "sparrow."

That's right, Bliss, and I'll tell you something else: Ole Cock Robin had a much better chance against that arrow than he would have had against bird shot—yes, sir!

Yes, he thought as the memory faded, *but this time whatever weapon he chooses let's hope that he misses*—and was jolted awake by the phone. . . .

Maybe, he thought, as he picked up the reciever, *we got to him after all.* . . .

"So you finally made it back," Wilhite said. "I've been waiting to hear from you."

"I knew you were," he said, "but I decided to relax a bit before I bothered you. What's happening with the members?"

"I guess by now they're grabbing a little after-dinner rest."

"Do you mean that they've already had lunch?"

"Since it's too early for supper and 'lunch' is what folks up this way call 'dinner,' I guess that's what we had."

"Good, and was there any word from our boy?"

"Not a word. How'd you make out?"

"Wilhite, I'm sorry to report that I drew another blank; and from the way things are going I'm beginning to feel that his secretary told him about our visit and he's on the run."

"I hope not, because if he has any idea of why we're trying to see him he'd see us. What happened to you?"

"Man, nothing! Not a single productive thing! No sooner do I step into the lobby than I run into that guard—the one Brother Provo wanted to choose— and got myself thrown out of the confounded building. The man made me wish that I'd let Provo go ahead and butt him a few times. It might have knocked some sense into his head—or into Provo's. Anyway, after that I went looking for a fellow I used to know hoping that he might be able to give me a line on our boy."

"Did he?"

"No, because hardly had I got started than I was grabbed in the middle of the sidewalk by a wild man—and I mean *physically*—who insisted that I was some kind of underground civil-rights leader. . . ."

Wilhite laughed, "A *what!*"

"You heard me: an 'underground . . . civil-rights . . . leader'! And not only that, he insisted that I once served time for rape!"

"Oh, come on, A.Z. *You?*"

"That's the truth. In less time than it takes to say it the man reinvented me, gave me a new name and a new philosophy, assigned me a new calling, *and* offered to help me overthrow the United States Government! For now that's all I can tell you, and please don't mention it to the members. I tell you, Wilhite, as soon as we complete this mission I'm getting out of Washington! How are the others holding up?"

"Pretty well, considering what we've run into. They enjoyed their meal in the main dining room—where the sisters had themselves a fine time criticizing the linen and the silver and comparing the service with the kind that's offered down home. . . ."

"Well, now," he said with a chuckle, "wasn't that to be expected? They've been washing and polishing the stuff long enough to think of themselves as *some* kind of experts. It's their way of feeling at home away from home."

"Oh, I wasn't being critical. In fact, I enjoyed hearing them identifying with the best the rich white folks can afford. Down home they do a lot of complaining, but being up here in the North they feel free to express their regional pride...."

"That's right, and their taste. The sisters might not be able to afford the best, but they sure appreciate it when they see it."

"You telling me? And that's why some of the brothers are so much in debt! So anyway, they had themselves a great time discussing the quality of everything. Then somebody brought up the way you were talking circles around that secretary and everybody got to laughing. What do you call it, A.Z.? Rhetoric, double-talk, or just plain shucking?"

Slapping his thigh, he laughed softly into the mouthpiece.

"Well, Wilhite, since she was forcing me to improvise like a jackass eating briars it was a little of everything. But *whatever* it was it didn't do us a bit of good. Not with her being so *un*-reconstructed."

"I know, but it wasn't because you didn't try. That guard was talking about old Provo showing off *his* moves, but he should have been there to hear you going through some of yours."

"Well, Wilhite, sometimes a man of the Word is forced to be simply a man of *words*...."

"Don't brag, A.Z., it's sinful. But, getting back to business, I was hoping that on your second try you'd make that woman stop pulling rank and listen. So since she didn't, what do we do now? What shall I tell the members?"

"There's nothing to tell them, and until we can think of something we'd better find a way of keeping them occupied. Meanwhile I'm hoping that the boy's secretary will have a change of heart and give him our message, therefore I'm leaning toward doing nothing."

"Yes, A.Z., but like you always say: Doing nothing *is* doing something."

"Sometimes that's true, so I won't argue. But here's an idea: How about taking the members sightseeing? Let them have a look at the city?"

"It's a good way of killing time—but will you go along?"

"Of course. That's what I meant, all of us will go."

"But what if he telephones?"

"So they'll take the message down at the desk and when we get back we'll return his call. Besides, a little waiting will arouse his curiosity. Meantime the members will be getting a little pleasure out of this trip and they'll have something to tell the folks back home."

"O.K., A.Z. It'll take time to get some transportation, so how about my setting it up for about an hour from now?"

Yawning, he looked at his watch. "Good! And while you're at it, I'm going to try and take a nap. So when you're ready, have them assemble in the lobby and give me a buzz."

[LINCOLN]

WHEN HICKMAN EMERGED FROM the Longview the brothers and sisters were already seated in the sightseeing bus and Wilhite standing at the curb beside its driver—a tall white man who watched his approach with undisguised curiosity—and a young white woman in uniform whom Wilhite identified as its tour conductor. And now, apologizing for being late, he followed Wilhite aboard to greetings of welcome from the brothers and sisters.

"Sit there, A.Z.," Wilhite said, indicating a seat near the driver, and as he moved toward the window and looked back Wilhite took a seat on the aisle near the rear. Then, with the young woman taking a position near the door the driver called out, "All set," and the bus moved from the curb.

Turning now to the view from the window, he watched streets become an accelerating blur of buildings and traffic, against the tempo of which crowds on the sidewalks moved in a dream-like flow of anonymity.

Yes, Hickman, he thought, *and Janey's little man could be anywhere among them. But even if you saw him how would you recognize him? And after all these years the same thing goes for the man he's after. But you still have to warn him, and here you are—may the Lord forgive you—sparring for time on a bus!*

And depressed by the thought, he turned from the window and gave his attention to the young tourist guide, who stood near the driver describing details of the unfolding scene through a small megaphone.

A petite blonde whose blue eyes were accented by mascara, the young woman wore a blue uniform and a white, black-visored cap, and as he listened to her voice above the rumble of traffic he recalled the days when he himself had used such a megaphone when shouting the blues above the moaning and groaning of reeds and brasses.

And now, closing his eyes and surrendering to reveries of days long past, he thought, *Those were times when bus rides went with being a musician. Days and nights of rocking-and-rolling through counties patrolled by sheriffs who were hostile, traveling hundreds of miles just to play one-night stands, and the roads rough, the dates far between, and the towns unfriendly. A time when no hotel would accept us—whether North, South, or in between—and with our own folks the only ones to take us in, many of them refusing because they regarded jazz as the devil's music and us his disciples. . . . And the tricks and skullduggery that went with the profession. Playing to halls packed with dancers, many of whom were gate-crashers. . . . Having local managers skip town with our pay. . . . Dances broken up by anything from drunks riddling the ceilings with owlhead pistols to jokers throwing terrified pigs and skunks through the windows.... The lives of men in the band threatened by jeal-ous country boys who thought we rode all those bumpy miles just to make big-city plays for their green little women.... Being late for dates in distant towns because redneck station owners refused us gas.... Served fat-back, greasy greens, and cornbread in greasy-spoon restaurants so often that we felt blessed whenever we lucked-up on good barbecue and chitt'lings.... Nothing strong to drink but rot-gut whiskey.... And that endless confusion over race and color, money and music—like that Christmas Day when the white owner of a black dance hall refused to let us perform until we agreed to parade through the streets like minstrel men playing "Dixie," which we had to do or be run out of town. Yes, and with me turning the tables by sneaking in that nasty, wailing obbligato of "Your Mama Don't Wear No Drawers" on which the others performed variations all along the way ... which made it not only bearable but side-breaking fun, with the local Negroes laughing and the white folks applauding and none the wiser.... It's a wonder we came through any of it alive—and yet sometimes there were the good things.... Like the quiet in which to remember my early days with my family ... and the pleasure of rolling past fields full of flowers and serene streams sparkling beneath clear blue skies. Or watching the soaring flight of blackbirds, quail, and doves.... The smell of wood smoke drifting from lonely cabins.... And that early morning in Virginia seeing red-coated horsemen riding to hounds over the broad rolling grounds of a fine white mansion.... And the tally-ho sound of a hunting horn floating through the air. Then on the rise of the hill ahead three bare trees looming lonely against the gloom of the sky—yes, and the air's sudden chill when my mind sang a blues evoking images recalled from my father's sermons celebrating the coming of Easter.... But finally we reached At-lanta, and no longer the need for quilts and pallets spread on the floors of cautious strangers.... And all that Saturday night excitement of women and whiskey and the joy of sharing down-home fellowship with those of our own kind—which was a bonus that came with making music.... White folks enjoy their put-down joke about what it means to be col-ored on Saturday night, but as usual they miss the challenge of the foxy truth hidden in it. Tally-ho! Maybe that's why they sneer at our styles and end up making them their own while refusing to admit it. Which is the living contradiction Millsap's friend Sippy was ex-ploiting when he went about creating what he considered an ideal white American.... What a character! First he takes a man whose white skin gives him room to maneuver and edu-cates him with a mixture of the best traits of both black and white. Then he trains his pupil to improvise on the unexpectedness of experience like a cross between a jazzman and a Texas politician—while he sits back and watches what happens from the shadows.... That Sippy! Only a great trickster would realize that in a land like this* nobody *has a patent on conceiving the wisest action or coming up with the most definitive blend of styles. So what's an American? Shucks, Hickman, it's all up for grabs! So sometimes it's us who're on target, sometimes it's others. And of ideal Americans there are only a few, and them mostly dead. As for us, we live in worlds within worlds, touching others cheek by jowl, and yet so far apart that when it comes to our ideals there's a* yes *in all our* no's, *and a* no *in all our* yeses.... *Black and white, we're all involved, but mainly it's the fault of folks who want to control everything and everybody but themselves. Still, it's a part of the game, and in spite of all the confusion it caused back in those bus-riding days our knowing exactly where the color lines were drawn made for a sense of security. We were young and adventurous, and having elected to perform in a land a-whirl with hostility there was nothing to do but deal with the world as we found it. No need for anyone to tell us the rules or the reasons, because there were always those* FOR WHITES ONLY *signs, their facial expressions, attitudes and quick-trigger violence. They were always there, and no matter how well we played, no manager—gentile or Jew—could have made things easier.... So with our manhood challenged on all sides we blazed our own trails, musical, moral and social, and used our outlaw music as our sword and shield. Sure, it was rough going; but by moving toward our own vision of the possible and trying to deal with the world as we found it we made the struggle a thing of self-affirmation.... So now, looking back, the bad part recedes while the good part advances, giving its memory a glow like the echoing hope of a rousing melody first phrased in the days of the old dispensation.... I wouldn't have believed it, but just as it takes two to tango it takes time, luck, and aging to see the effects of change. Which means that the bad part was the price we paid to get to the good part—So what's new? Given the tricky changes Father Time plays on the living we find ourselves constantly giving up some good things for other good things while exchanging old bad things for new. Which, perhaps, is the only reliable definition for that tricky notion called "progress."...*

And now, listening to the rise and fall of the young woman's voice he stared out at the passing scene with the events of the morning returning to mind, and when addressed by brothers and sisters excited by the young woman's comments on the scenery he replied with silent bows of his head.

Instead of being on this bus, he thought, *I should be in my room trying to work this thing out in my mind; at least I would be more honest. This way, after promising them bread, all I'm doing is giving them a pile of stones.... And I thought it would be so easy! We would see him and give him our information and those who knew him would have the satisfaction of watching his reaction to their gesture of peace and reconciliation, and then we would go back home and wait to see its effect on his actions. Just that. Not a lot of name-calling or accusations, but a gesture that would say: In spite of everything that's happened to you and to us since those old hopeful days, this is how we feel. And now may the Lord watch over thee and us while we're absent one from another. Instead, we ran into a wall within a wall, and here I am offering them nothing more than a diversion. And even if they find it refreshing it's far too little to even begin to compensate for the sacrifices they made to come up here.... Hickman, if you don't do better by them than this you'll never forgive yourself—Just listen to that young Northern white gal dishing out her canned version of what she's calling history! Spieling that stuff like a sideshow barker and doesn't even realize that she's addressing a glaring-staring part of everything she's omitting!*

And now, suddenly realizing that they had arrived near the Washington Mall, he leaped from his seat and surprised himself by ordering the driver to pull to the curb.

"Miss Guide, Mr. Driver, brothers and sisters," he said, "you'll have to forgive me, but I just realized that for all the comfort that's to be had by going about it this way, we can get more out of this trip if we go the rest of the way on foot.

"And don't worry," he said, turning to the driver, "you'll be paid your full fare...."

"I'm a little surprised, A.Z.," Wilhite called as he stepped into the aisle, "but that was taken care of before you came aboard. We paid in advance."

"Good!" he said with a smile for the puzzled young woman. "Most folks don't realize it, but that's usually the way it is when you go looking for history: You pay in advance and you get what you see and remember."

Then, giving Wilhite a blank-face wink and telling him to have the driver wait until their return, he moved to the door.

"So let's get moving," he called to the surprised members, "because from here on we're going to walk a while. And not only will we have our look at history, we'll do it while enjoying the cherry blossoms and the springtime air."

"Maybe so, Revern'," Sister Scruggs protested from her seat in the rear, "but what's your hurry? Some of us haven't even had time to get comfortable and now you're talking about walking!"

"Sister," he called with a laugh, "this is the first time in twenty years that I've ever heard of you riding in the back of the bus and *liking* it. So just come on out of there! Oh, yes, and if you're wondering why I changed our plans, there's no mystery: It's so we can commune a bit with nature while catching up with the progress of history."

"Nature and history," Sister Scruggs said as she struggled out of her seat. "Shucks, we have enough trouble in dealing with both of those down home! So what's so different about them up here?"

Hickman laughed. "I'm not sure, but maybe it's because up here we're free to enjoy a less *intimate* view. Now quit grumbling and come on out of there!"

Walking locked arm in arm between two of the sisters, he listened silently to the bustle of comments around him with a sense of relief. For in spite of his sudden change in plans the members seemed to be enjoying themselves. And now as they approached the Washington Monument their exclamations over its height and grandeur brought a feeling of reassurance. Moving silently among them now, he gave his attention to the sweeping view of the city as it wheeled serene and majestic as far as his eyes could see. And as the members gave voice to their excitement he was reminded of Juneteenth, their favorite of all the nation's holidays. And under the mounting spell of the unfolding scene the disappointments of the morning seemed to fade, and he was surprised by the extent to which some were identifying with historical events evoked by the scene around them.

For now they strolled along telling anecdotes which ranged from their grandparents' memories of slavery, the Civil War, and Emancipation to their own adventures during the Spanish-American and First World Wars. And listening to tale after tale unfold, he could hear that unmistakable blend of truth and fiction, tragedy and comedy, which marked it as uniquely their own, as Negro; a triumphant note which sounded in most of their accounts of difficult experiences

that had been transformed in memory by the passage of time and the sheer wonder of their endurance.

The triumph is in the telling, he thought, *so no matter what they felt at the time it was happening they endured the experience and made it their own. So while our role in much that happened has been denied or distorted in print, the living connections still exist. The truth lives on, if only in the minds and hearts of the ignored and forgotten.*

Reaching a spot with a distant view of the Jefferson Memorial he was reminded that several of the members were Virginia-born when Sister Gipson
grasped Brother Matt Jefferson's arm and held up her hand for silence.

"Brother Matt," she said as the group paused to listen, "now that we've
reached this place I think it's time for you to make a public and long overdue
confession…."

"Me?" Brother Jefferson said with a frown. "Confess what?"

"Nooow you know very well," Sister Gipson said, "so don't be wasting our
time!"

"Oh, no I don't," Brother Matt said, "I've been living a clean life, I pay my
debts, taxes, and life insurance, and Deacon Wilhite there can testify that I do
my bit for the widow women and orphans—so will somebody please tell me
what this woman is talking about?"

Placing hands on hips with a backward snap of her head, Sister Gipson stared
at Brother Matt with a frown of disapproval.

"Now look, brother," she said, "don't think you're going to get out of it by
talking like that. It's nothing recent that I'm talking about, it's something from
years ago."

"*Years* ago," Brother Matt repeated. "How *many* years ago?"

"Long enough, and I think it's time for you to stand up like an honest man and
confess it! And since we all believe that public confession is good for the soul I
don't think that you can find any more public place than where we're standing."

Brother Jefferson frowned, turning to Hickman.

"Revern'," he said, "maybe *you* can tell me what this woman is signifying
about. After all, this is neither a church, police station, or courthouse; and everybody here, including you, has heard me testify no more than a few weeks ago. So
what's she going on about?"

Amused and deciding to play along with Sister Gipson, Hickman returned
Brother Jefferson's stare with a blank expression, thinking, *Whatever she's up to it's got him feeling guilty, and since he knows it's impossible to live without wrongdoing he's racking his brain, trying to give whatever it might be a name.*

"I'm sorry, Brother Jefferson," he said, "but I'm afraid you'll have to put your
question to Sister Gipson. Now, as far as *I'm* concerned you're about as innocent
as a man your age can be, but it's the sister who's bringing the charges. And since
she's a bit older than me she knows a lot more about sin and sinning—but wait,
since I'm your pastor maybe she'll let me in on it. How about it, sister; what has
this brother to confess?"

"Revern'," Sister Gipson said, "I'm going to pretend that I didn't hear what you said about my age, but I'll be more than glad to tell you."

And with flashing eyes she whirled and pointed to where the Jefferson Memorial gleamed in the distance.

"Now," she said, "it's true that from time to time our brother here has testified to many a slip, wrong, and sinful transgression. Yes, sir, and yes, ma'am, he has. As a matter of fact, this man has a Sears, Roebuck catalog of wrongdoing that's so long and so outrageous that sometimes when he's confessing I've suspected him of doing some bragging!—Don't laugh," she said, throwing up her hands. "And that's not all, because I've also noticed that he's always done it amongst *us*, and that it's always been in the family where he *knowed* he'd be understood and forgiven—even though the good Lord might not have been so sympathetic. But all the time when he was beating his breast and going over his sins at the wailing wall there was a lot of folks who wasn't present...."

Pausing with a sly expression Sister Gipson nodded suddenly to a group of white tourists who were gazing toward the Jefferson Memorial with radiant expressions of reverence.... "Like them," she said softly, "over there. So this time I want the brother to stand up like a man and confess for real, and I mean out loud!"

"Confess *what*?" Brother Jefferson said.

"Aw, man," Sister Gipson said, "quit stalling! You know what I'm talking about! I want you to confess to claiming that you and that man standing out yonder in that monument used to be kinfolks!"

And now, shouting "What!" Brother Jefferson turned to him with an expression that wavered between exasperation and relief, saying, "Good Lord, Reveren', do you see what this woman is doing? Here she is standing right in your face and has the nerve to be bearing false witness against me—and I mean *boldly!*"

"Aw, man," Sister Gipson said with a scornful wave of her hand, "why don't you stop your weaseling and confess!"

"All right," Brother Jefferson said, stepping backward and facing the others, "I will!

"Brothers and sisters, for a second there I was worried that maybe this woman had something on me which I had overlooked, but now that she's made her charges I'm *glad* to confess—and here's my right hand raised to God: The only connection between me and that man out there that *I* ever heard about is the fact that my daddy, his daddy, and his daddy's daddy's daddy was *all* born in the State of Virginia! And as far as I've ever heard or seen they were all honest hardworking men and good Christians. Therefore I'm proud to be a part of their honorable line.... And here's something else: If Mister Jefferson out there owned any of them, or had anything *else* to do with our bearing our name, it rests between him and his God! So the sister here can worry about the mixed-up past all she wants to, but as for Matthew Morgan Jefferson... who's nobody else but me... he's looking to *tomorrow!*"

"Well, praise the Lord," Sister Gipson cried in the sudden silence. "Because for once our brother has confessed to both the daylight and the darkness of his complicated condition! Yes indeed! And this time his public confession shall cleanse his mind and make him whole!"

"And *free* him, don't forget that," Hickman added with a grin. "And that goes for all of us—at least in our hearts and minds, so don't forget it. For while all human knowledge is limited, the dimensions of truth are endless, complicated, and ever unfolding. And while there's no statute of limitation on the truth of how it came about, all we know is that our brother's name is *Jefferson,* which is as honorable a name as Jackson, Jones, or even *Gipson*—that's right, sister! So no matter who originally bore the name *Jefferson*—rich man, poor man, beggarman, thief, lawyer, doctor, or Indian chief—it's still our beloved brother's name. And like any other name, including our own, it amounts to no more or less than what *he's* made it. . . ."

"Amen," sang Sister Gipson. . . .

" . . . And he's been doing that the only way he can. . . . Which is by the way he lives. So let the past bury the past. All right now, and with the sister having heard his confession, let's keep moving."

"So where do we go next?" a brother called as he started away.

"Just come along," he called over his shoulder. "I realize that it's getting late and we have other things to do, but this discussion makes me realize that now is just the time for us to take a look at something each and every American should see at least once before they die. . . ."

"And what is that, Reveren'?"

"You'll see," he said, "it isn't far. . . ."

And now he walked ahead and alone. Behind him the talk and laughter continued, sounding with a regeneration of spirit evoked by Sister Gipson's playing joking with their past condition, the dazzle of elegant vistas seen through the springtime air, and moments of history memorialized. The members were enjoying themselves far more than he had dared hope, but now, recalling his own mixed emotions and conflict of mind which had left him shaken during his first visit to where they were headed, he had an impulse to draw Wilhite aside and suggest that they find an excuse for returning to the hotel. Perhaps, he thought, it would be better to preserve this moment of good feeling and return to the Longview. . . .

But now it was there before him, rising calm and austere in the ambient light. And as he stared in wonder it seemed to slow the scene's rhythm of trees, grass, and curving walks to a melancholy legato in which the distant, mechanical murmuring of traffic that marked the mindless rush of time was muted by the voiceless eloquence of impermeable stone.

"What place is that, y'all?" he heard as the others came to join him. "Revern', is that the place you mentioned?"

"That's right," he said, "that's the place."

"But what is it?"

"You'll see," he said. "Oh, yes, you'll see!"

And now, approaching the broad sweep of steps he moved upward toward the high-columned space with an uncanny feeling of entering a mystery being cast by the great sculptural form before him. And as its spell of place descended upon him an old, restricted part of himself seemed to fall away, giving him a sense of moving from the familiar world of the given into the misty sphere of the possible. As when, during his initiation as a green young musician his imagination had taken flight and he had suddenly found himself possessed of the power to create his own heartfelt patterns of soul-felt sound while riffing the blues on his battered trombone; or again as when, during the early days of his ministry, he had begun a sermon with dry, uninspired diction and had been arrested by the disappointed look in his mother's eyes and suddenly felt the power of the Sacred Word surging so rapturously within him that his mind, tongue, and elated heart sang forth with the poetic power of his native, slave-born idiom.

And now, with footstep slowed and heartbeat pounding he was looking upward, his right foot raised as it fumbled for the ultimate step that would raise him into the full force of the sculpture's mysterious power. Then, shaking with the sudden force of his emotion, his foot found the final step and moved him upward into the cool, shaded, and sonorous calm of the edifice, and he was passing with a dream-like slowness over stony floor and fluted shadows until, now, he stood facing the great stone image which sat with legs outstretched and arms extended as it relaxed in its huge stone chair.

And now in the hush descending around him he heard as from afar the voice of a single sister calling out in a tone of awed recognition, "Revern'... Revern'..." a tentative, questioning plea echoing in his mind with the slow sweeping motion of great wings flying... "Revern'? Revern'?"

Then he, Hickman, was looking up through the calm and peaceful light toward the great brooding face above him. He, Hickman, standing motionless as he stared up into eyes that seemed to gaze from beneath their shadowed lids toward some vista of perpetual dawn that lay far beyond infinity.

And gazing upward as though listening to the groping explanations of another he thought, *Now I understand: It was that brooding facial expression which caused his enemies to accuse him of being one of us! It wasn't the darkness of his flesh, the cast of his features, or what he did on our behalf—oh, no! It was that expression and what those sorrowful eyes reveal about what it means to be a man who struggles to reconcile all of the contending forces of his country out of a belief in simple justice. It was their sad revelation of what it means to be a man of vulnerable heart and floundering mind who found clinging to an elusive ideal more desirable than all the pride and glory of great wealth and great armies. Yes, that look in those eyes and the struggles which placed it there—those are what made him one of us, and him a most confounded and confounding American. . . . Yes, he was one of us. But it wasn't in the skin tone which made him a target of those dirty dozens which his enemies used in attacking his family and background, but in that look in his eyes. That look and his struggle against those who put it there and saddened his brooding expression. It was in all of that, in his being the kind of man he made himself to be. And it was in endur-ing the ordeal of it all that he became one of us. Oh, yes, he partially failed and came to learn that he could only take one short step along the road which leads to freedom. But in earning that look and the view of life to which it gave rise he joined us in what we have been forced to learn about living. And about what it means to be truly human in the face of perversity. In that too he was like us at our best. Because one thing we've been forced to learn is that when man is set down in all the muck and confusion of life and continues to struggle for his ideals he comes as near the sublime as any human being can ever arrive. So yes, he's one of us. And not only because of his act of freeing the slaves to the extent that the times and cir-cumstances would allow, but he freed himself and a good part of this nation of that awful inheritance of pride which denies us our humanity. And by doing so he became the one man who pointed the way for all who are willing to pay the hard price of true freedom—Yes!*

And as he stared upward into the great brooding eyes he felt a strong impulse to turn and share their distant point of focus, but was held fast, the eyes regard-ing him quiet and still as though asking a question. And now he was seeking to grasp the mystery of their secret life in the stone; aware of the stone, and yet feeling the presence of something other than stoniness. And as he probed for the secret source of the emotion which held him with a gentle but all-compelling power, the stone seemed to come alive, the great chest appearing to heave as though stirred at last by the aura of acts unfinished and promises unkept which he and his flock brought into its presence, and the sculpture had extended them a silent sign in recognition because of who and what they were; had chosen to reveal its secret life for those who still sought to live and survive by its vision. And then he, Hickman, was searching the stony visage as though waiting to hear it give forth with the old familiar eloquence which he knew only in the form of mute sounds and rhythms conjured by his ear from the printed page—when a sister's voice sang out as from a distance, "Oh, my Lord! Look, y'all, it's HIM!"

And now as her voice quavered and broke in a rush of tears he was silently addressing himself, crying in upon his own spellbound ears even as the sister's anguished, "Ain't that him, Revern'? Ain't that Father Abraham?" resounded in his mind like the cry of an old slave holler called across a moonlit field.

And too full of emotion to speak, he smiled. And in silence he nodded his confirmation, thinking: *Yes, with all I know about him and his contradictions—Yes! And with all I have learned about the ways of men, this country, and the world—YES! And with all I know about white men and politicians of all colors, backgrounds and guises—Yes! And with all I know about the things you had to do to be you and remain yourself—Yes! You are one of the few who ever earned the right to be called "Father." The Georges and the Toms and the Sams couldn't bring themselves to do it, but you did. So yes, before all our reasons for holding reservations concerning you—Yes! It's all right with me—Yes, sir! And although*

I'm a man who despises all foolish pomp and circumstance, and all the bending of the knee before false values that some still try to force upon us—Yes again! And though I'm against all of the unearned tribute which the weak and lowly are forced to pay to power based on force and false differences and false values—Yes! For you "Father" is all right with me....
Yes!

And now, still gazing upward into the great quiet face, he rested his hand upon the sister's arms; hoping to affirm by touch that complex of meaning which he was too full of emotion to convey by word, thinking as now he addressed the great man of stone: *Yes, and there you sit after all this unhappy time, just looking down out of those sad old eyes. Just looking way deep out of that old ugly but beautiful, storm-struck, windswept face. Yes, she's right, it's you all right; stretching out those long old weary legs as though you've just been resting a while before pulling yourself together again to go out and try to bind up all the wounds and injuries that have festered and rankled, and stunk up this land since the day they turned you back into that hard limestone from which you came. Yes, that's right, it's you; just sitting and waiting while taking your well-earned ease. Just getting your second wind before arising up to do all over again that which has been undone throughout all the long betrayed years. Yes, it's you all right, just sitting and resting while you think out the mystery of how all of this mess could have come to be. Just puzzling out how all this could happen to a man's work after he had done all one could possibly do, and then take the consequences for giving the world his all. Yes, it's you—sometimes, I guess... sometimes...*

And now he was saying it aloud, his eyes held by the air of peace and perception born of suffering which now he felt emanating from the great stone face, replying verbally to the sister now in a voice so low and husky that it sounded like that of another:

"Sometimes... I say, sometimes the good Lord in all His perfection gets disgusted with what's happening in the world and He goes ahead and takes his own good time and He makes himself a *man!* And sometimes that man gets hold of the idea of what the Lord intends for him to do on this earth, and he gets an idea of how to go about achieving that goal, and that particular and unique man lets his idea guide him as he proceeds to grow and struggle and stumble and sorrow, until finally he comes into his own God-given shape. And no matter what he has to go up against he goes on to achieve his own lonely place in this troublesome world. It doesn't happen often—oh, no! But when it does, then even the stones will cry out in witness to his vision, and the hills and towers will echo his words and deeds, and his example will live in the hearts of men forever!

"So there sits one of the few who have walked this land. The Master doesn't make many like that, and few that he makes achieve their purpose. Which, perhaps, is just as well. Because that kind of man is such a threat to the sloppy functioning of human affairs that he becomes like a grand dimension reality—which is something for which human beings have little capacity. Nevertheless that rare kind of man loves truth and justice even more than he loves his wife, his children, or his life. And that's because he knows in his heart, and accepts the burden, of having been designated and set aside to perform those hard tasks that ordinary men are too timid and weak of purpose to tackle. But though frail and flawed, and often blind in his purpose, that kind of man will toil and struggle in the interest of what he conceives as truth and justice until the earth yawns and swallows him down. Yes, but even as he dies, as all must die, his deeds persist. So now you're looking at one whose deeds will honor this land forever.

"So look at him a while and be thankful that the Lord allowed such a man to touch our lives, even if only a little while, then let us bow our heads and pray. Oh, no, not for him, because he did the Lord's work and transformed the ground on which we stand. For in the words which my slavery-born granddaddy taught me when I was a child:

> Ole Abe Lincoln digging in the sand
> Swore he was nothing but a natural man.
> Ole Abe Lincoln was chopping on a tree
> Swore a mighty oath he'd let the slaves go
> Free—And he did!

"So let us pray, not for him, oh, no! But for ourselves and for all of those whose job it will be to wear those great big shoes which he left for this nation to fill...."

And now in the sonorous shadows beneath his widespread arms they bowed their heads and prayed.

[RETURN]

PRECEDING THE BROTHERS AND sisters in their descent from the memorial, Hickman paused on its steps to look far across the Mall to where the broad Tidal Basin mirrored the sky. The banks of the basin were accented by trees whose branches were pale pink with blossoms, and above the curve of its southernmost bank the Jefferson Memorial loomed majestic and white in the sunlight. Then turning back to the steps below he looked beyond the reflecting pool to the Washington Monument and on to the far distant dome of the Capitol. Reflected in its pool Lincoln's marble-clad memorial rippled and swayed, and the reflections of visitors arrayed on its steps were bobbing and weaving in the breeze-ruffled water like figures in a dream sequence from a historical movie. And far beyond the pool and the Mall's stretch of stone structures and trees the nation's grand Building of State glowed in a brilliance of light that reduced scrambling people and lines of traffic to hazy meshes of fluid silhouettes.

The scene was marked by an aura of grandeur, but in viewing it now through the mixed emotions evoked by the great sculpture behind him he was suddenly disheartened. And as he continued his descent of the memorial's steps there came from somewhere behind and above him the choked sobbing of a sister who gave mournful voice to his depressed state of mind.

Nor were he and the mournful sister alone, for as he observed the others descending in silence it was as though they too were measuring the harsh realities which now shaped their lives against the high hopes inspired by the man whose image sat brooding behind them in stone. And this after he had anticipated that visiting the memorial would mark the high point of their tour through the shifty hall of mirrors called "history." But after assuming that a visual contact with its ambiguities would leave them exalted and refreshed for the task still ahead, he now realized that his thoughtless enthusiasm had been a mistake. For having long regarded the memorial as the nation's troublesome commemoration of its moment of high tragedy he had failed to prepare them for its emotional impact, and thus left them exposed to moods marked by grave doubts and deep sadness.

Yes, and he himself had darkened that mood with his own uncontrolled response to the edifice. Clearly, he was responsible; for in giving voice to a conflict of feelings inspired by the man whom he considered the greatest of the nation's heroes he had dimmed their hopes and defeated his motive for leading them there.

Yes, Hickman, he thought, *you were so eager to give them bread that you've ended up giving them stones....*

In keeping with Wilhite's arrangement, the bus was waiting for their return to the Longview. And after all were seated he climbed aboard and responded to questioning glances with smiles and nods as he made his way to the rear of the bus, where Wilhite and the brothers had gathered.

The bus moved slowly, stop-and-go in the now heavy traffic, and as he sat meditating on his response to the memorial he found himself listening, at first remotely and then with attention, to Wilhite holding forth on the subject of Abraham Lincoln's mixed attitude toward slavery and the consideration which the President had shown for the defeated owners of slaves. And suddenly he recalled looking up in the shadows of the edifice to see tears in his old friend's eyes.

But now a note of contention in Wilhite's argument suggested that his old friend was struggling to throw off the memorial's spell and sounding a warning, both to himself and his listeners, against confusing the emotion aroused by the sculpture with the present-day realities that denied in millions of contentious ways the cost in blood, sacrifice, and hopes unfulfilled that accounted for its presence, there on the Washington Mall.

Pretty soon, he thought, Wilhite will be applying an antidote like the one we used in the old days when we marched from the saddest of burials playing happy tunes to rhythms that swung. So after my dampening their spirits he'll try to give them a lift with an equivalent of "Oh, Didn't He Ramble."

"Looking at it hard and cold," Wilhite was saying, "and in the light of what's happening to us these days, no matter how a man might feel in his *heart* he has got to be at least as skeptical about what happened back there as Old Uncle Ned. . . ."

". . . *Ned*?" one of the brothers said. "Are you talking about old Uncle Ned *Wilhite*?"

"You can say that," Wilhite said, "although he was better known simply as 'Uncle' or 'Ned.' Now, I don't maintain that Uncle Ned was right, and in fact I know that he wasn't. But I *do* have to sympathize with him because of what was happening back there when the South and the North were fighting. Anyway, on this particular day Uncle Ned was struggling down a muddy backcountry road pulling his old bone-dry cow along on a rope that was hardly more than a string. He was looking for some grass and doing his best to get her off that road because it was used by white folks on horses. But as luck would have it, here come some Yankee cavalry men busting out of the woods, and after looking him over one of them yells, 'Hey there, Uncle, on which side of this ruckus are you?' And with that Uncle Ned knew he was in trouble. But when his ear tells him that they're *Northern* white folks he smiles and says, 'Yas, suh, Captain, suh, but before I tell you that kin I ask *you* a question?'

" 'Why sure,' says the Yankee in charge, 'go right ahead.'

" 'Thank you, Captain, suh,' says Uncle Ned, 'but before I tell you there's one thing I'd like to know. And that's if you ever seen two dogs a-fightin' over a bone?'

" 'Why, yes,' the Northern white man said, 'many times—but I can't see what that's got to do with whose side you're on. . . .'

" 'Naw, suh, Cap'n,' said Uncle Ned, 'but that's only because I ain't finished my questioning. So now heah's the rest: When them dogs was tryin' to kill each other in order to see which one would get it, did the bone jump in there and start taking sides?'

" 'Well I be dog!' the Northern white man said. 'I never thought of it in those terms. Uncle, you've got something there. Yes, sir!' And he took his men and rode away.

" 'You doggone right, I have,' says Uncle Ned, and headed down the road pulling his bone-dry cow as fast as he was able. . . ."

And while the other brothers laughed, Wilhite looked on with a blank expression.

"Now Uncle Ned was using his thinking piece," someone said with a laugh.

"Yes," Wilhite said, "and he got out of that one scot-free. But hardly are those Yankees out of sight than he looks up and here comes a bunch of Confederates riding out of the woods at breakneck speed.

" 'Hey there, uncle!' the leader of the Confederates yells as he leans down from his horse, 'Whose cow is that you leading?'

" 'She belongs to ole Mistress, Cap'n suh,' says Uncle Ned."

" 'Oh, yeah? And whar you takin' her?'

" 'Oh, just down the road a-piece, Cap'n suh; got to find her some grass....'

" 'Don't lie to me now,' the white man said, 'are you sho she belongs to yo' white folks?'

" 'Yas, suh, Cap'n,' says Uncle Ned. 'And what's more, she's the last one we got. The soldier boys done et all the others.'

"So the Confederate cavalryman looks Uncle Ned over a while then waves him on his way. 'All right,' he says, 'if that's the case, you can go; just see to it that you take good care of your white folks' property—you hear?'

" 'Yas, suh,' says Uncle Ned, 'and you can count on it 'cause I shorely will.'

"So Uncle Ned starts off—but, brothers, before Uncle Ned can get that cow's engine revved up and moving he hears the white man calling after him, 'Whoa up there, uncle, 'cause I got me one more question to ask you....' "

"Oh, Lord," one of the brothers said, "that cracker's done caught up with Uncle Ned!"

"Please, brother," Wilhite said, "*I'm* telling this truthful lie.... 'Yas, suh, Cap'n,' says Uncle Ned, and he looks that white man dead in the eye and says, 'I'm listenin'.'

"Then the white man says, 'Uncle, whose side of this war you on?'

" 'Me, Cap'n?' says Uncle Ned, 'ain't I heah taking care of ole Mistress and lookin' out for her cow and the chillen and all?'

" 'Well now,' the Confederate says, 'but that's what you niggers is supposed to do while us menfolks fight the damn Yankees. So what Ahm asking you is: Whose *side* of the war is you on!'

"So now with all those Rebels staring him dead in the eye, Uncle Ned starts to hemming and hawing and scratching his head, pretending to think—until finally he perks up and says, 'Cap'n suh, do you mind if Ah ask you a question?'

" 'Go ahead, ask it—but be quick about it,' the Rebel white man says, ''cause we got us some mo' fightin' to do up ahead!'

" 'Cap'n, suh,' says Uncle Ned, 'd'you ever see a couple of hongery hound dogs a-fightin' over a bone?'

" ''Course Ah have,' the white man said, 'so what about it?'

" 'It ain't you, Cap'n,' said Uncle Ned, 'it's *me*. 'Cause just this morning I seen a couple of 'em fightin' over one but for the life of me I *still* can't figger just which side that damn *bone* was on.' "

Suddenly Wilhite paused and shook his head with a mournful expression.

"Come on, Deacon," a brother said. "You can't just leave Uncle Ned suspended in the air like that—what happened?"

"Now, brother," Wilhite said, "you *know* what happened: That white man cursed a blue streak and charged Uncle Ned with being a no-good, nappy-headed, ignorant nigra. And before they dragged his cow away they told Uncle

Ned, 'Nigger, this will teach you what to say the next time a white man asks you whose side you on!' "

"Poor Uncle Ned Wilhite," Brother Roscoe said with a note of mock sadness. "He'd been thinking he was neutral, but now he was caught between a rock and a hard place, and in looking both ways he was forced to realize that neither side, North *or* South, was letting him get away as easy as that."

"That's right," Wilhite said, "And Abe Lincoln wasn't there to back him. So no matter what either side really thought about him, Uncle Ned was still a bone of contention."

"Yeah," Brother Roscoe said with a frown, "and even today they're still gnawing on him—which means that we're *all* Uncle Neds!"

But now, knowing the old story and hearing another voice take up the theme, Hickman ceased listening.

Looking back through the rear window he could see traffic creeping forward bumper to bumper. Up front the sisters were quietly talking, the young white girl reading a book, and from the look of his reflection in the rearview mirror the bus driver was cursing the traffic under his breath.

So now, he thought, *the brothers are protecting themselves from the endless complexity of our situation by laughing at stones. But while Wilhite was discussing Abraham Lincoln as a creature of politics—which he truly was, thank God, and no doubt about it—I was speaking of the man who changed history by executing God's will under disheartening conditions. Wilhite would like for him to have been a perfect hero and probably thinks of Robert E. Lee as a perfect villain—ay! But since perfection is reserved for God the Father, I'll take the man who did the best he could for us and came out the winner.*

Nevertheless, seeing the memorial in the presence of old friends and companions in Christ had affected him in ways that he hadn't foreseen. And now, back in his room at the Longview, he prepared to shower before dinner still brooding and troubled in mind.

But it wasn't for myself that I led them there, he thought, *and I certainly didn't intend to preach them a sermon. But then the spirit of the place took over and I lost control. And it wasn't as when you're playing your horn and get grabbed by a riff that sends you flying— or when you're in the pulpit working a familiar text and suddenly find yourself inspired by the Spirit and giving voice to a stream of eloquence that strikes fire in the hearts of your listeners. This was something else, and there was also that strange sense of insolation about it, as though I was struggling to purge myself of any conflict of ideas and emotions I held regarding the man's story. And doing it not so much for the brothers and sisters as for my own relief. But they were on the receiving end, and the effect of my outburst is yet to be seen— unless what Wilhite was saying on the bus is an indication. If so, getting their spirits back to where they'll be willing to face up to more disappointment is going to be a strain.*

Control, Hickman! Yes, and most of all, self-control! Because without it you try to make music and end up blowing wind! You try to lead the people by preaching the Word and you end up whooping and hollering and beating your gums. And then all you do is lead them into more trouble and disappointment! What kind of church did I think I was in—out there blowing my heart out without a lick of supporting rhythm or a single heartfelt echo of "Amen" to affirm my rambling? So without it they just listened, they just cried.... Well, I was never one for preaching "Take the World, Just Give me Jesus"—oh, no! This is His, our Father's world, and in our searching we have to find Him in it and through it. So maybe I made a mistake out there, but then again I'll have to wait and see. Maybe I blew better than I thought, and if I didn't, one thing is sure: I can depend on Wilhite to tell me....

Adjusting the shower, he allowed the water to flow over the back of his hand, testing the temperature before stepping into the tub. And now with water sprinkling down upon his head he grinned, thinking, *Hickman, you've already wasted enough water to baptize a whole church full of Methodists, where for a Baptist like you it's only the beginning of a shower bath. So I guess folks like us are much more steeped in sin.*

Then, grinning at his moldy fig of a joke, he stood soaping himself beneath the swift drumming of the shower and gave himself over to the ritual of cleansing.

At first he hummed inaudibly, his mind flashing with faces and scenes from his earlier years: St. Louis Square in New Orleans in springtime, Ma Rainey and Georgia Tom Dorsey crossing a street with a royal air in Memphis; Jelly Roll Morton seated at the piano flashing a thin-lipped, diamond-toothed smile; the dim faces of audiences seen from behind the footlights of the old State Theater in Chicago; Piney Brown and George E. Lee standing on the corner of Eighteenth and Vine in Kansas City; Jimmy Rushing in his less heavy days dancing a forgotten step called Falling Off the Log with his amazing, floating, fat-man's grace... John Bubbles of Buck & Bubbles singing "Make Me a Pallet on the Floor" to the pounding of Buck's piano; and a sad, broken King Oliver leaning wearily across the green felt of a pool table racking balls for a couple of hustlers because too ill to earn a living with his once famous horn.... Then beneath the random rhythm of the water's splash his mind flowed from half-formed thoughts to the mute lyrics of a song:

> *Well I was standing*
> *On the corner*
> *When I heard my bulldog bark*
> *Stackalee and Billy were gambling—*
> *Oh, yes!—In the dark.*

And suddenly aware of what was happening he paused, staring down at the soap-bubbling washcloth in his watery hands.

Hickman, he thought, *you must be nigh exhausted to let something like that slip out of you! Oh, how the sins of a man will find him out! That's one out of those wild, thoughtless, shimmy-she-wobbling times long gone.... Still, it was a good ole swinging tune. And amusing too, even though based on a terrible incident.... A ballad? No. More a blues-ballad or ballad-blues—but in those days who needed such fancy names? It sure wasn't an anthem or a hymning tune—Hey, now, Mister Preacher! Oh, yes, I'm guilty! Even made up my own version—added all those blams and slams. What was it called? Didn't know then, but learned much later and still can't remember—something like "onomatopo" something or other. Japanese-sounding Greek word. . . . We invent it, then the college boys come along and give it a name. Anyway, had the drummer taking rim shots on his drum to a fare-thee-well—"rim shooting"? No, fool, "rim shots," like I said—though probably then not in the dictionary. But the audience knew what was going on. Rim shots, as in the sound of pistols and sudden death; the agony of dying, farewell to life and death's confusion, the bang that ends the clamoring world. . . . Yes, and the knock of conscience and the roar of John Law the Tax Collector backed by Uncle Sam, the Regulator. . . . How did I have it? Well, a-rooty-toot-toot, I heard Stackalee shoot! And the drummer going Blam-blam-blam! Blam-blam-blam! Folks doing sixty in shoe and boot (Blam-blam-blam!) They call for the Sheriff / and his Black Maria / (Blam-blam-blam!) Stackalee starts running for that Dixie-flyer! / (Blam-blam-blam!) Billy's lying dead / Bleeding from his head / (Blam-blam-blam! Blam-blam-blam!) / After pleading for his life / for his chillen and wife / (Blam-blam-blam! Blam-blam-blam!) / Billy's poor lil wife / she's sick in bed / (Blam-blam-blam! Blam-blam-blam!)—that's right, and by now the drummer's hitting rim shots and kicking his drums like he's imitating cannons and civil war. And one night out there in K.C. the customers joining in and starting to knock on the tables with everything from knives to water glasses and pitchers of illegal corn. . . . Did so much damage that the boss docked me three days' pay—Blam-blam-BLAM! . . . Where was I? Oh, yes: When Billy's little wife hears all that shooting (Blam-blam-blam!) she screams and she cries, It's got to be (Blam!) murder / (Blam-blam!) / Or suicide! (Blam-blam-blam!) / Then up rolls the Sheriff / All puffed with pride / (Blam-blam-blam! Blam-blam-blam! / Then he sees all that blood / And believe you me / He's so shook up / That he has to pee! / (Blam! Blam! Blam! A-blammity-blam-blam!) / Sheriff yells, Suicide, hell / Y'all can't fool me / This here's cold-blooded murder / In the first degree / (Blam! Blam! Blam!) / And it's gonna cost that Stack his / Liberty! (Slam-blam-slam!) / Gonna throw his butt in jail / Throw away the key / (Slam-slam-bam A-bam-bam-BAM! / Keep his black butt jailed 'til he's as white / as me! / Slama-bam / A-bam-A-BAM!) Till black as he is he's white as me-hee-hee! . . . Then the whole band yelling choruses of:*

> Oh, you better run, Stackalee!
> Run, Stackalee
> Run! Run! Run!
> Stackalee, Stackalee!
> Just listen to the running and the jumping of
> To the hopping and a-skipping and the
> Digging and the gripping of
> That BAD
> MAN
> Stack-
> Ah-LEE!

Yes, he thought, *and you let some of the brothers and sisters hear you singing that stuff and it'll be Hickman who's doing the running.... But this boy, why is he still running from us? He must realize by now that we mean him no harm, so how long does he think we're going to keep being thrown out of places trying to see him before some newspaper reporter hears about it and gets the idea that there's more to our trying to see him than meets the eye?... What a terrible thing is power! Especially when it lets you forget how other people—poor people, weak people—can react to bad treatment. To being ignored and forgotten with promises unkept, to mean acts and casual insults.... But Hickman, you're forgetting that men of power don't have to know about such matters. In place of knowing and the feeling that goes with it they have a heap of unknowing, unfeeling folks on the payroll to force an unknowing, unfeeling wall around them. That's how it works. A high wall, like those around some of the buildings in this town.... That young secretary, now, she's a wall. Yes, and her being from way down home in her attitudes—another wall. A private untouchable wall in a public place that's been set up to make any black face a fool.... Thinks it's hidden, but a wall just the... Run, Stackalee!... Lord, it's so hard to tackle... and inside herself a stubborn wall.... Better turn on the cold, get braced for action—no, not yet. Relax. Cleanliness ain't godliness, but it helps.... Ho, a wall around a wall within a wall of white-walled womanhood—that's some kind of riddle, no? Holes for eyes a cotton sack and a gal now and a maiden then and a babe awash in the water, but no bulrushes there in Georgia! So where was Moses when the lights went out? But still the sparrow watches the watching of his watchers. Oh, he's somewhere out there, somewhere behind the walls within walls though no wall willing nor withering.... No seams, no runners, just bold defiance, narrow-nosed with folded arms trying to stare us down. Looking straight at us with eyes like pistol barrels but with no hint of savvy or sympathy.... Oh, speak the truth.... Crying, Please don't take my life.... Oh, I tried, I truly tried! Talked to her all that time, riffed about him and the shadow on the wall and kept back only what I couldn't say. So maybe that's why on the Mall I spoke the unspoken tongue but still split out with a busted lip and flubbed the notes.... Spoke to her earnestly, pleadingly and all but calling "O sinner come home," but she never heard a word! Oh, watchful dove—But no, it ain't gonna be like that! He stole the hat and the money, so she probably calls him honey.... Under the clock still deaf but not dumb with dumbness, eyes in the head but they see not. Just Caldonia-headed hard. Walled up in thick walls of attitude! It's in the grain, under the bark—and that's the bite! Yes, Lord! Words within walls within walled words and no word able to breach the wall.... And now the needles—cold! Brrr! God's gonna trouble the water, Yes! But this I must still confirm:*

Seek
Find
Knock
Open
Ask
And ye shall
Receive

Though no wall withering
Without resistance. . . .
But somehow, Lord, somehow. . . .

Soon, soon! But no wall can wall out or wall in the Word. For wherever the tree liveth the kernel sprouteth and leaves come forth to tremble in the winds of life, and now trembling is truly in order. . . . Yes, but Hickman, but do you realize that you have got the Word up against a wall? How so? Oh, boxed, boxed, boxed! But I didn't do it, or did I? Hidden within boxes without topses, that's our boy! Walled within a walnut wall and yet stirring, God willing, even though no one has yet heeded our cry. . . . Now that's it . . . cold . . . cold, needling cold. . . .

[CONTRAST]

AFTER SUPPER HE SAT in the quiet of the Longview's lounge fingering a copy of *LIFE* while Wilhite returned to his room for a long-distance talk with his wife. And as he waited for news of developments back home he thought of Janey, and how their presence in Washington had begun with her letter.

Poor woman, he thought, *if she's been trying to reach me I hope Sister Wilhite was at home. Because if her angry young man is still in her area it could affect what we're trying to do here. And if she's stopped her pouting long enough to talk some sense into his mixed-up head it could save us all kinds of trouble.*

And now, gazing from the subdued light of the lounge toward the lobby's brightness, he watched the coming and going of guests and visitors. The sounds of a string quartet were floating from one of the dining rooms and the lobby humming with lilting cadences of talk and laughter. And from the many couples streaming toward the elevators in evening dress he assumed that a formal dance or reception was being held in one of the ballrooms.

Marked by high spirits and elegance, the scene was warm and cosmopolitan, but although unfolding only a few yards from where he was sitting its actors were of a lifestyle so different from his own that they seemed to be inhabitants of a far distant world. And as he watched three brown-skinned couples joining a group of formally attired whites with an exchange of warm greetings, he noted that they appeared to be as unmistakably Negro American as he did himself. And with his sense of remoteness increasing, the scene took on a mocking dimension of mystery.

Change, Hickman, he chided himself with an ironic grin. *Endless change is the name of this American game! So there's no use in your speculating as to who those colored folks are, or how they happen to be here. They're HERE, and even a home-boy like you should know that with features standing out like headlines on a newspaper they sho ain't passing!*

Sure, in the old days you could spot most of us by color, occupation, and where we found pleasure, but up here in Washington times have changed so much that if you presume that you know any more about people like them than you know about the whites around them you'd be making a big mistake—which means that after years of being barred even from Capitol restrooms—Flies in the buttermilk, shoo, fly, shoo!—*some of us are welcome and becoming almost as mysterious as white folks—yes, and just as anonymous!*

Amused by his joke, he shook his gray head. But as he studied the style, dress, and manners of the interracial group before him, he was taken with a feeling that the clue to the mystery that united and divided them, one from the other, was a matter of perception. They were both individuals and members of groups, products of the past and of changes wrought by the present—which made for mystery that challenged the observer even when there were no attempts being made to deceive him. So for the outsider it was a matter of unraveling details of background and contrast that could work either way, depending upon what he saw or didn't. Like the whiteness hidden in blackness, or blackness concealed in the whiteness. Yes, and there's our American habit of adopting the styles and manners of groups other than our own. Which is a tricky form of freedom through which some folks are able to take advantage of our tendency to ignore the products of our diversity while refusing to see how common and extensive they really are. And with a chuckle he recalled a black scam-man from Birmingham who moved to Washington and found acceptance in segregated theaters simply by faking a French accent and wearing a turban.

But now, struck by the implication of the turban-wearer's feat, it occurred to him that Janey's shadowy young man might be somewhere within range of his vision. He turned and gave the lounge a searching sweep of his eyes.

But what he saw was a scattering of elderly men, some reading and smoking while others engaged in quiet conversation. And with a sigh of relief he turned back to his view of the lobby, but with an increased awareness that he, a brown-skinned Southerner and therefore an outsider twofold, was enjoying the rare privilege of being able to observe such an affluent segment of the Capital's life while seated unnoticed in a comfortable chair.

And now his eyes were drawn to a bellman dressed in a cream-colored, gold-striped uniform who moved into view bearing a huge basket of red roses for an elderly woman who hurried beside him cuddling a tiny poodle.

Thin, tall, and red of lip, the woman wore a flared black evening gown and a tiara sparkled in her hair, and as she spoke to the bellman with regal gestures her arms glittered with bracelets. Then, noticing with a start that her fluffy hair was tinted the same pale blue as that of her poodle he smiled, thinking, *Admire me, admire my dog. . . .*

Watching the grand manner with which the woman swayed beside the bellman he judged her to be about the age of Sister Gipson, but reminded himself that her dress was far shorter than Sister Gipson or any of the sisters would have approved of.

And yet, he thought, there was a time when several of the same sisters were proud to display their legs—oh, yes!—and strut their stuff with a seductive twisting of shoulder and hip. It's hard to imagine, but they were the same type that today's young men call "African Queens," and their hips and behinds were of the same shape and plumpness.

So Hickman, he thought, *there you go: The scene and the actors change, but the old story of Eden continues. And while the sisters went on to become pillars of the church and community leaders they also passed through the flapper phase like most young women of their time. And why not? They were only expressing what came naturally in what was then the acceptable style and trying to project an image that was as attractive and as American as they could manage.*

Oh, I wish I could shimmy like my Sister Kate. . . .

But then came the bodily and spiritual changes which come to us all, and they put that world away—and so completely that today just mentioning it would be like charging them with crimes committed while they were dream-walking, and during a time long gone and forgotten. And what right have I to remind them? Me, a preacher who enjoyed the pleasures of that wild free life? The main difference is that unlike the sisters I was cursed—or blessed—with a memory that forces me to remember things which they've managed to put aside. For all of us the song is ended, but for me its melody clings to my mind. And who knows, maybe the sisters' blackout of memory is a blessing that's left them less troubled in mind and more secure in their struggle with sin. . . .

And yet, as he watched a laughing group of young people enter the lobby, he questioned the sisters' stance of unquestionable rectitude. Especially Sister Gipson's. For while they were steadfast in their belief and conduct it was possible that the virtues of charity and sympathy depend as much upon one's memory of the past as upon one's hopes for heaven. Yes, and perhaps true conscientiousness depended upon one's ability to retain in memory—and without hypocritical regrets—the complex motives that led to a change in one's worldly ways. For perhaps true charity depends upon our memory as much as upon our willingness to identify with those to whom it's extended—which seems to be such a complex involvement of the past with the present that most Americans are unwilling to risk it. Maybe that's why we spend so much time looking down on others—especially the young—who repeat in slightly different styles the mistakes we made in the past.

One thing is sure, he thought, *Sister Gipson is perfectly willing to forgive our truant for committing his outrages, but not that woman with the dog—no, sir! Without the slightest idea of who she is or what she's like morally she'd probably find her a special place in Southeast Hell and say No better for you. . . . And no doubt Madame Bluehair would do the same for Sister Gipson. If so, they'd end up in a version of hell that's truly democratic. And while standing chin-deep in liquid fire and arguing over who deserved superior rights and privileges, the lost souls of other countries will be looking on and crooning, "Don't make a move or you'll get us all drowned. . . ."*

That's an unkind thought, but as the saying goes, women ain't gentlemen. What's more, both of these are American, so even in hell they'd probably keep depending on their difference in color to tell them who in hell they really were and weren't. But before you can see the other fellow for what he thinks he is you have to have the confidence of accepting yourself for who you are inside. Differences aren't necessarily negative or signs of inferiority—not by a long shot. And since diversity and variety are said to be the spice of life, maybe we've been blessed with such an abundance that we don't know what to do with it. Here I have the questionable privilege of looking at a style of life that not only requires more money than we've ever had down home, but one that springs from a different frame of mind and a different set of values. Not that it's better or worse than ours—beyond the question of justice and money, which are important—but they're different because they started from a different point in time and in place, and that long before this government got started. Anyway, this is a country in which the past and the present are mixed like the ingredients in a stew, and even when they fail to blend they come together in people from many levels and countless places—like it or not, and even if it's only touch and go, Madame Bluehair and the bellman are united by a purpose which will end in an exchange of clichés and hard cash. Then they'll go their separate ways, but each will have made an impression on the other that's bound to surface somewhere down the line. Then they'll remember and make a judgment and act on it. And I should know, because here now, up North off to the side and unnoticed in this fancy hotel—Hickman, are you listening to all those if's you're using?—this old cat can sit down while looking at the Queen! And what's more, he can do it without a horn in his hands! Which in the broader scheme of things doesn't amount to much, and it's costing me more than I can afford, but just knowing that it has come to pass clears away a little of the confusion that's accumulated through time and change.... Abe, old friend, are you listening?

And now, with strands of music drifting from the distance, he recalled the many occasions during which he played dances in such hotels as the Longview. Times when he had been forced to enter through rear doors and ride service elevators to the ballrooms—often after arriving hungry and tired from traveling all day by bus or by car. And then the torture of passing through a riot of kitchen aromas which drifted from the fine fare available to others but denied to him in spite of his ability to pay for a meal in good, In-God-we-trust American cash. And then the irony of watching from the bandstand as his music gradually took over and inspirited the activity of those whose power assigned him a pariah's place in society; watching their gyrations, graceful or wild, as they flung themselves with varying skills about the hard polished floor.

In those days, such people as these passing now through the lobby had seemed blissfully unaware that although they ruled him out of their dancing fellowship they had also given themselves over to his power to control, if only for brief, spasmodic moments, their most intimate moods and emotions. For although isolated there in the gray, undefined, and carefully avoided no-man's-land assigned to those like himself, they had an undeniable need for his talent as a dispenser of joy. And thus gradually he had come to recognize that he was not only the master of their revelry, but a lion tamer and intermediary who presided over the powerful instinctive urges whose attractions were undeniable but socially dangerous. He had come to view himself as an ambiguous figure whose role it was through the magic of jazz to provide an atmosphere which muted the threat of those powerful urges which his employers feared as too uncouth or dangerous for forthright display. It was a situation which he had come to dislike for reducing him to a black object of white convenience and assigning him a role like that of legendary Sam the shit-house man; or Frank, the Sabbath Day fire and candle-flame lighter. And yet because of his love for his art, his delight in performing, and the satisfaction which sprang from his ability to release the hidden pleasures of the dance, he had clung to jazz as to his innermost sense of his identity. Thus more often than not he had given his employers his best out of a recognition that one part of his dual role went with the other, and that no matter how deeply their artistic roles were examined, and regardless of their color or backgrounds, all entertainers—including opera singers and virtuoso violinists, were just that—*entertainers.* Like them he was an artist who served the whims of the anonymous public. But beyond that there remained those mysterious aspects of what one did through one's art which could not be reduced to terms of money, social status, or color. And somewhere in that mystery he had found the saving grace of his art.

"Sidemen," they called us and sat us aside, and though often a leader I was still set aside—and doubly.

Yes, but how many parties had depended upon his mood, energy, or condition of lip for their success or failure? How many marriages had he made or broken simply through the effects of his playing, his art? And on a more abstract and mysterious level, how many children, wanted or unwanted, had sprung into life through the coupling of lovers enthralled by the mocking spell of his horn?

How many dancers, experiencing dreams and emotions which their protected lives had left them unprepared to contain, had plunged for the first time into a quickened sense of those realms of life's complexity that lay beyond the narrow, respectable definitions of words while swinging and swaying, smiling and playing at the youthful game called "love"? He knew of some, had come upon their names in the newspapers now and then in his present life and wanderings. Famous names, important people, even a well-known minister or two. Perhaps things had changed since he left that life behind him, but who among the thousands for whom he had played had expected that even then he had been an observer? An inside-outsider who peered beyond any wall erected to restrict his powers of judgment? That although relegated to a platform at the back of society's glamorous room where he was ever cautioned to be more heard than seen, and where you were carefully ignored by the revelers who hired you and acted as though you didn't exist, or weren't governed by the same laws, whether moral or physical—even to the extent that when under the excitement created by your music secret intimacies which were so carefully hidden from their fellows' eyes were casually, even brazenly, revealed to your ironic gaze? Who noticed that you marked the groping hands, the hot surrendering of breasts, or saw limbs explored and caressed, even sometimes drunkenly defiled? Observed the infidelities of husbands and wives, the crude initiations of finishing-school girls by clumsy college boys made bold by bootleg gin? At first, back there, it had been so amazing that you felt invisible, because it was all there for a blank-faced band boy to see; revealed, exposed, even flaunted. And only because you were safely outside their scheme of things, their code of conduct. So if you smelled the hot odor of quivering flesh taking over the cloying of expensive perfume, so what? If you observed the signs of horny old Adam lifting his head, or caught sight of a flagrant Jezebel emerging from behind the mask of girls in debutantes' gowns—again, so what? Even if you intruded by riffing a snatch of "Squeeze Me," or "Meet Me in the Bottom" on your wha-wha-muted horn either as a taunt or warning they took it as no more than the envious applause of an outsider doomed never to be let in. So again, so what? Don't you wish you were as free as me was their only response. Or: Black boy, you can gaze at these peaches but you'll never shake this tree—so dream a while, Sambo, dream a while! No, you didn't count beyond the heat of the rhythm's beat and the lilt of the blaring horns....

Yes, but being human and still learning your way, you judged. You measured them as human beings against their dark opposite numbers, and you learned that in basic terms they came out no better or worse; just even Steven, just human. So you began to learn the protective and distancing attitude of irony, and slowly, gradually, you took on a bit of the Christian virtue called "charity." And even though you had no sense of what was happening to you at the time, you learned it; and then as a more experienced music maker you learned the power of art to confound the abiding scheme of things. Because you were forced to recognize that for all their pretending that you counted for nil in the glamorous room, you were *there*—both in body and spirit—and that within the limits of the role to which you were assigned you could still sound, shake, and even shatter the profoundest patterns of their self-confident lives....

Suddenly he shook his head, thinking, *No, Hickman. No! Because there's even a sin of pride involved in identifying pride. And don't forget: You were getting paid and were glad to be there, even if only for the fine acoustics. Besides, didn't you read somewhere that even Mozart sat beneath the salt? Yes, but at least he had a share of the salt!*

[FALL]

Turning from the bustle and flow of the lobby to the quiet of the lounge, he gazed at its scattering of guests with an increasing feeling of solitude. Here groups of men were talking and drinking and others sitting alone while smoking cigars or reading newspapers. And noting a group of men arrayed around one of its tables in stylized postures he thought, *But where's the photographer?* Whereupon with a coordinated shift to the right the men revealed the figure of a waiter who bowed at the waist while serving their drinks in tall frosted glasses. And now, drawing erect, the waiter became a white-skinned Negro whose features were unmistakably Afro-American. And as he moved along placing drinks on the table his guests responded by swaying left and then right as they avoided making contact with his darting white hand.

Hickman, he thought with a grin, *times may have changed but the old rule of "serve but don't touch" still stands. So while they wait for "George" to get done and fade from the scene they're adopting the postures of men of distinction. But since "George" is both black and white—and probably a student as well as a waiter—he knows that without him they wouldn't be playing that skin game they're playing. So while they fret for their liquor and sway like puppets he sidesteps and bows as though he were born to serve them.*

Not that the joker isn't concerned with the tips it'll earn him, but in the meantime he's having fun with the contrast between their pretensions and his having skin that's as white as theirs! As Millsap would say, the real-life black-and-white comedy of this country is truly outrageous!

But now, distracted by howls of merriment, he looked across the lounge to where a group seated near a window were cracking up over something being related by a grave-looking man with a drooping mustache who appeared utterly befuddled by his companions' laughter.

Well, Hickman, he thought, *what do you make of what's happening back there? There's a bunch that's acting just like fellows in a down-home barbershop, and although that old-timer who's stirring them up is pretending he's confused by what he's saying you can bet that he's spinning a lie that's so outrageous and yet true to life that there's nothing the others can do except laugh and grin as they say "Amen!" Well, that's how the good ones do it, and if things were different I'd be back there joining in the fun. But they aren't, so while they're enjoying good fellowship and laughimg at life's endless confusion I'm forced to sit here and worry about the fate of a high-flying rascal who refuses to see or even hear one of his oldest and most faithful of friends. . . .* And suddenly reminded of his motive for being in Washington, he turned away and tried once more to conceive a plan for snaring the high-flying senator.

But now his eye was drawn to an area of the lounge in which a section of a wall bore bright splashes of color that were accented by lights concealed in the ceiling. And assuming it to be an example of abstract painting, of which he was ignorant, he was about to look further—when, suddenly, the "painting" became a tapestry, and its abstract forms details of a landscape in which a curving headland looked out to the sea and the sky toward far distant mountains. In the foreground a lonely man was plowing a field that ended at a cliff that dropped far down to an inlet on which a large ship sailed toward the sea.

And the sea's blue-greenness extended past islands and rocks to a range of high mountains that loomed, luminous and white, in the distance. And seeing the sun's misty goldness lingering between the cones of two extinct volcanoes, the scene became so mysterious that in seeking an answer his eyes flashed back to the headland and the man who was plowing.

Wearing an orange loose-sleeved blouse beneath a gray cloth cloak, brown, tight-fitting britches, and a dark, circular cap, the man was striding behind a wooden plow which was hitched to a high-rumped horse. And while neat furrows curled from his plow like slabs of beef from a butcher's sharp blade, the man stared at the earth as though he were dreaming.

Well, Hickman, he thought with a chuckle, *he might be* dressed *like a prince in a fairy tale, but that horse and plow spell farmer.* Then, beyond the plowing man's shoulder he saw a meadow in which sheep quietly grazed while a shepherd with a bedroll hung from his shoulders and a large dog sitting beside him stood gazing at the sky with his head thrown back.... And stirred by the scene's pastoral air he recalled having arrived early at an empty theater for an orchestral rehearsal and heard the sonorities of Bach's "Sheep May Safely Graze" pouring from the theater's pipe organ and his surprise at seeing the usually irreverent, derby-hatted Fats Waller fingering the keyboard while swaying in time with the music. And now with Bach's melody echoing in memory he relaxed and gazed at the scene's images of peaceful labor with similar feelings of surprise and wonder.

Divided by a low green hedge, the meadow and farmland were bordered by trees through which he looked down to a steep green valley surrounded by tall shaft-like rocks, which were white in the tranquil light. And between the rocks and the headland the ruins of an ancient fortress arose from the sea. Then, far in the distance he saw the radiant towers and domes of a city that sloped down to the curving shore of a sea-carved bay.

Minature and white against a background of distant, cloud-capped mountains, the city appeared to lie under a magical spell. And far beyond, at the point where the sea met the sky, the misty globe of the sun, hovering at its center, endowed the scene with a feeling of suspense like that which often preceded a springtime storm. Then midway [in] the sea between the ruined fortress and the bayside city he saw three shadowy ships that leaned in the wind with white sails billowing. And far across the blue-green sea to his right the shores of a cloud-like island were awash with the foam-crested waves of a rising tide....

So there you go, Hickman, he thought, *just when you were thinking that everything you saw was quiet and peaceful you're reminded that while human life is ever-changing the earth keeps to its same old patterns. Put that farmer in Georgia—Lord help him!—and he'd be wearing overalls and driving a Missouri mule hitched to a John Deere plow, but he'd still be wrestling with old Mother Earth and counting on the sun and the rain for his daily bread. Yes, and whether ships move by sail or by steam engine the sea still gives sailors the same old problems. Progress brings changes in styles and machinery, but the worldly trinity of earth-sea-and-sky are ever the same. So, while life goes on being a process of permanence in change, human endurance is—and has always been—an endless matter of dealing with life's unexpectedness. Amen! Therefore, after sending the dove and the flood, God gave us hope and a warning with His rainbow sign—first by water but by fire next time.*

And with the lyric of the old song echoing in his mind the noise of the lobby and lounge faded to a murmur, and it was as though he were looking in upon the secret life of a long-vanished world made visible.

Clearly the clothes and equipment of the men in the landscape were of a much earlier time, and while the tile-roofed buildings of the seaside city reminded him of those he'd seen in Italy, the landscape's feeling of life's endless cycling was like that which came when looking down from lonely hilltops upon the troubled landscape of his own home country. There was even that feeling of a mystery unfolding which took over whenever he drove above the clouds through the Blue Ridge Mountains. Or looked into the sky on a star-filled night, or found himself marveling at the unworldly radiance of the rising sun. Here, too, the earth and the sun, the sea, the sky, and the weather were as they had been in the beginning. . . .

So could the landscape's feeling of suspense be nothing more than the effect of an approaching storm? Did that explain why the shepherd with his bedroll tied to his back was staring so hard at the sky? Most likely, because the sheep were grazing in a pasture that looked almost as dry as the earth on which the farmer was plowing. Could it be that the farmer and shepherd were praying for rain? And now as he stared at the headland more closely he became aware of other details that increased his sense of its ambiguity:

In a clump of bushes near where the farmer was plowing a man lay either asleep or dead; and there on the side of the cliff below the meadow a large bird looked down from a tree to where a man was angling for fish in the sea. . . .

And suddenly he asked himself, *Hickman, isn't it strange that except for that solitary bird looking at the man fishing not a living creature—farmer, shepherd, dog, or sheep—appears to be looking at any* other *living thing? I'm beginning to suspect that there's more here than meets the eye. It's like Negroes and white folks riding in a down-home streetcar from which they've just seen something terrible take place, but right away everybody's staring straight ahead because they all know the source of the conflict out of which it erupted so they're pretending that it hasn't really happened. . . .*

Then, recalling his shock at discovering a picture of Christ abandoned in a basement window he tensed, suddenly suspicious that what he had taken for a peaceful landscape might conceal similar details of shocking distaste. But despite his mounting feeling of unease the questions being raised by the scene before him demanded an answer.

For although composed of nothing more than colored threads and cloth, the details of the tapestry were amazingly like those of a painting, and the more closely he examined its composition the more the landscape seemed to pulse with some hidden meaning.

Whoever went about weaving this thing was truly some kind of artist, he thought, *but what was he up to, and what am I missing?*

Then, on a rock near where the farmer plowed he saw what appeared to be a knapsack and a clarinet—or was the "clarinet" actually a dagger? Which, considering the wooden blade of the plow and the fairy-tale clothing of the farmer, the shepherd, and fisherman, was far more likely.... Then among the many white grazing sheep he saw two that were black, and noted that behind the backs of the sky-gazing shepherd and daydreaming dog a single white sheep had strayed far too close to the cliff's edge for safety—a sight at which he stiffened and grasped the arms of his chair.

Only moments before, the landscape had come as welcomed relief from his mission's failure, but now the unfaithfulness implied by the shepherd's inattention aroused an uncanny feeling that the scene was edging him inward and toward matters that were painfully personal. And in the process of backing mentally away he found himself recalling a forgotten game once played among jazz fans on those who disrupted concerts by arriving during moments when an inspired jazzman was up and soaring. For then they were challenged to identify the original melody on which the soloist was riffing, and if they made a mistake in answering their punishment was gales of contemptuous laughter.

It was strange that such an ancient landscape should make him recall such a game, but despite their differences of time and of place the weaver of the tapestry appeared to be testing his ability to discover some message or story which was woven into the landscape. If so, just as tardy jazz fans were challenged to mentally "hear" the original melody which inspired the jazzman's soaring, he was now being invited to "see" and trace some hidden thread of a story which had been woven in threads.

In other words, he thought, by "signifying" with his needle and thread this man is *needling* me to get the point of the puzzle he's woven!

And now as he searched for the needling thread of meaning he grinned at his pun, but the hidden connection continued to escape him. And yet, the longer he stared the more certain he became that once he located the elusive clue it would lead to a parable or story—much as the original chords and melodic line that sounded unheard in a swinging jazzman's mind could move his listeners to a conclusion that was both inevitable and pleasing.

For being artists, the goal of both jazz musician and weaver was one of using their skills to arouse pleasure and wonder. And both did so by drawing upon that which was left carefully understated or concealed as a means for achieving a transcendent goal.

Brothers and sisters, he thought in ironic self-mockery of his role as minister, let us raise ourselves above the sheer sound and fury of that which is so faintly heard and so dimly seen so that we may COMMUNE, one with the other!

It was amusing, but whether by accident or design, he had stumbled upon a scene that challenged, so perhaps the key to the landscape's mystery lay in his accepting it as a game with unwritten rules and himself as a willing but uninformed player.

Whereupon he recalled that during his early jazz days he had learned that the success of a performance depended upon his enticing his listeners into participating in his act of combining familiar sounds and rhythms into patterns made rare and exciting. For it had been such mutual give-and-take that earned him their most enthusiastic response. A feat that was accomplished by blasting his listeners with freewheeling quotations from any musical forms with which he and they were familiar, whether it be ballads or blues, love songs, anthems, or spirituals. The trick was to move them with tonal and rhythmical excitement from the known to the unknown, and from the old and familiar into that which was new and still unfamiliar.

Indeed, the same technique prevailed when he preached before unlettered congregations. Establishing the mood with the Word as written, he quickly put the Bible aside and ranged orally through the familiar troubles and joys of the human condition while being careful to avoid learned abstractions while using rhythmical phrases to evoke images charged with emotions which they knew and to which they eagerly responded. After all, such a strategy for revealing the new in the old was traditional, and part of the art of persuasion. Thus he and the congregations became as one in the Word's graceful power. Which often depended upon his creating illusions, and which were indispensable aspects of all types of art, whether it be profane or sacred. It was a way of reaching the hearts and minds of his audience, and during his jazz days, when standing before crowds sweating and swaying as though possessed by spirits, he became a trombone-wielding agent through whom his listeners found musical transcendence. And if successful he was repaid with screams, applause, and dancing in the aisles, or bumper-to-bumper belly-bumping all over the floors of ballrooms.

But while on fortunate occasions such responses were truly inspired, on others he had simply gone through the motions of being possessed while relying on his acting skills to create a musical illusion. Nevertheless, such pretense went with being a jazzman and served as a lifesaver when true inspiration was lacking. To some extent all entertainers were actors, and that was true even of dedicated preachers, of whom spiritual eloquence and humility were not only expected but demanded. And wasn't it out of similar expectations that the storyteller near the window was pretending to be dumb to the meaning of the tale he was telling? That was his storyteller's way of flattering his listeners' intelligence while persuading them to a willing participation in his spinning of tales. Like a preacher, he mimed and "called" and his listeners responded. But in a deeper sense there was more to it than that. For while he hadn't thought of it until now, playing dumb was also a self-sacrificial act through which good storytellers prepared their audiences to receive and enjoy such hard-earned wisdom as might underlie the surface of his tale's comedy. And by pretending to be too stupid to recognize its underlying message, the storyteller assumed the burden of its underlying pain and embarrassment. Thus his listeners were freed to enjoy the comedy which such tales made of life's complexity. . . .

So, Hickman, he thought with a sense of discovery and relief, *perhaps by playing a wordless game of hide-and-seek the weaver meant to encourage the same type of participation. If so, I wish that his game were musical! Because then I could rely on my experienced ear and fairly good memory. As it is I'm eager and willing, but he seems to be playing a game on my ignorant old eyes—which puts me at a disadvantage, because beyond such things as biblical scenes, comic cartoons, billboards, and ads I'm ignorant of his kind of art. But now that I'm hooked I have to keep looking. Besides, if this tapestry is actually telling a story, I'm forced to find it or lose my self-respect as a wordman. Anyway, like jokes, jazz riffs, yarns, and sermons, stories have to move from a beginning through a middle to an end. The problem here is that while the figures and atmosphere suggest a movement toward some moment of revelation it's due to a soundless juxtaposition of forms and color. The farmer, shepherd, and fisherman are in the process of moving* without *movement—how about that! But perhaps by staring at the earth, the sky, and the sea they're still doing something that's suppose to move the story toward its invisible climax. My question is what does it mean, and how will I find it?*

As he frowned and stared, the answer continued to escape him; but now, as with the surprising patterns of melodic invention that enabled a swinging musician to keep his listeners' attention, new details were emerging out of the landscape's illusion of peaceful movement to tease his eye and his memory.

For, suddenly, the blue-green expanse of the sea was overlaid by airy images of glass insulators used on telephone poles during his boyhood. Such domed, translucent shapes had often served as targets for his slingshot, and though strictly forbidden by both the law and his father, he had found them so irresistible that years later, when coming upon young Bliss trying his hand at the game, he couldn't help but grin at his own hypocrisy while putting a belt to the little boy's bottom.

And now, with the airy image of the long-lost boy firing rocks at glinting insulators overlaying the landscape, new details of the scene brought a sudden sense of imminent discovery:

Below the cliff from which the man quietly fished the tall ship still steered for the sea through the inlet, but now for the first time he saw the miniature forms of sailors clinging high in its riggings as they reefed a wind-tossed sail. And now, looking midway through the watery distance between the stern of the ship and the base of the headland, he froze. For there, surrounded by a sun-reflecting splash, he saw the lonely legs and grasping hand of someone who appeared to have plunged headfirst out of nowhere and into the wind-ruffled sea. . . .

Suddenly spurred by his vague sense of a connection between the sprawling legs and the danger that had prompted his flight to Washington, he leaped from his chair and hurried forward, annoyed that it had taken him so long to notice such a shocking detail. And now, reaching the wall with a mounting sense of panic, he centered his attention on the sky-pointing legs and explored the landscape from highland to horizon and border to border—and paused with increasing confusion.

For now he saw that the tapestry's deep red border was embroidered with scientific symbols, steamships, automobiles, airplanes, submarines, space rockets, and miniature portraits of famous inventors and scientists, among whom he recognized Henry Ford, Albert Einstein, and Thomas Edison.

Hickman, he thought, *you were right about a story or parable being hidden in this thing! But now that you've found the clue you're either too dumb or uneducated to get its meaning—you, who have the outrageous nerve to interpret the Book of Revelation! But either way, from the size of the feet and shape of the legs it's plain that it's a man—so from where did he fall? It couldn't have been from the cliff, because he's too far offshore . . . and the fellow on the cliff is so busy fishing that he isn't even looking in his direction. And it couldn't have been from that ship because those sailors are acting as though he doesn't exist. Besides, if he'd fallen from there he'd have yelled for help. . . . So from where did he fall, and how long in his falling? It couldn't have been from an airplane, because in spite of all of those modern inventions woven around the border everything I see in the landscape indicates that he fell long before planes were invented. So could it be that he's supposed to have swum that far from shore to commit suicide? After all, the old folks did tell us stories about Africans who took their children and walked into the sea until they drowned. But they had a reason: because rather than live in slavery they chose to die. But this fellow's legs are white and he's far from any shore. . . .*

"A.Z.," he heard with a start, "what are you staring at?"

"Wilhite," he said, pointing a finger at the landscape, "what do you make of that?"

"Of *what?*"

"Those legs, man; those *legs!*"

"Well, I declare," Wilhite said. "What happened to him?"

"That's what *I'd* like to know. It's plain that he's going under, but from where did he fall?"

"You're the one who's been looking, so you tell *me.*"

"That's the point, I've been looking at this thing for at least twenty minutes and enjoying the view, but then, just before you got back, I see these legs! What gets me is that they were there all the time! Now it looks like I was enjoying myself while somebody decided to commit suicide by drowning. . . ."

"Suicide?" Wilhite said as he bent closer and stared at the legs.

"What else?"

"I don't know, A.Z., but I think that you're fishing in the wrong part of the creek."

"Why?"

"Because from the position of his legs there's no way in the *world* for him to be committing suicide by drowning. No, sir! Because it's simply impossible for a man to lift himself high enough out of the water to take such a plunge. Look at that splash!"

"So what do you think?"

"I don't know, but maybe we're looking at a religious allegory in which the plunge is supposed to be the one made by Satan after he got himself kicked out of the Kingdom...."

"Maybe so, but if that's what those legs are supposed to signify I'm put in the position of the fellow in that story you tell about the man who was being chased by a dog and had someone advise him to give himself up because the animal was a *police* dog: With him I'm saying, 'If he's with the police let him show me his badge, otherwise I'm gonna keep running!'"

"Oh, yeah? Well if you keep looking you'll discover that his badge has some pretty sharp points. But in the meantime, what about those legs?"

"I don't know, but if the fellow taking the plunge is supposed to be Satan, I want to see his hooves and tail! Which is only reasonable, because with that much of his body under water Satan's tail should be sticking up there between his legs—which it isn't. What's more, this fellow hit the water much too quietly and low-keyed to attract attention. That's probably why we can't see a single soul who's looking in his direction. Not the farmer, who's looking at his plowed ground, not the fisher or that unfaithful shepherd, nor anyone else—at least not as far as *I* can see. While we both know very well that if it was Satan he'd have been screaming loud enough to wake up all hell and Harlem!"

"Amen, A.Z., but don't go putting down Harlem. I've lived there and like most big cities you have to keep awake to stay alive. Besides, the serious questions remain: Who is he, and from where did he begin such a sad lonely fall?"

"If I knew that," Hickman said as he turned and started away, "I'd have the answer."

"You know, Wilhite," he said as they moved away, "I began looking at that thing while killing time waiting for you, but now I'm sorry that it ever caught my eye! That's right, because now that it has I'm liable to wake up in the middle of the night still worrying about who that man was and how he could have reached so high to fall so low.... This town, Lord, it looks like everywhere I turn there's something waiting to give me a fit! And I mean even in little things unrelated to what brought us here. It just goes to show that no matter where a man finds himself it's the things that aren't spelled out that give him the most trouble! Yes, and since any collection of things thrown together can signify far more than any one of them by itself, you have to keep watching out for the patterns they make when they come together. If the man's head was showing you could be satisfied in calling him Jonah—but then, Wilhite, where in all that sea is the vomiting whale?"

"A.Z.," Wilhite said, "you sound tired."

"I know it, but I still have my sense of humor. How are things going back home?"

"Nothing new, except for old Sister Caroline calling four or five time asking you to be sure and look up her brother."

"Good! Because after promising to look him up I'd forgotten all about it. How's she feeling?"

"She's holding on, but being as sick as she is she's anxious to see that brother of hers."

"So we'd better try and find him and get him on down there—even if we have to dig up his fare. Sister Caroline's a fine woman. Any word from Janey?"

"Not a word."

"Well," he said with a quick glance at the tapestry. "I guess that after setting up this wild goose chase she's sitting back

[HISTORY]

AND WAITING TO SEE what will happen. Wilhite, tell me the truth: Do you think we ought to give up on this mission?"

"After we've come this far! A.Z., what are you driving at?"

"I'm asking if you think we should give it up and return home."

"Are you serious?"

"That's right, I'm serious."

"Then you must *really* be tired! Anyway, now that he's alerted we have to keep hunting, and since we've missed him in the open why not keep stalking his secret hole—which makes sense to me. So instead of sitting here talking, why not give his woman's place another try?"

"Wilhite, this isn't some animal we're trying to corner, but a *man*. Which means that our trying to reach him through his lady friend was unethical, and since we failed I'm against trying that again. Besides, going there a second time could be dangerous. Maybe we should try once more to catch him at his office, and if we fail let's try something else."

"Very well, A.Z., but whether it's ethical or not, we'd better find a way of reaching him before it's too late."

"I know, and we'll do whatever we can, but rather than barging in on his mistress again let's try to reach him through somebody else."

"Okay, but who would that be?"

"Frankly, I don't know, but it might be the police...."

"The *police*! A.Z., I knew you were tired, but now it seems that you're losing faith. How could we go to them without revealing everything we don't want them to know?"

"That's the rub, my friend; that's the skin-scraping rub!"

"And you can say that again. The police would simply laugh at us, and we don't even know how to describe this young fellow of Janey's. So we're in the dark, and as usual with dark men caught in the dark we've got to find and follow our own path."

"Yes, but how? We've tried to see the man, we've been to his office and left telephone messages, but so far nothing has happened. I'm surprised that the members haven't gotten sick of wasting their time."

"Well, they haven't, because they remember that the man's life depends on our keeping after him."

"And is that how you feel?"

"Look, A.Z., I don't know what's gotten into you, but let's be frank about this thing. *I* know that you have a greater need to see this man than any of the rest of us. I understand that and so do most of the others, and we all respect your feeling. The truth is that yours is the really pressing need. Besides, you're the one who's setting the direction, so don't start talking about our giving up. Not at this early stage of the game!"

"I'm not, but I'm trying to consider the rest of you. Have the members been discussing any of this?"

"No—or at least not directly. But it could be in their minds."

"Yes, I know. And it would have to be, considering what's happened or *hasn't* happened. Still, if they've begun talking it could make a difference."

"Not necessarily. Because being faithful to you they're faithful to your idea and leadership. You loved that little boy, everybody knows that from way back. But so did the rest of us who knew him, and most of us still do. Anyway, it's been so long ago that it's gotten mixed up with other attitudes that are too complicated for me to describe. Anger for some, and for others it's their disbelief that anyone they knew could turn out to be what he's become. But I think that most of them won't *really* know what they feel until they see him face-to-face. However—and this is a big 'however'—if you'd given even a hint that you were losing interest in the mystery of this thing they would have been relieved to put it out of their minds. You didn't, so you kept the boy alive in their minds if not in all of their hearts."

Wilhite paused, looking into his eyes.

"A.Z.," Wilhite continued, "I hope you won't mind my saying what I'm about to say...."

Hickman smiled. "Of course not, old buddy. Coming from you the truth might hurt, but it won't kill me. I've suspected what you say about the members' attitudes for a long time. But now, what about you personally?"

"Now, don't tell me that you think that *I* might be faltering!"

"No, but I'd like to be able to judge the possible strain being put on our friendship."

"But why would you think of such a thing?"

"Because I realize that I've been asking you and the rest to go along with my personal craziness for a long time now.... Yes, and because this afternoon, after letting my emotions take over out there at the memorial... you might have felt... well, that I was losing my grip on reality...."

"... Do you mean because of what I was saying on the bus?"

He nodded.

"So that's it! But A.Z., I wasn't arguing against *you*, I was arguing with myself! I was trying to make some sense between what you made us feel about Abe Lincoln and the conditions we're living with today. Man, that's what was happening! Out there you had us under the spell of your vision, just as you did when we flew up here. We were being carried along by your faith and the power of your need to learn what had happened to that little boy. And we did it *willingly!* You didn't force a single soul. No, A.Z., that wasn't criticism, it was just a matter of my trying to straighten things out in my own mind...."

"Now, don't go making it light on me," Hickman said, "because I know I have cause to feel guilty. But I wasn't faulting you for what you were saying on the bus. How could I, when I know only too well that when it comes to Abe Lincoln there's a lot to be discussed on either side. And you must know that in spite of what I felt moved to say out there. There's still too much conflict between what I feel in my heart and what I think about the outcome of even the most well-intended human enterprise for me to lose sight of the other side. I mean the bad in the good, and the good in the bad that often gets coated with whiteness—at least when it's written as history."

"If you ask me," Wilhite said with a grimace as he sat back and crossed his legs, "that kind of history is a living mess. And thank God that we don't have to live in it, because just living is bad enough. It's a wonder we aren't all raving maniacs!"

"Easy, Deacon; easy! Because we're half in and half out of it. That's why it can feel as though we're walking around in somebody else's nightmare—and we both know whose! Seriously, though, history happens and men have a hand in it, or at least some of them do. Especially those who have the power to push other people around. The good thing is that they don't have as much control as they'd like to think. They draw a circle and say, 'Everything outside this line has no meaning and doesn't count.' But what's pushed outside can be anything from a springtime flood to a plague of boll weevils to a cotton-picking machine, or a bunch of Japanese flying plywood airplanes. That's why I feel guilty when dragging religion into the quicksand called 'history'—even though the big churches have been in it up to their steeples for centuries. Which means almost from the time they took Christ down from the cross. Still, it's all focused in mankind, and it's what our brooding hearts and minds try to make of what has happened irreversibly that moves me beyond all my powers to resist it. All the ifs and ands and the might-have-beens. Things that are sometimes more complex and contradictory than anything that's put down in the history books...."

"... I'm with you there, A.Z...."

"... I don't know, Wilhite, but maybe it's the fact that things in this world can get out of control so easily—Like when a war breaks out, or someone gets assassinated. Or when nature kicks up, like that flood back in '27, or that Dust Bowl drought. Things like that can cause a confusion that can take over people's hearts and minds. Maybe that's what makes the idea of history so appealing. Folks have such a need to rationalize what happens to them that they're willing to listen even if to somebody who claims he can cram life's complexity into a man-made jug with a fountain pen."

"Yes, but don't leave out the politicians! They do the things that satisfy their own interests and then they whitewash it and pay folks to tell the rest of us the meaning of what they've done and see to it that the unfavorable parts aren't included."

"That's true, but it doesn't even have to be intentional. After all, everybody likes to look his best, so it can depend upon who's involved and who sets out to tell the tale."

"Well, it might not be *intentional*, but when you have to stand outside and watch what they put down it sure can be confusing. And especially when you think *you* know what the truth really is."

"The truth, the whole truth, and nothing *but* the truth," he intoned with a grin. "But that takes in so much territory that a man has to lie even if he wants to be honest. Maybe that's what they mean by a 'legal fiction.' Nevertheless, there's always going to be folks who'll swear that they have truth by the tail. Actually, it's not white or black but a man-made game, so I guess we're complaining because we're ruled out of most of it by the rules they set up for themselves. But even for themselves there's room for choice, for selection. At least as far as the truth is concerned. And that's where the individual—whether he be judge, historian, or politician—steps in and pretends that he's the voice of God, which is their nickname for history. Then he sets out to re-create the world by word of mouth, and all that doesn't fit into the tale he wants to tell he leaves out. And that makes room for a whole world of complications that go unnoticed. So let's forget about Abe Lincoln and take a trip out of the jug of history and into the outskirts of town where there are plenty of gullies...."

"Okay, A.Z., but only if I can sit here in this comfortable chair while we're doing it."

"Oh, come on Wilhite, don't you know that up here in D.C. what were once the historical outskirts of town have become the *in*-skirts? Sure you do! Just like you know that things that used to happen only on the *outskirts* of town are now taking place in the so-called 'inner cities.' "

"All right, but what does that have to do with history?"

"I was just getting to that, because I'd like to know if you've ever heard of a Saturday night shooting-scrape being termed historical?"

"Which one?"

"Any one you can think of. Can you name me a single one—no matter how much blood was spilled—that went down in history?"

"Nope."

"And neither can I. But we've both heard about a few that folks still talk and sing about. For instance, when I was taking my shower I found myself humming words such as these: 'Stackalee, said Billy / Please don't take my life. / I got three little hungry black / Blue-gummed chillen / And a *very* sickly wife!'—now don't laugh—which was not only a plea worthy of going down in the history books, but enough to strike pity from a man with a heart of stone...."

"That's right," Wilhite laughed, "providing that he knew about those blue-gummed children! Those little rascals were so hungry that they ate up the cow and the calf and the railing fence, and if Stackalee hadn't shot their daddy they probably would have eaten him too!"

"Yes, and they might as well, because in spite of all their daddy's pleading Stack blew him away. Therefore if there hadn't been somebody on the scene to make up a song about what happened both Billy and Stack would have been long forgotten. And that holds true no matter how many others were on hand to hear that bulldog bark and the shooting start."

"Right, A.Z., but all you're doing is citing *outskirts* history. Which means that you're violating your own rules."

"I know, and I realize that I'm stretching my point a bit. But as I see it Billy and Stack were simply human beings, and therefore what happened to them should count down here on earth just as it does upstairs with the Lord. But since they weren't important and the argument that caused one to kill and the other to die didn't involve important people—unless it was the Sheriff—nobody considered what happened to them historical. So now let *us* praise two famous men. And as the boys in the pool hall used to say, 'Rack 'em back, Mister Gamekeeper, and set 'em up for one more round!' "

"A.Z.," Wilhite said with a frown, "before you became converted you must have been on your way to becoming a truly *great* sinner! So level with me now, were you there?"

"Who, me? No, sir! It was long before my time. I'm simply going by the account given in the song—which holds that the killing had to do with money—brand-*new* money, you hear me? Brand-new money and a Stetson hat. And it says that it came about because Billy was cheating at cards. Which raises the point I was making about history: Who knows exactly *what* led to the shooting? It could have been that Stack himself was cheating, or he could have used the situation to prove to himself that he had the nerve to kill another man—any man—and get away with it. Or maybe he was just anxious to try out his pistol. There were many possible motives, so who knows exactly what was on his mind when he pulled that trigger. All we really *know* is that there was a bang and a burst of smoke, then one man was dead and the other took off running. So while the who-shot-John of it might not be a question of history it surely involves a mystery...."

"You make a pretty frail case," Wilhite said, "but I wish you'd picked a better example. After all, those two were nothing but a couple of rounders...."

"... But they were also human beings...."

Suddenly Hickman sat up and leaned forward, resting his elbow on his knee. "Now, let's take a look at this thing in terms of the three men involved in terms of their possibility of becoming historical figures. Besides Stackalee and Billy there was also the Sheriff, remember? So by all means remember the Sheriff!"

"O.K., but Stack and Billy were the most important."

"True, but keep your eye on the Sheriff. So it all began with Stack and Billy gambling...."

"... Right..."

"Then Stack gets mad and shoots Billy...."

"... Right!..."

"... and Billy dies."

"So?"

"So then Stack grabs his hat and the money and takes off. Then, after a lot of mealymouthed talk about Negroes having no respect for law and order, the Sheriff tracks Stack down and throws him in jail...."

"... Probably after pistol-whipping him so bad that his legs roped like okra."

"That the song doesn't say, but we'll let it lay. So the Sheriff throws Stack in jail, takes his pistol, his bankroll, and the money that Stack had taken off Billy. But most important of all, he takes that Stetson hat which was supposed to have a magic in it which had gotten Stack out of all kinds of trouble. Such as run-ins with angry husbands, evil fancy women, knife-wielding gamblers, *and* the law. Now the song leaves it just about there, Stack's in jail and can't be freed on bail, but *we're* going to follow the action into the realm of what's called 'history.'"

"But it didn't make it that far, at least not the way I've heard it. So if you take it any farther you'll be blunting your point—whatever it is."

"Oh, no! Because now we want to take a look at that Sheriff. The Sheriff doesn't have much of a role in the song, but that's the way with history, and it didn't keep him from going on to rise into history on the magical power of Stackalee's Stetson hat!"

With a groan Wilhite got to his feet. "A.Z., I'm glad we've been sitting here by ourselves, because all of a sudden you've started to lying as though this fancy hotel lobby was a barbershop. I call that taking advantage of my good nature and abusing my sense of propriety!"

"Sit down, man," Hickman laughed, "because what I'm doing is in the interest of a larger truth."

"All right, I will, but you'd better convince me—and I mean in a hurry! Otherwise I'm reporting you to Sister Gipson, and you know how she feels about lying. So what's this about that sheriff and history?"

"Well, my friend, it went like this: The fact that he arrested a Negro as bad and tricky as Stackalee made the Sheriff a very famous man—even though it wasn't known that he'd stolen Stack's magic hat. Up to that point he's been strictly local, a redneck bully with a cheap reputation for being tough on black folks. But now he's known all over the state. Everywhere he goes white folks are greeting him, shaking his hand, and even slipping him jugs of illegal moonshine whiskey. So he ups and gets ambitious. And when the next election comes around he announces and runs for mayor—and wins!"

"Who told you that?"

"Never mind, it's the truth. He has no experience, he can barely write his own name—but he wins. He's dived headfirst into the murky waters of politics, and so now he's swimming strong with an overhand stroke. He was already in cahoots with the bootleggers and the madams, but now he's getting an even bigger share of the kickbacks from lawbreaking and has himself a swinging town in which he's admired by everyone except folks like us. His motto is 'Let the Good Times Roll!' So after two terms as mayor he takes off and runs for governor and gets elected—all on a reputation gained by arresting Stackalee and taking his magical Stetson hat!"

"A.Z., I'm going to pray for you, because anyone who'll tell a lie like this is truly in need of prayer!"

"So now the Sheriff is living in the Governor's mansion with two dozen convicts waiting on him hand and foot. What's more, he has two black convicts whose special duty is to hold up his head while he does his business in the bathroom. Now it's also true that by now even white folks are becoming a little leery about his conduct. Because they soon realize that if he hadn't been much of a mayor he's doing even worse as governor. But they're trying to overlook it because they're impressed and fascinated by the fact that such a no-good rascal could rise so high. After all, he's making the American dream come true. So now they're making bets and watching to see just how high he can rise by parlaying his reputation into further realms of power and glory."

"If it wasn't a lie," Wilhite laughed, "I'd have to cry. But if it wasn't the truth I couldn't laugh! Keep preaching!"

"Listen: So with all his success his ambition grows and he gains such confidence that when the next election rolls around he runs for the United States *Senate*! That's right! And since most of the white folks are backing him, he wins in a landslide what amounts to a job for life. And once in the Senate he keeps on winning, and winning, and winning! So today, right here in Washington, he's an elder statesman, the respected head of four or five important committees, and a sneaky millionaire. He drinks his whiskey with rich men, world leaders, and the President. And twice a year he goes to Paris, France, on government expense to check out its better bars, restaurants, and whorehouses—things that keep him so busy that today he drops down to his old stamping ground only once a year—which is at hog-killing time. That's because he also happens to be a dedicated chitt'lin' eater. He's a powerful and influential man, and all because two Negroes got into a Saturday night gambling game! And that, old friend, is how he made it into the history books!"

Pretending to collapse in his chair, Wilhite shook with laughter. "I know you're lying, but the way you tell it it could actually have happened."

"Not only *could*, but it probably *did*. And that's my point. We simply don't know whether it did or didn't, because you can be sure that when the Sheriff reached Washington he turned the damper down on the part Stackalee played in his rise to fame and power and only stressed his roles as mayor and governor. He doesn't say a word about the fact that he made his early reputation by kicking the 'nigras' around, or that he was once looked down upon by the aristocrats who ran the town. Oh, no! And now he swears that he was educated at Georgia Tech, read law under a man who studied with Jeff Davis and Huey Long, and claims that his good luck came from his being seventh son of a seventh son...."

"...What a country!"

"...While the plain, unhistorical truth lies in the fact that after all this time he's still conjuring around with that black magic which Stack had hidden in his Stetson hat!"

"Done stole the black man's power! Which raises the question as to why the respectable folks let him get away with it."

"Because, man, they're benefiting from his exploiting that magic! They're living off the prestige he's built up, and taking advantage of all those big grants and government contracts which he's able to bring into the state because of his position—and don't forget his seniority in the Senate. Sure, the other senators know who he is, but they aren't *about* to discuss it with outsiders. And as far as I can tell there's only two things that can possibly keep him from running for president."

"Like what?"

"The first is his age, and the second is Billy's blue-gummed children's blue-gummed children. Because while Stack didn't leave any offspring those little grandbabies of Billy and his sickly wife have their eyes on the Senator-Sheriff, and they intend to get Stack's Stetson back!"

Removing a handkerchief, Wilhite wiped his eyes. "A.Z.," he said, "if our reason for coming up here wasn't so serious I'd say that it was worth it, if for no other reason than the way these surroundings have set you to lying! How on earth did you get going about that Sheriff?"

"Just by trying to get at the mystery in history," Hickman said with a smile. "Just trying to look into what might have happened between the act and the shadow of the act."

"Yes, but you were talking about Abe Lincoln."

"That's true, I was; but it wasn't important. Let's get to work on the problem at hand."

"No, please. I'd like to hear what you started out to say."

Wilhite was earnest, leaning toward him with a slight frown.

"What I was leading up to was that in spite of all the interpretations for and against his policies, nobody really knows what went on in Abraham Lincoln's mind—at least that's how I see it. And that's where mystery laughs at history."

Stretching his legs, he gazed at the tapestry and crossed his ankles. "Maybe he doubted that freedom would work even if there was no problem of black and white to further complicate the situation. And maybe he preferred not to think too hard about it at a time he was trying to win the war. Or it could be that like Jonah he was trying to ignore God's command and the mess to be settled by history. But there *we* were, and so snarled up with everything both North *and* South that pretty soon he became so desperate that he threw us in to help do some of the killing. On the other hand, he might have realized if white folks went on killing one another in wholesale lots it might become a habit, and therefore it would be a good idea to have us on hand to remind the survivors of what all the bloodshed had been about. And if not that, then perhaps he decided that it would be a good idea to have us on hand to take the blame in the years to come. I think he was a great man, one of the greatest. But I can't forget that he was a *man,* and I'm trying to think of him as a man faced with difficult choices. A man with problems—and he did have problems! He was doing the best he could, so maybe he concluded that with white folks being unable to live together in peace, getting the black and the white to do so was just too big a problem for any one mortal man to solve. Maybe that's why he tried to cut things down to size by simply concentrating on keeping this fire-and-water, alcohol-and-gasoline, freedom-loving, nigger-hating Union together. And the fact that he did it was a miracle! A *bloody* miracle, but a miracle just the same.

"So who can blame him for not solving all of the problems? He kept the nation together—which was not only his dream and his hope, but a responsibility that went with the job he'd sworn to perform. How things went after the Union was secured was yet another mountain to be climbed, another stony row to be hoed. Some say that he couldn't bring himself to see a place for us here as a free people. Others say that he didn't even care, one way or another. . . ."

". . . Yes," Wilhite said, "I've read it and heard it said. . . ."

". . . And I've even heard one of our own kind make a joke about the statement Lincoln was reported to have made in New Orleans when he said that if he ever had a chance to hit slavery he'd hit it hard. . . ."

"And what was that?"

"That he wasn't referring to slavery exactly, but to a good-looking female slave who happened to be standing on a levee bound in chains."

"Oh, Lord," Wilhite said, "you mean that one of us would joke about something like that?"

"Wilhite, our people will joke about *anything,* including Christ on his cross! And what's so outrageous about it is the fact that it isn't because we're insane or stony-hearted, but because laughing at wounds and scars is the only thing that keeps us hopeful and sane! Like it or not, it's one of the few ways we have of keeping ourselves from being ground to a frazzle between the mysteries of life and the lies of history. We either have religion or we have the blues. And even our religion has to provide room for holy laughter...."

"I guess so," Wilhite said, "but for one of us to make that kind of joke—well, I don't know."

"But think of it this way: What if ole Abe *did* make such a statement and meant it? Would the statement blot out what he went on to accomplish? No! He was a man, and a man's instinct is not only without conscience but it gets mixed up into everything a man tries to do. So whatever is said about his motives we have to remember the one thing that can't be denied: He signed the papers that set us free!"

"Amen!"

"And no matter what that freedom has turned out to be, he made it possible. He wrote the words, and he signed them with his name, and that marked a new beginning. That's what I was thinking while listening to you fellows talking on the bus. I thought: Go ahead, brothers, and talk. Dispute your notions of history, and try to make some human sense out of what above all else was a *human* problem. But then remember that whatever conclusions you reach it was Lincoln who made it possible for you to argue about his motives, and that after the fact...."

"Oh, I knew that you were judging us, A.Z., even though you kept looking out of the window."

"Yes, but not harshly. I really wasn't. But the emotion I felt at the memorial was still with me, and I was sad because of the inadequacy of what I had said out there. You were speaking of him as a politician, and you were right. Considering the reason that brought us here, how could you help it? So I was thinking to myself, Yes, that's what he was, a politician. And considering the fact that *both* sides of the war were using us as a combination sign and symbol of what they were killing one another for as well as for what they both were trying to back away from fulfilling in the pact that this nation had made with God, he not only had to be a politician, he had to be more of a trickster-politician than any of those he was up against, both North *and* South. It was just our little bit of luck that something deep inside the man, something in him that probably had nothing directly to do with politics but still made the difference. It could have been something shameful, or it could have been something too glorious even for him to think or write about while trying to keep his feet on the ground and his eye on his target—but thank God for *whatever* it was!"

"Amen," Wilhite said. "Trying to think about it your way is like hoeing a straight row in stony ground, but Amen! Is that why you sound so sad?"

"Now, now," Hickman said. "Not after bending your ear. Wilhite, I don't know what I'd do if I didn't have you to talk with. For a while there I was worried that I might have gotten something going out there at the memorial that I couldn't hold on to. With my big mouth taking over I thought that with the problem of getting to this boy working in the back of everyone's mind— Oh, Wilhite, what I'm trying to say is that I think I'm over my head. If I'd known what we'd be up against I probably would have given up the idea of having us come up here. Right now I'm up against everything that my ignorance and lack of experience have left me unprepared to deal with. Even the manners and rules of this town are against us. It's set up in such a way that the man doesn't even have to do a thing to keep us at bay. Because everybody seems bent on keeping us from seeing him. They're so set on upholding on to the apparent arrangement of things that they won't even stop to think about what it might cost him if we *don't* manage to see him. They can't imagine the possibility that folks like us might actually have something to do with someone they are sure to go down in history. It makes a man wonder if they ever think about what those monuments scattered around this town might mean to folks like us."

"They don't, A.Z., because as far as they're concerned there's no connection!"

"Well, all I can say is that they should. Because whether they like it or not, Abe Lincoln dealt us into the game, and we're standing pat if only in thanks for all those on both sides who died to bring us here. So no matter how much ducking and dodging that boy manages to do, we have arrived; and I mean to see that we accomplish the mission that brought us here."

"Now you're sounding like your old self," Wilhite said. "What's our next move?"

Getting to his feet, Hickman removed his watch and checked the time. "It's later than I thought," he said, "and much too late to do anything about our boy. So in the morning we'll try reaching him at his office. In the meantime we'll have to pray that nothing happens to him."

"Good," Wilhite said with a yawn. "It's been a busy day."

"Yes, but it isn't over. So get up and come on."

"But you said that it was late, so what are you doing at this hour?"

"We're going to keep our promise to Sister Caroline and find Aubrey McMillen."

"But why?"

"Because Aubrey's a notorious white-folks-watcher. He's one of a kind who doesn't even think about it, he just watches how they walk and talk and eat and dress. And he keeps an eye on how they assert authority, drive their cars, bully other folks, and break the laws. He watches their pretensions and their need to measure almost everything they do against what *we* do. And years ago he learned down South that it's a good policy to watch white folks from their first soiled diapers to their last clean shirt. And that's because they like to pretend that colored folks are deaf, dumb, blind, and noseless...."

"All right, but why bother him tonight? Couldn't it wait until tomorrow after we've taken care of this other business?"

"No, because that's a good reason for trying to see him tonight. I want to keep our promise to his sister, and it just came to me that although he's a notorious liar and a dedicated white-folks-watcher he might be able to tell us something helpful...."

[MCMILLEN]

ENTERING THE TAXI WHICH Wilhite had summoned, Hickman settled back and turned his attention to the task ahead. The fact that his idea was inspired by a dying woman's desire to see her brother made him uncomfortable, but if Aubrey was still the dedicated white-folks-watcher he'd been years ago he might well provide clues that could save a man's life. So the problem was one of learning whatever he might know about the private lives of Washington officials without arousing his curiosity.

Staring at the flow of nighttime traffic he recalled that it had been during a summer visit to Chicago that young McMillen had been converted to the stylized manner of walking known as the "pimp's limp." A style with which, advancing along the dusty streets of the neighborhood one short step at a time, he had drawn attention as he swaggered and swayed in his crude imitation of Chicago's Southside types whose sporty clothes, fine automobiles, and good-looking women had struck him as glamorous. And while the clash between his new style of walking and his skinny, high-butted, teenager's body had made him a target for teasing, it soon became clear that his adopted style signaled his break with the conservative values of the respectable community and the pious ways of his parents. And it was during that summer of adolescent crisis that Aubrey adopted the attitudes of older outlaw types who were known for defying the unfair restraints imposed on their freedom by white folks. And by way of expressing his defiance he had become fascinated by the old Negro game of white-folks-watching.

Thus, in expressing his rebellion McMillen had become intensely concerned with white behavior, and especially with the behavior of those who were least likely to suspect that their personal conduct, carefree or guarded, was of intense interest to a teenage Negro whose expression was dull and his eyes heavy-lidded. Not that Aubrey was always able to grasp the complexity of what he observed, but like other youngsters of his group he became an observer of activities that dispelled some of the mystery which shrouded the ways of white folks.

Which in itself was not unusual, for the contrast between what whites said and what they *did* could be inescapable, even for children much younger. And given the close proximity of blacks and whites there was much to be seen, questioned, and evaluated; as he himself had discovered during his boyhood, viewed more intimately from the bandstand, and continued to observe as an elderly minister.

But then, for most hometown whites, even adult Negroes were hardly more than shadowy, inferior beings whose observations and opinions counted for little in the segregated world in which they themselves moved. On the other hand, circumstance both political and historical had forced Negroes to deal with the complex individuality of even the poorest of white folks. It was true that on the face of it some were friendlier than others, but underneath, *all* white folks required careful attention as to their individual backgrounds and characters. Indeed, the difference between living or dying could depend upon a Negro's knowledge of a white individual's values and dissents, and therefore white-folks-watching had become McMillen's way of protecting himself no less than a devious form of amusement through which, playing black cat to white king, he made a game of observing unwary whites while remaining himself unseen.

The game was dangerous, but that was part of its attraction. It was also a form of instruction through which a knowledge of matters not taught in schools could be gained, and a discipline in self-survival and social awareness which, once imposed, was never abandoned.

For not only was white-folks-watching a form of self-protection and an easy method of self-assertion, it was also a source of amusement. But as Millsap had insisted, white-folks-watching was basically a form of *people* watching. So along with laughing at the hypocrisies of others we should try to measure how much they are like us and we're like them. "And that, old buddy," Millsap had said, "is the eye-popping, color-grating rub!"

Indeed it is, he thought. *So if McMillen has continued his game and happens to know anything useful about our boy it's up to us to learn what it is without arousing his curiosity. . . .*

Suddenly aware that the taxi was slowing its pace, he looked out at the oncoming march of streetlights, and spotting the name of McMillen's street on a lamppost he directed the driver to let them out at the corner.

But after paying the driver and joining Wilhite on the curb, he stopped short. For instead of the slum he had unconsciously expected they had reached a quiet neighborhood which was marked by its graceful trees and well-kept houses.

"Hold it, Deacon," he said, "there seems to be . . ."

But before he could finish the taxi was speeding away.

So now, annoyed with himself, he stared into the flickering shadows beyond the streetlight and wondered if they had made the mistake of entering a white neighborhood so late after nightfall. But seeing no patrol cars or people he couldn't be certain.

"Let's get on with it, Wilhite," he said.

And now, moving ahead, they entered the dry, fragrant smell of a lane of tall trees and began checking the façades of houses.

Then, through the shadows ahead he saw a man approaching who appeared to be white. Carrying an equipment case of some kind slung over his shoulders, the man appeared to be talking to himself as he moved through the shadows and searched for something he had lost on the sidewalk.

"Look at that, A.Z.," Wilhite said, "wonder what he's up to?"

"I don't know, but keep moving...."

But now, becoming aware of their presence, the man paused, took a quick look behind him, and continued forward at a pace which sent the equipment case on his shoulder bobbing and swinging.

"Watch it, Wilhite," he warned. But in stepping aside he felt a blow from the case, saw the startled white face loom close to his own, grabbed the man in a bear hug, and in whirling him around was blasted in the face by the strong fumes of bourbon. And seeing the man's startled expression as Wilhite yelled angrily, "Who does he think he's bumping," he loosened his grip.

"It's all right," he said over his shoulder.

And releasing the man's arms he took a step backward, saying, "It's O.K., no harm was done.... Are you all right?"

"Why yes," the man said with a note of uncertainty, "but what's this about, what's happening?"

"Simply an accident," he said. "Just one of those things that go bump in the night...."

"Oh," the man said with a look of relief. "Nevertheless, it still has to be accounted for, understand? There's always an underlying motive, so we must consider the circumstance and get at the *facts!*"

"Facts," he said. "Man, what are you talking about?"

But instead of answering the man took off on the run.

"Good Lord, A.Z.," Wilhite said as they turned and watched the figure flash through the shadows, "he must have thought we intended to rob him."

"I don't think so," he said with a slap of his chest to make sure that his own wallet was still in place, "but that liquor I smelled on his breath might be playing tricks with his brain."

"So *that's* what it was," Wilhite said with a laugh. "And him talking about *facts!*"

"Well, Wilhite," he said as he watched the man rushing through the blobs of light and shadow ahead, "facts aren't everything, but they *are* important."

And now, watching the man become a small figure that listed to one side from the weight of its shoulder-hung case, he recalled Millsap's comment about the black-and-white drama of everyday life. And as he watched the figure staggering across the brightness of the street intersection and disappearing into the shadows beyond, he shook his head.

"Wilhite," he said as they turned and continued, "what puzzles me is how anyone who couldn't see somebody as big as me on this walk could get the facts about *anything!*"

"Yeah, A.Z.," Wilhite said with a grin, "but don't forget that he bumped into you in the *dark*."

Returning Wilhite's grin with a blank-faced stare, he said, "Let's get on with it," and continued south through the shadows. And now in checking the façades of houses, he saw the address which he had copied from Sister Caroline's letter and came to a halt. And in examining his notebook he gave Wilhite a look of surprise. For the address was that of a well-kept townhouse.

Built in a style which was common to early America, the three-storied dwelling seemed an unlikely residence for the likes of the McMillen he remembered, yet the numerals 369 that glowed on the glass of its fanlight were the same as those in his notebook. So with a nod to Wilhite he moved toward the entrance.

"What puzzles me," he said as he searched for a doorbell, "is how a fellow like the Aubrey we knew comes to be living in such a respectable neighborhood."

"Well, now, A.Z.," Wilhite said with a chuckle, "the rascal always hung loose and played the odds, so maybe he's got lucky and come up in the world. Still, I can remember a time when *I* would have thought twice before moving into a house with those particular numbers."

Pausing in his search for the entrance bell, Hickman stared at the numerals illuminated by the fanlight and frowned. Then, suddenly recalling that most dream books which were popular among gamblers during the old days had interpreted three-sixty-nine as the numerical sign for excrement and thus a potent symbol for life's unpredictable mixture of good luck with bad, he grinned.

"I see what you mean," he said, "because I can remember a time when all you had to do was to dream of stepping in some of what those numbers symbolize on a sidewalk—And *wham!* you'd rush to some policy joint and risk a week of your hard-earned pay."

"Not me!"

"Oh, yes, my friend! Because in those days you were such a frantic gambler that you'd bet on *anything*. But now since you're a deacon you can forget that foolishness and remember the parable of the honey and swarm of bees that were hidden in the stinking carcass of a lion. Yes, and the little book that was sweet to the taste but bitter in the belly. Because as soon as I find this bell we're wading in. . . ."

But the entrance had neither bell nor knocker, and finding the hopeful advice of a favorite spiritual, "Knock, and it shall be opened," to no avail he gave the knob a twist and a push, thinking, *All right, so it's a case of "seek and ye shall find"*—and was surprised to see the door swing inward upon a warmly lit interior.

For a moment he paused, giving Wilhite a questioning glance. Then, hearing no movement inside, he raised his shoulders in a gesture of "What's-there-to-lose?" and stepped into the spacious entrance hall of what appeared to be an upper-middle-class home.

Advancing over a thick carpet he saw near the wall to his left a tall porcelain jar filled with walking canes that had handles carved in the forms of men and animals. And as he beckoned for Wilhite to follow he saw, some ten feet ahead, the dark wood of a handsome grandfather's clock and heard it accenting the silence with the *tick* and delayed *tock* of its pendulum's swinging.

And again he paused, watching the pendulum's ponderous pulsing while listening for movement ahead. Then, suddenly aware of an odor which seemed oddly out of place in the setting, he frowned and looked back to the reversed numerals on the glowing fanlight.

"Hold it, Deacon," he whispered, "just in case we've picked the wrong house. Because why would anyone who's lived in Washington as long as McMillen go and leave the outside door to a place like this unlocked?"

"Oh, come on, A.Z., you checked the address yourself," Wilhite said, "so this *has* to be the place. What bothers *me* is what's a *home-boy* like Aubrey doing living here in the first place? Maybe he's only a roomer, so what do we do if he happened to have moved after writing his sister?"

"So now, way late, you're asking something we should have considered before barging in here," Hickman said. "Come on...."

But as he turned and looked past the clock he froze, surprised by the figure of a man who stared from a doorway ahead.

The man was silent but visibly upset, but as he opened his mouth to explain their intrusion he could see the man's lips mimicking his own, and realized with a shock that the "doorway" was a shadowy, full-length mirror, and the "man" his own startled reflection.

And suddenly it was as though his inner self had found his act of trespassing so outrageous as to materialize and charge its bodily flesh with violating all laws of privacy.

But look, man, he thought as he stared at his accusing reflection, *don't you go getting so self-righteous that you forget that we both walked in here on a mission of mercy! And don't* you *forget,* his reflection shot back, *about what might happen if somebody catches you messing around in here! So now either you tiptoe outside and find that doorbell, or get yourself together and sing out 'Is anybody home?' loud and clear and pray that whoever hears you doesn't call the police....*

Then, noting that the elaborate mirror was supported by pivot pins set between the curved mahogany uprights of a fantastic cloak rack, he saw, suspended beneath the mirror's frame, an upholstered bench the width of a love seat. And near the top of the uprights from which his mirrored image loomed he saw the prongs of two sets of deer antlers that appeared to sprout—now as he watched himself shift positions—from the sides of his own hatted head.

Good Lord, he thought, it looks like coming in here unannounced is going to be worse than getting thrown out of that office building!

But now with a glance at a grinning Wilhite he moved cautiously ahead—

until, suddenly, the wall on his left disappeared—and he found himself standing just outside the arched entrance to a short passage beyond which he could see to a hallway filled with silent people.

Moving forward a step at a time, he could see men and women crowding the floor before him and the steps and landing of a wide winding staircase which curved to the floor above. But except for a single man who turned toward him and frowned, the others were so preoccupied with peering into the open door of a brightly lighted room to the right that they failed to budge; even as Wilhite moved in to join him. And suddenly aware that the people were dressed in night-clothes, he grasped Wilhite's arm.

"Deacon," he whispered, "I don't know what's happening here, but it seems to have bounced these folks out of bed...."

And failing to see McMillen among the tense staring faces before him he decided abruptly to leave—only to be stayed by the touch of Wilhite's hand.

"A.Z.," Wilhite said, "do you smell what *I* smell?"

And with a deep breath he accepted the fact that the odor which had teased him from the moment he entered the strange building was the once all-too-familiar bouquet of fine bourbon whiskey.

And that, he thought as he recalled the man on the sidewalk and nodded agreement, *is all the more reason for our getting out of here....*

But suddenly, at a shout from within the room to the right the crowd surged against him, and he saw with a feeling of fatality the figure of a white man who loomed in the glaring light of the doorway.

Of slender build, the man wore a gray straw hat of the narrow, "stingy-brim" type favored by certain young men of his congregation, and seeing the metal badge on the man's lapel catch the light he thought, *a detective.* And now, slamming the door shut behind him, the white man took an abrupt step forward, shouting, "Didn't I tell you people to clear this hall! That was over fifteen minutes ago, and here I come back to find you still hanging around! So this time I mean it—MOVE! Get back to your rooms or you're all under arrest...."

"Under arrest for *WHAT*!" a shrill voice screamed from above, and whirling toward the stairs he saw a tiny brown-skinned woman in an untidy auburn wig whose body trembled violently as she glared at the detective out of large and extremely crossed eyes.

"So go ahead," the little woman added hysterically, "arrest us! Everybody knows you're just *burning* to get brutal! So what are you waiting for? You have your blackjack and gun, so go ahead and start getting your kicks! But before you start whipping heads you'd better remember that we're *citizens*! You hear me? What's more, this is our *home*! We pay our rent and taxes from here! This is part of our *community,* and whether *you* like it or not *we* have the right to know what you people are doing to our neighbors in there!"

"Look, lady," the detective man said, "if you don't want the law on your premises all you have to do is to keep them orderly! You people give us more than enough to do as it is. And as I told you before, there's a criminal investigation in progress and I have my orders. So that's it! I'm ordering all of you to get on back to your rooms and clear this hall!"

So that's it, he thought as he whispered to Wilhite, "Move out, Deacon, this is no place for us...."

But too late. For as he started away he saw the white man turn in their direction.

"Hold it, big fellow," the detective said, "and that goes for that fellow behind you. Nobody leaves this building without the chief's permission."

Sighing inwardly, he halted. And as Wilhite stepped beside him, he saw people staring in their direction with looks of surprise.

"Hey!" a hostile voice boomed from the rear of the crowd. "Where the hell did those two come from?"

And as he moved between two of the tenants near the entrance of the brightly lit room he saw the detective's expression become one of surprise.

"Saay," the detective said, "where *did* you come from? I didn't see you in here before...."

"That's right, officer," Hickman said, "we only arrived here only a second ago...."

"Arrived from *where?*"

"From the Hotel Longview."

With a sudden jerk of his head, the white man stared.

"The Longview, you say? What are you, one of the doormen?"

"Doormen!" the little wigged woman screamed. "*Doormen!*—Did you people hear that? The instant this stupid white man lays eyes on a big, fine, professional-looking black man he *low-rates him!*"

Now there's a woman with absolutely no sense of proportion, he thought as he said, "No, sir, I'm not a doorman; I just happen to be stopping there as a guest...."

"*You,* a guest at the *Longview?* When did they start accepting— Okay, forget it! Just tell me what you're doing *here* at this time of night."

"We came here to deliver an important message to a man who's supposed to live here."

"And who would that be?"

"Mister Aubrey McMillen," he said, stressing the 'Mister' as he watched the white man's reaction.

"Ah-ha!" the detective said with a gleam of triumph in his eyes. "I knew damn well that McMillen would be the connection! So you're just an innocent delivery boy who was told to give him a message and return with his answer in a big paper sack—is that it?"

Puzzled, Hickman studied the detective's face.

"I don't understand," he said, "what's this about a paper sack?"

"Oh, you get what I mean. Because you really came here on your own and expected to leave with McMillen's reply concealed in a bottle!"

A bottle, Hickman thought, and suddenly the heavy fumes of bourbon took on a vague but threatening significance. "I'm afraid I still don't understand," he said.

"Oh, I think you do. And you might as well know that we're on to McMillen's little game. You're probably one of his regular customers, so don't waste my time pretending otherwise."

"Customers? Customers for *what?*"

Studying his face with a look of contempt, the detective cursed under his breath.

"Now look, man," he said with a sudden change to an accent which was flat and insinuating, "don't try to snow *me,* you dig? Because, like, I've been *around*—you dig?—so I'm hip to the jive you're putting down. . . ."

"*Jive,*" he said, "What 'jive'?"

"The jive you black studs try to put down every time you get caught in the act! But with me it won't work—you dig?"

And suddenly realizing that a Northern white man was relieving himself of a tin-eared imitation of Negro speech it was as though he had been slapped back to the days of Stepin Fetchit, Jolson, and Cantor and rebounded to find the detective still crouched in the barefaced posture from which he had uttered charges that were intended to be personally intimidating and racially demeaning.

And it was working. For as he fought to control his own reaction the hall was resounding with the grumbling of tenants who stared at the white man with undisguised expressions of disgust that were usually directed at their own kind who degraded themselves in public.

A group of women on the stairs appeared physically sickened, and nearby the flared African nostrils of a glaring, light-skinned man were twitching as though he had been hit with the neglected contents of an ancient, four-seated outhouse.

And now, returning the detective's stare as through a wall of thick glass, he thought, *This poor man thinks his being born white brings with it the power of turning black in an instant—just look at that swagger!—and he's actually convinced that using a Southern accent he can disarm me of all the skills in lies and deception that folks like him have forced me to develop in just staying alive in this messed-up country! So forget it, Hickman, because if you take him on these folks who live here will suffer. He has that badge and it's an old, old pattern, even though he's so immature in dealing with human beings, black or white, that he thinks he can needle someone of your experience into playing his misguided game! Good Lord! And only a little while ago you thought your signifying riff on Stackalee and the Sheriff was nothing more than comic fantasy!*

"You'll have to forgive me, Officer," he said, masking his outrage with ironic politeness, "but while I'm doing my best to understand and cooperate, *you* seem to have something on your mind that I know nothing at all about. Nobody told us that Mr. McMillen was in business, so if you'd take a second and explain...."

"Oh, man, come *on!*" the detective said with a wave of his hand, "I dig the deal, so quit *stalling!* What do you take me for? He's into bootlegging and you damn well know it!"

"*Boot*-legging," the little woman screamed from the stairs, "BOOTLEG-GING! Do you people see what we colored folks are up against? This is what happens when the white folks send one of these young whippersnapper cops into our community! Never even *seen* Mister McMillen before and already he's done reinvented the poor man and set him up as a *bootlegger!* I'm telling you, this white man must be out of his mammy-grabbing mind! Here we are, living in a building that's so respectable that some of its dicty tenants even object when a down-home person like me wants to cook herself some *collard* greens! That's right, and you all know who I mean! And yet this ignorant white man is standing there signifying that folks like that would live in a *bootleg* joint!"

"If you have any doubts," the detective said in his natural voice, "just take a deep breath!"

"But officer," Hickman said, "my friend and I know nothing about McMillen's affairs, and whatever they are they had nothing to do with our coming here. That's the truth. We came here to deliver a deathbed message, and if it will help you understand, my name is Hickman, *Reverend* Hickman, and we came here..."

"No, Mister!" the little woman called from the stairs. "Hold it while I get something *urgent* off my chest!"

Turning from the detective, Hickman paused with a sudden feeling of disorientation as now he found himself the object of the little woman's cross-focusing eyes.

"Very well, ma'am," he said, "please go ahead."

"Thank you, darlin'," the little woman said with a toss of her wildly wigged head, "it's very considerate of you. And please understand that I don't mean to be impolite, not when I can tell from just looking that you two are real gentlemen. But like I was saying, there's something that I have *got* to get off my chest! And I mean right here and *now*—understand? This thing has been building and building...."

"All right, ma'am, go on...."

"Thank you, darlin', but before I do let me give you some good advice: Don't you go begging his pardon! Not his or any other white man's, you hear? Don't *do* it! Because *he's* the one who's trying to convince you strangers that Mister McMillen is a bootlegger! Which believe-you-me is a mush-mouth lie! Because as everybody knows Mister McMillen is a good, respectable, responsible, hardworking, God-fearing super! And I mean one who's known throughout the neighborhood for going out of his way to be helpful! And especially to us ladies."

"And if the stone truth was ever told," a man's voice boomed from the back of the hall, "she's telling it!"

"Why of *course* I am," the little woman said with an indignant frown, "but now, just because this rookie policeman has probably heard that the poor man takes him a drink every once in a while—which is true, darlin', but only when he's down in the dumps and his spirits need lifting—understand? So right away, and with no more evidence than a sniff from that crooked nose of his, this rookie cop has set Mister McMillen up in the *bootlegging* business!"

"What she means, my friends," the voice roared from the rear of the crowd, "is that through his maleficent act of gross hearsay and unfounded allegation this rookie detective has up and made the innocent man *ill-legitimate!*"

"That's correct," the woman snapped with an angry toss of her head, "he's up and made Mister McMillen a *CRIMINAL!* Why, it's enough to turn a person's stomach! Understand what I mean?"

Fixed by the little woman's cross-focusing gaze, Hickman nodded and braced himself for the detective's angry reaction.

With all the folks in this crowd, he thought, only a little Tack Annie of a woman like this would try getting away with defying a white policeman. But before the detective could respond the man's voice boomed again from the crowd.

"Now you're catching on to him, Maud," the voice called, "but instead of getting upset over something that ain't worth doodly-squat let me give you some advice— Hey! Y'all watch out the way and let somebody up there who has something to say...."

And through the stir of crowd Hickman caught sight of a fat black knot that had been tied in the frayed top of a woman's stocking to form a greasy do-rag, and beneath which, moving at a ponderous pace, a short, heavy-set man emerged from the shadows. And now as the man advanced, he saw that he was dark brown of complexion and that his improvised stocking cap fitted his huge head so tightly that the flesh above his popped, frog-like eyes was puckered like the skin of a sunbaked raisin.

"Now there, A.Z.," Wilhite whispered, "is an *old* billiards drinker if ever I saw one."

Recalling the old joke about a country boy who had pretended to be sophisticated by swaggering up to the bar of a big city pool and billiards parlor and ordering a glass of billiards, Hickman visualized the foamy-headed drink which the bartender had improvised for the imposter and silently shook his head. And appalled by the idea of such a character reappearing in such an exasperating situation as that in which they were now trapped, he watched the brown artificial fur of the man's bathrobe catch the light as he came aggressively forward, elbowing and bellying tenants out of his way. Then, reaching a spot directly behind the jam of tenants facing Wilhite and himself, the man paused, grasping a half-eaten drumstick in one fist and a can of beer in the other.

"Naw, Maud," the man called over his shoulder as he studied the startled white man's face with the jaded expression of a world-weary judge weighing a plea of innocence from a notorious, habitual criminal, "it ain't worth the sweat. Which you'll see once I explain what's *behind* this mess. Because then you'll realize that all this little cop is doing is looking for him a little... easy..."

Seeing the spokesman pause and thrust the fist-held drumstick high above his head, Hickman nudged Wilhite as the word "GRAFT!" resounded with an explosion of breath that left the spokesman's barrel-like body bouncing up and down as though set in motion by the sheer weight of his pronouncement.

"And that's all," the spokesman said with a lip-protruding grimace of absolute conviction, "the hell... it is!"

And here, Hickman thought, *after convincing myself that such characters disappeared with the player piano, I find one alive and bassing in Washington!* As now, relieving himself of a resonant belch, the spokesman took a quick sip of beer and glared at the detective.

"So now, ladies and gentlemen, here way early... in the mawning," the spokesman continued, "... he's got the un-*miti*-gated *gall* to try to hit a bunch of sophisticated, Dee-Cee folks like us with some ignunt *peckerwood* mystification—yeah! And doing it in the name of his undemocratic notion... of *law and order!*"

Hearing the hallway pop and sputter with an angry firecracker-flurry of agreement, Hickman stepped aside as the detective reddened and stabbed a finger at his accuser.

"Now you listen to me, Jack," he shouted, "there'll be no more of that! You hear?"

"You damn right, Jack," the pop-eyed man boomed with a scornful wave of his drumstick, "I hear you, but I also know my rights under the *Constitution!* Therefore before this court of my peers and these two brothers from down home I'm holding that Miss Maud up there has got no business letting herself get all worked up just because *you* want to put down your simple-minded hype!"

"... What? What was that," the little woman called with a hand cupped to her wig-covered ear. "What?"

"... Because all we have here," the fat man went on, "is a little *small*-time hustling!"

"Lonnie!" the woman called from the stairs, "LONNIE!"

"That's right, my clerical friend," the pop-eyed man said with a patronizing nod to Wilhite, "to you home-boys it might look complicated, but when you sift this crap down to the nitty-gritty all you get is a simple case—as the hipsters on the block would say—of the 'Man' trying to twist him a 'Boot' for some *loot!*"

"... All right, Jack," the detective interrupted, "you're asking for it, what's your name?"

"... And I'm one man who's willing and able to lay it out for you: The first thing he does in putting down this type of hype is to find him a tight *situation.* By which I mean some kind of double bind which he can go about naming anything he damn pleases—like larceny, loitering, spitting on the public sidewalk, littering, playing a radio with the volume high, or scratching his head and his behind at one and the same damn time—any damn thing you damn please.

"Next: He finds himself a 'Boot' who's in some kind of uptight predicament—which, as we all know, is liable to be true of *any* Boot at *any* time. Because after the way the white establishment have rigged the system it's more normal for a Boot to be *in* trouble than not. And being booted before he's out of diapers the Boot also knows that they rigged it that way so he'll always be up to his butt in some kind of trouble. Therefore, all the *Man*—of which you have a prime example caught in the act—has to do is find him a tight situation and a Boot to fit it. Then he goes about *terrorizing* his chump until he's willing to own up to any crime, no matter how trumped up and unreasonable, that he wants him to admit committing! And it don't matter if it's something as humanly impossible as peeping through a bedroom window when he's standing ten... flat-footed stories... below it on a stinking sidewalk! Then the *next* thing he does is to throw the Boot smack-dab in the middle of that kind of phony situation and force him to confess to being guilty—which, unfortunately—and *most* unfortunately, I must add—any unhipped Boot is more liable to do than not!

"And that, my friend," he said with a nod to Hickman, "is because when you get right down to it, your average Boot figures he's *got* to be guilty of *something*. Because otherwise he has no explanation—neither philosophical, political, legal—Yeah! That's right—or *theological* as to *why* his life in a country as prosperous as this could be as messed up as it usually is! Therefore, it makes it easy for the *Man* to find himself an iffy situation and force some innocent Boot to match up with it. And then, ladies and gentlemen, watch out! Because the *Man* has got it made!"

"That does it," the detective shouted. "What's your name?"

"BARNES," the pop-eyed man roared in a tone of high indignation. "The one and only, and well-known to the community! Are you satisfied? BARNES! LONNIE BARNES! And to you, *Mister* Barnes and a man who's *proud* to be of service to this community!"

"Now, Barnes, you listen to me," the detective began—but with a contemptuous wave of his drumstick Barnes whirled back to the crowd.

"So my friends—and as I was saying before I was so rudely interrupted—that's *all* that's happening. Therefore as your friend and fellow-tenant it's my responsibility to hip y'all to the scam that's going down!"

"A.Z.," Wilhite whispered, "I can't figure out what's going on, but from the way they *sound* some of these Negroes have got to be drunk! And this white man is right in there with them...."

"No, Wilhite," Hickman began, "it has to be more than that." But now, seeing the detective turn in their direction, he held up his hand for silence.

"Look, Officer," he said, "could we please get this over with? I've tried to explain that we came here to deliver a message, and that's the truth. . . ."

But suddenly the detective lunged, pushing him aside; and he whirled to see Barnes executing a dancer's spin that ended behind the protective bodies of his fellow-tenants, and from where, stabbing a fuzzy arm at the detective, he shouted, "As you folks can plainly see, he don't like the idea of my exposing him worth a damn. But as per usual that's what he's trying to do. Up to now he's been getting away with pushing folks around while he prepares to drop him a stinking shuck, but with a man like *me* looking him dead in the eye he don't know how. So now I'm spelling it out so that *everybody* will be forewarned the next time they see a scam like this going down:

"First he shows up here in the line of duty—that's right! But then, after casing the joint and finding nothing but *colored* folks, he decides to rename whatever it was that brought him here to his own convenience—which has *got* to be in the blurry category of crime. . . ."

"Crime," the little woman screamed. "*What* crime?"

" . . . and that's because he's a cop and, like it or not, cops live and *thrive* on CRIME! That's a fact, so take it from your friend Lonnie! No cops, no crime! No crime, no cops! Either way it's simply in keeping with the cops' unwritten law of demand and supply. So any way you look at a cop you're . . ."

" . . . Up against crime," a man agreed from the rear of the crowd.

"That right, brother," Barnes called with a slap of his hands. "These lousy cops eat crime, drink crime, breathe crime, and *thrive* on crime! And like that one standing there they buy their cheesy suits, shirts, shoes, ham hocks, and shinola with loot they make out of crime—and that includes everything from his funky drawers to the fillings in his snaggly *teeth*!

"So take my word for it, his true business is breaking the law in the *name* of the *law*! And when he finds him some kind of questionable situation the stage is set. Because then all he has to do is go poking around until he finds some black man who he can drop slap-dab in the middle of it—and, behold, brothers and sisters, ladies and gents, he's got it made!"

"Amen," a man shouted. "Give his butt hell!"

" . . . Thank you, brother, your 'Amen' is most welcome. . . . So now, my friends, the rest of you are probably asking yourselves how has he been going about it in this particular instance? Well, my friends and fellow-citizens, all you have to do is gimme your ears and I'll *tell* you:

"As you all know by now he's already picked Brother McMillen as his victim. And while I don't know what his buddies are doing to the innocent man behind those closed doors you can bet it ain't legal! Therefore, if I hadn't decided to speak up, that one standing there was all set and ready to go. That's right! Because between running out here and bossing *us* around he's been in there trying to trap Brother McMillen into confessing to some bogus, unfounded, and ill-conceived circumstantial evidence! That way he means to force our neighbor, Brother McMillen, to own up to it. And if *we* keep standing around and letting him get away with it he'll twist Brother McMillen so *hard* that he'll give up and give in.... And then, brothers and sisters, ladies and gentlemen..."

Barnes paused, shaking his head mournfully as he looked over the crowd, "all that so-called servant of law and order has to do is twist his Boot... and he's *got ...* his loot!"

"Now Lonnie, you listen to me," the cross-eyed woman screamed from the stairs. "You stop your referring to our people as 'Boots,' you hear me? Don't do it! Don't be giving that white man the immoral satisfaction of hearing you talking so common! Can't you see that that's his only reason for letting you run your big mouth? He's the kind who likes to twist and turn everything a colored person says and does wrong-side out! And if you'd stop running your mouth long enough you'd see it! He's just taking in everything you say so he and his friends can laugh about it! He's the kind that has so little respect for folks like us that if he sees us ladies being escorted a few times by different gentlemen he'll be calling us *prostitutes!* You know that! And that's because as far as *our* people go, he has a low-rating kind of mind...."

" ... And now, Maud," Barnes called with a judicious bow of his head, "you're catching on to him! You're getting his low-rating number—but it ain't uncommon. *And,* like I say, after he's yeasted a situation like we have here this evening to his own satisfaction he badmouths and blackjacks his victim 'til he confesses. Which is how he twists the Boot for the loot—that's right! And that, thanks to Maud's calling it to my attention, also goes for the *personal* loot of you beautiful ladies who're known far and wide for y'all's beautiful fine brown frames!"

"Lonnie," the cross-eyed woman screamed, "LONNIE!"

" ... However, it is my sad duty to point out that in the case of you *women*folks Buster there makes him a fine distinction. Because instead of busting y'all for breaking the law he'll be breaking down your doors demanding FREE TRADE! Which *I* would describe as his way of compounding the criminal offense of misnaming an iffy situation with the age-old crime of bearing false and malicious witness with an act of de facto—I said DE FACTO—bribery! In other words—twisting the Boot for some loot!"

"LONNIE," the woman screamed with a violent tug of her wig, "I HAVE TOLD YOU!"

" ... But that," Barnes continued, "is just one more way of upending a Boot for some loot or plunder—which ... in the special case of the *female* species ... I'd define as '*under-plunder*' or '*booty-loot*'!"

"A.Z.," Wilhite said in a whisper, "if I were superstitious and that woman was blazing at me like that I'd cross my fingers and spit in my hat! That crazy detective is letting Barnes' mush-mouthed legal talk upset him, but *she's* the one he has to watch—just look at those eyes!"

With a disapproving glance at Wilhite, Hickman looked to see the little woman stab a finger at Barnes.

"I'm telling you, Lonnie," she screamed, "if you don't hush up I'm going to *read* you! I'm warning you now: I'm going to READ you!"

"You're going to read *who?*" Barnes growled. "And where do *you* get the right to be threatening a man like *me?* Read me *what?* Hell, everybody in the community knows I don't go for no little skinny women, so what can you tell them about me? Besides, this is a free country and open to all *kinds* of opinion! Therefore I have a right…"

"…NO! And you listen to me, Lonnie Barnes! You listen to ME!"

Frowning, with his forehead wrinkling beneath his stocking cap, Barnes turned to Hickman.

"Hell, man, I been on to cops like him since I was a boy, therefore I know about his kind of hype better than anybody. So how come I have to listen to someone as ignunt as her?"

"I'll tell you how come," the little woman screamed. "In the first place, you're so full of bull doo-doo that everybody knows it excep' for that white man! And for another I want you to shut up so those gentlemen can listen to someone who *really* has problems!"

"So you've finally come up with something *intelligent,*" Barnes said as he turned to Hickman, "because she really does have some problems! But that's no sweat, because all she needs is some *orga-ni-zation!*"

"Organization," the little woman screamed with a stamp of her foot. "Go organize your mama!"

And surprised by her language, Hickman exchanged glances with Wilhite as he heard Barnes shout, "Dammit, Maud, that's going too far! What do you mean by bringing my mama into a discussion like this?"

"MEEE?" the little woman screamed. "It was you who brought her into it yourself by acting such a clown after all the trouble she had bringing you into the world! The only reason I mentioned your mother is because of your interfering with my telling these gentlemen my troubles! So think about that and keep your big mouth shut! Yes, and stop rolling those blood-shot eyes at me!"

"Why you little cross-eyed, nappy-headed, narrow-butted, piece-a—," Barnes shouted. "What makes you think you can talk to me like that? Why, I'll…"

[MAUDE EYE]

"OH, NO," THE DETECTIVE said, "there'll be none of that—and that's an order!"

"Order my butt," the little woman snapped as she eyed the detective with a stare of contempt.

"And forgive me, gentlemen, if I sound unladylike. But as you can see the only way I could get Lonnie's attention was by mentioning his mama. And then, after he's disturbed our peace in the middle of the night that big mouth beside him has the nerve to stand there yelling about order!

"Anyway, gentlemen, what I'm trying to tell you is that we're all out here at this time of night because something terrible has taken over this house—which is our home, understand? And when a thing like that happens it's awful, but especially when it come to a woman like me. Because then she has to have her some answers! So since that white man down there won't tell you what caused all this commotion I'll tell you the little I know:

"The police have Mister Rockmore, our landlord, and Mister McMillen, our super, back there in Mister Rockmore's apartment. And while I don't know the reason, it has to be *serious*. Otherwise that *big-time* detective, the one who's in charge, wouldn't be here. And now to go back a bit—and I don't mean to be meddling—but early this evening it sounded like some kind of *party* was going on in Mister Rockmore's apartment—which is truly unusual, because nobody here can remember Mister Rockmore's ever doing any *partying*...."

"And that's the truth," a woman called from the shadows. "He *never* parties...."

"Never!" the cross-eyed woman said. "And then there was a heap of stomping around and a woman laughing and carrying on...."

"... Yes," a male voice said, "and all that ear-busting music!"

"Right," the cross-eyed woman said, "and *dance* music at that! And pretty soon everybody's out here stumbling around trying to find out what's happening. And when I rush out to see for myself there's all kinds of *rumors* running riot, and I'm near knocked off my feet by the smell of *whiskey!* Understand?"

"Go on, ma'am," Hickman said, "Go on...."

"So with folks all excited over all these white policemen invading the premises I see one in uniform who's guarding Mister Rockmore's door. Which truly upsets me because *nobody* seems to know the truth about what's happening. And even after that white man down there comes out and starts ordering us around he refuses to tell us or let us get in to see for ourselves...."

"Right," Barnes said, "and that's because him and his buddies consider Jessie Rockmore just another Boot they can twist for some loot!"

"There he goes again, so ignore him, gentlemen," the little woman shouted, "because what I'm telling you is as much as we know. And personally I'm calling for your help because having a thing like this happen in the middle of the night makes me feel that I'm losing my mind.

"That's the truth, gentlemen! Understand? And being a natural-born woman it gives me the flashes, and I mean the kind that sizzle and blister! Like I say, it's terrible, and having to breathe this whiskied-up air is making it worse! Understand? What I mean is: When something like this hits a person like myself she doesn't any longer know who she is, where she's at, or what she's doing!"

"All right, lady," the detective said. "I've let you speak your piece, so now be quiet while I get on with my duties...."

"Listen, Mister White Man," the little woman screamed, "you haven't *let* me do anything—so forget it! Anyway, gentlemen, and as you can smell for yourselves, this building is *reeking* with whiskey! Which is strange, because other than for Lonnie this is a *respectable* building that's never been a hangout for any winos, bootleggers, or bums. But yet and still, and even though our landlord, Mister Rockmore, is a respectable gentleman who never entertains, there's been some heavy *partying* going down.... That's the truth, gentlemen. And so now, after going this far, I might as well tell it *all*—because what I'm about to tell you is *exactly* what's got this detective so upset: Some say that there's a *white* woman ..."

"Now there she goes," Barnes groaned as he looked at Hickman, "and it's *exactly* where I knew she was headed! She's invading the man's privacy and dragging his bedtime business down the middle of the street! Give these old maids even a *ghost* of a chance and they'll run off at the mouth like a broken-down faucet!"

"Oh, shut up, fool," the little woman snapped. "All I'm trying to do is give these gentlemen the *facts.* That's all I'm trying to do. So gentlemen, as I was saying, everybody who lives in this building knows that when it comes to *entertaining,* Mister Rockmore has as little to do with white folks as he has with colored—which is very little by *anybody's* standard. Therefore I have serious doubts about him partying with a *white* woman—because if that's what he wanted he has plenty of us colored to choose from.

"So I'm asking you gentlemen: What does it mean? We're crowding this hall because we want to help our good neighbors in their time of distress, but as things now stand we don't know its *name,* we don't know its *face,* and to be blunt about it, we don't even know its *race*! Which is truly upsetting. Because like any good neighbors we want to be helpful, but we simply don't know where to start. Our peace has been disturbed since around about midnight but all we can get out of that rookie detective down there is some stupid talk about Mister McMillen being a *boot*legger—which as all of us know is nothing but garbage! So now that you two fine, intelligent-looking gentlemen have stepped into this mess and haven't been here long enough to get confused, I'm asking you to please, *please* tell me something that I *personally* need to know—Which is, what shall we *dooo?*"

"What shall you do," Barnes shouted with a step toward the stairs. "Dammit, Maud, the answer is organize and pick you a leader! Which is what I been telling you Negroes for *years*!"

"Yes, gentlemen," the little woman said, "and Lonnie thinks he's a leader, but all he does is rant and rave and make threats like he has some kind of invisible army behind him. And then, when things come to a *showdown,* he's off in some bar swilling his beer! Which is probably the reason the white folks keep letting the old micturating clown run around Washington yelling about Marcus Garvey

628 · Three Days Before the Shooting...

and changing Old Glory from red-white-and-blue to red-white-and-*black*—so hush, Lonnie Barnes!"

"And that goes for you too," the detective said with a frown. "Cut the talk or I'm booking you for subversion and resisting an officer."

"Resisting an officer," the little woman screamed. "Man, what's the matter, can't you stand hearing the truth? Am I breaking the law by telling these gentlemen what's been happening? And besides, how're you going to arrest me—sprout wings and fly over the heads of my neighbors? Shucks, man!"

"I mean it," the detective said, "and when I do there'll be plenty of force to support me!"

"Yes, and then you'll brutalize me the way those others are brutalizing Mister McMillen!"

"That's right, Maud, tell him about it," a man called from the crowd.

"No, she's mistaken," the detective said, "because no one's laid a finger on McMillen, he's only being questioned...."

"That's what *you* say," the little woman snapped as she pointed a finger, "but we know better! And now, gentlemen, before I'm interrupted again I'd like you to answer me this: How *long* are our menfolks going to keep standing by while these white police run around dragging their filthy-dirty minds into neighborhoods where we colored folks are forced to live whether we like it or not? That's what *I* want to know! How long are our D.C. menfolks going to *stand* for it?"

"But, ma'am," Wilhite said, "why are you asking *us*? We just walked through the door...."

"I know, and that's *exactly* why I'm calling on you for an answer! I know you're strangers, but since you've shown up in the middle of the night and at a time when all this trouble's upon us you must have been sent here for a *purpose*...."

And suddenly with hands on her hips the little woman leaned forward and stared at Hickman with a sudden widening of her cross-focusing eyes.

"Wha... what happened to the other one, gentlemen? Why isn't he with you?"

"With whom, ma'am," Hickman said. "What are you saying?"

"With the *other* one, your *friend*..."

"But, lady," Wilhite said, "nobody came here with us—who are you talking about?"

"Oh, but yes he did," the woman said with a defiant toss of her warp-wigged head, "when you two gentlemen started out there had to be three of you. There *must* have been! So what happened, did he stop by the way to have him a beer?"

"Madam," Wilhite shouted, "what are you *talking* about! Who do you *mean*?"

"Oh, you know the one I mean," the woman said with a teasing smile and a wave of her finger. "Yes you do, and I *know* you do!"

"Now, lady, you listen to me," Wilhite said, "you're confusing us with someone *else*. You have to be, because nobody came here but the two of us...."

"And ma'am, that's the truth," Hickman said, "we came here alone."

"If you say so, gentlemen," the little woman said with a look of bewilderment, "but don't be too sure, because there's a sweet inner voice which tells me that when you started out there were *three* of you. So now I don't know, I truly don't—but all right, gentlemen, if you say so ... if you say so. But why is it that I still have such a strong impression that you usually travel in *threes*?"

And seeing Wilhite giving him a look of astonishment Hickman's mind flew back to their days as traveling evangelists and asked himself, *But how could she have seen us that long ago?*

"No, ma'am, only the two of us," Wilhite said, "because it's been years since we've traveled with anyone else."

"That's correct," Hickman said. "It's been a long, long time."

"Are you sure about that?" the detective said. "Because I have orders that no one is to enter or leave these premises. So are you sure that no one came in behind you?"

"No one," Hickman said, "and that's the truth."

"Forget him, gentlemen," the little woman said with a glare at the detective, "because even with one of you missing I can still see that good sign hovering over you. Therefore I'm sure you were sent to tell us things about our situation which none of us can see by ourselves. Lonnie there gives me a pain, but about one thing he happens to be right: We *do* need leaders of vision who can think for themselves. So while only two of you came here tonight I'm sure you were sent to tell us what's happening...."

"... Dammit, Maud," Barnes interrupted, "haven't I already analyzed this mess? So why go bugging some strangers when there's good leadership right here in the community? What you need to do is git yourself together and follow and pretty soon they'll come up with some answers."

"Fool," the little woman said as she wiped her glistening brow with the sleeve of her robe, "in all your dogging around haven't heard of the *change*? Because if you have you'd know that a woman like me doesn't have *time* for any more waiting! That's why I'm asking these gentlemen to tell me if what's happening here tonight is *normal*. And if it isn't, I want them to tell me if that's the reason for their being sent here in the middle of the night. And if it's to organize I want to be told what *I'm* supposed to do while in the meantime! And please, gentlemen, *please* don't say that we'll overcome in some future day. Because what *I* need to know right now is the time, the date, and the long-needed *way*!"

"Now, Maud," a woman called down from the top of the staircase, "that's *enough* of that! Because like Lonnie says, you're just letting yourself get all heated up over nothing. Why don't you get yourself some rest and let the law take its course...."

Whirling with her hands in the air the little woman turned to the woman, screaming, "What do you mean for *nothing*? Here I'm begging these nice gentlemen for help and you're telling me that there's nothing the matter? That's exactly the reason I'm calling on somebody who's not all mixed up in this mess like we are. We've been in it so long and been driven so blind that it's time for somebody to teach us to *see*! That's why I'm asking them to do it while there's still time for me! Understand? Being a woman you should. I'm calling on these gentlemen because they seem to be not only sober but *sane*. What's more, whether you see it or not, there's a hopeful light about them which promises to put my *mind* at ease! This building is reeling and rocking with trouble, but now with these two millionaire doctors of the spirit coming in the nick of time I believe to my soul that they came here to *save* us! And here you have the *nerve* to say that it amounts to *nothing*! Why, good God-a-mighty!"

"A.Z.," Wilhite whispered as the detective exchanged words with someone inside the room behind them, "did you hear what she called us? What's happening to that woman?"

"Search me," Hickman said. "Maybe she remembers seeing us on the revival circuit—but millionaire doctors of the spirit? May the good Lord help her!"

"So listen, gentlemen, and let me explain," the woman said. "When I woke up this morning I had this strong feeling that something terrible would happen— that's right! Because last night I dreamt of giving birth to three sweet little babies. And, Doctor Hickman—you did say that was your name, didn't you, darling?"

"Oh? Why, yes," Hickman said, "that's my name, but how did you . . ."

" . . . I thought so," the little woman said, "Hickman, *Doctor* Hickman. . . . Uh huh. . . . So, like I said, Doctor Hickman, I dreamt I had these three little babies, and I truly wish you could've seen them. One was black, one was white, and one was a nice 'riney red. And the wonderful thing was their looking so much alike that I could hardly tell one from the other! And gentlemen, it was all so *real* that I can't believe that it didn't happen. And to tell the truth, I *still* don't know whether it happened or didn't. Because from the way I feel it *must* have been real. It *had* to be. . . ."

"Oh, come *ooon*, Maud," Barnes said with a pained expression. "Dammit, woman, you better git a *holt* on yourself. Especially when you know damn well that you ain't even married!"

"Oh, but I'm *going* to be," the little woman sang on a lyrical note. "Oh, yes, indeed! My bridegroom ariseth and cometh! And besides, what's your stupid signifying got to do with it? What does it matter if he comes before or after, as long as he comes?"

"Before he *comes*!" Barnes yelled, his eyes bulging with outrage. "So was it before, or *after*—woman, do you hear what you're saying? What the hell are you *talking* about?"

"Just what I said, Mister Loudmouth Barnes! Is that too much of a riddle for you? And whether you believe it or not I gave birth to those babies, all three of them! And gentlemen, I was so *proud*! And what's more, I did it without all that labor and pain I've heard so much about. I did it, gentlemen, and my babies recognized me as their mother the second they saw me! They cooed and gurgled and looked at me with their sweet baby smiles, oh, yes! And I mean with little *Negro* baby smiles, of which there's nothing even close to being any sweeter!

"How do you like that, Lonnie Barnes? Yes, I birthed them and got right out of bed and I bathed them. Then I sprinkled them with talcum, and after pinning on their diapers I wrapped them real snug in their pretty blue blankets. And then I took them in my arms and hurried out on the street and showed them off to my neighbors. That's right! And told all the people how such a wonderful thing happened! Oh, but they were so beautiful, so sweet and so charming, such *dear* little babies!

"And then, gentlemen, this is what happened: At first, when folks saw me cuddling my dear little babies they couldn't believe they were mine. Then some of the doubters started laughing and said that I'd better stop kidding and take them back to their natural-born mother! That's what they did! And me so proud of my new motherhood! And even when I insisted that I *was* their mother they called me a liar!

"I tell you, gentlemen, today there's a heap of loose talk about us colored folks *loving* one another. Well, I hope that's true, I truly do, but it still doesn't stop us from treating one another unkindly. In fact, when it comes to being mean to our own kind we're *years* ahead of the white folks! Haven't you found that to be the case, Doctor Hickman?"

"To ... to ... some extent," Hickman stammered as he returned the fixed gaze with mounting confusion.

"So that's the way some of us are," the little woman said. "Anyway, to prove that I birthed my babies I took some of the ladies into a hallway and pulled up my clothes and I showed them exactly where they floated out in their life-giving flood...."

"Woman, what the hell are you saying," Barnes shouted. "You did WHAT?"

"Oh, yes, gentlemen, and I know it sounds shocking, but that's what I did! I showed them my boat in the bulrushes, my ... my ... bird in the bushes. I let them see *everything*, and I wasn't ashamed. That's the truth! I let them see the jolly O-boat in which my sweet little babes sailed to me bubbling and babbling! Because that was the only way I could make those ole Doubting Thomas women see what they were trying to deny just so they could insult me and ruin my good name! And then I went on and showed them the raw belly buttons of my cute little babies. I showed them *everything*, but instead of rejoicing over such a wonderful thing happening to a woman like me, those ladies, those members of my own sex and race, they *scorned* me!"

And as he watched the little woman's doleful expression Hickman was embarrassed by the lines of a blues which rang in his mind:

> *Did you ever see*
> *a cross-eyed woman cry?*
> *Well she cries so good*
> *out of just one weeping eye—*

And in seeing tenants turning to gauge his reaction his embarrassment became mixed with a shock of bewilderment.

"And, gentlemen," the woman continued, "those women weren't strangers. Oh, no! I've known some of those ladies for years and thought them my friends. But now they were calling me an ole draggle-tailed bitch! That's what my *own* people did to me, gentlemen, not the white folks but my very own people! And I want you to know that I was hurt to the core!

"Because here, after years of my wanting a nice little baby, I had been blessed with no less than *three*—not just one, but three—and those women refused to believe it! Oh, and they were such *sweet* little babies!"

And now, smiling triumphantly, the little woman began counting her long slender fingers.

"One-little, two-little, three-little, cunning-little, cute-little babykins! But instead," she said with a sigh, "instead of being happy and congratulating me on finally coming through on my womanhood—which *was* kind of late, and I admit it—they scorned me and called me a bitch.

"A *bitch*! How do you like that, gentlemen? And after my showing them all the evidence that anyone could ask for! After I went so far as to show them my bruised boat in the bulrushes they still called me a bitch! You hear me? A bitch! What kind of way was that to go treating one of their own after she'd just given birth to three triplet babies?"

"HOW ABOUT IT," Barnes yelled with a lunge toward the stairs. "What you did was a damn disgrace! And now you're tearing your drawers and downgrading the *race*! Yeah, and that's the reason you women up there ought to quit gawking and get her butt back in her bed!"

And seeing Barnes whirl to face Wilhite with his eye-bulging anger Hickman anticipated physical action.

"Hell, man, this woman's out of her cotton-picking mind," Barnes shouted. "Here at her age raving about having some kids! Hell, I've been knowing the witch since the Depression, and ain't no way in the *world* for a field as dry as hers to come up with that kind of crop! So how the hell's she gonna hit the jackpot this late in life? I tell you, man, this is AWFUL!"

"That's how *you* see it," the little woman called from the stairs, "but then, what does an old micturating bear who can't hold his water, his mouth, *or* his wind know about what I've been through?—nothing!

"And that's why I want you two fine, leader-type gentlemen to answer me this: Was I wrong? Am I a bitch for giving birth without having a husband? And was it any worse than it would have been if one of you gentlemen gave a woman a baby without being married? And if you did, would that keep her from being a *mother?*"

"WHAT!" Barnes roared. "Didn't I tell you ladies to get that crazy woman up to her bed? How can anybody do what she's claiming? Yeah, and how can a man give a woman a baby *without* making her a mother? That's what *I* want to know. Yeah! And how can any woman have a man's baby without his being a *father?* Hell! Let's have some *logic* around here!"

"Lonnie," the little woman sighed, "you're making me sick to my stomach. And instead of giving a woman the blues like normal men do you're giving me a sickening case of the belly-cramping *reds!* Well, I have the answer so it's for me to know and for you to find out! And in the meantime, Doctor Hickman, I'm waiting: Is it worse? Is it any worse than it would be if a woman was to give *you* a baby that you didn't know she was carrying? Tell me, darlin', because I'm truly in need of an answer!"

And seeing the little woman's eyes appear to flame brighter than the un-shaded bulb that lighted the stairs Hickman felt a tensing of nerves and sharp-ening of hearing that increased the scene's unreality. And as he stared at the little woman's anguished expression her questions took on a vague hint of per-sonal significance.

"But Miss Maud, what are you *saying?*" a younger woman called from the shadows. "You started out by saying that the babies were all part of a *dream....*"

"Yes, Thomasina darling," Maud said with a smile, "that's true, but you're for-getting that some dreams are *real!*"

"Oh, my God!" Barnes yelled. "Now she's trying to contradict a *contradiction,* turn the truth wrong-side out and talk a hole through our heads! Dammit, Maud, you have *flipped!* Ain't no doubt about it! If not, where the hell are the ba-bies? *That's* what I want to know, where the hell are those BABIES!"

"Fool, that's what I'm about to explain: Gentlemen, my babies were *stolen!* I was out buying them some soft little booties and such things as baby oil and talcum, and little safety pins for their didies. Yes, and some soft little brushes. And while I was gone some hardhearted kidnapper slipped in and took my babies away. The brushes are white with pink bunnies on them, and you can come up to my room and see for yourself. They're still right there on the top of my dresser. And gen-tlemen, when I came back and found my babies gone from their bed I rushed out and tried to find them by searching everywhere I could think of.

"Oh, I searched *everywhere!* All over the campus of Howard University, under the statues and trees in Lafayette Park. Up along the Mall, and around George Washington's monument and even the White House grounds. Then I hurried to Abraham Lincoln's memorial and I searched *everywhere,* including under the backs of his long bony knees. And then I searched all along the riverbank where people were fishing. But although I asked each and every one I met if they'd seen my little lost babies, not a single soul could help me. I looked and I looked, I searched and I searched, and then it started to pouring down rain, and even with my feet soaking wet I kept searching until I got so worn and weary that I barely could make it. And that's when I simply had to stop in the street pouring with rain and break down and *cry*!

"I tell you, gentlemen, I cried and *cried*! I cried so hard that I had to get off the street and come home for some rest. But by the time I got here I was so broken in spirit that all I could do was cry 'til I dropped off to sleep. And then, after all of that weeping and wailing, I'm bounced out of bed late in the night to find this house rocking and reeling with some kind of trouble. All that, gentlemen, and me now a baby-less, downhearted mother...."

Struggling to impose some structure of rational order on what he was hearing, Hickman caught a fleeting glimpse of the incredulous expressions of Barnes and the detective as now the little woman pinned him again with her cross-focusing eyes.

"Doctor," she called, "it's been terrible, truly *terrible*. So would you please, *please*, answer me this: Am I being punished this way because I wasn't married when my babies arrived? Is that the reason they were taken from me? And if so, do you call that *justice*?"

And as he groped for an answer he saw Barnes throw his hand in the air and yell, "Justice? What the hell's *happening* to this woman? First she waves her funky drawers in the air and insults our intelligence with a bare-assed lie about her birthing three bastard babies—three of them! And now she's got the unmitigated *gall* to be asking some down-home preacher about *justice*!"

"Yes, Mister Big-mouth, I am," the little woman screamed, "because I truly believe that he and his friend were sent here to shed some light on all this darkness—Speaking of which, let me ask *you* a simple question...."

"To hell with it," Barnes said, "stick with your down-home messiahs!"

"All right, I will," the little woman said, "but you might regret it.

"Gentlemen," she called, "did either of you ever have the pleasure of meeting Lonnie Barnes' mother?"

"His mother? Why, no, ma'am," Hickman said, "I don't think so—why do you ask?"

"Because if he interrupts me one more time I'll tell you something about her that you probably didn't know...."

"Woman, you never met my mother," Barnes yelled, "so what you gonna tell him?"

"Which is true, gentlemen," the little woman said with a mischievous smile, "I never met her personally, but I've been *told* that she has some cast-iron plumbing and a *bar-rass* washbowl!"

"*Wash*bowl," Barnes shouted, "Now all of y'all can see that this woman is out of her cockeyed mind! First she's raving about babies and diapers, and now it's *wash*bowls!"

"Yeah, Barnes, my man," a male voice called, "but this time she threw you one hell of a slow-breaking curve!"

"Curve," Barnes yelled as the man wheezed with laughter, "what the hell does that mean? Has she driven you nuts with her raving?"

"Don't tell him, Jerome," the little woman called to the man who had spoken, "and while it's traveling through that fat head of his maybe he'll be quiet and let Doctor Hickman answer my question. And *please*, sir, do it *now!* Because while I've been accepting what happened to me as no more than natural, I'm sure a man like you can give me a better understanding of how it all hangs together. I say that because if our good Mother Earth can give birth to all the blossoms and birds that come in the spring without being married, why do *I* have to be? Am I not a genuine, nitty-gritty daughter of black Mother Earth, who's the mother of us *all*—including that white detective who's standing there grinning?

"White folks like him are always trying to low-rate us colored women by calling us *earthy*, so why can't I just be my own earthy self and do what comes naturally? Why can't I, gentlemen? Why do *I* have to be a victim of this black-and-white mess? Tell me why, gentlemen, tell me WHY!"

Keeping an eye on Barnes' exasperated face, Hickman gasped. For now with the little woman's reference to washbowls and plumbing taking on the rhythmic beat of a chant he recognized the word play through which innocent objects were substituted for the crude terms which players of the dozens used when referring to the private parts of their opponents' mothers. And as memory supplied the rhyme's missing details he stared at the little woman with mixed feelings of dismay and barely controlled laughter.

Hickman, he thought, *what is this world coming to? She's too ladylike to call a spade a spade and yet has the nerve to defy a white policeman and insult this thickheaded bully by signifying about his mother! Woman,* he thought as he wavered between outrage and laughter, *thy name is Confusion!—Yes, but what have I done to deserve having her strike me head-heel-and-thigh with her questions and dreams?*

Nevertheless, desperate little Maud was one of his own, and as he scanned the bemused faces of tenants he felt compelled to say whatever he could to console her. Yet even as he surged with compassion his attempt to respond to her urgent appeal was mocked by its blatant, blues-like absurdity. And with her shrill voice grating his ears it was as though she were stretching his sense of reality to the point of breaking, much like a string on which a gyrating kite was threatening to fly free from all earthly restraints. And with the image of a kite soaring in his mind, little Maud, the tenants, and detective all seemed to fade, and he was standing on a sunny hilltop with Wilhite and the marvelous little boy who had once been their charge and constant companion. . . .

It was a holiday in June and they were enjoying a moment of pleasure, during which he and Wilhite were holding the boy's hands between them while looking high above a deep valley to where, weaving the air above a hill even higher, a handsome blue kite with a long spangled tail was dipping and diving in the bright summer sky. And as he watched the boy react with delight to the kite's lazy soaring he scanned the valley and far distant hill for a glimpse of the earthbound pilot who controlled its soaring. And there, outlined against the rocks and sparse grass, he saw a solitary man staring skyward as walking backwards with arms extended he fed the kite string from a spindle so long and curved that it looked like a dowser with which the man was searching for water in an unlikely setting.

Then as the kite soared ever higher on its lengthening white string, he heard a shout from the valley and looked down to see another man and small boy who were both staring skyward. And as he watched the kite sail high above the hill on which his own little boy was admiring the dream-like effect of its effortless soaring there came a sudden shift in the breeze which sent the kite plunging earthward in a deep-dipping dive. And as it recovered and climbed with a triumphant snap of its long sparkling tail he heard the boy beside him pierce the silence with a scream of delight.

And now, as they watched the kite flare in the sunlight, little Bliss began jumping up and down as he pointed to the silvery fish emblazed on its translucent skin. And as he smiled and stared upward he recalled the boyhood pleasure of watching the delicate motions of rainbow trout as they nuzzled the currents of clear mountain streams and heard himself saying, "Now there, little Bliss—and you too, Deacon Wilhite—we have an airborne sermon that's most worthy of our thoughtful attention. Because when it comes to lifting the spirits of earthbound folks like ourselves, who among our fellow fishers-of-men can even begin to compete with that silvery soarer?"

"Just give this one time, A.Z.," he heard as Wilhite pointed to the sky-gazing boy with a wink and a grin, "just give this little one time...."

Then came a sudden flash of bright summer lightning, and the sky and the hill were engulfed by a squall. And with rain veiling the valley and thunder shaking the hills he snatched up the boy in a run for cover—in the course of which, hearing a shout, he stopped and looked back to see a rain-drenched Wilhite pointing to the sky. And seeing the kite dipping and diving in the onrushing storm he pointed the boy's attention to its tail-lashing agony and was taken himself with a feeling of dread.

For now, whirling and tossing on its invisible string with its tail whipping the air like a withering water moccasin, the fish-emblazoned kite was battling the wind with bits of its skin flying from the fragile wooden cross that formed its skeleton. And as tatters of flayed skin whirled and took off in the wind there came flashes of lightning and loud claps of thunder, and fierce gusts of wind that sent the kite plunging earthward in a skin-flapping dive. And as he watched its thin wooden arm piece sag in the wind, the emblazoned fish tore free of its background and whirled in the sky like a bird on the wing. And as it circled high above the wrath of the storm he heard the boy beside him give a shrill cheer.... And with the boy's cheerful laughter echoing in his ear he snapped back to the present and stared at little Miss Maud through the scene's fading screen.

She stood as before, still waiting; and as he groped for an answer it was as though the wind-battered kite were struggling to rise and rejoin its free-flying emblem. But even as nebulous fragments of an answer struggled to take form in his mind, the intense expressions of tenants crowded around her increased his uncertainty that any answer he arrived at might well prove embarrassing, both to her and himself.

And suddenly it was as though he were taking part in a jam session, where with a crowd looking on he was being challenged to give melodic coherence to a progression of dissonant chords for which he was unprepared except for his musical ear and a grasp of tradition. Perhaps because jam sessions were battles of music in which the participants' skills at revealing old forms in the new and the new forms in the old were rigorously tested. And now, taking courage from his success in such musical encounters, he grasped at the possibility that the answer he sought might well be one that linked the little woman's frustrations and dreams to his own mixture of worldly and spiritual experience.

For as a jazzman he had become sensitive to such things as subtle timbres of voices, inspired variations on popular dance steps, tricky changes of rhythm and musical phrase, and had learned that spontaneous gestures were often more eloquent than words. And later, as a minister, he had learned to apply such knowledge when dealing with the sick and the dying, young mothers with infants, and spouses whose mates had defaulted; people whose array of problems, he realized with a pang, were inseparable from those that inspired the snarled emotions and motives that had brought him after prolonged resistance to Washington—yes! And into the improbable situation in which he was standing....

[LEGEND]

AND WITH THE LITTLE woman waiting it was though he were being challenged to give voice to an elusive melody which a mocking pianist had deliberately concealed in a wild outpouring of dissonant chords. And yet he suspected that the answer to her anguished appeal would be one in which her frustrations and dreams were linked to his own. But how proceed, when he had so little to guide him? As a jazzman his ear had been sensitized to subtleties of sounds and nuances of rhythms, and watching frolicking couples improvising new steps while dancing had taught him that bodily gestures and facial expressions could be most revealing. But how use such knowledge in this situation? And as he stared at his questioner's anguished expression, he reminded himself that in spite of its endless diversity, all human life was united by patterns that gave it coherence and unity. Thus as a minister he had applied his jazzman's knowledge when counseling the sick and the dying, young motherless children, or disconsolate spouses whose mates had defaulted. People whose assortment of sorrows, he recalled with a pang, were akin to the snarl of emotions and motives that had brought him at last to Washington—yes! And into the unlikely predicament in which he now stood....

And suddenly a moth's erratic circling of little Maud's head evoked a scene from a movie in which the petals and leaves of a wind-shattered flower had whirled in slow-motion retrograde and assumed the form of a lovely red rose. And recalling the legend of which the rose was symbolic he gasped at its being evoked by the scene before him. Yet even as little Maud held him fixed in her cross-focusing gaze the rose resurrected in memory was asserting itself against all that opposed it: the times, the tenants, the white detective, and his own reluctance in recognizing its presence in the wild cacophony of little Maud's dream.

And now with the legendary rose imposing tremulous order on the strident dissonances of the little woman's appeal, he felt a strong surge of emotion. And as he gazed at the scene he realized that far from having heard the mere retelling of a hysterical dream, he had listened to a dejected form of public confession. And one through which the pathetic little woman had given public voice to her hopes and despair. As a minister he had listened to countless confessions, but now he was so dismayed that he stalled for time by removing his glasses and mopping his brow with his handkerchief.

So, Hickman, he thought, staring upward, *even if her neighbors were aware of her fantasies, they're probably embarrassed by her exposing herself with this white man listening. Yes, and for a second even you felt that she was making you and Wilhite a target for mockery. But since she knows nothing about your reason for being here she's probably appealing to you because she senses that whatever it is that's upset her is of a nature that binds her secret heart to your own. Or it could be an effect of a woman's change-of-life crisis, but whatever caused it has to be terrible. And considering our helplessness, her appealing to a couple of strangers for comfort is a sad mistake. Even so, she seems to sense that we're dedicated men of the cloth, so who knows? Maybe she sees deeper and straighter with those focusing eyes than I see through mine with my glasses. . . .*

"You," little Sister Maud called from the stairs, "can't you see that I'm waiting! So why don't you give me an answer? *Tell* me!"

"Yeah," Barnes said, "so she'll stop bending our ears and go back to bed!"

And as the detective glance at Barnes and back to himself he gazed at little Sister Maude and asked himself, *Hickman, what can you tell her with all these Washington Negroes listening and this white man looking on like he's been caught in a three-ring circus full of sideshow freaks? Tell her that her dream strikes you as the distorted version of a legend of hope? And one she's made sound like an old sacred song played out of tune on a broken-down organ? Tell her that what happened in her dream is a version of what's happened to others, and usually with mixed consequences of pleasure and pain? Tell her that she's been gripped by a dream experienced in the full flowering of its mystery by one blessed woman, and that long ago? Stand before this upset crowd and tell her something she'll find acceptable concerning a mystery which I've had trouble getting across to my own congregation for years. . . .*

"What are you *waiting* for," she called. "Here I am, up to my neck in trouble, and all you're doing is standing there gaping like a catfish struggling for air! So, I'm telling you again: I need an *answer*! My brain needs it, and my *soul* needs it, and with everything in this house gone so crazy you can forget my brain and just speak to my *soul*! I'm begging you now for an answer because after being 'buked and scorned, now even this fool Lonnie Barnes is putting me down. So I'm telling you and that other gentleman too, that when a woman gets in my condition something like that makes for pain in her *soul*! What's more, it makes her feel *evil*! Which brings me to another question:

"Was I wrong—I mean when my own folks scorned me and called me a bitch—was I wrong when I told those women who turned against me, 'All right now,' I said, 'how many of you who call me a bitch have given birth to babies not because you loved them, but because you wanted to live free off Welfare? How many little saviors have you flushed down the toilet or thrown out with the trash because you were ashamed of how you got them?'

"That's right, gentlemen! I *told* them! I said, 'How many of you lost a chance to raise up a little black *savior* because you made your evil boyfriends or no-good husbands so mad that they kicked you square in your stomachs? Yes, and how many of you who have the nerve to give *me* a hard time lost your chance to help our race because after being given a little savior you didn't love and prize him enough to keep him alive?' Are you listening to me, Doctor Hickman?"

"Oh, yes," Hickman said, "and carefully...."

"That's good, because I want you gentlemen to understand what I believe in my heart, which is that one of those babies they miscarried might have been meant to be a great leader or savior—just as one of mine might have been, and might still come to be! That's right! Otherwise, why is it that when most women only have *one* I was given *three*? Even with husbands all they came up with was *one*, and then they wasted him and denied him his chance at leading our people. Which is what I told them, gentlemen. And I told them how much I loved my babies and how I intended to keep them, no matter what *anybody* thought about my doing it! So now I'm asking you again, was I wrong? Tell me, gentlemen! You, the big, fine-looking one! And don't bother straining for words—just speak from your heart to a poor black daughter of good Mother Earth who broke down on these Washington streets and cried!"

Moving on sudden impulse, Hickman felt the resistance of hot bodies as he pressed toward the staircase where little cross-eyed Maud waited with quivering lips as he heard the constricted sound of his voice saying, "No, ma'am, you weren't wrong—"

"The hell she ain't," Barnes bellowed. "And after hearing her talk up under those women's clothes you have the nerve to tell her she wasn't wrong? Man, what kinda goddamn preacher *are* you?"

"No, ma'am," he said with a quick glance at Barnes, "you weren't wrong, even though your way of putting it was uncharitable. It was mean, but while I'm not sure I understand exactly what you've been telling us I feel in my heart that it contains a mysterious truth. Yours was an experience which most folks will never understand, and don't *want* to understand. But *I* believe that your dream contains the meaning of a powerful mystery in which many *many* aspects of our people's experience have come into focus. And that mystery is so enduring that most of the time we're too confused to recognize the role it plays in supporting the slavery-born hope that's still working among us. So I bow to you, Sister Maud, and I pray that you'll be blessed with peace and understanding. Because I believe that in your pain and suffering you've seen the Promise that keeps us striving. You've seen it in your own tortured terms and accepted the responsibility of announcing it to your friends and neighbors, regardless of what they might think. Yes, and announcing it to me in my *own* confusion. You're reminding us of hopes and responsibilities that we as a people can't afford to forget. God bless you!"

"Oh, I knew it," Sister Maud sang from the stairs, "I *knew* it!"

And as he struggled to grasp the meaning of what he had said he saw others on the stairs moving aside from little Maud with mixed expressions of doubt, outrage, and wonder.

"I just *knew* you were sent here to bring me glad tidings," she sang with her arms thrust toward him. "I just *knew* you two would ease my condition!"

"Ease *what*," Barnes yelled. "Just what the hell did he say? Nothing! So now we have *another* damn nut on our hands! Folks, I don't know this ole burly Negro from Adam's off ox, but I swear he sounds as nutty as Maud! Next thing we know he'll be telling us how many babies *he's* lost! So all right, Mister Gentleman, go on and tell us how many whatnots, blowouts, washouts, and slip-outs you're supposed to have lost!"

And with the hall exploding with laughter Barnes turned to the white detective, his eyes bulging with indignation as he bassed, "Officer, if you take my advice you'd forget about McMillen and get both these fools into that nut house at St. Elizabeth's—and I mean in *straitjackets!*"

Gazing at Barnes with a calm expression Hickman felt an impulse to smash his face with a blow of his fist but restrained himself as out of the corner of his eye he saw the flicker of a grin on the detective's white face. How often had he seen such grins when white men were watching Negroes fighting one another? And hearing sounds of anger mixed with the laughter as he stared at Barnes he thought, *With a bone stuck through that knot in his stocking cap he could pass for a comic-strip cannibal, but inside he's dangerous. So grin if you like, but if this keeps up it'll soon turn against you.*

"Frankly, Sister Maud," he said, "I won't pretend that I have answers to all your questions, but never mind Brother Barnes, because as we both know, there's one like him around whenever our folks come together. He's the particle of truth in the lies other folks use to justify being against us. So forget him, Sister Maud, because... well, it's against my religion to call *any* man a fool, but I think you'll understand if I call him a *clown....*"

"Yes, darlin', yes! That's *exactly* the kind of fool he is!"

"... So you just forgive him and anybody else who's unable to grasp what you've been telling us. What happened to you has a deep meaning, a profound and *marvelous* meaning! I can't say that I fully understand it, but I'll tell you that I *feel* its truth deep in my heart. And because it speaks to my faith and says something comforting to my own troubled mind. And therefore I truly believe that if other folks would only listen to you with their hearts it would comfort them too. So cherish your dream and forget the clowns and the cynics. Folks like us are sustained by hope and by faith, so we have to put doubters aside and hold on to the promise and hope that's concealed in our dreaming...."

"Oh, yes, darlin', yes! And if you were close enough Maud would give you a great big hug! But don't stop now, darlin', because what you've said is so good to hear that I need more of it! *Much,* much more!"

And as little Miss Maud thrust out her arms to blow him a kiss he saw her robe fall apart and was shocked to see a tiny brown breast flip from the embroidered bodice of her scarlet nightgown.

"Watch it, you slut," a woman beside her screamed hysterically, "or you'll end up letting him see that boat in the bulrushes you been boasting about!"

"Oh, woman," Sister Maud said as she calmly rearranged her nightgown and robe, "you give me a pain in my bottom! Can't you see that's no ordinary man? Shucks, he's already looked deeper into womenfolks than the place you're so worried about. This man is looking into the depths of my *soul*!

"So please, darlin', don't stop now," she said as she fixed him again in her cross-focusing gaze, "because no matter what these others think about you, Maud understands. Just tell her some more. Tell her that she hasn't really lost her three little babies! Tell her it isn't so! Tell her—you hear me, darlin'? Tell her! *Tell* her! Good God almighty, darlin', say *something*! And if you tired, then let your friend take over! Tell me that stone is stone-gone stone! Tell me my flesh is still flesh with bone underneath it! Tell me I'm not awake and standing here in the middle of the night but really up there in my bed with my three little babies safe beside me while I wait for my righteous *bridegroom*! Speak to me, darlin', SPEAK to me!"

"BRIDEGROOM?" Barnes bellowed. "Now she's *really* blowing her store-bought wig!"

"... Tell me that pretty soon my righteous bridegroom will come tipping over that pretty blue carpet that Mister Rockmore had laid in my room, and that those pretty pink roses will still be there on my *wall*paper! Oh, yes! It'll be so *goo-ood*! So tell me all, tell me *everything*!"

"Woman," Barnes roared, "have you up and blown that beat-up wig you're wearing? Answer me!"

"Ignore him, darlin', and tell me! And after that they can do with me whatever they will, but you tell me! Speak to my soul! And then, darlin'..."

And extending her clasped hands in a gesture of prayer the little woman leaned toward him, crying, "Please answer a question which *no* good woman should ever have to ask: When will my bridegroom with those sweet, soothing hands start protecting us from white men like that nasty, stinking, little mammy-grabber who's down there doing his best to knock the foundation out from under our home! So you tell me now! I say, TELL ME! AND THEN SHOW ME YOU *MEAN* WHAT YOU SAY!"

Poor woman, he thought, *she's losing control, and from the stares they're giving this white man so are some of the men. . . .*

"Go ahead," Barnes said, "prove what she says about your being a leader by showing us how Uncle Toms like you and your buddy'll go about dealing with this D.C. policeman!"

"Very well, Brother Barnes, but I'll start by warning them against listening to an opportunist like you!"

"*Opportunist!*" Barnes roared with a jerk of his head. "Y'all heard him, folks, so y'all be the judge. I'm urging you to defend your God-given rights against a cracker policeman and he calls me a hustler! Hell, if that's his idea of leadership his friend Mister Charlie has him and his buddy bowing and scraping!"

"Listen, you," the detective said, stepping forward, "that's enough of that!"

"The hell it is," a man called from the stairs. "And what's more, we're tired as hell of being told to turn the other cheek for somebody like you!"

"Tell whitey about it," Barnes called. "Let the sucker know we're *tired* of that kind of leadership—yeah! And if this one and his buddy don't like it, I'll start kicking butt 'til they bleed like fountains! The nerve of them coming in here insulting folks like us with some Uncle Tom bullshit!"

"Well, now," Wilhite said with a quick step forward, "since it's your idea, why don't you give it a try?"

"No, Wilhite," Hickman warned, "we didn't come here for that!"

And seeing a man moving closer to Barnes with a hostile glare, he grabbed Wilhite's arm.

"I know, A.Z.," Wilhite said, "but it's time somebody taught this clown the difference between our character and the region we come from!"

"No, Wilhite," he said, holding on, "because he'll still go on thinking that all black Southerners are clowns and all white folks racists!"

"Hell, let the sucker go," Barnes yelled from a prizefighter's posture, "let's get it over with. . . ."

"Right on, Lonnie," a man called from nearby. "You take him and I'll take the big one!"

"Yeah," another man said as he moved to join Barnes, "and we'll see that whitey keeps out of it!"

"Oh, no," the detective warned as he unbuttoned his jacket, "not if you consider the consequences!"

And in looking past Wilhite, Hickman saw Barnes' defender's startled expression as suddenly those around him fell back at the sight of a gun in the detective's white hand.

"That's right," the detective warned with a gesture toward Hickman, "and before things get out of hand, you two get into that room behind you—now move!"

And seeing Wilhite still staring at Barnes, Hickman whirled him around and propelled him forward.

"Wait, darlin', WAIT," he heard from the stair. And seeing the detective facing the crowd with his gun raised for action, he pushed Wilhite into the room and followed.

[TERROR]

WHERE, PARTIALLY BLINDED BY the sudden intensity of light, he let go of Wilhite and heard shouts from the vestibule become suddenly muted by the slam of the door.

"This way," the detective said, "and watch your step, this place is a booby trap."

And hearing Wilhite and the detective moving away, he proceeded slowly forward by ear and by touch. And now, his eyes adjusting, he found himself moving through an aisle crowded with appliances and furniture and was surprised by the change of environment.

For now he was passing a collection of small circular tables and stacked wooden chairs, the carved headboards of mahogany bedsteads, an ancient washstand with a washbowl and pitcher. Two movie projectors stood surrounded by stacks of circular film cans, a tin weather vane in the shape of an eagle stood on a table with its wings spread wide above a troop of miniature Minutemen armed with flintlock muskets, a toy fire wagon drawn by galloping horses, a bugle, a banjo, and an old phonograph with a flared wooden horn. And in recalling the metallic sounds of such early machines his eyes were assaulted by the blinding glare of electric lamps.

Attached to the wall on his right, the lamps were fashioned in the forms of torch-bearing cherubs, and suddenly struck by their angelic smiling, he paused.

I get it, he thought with a surge of amusement: In case I'm here in all this blinding confusion in search for something important you little fellows will help me, but you're smiling because you know that otherwise I'd never lay hands on it.

But now, moving toward where Wilhite and the detective were standing, in what appeared to be the only clear space in the wall-to-wall clutter, his puzzlement was increased by the disorder around him. And as he gazed upward and wondered at the waste of electricity he realized that the source of much of the dust-filtered glare were four theatrical spotlights attached near the tops of the high-ceilinged walls.

"Officer," Wilhite was saying, "what *is* this mare's nest, some kind of store-room for second-hand goods?"

"I'm still not sure," the detective said, "but it's a hell of a mess to find in a historical building."

"*Historical*," Wilhite said, "are you serious?"

"Why not?" the detective said. "This is one of the District of Columbia's oldest areas."

"So there you go, A.Z.," Wilhite said, "the old saying holds true even up here in Washington. What comes around, *goes* around! So now here's a historical building that's ended up in the care of Aubrey McMillen!"

"That is if he's actually the janitor," the detective said, "and I doubt it."

"Either way," Wilhite said, "he's still in the picture. But what *I* don't get, is why everything out front is so neat while this part of the house is so junky. It reminds of my grandfather's advice when he gave me a pony. 'Take good care of him, Primus,' he said, 'because a man who doesn't appreciate his belongings is sure to abuse them.' "

"Yes, Deacon," Hickman said with a nod toward the detective, "and having been a slave he knew that even if the owner took care of his property other folks would abuse it. And all the more if his property was black. Because if he struck back the next thing he knows all hell would erupt with folks arguing over whether his property had human rights. And next thing he knows everybody's waving a gun in the air."

"Don't worry," the detective said with a shrug, "because at least this one's on safety. What's more, I agree with his grandfather's advice, a man *should* look out for his property. But as far as this gun is concerned I'd prefer not to use it. That's right, but since it could make the difference between living or dying I'm ready and willing to use it."

"I understand," Hickman said, "but would you actually have fired that thing in that hall full of people?"

"Only if I had to, but then, as a wise man once said, one never knows—*do* one?"

"No," Hickman said with a start. "One never *do*."

And, surprised that a man whose attempt at jive talk had been so inept would now take a potshot at proper English—and before two Southern Negroes—he felt partially disarmed. And watching the detective punctuate his remark by spinning the gun like a sheriff in an old Western movie, he chuckled.

"No, sir," he said, "one never knows, but it's unusual to hear a policeman quoting Fats Waller. So now maybe you'll explain why you hurried us out of the hall...."

"Because I have orders to learn what you two are doing here at this time of night. Which was impossible with that loudmouth exciting a riot."

"Oh, come on, Officer," Wilhite said. "Down South we call that 'barking at the big gate.' Barnes reminds me of a character I knew years ago who hobbled around Atlanta with empty pockets and broken-down shoes while claiming he was building a nationwide movement which would boycott General Motors until they renamed the Cadillac in honor of Abraham Lincoln and Booker T. Washington!"

"He *what?*"

"That's right," Hickman said, "I remember."

"I've never heard of such a character," the detective said, "but it sounds as though he and Barnes might be one and the same. Still, with his friends chiming in things were beginning to sound pretty serious."

"Sure," Wilhite said, "because most folks out there were already upset by having you policemen swoop down on this place in the middle of the night. But Barnes? Shucks, he's just putting on an act. And as long as anyone listens he'll woof and growl 'til he foams at the mouth. You heard him, he thinks he's a militant leader, so having an audience who couldn't escape he felt free to bass at the law and badmouth us strangers. That's what was happening, and if you two hadn't stopped me I'd have taught him a lesson."

"He needs one," the detective said, "but I had enough on my hands without you adding to it. What happened, did you two have a hassle with him on some other occasion?"

"Why, no," Hickman said, "this is the first time we've ever seen the man."

"And you've never been on these premises before?"

"Never!"

"And how about you?"

"Neither of us," Wilhite said, "and that's the truth."

"Then why..."

"Listen, Officer," Hickman said, "as I tried to tell you out in the hall, Aubrey McMillen is the brother of one of our members and..."

"... Members? Members of *what?*"

"Of our *church,* our congregation...."

"Are you telling me that you two are actually *preachers?*"

"Now let's get this straight," Hickman said, "as leaders of our church we work together, but *officially* my friend here is a deacon and I'm a minister. Which means that he assists me in everything from conducting sacred services to sharing the burden of seeing to the needs of our members."

"Very well," the detective said, "but my chief wants to know your personal relationship with this fellow McMillen."

"Good! And since we can save time by our telling him directly, where is he?"

"He's here on the scene, but since he's having trouble getting a fix on exactly what happened here tonight it's best that we don't disturb him."

"I see," Hickman said, "but no matter what happened he'll discover that we had nothing to do with it! And all we know is that we came here on behalf of one of our members who's terminally ill."

"And who would that be?"

"McMillen's sister, Mrs. Caroline Prothoroe. And since he's her only survivor she wants to see him before it's too late. That's why we came here hoping to persuade McMillen to see her while she's still alive."

"That sounds reasonable," the detective said, "but why did you pick this time of night?"

"Simply because we thought it would give us the best chance at catching McMillen at home."

Studying his face as though weighing his answer the detective removed a notebook and pen from inside his jacket.

"Reverend," he said, "give me your name and address."

"My name is Alonzo Z. Hickman, and I live with Deacon Wilhite and his wife at number —— —— Street, Waycross, Georgia."

"What does the 'Z' stand for?"

"For 'Zuber.' My mother's people were Zubers. . . ."

"And is preaching your full-time profession?"

"Yes, sir, preaching and performing the duties that go with my ministry. Such as coming here in the middle of the night on behalf of one of our oldest and most respected members."

"And that's your only reason for entering these premises?"

"No, not altogether. Because I also wanted to have a talk with a man I haven't seen for years."

"I see," the detective said as he wrote in his notebook and turned to face Wilhite.

"And your name?"

"Primus Davidson Wilhite."

"First born and son Number One, eh? And you came here with Doctor Hickman as a favor for McMillen's sister?"

"Yes, sir, and she well deserves it."

"Very well. But now, Doctor Hickman, I'll have to point out an inconsistency in what you've told me. Because while *you* say that you've never visited this house before, that hysterical woman out there seems to have known you. Can you explain that inconsistency?"

"I can't, but maybe it's because preachers have a certain look about them—with or without the collar. She might have guessed it, or heard me preach on some occasion."

"Heard you where?"

"I wouldn't know. Being evangelists, Deacon Wilhite and I do quite a bit of traveling."

"But you've never seen *her* before?"

"No, sir, not that I recall."

"And you, Deacon?"

"No, sir, before tonight I've never laid eyes on the woman. But I can tell you this: If I've ever seen a woman who's high-tensioned nervous she's one of the worst. And when a woman in her condition gets excited she's liable to see preachers and policemen *everywhere*. And the sad thing about it is that she's apt to confuse either one with some boyfriend she had, or *thinks* she had, or *wishes* she'd had—you heard that business about her having a bridegroom! That type of nervousness can cause a woman to see things which normal folks wouldn't even imagine. She's like a time bomb just waiting for something to explode her, so maybe something you said got her going...."

"Oh, no," the detective said, "I was only following procedures. But when I ordered them to clear the hall she got upset. Then you two showed up and she *really* got raving. I tell you, believe it or not, these days there's at least *one* screwball in every crowd, and with Barnes on the scene I've had the bad luck of dealing with *two*! But tell me, Reverend, how long have you known this fellow McMillen?"

"Since he was a boy," Hickman said, "but it's been years since I've seen him."

"It's the same with me," Wilhite added, "we both knew him as a boy, but when he reached his twenties he took off for Kentucky. And after a few years or so he stopped coming home, even for visits. Back in those days he was following the horses."

"Horses?"

"Racehorses," Wilhite said. "He worked around the racetracks."

"Now that's interesting," the detective said. "What was he doing?"

"I can remember when it was exercising and grooming," Hickman said. "Aubrey *loved* horses—but where do you have him? We'd like to give him his poor sister's message and get out of here."

Turning, the detective pointed to the tall double doors at the end of the room, "He's in there, being questioned."

"Is he under arrest?"

"If not by now, he's well on his way."

"And what are the charges?"

"That's depends on the chief, but it could be anything from bootlegging to something far more serious."

"Like what?"

"That's up to the chief, but I'd bet on homicide...."

"*Homicide!* So who did he kill—don't tell me it was his employer, his friend...."

"I'm afraid so, but that's not unusual. Homicide victims usually turn out to be close friends of the culprit, or members of his or her family."

Shaking his head, Hickman turned.

"Wilhite, does that sound believable, McMillen a *murderer*?"

"Listen, Reverend," the detective said with a burst of emotion, "these days there's *nothing* so outrageous that it can't be believed! Not when you see life from my perspective! Just last week, right here in Washington, a Southern congressman—who should damn well have known better—violated everything he holds sacred by turning up in a colored whorehouse where he gets himself beaten to a pulp, robbed of two thousand dollars, and thrown into the street—and I mean naked as a jaybird!"

"What!"

"You see? It sounds improbable, but it happened! Evidently on an earlier visit he rubbed one of the girls the wrong way and she complained to the madam that she'd been sexually molested. So this time the madam had a gang of pimps waiting, and once the honorable gent got stripped for action they broke into the room and gave him one hell of a whipping."

"They actually *whipped* him?"

"That's right! They made a premeditated attack on a United States *congressman* with rawhide whips!"

"What do you mean by premeditated?" Wilhite said.

"Planned in advance!"

"Oh, I know the meaning of the word," Wilhite said, "but I don't see..."

"Hell," the detective said, "it *had* to be! The whips were so new that they still had Kentucky sales tags glued to the handles!"

"Now I've never heard *everything*," Hickman said. "But it sounds as though he ran into some fellows who were making an act of personal revenge look like a new form of political protest. Which is most unusual, even for pimps...."

"Unusual? Not with fellows like Barnes politicizing everything from assault and battery to sleeping in doorways!"

"Maybe so," Hickman said, "but if a thing like that can happen in *Washington*, this country must be changing faster than I thought."

"And for the worse," the detective said. "Even the kids are losing respect for the law. Last week I picked up a ten-year-old *white* runaway and she came at me with a knife—and a *switchblade* at that! And only a few weeks earlier I had to arrest the teenage son of one of the District's wealthiest families for attempted rape of his *mother*! Which is incest! So don't tell *me* that there's anything unbelievable about a Neg... about... about a black bootlegger murdering his friend!"

Studying the detective's flushed face, Hickman leaned forward and frowned with the implications of what the white man had said, started to say, and left *unsaid* echoing in his mind.

"So you see, Reverend," the detective said, "you men of the cloth might know all about the human *soul*, but when it comes to what's happening in the area of *crime*, those of us who have to deal with it daily are much better informed. And by the way, if you ever think of reporting me for what I'm saying, my name is Morrison. Detective Morrison."

"I get your point," Hickman said, "but am I to take it that you're convinced that McMillen actually took his friend's life?"

"That's exactly how it shapes up for me."

"Then his trouble is *tripled*...."

"And what does that mean?"

"That in taking a man's life he's also lost a friend, and when the news reaches his sister it'll probably destroy her...."

"Well, at least you appreciate his predicament. Would either of you mind telling me if he had someone phone you to get over here?"

"Now wait," Hickman said. "Why would he do that?"

"To have you advise him... get him a lawyer...."

"But how could he? The man doesn't even know we're in Washington."

"By now he does, because he's been told of your being here on the premises. Still, he could have known that already. So how about you, Deacon?"

"Did somebody call me? Of course not!"

"There's your answer," Hickman said. "No one called either of us. So now, after coming here hoping to persuade McMillen to visit his sister, it looks like we'll have to find him a lawyer."

"He'll need one," Morrison said, and as the sound of loud voices arose in the hall he headed away.

"I've had enough of this," he called. "You two stay put and I'll be with you in a second."

"A.Z.," Wilhite said, "the deeper we sink in this mess the stronger it stinks! And Morrison probably stirred it up by trying to impress those Washington Negroes with his whiteness instead of using the authority that comes with his badge!"

"Whatever it was," Hickman said, "Barnes' big mouth or their being upset over what might be happening to McMillen and his boss. Either way, that's one white man who's being educated in what it's like to deal with our folks when we're truly upset and angry."

"Yes, A.Z., and he deserved it for bossing folks around and using slavery-time psychology with his Northern accent. And *then* he has the nerve to try intimidating a couple of old-timers like us with his jive talk! How long, A.Z., how *long* will it take white folks to accept the fact that we're just as American and contentious, as them?"

"As of now, Wilhite my friend, we'll have to leave that to heaven. But I'll say this: That act he pulled in the hall was so disgusting that for a second I had trouble deciding whether to laugh, cry, or get myself arrested for kicking his butt. But then, after he got us in here the poor man surprised me by sounding more intelligent—so maybe it's simply a matter of numbers. Having to deal with that many upset Negroes all by himself probably made him feel threatened. While in here and alone with only the two of us he felt more secure. Even so, there's something he's not telling us...."

"Like what?"

"Like his reason for thinking that McMillen would kill anyone, much less his friend."

"Right! And that *bootlegging* business. That new lady friend of yours out there denies knowing anything about it, but the way I see it that woman's either drunk or out of her mind—where on earth did she come up with such a cockeyed wig?"

"Shame on you, Deacon, you're forgetting your charity! How would *you* look if somebody roused you out of bed in the middle of the night? Besides, this place *does* smell like a still and we've been breathing the same liquored-up air that she has. And as far as her tale about losing babies goes, remember that we flew here chasing after a mixed-up dream of our *own....*"

Hearing the slam of the door followed by the sound of bumping and cursing, Hickman turned to see Detective Morrison hurrying toward them with his face red and taut with anger.

"Detective Morrison," he said, "it's getting on toward morning, so since we have little time in Washington and many things to do while we're here, couldn't you ask your chief to question us now and let us get some sleep? We'd appreciate it...." "Not now," Morrison snapped as he headed for the room behind them. "I'll be with you in a minute."

"A.Z.," Wilhite said, "it looks as though Barnes has finally got that white man up a tree, and now..."

But before Wilhite could finish Morrison called through the slightly cracked door, "Doctor Hickman, do I have it correct that the message you have is from a Mrs. Caroline Prothoroe?"

"Yes, Officer, that's right."

"And when did you see her last?"

"Two days ago," he said, moving forward. "Just before our group left home for Washington."

"*Group?* What group?"

"The members of our congregation who made the trip with us."

"And how many would that be?"

"Forty-four, including myself and Deacon Wilhite."

"And where are they now?"

"Getting some rest at the Hotel Longview—at least I hope so, considering all we've planned for tomorrow."

Suddenly Morrison swung the door a bit wider.

"And are you saying that all of you are stopping at the *Longview?*"

"That's right, Officer, all forty-four."

And amused by the note of white surprise in Morrison's voice he turned to Wilhite and winked as he added, "With such an unusual opportunity finally open to folks like us, how could we resist it?"

But now, turning back to gauge the effect of his needling, he saw Morrison writing with his notebook pressed high against the door's inner frame; and taking the opportunity of observing McMillen being given the third degree by a ring of white detectives, he peered past Morrison's shoulder and found himself looking at the face of an elderly brown-skinned man who stared angrily in his direction.

Glaring from a high, throne-like position, the man sat facing the door with his head thrown back and chin thrust forward as though shouting a protest at his intrusion. But as he strained to hear what the man was shouting there was only the scratching of Morrison's pen. And with an involuntary step forward he saw in a flash that the old man's torso protruded from the upper section of a decayed wooden coffin with his shoulder pressing the faded silk lining of its wide-open lid. And in noting the regal posture with which the man was sitting he snatched off his hat in a spontaneous gesture of respect for the dead....

But even as his mind recorded the imperious thrust of the old man's chin, his striped ascot tie, and the black braided lapels of his gray morning coat, he was shocked to see two gnarled, work-worn hands resting on the closed lower section of the coffin that were clinching the stem of a tall crystal glass and the neck of a half-empty bottle of Jack Daniel's whiskey!

And with the eerie juxtaposition of the coffin, the corpse, and the hands grasping whiskey awhirl in his mind, it was as though he were listening to a symphonic orchestra that had leaped without warning from a solemn requiem to a bebopping frenzy. And as he struggled to hold on to his sanity by trying to account for the man's elevated position, he realized with a start that the worm-eaten coffin rested high on a table, on the forward edge of which he saw a tray piled high with soul food: cornbread, baked yams, serving dishes filled with boiled black-eyed peas, fatback, and rice. Yes, it was hopping John! And in struggling to reconcile the nightmarish juxtaposition of corpse, whiskey, and the funeral-feast food of his Southern tradition he saw that the floor underneath was strewn with yellow-back banknotes, crumpled documents, and life-insurance policies. And suddenly recalling that white detectives were somewhere in the room, his bewilderment flared to anger.

Yet even as he willed to whirl and scan the shadows for a rational answer, his agitated eyes were stubbornly probing the coffin, table, and paper-strewn floor for the one missing detail which would reconcile the scene's mounting discord with reality. And although thwarted in finding that missing detail, he was certain that it would be no more unusual than a postage stamp, dollar bill, or birth certificate; and therefore so common to his everyday experience that even its sign, symbol, or echo in memory would be enough to exorcise the outrageous mockery of solemn ritual with which the scene was mocking and punishing his sense of reality.

Then as he stared from the paper-littered floor to the glowering corpse, its dilapidated coffin underwent an abrupt metamorphosis by suddenly taking the form of a wave-battered boat at which he was staring through the transparent pages of a huge open Bible. And with its airy pages of Scripture fluttering above the old man's head, it was as though he, Hickman, had summoned them up out of his desperate effort to provide soul-saving sails for a sailor atoss in turbulent seas. Then in a flash the vision had vanished, leaving him restored to that complex sense of reality which his life, both worldly and spiritual, had conditioned him not only to perceive but accept as the ever-unpredictable embodiment of all that was blues-like, enigmatic, and grave in human experience.

And now, surging with a mixture of terror and laughter, he thought, *Hickman, you'll probably never get at the secret that binds this pitiful mess together, but it has to involve some preposterous but soul-staking act of human frustration. See for yourself: There sits the man in his worm-eaten coffin while grasping those alcoholic spirits to ease the terror of his worldly departure. And there underneath lies his neglected cash and his death-canceled life-insurance policies. He even remembered to provide the traditional feast of hopping John and yams to be enjoyed by the friends he would soon leave behind him—And yet, being human and frail, he forgets his soul-saving Bible—good Lord! What a confounding parable of our worldly condition! But then, how else could we Negroes deal with life's hardships and stresses except with tears, prayers, and soul-easing laughter?*

And now, calmed by his Bible-and-blues-nurtured sense of life's birth-to-death cycling, he took a deep breath of the whiskey-laden air and realized that he might have been made the butt of a ghoulish joke being played by white detectives who were probably looking on from the shadows while cracking their sides in suppressing their laughter.

If so, he thought, as he stared at spots of dampness on the old man's sleeves, *they have no idea of how often even Negro preachers have to face the dregs of life's pain and squalor in doing their best when dealing with suffering.* And hearing someone approaching behind him, he waited for the next ghastly move in the gruesome game.

"Move in, Doctor," a calm voice said, "then take a closer look and tell me if you recognize that man."

Turning, he saw a blond, heavy-set white man of his own height and build who wore a blue sport shirt, rumpled seersucker jacket, and a tan summer hat. And as the man regarded him out of watery blue eyes, he saw a gold badge pinned to his left lapel, and beneath it a black plastic bar embossed with the words "Lt. Jeffrey Tillman."

"No, sir, I don't," he said.

And carefully avoiding scattered banknotes, documents, and a framed set of army discharge papers which lay among them, he moved toward the man in the coffin.

"No, sir, I've never seen this man before—but what happened, was it a stroke or heart attack?"

"As of now," the large man said, "all we know for certain is that he's dead as a doornail."

"But why is he sitting there like he changed his mind about dying in the midst of his funeral?"

"Now that's a good question," the white man said with a nod, "and if we come up with the answer it'll save me and the District a lot of time and expense...."

"That's right, Reverend," a new voice called from the shadows, "and a hell of a lot of trouble. As you can see, your friend there climbed pretty dam high for such an *old* guy—but then, not having the good Finnian luck of old Timothy the in-again-out-again Finnegan, he blew it. Even getting splashed with whiskey wasn't enough to save him. So now," the voice added with a mock sigh of sadness, "you'll never see your friend again—at least not *awake* again."

Offended by the lilting accent and self-satisfied tone of the new speaker's voice, he looked past the blond detective to see a younger man who looked back with a smirk on his freckled, college boy's face.

Finnegan, he thought. *With a dead man sitting here in a coffin this young clown comes up with a joke from an old Irish ballad I used to riff on my trombone back in my days in vaudeville? May the Lord forgive his wise-cracking soul!*

And turning from the joker with a snort of disgust he looked from the lieutenant to the man in the coffin.

"But Officer Tillman," he said, "I can see that he's dead, but why did he climb in there in the first place?"

"That I don't know," Tillman said, "but let's say that whatever his motive he turned out to be a bit previous."

Hearing the word "previous," Hickman stared, wondering if he were hearing more of a tasteless joke. But no, Tillman's face appeared to be grave and serious.

"*Previous,*" he said, "are you telling me that he climbed in there *before* he died?"

"Yes—or before his friend did him in."

And suddenly giving the shadows beyond the coffin a sweep of his eyes he thought, McMillen! I forgot all about McMillen!

"But what was he doing in there in the first place?"

"That's exactly what we're trying to determine. But as of now the one thing we *do* know is that they'd been drinking—the evidence is there in his hands. Are you *sure* you don't know him?"

"No, sir, I've never even *seen* him before. Who is he?"

"He's Jessie Rockmore, the owner of this cockeyed building. Did Aubrey McMillen ever mention him to you?"

"No, sir. The first time I ever heard that name was out in the hall. And as I told Detective Morrison, it's been thirty years or more since I had personal contact with McMillen.... But this poor man—can't we get him down from there, or at least stretch him out? No matter what happened it's disrespectful to leave *any* man's corpse in that position. And by the way, have you gotten in touch with his minister?"

"No, Reverend, nor with anyone else," the detective said. "All that has to wait until the medical examiner has a look at him."

"I see, but I hope it's soon, because leaving him in that condition is most *un-*

Christian. And now that I think of it, what about Aubrey McMillen? I was told he was here being questioned...."

"Take it easy, Reverend," the detective said, "I was just coming to that."

Then, moving toward the coffin, Tillman stopped beside a high-backed, slip-covered chair that faced the coffin and reached down.

"All right, fellow," he said, "turn around and let the Reverend here have a look at you. No! Don't try to stand, you might not make it. Just look around—and don't touch that table!"

And with the detective stepping aside he saw a man's blue-sheathed arm reaching around the high back of the chair. Then came a face that lolled as its chin came to rest on the chair's slip-covered top, and as the bleary eyes focused upward he was looking at an older but easily recognizable Aubrey McMillen.

"Hickman?" Aubrey said. "Are you really *A. Z.* Hickman, the slide-trombone man?"

"Yes, Aubrey," he said, "I am. I've changed a bit but it's been quite a long time since you've seen me...."

"Well, I'll be damn," McMillen said, "they been telling me you were out there! But hell, I took it for some more of their jive! But look here, let's get this straight: How come they called you Doctor? Now me, I been drinking, but hearing something like that is enough to confuse even Einstein and George Washington Carver! Because, hell, man, the Hickman *I* used to know was a gut-bucket *bluesman!* You mean to tell me the white folks done up and made you a Ph.D. of *gut-bucket* music?"

"Not quite, Aubrey," he said with a grin, "but as you know, even bluesmen can change. So I've been a minister for a long time now and I'm surprised that you haven't heard it."

"Well, I'll be damn!"

"I know," he said, "it's a strange turn for me, but believe it or not, today I'm a minister."

And as Aubrey's eyes blurred and returned to focus he was met with a pained expression.

"Now why would a man like you go and do a thing like that," Aubrey said, "especially when he was such a hell of a *fine* musicianer?"

"Aubrey, I was 'called,' you understand the meaning of being called, don't you?"

"Yeah—maybe... I guess so, now that I remember your daddy's being a preacher. But for such a fine *bluesman* as you to turn into one? Hell, Hickman, that's almost as bad as going on drugs or passing for some kind of African—which don't make sense, at least not to me. Still, a thing like that's a man's personal business—but you, *Hickman,* a *preacher?* It's hard to believe. It really is, so let it be. But with you gone religious I guess ain't no point in my offering you a drink—even for old times' sake?"

"No, but thank you, Aubrey. I gave up drinking long ago."

"Okay, 'cause I don't mean to insult you, but if it makes any difference this stuff ain't bootleg, no matter what they been telling you. It's *bonded*! We had us whole cases of one-hundred-percent, pure-dee bonded—which is what Mister Jessie ordered. And although a few bottles got busted there's still plenty left. What's more, I bought it at the *liquor* store. So don't let these white folks sell you some bull about me being a bootlegger."

"I believe you, Aubrey."

"And you can bet on it. But look, Hickman, these police say you brought me a message from Carrie—how's she doing?"

"Well, Aubrey, it's like this—and I'm sorry to be a bearer of sad tidings—she's as well as could be expected of someone her age, but now she's nearing the end. That's why she asked me to come here to persuade you to come home and see her before it's too late. Won't you please try and do that for your sister?"

Suddenly reaching for the table on which the dead man sat, McMillen attempted to stand, missed it, and tumbled back into the chair with a belch and a gurgle.

"And I mean to do it, I swear," he said, "I'ma start packing just as soon as I can get these officers to understand that I wouldn't harm *anybody*, much less a close friend like Mister Jessie."

"I know," Hickman said, "I know..."

"Naw, you don't, 'cause there ain't many like him to be known. But the man was a prince. A *prince*! You dig what I mean but these smart-ass police don't know a damn thing about his kind of colored man—and don't *want* to! Because after my telling them they still won't believe me. That's right! Just because I'm black and a little woozy from drinking all that fine bourbon they think I'm lying. Which goes to prove they don't know any more about a man like me than they know about Mister Jessie. But hell, Hickman, as you damn well know from the old days, I'm one hell of a *complicated* man...."

"Yes," Hickman said, "I remember."

"Sho, *you* do, but these police act like some of these ole dicty D.C. Negroes who see me as no more than an ignunt clown. Yeah, but unlike most of them *I've* been around, and around, and *around*! Oh, yes! And like that cat you used to sing about: I've wrassled me some bears and outfoxed me some hounds, and done heard me some sweet-talk from some mellow high-browns—but hell, you been knowing about me for *years*. So do me a favor: Tell these police about the kind of folks I come from. 'Cause as you know I'm out of some very fine people. *Honest* people, *respectable* people like Carrie. That's why I wouldn't even *think* of disgracing them by doing harm to Mister Jessie—and I *didn't*! That's right, Hickman, nobody did ... less'n it was the sight of that crazy white man...."

"*White* man! *What* white man?"

"The one who busted in here raising hell about buying back some kinda damn coffin! That's right, man! And a white one at that! Done up and color-segregated the goddamn *coffins*! Then the crazy dude claims that Mister Jessie bought it from somebody on one of his business trips down South. But then, when the sucker sees Mister Jessie sitting up there in that thing that's been stored in the basement for years he looks like he's seeing a ghost! It wasn't enough for Mister Jessie to be sitting in that beat-up thing which I warned him would bring us bad luck—oh, no! But then, all of a sudden, here comes this big-shot-looking white dude yelling about his having a *white* one!"

"And Hickman," Aubrey said with a weary wave of his hand, "that's the honest-to-God *truth*! Everything was going fine until that white dude showed up...."

"Showed up from *where*? And who let him in?"

"Hell, I don't know, but when I look up he's in here causing trouble! Hickman, we were just having a little party to celebrate Mister Jessie's birthday, when all of a sudden this white dude is in here raving. And before I know anything that crazy white gal..."

"What! Do you mean that you had..."

"... Oh, no! Not me, she was strictly Mister *Jessie's* idea. So get that straight! And when that fool gal starts doing her funky number I..."

"Yes," he said, "yes?"

But before Aubrey could answer, Tillman reached between them and swung him around to face the coffin.

"Reveren'," Tillman said, "that'll be enough for now, because as you can see he's getting overexcited again. So now we'll take a break and continue after he's calmer."

"But, Officer, I'd like to hear the rest of it—especially about this *woman* he mentioned. What happened to her?"

"Now listen, Reverend," the detective said with a sudden note of irritation, "you're getting into *police* business, so let it lay! And since I'm convinced that you and your deacon had nothing to do with this matter you're both free to return to your hotel. Just leave word as to where you can be reached in case we need you...."

"McVey," he said, turning abruptly to the freckled-faced detective, "go along and see that nobody stops them as they leave the building. That's an order."

So, Hickman thought, some things haven't changed: Just mention a *white* woman and the law slams the door.

And suddenly struck by the comic undertones that sounded in Aubrey's account of a white man invading a black American's disorderly house in a search for his coffin, he surged with amusement. Had it actually happened, or was it an example of Aubrey's sly skill in outfoxing the hounds by playing the dozens? Anyway, the whole thing's too wild for that man to have been our boy—No!

And now, watching Aubrey eyeing Tillman's restraining hand with a look of disgust, he turned to leave.

"Thanks, Officer," he said, "I'm much obliged. And for what it's worth I believe Aubrey's telling the truth. Because given the general disorder around us, how could *anyone* make up such a story?"

"Reverend," a voice called from the shadows, "didn't I advise you to stick to heaven and let *us* decide what's true or false in the area of crime?"

"Yes, Detective Morrison, I remember," he said, "but while you keep trying to get at the truth and can't believe what McMillen has told you, even an unworldly preacher like me knows that getting at the truth can depend upon asking the right party the right questions. So maybe if you forget your theory about McMillen being a bootlegger and ask his friend up there in the coffin the meaning of that cornbread, those yams, and his black-eyed peas and rice and you might get your answer."

"Thanks for the brilliant advice," Detective Tillman said. "Now get the hell out of here!"

"So long, Aubrey," he called. "I'll get in touch with you as soon as possible. Just keep telling the truth and you'll be all right."

"Come on, you," McVey said, "let's move it."

"I'm with you," Hickman said. And with a final look at the man in the coffin he put the scene behind him and moved through the shadows and focused his mind on the day ahead and the problem of seeing the Senator.

But now, having followed McVey to a point near the door, he was brought to a halt by the sight of a woman who lay stretched on her back in a lounging chair. And as he watched her white skin and features emerge from the shadows he thought, *So here's the woman that caused Tillman to shut Aubrey's mouth!*

Apparently asleep, with a bare arm curving above her head, the woman lay beneath a blue policeman's jacket that stretched from the tip of her chin to the cleft of her thighs. And as he gazed at the odd fringe of yellow paper that protruded beneath the end of the jacket he realized with a start that the woman's silk panties were adorned with depreciated twenty-dollar bills like those on the floor near Jessie Rockmore's coffin. And as he looked back to the woman's face he felt a jerk on his arm.

"Let's move it," McVey shouted, "and I mean now!"

"All right," he said, "all right!" But not yet. For at the sound of his voice the blue-shadowed eyes popped open and flashed from his face to McVey's—and he was watching the motion of the woman's hand as it reached for the jacket and drew it aside with a stripteaser's gesture—and except for its flip-tail skirt and high-heeled shoes he was staring at a female form which was completely bare.

But what better costume, he thought, for somebody performing a "funky number." And with McMillen's term echoing in his ear he saw the woman smile and extend her manicured hands in his direction.

Instantly insulted and alarmed by a white female's signifying play upon taboos that could trigger many white men to violence, he snatched his arm from McVey's grasp as the woman spun to her right and attempted to stand. And now, rocking and reeling against the counter-swinging of her bulging breasts, she kicked the jacket aside and turned to McVey with a challenging smile. Whereupon, sensing an eruption of movement, he whirled to see McVey reaching down and shooting erect with the abandoned jacket stretched in his hands; and as the young detective sprang forward with a grimace of distaste the scene became a distorted version of a chapter from Genesis, and he was transfixed by fleeting images of Shem and Japheth hurtling backwards with a billowing blanket between them. And with details of the post-Deluge story flooding his mind, he realized that neither the likes of wine-drunk Noah nor the son who had witnessed his nakedness were anywhere to be seen, heard the woman explode with obscenities, and saw McVey's improvised blanket resume its mundane form as it flew like a fisherman's net toward the woman's red head.

And as he listened for Tillman to take over, he saw McVey closing on the woman with the sleeves of the jacket flapping like the wings of a hawklike bird. He thought, *Hickman, as one of his so-called sons you've always questioned Ham's being punished for looking too hard at his father's weakness, but drunk or sober this woman's no Noah, and McVey's no Shem or Japheth—so how is it that way late, and here in this crazy Washington house of all places, you're being forced to suffer Ham's sin and his fate once again?*

And as he restrained a sudden impulse to grab the jacket and allow the woman to deal with her own bawdy nakedness, he was amazed to see her snatch McVey to her breasts and assail his crotch with a fierce bump-and-grind.

Yes, he thought, *but that's far too simple for a final answer. So much for Noah, so much for Ham, and so much for Ham's son, Hickman.* And collapsing with laughter he heard a disgusted Tillman roaring behind him, "McVey, handcuff that strumpet and get that goddamn preacher out of here—and I mean NOW!"

"Right," McVey called, "right!"

But as he laughed and watched McVey struggling to break free of the woman's embrace she glared at him over the detective's shoulder.

"That's it, Dad," she called, "laugh your chitt'lin'-eating head off if you think it's so funny, but this is one frigging gig that's been *tra—uuul-ly* maaad!"

At which, cursing and breaking her hold with a thrust of his shoulder, McVey leaned forward, and in raising the jacket received a backhanded slap across the bridge of his nose as the woman screamed, "Get your hands off me, you sonofabitch!"

And as McVey paused and stood shaking his head, she snatched at the jacket and screamed, "That's right, Dad, the whole frigging deal has been mad as a hatter! We were having . . . one . . . wow of a time . . . just the three of us . . . spreading a little joy . . . as you boot boys say . . ."

Bump!

"Take that, you little bastard!—I say, stop it, you clown!—But then some bigshot *coffin*-freak shows up—how about that!—and before this ole gal could yell hooray the hell for Jackie Robinson he's gone and a gang of creeps like sonny here come barging in! And then, Daddy-O, all *hell* broke loose! And with the Boots and cops going at it like the Dodgers and Giants, the whole frigging scene turned into a saaud, *saaaauud* maaud!"

And now, giving McVey a stiff-arm thrust to his chest, she threw up her arms and fell backwards into the chair; from where, giving a flaunting flip of her bank-note skirt, she exploded with laughter.

And now, slamming her face with the policeman's jacket, McVey whirled and seized his arm. And gasping with laughter he was being rushed through the narrow aisle of the room, banging against objects that creaked and tilted as McVey propelled him into the door that led to the vestibule; where, now, he could see Wilhite looming closer with his mouth agape. Then they were there and McVey wheeling Wilhite around and snatching open the door to the vestibule—and as cross-eyed little Maud screamed from the stairs, "Wait, darling, wait," they were both being rushed through the jam of wide-eyed tenants, past the grandfather's clock, and onto the steps—where, relieving himself of an encyclopedic explosion of anti-Negro profanity, McVey released their arms and rushed back into the hall, which was now roaring with the shouting of angry Negroes.

"A.Z.," Wilhite said as he gasped for breath and stared at the door, "what was *that* all about? What happened in there?"

"Later, Wilhite, because it will take a whole *book* to tell you—but I found her!"

"Found *who?*"

"The *woman*! Those detectives had me playing what my young friend Millsap used to call the American game of *cherchez la femme*. I thought little Sister Maud was mistaken about a woman being in on this thing, but at the last minute I *found* her!"

"Wait, man; wait! What woman are you raving about?"

"The one those folks said McMillen and his boss were entertaining! The *white* woman!"

"What!"

"Yes! And now it seems that most of what they said about what's been happening in this crazy place is true!"

"Are you telling me that there's really a . . ."

"Wilhite, didn't I just tell you that I *saw* her? Those detectives had her stashed in the shadows, but she's there—I swear. And I mean sloppy drunk, half-naked, and so foul-mouthed and disorderly that she even amazed an old sinner like me!"

"Good Lord! And what about McMillen?"

"Half-drunk and being questioned, but physically unharmed—at least as far as I could see. Which appears to be true, because while those white detectives are treating him like a clown he's easing them into the dozens and getting away with it."

"Well, at least that rascal hasn't changed—but what about his boss?"

"Wilhite, the poor man is done with this world...."

"... Dead?"

"Dead? Yes! But *murdered*? I doubt it. Because—now listen to this—he's sitting up on a table looking like a king holding court in a worm-eaten *coffin!*"

"A coffin? Come *on!*"

"Yes! And dressed in a morning coat and ascot tie! Man, let's get ourselves back to the Longview before we *both* lose our minds!"

"I'm with you," Wilhite said. "Let's get out of here!"

And with a quick look at the glowing 369 on the fanlight he shook his head and hurried away.

EDITORS' NOTE TO "HICKMAN IN GEORGIA & OKLAHOMA"

"HICKMAN IN GEORGIA & Oklahoma" consists of two sets of files that Ellison gave their own distinct tables of contents. Ellison appears almost certainly to have intended the sections to follow one another. The evidence for this is both narrative and textual. The Georgia sequence ends with Hickman leaving for the airport, while the Oklahoma sequence begins with him landing in Oklahoma City. Further corroborating the connection, Ellison's archive at the Library of Congress includes a printout with continuous pagination running from the last Georgia file to the first Oklahoma file. To respect their close connection, we have elected to treat them as a single sequence. Together they constitute the most sustained narrative from the last decade of Ellison's life.

This sequence begins with Hickman at his home in Waycross, Georgia, going through a stack of mail. Among the letters is one from Janey Glover, an old friend from Oklahoma for whom he'd long harbored an infatuation and who, we later find, is connected both with Sunraider and Sunraider's estranged son and would-be assassin, Severen—whom Janey had raised from infancy much as Hickman had Bliss. The sight of her name on the envelope sparks in Hickman a series of reveries, and inspires him to return to a thirty-year-old report from a man named Walker Millsap whom he had enlisted to find the young man Bliss. When he gets around to opening the letter, he discovers that Janey is in great emotional distress, the precise cause of which is unclear, but somehow related to the one she calls Hickman's "little man": Bliss/Sunraider.

When Hickman arrives in Oklahoma City, he makes a series of visits, including ones to Janey and to a half-Indian, half-black shaman by the name of Love New. The section ends with Hickman visiting a bar called the Cave of the Winds, where he listens to a wild improvised story told by Cliofus, a kind of savant who was raised by Janey alongside Severen.

Oklahoma, the place of Ellison's birth, remained a source of enduring fascination for him throughout the decades of the novel's composition. He imagined Oklahoma as the site of the novel's governing mystery and motivation. In notes likely dating from the early 1950s, when the novel was little more than a notion, he mapped out a three-part structure that would commence with Oklahoma. "The first book is that of the frontier. // The middle book that of the city. // The third book that of the nation." Fragmentary typewritten drafts dating from the 1950s and later place an emphasis upon Oklahoma as the scene of action in ways not found in the Books I and II typescripts. Some of these drafts show McIntyre visiting Oklahoma in the aftermath of Sunraider's assassination seeking clues to unlock the mystery of the violent act. In the computer sequence that follows, Ellison has substituted Hickman for McIntyre and moved events back before the Senator's shooting.

These changes would appear to signal his intention of placing Hickman's visit to Oklahoma first in the narrative sequence to correspond to its temporal order. Yet his notes continually reaffirm his decision to begin the novel in Washington, D.C., with the prologue. This is perhaps the most significant of the textual decisions Ellison left unresolved. Thus, it appears likely that Ellison never composed the textual bridges that would connect D.C. with Georgia and Oklahoma, and both of these sections with the complete McIntyre computer text.

HICKMAN IN GEORGIA & OKLAHOMA

[GEORGIA]

[SISTER]

THE LETTER ARRIVED IN the morning's mail. Hickman was working at his desk facing the window when Sister Wilhite came in with it cradled in her arms.

"Reveren'," she said, "you busy?"

"Yes, ma'am, I am," Hickman said, "I'm right in the middle of something."

Sister Wilhite sniffed. "Middle," she said, "you're always in the middle. That's your middle name...."

"No, ma'am, it's *Zuber*, as you well know."

"Yes, but you know what I mean. You're always in the middle and forever pecking and scratching away on those sermons which you write down one way and then stand up there and preach the way you really feel it. If you would write it the way you *say* it maybe folks would want to read it, but even if they didn't you would surely save a heap of time...."

Hickman dropped his chin to his chest and sighed.

"Sister Corrine," he said, "I'd be so thankful if you'd—"

"All right, all right," Sister Corrine said, "but I won't drop dead. And what's more, I can wait even though some others don't seem to be able."

"Thank you," Hickman said, "and just drop the mail on the table there and I promise you I'll go through it as soon as I'm finished."

Without a word Sister Corrine placed the pile of mail on the table and swept out of the study with the offended dignity of a Bantam pullet.

Hickman stared at the words on his interrupted page, thinking, *Why can't she understand that there's more behind a thing that's said than mere feeling? That it's the conception* behind *what's being said that gives it vibration? It's a good thing she wasn't around when God was making the world, otherwise she'd never have let him get finished. Come to think of it, maybe she was there.... I'll have to ask her....*

He smiled, thinking, *And I'll have my chance because Sister Corrine has something in mind, and it probably has to do with the mail. And with a woman, just as it usually is. . . .*

He had never married, and back during his early career, at a time when husband-hunting and shamelessly adventurous women were a threat to his relations with his congregation, he had thought to protect himself by asking Deacon Wilhite and his wife to share the parsonage. Wilhite was an old friend from his boyhood, and Sister Corrine turned out to be not only an excellent cook and housekeeper, but a mistress of the house who took over such entertainment as was expected of him as a minister. She had been a godsend in many ways, for years ago, before his foster son ran away, she had also provided the woman's touch that was necessary in raising a child. Thus she had won a permanent place in Hickman's affections, and this even though she had come, over the years, to bully him almost as much as she did her husband. Nevertheless, it was a satisfactory arrangement, and before the boy ran away it had given the parsonage much of the warmth of a true family unit. Sometimes, however, he regarded Sister Corrine's bullying as a self-inflicted burden that was made bearable only because of his friendship with Wilhite and her contribution to the success of his early ministry.

When he was assigned to the congregation, certain of its members who knew of his past as a jazz musician had objected. For not only did they consider him unsuitable, but they desired a leader who was married, and preferably one with children. And even though he had a foster son, his lack of a wife had been against him. Some of the most important members had considered it a most crucial issue, in maintaining tradition, certain ceremonial duties and leadership functions connected with the church were the responsibility of its minister's wife.

And even more important, at least to some, was the assumption that marriage automatically afforded a minister a keener insight into the many problems afflicting families. Especially the inevitable contentions that arose between husbands and wives and parents and children. Here at least his background as the son of a well-known minister had been in his favor, but there was a related objection that proved so thorny that it appeared that he would lose his assignment. For while he could feel its presence behind the questions put to him by the head of the board of trustees—a head waiter for the leading hotel—the man seemed to find the subject as delicate to deal with as the unzipped zipper of an important guest, or a bluebottle fly in a carefully prepared vichyssoise. Then it turned out that some of the trustees considered marriage as an indispensable safeguard against a minister's becoming profanely involved with ladies of the congregation. And though most were experienced enough to realize that such a safeguard didn't always work, they felt that it *did* place certain constraints in the way of temptation. Fortunately, what counted most was a minister's ability to move them with the Word beyond the limitations of words, and he passed the test. They had liked his personality and style of delivery well enough to give him a chance, and with Sister Corrine taking over to fulfill the duties of a minister's wife he had earned the respect of the congregation, men and women, married and unwed alike.

[JANEY 3]

WHEN HICKMAN READ THE name and return address on the thickest envelope he paused, weighing it in his hand as he thought, *What on earth is going on with Janey? This thing looks like she's taken off on some kind of writing jag. Just look at all the stamps!* Then, shaking his head, he placed the envelope on his desktop and read rapidly through the rest of his mail.

Ripping the envelopes open with his fingers, he discovered among the bills and solicitations for funds three letters from former members who had moved to the North; the first asking his aid in securing a birth certificate from a small nearby town. *I'll try,* he thought, *but it's probably impossible since at the time they weren't issuing many to Negroes. But I'll see.*

The next was from a former member who had just lost her husband in New Jersey, saying that she expected him to conduct the burial ceremony, and would he see to it that her old family plot was made ready by the time she reached home with her husband's body.

Of course I will, he thought, *and the plot's no problem, because just last week I was out there and noticed that somebody—probably a member of the family—had looked ahead and given it their attention.... Oh, but how time leaps ahead of memory's markers—here I've been remembering her as such a cute little girl and now she's a widow!*

Opening the next letter, he read a few lines and smiled. It was from a couple asking that he conduct the marriage ceremony of their daughter, who had just graduated from college, and informing him that for the occasion members of their widely scattered family would gather for a reunion during which they hoped he would make them welcome and do them the honor of baptizing two of its youngest members.

Hickman smiled, thinking, *Of course I will, and it'll be a pleasure to see what's happened to the old-timers.... Let's see—already there're four family reunions scheduled for late summer and this makes the fifth. So there'll be well over eight hundred natives and their in-laws returning home to the briar patch. I wouldn't miss it for anything. Tempus certainly fugits, and that's no lie. I used to play hooky with that fellow's daddy, and now his engineer son will be bringing his grandkids home to show them where he started from. Couldn't stay in the South, but thank God he still loves our part of it.*

And now, putting the request aside to be answered along with the others, he stared at Janey's thick envelope with his head cocked to the side; then, picking up an old ivory-handled switchblade knife from his desk, he snapped it open, examined its edge, and shook his head with a sense of irony. For although he now used it as a letter opener there was a moment during a robbery attempt when his life and death had swayed and balanced on the point of its razor-sharp blade. Like two locomotives plunging head-on toward a single junction, things might have gone either way but for the Lord's throwing the switch in his favor and allowing him to wrestle it out of the young man's hand. In the struggle his own hand had been cut and in his anger and outrage over someone he'd known since childhood doing such a thing he'd had an impulse to repay him in kind. But in forcing the overgrown boy to explain his action and learning that it was out of a desperate effort to reach his dying father, he had let him go and kept the knife in exchange for railroad fare to Chicago. *Hickman*, he asked himself, *would you have used it? No, not really, but I might have broken his arm. But, thank the Lord, he gave me a way out and this "deadly weapon" was turned into a two-way ticket which took the boy to Chicago, and me safely home with a fine letter opener. Truly, the miraculous thing about miracles is their ability to escape our awareness. So blessed be the knife that binds instead of severing!*

Slitting the envelope, he removed a sheaf of ruled school-tablet paper and gave it a rapid flip-through of his thumb. There were fifteen pages, all covered with Janey's careful schoolgirl's writing; and now, settling back in his desk chair, he began the slow process of reading.

"Dear Alonzo," she began,

> This leaves me well in body but troubled in mind. Because although I have been in pretty good health since we were last in touch there are things taking place out here which have me worried, and I think that they are things you ought to know about. Now it will probably take me a whole week to get them all down on paper, but since my handwriting is still almost as good as it was when I was a young woman I do not think it will take you that long to read my letter. I smile when I write this because anybody who can read those little fly specky music notes like you ought to be able to read *anything*. I surely hope so, as I am going to try and give you the *feel* of things, and since they are speeding up I hope you will give it your full attention. Besides, you will remember that you used to give me the devil because I did not write much in my letters, and said that for folks who knew how to put a pen to paper but did not was a sin. That's right. And you also said that not writing was one of the real reasons that we as a people know so little about what is happening to us after we get scattered from the places where we were born.
>
> Well, when I consider what has happened to some of us I do not know whether you were right or wrong, because it might be better that those we left behind did not know. Because otherwise they might get discouraged. But all right, you wanted me to write, so I

am going to write you the longest letter of my life, and I want you to read it carefully and think about what I'm trying to say. I hope also that you will please forgive this purple ink, which is due to Cliofus. I sent him to the store for some blue and this is what he brought back, but since time is pressing I have to use it. Cliofus says it was all they had, but knowing him like I do I believe that he got it because he knew that I was writing to you. You will remember that he never forgets a thing, even if it is only something he has just heard about. So I think it is his way of signifying and teasing at me. Anyway, I had better get started with my long distant letter.

Remember how it was when you were living out here and folks had a way of running everything into the ground? The white folks did it and so did the Indians. Also the Natives like that old rascal who calls himself Love New, remember him? Anyway, our folks were probably the worst. Folks from other states used to call us wild, and Texas white folks insisted that it was because we did not know our place or anything else, including how to empty a rained-in boot (Smile). They said that giving the Territory statehood was a mistake because it gave us Negroes an inch and we were taking it and stretching it mile by mile. Maybe that is why so many of those thugs and musicians you used to hang around with rushed up here from San Antonio and Dallas. Like a lot of folks from all over the South they knew a good thing when they saw it, so they came up here to run wild. But it would seem that in those days no matter where you came from things out here were just too unorganized, and with all the new freedom to deal with folks had not yet learned how to keep themselves or anything else in reasonable order, therefore they just overdid everything.

And not only the people, because even the weather went to extremes. Sometimes the sun would be shining on one side of the street and the rain falling on the other, all at the same time. It was like there wasn't enough sky and space and earth for any one kind of weather to have its own fair turn. Sometimes we had rain, snow, sleet, hail, and sunshine all coming down together. Therefore the weather itself must have encouraged people to act in the same disorganized fashion. So being that kind of country it attracted that kind of people.

Which you ought to know because, come to think about it, when it came to overdoing things you were Mister A-Number-One. And maybe if you had not been we would have got somewhere together. But oh, no! You *ate* too much, and you *drank* too much, and you *gambled* too much, and danced and played that horn too much. And what's worse and which sorrows me to say, you chased the "chippies" too much. Yes, sir; you went after the young women like a buck-duck after a june bug—especially the draggle tails. And on top of all that, not only did you let them *chase* you, you let them *catch* you! And I mean so easy and so often that it is a wonder that you did not kill your fool self or cause somebody else—man, woman, or green-eyed boyfriend—to get mad enough to do it for you. So praise the good Lord that you finally turned around and got yourself saved!

Now please, Alonzo, don't go swelling up and taking me seriously. I'm joking in order to say that just like back in your time out here things are still ripping and tearing along like they do not know where or when to stop. And my reason for this letter is that recently they have taken what I consider to be a very strange turn. Now it could be that it is only me and the results of my reaching the time of sad good-byes. I say this because hardly a week goes by but there is another old friend passing from the scene. Naturally I hate to see it happening, but I know it is a part of life and has to be. Like they say, we all have to go when the wagon comes, and some day soon it will come for me. So that in itself does not worry me, for I know that we all have a time to die. But what does have me bothered is some of the things that have been showing up in the train of some of these passings. It's not the deaths—which so far have all been due to natural causes—so much as certain signs of unseen things to come which have appeared with them. And before I go any farther, please do not go acting the preacher and start putting me down as superstitious or anything like that. Just remember that if *I* can believe in the water turning into wine and in the raising of the dead—which I surely do, and probably even stronger than you do—*you* can go along with me and consider that sometimes things have strange connections with things to come which are revealed in the form of warnings.

Like recently, when I had this dream of fire—which for me is always a warning dream. In it I saw a big house that was swirling with sparks and filled with smoke, and I mean black smoke and white smoke. And the fire inside was so hot that the glass in the windows was crackling and popping like popcorn, and through the windows I could see the smoke fairly boiling. It was a very big house, a white one, and such as I have never seen in all my waking life. So it must have been the house of a very rich person, and there were a heap of folks in there yelling and screaming and calling on the Lord. And yet with all that yelling and praying I could not see a single fire wagon in the entire dream. Neither were there any policemen or doctors or men in white coats running around trying to get them out. In fact there was nobody else looking on but me. I was by myself and alone, just standing there in a big wide street and feeling that I was being called upon to do something for them, but unable to move. Alonzo, you are a naturally smart man and gifted with vision, so I hope you will think about this dream. Oh, yes; I almost forgot to tell you that back beyond the house and off to one side a little piece I could see a river winding down a hill, and the water was sparkling in the sunshine and rippling along but it was too far away to be of help in the fire. Not even if someone had been there to use it. And on the other side of the river there was some kind of park with statues and some lovely trees. But the main thing I remember is the burning house and the smoke and all those pitiful screams.

Now, even though I finally woke up and realized that it was only a dream, a situation like that is bad enough to worry anybody. So if you want to dismiss it and say that I am just getting old or maybe just jumping at shadows, I can go along with you. But then I must ask, what do you make of what happened soon afterwards?

Only last week come Tuesday I went to see one of my old friends laid to rest, and on the way to the graveyard, which you will remember because except for having so many more folks buried in it is the same we used when you were living out here. Anyway, we were on our way out there when something terrible happened, and I tell you truly that I have never seen anything like it in all my born days.

There were fourteen or fifteen big limousines in the procession and considering how the undertakers try to rush folks into the ground these days they were moving not too fast and not too slow, even though we were already past the city limits and still had the graveside ceremony to go through with. Therefore everybody was still feeling sad about our old friend's passing and thinking on final things. Not a soul was talking, at least not in the car where I was riding, and I could hear the engine and the tires working their way to the graveyard the same as they had so many times before. Yes, and like I have done before. So I was sitting there on one of the little folding seats behind and to the left of the driver, and as we rolled along I was looking into the side mirror and thinking of times that had been and at the same time I was watching a little white child bouncing a big blue ball in a yard along the way and the ball bouncing less and less and the child getting smaller and smaller while the fields and trees kept flowing past like they were part of a different and safer world.

But then, just as the procession started to take a wide curve in the highway, I could see the hearse in which the driver was sitting up straight behind the wheel with his cap tilted on the side of his head, looking a little sporty but in his way almost as dignified as the undertaker sitting there beside him wearing a shiny stovepipe hat. I mention this because off the job this particular driver is known as something of a liquor-head, but get him behind that wheel and he's sober as a judge and on his best dignified behavior. So watching him made me think on how mixed life and folks can be, and how the very blackness of the hearse with its gleam and scrolls and church-style windows together with all those fine limousines strung out behind it can make for a sight that is both fine and grave and yet so awfully sad. And I swear, Alonzo, it was at that very moment that I saw *flames* flare up in the back of that hearse!

For a second or so I think I'm dreaming, but before I can get my thoughts together the rear section of the hearse with the flag-draped coffin and wreaths and flowers is filling up with smoke and flames, and right away I know that it is not a dream. No, sir! Because now the driver is yelling to the undertaker and wrestling the hearse to the side of the road, and the two of them are leaping out and waving like mad for the rest of the cars to stop.

I tell you, the sight of it was a pity and a terror and an ice-cold chill to the heart. There I was, still holding on from bucking back and forth from our driver's slamming on the brakes and hearing the other limousines skidding and banging and bumping to a stop. And then everybody is tumbling out and rushing to the hearse to try to help out. But before we can get close enough to do anything the fire gives out with a roar that freezes eveybody dead in his tracks. And me among them, because I will not lie. That fire goes leaping up so fast and so fierce that all we can do, whether man or woman, young folks or old, is to just stand there on that lonely highway and watch our old friend go up in smoke. Folks are weeping and wailing and wringing their hands, but in the face of that fire all of us are as help-less as newborn babes.

And it isn't that the undertaker and his drivers aren't doing all in their power to get the poor soul's body out of there, no, sir! They're dashing around and spraying stuff out of those red fire extinguish-ers and hitting at where it was shooting out with their caps and coats, but it had about as much effect as spitting into a cyclone. Those flames caught on so swift and got so hot that they wouldn't let the poor men get close enough to even open the rear door. And when one of them manages to break one of the big side windows with his fire extinguisher the flames leap out and catch him so that the others have to tackle him and roll him on the ground to save his life. And too, since it's a kind of windy day, his breaking the glass makes the fire burn even faster.

So for all the poor driver's trouble and pain the next thing we know our old friend is nothing but some smoking ashes. And in another few minutes all that's left of the hearse is just plain junk. That's the sad truth. What's more, it's lucky for us moaners that the undertaker remembers about the gasoline tank in time to warn us to back away from there. Because sure enough, hardly before we could scatter that fire reaches the gas tank and the hearse explodes. Then folks are running and screaming and pieces of glass and patches of burning stuff are whirling all over the road, and it looks like somebody is burning off last year's grass on a windy day. Or maybe firing a field to get it ready for planting a new crop of some kind.

Now, I think you will understand how we all felt over such a thing happening when you remember how in your days out here you musicians used to leave the church and march the body to the graveyard playing dignified and slow, but then after the burial was over and done you all would lift the moaners' spirits by strutting back to town hooraying and sassing the devil. That's when you liked to play such sinful lowdown trash as that "They Picked Poor Robin Clean," and "Oh Didn't He Ramble." Oh, yes, I'm sure that now you are a preacher you will want to deny it, but you played it often enough, and unlike me there were those who liked it.

Well, let me tell you something—after seeing what happened to our friend *nobody* would have been up to any of that kind of old foolishness, even if they were years younger and had the best band in the land to raise their spirits. No, sir! We were numb and dumb and shaken to our very roots. And who wouldn't be, with old Death erupting in the form of fire to claim twice over the blessed and prayed for but still uncommitted dead? And I mean even before the minister could say his Ashes-to-ashes-and-Dust-to-dust!

Anyway, it was a terrible sensation and when it was all over the word spreaded like wild fire and folks are still talking about it—and will be, if I know anything about our people, for years and years to come. Because a thing like that is enough to get even a hardened sinner such as you used to be all shook up, but if you ask me there are some who are by no means shook up enough. So we now have a scandal, with some saying that the fire was an act of God, while others insist that it happened because the Devil was in such a hurry to get his scaly hands on our old friend that he could't even wait 'til after the minister had had his say and the poor man was put six feet under. So as usual the sinful ones are sneering and cracking wise, but the truth is that they are talking like that only because way back before you left town and got your own sinful self saved this poor friend of mine used to bootleg a little Choc beer and whiskey. This is not gossip but the Lord's truth, and I am sure that you would recognize him if I were to call his name, which I will not. I will only say that since those days when you were out here lowlifing like a dirty dog the man reformed and went on to live a fine upstanding life. So it is a sin and a shame that as far as those doing all the talking are concerned it went for nothing. But then they are the kind who never seem able to forgive and forget the other person's transgressions. Which is a sin and a shame and downright hypocritical, because I can well remember a time when some of them that is cracking wise about him was in the joint he used to run every time he opened the door. And I mean in there lapping up his booze like hogs turned loose on a swill barrel, and some on credit. Therefore, Mister Preacher, I ask you, who are they to be scandalizing the poor man's good name? My guess is that while the good Lord forgives, some folks are just too ornery, even in the face of such a terrible warning. That's right, I see it was a warning and even if you do not just keep reading and I'll tell you why.

As I say, things out here are still running toward extremes like in the old days and nothing seems to know when or where to leave off and give us a rest before rushing on to something else. And just when they appear to be quieting down and I think they're getting back to normal, something even worse and more upsetting breaks out. And when it does folks and things that you never thought of having anything to do with one another are revealed as being twisted together like a barrel of rattlesnakes that have had their rattles wrapped in cotton. Then you are shocked to discover that although you couldn't hear it they have been rattling away all the time.

Which is to say that some other things are happening out here that appear to have connections that I cannot figure out. Maybe it just seems that way, but I cannot tell. Now I know that I am too old a hen to be acting like Chicken Little in the storybook, and as you well know I have never been chickenhearted. But yet and still with all that's happened I have taken to keeping an eye peeled on the weather even when it appears to be bright and sunny. You have heard about that cloud that starts out no bigger than a man's fist and then sends houses and buildings crashing down? Well, I have not seen the cloud but I *have* seen a man. And he showed up right after all the other stuff I've told you about. He came out of nowhere and has been going around asking questions and looking up names that have faded from most folks' minds. And what worries me is that some are names from way back yonder when you were out here. Some are names you know and some I had forgot, and still others I never even heard before.

But what worries me even more than the names is the one who keeps bringing them up. This is because he looks a bit like one of my little lost lambs might have grown up to look if he had been brought up Northern and rich. And that is exactly what he lets on that he is, *and* what Cliofus thinks he is. But to tell you the truth, *I* am not sure of anything about him. If he was one of mine it has been too long for my memory, and besides that he is so different in his ways from anyone who I have raised. So at the moment he could be Mister Anybody from Nowhere or Mister Nobody from Anywhere.

And it's not just his color, or the way he dresses and carries hisself. By which I mean to say that he is of a different style from all the others who have lived with me, and is much more educated. Therefore the only thing I can be sure about is that he is out here going from door to door and asking questions. He's even been seen in the barbershops and bars, especially in the one where Cliofus has this sinful job telling stories and saying filthy toasts for the customers. And he is making himself busy stirring up ashes which I feel ought to be left strictly alone. That is why I have this feeling that nothing good can come from what he is doing. You remember that Bessie Smith used to sing a blues about trouble? Well, when it comes to trouble I'm like her, because I've had it all my days. So if this little man is bent on raising a new crop of trouble from some old dead roots it is too late in my life and I cannot use anymore.

Yet what can a person do? It is not the way of trouble to knock politely at your door and say Please, Mam, can I come in? No, sir! You just happen to look from peeling onions or stringing beans and there it is looking you dead in the eye. That is why this little man has me so upset. And it's not that he isn't polite, because he is. He even seems to have a special good feeling for me, but I don't know his intentions and he ain't saying. So I am praying that I am just an old woman who is making one more mountain out of a mole hill and that he will soon settle down and get interested in other things.

Or, which would be even better, that he will go away as quiet as he came. I really wish that he would because whether you think I'm superstitious or not I feel that he has the smell of death about him. That's right, and if he doesn't go away soon I'm afraid that after all these long years that old snake-whip that was lashing out back in you know when is going to start lashing again.

I am serious about this, and you had better take it that way. For no matter how dry and old a dead root might look to the naked eye it ain't necessarily dead. You just let the right kind of rain heat the ground up a bit and when you least expect it will start putting down fresh roots and sending up new shoots, some with thorns. What is more, I have once heard tell of a man who cut off the head of a rattlesnake, a diamondback, and he thought it was dead and the danger past, but as it turned out that head had enough life left in it to bite him. Got him straight through his leather boot and held on. So while I know that you learned long ago that this is a country in which strange and pitiful things can happen and do, I am passing along this information so that you will think long and hard on the little man and the signs and symbols that came before him. Knowing you I do not have to remind you that 2 plus 2 do not always add up to 4. Because sometimes when you look close and consider how they come together they add up to 22. And the same goes for 22 plus 22. Put one on top of the other and they make 44, and if you put them side by side they can add up to thousands. Especially when it comes to paying debts. So in light of such possibilities I am looking carefully at the way the numbers are falling together, and I advise you to do the same.

To repeat, this little man is bothering me and I am calling on you, my dear old friend, to help me add it all up. Not that I aim to burden you with all my fears, because you get enough of that from your congregation. And especially the women. It is just that I feel that even if you do not have any answers it is still something for you to know. Sleeping dogs are awake and beginning to dig around for old bones, and what looks to have been a long lost lamb is back on the scene with horns. I don't know what it all means, but from the way he is acting he don't mean to stay here long once he gets whatever it is he's after. But whether he does or don't I think you ought to know. Therefore I want to stress that his questions are flying and some folks are beginning to try to play like they know the true answers. And naturally they are doing it not because they *know* anything, but because they want to find out what it is this little man is up to that he will not explain. Some even think he is somebody in the oil business who's looking to buy up some leases, which is foolish since it is well known that they quit drilling when the oil ran out years ago. But I guess some of them have seen the expensive way he dresses with his fine clothes and shoes with little silver horse bits on them so they think they smell money. Me, I think they smell something all right and its name is Trouble.

It is ever the same, old friend. Some folks find it hard to mind their own business and therefore like some of these out there they make up lies and don't seem to care what will happen from it or even if somebody gets hurt. So while I don't think that they can really tell the little man anything with teeth in it, and I am sure they cannot, still you never know. Because when a sleeping dog raises up and sticks his nose in the breeze and starts to sniffing around he can sometimes come up with all kinds of information that you didn't even know to be in the wind. That is what I fear, and while it might not mean a thing, only time will tell. Anyway from out here time seems to be stumbling all over itself, and therefore I am doing my Christian duty by letting you know so you can look into it. Then if you think it wise you can drop the word where it can do the most good. Understand? What I mean is that if you can unravel all this which I'm sending you and know the right place to drop it, then drop it. And I mean fast.

Old friend, it has been years since these old eyes have looked upon you in the flesh but I want you to know that I still think about you and our old times long past. This leaves me well and I hope you are in good health and still standing firm in the Spirit. Trust in the Lord!

I remain your sister in Christ,

JANEY

[JANEY.ALZ]

THINKING, *I DON'T LIKE IT, I don't like it at all,* Hickman dropped the letter to his desk and stared between the curtained window into the sunlit morning. *No, sir,* he thought, *I don't; and for the moment I'm not even prepared to ask myself why....*

Through the window the backyard appeared peaceful, but from the street beyond the house he could hear the cries of boys skating back and forth over the concrete roadway. *Who on earth schedules the seasons for boys' games,* he thought. *In the spring it's shooting marbles, spinning tops, and roller-skating along with flying kites; then comes summer and it's baseball, baseball, baseball until fall, and then it's football. Yes, and with all the aches and pains picked up along the way. There was a time when you could tell the time of year simply by counting the number of boys with rock-raised hickeys on their heads. If there were more than two or three you knew that winter was over and rock-chunking time had arrived. But it wasn't simply a matter of the seasons, because while Christmas brought a few gifts of toys, the boys seemed to put them to use according to some kind of seasonal cycle whose logic I've long forgotten. And yet I did it too, and picked up some of the same scars and scratches and cuts and bruises that those youngsters yelling in the street probably have. Maybe it's simply a matter of giving and recieving enough scars to prove that you're a boy of a certain age—but that isn't what's bothering me, so why am I thinking it?*

From their bangs, clatter, and cries the boys were probably playing coon-can hockey, trying like mad to see which side could knock a Pet or Carnation milk can across the other's goal line by clubbing it over the street with sticks. It could be a rough game because if you got too excited the sticks could land against your head or shins. Oh, but what a feeling you got from sprinting and guiding a can toward the goal on skates!

And now with a smile he saw himself as he'd been at that time of his life. Larger than most of the others, his bare upper body gleaming with sweat above the loose corduroy knickers that whipped beneath his pumping knees, the bill of his cloth cap turned to the rear as he sped into a knot of straining players who yelled and moiled, whirled and skittered as they formed a thicket of skate wheels, legs, and thrashing sticks—out of which a battered tin can suddenly exploded in the direction from which he'd sped. And now, crouching, pivoting, and pumping, he caught up with the can with his stick on the ready, and sent it straight as a bullet across the goal line. And then slaps on his back and yells from his teammates.

Once in a tight game he had swung at the can with such force that in missing he had splintered his stick against the curbstone, sending his skates from beneath him and gashing himself with the end of the shattered club just below his right ankle. Delivered with both hands, the blow had been less painful than the sight of the gash left in his flesh, and after stopping the flow of blood he had returned to the game. The wound had continued bleeding but with his team only a point ahead he had ignored it and helped with the winning goal. In those days the excitement of winning was enough to numb the pain, and within a few days a thick, puckered scab surrounded by a slight swelling was all that remained. And since it pained only when something pressed against it he moved carefully and forgot the wound.

But then, two months later, when rubbing at the itchy new skin that had replaced the scab he was shocked to see it burst with a watery spurt of fluid. And when he gave it a squeeze, what appeared to be the sodden head of an insect had slowly protruded from the joint of his ankle like a worm emerging from the pierced skin of an apple. And with the strange object setting off fantasies of blood poisoning the effect had been far worse than the sight of the original gashing. But then, more fascinated than frightened, he had continued squeezing and watched with awe as two slimy inches of splintered pine wood emerged from the smelly, pus-filled wound. To his relief there had been little pain, but during the days that it took the wound to heal he had lived with the fear of tetanus.... *That too,* he thought, *but the worst of it was realizing that I'd lived that long with that thing buried so deep in my flesh and didn't feel it or even know it was there. I must have been no older than nine years at the time, but I still have the scar*—And suddenly aware that he was thinking less about his early accident than about the strange letter from Janey, he thought,

Yes, it was a way of thinking about it while not approaching it too directly. It didn't work, but sometimes you can be hurt in such a way that you can't bear to face up to the full extent of your wounding. Like my being so afraid of blood poisoning that instead of telling my mother I simply refused to feel what was left in my ankle. So you slick some hurts over with forgetfulness and try to get on with your life as though nothing has happened, and after a time the body forgets what the mind refuses to acknowledge. And while the processes of the blood carry off any poisons that might have formed, the mind turns to other problems, other fears.

But not always. Sometimes something happens and years later you're forced to realize that something alien, something you couldn't deal with at the time it happened, remains buried beneath scars you've long forgotten. Like bullets or pieces of shrapnel beneath an old soldier's skin long after the war in which he recieved it has been won or lost. Then you have to recognize that whatever caused the wound has become so much a part of you that you re-member it only when you bend the wrong way or accidently strike the scar. Some old wounds to the flesh act like barometers announcing changes in the weather, but wounds to the spirit can become encrusted in such a way that they lose all sensitivity to the pressures of time and change, becoming like embalmed shafts of experience that are armored against change but still capable of acting up when you least expect.

And suddenly he understood why Janey's letter disturbed him. It wasn't its message so much as the voice which it evoked in his ear; a voice that clashed with the emotion-encapsulated image which was buried deep in his mind. For while the image was that of a girl whom he'd first known in the fresh bloom of womanhood, the voice which sounded from the letter was not only that of an elderly woman, but of a woman schooled in the suffering and uncertainties of living. It was having the two, the young image and the old voice, brought into unexpected conjunction that was disturbing. For it was as though an elderly woman were addressing him through the form and figure of a young girl—or as though a young girl had addressed him with a voice that echoed the experiences of age. That voice, issuing suddenly from the page, had assaulted a memory that had been inviolate for years, and he was shocked by the extent to which he had sustained an image of a reality that had long since faded.

Years ago there had been a moment when the girl of the image had caused him such unhappiness that he had thought he would never recover, but in time the pain had dulled through the mysterious process by which memory selects that to which it clings and that which it puts out of mind. It was as though he and the image had been part of a motion-picture sequence in which at the moment he'd attempted to embrace a smiling Janey she had snatched out a pistol and fired at his heart. Her impulsive, unanticipated gesture had not been in the script he thought he was enacting, so with the action completed, he had carefully clipped the frame in which her smile glowed its brightest and set fire to the frames that recorded the disillusioning sequence in which she'd fired at his heart. Then, having encased that single frame in thick crystal, he had hidden it away in his trombone case. Shortly afterwards he had left town, but while over the years his image of himself had changed—and in many ways as drastically as it might had Janey actually fired an unfatal bullet—in his private relationship with the cherished image of the girl in the frame it was as though the two of them had been transported into a realm beyond duration and fixed in a deathless posture of appeal and rejection, with himself ever reaching out and Janey ever turning away.

Not that there had been no period of trauma, for again and again he had re-lived the painful moment of her rejection. But usually it was enacted in the breathless pantomime of dreaming. Then he had trained himself to return to sleep and dream of other women, other loves. And later, when the experience of rejection returned to haunt his waking mind with fantasies in which he appeared abject and prideless, he had learned to blunt his anguish with the same irreverent laughter which was evoked when he gave voice to the blues. The process had been something of a desperate maneuver, a blues-like laughing at pain. For gradually he had come to see that desperate emotions required antidotes that were drastic and had been so successful that he no longer thought of Janey even when singing or blowing the blues.

Then in his travels he had come to associate his experience with a stage routine performed by the Zephyrs, a team of dancers who were famous for a comic dance of epic chase and combat performed on a shadowed stage. Where, bathed in the flickering of stroboscopic lights, their violent, ultra-slow-motion, larger-than-life gestures took on the illusion of a fluid and dream-like struggle in which the two men danced out a riddle in which failure was a success, and a success a failure. The choreographed story of which presented the agony of a worm turning into a hero and a hero turning into a worm, a battle in which there was neither winner nor loser, but only a cycle of engrossing action. Clashing on the stage in soundless give-and-take, the dancers appeared to acquire a weightlessness discovered later by the men who walked on the moon, with the split-second flashing of the strobes endowing their exaggerated gestures with the appearance of a magical domination of time and space, gravity and pain. For as they fought with a flashing of knives, the imaginary wounds they dealt and sustained were no hindrance at all to their will to dominance. There was a magic evoked by the act and he, like the audience, had loved it.

And yet he knew that much of what the Zephyrs appeared to do took place only in the eye of the viewer. That each of their leaps, their blows, their turns, falls, and soundless winces, their snarls or cries, were but near-immobile segments in a pattern of carefully controlled and juxtaposed movements that were as carefully synchronized as those of puppets animated by invisible strings. Each gesture, raised leg, up-flung arm, dodging head, or falling body, was executed according to a strict count like that required when performing classical music or an arrangement by Ellington. Each movement was followed by the next and appeared to flow from it, but actually depended upon the flashes of light which filled in the blank spaces between and connected and gave them the appearance of a continuous flow. It was all illusion which depended upon the Zephyrs' marvelous body control and sense of timing. Yes, it was an illusion assisted by the hypnotic lights that had given reality to the impossible and defied time, space, and the laws of gravity. But it was not that their success was due to the lights alone, for often he had watched them rehearse without strobes and was still impressed by their ability to make their bodies defy the laws of time and space. They had made him laugh with admiration; and, better still, they had taught him how to exorcise his pain by allowing him to laugh with admiration at the endless rise and fall of pride. And the point of his self-directed joke was that he, by having reached out for a love that was no more than a flickering light in his own self-hypnotized eyes, had been the composer of his own sad song of failure. It was a strange form of instruction, yet by associating his failure with the triumph of the Zephyrs' illusion he had relieved his anguish. And he had learned that in some matters atmosphere and sheer timing were the key to success; just as selective forgetting was one way of dealing with heartache. Thus, by repressing his pain he had been able to retain Janey's youthful image in a state that was illogical but invulnerable to time. Thank God, he thought with a smile, for the Zephyrs....

Now, riffling through the letter's tightly written pages, he frowned and thought, *Here she's given me a burning house and then a burning hearse, a snakebite and somebody she calls a "little man" who's going around disturbing buried secrets. But what secrets, and whose? Why all this hinting and signifying? Yes, and why did she save the part about the "little man" for the last? Why not give him a name? After all, she's used that phrase for years and it was always for one of those homeless boys she's taken in and cared for until they went off on their own, or were removed by social workers or their parents. They were always her "little men," never her sons. And neither did she allow them to call her "Mother," come to think of it, even though there's no question that she loved and mothered each and every one of them. But maybe it was her way of helping them keep their parents alive in their memory. Yes, and if I'm not mistaken it was her way of making it known that looking after them was her way of fulfilling her responsibility as a Christian. That Janey! That husbandless, virginal mother! For years, by taking in washing, sewing and cooking, and doing housework, she's kept her house full of otherwise homeless boys. And not only feeding and clothing them, but sending them to school—and all of it, except for the help she got from a few friends and neighbors, out of her earnings. Hickman, that took far more than faith and charity, it took a kind of love that's past most understanding.*

And at her age she's still at it! Because this Cliofus is a grown man now—at least in age—and he's been with her since the day his folks got discouraged and threw up their hands. Well, time and Janey's love have proved that he's not the idiot they thought he was, but even with that admitted that Cliofus is one strange *fellow! Thank God that the others she took in have gone on to make comfortable lives for themselves and are doing what they can to help her along, especially the one with a reputation for operating outside the law. He makes her uneasy but she loves him along with the rest, and no matter how big and rusty or smooth and educated they've grown up to be they're still her "little men." Talk about your matriarchs and extended families, Janey's a one-woman institution!*

Her "little men," his mind repeated, and suddenly, echoing an old spiritual, it was as though the phrase was trying to tell him something which he had no desire to hear.

Oh, death is a little man who goes from door to door, he hummed. Then with a shrug he said aloud, "Now she's got *me* doing it!"

But why doesn't she know if this fellow in question is one of hers or not? Nothing else in here indicates that she's lost her memory. And even if it happens to fail her once in a while, why didn't she ask Cliofus? Because far from being an idiot he's been blessed (or cursed) with too much memory, and she knows it! Why, that fellow remembers everything he's ever seen, read, done, or heard talked about. And once he gets started on a subject he drones away at it like a talking robot. So if he says that this stranger—if he is *a stranger—is one of hers, he must be. Because that Cliofus is a walking depository of happenings, whether they're organized or unorganized, classified or beyond all classification. Say something to him and it's like dropping a nickel into a slot machine that's sure to pay off. But instead of producing the usable cash you hope for, any and everything comes pouring out. So by now he's probably spilled every detail about whoever this man is, from his arrival at Janey's to the times he was spanked, given castor oil, or had his diapers changed.*

So who does Janey think she's kidding? Why write that she's uncertain about this particular *fellow? Could he be one of her strays who wandered away and she wants to forget it? If that's the case, then she* isn't *uncertain and expects me to recognize that she's not. Maybe that's why she's skipping around her real meaning like one of these beboppers who try to stand a melody on its head and then turn it wrong-side out so that the listener will be more impressed with his flying and stuttering over the keys than with what he has to say. And yet she's basically serious, too serious for her own good, so it might be her way of warning me to probe between the lines for her meaning. . . .*

But why? Is she protecting something or somebody, or simply having fun? If so, Hickman, you'll have to face up to the fact that for better or worse the ways of slavery are still with us even in the way we talk. So use what you know! You were a word man—even if it was *mostly for the dozens—long before you became a man of the Word, therefore you know that our people like to talk* around *a subject even when there's no danger. They enjoy it, and if they know you well enough they're apt to leave their true subject unstated so you'll have to supply the missing meaning. And even in music. Didn't you sing something called "Squeeze Me" and look all innocent, when anyone who'd been around recognized that you were really giving them "The Boy in the Boat" and automatically supplied the words? Sure you did, and thought you were having it both ways, because it was too funky a subject for polite society, and that whether the listener knew about woman-lovers or not he could still enjoy the melody. Sure, it was a worldly, gut-bucket subject, but the fun was in communicating with the insiders while leaving the innocent untouched in their innocence.*

"Are you with it," the drummer would yell, and you never knew who was or wasn't. That was the fun of the game, and deep down the point was cautionary as the Ten Commandments—even for those who loved to play it. Besides, there was always a risk in such signifying. Because you could direct it at someone you thought uninitiated, and he kept a straight face and turned it back on you....

Like the barber in the crowded barbershop who assumed that the schoolteacher whose hair he was cutting would consider the food he'd had for dinner low class deciding to have some fun by using double-talk in describing his meal to his partner. There he was, showing off and talking with straight-faced deliberation as he went into detail about everything except those "things" which he had eaten as his main course, and being urged on by the barber working in the next chair feeding him questions that had all the customers grinning. "How did you find those things she served?"

"Well now, I'll tell you: The first were only fair to middling. But, man, man! that second serving was something else!"

"What you mean, something else?"

"I mean that seeing how fast I put away the first she must have decided to dig way down in the pot and give me some real action. Because on that second go-around she really came on with the come-on. *That woman dived into that pot and when she came up those things she hit me with were pure-dee out of this world!"*

But then as he gave a self-satisfied wink and began removing the neck-cloth, those "things" he'd left unnamed backed up on him. Because after the teacher had stretched and paid for his haircut and added a tip, he snapped a dollar bill between his hands and took a step back so that everyone could see as he applied the hot sauce.

"My friend," he said, "I enjoyed that description of your meal so thoroughly that on one simple condition this is yours...."

"Why thanks," the barber said, looking surprised as the shop got quiet, "what's your condition?"

"That you'll be so kind," the teacher said, "as to give me the name and address of the good lady who serves such excellent chitt'lin's."

And with that even the barber broke down and joined in as we laughed at the teacher's reminder that it's a mistake to judge a man's knowledge and experience by his job or appearance. But what's this got to do with Janey's little man?

Suddenly tossing the letter aside, Hickman went to his old oak-wood file, removed a worn manila folder, and returned to his desk.

It's been quiet for a long time, he thought, *but now it seems to be stirring again. And* removing a faded sheaf of papers, he leaned forward and stared at its fading typescript.

[SIPPY]

HE HAD RECEIVED THE report, undated and stamped "Confidential," during the early twenties from Walker Millsap, a young college student whom he'd hired whenever his regular drummer was unable to make a string of one-night stands. *Too bad,* he thought, *that a young man so good on the drums would let himself get hung up on liquor.... Personable, too, and at the time I felt that if he'd been more interested in music than in books and his abstract ideas he might have ended up with one of the big bands. But what did I know, me who thought that playing music and chasing women made the best of all possible worlds? And when I learned that he aspired to become something as unglamorous as a college professor, the very idea was such an outrageous challenge to my own untested notion of possibility that I tried to discourage the man. Treated him as though he had no right to reach out for goals in which I had no interest.... So what happens? After giving him hell for reading so many books and preaching to him about the rewards he'd receive if he stuck to music I almost lose his respect by becoming a man of the Word! Mr. Ignorant Arrogance, thy name was Hickman! Instead of encouraging his hope in the possibilities of life I took his ambition as a threat to my own timidity and self-satisfaction. Talk about pride and fear of the unknown parading as wisdom....*

For a moment he stared into space, marveling at how things had turned out and the price in ridicule his own change of role had cost him. But now as he began reading he recalled the complications that had led to his change of life, and the old mood of hope, frustration, and wonder which caused him to turn to Millsap for help.

"Dear Hickman," he read,

> It is interesting that you should write in regards to that incident in which we were involved so many years ago. For it so happens that I, too, had been thinking of it quite recently while going through an old notebook which contains some of the observations which I made during my investigation. Even so, I'm surprised to learn that you're still interested in such an old cold trail. And all the more when I realize that by now the young man who was the focus of our interest must be well into his fifties. Over the years I have often puzzled over the events of that period and wondered why you, who had knocked me for a loop by becoming a minister, could have become so mysteriously interested in such a questionable young "peckerwood." And please, let me assure you that I use that old down-home term without bias but by way of expressing the attitude which I held

at the time—yes, and an attitude that was increased by certain resentments which I felt over being drawn into your mysterious problem. And especially the disappointment I felt after I had sniffed around and thought I had spotted your man, and then had you instruct me to watch his every move but keep out of his sight.

Which made my task all the more difficult, because in order to keep him in sight I had to risk being *seen,* and if he became aware of my scrutiny and I remained silent as you instructed it might have aroused his suspicion and anger. Fortunately, there were others of us in the company he kept who disliked him because of his color, and since there was a possibility that he might well number me among them I used that possibility as a cover under which to operate. I didn't like it, but because of you and the mystery involved I kept on his trail to the best of my ability and hoped that in learning more about him I'd discover what the hell you were up to.

Now, however, I can tell you quite frankly that I hoped that somewhere along the line you'd tell me what you had going. Instead you remained silent, and since I was hooked it seemed better to wait, use my eyes and ears, and ask no questions. It rankled me, but perhaps that's why certain details of my "investigation" remain so vivid in my mind. You seemed to be playing a game of "ask me no questions and I'll tell you no lies," so I was forced to look, listen, and wonder. Still, you were certainly shrewd in asking someone with my inclinations to play detective. For while I had an endless curiosity about the unseen underside of this country it was too restricted in its range and you provided an opportunity to extend it. And then to my surprise I found myself going about playing your detective-observer in such a fashion—and enjoying it—that it seemed fairly natural. What's more, by getting me out of the library and into the streets the experience proved helpful in pursuing my studies, and for that I thank you.

But you've asked me to refresh your memory as to my findings; so now, assuming that you know most—if not all—of our little saga, I'll do my best:

After you offered to pay me for keeping an eye out for any youngster showing up in the Negro sections of this area who matched your rather vague description I finally spotted a likely candidate and started checking him out. Having so little to go on I still wasn't sure of my quarry, but by stretching your description a bit (and allowing for the rapidity of adolescent change) I chose a likely prospect. And here, I must confess, luck and intuition played a significant role. *Luck,* in the circumstance that this young fellow started showing up at one of the joints where I hung out after classes; *intuition,* in the sense that something about him—perhaps his mixed, kind of improvised character—told me that he just might be your little man. But as I say, I was uncertain and so remain.

Anyway, I spotted a likely suspect and the best way to proceed is by saying that in the beginning he struck me as some kind of poor orphan of a white boy who, as a child, had passed through the loving hands of some Negro nursemaid or cook who treated him as one of her own. Which meant that he had the good luck of having had not one mother but two, and thus had been doubly loved. And, since it happens so often, I figured that his dark mother may well have spoiled him by treating him like a little prince. Incidentally, as I look back I find it interesting that my imagination was so involved in fleshing out the maternal roles in his background that I was on the point of completely overlooking his *paternity.* For other than entertaining the vague possibility that he must have been a man of substance who had strayed, died, or been enticed away, I was unable to provide the little bastard with a father!

I guess I simply left the matter of his daddy's identity and character up to you. But if my assumption that the boy was without blood relatives was correct, it followed that he'd also had the bad luck of being twice orphaned; first physically, and then psychologically. Because given his footloose condition, I speculated that his white mother had actually died, while her black extension had survived. And that then, following the normal course of such relationships, the boy would have presumed to have outgrown his black mother and cast her aside.

As you can see, I was improvising a scenario out of very thin air. And yet I was keeping to a well-known pattern whereby such a child lives for a time in a kind of Eden that is bright, shaded, and full of wonderful colors—then *WHAM!* and he or she reaches adolescence and the world becomes strictly white or black. Then the child is forced to withdraw his or her affection from its black protectors and adopt attitudes more in keeping with its acclaimed racial superiority. Nor does it matter a damn that its black relatives are resentful, or that its second "mother" feels deprived and betrayed. Obviously, my improvised application of this sad old pattern ran the risk of being farfetched, and yet something about the boy gave me the feeling that it was valid, but that there had been a twist to the pattern in which, after losing his natural mother and rejecting her dark counterpart, he had become a rather unique type of "motherless child."

Whether this projection of his possible background was false or true I was never to learn, but it seemed a likely seedbed for what I identified as such an unmistakable air of defiant loneliness that I thought of him as a young, mammy-made Ahab. It would also account for his habit of hanging around Negroes so long after the normal period of initiation into his role as one of superior racial and social status. Indeed, the fact that he continued such relationships stirred my suspicious imagination. But while I felt safe in projecting him as mammy-less, something about him, an echo of style and a quality and volume of sound behind his laconic silence, suggested that he was far from being fatherless. Therefore I asked myself, "Why, if it is possible that he could have two mothers, couldn't he have also had *two* fathers? One to plant the seed which shaped his physical image and connected him to his biological past, and still another to endow him with a certain attitude, and cultural style?" It was then that I decided that it really didn't matter if the influence of one of his fathers was merely spiritual, or if his influence were good or bad! In other words, I concluded that even if it appeared obvious that none of *us* had strayed into the boy's "genes" pile there was no question but that we were hiding in his "style" pile!

Hickman, the idea was as shocking as that of a monster with two heads inhabiting a single body, and yet it seemed to fit my original assumptions. For where there's an Eve there has to be an Adam, and where there's a Hagar it's likely that there's an Ishmael with his hand turned against all mankind. Therefore I speculated that it was probably through the very kindness of his Negro "mother" that the poor fellow had failed the test of putting her and all her kind behind him, and that thanks to her he was stuck to Negroes as tight as Brer Rabbit to Tar Baby. Therefore I concluded that it was through his black "mother" that he'd come under the fateful influence of some Negro stud of a type who fills white children with delight, but whose very existence their parents prefer to ignore. If so, it would have been precisely through the boy's association with such a fellow that a white boy suckled at a Negro woman's breast would have fallen into the confusion that left him unable to make the traumatic break which white kids brought up among us are forced to make come adolescence.

Hickman, my preacher friend, here I must confess that lacking your Christian virtue of total forgiveness, I'll never really understand the nasty, sadistic business those kids can come up with when they reach that stage of their development. Such as their adolescence-

triggered insistence that even the adults who've loved and protected them from infancy must address them as "Miss" or "Mister."
Then there's their contemptuous name-calling and calculated
rudeness—not to mention the boys' sexual exploitation of Negro
girls with no social risk to themselves. It's the direct opposite of
what they're taught in regard to their own, and yet many appear to
make the change from relations to us as friends (if not as members
of common families) to assuming the roles of social and spiritual
superiors as easily as falling off a log into a warm pool of water. But
since they are Bible-belt human and possessed of some sense of
morality there *has* to be some kind of masochism involved, some
form of nagging guilt if not of self-hatred. And this even though
they are supported in their rejection of their racially and culturally
ambiguous childhoods by all the laws and customs, religious and
civic, that support the crooked color line.

So as I mulled over these notions I came to feel that in the boy's
case something unusual had short-circuited the process. And I suspected that it had to do with the strength of his early physical and
emotional bonding. Something that left him unable to ignore the
difference between what was *said* about his old associates as members of a rejected group, and his own complex memories of them as
individuals. In fact, I see his early bonding as having an effect like
that of the religious rite which you call "a laying on of hands," for
while it was by no means "sacred" it is so powerfully human and
tenacious and affective that it appears to me that many white
Southerners spend the rest of their lives struggling with its traces
even as they deny its source.

Anyway, following this line of conjecture, I imagined that my
suspect's choice of Negroes as companions began early in his life in
the person of some son, husband, or boyfriend of his black mother-
figure, and that he in turn was most likely a worldly and utterly
irreverent hustler and con man. Not a professional, mind you, but
one of a type familiar to us but least suspected by their white
victims. Here I refer to that home-grown variety of rascal who
operates behind the mask of a genial but not too intelligent butler,
waiter, bellhop, chauffeur, or yardman, but who will manipulate
anyone rash and arrogant enough to confuse his personality with
his job or his color and social status with his intelligence to a fare-
thee-well. Those who make such mistakes are his natural prey, and
he'll lure them into a serene quicksand of black-and-white illusion
and leave them as naked as fledging jaybirds while strutting like the
king who wore no clothes.

But hell, Hickman, you know the type better than I do. Therefore you know that such a trickster will let white folks knock themselves out over chicken-stealing jokes in which he is quoted as asking, "Who dat who say who-dat when Ah say who dat?" and grin like the Cheshire cat. But never in this world will he reveal that when necessary he can speak schoolbook English, understandable French, Spanish, and Yiddish—or that he is knowledgeable as to which of their best friends are having affairs with their supposedly faithful wives.

Since there are many musicians among them I'm sure that you know the type I mean. They can be found in almost any town large enough to provide the conflict of values and stereotypes based on notions of racial superiority that form the social briar patch in which to operate. Playing dumb, they can be quick-witted and even wise; though perceived as cowardly they are capable of a reckless, life-risking daring when the chips are down; and though treated as inferior beings, they delight in taking advantage of such misconceptions of their humanity by infiltrating the most private areas of their employers' lives. And once there they can manipulate the stereotype role thrust upon them like a magician drawing doves, rabbits, and white elephants out of a hat.

Here—not that he did any of that—I'm reminded of a slave-servant who appears in a book in which two paintings of George Washington are reproduced. In the first the General stands before a field tent holding a scroll of papers as he strikes a pose, à la Napoleon, with his left hand stuck in the breast of his jacket; while in the background, wearing a plumed turban, his round-cheeked, white-toothed young servant holds the bridle of his master's horse and grins as he looks back knowingly at its docked, high-lifted tail. Incidently, the portrait was done by a Frenchman who was probably as familiar with the natural ways of horses as the slave boy with the ways of his master. . . .

The second painting is actually a family scene in which, resplendent in dress uniform and boots with spurs, General Washington sits crossed-legged beside a table upon which his hat and the hilt of his sword rest upon a large military map. The map covers most of the table but the General appears to be staring far into the future as, to the right of the table, his young grandson stands close by with a hand resting on a globe of the world which sits on a convenient stand. And as the boy looks on, his willowy young lady of a sister (who sits across the table) is holding a furled end of the map in her delicate fingers so that Mrs. Washington (who sits beside her, richly bedecked in a ribboned bonnet, lacy scarf, and silken dress) may trace what appears to have been the course of one of the General's battles. I'm not sure of what she's doing, but whatever it is the map is the focal point of the painting. For with the map as its axis the ladies and young boy are portrayed as sweetly genteel and the General relaxed and peaceful. Which was most suitable for a Tory aristocrat who opted for revolution, fought difficult battles, and triumphed against great odds. The General stares from the canvas as though contemplating the invisible viewers who would inherit it, and if so, he was right on target.

Because across the table and in a corner behind the elegant ladies there hovers a shadow of the past—and that shadow is the point of all my bumbling attempt at description.

Because the embodiment of that "shadow" is none other than the man who had been the young boy who appears in the first painting. Presented in semi-profile, he stands erect and attentive with his left hand thrust into the bosom of his vest and his eyes properly averted. His name was William Lee, and though no member of the family he, he's there because the General must have insisted that his friend and companion through war and peace be included to give depth to the scene and convey some of its historical complexity. Who knows, maybe Washington recognized that William performed an important service which, for one in his own heroic position, could be rendered best by a man beyond the pale. Maybe the slave kept the hero's feet on the ground and warned him against becoming puffed up with pride. Perhaps he served his hero-master as well by being an ever-present reminder of his human mortality, and thus helped deflate any illusions he might have had as to his infallibility. For after all, the length of his shadow may inspire questions as to the true measure of *any* man, even as it adds texture to and helps define the scene in which he acts. So it is that not only does Lee deepen the painting's historical perspective but foreshadows other "shadows" to come. What's more, he's standing right behind Miss First Lady Martha—which must have been one hell of an observation post! Because if I know anything about our people, old Bill has his eyes and ears wide open to what's going down, and *nobody,* not even the surveyor, slave-master, general, and father of our country, knew what the hell he was *thinking*—much less the influence for good or evil that he might have been having on the first family's grandchildren. And here you might recall that the father of our country fathered no children of his own....

Black William Lee was with George Washington for thirty-one

years, during which time an undeclared independence of observation was, perhaps, his only self-defining area of freedom. But don't forget that although a slave he was still privy to many matters having to do with affairs of family, state, and politics. And if interested he might well have used his shadowy position as unsurveyed landscape for self-exploration, or a dimly lit stage upon which to perform the kind of playacting which is the speciality of the type I mentioned above. And like the type he could have been quite fascinating to children; perhaps because in the eyes of the children of that day the slaves were natural allies in a silent war with powerful forces that limited their own freedom of self-assertion. A similarity of situation which makes for a potent point of mutual identification and ground for all kinds of rebellion, and perhaps explains why their parents insist that they break with us once they reach the stage of self-discovery and procreation—which is adolescence. No wonder white kids are admonished not to act like "niggers"!

Hickman, I suspect that all this abstract speculation is bugging you, so now, back to the boy. While keeping clear of any eye-to-eye contact of which I was aware I scouted around for some down-close down-home contact of color who might fit the type I've been describing—and by George it worked! For by keeping an eye on our strange bronco stray I finally tracked him to a most unrighteous stud! And in the course of my investigation I learned exactly what type of Negro had taken him in charge. I must warn you, however, not to take my "exactly" too seriously, because this character who I finally connected with the boy was so tricky that he could walk straight through a plate-glass window without a scratch, or dive through a sieve without leaving even a microscopic shred, thread, or bubble!

[PAIRS]

This was a guy who went by the name of "Missippy Brown," or simply "Sippy," a self-bestowed moniker which sums up the mocking irreverence of his character. But if Mississippi missed the rascal it was only because he eluded some irate mob by being so fast on his feet. At the time he came to my attention he was supposed to be the butler of a young multimillionaire, but the moment I laid eyes on Sippy I doubted that he'd ever worked for anyone except *himself*— and I was right. For although quite personable, he turned out to be of the type who never loses sight of the "bread" or the side that's spread thickest with butter. And even if the "bread" is tossed past them and out of a ten-story window they'll be there waiting to grab it before it can hit the ground. So while I'm hopelessly fascinated by maverick types (being something of one myself) I found Sippy's character so unusually outrageous that my initial impulse was to steer clear of him and all his exploitations. I was already having enough trouble trying to bring a college course in Culture and Civilization into line with the reality around me, so why make matters more confusing by introducing a rambunctious embodiment of living chaos into the neat symmetry of my textbook? Nevertheless, out of respect for your interest and spurred by my own irrepressible curiosity, I felt compelled to investigate Sippy's connection with the boy. But again I must confess that my decision was also influenced by sheer chance.

Shortly after our long-distance conversation I happened to pass a music-store window in which was a publicity photograph for Ted Lewis's version of "Me and My Shadow," wherein a strutting Lewis wearing top hat, tails, and silk-lined cape is pointing his clarinet skyward as he plays pied piper to the little brown-skinned boy whom he featured in his act as "Ted Lewis Junior." Dressed in miniature top hat and tails, the kid enacts his role of "shadow" a short distance behind his partner, and as he dances to Lewis's reedy noodling he has a signifying grin on his face which reminded me of the way young William Lee had grinned when eyeing the raised tail of George Washington's horse. The coincidence was, as the saying goes, a "gasser" which damn near knocked me out!

Hickman, I had been passing the shop for weeks without any conscious reaction, but this time those two familiar characters leaped from their position beneath pedestals bearing busts of Bach, Beethoven, and Wagner and threw me slap-dab into the middle of that murky context of relationships between children and adults, blacks with whites, and whites with blacks, which your problem had triggered in my mind. It was as though the two, man and boy, had been *waiting* for me! And once they caught my attention they were like pied pipers in summoning up other couples like themselves to join them in a game of firing jeering riddles at me that were so outrageous that I felt like kicking my own behind!

Recalling how you kidded me for wasting my time reading for pleasure, my fascination with such characters will probably have little meaning for you, but while the idea might disgust you they did, nevertheless, play a significant role in my investigation. Starting with George Washington and William Lee and continuing through such characters from books as Uncle Remus and his little white friend, Uncle Tom and Little Eva, Captain Ahab and his cabin boy, Pip, and especially those famous runaways, poor white and slave, Huck Finn and Jim. If you remember any of them (and I'm sure you do), perhaps my agitation over the similarity between their relationships and that of Sippy and the boy will become a bit clearer.

For one thing, each of the pairs had relationships which bridged the color line—you might say that they performed feats of daring on an invisible high wire that stretched dangerously above the gap which separates the races. For another, each of the pairs sported and spieled within areas that were usually taboo. Therefore one could say that they operated on privileged ground—or at least the *Negro* members of these unusual duos did. In a sense these couples were innocents who lived in a screwed-up Eden after the Fall—no, not the Fall you preach about but the Civil War, Reconstruction, and all the other mess which was its aftermath. With all the hostility around them they lived charmed lives which made them invulnerable to the taboos which defined their friendships as threats to social order.

Talk about being elected and set aside! Hell, they were deodorized, dunked in a hyssop-and-myrrh bath of sentimentality, and treated as though no more than floaters in their beholder's color-confused eye! And if you think I've blown my mind consider this: When a simple "a" and "n" are added to the titles of those most famous of black Southern "uncles," namely Remus and Tom, they are quickly stripped of their deodorant and amenable masks and become—Lord help them—"Uncle(an) Tom" and "Uncle(an) Remus"!

Now I *know* that you're laughing, but this hilarious hint of a secret stink that lay barely detectable beneath the title of affection bestowed upon kindly Southern Negro men has bothered me from the moment it reached out and slapped me for blundering into its secret—which happened through my drunken mistyping of "uncle," a word so familiar that we seldom think of its slippery connotations. But with that blunder I penetrated the cover of that tricky, Bible-and-Constitution-quoting snake in the grass. He's been there waiting all the time, and when there's an avuncular relationship between a black adult and a young white friend the joker asserts himself with such rattling mockery that we pretend that he doesn't exist. It's no wonder that some of our folks who don't read books are offended by the very *idea* of poor old Uncle Tom. Perhaps it's because they've been so conditioned to listening for what's said by being left *un*said that they hear implication which others find it more comfortable to ignore. So for all of Uncle Remus's skill in telling our own folktales they find him suspect. And despite poor Uncle Tom's loyalty to the Christian virtues which guide their own lives they reject him as vehemently as they reject Simon Legree.

Which is ironic, since that worthy uncle (who, by the way, was patterned after a man of your profession) appeared in the book which President Lincoln praised for its role in arousing support for the war which led to our so-called Emancipation. Come to think of it, maybe there was an echo of the same ambiguous uncleanliness at work in the game we played back during the days when horse-drawn wagons made the steaming evidence of life's irrepressible stink and cycling a property of every street and roadway. Coming upon it we'd step aside with giggling chants of "Never kick a horse turd 'cause it might be your uncle." A boy's silly joke, true; but one in which a philosophical idea of one of your distinguished forerunners, Nicolas of Cusa, found verification. Much as our boyish fascination with death and dying, resurrection and immortality found comic relief in the arcane doings of tumblebugs.

Okay, Mister Preacher, so I'm being childishly excremental, but it's by way of giving you an idea of the vein my mind was set working in following your assignment. For when Sippy, the boy, and the sight of a white man and black child cavorting in a publicity photograph became linked in my mind, I was forced to ask myself what exactly did such a recurring juxtaposition of the generational and racial, the innocent and the worthy but somehow unclean really mean? Out of what mixture of motives and complex needs did they arise? And why did the figures who embodied those needs and motives keep turning up in books, stage plays, and movies? (Hell, Hickman, it just occurred to me that when Shirley Temple and Bill Robinson danced up and down the stairs they were a more recent instance of the same ubiquitous pairs! And what about Matt Henson and Admiral Peary?) So I asked myself what was the real function and hidden connection of such pairs in the psychological processes of everyday life? And then in my frustration I asked myself how the hell did you, an old jazzman and former barbershop cynic, come to be so involved in such a relationship? Quite frankly, I was so snarled in the mess that pretty soon I found myself thinking of you as "Uncle(an) Lon"!

Now if you assume that I began thinking along this line while in my cups, you're right; I was indeed. But even so, the characters who reached out and grabbed didn't spring out of a bottle; instead, they exploded out of a bunch of books which I had read for pleasure no less than for college credits. Thus, thanks to you, Sippy and the stray white boy roiled the placid waters of my academic studies. And, just as I feared, the two of them caused me one heap of confusion.

And that confusion began to spread when I learned that my snap judgments as to the connections between Sippy and the young man wouldn't stack. For it was soon clear that whenever and wherever he had been touched by the gentle hands of his blessed Hagar—and I still think it was down South—the boy had actually run into his Negro con-man-gambler of an "uncle" up North. And at—of all places—a famous racetrack. Just how he came to be in that particular scene remains a mystery, but it seems that being hungry and down on his luck he'd hit on Sippy for some eating change, and that was the beginning.

Being flush with his own winnings, and always a free-spending sporting man, this Negro gambler had not only given the boy a stake but had added a tip on a winning horse which paid off at the rate of eight to one. And then, taking a whimsical liking to the boy, Sippy offered him a place to stay and the boy accepted. I understand that Sippy was both pleased and surprised, because he was testing the boy's attitude toward his racial identity and had anticipated being turned down. But then, heaven help us, after discovering the kid's unusual intelligence, Sippy decided to use him in a cockeyed experiment that only a black rascal like himself could have conceived.

Which was no less—now get this!—than to make the young man over into Sippy's own larcenous freebooter's conception of what an ideal American should be! Don't ask me what put him up to it, because such insight is too far beyond my limited range of vision. But since I've finally come to recognize you as one of those whom a professor once described as "past-masters of profane ecstasy" who have been self-transformed into "latter-day celebrants of religious exaltation," I'm hoping that you can do better. For I assume that the experience of such a mysterious transformation will have provided you with privileged insight into a wide variety of life's dog-assed aberrations.

As for me, Sippy remains a mystery, but I *imagine* that after working from boyhood inside the walls of white folks' bedrooms, bathrooms, dining rooms, country clubs, and various kitchens, he simply decided that most white males not only failed to measure up to what they claimed to be, but fell far short of his own high, if garbled, standards. (Incidentally, he had an ironic, debonair respect for most white women, and this despite the role of goddess-trollop imposed upon them by some of their menfolk—but I won't go into *that*!) The point here is that Sippy seems to have set out to create himself a white man who measured up to his own high, if mammy-made, standards! And this, I take it, was the logic behind his experiment. In other words, Sippy was out to create himself an ideal white American male in his own mammy-made image!

But once again, please don't ask me as to what precisely put such an idea in Sippy's head, because I don't know. All I can say is that from working around the affluent he seems to've become obsessed with the mystery of manners, style, and power. But most of all with *power.* And here I mean a dimension of power that ranges so far beyond the limits of finance, science, or politics that it takes on connotations of the mystical. Sippy seems to've considered such power an extra portion that is available but to the precious few who are blessed with his own rare powers of perception while remaining elusive to those who were otherwise in control of the good things of life, and he resented the situation. Therefore I suppose that it was probably some minor incident, some sneer or snub or snide remark, that provoked him to take a detached, irreverent outsider's look at the assorted types of whites with whom he came in contact; and after comparing *their* opportunities, accomplishments, and approaches to life with what he saw as their wasted *possibilities,* he then compared their assets with his own and made his cockeyed decision.

Therefore I imagined that Sippy—who incidentally was given to speaking of himself in the third person (a characteristic of his type's rampant, self-centered myth-making)—probably told himself, "Now here they are, living on the tip-top of the greatest country in the world, bragging and lording it over everybody else but got no more sense of the swinging *style* that's needed to go with such good luck than a gorilla knows what to do with an Omega watch or a flying machine! And yet they have the nerve to treat Sippy like *he's* a clown! Done completely ignored the fact that if you do it to others they'll do it to you, 'cause in the game of life it's a Golden rule that everybody on earth is *somebody's* fool!

"So all right, in this kooky country what you see is what you get, and what you *don't* can get you *got*! So as far as *they* can see Sippy's just a nowhere nobody who they don't have to see, and that mistake will finally get them. Because they're missing the simple human fact that Sippy just might be as smart as they claim to be *and* have a mind and eyes of his own. So for all their attempts to ban him from the action he's still in a position to see a hell of a lot about the scene which they keep overlooking. Starting with the fact that Sippy's a natural-born gambler and a cool, homegrown American cat who don't belong to nobody but his own hard-cutting *self*! Therefore he's not *about* to waste his precious time blaming all his troubles on something which happened so long ago as slavery. 'Cause judging from everything that Sippy can see, only those who free *themselves* can be truly free!

"Therefore he's not taking low for *anybody*, and neither is he leaping off the sidewalk for a bunch of ignorant squares who can't see that it's by trying to keep *him* from having a fair share of democracy that they keep crapping out on their *own* liberty. Neither is Sippy wasting time moaning and groaning about the way life's deck of cards is stacked, because since that terrible day when Abe Lincoln dropped his guard and got himself wasted, the odds have been against him. That's how the deal went down and nobody can undo what's already happened. So from then 'til now they've been in charge of the game and standing pat, but since the Constitution guarantees Sippy a chance at the cards he's going to lay in the bend and grin while he plays his hand the best way he can. And it don't matter a *damn* to Sippy who's in charge of the jive-assed dive, just show him another five—just a lousy *five*—and not only will he use what they overlook in order to stay alive, he'll do it in a true In-God-We-Trust American style! Meanwhile, if they insist on being top man on the country's totem pole, then let them compete and not only *act* like they deserve all that freewheeling power, but let them convince Sippy that they mean to *use* it in the way it was meant to be!"

(You'll note, dear Hickman, that this is only my interpretation, but right or wrong, Sippy seems to have kept an unblinking eye on the difference between reality and an as-yet unfleshed ideal. Therefore he hoped for the best while expecting the worst and kept an eye peeled for the joker. And if I'm not mistaken he knew damn well that a "five" is both a playing card and the banknote graced by the image of Abraham Lincoln. The man was devious even in his hopes!)

So it appears that after a brief period when he drifted into prize-fighting and footracing (he once beat the then champion, Bojangles Robinson, at running backwards by a yard and scored a dozen knockouts as a middleweight before hanging up his gloves), Sippy became a hustler. As such, he gained a flamboyant reputation as an ace prizefighter, footracer, whoremaster, and chippy-chaser; a reputation which he glamorized by sporting tailor-made suits, hand-made shoes, Barcelona hats, and raccoon coats, and driving a lavender Marmon roadster, a red Pierce-Arrow convertible, and a white, suede-topped Lincoln touring car; in which, weather permitting, he enjoyed showing off his huge, blue-eyed black-and-white Great Dane dog—all this by supplying some of the most powerful men in the country with bootleg liquor, advice on horse-racing, prizefighters, and tips on the stock market obtained from mysterious sources. But being a resourceful con artist, he was *also* pretending to work as a waiter; a strategy which allowed him to make useful contacts with important guests and pick up quick bits of easy change by gambling in the locker rooms of various high-class clubs and hotels.

[SIPPY]

In fact, it was during that phase that he was given the job of butler by the millionaire, who was only a few years younger but light-years behind Sippy in experience. And here, thanks to their black-and-white relationship (which violated every nuance of the nation's established code), I must give you a few words about this young millionaire.

It seems that Sippy ran into the young man when working at a certain exclusive club. It was during a big champagne party at which the young man got crying drunk, wandered into the kitchen, and made a nuisance of himself by sitting on its range and beating a saucepan with a wooden spoon. Naturally this caused a crisis in the kitchen, because such unusual conduct was disgraceful. And especially from a young man who was usually quite gentlemanly. Therefore the kitchen's orderly routine was brought to a halt, with no one—cooks, chefs, tuxedoed headwaiter, white-jacketed waiters, or astonished busboys—knowing what to do about it.

Drunk as a coot and mad as a sorehead bear, the young man was calling everybody names that made some of the churchgoing older waiters want to break his neck. Then, from beating on the pan he turned to cursing and striking at anyone who came within range, but out of respect for his wealthy family no one was willing to lay a hand on him—until, that is, Sippy wandered into the kitchen from a party which he had just finished serving on an upper floor. Then, hearing the commotion and seeing everybody crowding around and doing nothing, Sippy recognized the young man and took charge.

"Mister So-and-So," Sippy said, "what the hell do you think you're doing, sitting on top of that range like a goddamn clown on a throne? Who do you think you're kidding, perched up there like all of a sudden you're some kind of iron-assed devil? I want to know, and I mean right this minute! Because by now even the dumbest stud in this kitchen knows that if that range was fired up your butt would be blistered—which it ought to be—and burned ten shades blacker than mine!

"And just look at what you're doing to that fine tuxedo! Good Lord almighty, man, what's come over you, the son of a son of a *Virginian*, that you can't handle your liquor any better than that! Do you know what your daddy will do when he hears about this? Hell, I'll *tell* you what he'll do, he'll bust a gut and then go upside your head, that's what he'll do! So now you come down off that dam' range and let me bring you back to your senses!"

Well, with that (and to everyone's surprise and relief) the young man broke into tears and allowed his newfound friend to guide him out of the kitchen and into an unused dining room, where Sippy forced him to drink a concoction which left him pale, watery eyed, limp-legged, and sober. This incident, which has long since become local barbershop legend, was the start of the young man's relationship with Sippy. And from there he went on to psych the poor man out of his mind and beyond all rational belief. Sippy worked more changes on that poor rich boy than those African masks worked on Picasso! What's more, he seems to have worked a major change in the young man's life and values. And what a backflip of a change that had to be!

For I was told that after attending an expensive prep school, Sippy's boss had graduated from Harvard, where he played football, and that at the time of the incident he was enrolled in a divinity school where he was said to have been a top student and an excellent classical pianist; a gift which Sippy, a self-taught piano man, embellished by teaching him ragtime and stride. Then, by way of making him more aggressive, Sippy taught him boxing. Because, thanks to a pious but domineering father and despite having a pile of money inherited from his mother's father, the young millionaire was somewhat depressed and inhibited. During your jazz experience you must have encountered hundreds of the type; who for all their whiteness remind me of nothing so much as those Negroes who wear their hair defiantly long and bushy but then walk around with hangdog expressions. But be that as it may, in Sippy's eyes his young employer's timidity was the result of a misdirected upbringing and sexual immaturity, so he seized these as an opportunity for taking his boss in charge and improving his character.

This feat Sippy accomplished with the enthusiastic cooperation of a couple of his women friends, a teasing brown and towhead blonde respectively, who were paid far above the going price for initiating the millionaire into the subtleties of bedroom mechanics that turned out to have some of the liberating effects of a lengthy psychoanalysis. After that he became what Sippy termed his "main man." And with the shredding of one inhibition leading to the loss of another, the wealthy divinity student got rid of his shyness, broke with his father, and lost his religion.

More important, he was so thankful for his liberation that he regarded Sippy as more of a companion than a servant. And since Sippy was of light complexion and indeterminate racial features (unless of course one was from the South and familiar with types produced by its after-dark activities), he was often the millionaire's companion at sports events, stags, poker games, and interracial carousels. But remember, this was during the so-called Jazz Age, when things were hanging loose, at least among the rich flappers and jelly beans. So while members of the millionaire's social set were aware of the companionship, few objected. And of course its Negro observers just laughed and got a kick out of watching Sippy give the man a freewheeling Ph.D.'s instruction in subjects whose basics Uncle Remus had taught the one little white boy who absorbed his wisdom. Besides, the white man was so rich that under Sippy's influence he discovered that he could do anything he wanted and dare anybody to try to stop him. It was as though he enjoyed flaunting social conventions and was using his wealth to rise above them. And naturally Sippy was right in there with him!

That Negro even had that white man kissing women's hands and bowing Continental style, and taught him to dance, swing, strut, and jive! I tell you, that Sippy was *slippy*—which should have been his name! And then, having taken the millionaire over with such success, the rascal went to work on your boy—providing, of course, that he *was* your boy.

Nevertheless, from what I could glean the young man took to Sippy's instructions like a duck to water. And as you'd expect of somebody who, as I gather, had been well prepared by his early association with you, the boy was a quick and willing student. By which I mean to say that he was already something of a natural-born actor and potentially a man-of-all-situations, and therefore made to order for Sippy's ultimately subversive plan.

Hickman, before long this butler had shaped the boy into his idea of a white American gentleman! Bought him clothes and taught him to wear them, worked on his manners, and had him reading all kinds of books so that he could hold his own among the educated. However, after discovering that the kid could change his modes of speech with the facility of a traveling salesman or a world-traveled mynah bird, Sippy left his speech alone. Instead, he drilled the boy in the vernaculars of baseball, boxing, gambling, and in Harlemese, Brooklynese, and the bits of Yiddish which he himself had picked up while working for a Jewish agent whose specialty was booking vaudeville acts and jazz orchestras. And finally, being as good at the craft as you were back when I backed you on the drums, Sippy steeled his student against any easy provocation, whether from hostile individual, error of choice, or circumstance, by coaching him in the finer points of the dirty dozens. In fact, it was the boy's familiarity with that form of contentious discourse that strengthened my suspicion that he was indeed your man.

Well, as far as I can recall I left town for a semester to continue my studies at Chicago and thus lost contact with the experiment. But by the time I returned Sippy had come up with a Falstaff-Pygmalion feat of transformation that can only be described as a combination of Thomas Jefferson, Benjamin Franklin, P. T. Barnum, George Washington Carver, Groucho Marx, Billy Sunday, Yellow Kid Weil, William S. Hart, Teddy Roosevelt, Warren G. Harding, Gaston B. Means, and Lon Chaney—*plus* our own dam' Sam, John Henry, *and* Brer Rabbit. A creation which turned out to be so swindle-prone, fluent, and shifty that absolutely *no one* could get him into focus. And that goes for most cynical and worldly-wise Negroes who happened to be tracking his progress.

Because even under the most rigorous scrutiny, the rascal's image simply kept fading in and out of focus and reforming and realigning itself into so many ungraspable and shifting shapes that even the most knowledgeable and sociological of observers were utterly confused! Those two, mentor and student, operating as master and servant, Arab sheikh and interpreter, con man and shill, could charm the tail off a brass monkey or raw beefsteak out of the jaws of a hungry hound. They worked more scams than Houdini performed escapes, and were reported as having been seen from time to time on every level of white society. But what was so amazing to me was that most folks saw in them, and especially in the boy, whatever it was they *wanted* to see. All they had to do was think it, and there he'd be in the charismatic flesh!

And aliases? Hell, he had enough to fill an *encyclopedia!* Name a place and he was from it, accent and all. And with the manners and costume to fit. Sometimes he wore Texas boots and a cowboy hat, sometimes a derby, chesterfield overcoat, and spats; sometimes an opera hat, white tie, and tails; or, as the occasion or ploy demanded, high-rise gamblers-striped pants, spats, and an Oxford gray cutaway morning coat with its braided lapels adorned with a white carnation. And on one occasion, during which he must have been in the grip of some reckless frenzy of larcenous fantasy, he was seen ambling along the streets of New York's Lower East Side wearing a prayer shawl and yarmulke!

Apparently the boy was driven by some obscure need to transform himself into any and every image of possibility that entered his Sippy-scrambled mind! Because once when I'm visiting my old church back in Dallas, I look up and there he is, up in the pulpit preaching a fire-and-brimstone sermon—and I mean rocking the church with such effect that I didn't know whether to laugh, cry, scream, or expose him! Of course I didn't, both out of respect for your concern and the kick I got from just watching him operate. In fact, watching him confirmed what I'd been taught during my excursions from the classroom, which was that in this country the most instructive drama is not to be found in the theater—where most of what you get is souped-up soap opera having nothing to do with the life we know—but in the street. And Hickman, I assure you, those two transformed the streets of every good-sized town and city in the country into their own reality-defying stage! Or so it seems, because I was often unable to keep an eye on them and had to depend on others for my information.

In fact, after that pulpit bit, it was a year or two before I saw them again, this time in the North; and by then something must have gone wrong between them. Because I learned that Sippy was serving time for cracking some thug's head with a billiards cue. It was said that he had acted in self-defense, but that for some reason the boy refused to supply him with a lawyer. This ended their friendship, and shortly afterwards the boy disappeared. I asked some of my friends with whom I had been enjoying his and Sippy's career what had become of him, but none would admit to having seen him—probably because they put him down for betraying Sippy. Nor was I surprised, because as I said earlier, Sippy was the type who always looked out for number one, and since he'd fashioned the boy in his own ideal image some such parting of the ways was to be expected. So, having lost his trail, I finally gave up; both out of frustration and because my fellow observers were not your ordinary variety of change-shocked and color-blinded citizens, they were experienced, people-watching *Negroes;* men who worked for all kinds of businesses and institutions, and included Pullman porters, dining-car waiters, and truck drivers with whom I patronized the same barbershop. Therefore I concluded that he had taken off for Europe, or perhaps Hong Kong. However, during the same period a Pullman porter friend did tell me of an incident which you as an old jazzman might find amusing.

It seems that one night when on a trip to the West Coast he looked into a parlor car to check it out and saw a white songwriter of some reputation who was drunk and down on his knees at prayer. So seeing the situation, my friend said that he was about to close the door when something the songwriter was mumbling pricked his ear and stopped him dead in his tracks. He said that in the first place he was surprised that the man, who he had served before, even *believed* in prayer. But what stopped him was hearing a white man asking the Lord to make his latest song a success by having it fall into the hands of *Louis Armstrong*!

After I recovered from a fit of laughing I told my friend that he *had* to be lying, but he swore by his mother and Alberta Hunter that he was telling the truth, and went on to tell me in all sincerity that this celebrated composer and lyricist was not only laying his case before the Lord with the passion of a true believer, but that he was pleading with Him to "please, please, *please*" (these were my friend's exact words) "make that gravel-mouthed nigger listen to Thy divine will and do right by my beautiful song." This I give you for what it's worth, but who knows? Certainly there is enough evidence around to suggest that maybe the Lord responded and gave ole Satchmo a nudge. What's more, to my faulty ear that mocking, "Oh, yaaas!" which Satch uses to end some of his numbers sounds suspiciously like an ambiguous "Amen!" Anyway, I suspect that if you scratch an old-time Negro jazzman deep enough and hard enough you'll find yourself a strayed apostate preacher!

However, and all joking aside, I couldn't recall your having said that your young man possessed musical talent and thus concluded that he couldn't have been the prayerful songwriter. But then, sometime later, when getting some gas at a filling station, I saw this chauffeur who was sitting behind the wheel of a big limousine dressed in a finely tailored gray uniform. At that time there were plenty like him around so that in itself wasn't unusual. Conk-haired Negro chauffeurs were comporting themselves like brown-skinned Valentinos all over the place, gold slave(!) bracelets, guardsman's overcoats, English riding boots, and all. But this was no "blood," at least not an ordinary one, because he looked like a movie star and it was obvious that he had something going with the high-class lady in the backseat. Therefore I took a carefully guarded second look, and dam' if it wasn't that boy again!

This time, from what I could learn from the station attendant who was servicing my car, he was employed by an elderly but powerful politician, a really old one. And when I took a second look at the woman (a middle-aged strawberry blonde) and then at the limousine and your boy, I said to myself, "Now *there* sits a car that's in for some hard, fancy driving, and a fool of a woman who's had some fancy 'tampering'; so somewhere in this town there has to be a husband who's in plenty of trouble!"

Later I checked the address of the old man's estate and drove out to look it over, and it was what you'd expect of a Southerner who'd started out on grits and greens and rose up to spend forty years in Congress. It had fine lawns, a swimming pool, and tennis courts that were suitable for the Olympic games, and a servants' quarters which, given its own site, would have looked like a small mansion. But although the main house was staffed by a large staff of servants, including a French maid and a slew of us, the servants' quarters were strictly the domain of your boy. One night when I drove through the alley there seemed to be a party in progress but although the phonograph was blaring "Some Sunny Day" I saw no one. And since he no longer visited his old haunts, probably because of his break with Sippy, I was unable to check his movements. Then the old man and his wife took off for Europe and I assumed that once again I had lost contact. Which except for one final, somewhat bizarre, incident which came about through my constant need for funds to stay in school, was true.

That summer I was waiting tables in Maryland with a fellow student who told me about a movie based on the Civil War that was being shot on a nearby historical site where one of the battles had actually been fought. At first I thought, "So there they go messing with history again," but I became interested when he told me that the producers were having trouble hiring Negro extras to act as slaves. I asked him why *he* didn't give it a try and he said, "Hell, man, I have enough acting to do in just holding down this job. And besides, who the hell needs a second go at slavery?"

I approved of his sentiments, but since I needed extra cash and he assured me that it would only be a two-day deal which required no special experience, I rushed to Antietam and was hired.

Hickman, you would have died laughing to see me, a college man and aspiring intellectual, marching down a dirt road wearing overalls and carrying all my earthly belongings bundled in a red bandanna; but, as the old folks say, hard times will make a black rat swallow his pride and eat raw red onions. There were over two hundred of us, young and old, men and women, struggling along a road full of mule-drawn wagons, cannon, caissons, and panicky Northern soldiers in retreat from Southern cavalry. It was one hell of a scene, with cannons roaring, rifles crackling, and cavalry charges in which horses were rearing and neighing and kicking up dust as though they were caught up in the real thing, whether we humans recognized it or not. For as far as those animals were concerned us human beings had gone stark raving crazy. And it didn't matter who the hell they had in their saddles. Because they were being ridden by everybody from ex-cavalry men to cowboys, jockeys, and society equestrians—or anyone else who was willing and able to act the roles of that rip-roaring Johnny Reb cavalry. That movie crew reproduced the Battle of Bull Run in every detail they could come up with. From variations in the weather to the spectacular spilling of blood, sweat, and tears, to military equipment straining, banners flying, bugles blaring, wild-eyed, bit-chewing horses a-foam and lathering, sabers flashing, and men and mule turds falling—all timed to an array of real-life sound effects. They even shot a scene in which some Northern congressmen and their wives, dressed in the costumes of that period and carrying parasols and picnic baskets, came out to watch the action as though the battle was some kind of athletic contest. You should have seen them haul ass when those Southerners made a dash toward the Capital with those minié balls flying!

It was so realistic that in the thundering, ear-banging excitement I had to remind myself that for all the dash and slash those Southern horsemen were laying on the boys in blue, Time hadn't *really* reversed itself and transformed me into what I might have been if instead of winning the battle (which in fact it did) the South had been beaten back, redeployed, and then gone on to win the war.

Then it occurred to me that under such circumstances "history" didn't exist but was an afterthought imposed later as an explanation. History was a picture of events that were juxtaposed, recorded, and given meaning during the shooting of a given scene. It was not a product of destiny, but of the sound and fury of man-made, man-controlled action that was taking place in a fabricated context of events in which such mortal matters as birth and death, duration, change, and chance—those defining limits of human experience—were safely absent.

Because I was there, sweating and straining on a once bloody ground of political contention while taking part in the shooting of a movie that proposed to conjure up the past with optics, cogs, and film. But in fact neither the scene, the action, nor the "me"—the nonactor who was performing the part of a slave—were real. I "was," but was not; the war "was," but not truly, only "reely"! Because in fact my "role" was a nonwinnable "non-role"; something like that of a bone over which two dogs are fighting to see which one would eat it.

So it came to me that what is called "history" is to the actual as a reel of film to the scenes and action that we see unfold when we sit back in a darkened theater and watch lifelike shadows make their moves on a wall-sized screen. All of it, actors, scene, and action, lack life's depth and endless concatenation of detail and changeability and thus are without the consequences of mortality. It's something like the difference between disemboweling oneself in the Japanese ritual of *hari-kari* and pretending that you're Harry Carey chasing bad men and stray cattle in a Wild Western movie. And this despite a movie's ability to arouse and structure emotion. History is a tale told about the joys and anguish of survivors, winners or losers, by those who weren't there or even born when the actual events occurred.... But oh, how taking part in a historical movie can make you reel! And without your being aware of how and where you're tilting!

But such conjectures didn't stop me from going the full course. Besides, taking part in it turned out to have been far more instructive than reading the history book I consulted later to learn what the battle was all about. However, the point of all this speculation— which is a matter of notes I made at the time and not necessarily a matter of my present thinking—is to modulate to the incident which grew out of my venture into acting.

Two days later, after the shooting was over and I was standing in line waiting to be paid, I received a most unexpected bonus. It wasn't anything like the forty acres and a mule the real slaves were promised and then refused, but I happened to look up to see the famous star of the movie and a bunch of his supporting actors passing by and got a shock—yes, you're right on target! There he was again, this time swaggering along beside "Jeb Stuart," dressed in Confederate gray, carrying a saber, and wearing a foot-long feather in his hat!

Hickman, I swear, I was so disoriented that for a second I didn't know where I was, whether in "now" or "then," in the present of

Antietam or lost in movie-confused "history." And as I stood there wavering between making myself known or following my old routine of fading into the background where all such matters become blurred, a strange thing happened. For even though I was in blackface, filthy as could be, and still wearing the overalls and bandanna which they'd given me for a costume, I didn't have a chance. Because at that very moment he turned in my direction, stopped in mid-stride, and looked me over. That's right, he *recognized me*! And for the very first time in all the years that I'd been on his trail he indicated that he knew who I was. I say this because during the second our eyes met I could see a little smile playing around his mouth. Then he winked and gave me such a sweeping salute with his Confederate hat that its feather trailed in the dust, and I stood there looking down at the lacy marks it left like a chicken does when hypnotized by having its beak pressed into the dirt. And then to make sure that I would know who he was, he swaggered off after the Jeb Stuart character by doing a cute little hustler's limp!

It was as though he were telling me, "So all right, sport, we have finally met on neutral ground and therefore it's checkmate. But when you get in touch with Hickman don't forget to tell him that *I* let it happen. And if you should bump into Sippy you can give him my regards."

Hickman, all I could do was to stand there sweating more real sweat than I had during all the ruckus and strain that the movie director had put us through. And not so much because he had recognized me as from the shock of finding him slap-dab in the middle of a made-up world. It was upsetting because up to then I'd always found him acting in a world which I accepted as "real," but here he was acting in the middle of a made-up time and place; otherwise he would have been a Rebel officer and I would have been a slave. Therefore I had to ask myself where illusion ended and reality began, and what would happen if he ever stopped acting and decided to limit himself to a single role? I guess I'm trying to say that for the first time I had a sense of the frightening possibilities of the worlds, real or illusionary, in which he chose to operate and its possible consequences. What would happen if he operated in an actual job as he'd been doing in his endless con games? You'll understand when you consider how a movie actor can start his career playing bandits and horse thieves and end up playing sheriffs and judges, begin as villains and end as heroes.... But here I go trying to think again and I'm no more prepared for it now than I was back when I was playing your young man's shadow. However, I can say that my face-to-face encounter with him raised questions which cooled my enthusiasm. I think it was because I was already too uncertain about my own life and living too close to the edge of my own form of hell to keep prying into such mysteries....

That's my report, and I'm sorry I have nothing more to add, because without threatening me outright he managed to convey a warning that I should keep off his trail. And since I'd come to believe him capable of damn near anything I decided that it was best to leave him alone. That explains my silence and I'm sure that you must have grasped what had happened. I lost the game, but I had done my unskilled best against one hell of a player—or so I consoled myself whenever I felt guilty.

Other than that I'm doing fairly well and still fighting my habit by making do, for the most part, with what you used to call "dark-complexed coffee." And for all the frustration it's brought me I'm still studying and supporting myself by teaching a few courses in night school. I've also gone back to music. Nothing big-time, understand, but when I'm on a gig with a group of old-timers the excitement returns and it makes me wonder why anyone as good as you were could have given it up for preaching. For as I see it, you probably influenced far more souls for the better with that trombone than you'll ever do as a preacher. But don't get me wrong, I respect your decision, and while I'm thankful for the entertainment and instruction I received from trying to keep up with that character of yours—and was well paid for doing so—I hope and pray that one day you'll relent and tell me just why in hell, and where in hell you became interested in his activities.

In the meantime I must confess that back in those days when we were performing together I was so ignorant as to think that someone like you wouldn't understand the ideas which were rattling my booze-confused brain. But now I feel free to write you to the limits of my capacity because I've entered the age where I'm forced to recognize that experience is experience long before words can impose the unstable meanings for which they're employed. Therefore I realize that wisdom is wisdom, no matter how it's gained, and no matter the words through which it finds expression. So now, having done the best I can, I'm sure that you'll read right through my words and supply your own meaning. But words are no substitute for the pressing of the flesh, so if you're ever up this way please look me up. For not only would I be glad to see you, but there are still a few old-timers who refer to you fondly as "King Kong the Baptist" or as "Big Lon the Signifying Revealator" who'd like nothing better than to see you.

And come to think of it, Sippy is still around and living, some say, on some kind of pension set up by his millionaire. Should you have an interest in meeting him I would try to make it possible.

[DECISION]

So, Hickman thought with a grin, *you were not only "King Kong the Baptist," but "Big Lon the Revealator." Which wasn't so bad, considering what could happen to a man when fellows like that put the badmouth on him. What's more, there are still a few around who'd probably be pleased to come up with something far worse. Since Millsap proved to be so dependable I guess I should have told what it was all about, but what he didn't know didn't hurt him. In fact, not knowing might have saved him the burden of more hopeless knowledge—who knows?...*

But that boy he was trailing tried everything! Not only his stunt in that Dallas church, but others in Chicago and Lord knows where else. Playing small Southern towns with Lasses White's Minstrels, then up in Vermont with small carnival shows . . . sometimes playing Mister Bones in blackface, sometimes Mister Interlocutor with the barest of makeup. Then that hairdresser telling me about his being secretly in business making bleaching cream and hair straightener which he hired a bunch of attractive young women to peddle from door to door. Then he expands his business with wigs, hairpieces, and straightening combs which he labeled with the picture of a pretty, brown-skin Queen Cleopatra combing snakes out of her hair! And when that pays off he tries his hand at designing ads for the cosmetics trade. But there he slips up, because his ads were so ambiguous that after a few turned up in the comic section of a white newspaper he had to grab a freight train out of town. Maybe that's what led to his turning up in the movies, because even before Millsap's report turned up one of the members had spotted him in Virginia dressed in Rebel gray and riding a fine horse while taking part in a scene being shot near Richmond. So when the movie was premiered we rushed to see it, but sitting up there in the peanut gallery even I was unable to spot him among all those hard-riding Rebels. So for a time we lost both the man and his shadow. . . . Millsap would have liked it otherwise but I doubt that the boy could have been the fellow who was heard praying in the Pullman car—and yet I did hear that he'd cooked up a batch of what he tried to pass off as blues lyrics and was brash enough to try to palm them off on a famous white woman blues shouter. . . .

Hickman, how could it happen? What did you ever do to let such a rascal loose on the world? Once he ran away and stepped over the line he seems to have become like a kite broken loose from its string. Dipping and diving and whirling about, first rushing away from us and then making unexpected feints in our direction and darting away. And for all we were doing to keep an eye on the rascal it was as though each time we decided that he was going too far and agreed that we'd either bring him back to the fold or expose him, he sensed it and disappeared.

As he did after that terrible thing which happened to the young woman Janey told me about. I hoped and prayed that he'd make peace with himself and come home to rest, but it wasn't to be—at least not then. He just turned up again in other places and on other levels, and always exploiting and debasing the very best things we'd tried to give him. Conned and bankrolled his way to where he is today by using whatever it is he rejects in himself simply because it came from us. And as though that isn't enough, and in spite of our silence, he still keeps acting as though this country is a plantation which he owns and us, his old friends and guardians, no more than field hands to be denied and exploited. And what makes it so hard to bear is that he seems to be punishing us and anyone like us. Us, who gave him our love and who still hold true to our early commitment. So whatever's eating on him has to be something other than a madness for power. Maybe it's metaphysical, some kind of irrational need to deny his connection to us while taking revenge on whoever and whatever was responsible. Maybe he wants to turn back the clock so that he can be present at his own conception, observe the penetration, belly to belly, skin to skin; would listen to the sighs and moans, inhale the smells and feel the moisture.... Or even more desperately it must be the colors of skin-pressing skin that he yearns to see! He would recreate circumstances which are so far beyond his knowing—and mine—that they can only be accepted as an act of God and borne as an act of faith and self-acceptance. Maybe the explanation of his arrogance and restlessness lies in his desire to be the total product of his own creation—Bliss immaculate! If so, then it's his own self-chosen form of living hell. Yes, and just as being bound to him is my retribution for the sin of misguided pride.... May the Lord forgive us, him and me.... Amen.... But the sad, fly-in-the-milk joke of it is that I hoped to do good. Like the character in that high school play proclaimed, I've been true to our dream. So if now the time has come when I'll have to pay for my dreaming I'll see it through to the end....

Say me some Shakespeare, Daddy Hickman.

You mean to tell me that you want to hear me do some spear-shaking, Bliss?

Yes, sir.

But why?

'Cause it sounds so good.

Okay, so just give me a minute to think—how did it go? Oh, yes:

> *Mine honesty and I begin to square*
> *The loyalty well held to fools does make*
> *Our faith mere folly; yet he that can endure*
> *To follow with allegiance a fallen lord,*
> *Does conquer him that did his master conquer*
> *and earns a place in the story...*

And I thought the teacher who made me memorize such words was making an ass of himself and a fool out of me! Now look at me!

Replacing the report in its folder, he went to the closet and returned with an old alligator-hide briefcase from which he removed a batch of orchestral arrangements and sheafs of newspaper clippings. Fading and falling apart, they were notices from the Negro press of dances and theatrical dates of his performances, each displaying a publicity photograph of himself as an arrogant, cock-sure young man. Placing the clippings carefully aside, he searched deeper into the briefcase, removing papers and mementos until he found a small bundle wrapped in pink tissue paper, from which he removed a packet of photographs and began flipping them to the desk as though dealing himself a hand of solitaire—until, coming to a snapshot of a young couple with a nineteen-twenties touring car in the background, he paused and recalled the spirit of adventure, good times, and success which it held in timeless suspension.

Young, tall, and robust, he stood before the car's high convertible top with his arm around the waist of a pretty young woman who snuggled against him in her short fur coat. In the brilliant light his homburg tilted backwards, lending his image an air of self-esteem which caused him to grin now as he noted how pleas-antly the young woman had smiled and how brightly the car had gleamed in the sunlight. *It was a Dodge,* he thought, *and that fur coat she's wearing was called a "chubby"—but though huggable she sure wasn't chubby. If anything she was lean, keen, and unexpectedly mean. Built for speed but lacking the usual down-home warmth of our sweet teasing browns....*

How did it begin? You remember: In that riverside park where spring floods finally caused the white folks to turn it over and then make jokes about its being "the nigger Eden"—where else? It was the Fourth of July with you sitting high on the bandstand with members of the Elks band playing everything from patriotic marches to ragtime and jazz. And as usual your big glad eyes were ever a-roving—remember?

Yes, and the crowd of folks enjoying an afternoon of freedom. With some listening, some strolling, and others at the far end of the park yelling as they watched a baseball game. And far down the slope to the left of the bandstand girls in long skirts, headbands, and white blouses, and boys in white flannel trousers chasing tennis balls darting about the red clay courts with racquets. And beyond the crowd around the bandstand the backs of young men sporting sailors' straw hats and striped silk shirts strolling toward the trees with laughing young women who saunter and sway twirling parasols. And others like them, coming toward the bandstand with the wide brims of beribboned picture hats bowing gently around spit-curled, beauty-spotted faces as they smile and flirt with beaus who move with a silk shirt flouncing, "strutting-with-some-barbecue" swagger. And far beyond their spoony bantering small children are rising and falling—See-saw Margery Daw—or whirling in dreamy de-light on the park's carousel. And farther still beneath the low-branched trees families are gathered around tablecloths loaded with food and picnic baskets. And as you view the bustling activity around carts selling hot dogs and hamburgers, ice cream and lemonade, popcorn and spun cotton candy, you see the tug and toss of inflated balloons clustered on a string attached to a candy-striped cart. Then in standing to take a solo you see a single red balloon floating toward you over the heads of a young man and two young women. And as the three draw near, nodding their heads to the beat of the rhythm, it happened—

And there she was, with the warm, peachy bloom of her brown complexion bugging your eye and heating your horn and the music. Yes! And then with sly growls and bluesy moan-

ing you were riffing thirty-two bars of trombone sweet talk—all for the sweet young lady under the red balloon, saying:

I like them!

Like what?

Them!

Them what!

Lovely peaches!

Get on with it—what peaches?

Those peaches!

WHAT! Them lil' ole things? Them little Albertas?

Don't care!

But they might be canned!

Don't care!

But they might be clingers!

I don't care, I don't care, I don't care!

And if they're freestones?

It don't matter because freestones are sweet-sweet-sweet to my hong-gone-gongrey taste!

So?

So ooooh, aaaah! Oh-ho-ho! How I'd like to shake . . .

Yas?

I said I'd like to shake . . .

Yas?

. . . The leaves of that love-love-lovely . . .

Yas?

That lovely little, peachy little, unplucked a-little . . .

Yas?

'Cause just gimme one little shake and she'll never have to say say—Oh, no!

Now say it, SAY it!

If you don't like my peaches . . .

. . . Keep a-coming! Keep a-coming!

Just a-let my a-peach a-tree a-be!

Well a-yass, yass, a-yas-yass-yaaas!

And then giving her that snappy, horn-flipping bow and your signifying "It-was-all-for-you-darling" smile you looked straight into her curious big brown eyes. And then at the end of the set you made that tap-dancer's "How's-this-for-a-big-man" leap from the bandstand and it was: May I introduce myself, you said.

Oh we know who you are, he said.

Fine! But how about you, young lady?

Her too, he said, hugging the girl on his right. Any girl of mine has to know about you!

Now that's really good news, and I thank you. But how about this other young lady?

I'm not sure, she says, but I think I've heard of you.

Is that right? Well let me make myself known, it's Hickman. Alonzo Hickman. And yours?

Oh, go on, girl, he won't bite you! So tell him!

Oh, I know that—Mr. Hickman, it's Janey . . .

And what a sweet name for such a pretty lady. It's a pleasure to make your acquaintance, Miss Janey, and I'd like nothing better than to see more of you—is that possible?

But Mister Hickman, I've just met you . . .

I know, but I have plenty of patience—oh, Lord! There they go, signaling me back to the bandstand. So before I go, is there any way that I may get in touch with you? And before you answer, think about this: If I don't see you again, and soon, I'll simply wither away and away and away until there's nothing left but a wee tiny voice whispering Janey, Janey, oh, please, Miss Janey!

And then with a giggle she'd surrendered her address, and you returned to the bandstand thinking everything was coming up roses. The very next day you paid her a visit, met her parents, and escorted her to several parties before leaving town for a series of Northern engagements. Then came your return during the bright fall weather of the photograph, and the fateful church social in which your luck turned bad. Thought everything was copacetic, then one of her friends' parents looked up and recognized you and informed her parents of your reputation, and that was the beginning of the end. For in spite of your—no his, your old self's—pride over his way with words, you could get no farther. Not even when you proposed marriage. So you reaped what you sowed, after climbing many a wicked, easily climbed mountain you finally looked down upon a lovely valley and got turned away. . . .

Dropping the photo to the desk with a rueful smile, he shook his head, thinking, *It's been so long ago and so much has changed that it's hard to believe that it ever happened. But whatever she's asking of me I have to answer. Her "little men"! Maybe that was the real trouble, you were simply too doggone big, loud, and aggressive!*

But as he returned the snapshots to their wrapping he realized that his troubling, apprehensive mood was being generated by overtones which played between Millsap's old report and Janey's letter. Reaching for it, he began reading it again; but suddenly aware of the edgy sound of Sister Wilhite's second call to lunch, he replaced the report, clippings, and snapshots and returned the briefcase to the closet. Then, thinking abstractly of Millsap and Janey, time zones and distances, he made his way to the bathroom, washed and dried his hands, and inspected his beard in the mirror.

Stroking his chin, he thought, *A boy learns to shave by watching his father—at least I did—but what do boys do who have no fathers? Like Janey's little men? Hickman, they experiment, scrape and nick. Keep their eyes open in barbershops. Safety razors helped a lot, but with fathers or without, boys must make up a good part of themselves from observed examples. We are formed or left unformed by such small and unnoticed things. Because at that time of life everything from games to catechisms serve as rituals, whether in the streets or at the dinner table. So boys, unlike girls, are formed catch-as-catch-can, no matter what parents do to guide them. They're formed more by accident and so much slower than little girls—but I know that he watched me shave, even played at it, using soapsuds and a butter knife . . . asking me why I puffed out both cheeks like I was blowing my horn when I was only shaving. . . .*

I said, Because stretching the skin a bit makes the shaving easier....

And why don't ladies shave?

Some do, Bliss, but only a few, far and in between.

Between what?

Why between the times they shave. You know something, Bliss? You ask a lot of questions—hand me that towel.

How come?

You mean why ladies don't shave? Because, Bliss, most of their hair is on their heads where everybody likes for it to be. And since any hair that they might want to shave takes a long time to grow back they just leave things as the good Lord made them....

His will be done?

Yes, Bliss, His will be done....

Reaching the table, where Sister Corrine in a hard-starched blue gingham apron and Deacon in white suspenders and open collar were already seated, he said grace, picked up his napkin, and turned to Sister Corrine, who was serving his plate, and said,

"Sister Corrine, you were right...."

"Of course I'm right," she said with a pert jerk of her head, "but what about?"

"Oh, come on," he said, "quit stalling; I mean about the letter...."

"Oh my Lord! Is she sick?"

"No, or at least she didn't say so. It's something else...."

"So tell us, what did she say?"

"That's the point, it's not so much what she said as what she *didn't* say...."

"Quit making riddles, A.Z.," Wilhite said. "Is it something to do with that boy?"

Suddenly Hickman sat back in his chair, his fork in the air.

"*Boy,*" he said, "what on earth would *he* be doing out there?"

"I'm only asking," Wilhite said, "but as you know, he has a way of turning up almost anywhere...."

"That's right," Sister Corrine said, "and you remember that she wrote you years ago about his being out there."

"I remember," Hickman said, "but you can forget that because this time she said nothing about him. Besides, why on earth would he go into Janey's area? She's the last person in the world he'd want to run into. Especially now that he's sitting on top of his world."

"Well, I wouldn't be so sure about that," Sister Corrine said, "because there's still such a thing as conscience, even for someone like him."

"No," Wilhite said, "A.Z. is probably right. He wouldn't risk it."

"So all right, Revern'," Sister Corrine said, "instead of all this speculating why don't you tell us what she said? What's bothering her?"

His appetite gone, Hickman put down his fork. "To tell you the truth, she wrote me a small book of a letter and after reading it twice I still don't know exactly what she's getting at."

"So what's so strange about that?" Sister Corrine said. "She always liked to play the coy one. At least that's the way she's always seemed to me. One way or another that woman has been stringing you along for *years*!"

Wilhite struck the table. "Corrine," he said, "shut up and mind your own business!"

"I am! Because it's my God-given duty to look out for *both* of you hicky-heads, so don't you go raising your voice at me!"

"Please," Hickman said, "the last thing I need is for you two to get going at one another. So if it will do anything to quiet you, she seems to be worried about some fellow whom she thinks to have been one of her charges. One of those she refers to as her 'little men.' Heaven only knows why she's being so vague about it, but she says that he's out there asking questions...."

"And didn't I know it," Sister Corrine said, "she's after you ag'in! A woman like that will say *anything* to get a man's attention!"

"No," Hickman said, "it's nothing like that. And even if it were, where's your charity?"

"Charity? It's not charity she wants, it's *you*."

"So what are you going to do about it, A.Z.?" Wilhite said.

"I guess," Hickman said, suddenly making his decision, "that I'm going west about it...."

"And like I didn't already know it," Sister Corrine said, getting to her feet, "so instead of sitting here listening to you two making up excuses while this food gets cold I'm going to do some packing."

"A.Z.," Wilhite said, "don't you think you should let me do it? I could scout around without many folks recognizing me...."

"Thanks, but it's better that I look into this myself. And face-to-face. Anyway, I doubt that Janey would talk to you—And no matter what Sister Corrine thinks, she's not playing games. Signifying, yes; but it's something serious that's bothering her."

"Did this fellow threaten her?"

"No, but she sees some kind of threat in his showing up."

"So it has to be that boy, he's on the move again!"

"No! Why do you keep bringing *him* into it? He was never one of her little men, he was ours!"

"Take it easy, A.Z., I was only asking. And I have this feeling that he's mixed up in it. Big men make little men, remember? And have women who birth them."

"True, Wilhite, but he'd be crazy to show up out there."

"And that's what I'm afraid of, A.Z. And since it's come up, I might as well say it: I think the game he's been playing has brought him to the point where he'll do *anything*. So far he's been getting away with it, but there's a limit to everything."

Hickman leaned forward. "What was that you said about a woman?"

"I didn't, I said 'women,' and I was thinking about that mess he made back when he was exploiting folks with those mammy-made movies. Don't tell me you've forgot it."

"No, I haven't, how could I? Naw, Wilhite, it's simply something that I wasn't allowing myself to remember."

"So you see what I mean?"

"Yes," he said, getting up from the table, "and it's all the more reason that I have to get out there. Will you drive me to the airport?"

"Who else?"

"Fine! So I'd better tell Sister Corrine that I'm traveling light and get myself ready."

[BUS TRIP]

WITH THE PLANE SLOWLY circling as it began its approach to the airport, Hickman looked out to see networks of streets wheeling below. Tall buildings thrust skyward from the heart of the city, and far to the northeast the domeless State Capitol revolved in its setting of green lawns, oil wells, and derricks. Then from a wing-tilting slant southward the North Canadian River flashed into view, etched in the landscape like the scrawl of a child.

Shimmering low in its banks, the river appeared peaceful, but in following its course from the air he recalled accounts of a spring when without warning it had raged through the lowlands destroying homes and uprooting trees in a flood filled with debris and drowned animals. That no human lives were lost was seen as a miracle, but people caught in its path were forced to flee its destruction in skiffs and canoes....

But now the river's tranquillity muted his memories, and as he turned away to see the FASTEN SEAT BELTS sign flashing, he obeyed. And in thinking of Janey he recalled that her mysterious visitor had also arrived without warning and wondered if it were that which she found so disturbing.

But now, hearing a roaring reversal of engines, he felt the plane descending. And with a belt-tightening bump it struck the runway and he was cruising toward the airport ahead like a shot from a cannon.

Leaving the plane, he retrieved his baggage and made his way through the crowded terminal to wait outside for the downtown bus. Where, standing in the shade with his panama pushed back from his brow, he watched a steady stream of cars and taxis discharging and taking on passengers. Marked by a hubbub of idling engines and excited voices, the scene was punctuated by the *slam-bam*, "Thank you sir, Thank you ma'am" of skycaps loading and unloading luggage. And as he looked on he recalled his last trip to the airport. For then he had enjoyed reminiscing with three of its veteran skycaps about dances for which he had played during the old days. But as he scanned the scene nearby to see if they were among them there came a flash of memory in which it took on details from the past, and with it a disturbing sense of his aging.

For increasingly such flashbacks were accompanied by interior dialogues in which a voice from his life as an irreverent young bluesman mocked his present role of spiritual leader and reminded him of his lingering worldliness. Marked by a conflict between his past and his present, it was an ongoing dialogue in which the younger self badgered and teased while his older self stubbornly asserted its spiritual authority. But while their interchanges were often amusing and helped in clarifying his thinking, a busy airport was no place for such distracting argument. So now, still hoping to pass a few words with somone from the old days, he concentrated his attention on a group of skycaps who were loaded down with the baggage of passengers as they headed for a plane which was loading. But again none were familiar.

And with a shrug he turned away, thinking, *Forget it, Hickman. And remember that it's been years since you've seen them. So if they're still alive they've probably retired or gone on to other jobs or professions. In those days it was common for college graduates—including Ph.Ds.—to work as skycaps, bellhops, and waiters, but now times are changing. So who knows? Maybe the old-timers you remember were college trained and the war finally provided them opportunities for using their knowledge. . . .*

Yes, he thought, *the war was terrible, but like the Depression it brought new opportunities. Which is what Daddy meant by such events being forms of "left-handed democracy." And he was right, because they have indeed brought important changes. They're unpredictable, but even when they appear totally negative their effects can be mixed and deceptive. That's why Daddy was always advising folks to keep alert in case something which appears completely disastrous turns out to be a blessing in disguise. Yes, and gets exploited by others before our folks even realize what's happening. Young Millsap called it "a unity of opposites"—which was just another term for the unpredictable unity of good things and bad.*

And now, watching a handsome black chauffeur assisting an elderly white couple into a gleaming Rolls-Royce, he recalled reading Millsap's hilarious account of what he called his "Civil War experience" and shook with a sudden upsurge of laughter.

What a devilish example of how man-made illusions can play jokes on reality, he thought. *First the real war leads to the end of slavery and promises Millsap's grandparents their freedom. And although it turned out to be far less than they expected, they encouraged their children to look ahead with fairly high expectations. Then, with the war assumed to have ended, Millsap is born and his parents train him to be a responsible citizen. And out of a stubborn hope that whenever equality did arrive he'd be prepared to make the most of it, they sacrifice to give him a good education. So although the road was still rocky and dangerous he was sustained in his struggle by his parents' faith in democracy.*

But when he's finished college and things seemed to be becoming a bit more hopeful, times change for the worse. He's on his own, out of work, and so low in his educated mind that he's plumb disgusted. And then, just when he's beginning to wonder if conditions were any better than they were for his grandparents—up pops the War between the States—which was anything but Civil—to set back the clock and confuse him!

Only this time it's taken the form of a movie, and about which he hears from his buddy who, like most of our folks, wants nothing to do with a war in which thousands of white folks were killed fighting over slavery. Yes, and over which they're still fighting, whether they know it or not up there in Washington!

So while his buddy rejects risking the embarrassment that could come from taking a job in the movie, Millsap faces a tough decision. Because having studied books on the war and lived its results he can either follow his friend's example and feel morally victorious, or refuse to let the past get in the way of his dealing with his present condition. So, deciding to be practical, he rushes to Antietam, a place where some of the worst of the killing took place, applies for a job, and feels lucky to be accepted.

Then next thing he knows he's been cast backwards in time and being told how to act like an ignorant slave by a white director—who was probably born somewhere in Europe—and ends up with his educated mind in a whirlwind. Because after all the years and the struggling he finds himself being fed at long range by the same war which led to his being born half-free and now educated and hungry!

What a war! And when you consider who turned up playing the part of a Confederate officer, what a mind-boggling joke for history to play on us descendants of slaves!

Yeah, Hickman, an inner voice answered, *it's crazy, but as you keep telling the brothers and sisters: Every "yes" has its "no," and every "no" its "yes." And just as you keep insisting that mankind's distress is God's opportunity, this country's hard times—like its love of easy living—often work to our advantage. It's like improvising jazz, but given all its commotion, sour notes, and off-beat rhythms, if you don't keep the hope-inspiring melody it began with ever in mind, life can be a tough tune to follow.*

So if you want to keep riffing you have to keep thinking and making tough choices, and not only looking ahead, but up, down, around, and behind you! Yes, and watching out for all kinds of discords and accidentals. Talk about blessings coming wrapped up in calamities! Still, that's how it always was, is now, and shall probably continue, world without end as it was in the beginning.

Yes, he thought, *but these skycaps are youngsters, and even if I were to remind them of such complexities they're probably too busy making money to let it bother them.*

Like me in the old days. When you're young and not only getting by but enjoying a few of the good things of life, who wants to think about the close connection between good times and bad, the past and the present? It's too gloomy, too depressing. Satchel Paige said, don't look back because something might be gaining on us. Yes, but no matter how fast you keep running something is always *gaining on you, even if it's nothing but Time.*

Time, now that's *the joker in the deck—just look at those fellows racing against the clock as they hustle those tips! Wonder how they think about themselves in terms of ambition and training? Students? Ex-war pilots? Airplane designers—like the fellow working as a porter at that airfield in Dayton? Which reminds you that the difference between a man's sense of himself and how he's viewed by others can be as different as the contrast between midnight and morning....*

Get an education, they tell us.

And we try.

Then they say, Now make yourself worthy.

So we try and sometimes succeed, at least to our own conception.

But then they tell us that we're not really ready, and no matter how hard we dispute them we learn that we have to wait for a war or depression to strike the whole country before we can move on to our next slow stage of advancement.

Still, there's no question that toting bags is better than chopping cotton—which a lot of folks back home are not only still doing but making the best of it. So where you are still makes a difference. That's why so many took off for places like Chicago, Denver, and Kansas City—Sorry, baby, but I can't take you. And before that those like Janey's folks left the South and came out here where the land was less settled and living less contentious. But all too soon they learned that they still had to keep watching their steps. Because when the land got settled and the towns established and more of us kept arriving, doors started slamming and we were pushed off to the side, across the tracks, and down to the bottoms.

Which was already happening by the time I arrived in this town. First they pushed us out of certain types of jobs, then out of the parks and the movies. And then, after labeling us "animals"—lo and behold!—they denied us the freedom to visit the zoo!

Janey still complains about how wild we musicians were back in the old days, but wildness went with the territory and was part of our freedom. Still, she's right about that being my reason for hanging around towns like Kansas City so long. In those days they were places where a musician could develop his music and make it sound in ways that gave him fulfillment. Yes, and still make a living. And that was possible because everybody and everything was so wild and woolly that our hard-driving style gave a little more order to what even white folks were feeling. Gave form to all that freewheeling optimism and told folks who they were and what they could be.... But then up jumps Time, that ever-waiting joker, yelling, Get back to the beginning and take it from there! Yes, and now here it comes again, leaping at you now in the form of a bus....

Once the bus was parked and taking on passengers, he paid his fare, gave the driver his luggage, and climbed soberly aboard. And brooding again over his coming encounter with Janey, he took a seat in the rear next to a window. Where, settling back, he waited impatiently for the bus to be under way. Its first stop would be a famous downtown hotel, and from there he would head for the East Side and find a room somewhere in his old stomping ground before making his way to Janey's.

And now with his hat tilted over his eyes he watched the entry of two young Negro men whose casual air was belied by the alertness with which their eyes flashed over the seated passengers before selecting seats in the left front row.

Times might have changed, he thought, but as in the old days they're checking opportunities against custom, and watched the two deliberately taking their time in getting seated while keeping a lively group of young white men and women waiting.

Studying the young whites he thought, *They're probably college students. Unso-*

phisticated and having a good time enjoying the freedom of doing what for them comes naturally. About the same age as the two blocking the aisle, having no need to check out the scene before taking a front seat on a bus or anywhere else. . . .

But now he was watching two white youngsters wearing cowboy outfits topped by ten-gallon hats who flopped with a stylized nonchalance into seats several rows ahead.

There you go, Hickman, the blues voice said: *Just when you decide those young brown-skinned bloods were putting on an act, here come two young white dudes about the same age dressed up like cowboys. Yeah! And from their looks they've probably never seen the smoke of a red-hot shoe being pressed to the hoof of a horse. And unless I'm wrong they'd probably consider the practice of getting a mule's attention by busting his head with a whiffle tree a crime against nature!*

So with one bunch pretending to be sophisticated citizens of the world and the other pretending to be something out of a cowboy movie, which of the two is being forced to act, and which is giving free rein to their fantasy?

But now his eyes were drawn to the bustling entrance of a young Indian woman wearing a bright blue dress and carrying a plump young baby, a nursery bag, and a fresh bouquet of red roses.

Now *that* appears to be the real thing, he thought, and two generations of it, times and change notwithstanding. And as the young mother moved past, the baby turned and stared into his face out of black, sharp-focusing eyes that seemed to ask questions.

Then seeing the door filled by a tall, narrow-eyed official-looking white man dressed in a Western hat and a corduroy jacket that bulged at his hip. And as the doors closed he watched the man survey the bus from front to rear before taking a seat on the right near the driver. Then the driver shifted gears, and as the bus moved into traffic he rested back with Janey's letter again troubling his mind.

But now, with the bus on the highway and picking up speed, there came a protesting cry, and looking to the rear he saw the Indian baby squalling on its mother's shoulder.

So, Reverend, the blues voice said as he turned and looked ahead, *it seems that whoever said Indian babies never cry was telling a lie. Am I right?*

Could be, came the answer.

Yeah? Well don't leap to conclusions.

Why not?

Because it's probably that little fellow's way of protesting over having to ride in a bus loaded with all these blackfeet and palefaces. . . .

Now you listen. . . .

. . . But on the other hand, Rev, it could be that after staring at you he still can't decide whether you're King Kong the Baptist or Peter Wheatstraw. You remember Wheatstraw, the Devil's son-in-law, who was always challenging you to gamble back in the old days? So if the papoose is right about his being on this bus, are you prepared to shoot him one?

Not when I'm out here strictly to help Janey. If I were at home I'd be preparing a sermon. Besides, being challenged by the Devil goes with my job. So knock it off!

Poor Janey, he thought, *she's upset over some stranger showing up in her neighborhood without her permission. What did she call him? Oh, yes—it was "Mister Noname from Nowhere." Which simply means a mysterious stranger. So let's hope it's a case of his giving her nothing more to fear than what F.D.R. called "fear itself."...*

Now that sounds like a promising text, so take it and git while I sit back and listen....

... Oh, yes, my friends, but while F.D.R. was speaking of "one world" and raising our expectations, I must remind you that one of our worst problems comes from being forced to live in a world within *a world. That's right! And with ours small and familiar and the one in which it finds existence so much bigger that it seems overwhelming.... It has also been said that a house divided against itself cannot stand—but don't you believe it! Because given enough space, strength, and worldly resources it can. Yes, but only with the injustice and violence with which we ourselves are all too familiar. Therefore we're stretched between a world in which we know our way around fairly well and another in which we're constantly at the mercy of those who would keep its ways and motives a mystery. Yes, my friends. And although I don't actually know this, it appears that those who structured the world around our world have set up ways-and-means committees just for keeping folks like us in the dark!*

Oh, yes! As far as we're concerned their policy has long been one of out of sight, out of mind—just listen to that little baby and ask yourselves who back East or in Washington ever thinks about the Indians these days other than as actors in cowboy movies. And yet out here there are many different tribes of Indians—yes, and some with soggy, uncomfortable diapers!

Therefore the idea of putting the Indians on film and forgetting them hasn't worked— oh, no, because those diapers keep filling! And what's more, they keep messing up the claims of Christopher Columbus! And by the way, the Indians say that they had no need to be discovered by the likes of Columbus....

So as I say, the powerful are forever trying to keep the connections between their world and ours under cover and in the dark. And so intently that when some person, or force, or sickness from the big world shows up in the smaller—or from the smaller into the larger— it plumb upsets the landscape of the mind and all its crannies and regions. And what's worse, it charges everything with uncertainty.

"What's that smell? Where's it coming from?" we ask ourselves. "Who's responsible?"

And pretty soon folks in the big world start wrinkling their noses and pointing at those in the smaller. And those in the smaller start shaking their heads, because after all this time they think they know not only who's a friend, enemy, or neutral, but exactly who it is that's so chronically upset in his bowels. Therefore they figure that they know the source of the smell all too well, so in order to keep their sanity they try not to think too much about the goings-on in the bigger world if only because they have only so much God-given time to stay alive. Therefore they try to get their cornmeal made and enjoy a little happiness.

Yes, my friends, but the stink keeps spreading and fuming, so don't relax too much and keep a Kleenex handy. Because when the big world rumbles the little world quakes. And when that happens things get thrown off balance and knocked out of scale. And then, Lord help us, if we don't hold on tight to the values which our small-world experience has taught us. Otherwise it can leave us helpless. And when the lines between the two worlds blur, everything and anything can become threatening.

Like shadows, or gifts, kind words, or simple politeness. Even acts that would seem to have nothing directly to do with us in the quarantined, pesthouse world of our semi-isolation. Because as you all well know, very often mistakes of identity or misinterpretation of events make for mistaken intentions and unexpected reactions. Maybe that's what our sister Janey is up against—not something KNOWN, but something NOT known. And that's what I'm up against, and of that I feel sure. So we ask ourselves, What's to fear and what's NOT to fear?

My friends, it's like living in a blackout of a big city, where every shadow or movement or sound in the dark can mean danger. Or to bring it closer to home, it's like being caught at night on the only piece of high ground when a springtime flood sends snake and possum, raccoon and deer up out of the bottoms to join you. That's when you find yourself slap-dab in the middle of what's been dreamed of as a "peaceful kingdom," a situation in which man and beast forgive one another their differences and live in peaceful coexistence—yes, but the truth is that when man and beast come together they are both immobilized by fear. For when the UNEXPECTED becomes the expected, and the ideal threatens to become FACT, all KINDS of nightmares start romping wild in the daylight, and nobody dares drop his guard.

I am reminded of a time years ago, when our jazz band was traveling by automobile through the flooded countryside of Kansas. Being young and brash we considered ourselves streetwise and worldly, but soon we would find our worldliness tested by reality. For as our slow caravan of cars made its way along a road flooded by a swollen river we saw in the distance a magnificent tree.

Brothers and sisters, it was a MAGNIFICENT tree! Tall with widespread branches, and so bleached by the sun and so warped by the weather that it gleamed in the air like a candelabra of silver. Spring had sprung and the fields on hillsides were bright green with promise; but then, rolling closer, we entered a stench and saw that the river was filled with the carcasses of animals. Hogs and horses, cows and pigs, all floating belly-up in the swirl of the current. And then, hardly before we could react to this bloated evidence of natural disaster, we looked skyward and saw that the tall magnificent tree before us was covered trunk, branch, and tips of limbs with snakes! And POISONOUS snakes they were!

Snakes were EVERYWHERE! Black snakes and copperheads, diamondbacks and moccasins! So many snakes were clinging to that towering tree that we stopped the cars and watched them coiling and wiggling and flicking their tongues as though they were testing God's radiant sunlight for some unnameable danger. And suddenly before our awe-stricken eyes that familiar object of nature became a gnarled elderly white-haired woman, who wore snakes for a wig and more snakes for her shawl!

It was and it wasn't. It was both dead and alive. An optical illusion yet one that was alive with deadly potential. And so before our disoriented eyes the real, the natural, had become an illusion, and the illusion a thing of natural and unnatural terror!

Thank God that we rolled on rubber! Thank the Lord that no sparkplug misfired nor car engine sputtered as we rolled away gazing backwards! . . .

... Yes, Hickman, and thank the Lord that for once you were stone-cold sober, in your right mind, and able to drive that half-paid-for Dodge through all that muddy, floorboard-deep water! ...

... Beat it, Buster!—Oh, yes, my friends, we live in a bisected double-world, one part fairly small and the other so large and complicated that it can seem foggy-formless. And while we can control the smaller world to a limited extent, the other is in the hands of folks who try to act as though there's no possible connection between us and them. Therefore, when something from their larger world enters the life of someone like our sister Janey, everything gets charged to the breaking point with uncertainty.

And that, my friends, is because in a certain sense this country is an unsteady contraption of wheels within wheels, or gears within gears, and the problem arises because too few of its gears are truly meshing. Therefore instead of running smoothly, and under the attention of wise and perceptive attendants, great worlds of energy are wasted in denying the connections that do exist, and must exist, between them.

And they DO exist, even here on this bus. So whenever something happens to make us aware that the gears are slipping, our world starts to banging away within the larger world like a locomotive stored deep in the hold of a seagoing ship that has broken loose from its moorings. And that's when that larger world finds that it can't zig for zagging. And then its gyroscope spins backwards and the entire country starts to wobble and shake on its axis. And while the big men up on the ship's bridge might or might not know what's happening, we down in the hold are filled with anxiety. That's when we sense all kinds of dangerous possibilities and life becomes a matter of living in the dark, or perhaps it's like being crazy—paranoid, I think is its fancy name. Then everything seems to become either all Black or all White, even though the real world remains as gray as it always was. And that's exactly the time to remind ourselves that Ezekiel saw the WHEEL! And that while the big wheel ever has trouble turning according to Constitutional law, the little wheel turns—oh, yes—by the grace of God!

My friends, my sisters and brothers, I'm reminding you of all this because discomfort and danger are abiding aspects of life. For indeed if we aren't careful many familiar things, many familiar forces, can become filled to the brim with danger. Such as food and drink, entertainment and family relations, patent medicine and tobacco, even self-confidence, modesty, and well-deserved pride. Yes, and even the most sacred of joyful music. For given the wrong combination of circumstances any of these can lead to destruction!

Therefore, my friends, we must get ourselves together and learn more of the larger world in which we are living! Because what we don't know can do us in! Not that there aren't plenty of things in BOTH worlds—and especially in the blurred and concealed connections between them—to justify ANYBODY'S being skittish.

Indeed, our problem is one of knowing of what, exactly, to BE afraid. For recognize it or not, there are real dangers hidden in the shadows used to limit and control us. For always we see as through a glass darkly, and I don't mean those fancy things those young folks up ahead are wearing.

For even fashion can blind us, and one of the worst things to have happened to this country is that today people are being deliberately taught to fear harmless situations and people while being urged, badgered, and exhorted to grab fearlessly onto things that can destroy *them. Oh, yes! Somewhere along the way that old earthly wisdom called "common sense" went plumb out of style! Yes, and with it the obvious fact that while fear can inhibit action it has the function of preserving life. For as we all know and forget at our peril, it takes COURAGE to be afraid of real danger and stay alive! Did somebody say "Amen"?*

So here, as in other ways, we have fallen below the level of the birds and the beasts, who never forget that just being alive is precarious and precious! And yet if we would use our eyes and minds and remember that up there above us all HIS eye is on us even as it is on the sparrow, the heron, and the whale. Therefore, in using our eyes and minds we are prepared to live neither in cocksure daring nor in sheer fear and trembling, but in faith. Otherwise we are so much at the mercy of the many, many things and circumstances that can kill us that we are unable to perform even the simplest acts that make us human.

For memory can kill, and forgetfulness can kill, and the deliberate rejection of memory which is practiced in this country can be most deadly. Oh yes! As deadly as arsenic, rabies, or internal war. For it can come at us on our blind sides and kill us in unexpected ways. It can erupt out of things as innocent as a handful of dust, drops of water, a shaft of sunlight, a splinter of glass, a misguided leap, stumble, or fall, a needle in the flesh, a sniff of powder, or explosion of noise on the eardrums.

And shortsightedness can kill, as can staring at one point in a total scene as we look backwards while traveling ahead. Or staring at a single segment of a complex action while ignoring the expanse of the whole—this too can kill.

And ignoring the possible connections BETWEEN actions and their results. Or between causes and effects. Or the tricky, distorting web that time itself spins between past wrongs, forgetfulness, and present-day resentments—these can kill.

And reducing complex events to simplicities and calling it "history" can kill. And I mean long after such distortions have been lied about so often that they become meaningless. For then such so-called "history" can be far, far more deadly than war.

And blind power and arrogance can kill—as can impatience before human complexity.

And ignoring the fact that we can reap what we sow. Or that what goes up has to come down. Or that the higher a monkey climbs the more he shows his . . .

. . . No, no, Hickman! Because while true it wouldn't do! But keep riffing . . .

. . . Or that the last shall be first and the weak be made strong, and that the meek who endure shall inherit whatever the hell is left of all the confusion created by the inevitable downfall of arrogant pride.

Oh yes, my friends, my sisters and brothers, many things can kill. MANY things. But nothing is more deadly than forgetting that ALL men are brothers who possess the same instincts, emotions, and dreams. And if we ignore this it can kill us most cruelly. As cruelly as lynch ropes, gasoline, and torches.

But why stop with such extremes? Why stop there, when pretty women can kill? And airplanes, bucking horses, careless physicians, and bad, uncommitted teachers—yes, and sinful, fore-day-creeping, rabble-rousing, money-grubbing publicity-seeking PREACHERS—yes, that's right! They too can kill! As can prejudiced politicians and unjust judges! All these can kill—and do, and in wholesale lots; whether in bed, in the air, the schoolroom, pulpit, ballot box, or at high noon on an empty sidewalk!

And IDEAS can kill—yes, that's right! For in this weird, cantankerous country of ours with all of its newspapers, books, radios, and television bringing all kinds of information to all kinds of unknown, cranky, and volatile people . . . even the NEWS can kill.

For just as the world is made up of different peoples with different strokes, the news means different things to different folks. Therefore the same ideas that have the power to quicken one man's mind, strengthen his will, and make him hale, hearty, and whole, can make another man mindless, dead, and forever still!

And a lack of charity can kill. For refusing to share with the weak and homeless can lead them to discover their potential power and allow some con man to use it and organize their resentment against you.

And the same is true of condescension and self-righteousness. For it is in our nature as human beings, men, women, individuals, and groups, to bring down arrogance and pompous, puffed-up Pride. Therefore even though it is our tradition to punish such things with laughter and scorn it remains most deadly.

And brushing aside the opinions of the weak (like those of that little Indian baby) or the weaknesses of the strong, or the vision of the blind, or the blindness of visionaries, or the holiness of sinners—all or any of these can lead to deadly confusion and to death by confusion.

And ignoring the justified complaints of our fellow human beings can kill—even as playing too long upon the guilt of the strong when we press our just claims against them. For then it can backfire and make them even more steadfast and unyielding in their unjustness. And in defending their acts and wrongdoings they will kill us in the name of the very ideals and principles upon which we base our just claims.

For if driven into a corner and deprived of the slipperiness of words, they will turn upon us in anger, saying, "Yes, so all right, you've made your point, but we kill you in the name of DEMOCRACY!"

Or they will say, "Yes! What you say is true, for we see your suffering and sympathize. But nevertheless we must deny you freedom in the name of a future freedom, one which is higher and more GLORIOUS!"

And then if we keep pressing—as we have to do, oh, yes!—and cry out and appeal to them in the name of Almighty God, they will shrug their shoulders and perhaps even smile as they inform us in the most reasonable of language, "Ah yes, you are right again. But you must understand that WE have OUR history just as YOU have yours, but unfortunately both are against you. Therefore you must understand that there is nothing personal in what we do, because we kill you in the name of our God, who in all things is most JUST and GENTLE!"

So while we stand confounded by their insistence that God's will and what they call "history" are one and the same, they will rear back and kill us in the name of their God, and feel not only justified in what they've done but as innocent as a babe and hound-tooth clean! . . .

Okay, Rev, if you insist, but we're almost back to the real world, so you'd better pull that hound's tooth and get it over with. . . .

That, my friends, is the bind we're in. But the saving grace is that we see the lay of the land and the structure of his lie, just as we see the joke in his thinking that we willingly accept it. But here we must remember that if we hate our enemies for rejecting our humanity we'll end up participating in our own DESTRUCTION.

So let us remember the ties that bind us to this land and to those who oppose us—not for their sake, but for the sake of our own salvation. And since blind blackness can kill no less than blind whiteness, and just as self-righteously, there's no lasting satisfaction to be found in blind retaliation based on our blackness. Yea, we must love our enemies as ourselves—not because we bow down before their will—oh no! But because both we and they are committed to the same transcendent ideal. Yes, and it is in the name of that unifying ideal that we both toil and suffer, and it is precisely because of that shared ideal that they shall fail and we shall prevail.

Therefore, my sisters and brothers, let us cling to OUR version of the all-encompassing vision and heed the glad tidings that bind us to this land. Let us survive and give hope to ALL its people....

...In other words, dear sisters and brothers, he's telling you to quit all your messing around and get your black selves TOGETHER!

Feeling a loss of motion, he opened his eyes to find the bus rolling through the downtown streets of the city, and shook his head as he thought, *Hickman, urging folks to live in faith is fine, but hitting them over the head with poorly organized ideas is something else. So since that's about the* homeliest *homiletic you've ever come up with, you'd better remember that corny sermons make for gloomy Sundays and half-empty churches....*

Now that the bus was parked before the famous downtown hotel, the aisle filled with passengers. And as they made their departure he remained in his seat and looked out to see them take off in various directions. Some with their luggage were hailing taxis while others moved toward the hotel to the jovial welcome of its uniformed doorman. And as he watched people on the sidewalk approaching the hotel from both directions he was reminded that he faced the annoying problem of finding a room before proceeding to drop in on Janey.

But now, looking to see the young Indian mother moving past with her baby peeping over her shoulder, he recalled his joke about the infant puzzling over his identity and surged with laughter.

No, little Chief, he thought, I'm neither Peter Wheatstraw disguised as King Kong the Baptist nor King Kong disguised as Wheatstraw, I'm Hickman. And with a wave to the baby he cooed, "Bye-bye, little bright eyes, it's good to have seen you."

And with a bubbling burp, the baby waved back, and cooed, "Goo-goo!" with a smile.

[VISIT]

LEAVING THE BUS, HE recovered his baggage and became aware that the business area was far more crowded than during the old days. Across the busy street people were hurrying along, exchanging comments with voices raised against the roar of traffic, groups arriving in cars, taxis, and limousines were joining those entering the hotel in a mood of excitement, and while others waited patiently to follow the scene became one of good times and well-being.

And now, thinking to find a room as quickly as possible, he crossed the street and began edging his way along the crowded walk toward an idling taxi; until, seeing the face of its driver, he veered and kept walking.

It would save time, he thought, but even if he accepted me as a passenger it's unlikely that he'd know where rooms are available on the East Side of town. Then, as he scanned the curb ahead for an empty taxi driven by a Negro, a detail from the scene behind him loomed in his mind.

And again he was approaching the hotel, baggage in hand, but this time seeing several passengers from the bus among the crowd waiting to enter, and in moving past the burly white doorman dressed in the uniform of a Prussian general he could see him smiling as he welcomed the young Indian mother and her alert young infant. . . .

Yes, he thought, *it happened, but still living under the spell of the old days I was so busy protecting myself from the indignity of rejection imposed by both law and custom that I refused to see it. . . .*

And suddenly it was as though he had willingly cooperated in making himself the butt of a game played by the past on the present; a malicious game in which the dead challenged the living to run the risk of reaching the ever-receding frontiers of freedom and face up to its mysteries. And now, frowning at the thought, he stopped in his tracks.

Hickman, he thought, *you've been away a long time, so exactly how much things have changed in this town is debatable. But let this teach you to remember that these days wherever you happen to be in this country and see doors opening to others you're obligated to run the risk of giving them a try—otherwise how can you assume that you'll be rejected while placing all the blame on white folks?*

And with an abrupt round-about-face he proceeded at a resolute pace to retrace his steps to the hotel. Where, with a nod to the doorman he entered the lobby, took a quick look at the guests in the lobby, and bracing himself for the possibility of being turned rudely away, or grudgingly accepted, strode straight to the reception desk and slammed down his baggage.

But no, without the slightest hint of hostility, the reception clerk asked him his name, address, and home phone number, wrote it down, assigned him a room, and signaled for a young, brown-skinned bellman to escort him. And to the bellman's polite "This way, sir," he pointed to his luggage and moved toward the banks of elevators where groups of passengers were waiting.

He noted with an old performer's sensitivity to the moods of audiences that no one in the group was paying him more than casual attention—until, drawing closer, he saw a robust elderly man give him a quick double take, and the scene became charged with uncertainty.

Then, as he prepared for a verbal assault, he heard the man exclaim, "Why, I declare, if I'm not mistaken it's Big Lon Hickman!"

And stifling a gasp he stopped short in amazement.

"No, sir, you aren't," he said, "but..."

"...How did I know about you?" the man said with a grin. "Well, I do, and I'm delighted to see you."

"Why, thank you, sir," Hickman said, "but I'm afraid..."

"...That you don't remember me?"

"That's it, and while I wish it were otherwise, I don't."

"I know, but it doesn't change the fact that there was a time when you gave my wife and me a great deal of pleasure."

"Now that's a pleasure to hear, and it's most kind of you to tell me."

"No, I'm not being kind, I'm only trying to redress a wrong I committed years ago when I simply cheered from the crowd instead of telling you personally. Understand? Because things being what they were I simply didn't know how to approach a man like yourself. Come *on*, Big Lon, you know what I mean! It took *time*, and that's what this country needs more of: time. When we danced to your music our attitudes were different, but now times have changed, so I'm free to tell you. Hell, yes! And I'll add something else..."

"All right, I'm listening."

"That I felt that you and others like you were not only fine artists, but national treasures!"

"Now, that really *is* a surprise! And I'm honored, but I'm not sure I deserve it...."

"No buts about it, you were good, *damn* good! So since I'm too old to go fencing with words, let's just say that there are still a few like me around who appreciated your music. That's right, and I'm one who's delighted to tell you."

And now, with the elevator arriving and passengers piling in, the man stepped aside with a gracious, "After you, Big Lon."

"Thank you," Hickman said, and with the door closing and the car ascending he felt the probing of curious eyes.

With the elevator coming to a stop on the fourteenth floor, the door slid open, and with a nudge from the bellman he turned to his admirer and nodded.

"Sir," he said with a smile, "you've really made my day."

"And you mine," the man said, "so take care, and good luck."

"Thanks, and God bless you," Hickman said. And in turning to leave he was met by the intense stare of a young, blue-eyed man whose expression appeared to be one of surprised recognition.

Moving down the hall and seeing the bellman giving his battered leather briefcase a look of approval, he asked, "Who was that gentleman?"

"That was Mr. William Callahan, who's better known as Wild Cat Bill," the bellman said. "He's a big oil man who got rich during the old days. Owns two of the tallest buildings in town and a big estate in the suburbs but prefers to live here with us. I wish there were more like him, because unlike some of the others he's nice to have around."

"He certainly seems to be," Hickman said.

"And you can believe it," the bellman said. "Not only does he tip well, but he gives a lot of money to things like museums and symphonic orchestras. But if you don't mind my asking, how'd he come to know you?"

"He didn't, he only knew me as a musician."

"Were you a rock man?"

"Oh, no, I came along much too early for that. In my day we were mostly bluesmen, stompers, and swingers."

"Those must have been some pretty fine times," the bellman said, "and according to Mr. Callahan you must have been good."

"At least that's his opinion," Hickman said. "Anyway, it's good to be remembered."

And now, entering the room assigned him, he stood watching the smooth swinging style with which the bellman placed his briefcase and suitcase expertly on a rack at the foot of the bed with amusement. Then, as a compliment to his guest's importance, the young man danced out a gracious expression of the hotel's concern for his comfort, snapped on the lights in the bathroom, and adjusted the air conditioner.

And now, moving with a graceful it's-a-mere-courtesy-of-the-house stride toward the door, the bellman smiled.

"That should do it," he said, "and if there's anything you need—food, drinks, or whatever—just buzz the desk and I'll come running. Yes, and if you need help in finding your way around town I'm also pretty good with directions."

"Thank you," Hickman said as he extended a tip. "It's been quite a while, but I'm pretty sure I still remember how to get where I'm going."

"Good," the bellman said, "and thank you. But if you haven't been here recently, watch your step; because they're tearing things down even faster than they're building them up."

And with a smart salute the bellman was gone.

Removing his jacket, he hung his suit in the closet, stripped to his waist, and made for the bathroom with his traveling kit. Where, after bathing his hands and face, he began combing his head as he stared at the mirror. And suddenly reminded that the young Indian mother had been responsible for his being in the hotel, he recalled her baby's response to his greeting on the bus and erupted with laughter.

Hickman, he thought, *the way that little rascal gooed at you sounded like he actually overheard that half-awake sermon as it ran through your mind. And if so, he was right on target. Still, just in case you go crazy and try converting some Indians you should ask to hear one of* his *sermons. After all, some babies are born leaders; wasn't Bliss but a few years older when he began preaching?*

Returning to the bedroom and noticing the telephone sitting on a table, he settled down to phone Janey to let her know that he would soon be on his way but decided against it.

No, he thought, *she'll only get herself worked up. So it's better to simply appear and go on from there. . . .*

Leaving the hotel on foot, he headed east, expecting to cross the maze of railroad tracks which he remembered from the old days and continue uphill and then down to the Negro business-and-entertainment section. But to his surprise he discovered that the tracks were now elevated, and found himself walking through the cool shade of an underpass toward the bright rise of the sidewalk ahead. Then as he emerged into the heat he was again surprised to see that the area once occupied by an ice-cream factory was now given over to empty lots marked off for parking.

And this, he thought, after they became famous for making the best ice cream in town. Good butter-pecan, strawberry, and that blue specialty they made from hawthorn berries—blue haw, they called it. . . .

Continuing east, he remembered the block as a mixture of rooming houses and family dwellings, but although the walk was still shaded by some of the same trees, most of the structures were gone. And suddenly remembering that the railroad had run parallel with the street that divided the eastern section of the city from the white business district, he turned and looked down the slope from whence he'd come. And yes, although now overshadowed by elevated tracks, the street was still there.

But you have to watch them, he thought, because when they start expanding they go about it like the joke about bathing with nothing more than a washbowl and a pitcher of water: First you wash *down* as far as possible, then *up* as far as possible, and then in a rush to get it over and done you wash "possible."

So first they divide a town and move as *far* from us as they think possible, then they build as *close* to the dividing line as they think possible, and finally as the town keeps expanding they say to hell with you folks and go about bulging the line until they've crowded us off in a corner. . . . So much for them, us, and the unwashable impossible possible!

And now on sudden impulse he began crisscrossing the street, taking long strides and avoiding passing cars as he looked for more signs of change.

To the north whole blocks had been razed, and although he remembered nothing impressive about what was gone he felt a stab of sadness that was relieved by the sight of a single construction site on which workmen were busy erecting a building. Then as he continued toward the corner ahead, the broad stained-glass windows of a familiar church loomed against the sky and he hurried toward it with a sudden sense of urgency.

Reaching the corner, he paused and stood staring at the tall brick structure and thought with a sense of relief, *Thank God it's still standing.* For having seen many such neighborhoods destroyed, he knew that churches were the last structures to be demolished and took the fact that Janey's church was still standing as a reliable indication that the old neighborhood was enduring the stresses of change.

For now, as in years before, green grass grew on the slopes of its high embankments, its broad oaken door and brass handles and hinges gleamed in the sun, the black handrails leading up from the walk below newly painted, and the old haven of a church loomed like a time-battered rock in a turbulent land.

In the old days Janey would've had to knock me in the head to get me in there, he thought, but now I'm overjoyed to see it. Like that man Callahan said when he surprised me, it took time. But Time is both change and stability—so now let's have a look at what's happened to that once famous hall where we played all those dances. . . .

Then, crossing the intersection and moving down to his old stomping ground, his sadness returned. For as he moved past the old corner hotel and the brick lodge headquarters beside it he saw that both had fallen into decay. As had some of the block's once well-kept houses and lawns.

And now, increasing his pace, he descended into the area where many years before he had lived, worked, and gambled, and saw that the once crowded sidewalks were empty, and except for a few parked cars and a trickle of traffic the street appeared lifeless. The corner hotel where he had roomed was now shabby, the windows of once busy shops were now boarded, but even worse, the famous theater which had stood beside it had been demolished. Even his favorite barbershop, pool hall, restaurant, and barbecue shack were gone. As was the shoeshine parlor where he had joined in jam sessions, drinking, gambling, and enjoying good lies. And the funeral parlor on the corner had disappeared as though gone underground with its corpses. And feeling angry and hopeless over a section that had been so full of life being so ravaged and dead, he increased his pace, thinking to get to Janey's as quickly as possible—but then as he looked toward the street for a taxi he paused and stared down.

Near the curb ahead, where water from a fire hydrant trickled in the sunlight, a black, long-haired spaniel lay in the shade of a building nursing her three black-and-white puppies.

So there's at least one sign of hope left on the scene, he thought with a smile. But as he looked along the street for the dogs' owner the only evidence of one were the remains of a can of dog food that had been dumped on a sheet of newspaper.

Things appear to have gone to the dogs, he thought, *but at least not completely.* And as he watched the prostrate animal nursing her pups he smiled. Then, bending and giving her a pat on the head, he resumed what had become a most sorrowful journey.

Approaching the hill which led to Janey's home, he slowed his pace and took a look at the quiet, tree-shaded block. The houses neat and the sloping lawns with steps leading down to the brick sidewalks well-kept and green in the sunlight. Across the walk from where he stood, cinder blocks which formed an embankment for the lawn above were wet with dew, a line of red ant hills edged the sidewalk below, and high above in a locust tree a songbird trilled.

It looks much the same, he thought, but after coming all this way I hope there's nothing really serious going on inside. If not, I'll hear her out and catch the next flight back to Georgia. Not that Sister Corrine might have been right in saying that Janey did all that signifying just to get a little of my attention. She's not like that, so no matter what led her to write she's upset and I'm obliged to do whatever I can to calm her....

Then, suddenly hesitant, he looked around, thinking: *So here I am, but now such a stranger that my trying to help her is as risky as a physician treating a member of his own family: There's too much old emotion and memory to get in the way of his better judgment. And betwen Janey and me there's too much wreckage from the past, too many ghosts of what might have been.*

There was a time when we could have been closer than I've ever been to anyone in my life—then it was over. Time passed and with it we changed. So now there's only the memory of what might have been and a long-distant friendship based on our fidelity to old, frustrated dreams which she chose to reject. Then I changed my ways and grew older and colder, but while I made my peace with what happened between us I could never forget that peach-brown girl with her arms full of flowers...

Yes, Hickman, his blues voice interrupted, *and that sunny backyard's fenced-in greenness filled with the scent of honeysuckle and roses and you being careful not to bang the balls too hard as you played croquet with that willowy daughter and her prim hourglass of a mother. And there you were, acting the courtly, well-bred gentleman with your horny mind as usual on a more earthly game. Then getting your big foot caught in a wicket and high-collared, white-dressed, tight-corseted, blue-sashed mama-chaperone with that gold watch pinned to her pouter pigeon's bosom revealing both the lay of the game and time of day by laughing like a flute as she swatted the balls and scored. And afterwards, watching you out of her shrewd card-sharp's eyes while serving you an ice-cold glass of lemonade, she paused and plopped in a red, signifying cherry. Made you, a gambler who had played high-society and barrel-house dances, feel like a yokel just come to town. That's when you realized how much more dangerous dealing with strivers like her was than performing dances where hot young gals crowded the bandstand and smiled to attract your whiskey-eyed attention.... Lips that touched wine shall never touch mine, Janey said, and she meant it—as though a rascal like you could reverse all prior time in order to get married.... And you wanting to give it a try, thinking like a fool that a bluesman could become a saint and a jazzman change into a one-woman monk.... Why didn't Eve come equipped with a chastity belt, Yale lock, and cast-iron bloomers?*

Once Millsap argued with you that underneath most black Baptist preachers there's a vestige left by the old fertility gods. Said that it made them so hound-dog randy that even dumb young women knew it instinctively.

Underneath where, you said.

The skin, Millsap said.

No, you're wrong, you said, because although a true minister's flesh might quiver it's only his response to his testing, his prick of conscience. And if he ignores it he fails his test. But when he lets that happen even the most compliant females will condemn and reject him.

And you can say that again, Millsap said. That's the way they are. Some come and condemn, while others come and then condemn—and if I'm wrong, what's all this business about celibacy?

It's to keep the flesh under control and the mind on the saving grace. It's a discipline. Remember Jack Johnson's advice when asked how an ordinary man should deal with the likes of those hot-tailed gals who were always hanging around him? Eat pickled walnuts, take cold showers, and think long-distant thoughts. That was his formula, a matter of mind over matter. But it was nothing new, because dedicated ministers always followed that rule. Saint Paul taught them, so if you'd like a reference read your Bible.

Yes, he said, but old Jack wasn't a minister—unless you want to call his upper-cutting and left-jabbings some kind of preaching. Instead, he was what all the gals knew by instinct—a strapping black fertility god dressed in boxing gloves and form-fitting tights. That's why he raised so doggone many underskirts, not to mention that sea of white hopes.

And you said: Coming from a little two-bit Satan that's pretty good, but get thee behind me just the same!

Then he laughed and called the waitress over.

Delois, he said, my man here looks like he's not holding up so well under the jive I've been laying on him, so maybe you better give him a booster shot....

A what?

A booster shot...

And what the dickens might that *be? she said.*

Another serving of ribs, you Eveish creature, Millsap said. Give my man another slab of RIBS! Then he stared at you to see if you got the joke....

Jazzmen, jazzmen, Hickman thought as he chuckled and started toward Janey's, *they'll turn anything and everything into something else. Just give them a couple of beats and a progression of chords and they'll turn the "Star-Spangled Banner" into "Don't You Feel My Leg." And get away with it, too, because they're such masters of chaos and fluidity that either folks don't notice what's happening or they don't know what to do about it. What moneymen do with political influence and cash they do with horns, rhythm, and reeds....*

[BLURRING]

BEHIND ITS SHALLOW, FRESHLY mown lawn the six-room house was much as he remembered: its wide front porch supported by four wooden pillars, to its left a swing suspended from its roof by chains, four white wicker rockers, and pots of pink geraniums arranged on its railing.

All right, he thought, *it looks much the same, so now let's get going and see if she's home.*

And making his way to the screened front door he pressed the doorbell and was surprised by a faint sad sound of chimes. Then came a rapid clicking of locks and Janey was peering through the slightly cracked door.

"Thank the good Lord," she cried, "it's Alonzo!"

"That's right," Hickman said as the door flew open, "he's back again."

"Yes," Janey said, unlatching the screen, "and I knew you'd come! I just *knew* it!"

"You did, did you," he said. "So instead of writing me all that double-talk, why didn't you come right out and invite me? Anyway, I'm here, so now that you've seen me, what's a man supposed to do—rush back home to his duties, or wait out here in the heat until you decide to ask him in?"

"Shame on you, Alonzo; you know you're always welcome. But first let these old eyes have a good look at you! How *are* you?"

"Fine," Hickman said, "except for being confused and a bit upset by that letter of yours. Otherwise I feel fairly fine."

"And you look it," Janey said, "you really do. But I guess you know that from all those ladies you have around you. . . . Come in and get out of that jacket. And don't go reading anything into the shades being down. I have them drawn against all this heat. I hope you don't mind a little darkness."

"Not at all," Hickman said as he moved into the living room. "Being a dark man I've seen many a dark day, so as soon as my eyes adjust I'll be in my element. Meanwhile, Miss Janey, Janey, Jane-Jane-Jane, tell me how are *you*?"

"Now don't you go jadda-jadda-jing-jing-jinging me, you old rascal! Anyway, I'm pretty good, or at least I *feel* good if not pretty."

"Well, you look both," Hickman said. "Where shall I sit?"

"Take that big chair right there. It's Cliofus's, and if it can hold him it can hold anybody, even someone as big as you. Give me that jacket and make yourself comfortable. Would you like something cold? I just happen to have some homemade strawberry ice cream, or if you like I can make you some ice tea or coffee."

"You really did know I was coming, and as always I'm tempted. But nothing right now, thank you. And with this having to be a short visit we'd better get to what's bothering you. Sit down and tell me what's been happening. Who's this little man you wrote about?"

Sitting on the sofa and cooling herself with a cardboard fan, Janey frowned.

"Alonzo, I don't really know," she said, "and that's the problem. I'm not sure *who* he is, and I'm not even sure that I want to. That's why I wrote you about his being out all of a sudden. He *claims* he was one of my little men, but if he *was* then he's the son of a young friend of mine who killed herself years ago. . . ."

". . . *Killed* herself? Who was she?"

"You wouldn't have known her, Alonzo, but she was a fine young woman who got herself ruined by a fast-talking man. . . ."

"Did you know the man?"

"Not really, but he went by the name of Prophet. At least that's what he was calling himself when my young friend had a baby boy by him."

"And what happened to the baby?"

"He became one of mine. I didn't know what she was up to, but when she decided what she was going to do and asked me to look after him awhile I promised her that I would. And I did...at least as long as I could...."

"But what about about his father, this fellow Prophet? Who was he and where did he come from?"

For a moment Janey was silent, staring at her motionless fan. "Alonzo, I don't truly know. But if you'll forgive me for saying it I think he had certain connections with you...."

Hickman sat back in his chair. "With *me*? Now listen, Janey, I didn't come all the way out here to play games...."

"Oh, hush, Alonzo! I'm not playing games, I was referring to that boy...."

"Boy? *What* boy?"

"Now don't go pretending you don't know, because you had him with you at the time you were out here putting on a circus sideshow and calling it a *revival* meeting. I never let on but I heard about it, and one night I made it out there to see you putting on your act with that poor child in a coffin. It's a wonder the good Lord didn't strike you dead, right then and there...."

Folding his arms, Hickman sighed.

"Janey, I swear, you never forget or forgive. And what's even worse, you reject anything that's slightly unusual! But you have to remember that in those days I was fresh out of show business and assuming my role as a minister. It was new, so I was using whatever I could to save souls. I was still learning, and in spite of what *you* might have thought about it the fact remains that our bit with the boy in the coffin converted a few souls. And they *stayed* converted, ask any of them who're still alive. Yes, and we caused many more to think about how they were living."

"That's what *you* say...."

"And that's the truth! So while you condemned us for using a gifted child in dramatizing the gospel—yes, and outdoors under a tent—don't forget how peacock proud you were to be a member of that fine church with biblical stories in its stained-glass windows. Oh, yes! You loved being a member but you managed to forget that in his day Christ didn't *have* a fine cathedral. All he had was the Word. So if he and his disciples hadn't acted out the gospels your church wouldn't have had any stories to tell in those stained-glass windows. So now try to forgive me for what I did years ago and tell me what my boy, my little assistant preacher, had to do with your friend?"

"Well," Janey said, "you might not want to believe it, but after he was grown he and two other men, two white ones, turned up out here making a movie...."

"So?"

"So even though I hadn't seen him for years I recognized him."

Hickman frowned.

"Now that's interesting, making a moving picture! Why can't I recall your mentioning it before? But let's not get into that just now. Yes, after the boy ran away he was up to all kinds of devilment, and as he grew older he often back-tracked over the circuits we covered. When was he out here?"

"Sometime back in the early twenties," Janey said. "And like I said, he and the other two men were around here for weeks upsetting folks with that picture. Yes, and socializing with anybody who fell for what they were doing. Can you imagine folks *paying* their hard-earned money to be in a junky, made-up movie?"

"They made them *pay* to be in it?"

"Yes!"

"Well I'll be," Hickman began and broke off with a chuckle. "But Janey, this is the U.S.A., and most folks believe in its do-it-yourself tradition."

"Maybe so, but in this case it was more like a bunch of stupid lambs being led to slaughter. Because a heap shelled out their hard-earned money to be in it, and after that boy and his friends grabbed all they could they left town. But not before he got my young friend into trouble...."

"But how can you be so sure that he was responsible?"

"Because I could see it coming and tried to warn her, that's why. But by then he'd got her so excited that she wouldn't listen, and she was too green to know what was happening. Even greener than me when *you* came along...."

"... But not as sensible and virtuous, is that it?"

"I hear you talking but it's the truth. So she got caught, and by the time the baby came he was long gone. She told me that he came back shortly before it was born, but then he took off again. And as far as I know he was never seen around here again."

"And you're sure that he'd been the boy in the coffin? That he was responsible?"

"Yes! Because she *told* me and she didn't lie."

"And did you think it was my boy simply because this fellow Prophet reminded you of me? Think about it now, because when you saw him with me he was not only a youngster, he looked white...."

Tensing, Janey leaned forward.

"Oh, he was the one! He had your mark all over him! And what's more, with most folks thinking he was white he insisted he was black. And there I believed him, because he had your walk and way of talking and carried himself as much like you as someone who looked white ever could! Oh, yes! He was the one in the coffin all right. Your mark, your style, was all *over* him! And that's why his doing what he did to my young friend upset me all the more. Until that fast-talking floater showed up Lavatrice was a *good* girl. She didn't play around. Yes, and I'll say it: She was a virgin! Then he and those other two showed up and got folks crazy over playing in that movie. Some of the younger women went plumb out of their minds over his looks and manners and his way with words. And Lavatrice worst of all. And after he got the poor girl big-eyed by giving her a leading part in that movie he left her waddling around with a great big belly."

"But Janey," Hickman said, "a lot of what you're telling me has to be guesswork. I don't mean about the girl, because whoever was responsible, what happened was terrible. Terrible for the girl and a disgrace for her family. But I still can't understand why you didn't mention her or this Prophet in your letter."

"It was because she's dead and I felt that it was enough for you to know that he'd been through here again, that's why...."

"But wait! Janey, you've got me confused again—I thought you said that he left here years ago and had never been back! So what's the connection between what you're telling me now and what you wrote?"

"Alonzo, it's a matter of chickens coming home to *roost*! I'd seen the signs, but after he ran away and you couldn't find him I felt that you'd suffered enough. So why should I tell you what he'd done—especially about the baby—and make it worse?"

"But Janey, you're not making sense! Why would he come back here when he knew what..."

"...Not *him*, Alonzo; I'm talking about the *baby*! About the *child* he had by Lavatrice! *He's* the one who came back. *He's* the one who's been asking all the questions. Don't you see?"

"You're not making it easy," Hickman said, "but I think I'm beginning to see the pattern. First the father arrived, ate some forbidden fruit, and disappeared. And now you're telling me that the son has turned up with his teeth on edge— is that it? But where had the son been? And since he'd lived here with you, why wouldn't you know him?"

Clasping her hands and resting her forearms on her knees, Janey leaned forward.

"Wait, Alonzo," she said, "let me go back and start all over:

"This mess that I'm getting at began years ago; then, after I thought it had quieted down and been long forgotten, it ups and starts stirring again. I didn't realize what was happening until a few days ago when I came home and found Cliofus sitting on the front porch talking with a white man. I had come up the alley and through the backdoor, and when I heard them talking I eased up here and took a peek at him. At first I thought he was one of these young white professors from the university who've taken to coming out here wanting us old-timers to talk about the early days so they can record it. So I said to myself, 'Not today, young man. I've got no time for your questions.' Then I tiptoed on back to the kitchen and started blanching some tomatoes.

"But a little later I could hear Cliofus talking a mile a minute like he does when he gets excited. So not wanting to have him getting sick on my hands, I eased back up here to find out what was happening. That's when he saw me looking through the screen and said, 'Miss Janey, are you just going to stand there? *Behold* this man! Take a good look at him!' And before I know what's happening this white man has opened the screen and he's hugging me! *Me,* who'd never been hugged by a white man in all my born days!

"Well, Alonzo, with that I turned cold. And although something inside me seemed to recognize the man my mind said NO! IT CAN'T BE! But when I pushed him away he still held on to my arms, so all I could do was stare and try to see if one of my little men was hidden in his blue eyes and white skin. I was trying so hard, so awfully hard, and while this is happening Cliofus speaks up and names him.

" 'Miss Janey, it's *Severen,*' he says. 'It's our little ole Severen!'

"And I thought, Yes, it could be. But although a part of me was trying to accept him as one of mine, as one of my lost little loved ones, it had been far too long ago and I was much too unprepared...."

"Just take your time," Hickman said. "I didn't mean to upset you. Why don't you rest a spell?"

"No, I'll be all right, and it's a relief to relive it in words.... So there we stood, and although the weather was hot I was ice-box *cold*! I wanted him to go away, to vanish. And while he's standing there smiling with tears in his eyes something deep inside me was waiting to hear him cough and see smoke curling around his head and into my own eyes and lungs. But he was still holding on to me, still smiling. Yes, that's how it was, and I thought, No, this can't be, it's not him—no! He wouldn't come back all this way, not without a warning. No, it's impossible. Because he wouldn't have the memory, the desire, or the forgiveness to find his way back. Just as I can't and won't and can never receive him, or have him back...no...."

"Then Cliofus said, 'Gee, Miss Janey, I guess it's too much of a surprise for you. So come on, Sevie, let's get her in the house so she can get her bearings.' And that's when the two of them helped me inside.

"So then we were inside here with me fumbling into my old rocker and looking at him and trying to accept the fact that I *did* remember him and that all I had done years ago was falling apart right here before my very eyes. That across all that long time and distance and his change in circumstance he had kept me, kept us, in his mind. And worst of all, in his heart. That was the terrible part...."

"...But why?"

"Why? Did you say WHY?"

"Why, yes, was that unreasonable?"

"Alonzo, how can you sit there and ask me that? Haven't you understood anything I've been telling you? Because he was WHITE! And had been white for *years*! White for so long that as I stared at him it came over me that maybe by coming back he was just being white-folks cruel, and his way of letting me know that he had risen above all those smoking smoldering coals I'd used in my attempt to destroy those family ties which by now should have been long dead and forgotten. It was like he was getting down on his knees just so he could rise above us.... Like he was bragging to Cliofus and me about his charity and forgiveness. So I said to myself, No, it simply cannot be!

"But there he was, a grown white man smiling at me through his tears while my body was turning to dust and my clothes into sackcloth and ashes. And then my eyes blurred and I couldn't see him, both from my tears and my mind rejecting what I couldn't bear to remember...."

"But why were you resisting what should have been a happy reunion for all of you?"

"Because I simply couldn't bear having that dear little boy who I had known and loved turn into this grown white man who was claiming to be both himself and that child! Because even though my eyes were blurry I could still smell his smell and hear his emotion, and sense his need as he talked to me. But for all my straining I simply couldn't hear anything in his Northern white folks' educated voice that sounded like the child I had known and loved. Do you understand? I couldn't even *hear* him!"

"But, Janey, he had come..."

"...Back! Yes, he had! Yes! Against all the pain that my plan had cost us, and against everything I had done to see to it that he wouldn't even think of it or want it, he had to come back!"

"Janey," Hickman said, "you're leaving something out...."

"I know, I know, and it's not doing a bit of good. So now in order for you to understand you'll have to listen to a terrible confession. And if you do you'll have to remember some of the things which that cross on your watch chain stands for and try to understand my position... my condition. And maybe then you will remember what the spiritual says about a man like you: That he shall lead his flock like a shepherd and shelter the young lambs in his bosom.... Yes, and remember too that when there are orphans and no man to help her a woman has to take over and do whatever she can to be not only motherly, but also as fatherly as a woman can manage—which is what so many of our women have always had to do, and which is what I tried in my mistaken way to do."

"All right," Hickman said, "I remember and I'm willing. But since I know so little, why don't you explain why you didn't write me about this girl... about his mother?"

"It was because I felt that it was enough to warn you that old bones were being stirred. And I felt that when he, the father, first ran away and you had tried so hard and couldn't find him, you'd suffered enough. So years later why tell you what he'd done out here? And especially about the child—which would have made it still worse."

738 · *Three Days Before the Shooting . . .*

"But since we're friends, why didn't you let *me* be the judge of that?"

Sighing, Janey shook her head. "Oh, Alonzo, hadn't I already caused you enough misery? It wasn't that I didn't *think* about telling you, but what good would it have done? Could you have brought the child's mother back from the dead? Could you have made the father come back here and own up to his child?"

"But I would have *tried*. I would have done something for the girl and the baby. . . ."

"Yes, but we weren't seeing each other during the time it was happening. And you couldn't catch up with the one who ruined her, even though you were trying. And since he must have known what happened, that she had killed herself, he probably would have figured that if he turned up out here again somebody would have cut his throat for him just as she cut her own. . . ."

Feeling suddenly numb, Hickman leaned forward, gazing into Janey's tear-wet face.

"When did all this happen?"

"Back in the twenties; the early twenties. . . ."

"And you mean to tell me that for all those years you let me come in here and play with that white-looking child and wouldn't tell me who his daddy was . . . I can't believe it. . . ."

"No, Alonzo, I didn't. But I would have; I was always prepared to tell you, and that's the truth. All you had to do was ask. That's all you had to do. Every time you came—and remember it wasn't often in those days—I was just waiting for you to look at that child and say something about his resemblance to the other one when he was about the same age. And if you had I was prepared to tell you. But you didn't, and therefore I decided to just let the dry bones rest while nature took its course."

"Well, you did, but now it's *human* nature we have to deal with. . . . Why didn't you tell me?"

"Because I didn't want you to know what that boy had done. . . ."

"You were protecting *me*?"

"Yes, I guess I was. But I also remembered your saying something about what ought to be done to white men who ruin colored girls, and hearing that I was tempted to tell you then—just to hear what you'd say when you found out that it was him who had done it, that he was the child's father. I wanted to hear what you'd have to say if the man only *looked* white, or if it was a case in which no one knew or cared whether he was white, black, or in between. But then I asked myself why should I hurt you some more. At the time you were very upset about something that happened back in Georgia, so why add something that nothing could be done about? Besides, I felt that it might have turned you against the baby, and I didn't want that to happen.

"Anyway, and no matter how this thing turns out, you have to understand that I loved that baby. I loved him just as you loved his no-good father. I loved him and looked after him as I would one of my own. And as far as I knew at the time his father could have been dead, or turned into a hobo like some of these old pudding-headed white men who're always knocking on the back door asking for something to eat. That's right! As far as I knew he could have been like one of them who'll beg a colored woman for something to eat and then be too white-folks proud to come in and sit down and eat it like a decent human being...."

"I thought that kind of thing—hoboing, I mean—stopped with the war. Is it still going on?"

"Not like back then, but it still happens."

"And are you still charitable?"

"Now, don't you go starting in on me, A.Z.! Yes, I am. My religion teaches me to help the poor and the needy, and I do. They're always welcome to share what-ever I have. But you might as well know that I won't feed them unless they have the decency to recognize themselves as my guests. It's simply a matter of shar-ing whatever the good Lord put here in this house to be shared. But as dirty and down-and-out as most of them are, some are just too prejudiced. Not all, be-cause some have enough decency to respect me as a sharer and have been known to come back for more. That's all I ask, but although I'm ashamed to admit it, whenever one comes knocking with his hand out and then refuses to come in and sit down like he's been taught good manners, I think about that child's father and it fairly ruins my day."

"So now you can't accept your young friend's son because you hate his father, is that it?"

"No, that's *not* it! It's because he's changed. I loved that child, and after he was taken from me there was nothing I could do but accept it. So I tried to make my-self forget him. I even told myself that after what I did to him he'd never *think* of coming back. But after all my years of hoping that he'd found some kind of hap-piness by living with his own flesh and blood, he's back here asking me about his mother and father...."

"So I take it that you didn't throw him out, that you talked with the man...."

"Yes, I did. I finally calmed down enough to be polite, which Cliofus helped by being so happy to see him."

"And what did he want?"

"He wanted me to tell him about his mother, and then he wanted me to tell him who his daddy was...."

"And so?"

"About his mother I was able to tell him the truth, that I knew her from the time she was a baby. Back when her folks used to bring her along when they drove into town for visits. It wasn't so often, because being Natives they lived on one of the reservations with their Indian kinfolks. But when he asked me how he came to live with me, I had to lie. I told him that when his mother realized that she was going to die she asked me to take him so that he could be brought up in the city where the schools were better. The truth was that she gave him to me out of shame. Shame over what had happened to her, over what that boy of yours had done to her. Can you understand why I felt that I had to lie?"

"Yes," Hickman said, "I think I do—but what did you tell him about his father?"

"What *could* I tell him, Alonzo? I told him that I didn't know his father, that I never met the man. Which was the truth. I never did. But then I had to lie again by telling him that at the time his mother died his daddy was away somewhere working on a job—only I didn't tell him about the moving-picture part. And when he wanted to know why his mother hadn't left him with his father instead of with me I had to lie again. It meant protecting that scoundrel but I told him that I guessed that it was because losing his wife had broken his father's heart. That after hearing about his young wife dying so sudden he got so upset that he couldn't stand to see this town again. But for all my lying it didn't work...."

"He already knew the truth?"

"Maybe not for sure, but he sensed it. Because the next thing I know he's asking me if his parents were married...."

"And what did you tell him?"

"With him coming at me so sincere and so sudden, what could I tell him? I told him that they weren't but that they intended to be, and that the reason his father was away when his mother died was that he was off raising money so that they could get married and set up housekeeping. A.Z., I know how terrible it sounds, but I had to tell him *something*. So I lied, but for all my lying I don't think he believed me. He just looked kind of sick and strange and didn't say anything for a while. So I tried to lift his spirits by recalling how things were after he came to live with me. Cliofus took over at that point, talking about things he and the rest of the boys used to do. And then I told him of how after a while his father got on his feet and began sending me checks so I could take better care of him. Which was

[SMOKING]

THE TRUTH. I GAVE the devil his due for that, but I didn't go into the rest because now that the boy had found his way back home I figured that he remembered...."

["But why?"*

Suddenly Janey looked up as though she had forgotten his presence.

"Why?" she said. "Did you ask me *why?*"

---

* The bracketed passage from page 740 to page 745 is an extremely close variant of the passage beginning "But why?" on page 736 and ending "that he remembered" just above.

"Yes, why," Hickman said, seeing Janey's eyes widen as she struck the table with her fan, shouting, "WHY? Alonzo, how can you sit there and ask me that? Haven't you understood anything I've been telling you? It's because he's WHITE! And has *been* white for *years!*"

"But, Janey, didn't he always look..."

"...No, Alonzo, NO! Not that kind of white, that's not what I'm talking about. Back then he was white-*looking,* yes; but he was one of us, a Negro; now he's white and one of *them.* Then he had *our* manners and *our* ways; now he has theirs—you know what I mean! I'm not talking about skin color, I'm talking about attitude, about what a person expects out of life and what he stands for... what he has come to stand for through living. Back then he was just a white *colored* child, but now he's a white *white man*—don't you see?"

Poor Janey, Hickman thought with a nod, *somehow she's stumbled through the curtain of color and landed up to her eyeballs in all the old race-based confusion—Bliss again.... Take away the lips, the hair, the talk, the rhythm and high behind—and what do you have? A mammy-made American Adam shaped out of this terrible American confusion.... Neither white nor black but as much a mystery as when some folks hear thick lips give voice to Shakespeare, Lincoln, or the Word....*

"...He had been white for so long a time that as I stared at him and tried to get myself together it came over me that maybe he was really being white-folks cute and mean. That by coming back here unannounced he was letting me know that he had risen above everything I had done to do away with his connections to us.... That all that smoke from those smoldering coals which I lit in trying to make his leaving easier hadn't meant a thing. I did it for his own sake, thinking that any memory he had of his life here with us would have been long dead and buried, but now it was like he was getting down on his knees just so he could let us see him rise above us.... Like he was bragging to me and Cliofus about his charity and his forgiveness. So I told myself, No, this simply cannot be!"

"...But wait," Hickman said, "you're going too fast—what's this business about fire and smoke?"

"...Still, there he was, a grown white man looking at me with a smile on his face, and all of a sudden my body felt like it was turning to dust and my dress and apron become sackcloth and ashes. Then everything got blurred and I could only see him in outline—not only because of my tears, but because my eyes no longer wanted me to see what my heart couldn't bear to accept...."

"But I don't understand," Hickman said. "Why were you so upset by what should have been a happy reunion?"

"It was because living white had *changed* him, that's why.... And because I simply couldn't accept the idea of that dear little boy who had been one of us, the little boy I had loved and cared for, turning into this grown white man who was standing there in his fine clothes claiming to be that child! It was enough to drive me crazy!

"Still, even though he was only a blur I kept trying to get holt of myself and deal with his claim, but my nose kept smelling his white folks' smell, and my ears kept being jarred by that Northern white folks' talk they were hearing in his tone of voice and his accent—all of which was happening at one and the same time. But for all my straining the one thing that I *couldn't* see or smell or hear was a trace of the child I had loved. Do you understand? I could neither hear him, or see, or feel him!"

"But, Janey, he *had* come back. . . ."

". . . Yes! That's right! Yes! After all that pain that his leaving us had cost both of us, and against everything I had done to see to it that he wouldn't even *think* of it, much less *want* it, he had to come back!"

"Janey," Hickman said, "you're leaving something out; you have to be. . . ."

"I know, I know," Janey sighed, "and it's not doing a bit of good. . . ."

"So why don't you tell me?"

"Because if I did you'd have to listen to something terrible. . . ."

"Well, I'm here, and I've heard terrible things before; even things like rape, incest, murder, and lynching. It goes with my job; so since I've heard of unwed mothers, why don't you go back and fill me in on this girl you didn't mention in your letter. I take it that she was his mother—why didn't you write me about her?"

"Because I was upset and felt it was enough to warn you that out here where you least expected it some old bones were being stirred up. But I didn't want to go too far because I felt that when the father ran away and you tried so hard to find him and couldn't, you'd suffered enough. So why tell you what he'd done out here and make it worse?"

"But since you are my friend, why didn't you let *me* be the judge of that?"

Sighing, Janey shook her head. "Oh, Alonzo, hadn't I already caused you enough misery by turning you down? It wasn't that I didn't think about telling you, but what good would it have done? Could you have raised the child's mother up from the grave? Could you have made that man come back here and own up to being the child's father? No!"

"But I would have tried, I would have at least done something for that baby. . . ."

"Yes, but you forget that when it happened we weren't in touch with one another. And what's more, you couldn't catch up with the one who ruined her, and since he must have known what happened and that she had killed herself he probably figured that if he turned up out here again somebody would have cut his throat for him just as she had cut her own. . . ."

Feeling suddenly numb, Hickman leaned forward, gazing into Janey's tear-wet face.

"When did all this happen?"

"Back in the twenties, the early twenties. . . ."

"And you mean to tell me that for all those years you let me come in here and play with that baby—the light-skinned one—and wouldn't tell me who his daddy was? I can't believe it...."

"No, Alonzo, I didn't. But I would have; I was always prepared to tell you, and that's the truth. All you had to do was to ask. That was all you had to do. Every time you came—and you remember that it wasn't often in those days—I was just waiting for you to look at that child and say something about his resemblance to the other one when he was about that age. And if you had I was prepared to tell you. But you didn't, and therefore I decided to just let the dry bones rest in peace while nature took its course."

"Well, you did, but now it's *human* nature we have to deal with.... Why didn't you tell me?"

"Because I didn't want you to know what that boy had done...."

"You were protecting me?"

"Yes, I guess I was. But I also remembered your saying something about what ought to be done with white men who ruin colored girls, and I was tempted to tell you then—just to hear what you'd say when you knew that it was him who had done it, that he was the child's father. I mean what would you have said if the man only *looked* white, if it was a case in which no one knew or cared if he were white or black. But then I asked myself why should I hurt you some more. At the time you were very upset about something that had happened back in Georgia, so why add something that nothing could be done about to it? Beside, I felt that it might have turned you against the baby and I didn't want that to happen.

"Anyway, and no matter how things turned out, you have to understand that I loved that baby. I loved him just as you loved his no-good father. I loved him and looked after him as though he was my own. And as far as I knew at that time his father could have been dead, or turned into a hobo like some of these ole puddn'-headed white men who're always knocking on the back door asking for something to eat. That's right! As far as I knew he could have been like one of them who'll beg a colored woman for something to eat and then be too white-folks proud to come in and sit down like a decent human being and eat it...."

"I thought that kind of thing—hoboing, I mean—stopped with the war; is it still happening?"

"Not like it was back then, but sometimes."

"And you're still charitable?"

"Now don't you go starting in on me, A.Z. Yes, I am. My religion teaches me to help the poor and the needy, and I do. They're welcome to share whatever I have, but you might as well know that I won't feed them unless they have the decency to recognize that they're my guests. It's simply a matter of sharing whatever the good Lord put here in my house to be shared. But as dirty and down-and-out as most of them are, some are just too white-folks proud to act decent. Not all, because some have enough sense to respect me as a giver and have been known to come back for more. That's all I ask, but although I'm ashamed to admit it, whenever one comes knocking with his hand out and then refuses to come in and sit down like he's been taught good manners I think about that child's father and it fair ruins my day."

"So you couldn't accept the boy because you hate his father, was that it?"

"No, that's not it, it was that he had changed. I loved that child and after he was taken from me there was nothing I could do but accept it. So I tried to make myself forget him. I even told myself that after what I did to him he'd never come back, but after all the years of my thinking that he had found some kind of happiness by living with his own flesh and blood, he's back here asking me about his mother and father...."

"So I take it that you didn't throw him out, that you talked with the man..."

"Yes, I finally calmed down enough to be polite; which Cliofus helped by being so happy to see him."

"And what did he want?"

"He wanted me to tell him about his mother, and then he wanted to know who his daddy was."

"And?"

"About his mother I could tell him the truth, that I knew her from the time she was a baby; back when her folks brought her along when they came to town for a visit. It wasn't often because being Natives, they lived on one of the reservations with their Indian kinfolks. But when he asked me how he came to live with me I had to lie by telling him that when his mother realized that she was going to die she asked me to take him so that he could be brought up here in the city where the schools were better. There I lied, because she gave him to me out of shame over what had happened to her. Can you understand why I felt I had to do it?"

"Yes," Hickman said, "I think I do—but what did you tell him about his daddy?"

"What *could* I tell him, A.Z.? I told him that I didn't know his father, that I never met the man. Which was the truth. I never did. But then I had to lie again by telling him that at the time his mother died his daddy was away somewhere working on a job—only I didn't tell him about the moving-picture part. And when he wanted to know why his mother hadn't left him with his father instead of with me, I had to lie again. It meant protecting that scoundrel but I told him that I guessed it was because what happened had broken his father's heart. That after he heard about his young wife dying so sudden he got so upset that he couldn't stand to see this place again. But for all my lying it didn't work...."

"He already knew the truth?"

"Maybe he didn't *know* it, but he sure *sensed* something. Because the next thing I know he's asking me if his parents were married...."

"And what did you tell him?"

"With him coming at me so sudden with so sincere a question, what *could* I tell him? I told him that they weren't but that they intended to be and that that was the reason his father was away when his mother died. That he was off raising money so they could get married and set up housekeeping. A.Z., I know how terrible it sounds, but I had to tell him *something*. So that's what I told him. But for all my lying I don't think he believed me. He just looked kind of sick and strange and didn't say anything for a while, so I tried to lift his spirits by recalling how things were after he came to live with me. Then Cliofus took over, talking about the fun he and the rest of the boys used to have, and then I told him of how after a while his father got on his feet and began sending me checks so I could take better care of him. Which was the truth. I gave the devil his due for that, but I didn't go into the rest, because now that the boy had come back I figured that he remembered...."]

" 'The rest'? What are you talking about?"

"About how he was taken from me and what I did, the thing that made his coming back so upsetting. He was so young at the time that I hoped he'd forget it, that it would be blotted out of his mind. In fact, that was my reason for doing it and now that I know that he remembers it's about to kill me...."

Suddenly Janey buried her face in her hands, rocking from side to side.

"Janey," Hickman said, "are you all right?"

"No," she said, "and I doubt if I'll ever be again...."

"But why? What did you do?"

"The worst thing I've ever done in my entire life, A.Z., and may the Lord forgive me. I was trying to make things easier for the child, but now it turns out that I made things worse for everybody. Do you understand? That's why I couldn't deal with his showing up here again, why I don't want to recognize him as one of my little men...."

"Janey," Hickman said, reaching out to touch her hand, "I'm here to help, so tell me...."

"I know, I know you are; but give me a little time...."

"Of course, take your time and then try to tell me from the beginning...."

Waiting in the quiet for Janey to continue he became aware of approaching music. A faint bright frill of sound, it floated in from the street like the sweet-sad echo of a distant carnival's calliope tune he had heard long ago during a lonely walk in the dark. And as it drew closer and was joined by the rumbling note of a slow-moving van he was listening to a playful fuguing of *Three Blind Mice* and the gleeful, "Mommy! Mommy! Ice cream! Ice cream!" of a delighted child. And now as the bright tones skipped and frolicked across the air he relived an early visit during which he had hailed such a passing vendor and treated each of Janey's little men to triple-dipped cones of ice cream; a treat at which, dangling bare legs and feet from the steps of the porch, they had licked away in grinning contentment....

Then while Janey looked on with a smile, there were seven young boys gorging on ice cream and me having fantasies of what might have been. . . . Cliofus and the one she's worried about were among them, but where are the others? Where have they gone?

"Alonzo," Janey said, "this is the way it was. On the first of the month this letter came, just as it had been coming all along. . . ."

"You mean that he had been writing to you?" Hickman said.

"Not him, A.Z., his lawyer. . . ."

"From a lawyer—and where did this lawyer write from?"

"Always from Boston—but I didn't mean to say that he wrote me letters. Actually they were just envelopes with the checks he had his lawyer send me."

"What name was he using?"

"That I never knew, because it was always this lawyer, Mr. Delano, who made out the checks."

"But didn't he ever send you some kind of message?"

"Only in the first one, and even that was from the lawyer, who explained that the money was for the child, and that from then on they would be coming once a month. Which they did. He kept his word. Those checks came as regular as if they were sent by somebody paying off a debt on the installment plan, but there was never anything else. Never once was I asked what I did with the money, or how the child was getting on. But come the first of the month and I could expect a check folded in a blank sheet of paper. . . ."

"For how long did you receive them?"

"For about seven years. Seven years of nothing but checks, and then I *did* get one with a letter in it. It was from this lawyer, and like always there was a check, but this time he wrote me that the child's father had other plans for him and that I was to get him ready to leave here. He didn't say why, when, or where they were taking the child, only that I was to get him ready. A.Z., I tell you, I was so torn apart that it was like they had gone up in an airplane and dropped a bomb on the house the way they did when they had that riot in Tulsa. I was just about blown apart with the misery of knowing that the child was going to be taken from me.

"And not only that, because there was the problem of how I was going to go about it. How was I going to make the child understand that after all that time when he hadn't had anybody but me, his father had come to life and decided to take him from the only home he'd ever known? How was I to tell him, much less explain, how it could happen or why? I didn't even know if the man had the legal right to take him—which I doubted—but then I figured that he did because this lawyer had been handling things for him all along. . . ."

"But didn't you try to get some advice?" Hickman said. "I can understand why you didn't get in touch with me, but didn't you consult your pastor?"

"No, A.Z., I didn't. I wanted to, but that would have meant telling him about the child's mother and all, and about things that happened out here long before he came to town. So I didn't. . . ."

"So what *did* you do?"

"They didn't give me time to think, A.Z. A day after this letter arrives this lawyer, Mr. Delano, shows up..."

"...You mean that he came to see you?"

"That's right. He turned out to be a Northern white man who drove out here one day in a taxi at a time when all the boys were at school. I guess he must have timed it that way so he wouldn't be overheard. Anyway, he knocked on the door and when I went to answer I knew right away who he was.

"He was a middle-aged white man, and a very polite one, so although I dreaded what would happen next I asked him in. And like I say, he was smooth and polite and continued to be as he went about explaining what was to be done. Told me that the child's father was now a wealthy man and wanted him to be brought up in a way that he couldn't be out here with us—probably meaning with 'niggers,' but he was careful not to say so. He then said that the boy had reached the right age for the change, being in the second grade and all. So up to that point I just listened while I asked myself where was this so-called father when the boy had the whooping cough? What was he doing when I was bringing him through the measles? Where was he when the child was learning to read and deal with other children who teased him about his looks and color? I was getting a bit worked up, so I told him that while I could understand how the father might feel about wanting the best for his child I couldn't for the life of me understand why the man didn't bring himself on out here so he could get to know the child and let the child know him before snatching him away. Because as things stood the poor child didn't even know that he *had* a father. And as far as he knew he was just another one of my little men, my orphans.

"Well, the lawyer—this Mr. Delano—explained that the child's father was a very busy man, but that he was sure that once the child got to his fine new home and saw how nice it was everything would be all right. It was like asking me to tell some poor traveler that when he reached a certain spot up the road a piece he'd be able to see the Promised Land but to leave out the fact that he'd have to climb a mountain just to get near the spot.

"So that's when I sat back and asked him real quiet: 'But how about me, Mr. Delano? How am I going to find the words to tell the child? How am I going to *prepare* him?'

"So with that he just sits there looking up at the ceiling and a-twiddling his manicured thumbs like he'd never even given it a thought. Until finally he gives me one of those there's-nothing-to-be-worried-about smiles and says, 'Oh, you'll find a way. Since you care for the boy and it's to his advantage, I'm sure that you'll make it easy for him. And by the way,' he says, 'my client, his father, instructed me to tell you how much he appreciates what you've done for the boy, and that he regrets being unable to tell you in person. And naturally, he expects to reward you for all the trouble you've had in seeing after the boy. And you can take my word that he'll be most generous.' That's what he said, sitting there talking like some kind of Northern honey-dripper in that fancy accent of his.

"Well, A.Z., all I could do was look at him, sitting there all calm and smiling. It was like they thought I had been taking care of that child for that low-down floater instead of trying to do my Christian duty. And I mean both for the child and for his poor dead mother. I did it on my own, just as I took on the others on my own. But there I was, with this rich white lawyer sitting here with his smooth blue-veined hands running off at the mouth as though instead of discussing the future of a human child we were deciding the best way to dispose a brood of chickens . . . or maybe send a calf to market. And while I'm listening to his trying to sweet-talk me I'm thinking, What am I going to do? What *am* I going to do!

"So now I'm sitting there feeling like he'd struck me on the head with the flat side of an axe while the pain was standing somewhere off in a corner just watching and waiting to rush out and knock me down. I could feel it building up strength to crush me, and I knew that as far as those two men were concerned what happened to me wouldn't matter a damn. Because it was plain that in their way of thinking I had no claim or say-so whatsoever, no matter how long I had loved and looked after that child. So in a way of speaking they were telling me, Janey Glover, 'We appreciate what you've done for the boy and all, but as far as we're concerned you're nothing but a handkerchief-headed mammy, and it's better that he leaves you behind him.'

"Well, I might look like a mammy to them, but Janey has her pride. So I told him, I said, 'All right, Mr. Delano, you and that man seem to have made up your minds, so what has to be has to be. But how that man came to think that this is any way to go about doing whatever it is he plans to do is beyond me. In fact, I'd like to ask him personally, by long-distance telephone. What's his name,' I says, 'what does he call himself?'

"And do you know what this Delano said? He said that he was sorry but that his client's name was 'confidential'—that's what he said. Yes, sir, and that's when I knew that the name he was using when he was making that movie was as false as a six-dollar bill. . . ."

Suddenly Hickman tensed. "What name was that?" he said.

"Prophet. He called himself Dewitt Prophet, or Prophet D. Witt. Anyway, when he said that about his client's name being confidential I asked him what he meant. 'How does he get his mail?' I said. 'How does he let the government know that he's paid his taxes?' I was beginning to get hot under the collar. 'Mr. Delano,' I said, 'you might know all about the law but *I* know about children, and especially boys. Children are known to ask questions, and the child we're talking about is a very bright child. He knows about trains and horses and airplanes and all kinds of games, and he's the type who asks questions about *everything*! So with that in mind, what am I going to tell him when he asks me who's taking him away—Mister Noname from Nowhere?'

" 'Oh,' he says, 'but that won't be a problem because I'll take care of it in advance. And I assure you that while his father plans to reveal himself in due time, just now for personal and business reasons he prefers to keep his identity strictly private.' "

" 'Private,' I says. 'What's he afraid of? That poor girl's folks are dead and gone, so they can't harm him. And as for me he can forget it, because for the boy's sake I wouldn't touch him with a ten-foot pole.' "

"So he laughs like I was telling a joke or something. Says, 'Miz Glover, it isn't that he's *afraid* of anything. Fear has nothing to do with it. His reasons for remaining in the background are personal, and that's why I've always handled this matter for him. So please try to understand that for a man in his position privacy is most important.' "

" 'Well,' I said, 'this is surely a fine time for him to start thinking about that. Why didn't he remember to keep his privates personal back when he was out here getting that child's mother into trouble? *That* was the time to think about his privacy.' "

" 'Yes, and I agree,' he says. 'Perhaps with hindsight you're right. But passion makes for all sorts of complexities, and that's why lawyers are needed. So you must understand that I'm only the middleman. I carry out orders, *his* orders. I don't know how or why this situation arose, and I don't want to know,' he says. 'And in fact I don't know as much as you and it'll have to remain that way. I'm just a lawyer who was brought in to pick up the pieces, the stray ends, of another man's life....' "

" 'Not just a *man's* life,' I said. 'There was a girl in it too, remember? Because he sure didn't have that baby by himself.' "

" 'No,' he said, 'I'm sure he didn't,' and for the first time he looked uncomfortable.

"So I told him, 'Mr. Delano,' I said, 'In a way I understand your position, even though I can't figure what the child's so-called father's may be; not after what he did and walked away from it. So now he's sent you to clean up after him, and since you're a lawyer I guess it's legal. So all right, like I said, what has to be has to be. Therefore I'll do whatever I can to get the boy prepared, but may the Lord have mercy on us all—and that includes you, Mr. Delano,' I said.

"And do you know what he did, A.Z.? He sat there and *smiled*! Yes, sir, he smiled and shook his head. Then he said, 'I agree with that, Miz Glover, and I trust and believe that you'll find a way. And I'm also sure that you'll make it as easy for the boy as you possibly can. That's because over the years you've proved yourself a loving and responsible foster parent. I must leave you now, but before I do I assure you again that we're all concerned with the boy's welfare and agree with you that he's the whole point of this rearrangement.'

"So he got up then, and I showed him to the door. He had a taxi waiting and after watching him climb in and leave, I locked the door and pulled the shades and then sat down and started to cry. Oh, how I cried! I cried over the prospect of the child's being taken from me, and then I cried over my being unable to do a thing *except* cry. And then it came to me that it would have been easier on everybody concerned if both me and the boy had been in slavery and standing on the auction block. Because if we had, the child would have at least grown up knowing that he could be taken away. But like I say, he didn't even know that he *had* a father, much less one who had deserted him and his mother without even once looking into his little face. Therefore what was the child going to do when I told him out of the blue that this man who he'd never even heard tell of had decided to snatch him away from the only family he'd ever known? And not even do it himself. Not like a man making amends for a wrong he had done, but having some lawyer do it for him. A.Z., I tell you, I felt sick to my very soul! So sick that I just wanted to take the child and leave town—which was out of the question because I had all the others to look after. So I was trapped, A.Z. I was trapped by time and by the little good I tried to do...."

So, Hickman thought as Janey's voice trailed off, *Cliofus was right, this fellow had become strange to Janey but he was more than a stranger, and now this whole thing is drawing close to me....*

"Janey," he said, "I know that it's pointless to ask, but why didn't you get on the phone and call me? I could have at least tried to put some pressure on that lawyer, and even better, I might have caught up with that runaway of mine...."

"But I was so upset that I didn't think about you, A.Z. What's more, I had been doing for myself for so long that I just naturally kept my troubles to myself. And since I never had a man to turn to I didn't think in those terms...."

"No," Hickman said, "and you didn't want me to know about the child's father. I guess if you keep saying 'yes' to 'no' that 'no' turns into the very 'yes' that you were trying to avoid. So then what happened? What did you do—no, stop and rest a while, you must be tired...."

"No," Janey said, "now that I've started I have to get it all out... if you're willing to listen...."

"That's what I'm here for, so go ahead."

"Well, that afternoon when the boys—he and Buster and Cliofus—got home from school I was puttering around in the kitchen still brooding over how to prepare the child for what was coming. I had made them some sandwiches and was pouring them their glasses of milk to take out to the backyard where I could hear them playing and arguing. At first my heart was so full and my mind so occupied that I wasn't paying them much attention, just listening to the sound of their voices. But then I realized that they were teasing one another about the kinds of *blood* they had, and it stopped me dead in my tracks.

"The child was insisting to Buster and Cliofus that he was part Indian—which was true, even though he didn't look it. But like I said, his mother was a Native, and not only did she *look* like she had Indian blood—which a heap of us have—she was a pretty little thing who had both an Indian name and what they call tribal rights. I know because back there when the government handed out all that money to the various tribes her folks got their share. Few of them knew what to do with it, but with all that money Indians and Natives were riding around in everything from Cadillacs to brand-new fire trucks and hearses. But I never told the child any of this, so right away I thought, Who's this child been talking with? And right away it came to me that it must have been that old rascal Love..."

"...'Love'? Is that somebody's name?"

"That's right, Love New. He's been around here so long that I thought you might have known him. Anyway, he's one of the biggest liars that ever walked the earth, *and* a hard-shelled heathen on top of all that. I've been knowing him for years and have tried to keep the boys away from him because he has no respect for our religion or much of anything else. But for all my trying it did little good because those little boys just *loved* to hear his lies.

"So when I went out to take them their after-school snack what the child had said was working in my mind. They were under the tree and Severen was bent over a tablet drawing Cliofus a train—you might remember that as a child Cliofus was train-crazy and still is. So I just stood there looking at him draw, wondering what would happen to Cliofus when the child was no longer here to help Buster take care of him. And when I gave them their snack and got back in the house I started to thinking about how much like slavery times our lives continue to be, and about all the terrible things that happen through black folks and white folks and Indians being thrown together.

"I mean with the whites always managing to get the best of everything and the Indians and us Negroes getting the leavings—and not always even that. Ole Love claims that being black among the Indians made him something special. Claims that with them black is more spiritual than white because they believe that black is closer to the spirits. Can you feature that, A.Z.?"

"I'm not so sure about the spirits," Hickman said with a chuckle, "but sometimes I have a feeling that white folks have a sneaking feeling that we're closer to the *spiritual.* Did he really say that?"

"Yes! And so I said, 'Maybe so, but why is it that ghosts are supposed to be white?'

"So he says, 'They are, but a black shaman can see them better and truer.'

"So I says, ' "Sheman," what on earth is a "sheman"?'

"And he gets all puffed up and says, 'I didn't say nothing about any "sheman," I said a "*shaman*"!'

"He sounded all riled up—which was exactly what I wanted him to be, so then I said, 'All right, so you said *shaman,* but what is it?'

"And he says, 'It's an Indian medicine man.'

" 'Well,' I says, 'I don't know anything about your medicine man or your so-called shaman man, but now that you've told me about him I can tell you a well-kept secret....'

" 'What's that?' he says, looking huffy as a bantam rooster.

" 'It's that you, Mister Love New, are one out-and-out sham! That's right! And you're probably making up a great big lie when you claim that those Indians of yours think that black is spiritual!'

"Well, he just laughed at me then and said something in his old high-pitched voice in what he claims is Creek talk—oh we have some hot arguments. . . . But when he left I thought to myself that if he was telling the truth, then the Africans and Indians must be the only folks on God's green earth who didn't see being black as a sin. But Love says that even when he was a kid they understood his being so black as giving him special insight into things. And he claims that when he was a young boy they had one of their medicine men teach him how to see the spirits and to go into trances and do other spiritual things like healing the sick. He sure does know how to cure sick horses, that I know. Because back in '22 he cured my Princess. He also claims that being a medicine man makes it impossible for him to ever be a Christian, and makes all kinds of fun at the story of Ham and Noah. And Moses? He says that Moses was nothing but a jackleg medicine man! The old heathen!"

Suddenly Janey threw up her hands and stared into his face, saying, "Now how did I let *Love* get into this? Anyway, while this problem with that lawyer is running through my mind I hear the boys going at one another again, with Severen sounding like a little jaybird. Now he's telling Buster and Cliofus that his father was a big rich white man who lived up in Chicago. That's right! Said he was over six feet tall with red hair, and that he was an engineer who built tall buildings and railroads and that he always wore army britches and shiny boots, just like General Black Jack Pershing, and that he always smoked big black cigars. . . .

"Well, I tell you, A.Z., when I heard that about army britches and boots I pricked up my ears and wondered how he'd come up with such truck as that. Because I was sure that even an old troublemaker like Love wouldn't tell him anything like that. The others were telling him that he was telling a whopper, but the more they teased the more he insisted. Said that not only was his daddy a millionaire, but that he was also an auto racer who could drive faster than Barney Oldfield. At that I decided that he was making it up out of things he'd seen in the newsreels at the movies. And I guess it was his making up a father who was like somebody he'd seen in the movies that gave me the idea of how to go about doing what I had to do. . . ."

Suddenly Janey paused, her lips pressed tight as she shook her head and closed her eyes.

And now it's coming, he thought, *out of child's play to become grown-up trouble. . . .*

"Which was?" he said.

"So with that I realized that whatever I came up with would have to be done the hard way, and even harder on me than it would be on him. Then I remembered a white girl telling me that when she woke up one morning and showed her mother the fresh evidence of her coming into her womanhood, her mother had slapped her across the face with it and then broke down and cried. She said that she didn't understand at the time, but that as she grew older she realized that her mother was just preparing her for all the trouble that went with becoming what she'd always wanted to be. She got what she wanted, but it turned out to be other than she expected. I realized that the two cases were different, but I decided that whatever I did with the boy would have to have the same effect. That it would have to be done the hard way, as though he'd got his wish and would have to pay for it in ways he didn't expect. Which meant that it would have to be done in the most drastic way that I could think of...."

"...I understand," Hickman said, "I understand, so what did you do?"

"I told myself that whether I liked doing it or not it would have to be done in a way that was so final that the child wouldn't spend the rest of his life looking back at what he had been before it happened. Because I knew full well that he was going to suffer, there was no way in the world to prevent that. But I didn't want him to suffer more than once, and therefore when the break in his life came it would have to be sudden, and sharp and clean. And as painful as when a doctor puts a red-hot iron to a person's flesh to cauterize a snakebite. I warned you that this would be terrible, A.Z.; I *warned* you. Because I took what started out as daydreaming and turned it into a nightmare.

"I had no way of knowing whether he had hit upon a true idea of what kind of man his father was or not, but whoever and whatever he was leaving us for I didn't want him to go and then be looking back and grieving over what was past and done. Neither did I want him to be always looking back like Love and talking about what used to be. Therefore, since he *had* to go, I wanted him to go and be done with us. And when he took on his father's race I wanted him to do it without pain and be peaceful in his mind. So although the pain had begun to bear down on me I hardened my heart for what I had to do. And as you know, A.Z., when there's need for it in protecting me or my boys I can be truly hard."

"I remember," Hickman said. "I'll always remember...."

"But I mean hard on myself as well as on the child," Janey said. "Because I wanted him to never have to even *think* that he might have been better off here with us than he would be where he was going. Or that I might have loved him more than anyone he was leaving us to make his life with ever could. So with that in my mind I steeled myself, A.Z. I dried my eyes on my apron, and while they were still yelling and teasing one another I go rushing out there to do what had to be done before I went soft and changed my mind.

"Those children didn't even see me coming, so I was almost on top of them before they looked up—and when they did, may the Lord have mercy on my soul!

"A.Z., those children weren't even mad at one another, that I could plainly see. They were just having another one of those tiz-and-taint arguments that kids will have. Severen was saying that although he was a red man he was just as black as Buster, and when I heard that I leaped on that single word, 'black,' and used it against him like Judgment Day. Oh, but yes I did!

"I yelled at the child as loud as I could, 'Boy, what's that you're saying?, and he almost jumped out of his skin.

" 'Nothing, Miss Janey,' he says. 'We were just playing. . . .'

" 'Yes,' I yells, 'but you were playing those dirty dozens, I just heard you!'

" 'Oh, no, ma'am,' he says, 'I wasn't doing anything like that, no ma'am! Buster and Cliofus were teasing, calling me 'white folks' and I said that I was just as black as them, but none of us meant any harm. . . .'

" 'Oh, no,' I says, 'that wasn't playing; not the way you said what you said to your brothers. That was *slave* talk, and the worst, most miserable, low-down kind of slave talk at that! You said it like the kind of slave who didn't have any respect for either himself or his people!'

"Well, with that Buster and Cliofus started trying to defend him, but I wouldn't hear it, and then he started crying and pleading his little case. It was terrible, and seeing him cry made me ashamed of myself, it really did. But once I had begun there was no turning back. . . .

"A.Z., I don't know what came over me, but now that it had started the whole thing became *real*. The child rushed up and hugged me around the legs and buried his little face in my apron, but even though I wanted to take him into my arms I couldn't. Instead I said, 'No, I can't forgive you. You've been acting like a slave, and for that I'm going to *treat* you like one. Now all you git into the house before our neighbors can bear witness to this disgrace you've brought on yourself and us!'

"Oh, it had started to happen, the reality of what I was doing was taking me over. It was like something was pushing me against my will. And like I say, what I had decided to do and my reason for doing it had become *real*. It was coming down on top of me like a mountain. And as I followed the boys into the house I didn't even know what the next step would be. I was fighting to keep from crying and my mind was going like a house on fire, but it wasn't until we were all in the house and passing through the dining room that I knew the next step. That's when I happened to see that big potbellied stove which I used to have and was reminded of something I heard my grandmother tell about when I was only a little girl, and I thought, *No, please, not that*. But now it was like that stove had come alive and was hypnotizing me . . . that it was talking to me. And that's when I knew the next step I was going to take . . . when I knew what I was going to do, and *had* to do. I was going to punish him the way my grandmother said they punished slaves—I was going to smoke him. . . ."

Suddenly Hickman found himself on his feet, shouting, "You WHAT?"

"Yes, I know, A.Z., it's terrible. Terrible, terrible, TERRIBLE, like I told you.

So sit down and listen and try to understand, because now that I've started I'll have to tell it all...."

"But you can't mean that," Hickman said, dropping back into his chair. "Not you..."

"Oh, but I did," Janey said, "and I can't undo it. I ordered the child to fetch me the big canvas laundry bag in which I kept my quilting material, and while he was fetching it I had Buster bring me a gunnysack and some old rags and excelsior from the chicken house. And when he came back I had him rake some live coals out of the stove into a big shuttle we used to have. Cliofus was just sitting there looking on because he was too clumsy to do anything, but from the way he looked at me he must have sensed what was coming. So when they'd brought the bag and the gunnysack and stuff I got busy making a real smoky fire. The boys didn't know what was happening but they knew it wasn't the kind of fire I'd taught them to make, so they were both puzzled and fascinated. I know it was terrible for them because it was killing me.

"And all the time the child was crying and pleading and saying over and over again that he didn't mean any harm, and me saying, 'Yes, you did! I heard you, and you were all of your family and friends! So now to see that you'll remember never to call anybody black in that tone of voice ever again you're going to be smoked!'

" 'But why, Miss Janey, why?' he cries, and I say, 'For your own sake, and because if you don't learn it now while you're young you're liable to call somebody black in the wrong tone of voice and in resenting how white-looking you are they'll up and *kill* you!' "

"... But you were simply threatening him, weren't you? Surely you weren't actually going through with it. I can't believe that you'd actually *smoke* the child to prepare him for being white."

"But I *did*, A.Z., I couldn't do it today, but I *did*. And may the Lord forgive me because it was probably the cruelest, most useless thing I've done in my entire life. I thought I was preparing him for his new life, but even as I was doing it I wished that none of it had ever started.

"Because by then not only was the poor child crying and begging, but both Cliofus and Buster were joining in. And if you've ever heard someone who's afflicted like Cliofus cry you have an idea of how terrible it was. And I mean for all of us. It was terrible, *terrible*! And when I made the child undress and get into a nightgown which a lady with a family of older girls had given me, it got even worse. The child hated that gown because it had been worn by a girl, but I made him put it on so that he'd know how it felt to be a shirttail slave with nothing else to wear...."

"Dammit, Janey," Hickman exploded, "you weren't preparing that boy for a new life, you were *castrating* him, denying his manhood!"

"No, and if you were to see him you'd know that didn't happen. He might be strange but he's a real man. Besides, I thought I was *teaching* him to be a real man—and a *free* man. So I made him dress like a slave so that once he was taken away he wouldn't even *think* about coming back. Which would have ruined his life because where he was going would be so different. He would dress different, eat different, talk different, and have different attitudes. He'd feel different and act different, and soon he'd come to look on folks like us with a different eye. So I didn't want the poor child holding on to something he'd left back here with us who would no longer have a place in his life.

"No, since he was going to live in his father's world then let him forget us and be done with it. It was a terrible thing I did, but I insist that I did it out of love and only because I knew of no other way of seeing to it that his last memory of us would be tied to something cruel and inhuman. I only hoped to set him free, Alonzo. That's all I wanted, and while I knew that it would break his little heart for a while I thought he would get over it and forget that he was ever one of us and called a Negro...no, don't stop me now; just listen:

"So when he was in the gown I made him step into the center of that gunny-sack, and then I pulled it up over his head and tied it with a piece of rope—yes, I did it! I tied him in there. And then I called to Buster and Cliofus to come and place their hands on top of mine as I lifted him and held him over that smoldering fire. Yes, I made them a part of it. And I held him there until the room was so thick with smoke that it had all of us coughing and choking and crying so bad that we couldn't stand it. Then I untied the sack and rushed him and the others outdoors to get some air.

"By then the poor little thing was so blue in the face that I thought I'd have to call the doctor, but finally he was able to breathe normal again, and with that I got enough control of myself to take him inside and put him to bed. So there you have it, Alonzo. That's what I did, and to the end of my days I'll never forget the look in his eyes. Yes, and that's why I can't accept his returning."

"But Janey," Hickman said, "how could you bring yourself to do that to *any-body*, much less a child? How could you punish him for something he had nothing to do with?"

"A.Z.," Janey said, "there's a world of difference between what I knew and felt then and what I've learned these last few days. But at the time I was able to do it because I *loved* him and wanted to help him. I had learned the pain of regret long before it happened, so I knew what it meant to want something that could never be mine. You never get over such a loss, so I didn't want that child to go through any of that. And I believed the lawyer when he said that the child would be going to a better life. And who was I to dispute him? The child was to be one of them, so since I didn't want him holding on to us and spoil his chances I did it. I tied him up in that awful bag...."

Was there ever a crime, Hickman thought, *that somebody didn't commit in the name of love? That wasn't justified and defended in the name of love? Love of family, of religion, of country, of loved ones? Janey, poor Janey...she sacked that child in the name of...*

"...A.Z.," Janey sobbed, "try to understand my situation. From the time Lavatrice died I tried to be a mother to her child, and I believe I was doing fairly well. But then all of a sudden, and out of nowhere, here comes a couple of strange white men treating me like I was the child's *mammy....*"

"What do you mean, his *mammy?*" Hickman said. "You were never a 'mammy' to any of those boys; you were their guardian, their *mother....*"

[BLUR TWO]

"LISTEN, A.Z., I KNOW what I'm talking about. Of course I wasn't a mammy, but that's how they treated me. It wasn't exactly the way they do it down home but it amounted to the same thing. They lived up North but like most Southern white folks it didn't matter to them that a black woman could be as loving to a white child as she was to one of her own. As far as they were concerned she was nothing more than a convenience—that's all she was!—and as long as the child was small and helpless they used her to raise it. She taught it to walk and to talk, taught it good manners and to respect older people, things like that. But when the child reached the right age they took over. And with that they started teaching it that she was inferior. And although she'd been caring for the child since it was born and loved it they didn't give a damn about hurting her feelings. The child was white and she was black, so they taught it to treat her like they did. Which was like a slave who earned wages.

"And what's more, all the other white folks, from teachers to preachers to cops on the beat, saw to it that the child would treat her the same way they did. So no matter how much the child might have loved the poor woman they went about doing everything they could to make it deny her.

"And it works, because not only does the child turn against *her,* it turns against everybody *like* her, against *all* of us! And it begins having its full effect as soon as the time is ripe. Which is just about the time when young folks start smelling themselves and don't know what's happening to their bodies. Then they get confused in their minds and the poison takes them over...."

Suddenly Janey sat back in her chair, whispering, "Oh, my Lord..."

"What is it?" Hickman asked.

"Now that I'm talking about it I just realized where I made my mistake...."

"What are you getting at? *Which* mistake?"

"The mistake I made in overlooking the fact that in order for their nasty business to work the child had to *deny* me! That's the pattern: First they have to reach the age when the sap starts rising, and then the grown folks encourage them to begin acting like white folks instead of people. Because that's when this grown white folks' devilment takes over and the children begin turning their backs on their black mothers...."

"No, Janey, not always, because I know some who were loyal to the end...."

"All right, not always—maybe—but that's exactly how it usually happens, and that's where the boy was different. He was too young and had no white folks close enough to corrupt him. So the child never denied me; what happened was because of his daddy and that lawyer. *They* were the ones who raided my house and treated me like a mammy. And it was because of *them* that I was forced to deny my motherly love in the name of one that was deeper. It almost killed me, but when that lawyer showed up I had to do *something.* So to make it easier for the child to leave us and become his father's son I decided to wean him. . . ."

Suddenly grasping his thighs, Hickman leaned forward shouting, "*Wean* him! . . . Are you telling me that by smoking that child you were preparing him to become *white?* That with a single stroke of slavery-time cruelty you were initiating him into an attitude for which he had no white folks to teach him? Was that your way of making him accept a condition which most folks in this country consider as being the best in the world? Teaching him to hate you and our people so he could accept living as white? How on earth could you even *think* such a thing?"

"But Alonzo," Janey sobbed, "you have to understand that I wasn't thinking, I was *acting!*"

"*Acting!* But why didn't you just make him wash his mouth with soap, or give him a whipping? Confine him in the chicken house for a while? As I remember you were proud of raising white Leghorns about that time, so why didn't you make him spend a night roosting with the chickens?"

"Because none of that would have been drastic enough, A.Z. When you have a strong cord to cut you have to use a sharp knife. And think of the position I was in—all of a sudden that lawyer shows up and turns everything into the opposite of what I expected, both for me and the child. Like you say, I should have been happy for him; happy to see him enter into his fine new life and good fortune. But I wasn't. Instead I reacted like a sinner who was questioning the wisdom of almighty God. So as you've accused me for years, I was arrogant. I admit it, but when the meaning of what that man and his lawyer were doing started getting to me I felt all of a sudden that no matter how little the child had here with us it was better than anything he was going to. Poor and humble, yes; but better because I *loved* him. . . . We, me and the boys, we *loved* him. So although I knew both in my heart and in my mixed-up mind that there was nothing I could do but give him up, I said NO!"

"Yes," Hickman said, "but you didn't stop it from happening, and now it seems that you made matters worse. Maybe that explains your being so upset by his coming back—you couldn't accept the idea that you'd done him wrong and he'd forgiven you. But now that you've finally seen it, let's leave it at that and get on to what else happened—what was he like?"

"I'm still confused," Janey said, "I really don't know. But for one thing, he wasn't like anyone around here—white *or* colored. . . ."

"What do you mean?"

"He was so *white*, Alonzo; so *ofay*-acting."

"But you should have expected that...."

"I know, but before they took him he talked and acted like us, while now he has their manners...and...and..."

"And what?"

"Well, A.Z., the only way I know to put it is to say that he acted crazy...."

"Was that how Cliofus reacted?"

"No, but Cliofus wasn't here to hear our talk, he had gone to see his doctor."

"All right, so you say he sounded crazy. But what kind of crazy? Crazy insane, or crazy odd? Or was it something like when a white man tries to communicate with one of us and gets his words scrambled and his signals crossed?"

"Something like that. It was like we lived in two different worlds and spoke different languages. Maybe instead of 'crazy' I mean 'emotional,' but he sounded like one of these spoiled white kids. And like some who're much younger than him; the rich ones who have everything and don't know what to do with it. I guess what I'm trying to say is that he acted *mad*. I mean like he was angry mad. Not loud and noisy mad, but like a person who's been hurt and cried over it and then stopped crying and got quietly mad at the world...."

"So what did he say?"

"Alonzo, it was something that nobody who'd had the right upbringing would ever even *think* of saying. And more than his coming back it was that which upset me. After asking me to tell him who his father was and I couldn't he said, 'If I ever find the son of a bitch who gave me this color I'll *kill* him!'

"...*Kill* him? He actually said *that*?"

"Yes! Those were his very words, and I don't have to tell you what it did to me. I was knocked off my feet because it was the last thing I expected to hear him say about his own *father*. And all the more because for all those years I had thought he'd been *living* with his father. But I tell you, the way he said it made my blood run cold. He sounded like he really meant it, and now you know why I wrote you. Anyway, I tried to tell him that he ought not to say things like that, but he was so worked up that after asking me what right *I* had to be telling him such a thing he rushed out of here like I'd slapped his face...."

"Are you sure that he wasn't just blowing off steam, saying it out of frustration?"

"As sure as I'm sitting here. He had a look in his eyes like he meant what he said."

Shaking his head, Hickman was silent as he listened to the barking of a dog somewhere in the street.

"Alonzo, what are you thinking?" Janey said.

"I'm thinking that he might have come back with more than one purpose in mind. And if he did—well, this thing is more serious than I expected...."

"But of course it's serious, A.Z., why else did you think I wore out my fingers writing you that letter? I couldn't give one hoot in hell over what happens to that scoundrel of a father, whatever he calls himself, but I don't want that boy to get into trouble. No, sir! I have enough on my conscience as it is. Therefore I was hoping that you'd know how to get in touch with that man and warn him. You do know how to reach him, don't you?"

For a moment Hickman was silent, asking himself, *Do I? After all our attempts to keep tabs on him, do I really?*

"You do, don't you? Because I truly hope so...."

"I'm not so sure, but I think I might."

"Why 'might'?"

"Because to tell you the truth, he's kept out of my sight as carefully as he seems to have avoided his son. Did the boy say where he'd been living after all this time?"

"No, we didn't get into that. I guess he was too mad. But after thinking about it I figured that what they did was to take him from me and put him in the hands of somebody else, some white person up North. He sure dresses well and doesn't appear to be having any money problems. In fact, he looked wealthy. And I mean white-folks wealthy."

"It's possible, because the father has money—but why would the man refuse to make himself known, uproot the boy from the only life he knew and then keep behind the scene and out of the picture? Why play hide-and-seek with his child?"

"But A.Z., wasn't that what he did to you?"

"Yes, I suppose he did. But as you remember in those days life in this country was much harder for us than it is today. And besides all that he was rebelling against me. I suppose after working the revival circuits with me and seeing how unfair life could be for folks like us he decided that things would be better on the other side of the line. So after a while I came to accept that as his reason for crossing over. And whether he was right or wrong we have to consider that he had a choice that's denied folks who look like us. And so, having the credentials for crossing over, he used them."

"Yes, and betrayed you."

"Call it what you will, it happened and I suffered. But what I can't understand is why he would uproot the boy, his own child, and place him among strangers, and then *abandon* him. If what the boy told you is true, he didn't even give him a concrete cause for rebellion—or at least not a healthy one. Did the boy leave town?"

"Oh, no, because the next day Love told me that he'd been asking him the same questions about his mother and father."

"And was Love able to tell him anything?"

"All I know is that he could tell him a lot about his mother, because they were both Natives. But I doubt if he knows much about the father. Although he *was* around town when they were making that movie. What worries me about his going to Love is that Love might have loaded him down with some of his lies...."

"Did the boy come back here after talking with Love?"

"Not to the house, maybe because he's sorry he left here so angry. But I've seen him standing across the street looking over here like he wanted to. Made me so nervous from worrying over what he might do that I wrote to you. Which ought to explain why I didn't feel that I could come right out and tell you what he said about his father. I would have been committing the sin of bearing false witness, because after all he hadn't done anything except say what he'd *like* to do. I'm so thankful that you read between the lines, A.Z., so very thankful."

"Even so, *I'm* the one to be thankful; because although I don't know this little man of yours I'm much more mixed up in this thing than you could ever be. Maybe I should have a talk with Love...."

"That old infidel lives! Why bother with him?"

"Because he might be able to tell me what the young fellow is thinking...."

"Well, if you do may the good Lord help you...."

"Now, Janey, as you very well know, the Lord's will is His will—so what's bothering you?"

"Because Love is one of the biggest liars that ever made a mess of the truth, that's what! And whatever he told that boy or decides to tell you is bound to cause trouble...."

"Why trouble?"

"I don't know, A.Z., but Love's the kind who'll insist that black is white and white is black and set out to prove it. And being a Native he thinks he's so much better than anyone else, white, colored, or in between, that he'll tell them *any-thing* and expect them to believe it."

"You make him sound like a true, dyed-in-the-wool American, so I'll keep that in mind. But after what you've been telling me, our learning what he said to this visitor of yours might be important. Where can I find him?"

"Find who?"

"This Native who's called Love New."

"Right here in town, Lord help us. He lives in a section called Whitby's Court, but if you want *my* opinion everybody would be better off if the lying old heathen was still living with his Indians!"

[LOVECOU[R]T]

FOLLOWING JANEY'S DIRECTIONS, HE walked north and then east, feeling the heat as he made his way through streets that were vaguely familiar.

So, Hickman, he mused, *you fly out here on what you expected to be an overnight visit and now you're finding that things are much more complicated than you expected. And all because a white-looking stranger turns up at Janey's claiming to be the child she lost years ago. But while Janey rejects the man's story and seems unyielding, Cliofus accepts him as his childhood friend—and that raises a few troublesome questions.*

Why would a stranger present himself as Janey's lost "little man"? And if he wasn't, why is Janey so upset by his visit? Is it because the child in question looked white and she still feels guilty over what she did to make it easier for him to leave her and his foster brothers? Because any child who'd been tied in a bag and smoked like a ham is unlikely to forget it. Therefore if he was that child he's probably forgiven her. So what's keeping her from accepting him?

But then there's the question of why, after living all these years in the East, he now claims he's never laid eyes on his father! What kind of man would separate his son from the only mother he knew, have a lawyer tell her that it was being done so that the little boy could have the advantages of living in a white environment, and then abandon him to the care of strangers? Which must have been upsetting for the child, but that the man would then refuse to have personal contact with his son is so unbelievable that the son's telling Janey that he'd like to find the man and kill him makes it sound true. And then, heaven help us, things proceed to take a truly weird turn in my *direction.*

Because while Janey rejects her visitor as though he's some kind of counterfeit prodigal son, she then adds to the confusion by suggesting that the child taken East by his father's lawyer might have been the illegitimate son of the man I began training as a minister when he was a child. . . .

What a mind-blowing mess! Years ago that marvelous little preacher of mine runs away, and now, way late, this grown-up "little man" of Janey's turns up in search of someone who might or might not have been his daddy. So with him seeking a father and me seeking a son the old game of hide-and-go-seek turns into a footrace with none of the players having the slightest idea of where the finish line lies or what will take place once we reach it. . . . But one thing is certain: If Janey's visitor ever finds his father and fulfills his threat . . . well, may the good Lord help us, fathers, sons, and everyone who's involved in this nasty confusion. . . .

Which makes a man wonder if there were ever creatures on God's green earth more mixed up than us Americans?

No, Hickman, never! Because given their mammy-made tendency to go berserk over questions concerning their mixed blood and scrambled identities, they turn reality into a raving nightmare!

Just look at this thing: Here we have a fellow who claims to have been the white-looking baby who once lived with Janey. And now, years after being taken East where he had the good fortune of growing up as a well-fed white boy, he's back here telling his black foster mother that he'd like to kill *the man who made it possible by giving him a white complexion! How's that for turning things inside out and upside down?*

Maybe that's what educated folks mean when they talk about this so-called American dilemma. Because usually when a light-skinned Negro gets mistaken for white he keeps quiet and exploits it as a means for going after freedoms denied people of darker complexions. As a white *black American he makes his peace with being accepted as one thing on the outside when he's something else—whatever that might be—on the inside. Which could be unsettling but in many ways rewarding. Then, like the little fellow I thought I knew fairly well, he covers his tracks and leaves the question of his true identity up to the eyes of his various beholders. Meanwhile, he thinks, Behold the man if you can, and gets on with his living.*

Yeah, but what about his opposite?

Now that's somewhat different. Because if a white *white American has a hint that his blood contains a* black *gene or two he'll foam at the mouth and go looking for scapegoats. And I mean with anything from Supreme Court decisions to high-powered rifles.*

Right! And that's the grain of truth in that barbershop lie they told during the Depression about a passenger in a train wreck who had his brain mangled so bad that it almost killed him. You remember?

How can I forget since you enjoyed it so much? With the wreck taking place down South in unsettled country, the doctors who rushed in to save the man were forced to replace his brain with whatever was handy. So they improvised, and after hours of sawing and stitching they performed the first brain transplant in medical history. And so successfully that it was acclaimed a miracle.

So everybody was amazed, and especially the patient, who praised American medicine for making it possible for his being alive and kicking. Then he bragged about being reborn with faster reactions, clearer vision, a sharper nose, and more sensitive hearing. But then the news hit the papers, and when he learned that he'd been saved by the brain of a hound—and a black *hound at that—right away he was out on the street raising hell and threatening to sue the railroad and kill his physicians.*

Why? Because now he claims that a few days after he recovered he was blasted by sensations so strange and inhuman that they damn near undid him. Then he squalls like a baby and howls like a hound, and when he's pressed to explain he replies with tears flooding his eyes that now not only does he have a powerful urge to chase rabbits, but that no matter how hard he tries to resist he's obsessed by a notion that bullshit is health food!

Yes, Hickman, you have it. But whoever made up that lie went after his point with a baseball bat!

Amen! But sometimes telling jokes to ease the stress of life in this country is like trying to perform music which some harmony-hating joker has deliberately messed up with discords. It's like listening to a symphony played out of tune because some soreheads in the orchestra disagree with the composer's conception. . . . Maybe that's why the so-called "harmony of the spheres" was considered ideal: There were no human beings up there either to take part or listen—otherwise the Tower of Babel would have reached the high heavens.

Which of course it did, because whatever else it might be, these United States are the Tower of Babel reinvented. And that's the reason our ancestors developed gut-bucket and blues. In protecting themselves from all the craziness around them they needed the sound of reality reformed in a way that makes life a little more bearable. Therefore my friends ivy me music unless it's been Boldened by Buddy and Wallered by Fats!

Which isn't much of a pun, but when it comes to music we do *have our own special needs and high standards. Besides, old Buddy and Fats might have even helped Charles Ives reach the top of the wall he was climbing. . . . Somebody called jazz music the sound of surprise, but more than that it's also the sound of a receptive state of mind. Therefore, if music is to keep up with this country's confusion it has to shake, rattle, and roll, hang loose and fly high. Otherwise its message gets lost in our stumbling and grumbling. . . .*

Poor Janey and her confounded signs! *What are they—the ghosts of wishes, omens, or intuitions? Hidden wishes? And what else is hidden behind her refusing to accept a young man who obviously loves her? Anyway, I'm here; and if this thing gets to where it seems to be headed—which is probably to that lost boy of mine—I'll have to find him and show him my face. Give up my pride and confront him in some bright spot where he'll have to see me even against his will—no! He'll have to see* us, *that's the way it should be. Because by hope and by faith the members have earned the right to see him and be seen—whether he wants it that way or not. . . . Not to judge, but to warn. Just that, and maybe to marvel that he could make so high and so reckless a leap. . . . But right now there's the problem of finding this man Love and learning what happened when Janey's little man came to see him. . . .*

Approaching the block in which he expected to find the address, he was surprised to find himself looking across a broad avenue glinting with trolley-car rails to a broad, park-like space.

Bordered by towering cottonwood trees, the recently mown area extended into the distance; and on a wooden bench beneath the trees to his left two elderly men leaned together as they argued and gestured. Then in the shade behind them he saw a concrete path which led to a series of shingled-roofed houses.

Painted white and shingled black with low sweeping eaves, the houses sat behind individual lawns, and across the greensward to his right a parallel path led to a row of houses that faced them. And now, crossing the avenue, he entered the park-like area, which ranged for what he judged to be the length of a football field and a half to a high, vine-covered wall. And as he moved slowly ahead a gate in the wall swung wide, and he was watching a brown-skinned young woman dressed in blue float into view with the sun in her hair and her arms full of flowers.

The flowers were red and probably roses, and entranced by her graceful, hip-swinging motion he stopped in his tracks and stood watching until, reaching the entrance to one of the houses, the girl disappeared. And as she faded he smiled at the image of loveliness which remained alive in his delighted old eyes.

And now, entering the park-like area at a leisurely pace, he began his search for Love New while breathing the odor of freshly mown grass and admiring the extended array of well-kept houses.

Thank God that they did, he thought, but why on earth would the white folks let such a pleasant spot get away when they might have done better—yes—and found life more interesting if they'd relaxed and chosen to share it? Not a single rattletrap car parked in a yard, no washing machines displayed on the porches; and although that stereo is a bit too loud, it's not rock-and-roll but Duke Ellington. . . .

And now, seeing a house with numerals that matched the address, he paused, thinking, *So this is the castle of the man Janey calls "the king of black liars." But what better place could he choose than a courtyard?*

Knocking on the door, he waited and was surprised when it was opened by a small man whose translucent black skin bore an undertone of deep red. And as the little man stood looking him over he noted that his hair was braided and hung to his shoulders, that his neck was hidden by a deep purple scarf, and his shirt made of denim. And reminded of Indians whom he had encountered in the past, he was instantly curious as to what idiom of speech and timbre of voice would emerge from a black man dressed in such a costume. Would it be Indian or Negro? Yes, and given the changes of time, perhaps even Harvard?

"Would you," he asked, "be Mr. New?"

"That's right," the little man said, "a bit older, but still New to you. How can I help you?"

And hearing a trace of black Southern idiom in the high Indian timbre he smiled, thinking, *Whatever this fellow calls himself he's some kind of mixture,* and extended his hand with a smile.

"Mr. New," he said, "I'm a friend of Janey Glover...."

Ignoring his hand, the little man stared at the cross on his watch chain.

"A friend of Janey's, are you? So then you must be Hickman, that preacher she's always going on about. She send you over here?"

"Oh, no," Hickman said, "but she did tell me how to find you...."

"Well, that's good enough for me. Anybody who's put up with Janey as long as you is welcome. Come on out to the back and tell me what's on your mind."

And now, following his host, he found himself moving through a medium-sized living room furnished with two upholstered chairs, a worn leather sofa, and a small cocktail table. A brass spittoon gleamed on the floor next to a wooden reclining chair, and a floor lamp topped by a translucent shade fringed with tassels stood in a corner. Framed color prints of game birds hung on the wall to his right and were joined by an ancient army canteen, a riding crop, and a Remington rifle. And as he glanced to his left he was surprised to see a bookcase loaded with books.

Protected by horizontal glass doors, the books were flanked on one side by a huge globe of the world, and on the other by a huge Webster's dictionary which rested on a stout wooden stand.

So, he thought, it appears that along with his lying this little fellow also reads books—which is something Janey never bothered to mention. And suddenly on impulse he paused to have a look inside the bookcase. But seeing the silhouette of his host waiting in the doorway ahead, he moved to join him and found himself on what turned out to be a wide screened porch. The porch looked out to a neat grassy yard with towering trees through the limbs and green leaves which the afternoon sunlight filtered.

Pointing to a pair of large, throne-like chairs, his host said, "One of those ought to hold you." And noting that the chairs were fashioned from the curved horns of steers, he thought, *Come to this little fellow with a dilemma and right away you're sitting on horns.* He settled himself and found the chair comfortable.

"So," his host said, "you're the Hickman I've been hearing so much about."

"Yes," Hickman said, "and after all this time it's a pleasure to meet an old friend of Janey's."

"Friend my foot," the little man said. "I'm more her substitute for a sparring partner and a punching bag than anything else. But before we get started, how about a beer? I've got some pretty good Choc, if it ain't against your religion...."

"Choc!" Hickman said, "Now that's a pleasure I haven't tasted for *years!*"

"You will now, but don't you tell Janey. That woman's favorite drink is croton oil—or at least that's what she'd like mine to be. I won't be but a minute."

Watching his host move away, Hickman noted his quickness of movement and saw that the texture of his hair was more Indian than African. And amused by the game which the little man seemed to play with his mixed background and color, he smiled as he recalled a football backfield man who had been about the same size.

Also an Oklahoma Native, the young college athlete had been famous for his spectacular skill in receiving passes and for his speed in evading his would-be tacklers. Yes, he thought, but the reason this fellow Love brings him to mind is the fact that he was also a natural-born showman who got a kick out of outrunning pursuing defense men. And once free of the pack he'd excite the crowd by throwing off his helmet and galloping to the goal line, tossing his head of black hair like the mane of a colt at play in a pasture....

"You know, Hickman," the little man said as he returned with two chilled bottles of beer capped with tall glasses, "this'll be something new for me. I've drunk with cowboys, outlaws, and gamblers, but never with a preacher. What do you know about Choc?"

"Choctaw beer? Didn't Janey tell you that I wasn't *always* a minister? Why, during my day out here as a musician this town had more Choc-joints than Rome, Italy, has churches."

"Yao! And more good times too, because so many State folks hadn't trooped in to spoil it. How's that Janey doing?"

"Physically she seems fine, but she's upset in her mind. That's why I flew out here.... Besides, I've wanted to meet you."

"And me you," Love said as he extended a glass filled with beer. "But it's really about that boy coming to see her after all these years. Is that it?"

"I'm afraid so."

"Well, cheers anyway, because as you know that Janey loves nothing better than worrying."

"I agree, but right now I'm enjoying this Choc, which is excellent—so maybe you should send her a bottle...."

"... And get crucified? Not me! She's against any kind of liquor because of her religion, so let her. And if she wants to let some old Hebrews tell her what to do and what not to do she's welcome. But like I tell her, those suckers couldn't have lasted a year in this country. Talking some foolishness about a goddamn snake causing all the world's trouble—Hickman, you know what we did with snakes when I was living amongst the People? Hell, we'd grab the bastard by his tail and snap off his head! No offense to Adam and Eve—or you either...."

"And none taken," Hickman said, "as you can see from my grinning. What's more, my granddaddy did the same back in Georgia, and his snakes were rattlers. But what can you tell me about this young man? What did he want?"

"What most orphans want, which is to know about their parents. That and maybe to see me again. Years ago he used to visit me whenever he could get away from Janey, who was against it. She was always warning him and the others that I was a heathen and a bad influence for her little Christians—ha!"

"I can understand her concern, but why did he come to you? Were you able to tell him anything?"

Settling back, Love gazed at the beer in his glass, and now as he spoke again his voice became more like that of an Indian.

"This is the way it was: When he was taken from Janey he was only a cub, but he still remembered enough to know that if there was *anyone* around who could tell him what he wanted to know it would be me. So he comes to Love. And, Hickman, dealing with what he wanted to know gave me one hell of a time...."

Pausing, Love held up his glass and stared at the beer with a thoughtful expression.

"You know, Hickman, this Choc is a drink blessed by the spirits. That's why the People treat it with ceremonial respect. It takes charge of time and brings men together like the sacramental wine of your churches...."

"I understand," Hickman said. "It's not what folks *drink* but what they do *after* drinking that makes the difference. You say that the boy gave you a hard time— what did he want?"

"Wanted me to tell him who his father was. But when he's asked a question like that, how can *any* man be sure of his answer? Only the mother would know, but in his case that's impossible because she put the knife to her throat when he was still too young to even know about death. So while she was the kind of woman who would have known, there wasn't time for her to tell him. Then Janey took him and started raising him and loving him like she did all those others, and even though he was taken from her years ago she still wouldn't give him the answer. Not even if she knows it. Because telling the boy would mean giving up more of the little she has left of him... memories of him as a baby and all. And that's because she don't like the idea of somebody else being more important to any of those boys than herself.

"Hickman, I think you already know, but I'll say it: Janey's the kind of woman who can never bring herself to give in to a man but can't live without children around her. And so back in those days she started picking up all the orphans and strays she could find and went about raising and feeding and loving them. Yes, she loves them, but the woman is so damn proud of what she does that she refuses to share it. Especially with women who have a chance to give birth but refuse it. That's her way. She wouldn't tell the boy what he wants to know even if she knows it. So when she refuses him he comes to me.

"After all those years he comes to *me,* Love, who's sometimes known as old *Loveless* Love. And seeing how disturbed he was, and knowing how long he'd been carrying that question around inside him, I tried to help. That was my first mistake—if it *was* a mistake. Because I had no idea that he would go beyond me, or that the road he's taking would wind around so far and spiral so high...."

Suddenly Hickman leaned forward, saying, "*High?* What do you mean?"

"Hickman, you'll just have to listen and draw your own conclusions, because now I'm speaking in words that leap back and forth as they wrestle with time. Are you willing to listen?"

"Of course, and excuse my interruption...."

"Done! So as I was saying, what happened will happen, 'cause like you preachers keep repeating, in the beginning was words. So I told the boy what I knew, and even though I went at it at an angle, like when you use a parable to say something that you'd rather not run the risk of saying straight out. So he got something from what I said, and when he finds his man we'll both know the rest. I feel sure that he will, that he'll keep on the trail until he gets satisfaction, but I can't be too sure.

"Hickman, as we both know, the truth has penalties. Maybe that's why it's truer when it's told in circles. All this talk about truth being straight ain't no more than what the great bull left steaming in the field behind him. Therefore I went about tracking it for the boy in circles, when maybe I should have looked deeper into what lay in the road ahead. Instead, I looked so far into the past that I failed to question the future. And that's because the boy's story cuts across my own and touches on the fact that I died a bit with the dying of the People and surrendered the sacred medicine they invested in me— Hickman, drink up and let that Choc help you in understanding what I'm saying."

"Don't worry," Hickman said, "and if I look puzzled it's because I'm trying to see where you're going."

"Good, because when medicine men consult in earnest good Choc makes the talking flow smoother."

With a quick look at Love's mask of a face, Hickman smiled.

"If I'm hearing you right that's a compliment, and I'm honored."

"And I'm serious. I don't know what kind of ordeal *you* had to endure to earn your credentials, but when I speak of medicine I speak of knowledge I had to earn by being sent to die on a mountain. Yao! I had to *suffer* to earn it. And in the course of my instruction the Eagle, my totem, entered my skull and left my young body of flesh lying on the stone of the mountain."

"I see."

"No, you *don't* see, but that's how I learned to soar with the Eagle's wings, see with his eyes, and hear with his ears. Then, after I had learned that powerful part of the People's medicine, I was given the responsibility of using it wisely. But then years passed, and with the world changing I thought I had put all of that behind me. But here, way late, that boy turns up and I forgot to look through his returning and into the unfolding of things yet to come...."

Hickman leaned forward. "Mr. New, are you saying that you have the gift of second sight?"

"Just call me Love—no, it's not me, but that which speaks *through* me. And if you don't believe what I say about the eyes, ask any of the old-timers around here. They'll tell you that I speak the truth. They used to make bets on my vision, and on my hearing too. Even today I can tell from across a good-sized room which of two watches is ticking the loudest. With the State Negroes that's something unusual, but I had to earn it. Yao!

"Like I say, when I went through my trials on the mountain I died, and when I returned I was of the Eagle—which is something I don't expect you to understand, much less believe. Not as a preacher of the State Negroes. But even though the State people, the Americans, won't believe it, there are other ways of living life than the one they pursue. They insist that their way is the *only* way, so I don't argue. What I know, I *know;* and I am older than most of them. Not always wiser, but much older and more experienced. My name is New, yet I am older than the hills and the rivers. A man of the People's medicine sees what he trains himself to see, and if I put my mind to it there are still things I can foretell. So what happened between me and the boy came about because I'd put my Eagle's knowledge aside. So maybe in trying to spare him I harmed him. We shall see.

"So he came asking me who was his daddy and I believed that I knew the answer. But how could I tell him? He'd been gone all these years and now, all of a sudden, he's back here asking that kind of question. I thought to myself, What kind of man has this boy become? He's still young, but even so he's old enough to have learned that some questions are better left unasked—or if you just *have* to ask it's better not to wait for an answer.

"Because just as shorely as thunder breeds lightning, somebody's bound to come up with an answer, whether they know the truth or don't know it. And that's just the beginning of more confusion. So why the hell would he come back here for that after he'd been gone so long? Sure, anyone might think of asking it at one time or another, but you'd think that after all this time he'd have made his peace with that question. But no, he had to *ask* it.

"Better that he'd forgot it. Better that he'd said, I am me, myself, and that is sufficient. And even better if he'd said, I am my own father, and gone on from there.

"For many have said it and done pretty good, have gone on to make up whatever was missing, mother, father, and family. But no, he's dying to discover an answer, so that afternoon here he comes, a fine-looking stranger. And no sooner than I recognize him as the boy I used to know through Janey, I offer him a welcoming drink of hard liquor, some cigars, and pipe tobacco. Then the minute he's settled in his chair he asks me, Mister Love, who was my father?

"Hickman, it was the last thing I expected, and when he asked it this old nose of mine starts to twitching so hard that I had to sit back and study him.

"Now if he had given me a little time I could have prepared, but with his coming at me straight as an arrow he caught me off guard. He reversed time and space without warning and I was left hanging on air. I say that because except for now being grown with a voice that was deeper he sounded just like he did as a kid. Like the kid he was when he had the habit of stopping strange men on the streets and asking the very same question.

"That's right. A man would be walking along minding his business, when all of a sudden there'd be this little nice-looking kid grabbing his pants leg. And when he looks down the kid's looking up like he's holding a pistol, saying, 'Mister, are you my daddy?' "

"He did *that?* Why, the poor little fellow!"

"Yes, and he asked it over and over without receiving an answer. So how about you, Hickman; did he ever ask you?"

"No! And what's more, I was seldom on the scene at that time. And later when he saw me at Janey's he could see that I wasn't exactly the right color."

"*Color?* Hell, Hickman, the boy didn't care about color, he just wanted his daddy! But black, white, or Native, any man he hit with his question had to be surprised and flattered, because he was a fine little boy in spite of it. Fellows used to joke about his confusion—not that they disrespected his mama—but because he was raising a question which a lot of folks would be within bounds of reason for asking, even some who might not have thought so. What's more, there was many a fellow who would've been proud to say truly, Yes, son, I am, and rush to pick up the burden.

"Because, you see, his mother was a woman of stature. That's how the people of my tribe described her, which is after the Spanish. Oh, yes! And as you preachers like to say, I tell you verily that she was something to see. Naturally pretty and lovely, and even prettier from the process of giving birth to a baby. So she was the kind of girl that many a man would have been proud to tie the knot with—and I mean for the rest of his life. But when the boy asked me, 'Mister Love, who was my daddy?'—no, 'father' was the word he used—well, I looked at him a while and knew that I was getting old."

"But since you *did* know his mother..."

"Because being that which I am I should have seen his question arriving and been prepared to turn it away. But I *didn't*, so I was caught. Then as I sat there staring and remembering I felt my nose bleeding. What's more, I could feel it grow cold the second it touched the back of my hand. But even that didn't warn me in time.

"So being of no mind to lie, I just looked at him in a state of suspension. And then all of a sudden I entered a state of mind like I had when I lived among the People. Of that kind of attention, and when I saw the look in his eyes my mind whirled up and took flight. Because in his eyes I saw fear and hope and insistence, so I flew up and around and climbed to the zone of the Eagle. Then in my mind I was back to the town as it was in the old days, seeing streets full of people and wagons, the tents and shanties they lived in. Yes, and the trees and the gardens, the red clay, and tracks in the dust on the roads. Then I was back to the times of the old Territory—

"Hickman, I was living in this land long before there was such things as states, railroads, or cities. And then I was southwest and up in the mountain where I had died in my young days. Yao! And I could see myself stretched on the rocks with my head to the east, my feet to the west, and my arms to the north and the south. I was there, where I'd been for many days without food or water, naked to the sun and the wind and the rain. There, where the Eagle finally came to rest upon me, speak to me, and give me the medicine meant to stay in my keeping and be my responsibility until I died the death you call natural.

"All this happened in a flash, you see? You understand? But with such a great slam and bang of my spirit that I was disturbed. Truly disturbed. Because that was the first time I had left my body and soared since I settled here in town and gave up the ways of the People. And that it could happen these days is still a mystery, because the elements that go into such a happening—the earth and the weather and the blood and atmosphere—weren't of the right proportions. Sure, being the son of his mother the boy bore some of the blood of the People—just as a heap of State Negroes bear a trace of the blood—but he was not, and had never been, of the People. What's more, his were now the ways of the East, of the white State people. And yet something he brought into the room caused me to take flight, so I found myself soaring and returning to a scene which existed shortly before he was born.

But there I was, hovering over the streets and looking at his mother, Lavatrice, as she was at that time. She was just a slim young thing who was getting into a strange-looking auto. One of those with a slanting hood over its engine, broad running boards, and reversible cloth top. Yao! It was her, climbing in, looking over her shoulder at some of her young friends standing on the sidewalk, there in the sunlight, and all of them smiling. She was a beauty, and that's the truth even in the eye of the Eagle.

"Hickman, it was as though the Negro and the Indian and the white Sooner blood, the black and the white and the old Native red, had settled together in just the right mixture to produce the finest young woman those three warring, dog-assted bloods could possibly come up with. So there she was, climbing into that touring car—Yao! Into *his* car. Because while I couldn't see who was behind the wheel—the Eagle didn't mean for me to see him, understand?—I'm sure that he was the one.

"Hear me, Hickman: She was dressed in a long black skirt and wine-colored blouse which was full in the right places and narrow in the places where a young woman should be narrow and thin. Yao! And that jet-black hair of hers was done up in the style young women of the time were proud to be wearing. And when she bent over to get into that car a necklace of blue turquoise—stones of truth, the Navahoes call 'em—swung down from her neck to her bosom. Then a teasing little breath of wind made her black skirt flutter and swing, and everybody on the scene stopped what they were doing to take a look and admire her.

"Me too, back then and now as I hung poised there in time and space over her head. Yao! And that's when I felt hate for that fellow who brought that one-eyed contraption to this town...."

"Wait," Hickman said, "what's this about a contraption?"

"That lying camera," Love said. "That three-legged thing with a single eye which was its owner's snare and the source of all his illusions. I really hated him—Yao! But how could I tell that to the boy? He was sitting with his head cocked to the side, looking me straight in the eye. Even looked a bit like his mother, but now he had the ways of the Eastern white State folks.

"So I said, 'Boy, are you asking *me* about your daddy? Didn't Janey Glover raise you?'

"And he said, 'Yes, she did until I was taken away. But she wasn't my mother.'

"Well, I didn't say anything to that, I just crossed my legs and looked at him a while. Then something struck me a sharp blow behind my right eye, and the moccasin I was wearing fell off my right foot and I felt the tears well up but managed to control the pain that it dealt me. I had to, because it was the Eagle that did it. He'd showed up and his peck was a warning. And that's when I knew I was really in trouble.

"So I told the boy, I said, 'I know all that. Sure, Janey mothered you, but she wasn't your mama. At least not of the flesh. Anyway, you're asking about something that happened a long time ago. Many moons ago.'

"Then he said, 'Yes, but not too long for you to remember, so please, go on and tell me....'

"So then I said, 'I'm old and well-preserved but not all-knowing. Did you ask Janey?'

"He said, 'No, because Miss Janey is a woman, so naturally she wants to protect my mother's memory. Besides, I don't think she knows. Any more than she really knows who took me from her and sent me to live in the East—but I think *you* might know.'

"So then I looked into my glass and again felt the pain, this time behind both of my eyes. And my nose was bleeding again. So I looked out to the yard, and sure enough, I saw the Eagle. There he was, circling the air like he was about to plunge into the yard after Mrs. Gresham's chickens. I knew then that he was warning me of my oath and that no matter what had happened in the meantime I was still of the People.

"Hickman, what I'm telling you is true, all of it. He was reminding me that I had gone West and come back from the dead. So I looked at the young man and managed a smile. I myself would have liked to have been his daddy, because then I could have trained him in the ways of the People. Anyway, about that time one of these double-winged airplanes flew low over the houses and I could see the Eagle resting in the top of a tree with the sun glinting on his neck and the point where the white and black feathers formed such a fine pattern. He was looking at that man-made bird with contempt, and then he stared across the yard and into the house at me. So then not knowing what was going to come out I said, 'I can remember a time when folks used to run out of the house to see one of those—do you remember?' And he shook his head.

" 'I do,' I said, 'just like I remember when the picture shows, the movies, first came to town. But that was long before you were born.'

"So he just looked at me and remained silent. Then I rocked a bit in my chair and looked out to where the sun filtered through the leaves of the trees. By now my right foot had started itching and aching, and on the rug my big toe began drawing a circle—as though it was remembering and meant to get on with the ritual even though I was reluctant.

" 'That's Mrs. Gresham's chicken yard over there,' I said, 'and there's an eagle hanging in the sky above it. . . .'

"So then he bent over and looked out, and after a while he said, 'Where is it? I don't see it and neither do those chickens.'

"So I thought, Well at least he hasn't forgot everything he used to know. And sho enough, when I looked out those chickens were scratching the ground and dusting their feathers undisturbed. But when I took a look at the sky the Eagle was still there. And by that I knew that he was *my* Eagle, the Eagle of the People, and the same who instructed me after I had died and been chosen to possess the People's Medicine. I knew then that I was really in trouble. . . .

"So I told the boy, 'Although you don't see him and can't, I do. He's my own Eagle, the one who instructed me after I died and whose spirit entered me when I was chosen to be the vessel of the People's medicine. I told you about it when you were little, but you don't remember.'

"To that he was silent, but he looked at me with doubt in his eyes.

"So I said, 'Here's how it is so there'll be no confusion: You call it science, psychology, and other such words, but the People put them all together and call it medicine.'

" 'I understand,' he says, then he gets quiet but he's pressing me hard.

" 'I believe you do,' I says. 'You've read some of those cowboy-and-Indian stories and seen moving pictures, so you have that kind of understanding. But I'm speaking of something more serious. What I mean by medicine is the feeling and understanding that connects a man both to his people and to those who came before him. To the elements and animals, and to all that lies deepest in his own mind.'

"Well, to this he just nods his head, but he keeps asking me with eyes that keep pressing. So I look out again and see that the Eagle is still there, hovering in the air like a kite against the sky. The chickens were still there too—white leghorns and demoniacs, but they were all the boy could see. Being of the People, I could see both, and therefore I was still being reminded of my oath and my duty. And that's exactly where he had me, and had me even though he didn't know it. But I understood. He was pressing me because he was desperate and I was old and had been here and known his mother. Yes, but he couldn't see the Eagle who was helping him. Then I tried to con myself. I told myself that maybe I was caught up in a coincidence, because I couldn't see where the boy fitted into what was happening. That maybe the Eagle had returned for other reasons.

"So I said, 'Old friend, why'd you come back?'—speaking to the Eagle—but not understanding what was happening the boy said, 'Because I *had* to.'

"So I nodded to the Eagle and looked at the boy. 'Drink your whiskey,' I said. 'Or if that man's drink is too strong there's some soda pop in the icebox.'

"Which made him look up like he'd been challenged—which was true—and he took a drink of the liquor.

"I said, 'One day there were three men who drove into town in an automobile. They came from the East, and I was standing down there in front of the drug-store talking with the man who published the newspaper we had at the time. So I had a good look at the three and at the car.

" 'On the backseat where one was riding they had a lot of round shallow cans all strapped together, and strapped to the running boards there were big lights on black stands and what turned out to be a movie projector. . . .'

"Then I stopped and studied his face and saw a puzzled look take over his eyes. But he didn't break the silence, and when I looked out and saw the Eagle I knew by that I would have to keep going.

"So then I asked the boy, 'How old are you now?' and he said, 'Twenty-six.'

"Then this was sometime before you were born,' I told him and waited. In fact, it was no more than nine or ten months before. But since even men who are conceived in the light are born in the dark, I didn't feel it wise to go further. Because even though what he wanted to know was things that could be seen in the daylight, daylight has its own dark places and shadows.

"I said, 'These three fellows from the East brought along some presents; Kewpie dolls, and little bottles of five-and-dime perfume, chocolate candy in boxes tied with red ribbons, shiny pictures of actresses and actors, and other such junk.

Stuff they must have got from bankrupt carnivals and circuses. Later we found out that they meant to give it to the young women.'

" 'What kind of men were they?' he said, and I told him. I said, 'That was Editor Dunhawse's question, who said, "Tell me, Love, what manner of men are these?"' And I said, 'Well, Editor, there's three of them and they come here from the East, so draw your own conclusions.' Then Editor slapped me on the back and laughed. But the boy just stared and kept pressing.

"So I said, 'We could see that there were only three of them and they all looked white. Later we learned that one was a Rebel, one was a Jew, and one was black. Or at least that's what he *said* he was, even though you couldn't tell it from looking at him.

" 'In looks he was like the others, but not in his actions. Wore the same high-laced boots as the others, the same khaki shirt and britches as the others, and like them he wore his cloth cap with the bill turned to the rear, like he was looking backwards while walking forward. And like them he wore the same kind of goggles on his forehead like he was keeping a weather eye out for bad weather. In all this he was like the others, but although he was always in an agitated rush like a caged badger he was more inward and quieter than his buddies. And it turned out that he was also the leader and the shrewdest among them. He was as white as them too, even though he said he was black.'

" 'What did you think?' the boy asked me, and with that I knew he was hooked.

"I said, 'Look at me: To the eye I'm black, and before you were taken from Janey folks considered you black. So think about the difference between us. There are many ways of being black. There are the ways of the skin, and the ways of custom, and the way a man feels inside him. So I had no way of knowing how this one felt inside, but if he could appreciate the hardship and rewards—Yao!—and the honor of being taken for black it was fine with me. But *whatever* this fellow happened to be, I could see that he was definitely different. A heap of other folks did too, and they accepted it as being due to his being black behind a white skin. Some of the religious State Negroes were even glad that he was black because it made the three seem more like those wise men who were supposed to come out of the East.'

"At this the boy laughed and I joined him, because it was good to join him in a joke after so long a time. But while I was laughing I could see the Eagle making agitated movements high above the trees, where he was plunging and rising and beating his wings like he was attacking a sidewinder or rattler. Which meant that I had to keep going.

"I said, 'The three fellows didn't spend much time in the street that evening. For a while they just sat in that auto looking out from behind those goggles, then they got out and stretched and began asking questions. That was about all. Then the tall one, the one who had been sitting in the backseat with the camera, he came up to me and was about to ask me a question when something in my face stood him off. So he veered away and put his question to the crowd that had gathered.

" 'He wanted to know where he could find the moving-picture house, and before anybody else could tell him, Logan's little bowlegged boy was out in the middle of the street pointing down the block to where it stood. At the time it was only a sheet-metal shed, but Logan's little jaybird of a boy was yelling, "There it is, Mister, it's right down there. We have us a keen one!"

" 'So the three fellows took a look and exchanged a word or two between them.

" 'By now the crowd was all set to pile after them, with Logan's little boy in the lead. But instead of giving the place a closer inspection—its name was the Sunset—they climbed back into that car, a Franklin, and drove west, up the hill and down to the main business section.'

"So then the boy said, 'Why are you telling me this?' and I tightened the reins.

" 'Just listen,' I said. 'I don't know where they went down there, but they came back in the night. Because when I went out the next morning they had posted their paper on every fence, building, and lamppost in the section. Even on a few of the trees, the big ones.'

" 'Paper,' he said. 'What kind of paper?'

" 'Posters,' I said, 'playbills. Back when I worked with the 101 Ranch we called it paper. The ranch had the names of the top acts and pictures of cowboys, Indians, and circus girls on them. There's one with a picture of Bill Pickett on it tacked to the wall over there.'

"So he got up and took a look. Then he sat back down and said, 'I remember Pickett, he was a bulldogger.' "

"Me too," Hickman said. "I saw that outfit any number of times, but what were they doing with the 101 Ranch?"

"Training horses," Love said. "The boy asked me the same thing and I answered him with a question. I said, 'Don't you remember Astarte, that gaited mare of mine? You ought to, because you used to tag along begging me for a ride.' So then he remembered how I used to exercise her in the afternoon, and how all the younguns would come running to watch me put her through her paces. He seemed to get pleasure from remembering how she high-stepped, waltzed, and cakewalked along the street while younguns like him sang her the music. But then the smile died on his face, so I got back to the three strangers.

"I said, 'So next morning they had posters up announcing that they were making a movie....'

" 'A moving picture,' he said. 'What kind, and why make it out here?'

" 'That's just it,' I told him. 'The posters didn't say what kind it would be, but what got everybody so excited was the news that they'd be using neighborhood folks for the actors, and that they'd be running a contest to see which of the young women would win the part of the leading lady.'

" 'The leading lady,' he said, 'well, I'll be damn!' 'That's right,' I said. 'The young woman who raised the most money by selling the most tickets would end up playing the part of the female lead.'

"So with that he got still and sat there staring at me. Then my nose started bleeding again and I wiped it away and wondered what he was making of what I was telling him. Because after all the time that's passed and all the things that's happened, when you tell a youngster a thing like that it sounds like a lie and the damndest gimmick those three could have come up with. But that's always the way it is when you put one thing after another in words. You have to leave out all the things that surrounded it at the time it was happening. It's like looking at a stuffed grizzly after all the power and the fierceness is gone. So I studied the boy's face, but all I could tell was that he wasn't letting up the pressure, no matter how much he might doubt what I was saying. He was still pressing, forcing me back into those days and times. Then I saw the Eagle again and knew I was wrestling with him as well, because I had no way of knowing if I was getting at the boy's question.

"So I hushed for a while and took me a drink and just let myself climb back to those times so that I could see things more clearly. And right away I was looking for the girl who became his mother. But it was later, after the three fellows had whirled through here and took off. By then she'd got caught, missed her monthlies, and with the boy on the way she came to me for advice. That's how it was. . . ."

"But why *you*," Hickman said, "instead of a doctor or Janey?"

"And you call yourself a man of medicine? A man of both worlds? Hell, it was because she was ashamed and protecting her secret. I was not of the town, so maybe she came to me because at some time or another her folks on the reservation down at Anadarko had told her that I was of the Eagle; I don't know. But she came to me in much sorrow and pain of her spirits, so I told her:

" 'So this thing has come to you which according to some is a very bad thing. But since the seed has sprouted and taken its root, you can't dig it up. So without instruction you have entered into the mystery of womanhood, and being a man I have no knowledge of how to undo what has happened, and wouldn't even if I did. For while you're of the town you are also of the People, and that is not our way.' Then I shook my head and waited.

" 'But what shall I do?' she said, and I told her. 'Think about it a bit and you'll see that it's the State part of you that's unhappy, not the part that's of the People. That part is happy because a beautiful girl has begun the cycle which connects her with them and to the things of nature. You are both of the People and of the State Negroes, so use it to your advantage. While you wait for your time stretch out your arms to nature. Listen to the singing of the birds and don't worry about the gossip of those who are mean and narrow. You have education, so now is the time for reading good books. Read all you can of the best you can find and do not worry. Because what is happening will happen as it has happened to others. It will be a trial but not important because you are young and healthy. So watch the rising of the moon and the sun and their setting, and give yourself up to their rhythms. Listen to the shrill of the hawk and the call of the quail at sundown,' I told her. 'And watch how the smoke weaves in the sky in the quiet of the day, and hear the story told by the wind as it passes through the fields and the trees. Listen to the talk of the trains in the nighttime, and to the argument between the wheels of the freights and the sleepers lying under the hot steel rails. And study the stars. Study the stars and learn tranquillity and the long view of life, the view of the People. Yes, and drink of the clear water and warm milk. Go sit on the earth alone and think in the moonlight so that you can communicate with yourself as you listen to the thunder of the great drum in the sky.'

"She said, 'Why must I do all this, Mister Love?'

"And I said, 'Because it is good, and the best medicine for the seed that's growing inside you.'

"And she said, 'For the seed? What do you mean?'

"So I looked at her for a while and searched for words to span the distance between the ways of life she straddled, the ways of the State Negroes and the ways of the People. And when I spoke my tongue took over and said, 'That that's growing inside your belly, do it for your secret seed.'

"And then she blushed the ripe color of Alberta peaches, and her eyes were black with the longest of lashes, and she said, 'Mr. Love, you oughtn't to talk like that to me.'

"So I shook my head, knowing that in order to help I would have to hurt her, though not hard but gently.

"I said, 'There's no need for you to try to hide from me, because I am not of this town or its people. I talk to you straight in order to cut away the shame you are feeling. So don't feel bad. The seed is there, and I am sorry over how it happened, but what I tell you is good and good for the seed.'

"I said, 'Now you must look to the future and give what you carry within you love and consideration. So listen to the good voices around you. Listen to the good deep laughers of laughs, the bright laughers like old Deacon Turner who gets laughing-happy in that church you go to. Listen to him because his laughter is holy and he's a man who is kind and good. And even though I reject his religion he's one of the best men I know. What has happened has made you alone, so sit still sometimes and be by yourself and think about the world, about the great spaces and the clear distances now in this springtime. Listen to the growing of the grass—yes, that is possible if you try—and breathe the perfume of the flowers,' I said, 'because you are making a man. You have just got him started, and with his daddy gone he will need all these sights and sounds and feelings more than other children. To deal with the stresses of the world he will need a deep passion and strong sense of life, just as the trees of this country must be flexible and stand strong against the big winds, the cyclones and tornadoes. You're making a man, so shape him like the arrow that flies high in the sunlit sky.

Mold him to respond to the best in this confused world of confused people. Learn, and teach him the wisdom of solitude, and the rare greatness which is possible for the best of men and women. Start now, Lavatrice! Start now, and make him a man of stature as you yourself are a woman of stature. And close your pretty ears to the gossip that will soon come like a sandstorm to pelt you and blister you, and you'll give him the strength to stand firm and endure....'

"So as I say, Hickman, by now I had stopped speaking to the boy. Instead I was climbing back through the past on my lookout for the girl, his mother. But everywhere I looked I kept seeing those goggle-eyed fellows and those streets full of confusion.

"They wasted no time. They had tickets printed and given to all the girls and women who wanted to be in the picture—men too, but not so many, at least not in the beginning—and the contest was on. Most of the best-looking girls were in it, and even a few ugly ones; girls who were glad to compete because they knew that good looks are no guarantee of intelligence or talent. Even some of the whores from down in the red-light district got in it. And church women, house-maids, and cooks, and some of the big-busted sudsbusters, the strong washer-women. Everybody was out peddling those tickets, if not for themselves, then for friends they were backing. And pretty soon the news spread so far that a crowd of oil-rich Cherokees showed up riding in hearses and fire engines just to see what was happening. You with me, Hickman? You getting the picture?"

"I think so, although I'm finding it a bit confusing. But I'm still with you."

"Good," Love said. "So let's backtrack a bit: The goggle eyes rolled into town that Friday afternoon right after it was struck by thunder and lightning. For a while it seemed like a cloudburst, but it didn't last. Then all day Saturday they were out hustling in the streets. The black-white one stopped in at the theater and had the manager announce the contest during the break between the movie and the newsreels. Then he talked to the businessmen and got them all excited. And when I saw him talking a mile a minute to the fellow who ran the Elite, which was a social club for young men and women, I could feel how it was going. Because the fellow who ran the club was so flattered by his being considered im-portant enough to take up more time than it takes to say 'Howdy.' Those goggle-eyed fellows were running around all day, talking with folks and looking at the buildings and the dance halls and lodge rooms and churches.

"Then to sweeten the pot they unleashed that camera and started training it on the streets and on the buildings like they were surveying the town. But mainly they shot at the people. They'd shout orders back and forth to one an-other, and then consult among themselves and argue back and forth and go back and point that one-eyed man some more.

"So with that the boy wanted to know which of the fellows was one-eyed, and when I explained that I meant the camera, he laughed. Said, 'You make it sound like Polypheman'—or maybe he said 'Polyphemus.'

"'I never hear of him,' I said, 'but you should have seen what that one-eyed thing was doing. He collected such a crowd that soon you'd have thought that folks had nothing to do except follow those strangers and that three-legged contraption around the streets. It was like it had stirred up a storm and folks couldn't run for watching it. And those fellows treated the damn thing like some kind of totem.'

"With it standing on those three wooden legs one of them would squint through its eye and wave his arms to warn the crowd against getting too close. Then one of the others would have *his* head down looking through it, and his buddies would have the crowd walking in front of it or crossing the street and doubling back. Sometimes it looked like they were having a roundup and the folks were the cattle.

"First the goggle eyes were polite about it, but when they saw how fascinated folks were by what they were doing in front of that one-eyed bastard and how pleased they were in doing it they started ordering them around in a pretty round way. In fact, I've seen men killed just for using the tone of voice they were using.

"But not this time—hell, no! Folks were not only taking it, but liking it. And when the goggle eyes finished working on one end of the street one of them would pick up that contraption and carry it to another spot on his shoulders. And when he sat it down it was like he was settling a pregnant woman on a cot or a child on a potty. Then they'd spread its legs and start aiming it again and giving folks orders.

"Then they took out a little slate like the kind used by children and a piece of white chalk. And after they'd aimed the one-eyed contraption at the crowd and cranked it a while they'd write something on the slate and hold it in front of it and crank it some more like they were feeding it something rare and special.

"Hickman, now-a-days that kind of fiddling wouldn't mean much even to country folks, but back then it was heap big magic. So those fellows were causing no end of excitement because nothing like it had ever hit town. Folks were getting so drunk from just looking at them fiddling that pretty soon they began to act like they were no longer themselves. It was like the whole bunch had et a meal of loco weeds. Even old folks, and folks you'd have thought would know better got to making excuses for going out into the street to walk in front of that damn hunk of glass mounted on stilts.

"At first they'd walk natural, but then they'd double back and give it another try. They'd walk fancy and they'd walk lame. They'd strut and they'd creep. They'd walk tall and proud and then low and beat down. It was something to see. Verily, it was something to witness.

"And then it began to affect the kids. Because when those fellows would look through the one-eyed man they always had the bills of their caps turned to the rear, so pretty soon all the little boys—and a few of the grown ones too—they went in for the new style of cap-wearing. So that now they were walking around looking like somebody had cut their heads off and stuck them on backwards.

"Hickman, before those goggle eyes showed up only some of the pool sharks and hustlers went for that kind of style, and if a respectable woman was to see her boy wearing his cap that way she'd break his neck. Yao! But now they were glad to let the younguns get away with it. You'd have sworn that every cap-wearing boy in town was walking around backwards. Never in my life have I seen a hunk of glass cause so much confusion.

[CYCLOPS 1]

"Damn near everybody was talking about this movie. I stood in Speed's place listening to Jonas Ironwine going on about how it would benefit the community. According to him it would win nationwide attention and develop young actors who'd end up in Hollywood making movies with stars like Pearl White, William S. Hart, and Hoot Gibson. He said, 'Hell, gentlemen, this thing'll inspire the entire country!'

"So with that Editor looked at me and I looked at him. Because let something new come along, Ironwine'll grab it and try to promote it. And he'll do it even though he knows nothing about it or the folks behind it. In other words, he's a self-promoter. And true to form, when Editor asked him to describe the movie the goggle eyes had in mind he comes up empty. So then Editor asks him if he didn't think it a good idea to find out before things went any further.

" 'Not with such experts as these behind it,' Ironwine said. 'They're gentlemen of vision who know what they're doing. Besides, what's important is that they're making a movie right here, in our part of town, with *our* people doing the acting.'

" 'I understand,' Editor said, 'but acting what roles? Because after what happened with *The Birth of a Nation* that's also important.'

"Well, that got Ironwine hot under the collar. Said, 'Let me tell you something, Editor, you're running true to form. Let something good come along which *you* don't have a hand in and you'll try to kill it. Oh, yes! You're a great one for badmouthing another man's ideas, but this time I'm putting you on notice: You interfere with this once-in-a-lifetime chance that's come to this town and I'll see to it personally that the entire community boycotts that crummy paper of yours!'

"Well, at this Editor shook his head and grinned.

" 'Ironwine,' he said, 'I've always taken the knocks that come from expressing my opinions, both editorial and otherwise, so don't worry about me—unless you're making this personal.'

"And with that Ironwine draws in his neck. Because like I told the boy, Editor was both a man of words and a man of action.

"Hickman, I once saw a bully twice his size go after him, but instead of backing off he bent the man double with a butt in the belly and then pistol-whipped his head with a Colt forty-five.

"So, knowing all this, Ironwine rushes out of Speed's like he has an urgent appointment. Then when he's halfway up the hill he starts yelling and giving Editor hell. Called him everything but a child of God.

"But Editor just laughed and said to the rest of us, 'Gentlemen, I thought I was asking a sensible question. Because while the picture these strangers have in mind *might* be a good one, I think it's reasonable to consider what might happen if it's not.'

"So that's the way it went, with folks laughing at Ironwine talking low but forgetting about Editor's question. So things kept building.

"All day Saturday those three fellows were driving around pointing that one-eyed contraption at everything from churches to outhouses. They didn't even miss the animals—I know because they pointed that thing at my mare with me in the saddle and she up and bolted.

"Everywhere you turned they'd be there, and with folks falling over one another asking questions and getting in the way. This went on until it got too dark for the three-legged bastard to see, and even then they hung around under an arc light which used to hang over the center of Bailey and Giles, pointing that bug-eyed sonofabitch at the shadows. Then they slipped a leather hood over its head and disappeared downtown in that Franklin.

"That evening after supper, I went down to Speed's to get me a plug of tobacco, and there was Tom Jornigan carrying on about how this movie would help business, and how lucky we were to have the goggle-eyed fellows pick our town for a movie. So I asked him if anyone had found out what kind of picture they had in mind, but that he couldn't tell me. And neither could anybody else.

"Well, the next day was Sunday, and since I'd promised to let Janey drag me to church I figured that except for the usual yelling and singing it would be more or less peaceful. Now don't get me wrong: Being of the People I know how powerful religion can be. But Hickman, I swear, the uproar which some of the State Negroes set off in church on Sunday sounds like all hell is erupting. So thanks to Janey I'm prepared for that, but I'm dead wrong in thinking that otherwise things would be peaceful—which I began to discover when I pick up Janey and we start walking to church.

"By the time we head uphill the service had already started—which is how Janey likes it. Because with folks yelling their heads off and the organ blasting she can grandstand a bit by marching down to her pew in step with the music. And if it's 'Onward, Christian Soldiers,' she likes it even better. Because then she takes a grip on my arm and pretends she's captured a heathen and means to convert him. So since I'd been through it before I'm prepared to go along—only this time things take a turn I least expected.

"Hickman, as you know, those steep stone steps which lead up to the church have three landings with railings...."

"Yes, and I've climbed them."

"Well, just as we round the corner and head for church I see what looks like a big bundle which some ornery coyote—be he laundryman, hobo, or thief—has dumped square in the middle of the topmost landing. And as we draw closer folks heading for church are squeezing past it and looking back with puzzled expressions. Then, as Janey and me reach the steps and start up, I see that this bundle is silk and a deep tone of purple, and I know right away that I'm staring at *trouble*—Yao! But since it's too late to escape from Janey I have to keep climbing. And just when we're about to reach it the damn thing moans and relaxes and I'm looking at the form of a man!

[CYCLOPS 2]

"A *MAN?*"

"That's right, and from the signs on the steps and the landing he'd been so hell bent on making it to church on time that after being knocked to his knees he kept going by crawling...."

"What led you to such a conclusion?"

"The signs, Hickman, which are always around to be read. Like the cigarette ash on his elbow, the dust on the hem of his robe, and the black shoe polish scraped on the steps behind him. So I figured that at the point where he fell whatever hit him the first time backtracked and knocked him colder than a well-digger's butt in December.

"Anyway, when we reach him he's all doubled up with his head under his arms like he's hiding, and he's clawing toward the church with his long white hand. So, seeing State folks high-stepping and frowning like he's something contagious, I'm reaching down to help him when Janey—your good Christian friend and mine—jerks me away. So either I land on top of the man or let her drag me up the steps beside her. Which I do.

"But while this is happening folks behind us go into action, and when I look back they're rolling him over. And Hickman, when you hear who he turns out to be you won't believe me."

"I don't doubt it, but what do you mean?"

"Because this man, this poor weary pilgrim, is the head man of the strangers in goggles and leggins..."

"...Now wait! Do you mean the *moving-picture* man?"

"Right! He's the black-white one! And not only is he dressed in a purple silk robe and fancy black gaiters, around his neck there's a heavy gold chain—Yao!—and dangling from the chain there's this figure in ivory of a white man who's nailed hands and feet to a heavy black cross..."

"...A *what?*"

"A crucifix, Hickman, a *crucifix*! And when the boy hears about it he falls back in his chair with a 'Well I'll be damn!'—which is how I felt when I saw it. So if you want to join us you have my permission."

"That's considerate of you, Mr. New, but no thank you. Then what happened?"

"So naturally the boy wants to know what this fellow was doing dressed like that on the steps of a church—which was the question on everybody's mind, including folks inside the church who'd passed him before Janey and me arrived. Anyway, now he's lying on his back with his eyes closed, and as folks gather around he begins mumbling what sounds like a prayer in the unknown tongue— you getting the picture?"

"I get it, so then what happened?"

"So while Janey hustles me up the steps and into the church, four men lug this fellow inside behind us. With folks on their feet singing 'Praise God from whom all blessings flow' they're trying their best not to disturb them, but as it turns out they have no more chance than a snowball in hell. Because just as they stretch the white-black one on a bench in the rear his foot bangs the floor, and when folks whirl and see him lying there dressed in that long purple robe it's the start of a strange Sunday morning.

"Not that it stops the singing, but with some of the squaws—old, young, and in between—having seen this fellow and his friends working that one-eyed contraption, they start itching to get back there to nurse him. And now folks all over the church are asking themselves whether he's dead or just ailing, and how come he's dressed in that purple costume—Yao! And what the hell was he doing stretched on the steps in the first place, and how he managed to get there without being noticed? But whether it was by trick or by whirlwind, the white-black one was *there,* and even lying flat on his back he's taking them over.

"Meanwhile, up in the pulpit the minister, Reverend Caruthers, is still in control and means to stay in control, no matter what the hell's brewing back in the rear. So to make sure everybody keeps their eyes on the pulpit and their minds on the service he takes over the singing. And pretty soon he's damn near busting a gut yelling 'Amazing Grace.' Which was a good choice, because being an old favorite everybody except me joins in and goes hymning away like they're seeing a vision.

"So now Caruthers is standing in the pulpit with the choir and the organ roaring behind him. To his left the sun is beaming through the big stained-glass windows, and especially through the clear pane they were forced to install after some rock-throwing boys knocked out the section with the heads of Saint Paul and John the Baptist on it. And as he leads the singing and waves his arms in time with the music he's keeping his eyes on the rear like he's mapping a strategy. And it seems to be working. Because even though folks have to be wondering what's happening behind them they're looking straight ahead and getting on with the singing.

"But the tension keeps rising. So then the head deacon steps up to Caruthers, buzzes his ear, and gets told to get lost. Then, with folks fidgeting and turning to see what's happening behind them, another deacon steps up to offer Caruthers some assistance.

"This time it's a tall, lanky fellow who looks like a grasshopper with frost in his bones who comes tiptoeing across the platform in his swallow-tailed coat, gambling-striped britches, moleskin vest, and rimless glasses. But without missing a beat or turning his head Caruthers waves him away and keeps sweating and singing.

"Meanwhile, with everybody's eye on Caruthers, the tension keeps building. And that's where being both an outsider and a heathen works to my advantage. Because while everybody else is looking forward and stewing I'm sneaking looks to the rear to see what'll happen when the white-black one makes his next move. I'm also beginning to respect the way Caruthers is handling his problem, because even though he hasn't yet come up with a solution it's clear that come hell or high water he means to stay in command.

"So now he turns and whispers to the head deacon, no doubt telling him to get that movie-making fellow into his study, which is in a room just back of the choir and the organ. Or maybe it's to get him the hell *anywhere*, as long as it's out of his sight.

"And he damn well needs to do *something*, because by now all those women dressed in beaded dresses and wide-brimmed hats have gone to waving their fans so hard and fast that it sounds like a storm blowing in from the prairie. Even the organist sitting with his back to the pews is feeling the tension, because once or twice he loses control of his fingers and something which ain't exactly church music reels from the organ. But Caruthers keeps singing, and with that muledriver's voice of his getting stronger and stronger I'm beginning to think he'll come out the winner.

"But I'm wrong, because now the tune runs out of verses. Then as he stands waving his arms there's a pause which ends with the organ easing into a high, smoke-curling tune that's dream-like and peaceful. But there's no peace for Caruthers.

"Because by now he's so frustrated by what's been brewing back in the rear that instead of getting on with his sermon he's dabbing at his face with a big white handkerchief and looking desperate. And that's exactly when one of the old ladies down front on the mourners' bench goes into action.

"Hickman, this one was a shouter of note and wide reputation, and like always she's been waiting for Caruthers to get preaching so she can add her bit to the shouting excitement he's well known for igniting. So now she starts tapping her foot so fast that it sounds like a drumming contest between a cock prairie chicken beating his wings and a rhythm-crazy drummer beating his cymbals. And wouldn't you know it—right on the beat a leading deacon comes out of a door that's to the right of the pulpit and marches up the steps as he heads for his chair on the platform.

"This one is big, burly, and dignified; and being late, he's missed what's been happening. Also, being a leading mortician he's unusually pious. So now he kneels in front of his chair and sweeps his coattails aside with graveside decorum. Then, with his britches bulging and aimed straight at the gathering, he bows his head over the seat of his chair, clasps his hands, and starts praying. And right on the beat the black-white one starts stirring.

"At first it's no more than a rustle, but it turns me around just in time to see him rising up like a corpse from the bed of a river and taking off on a slow-motion float down the aisle. And Hickman, that's when things *really* start happening.

"By now I'm watching with my sharpest attention. With the church gone quiet as the flight of an owl the black-white one moves forward by putting one foot after the other careful and slow like he's unsure he can make it. Then, with his arms stretched out and his long fingers touching, he trains his eyes on the ceiling, and as he advances he's mumbling and nodding his head.

"So now except for the smoke-curling music—Yao!—and that *rat-a-tat* racket being made by that old lady on the mourners' bench who's gone to tap dancing sitting down—it's got so quiet that you can see folks straining to hear what the white-black one is mumbling as he advances like a sleepwalking turtle. All eyes are upon him, and I mean all the way from the choir to the balcony.

"Up in the pulpit Caruthers and the deacons are watching. On the floor just below twelve stewardesses and stewards are watching as they lean over the long collection table—Yao!—and looking madder and madder as he makes his way closer. Which you'll understand, because not only is this camera-grinding stranger upsetting a Sunday morning service, he's doing it before they've even made the *first* of their regular collections.

"But while they stand there looking like they'd gladly put him out of his misery, the white-black one keeps a-coming and coming with his eyes on the ceiling. And next thing I know he's heading for the pulpit like a slow-motion arrow. And then, Hickman, I bat my eyes and it's like he's shifted from walking to *gliding*.

"Because all of a sudden he's up in the pulpit, where the deacons stand frozen in their tracks and Caruthers bending forward with his hands on his hips looking like he's wondering what the hell's happening.

"Which he learns in a second. Because before the black-white one makes his next move he starts shaking and shivering. Then he makes a fall to the floor that sends that purple robe collapsing like a circus tent after some joker snatches the pole that supports it. Then he's lying in front of Caruthers and reaching out and grabbing the poor man's feet in his long white hands. And with Caruthers staring down and the church gone quieter than a mouse leaking on cotton he gives a sigh that echoes off the walls like far distant thunder. And next thing I know he's intoning in a voice so penetrating and pleading that even folks way up in the balcony can hear him:

" 'Bless me, Reverend,' he pleads. 'Bless me with the laying on of thy most holy hands'—Yao!

"Hickman, when Caruthers hears this he's so flabbergasted that before he can think he's doing it. And when he makes contact with the black-white one's head it's like he's laid hands on a red-hot stove! And with that the black-white one starts shaking from his head to his feet like he's been hit with a fit of buck fever!

"And that's when another of the old shouting mourners' bench sisters gets in it. This one's been waiting for any excuse to cut loose so now she grabs it.

" 'Have mercy, Jesus!' she yells, and claps her hands three times so loud that it echoes like a rifle going off in a canyon. Then I hear somebody way in the back yell, 'AMEN!' And with that the church explodes like a ballpark after the home team scores on a three-bag homer.

"From all over the church I'm hearing shouts of 'Thank you, Jesus!' and 'Do, Jesus, *Do!*' to such a clapping of hands and stomping of feet that it sends the whole church rocking and reeling. It sounds like the entire congregation is having a catharsis and giving Caruthers's blessing of the black-white one their hearty approval. So no matter what poor Caruthers really feels about what's happening all he can do is raise his hands and try to quiet them.

"So now he steadies himself against the lectern with the big Bible on it and hiccups something or the other about being pleased to welcome the 'distinguished visitor' but unfortunately he hasn't yet had the pleasure of learning his name.

"And that's when a fellow who'd seen the three goggle-eyed strangers shooting up the neighborhood jumps to his feet and yells, 'Reverend, that's the famous Mr. Eddy Shaw Prophet'—or maybe he called him 'Prophet Eddy Shaw.' Anyway, Caruthers thanks him. And with folks all excited he decides that the best way out of his bind is to ask the black-white one if he'll say a few words.

"Hickman, up to this point this Eddy Shaw fellow is still on his knees, and with that big crucifix weighing him down like it's over his shoulder he's looking like he's just been caught dead in the act of tomahawking his daddy and chasing his mama up a dry hollow log. But now he draws to his feet and bows, first to Caruthers and then to the deacons, who nod their heads looking damn disgusted.

"And then he bows to old Reverend Turner, the presiding elder. To which Turner leans forward and takes him a long hard stare at that purple silk robe. Then he slaps his thigh and lets out a belly laugh that makes the pulpit rumble and tremble. Yao! And while it goes booming and echoing you could see folks looking at one another like they're trying to decide the best way to react to this further confusion old Turner was adding to what was already a strange Sunday morning.

"Hickman, having been a jazzer (and probably more of a heathen than me), you might have missed old Elder Turner, but not the boy. Because along with the rest of Janey's kids he liked it whenever Turner erupted in one of those religious fits which the State Negroes out here call getting laughing-happy. And me too, because considering all the hell the white State folks give us of the People in the name of religion it was a comfort to think that the *black* State folks' God had their sense of humor—Yao! Because no matter what anybody else thought about it, when Turner's God told him to laugh he'd cut loose and laugh 'til the tears came down. And keep at it 'til everybody else was forced to laugh and cry along with him. Then he'd pace the pulpit laughing and shouting, 'Praise the Lord, ha! ha! ha! Whooo-eeee! Praise his holy name! Good God almighty—ha! ha-ha-ha!'

"Hickman, he was marvelous to see and to hear. He was as tall as you and about your size, and when he laughed it was from deep in his belly to high in his head. And when he got to praising his God even an outsider like me had to admire him. Because for him the State folks' God could be praised by laughing as well as by crying. Which made more sense to someone who'd lived the mixed-up mare's nest of a life I've lived than the white folks' God ever could. And no disrespect intended.

"I remember a cold Sunday morning when I heard Turner preach from the Book of Job. Times were hard, folks out of work, and snow on the ground, but when he came to the part where old high-class Job was complaining about all the boils on his butt Turner broke down and laughed for ten straight minutes by the church-house clock.

"Yao! He was a *mighty* laugher. He laughed and cried over Jesus' weeping, and over Jonah rebelling in the belly of his whale. He laughed over Mary Magdalene's transformation and a few loaves and fishes feeding a multitude of people and simple drinking water being turned into good-drinking wine. And he laughed 'til he cried like a baby over his beloved Jesus crying on the cross like he was no less human than the poor natural men he was dying to save.

"Being a heathen I'm untrained in such matters, but I guess Turner's laughing amounted to what Janey calls the sign of a mystery that's holy. Anyway, he was a good man and a deep believer in his religion. Therefore I tell you verily: I have puzzled long over Turner's life-easing laughing—and you can believe me!

"Anyway, while Turner goes on laughing this Prophet fellow waits politely until he quiets down and starts wheezing. Then he raises his long white hand like he's giving him a blessing and would like to embrace him. Then, after bowing to Caruthers, he makes a turn and bows to the congregation, who by now are sitting in their pews looking dazed and exhausted.

"Maybe because by now Prophet looks even whiter than he did on the streets with that camera. But he just stands there with his crucifix dangling and his purple arm resting beside the big Bible while things get quieter and quieter.

"To me it's like he's turned Siamese twins and gone to debating what he'll say—Yao!—and out of which of his mouths he'll say it. Then some old fellow lets out with a snore like a buzz saw and gets punched in the belly, and when he rattles his dentures and yells 'WHO? WHERE AT?' some of the little boys let out with a snicker. And that's when the white-black one, Eddy Shaw Prophet, goes into action.

"Hickman, I want you to see him through the eyes of a heathen: He's standing up there in that silk purple robe, and with that crucifix resting on his chest he looks like some kind of priest who's strayed into the wrong part of town, landed in the midst of the wrong congregation, and finds himself facing us down out of sheer white-skinned gall and presumption. And as he looks out to the pews he sort of sways like he's thinking deep thoughts on life, death, the final reckoning. Then he raises his arms and stares at the ceiling with his palms toward the pews and the wide sleeves of his robe making a wing-like flutter. And then, just as folks begin giving one another looks as if to say, 'What's happening?' he speaks. Yao!

"And when he speaks he *moves.*

"And when he moves, I swear, it's like I'm watching one of these jazz musicians who carries himself like a college professor.

"You know the type: On the street he's a model of high-toned deportment, and when he's sitting down playing along with his buddies he's cool and collected. But give him a solo, and *Wham!* Next thing you know he's up in the spotlight shaking his butt like a loose-jointed bear, honking like a gobbler and stomping the bandstand like he means to reduce it to kindling and set it on fire. Then, with folks still applauding, he's tucking his horn, his weapon, under his arm with a bow. Then in a wink of your eye he's back in his chair and a professor again—conked hair, sweat, and horn-rimmed glasses!"

"Oh, yes," Hickman said. "Not only do I know the type but I'm now beginning to see why folks call you Love the Liar."

"Maybe so, but being different from them, how would they know me? Or you, who you calls yourself a *Christian?* Anyway, that's how it was with Prophet. Black-white or white-black, which*ever* the hell he was, he preaches up a storm. And as you'd expect, he starts out warning folks not to waste precious time in grabbing what he called their God-given chance to be *born* again. Yao!

" 'My friends,' he says, 'you must seize the day, and seize it *nooooow!*'

"And with that old Turner shakes his cotton-white head and stares at Prophet like he can't believe what's happening. Then when Prophet stretches out his arms and cries, 'Please, sinners, *please* don't let this harvest pass!' that purple robe flounces and swirls like a cape in a bullfight. And with that Turner falls back in his chair, and I swear, it's like he's exploding with laughing gas. That's right, but out of respect none of the deacons bothers to stop him.

"So then with things quieting down a bit Prophet turns and looks at Turner like he's decided right then and there that if he can't beat him he'll use him. So he stares at the ceiling like he's filled with emotion, and when Turner takes off again he's all primed and ready. And sure enough, before he can get rolling Turner lets out a laugh, and right on the beat Prophet sidesteps the poor man and downs him by switching his text from Matthew, Peter, and Paul to what he calls the life-saving role of holy black laughter, its uses and abuses. And Hickman, the way he uses old Turner to accent his thesis sounded like they'd rehearsed it. And I mean for whole *months* of Sundays!

"Next thing I know he has the church rocking with such a masterful example of State Negro preaching that folks are eating it up—skin, bones, and what's left over!

"Hickman, not only did Prophet have the State Negro *style* of preaching, he had the *movements!* And what's more, when he gave them hell about the way they laughed when they should have been crying, and cried when they should have been laughing, he even had the full range of State Negro *sound.* And I mean from threatening basso profundo to falsetto pleading! He rumbled like an engine and shrilled like a whistle, and once he'd laid down the cross ties and rails for his highball of a sermon he dragged Turner aboard and took off for what he called the promised land of true fulfillment. And with Tucker stoking the engine and ringing the bell he swept folks along like leaves in the draft of a Santa Fe special!

"He rocked and he rolled, he highballed and rambled, and next thing I know he has those State Negroes clapping their hands and yelling 'Praise the Lord,' and 'Have Mercy sweet Jesus!' And before he's through he has the whole church swinging and everybody—choir, organ, congregation, and deacons—shouting *Well-a rock-a my soul in the bosom of Abraham!*

"Where the hell Prophet learned to preach like that was a mystery, but *wherever* it was it made him the talk of the town. The word spread like lightning, and even folks who missed his performance were pleased and surprised. And the fact that this white-black one of the three from the East with the camera not only talked their talk but was a master of their style of preaching they took as no less than a miracle. Next thing I know he's being invited to preach in other big churches, bootleg joints are serving him and his buddies drinks on the cuff, and sassy gals doing them all kinds of favors. All this I described to the boy who sat listening with interest, but by now my nose was bleeding again and the day getting shorter. So since anything serious demands a certain amount of strength and discipline I sat there staring at the boy and wrestling with the Eagle, my totem, against having to keep going.

"So I told him to ask Janey how it was, because being a woman she'd remember the things I didn't. 'Maybe so,' he said, 'but she'll never tell me. Can't you go on?'

" 'Not today,' I said, 'because I'm worn out with remembering. So go see her and come back tomorrow.'

"So he left, and so did the Eagle, and my nose stopped bleeding.

"Hickman, I was tired as hell, but once the boy was out of here a strange feeling came over me. And I mean strange even for a man given to strange feelings. But this was different, a feeling I hadn't had since the People were still together and vigorous. Like back there when it seemed possible to work out a way of life which would suit us even with the white man overrunning the land. Of course it was a mistake; either that or we didn't try hard enough after our warfare and resistance had failed us. Or maybe we lost courage and didn't try hard enough out of our own inner rot, our demoralization.

"Then there was the greed and restlessness brought here by the State folks from the East. Over the years I had resigned myself to the great changes, had seen the results and lived alongside it. But just the same, after the boy left I felt some of the old promise returning.

"It had the feeling of times long past when the skies were so clear that the eyes could range unobstructed for miles. Hickman, this land is called flat, yet to the south there are mountains. They seem blue from the distance, and in the old days I've seen cattle grazing the grass high upon them. In those days there were great herds of deer, packs of wolves and coyotes, and great flocks of turkeys. There were pecan, pine, and hickory, and cottonwoods like those in the courtyard grew everywhere. And in the spring the blossoms of blackthorn trees drifted like snow and the perfume of it sent many a young buck out on the prod. There was blackjack, walnut, and wild persimmon, and endless cover for quail. Doves came in clouds and prairie chickens beat their tom-toms like Crackshot McNeal, the Blue Devils' drummer, beating on his bass drum, cymbals, and snares. Yes, and there was coon, rabbit, and possum, and plenty of bear—

> *Ho! Yah! Big brown brother of the shiny nose*
> *Our guide to the honey that's hidden in hollows,*
> *Ho Yah!*
> *Thy velvet paws seek out the sweet hidden gold*
> *in the bee-trees, Ho!*
> *And thy black eyes gleam and you laugh when you*
> *raid the barrels of beer of the Choctaws—*

"That's what the kids of the Bear clan used to sing. And Hickman, you can believe me when I tell you that bears around here used to raid every mash barrel they could find. Come Choc-making time and you could see troops of them staggering through the woods like black Shriners and Elks on the Fourth of July.

"Anyway, after the boy left I felt like I did in those times of many horses and had hopes those days might return. With the sky clear and the game roaming the land undisturbed. A time when men would be at peace, and our way—the way of the People—secure against a way which for all its iron and noise, its money and bigness, is no fit way for mankind to live.…

"So having the boy return seemed like a good sign. And the same with the Eagle. After all, some things in life do continue, no matter how much men think they've changed. And that's true no matter how much the State people junk up the land, kill off the game, and tell big lies to justify their viciousness and failure to achieve true civilization. Of course I was dreaming, but awake or dreaming, I am not of these, the State people. No, I prefer to be brother to old honey hands, Big Brother Bear. Yes, and servant to the Eagle. The dream I dreamed was empty, and when I awoke I thought of the street where I lived at the time the boy was taken away; and there where I killed my first deer, a buck and a big one, I saw a parking lot filled with junk and signs screaming, 'Big John Krackenbaum's Place', 'Let's Make a Deal!' "

"I know," Hickman said, "it's sad, but life is change, so get back to the boy and the movie men. What happened after Prophet preached?"

"Here's how it went: The next day he's out early, shooting up the streets and talking more crap than the radio—Yao!—and stacking the deck like a riverboat gambler. And with folks even more excited by the news of his preaching they can't wait to see samples of the shots he'd been shooting. So he takes some of the shots and joins them together then makes a deal with the Sunset's manager to show them on the screen between the first show and the second. Then he spreads the word that for the price of the regular admission anyone can see first-hand how they'd look in the movie he's planning.

"Hickman, Prophet and his boys were working like beavers and the State Negroes were stumbling over one another to be with them. That afternoon I get to the Sunset shortly after the main movie had started but had a hell of a time finding a seat. So I'm sitting there reading the captions as I try to catch up with the action of a Western in which the hero and his sidekick shoot it out with about sixteen outlaws in a dispute over range land and water. Now it happened that the actor playing the hero was Jack Hoxie, and the one playing his sidekick was a fellow named Morman Jackson—which is important. Because Jackson was a State Negro out of Kansas who broke into the movies years before by passing for white. So unknown to white folks he'd been acting any part he could adapt to, which turned out to be everything from renegade Indians, Rebel generals, railroad detectives, outlaws, sheep herders, Tex-Mexicans, to cowboys, Chinese laundrymen, and Yankees.

"Which made him a real-life hero for State Negroes who got a kick from seeing him turn the white folks' game against them. Put Jackson in a movie and right away they had them a plot within a plot, a double feature which they could enjoy for the price of a single admission. And underneath whatever else was happening they had them their own kind of comedy!

"Anyway, at this point when I'm watching the outlaw tiptoeing toward Hoxie and Jackson with his gun cocked and ready, all hell breaks loose in the balcony—Yao!—and years before it was invented a movie in the Sunset exploded...."

"With *sound?*"

"Yao, with sound! Because when a damn sign painter by the name of Tackett sees the Hoxie and Jackson characters in trouble he loses all control of his senses. Did you know Tackett?"

"Not that I remember."

"Well, he was tall and skinny and black like me, and having a mouth full of gold he was always grinning—which *ain't* like me, because my teeth are natural and I do little grinning. Anyway, when Tackett sees this outlaw slipping up on Jackson and Hoxie he's fit to be tied. All at once he's yelling, 'Watch out, y'all, there's one slipping behind you!'

"Hickman, the fool has leaped square into the action with a gun in his hand. And next thing I know he's leaning over the railing blasting the screen with a forty-five flashing. And in ten seconds flat nobody's left in the place but him and the fellow back in the projection booth—and he's there only because in trying to escape he twisted an ankle. Then with the crowd spilling out on the sidewalk the law leaps in and Tackett gives the Sheriff, his deputies, and six *Irish* policemen one hell of a struggle before they get him out of the Sunset and back to reality.

"It was so awful that if Prophet hadn't made his deal with the Sunset's owners they would've locked the doors and called it a day. Then folks would have cleared out and ended up laughing. But after coming to see themselves in the sample Prophet had been taking for his movie, and with all the excitement he stirred up with his preaching, not even an earthquake would have caused them to leave. So they crowded in front of the Sunset and argued and threatened until the manager gave in and got on with the show.

"And Hickman, the way those State Negroes reacted to seeing themselves blown up on that screen was like they'd been given a compound cathartic that worked on the mind—Yao! It was as though after waiting most of their lives it finally had happened. Maybe because after coming out here with high hopes of enjoying a new state of freedom they found mostly the old ways of the past. They'd made their way West but found their new state just as Southern as most of the white folks who rushed here to claim it. So after taking a step West it left them suffering big doubts as to where they were, what they were, and who they were.

"I wouldn't know, but when they sat in the dark watching themselves walking along crowded downtown streets and into fine stores, big banks, and places like the opera house, which were usually off-limits, they seemed to confuse those shadows on the screen with reality. It was as though seeing themselves ballooned on the screen finally convinced them they were really living in a new state, in a real town, and amongst other real people.

"Maybe it was like when you see yourself in a photograph and can't be certain it's you. Maybe you don't recognize the mood you were in at the time it was taken, or the look in your eyes is like that of a stranger. In other words, we don't see ourselves; and since the self is a smoke-like thing of the spirit, most of what we know about who we are comes from the inside. So when we look at our images shiny and frozen something important is missing. But just as man and the animals are one with the earth, man's body and spirit are united but separate. So there's always a question as to which is in charge. Is it body or spirit? Still, as some insist and others deny, all men are brothers and must depend upon others to help them define who they are. This is true of all tribes and that leaves them uneasy. And for State folks who are black this is especially urgent, because they think one thing of themselves while their white brothers insist that they're exactly the opposite.

"Anyway, after they were gobbled and vomited by that one-eyed, three-legged contraption, folks in the Sunset could finally see themselves with a sense of objectivity. Laughing and clowning with other folks they recognized from the outside gave them a sense of security and a different perspective. So in a sense it was like they'd been wandering in darkness, and when the goggle eyes pointed that camera in their direction they reacted as though they'd heard the spirits shout a command of 'Let there be light!'

"That's why what happened in the Sunset was so different. And maybe the main thing was movement. Folks could see their bodies ripping and romping and their mouths whooping and yelling, and could recognize themselves by who they were with. Even the absence of sound didn't matter, because all they had to do was remember who they were with. And seeing themselves move let them know who they were even though they'd been reduced to overblown shadows. I tell you truly, it was big medicine and *powerful*!

"After it was over, with folks excited and asking for more, Prophet was so pleased that he ran off some of the reels he and his crew hadn't yet edited. And next thing I know I'm sitting there watching folks watching themselves floating down streets in dream-like slow motion, then streaking around houses and buildings like hounds with cans tied to their tails. Then they're watching themselves inflated into images as wide as the Courthouse or Capitol, then walking forwards, running backwards, and dancing in circles. First in slow motion and again at the speed of a whirlwind. In fact, the goggle eyes showed them doing every damn thing they could get away with in public except making love, looking sad, and crying.

"It was nothing short of medicine, *big* medicine. And sitting there listening to what State folks around me were saying it seemed that they liked what they saw. And liked it even though those of our color came out looking like ghosts. I understand it had something to do with the film, which was made with white-skin folks in mind and white folks only. So maybe being forced to swallow all that rainbow of State Negro colors gave the one-eyed bastard, the camera, an ache in his belly. Still, his magic kept working, because fellows as black as me didn't seem to mind looking like ghosts.

"You would have thought that this would have turned them against the goggle eyes and Prophet, and at first it was clear they were shocked. I could hear them reacting all over the Sunset, but I guess the excitement of seeing themselves moving and strutting and parading and dancing overpowered the shock of their changes in colors. Maybe the way they moved was more important. Maybe they were going by the cut of their clothes and their styles and their rhythms.

"Anyway, after seeing Prophet's patchwork of a sample they were hooked. They took the bait and were raring to get on with raising the cash to pay for his movie. And with that the sly men from the East had it made.

"Pretty soon folks were struggling to see who'd raise the most money. Friendships and families were broken, pawnshops emptied of dresses, military uniforms, swords, and badges—which they hoped to use as costumes. Maids and cooks, chauffeurs and butlers got fired for sneaking out the best evening clothes of the white State folks they worked for to wear in front of that camera.

"A cocky young janitor out at the Statehouse, the Capitol, got himself in deep trouble by sneaking the goggle eyes and the camera into the Blue Room to shoot scenes for a make-believe ball. And along with make-believe guests wearing borrowed evening gowns and white ties and tails Prophet even managed to sneak in a six-piece orchestra. So while the musicians went through the motions of playing make-believe music the make-believe guests strutted and danced, sipped ginger ale and Coke, and pretended they were high on champagne and bourbon. And with couples flirting and whirling and musicians going through the motions of blowing up a storm, things seemed to be working. But then the scene reels out of hand.

"Thinking to make things look more realistic, Prophet has one of the male dancers go through the motions of slipping the drummer a sip from a silver hip flask so the one-eyed man could do a closeup shot of him drinking. But while the flask was filled with warm Coca-Cola, Prophet had no idea of the headache his strategy would cause him. Because it turned out that the drummer was the type who gets roaring drunk from just the *idea* of drinking hard liquor. So once the flask touches his lips he starts banging out a rhythm that's so wild and compelling that the other musicians join in. They forget Prophet's instruction, and before he knows what he's done they're blasting the roof off the Statehouse, Capitol.

"Then with the smuggled-in guests either forgetting that what they were doing wasn't real or deciding to make the most of a rare opportunity, they ended up making so damn much noise that the guards rushed in and started throwing them out, funky dresses, sweaty tailcoats, and dusty shoelaces!

"But it didn't stop Prophet. He simply had his goggle-eyed crew back off a piece with the camera, and while the guards went about rounding up the State Negroes and throwing them out they aimed it at the action and took pot shots at all the scrambling confusion. Then, when the Blue Room was cleared, Prophet convinced the guards and the janitors that if they forgot what happened he'd give them important parts in the picture, and they were so pleased that they let the whole crowd of them go."

"I'm beginning to get the picture," Hickman said, "and I'm glad that since I was a musician back in those days I was somewhere safe in Georgia. But let's get back to the boy's mother. Was she one of the dancers?"

"No, but about that time she'd got herself all worked up to be in the movie, and some of her young friends kept urging her to do it. And since she was pretty and popular they felt that if they dug in and sold enough tickets she had a good chance of being picked as one of the stars. Then when Janey told me about it I tried to discourage her, but the numbers were against me. Along with Editor Dunhawse and one or two preachers I was among the few who didn't think too much of what was happening, but the gal wouldn't listen. So she entered the contest and won it, and that led to one of the goggle eyes getting to her...."

"I see. And did you tell the boy about this?"

"Of course not! It's not the kind of thing you tell a man about his mother. Besides, she was a young woman of stature and I admired her and wanted to help her. But she was innocent and untried by the ways of the State folks, so she got caught in the swindle, the madness.

"Hickman, it was a madness which was building like a storm to bloodletting. I could feel it building, but she and the State folks were so excited over the chance for pretending that they were somebody else, of playing a part, that although I tried to stop her I was too slow."

"But what about your Eagle? Didn't he make an appearance?"

"Oh, no, he kept far away. Because, you see, it was not an affair of the People. So knowing it was State folks' foolishness he kept to high places and far out of range. I myself had been watching this thing develop from the time the men from the East showed up and got going. Yao! And the State Negroes were ripe for the picking. Out here they were wild and not like they'd been back South and East, where most of them come from. And of a special wildness. They'd come out here expecting more freedom of movement because it was a wide-open country without too many of the old customs and laws to restrain them. But when they had their new freedom they didn't understand the form in which it existed. Which was deceptive, so either they didn't recognize it, or couldn't grasp its nature and dangers. So they confused it with *having* things; in owning things that the others, the rich white ones, had back in the old towns and cities. I guess that was at the heart of the confusion the goggle eyes stirred up with that camera. And the lights they focused on the State Negroes distorted their eyes so they became like little animals caught in the headlights of fast-moving autos and trains. Looking into the eye of that three-legged contraption made them think they were looking up at the stars, when in fact they were really looking at a fire which was set to consume them—Yao! I tell you truly, they were confused! And before they got back to their normal confusion some of them were ruined, and the fellow who won the right to play the hero got himself unmanned…”

“Unmanned?”

“Unmanned, yes!”

“How unmanned?”

“By his woman, who got jealous of his playing the boyfriend of the boy's mother. So she did him in with a razor.…”

“WHAT!”

“Yao! The bitch lopped him, she pruned him—hell, Hickman, she hacked off the head-end of his manhood, his root, the barrel of his precious begatter! But that would come later, after other State folks were already damaged.…”

“So he couldn't have been the boy's—”

“…Not with his works in a sling and his rifle barrel busted! I tell you, the confusion leading up to the man was something for thinking long thoughts about. Fooling around with those fellows and that gadget seemed to make the State Negroes lose all sense of time. And soon the white part of town was in an uproar because the cooks and the maids and the porters and waiters weren't showing up when they were supposed to. A damn white woman, an old maid who lived way over in the other part of town—she hears about what's going on and damn if she doesn't bring a bunch of young white people over here to act in the movie. That's the truth! And when she gets nowhere she comes back with the Sheriff—who was her brother-in-law—and tried to *force* her way into it. And the only thing that keeps her out was the Sheriff's being from down South and dis-liking even the idea of her being mixed up with that many Negroes, even in a mammy-made movie—ha!”

“Forgive me for laughing, but maybe she thought they were making *The Re-birth of the Nation*—which reminds me, what was the movie about? What story did it tell?”

“Hell, man, that was part of the mystery, the attraction, the come-on. Those goggle-eyed fellows were shooting up the town at random, inside and out, like drunks on a spree. And ordering folks around like cracker policemen. But in-stead of resenting it and insisting on being told what they were doing, folks were fighting and feuding and lying and stealing to be in it. But still nobody knew what kind of picture they were making. Some said it was one thing, and some said it was another. Everybody had a different idea because those fellows were pointing that contraption at just about everything in sight. They'd shoot a little of this and a little of that, and when folks kept asking them about it they said it was a secret which would be revealed after they finished shooting and put what they'd shot all together. So, being taken in by the glass-eyed magic, folks went along.

“Maybe they didn't care about the story because they were glad to be doing something they didn't do every day. Some of them got so worked up that pretty soon the goggle-eyed fellows were making money hand over fist by selling little strips of the film they'd shown in the Sunset. Folks wanted to study how they looked and went around showing off those little bits of film to their friends. You could see them standing in the street holding the stuff up to the sun and saying to anyone who would take a look, 'See, that's me. I'm the one standing next to Choc Charlie.' Or, 'Look at the way I'm walking the dog with that high gloss polish on my best pair of shoes.' It was as though they felt they were looking at themselves and yet *not* at themselves, so they needed somebody else to tell them, to make them feel sure of who they were.

"The next day on the street it was even wilder. I watched them, Hickman. I gave them my closest attention. The sun was bright and the air was clear, and after those three fellows stirred them up the State Negroes started parading in front of that one-eyed contraption like it had reached out and grabbed them by the short hair. It was like it had them under a new unheard-of spell. I don't know what else to call it, but like it says in the Bible, I tell you verily, its effect was something to see!

"And naturally it started with the men. After they listened to whatever those three fellows told them to do for the camera they went into action. First they'd walk past the damn thing cool and slow, with each man carrying himself according to his own home-grown notion of dignified decorum. And then, after they got down the street a piece, they'd double back and try it again. But this time real fast and agitated, like they were urgent. Then some of the others who'd been looking on and didn't want to be outdone—*they* took off in front of that thing and it was like somebody being chased by the Klan, the police, and a sheriff and his posse—or maybe the Devil hisself. Then the same fellows would circle around and come past it again. Some would be strutting and walking the dog, some walking tall and proud like soldiers, and others kinda dipping and swaying like they were marching in church and the music was solemn. Then a bunch staggers past with their arms around each other's shoulders, pretending to be drunk and disorderly. And right behind them comes old 'Fatty-Come-with-Fleas,' a nickname which some joker came up with for *Fait accompli,* which was the French nickname some white politicians gave him after he stole the State Seal from the old Territorial Capitol at Guthrie and brought it down here in the plot which made this the state capital.

"Anyway, Fatty-Come-with-Fleas walks past a few times smoking a five-cents cigar and tipping his hat real grand to the crowd. And I have to admit that with each pass he makes he looks more and more like the woodpile politician and the historical figure some folks like to believe him to be.

"Then here comes old pop-eyed lawyer Jerkins, looking like a pouter pigeon with that elk tooth dangling from his watch chain. And Tommy and Brilliantine, the two fat, high-yellow aristocratic-looking whores from down in the Bottoms. They're dressed to kill but as usual they're loud and disorderly. Then right behind them here come four big, strong, double-jointed butchers who worked on the killing floor at the meatpacking plant. They're high-stepping along dressed in stocking caps, rubber boots, blood-stained aprons and carrying meat cleavers, cattle prods, and butcher knives and looking like they have the world by the tail with a down-hill swing and dare *anybody* to deny it. That's when I look around and see that other folks besides me are staring at all that steel like they were asking themselves some serious questions about what might happen next. But then, here comes a quartet of Pullman porters singing 'Oh Didn't He Ramble' in barbershop style, so they forgot to come up with an answer. But by now all kinds of folks were passing back and forth before that goddamn eye, and each and every one making sure to give himself a second chance—and I mean a *heap* of second chances!

"Because after making the first few passes they'd stand back a while and stare at that three-legged thing like it's the unblinking eye of the universe—Yao!— and they're thinking up the next thing to do that will please it. So they kept going and coming and trying to satisfy that one-eyed contraption.

"And Hickman, I tell you, they really walked some walks and cut some capers—and I mean all *kinds*! And since the goggle eyes kept on pointing and grinding that contraption folks kept reversing the field and doing something different. Then with the womenfolks joining in it *really* got confusing. And to make it worse, some clown up in the second floor of a rooming house sticks the horn of his phonograph out the window and started to playing 'The Bugle Call Rag.' And next thing I know a bunch of thugs are swinging past singing 'There's a Soldier in the Grass' at the top of their voices. And when the war veterans in the crowd hear them yelling 'Pull it out, Uncle Sam,' it's like some strict, no-bull-dodo master sergeant had yelled a command for everybody to fall in and act the fool. Because with that they grab the women for partners and got to doing just about every dance step they could think of.

"Oh, it was something to see! They balled the jack and bunny hugged, they eagle rocked, two-stepped, waltzed and turkey trotted. And when they ran out of those they started making up steps never seen before, whether in dance hall, whorehouse, or gospel meeting. But no matter what kind of steps they came up with they made sure that camera was taking them in.

"And then, running true to form, they did what State Negroes are apt to do in any situation from baby-naming rites to public funerals—they turned it into a *dancing* contest. And when one tap-dancing joker does a routine and yells 'I'm no goddamned amateur,' he was speaking the truth for a heap of the others.

"Hickman, I look up the block a few yards and I see four dressed-up couples lining up in a row, with the men squatting low to the sidewalk like a flock of penguins. And then when the women squat beside them with their hands on hips and skirts hiked above their knees, one of the men gives a signal and their friends on the sideline start beating out the rhythm with their hands. And that's when they take off doing something they called the funky walk—Which wasn't much of a walk, but it sure in hell was *funky* funky—or maybe funky goosey! Because that was the way they moved.

"First a long lean fellow shuffles to the front with his head high and his chest stuck out like a gander's. Then with his shoulders squared and his elbows raised and his fists pressed tight together he moves forward, swaying from side to side while fanning his thighs in and out like his crotch is on fire. And after he wobbles his way a few feet in front of the others he halts, still fanning his thighs and nodding his head, while the gal who's his partner starts fanning her big fat thighs and duckwalks up to join him. And then, one by one, the others take their turn, grinning and fanning up a storm of funk.

"Then—*a-hup-a-hup-a-hup!*—they all fan out in a row and come shuffling forward until they reach a spot where there's no way in the *world* for that camera to miss them. And then with the crowd urging them on they squat there with their arms over their heads, snapping their fingers and fanning their thighs. And then, staying close to the ground with their hands on their hips, they take turns spinning and kicking their feet from a sitting position.

"And then, Hickman, right before my mixed-up eyes, they're up and dancing themselves into ducks and drakes, boar hogs and sows, seed bulls and cows, stallions and mares, bucks and ewes, roosters and hens . . ."

"Wait! Hold it," Hickman said; "they were doing *what?*"

"Mating dances, Hickman; *mating dances!* And with the bucks on the prod and the females willing but teasing. Then they all go Cuban by dancing a dance called shoeing the mare, with each gal twisting her hips and smiling a come-and-get-it smile and the fellow spinning at her feet 'til he corkscrews erect and begins circling around her, bucking his shoulders and head with his feet pawing the ground like a stud in white heat. Which turns out to be one hell of a performance, and done with so much spirit that everybody in the crowd is clapping and yelling. Yao! And admiring those teasing views provided by those hip-swinging ladies.

"But then, not to be outdone by the sinners, a little old church sister catches fire and shocks everybody by pulling off a pretty fair high-kicking cakewalk—and I mean showing off her linen and everything. She was known for being a strict fire-and-brimstone Baptist, but under all those petticoats and 'touch-me-not' bloomers, she's wearing some red silk garters—maybe to warn herself that she's still a woman with sin-juice left in her bony little frame. Anyway, when the others see a woman of her reputation cutting loose it's like they'd got a signal to go rip-snorting wild. Because quicker than you could say 'Bojangles Robinson,' everybody and his brother, cousin, and mother-in-law is joining in the breakdown.

"And with that one-eyed contraption and those goggle eyes in full command, that was just what it turned into: a breakdown. It was like they'd put something powerful in the drinking water that was driving those State Negroes out of their minds. And with all the commotion the news kept spreading.

"Next thing I know an undertaker turns up driving his hearse but he can't get through, so he curses up a storm over having to drive backwards for more than a block. Then right behind him, and twisting up a breeze, come sixteen whores from the red-light district. In all that heat they're sashaying along sporting silver-fox fur pieces and with those Hudson-seal coats they favored pulled up tight to advertise the full nasty action of their rumble seats. And as they come on they're looking down their noses and batting their gooey eyelashes like vamps in the movies. You should've seen the respectable folks, especially the women, giving them room!

"I tell you, Hickman, before it was over almost everybody in the section was out there acting the fool before that damn one-eyed contraption. But now as I think about it, they were doing no more than folks do today, when they'll knock one another down trying to sneak them a split-second on television news. In fact, about the only ones who didn't join in were the undertakers, the doctors, the teachers, and the preachers. And with a few of them it was only because they didn't want to be seen associating with the riffraff, whether by their neighbors or that one-eyed contraption.

"Hickman, like I say, I'm of the People and old as the mountains, but I tell you verily, it was like nothing I'd ever seen. And you can believe me, because I've seen shoot-outs, I've seen lynchings, I've seen roaring-drunk Apaches on the prod. I've seen dust storms, springtime floods, cyclones and tornadoes, and out of control oil wells burning like eruptions from hell. I've seen State folks hold those powwows they call revivals and get so worked up by all the yelling and singing that they rolled on the ground and foamed at the mouth. I've witnessed a big Fourth of July dance ruined by a reefer-headed whore who got mad and snatched the bandleader's golden horn out of his hands and smashed it on the floor just because she didn't like the way he winked his eye at another whore when the band was playing 'Mama Loves Papa!' I've heard Billy Sunday preach and seen him beat the hell out of his Bible and go jumping up and down until he had a whole tent full of *white folks* staring in a drip-lipped trance—and I could keep going for hours. But Hickman, I swear: Of all the things that have driven the State Negroes loco—like gambling on the numbers, driving secondhand cars as though they were chariots, dancing the Lindy, the Charleston, and the one-butt shuffle—the way they performed for the eye of that camera was

[NATIVES]

BY ALL MEANS THE damndest!"

"Yes," Hickman said, "and as you relate it you're still amused over those poor folks being so gullible. But while I share your reaction I'm appalled by the tragedy."

"Tragedy?"

"Yes, if you consider what happened to that young man and young woman. With no experience *whatsoever* as an actor, he wins a contest and thinks he'll be the hero of a movie. Yes, and one contrived by three strangers. But then the movie turns out to be nothing more than a swindle and he ends up—well, let's say, with his 'head' on a platter.

"And as though that wasn't gruesome enough, the young woman gets so excited over winning the role of a leading lady that she gives in to one of the swindlers and turns up pregnant. Then, after nine months of being humiliated by all the backbiting and staring, she's so distraught that after giving birth she *kills* herself and leaves behind a motherless baby."

"All right, Hickman, if that's all you make of what happened, call it tragic. But from where I stand it was the fruit of State Negro foolishness. So before you preach me a sermon about pity and terror..."

"*Me*, preach to *you*? Forget it!"

"...Remember that you're a medicine man and accept the fact that the evil no-see-ums spawned by that hungry-eyed gadget are still around buzzing and stabbing."

"And you find that so amusing that you can forget the rest of it?"

"No, but the rest is important. Think about it: After the hero got butchered he moved up North and took a new name. But that didn't help, because today he's still so mad over being scammed by those goggle-eyed strangers that he hates *all* white folks, whether they be men, women, or babies. So now he wears African clothes, calls himself the new Marcus Garvey, and tells anyone who'll listen that before he was reclaimed by what he calls his African heritage he was on his way to becoming famous as an actor in movies—Yao! But not a peep about his foolish pride or the woman who pruned him!

"Then take a look at what happened to the child of Lavatrice. Until he's snatched away by his father's smooth-talking lawyer, he's mothered by Janey. Then taken East, he grows up living the life of a rich white American. But now, after all his years of such living, he's back here among the black State folks and pressuring Janey to come up with answers to unanswerable questions!"

"Yes," Hickman said, "I get the irony, and it sounds like a blues howled by an idiot. And what makes it so terrible is that it all ties together, the past and the present, the hope and the terror...."

"Aye! And don't forget this, my brother in medicine: You're sitting in that chair because of that camera. You want to continue?"

"Of course. But since most of what you're telling me is new, please do me the favor of not being annoyed if what *you* find amusing leaves *me* torn between laughing and crying."

"Hell, Hickman, I'm trying to give you an idea of the mess the State people have made—and keep making—of life in this country. So the only thing *new* about it was what those goggle eyes did with their devilish gadget. Anyway, if I go on we'll be needing more Choc—you with me?"

"Yes, thank you, and as long as you talk I'll give both you and your beer my sharpest attention."

"Now *that's* the way of a hunter! When tracking game in deep cover he must see with his ears, hear with his eyes, and feel with his mind and his smeller!"

Yes, Hickman thought, *and it's also sound advice for my dealing with you....*

Love New—what outrageous names for such a sly little rascal! Because old or new, he's anything but loveable. And if as he claims he grew up among Indians, all those volumes in his bookcase suggest that he's as much of a reader as my old friend Millsap. Which makes for a mystery because most folks don't expect a Native to be familiar with books. That's why in making himself even more mysterious he shuffles his idioms and makes allusions to any book he can think of in ways that mock those who assume to be of superior intelligence. Which was exactly the way of that down-home character who was known as Sam, the Truth-defying Signifier!

Yes, Hickman, an inner voice chuckled, *and at some time in his life this little Choc-drinking rascal jumped the reservation and went rambling in pool halls, beer flats, gambling joints, and other not-so-green pastures. And along the way he matched wits with fast-talking barbershop lawyers, past-grand-masters of the dirty dozens, and maybe a few worldly-wise preachers like you. But now, being old and ornery, he gets a kick out of blur-ring his image and background with talk about being of a son of "the People."*

All right, so he's an Oklahoma Native, but of which of the tribes—Seminole, Choctaw, Chickasaw, Cherokee, or Tuskegee-Creek? That's the the high card hidden in the deck he keeps flashing and shuffling.... He's like that New Orleans piano man who tolerated white folks calling him a "Negro" as long as they enjoyed and praised his music. Yeah, but let one of us homeboys question his background and he'd French-fry his accent and swear to being unadulterated Creole by blood and by breeding!

Which was like saying he was a mulatto who had not a drop of African blood. But so what? When we were paid for a gig and divided the kitty it didn't earn him an extra plugged nickel. Any more than it did when it came to voting, or taking part in anything else ruled off-limits to us nappy-headed descendants of Hagar. So Creole or no, in the eyes of white folks he was just another "boy" with a talent for a new type of music.

Yes, Hickman thought, *and I've known quite a few like him, and sympathized—sometimes—with their attempts to make the most of their hair and their features and color. Even so, out of all of those I've known who tried to have it both ways, this Native, this Love, tops them all!*

What a character! Knowing full well that the truth is seldom as simple as we'd like it to be he laces what he says with lies and dares you to find the truth in his lying. And along with his ducking and dodging, play-acting and jiving, the little poker-faced rascal has the nerve to play the dozens with my religion as a way of getting my goat the way he gets Janey's. And in turning his tongue against what he calls "State folks" he's acting an Ishmael straight out of Genesis—yes!—and with me listening and staring him dead in the eye!

Well, he has his ways and I have mine, and just as a musician's background comes out in his music, whatever this little joker's true identity happens to be sounds in the styles he combines in his lying. Like those echoes of Hiawatha which keep accenting the beat of his riffing. And while he tries to make what happened out here a case of "either/or," what I'm hearing in what he's relating is the age-old, ever-present "this-plus-that." Wonder what he'd say if I mentioned Will Rogers, who was both of the People and a star on Broadway? Or that other sons of the People, such as Jack Teagarden and Big Chief Moore, are famous for their skills in playing State Negro music?

What a mockery we make of democracy! Here's a black, mixed-breed Oklahoma Native having fun watching what he calls "State Negroes" fighting with white folks over which of them is truly American. And while he looks on from behind his cigar-store Indian façade he's probably cracking up over the idea of white folks going crazy thinking up ways for keeping us from mixing our blood with theirs. When the outrageous joke of it lies in the inescapable fact that it's our rhythm and style which keeps taking them over! Yes, and what my bookish boy Millsap calls our grace under pressure. And as Millsap argues, many whites do draw hope and courage from our insisting that this country live up to the ideal of freedom which they deny us. . . .

Hearing a hearty "Here we go," Hickman turned to see Love standing with two bottles of beer. One of which the little man placed on the table before him and returned to the swing; where, taking a long sip of beer, he stared at his glass.

"Hickman," Love said, "when it comes to beer, not even the *President* can drink anything better than this."

"Yes, Mr. New, I believe you, but if you tell the white folks they'll grab it."

"Yao! Then they'll slap on a tax and label the bottles with the picture of a white man propped on a horse. And next thing you know everywhere you turn there'll be billboards telling the world that the best beer in the world is George Washington Beer. Done blanked out the fact that it was the Choctaws' gift from the spirits. So I say let the State folks stay ignorant! And don't even mention it to Janey, because she'll phone her pastor and next thing we know he'll be up in the pulpit ranting and raving about Choc being brewed by the Devil. That woman wants to ruin my life just because my ways are different from hers. Where'd I leave off?"

"You were saying that the boy came back the next day, but before you get into it, I'd like to ask you a question. . . ."

Suddenly motionless, Love looked out into the sky above the backyard then back with a stony expression.

"Okay, Hickman, shoot," Love said, "but be warned that I'm a fast-moving target—which a man like me has to be in this country. What's your question?"

"I'm curious as to why you call folks like me 'State Negroes'?"

"Hell, Hickman, it's because you people let our being about the same color blind you to all the differences between us."

"What differences?"

"Hell, man, the difference between our backgrounds and experience."

"But that is true of everybody—at least in detail—so what do you mean?"

"That you State folks tend to see color before you see individuals. That you reduce a man to his color and overlook his uniqueness, his culture. That you State folks tend to see in the way of the shotgun, which scatters its shot in loose patterns. Which is fine for bringing down birds, but not worth a damn for stopping a man or a grizzly.

"For such the way of the rifle is needed, and even better, a telescoped rifle. One which can isolate details of camouflaged shapes, detect the slightest degree of uncontrolled tension, and allow a hunter to see through the shadows surrounding his target. Because when he's dealing with those who enter the field of his vision such attention to detail is imperative. Aye! And when they speak with forked tongues it helps to have ears tuned to detect what's being said and what's *not* being said. Which is my way with men of all shapes, forms, and colors. A way which makes a hell of a difference between me and you State folks—you with me?"

"Oh, yes, and I'm learning."

"You keep at it, because between us there are also the many differences in experience which go back to the time when the Yankees and the Rebs got tired of their killing and your folks came under the command of the United States government...."

"All right, but what about *your* folks, your father and mother?"

"In the beginning they were like the parents of your parents, human beings who'd been sold into slavery—Yao! But sometime before that Reb-Yank ruckus erupted my parents escaped and came West. Came to what was then known as the Old Territory, and here the tribes of the People made them welcome. So with that they were no longer slaves. And that began the branching of what in the beginning had been the common stream of life which was shared by your people and mine.

"Then time passed and the Rebs and the Yanks went to war, and when slavery was supposed to have ended my folks had a choice which yours didn't. Because yours were still rooted in the ways of the slave states, and though no longer slaves they were left without options. But mine remembered what their lives had been under the feuding government in Washington and chose to remain with the People. Which means that they were never of the State people and had no need for the mockery of freedom which the North threw at the State Negroes, who by then were called freedmen...."

"Why not?"

"Because by then they were *already free*! And Hickman, they were *self-freed*— which is as different from being freed by the whites who enslaved them as darkness from daylight. Living among the People my folks had tribal rights and a voice in the councils. They had the same freedoms and responsibilities that were shared by all of the People—Yao! They were governed and ruled by the same laws and customs, and having put aside the white man's religion they were also free in spirit, free to worship the gods of the People. Which they did."

"But even so, and forgive me for smiling, they were still colored.... Still mixed bloods living in the U.S. of A...."

"Yao! And had to keep well out of the way of the white man. But living on the reservation they were able to avoid most of the crazy color confusion in which the State folks—black, white, and mixed—are tangled. And remember this, Hickman: They were here in this country long before the State folks rushed in and ruined it...."

"Are you saying that before those you call the State folks arrived this part of the country was another Garden of Eden?"

"Oh, no! That's just some more State folks' foolishness. This was no Eden, and neither was it a 'New Jerusalem'—which was another childish misnaming. It was simply a country where mankind, the earth, and the animals could live together in some kind of peace. But then the State folks came crapping and destroying and ruined it.... They *ruined* it!"

Hearing a note of anger, Hickman looked up to see the old man shaking his head. And now as the ancient eyes focused on his face, Love's voice returned higher in pitch and more nasal, sounding with a mixture of Negro-Indian idiom that was edged with a bitterness long held in memory....

So now, he thought, *he'll get back to the moviemaking and to Janey's little man whose questions got him started. Yes, and come to think of it, where's the boy now, and what is he up to?*

"Like I told the boy," Love said, "the State folks had invaded this country all of a sudden, gusting through the land like flames through the prairies. Came fast and from many far places, and most of them wild as sage hens drunk to the gills on fermenting berries. On they came making waves. Came in the nighttime, and came in the daytime, with few knowing what to expect but all leaping along with heads filled with some raggle-tag notion of unlimited freedom.

"They came riding and came walking, on horseback, on foot, and in wagons. Yao! And some of them hoofing it all the way from Tennessee and Virginia, Alabama, Mississippi, the Carolinas, and Georgia. These were the ex-slaves, the so-called freedmen, the State Negroes.

"So to bring things closer to the times the boy knew when he was living with Janey I asked him, 'Do you remember the Watsons, the Hunicutts, and the Rogans?' And he said, 'Yes, I played with some of their kids. They were relatives, weren't they?'

"I said, 'Not unless it was through hoofing it all the way from Tennessee. Anyway, folks like them were different from the others because in remembering what they'd left behind them they came in hope but were prepared for the worst. But I was speaking of those who rushed here seeking "free land"—how the hell could this land be *free* when it belonged to the People? But that's what most of those who came walking or riding behind mule teams and oxen were seeking. So like a party of braves who had run many days and nights with a war party of hostiles dogging their trail, most arrived rest-broken and weary. I watched them come, and I tell you, the sight they made was alarming.

" 'Even sitting still on their exhausted behinds they seemed nervous and restless, still on the move. And as they increased in number most seemed on the lookout for something which kept to the shadows behind them. Something hostile and biding its time before springing to attack them. Something which moved only at night, or during that time of day when the sun pounds a man's eyes like a club on a war drum. But the State folks kept coming and coming.

" 'They streamed here from the old country seeking what they told themselves was a new land, but which was by no means a reality. No, it was only unfouled. It was just not in disorder. And that's because the People respected the earth and replaced what they used of it. Sure, being men they did what men do, both to the earth, the game, and each other. But when this land was the People's it was untouched by the treacherous sickness which the newcomers brought to it. It was unspoiled by the hate and the greed and color confusion that those of the desperate blue eyes brought here from the old land. Those who were sick with a self-disgust which made them think in ways other than those of the People. And besides, for the proud invaders our ways didn't count, because in considering us heathens they denied our humanity!

" '*They* who came here bringing their messy ideas and stinking up the land, step by step, as they made their way westward!

" '*They* who came like packs of wild dogs that piss-marked and shit-kicked every stone, bush, and tree on the landscape—Yao!'

"I said, I told the boy, 'They claimed that they were here seeking freedom, but I think that they were really on the run from themselves! Why? Because behind them they'd left that big bloody war and all the killing and stealing that followed. Yao! And all the lying and cheating and betrayal of that much too short a spell when Yankee armies guarded the human bones of contention that had led to all the bloodshed and lying. Then they declared peace, a peace which turned out to be tall like a pine, squawked like a crow, and talked more crap than the radio!

" 'Even so, it was a peace enforced by rifle and cannon, and for a while there appeared to be a possibility of making a life in which men on both sides, black men and white, could walk tall with their heads erect on their shoulders. But then the white man's belief in what he calls "freedom" and "justice" went limp as a flag in a skin-soaking weather. Then he turned his chicken-shit weakness westward and his back on that which he should have done in justifying all the bloodshed, the killing, and arson. Yao!

" 'But just at the time when he should have been strong and determined, he collapsed like a brave debauched by syphilis and whiskey. Then he demonstrated his strength to be mainly of numbers, guns, and bloodthirsty ruthlessness. But because no group of men can live out their seasons perpetually at war—not even these, the proud ones called Americans—they became uneasy. Aye, for a greater strength, a strength of the spirit, was needed. And this the white man did not have—and still doesn't!'

"Well, when I said that I could see the boy's face turn red as an ember.

"He didn't like it, but I continued. I told him, 'For even in so powerful a country as this, peacetime is harder, much harder, than wartime. And even harder for men like these who had turned what they called peace into a nastiness that's in many ways much worse than armed warfare. They corrupted the spirit of the words they claimed to hold sacred until they were like words scribbled on scraps torn from catalogs and newspapers, which in the days before bathrooms they used on trips to the outhouse—Yao!

" 'So, as I say, when they could no longer stand the stink they'd made in the East they rushed here and invaded this country. The humiliated ones, the greedy, and the mean, dog-assed, bloodthirsty ones—yes, and even a few, though only a few, of those who were truly brave and well-meaning. And I name only the best of a crew that was sorry.

" 'Because all that can be said even of the best, both the black, the white, and the stewpot mixture of Africa, Europe, and Asia, is that when the jagged blade of their bloody transgressions was pressed to their throats, when the consequences of their misdeeds could no longer be disregarded, they tried to leave the past and all their misdeeds behind them. They took off. They ran—Yao! And they had a heap to run from!

" 'Like the death and destruction left by that cowardly scum dressed in hoods rigged out of bedsheets who rode through the night killing and raping. That mangy scum mounted on horseback who prowled the countryside by the light of tar-burning torches carrying ropes noosed for hanging—yes, and lynching and burning you black Christian State folks on tree limbs and crosses...' "

"But..."

"No, Hickman, don't say it! Don't tell me that they were only a few! *All* the bastards were guilty! All of them, North and South, who benefited from slavery, which was a violation of their own ideals, which turned life into something that stank like the body of a dead horse being worked from asshole to eyeball by buzzards—and the land was the horse and they were the buzzards!

"So they swept out here in a leg-pissing panic. Because after a brief time of hope they had seen the face of freedom turn into a mirage, a mask hiding evil. Then a pestilence arose and polluted the old land, a pollution that ballooned, farted, and drifted until it was impossible to look anywhere, but they saw its effects and felt it and breathed it. Yao! This was the new life that had been bought, back there in the North and the South, with so much bullshit and bloodshed. This, Hickman, was the life your folks, your grandparents, the emancipated freedmen, came into after that war. And it was very different from what mine knew with the People.

"This was the new peace, the new morality and justice. And though they were running there was no escaping. Because those who came West, even the good ones, brought along their sickness like pox in the bloodstream.

"So you see, after the State Negroes endured slavery and survived the war they were betrayed by those in the North who made a deal to undermine the so-called Reconstruction—which was no more than a new form of slavery. So now they were little better off than when they were slaves. And as though all of that hadn't been enough testing, enough of an initiation into the white man's freedom, the State Negroes learned that they now had to deal with tar, lynch ropes, and fire as other men dealt with the cost of their food and their shelter.

"And like I told the boy, some came here even before statehood was established. They came in hope, but now hoping was even harder than when they were slaves. Because the hope which had once been a life-sustaining vision had shrunk like a spring gone dry in a drought. And the same with their belief in their strength to endure—oh, yes, they had survived, but they had been seared, maimed, and their vision distorted. So they came here. Came walking, came riding, came running—Yao! And like the old slave song has it, some came crying in the name of your Jesus—ha!

"Yes, but now they were folks of cloudy, color-warped vision. No longer did they possess the clear eyes and high hope mixed with caution which guided those like my pappy and mammy after they killed and escaped bloodhounds in making their way to the People. Theirs was an old, *old,* hope, a hope as old as the giant sequoias. Secret, yes; but undulled and unblemished by what would come after the end of the Reb-Yankee war. And Hickman, it was probably a hope which your grandparents shared. Not a hope for what you Christians call Eden, no. But simply a yearning for a place where they could be themselves whatever their color.

"My pappy used to sing about going to the Nation, going to the Territory, and after he made it here and found his place with the People he kept singing that song until he died and went back to the earth to join his ancestors. For him it was a song of promise, a song of fulfillment—Yao!—an incantation to the gods on which he and my mother had staked their lives and found contentment. They had planned long and thought hard, and took the risk of stealing themselves—clothes, bundles, and hopes for freedom—then made their way here to become part of the People. For them that was the way it was, and they lived in peace and died in dignity, right here in what was then the Old Territory....

"But with the State folks it was different. Something inside must have been killed off as they made their way West. And I mean most of them, and especially the white ones. Maybe they died in spirit as did many of the People on the long Trail of Tears. Because it was back in those times that we began to unravel. First in the old land—in Alabama, the Carolinas, Florida, Mississippi, and Georgia—and then along the trail that was watered with tears. And once in this land the dying continued, a cruel slow dying during all the long years.

"So maybe the State people who came later were already dead, were zombies, who didn't realize they were no longer human. Perhaps all that which had happened, all that they had done during the Reb-Yankee war and after, had been like something that scrambled their brains and shriveled their hearts. And perhaps because of their crimes they were made to go on as though they were human. I do not know, although I have thought on it for a long, long time. But suddenly they were here, still moving and building and ruining. And with my own eyes I saw them. Hickman, I am old enough to have seen many generations rise up and go West, but I do not believe that most of them are human. . . ."

Pausing, Love shook his head. "Like I told the boy, I know what I say is not generous—Yao!—but I stand by it. Truly I don't think they are human. They are something else, for them another name is needed. And to this the boy grinned and said, 'How about "supermen"?'

"And I looked into his eyes and I said, 'No, that is now a name for the funnies—which are no longer funny—or for cartoons printed on the editorial pages of newspapers. Besides, if you were in the last war you would know not to laugh at the type of men who call themselves super.'

"And the boy said, 'Okay, so I made a bad joke.' And I said, 'By helping us deal with the truth joking helps keep us alive, but in this I am far from joking. No, because I think seriously that they're something else, and therefore some other name is called for. For they are people who violate both their own gods and the rules of their gods. And though they are many and powerful, no tribe has been known to violate its gods and go unpunished. For sooner or later something revolting takes over. Something small which they overlook or dismiss with a sneer of pride will defeat them. . . .'

"And to this the boy shook his head, and I said, 'Do you think I'm overstating my case?'

"And he said, 'I think you're making it all black and white, or all white and red. If not, where do *I* stand in all of this?'

"I said, 'That is for you to say. It's been many moons since you left this country and Janey, therefore you, yourself, must decide where you stand. What you are is hidden behind your eyes and under your skin; but you are young, and young men who look like you have the best of choices—though not for long. I can only tell you that you are not outside of it, no matter how you might feel.' And the boy said, 'Yes, that's true.' And I said, 'I know that it's true.'

"Then I told him, 'Yes, it is true, and maybe it'll remain true until the problem of the black and the white and the red man is considered in terms other than it is today. Maybe then the State folks will make peace with who they are, and what they are, and again become human. But today as in days gone by there is great trouble brewing among the State folks, and great inner division. And while they have some sense of what's happening they ignore it. Otherwise, why all their endless arguing and fighting over what and who they are?

" 'Now there,' I told him, 'is your true comic strip alive and kicking—your Moon Mullins, your Maggie and Jiggs, your Katzenjammer Kids! The State folks have confused human life with the comics and don't even know it. They don't know or recognize themselves, and when they think it's to their advantage, some of the State white folks will even claim to be of the People! And even some of the black ones—not Natives like me, but State Negroes—will argue over who *they* are. But how could this be a problem? Are not they men with other men, their fathers, behind them? And are they not men born of mothers? Beings connected to the land? For being human, how can men *not* know who they are, or from whence they came? When you stop and think about it, it's all very odd, very strange. As strange as calves with two heads and one body—which I have seen—or Siamese twins, which I have also seen, and which is a good name for the State folks. But I think you know that I speak the truth truly.'

"And then the boy was pressing me again. He said, 'Perhaps it's true. But tell me, Mister Love, Mister New, where do *you* stand in all of this confusion?'

" 'Hell,' I said, 'exactly where I've stood for many a long year: outside the lousy corral.' And he said, 'But I've known you for years, right here in town.' And I said, 'Yes, here in the flesh but outside in spirit—Yao! And a world apart from people who believe that a good life can be built on a lie, and that men can kill without taking responsibility for those they destroy. Because for all their differences all men are brothers, and to kill without compassion and pity is a crime against nature. It hangs in the mind like a snake gashing his own tail with his fangs. It bleeds in the night and rampages in dreams, where it slashes the dreamer like tomahawks and knives. And the children inherit it through the milk of their mothers, and when they grow up it sounds in their actions like fear in the boastings of cowards.'

"Like I say, we were drinking whiskey, and by now the boy's had run low, so I got up to refill his glass. And that's when he looked up at me like a smart-assed Sooner district attorney questioning a criminal and says, 'This is fine bourbon, but isn't it illegal to sell whiskey to Indians?'

"So I said, 'Indians? Why yes, but laws like that don't apply to me, Love New.'

"And he said, 'But you keep saying that you're of the People, an Indian....'

"And it's true,' I said, 'but you're overlooking one important detail....'

" 'What's that?' he says.

" 'Hell, boy,' say I, looking him dead in the eye, 'when I'm drinking my whiskey I'm *colored*!—a Negro.'

"So then, laughing like you, he says, 'I get it, you really do fall between definitions.' 'Yes,' I said, 'and if I didn't folks would crush me the way they crush the State Negroes.'

[FLIGHTS]

"THEN I WENT ON, I told him, 'It's a crime to kill without brotherly feeling, because when you do there's nothing left inside to restrain you. All men are human, so when you fight with someone you recognize as being a man like your-self you might hate him but you're bound to him by human feelings. So that being true, you don't set out to kill the things which bind you. Neither do you call him an animal to justify killing him, because you'll be killing part of your-self.'

"Then I said, 'In war, soldiers are bound by their common condition as men facing death. That's why they try to fight according to rules that respect their enemies' humanity. But when you fight somebody and tell yourself you have nothing in common with him or his brother, or his father, or his mother, wife, or children, you feel free to go on a rampage of killing—Yao!—but later on the killed and the killing will come back to haint you.'

" 'And that kind of killing has been going on in this country for years. There's been too much of it, and those responsible tell themselves that they have noth-ing to do with those they destroy. That's the lie they tell themselves and tell oth-ers. Meanwhile, the land they've been trying to build a good life on has turned to bloody quicksand.'

"And Hickman, you know what the boy said to that? He got real Northern and white and said I was talking abstract ideals and that historical necessity— that was his word, has little to do with truth! Oh, he was hot as a pistol, so I got quiet and let him have his say.

" 'Look,' he said, 'you're talking as though a great nation is no more than a single man, but it's not. Because a great nation is a collectivity of diverse individ-uals that has to operate by rules above and beyond the rules that govern individ-uals. That's why great nations do whatever they have to do in order to survive and fulfill their destinies.'

" 'Is that right?' I said.

" 'Yes,' he said, 'and when a few hostile tribes try to impede a great nation's progress and it wipes them out, in the broad scheme of history it's no more im-portant than if they were struck by an earthquake.'

"He said, 'You might not like it, but as things stand what you call quicksand seems fairly firm, because a great nation has been built on it. So whether you like it or not, it's here.'

"So I looked into those blue eyes of his and I asked him, I said, 'But what will you do when you wake up one morning and find this proud nation of yours ex-ploding and you're lying under some wreckage? Hell, you talk to me about something called history which I think is phony. But now you listen while I tell it as it would be told by the People:

" 'First, folks arrive in ships, and after shaking the hands of the People and ac-cepting their succotash, fish, and tobacco, the white foreigners get settled. Then, after seeing what a wonderful land it was they turn on the People and begin killing off the tribes to the east. They beat them away from the sea and took over their homeland. Then they lied to themselves about what they'd done and tried to build a good life on the lie. By this time they were calling themselves Americans, and they came like a plague to the South and killed off more of the People and beat them away from the shores of the ocean. Then they lied to themselves again and built some more on the lie.

" 'Next, after calling the Chickasaws, the Choctaws, Cherokees, Creeks, and the Seminoles the Five civilized nations they turned on them. Then that great democrat Andy Jackson forced them west on a trail that was so lone and bloody that it was known as the Trail of Tears—and all this after they had taken the solemn oaths to be bound by the treaties and smoked the peace pipes and exchanged peaceful words with the People. So with all of that turned into a mockery they then went on to build some more on the lie....'

"And he said, 'What lie?'

"I said, 'The biggest lie that men can tell themselves: that they were innocent. That they acted out of what you call necessity and did what they did in the name of their god.'

"And he said, 'I see.'

"I said, 'I hope so, because that's what happened. And with all the lying and stealing and abuse of the land, why blame it on God? Hell, they had superior weapons and ships to supply them with food and machinery. They had livestock and horses—Yao! And by then they had the black man shackled and bound to the hoe and hitched to the plow. And with every incoming tide more ships were bringing in slaves! And on top of that they were breeding like rabbits and moving West at the rate of seventeen miles a year. Not only that, they were swarming like locusts and grabbing more land than they needed or had men to settle. But when Black Hawk ... when poor old Black Hawk tried to hold on to his land so he could feed his people, the God-fearing Americans went to *war* against him! All that many against so few.

" 'And let's not go into what they did down in Mexico,' I said. 'Let us leave that alone. Let us just say that they were not satisfied with the peace they had forced or with all they had stolen. Let us accept what they say about it today, which is that they were innocent and couldn't help themselves. That they were helpless in the grip of their manifest destiny, which was sending them speeding west to the Pacific—Yao! But the truth is that inside their lies and killing was boiling, and that they were forced to lie some more and kill some more to justify their killing. Some manifest, some destiny!

" 'And it was becoming easier, because by now the People were divided and weakening. So then the State white folks turned to killing each other over the spoils. And with that even *I'm* forced to admit that for once in their bloody time in this land they were fair and evenhanded. Because when they turned against one another in that family feuding of theirs they *really* did them some killing!

" 'Along with rifles and cannon they killed with food and machines, engineers and medicine. They killed in the name of freedom, and in the name of slavery.

With one side insisting that freedom was the right to keep breeding slaves, and the other insisting that it was their right to be rid of slavery. So they killed and killed. They killed with iron ships, and they killed with locomotives and with factories. And one side killed using farmers to feed their fighters, and the other side killed using slaves in the fields to supply theirs with rations.

" 'Then Rebs began to get the best of the Yanks and the Yanks moved South and started burning Reb cotton fields and gardens. And when the Rebs kept fighting, the Yanks cut loose from their bases and killed whole countrysides and cities. And before the two were through they'd shed so much blood that even the rivers ran red. And so it went, and it wasn't until men were falling like corn before the blades of a reaper and the dead stacked up like logs did they finally become afraid that they'd gone too far. And that's when they made the lying arrangement they called peace—Yao!' "

"And is that the People's view of the Civil War?" Hickman said.

"Hell, yes! And they don't give a damn whether you call it the Civil War, the War Between the States, or a fight between two different nations!"

"Okay! Okay!"

"I said, I told him, 'But no sooner than peace was signed they broke it. Then they murdered their one great man, Old Abe. And then they lied to themselves again and set out once more to build a good life on that bloody pyramid of bodies. That's some of the truth, if there's a place for it in what you call "history"— Yao! But like they say when they go hunting and fail to hit a target that's sitting: A miss is a mystery, while a hit is history.

" 'Which means that a hit puts blood on the ground and meat on the table, while a miss becomes the subject for lies that are endless!

" 'But change the words around, and what do you git? Hell, you'll have the *hit*, the kill, as your mystery, and the miss as your history! So I stick to the facts and try to remember the mystery that's made of what really happened by those who do all this talk about history. They can stretch and quibble all they want, but it's still a fact that Ole Abe died just as much from all that had happened *before* his time as from that bullet in the back of his head. They knew it too, but they couldn't face up to it. So after putting down their guns they started fighting with words and blaming all that happened on those who they'd now made outcast and homeless. They made what they called the white man's burden their Balaam's ass but wouldn't listen to what he was telling them. And he was braying as loud as thunder! Hell, to let them tell it the half-shackled Freedmen were the cause of it all. And to prove it the white State folks claimed that those ex-slaves were more powerful than cyclones, drought, smallpox, and tuberculosis put together. Yes, and faster than greased lightning, and slicker than Houdini on a blacked-out stage. With X-ray eyes, fingers like feathers, and an urge for white women that drove them loco. That's some of the mystery hidden in your manifest destiny, your made-up history. But with all that to hide behind they didn't even have the decency to do something about those polecats who murdered Abe Lincoln!'

"So the boy took a swig of whiskey and spoke up.

"Said, 'That's not true, Booth and the others were caught and hanged!'

" 'Yes,' I said, 'but something more was called for. Today there are some living where the ringleader came from who still brag about that killing and praise the one who pulled the trigger. They call him a brave big man, a patriot and a hero. Well, the people would have known what to do about his kind of bravery. For that they had strong medicine and would have dosed him until it ran from his eyes, ears, nose, and throat like spray from a geyser. And like I said, what they think is past is still present, and what I have told you is history as known by the People, a history that will come back to haint you.'

"So to that the boy said, 'You're forgetting that I wasn't even born.'

" 'Even so,' I said, 'its mark is upon you. And just like it haints the spirits of those who did the murder and those who refused to do the right thing after it was done it haints their children and their children's children....' "

"Now you're beginning to sound like a Christian prophet," Hickman said.

"Hebrew," Love said, "but I'm not kosher. Anyway, no matter who gets a hand on it and lives to see it in action, wisdom is wisdom. Hell, everybody except you State folks know that when a powerful man is sacrificed he has to be worthy of it. And when he's killed the land gets sick, and to cure the sickness proper things must be done to redeem his sacrifice and appease his spirit. In picking ole Abe they had the right man, but after he was killed, was sacrificed, the proper things were not done. Instead some of the State folks blamed *him* for being murdered—him, the war-proven chief and unyielding shepherd! Him, murder-sacrificed while he was having a little relaxation after doing all he could do to keep his crazy nation together! So not only did they fail to do the proper things to appease his spirit, they *lied* about it! And that's what made for this deep sickness that's in this land and in all the State people—Yao!

" 'You call the People heathens, but even we know that when you plant a great man some great good should come from it. But for this to happen the right things, things great and solemn, have to be done. But like I say, they were *not* done, and since then there's been a harvest of trouble. *Great* trouble, and easy alibis.'

"Hickman, since I made peace with this town and came here to live I've sat through a thousand movies just waiting for simple justice to be shown, not done. Because I have no hope for that, but just shown in the moving shadows. Just unfolded in the dark places where no man has to look his neighbor in the eye. All these years I've been waiting for a little of the truth to be told. But no, even in the places of play, of make-believe, it's all been lies, compromise, and equivocation.

"And what do they say, how do they tell it? Hell, the red man was a thief and a savage without rights to his own country. The North was weak, hypocritical, and pompous, the gray boys, the Rebs, all heroes, and the black man childlike and a coward. And even we of the People are expected to accept this version of history and despise ourselves and our ancestors!

"Even on the reservation the pictures are always the same. I have seen them, and I'm ashamed to say that they even excite some of the young of the People. But being old and one who falls, like the boy says, between most definitions, I've always seen such pictures from the outside. I am not like those who cannot see reality because they are inside the corral, or like those who accept the lie out of weakness before the harshness of truth. Or like those who have no stomach for the truth of their own acts. Or the cost of living inside the pox-ridden corral. Nor am I like those who hope to get in, those who can't look truth in the face because if they did they'd no longer have hope.

"But there are State folks of my complexion like that, people who swallow the lie whole because they know no other way. Or who can only counter the State whites' 'Aye' with a State blacks' 'Nay'; lie for lie, black blindness for white blindness. Nor am I like any of those who hate themselves and all men who are different, nor like those who believe in nothing.

"And Hickman, that's when my nose started to bleed again, and as I took out my handkerchef to wipe it away the boy said, 'Okay, but where do you really stand in all of this?' and I could feel the hairs stand erect on my neck.

" 'Hell,' I said, 'I'm outside the enclosure. Off the reservation. In solitude. That's where I am, and where I choose to be. I'm by myself, alone in the town. All that is me! Yao! And I believe in the Great Spirit by whatever name men choose to call him. And I even believe in enclosures, but not in *this* enclosure.'

"And he said, 'But since men are social beings there have to be enclosures.' And I said, 'Yao! But there are enclosures and enclosures. The question is what's inside. What goes on inside them.' And then, Hickman, I told him a tale from my life with the People.

" 'Once,' I said, 'we were herding some ponies up from the south. We had ridden hard a long way and for many days and were now very tired. So for the night we hobbled the animals near some boulders and thought we were safe. Well, the next morning we found that the rocks contained the den of a cougar.' So the boy gave me one of these oh-come-on grins and said, 'I can see where you're headed, but I'd think that the difficult thing would be to recognize what is or what isn't a cougar.'

" 'You're right,' I said, 'it goes with the deal, and it's always the same. Because all big enclosures must contain cougars and snakes and coyotes and buzzards. But in your enclosure they wear masks and costumes. Many are not what they pretend—By their acts ye shall know them, Yao! But a heap of times they hide their actions with words and disguise their stink with the powerful perfume of money. So a man has to have a strong stomach for truth in order to accept what his eyes and nose tell him is snake or cougar—unless you happen on one of the big fat cats with his britches down—Yao! Because then even a snot-clogged nose will tell you. It will identify him, and if you've ever come on one in the right position you'll know what I'm saying.'

"And the boy grinned and said, 'But men are different.'

" 'Yes and no,' I said, 'different but similar. Men hide in the ignorance and greed and carelessness of towns and cities just as animals hide in tall grass and thick trees. Anyway, you asked me where I stand and I've told you. I'm outside the corral, the enclosure. And from where I stand it seems strange to me that you State people can believe that a good life can be built on the lie you make your livings by. I know it's odd when you think about it—if you can bring yourself to think about it—but that is the way it is. And when you think honestly about it and accept the fact that past times go on living in the generations that follow you will recognize that truth is always stranger and more difficult than fiction. But when a man thinks about how the things that happened—or weren't recognized as important—can hold on and become snarled in the things of the present, the truth is even stranger.'

"I said, I told the boy, 'When you look back on what I've told you it might seem like a lie, but you have to remember that times have changed and many of the folks who were here in those days are now gone. Now folks don't dress the same, and there are few horses and many autos, unlike the days when cars were so scarce that spooked horses gave the hoof to runningboards, windshields, and bumpers. Today many things that were rare are now common, but the old troubles hang on and are mixed up with what seems new. The old lies are still being told, and the old debts unpaid—Yao! So the State people are a strange people; very strange. They seem to forget what lies behind them, or at least they refuse to think upon it. So like I say, they're in deep trouble. *All* of them are in trouble. In fact, they remind me of a man I knew many years ago when I was still a greenhorn at my profession. I was just an apprentice, and it was shortly after I achieved my first flights. . . .' "

"*Flights?*" Hickman said. "You've lost me—what do you mean by flights?"

"A trance in which the soul leaves the body and climbs to the world of spirits," Love said, taking a sip of beer. "I mean as a medicine man. It was after I had completed my trials and the Eagle had finally revealed himself to me."

"Now I understand," Hickman said. "So what about this man?"

And now Love focused his eyes on the trees outside the porch as he said, "He was a man of the People, the son of our Chief by a mother who was the daughter of a chief. A fine young man and much admired by the People. Yes, but he was one to whom strange things would happen—in your religion you would say that he had been 'designated and set aside.' Anyway, I have it from my pappy that when this young fellow was still a papoose, a baby, his mother took him along when she went with the squaws to pick berries. And Pappy said that she left him lying under a tree where she could keep an eye on him while she and the other women worked the bushes for berries. But then, being a woman talking woman's talk with the others, she forgot about him until she happened to look up and see a bear disappearing in the woods with her child under its arm. With that she and the other women started screaming back to the camp and the hunters set out for the bear. But they never found him, not even a cave. So for the People it was a terrible time of great sadness, but there was nothing to do but mourn the baby—which was done with grave ceremony.

"There was great mourning, and everybody was sad. And not simply for the loss of the baby, but because this was the Chief's only son, and a son who would have become a chief like his father...."

"As a minister I understand what such a loss can do," Hickman said. "It's terrible. But was any trace of the baby ever found?"

"Not at that time," Love said. "But sometime later, after there was no longer talk about what had happened, a tall gray-eyed white man came to the village. Pappy said that he was dressed in black with his white collar worn backwards, and that he had a high voice and the soft white hands of a woman. This man brought the baby back all wrapped in the hide of a bear which a strange white man had brought down with a shot. A bitch bear..."

"...And was the child alive?"

"Alive and kicking—except for a broken leg, which the tall man had set and put in a splint. Pappy said it was a strange sight to see a baby kicking with its little leg in a splint, but the man had done his work well and the bones soon healed and were strong...."

"Who was this white man who returned him?"

"A preacher, a missionary. Hickman, there were many who came here in the old days. And through them some tribes took up the white man's religion. Like the slaves and the Nez Perce under Chief Joseph they embraced it—Yao! And for all the good it did them. Still, that's part of the story, because that was the end of what the Nez Perce had been. Anyway, when this white man appeared with the Chief's son there was great joy because the son would someday be a chief himself. So naturally everybody felt grateful toward the tall man. They felt in his debt, so when the tall man asked the Chief to let him take the son away for a while to educate him in the white man's ways, the Chief consented. He was that grateful for having his son back alive. After all, the bitch bear had been defeated, and his son was strong and healthy. And some of the elders thought that it was possible that the baby had special powers. Because like Pappy said, until the tall man found him he had lived mainly on bear's milk.

"So with the tall man having rendered such service to the tribe it was according to custom that his wish be granted. Pappy said that both the Chief and his wife hated to give up their baby so soon, but they said yes. So the little boy was taken East by the tall man, who swore on his Bible that he would bring him back in five years.

"Well, the tall man welshed on his word. The five years came and things were made ready, but the white man and the Chief's son didn't appear. It was during that time that I was born and learned to walk but not to talk. Hickman, as a child I was very slow to talk—but that is another story...."

"Like I say, the promised five years passed, and then ten more, and then fifteen years came and went but still no son. The People had been patient, they had kept the faith and held on to hope and been disappointed. So now it was decided that the Chief's son had died. Died because the ways and the food and the customs of the white men in the East had been too much for his nature. Some of the elders even advised a ceremony of mourning, but that the Chief was against. Other elders advised him to take another wife and have another son while he was still in his vigor, but the Chief wouldn't have it that way. At the time I was too young to understand what was happening, but the People had fallen on bad times and worried over what would happen in days to come. Their leader was in trouble and the State folks were moving closer and closer. Then another year passed and then another, all cloudy and sad....

"But then, in the eighteenth year of his leaving, and about the time I began reading books, the Chief's son came back. He returned in the evening, and the next morning we all saw him. He was now very tall like his father, and very handsome. And except for a black Stetson which he wore peaked in the crown—which was the fashion of the few People who took to hat-wearing—he was dressed like a white man from the East. There was great excitement because his coming back was like a miracle, in fact it was like a *second* miracle, because he had already been returned from the den of the bitch bear. So now his return set off a time of rejoicing and feasting. A time of ceremonies through which the Chief's son would be fitted into the life of his people.

"There was great concern that he have the traits of our Chief, his father, who was a great leader. So the young man was tested, and it was soon clear that he was a fine marksman with the rifle and that he had the instincts of a great hunter. This pleased everybody because it had been expected that the tall man would train him as a preacher, a missionary. But it turned out that although it had taken the white man more time than he promised, he'd had the boy study veterinary medicine so that he could return with gifts and knowledge which would benefit the tribe.

"Like I told the boy, in those days we were great breeders of horses, but with the State folks crowding the range we were losing too many foals to sicknesses they brought here with them. So in time the Chief's son was able to stop it, and he taught even the old horsemen things that they didn't know. And after a while the bloodlines of our horses were much improved, and we were doing well in our trade with the State folk's army.

"So I asked the boy if he'd heard of the Buffalo Soldiers, and he said he hadn't. 'So,' I said, 'you talk to me about history, but like most State folks after being born out here you don't bother to learn what happened.'

"So he asked me why he should know about that particular group of Indians.

" 'Because,' " I said, 'they weren't of the People; they were State Negroes, that's why. Black cavalrymen who fought against the People. Hell, Janey Glover had a brother who served along with them. Fellows who fought against the People when they should have joined with us. Things might have been different if they had—but it wasn't in the stars, because they were State Negroes and black-white men in their customs and thinking. So they couldn't see the advantage or irony. The machines and the gadgets had bit them, so that was that.'

"But Hickman, I tell you, there were some good years that followed the Chief's son's return. And during that time I grew up, and like everybody else I thought of him as a hero, as a great leader. But by that time the life of the People was fast changing, too fast, and for a while he helped keep things in balance and helped ease the passage from the old way to the new. And it was felt certain that when his father stepped down or passed on he would be our next chief. So the People were happy and much too satisfied. Because soon bad times fell upon us. Very bad times. And soon it was felt that in being eager to make up for the time he'd lost while away from his people the Chief's son had broken some powerful taboo. Not that anyone knew that he had committed a crime or when he had done it, but one morning he showed all the signs. . . ."

". . . *Signs?*" Hickman said. "What kind of signs?"

"Indications that he'd been taken over by angry spirits. And in cases where a man has violated a powerful taboo you could tell from just looking for the signs. First he refused to eat—which meant that he was accusing himself. Next, the sick one covers his head with his blanket and punishes himself by refusing to eat, to speak or move. And he stays that way until death finally overtakes him. . . ."

"But didn't someone try to help them? Did you simply let them die?"

"Yao! Because among the People the guilty one knows of what he's guilty, and that in breaking a powerful taboo the rest must follow. You State folks call it 'self-indictment.' But this time it was different because the elders felt that the circumstances called for special consideration. This was the son of our Chief, and through his experience the son of a bear woman—Had-Two-Mothers was one of his names. Yes, and after his life as a bear cub he had returned to do great good for the tribe. So instead of following the usual course and letting him die, which would've been the just and proper thing, the elders suggested that he be saved and it was agreed."

"Thank the good Lord for that," Hickman said.

"Listen before jumping to conclusions," Love said. "Because I speak of the world of the People, of a world that's in your State folks' world but hidden to your unseeing eyes. Everybody was upset over what had happened to the young man, and the Chief even offered to die in his son's place, which was his right as a chief. For among the People a chief had the power to step between a guilty man and his punishment. Just as he could offer sanctuary even to murderers. It was the right of the Chief to take punishment in the place of the guilty, so this was another reason for trying to save the sick son. For we loved our Chief, who was a great man and good.

"So, Hickman, after much powwowing and debating it was decided that some of the elders would take the sick son on a many-days' journey to the south. Far to the south, where a powerful old shaman, a medicine man, lived in the mountains, in hope that he could make the sick man well."

"Where in the South?" Hickman said.

"Near Mexico, and as a young apprentice I was allowed to go with them. This would be my first participation in anything so serious, and my first real testing in my profession. So I was there to witness that which I'm telling you with my own eyes—Yao! And in my mind nothing that happened has lost its sharpness. With my own eyes I saw that old medicine man, that shaman, and he was truly powerful...."

Pausing, Love smiled, shaking his head as he fingered the bright scarf around his neck.

"Yes, Hickman," he said, "this one was of a wisdom that you wouldn't recognize today because you don't respect wisdom unless it comes in a certain kind of package. Or unless it wears a certain cut of clothes and operates in places staffed with young gals who answer telephones. Places with framed sheepskins hanging on the walls. Yet wisdom is wisdom, and it is always so hard to come by that few possess it. Yes, and maybe the first step to achieving wisdom is to recognize it in whatever form and place you find it. Yes, and it is only men who have forgotten from whence they came who forget this.

"No, don't answer, just listen and don't feel too bad at what I'm saying. Because I say this not out of anger, but to keep close to our subject. Hickman, this old shaman was an Einstein among medicine men, and my being able to watch this Old One's medicine was a great privilege. Maybe as great a privilege as it would have been if you could have watched old Moses operating in Egypt—ha!

"It was a long, hard journey, slow to begin, but a journey of hope. And after the elders roped the sick man to the back of a blind pony we set out on our horses and traveled south by the moon...."

"Why a blind pony?"

"Because with only the trail to concern him he wouldn't be shying at snakes or shadows—understand? It was best for the sick man."

"Yes," Hickman said. "It was the same logic as using blind mules in coal mines."

"You have it," Love said. "So as I was saying, we traveled by the moon. At first we rode the well-traveled cattle trails. One was the old Chisholm, which ran past the old State Fairgrounds, and once we got started we pushed our ponies for all they were worth.

"It was a strange journey, very strange, and butt-busting long, with the roads rugged and the heat hellish, and the sick man screaming obscenities aimed at everything from the earth to the gods and the weather. And while this went on the rest of the party rode silent and sad that such a thing could happen to a fine young brave. So for mile after mile there was only the hoofbeats of horses and the sound of his blasphemy.

"It became so bad that even the elders became afraid of what it might bring down upon us. So finally the leading elder halted the party and gave orders that the sick man's mouth be muffled with a gag. But the gag only muted his cursing, for now as we rode he growled like a wolf with his jaws in a trap, and his eyes were on fire with his madness.

"Like I say, it was a strange, difficult journey. With old men, the elders, punishing themselves and their ponies each day to their limits. And then we were far to the south, where with the sun even fiercer and water holes scarce it was impossible to go on in the daylight. So now we kept to the shade and rested until the sun slanted westward and then it was back to the trail—Yao!

"And then we rode in the dark and under a blanket of silence out of fear of what the Chief's son's sickness foretold for the tribe. Together we rode and thought and suffered as we moved farther south. Then at last the mountain for which we were seeking arose before us, and we slowly ascended to that place—not of history, Hickman, but of mystery. . . .

"Seen from a distance it appeared like any other mountain, harsh, sunswept, and high—Yao! A place for eagles! But now, in the westward dropping of the sun, in the dying of the light—*that* was when it revealed itself. Seeing it at the distance from which we saw it I expected thunder and lightning. It was like a god, suspended there and waiting. And when a man approached it in the dark he could feel it filling up the night with its presence. From miles in the distance you could feel it, and that was a part of its mystery. And when approached in the dying of the light it stretched forth its power and a man could feel the hair on his neck spring erect like the hair of a cat caught in static discharged by a storm of thunder and lightning. His eyes became unsure of distance and form and his ears heard the sound of silence. That's how it was with me, and between my knees I could feel my pony shy and tremble.

"That was the kind of place into which we were climbing, and suddenly the sick man broke the silence, mumbling and screaming behind his gag. Up we went, up and up, tugging our ponies by their bridles. Up and on, until our legs were trembling from fighting the overgrown trail. And then, just as the sun died with a splash in the night, we arrived.

"Just where we were I could not tell exactly, for before me I could see only the rocks and the shadows. We were panting, and me no less than the elders. I remember the nervous blowing of the ponies as they expelled the hot air from within them. They too felt the presence, and the air had become both rare and cold.

"That was when the leading elder climbed some hundred yards ahead of the party, where he gave the call of the great horned owl and waited. At first there was silence, then a tired pony stamped its hoof on the stone, and among the towering rocks I could hear the elder's voice echoing and dying.

"Then, giving the lonesome call of the owl, he said, 'Shagatonga! Old Wise One, we need you....'

"And again the voice echoed among the rocks, echoing sadly with the motion of a discarded feather floating high in the air.

"Then one of the elders broke the silence.

" 'Perhaps we arrived too late,' he said. 'After all, the Old One was ancient.' And another said, 'Yes, that could be true. Because for all his power he was still a man, and all men die.'

" 'No,' the first elder said, 'for him to hear the voices of men takes time. It always takes time, because he must come a long way through the silence.'

" 'This place,' another of the elders said with a shiver, 'I do not care for this place.'

" 'Nor I,' one of the others said.

" 'Silence,' the leading elder said. 'We did not make this journey for you.'

"And it was then that I stepped out of my place, that I violated protocol. 'Yes, it was for us too. For all of us,' I said, which drew their eyes. And lucky for me it was then that the Old One emerged from his hole in the rocks.

"Hickman, at first there was only the wall of stone, bare in the shadows. Then a pebble rattled against the earth and he was there, tall and like a rock in his stillness. No one spoke, for it was as though a slab of rock had detached itself from the mountain and taken on the form of a man. A man who was ancient and tall and of great dignity, and whose eyes were hooded and strange. He was very tall and very ancient, and of such power—I tell you verily—that having him around would have been like living in close quarters with an elephant, or trying to tame a roaring cyclone.

"That's why his tribe lived below and on the opposite side of the mountain while he lived high in the rocks alone. Which was his choice. And each day they left food outside the cave, great mounds of it, so he could take what he needed. Which wasn't much, because a long time before I saw him he had lived a life of dedication and put most of the needs of men behind him. But although he had been slow in answering the leading elder's appeal, the moment he saw the sick man tied to the pony he knew what was expected. So with a gesture he invited us to enter the cave.

[CAVE]

"After coming so far and so fast I thought there'd be time for resting, but when he took a closer look at the sick man the Old One became urgent. So we hurried below and dressed in our buckskins, feathers, and beads before painting our faces...."

"Painted your faces?"

"Yes—with the shapes of the plants, animals, and birds used by our totems.

They are symbols of our connection with the earth and the world and the spirits whose help we ask when making our medicine. This demands careful attention to everything from our costumes to our rituals, otherwise our medicine will fail. In a sense it's like your High Court up in Washington."

"Now you're kidding again—what's the Supreme Court got to do with what you call totems?"

"Hell, Hickman, think about it. Up there the medicine men are called justices, and their totems have names like the Declaration of Independence, the Bill of Rights, and the Constitution. Which are totems of words but more powerful than armies—Yao! and they're T.N.T. touchy. That's why when your white medicine men, your justices, call on their totems when making the medicine called law they have to do it with a special dignity, and in a style that includes all of their people. And that's why they dress in black shoes and black robes—Yao!—and write with black ink on white paper.

"That's how their totems give them the double-tongued power to say the 'yes' that means 'no,' and the 'no' that means 'yes.' In the North their words mean one thing and in the South the opposite. They speak out of the right sides of their mouths for State folks who are white, and out of the left sides for those who are colored. But for such volatile medicine to work it has to be made under certain conditions and with grave ceremony—drink your Choc, Hickman, drink your Choc!

"So, dressed in our feathers, buckskins, and beads we returned to the cave of the Old One. Suspended from a rack at the center a big smoky kettle bubbled and steamed over a low flame of embers, and against the wall nearby the sick man lay twitching in his sleep as though being punctured by powerful stings. And when the Old One ordered us to sit in a circle I took my place with mounting excitement. Because as I say, I had never taken part in making a medicine of such crucial importance.

"The Old One began by preparing a pipe, which he raised above his head for his totem's approval. Then, after taking seven slow puffs he passed it among us. And while it began circling from elder to elder I kept my eye on the sick man. We had hoped he would become a great chief, but now, seeing him lying with his braids in the dust and his spirit divided, I felt downhearted and sad.

"But this was no time for sadness, so when the pipe came to me I puffed it, and through the smoke I studied the Old One. Looking back I don't think that he had as much concern for certain minor details as others I have seen, because things went faster than I expected or later experienced.

"After the pipe came the drinking of a powerful liquid brewed from a formula handed down long ago for such crucial occasions. Then hardly without a pause the Old One asked to be given an account of the Chief's son's life and the background of his sickly condition. And as the elders took turns in telling his story I listened with special attention, for it was also a part of my beginner's instruction.

"They began their account with six chiefs behind our Chief, the sick man's father, and told of their characters and what they had done. How the tribe had fared under their leadership, of battles won and battles lost, and of the conditions of the hunt and the game and the horses. They gave each chief credit for his gains and his losses, his days of honor and his times of defeat and of sorrow. Then they told of the Chief, the sick man's father, and then of the sick man's capture by the bitch bear who made him her cub. Then of his being found and taken East by the tall white one, the preacher. They spoke in detail, and in listening I could see the life of the tribe spread before me for six generations, and in the drifting of smoke and weaving of words I relived it.

"But while all this was being related I kept my eye on the Old One and watched his hooded old eyes glow up behind his wrinkles and gleam through his thick brows and lashes. Hickman, I tell you verily, that was a face! Today you see few of such faces because it takes too much living and thinking to make one— Yao! It was a face that appeared to have risen out of the young manhood of the world, and its eyes burned with the original fire that flamed when the sun exploded. They were eyes that were young when the father of men first stood erect and walked on his legs—Yao! And I am sure that they saw the double-faced joke hidden in all human experience and foresaw its results—but that is a matter that's still unfolding.

"As I say, I could see the Old One's eyes glow up behind his lashes, and when he raised his hand the elders became silent. Then he spoke in an ancient voice heavy with quavers in which he warned us that there was no time to lose, and therefore he would begin the medicine the moment the night became pregnant. Then he motioned for the sick man to be placed near the fire and the cave be emptied.

"So I arose with the others, but as I started to leave he placed his hand on my shoulder and indicated that I was to stay, that I was to be one of the three to sleep there in the cave. Which meant himself, the sick man, and me.

"And now, with the elders gone, the Old One sat by the fire near the head of the sick man who lay on the floor still bound and gagged for his safety. And as he twitched in his sleep and the Old One sat nodding, the cave became truly mysterious. So much so that for all my tiredness sleep was denied me, and as I studied the Old One I wondered why out of all the others he had chosen me to assist him. Because there in that place I could take nothing for granted.

"Hickman, I was like a man who sets out for a far distant village and becomes lost in the dark. Footsore and weary, he's come a long way, and as he advances the terrain becomes steeper and steeper and the trail more uncertain. Several times he stumbles and feels discouraged. Then as he falls and regains his footing he's surprised by the flickering of lights that gleam far in the distance. And with a sense of relief he tells himself, There! There it is at the top of those hills!

"So with his confidence restored he increases his pace and climbs in the dark with fresh energy.

"Ah, but soon he's overtaken by doubts that keep dogging his trail. Because now he notices that with each step he takes forwards the lights appear to move backwards, and as he slowly advances they retreat and rise higher. But being committed and still desperately hopeful, he keeps climbing and climbing. Until with the trail becoming even more resistant and the air ever thinner and colder he realizes with a stab of despair that it is not to the lights of a village toward which he's advancing, not to a community of men, but to the far distant world of the stars. . . .

"Well, that's how it was, there in the cave with the Old One and the Chief's son, the sick man. I lay with my head on my arm, and beneath the kettle's bubbling and hissing I could hear my heart's drumming. And as I studied the shadows at play on the wall I questioned the goal toward which my life seemed now to be pressing. Then I thought of my mother and father, maybe because when a man becomes aware of the uncertainty of his existence his mind tends to turn to thoughts of those who begat him.

"So I thought of the stories they told of the escape they made so that I could be born among the People, and of the desperate crime they committed in achieving their freedom. . . ."

"A crime?"

"Yes, a crime—or at least in the eyes of the State folks. Because being slaves they were forced to kill and flee for their freedom. Yao! And their decision was by no means easy, especially for my mother. . . ."

"Why especially for her?"

"Because the man they killed was not only her master, the man who owned them, but her father, the man who begat her."

"Good Lord!"

"So I thought of their killing this man, this proud hypocrite of devious identities. A slave owner with a white wife and children who begat a black line of offspring out of a slave who herself bore the blood of the People. I thought of that confusion of bloods, which was also mine, and what it did to those who possessed it, and how what my parents did defied and questioned the easy distinctions State Folks make between rightness and wrongness, blackness and whiteness. Given such conditions what's crime and what's justice? And I thought of how in the long, slow whiplash of its spiraling, time had led to my being holed up in that high dark womb of the world. And as I listened to the kettle's bubbling and hissing I wondered at the fate of men in this land, and at the treacherous currents that surge beneath the frantic flow of their fucking and fighting.

"I only knew that I was there, and that by background, temperament, and what State folks term 'history' I had been destined to be there. I was of the People and a servant of the Eagle, but while I could ransack the past and the present for wisdom there'd be no turning back on the road I now wandered.

"Hickman, I had been chosen by the Old One to be there, and I believe that if I'd tried to leave my legs would have refused their burden. Besides, where would I go? Certainly not to the place my parents had left to find freedom, because now in many ways it was worse than it was when they left it. No, I was of the People, a servant of the Eagle, and here was the cave. Here was the sick man, the fire, the smoke, and the Old One. So I lay like a man in a trance, or like a child whose eyes remain open long after sleep takes over his body. I don't know how long I lay like that, but suddenly I was awakened by the Old One beating a small drum to which the sick man was now fitfully stirring.

"Because while my mind wandered between the past and the present—or what you'd probably call the gap between the Old and the New World's dispensations—the Old One, the shaman, had removed the sick man's gag. And now as he tapped on his drum the sick man responded with a strange confusion of voices which the Old One seemed to ignore. But since I had never heard such sounds from a single man's mouth I was amazed and bewildered."

"What was it like?"

"Sometimes it was like the fretful voices of a child and his twin, then the angry voices of men who were quarreling. Sometimes they barked and snarled like animals, and yet again they were the voices of a man and a woman—Yao! A woman full of discord and malice whose voice shrilled and attacked the ear like a boreworm. It was a voice that lacerated like thorns, and of all the voices that raged in the dark it was the most eerie. It was sinister. It shrilled and it scraped and it stabbed, and as I listened it finally took over. It dominated the others and became most obscene. It knifed and it slashed like a cougar attacking a stout cage of saplings. And as it raged the sick brave began shitting his britches and the sight and the stench were disgusting.

"But then, slowly, a new voice arose. At first I took it for one I'd heard earlier, but somehow it was softer and different. Then I looked at the Old One and realized that he had begun speaking, and as his voice grew stronger it seemed to issue from the mouth of the sick man. And as it wove between the earlier voices of the men, the child, and the woman it became calmer and soothing. Then it became an incantation which echoed in the cave like far distant thunder, only gentle and moist with the promise of rain.

"Hickman, Janey tells me that before you were a medicine man you were a musician, so tell me this: What do you know of the music of Spain?"

"Of *Spain?* Only a few military marches which I played with an Elks band in Chicago."

"What about the music of Gypsies?"

"Only what I heard when watching them dancing in circuses."

"So then you've heard the magic with which they can evoke landscapes and weather with no more than the sound of their voices. How a master of *cante hondo* can unroll the great spaces, the miles of fields and towns in the moonlight with the passion of his singing, and how he brings alive the prancing of bulls and hoofbeats of horses with the rattling *stampada* he makes with his hands and his boot heels."

"The pictures escaped me, but I've heard the sounds and seen the dancing, and after listening to you I'll be more attentive."

"You do that, because I have seen such scenes evoked many times by Chico de la Matrona, a Gypsy I knew when I rode for the 101 Ranch. Anyway, that's the kind of magic the Old One produced in the cave with his voice. It was high-pitched and thin but in it I could hear the sound of peace and goodness, times of much game and droves of fine horses. And soon there was a kind of debate in progress between the Old One and the warring voices of the sick man's spirits. I listened carefully so that I could instruct myself and soon, one by one, the others faded until only the voice of the woman was left. And as it ranted and raved the Old One's voice grew more stern and warlike. Then the voice of the woman became defiant, blood-curdling and pleading. And that was its tone when the Old One called first upon the sick man's spirits and then upon his ancestors. And as he attacked with his medicine a very strange thing took shape in the cave: As I watched I saw with my own eyes the figure of a two-headed animal that suddenly appeared above the sick man's head. . . ."

"You saw *what*!"

"Yao! Two heads cursing and howling out of mouths that were foaming with blood! Up to then I had been lying stiff on my blanket, but when this strange thing arose I bolted erect, only to have the Old One order me down. And with that a turbulent mixture of nightmare and dream fell upon me.

"Hickman, I flew out of my body and found myself in places about which the only thing I remember is that they were bad. They were places of confusion in which every word meant its opposite, and where intended actions led to results unintended; places in which men in pain screamed screams that were soundless. Then I must have screamed myself, screamed in the flesh, because the next thing I remember I was being shaken by the hand of the Old One. So now he indicated that he was ready to begin and that I was to assist him. There were small deerskin bags to be arranged on a blanket near the sick man's head. Then the Old One pointed to two medicine bags which sat near the wall behind him, and when I fetched them he removed a sharp knife and a small bow of the type used for drilling. It had a rawhide string and a short, wooden shaft which was tipped with a stone of great hardness. Then from the other bag he took out a branched twig of a tree that was covered with the thick webs of spiders and the polished horn of an animal which was filled with a powerful paste. Then at his instruction I placed all of these on the blanket and waited.

"Hickman, imagine the scene in your mind: The mouth of the cave is covered with blankets and the walls dancing with shadows cast by the fire that glows beneath the black kettle that hangs at its center. The sick man lies on the floor in front of the Old One, and except for the bubbling and steaming made by the kettle the cave is as quiet as a tomb—Yao!—and the air's become heavy and foul. So now as I wait for the Old One's instruction the sick man wakes up, and all at once I'm listening to a free-for-all between his arguing voices and the soggy eruptions of his unruly bowels.

"Hickman, of all the strange sights I've witnessed that of the cave was the most revolting. But I had to endure it, because now the Old One kneels directly behind the sick man's head and begins swaying to the words of an old incantation. Then he points to one of the bags, and when I open it he removes the kernel of a nut that's green and round like a marble. This he holds between a finger and thumb of his six-fingered hand, and when the sick man's mouth gapes wide with his screaming the Old One drops the nut on his fluttering tongue.

"For a second the sick man goes quiet in wild-eyed surprise, then he gags and the nut lands in the fire. So now the Old One waits patiently and tries it again, and once again the sick man spews it out and returns to screaming in a contention of voices, of which that like a woman is the most obscene and loudest.

"Then the Old One becomes rigid as a man made of stone, and after muttering an incantation of which I was ignorant he turns to me and says, 'Now, Black One, as you would with a pony that's sick—' "

"Why did he call you that?"

"Call me what?"

"*Black One.*"

"Hell, because I am black if not comely. Besides, what's a better match between a man like me and his name? Among the People I'm known as Black One, among State folks as Love New, and for myself I have a name which they chose to ignore...."

"And what's that?"

"You don't know?"

"No."

"Well, it's Part White One, because like you I share the blood of a slaver. Are you through?"

"Oh yes, and pardon the interruption."

"Hickman, are you one of these State folks who's ashamed of his color?"

"No, I'm not ashamed, but it does cause me trouble."

"Sure, but that comes with the package, and the spirit's what counts.... Anyway, when the Old One said, 'Now, Black One, as with sick ponies,' I understood, for I am a tamer of horses.

"So I took another nut from the bag and holding my breath against the stench of the sick man I forced open his mouth and dropped in the medicine. And when he spewed it out I waited for the Old One's instructions—which came with a growl of impatience.

" 'Black One,' he said, 'you call yourself a man of the horse, so why are you waiting?'

"Which was a rebuke, and as he intended it shamed me. So I tried it again. But this time I crushed the nut with my teeth until it was soft like dried beef intended for babies, being careful not to swallow its sleep-making juice. Then I forced the sick man's jaws open and passed the wet pulp from my mouth to his. Then I clamped his jaws tight between one hand and my knee while stroking his throat with the other. But still resisting, he refuses to swallow.

"So suddenly the Old One pushes me aside and calls out the name of the sick man's mother, and with that his body contracts like a king snake downing a rabbit, and the medicine flies down to his stomach. And with that the Old One begins chanting again, and as his voice keens in the cave the sick man begins having visions, and with his body reacting it was a very sad thing to witness.

"First he was eating the tabooed flesh of wild animals, then nursing his mother. And then with great violence and foam on his mouth he's eating of her body—which was most shameful to witness. And then he was singing the puzzling words of a song that's so strange that I'll never forget them:

> *This is the land and this is my mother*
> *This is a hill and it is my father*
> *This is a hole in the ground and the trees*
> *And the blades of grass are the hairs around it*
> *And I run in and out of the hole like a weasel*
> *This is a hole with a lake in it, and I am a snake*
> *in it—bass, pike, and petticoats!*
> *Take out the legging and drop in the hammer,*
> *There are plums in it, blue plums are in it*
> *This is the hole and I am a kingfisher*
> *I dive in the hole and wiggle my tail feathers*
> *As I dive for the fish in it*
> *That makes the fish and the cornmeal bubble!*
> *This is the land, and this is my mother...*

"Hickman, that's what he sang lying there bound on the floor of the cave. And in it there was a meaning for which I had no stomach. Something sick and most private even though it was a mix of things most us knew. Still, I was of the Eagle and it was my duty to bear witness and be of assistance to the Old One.

"And the sick man kept repeating himself as though he were trying but unable to remember the ending. Sometimes he was a bull among heifers, then a boar hog and stallion—and he went on and on until the Old One nodded and motioned for another of his strange little bags.

"In this one there was a dark paste in a piece of armadillo shell, and I watched him take up a porcupine quill over which he uttered a formula before dipping it into the paste. And then, making an incantation, he pricked the sick man in the pit of his arm, the left one. And for a second the sick man became even more violent, winding his hips in barnyard motions and making smells that were truly disgusting. Then he became quiet, and when his breath had almost faded the Old One pointed to still another quill which he coated with paste. This time he stuck the quill into the skin at the back of the sick man's neck, and it took effect like a bolt of lightning.

"And now as he chanted the Old One motioned for me to fill a calabash with the brew that steamed in the kettle. I thought he would drink it, but instead he leaned over the sick man and began bathing his face, neck, and head. Then he gazed at his face with deep concentration.

"Then he seemed to drift into sleep with his eyes wide open, and when he began shaking like a man with the palsy I knew that I was now in the presence of his totem, the source of his power. And with that he began singing, and as it grew stronger I realized that it was also coming from my lips as though of its own accord. You'd probably say that I was in a state of possession, but that is often the results of the People's medicine.

"I had no idea of how long this went on, but when the Old One looked at me again he had become much stronger. He has released within himself some new store of energy like that which comes to those taking part in a powerful dance.

"So now he took up the knife and the small drill with the tip of hard stone, which he raised and asked for the blessing of his guiding spirit, his totem. Then, Hickman, my black State brother in medicine, I became truly frightened. I watched him measure a spot just below the sick man's hairline and rub it with a powerful salve. And suddenly I seemed to know what he would want with no need for words or for gestures. It was as though I had helped him make such medicine before. So reaching into the fire I removed an ember and handed it over, then sat back and watched him press its glowing tip to a spot in the center of the sick man's forehead. This brought a swift puff of smoke, but although I could smell his flesh scorching the sick man gave no sign that it pained him.

"Then the Old One looked at me and I picked up a long thong of leather, and with his eyes he instructed me to bind the sick man's head at the temples. And into this I put such strength that I could see the thong knifing so deep that it ridged and puckered, as when boys tie strings around the skin of half-ripe tomatoes.

"And with that the Old One picked up the knife. Then things went swifter than the eye could follow: The blade moved along a course just beneath the sick man's hairline, then down a straight line just above the center of his right eyebrow. All this was very swift and light, like a drop of rain flowing down the pane of a window. But the only blood was in the form of small welling drops in a fine straight line. Then as I weakened at the sight the Old One uttered some words, some formula, and leaning over the sick man he made a downward movement with his hands—Yao! And when I looked again a neat flap of flesh lay over the sick man's nose.

"Hickman, it was as though a squirrel had been skinned in the wink of my eye, and a good thing that I was still under the Old One's power and had no time for thinking. For now he moved very fast. He motioned for the bow drill, which was ancient and small and with a point of a kind I'd never seen. Rising to his knees he placed the stone that guided the drill in the palm of one hand, then seized the bow with the other and began.

"Hickman, never in my life had I seen such medicine. The Old One attacked the sick man's skull without hesitation and sent the point of his drill whirring into the network of veins and bone with a surgeon's precision. And knowing that the living brain, the father of nerves, lay beneath the bone, I watched without breathing. And knowing that life and death teetered on the tip of that drill I watched with great suffering as I thought of the Chief, the tribe, and of the sick brave's mother.

"But such was the Old One's skill that the sick man lay like a statue, without flinching. The bow buzzed and the blood welled up around the point of the drill like water when you dig into ground that is swampy. And as the Old One bore down with the weight of his shoulders I could hear the hum of the bowstring. Then I could see the point sinking in. At first with the bone resisting it was slow, then faster and deeper.

"And I thought, If he goes any deeper he'll stir up the gray stuff—and then what? But the Old One drilled on, like a scout who knows his goal in the dark and how long it will take to arrive. Then he was done, and in the center of the sick man's skull I saw that the hole was small, neat, and bloody.

"Then the Old One's movements were even swifter as he asked for a fresh quill and the webs of the spider—which I handed over and watched as he wound them on the tip of the quill and placed them into the hole. This he did with great delicacy, but Hickman, when I saw that web-covered quill enter the skull my legs turned to water! Yao! And my stones flew up to my chin, and it was like I'd been gelded. But I remembered that I was of the Eagle and settled down as I waited for the Old One's command.

"Now I watched him plug the hole with spiderweb, a heap of it. Then he applied balsam to the underflesh, and lifting the flap of skin from the sick man's nose he placed it back beneath his hair line and smoothed it. Then he covered the incisions with more spiderwebs and balsam. Then he looked at me then and said, 'Now, Black One, it is for you to finish,' and I leaned forward and began removing the thong. This took some time, and when I was done the Old One handed me some strips of white cloth and I began bandaging the sick man's head. That's how it was. . . .

"When I looked up for the Old One's next instructions he lay on his side like a dead man. He had gone into a trance with his old hooded eyes staring straight ahead and the fine wrinkles of his face become smooth. But when I listened for his breathing it was gone like that of a bear hibernating in winter. So in a sense I was by myself, there in the cave.

"Before me the Chief's son lay more like a log than a man, and with the dying of the fire even the pot had become silent. Then in the darkness of the cave I had a spasm that sent bitter vomit spewing into the ashes. Then sleep came down, striking like a boulder. I don't know how long I slept, but when I awoke I was under a blanket. The Old One was gone, and finding myself alone with the sick man I sat up in alarm. Then hearing sounds of excitement outside the cave, I knew that he had survived the strange form of medicine.

"So in the first light of morning we made a litter for the Chief's son, and after saying farewell to the Old One we made our way down to his people who lived below. Here we stayed until our patient was again able to travel, which with the Old One's medicine still in his veins took a few days. Then we set out for our village on what was to be a slow, hard-riding journey...."

"How long did it last?"

"Seven days and seven nights."

"And him asleep all that time?"

"Like a dead man, but still under the spell of the medicine."

"So how did you know he was still alive?"

"We didn't, but such powerful medicine calls for great patience, so we waited. Waited and hoped—Yao!—and kept the faith, just like you advise your people. Then we spent three more days waiting for the time when his thongs could be cut...."

"Thongs? And what about his stitches?"

"Stitches? What stitches? I didn't say that the Old One had stitched him. No, the healing was done with bandages and pressure, and with something in the balsam. The thongs were around his wrists and ankles. This was because Shagatonga, the Old One, had instructed us to keep the sick man bound in case he returned suddenly and injured himself. So we obeyed and spent the time waiting for his recovery in preparing a great celebration. Many cattle were slaughtered and much game, enough for a great ceremony.

"Then the day finally arrived, the Chief's son awoke, and with a beating of drums the period of feasting began. All the tribe and kindred tribes were there. The meeting ground—the council space—was packed, and there was much dancing and eating and drinking. It was all spread before us.

"Here," Love said, making a crescent in the air with his finger, "were the elders, and on this side beside the Chief, his father, was the sick son, the recovering patient. Now he was awake and smiling. Although sitting with his hands bound behind him he was smiling. Yes, and his eyes were bright as a raccoon's in the light of a lantern. Yes, and his spirits were high as the tallest of pines.

"All during the celebration, the games, and the dancing, the People had been coming up to greet him, even the children. And he sat in his place, silent but smiling. And except for the thin scar on his forehead he looked very handsome. The scars were still healing, and since I knew their secret I wondered what was happening behind them. But with the barbecue and the corn making such a fine smell in the air I rested easy while keeping him in range of my vision. Then the squaws began serving the food and I watched his bright eyes grow even brighter. I watched him carefully, for that was my responsibility, and soon realized that some of the old men were also watching and exchanging comments between them.

" 'Look at the Chief's son,' one of them said. 'The sight of food puts flames in his eyes.'

" 'Yes,' one of the others said, 'and that's a good sign. The sight of roast bear makes his eyes shine and glimmer.'

" 'You speak true,' the first old man said, 'his eyes shine like a hungry bear's when it plans a great strategy.'

"And then still another old man cleared his throat and said, 'Yes, you both speak the truth, but I think his eyes are bright for all of it. They shine for the beef and the squash and the corn, and for the possum and beans as well as the bear meat. For as we all know he's been many days without food.'

" 'For how many days has it been now?' one of them said.

" 'For many nights and many days,' he was answered. 'More than enough to starve a man who's not under the spell of great medicine.'

" 'That is true,' the first old man said, 'so it is good that his hands are tied, because otherwise he could do himself great damage.'

" 'Yao! You speak the truth,' one of the others said. 'First to the food and then to himself!'

"Then another old man, a famous drunkard, lets out a yell and says, 'Ayee! Just look how his mouth is watering! If he keep that up he'll soon make a flood!'

" 'And I will join him,' says another, 'because mine's watering too—why don't those squaws with the legs of terrapins shake themselves!'

"Then another old man frowns and says, 'Those old women? I don't think you would like that. No, that is something I don't think any of us would like.'

" 'But look at the man! I think that if they don't feed him soon his eyes will burn right out of his head!'

" 'Me, I sympathize with him,' says the oldest of the old men, 'because a man in his condition shouldn't be fed too suddenly. This requires great discipline, for he must approach his first meal in the correct manner. . . .'

" '. . . Correct *manner*,' says one of the others, 'what is this about correct manners?'

" 'The correct manner after so many days,' the oldest one says, 'is that he should first take of the broth. Just the broth alone. After so many days that is the way. First the broth, then a little of the boiled meat. . . .'

" '*Boiled!*' an old man who has been listening said. 'Boiled meat is for old women and babies, not for a Chief's son. He should begin with meat that is red!'

" 'No,' the oldest one said, 'not at the start. In my young days I suffered a bullet in my gut, so from that I learned of these matters. First he should have the broth, and then, after his bowels have begun to adjust, and after the wrinkles have smoothed out a bit he should rest and relax. And then, after he has his second wind—*that* is the time for the red meat, then and then only!'

" 'But not too fast,' somebody said in agreement.

" 'No, not too fast,' the oldest one said. 'There should be no rush about it. First the boiled meat, then he should rest. Next, some of the half-rare roast of bear that comes from up along the backbone....'

" '...Then he should rest some more,' the second old man said, nodding his head.

" '...Or maybe some liver of the deer...'

" '...Then he should rest some more, maybe with a sip of beer...'

" '...Yes, but then before proceeding he should rest...'

" 'Rest, rest, rest! This is too much resting for me,' the third old man interrupted. 'In all this resting my stomach would grow the teeth of wolves, all fangs!'

"To this the second old man made the ugly face of a carved coconut and frowned. 'In his youth,' he said, 'this one was a notorious masturbator, so that now his is the limp wisdom of second childhood. So we can ignore him. Understand?'

" 'Who?' the impatient one said. 'Who are you insulting?'

" 'You,' the eldest said, 'so be quiet while the rest of us continue our discussion of eating. As I say, in these matters a sick man must take it slow. Very slow....'

" 'I agree,' the second old man said, and began looking out across the heads of the crowd as he pressed his stomach with his hands, from one of which he'd lost the middle finger. 'But not too fast,' he added.

" 'No,' the eldest said, 'but at a canter, a slow, steady pace. He should be moderate, like an elk when it feeds on the leaves of trees in the spring—and with equal dignity. Proceeding in this fashion he will be eating and still restoring his strength long after the sun goes down.'

" 'Now you have touched the fringe of the truth,' the impatient one said, 'and at last you have said something! Because at the rate you having him going he wouldn't get started by the rising of the moon! Nor us either! Where the hell are those squaws! Bring on the bear meat! Bring me the turtle, the corn, and the onions! Bring me the red meat before I give up the ghost from starvation!'

"He was working himself up and acting a fool, so the others ignored him. For he knew as they all knew that when you ate with the chiefs you were the last to be served. That was the custom. Besides, they were whetting their appetites by discussing how the Chief's son should break his long fast.

" 'That is the way he should begin,' the eldest of them repeated. 'Only after he has eaten some of the rest, the preliminaries, should he eat of the red meat. Then he should have plenty. The red meat of the bear. The red meat that lies between the short ribs of the steer—and *plenty* of it! Then he should have the rare red meat that is streaked with fat and greasy when it's cut from the bone with your knife. The tenderest of red—that is for a man!'

" 'And for a future chieftain,' the second elder said. 'Just look at his eyes as he follows the movements of that squaw serving that fine roasted quail! I wouldn't like to be in the place of that quail!'

" 'Or in the place of that squaw with the hamstrung legs,' the impatient one said. 'Not unless she canters herself and serves him!'

"And then, noticing that I was watching, he pretended to work up a great anger. Throwing back his head and beating his chest he yelled, 'Bring me my Colt of the blue-tempered steel! Hand me my club with the six-pound head! Bring me my horse and my death-dealing rifle and I'll feed these turtle-legged teasers of appetites a big meal of lead! I, Starving Konukno have spoken, and to this I swear!'

"That's when one of the others winked at me and said, 'Pay him no mind, Black One, he has only a few teeth left and is always impatient of the gut and the bowels.'

"So then they proceeded to discuss the proper places to tickle the serving squaws to make them move faster. But there is no need to recall what they said, because after all the years and great changes you can hear the conversation continued in the barbershops of the State Negroes. Those old men had been around too long to worry about their dignity, so old Konukno could allow himself the impiety of boasting—which in a younger man would have been in bad taste. It was part of their joke and as they kept working themselves up for the feasting I enjoyed listening. At their age there was nothing left for them to do except eat, drink, talk, and tell lies. Yes, and disagree with how everything was done by men who were younger—which is the privilege of old men—Yao!"

"If you say so," Hickman said. "But what about the sick man, did he ever get fed?"

"I was coming to that," Love said as once more he took a long, high look into the trees.

"At this point I looked up and saw the Chief helping his son to his feet. He was smiling, and I watched him pat the young man on his left shoulder with great tenderness, then he stepped around and with his knife he cut the thongs from the young man's wrists and ankles. Hickman, you should have heard the shouts and whooping that greeted his action. Then came a glad thunder during which the son stood smiling and rubbing his wrists. And as the noise grew louder, he spread out his arms like a true chief and smiled. And in that moment he was like something that was very young and innocent, and his smile was like the pure smile of a child while it's sleeping. With that the shouting really soared, and it went on and on until the old Chief raised his hand. Then the Chief helped his son to take his seat and the feasting began.

"For a while I was so busy eating that I had no eyes for the sick man or anyone else. For during the period when Shagatonga's medicine was working I had eaten very little because of my being as one with the sick man. His burden was mine. And to the extent that it was possible it was my task to endure what he endured and feel what he felt. It hadn't been easy, so by now I was nervous and hungry. So when the Chief freed the hands of his son he freed me of a great burden. So now, as I say, I was eating. Eating with the concentration of a starving animal, when I became aware that the noise of celebration had become so quiet that I could hear the faraway howling of a dog. And when I raised my head I saw that the Chief was now standing and looking down upon the head of his son. All eyes were upon them, eyes of the old men, the young braves, the women, and the children. Some held pieces of food in their hands, and there were strange expressions on their faces. Then as I narrowed my eyes and looked at the son I understood—and Hickman, that moment was terrible...."

"What happened, man?" Hickman shouted. "What's all this bopping and stopping?"

"Hickman, he'd *changed*! Right in the midst of the feasting he had *changed*...."

"All right! But how? In what way?"

"From what he'd been. Changed as the weather changes between seasons. Changed as winter is different from summer. Changed and become different as a ghost is different from the living. Only as it turned out he could still walk, talk, and eat, and even hunt, but his humanity had left him...."

"His *humanity*," Hickman said. "Man, talk like a State Negro and tell me what you mean!"

"Hell, didn't I say his humanity was gone? What are we discussing—bears? Is that what you think I've been talking about? Don't you admit that we of the People have humanity?"

"Of course I do, otherwise I wouldn't be interested. I just want you to be more specific so I'll know what you mean."

"And you call yourself a man of medicine! Hickman, I mean that he had lost that which makes man *man*—now do you understand? He was no longer the man that he had been, and he had forgotten his name—which is one of the first signs of the living dead. A very bad sign."

"Do you mean he had amnesia?" Hickman said. "There was a faithful member of my church who had that, so I understand something of amnesia."

"You do, do you," Love said. "Well, I hope you do and that it's not a matter of you State folks giving a thing a name and thinking you understand it. Yao! And I hope you understand the rest of it."

"So try me, what is the rest?"

"His loss of control over his body's urges. He was here and not here. He was well-named and no longer knew his name. He was now neither man or animal but some strange untamed thing of no specific name. He was sitting there with all the clans watching, and with his father the Chief looking on he began devouring everything in sight. He was stuffing himself until his cheeks puffed like balloons and his eyes burned like embers! With unchewed grub spilling from the corners of his mouth and falling to the ground. He was running amok with eating, and not even the silence and dismay of the crowd could stop him. I watched him reach for water and when he drank it was with the thirst of a horse that had covered many miles in the desert. And just as noisy. He snorted spray from his calabash like a mule, poured water down his throat until it distended his belly, and he kept snorting and drinking until he pissed his britches. And all of that before the eyes of his people! He had changed, I tell you, he had *changed*! But as we learned in the days that followed, that was not all.

"For now there was no moderation left in the man, neither in the matter of taking in or giving out. When he gave, he gave everything—horses, dogs, blankets, his knife and rifle. Even pairs of his Eastern shoes with the thick soles and scotch-grain uppers. And when you offered to share with him he left you nothing. In everything he did he was like a locomotive running on a downhill grade with the brake shoes busted, the fireman and engineer both dead, and the brakeman twenty cars back lying lap-legged drunk in the tail-end caboose. So don't try to pin him down with some simpleminded word like 'amnesia'—hell, the man was a walking *calamity!*"

"I withdraw my suggestion," Hickman said. "It had to be more than amnesia."

"Yes," Love said, "and even worse, you could hear and smell him coming even from a great distance because of the violence his bowels did to his britches. Whenever it was possible we tried to keep upwind of him, because when the stench of him blew in your direction the smells that blow now from the packing plant out west of town would have been no competition. Amnesia? Who ever heard of such an amnesia?"

"All right," Hickman said, "so I was wrong and it was something else."

"Are you telling me? As old as I am I have seen only one case like it. The man was out of control! In all things he was like a stampede of wild horses! And while his explosions of energy might have been to his advantage with women, no squaw in her right mind would risk such wear and exhaustion. With women lined up in sufficient numbers—Yao!—and with thick enough colds in their heads to keep out his stinking, he could have fathered a whole tribe in the course of nightfall and morning! He would have been like a stallion among the mares, a seed bull among the heifers. This is mere speculation, but Hickman, there's no need for guessing when it comes to his hunting.

"When he hunted anyone could see the damage he created, there's no guessing about it. For one of the strangest effects of his condition was that he had become even more deadly as a marksman than he'd been before, and he was one of the best. He killed and he killed. He lay waste the game. He brought down more animals than the hoof-and-mouth disease. On the hunt he was like a blast of fire. And soon the game flew before him as though they'd been given the word. The fish deserted the streams or lay still in the shadows. Or maybe they went on a diet and became vegetarians. The birds found distant cover or learned to feed in the nighttime.

"So bad days came to the People, and all because of this Chief's son who had lost that which makes a man human.

"Hickman, I have thought on these matters for a long time and I appreciate your being willing to listen. I told it to the boy but I have no idea how much he understood. Maybe for you, being a preacher, there's a worn-out moral in it. But think on it anyway. First there was his time with the bitch bear. Then his life in the East, about which I know little. Then came his return as a great hunter and teacher who improved the crops and the bloodlines of horses. Then came the broken taboo and his being taken over by spirits that were evil. Everything that we knew to do was done to save him, but for all of the wise medicine of Shaga-tonga, the Old One of the mountain, there was nothing left to be salvaged. We did our best, but the evil spirits took him over. . . ."

"Once," Hickman said, "I played a concert at an army hospital that was full of fellows like that. It's a sad thing to happen to anybody, and a terrible thing when it happens to such a promising young man. What was finally done about him?"

"For a time we tried to live with what had happened, for this had been a much-loved young man—Yao! But soon, under the lashing of the hard times that followed, that love began to change into its opposite. So the council made up of the chiefs and wise men of all the clans came together, and for three days they discussed the problem. And so it was agreed that since everything that might have appeased the angry spirits had been done but failed to save him, the Chief's son would be escorted to the high sad place where the cliff overlooked a deep valley. That was their sad but final decision, and in the interest of all the People the old Chief agreed. . . ."

With the thought, *Absalom, Absalom, my son,* Hickman looked up to see Love staring into his face with eyes so bright that he felt a chill. Then the high-pitched voice continued.

"All through the night the old Chief sat by himself in the council lodge, smoking and singing a certain sad song of anguish. Then, before day broke the next morning, the party assembled and set out on its journey. . . ."

"Did you . . ."

". . . Yes, I went along. The old Chief led the way, and the one who had been his only son rode on horseback behind him. The Chief set a slow pace, with his sad eyes turned to the hills as he led the blind pony by its bridle, and the son came swaying and rolling behind him. He had been barbered and bathed and dressed in his buckskins, beads, and feathers, and wore on his braided head the black Stetson that he'd worn when he returned from the East. To divert his attention one of the elders had given him a great melon which had been chilled in a spring, and he rode with it cradled in his arms. Rode with his head lowered above it, giving it such attention that he had no eyes for the trail along which he was traveling. This I know because I was riding as the last of seven medicine men arrayed in a row directly behind him. He was totally involved, caressing and babbling to it, and when he bit into it and began eating, some of the elders became upset by his affair with the melon.

" 'Such a thing should not be permitted,' one of them said, 'for it is not right for a man to be eating at such a time as this!'

" 'Maybe not,' another said, 'but at a time like this what does it matter? Why not let him have his pleasure and think of how glad he made us during that spring of his returning?'

" 'I remember,' he was answered, 'I remember it all too well, but that springtime is long gone, and this time is a time of winter in summer. His is no way for a man to act in such a time.'

" 'Why not think of his father and what he has to do?' I said. 'Think of what he must be thinking. He is a good Chief and a good father—just look how he holds up his head.'

" 'That is true, Black One,' the elder said, 'but on such a grave occasion as this he should not be allowed that melon.' And so it went.

"We were climbing into the hills by now, and I watched the Chief's son with full attention. Sometimes he would look into the sky and smile, then he would lower his head to the melon again, and it went on like this for miles and miles, until we were close to that special place. It was high and eerie, and when we reached a certain point the Chief went ahead of the party, leading his son by the blind pony's reins to a spot at the edge of the cliff.

"Now the rest of us formed a tight group some distance behind them and sat waiting quietly on horseback. The light was gray and beyond the edge of the cliff huge cloud-like shapes that were threatening were slowly arising. Then in the foreground ahead the blind pony of the sick man let go with some droppings, and in the chill of the air I could see it steaming and drifting. And yet, there in the cold air, I was shivering and sweating.

"For in that moment I was one with the son, the doomed man, with all of my powers. And with the Chief, his father. Sitting there astride my pony I trembled, and with blood running from my nose I could see drops of it falling upon my hands and feel it cooling. Then I was watching the Chief dismounting and helping his son to dismount from the pony. And as I watched I swayed on my pony. I remembered the night in the cave with Shagatonga, the Old One, and how the story of the life of the tribe and the deeds of the sick man's fathers had unfolded before me, and how the under-flesh of his skull had looked when the peeled skin of his forehead had covered his nose. Yao! I remembered, and thought of the change in the times and feared for the life of the People.

"And in wanting to help I was concentrating so hard that my blood was dampening my temples. And since my duty prevented me from fainting I passed into a state that was rare—not of unconsciousness, but somewhere beyond. And yet I was still there with the others. I could see, smell, and hear, but it was like looking at a scene unfolding through fire. I was with the sick man, watching his swaying from side to side as he mouthed on the melon. And in that last moment I tried with all of my powers to return him to normal.

"Hickman, I *tried,* I tried! With all my powers of mind I tried to make him drop the melon and take his place with dignity—Yao! Because for a people who had been taught to live and die with honor it was his moment of ultimate dignity.

"But I failed, I was unable to help him. And with blood dripping from my nose I watched him eating as I surrendered him to his ancestors and felt defeated and sad that the tribe had lost an exceptional young man.

"Hickman, he never stopped eating. When we lifted him from the back of the pony he was eating. And as we guided him to his position near the edge of the cliff he was eating. And when the old Chief his father began addressing our gods in a voice that echoed and quavered he had his face deep in the rind as he snuffled and gobbled the meat of the melon—Yao! And when his father turned him to face the west he stumbled into position and kept eating. Aye! He was *eating*! And as I watched the Chief retreat a short distance before raising his rifle and sadly taking aim he was so busy eating that he paid no attention. And when the rifle rang out in the silence his head jerked back in surprise as though he'd heard his name called in a crowd while moving among strangers. And as he slumped to the earth he was still grasping that melon in hands that were dying.

"Then, as though blasted by cold winter winds, I shivered and lurched on my pony. And with teeth chattering like dry seeds in a gourd I shuddered as I watched the old Chief raise his arm to the skies in fulfillment of his duty. Then as he turned and retreated from the edge of the cliff, I could see a bloodred sun rise up in the distance. And as the Chief bowed his head and began descending the mountain alone, we moved to the son through the red dawn of morning.

"I was the first to reach where the dead son had fallen and there was a smile on his face, and just below the thin bluish scar which puckered the skin of his forehead I saw a single seed of the melon which glowed ghostly white in the dawn of daylight...."

[EGYPT]

WHAT A TERRIBLE SACRIFICE for a father, Hickman thought, and in a scene evoked by the incantatory rhythms of the old Native's voice he imagined the old Chief standing alone on the mountain as he gazed into the sky above an ancient, bloodstained pyramid such as those Millsap once described after a trip to the Aztec region of Mexico. Then, hearing the clatter of trolley cars passing in the street blend with the drone of a plane overhead, he found himself standing dangerously close to railroad tracks along which a tandem of two huge locomotives were speeding with a train of rumbling boxcars.

It was strange, yet here he was, pinned on the wrong side of the track with boxcars sweeping past to a rhythmical pounding of wheels on rails; while there, far in the distance, where the tracks curved to the left, the two engines were speeding toward a trestle which spanned a wide-yawning gorge. And looking back to the void out of which the train was emerging he could see boxcars still flying toward him while smoke pouring back from the engines swirled in the air above them like a message being written in retrograde. And now as he took a quick look back to the trestle toward which the engines were plunging he seemed to be standing nearby and watching the gorge stretch ever wider and wider in what appeared to be a race between locomotive and chasm, engineers and time—then, with an earthshaking rumble, the locomotives raced over the trestle, and he found himself back at the crossing and thought, *Hickman, at the speed it's tooling it'll soon be past, so get set to get going*—but as he stared at the cars sweeping past he froze with uncertainty.

For suddenly increasing their speed the cars were hurtling past so fast that the signs and symbols displayed on their sidings seemed to hang in the air: A shield striped with the red-white-and-blue of Old Glory, a buxom white woman with a white banner displaying the words NOLI ME TANGERE streaming from her shoulders, a smiling young Indian named "Snookums" who held a large ripe orange in his hands, a green Gila monster, a bronco, a bull moose, a hump-shouldered bison, a white haloish circle in the center of which a black cross tilted at a precarious angle, a Christian cross blazing with flames, and a figure dressed in a white robe and a hood that had black holes for eyes—all flying so fast that they appeared to move without moving.

And now, as the wheels of the cars began to screech and lose traction, the names and shapes of regions and states, and the initials and symbols of nation-wide railroads hung before him like a multicolored map which the highballing engines were creating in a headlong plunge across a landscape which was being rapidly girdled with copper and steel.

And just as he thought in despair, *Not even a veteran hobo could find his way through all this confusion,* the boxcars gained traction, and with a blues-like blast from its engines the train shot ahead in a jubilant crescendo of whistles and bells. And now as he whirled, wondering what would follow, he saw the red caboose flying toward him. And now, seeing a brown-skinned man wearing an engineer's cap leaning out of a window he stared in wonder. For while the man sat in the hindmost car of the freight train his posture was that of a skilled engineer. Then, with the caboose flashing past, the man threw him a salute and roared with laughter—whereupon the scene became even weirder.

For now the rails over which the train was advancing were no longer affixed to the roadbed but spurting backwards to land under its wheels as though being extruded by the frantic exertions of the engines which were now far in the distance and rounding a curve. Then, seeing the caboose skip up the tracks like the tip of a whip, he thought with a sigh, *So now you can get on to wherever it was you were going....*

But just as he moved to cross over the roadbed the scene vanished, and with a start he found himself sitting once again in the old antlered chair...from which, now, Love was sadly intoning, "That's how it was...."

And to which, sitting up in surprise, he heard himself adding, "As it was in the beginning, is now, and ever shall be...."

Then, in the silence that followed, Love's account of the Chief and his son began echoing in his mind with implications so increasingly personal that he snatched off his glasses and leaned forward, listening with a sense of dread for Love to sound some amen of resolution that would confirm or deny the mounting confusion of dream, reality, and dread through which his memory was stumbling. But Love remained silent, and through moist eyes he watched the old Native gazing out into the tops of the trees behind them.

Hickman, he told himself, *not only is* he *tired but if* you *don't get out of here you'll embarrass yourself*—and was interrupted by the clear call of a bird, sad, sweet, and lonesome, which was quickly lost in the clatter of a trolley car passing in the street beyond the courtyard. And at last he saw the owl-like turning of Love's braided head.

Then with the old eyes focusing upon him, he heard himself saying with strong emotion, "What a pitiful thing to happen to such a good man and loving father, it was terrible!"

"Aye," Love said, "but it's the duty of men of our profession to take part in experiences that are not only sad but ridiculous. And by now we both know that if any story continues long enough even the happiest has to end in the sadness of death and dying."

"Amen," Hickman said, "and that's why it's our duty to try and understand how such terrible things can happen. But even when we can't we're still bound to provide the sufferers whatever relief we can offer. Was that what you were doing for the young man?"

"If you say so," Love said. "Yes, I was trying to warn him obliquely, to divert his mind to other possibilities. To suggest different paths and remind him that no matter how long or short, happy or sad, pitiful or terrible it happens to be, all life finally ends in what State people call a death sentence. Therefore he should stop and think about his condition. That he should weigh it, and weigh it calmly. Because now he's still trying to pressure his vague feeling into an idea, and that is a danger to himself and to others...."

Leaning forward, Hickman grasped the arms of his chair.

"Why do you say danger?"

"Because now his are the ways of the white State folks, for whom ideas are things to be approached with fear and distrust. So when they're called for they leap to turn their feelings into action. And violent actions at that. Now he is one of those who would rather act than think, so instead of thinking and arriving at a state of reasonable resignation before what's hounding him he'll keep searching for a target. And when he's found one he'll blacken or whiten or redden its face and press his attack. That is the danger, because when he thinks he's found his target he'll shoot from the hip. And even if it happens to be in a steel-plated room he'll ignore the fact that bullets can ricochet and bring down the gunman."

"I hope not," Hickman said. "Even if it's only a figure of speech, I truly hope not."

"My words speak of the possible," Love said, "so since he's only prowling through the past of this town there's room for hope. But remember that he is now of those who try to solve every problem with guns and machines. They turn to guns and machines as in the movies they use Gatling guns against the People who were armed only with knives, tomahawks, and rifles. And in peacetime they kill with telegraph wires, newsprint, and the radio—Yao!—and with cash registers! But as I say, for him hope remains possible."

"Well," Hickman said as he replaced his glasses, "I hope you're a good prophet, because I had no idea of what was going on out here. And now that I've talked with you I'm truly worried."

"Why now, more than before?"

"Because when Janey wrote me I thought that she was just imagining things, and that the boy probably came back because he remembered his life with her and simply wanted to see her again. But after talking with her in person, and now with you, I see my mistake. Which leaves me lost in the woods without a compass and up the creek without any sign of a paddle.

"So you tell me, Love: What's *bothering* this young fellow? What's got him so upset? I'm sure you understand how important it is for me to learn all I can. So even though you must be tired I'm still asking you to give me a few more minutes of your time, and then I promise to leave."

"Hickman," Love said, "are you signifying that I'm too old to go on talking?"

"Oh, no! But while I've been listening I realized that if *I* had to preach a sermon even half as long I'd have my associate minister, the presiding elder, the head deacon, and a bunch of stalwarts sitting on the mourners' bench to fill in the pauses and help me. But while you've done the talking all I've been doing is listening and trying to understand what happened."

Gazing into the trees, Love grasped the chain of the swing in his ancient hands and set it gently in motion.

"Okay, Hickman," he said, "this boy is really upset because something which began bugging him back when he was living with Janey has returned to haunt him. It showed up first when he was still a yearling in the use of words, but it wouldn't give him its name. But when he was taken to live in the East it went along with him. And there like the young of the cicada, the seventeen-year lo-cust, it burrowed so deep in his young mind that he could ignore it. But that nameless thing didn't die, it just lay in the underground of his mind like a larva, a maggot. And there it underwent a slow series of molts and gradually took on a new form which drew its strength from the confusion bred by his rebirth into a scrambled experience—why are you smiling?"

"Because you speak of his being reborn and I hadn't thought of rebirth in the context you give it. . . ."

"Well, think of it now. Men are born as old as the hills and the oceans from which they evolved, yet when they put it into words they say they arrived on earth as newborn babies. But have you ever taken a good long look at a newborn baby? Hell, man! Those little wrinkled things look *old*! Boy or girl, male or fe-male, they look as old as the earth from which they sprang! Many look older than they'll look when they die, but still we call them 'babies' and term their arrival 'birth'—Yao!—when it's clear from their looks that they're only setting out again on a journey that they've taken before. And I mean a journey through which they'll go from being old to being young to being old once again—if they're lucky. And each leg of the journey marks a new beginning in which new sight-ings must be taken, and new strategies devised for coping. Each stage of the jour-ney has its own revelation and surprises, its own rewards and its dangers. Therefore the initiations that men undergo are endless. So when a child is snatched from a way of life to which he's been adjusted and set down in one that's quite different it's like he's being born again.

"That's what happened to the boy. When he landed in the East he underwent a second childhood during his childhood. Because out here he lived in the brightness of Janey's darkness, her blackness. But now he was living in the shadow that goes with his whiteness. And being forced to learn how to make his way with black-seeing eyes while undergoing the pressure of becoming a white child.

"This took much time, so for years the unnamed thing left him in peace—yes, but soon he became a young buck of a man. And then some smell, or sound or sight, some taste of food, echo of memory, or shape of shadow roiled up the un-derground of his life with Janey and that which was sleeping awoke. . . ."

". . . So it awoke," Hickman said, "but what then?"

"It awoke, that's right, and like the cicada, the harvest fly, it surfaced. . . ."

". . . Which means that it crawled to the surface and left its old shell clinging to the branch of a tree like the shell of a locust. . . ."

"Yao! It split the back of its shell straight down the middle and climbed out beside it. Then, stretching its wet limbs to dry in the sunlight, it began buzzing and humming. . . ."

"So in the East it took on new life?"

"Yao!"

"...And found its voice and began singing a bebopping song like a mocking-bird?"

"Aye! And because the boy was now vulnerable to the ghosts of the past he heard it...."

"...He heard it!"

"Yes, and he heard it *loud*, but by no means did he hear it clearly. So with that his white life took on some of the color-feeling that's described in a song I've heard you State Negroes sing...."

"Now wait, man," Hickman said, "what song would that be?"

"Just listen, Hickman," Love said, "and since you're turning this into some kind of a medicine man's prayer meeting, why don't you go on with your medicine and use your mind? What else would it be but the one about the blues jumping on the back of some rabbit-assed rascal and riding him ten thousand miles?"

Slapping his thigh, Hickman laughed.

"Now that one I deserve," he said, "even though I was trying to give you a little old-time Baptist support. Even so, you have *got* to be kidding!"

"Me, kidding? Haven't you heard that us Native Americans have no sense of humor?"

"Oh, yes, but those who have some of my down-home blood in their veins are different."

"Maybe so," Love said, "but what you're hearing is the jibing of words, the joke that comes mixed up in language. So listen to *me:* This thing out of the boy's past has jumped him exactly the way the blues jumped the rabbit. And once in the boy's white skin of a saddle it dug in its spurs and took off hell for leather...."

"...Riding like a cowboy..."

"Yao! And with a grip of steel on the reins and the bridle. And by now it's been spurring his white skin of a saddle so hard that he's almost decided that getting rid of his skin is more important than having the protection and comfort it brought him."

"I hate to admit it," Hickman said, "but at the rate you're going I can't tell the horse from the saddle, the saddle from the rider, or the rider from the whip and the spurs. But if I'm anywhere close you're saying that the boy's in a bad, bad way. Which in my down-home idiom means that spiritually his head is knotty, his nose is snotty, and his butt is dragging the ground...."

"Okay, except that in his case his butt is bumping the sidewalks and curbstones. Hickman, there are many way of describing the human condition, but since most are inadequate, you stick to yours and I'll stick to mine. Either way, that's how it was. The boy's up to his eyeballs in trouble, and no matter how much his flesh keeps festering, and no matter how much he'd like to be free of his burden, he's in the race and thinks he's forced to hold his position and keep pace with the bit-foaming pack."

"Which means," Hickman said, "that he's being ridden in the race of races."

"If you insist," Love said. "And now his devil of a jockey has ridden him here, two thousand miles to the west, in search for the scenes and the acts of a time and place which faded with his coming into the world. Deep inside it's made him wild, and when he's calm he knows it, but still he keeps festering. Therefore he'd like to do something, anything, to stop the nagging, the strain, and the itching. Many times he's tried to put it aside, tried to ignore it, but it keeps at him, winter and summer, midnight and noon. So now, far out on the cloudy edge of his mind, he's decided that if he's ever to learn the truth, it's not only a matter of finding a simple answer but one of forming the proper question to ask those he keeps pestering. So as bad as things seem there's still reason for hope."

"That's something I've been waiting to hear," Hickman said, "but why is there hope?"

"Maybe it's because he's coming to realize that what's eating on him isn't a fully formed idea. That instead it's a swarm of vague feelings that refuse to come into focus. A hit-or-miss mix of memory and feeling which refuse to be anything but fragments. Fragments that keep swirling in his head like a swarm of *no-see-ums*...."

"...Of *what?*"

"Of gnats, of flying things from which he has not protection because they refuse to stay still and give him a target. Yes, but they won't leave him alone, and when his mind is on something else, even something pleasant—like a beautiful girl, or a hunt for pheasant and quail—they strike him from ambush and take off like rockets. And just when he thinks they're gone they swirl back and strike him like sharp grains of sand in a whirlwind. That's how it is, they punish him morning, midnight, and noon. They pursue and harass him, they tease, taunt, and thorn him.

"So he thought he'd find relief out here, that if he returned to this place where he first saw the light his torment would end. That he'd find both his question and answer and know his next move. So he came with his torment to Janey, and when she couldn't help him he turned to old Love. And Hickman, that's my reason for giving him my time and attention. He remembered me, he came to the same old heathen who Janey tried to keep him from knowing when he lived here in this town. He came to one who lives outside the State folks' corral, to one who has contempt for both the thing that rides him and those who make it important. Such is the weight of his burden. So he was here and we talked—or at least I talked while it was mostly his *ears* that listened."

"Only his ears?"

"Yao! Because even as I talked I could see that his mind was already searching for others to question."

"For instance?"

"That's the question I put to myself, so I addressed myself to the Eagle. 'Old

Father,' I asked him, 'where will he go after talking with me? Will it be to some lawyer, some doctor, some jackleg of a preacher who knows even less about what's bothering him than either Janey or me? Will it be to some rich man, poor man, or pool-hall hustler? To some white downtown insurance agent who got so rich from milking nickels and dimes out of the death-fear of State Negroes that he thinks that he's an authority on everything that goes on among them? Or will it be to Janey's pet, that Cliofus? That strange one whose wires are so scrambled that he even gets what he had for this morning's breakfast confused with some damn Easter eggs that Janey dyed for him twenty-five years in the past? Will it be to that cock-eyed, loose-tongued, word-drunk oracle, who mixes what really happens with tales he's been told, books he's read, and stories he makes up until he can't tell the difference between life-and-death facts and Uneeda Biscuits?"

"And what was the answer?"

"The answer was, Yes, Black One, he'll go to him too. He'll give all of them a go at his question. So spoke the Eagle, and so it is and shall be.

"And then, Hickman, I guess he'll try to put whatever they tell him together. He'll be like the greedy monkey who got his paw so full of candy that he couldn't get it out of the jar it was stored in. Then he'll twist and tug, trying to get rid of the jar so he can arrange whatever he gets hold of. Then he'll see that in order to get free he'll have either to empty his hand or break the jar—which means that he'll run the risk of spilling blood, *his* blood—Yao!"

"His own?"

"Yes, because if blood is spilled, some of it, one way or another, will be his own. That is the danger, but even though I warned him that seeking time's faded shapes is a *waste* of time he refused to listen.

"So I told him again. I said, 'The time you seek is *gone*! Gone like a long broken pitcher of the Navahoes, with pieces of it buried, some ground into dust so fine that it's blown worlds away, while others passed through the guts of migrating birds and dropped in far distant lands. That is the way it is, but in spite of all such shifty processes of time you still come here hoping to pick up the broken pieces. Aye, and I understand your need. You'd like to brood over them, shift them around, and bring them together. And you think, you feel, that if you could only put them together again you'll have some peace. That desire, that need, has taken you over like drugs and can prove just as destructive. For like I say it has set you in search for lost shapes of time and numbed you to the fact that time is to the doings of men as the air of a balloon to its rubber. The air gives it its shape and its ability to bounce, soar, and give pleasure to youngsters. Air is its soul, its ghost, its spirit, and when the air escapes through a leak or a puncture it dies. Then all that's left of its bobbing and weaving are memories stirred by the sight of its deflated skin clinging to its pale bamboo stick. And even though you manage to patch the hole you can never inflate it again, not with the same air which was its soul.' "

"Amen!" Hickman said, "and amen again. . . ."

"And the same with men. For when they run out of time they become like balloons without air, lifeless and hard to imagine as they were when they soared and gave pleasure. Memory helps, as do pictures...."

"Yes," Hickman added, "and the words of those who knew them and remembered the clothes they wore and the houses they lived in, and the things they did do and didn't...."

"Aye," Love said, "but the sound and the feel, the smell and the sweat of their living is gone now forever...."

"Amen!"

"...For now like the air of the balloon, the mind has left the body, and the rest, Hickman..."

"Is memory?"

"No, it's what you call *history*. For men live in time as they live in air, and run out of air they run out of time. But remember: Whether pure or polluted, air is always air and time always time. So while men come and go, time remains as the earth and the earth and the stars remain. And whether you speak of it as time-present, time-past, or time-future, Time goes on being Time—Yao! For that is the eternal joke of Time on the presumptions of man!"

"Now there, Mr. New," Hickman said with a slap of his thigh, "your preaching is leaning in *my* direction!"

"Just listen to what I said to the boy," Love said. "I told him—these are my words: 'For men exist as *men* only in time, and while they leave traces of their acts and beliefs behind them the meaning of what they did and did not do—Yao! *That's* the mystery that gets left out of what the State folks call history! You say that you're looking for peace of mind, but what the hell do you mean by peace? Is it anything more than a quiet spell in the endless struggle of living? An endless war that's carried on in this country according to a strategy of self-serving rules, stacked decks, and lawyers instead of bombs, cannon, and rifles?'

"I said..."

"...You told him..."

" '...Hell, boy, today this country is supposed to be at peace, and yet you, a man who has a fair share of the best of it, you come to me, a dispossessed man of the dispossessed People, all agitated. You returned here that way. From the outside you look like a healthy, wealthy young white man. Yes, but behind that gentleman-of-distinction expression of yours your mind is as jittery as a wild captured badger. A handsome, fine-furred badger that tries to escape its cage by loping around the floor in endless circles. And when it gets frustrated and tired it does side flips and begins retracing its path by turning barrel rolls over the same futile circles. Then it foams at the mouth and turns to pacing back and forth like a young circus tiger—only with you there's a difference, because while the badger and tiger know that their cage is outside their bodies, yours is in the mind that controls your body....' "

"...And that's how the corn pone crumbles and the eggs get scrambled!"

"True, and although I didn't like saying it, that's how it is. But I told him, I said, 'But it doesn't have to be, not for you. Not for a man of your appearance. Not in this mirage of a country with its ever-shifting shapes and confusion of people. Because except for the whirling in your head, the noise of ghostly cicadas, you're free to come and to go. You can fly here, fly there—and do it first class. You can walk where State Negroes like Janey are not allowed, say things which for them is too dangerous, buy in places in which neither their money nor mine has enough value. So as I say, you are free. But the real question is what is this freedom? What are its boundaries?"

"Now that's a good question, what is the answer?"

"Hell, Hickman, it ain't a thing in itself—as you damn well know—neither is it a simple, one-way process. Because freedom has a twin, and to make life more complex its twin is *Siamese....*"

"And the name of this indivisible twin?"

"It's Slavery! What the hell else could it be?"

"Talk to me!"

"And as I told the boy, 'The privilege of freedom comes at a price even for a man who's no longer shackled by all the color confusion that haunts this country. Because if you accept the fact that you're neither black nor white, Gentile nor Jew, Rebel-bred nor Yankee-born, you have the freedom to be *truly* free. Which is something much different from mining for the fool's gold that's supposed to be waiting at the cloud-hung end of the State folks' rainbow. For you there's the true freedom of choosing goals that are more human than most of them have the good sense to seek—Yao! And yet they laughed at those of the People who once used funeral hearses as vehicles for pleasure. They sneered because they couldn't see that the laugh, the joke, was on themselves. So unstrap your saddle and step back and take a good look around you. Then you'll see that the question of freedom is all up to you. You have neither to ride nor be ridden in this race of races, but you must make a choice. Continue racing in the way of the crazy State people and you'll remain like the badger, turning barrel rolls and pacing in a cage of your own choosing. Take the risks of identity that go with true freedom and you can be your own man. Then when your value, your manhood, is measured by the whiteness of your skin you can laugh as the State Negroes laugh whenever they decide to stand back and measure themselves and their ways against the myopic standards of others. And if someone happens to suspect that you're what you are because you once shared the life of States Negroes like Janey—which many white States folks do, even if they're too blind and stupid to admit it—you can be proud of being a pure, mammy-made, Janey-made American! Aye, and the son of a daughter of the People who was a beautiful woman of stature!'

"I said, 'So now listen and hear me: You stand on the edge, you straddle the line which divides the States people and drives them loco. That is your time-shaped advantage, and you should be proud and accept it. Yes, but with all that precious gift which human fumbling and time has left you, you go on letting your search for the answers to unanswerable questions act like a water-soaked thong that keeps shrinking your head in the heat of your searching, shrinking and causing your ability to deal with reality to run wild in your head....' "

Pausing, Love looked into the tree, then took a sip of beer.

"That was good advice and strong medicine," Hickman said. "In fact, so strong that you could make it as a black Baptist preacher. So how'd the boy take it?"

"Without a word. He just sat there looking at me for a while, then he left without a word. But he'll be back, and right now he's probably somewhere downtown with me on his mind."

"So after he left, what did you do?"

"I felt exhausted and sad— Hey! What the hell are you up to? Trying to be some kind of detective?"

"No, my friend, I'm only trying to do something for Janey."

"As a black Sherlock Holmes and me as your Watson?"

"No, as a minister, or as you say, a man of medicine."

"I know that, but what the hell else are you?"

"All right, so I was once a bluesman."

"Hell, I already know that! So what else are you, and how come you're so interested that you've been sitting here all this time listening to old Love run his mouth—Yao, and staying even when he takes potshots at your religion?"

Hickman laughed.

"And me thinking you were wearing out your vocal cords. So now I discover that you're still full of devilment. So all right, since you've told me something about yourself, I'm a father— No! I'm a *foster* father who lost a beloved son."

"That's better," Love said, "*much* better. And what else are you?"

Thinking, *He never lets up,* Hickman climbed out of the antlered chair and stood staring down into Love's challenging eyes.

"All right, if you insist, I'm a grown old man who's as confused in his own way as that lost boy of Janey's."

"Yes," Love said, "and even a heathen like me can say amen to that! But at least you learned something from all my talking. So now get the hell out of here, because as you States Negroes say I'm dry as a bone and beat to my socks. Then when you see that Janey, give her my heathenish blessings. And now that you've become my brother in medicine, when you know more about what the boy's up to, come back and *I'll* do the listening."

"I'll be glad to share whatever I learn," Hickman said. "And this I can tell you right now: One thing that I learned as a musician was how to listen. So when it comes to you I'll listen, and carefully, to anything you have to say. Even if it's again about that poor man and that melon. Because as one who preaches funerals and arbitrates family matters I *know* how terrible it was."

"Yao! And probably more pitiful than anything you've heard or experienced. But that wasn't my reason for telling the boy about it."

"No, but on my way back to Georgia I'll be haunted by what performing such a task must have been for the poor man's father. It must have been terrible."

"For all of us, the Chief, his wife, and the tribe. It was a devastating end to a very strange story. First the Chief and his wife lost their papoose to a child-stealing bear, who lost him to a white States man from the East, and after returning to the tribe as a fine young man he fell into trouble and was lost to the spirits.

"But I told the boy the Chief's son's story because I had seen the same feverish look in the sick son's eyes that I saw in the eyes of the States folks who flocked here to settle. Like him they had forgotten their names, or were trying to forget them, and they were breaking their own laws and taboos as they took over the land. So by the time the goggle eyes came they were ripe for the confusion released by the camera. So now the past has spiraled back to the present, and what has to be has to be. . . ."

"*What* has to be?"

But now, staring into the trees as though seeing a vision, Love did not answer.

"What is it that *has* to be?" Hickman said, and hearing no answer he arose from his chair. Then, seeing a drop of blood gleaming as it dripped from Love's nose, he reached for his handkerchief to wipe it away. But stopped by the thought *He's too tired to be disturbed,* he denied his impulse and with a silent *God be with you* made his way through the quiet of the house, out into the green of the courtyard, and on into the noise of the street.

Reaching the hotel, he picked up his key at the desk and joined a group of guests who were waiting for elevators. And among the passengers leaving the first car to descend he recognized the young white man who had been so attentive when hearing the old jazz fan address him by the name Big Lon. Then as the young man left the car and greeted him with a smile and a nod he turned to respond, but the young man was gone.

Oh well, he thought as the car ascended, *He's probably some young fellow who's interested in early jazz and thinks of those times as a golden age. So why not? Golden it wasn't, but it sure was exciting.*

Back in his room he stripped to his shorts, and as he washed his hands and face his mind returned to his visit with Love.

What an ornery little rascal, he thought. *The man's mind moves like an eccentric dancer and he plays with words like a mockingbird imitating the song of anything around it. Yes, and even when being serious he couldn't help playing the dozens with my religion and giving Negroes as much hell as he gave white folks.*

But whether he's a medicine man or not, he's surely one hell of a talker! Hickman, what are you supposed to make of a little fellow who says his blood is a mixture of black, white, and

Indian and claims he's a shaman? That's as confusing as an Afro-American claiming to be a Rabbi. Still, when you think about it it's no more confusing than a jazz and blues man like you turning into a Baptist preacher. So keep in mind that this country is a place that's so fluid, changeable, and mixed up that most of its confusion goes undefined and unnoticed. But thank God that even in this Babel of a country the blood of the Lamb comes in many colors and speaks in many tongues and accents. . . . A little black book-reading Ishmael whose hand is turned against State folks, that's Love. Still, he has compassion for that boy and a real friendship for Janey—should you call her? Yes, I'd better. . . .

When Janey finally answered the phone her voice was guarded.

"It's all right, Janey," he said, "it's me, Alonzo."

"Thank God," Janey said, "I hesitated to pick up the receiver because I thought it might be him again."

"Are you saying that he's been calling you?"

"No, but not long after you left I looked out and saw him standing across the street. Did you learn anything from Love?"

"Yes, I think so. But it'll take a while to figure out exactly what it was. He's quite a talker."

"A liar is what you mean, the old heathen. But I warned you. Did that white man go to see him?"

"Yes, he did, and Mr. New tried to help him. . . . But tell me, how can I get hold of Cliofus? Is he at home?"

"No, he's not! What you want with *him?*"

"I just want to talk with him. Maybe he can help me understand some of the things Love said about your visitor. Where can I find him?"

"I can tell you, Alonzo, but I don't think you'd want to be seen in the place where he works. . . ."

"What do you mean?"

"I mean that no self-respecting preacher would want to be seen in that kind of den."

"What kind of den?"

"They call it a nightclub, but night or day it's always full of lowlifers and whores."

"Well, and as you never let me forget, I've worked in a few myself. What does Cliofus do in this den?"

"You won't believe it, Alonzo, but he has a job of saying filthy toasts for those drunkards and telling them *stories!* Yes, and he makes pretty good money doing it. But if I hadn't raised him and took care of him since he was a baby I'd throw him out of my house for doing it."

"Did you ever hear him perform?"

"*ME?* I should say not! No self-respecting woman would *ever* let herself be seen in a dive like that. Besides, I've been listening to Cliofus run his mouth for most of his life, and since he's always suffered from some kind of talking sickness

I've had to live with it. But even the idea that anybody would *pay* to hear him is a sure sign that we're living in a brand-new Babylon!"

"I won't argue with that, but who does he work for?"

"......"

"Janey, are you there?"

"Oh, yes, I'm here...."

"Then why don't you answer?"

"Because I'm ashamed...."

"Ashamed of what?"

"To have to tell you that Cliofus works for Buster."

"And who's Buster?"

"You remember Buster, he's another of my little men. I raised him, but now after all I did to point him in the right direction he's operating that den of the Devil. And because he liked the stories Cliofus used to tell him and the others from the time they were little, Buster decided that they could make some money by entertaining the riffraff."

"Now, that's most interesting."

"No, it isn't, it's terrible! Although I do have to say that it's the first and only job Cliofus ever had."

"I can see your objections, even though they're both grown and on their own. Still, considering the stories I used to hear in barbershops, the idea is interesting. But in my barhopping days there was too much noise for that kind of thing. What's the name of this place?"

"It's called the Wind Cave, but I'm told that folks who go there regularly have a different name for it."

"What is it?"

"Alonzo, you won't believe this, but they call it Buster's Funky London! Why are you laughing?"

"Because hearing you say 'funky' was so unexpected that it shocked me."

"I bet it did after all your days of hanging around with such riffraff."

"Yes, but that was long ago. Anyway, Janey, I'd better hang up now and get some rest. Then I think I'd better have a talk with Cliofus about your unwelcome visitor. Meantime, keep an eye out for him and let me know what happens."

"And you be careful, you hear me?"

"I hear you, and so long for now."

Stretching out on the bed with his eyes on the ceiling, Hickman tried to make himself comfortable, but now his mind returned to Love's account of the ill-fated movie and its connection with Janey's young visitor. Did Love know about the terrible thing she had done to the young man when he was a child and about to be removed from her care? Probably not, otherwise Love would have mentioned it, or maybe he didn't out of his regard for their friendship.... And the young man—where was he now? Had he talked further with Cliofus, and did he know about Buster and the nightclub?

When the sound began he was cautiously climbing a steep mountain trail toward a point which offered the broadest view of the landscape below him. Beginning pianissimo, it was like the

[WINDCAVE]

HUM OF AN INSECT, *a drill or a buzzer, and as he continued to climb he ignored it. But now, just as the top of the trail came into view, the hum became a fortissimo roaring—whereupon he found himself spiraling feet first in a fall that seemed endless; and as he plunged downward he told himself to relax, to hang loose, hoping to lessen the impact when at last his body struck the earth, rock, sand, or vegetation to which it was falling. I'll probably be smashed into pieces, he told himself, but suddenly the fall took a horizontal direction and he was flying backwards along the landscape with a bounding floor underneath him. Then he was teetering on the rear platform of an observation car attached to a speeding passenger train and dancing desperately to stay on his feet—yes! But now as he grabbed wildly to steady himself by grasping the brass safety rail the rail flew away and he realized that with the train traveling at breakneck speed his staying alive depended upon his entering the car. And then, if successful, he would figure out both the reason for his fall and backward plunge into the unknown. Both answers were urgent, but for the moment there was no head-heel-toe of time for anything other than turn-turn-turn to face the door face face the door which was both before and behind him. And quickly, because the platform was narrow and the train's clickety-clack speeding so jolting that turning to face the door was like willing himself to move without moving. Yet turn he must, and as he bounced and twisted he was taken by a feeling that wrestling against the train's forward propulsion was as futile as engaging in a grappling match with an adamant bear. And as he lurched from side to side in keeping his balance, that image of his situation was becoming ever more real and embarrassing. Nevertheless, it was a case of do or die, and now he fought against the train's headlong motion by thrusting his right arm toward the door behind him in search for its handle.*

At first there was only the smoothness of glass and the coolness of metal. Now, *he thought,* now! *But just as he touched the curved shape of a handle the train lunged forward, and as he banged against solid steel the handle slipped from his hand and sent him reeling. And saving himself by leaping backwards against the door, he rocked and swayed to the train's pounding motion with the rhythmical clicking of wheels on rails sounding like the challenge of a disdainful drummer daring him to abandon the written score of a piece of new music and take off on a flight of syncopated riffing and swing the band to his personal rhythm. The sound was reassuring. And now, as he countered the train's rattling advance with a side-to-side swaying, he looked back to see the landscape wheeling past to become a succession of tranquil scenes which flickered and faded in the blue-cast haze behind him. And with the train bearing him relentlessly backward he thought with a sense of wonder,* These scenes I see are not the scenes into which I'm plunging, nor can they ever be again the "where" out of which I'm being carried, or the "when" that lies ahead.... *Then, bracing himself at a backward slant he reached over his head, clutching the top of the door frame with one sweaty hand, found the handle again with the other, gripped it, and gave it a tentative turn.*

But this time, squirting from his fingers like a wet cake of soap, the handle flipped free. And, annoyed at his failure, he wiped his hand on the seat of his trousers. Then, finding the handle again, he gripped it firmly, and with a grunt applied all of his strength in giving it a teeth-gritting tug. Come on, Come ON! he gasped, but though firmly clutched in his hand the handle resisted. Then, gasping for breath, he tightened his grip and tried once again, but still no movement. Then, giving a final tug of futility, he accepted the now obvious fact that the door had been locked from the inside.

And now, confounded by the sudden sound of dim laughter, he was furious and raising his right leg kicked backwards against the door three thundering times but heard no answer from inside the car. Then, in an effort to see if there were actually passengers inside, he gave a violent twist to his body—whereupon the train's headlong advance was suspended. Then the distant engine seemed to reverse its motion, causing the cars to contract like the retracted pleats of an accordion's bellows—until with an earthshaking roar the train leaped down the track and he was forced to save himself by hanging again on to the handle.

First he was flying along at a slant with his feet banging the platform, then squatting in the position of a Cossack dancer with arms stretched over his head. And as he held on he found himself looking back with a sense of dread as twin lines of track-side telegraph poles accented the landscape like an ominous parade of wire-supporting crosses.

This is awful, he thought, but since it seems to be the only way to wherever I'm headed then I'll have to hold on 'til I reach it...

Then, with a sigh, he began consoling himself by counting the crosses. But hardly had he begun than a tall, leafless tree loomed into view above the landscape, and at such a precarious slant that it threatened to topple onto the tracks. And there, sticking through a hole high at the top, he saw a small furry head which at first he took for that of a puppy and then the head of a child's teddy bear. But no, it was the head of a fox! A fox with its red tongue dangling as it peered below as though on the lookout for hunters and hounds. And as he looked down to see what threat of man or of beast could have chased a fox into so desperately high a hiding place, he saw a small child emerging from a tumbling clump of tumbleweeds and crawling rapidly toward the tree. Yes, it was a child dressed in a diaper! A child who now paused and, looking over its shoulder, disappeared into a hole in the base of the tree. Then from far in the distance came the lonesome wail of a whistle followed from high above by the eagle-winged swoosh of an airplane descending—which, approaching at an angle, swept over his head with an eerie, high-pitched whine—but how, he thought, can a child that small tree a fox? And the scene vanished.

And now as he stared up at vague shadows cast by an early-evening glow of street signs and traffic he asked himself the puzzling, blues-echoing question: Since you heard a WHISTLE blow, why were you buzzed by a PLANE? And as echoes of whistle and whine combined in a tremulous chord there came the clanking and sliding of elevator doors and with voices moving past in the hall raging in heated argument images of wild-eyed white men, black men, and Indians recalled from his visit with Love reeled through his mind—whereupon he rolled over and stared sleepily at the blue glow of the clock on the dresser and thought, *Thank God it was only a dream, but what terrible people for a man to have around when he needs them!*

Yes, Hickman, a taunting voice from the past said with a chuckle, *but remember that you were the one who was doing the dreaming and you never got a look inside that car. So while it was un-Christian for its passengers to ignore your situation, maybe the dream was your way of punishing yourself in the eyes of your enemies. That way you could punish anyone who might or might not have harmed you.... And if you really want the truth, that's it!*

But you know, he answered, *that I've always been willing to pay for my falls from grace—so at a time like this why would I dream such a dream?*

I knew you would say that! Why can't you face the facts without bringing me into it? The truth is that Janey's problems and all the changes you're seeing out here on one of your old stamping grounds has you feeling old and discouraged. So now you're punishing yourself for all those times you sinned against the dignity of your body at the expense of your spirit. Times when out of pride in your musical skills you'd cut comic dance steps while blowing your horn. Times when you amused the crowds by pretending to have so little body control that your trombone slide would become detached and go spinning into the air like a drum major's baton. And while it whirled cartwheels through the air overhead you'd pretend dismay and blow hysterical riffs on that Rudy Muck mouthpiece which you prized as much as Stackalee prized his magical hat.

And what did you blow in your clowning? I'll tell you: It was that vulgar "I Know Something That I Can't Gonna Tell You Blues"! Which wasn't a true blues at all but a childish piece of doggerel about somebody's backside smelling so loud that the gnats and flies were giving it hell!

Now you can admit that something like that was a mean, low-down, dirty, ungentlemanly thing to do, even for the you of those freewheeling days. So even though those dumb, condescending white folks didn't understand your signifying, it was still disgusting and unworthy, and you knew it! Still you kept spraying them with it, and then you went wriggling and twisting across the stage until you were under that tumbling gold-plated slide— which you were not about to drop—and caught it in what looked like a last-minute save from disaster. Then you snapped that bell and slide back together and ended your disgraceful act by sinking to the floor in a stiff-legged, britches-busting split! Yes, and with that trombone held high overhead and the poor, bamboozled crowd applauding your clowning!

All right, all right! But in those days that kind of caper was a part of show business, and if performers like us didn't come up with something that left them comfortable with memories of minstrel shows we didn't work....

Yes, Hickman, it's true that the minstrel show was alive and well in a lot of things, including the movies, Uncle Ben's rice, and Aunt Jemima's pancakes. Just as it still paid off for white performers to pretend to be black, and for Negroes to pretend to be blackfaced white folks pretending to be black. All that's true, but you were using it as a form of guerrilla war-

fare. Because you were playing with the crowd's reluctance to reconcile your dancing skill with your size, or your gifts as an artist with the negative rating they placed on your race and your color. That you resented, and in retaliation you acted the clown and told yourself that it was a way of getting back at them. So now as you say from the pulpit: In sinning against them you sinned against yourself and against all your people. Because in hiding behind your skin, grin, and antics you thought you were only manipulating their smug feelings of superiority. And like the hep cat you claimed to be you toyed with their mixed expectations like a black cat playing with a nest of mesmerized white mice like the ones that they use in scientific experiments. And when you took those "Thank-you-boss" bows in response to their applause you were anything in this world but humble. No, because behind your grin you were sneering with contempt and exulting with pride over compelling a bunch of misguided human beings to swallow a color and style they despised along with the slavery-based, mammy-made art they couldn't help but admire and envy. . . .

Hey, he asked himself, *where do you come off preaching me a sermon! And given what I was in those days, why should I have been more gracious than those who looked down upon me?*

Hickman, you're the preacher, so ask yourself. Because I'm only the self you left behind. But since you've been dream-shocked into enough humility to ask, all right: Maybe it's because your gifts and suffering should have taught you not mere forgiveness, *but insight into the pathetic pretensions of humanity—and I mean your own as well as that of others. But instead of reacting out of the deeper wisdom of the experience you inherited, that tough experience which carries with it the obligation of Christian forbearance before provocation, and a tolerance of childish vanity, you were pulling a two-faced act in the name of revenge. So you ended up committing an act of self-abasement. Then you told yourself that you were doing the world a service by feeding your enemies their own fires of destruction. What do the radicals call it—"boring from within"? Or was it construction by debasement?*

Are you through?

Yes, I'm through until the next time you disturb my rest with some crazy dream.

Good! But before you go, what was the meaning of the baby, and that fox in the tree? Who was I punishing with that?

Hickman, that wasn't punishment, you were putting that fox and baby to the same use you put me—which is to avoid facing up to what's staring you straight in the face. The rest is silence—go somewhere and relax, have some fun.

Sitting up, he looked about the room with a feeling of disorientation, then Janey's voice sounded in his head and he thought, How did she put what that mixed-up boy, her denied prodigal, had said? "If I find the one who gave me this color, I'll kill him." . . . Yes, and that was my cue—let me get out of here and find that Cliofus!

And now, gazing abstractly into the bathroom mirror as he went through the ritual of shaving, his mind went back to the time when he had found Janey mothering Cliofus.

And what a time that was, he thought. *I hadn't seen her for three or four years, and when I did it made me realize that not only had I failed to understand her, but that I didn't know the first thing about the basic female nature of any of the other women I'd known. Because long after giving me my walking papers I discover that not only is she still unmarried, but she's supporting five young children and they're all boys. And when I saw the youngest I was so confounded and felt so guilty over what happened between us that I wondered whether she hadn't taken him as a way of punishing me for not being acceptable as a husband. Not only was he the biggest baby I'd ever seen, but even for a baby he was so awkward and ugly that I asked myself if it were possible that adopting him was her way of signifying that he was the kind of child we would have had if we'd been married. Took it so personally that right then and there I decided not to see her again. Yes, but after seeing how well she treated the boys I changed my mind. Still, there was no way that I could ignore the fact that he was a strange baby, and while I had sense enough not to say it I doubted that she was prepared to fulfill the obligation she'd taken on. So I kept my mouth shut and hoped for the best. Then, three years later, I returned to find that he hadn't learned to talk, and that Janey had made up her mind that he was deaf and dumb. By now he was a giant of a baby and giving her twice the usual trouble as well—but, being Janey, it only made her more determined to finish the job of raising him.*

What was it, Hickman, a case of frustrated mother love? Her spirit compensating for her denial of your wayward flesh?

Who knows, it could have been—but by then, thank God, I had entered my ministry and was learning to wonder about such things, so I decided that whatever her reasons were for taking him on might have been she was managing to deal with him and her other boys—yes, and was keeping me informed about them....

Inspecting his image as he wiped the foam from his ears and applied shaving lotion to his cheeks, he gave himself a slap that erupted into a spasm of body-shaking laughter as he thought, *Then came that Thanksgiving Day dinner when she served the other boys a second helping of her fine sweet potato–yam cobbler and forgot to serve ole Cliofus—and what a mixed-up day of thanksgiving it turned out to be!*

She said it was then that the rascal spoke his very first words, and swore that when she heard him it almost gave her a heart attack! Yes, sir! And don't forget that when she told you about it she wanted to kill you for laughing. But what did she expect from someone with my sense of humor? Reminded me of the lie about the iceman's horse who could talk but wouldn't let on because he was afraid that if he did he'd have to climb all those long tenement stairs delivering ice and have some woman refuse it because it wasn't as cold as a white iceman's ice—wow!

Yes, sir! After three long years of playing possum, old Cliofus ups and starts talking— and it wasn't baby talk but in the polite down-home idiom she'd been teaching the others. And when he said, "Miss Janey, ma'am, I think I'm ready for my second helping of pie," poor Janey couldn't believe her own ears. But he'd said it so clearly that while she sat there wondering whether she'd really heard him, her other boys had got the message and were cheering and asking Cliofus to talk some more. Yes, and that's when ole Cliofus demonstrated without a doubt that he was neither a deaf dummy nor a mindless fool!

Because while the others were going out of their heads with excitement the rascal just sat there, crammed into that high chair and looking around as though he hadn't said a mumbling word—and it wasn't until Janey finally listened to the others repeating what he'd said and came across with more pie that he spoke another word. And when he did she was so sure she'd witnessed a miracle that she called in all the neighbors to witness it. And that's when ole Cliofus came into his own! Talked so much and so well that everybody who'd been saying that Janey had an idiot on her hands had to eat crow. And I mean with hot sauce!

Now let's see, he thought as he returned to the bedroom, switched on the closet light, and selected a shirt and underclothing from the dresser, *she always mentioned him in her letters, but the next time I actually saw him he'd grown into a clumsy, oversized teenager who walked like an agitated robot, and his small child's fascination with railroad trains was causing folks to treat him like some kind of harmless idiot. By then I knew that he was far from that and tried to get the idea across, but with our folks being no kinder to their own than other folks are to us he had to suffer for being different. Even worse, he had so little control over his mouth and movements that he became an easy target even for kids who were smaller than himself. Those were the days when every letter from Janey had a complaint about his being punched, teased, or forced to buck-dance for older boys. And that wasn't the end of it, because a few years later his word trouble had reached the point that he was making grown folks uncomfortable because they were afraid that his uncontrollable mouth might reveal things which he might overhear them say or see them do. Treated the poor fellow like he was some kind of unblinking eye of community conscience—what a terrible trial it must have been to find himself speaking the truth in all innocence of evil intention and having to pay for it! It must have been like having a mouth like a running sore, with folks fascinated by what you might say but being too repelled by the smell to really want to listen. For a youngster with a mouth like that the heaviest cross he could ever think of being forced to bear must have been a cross of unruly words!*

Then as he smiled at the confusion created when Cliofus decided to speak for the first time he shook his head, thinking, *Yes, Hickman, but as you have now come to know all too well, the WORD itself is a cross. And since even sacred communion itself depends upon our communicating through word and gesture, why should the innocent offspring of the Word be free of agony? And least of all for those who were given an unusual gift for using them? When old mouthy Love talked about that denied little man of Janey's going to Cliofus for information about his father he called him a "word-drunk oracle," but that's something like a copper kettle having the gall to low-rate a black iron pot for being smoky. So now just as I went to him I'm going to that same word-drunk Cliofus in search of a word or gesture that might save another man's life.*

Selecting a dark blue suit, he dressed quickly and made for the lobby, turned in his key, and left the hotel. Heading east on foot, he hailed a passing cab and asked the Negro driver if he knew how to reach a bar called the Cave of the Winds.

"Why sure," the driver said, "if you mean the one they call Buster's Funky London—would that be the one?"

"Why not," Hickman said, "since like they say, a rose by any other name—"

"Yeah," the driver interrupted with a laugh, "but it wouldn't be even *half* as funky! 'Cause I tell you, man—and you better believe me—*Jimson weed* would be more like it. Yes, sir! Because I've been there a few times myself and the funk was so thick that you could've cut it with a paper napkin!"

"I understand what you mean," Hickman said, "but, according to an experienced friend of mine, when it comes to good down-home entertainment, 'No funk, no fun' is the rule! Of course that was just my friend's way of saying that no matter what's happening the flesh still plays host to the spirit."

"Hey, now!" the driver said with a thoughtful glance in the mirror, "that friend of yours was *on* to something! Because no matter what's going down, whether it's work or play—yeah, and no matter what's being said by his mind and mouth—the rest of a man's body insists on speaking *body* language. Hell, yes! And you know something else? All this high-priced perfume you see in these ads ain't nothing but the extract of some overeducated *funk*!"

Hickman laughed, throwing up his hands before the rearview mirror. "Brother," he said, "*you* are a man with an educated smeller!"

"Who you telling," the driver said. "And while I might be yeasting the biscuit a bit, it's still the truth. Hell, man, those people distill that junk out of stuff like *whale* puke, *polecat* juice, *skunk* oil, *bear* grease, *snake* shit, *bat* crap, *muskrat* sweat— yeah, and that doggone Spanish *fly*. And by time they get through adding alcohol and flavoring it with sweetening—hell, a female buzzard could spray it under her arms and come up smelling like some kind of de-funked Miss America!"

"Hush," Hickman said, "hush, or you'll get us both thrown in jail for revealing classified secrets! What are the best nights at Buster's?"

"Saturday and Sunday, that's when that joint really jumps. But tonight's not bad if you like to hear some good lies. You ever hear that fellow Cliofus perform?"

"No, but I've been told that he's something special."

"And that's no lie. I don't know where they dug him up, but, man, he's *something!*"

"What do you like about him?"

"I like the way he puts himself into those lies he tells. When he's telling about something sad you can see him crying, and when he's describing something ugly he looks ugly and you can hear the ugliness in his voice. It's the same way with happy things and funny things, you can *hear* it. And when he looks down from the stage and sees how his audience is reacting it's like he's watching those words of his come alive. And it's like what he's telling is as new to him as it is to the rest of us. He swears that his words are in control of him, and damn if I don't believe him! It's like he's one of these spiritualists who claim that the spirits speak through their mouths...."

"Do you mean that he tells the future?"

"Hell, no! You think I'd go for that? No, it's not the future he tells but things that happened—or maybe should have happened in the way he tells it. By which I mean that he tells things in such a way that he takes the edge off and lets you think about them and even laugh...."

"Well, now," Hickman said, "I could stand some of that. I could stand a *heap* of that!"

When Hickman entered the Cave of the Winds it was hot and packed with noisy customers. Painted a deep blue, the room was spacious, with a high ceiling and circular walls that curved forward to embrace a performing stage which he glimpsed over the heads of the crowd. An elbow-to-elbow-crowded bar stood near the entrance, and in the dining and dancing area men and women sat with drinks before them at tables arranged to provide the best view of the entertainment. Aglow with lights, the stage reminded him of the many on which he'd performed in the old days, but since it was empty and the customers appeared to be enjoying themselves he concluded that he had arrived during an intermission and relaxed as he looked them over.

Warm and friendly, the room's atmosphere was alive with that tension of hopeful expectation which he knew to arouse the best efforts of jazz musicians. Yes, and the best revival meetings. For both shared some of the same hopeful anticipation of joyful fulfillment. And looking over the crowd for a familiar face he thought, *Hickman, what was once your worldly bread and joy is now your competition,* and decided with a mixture of relief and disappointment that there was no one present, whether churchgoers or old-time sinners, to recognize him from the old days. Most of the customers appeared to be working people, the rest fashionably dressed members of a younger sporting crowd; an impression which increased his feeling of lonely but comfortable anonymity.

Then, suddenly reminded of his dual mission by observing the presence of a handsome waiter with Anglo-Saxon features, he scanned the crowd's faces more slowly and was relieved that he recognized not a single "white" white face among them.

So, Hickman, he thought, *it seems that the confusion of social change hasn't caught up with this particular sanctuary, but what if the boy has been here and gone? Or is it possible that he hasn't learned about its connection with Cliofus?*

Squeezing toward the bar, he ordered a beer, paid for the cold, napkin-protected stein, and retreated to a spot near the entrance. Then as he sipped his beer, he saw a man in an invalid's wheelchair being rolled onto the stage.

Immediately a burst of applause erupted, and he was staring at a big, dark brown, bald-headed man who wore a white short-sleeved shirt, red fireman's suspenders, and the gray, black-striped pants that were once the favorite of old-time gamblers and jazz musicians. Below his trousers' flesh-bulged legs the man wore a pair of black, highly polished high-topped shoes, and he thought, *Not much of a costume,* then noted that with the rays from a spotlight playing around his head the huge man in the wheelchair sat gazing into the crowd with the dignified immobility of a circus fat man, or with that air of self-acceptance displayed by the physically deformed who are confident that they are of far more worth and interest than can be seen by the unknowing eye.

Then as the rhythmical applause increased he watched a waiter appear with a small table which he placed at the huge man's side, then shot offstage to reappear bearing a tray with a pitcher of ice-cubed water, a glass, and a white bath towel, which he arranged on the table with a flourish, gave a curt bow, and disappeared.

And now as Hickman studied the play of light and shadow upon the stage he was struck by the ironic development of the boy who had been the strangest of Janey's brood of little men.

So, he thought, *after years of being considered some kind of natural-born clown, he's found a setting where he's recognized as an entertainer—which I guess he's always been, whether he liked it or not. So through all the flipping and flopping of fate which set the rest of us running, HE ends up on a public stage, while I in my need am here to hear to him. And what's important beyond all appearances isn't whether he's now a stand-up or sit-down comedian—no, nor whether he should be doing whatever he does in a place like this—but what he might say that might cause trouble or save a life. That's what's important, and if I can learn what he told that mixed-up boy I'll be on my way to do something about it....*

And now as he turned to see a group of noisy customers entering the door behind him he thought, *Hickman, it's a cliché, but life remains a puzzle within a puzzle and a mystery within a mystery, and try as you can it's hard to predict what will happen or grasp what it means after it happens. Years ago you lost a son who was to be lost by a son, and now both you and the son of that son are trying to find him, while sitting up there in the spotlight is a fellow whose parents denied him both their love and protection because he was unlike his brothers and sisters. And yet, thank the Lord, he survived their lack of love and faith. And then comes the twist: They thought he was dumb, but while obviously strange he turned out to be an odd but exceptional talker. They thought he was mentally retarded, but he turned out to be more intelligent than many who put him down. For they approached him with unseeing eyes and listened to his speech with unhearing ears. Because in spite of their erring, both speech and intelligence were there all the time. And not only there, but just waiting for recognition in the form of a little love and understanding. So thank God that Janey took him in and gave him the love and encouragement he needed to accept himself and his world. Yes, Hickman, you're beginning to understand—maybe—but don't forget that he needed both a carrot and a stick to do it! And it turned out that the carrot was nothing more than a second helping of dessert! Like any kid he had to be punished before he could discipline himself, and after he started talking Janey knew that his way with words was a reward for her charity. So thanks to her faith and love this is what Cliofus has become.*

And now, as the applause increased in volume, he looked up to see the man who had rolled Cliofus onto the stage emerging from the shadow behind him with a smile on his face and hands in the air.

So this must be Buster, Hickman thought, *and what a little devil of a boy he was! With that liar's gap in his upper teeth and knots and sores on his head from protecting Cliofus from boys who tried to pick on him. So now that rough little rascal has turned into this smart-looking dude in a tuxedo!*

"Ladies and gentlemen," he now heard Buster call out from the stage, "welcome to the Cave of the Winds! And if there are any of you who wonder why we gave it that name, it's because this is a place of *good* food, *good* drinks, *good* music, *good* talk, *good* feeling, and plenty of all those *good*-bad winds of satisfaction that come and go with them! In other words, this is *the* place for the *good*-bad and the *bad*-good folks. And if you don't dig that, don't ask me, because I'm ignorant!"

"What you mean," a voice called from the bar, "is that this is a place for righteous funk-busters!"

"Yes, sir," Buster called, "and may God bless 'em! And that said, let's get on with the show. And now it is with pleasure that I turn the evening over to the Great Cliofus. He's waiting to entertain you, and you know the rules: Give him a theme and he'll take it from there. He'll tell you stories, he'll give you toasts as juicy as our good beef roasts. He'll give you speeches, poems, and orations—hell, if you want it he'll even give you the United Nations, discord included! He'll give you Abe Lincoln and Frederick Douglass, he'll give you Booker T. Washington and W.E.B. Dubois, he'll give you Franklin Roosevelt, the Happy Warrior, or the Sermon on the Mountain—but *you* know, and *I* know that that's not why you came here to the Cave of the Winds! So now the joint is yours to call the tune."

And as he watched Buster take a bow and retreat into the shadows Hickman thought, *That fellow would have known Janey's returned prodigal as well as Cliofus—so what if he's been to see him?* and broke off as he heard a gravelly voice calling out from the bar, "Hey, Cliofus, hit us with some *Shine!*"

And as he thought, *What! And with these women present,* and looked toward the stage to see Cliofus thrust his head in the direction of the voice and begin spieling with a machine-gun burst of words: "*You* shine, *I* shine, we *all* Shine-shine in the sunshine's shine!"

"Hell, man," the voice yelled over the explosion of laughter, "that ain't the Shine I'm thinking about!"

"And it serves you right," he heard from a table off to his left, "because after that you'll be wanting to hear some juvenile crap like the Signifying Monkey! Every time a man comes in here to enjoy himself some of you clowns are asking Cliofus for that or for *Shine!* Hell, you need to go somewhere and get *educated!*"

Me too, thought Hickman, *and the last thing I came here for was to witness a fistfight or a riot....*

Then: "Gentlemen, GENTLEMEN!" he heard Buster calling from the shadows. "Let's keep it cool! And remember, you don't *command* Cliofus, you give him *suggestions!* Yes! And then you wait to see what comes out. Cliofus is a man of *words,* remember? So now to get him started I'll suggest that he give us an account of his reaction to a visitor he had just yesterday. How about it, Cliofus?"

Watching Cliofus silently grasping the arms of his chair, Hickman stiffened, thinking, *What's going on in here?* Then, seeing Cliofus lean forward with a jerk of the head, he realized that the bright eyes were staring straight at him and thought, *He's recognized me! Which means that Janey told him that I'm in town and now both he and Buster know why I'm here....*

Then seeing Cliofus gazing down at customers near the stage he waited to see what effect his presence might have on whatever was offered the crowd. And now, sitting back in his chair and taking a sip of water, Cliofus began:

"When this fellow turned up those words started coming out of me so fast that I thought I was being hit by one of my worst talking spells—"

"...Now wait," Buster's voice said over the loudspeaker system, "hold it right there! And before you go a step farther give the folks some *background*—yeah, and some *characters*! Tell them where you were and who—"

"I was sitting on the porch drinking lemonade...."

"Good! And who else was there with you?"

"A stranger—or at least someone I didn't recognize...."

"Fine! So now we're getting somewhere! What did he look like?"

[WORDS]

"HE WAS TALL AND white with a sunburned skin, wearing a panama hat, a gray summer suit, white shirt, blue tie, and black-and-white shoes. He had a ring on his finger and a watch on his wrist, and white silk socks with thin black arrows for clocks...."

"What *is* this, Cliofus," Buster called, "a magazine ad? Cut the stalling and get on to what happens when the man hits the scene."

"What happens, ladies and gentlemen," Cliofus said, "is that my visitor gets grabbed by *words*! He gets grabbed by those confounding words!"

"Thanks, Cli," a man called from the bar, "but since we know about you and your words what did they do this time that's so different?"

"Tell him, Cliofus," Buster called, "and since there might be folks present who're unfamiliar with your condition, fill them in."

"Hey, Buster," Cliofus called over his shoulder, "are you going to let me do this *my* way or not?"

"That's up to you, Cliofus. All I'm asking is that you tell the folks what happened to your visitor, and *why.* Do that and I'm keeping quiet. So let's have it...."

With a quick look in Hickman's direction, Cliofus threw up his hands and said, "Ladies and gentlemen, and any *strangers* who might be among us, please understand that I have an unusual problem with words. But on top of all that,

Buster back there is always trying to tell me how to handle it! Which is like a blind man trying to tell an acrobat how to swing through the air on a flying trapeze....

"Anyway, the second my visitor steps on the porch I begin to feel a boiling inside which comes whenever my words start to bug me. So while I'm wondering who this man is, those words go at him like he's a long-lost friend and I'm sitting there trying to catch up with what's happening. And while he's smiling and listening *I'm* struggling to catch up. Which happens so often that Buster calls me the reckless word man. So before any strangers among you decide that I'm some kind of nut, let me say this:

"Ladies and gentlemen, you've heard it said that people misuse words, and I agree. But due to my condition, I'm forced to look a little deeper and recognize the fact that very often it's *words* which misuse *people.* Because frequently when you think you're saying something which you intend to say, what comes out is what the words stored inside your head *force* you to say. And a good example of that is what happened to a piano player who claims that when he's in his liquor he doesn't worry about how his music sounds because he leaves it up to his educated fingers, and that when his fingers take off he just sits back and goes along to wherever they take him.

"Which I believe, because once upon a time after he staggered into the biggest white folks' church in town they took off and got him thrown in jail for knocking out the Jelly Roll Blues on the God-box!"

"Hey, Cliofus," a man shouted through the roar of laughter, "I remember that! You're talking about ole Derby Brown, the piano player—but what's a *God-box?*"

"A God-box? Why, that's the great Fats Waller's name for a *pipe* organ."

"Now I remember," the man called from the bar. "It was in all the newspapers!"

"That's right! And that's another reason the judge threw the book at ole Derby. He told the judge he really started out playing 'Nearer, My God to Thee,' but his fingers got to swinging and he couldn't stop 'em. Made the judge so mad he gave him thirty days for breaking and entering, fined him fifty dollars cold cash for being drunk and disorderly, and hit him with another fifty for contaminating a holy instrument with barrel-house music!

"Which is a good example of how words can cause confusion. And in Derby's case it goes to show that even the words on a church organ's stops—such as *Vox Excelsis* or *Vox Angelica,* can get you into trouble. Especially if your fingers start messing around like Derby's did. And it doesn't matter that the organ stops are labeled with the Latin words for the voice of angels and the voice of heaven.

"So like I say, words can be tricky! But in *my* special case they can take off like I'm some kind of walking talking machine which was put on earth for their special convenience. And when they have their habits on it doesn't matter what *I* intend to say, be it ever so humble, because they just thumb their noses at me and come up with whatever they like. That's right! And although most folks won't admit it, it also happens to them.

"Words are so unreliable that when you really want to *communicate,* signs and gestures are about the only things you can depend on. That's because no matter what it is you try to say words can only *signify* and hint at your meaning."

Suddenly staring in Hickman's direction, Cliofus made the sign of the cross, then with a rapid play of his fingers followed with a mixture of the signs and gestures used by deaf-mutes and Indians.

"Better go slow with that sign language, Cliofus," Buster's voice warned, "or you'll make a mistake and insult somebody...."

"I'll take my chances," Cliofus called over his shoulder. "And that, ladies and gentlemen, is because I've learned that signs and gestures are safer than words.

"For instance, when you wave your hand at somebody, they'll know right away that it means good-bye. Throw a kiss, or hold out your arms like this, and even a *baby* will get the message. Yeah, but if you say it in *words,* watch out! Because right away you'll resurrect the Tower of Babel and have the grapes of wrath pouring down on your head! Don't laugh, because *most* words tend to be ambiguous, and damn near all spoken words end up as *double-talk!*

"Sometimes even the words you hear in church are spoken by preachers who're unable to speak the Word truly and clearly. That's why when the words are giving me a fit I often think of a mysterious line I read in a poem which goes,

> *The word within a word, unable to speak a word,*
> *Swaddled with darkness. In the juvescence of the year*
> *Came Christ the tiger.*

Then I wonder about my problem with words and remember stories about a little boy who was said to be a master of words and who preached in this town...."

Feeling sweat erupt from his brow, Hickman moved closer with the thought, *That was Bliss! But what on earth is he getting at?*

"Like I say," Cliofus said, "my words cause me all kinds of trouble, but signs are different. But in everyday life if you bow your head and smile, even folks who don't speak your language will get the idea and smile back—providing it's not a thug or a redneck. And ladies and gentlemen, I don't have to remind you that all you have to do is *whisper* 'peace' and that right away you'll have somebody claiming you've declared war and be out to *kill* you. And I mean with the first thing that's handy!"

Yes, Hickman thought as the room echoed with shouts of amusement, *but while he's praising signs at the expense of words he's also double-talking his audience by sending me one kind of message and them another*—and was interrupted by a shout of "Yeah!" and saw a tall, heavyset man struggle to his feet from a table near the stage and stand scowling at the audience. And as he strained to see what was happening the man turned, shaking with emotion as he bellowed, "Cliofus is right, and I'm here as his witness!"

"Aw, man, why the hell don't you take Bert Williams's good advice and go way, *waaaay* back and sit *DOWN!*"

It was a customer at the bar who swayed from side to side as he waved a hand in annoyance.

"That's right," a woman called from the other side of the room. "We didn't come here and spend our money to hear about your mammy-made problems!"

"Okay fellow," the big man called to his critic at the bar, "you just gimme a second, and when I'm through I'm coming back there and streamline your ignorant butt—you hear me?"

"Oh, I'm listening," the critic snapped back, "but all I'm hearing is a nowhere stud trying to get him some easy publicity!"

"Oh I'll have plenty of that after I'm done with you," the angry man called as he reeled and recovered, "but just now I want to tell Cliofus and the rest of these *un*-ignorant folks about something which proves what he's saying—

"Which is this, ladies and gentlemen: I've worked for this man I'm about to tell you about for over fifteen butt-busting years. And even if I do say it myself I'm damn good at my job! Anyway, just the other day my boss's wife was operated on for cancer. You understand me? It was for *cancer.* So on hearing about it all of us in the crew—black, white, Mexicano, and whatever—we felt sorry for the man. And naturally I felt even sorrier for his wife. Because . . ."

Pausing to take a quick drink, the man glared toward the bar. "Because while I'd never *met* the lady, I've been told that she has a cast iron—no, that ain't it. Forgive me. What I'm trying to say is that I've been told that she has a nice disposition—*very* nice—and a heart of gold. So putting myself in her husband's position, I felt real sorry for him and the lady. Yeah, but when I tried to show how I felt by asking him how she was doing, you won't *believe* what happened. . . ."

"All right," the critic called from the bar, "so what happened?"

"The cat jumps *salty!* That's right! Then after looking me up and down like he wants to jump me he changes his mind and threatens to *fire* me!"

"I *knew* it," a woman screamed with a glass rattling bang on her table. "Them folks know less about good manners than a rattlesnake!"

"But wait," Cliofus called, "wait! Let's get this straight—he did *what?*"

Swaying slightly, the man bowed his head, shouting, "You heard me, Cli! He threatened to *fire* me! And you want to know why?"

"Hell," the drunk called from the bar, "anybody looking at a stud like you would know the answer to that. . . ."

"Hey, you back there," Cliofus called, "let him finish! So now, my friend, why did he do it?"

"Because," the big man said with a throb, "he claimed I was talking . . . up under . . . his woman's . . . *CLOTHES!*"

And now as the room exploded with silence Hickman heard the musical gurgling of liquid being poured from a shaker, then someone broke the spell with a snicker which ignited a roar of laughter through which a masculine voice shouted, "I never met his woman, but I been told she—Lawd, Lawd, *LAWD!*" and the laughter roared even louder.

"Man, *man*," the hoarse voice called, "either you're lying like a lawyer, or that boss of yours is some kind of *mind*reader!"

"Listen, fool," the big man shouted, "this ain't nothing to joke about! He wanted to *fire* me—and still might do it—when all I was doing was being *friendly!*"

And now, muttering a curse, the big man took an unsteady step toward the bar, then, changing his mind with a wave of disgust, sat down.

And with a sigh of relief and a quick look at Hickman, Cliofus threw up his palms and said, "So there, quod erat demonstrandum, ladies and gentlemen, you have an example of what I was saying! The woman's husband couldn't hear *what* our friend here was saying simply because his *words* took over and put a label on *who* was saying it! All our friend meant to do was express his sympathy, but once *his* words landed inside his boss's head they hit the poor man with some simpleminded static and *colored* up his intention and his meaning! It happens *all* the time! So with words confusing human relations with that kind of crap it's no wonder that what folks call social communication is as rude, crude, and snafued as the words historians write down and call history. Words are the root of it all!"

Watching Cliofus sigh and take a sip from his glass, Hickman listened to the discussions set off by the big man's experience and thought, *I have doubts about his theory of words but he certainly has this crowd under control. And if I'm not mistaken he seems to inspire some of them with a freewheeling urge to make public confessions....*

"Ladies and gentlemen," Cliofus said, "I know what our friend is talking about, because for a man in my condition it can be even worse. That's why whenever I find myself in a tough situation I say to hell with words and fall back on gestures. But since I'm not always able to control my body even my *gestures* can make me look like a fool. Nowadays it's not so bad, but when I was a kid going to school it could be *terrible*.

"For instance, I was late getting enrolled in school because I was unusually big for my age and not very social. And while my foster mother had done her best to teach me good manners long before they let me attend school, when they did it made for all *kinds* of problems. Because while Miss Janey, the dear lady who raised me, knew that I wouldn't hurt anybody, the other kids' parents *didn't*. So that left me open to all kinds of tricks and foolishness in which my own ornery words took part...."

Seeing Cliofus stop abruptly and stare into the crowded audience, Hickman thought, *He's counting the customers.* Then, resting back in his chair, Cliofus continued in a voice which resonated with an undercurrent of self-amusement.

"Like the time when I was in the third grade and already so big that when I sat at my desk my knees stuck out in the aisles and my head so high that it made the best spit-ball target of anyone in the class. So there I was, when without a word of warning Miss Kindly, our teacher, points at me and says, 'Cliofus, *whooo* was the faa-ther of our coun-tree?' Just like that.

"So I said, 'I don't know, ma'am,' because I really didn't.

" 'You don't *know?*' she says. 'Then think a bit, Cliofus.'

"So with all the other kids staring at me like I was a fool I give it a try and say, 'Miss Kindly, ma'am, is it Him who art in heaven?'

"Well, when Miss Kindly hears that she starts to grin and tries to hide it, but she's too late because the kids have seen her. And right away all those outlaws like Buster—that's right, the same Buster, my adopted brother who runs this joint—and Leroy, Tyree, and Tommy Dee are already banging on their desks yelling, 'Cliofus is a dummy! Cliofus is a *pure* fool!' And Miss Kindly is looking at me real disgusted. Then she yells, 'Quiet, class, quiet!' and starts to frowning so hard that I'm truly confused and embarrassed.

"Then Miss Kindly says, 'Cliofus, it's important that you learn the *history* of our country.' Just like that. And I say, 'Yes, ma'am.'

"But being confused, and thinking she's talking about a *Mister* History who was also the father of our country, I say, 'Yes, ma'am, Miss Kindly, I'd be pleased to meet him, ma'am.' But even before the words get out of my mouth I know I'm up the creek without a paddle. And *doubly* sure when I hear Jack BooBoo Beaujack yelling, 'Hey, y'all, just listen to ole Cliofus! He's one sho nuff *bad* granny-dodger this mawning!'

"But although I hear him as plain as day by now I'm losing ground to those ornery words so fast that I hear myself saying, 'But Miss Kindly, do you think Mr. History would have time to be bothered with somebody like me, ma'am?'

"Not that I was being sassy, you understand, but being so big and clumsy I felt I was a living example of what folks meant when they referred to something as being what they called so doggone unnecessary. For after all, folks had been calling me a fool as long as I could remember, so in those days I didn't know whether I was or wasn't. And if I was I didn't know exactly what kind of fool I happened to be. I just figured that I was pretty lucky to be attending school with the rest of the kids. So you see, the words had betrayed me twice over, and now those fiends in the class were really laughing at me. In fact, it was like during a springtime recess near the last day of school and they'd already busted out most of the window lights.

"So when Miss Kindly hears my question she slams a book on her desk and yells, 'Boy, what do you *mean!*' I really didn't know what those words of mine would come up with. Then I could feel pain bursting out in the back of my head and everything around me started rushing away like a fast freight train leaving a tramp. And right in the middle of it all I could hear a voice that sounded exactly like mine saying, 'Why, shucks, Miss Kindly, I'm so full of history that even the *dogs* know about it!' And for a second I thought my words were playing a new mean trick on me. But then I realized that it was really Jack BooBoo Beaujack throwing his voice from the back of the room as a signal to those buddies of his to start raising hell. And ladies and gentlemen, if you think kids these days are unruly you ought to have been there!

"Next thing I know Buster jumps out into the aisle doing a buck-dance and singing,

> *Well, if at first you*
> *Don't succeed*
> *Just-a keep on a-sucking*
> *Till you do suck a seed!*

And before Miss Kindly can call for order ole Tyree jumps up on his desk and after spreading out his arms like a Cicero or Calhoun he yells, 'Friends, Romans, and countrywomens, lend me your ears: This here Cliofus is a big ape-sweat with too much *mustard* on his bun!'

"Then he slams his fist in his palm, frowns at me like he's a judge, and rolls back his lips and shows his teeth like a bad bulldog. And with the other kids yelling and acting up it was truly confusing.

"Because in those days an ape-sweat was what the kids called a certain kind of hamburger patty that had bear meat in it. So when outlaws like Tyree were eating hamburgers and didn't want anybody to beg them for a bite they'd wrinkle their noses and say, 'Hey, man, this damn ape-sweat is *terrible*' and eat even faster. But now they sounded like an ape-sweat was the nastiest thing they could think of while wrinkling up their noses and the other kids were scraping their fingers at me and yelling, '*Phew!*' and 'He ain't on *my* mama's table'—which was what they did when they smelled something that stunk like a skunk.

"Then Boo-Jack yells, 'Tell us some more, Tyree,' and Tyree flaps his arms and struts in a circle and starts pecking his head back and forth like a rooster. Then he frowns like a judge and yells, 'Honored brothers and sisters, and all you grand-mammy dodgers, Cliofus is a rotten goose egg and soft horse-apple!'

"And with that everybody started clapping and yelling, 'Yaaay! Cliofus ripped it! He ripped it! He really ripped it like a *foool!*'

"Then somebody hits the blackboard with a biscuit soaked in molasses, and a big baked yam misses my head and squashes all over the map of the United States which is hanging beside Miss Kindly's desk on a stand. That's right, but with all that insurrection erupting, all Miss Kindly was doing was glaring straight at *me*. The woman didn't even dodge! Then she yells, 'Young man, you march right up here and apologize to me and to the rest of the class!'

"But before I could even *move* Boo-Jack spoke up in his natural voice—which was already as rough as Louis Armstrong's—and said, 'Miss Kindly, how come you want Cliofus to apologize? All he's saying is that he's chuck fulla *brown,* and that's a natural fact. You don't believe him, *sniff* him!'

"And with that the whole class exploded, including those little twin sisters whose mama wrapped their braids in gingham rags so tight that they could barely blink their bright little eyes, while the boys were shooting cap pistols and bouncing blackboard erasers off my head.

"Then Boo-Jack yells, 'Cli's a good ole boy, but he's got no brakes or steering wheel,' and something slimy hit the back of my head and oozed like a snail down the nape of my neck. And when I turn to see what's happening a barrage of over-ripe grapes hits me square in the face.

"Oh, yes! They really had my range and were right on target. And with plenty ammunition, thanks to Boo-Jack supplying his outlaw buddies with a whole crate of over-ripe Concords which he swiped from a nearby produce house. So with me twisting and turning and them firing away I could see my white sweater turning purple right under my eyes. It was like it was being stirred in a big tub of dye and the sight started me to gagging. Because I dearly loved that sweater which Miss Janey knitted with her own dear hands. Then as though that wasn't enough of a disaster, I could feel one of my spells coming on—which wasn't helped by the way Miss Kindly was banging away on her desk. Because in spite of my condition I also had my sense of pride, therefore I would rather have *died* than be hit by a spell with all those clowns watching me. So I turned to Miss Kindly and held up my hand the way we were told to do when we needed to be excused. But then my doggone *fingers* turned against me.

"Because instead of opening they clinched and made it look as though I was shaking my fist at Miss Kindly. And right away I could see her face turn a deep gallish green. Then her eyes started to pop, and with everything around me growing dark I had a feeling of falling. Then I was lying in the aisle with every-thing around me whirling in circles. And as I struggled to get up I could hear Miss Kindly yelling, 'ORDER! ORDER!'

"Which she sure as hell didn't get, because by the time Miss Janey got the news and rushed there to get me the kids had smeared paste in my hair, poured ink in my ear, pulled the legs of my drawers out of my stockings, and powdered my face with dust from the blackboard. And when Miss Janey saw my condition she gave the school, the kids, and all the teachers hell!"

And I bet she did, Hickman thought as he joined in the laughter, *but with a class like that the teacher should have used a baseball bat. . . .* Then, seeing Cliofus hold up his hands for quiet he leaned forward.

"Ladies and gentlemen," Cliofus said, "did you hear what just happened to me? Here I start out to tell you about what happened between the words and a visitor I had just the other day, but instead I end up telling you about some class-room monkeyshines that occurred years ago. That's one of the ways my words take over, which makes me a man full of word who can't get in a word although he's doing the talking. So now from the way a certain distinguished visitor back in the rear has been listening I'd better get back to where I started...."

So he does know I'm here, Hickman thought, and moved from the bar to a closer position.

"At the time this stranger I was telling you about came up on the porch," Cliofus said, "I was sitting there—so to speak—batting at the flies around my rocking chair and thinking about our condition out here in this 'New Jerusalem'—which is Miss Janey's pet name for our state—and I kept thinking these words of a poet I'd read:

> *Bring me my bow of burning gold!*
> *Bring me my arrows of desire!*
> *Bring me my spear! O, clouds unfold!*
> *Bring me my chariot of fire....*
> *I will not cease from mental fight,*
> *Nor shall my sword sleep in my hand.*

"So naturally the words had to get into it and came with 'Till we have Miss Janey's Jerusalem / In this flat crazy western land.'... But while the words of the poet were dancing in my mind like gnats around the eyes of a hound dog this fellow came on towards me not saying a word. Then he stopped beside my chair and stood there, just looking at me. And before I knew what was happening those words went after him like he'd asked me a question they didn't want me to answer. And I mean before I had a chance to say Howdy.

"But like I say, those words didn't need me. They seemed to've been waiting to get out and didn't give a damn about how they did it. I know now that they'd recognized him long before I did, maybe by smelling him, or hearing him coming from a long way off the way dogs do. But even after they go to working on him I still didn't know who he was.

"And I should have, just by his standing there looking poker-faced and listening. Which alone should have told me that he was someone who knew something about me. Because with me sitting there weighing over three hundred pounds and talking all disorganized from the words taking over, a true stranger would have listened a second and then backed down those steps and cut out. Wouldn't even have taken time to tell me good-bye.

"But, no, this fellow was still standing beside me. And what's more, I could see definitely that he wasn't an insurance collector or a recruiter for some kind of religion. I was sure of that, because instead of looking like he was getting ready to scare the hell out of me in order to save my soul, whether I wanted it saved or not, or working out a strategy for taking advantage of a fool, his eyes were asking questions. In fact, even though those words were working up such a head of steam that they had me stuttering he's looking at me as though I was normal.

"Which is another reason I should have recognized him. Because from the day I first knew him and until he was taken to live somewhere up North he always treated me like I was no different from anyone else. But I swear, apart from those words I didn't know him from Adam—or Lazarus, which is more like it, since Adam had only one time to die while Lazarus had him at least two.

"So, having said that, I might as well tell you that this fellow had been gone from this town so long that I thought he was dead. But those words knew different and were going after him like he was a long-lost friend suffering from amnesia or the loss of his memory. So when I hear them saying, 'There was the big one in the union suit' I just wanted to get out of there and ease my mind by watching me some trains rolling for parts elsewhere.

"But instead of looking surprised at the way those words were going after him this fellow just looks at me with a funny expression in his deep blue eyes. And then as in answer to a question that had never been asked those words took off.

" 'That's right,' they said to this stranger. 'You know, the big one in the union suit. You remember Boo-Jack, the guy who got so worked up by seeing Miss Theda Bara smiling and blinking her great big eyes in a movie that he yelled, 'Hey, Lawdy Mama' so loud and urgent that he caused a panic? Boo-Jack, the one who was always as clear and present a danger as you ever would see, and I mean far beyond the faintest *shadow* of a shadow of a doubt. . . .'

"But even with such disconnected stuff as that coming at him all this fellow does is frown. And while I'm trying to catch on the words kept after him.

"Jack Beaujack, the words insisted. BooBoo Beaujack! You remember *him*. The big one, the burly one. The one the boys used to call Ole Sacka Fat, Ole Funky London, Mister Loud Fart in a Cyclone with a Derby On! Hell, you remember: Jack BooBoo Beaujack, Weinstein's Bear. . . ."

Suddenly Cliofus paused, taking a sip from his glass as he listened to the laughter. Then, looking back at Hickman he raised his hand for quiet.

"Ladies and gentlemen," he said, "at this point I'd better explain that in those days there were so many great big colored guys nicknamed Bear around this town that they had to be identified by the businessmen who gave them jobs. So there was Helpler's Bear, Ruby Lyon's Bear, Lowinstein's Bear, McDonald's Bear, and a heap of others. But Weinstein's Bear was the most notorious. You've heard talk about what can happen when a bull turns up in a china shop? Well, although he was from Chicago and had a Phi Beta Kappa key to boot, Weinstein had him a *bear* working in his *jewelry store*! This was the BooBoo Jack-the-Bear Beaujack that those words of mine were going on about. And until he was finally forced to fire him Beaujack gave Mr. Weinstein (who, incidentally, was an underground member of the N.A.A.C.P.) a lesson in what I'll define as passive resistance to honest, paid-for labor.

"For one thing, Beaujack wouldn't keep all those clocks in Weinstein's stock running on time. For another, he wouldn't keep all that gold and silver polished and shining. And then, when Weinstein refused to give him a raise, he bought up a batch of cheap rings from the five-and-ten and passed them out to his girl-friends and henchmen. Then he spread the word that it was some hot stuff which he stole from Weinstein's finest stock. So before Weinstein caught on to the fool, BooBoo had more green, brass-cankered fingers fumbling and sneaking feelies around this town than there're Okies in all Los Angeles. What's more, he damn near *ruined* Weinstein's reputation among the high-school-graduation trade, both black and white....

"So this was the Boo-Jack those words were whipping my visitor's ears about, and they got to him. Because finally he frowned and asked me, 'Where did he live?' And that's when I heard those words saying:

"'Where else but down in the Killing Floor section with the rest of the rough folks? Back in those days he was already a very famous character and was the same outlaw who threw his voice and wrecked Miss Kindly's class. Boo-Jack had a sweet tenor voice and could sing like a songster but liked it better trying to sound like Satchelmouth Armstrong with a bad cold in his throat. Once he grabbed your marbles, remember? Came storming across the schoolyard yelling "Snatch-grabs" and kicking up dust and striking unholy terror among the little kids by knocking them down just to see them falling. Made you so mad you just lay on the ground and howled!

"'You *can't* forget Jack BooBoo Beaujack! The fool and his henchmen had been stealing and drinking the Communion wine out of seven churches for three straight years before the preachers and members laid a trap and caught him. And when they asked him why he would do such a thing he laughed and said he was just testing to see if the grape juice had actually been changed into wine. Then he got sassy and said that he was teaching them that the only true and correct reason for drinking wine was raising hell.'

"Yes, ladies and gentlemen, and our distinguished visitor, I know it was out-rageous. But that was back in the olden days before the mayor hired those fine colored cops and brought some civilization to our part of town....

"Well, when the words told my visitor about Boo-Jack and the wine he gives a little laugh and shakes his head. So I said, 'What's the matter, you still can't remember Boo-Jack? If you can't, something terrible has happened to your memory....'

"'Mainly it's time, change, and different scenes,' he said. 'And the shock of re-turning. After all, it's been over twenty years. But nothing seems wrong with your recall....'

"'That's right,' I said, 'but I can't take credit for that because it's not my rec-ollection that counts, it's what I can't keep from saying. That's why folks call me things like the Talking Fool, and the Reckless Word Man, and tell one another, "Don't ask Cliofus anything, because he'll tell it like it is."'

"So he laughed and said, 'Does that mean that you always tell the truth?'

"'Oh, no,' I said, 'but the funny thing is that most of the time the truth man-ages to turn up in it. Maybe that's why folks take a gamble and listen.'

"That made him laugh, and when they heard him those words took off after his memories of the olden times. Said:

" 'Remember the little children sitting in rows, sniggling and snotting, snorting and stinking, and almost all of us knotty-headed, pee-pee-legged, and wearing corduroy breeches or gingham bloomers? And everybody stealing bites out of their lunch bags whenever Miss Kindly turned her back or dropped her weary old maid's eyes? All small, most of y'all, but with Beaujack and me the biggest in the class?

" 'Miss Mable Kindly was her name, and teaching unruly kids her city-wide fame. She talked real proper, rolling her rrr's and bugging her eyes, wore her hair rolled up in three big buns out of which the fat felt rats peeped where the hair was skimpy. She had a little bosom which was ironing-board flat and made up her face with so much powder and rouge that it looked like some kind of Anglo-African-Indian mask. Then she swore that us kids were outlaws and heathens and the burdensome cross she had to bear. That's right, and ole Beaujack did his best to prove it!

" 'One fine spring afternoon when he sees her taking a ladylike stroll dressed in robin's-egg blue, white gloves, and a pink parasol, Jack ducks behind a tree and yells, 'Cherries are ripe! Cherries are ripe!' Then, being a master whistler and ventriloquist, he thrills the air like a robin redbreast on the prod for his mate. Took me *years* to understand why his yelling about cherries got her so upset, but when Miss Kindly hears him it's like he's yelled her most *secret* secret business to the wide wide world.

" 'First, she jerks around to see who's putting her down, then her white-gloved hands start flying over her hair, her neck, bosom, and butt, and it's like she's having a spasm. And next thing I know she's cutting out of there in double-quick time, and her face had turned red as a maraschino cherry!

" 'Shucks! You remember Dust-mop Mable, which was what those bad big gals used to call Miss Kindly as they shagged their hot young nasties up and down the schoolhouse halls between classes.

" *'Oh, Dust-mop Mable,*
She swears she would if she could,
But she just ain't able!'

That's what they sang—and there she was, trying to teach us arithmetic and algebra!

" ' "What's the difference between a multi-*plier* and a multi-pli-*cand*," her question was—and shame on poor Miss Kindly!

" 'There we little heathens sat, looking all innocent and bland behind our second-grade desks, when Beaujack—who's being punished by having to sit facing the class—wakes up and gives Miss Kindly *his* kind of answer.

" 'First the fool lets out a sigh and slumps way forward in the seat of his chair, with his arms dangling like he's throwing a faint. Then he gives a heave and a grunt and does a gut-bucket bump. And like magic a big, hickey-headed pickle flips out of his fly, and the effect on Miss Kindly is damn near explosive!

" 'The poor woman's eyes stretch so wide it's like she's seeing the Devil come straight from hell. Then Jack aims the pickle at the electric lightbulb, and every eye in the class is watching it fly, break the bulb, and skid across the ceiling. And when it slams down on the desk and squirts juice all over poor Miss Kindly's hands she stares and lets out a horrified a yell of "Oh, oh, OH!," like she's been hit square in the belly with a baseball bat. Then she leaps backward—*wham!*— against the blackboard and the map; and before we can blink she's out in the hall, screaming "Rape and resurrection" at the top of her voice—no, don't ask me why, because "rape and resurrection" was exactly what she cried.

" 'Then, while she's throwing conniptions out in the hall, ole Beaujack is rolling on the floor and laughing like he's having a fit, and everybody except me is on his feet and roaring away like a football crowd on Homecoming Day.

" 'Oh, but then, filling the doorway like the Angel of Doom, there stands Dr. Peter Osgood Ellicot, our strict and respected principal. Usually he looks as majestic as a bronze general astride a granite horse that stands two hundred hands high in the air, but now his iron-gray hair is standing up on end, his bowels grumbling and rumbling up an earth-shaking storm, his false teeth rattling like a telegraph key, while his right arm stabs the air like he's wielding a saber and us kids are the enemy in a cavalry charge.

" 'Ole Doc's fairly foaming at the mouth, and before he stops to get his breath he's put the whole class under a combination order of quarantine and house arrest, charged all the boys with flipping the pickle, playing the dirty dozens in a public school, writing nasty language on the schoolhouse walls, and breaking his iron-clad rule against saying *spit*, which for him was the dirtiest word in the dictionary. And when he runs out of charges of misconduct he does a smart roundabout-face and rushes out yelling for his fearsome lawman.

" 'Then, before we can blink our bewildered, bugged-out eyes, in leaps the Right Reverend "Blue Goose" Samson with his razor-skinned head. And without a word of explanation he goes into action with that half-a-tree limb he was always dragging behind him. He doesn't say who, wherefore, or why, but before he's through he's not only whipped *Beaujack's* tough butt to a fare-thee-well, but the tender behinds of all the boys in the first five rows—and few of us knowing what it's all about or able to believe what's happening before our own dear eyes. I tell you truly, that was one day when Justice was not only stone blind, but deaf, dumb, and *vindictive!*'

"Well, that's when my visitor broke out laughing just like you folks are doing and said, 'I remember Blue Goose, he was the truant officer.'

"And I said, 'Well, it's about time.'

"Because he was right, and I knew right then that I had to catch up with all that action which those words were digging up and stretching out—but I didn't let on to him.

"I said, 'How could you forget him? When he used to make his regular rounds by knocking on classroom doors and saying to the teachers, "Miss So-and-So, you have any boys who need my attention?"—and he wouldn't take no for an answer. He'd just start to squinting and pointing like he was picking sides to play some kind of game, yelling "You . . . you . . . and you, over yonder on the aisle—get on your devilish feet and march!" Then he'd stand there trembling in his tan striped suit, brogan shoes, and that dusty brown derby he wore for a hat, while his snuff-colored eyes threw sparks like an anvil.

" 'Yes! And if the teacher said, "But not him, Reveren' Samson, he's a *good* boy who makes all A's for his grades," Blue Goose would tell her, "Is that right? Well, I aim to keep him going good, and what I'm giving him won't hurt his A's or B's a single iota. Because, believe me, ma'am, I don't aim to touch 'em!"

" 'And then for no good reason that we could see he'd march us down into the basement among all those pipes, urinals, and toilet bowls, and lined bottoms up with all our britches hanging down he'd lay on that strap—*strap?* Hell, no! It was a thick, solid rubber tire he'd taken from the pedal wheel of a big tricycle and it raised welts on our butts like alligator hide!

" 'Damn his soul! Damn his bald-headed soul to hell! Calling him Blue Goose wasn't much revenge, but it was about all the little kids could get away with. Sure, those fast, fleet-footed runners like Buster would wait under the viaduct for him to ride his bicycle over it and yell, "Blue Goose is a loose goose" and take off. Or on Sundays when he was preaching some would hide outside under the windows of his church and honk like ganders, but I could never move with enough control to risk joining them.

" 'Blue Goose was a holy *terror!* Why, one time he whipped China Jackson so bad that ole China ran down the railroad tracks home and came racing back with his daddy's forty-four and shot at Blue Goose six straight times, raising up steady and leveling down slow, and busting those caps like a young Jesse James—Wham! Wham-wham-wham-wham! Yeah, but he missed the snuff-dipping bastard every damn time!

" 'Because, you see, poor China was pulling the trigger with the barrel pointing at twelve o'clock noon instead of at three P.M. because he'd been watching too many of those shoot-em-up movies. Which was too bad, because if he'd only pulled the trigger with the barrel pointing at one he would have drilled Blue Goose a third beady eye; or if he'd squeezed it pointing a little bit lower he would have hit him in his spareribs or chitt'lings; while nine o'clock or three would have hit him in his heart and called right then for the undertaker to dress him in his last clean shirt. But it wasn't in the cards—Blue Goose choked to death on the glorious Juneteenth while nibbling on a catfish bone at a party.

" 'But ole China did much more than fire a blank, because when all that gun-fire erupted, Blue Goose took off honking bloody murder for a fare-thee-well. In fact, he ripped his britches, swallowed a big lip full of Garrett's snuff, and busted all the seams in his brogan shoes. And when he finally stopped running and found he was still in one piece he threw back his head and preached the Book of Revelation down on poor China's soul. What I mean is, Blue Goose put the badmouth on China and all his kinfolks. And *then* he cursed him the way that cruel old prophet, cruel Jeremiah, cursed those little kids who yelled "Go down, ole Baldy" at him. And as you'll remember, he had them eaten up by bears!

" 'Ah, yes! But China boy, while both you and Blue Goose are gone forever those bullets are still up there in the ceiling to mark your day of glory. A little snot-nose kid who lives up the street told me the other day that it was some Indians who put all those bullet holes up there in the ceiling. So I said, "Well, if that's the truth, then one of them had to be named Chief China Lee Jackson." And then I told him that he'd better remember things like that because out in this part of the country folks tend to make up history as they go along. Either that or they think that all the lessons are written in books and believe that everything happened the way somebody writes it....' "

"Hey, Cliofus," a man's voice called, "forget history, what I want to know is what happened to that cat in the *union suit!*"

"Now that's exactly what my visitor wanted to know," Cliofus called back with a quick look at Hickman, "and those words rushed out to tell him.

"They said, 'You remember the time Miss Kindly marched the class down to the Santa Fe crossing so we could see the great whale? Marching two by two, we had to hold hands, remember? And you held mine wearing mittens which were pinned to your sleeves with safety pins. It was a long cold walk for the littler kids, but with plenty new strange sights to see.

" 'Like when we came to a tall factory building where the shadow of wings was shading the sidewalk. And when we stopped and looked up there was this great big statue of an American eagle sitting on top of a globe. The globe was the earth, and while we stumbled ahead looking backwards and wondering what it was all about we could see the eagle's sharp eyes glaring like the globe he's sitting on is really the world and he's in charge.

" 'Then when we came to an ice-cream factory and Miss Kindly snatched us kids up the walk like she was herding cattle and us the rawhide whip she was snapping. And next thing we know she's hustling us through mouth-watering smells of roasting coffee and hot baking bread. Then after passing machine shops, warehouses, and other strange places we reach a little red shack with a tall smokestack which sat beside a railroad crossing with so many tracks that the city had to have a watchman to guard it. And way down there in the bowels of downtown we had our first look at the whale.

" 'He was rubbery and black and so big that it took three flatcars to support him, while the cars were covered with canvas that looked like seawater billowing with whitecapped waves. And lying there near the crossing the great whale looked as big as three locomotives hooked head to tail for a trip through the Rockies. But instead he's resting on the railroad siding, and not only as far from the ocean as we could ever have dreamed, but looking like a holiday float that got left behind during a holiday parade. Yeah, and so full of embalming fluid that the air around him was filled with a sick-smelling sweetness that at first gave us trouble in breathing.

" 'But that didn't bother Miss Kindly. She just made us gather around like she was about to lead us in singing "Praise God from Whom All Blessings Flow" while she gazed up at the whale with her head cocked to one side and her eyes looking dreamy.

" ' "Chill-dreen," Miss Kindly said, "now that you're enjoying the rare good fortune of seeing the great whale you must *observe* it!" and we stood there with our heads thrown back as though the great whale was floating like a dirigible two miles in the air.

" ' "See the great whale, chill-dreen," Miss Kindly said, and we answered, "Yes, ma'am, Miss Kindly, we sees him, ma'am," and stood there gawking with our eyes bugged out.'

" 'Oh, no!' said my visitor, but the words kept going.

" 'Remember how the great whale had lightbulbs suspended above him from head to tail, and the two big red ones which stuck out of the sockets where his eyes had been? With one bulging from the right side of his head and the other so far on the left that we had to take a walk to find it? And how all those rope-dangling harpoons stuck in his hump trembled whenever a truck rolled past? And how a little girl giggled and said, "Why, he looks like a giant pincushion with knitting needles sticking in him"? Yeah! But great God-a-mighty, what a hell of a catch he'd have been for a catfish fry!

" 'But Miss Kindly had other things on her mind. Because after she let us study the whale for a while she gets real frisky and comes on with some teaching.

" ' "As you can see, chill-dreen," Miss Kindly said, "the great whale is made of blubber."

" ' "Yes, ma'am," we said, "us sees all that rubber."

" 'And then Miss Kindly arches her eyebrows and puckers her lips like she's sucking a lemon as her hand falls backwards in a limp-wristed flip.

" ' "The whale, chill-dreen," Miss Kindly says, "is an ani-mule—do you understand?" So in unison we all chime in and say, "Yes, ma'am, Miss Kindly, whales is *ani*-mules!"

" ' "That's right, chill-dreen," Miss Kindly says, "and therefore little whale babies are nursed on the good rich milk of their mothers! Isn't that wonderful?"

" ' "Yes, ma'am," we say, trying not to giggle, "good rich fish milk is good for whale babies—yes, ma'am!"

" ' "That's very good," Miss Kindly said. "And now, who would like to ask a question about our great big beautiful whale?"

" 'But while she's fishing for an answer she doesn't get a bite. So while we all look dumb and try to think up some questions Miss Kindly arches her eyebrows and makes big-eyes at the whale and starts prancing back and forth while looking as proper as the Queen of Sheba.'

"By the way, ladies and gentlemen, Miss Kindly was a fool for classical music, tea parties, and high-class manners, especially for the girls. So when nobody comes up with a question all of a sudden she struts back and forth and drops her handkerchief on the cinders right in front of me. And when a little girl in an apple-green dress reaches down to pick it up Miss Kindly stamps her foot and sings out in a voice as high as a flute, 'Nu-nu-nu-nu NU!' Then she stamps her foot again and that little gal freezes like she's been blasted by a blood-chilling wind.

"Then, looking as bossy as Queen Victoria, Miss Kindly points straight at me and says, 'Let *heem* pick it up, for *you,* my deah, are uh *lay-dy!*'

"And so I stoop down to get it, but being big and clumsy I land in the cinders flat on my face and have to listen to all the snickering around me until Miss Kindly goes back to picking on that poor embalmed whale.

" 'Well, chill-dreen,' Miss Kindly says, 'I'm still waiting for questions—so use your imagine-*naay*-shons!'

"And that's when a little high-butted, freckle-faced, mariney-colored son-of-a-gun named Bernard ups and volunteers.

"He says, 'Yes, ma'am, Miss Kindly, I got me one,' and Miss Kindly's eyes light up like a Christmas tree.

" 'Now that's veeer-ree, veeery good,' Miss Kindly sings, 'because we learn by asking *questions!* And indeed I'm most disappointed that after this marvelous wonder of nature has been brought all the way from the ocean for your instruction you chill-dreen have asked so *few* questions about our great big wonderful whale! So now I want you to listen to Bernard and learn from his enriching curiosity. As you know, Bernard is *highly* intelligent. So now speak up, Bernard— what is your question?' And ole Bernard really puts it to her.

" 'Now Miss Kindly,' he says, 'if that there whale is an *animal* what gives rich *milk,* what I want to know is: Where do she carry her *tits?*' "

Pretending to be surprised by the outburst of laughter, Cliofus sighed. "Ladies and gentlemen," he called, "when those words came up with that I had no idea of what my *visitor* was thinking, but *I* was relieved that ole Bernard hadn't asked Miss Kindly the meaning of '*sperm.*' Anyway, the words went on to explain that when ole Bernard asks her about the whale's tits, Miss Kindly reacts like he's turned into a twelve-foot monster with horns on his head. And him looking like he's demanding an answer!

"But luck is with him, because just then the door to the little red shack with the tall smokestack that was used by the guard in charge of the crossing bangs open. And before Miss Kindly can scream, faint, or kick Bernard's butt, out steps a little old white man, and in his mouth there's a corncob pipe turned upside down. And as we stare in wonder at his being there he picks up something that looks like a spear dangling on a rope and comes hobbling toward us on a short wooden leg.

"He's about four feet tall, has eyes like an eagle, and wears a blue sailor suit that's seen better days with a fisherman's hat that's ancient. And when he finally makes it to where we're standing, right away he's telling Miss Kindly in Yankee talk that not only do us kids owe him a nickel apiece for just *looking* at the whale, but ten cents more for listening to the lecture he's about to give us about the history and habits of the great sperm whale.

"So maybe being glad to avoid answering ole Bernard's question, Miss Kindly gives the little man the money and he's off and running.

"First he tells us that catching the great whale was as easy as digging for crawdads or falling off a log. Then he turns right around and swears that after he harpooned the whale from his boat and got dragged through foaming seas for two hundred miles and a quarter, the whale jumped salty, knocked a hole in his boat, and bit off his leg. And while we stood there listening with our mouths gaped wide he swore he'd given the whale such a fight that he was still able to land him. Then he threw back his head and sang us a solo. Something about us kids being cheerful and not having heart attacks when we watched a bold harpooner like him go after a whale! And he ends up by dancing a wobbly jig on his old wooden leg.

"Which we enjoyed. But while some of us are still undecided about his really catching the whale, Miss Kindly bugs out her eyes and asks him to do some more lying!

"So now while he hobbles from the poor whale's head to his tail, and around and about and back again, we have to listen to him lie a mile a minute about Jonah, whale oil, the whalebone used in women's hairpins and corsets, and about carving scrimshaw ivory and other stuff. Such as Eskimos and igloos, polar bears and Arctic seals, whaling ships and American history. Then he goes and gets a big sticky-looking hunk of something he swears to be ambergris. We'd never heard of the stuff, but it looks and smells like something he'd fetched up from the profoundest depths of the sea and should have been left right where he found it. And sure enough, when he passes it around he makes the mistake of going too far for some of us children.

"Because after ole hoarse-voiced Tyree wrinkles up his nose and gives it a real close inspection he lets out a protest that's so loud and contentious that everybody halfway to the capital can hear him.

" 'Hey, y'all,' he says, 'y'all can believe what you want to, but far's *I'm* concerned that there stuff ain't nothing but whale puke! And I don't care *what* that white man says about it!'

"And here the man had just explained that the stuff was worth ten times its weight in gold and was used in making the very finest of high-priced perfume! But while the little man stands there trembling on his wooden leg and looking at Tyree like he wants to kill him, Miss Kindly swallows whatever it is, hook, line, and sinker.

" 'Now, isn't that *amazing*, chill-dreen,' Miss Kindly says. And to keep the peace we all chime in with a loud, 'Yes, ma'am, Miss Kindly, we 'mazed.'

"And while Miss Kindly is beaming and cooing, the little man hobbles to the shack and pulls a switch, and the next thing we know the great high-headed whale is winking and blinking his lightbulb eyes.

" 'Now, isn't that wonderful,' Miss Kindly says. 'Observe the great whale's eyes and see how they're *blinking*! Which proves that whales are not a fish, but ani-mules!'

" 'Yes, ma'am, Miss Kindly,' we all chime in, 'we sees him winking his great big bulbs....'

" 'And therefore, chill-dreen,' Miss Kindly says, 'how do we classify this wonder of nature which is known as the great sperm whale?'

"And that's the start of a great argument; with some saying he's a fish, some a blubber mule, and with others insisting that he's either a great sea elephant or an animal-eyed fish. Which has Miss Kindly's head swinging on her neck like a pendulum.

"Then, as the little man watches some boys fighting over the true nature of the whale he takes him a chew of Brown's Mule tobacco. And after chewing it a while he spurts a stream of tobacco juice that's so hot that it steams when it hits the cinders. Then he ducks under the whale on the flatcar and gives a twist to some kind of valve. And the next thing we know water is spouting from a hole in the top of the great whale's head and coming down like spray from a fountain. And while Miss Kindly is outrunning the fastest runners in the class in a dash for cover the little man is waving his harpoon in a rainbow of spray, whooping and yelling, 'Thar she blows!' "

Joining in the laughter, Hickman watched Cliofus take a sip of water and shake his head. And with customers pounding the tables and stomping the floor he thought, *Who would believe that* anyone *could get away with stuff like this in a nightclub!*

[STATION]

"AND NOW, LADIES AND gentlemen," Cliofus said, "if you're wondering what my visitor was doing while those words were bending his ears, I'll tell you: He was laughing, and I mean in a genuine down-home style. In fact, he sounded like a home-boy. And while I'm wondering how someone like him came up with a laugh like that, he offers me a cigarette. So, since I don't smoke, I thank him and tell him to go ahead. But after taking a puff he starts laughing and coughing on the smoke. And next thing I know he's sitting on the porch crying like a baby and shaking his head. And when I ask him what's happening he just looks at me. Then he sighs and says real sad, 'It's the *whale*, Cliofus. It's what happened to the whale!'

"Then he gets real emotional and says, 'One of the prime wonders of the animal kingdom, out here, thousands of miles from the ocean, stranded on a flat-car with his natural eyes replaced by *lightbulbs!* And as though *that* wasn't enough of a crime against nature, a little con man of a railroad watchman sees the whale and decides to make a few nickels and dimes out of anyone who'll pay for listening to his cock-and-bull rant about whales. Then to make his scam more effective he connects the whale's lightbulb eyes to a power line, uses a water hose to connect the poor animal's airhole to a fire hydrant, and lays in wait for his victims. Among the first of whom turn out to be a bunch of little kids and their teacher. And after snatching their nickels and dimes he's off and lying like a circus barker.

" 'But when some of the kids turn out to be too smart to accept some of the things he tells them, he reacts by opening the valve that's connected to the whale's head and punishes the whole class by making it appear that the long-dead animal is spouting them with spray from its airhole—good Lord!'

"He really sounded sad, but right away he mumbles something about innocents refusing to be slaughtered and starts laughing and crying again. Then he asks me what Jack the BooBoo Beaujack was doing while the whale was spouting, and before I can get my memories together the words took over.

"They said, 'Hey! Don't you remember *that?* When the little one-legged man made the great whale spout we ran down the tracks a-ways to escape the spray. Then as we watched the rainbow it made in the air we see Miss Kindly herding the class back to school and decide to play a little hooky. And with me being a fool for watching railroad trains and the Union Station just up the tracks from the whale, we decide to be there when my number one favorite, the Santa Fe Chief, comes rolling in.

" 'So we get to the station, and who do we see in the crowd of passengers and red-capped porters but Jack the BooBoo Beaujack, who's doing his thing. With his mother and his teenage sisters, he's standing smack in the middle of the crowd, and we're just in time to see him throw back his head and yell, "Here we is in the Union Station, and we all dressed up in our *union* suits!"

" 'That's right! Standing in the center of all that hot public space the fool's talking up under the clothes of his own dear mother and his sassy big sisters! And when his poor mother sees passengers stopping to stare and porters scowling like they're trying to decide who to kill first, Beaujack or a big white man who's pointing at his mother and laughing, she's so shocked and embarrassed that she damn near dies!

" 'But that doesn't stop ole BooBoo, because by now he's reading off the station's billboard signs like some kind of a runaway foghorn that's done gone on a toot:

FINANCIALLY EMBARRASSED?
SEE HARRIS THE BANKER.

RADIATOR LEAKY?
SEE PUCKETT, THE TINKER!

FEELING RUN DOWN AND OUT OF LINE?
FEEL FINE WITH BEEF IRON & WINE!

LADIES, DO YOU HAVE BEARING-DOWN PAINS?
LYDIA E. PINKHAM'S IS THE ANSWER!

LOSE THAT OLD BLOATED FEELING,
THAT PAIN IN THE HEAD WITH BROMO QUININE!

CHEW BROWN'S MULE TOBACCO!

DRINK BEVO, THE SPARKLING BEER!

" 'Then he points his finger and yells, "Look a-yonder, Ma, that one over there reads Carter's Little Liver Pills! Hey! Mine's kinda little, so maybe I could use me some...." '

"So with that my visitor asks me a question which I don't hear. Because all of a sudden I realize that after starting out with Jack upsetting Miss Kindly by flipping his pickle, the words had reduced him in age and in size. So naturally I'm puzzled, because there was no way in the *world* for the BooBoo in the station to have been the size he was in the classroom. Not if my visitor was actually the kid who'd been with me at that time. Anyway, with those words building up steam there wasn't time to figure it out. So while my visitor listens with tears in his eyes they began filling him in on Jack the BooBoo Beaujack's mother.

"They said, 'Now, Jack's poor mama was truly peacock-proud of his being able to read so good, but with him proclaiming those cures for ladies' bodily complaints and his sisters blushing and giggling, she claps her hand over his mouth, and next thing we know she's rushing him and his sisters out to the street.

" 'So with that excitement come to an end we hurry out to the platform that faces the tracks just in time to see that Santa Fe Chief come rolling in. And that's when we spy this man who's leaning out of a dining-car window with a fat greasy bag in his great big hands.

886 · Three Days Before the Shooting . . .

" 'Dressed in a white cook's jacket and a tall chef's cap, he's the one who kicked a waiter by the name of Sam Shagwaugh square in the butt for saying that he had hands so big that if either one was baked and served with sliced pineapples and a light-brown sauce it would look so real that anyone would think it was the ham on the menu which had been misspelled S-m-i-t-h-f-double-e-l!

" 'Now, this handy ham-man was Mister Big Smith the chef, who was the number one cook on the Santa Fe Chief, and he's looking out the window for his pretty little wife and his six little children. Then, as the Chief rolls closer, a commotion breaks out in the crowd behind us and we see six little boys pulling little red wagons come bursting through the door. There's a lady dressed in blue right behind them, and when they spy Mister Big Smith holding that big greasy bag they let out a cheer like it's already Christmas and he's Santa Claus. Then the train comes to a halt and they all run to greet him, and when we draw closer we see Mister Big Smith look his missus in the eye and start laying down some jive.

" 'He says, "I brought it to you, baby, all the way from Chi!"

" 'To which his little missus bats her big brown eyes and says, "Oh, you did, did you darling? Well, now, that'll make the crackers more crumb-rum-bumbling and the cheese taste fine! But how come you treating me so gentlemanly kind?"

" 'To which Mister Big Smith smiles and says, "It's because I loves you, baby, better than I do my handsome self."

" 'To which Missus Big Smith then replies, "But that's "how it's supposed to be, considering that all these hungry younguns truly happen to be ours."

" ' "They sho is, baby," Mr. Big Smith says, "and that's exactly how come I brought it all the way from dear ole *Chi*."

" 'At which the six little children start to licking their lips with a gleam in their eyes.

" 'And that's when Mister Patrick O'Sullivan, the Santa Fe Chief's chief steward, sticks his red head out of a window with his Irish up.

" ' "Tell me something, Smith," the chief steward says, "how could you bring it *from* Chicago when we both know damn well that it was already sitting in the freezer on our way up North? Aye, and begorra, it was there and getting bigger on the morning we arrived!" And when we hear him squawking in that angry tone of voice we almost run for cover.

" 'But we don't, because with Mister Big Smith's madam and boys all standing there listening we're much too curious as to what will happen next. So we move a little closer, and when we hear it we have visions of a race riot breaking out.

" ' "Man, what the hell you talking about?" Mr. Big Smith says. "Why, you make this Santa Fe's Chief sound like some kind of one-hoss, one-way line— which it sho to hell ain't! Therefore like I say, I brought it here from Chi! Which even *you* ought to know is the boar-hog's special hangout and the she-pig's grazing ground. And besides all that, why else would I be slaving on this railroad 'lessen it's to fill all these hungry bellies which I swore to God I'd feed?"

" 'Then, turning ruby red and blinking his eyes, the chief steward says, "Just exactly what the Santa Fe railroad has to do with how you spend your nights at home is too much of a riddle even for a traveling man like me—but if you have an honest answer you'd better let me have it!"

" 'And that's when Mister Big Smith starts preaching him his answer in a deep bass-baritone.

" 'He says, "When you hired me for this job, didn't you insist you had to have a man who was *fast* with his hands and *steady* on his feet?"

" 'And the chief steward glares and says, "That's right!"

" ' "Well that's *me*," Mister Big Smith says, and to which the six little children yell a loud "Amen!"

" ' "And didn't you say you wanted a *strong* man who could swing and sway like What's-his-name on the radio and bring it in the cold of December and the heat of July?" Mister Big Smith says.

" ' "That I did," the chief steward says, "that I did...."

" ' "And in the light of day and the dark of night?"

" ' "Right!"

" ' "And in Kansas windstorms, Oklahoma sleet, and in all that hellish Texas heat?"

" ' "Right again," the chief steward said, "that's the man this line requires!"

" ' "Well, so you got him," Mister Big Smith says, "cause *I'm* that man!" And the six little children yell, "AMEN!"

" 'Then, trying to switch the argument back on the track where it started, the chief steward holds up his hand to get him in a word. But Mister Big Smith won't let him do it, not even edgewise.

" ' "Naw," Mister Big Smith tells him, "you started this mess so now *I'm* gonna finish it: You said you wanted a *family* man who'd be forced to keep on the job and stay on the ball—and that's *got* to be me! Take a look at all those kids down there, every damn one has a gut as vicious as a tiger...."

" ' "...And grinning like they were truly tiger cubs, the six little children yell, "*Aaa-men! Aaa-men!* And agin *Aaa-men!*"

" ' "What's more," Mister Big Smith says, "they have to have clothes and the other necessaries! Like schoolbooks, pencils, and yellow writing pads! And pretty soon they'll have to take off and go to *college!*"

" ' "They'll have to do WHAT?" Chief O'Sullivan cries, and he stares down at the crowd like Big Smith's either telling lies or hitting him with a corn shuck that's steaming hot and nasty.

" ' "You heard me, man," Mister Big Smith says, "just like those kids of your'n they have to git to college! That's how come I have to skimp like hell and lay away the cash!"

" ' "Well, I'll be damn'," Mister Pat O'Sullivan says, and as he stares at Big

Smith's kids he starts to tremble. Then his eyes stretch wide like he's been hit with a vision of train wrecks, arson, and national disaster.

" 'Then he stares at that big greasy bag in his chief cook's hands and says, "Dammit, Smith, I've been waiting to hear the connection between what you're saying and what you have stashed in that *bag*! So now tell me in plain English, what the hell is it?"

" ' "If you need more of an answer," Mister Big Smith says, "that's up to you. Because since you were smart enough to hire a man who's loaded down with all this weight *I'm* carrying, then you ought to know without being told that he's got to make ends meet so his family can eat, and his kids can be strong enough to face up to the future! So now I repeat, this here greasy bag and all what's in it is *mine,* yeah! And I brought it all the way from what you call *Chur-caa-ga*!"

" 'So by now the chief steward's idea of geography is so warped and scrambled that he can't tell north from south. And with all those college degrees and dollar signs whirling in his head all he can do is stare and stammer like he's up and lost his mind. While Big Smith, who's blasted the poor man's logic with his different point of view, stares back with a look of firm conviction in his eyes.

" 'Then we see the chief steward start looking uncertain as he tries to find a flaw in Big Smith's argument, but it gets him nowhere. Because pretty soon his body starts to sag and his face begins to quake, and all at once he's grinning like a possum with a bad toothache. And with that we see Mister Big Smith give his six little tigers a wink and a grin. Then he slaps Chief O'Sullivan on his back and whispers in his ear. And the next thing we know they're laughing and wheezing and pressing the flesh, and it's like watching a couple of close soul buddies out on a spree. So with that, after they'd engaged in a war of words and had us thinking that the next step would be a hard-fought, head-knocking, butt-kicking Battle of the Greasy Bag, it was done and over—or at least reached a truce....' "

"And that's all it was, a truce," a man yelled through the roar of applause, "and you better believe it!"

And as Hickman watched Cliofus waiting to continue he smiled and thought, *They're really enjoying it, but I doubt if it could have happened that way. But now let's stop the noise and let Cliofus—or whoever it is that's inventing this lie—get going so I can learn more about Janey's visitor....*

"Thanks, ladies and gentlemen, I appreciate that," Cliofus said, "but some of you might be thinking that my little buddy and me were being too optimistic. But don't forget, ladies and gentlemen: Both Big Smith and Chief O'Sullivan were dedicated *railroad* men. And although members of segregated lodges and unions they were *also* good Scottish Rite Masons in the thirty-third degree. Which in those days—if you dig what I mean—was far more a cause for hope and understanding than if they'd simply been blood brothers who happened to have black and white skins...."

"Oh, we dig you, Cli," a voice called from the bar, "because on the job those cats could be one thing and something completely different when they met on the sidewalks! Which for us is ancient history. So what we want to hear *now* is the rest of what the words had to say to your visitor and how he took it!"

"That's what I'm waiting to tell you, man," Cliofus called back with a frown, "but the words aren't concerned with history, they deal with what really happens to folks before history gets written!

"Anyway, since I knew better than to interrupt what the words were saying to my visitor I listened, and this is what they said:

" 'So when he stops laughing the chief steward gives the chief cook the high sign and decides to hang loose. But since his wise Irish mother didn't raise her a fool, he takes a good look at Big Smith's kids and their little red wagons and thinks warm thoughts about his own little kids and his wife's nice disposition, her fine corned beef and cabbage, plus her sweet, sweet jelly-roll. Which reminds him why he has to work hard and look out for them and their best interest. And especially his job.

" 'So he rushes off to check out his meat box, his storeroom, and his bin of fresh vegetables. And this leaves Big Smith time to spend with his six little children and his pretty little missus before the Santa Fe Chief takes off for Texas. And now as the kids focus on that big greasy bag they start firing him some questions.

" ' "What'd you bring us for supper, Daddy?" the six little children say. But although they're fishing like Trojans they aren't about to get a bite. Because by now Big Smith the daddy has gone to gazing at their mama with genuine larceny, and she's smiling back with what they'd come to understand is a sleepy bedroom look in her eyes. So then they start making them some wishes.

" ' "I hope it's roast beef," the oldest one says.

" ' "I hope it's mutton," the second oldest says.

" ' "I hope it's corned beef hash with some good ole giblet gravy," the third oldest of them says.

" ' "Now me," the fourth one says, "I could use some good ole sausage, and I mean the Brookfield kind."

" ' "Shucks, I hope it's round steak cooked as tender as Jim Jeffries' head after Jack Johnson got through right-crossing and left-jabbing," the fifth one says, "and a great big bucketful of good ole onion gravy—yeah! And a skillet full of cornbread, and some good ole turnip greens with the turnips on the side."

" ' "Then the little Big Smith baby sticks out his tongue at his brothers and says, "Shucks, all of y'all ain't nothing but some greedy greedy-guts. But I don't care *what* Daddy brought us in that bag, long as there's some sweet Virginia *ham* hidden in it. And you want to know why? It's 'cause I got this brand-new tooth which needs something truly *special* for me and it to try...."

" 'So pretty soon they get so worked up and hungry that they almost get to fighting. But then they hear the Chief's engine shooting off steam and ringing its bell and turn to have a look before the long train leaves the station.

" 'Because by now the fireman is in position with his big scoop on the ready, the engineer sits gripping on the throttle with his white-gloved hand, the steam domes, the sandbox, and the long bulging boiler are all bright and gleaming, and its valves are jetting steam. While lined in a row near where we're watching, the waiters in white and porters in blue are looking stern and handsome like the Coldstream Guards we used to see marching side by side in the newsreels.

" 'So now, with the passengers all seated with the crew in place and the big stationmaster standing at attention with his megaphone in hand, here comes the conductor who's in charge of the Chief's long journey, who's stepping like he's listening to a band.

" 'Dressed in a blue uniform with his jacket rowed with medals and the black visor of his cap aglow with golden braid, he's strutting like a general on parade. And when he comes to a halt he throws back his head, and when he sings out "AAAAL-ahhh-BOARD!" he reminds me of how Miss Kindly tries to encourage us to like classical music better than jazz by having Enrico Caruso yell *Aida* through the horn of her Victrola!

" 'Then down the tracks as far as we can see, the signal lamps and semaphores are glowing green, green, green. And that's when Mister Big Smith beams down at his chair-step children as proud as a king. Then he turns to his pretty little missus and looks very soulful as he says, "I want you to save it, pretty mama, and I mean all of it, for me!"

" 'And Missus Big Smith says, "Oh, that's no trouble, no trouble a'tall. Not as long as I get your kind attention on your next trip through!"

" ' "And if I don't, I truly hope," Mister Big Smith says, "that something big and mean will bite me!"

" ' "Never you mind all that innocent-sounding jive," Missus Big Smith says, "'Cause *you* know, and *I* know there ain't nothing that big and reckless even down there in Dallas! Anyway, after all your endless traveling it's time you had some rest and quiet diversion. So you hurry home and *see* me, you hear me?"

" ' "Oh, yes," Mr. Big Smith says, "but 'til then you save it, pretty mama, 'cause I'm really going to need it!"

" 'Then, with a hug and a kiss, he presents her with that big greasy bag, and tosses the six little kids some hard rock candy of the kind that's flavored with peppermint and cinnamon, and they go racing down the tracks so they'll be there waiting when the Chief comes rolling south on its way to Texas.

" 'So then we take off down the tracks a piece so we can have a better view. And my, oh, *my*! When it hits that back-o-town grade it's a-huffing and a-puffing and a-ringing its bell. And when it takes that sweeping curve past the cotton-seed mill the little Big Smith kids are already there with their little red wagons. Then, as the dining car gets closer it starts to belching out this eye-bugging bounty of pork chops, lamb chops, veal chops, and mutton, beef steaks, calves' liver, and bacon, and crates of chitt'lings—which Big Smith *had* to get in

Chicago, or else K.C., 'cause even the richest white passengers of the Santa Fe Chief weren't up to being served such special colored folk's food as chitterlings. And next thing we know those six little Big Smith children are hustling along the tracks snatching and grabbing as they gather in the grub. And when they come dragging their wagons back all loaded down with loot and the oldest sees us gawking like we can't believe our eyes, he wrinkles up his nose and sings out real sassy,

> *I don't know about* y'all's *daddies,*
> *But* ours *treats us truly fine*
> *'Cause he's the best chief cook*
> *On the Santa Fe line!*

" 'And as though to prove he's not telling us a lie, when we take our last look at the Santa Fe Chief, Mister Big Smith, their dear ole daddy, is leaning out the window waving to his missus and his boys with a big loving smile on his face. And as we watch him fade down the tracks we both want to cry. Why? Because it's made us understand far better than we can say about what we've missed by being orphans....' "

And now, as Cliofus suddenly paused to stare in his direction, Hickman watched openmouthed as the big man in the wheelchair clasped his hands in a gesture of benediction. Then, spreading his arms like a dedicated preacher, Cliofus said with a throb in his voice, "Ladies and gentlemen, I still don't know what those words were up to or how my visitor took them, but take my advice: Whenever times get so hard that you doubt your earthly mission, just remember Big Smith the chef and his family! Yes, and keep the spirit of its mother, its father, and its six little children in your minds! Then give praise to Glory for sending us such a self-persevering, hope-inspiring example for our instruction!"

And as Hickman whispered Amen and joined the crowd's applause, he felt a gentle tap on his shoulder and turned to see the driver who had driven him to what had turned out to be a cave of surprises.

"Didn't I tell you he was something else?" the driver said.

"You surely did, my friend," Hickman said with emotion, "but even after your warning I wasn't prepared for anything like what I've heard here tonight. And would you believe it, after seeing me in the audience he signified at me by ending his wild parable of a tale like it was some kind of *sermon!*"

"Yeah, but you liked it, didn't you?"

"And you'd better believe it. I liked it almost as well as some of the wise old lies I heard in barbershops and pool halls back in the old days. But hearing that kind of thing in a nightclub makes a man wonder what's happening to this country and us as a people."

"Oh, we'll make it, and you can bet on that. But what about Cliofus?"

"Well, even after knowing him since he was a big clumsy infant I'll have to say that he's turned out to have the strangest way with words that I've ever heard. But who knows? Maybe he's not only a man who's plagued by his words, but a man of the Word transcendent...."

[MOVIE]

AND NOW, AS HICKMAN watched Cliofus throw his hands above his head and bow, the room rang with cheers and applause. Then, feeling a tap on his shoulder, he turned to see a grinning face within inches of his own.

"Didn't I tell you he was something else?" the face said, and he recognized the taxi driver.

"You surely did," Hickman said, "but I wasn't prepared for anything like this, not in a nightclub...."

"Yeah, but you like it, don't you?"

"I'll have to admit that I do, almost as well as I did in pool halls and barber-shops. But hearing this kind of thing in a nightclub is still pretty strange...."

Suddenly, through waves of applause and shouted requests for *about the Big Smith family, Hickman was surprised to hear Cliofus call out, "Hey, you! The big gentleman back there in the rear! Now that these words of mine have their nasty habits on, what would *you* like to hear?"

Surprised, and seeing customers turning to stare at him with expressions of amusement, Hickman hesitated.

"Go ahead, Ace," a freckle-faced man said with a friendly nudge, "tell the man...."

"Oh, no," Hickman said, "he doesn't mean me...."

"The hell he don't! You're the biggest one back here, so he *has* to mean you. Tell the man, and he'll give it to you."

"Okay, so now we'll see," Hickman said as he called to Cliofus. "Was your question meant for me?"

"Yes, sir," Cliofus called back—"that is, if you're the one I think you are. Aren't you in town to visit a certain lady?"

"Why yes," Hickman said, "as a matter of fact, I am...."

"I thought so," Cliofus said with a nod. "And you dropped in here because you knew Buster and me from years ago and you wanted to see how we were doing—isn't that right?"

"Yes, that's true...."

"Right! But that's not all of it, because the words keep telling me that you're really here because you have a question that's weighing heavy on your mind,

---

* In the typescript, between "for" and "about," one or more words are apparently missing.

and somehow it's connected with the fellow who got them started the other day. So now that they know you're in the room they want to get out and get on with it. If I'm right, just say so and maybe they'll let both of us have a little peace."

"Very well," Hickman said, "and if it wouldn't interrupt your regular routine too much I'd be grateful if you'd have your words give us an account of a moving picture which was produced out here many years ago—or so I've been told...." And as he waited for the big man's reaction he thought, *So there, I've asked what Love would probably call the wrong question of the wrong man, in the wrong place....* Then he saw Cliofus nod, slap his thigh, and lean forward. But just as Cliofus was about to answer an elderly woman who sat at a table just below the stage whirled in her chair.

"A *moving picture*," the woman shouted. "Mister, I don't know who you are, but I've lived here since I was a young girl and never in my *life* have I heard about anything like that!"

With a sudden forward movement Cliofus looked down, saying, "Now wait! *Hold* it!"

"That's right," the woman shouted, "never!"

"But madam," Hickman called with a smile, "while I'm sure that you haven't, couldn't it be because you were too young?"

"Oh, no, Ace," the freckled-faced man beside him said, "I know for a fact that Anna there has been here since Adam messed up with Eve, but in those days you're referring to she was always out in the country picking cotton...."

"Now that's a cotton-mouthed lie," the woman shouted. "I was never even *near* a cotton patch!"

"Don't tell *me*," the freckled man laughed, "'cause you spent more time picking cotton than you did in school!"

"And that's another cotton-mouthed lie! I've never picked cotton!"

"Now, I wouldn't know about that," Cliofus called down from the stage, "but according to Miss Janey you can take some folks out of the cotton patch, but you can't take the cotton patch out of their kids. What's more, you're suggesting that the gentleman who mentioned a movie is telling a lie. Well, I'm telling you that if he tells you that a hen dips snuff all you have to do is look under her wing and you'll find a can of *Garrett's*!"

"And just how I'm supposed to take some stranger's word about a movie?"

"Because he's a man of his *Word*," Cliofus said, "that's why! But if you won't take *his* word about that movie, take mine. I was just a kid but I remember a few things about it, and since the gentleman has admitted that the words are onto something, why don't you just listen and see what they come up with?"

"Hey, Cliofus," a man called from the bar, "that's not fair! How come you letting a stranger who nobody's ever seen before break into your regular routine?"

"Don't blame it on me, Lonzo," Cliofus called, "it's the *words*—and besides, that man is no stranger, because I remember him from when I was a kid...."

"Get on with it, Cliofus," Buster called over the sound system. "Time's a-wasting, so get on with it."

With a sudden twist Cliofus stared into the shadows behind him, shouting, "Now just what the hell do the words care about *time?*" Then, turning and stabbing his finger in Hickman's direction, he continued.

"Anyway, as I recall there *was* a movie made out here. And it happened back in the early twenties when three men showed up with a car full of moviemaking equipment and spread the news that they were going to make a moving picture. That's the truth, and it got everybody excited. . . ."

"So what was so strange about that?" a voice called from a side table. "This was cowboy-and-Indian country and plenty of movies were made out here."

"Yeah, but this one was different," Cliofus said, "because it was to be one in which anybody who wanted to could play a part."

"You mean folks like *us?*"

"Yes, and what's more, it was made right here in our neighborhood."

"Now I *know* it didn't happen," the elderly woman said, "because the folks in charge of things wouldn't let it and they didn't! I don't know that man back there, but next thing we know he'll be telling us that it was a movie about Marcus Garvey chasing Tarzan and all those apes out of Africa!"

"Ace," the freckle-faced man said as he nudged Hickman and laughed, "if this was a ball game she'd have you swinging at a vicious curve that sailed dead over the plate!"

"And that's no lie," Hickman called above the laughter, "but while I'm sure that the lady knows what she saw and didn't see, I can remember a time when movies about us were being shown right here in this neighborhood. They weren't *made* here, but there was a man by the name of Micheaux who was in the business, and I've seen some of his movies that were shown in the Sunset. So, madam, while *you* might not be interested in hearing what Cliofus and his words have to say, would you mind if the rest of us listen?"

"No," the woman said, "I just hate to see folks come here to hear some lies that get at the truth be mixed up by some that will be nothing but lies."

"I think I understand," Hickman said, "but isn't it possible that the kind of truth you want depends upon the way a lie is told? That the truth lies in the telling? You say that no such movie was ever made, while I've been told that it was. Therefore, since Cliofus agrees with me, maybe the best way to settle our argument is to listen to what his words make of what happened or *didn't* happen. . . ."

"That's right!" the freckle-faced man said, "and if you want the truth go to church! Hell, this is the Wind Cave and the rest of us came here to hear Cliofus entertain. We don't give a damn whether he blows up a lie until it sounds like the truth, or if he gasses up the truth until it sounds like a lie. All we want is for him to get started and do some *blowing!*"

"So how about it, ma'am," Hickman said. "Do you mind if we hear what Cliofus has to say?"

"Oh, yes, I mind," the woman said, "but since I'm outnumbered, go ahead, Cliofus."

"Thank you, Miss Anna," Cliofus said, "but I want you to know that the words are a bit upset over your hinting that the truth's not in them. They say that it's like arguing that since the Bible wasn't written until after the things it tells about had already happened it has to wait until somebody reads it out loud or be caught up somewhere between the truth and a cotton-mouthed lie...."

"Now you just wait," the woman shouted. "Don't you go putting words in my mouth...."

"...Or since all the words in the dictionary happen to be printed in *black* ink on white paper rather than with *white* ink on *black* paper, they're incorrect...."

"I didn't say that," the woman shouted. "I didn't say anything that was even *like* that!"

"I know you didn't," Cliofus said with a grin, "I'm just reporting what the *words* have to say about it. You didn't say it, and what's more, you know that sometimes the Bible rings truer when a preacher lays it down and goes about dressing up its message in things from his own background, and in his own words and experience. That way it can come so alive that you don't have to sit there wondering if things would have been any better or worse if Jesus had been black. But don't get me wrong, that's the way the words look at it, and since they're mine I apologize."

"Now don't you be trying to jive me, Cliofus," the woman said with a wave of her hand, "because everybody knows that you're nothing but a long-winded fool!"

"And I thank you kindly," Cliofus said with a laugh. "But yet and still a movie was made around here, just as that gentleman said. A black-and-white one, and the men who had the idea were some strangers who showed up on the last day of June, when a big rainstorm was in progress. It rained and rained, but instead of cooling off afterwards as it usually does, when this particular rain stopped it got even hotter. In fact, it got so hot that some folks thought that the men would give up on the idea. But the opportunity for being in a movie was so unusual and so exciting that most of them made it clear that come hell or high water they wanted the men to go on and make it...."

"Could you tell us who these men were, and where they came from?" Hickman called.

"Out of the East," Cliofus said, "where else? And all three were white. One had a Southern, one had a Jewish accent, and the one in charge had so many ways of speaking that *nobody* was able to pin him down...."

"Yes, honey," a woman said with a slap of her hand, "and I'll bet a dollar against a doughnut that he turns out to be the sheet we have to bleach! Yes, and the one we have to watch!"

"Maybe so," Cliofus said, "but that wasn't bothering anybody, because the three of them were giving folks a chance to watch themselves act in a movie. So with that kind of opportunity knocking they weren't worried about accents or even color. But there *were* a few complications—which," Cliofus said as he took a sip of water and stared at Hickman, "you'll need a little background in order to understand.

"The problem arose when the movie men explained that on account of having pressing business out in Hollywood they would have to push the calendar ahead a bit. Which meant that while the story was supposed to take place on Halloween they would have to shoot it on what was *actually* the Fourth of July. So with it already being close to the end of June, and as hot as blazes, I don't have to tell you that the idea met with some heated objections.

"Because for years most of our folks had been juggling the calendar to fit their special needs, so naturally they didn't want some white strangers messing with their schedule. This was by celebrating Emancipation Day—better known as Juneteenth—on the Fourth of July. . . ."

"Hey, Cliofus, how come they call it Juneteenth?"

"That's a good question," Cliofus said, "and it was because while Abe Lincoln signed the Emancipation Proclaimation in January, the good news didn't trickle down to many of our folks until the middle of June. And since they had learned to trust the calender more than what was written in the law books, and very little seemed to have changed, they came up with 'Juneteenth.' But they discovered that the fourteenth of June was usually a working day on which their bosses weren't *about* to let them lay down those rakes and hoes—and especially when it meant that white folks would have to stand by and watch a bunch of Negroes knock themselves out celebrating an event which they considered the worst thing to ever happen to the United States. Naturally our folks disagreed, and some went so far as to argue that by celebrating Independence and Emancipation on the same day they were making the Fourth of July both more glorious *and* more truly American. That's right, and some even argued that it was one of the few ways they had of giving the so-called Glorious Fourth some *color*. So for a while there it looked like the movie was out. . . ."

"And they were right," a man shouted, "because we have to see things from our *own* situation! Hell, some of these white folks still think that the only time a black man ought to celebrate is on Saturday night!"

"You're right," Cliofus called above the laughter, "but after listening to all the objections, the movie man with all those accents was finally able to convince folks that since the Glorious Fourth was the one holiday on which most folks didn't have to work, even more of them would be free to take part in the picture. That turned the trick, and soon folks were agreeing that not only would the picture help put the city on the map—which was what the movie men said—but that by combining Independence and Emancipation Days with Halloween they would be stretching *three* holidays into *four*.

"So once that sheet was washed and bleached the movie men really got folks excited. They put up posters announcing the movie and ran a contest in which the winning man and woman would be picked to act the leading parts, and pretty soon everybody and his brother were knocking themselves out in anticipation. Even folks who were still a bit leery over the whole idea lent a hand. Some let the movie men use their front yards and parlors for some of the scenes. Some of the ladies lent their furniture and donated flowers and other things. And the local butchers, both black and white, donated racks of ribs for the big barbecue and chitt'ling strut which was to be a part of the story. And the men who ran cafés and lunchrooms donated things like hot dogs and chili and sandwiches and soft drinks.

"The idea of acting in a movie really caught on—even though nobody knew what the story was all about, or even what parts they would be acting in it. But the movie men took care of that by explaining that they planned to hang loose and let the local folks use their own creative imaginations in helping them make up the story as they went along. That way, they said, they could discover each and every body's special talents and use them. In fact, they made making a movie sound like some new kind of game...."

"Yeah!" an old man's quavering voice called out, "and a hell of a game it was!"

"That's right," Cliofus called with a nod of his head, "but it stopped the objections and raised the excitement. Even some of the so-called *society* folks caught the spirit, and that included some of those who were leery and a bit uneasy over the idea of associating with the local riffraff—who were knocking themselves out over the idea of acting in a moving picture.

"And even when the old folks held back, some of their kids liked it fine. Like the grandchildren of a man who they swore to have been a hero back in the Civil War. They really went for it, even though nobody could find his name in the history books. But they insisted that he'd been a sailor and a spy for the Union Army, and that he'd been praised for stealing a battleship from the Rebels. So now that they had a chance to give the old man some publicity they dug his old navy jacket out of a trunk that hadn't been open for fifty years or so, and even though it turned out to be much too big, one of the boys wore it for his movie costume. The other problem arose after he got it on and discovered that he didn't know the *first* thing about what kind of man his granddaddy had been. So then he asked the older members of his family how a slave who had been a sailor *and* a hero had carried himself and he found that they had no more idea than he did. What's more, the kid had never seen an ocean or a battleship!

"There were others who had similar problems, but in all the excitement and expectation it turned out not to matter. And since most folks had come out here from all over the South it was hard to dispute what they said that they and their old folks had been before they came West. One fellow said that his great-grandmother was a slave who invented Coca-Cola and that her master took it from her and sold it as his own. Another swore that his granddaddy was a painter who had once had a contract to paint all the public buildings in Nashville, and when he was kidded about it he reeled off the names of a lot of buildings and produced the torn and faded contract. One woman said that she was related to Daniel Boone on her mother's side, and another claimed to be kin to Thomas Jefferson, and so it went.

"But whoever and whatever they and their grandparents had actually been down South, they were putting just about everything they could think of into dressing up for the parts they hoped they might play in the unplanned movie. Soon it turned into a costume contest, and a few even dressed up their dogs in things like little clown suits and eyeglasses. One fellow had his old bob-tail bull-dog walking around with an underslung pipe in his drooling mouth. That's right! And with the pipe bowl stuffed with red cotton the damn dog looked like he was actually smoking!

"One old man's costume was nothing more than a pair of blue-jean britches with a piece of clothesline for a belt. The rest of him was naked except for some sandals he'd made out of auto-tire rubber and some rusty skid chains which he wore draped over his shoulders. He swore that he got the chains back in slavery times, but some of the other old men who had actually been slaves put a stop to that lie by forcing him to admit that he hadn't even been born during slavery. And when he did they told him to get himself another costume or get lost. Otherwise he'd be in trouble.

"With that he argued that since he was black it didn't matter, and that they were messing with his civil rights to be whoever the hell he wanted to be. Then he threatened to go home and come back dressed as General Robert E. Lee. Which was such an outrage to his critics that they told him to go ahead and that they'd be waiting dressed up like U. S. Grant and William Tecumseh Sherman and would proceed to stomp his ignorant butt until it roped like overcooked okra and as raggedy as a bowl of yakami. They meant it too, but they never did find out whether he carried through his threat, because when things got going at least *three* guys showed up dressed like Robert E. Lee, and not a single one would take off his hat, whiskers, or Halloween mask.

"Folks showed up in all *kinds* of costumes. Some came as African kings carrying shields and spears, some came as Indian chiefs wearing warbonnets and arrows, Indian clubs, and prizefighter's skipping ropes. One fellow came dressed like Uncle Sam and went strolling through the crowd on stilts. He claimed that he had been in the circus and minstrel shows, and proved it by whirling the hell out of a drum major's baton. Another fellow dressed himself in tights and did all kinds of acrobatics that nobody ever dreamed he could do. And like here there were others who used the movie as an opportunity to show off skills which they'd put aside years before—and among them even some old-time musicians who were working as handymen. But hardly *any*body came dressed as his own dear self—except some of Jack BooBoo Beaujack's henchmen. Such as Tyree,

Yella Pea Mitchell, Sad Rag Doll Green, and Duck-Dinner Jones. The rest came in masks and fancy costumes.

"In fact, folks got so enthused that they damn near started a business boom in the hock shops. Pretty soon, as the pawnshop owners tried to keep their supplies in pace with demand, they found themselves making money hand over fist. But then Little Sammy, who owned a popular shop, almost killed it. That's because when he realized that folks were buying and renting things that they'd never even *looked* at before, he made the mistake of letting one of his customers overhear him say that the *schwartzers* were going crazy from trying to be like the goys. When folks heard about that they wanted to kill him, because after all Little Sammy was a midget who sported a monocle and strutted around trying to impress white folks as well as black with his phony aristocratic manners. Naturally, he lost his colored trade, but before he put his pigeon-toed foot in his mouth he'd been reaping the benefits along with Uncle Jake—who was the favorite— and Uncle Nate and Uncle Moe. That was because instead of hocking their jewelry and threads as they usually did, Negroes were buying and renting all kinds of suits, coats, hats, and boots, spurs, helmets, sabers, and medals.

"One guy bought every medal and ribbon he could find and pinned them up and down the front of his Prince Albert coat. And for a walking cane he carried a flag on top of a tall thin staff. But since they were taking part in a cross between the Fourth of July, Emancipation Day, and Halloween, many of the would-be actors tried to combine the three themes in their costumes. And since they didn't know exactly how their costumes would fit in the movie they just let their imaginations go for broke.

"They came up with all kinds of airplane pilot's goggles, leather jackets, flying helmets, and leggings. And enough smooth and woolly cowboy chaps and britches to outfit the entire crew of the 101 Ranch. Some came up with some old leather fire chief's helmets, and those striped railroad engineer's caps were selling like hotcakes. One war veteran wore a spiked German helmet which he had brought back from France. Two others had army gas masks dangling from their necks, and wore overseas caps with long red feathers stuck in the folds. And still another went parading around all wrapped up in a webbed machine-gun belt that was full of old corroded bullets. The damn thing was so heavy that he looked like ole Uncle Jack, the jelly-roll kind, and since he had a hump in his back folks kidded him about being too old to shake that thing. The jokers were really giving him a hard time, but when another old fellow turns up dressed like an angel complete with a halo and some beat-up wings and starts to quoting the Bible at them they let him be and went to teasing some of the women.

"And there were plenty of them. One bunch of women came dressed as Red Cross nurses, and so as not to be outdone, another bunch shows up dressed as *Black* Cross nurses, and wore pictures of Marcus Garvey pinned to their uniforms. One young high-yellow woman decided to play the part of Harriet Tubman, so she did up her face in lampblack, put on a bandanna for a turban, and marched around with a corncob pipe between her teeth, a Civil War rifle over her shoulder, and a waving railroad lantern in her hand.

"Then folks with reputations for having loose screws got into the act. For instance, there was this fellow called Gone Grease Thompson, who was supposed to have gotten his brains scrambled after selling his two-hundred-acre farm near Okmulgee and turned most of the money over to Marcus Garvey with the idea of going back to Africa—where, being part Creek Indian, part South Carolina Geechee, and a good deal Georgia cracker, he'd never been except in dreams. But then, after his money was gone and Garvey was deported, he learned that the lower forty acres of the land which he'd sold for a song was swampland soggy with high-grade oil and it snapped his cap. Well, Gone Grease Thompson turns up wearing striped pants, pearl gray spats, a long-tailed coat, a high silk hat, and carrying a silver-headed walking stick—all of which he'd rented from Little Sammy's pawnshop. I don't need to tell you that folks gave him hell....

"Then here comes a woman dressed in a pair of overloaded army britches with a reinforced seat that's as wide as a barn door, and some high laced boots that are under one *hell* of a strain from trying to contain her great big calves. She's also busting out of a leather pilot's jacket, and on her head she's wearing a flier's helmet and a pair of goggles exactly like the ones the three movie men were wearing. She's moving along real proud, and when some jokers asked her to explain her costume, she cussed them out for being ignorant and proclaims that she means to get some true history of the colored flying woman into the picture. Then she drew herself up like a balloon and declared that she was the living spirit of Miss Bessie Coleman.

" 'So who the hell was that?' one of the jokers asked her, and she drew herself up and said, 'Why, she was a famous colored lady *air*plane pilot, that's who! And you better believe it!' And then to make sure that nobody missed the part she was playing, she went home and came back wearing signs on her bosom and her back which read BESSIE. She must have also taken a look into some book, because now she was walking with a terrible limp, which she said was the way Miss Coleman had to walk after busting her leg while test-piloting a German airplane. The joker didn't want to believe her but she had a faded photograph of Miss Bessie to prove she wasn't making things up.

[COSTUMES]

"OH, IT WAS SOMETHING to see, especially since I was only a kid. Men in lodge uniforms, with their ribbons and sashes and Sam Browne belts, and their cocked hats crowned with snow-white feathers. Ole Zebedee Richardson, who's as big as me and as dark-complected, turned up wearing a white suit, white shoes, a big broad-brimmed white hat, and the kind of flowing tie that you see in pictures of those old-time poets. He was really strutting his stuff and shaking hands, and swore that he was the spitting image—nose, mouth, chin, and cheekbones—of Senator Carter Glass. And when some joker asked who the hell was Glass, ole Zeb frowned like he was outraged and said that he was an important politician he used to know back in Ole Virginia. So then the joker said that he'd never heard of any such senator, but that if he looked anything like Zeb there was no way in the *world* for him not to have been a white, unreconstructed ink-spitter. That's when I thought I was about to see a fight, because up to that point Zeb was only clowning, but when he heard himself being signified at as a black ink-spitting Uncle Tom it made him so mad that it took four big strong men and a pint of whiskey to quiet him down. And with that things really started getting out of hand.

"When the news about a movie being made in this part of town reached the white folks, a big-shot politician decided to exploit it. So he donated a whole *herd* of pigs, carcasses of beef, and a young boar bear to be barbecued and served to all those taking part. Back in those days not many of us could vote, but he figured that by casting all that meat on the streets things would get so greasy that come the fall election all the colored votes would come sliding to him. But he made one big mistake. His only link to folks out here happened to be a con man of a jackleg preacher whose ace-in-the-hole hustle was operating a beat-up old-folks home. And it was this con man who convinced the politician that with all that barbecue to work with not only could he deliver the vote for the entire district, but he'd even get the Lord to send the white man straight to Congress. And it worked. That's right—yeah! But then instead of the rascal turning the meat over to the cooks to be barbecued as he was supposed to do, this con man crams as much of it into the iceboxes of his congregation as they could hold and stashes the rest in some crates and hid it in the basement of his old-folks home. Then he loads the rest in a wagon and heads for the little nearby towns and farms, where he peddles it at prices way below those of the markets and grocery stores.

"Up to this point his plan was working smooth as silk, but he overlooked two details. The first was that the news of the barbecue had been announced in the newspapers, and the second was his forgetting about Jack BooBoo Beaujack and what could happen when the doctored-up liquor which Jack was dispensing free to anybody who had nerve enough to drink it took effect. But by now the moviemaking was well under way, and when all that liquor started working its spell in all that July heat, folks began to be agitated by the bite of all that booze in their empty stomachs, and that's when hell erupted.

"If they could have eaten they wouldn't have drunk so fast, and if they hadn't drunk so much they might not have got so doggone high. And if they hadn't been pretending to be somebody else and living in different days and ages they wouldn't have begun to believe it. But with everything going at sixes and sevens, they lost control. So yes, ladies and gentlemen, the answer is yes: It all began to come apart when that movie camera became red hot from all its grinding....

"That's right, sir," Cliofus laughed as he waved to Hickman, "I was there and saw it steaming! It was as hot as Hoot Gibson's pistol, but although those movie men had been cramming folks into it for hours they still weren't telling them what they were supposed to do.

" 'Just act natural,' they told them, and went on to explain that for the time being they were just shooting some background scenes so that folks would get used to the idea of being actors. And therefore they could feel free to do anything that came to mind. So with the streets all decorated and renamed for some local characters who had long since passed away, folks lost their bearings. And with all those masks and costumes mixing them up as to who they were, they started cutting loose like mile-high kites in a strong March wind. And by the time Beaujack's liquor went to work, all some of them knew for sure was they had to have some food to eat. So the stage was set, and when a gang of them burst into a restaurant and can't be fed, one of them gets the others all worked up by yelling, 'What? No *barbecue*! So how the hell are we supposed to act our best on empty stomachs?' Then the others join in, yelling things like, 'Who the hell stole all them ribs and the bread with the hot-sauce on it? Where the hell's our rightful share of them red beans and fluffy rice?'

"And when the cooks couldn't produce and told them why, they took off looking for that jackleg preacher, with the one in the lead waving a beat-up Louisville slugger in the air. Quite a few took off with them, but with so many people in the street the movie men didn't mind. Because even though they'd been rolling that camera since sunup, they hadn't even *begun* to run out of raw material, and more folks in masks and costumes were appearing.

"Pretty soon it was like watching a parade. Here comes a little short guy wearing an oversized cowboy hat and some boots with turned-up toes that looked like somebody had shot their heels off with a blazing forty-five. He's pretending to be a marshal or a sheriff and doing a John Wayne strut, but the star on his chest is made of tinfoil, and instead of six-shooters he has a couple of rolling pins dangling from his cowboy belt.

"Then here come three drunks dressed in black choir robes and wearing lensless glasses who're pretending to be judges and carrying ball-peen hammers for gavels, and beat-up copies of *Captain Billy's Wizbang* and the *Police Gazette* for law books. They're marching along all dignified, but talking more jive than a reefer-headed disc jockey at five o'clock in the morning. But it worked because folks got a kick out of identifying them with judges who were actually sitting on the courts. The crowd gave them star-quality attention, but then—here come a dozen of Jack BooBoo Beaujack's buddies and they steal the judges' thunder.

"These thugs are all dressed up in long, pioneer women's dresses and wearing poke bonnets like the Old Dutch Cleanser woman on their heads. And not only are they wearing death-head masks, but they have pillows stuffed under their dresses to make themselves look last-minute pregnant. This gets the crowd to laughing and calling them the various kinds of mothers which on any normal day could get you killed. But instead of getting mad, Jack's henchmen just start dancing in a circle and singing 'Little Sally Walker,' with a tall skinny fellow standing in the middle. And when they come to the line 'Turn to the east, turn to the west, turn to the one that you love the best,' he falls down and starts to screaming and rolling on the street like he's about to have a baby. Then he snatches off his bonnet and screams like he's in body-wracking pain, and the others close in on him while holding up their skirts to give him privacy. And the next thing we know one of them kneels over him and comes up holding a little suckling pig by its hind legs. The little pig is as wet as a circus seal and squealing for dear life, but they're oohing and aahing over it like a bunch of women; and the next thing I know they're dressing it in baby clothes! And I mean including a little bonnet—which they must have swiped off some little girl's doll. Then after they get it dressed they shove a baby bottle of milk into its squealing mouth and the little pig goes to work on it like it's his mama's tit and nipple.

"Those clowns really had it all worked out, because after they pass the pig back and forth between them and oh and ah over it, they ask the one playing the mother the name of its father—and right away here comes a guy who's dressed like a preacher, except that instead of wearing britches he has on a great big diaper. Then after he chants some mumbo-jumbo which he pretends to be reading out of a book, he pulls out a pint of whiskey, and as he sprinkles the little pig's head he gives it his blessing by saying, 'My dear newborn chile, I bless you now in the name of the butcher, the brush, and the football maker, the mud, the moon, and the barbecue pit. But most of all I bless you in the name of all those fine folks who like their pigmeat greasy!'

"And as you would expect, this really sets off a roar of hooting and hollering, especially among the hustlers. Because 'pigmeat' was their special name for young women's most precious gift and burden. And then, right in the midst of all that noise, here comes Jack BooBoo Beaujack in all his unrighteous glory....

"Ole Jack has been laying low and playing it cool, but now with that camera grinding away here he comes. Strutting along in his deep-wine-red bully-woollies; which, being him, he's wearing with the drop-seat gaping. And behind him the fool is pulling an old billy goat which he stole off the grounds of the hospital where its blood was used for making serums.

"Jack's wearing a black derby hat and smoking a big black cigar and sweating up a river as he drags the goat along. And quite naturally, with the poor goat being upset by all the noise and people, he's butting at anything that moves and smelling up the sidewalk like a crapping machine.

"*Oh, the lamb misused breeds public strife*—that's from a poem I've read, and from all the fancy footwork folks were using in getting out of his path it's doubly true of billy goats.

"Anyway, by now Halloween is everywhere. Folks are wearing costumes right down to the bricks. With women dressed as men and men as women, and with all kinds of foreigners being represented. Because when it came to masquerading, folks were forgetting their prejudices and trying anything and everything on for size and feeling. But just after Jack and that goat showed up some powerful conjure woman—probably old Miss Mildred Merryweather—must have dropped the shuck, cussed it, and set it on fire.

"I say that because when Buster and I came down the hill to watch the fun we heard Mr. Pulliham's big black dog cut loose with a bark which he followed with a lonesome howl. Then from up in the corner dance hall where the band was tuning up we heard the trombone player stick his horn out the window and blow some pure gut-bucket down the crowd. And that's when we see Jack stop pulling on the goat and do a nasty mess-around. Then he throws back his be-derbied head and yells, 'Aw, put us in the alley, love'—which was his nickname for everybody, both men and women, white folks, Indians, Chinese, Mexicans, and Jews. And he got away with it too, because he always winked and grinned so that nobody knew what the hell to do about it. So now with folks yelling and shouting to encourage the fool, the three movie men were cussing like sailors because folks keep getting between Jack's clowning and their camera lens.

"With the camera set up in the intersection of the street they had been making some shots of the leading lady and the leading man, but now, with Jack cutting the fool, the one with the Southern accent was trying to herd everyone who wasn't in the scene off to one side. He's trying to use some slave-master psychology, but it won't work and it's about to get his Rebel up. But then the one with all the accents, who's directing from on top of a big moving van, finally gets folks to move out of the way. Then through his little megaphone he tells the leading man and lady what he wants them to do. And since they don't know the beginning or the end of the story, he explains that the hero is supposed to be a young lawyer who's new in town, and that he hopes to make his fortune by helping to bring some law and order to the wild and woolly frontier. And although he's only seen her passing in the street he's supposed to be falling head over heels in love with the fine southwestern pioneer gal who's being acted by the little leading lady.

"So now the leading man is supposed to be out on the streets trying to get her in his sights, but he's not supposed to let her see the extent of his true feelings. Just pretend that you're walking past the ice-cream parlor where she's having a soda, the director says, and when she comes out, pretend that you just bumped into her accidentally. Then you give her the glad eye and sweet-talk her into going back inside to have a chocolate nut sundae.

"Speaking down from the top of the moving van, the director explains the action to the nth degree, how they're to walk, look, and carry themselves. So while the crowd stands gawking and making jokes, the leading man and lady get all set to act.

"Now, for this scene both the leading man and lady are dressed in normal everyday clothes, except that hers are sparkling new. From the shoes on her feet to the ribbon in her hair, which is black and glossy like an Indian's, she's dressed in the latest fashion. She's also young and very good-looking, and now as she comes sashaying up the street to the ice-cream parlor the cameramen are grinding like they're grabbing at a dream that's walking. Then some jokers standing across the street in weird costumes start yelling, 'Whooo-wheee!' and 'My, oh, my!' and 'Now did you ever!' But she pays them no mind, because after all it had happened so often in her everyday life. So she just heads into the ice-cream parlor like the director said and disappears. . . .

"So then the director signals the leading man, and here he comes from the other direction, tipping along with a smile on his face and pretending that he didn't see her. He's just strolling along with a smile on his face and trying to play it cool in just the way the director is instructing him through his little megaphone. And for a hotel waiter who'd never done that kind of acting he's doing fine—yeah, but then the worthy BooBoo Beaujack strikes again!

"Just as the leading man reaches the ice-cream parlor, here comes a bunch of drunks running like crazy as they splash around the corner pulling and pushing a big dirty barrel in a beat-up baby buggy. Nobody like them is supposed to be anywhere *near* the scene, but when the cameramen yell for them to get the hell out of the way the director yells orders for them to let the drunks proceed and to keep on shooting—which they do. The drunks still don't know what it's all about, but when they see all the folks on the other side of the street they realize that something unusual is happening and skid to a stop. And when they look around and see that the leading man has neither a false face nor a weird costume, they figure he's fair game if only because he's looking and acting different.

" 'Hey,' one of them yells to the others, 'this here dude must be some kinda freak, so let's give him the treatment!' And before the poor movie hero knows what's happening, they grab him and force a dipperful of BooBoo's hyped-up Choc—which was what was in the barrel—down his throat. And with that things *really* started going to hell.

"Now, as all you old-timers know, Choc beer has been scarce ever since Repeal, but in those days it was plentiful. And not only did it have a fine taste and bouquet, it had a kick like TNT. So when the crowd gets a whiff of what the BooBoo's henchmen were forcing the hero to drink they react like they're witnessing a long overdue initiation into a fraternity and rush across the street. And in a second they're making such an uproar that when the little leading lady looks out the window and sees what's happening to her leading man she figures that once the drunks gets through with him they'll be coming after her. So she slips out of the back door and disappears.

"But although the scene was getting truly rowdy, the drunks were simply using the leading man to have what they considered to be some innocent fun. It's when Miss Brilliantine shows up and decides to go them one better that things get really nasty.

"Like her twin sister, Miss Thomasina, Miss Brilliantine is big, overbearing as a lady bear, good-looking in a damn-near-white sort of fashion, but far from bright, and the kind of woman who'll do *anything* just to be outrageous. So when she spies the movie director standing up high against the sky while his buddies below are busy pointing that camera like they were a couple of mad-dog machine-gunners who had orders to shoot anything that moves and intend to do it, Miss Brilliantine decides to steal the entire scene by bringing the movie hero down. That way she figures to get herself both some cheap notoriety and demonstrate her talent for acting.

"So with that hungry camera swinging up and down and around and around like the unblinking eye of ever-watching God, Miss Brilliantine starts knocking folks out of her way until she reaches the leading man. And when the drunks give way so they can see what she's about to do, she puts a headlock on the poor man and goes into her act.

"First she yanks the man around and yells, 'Come to mama, good-looking, and let's swap some slobber!' Then she makes him kiss her square on her nasty-talking mouth. And then, with the crowd urging her on by making juicy kissing sounds, she purses up her lips and blinks her big mascaraed eyes and starts pretending that she's as shy a young gal as the little leading lady—only with great big ants in her great big pants. Then, squeezing him in a bear hold, she does a take-off on Theda Bara by tossing the crowd a high-toned over-the-shoulder stare. Then she says to the poor bewildered bug-eyed man, 'Kiss me, you fool!' And then she gets to giggling and tries to smother the man with her great big pair of jugs while she blinks her eyes and coos, 'Oh, please, *please* be good to me, daddy, 'cause I'm really very young.' Then she grabs his head and damn near suffocates the man with a half a yard of tongue! And when the crowd applauds she hugs him even tighter while she does the shimmy and whines, 'Oh, daddy, daddy, *daddy,* I've never, *never* had it so fine!' and tries to break his back with a double-Georgia grind!

"With this the crowd screams even louder and the poor man looks like he wants to hang his head and die, but being a gentleman and realizing that she's playing to the crowd and clowning for the camera, he just shakes his head real disgusted. But with the crowd begging for some more, Miss Brilliantine decides to knock them for a loop by getting real lowdown and personal. That's right, and the camera keeps on grinding.

"So now she looks at the hero with those phony goo-goo eyes and starts to fumbling for his fly. And even though all that Choc has left him groggy, he puts up some resistance—which is exactly what she's hoping for. But when she looks around to see if the camera is recording what she's doing to the man, all at once she throws back her head and starts screaming bloody murder at the three white movie men. But the camera just keeps on grinding.

"Now she has the hero in a bear hug and holding on while he's still acting like a gentleman even as he tries to get away. But then the crowd whirls around and he sees it gawking and making room for something that's beyond his range of vision. And the next thing he knows they're laughing and scraping their fingers at Miss Brilliantine—because all of a sudden the camera's deserted her and gone to pointing toward the *ground,* where it's making eye-to-eye contact with a long, lean, blue-tick hound!

"That's right," Cliofus laughed as he paused to sip some water, "she's been upstaged by a *hound*! Now, no one knows where he came from, or just when he hit the scene, but with so many weird-looking humans cutting the fool he has his tail between his legs and his ears drooping down. And as he stares from mask to mask he looks pure-dee bewildered. But then he sees that except for this one big woman who seems to want to lynch him all the rest are warm and friendly he decides to hang around. And besides that, he's reminded that he's hungry and would like to eat when all at once he smells some red-eye gravy on somebody's smelly feet. So even though Miss Brilliantine is still after his hide he realizes that the camera is recording his each and every twitch, and he makes a decision which for a dog in his position is a very serious move. Meanwhile the camera keeps a-grinding.

"So now with Miss Brilliantine still ranting and raving and demanding his meat, he stakes his life on a policy of do-or-die and decides to do a number in the style of Petey, the white-haired bulldog of the *Our Gang* comedy fame, the one with a thick black ring around his eye. *And* since it's his first performance before an audience of such overwhelming size, he decides that the best way to please both the camera and the crowd is by doing what comes naturally. So with his brow wrinkled up and his ears laid back he starts turning second-hand slow in a perfect circle. Then, pointing his nose upwind and buckling down in what turns out to be a spectacular feat of concentration, he proceeds to demonstrate his finest form in laying down a doggie-do which would have been worth a cool fifty dollars if the dog-catcher caught him at it.

"Well, the crowd was amazed, but when Miss Brilliantine gets a glimpse of his heroic production she damn near busts her britches. But all her cursing and screaming at the hound could hardly be heard as the crowd goes wild over his bit of natural acting. And with folks applauding his mighty effort on each and every side, the hound gives himself a whiplash shake which travels from his head to his tail and fairly beams with pride.

" 'Somebody better get that nasty son-of-a-bitch away from here,' Miss Brilliantine screams as she aims him a kick, but she truly fails to appreciate the effect of a little public recognition on the ego of the hound. Because now that he knows that he's the focus of the camera and the crowd's attention he's not *about* to lose it. Oh, no! So before Miss Brilliantine can knock enough folks out of her way to get at him he starts to reeling off tricks faster than a riverboat gambler dealing educated cards.

"He rolls over, plays dead, turns a double somersault, and stands on his head. He walks on three legs and then on two, whirls on his toes and runs his big wet nose up Miss Brilliantine's thigh and sniffs it. Then he hits a house fly with his tail and cuts it straight in half, crawls on his belly and wiggles his ears, and bows to the crowd for their thundering cheers. Next he runs backwards faster than the great Bojangles in his prime, slams on brakes, and stops on a dime. Then flapping his ears like he intends to fly, he reverses the field about twenty paces, cocks his leg, and without squinting an eye he knocks an iron fire hydrant straight up into the sky. And when it makes a curve and starts rocketing back to earth, he sets it a-tumbling with a vicious second burst. Then with the damnedest display of marksmanship the crowd has ever seen, he washes it down until it's not only hound-tooth clean but changed in color from a firehouse red to a glistening green while it's still up there circling like a fat woodchuck among a flight of pigeons. And *then,* while the crowd is running and ducking from the fall-out of his stream, he does a Houdini in the heavy cloud of steam—and the camera keeps on grinding.

"With that the mystified crowd is arguing and cussing. With some saying, 'He went *here,*' and others, 'He went *there,*' but of the hound himself there's neither hide nor hair. Exactly *where* he's gone nobody really knows, but according to this Geechee gal known as 'Miss Heavy Toes,' he's long, long gone and headed South so the city can't sue him for damages. Then there's a loud difference of opinion on various grounds as they argue whether according to man-made law, or even the Bible, a hound could really be held liable for obeying the laws of his doggy nature. But then when things start to getting real contentious, with some folks cussing and others quoting Scripture—there stands the hound, and he's giving them a grin as he poses like a star for those moving-picture men—and the camera keeps on grinding.

"And what gives weight to Miss Heavy Toes' theory is the indisputable fact that he has his tail pointing north and his nose pointing south, grits on his chin, *and* red-eye gravy on his long lean mouth! But although everybody's amazed and delighted, he gives them no time to figure out just where he got it. And maybe to remind them of the true spirit of the day they're celebrating he starts beating time with his tail, which is as stiff as a rail, and with a-one, a-two, a-three, he throws back his head and it's 'My Country 'Tis of Thee' that he howls.

"He really sends the crowd with his mastery, and when they give him a great big hand he takes a bow-wow bow and gives them the radiance of his canine smile. And when Miss Brilliantine protests and causes the crowd to boo, he proves for all his admirers that he's by no means through. Sitting up on his haunches ramrod straight, he starts to covering first his eyes, then his ears and his mouth at a mind-spinning rate as he flashes his paws and imitates those three wise monkey boys of yore, who were known as See-no, Hear-no, and Speak-no Evil.

"It's an eye-popping performance, and smooth as silk, except that when he covers his eyes his hackles rise, and when he covers his mouth to everyone's surprise he looks straight at Miss Brilliantine with a sweet soulful expression in his big brown eyes—which proves again that he's one lo-mo signifying hound, while the cameramen keep on grinding.

"Yeah, but his fine performance and the sniff he gave Miss Brilliantine didn't help him one bit. Because with the crowd knocked off its feet by his fine performance she's fit to be whipped and tied. She tries to get at him once again, but the crowd won't let her. And when she sees the movie men still grinding that camera at the hound she rears back with her hands on her hips and starts reading them some uncensored chapters from her very filthy mind. But just when she's about to bust a gut from dishing out such smut, it's Jack BooBoo Beaujack who comes out of nowhere to cool her down.

"First Jack grins and pats the hound on the head and lets him smell his funky fingers, and as drunk as he acts he sounds stone-cold sober when he straightens up to address Miss Brilliantine.

"He says, 'Woman, how come you badmouthing and abusing these innocent movie men? Are you trying to make out like what they're doing is some kind of sin? If so, I'm here to tell you that they're only doing their duty just the way this dog was doing hissen. Which is a hell of a lot more than can be said for you! Why, the way you been acting is a crime, a sin, and a damn disgrace, to the state, the country, and the whole human race. And that includes your own funky butt and all of us who been watching you tear your nasty drawers in a public place. Just who the hell you think you kidding, when everybody knows for a fact that the only reason you were trying to make that leading man look like a clown was because he's a gentleman and wouldn't fight back. If it had been me and you wasn't so plump I'd lost my foot in your big fat rump! You tried to play the poor man cheap, and when the joke goes against you, you start acting like some Northern creep, who thinks all the folks in this part of the country is ignunt!'

"And when Miss Brilliantine gives him a drop-dead stare he basses at her deep and loud, 'Don't you roll those bloodshot eyes at me! 'Cause I'm big as you and twice as evil! Yeah! That's what I said, and if you don't like it I'll go upside your ignunt head!' Then he balls up his great big fist and sniffs it.

"Jack sounds like he means it too, and for once Miss Brilliantine pays some heed to a man and just stands there pouting and glaring. So then Jack sees the director standing way up high as he directs his buddies where to point the camera and decides to gives Miss Brilliantine the benefit of his philosophy:

" 'Woman,' he says, 'you've got a lot to learn about the game of life, so you better give strict attention to this sound advice, because from now on these are the rules of the street that you better follow:

" 'Number One: When you trick a sucker, take what's yours because you won it fair. But don't rub it in and mess with his pride unless you aim to commit instant suicide.

" 'Number Two: When you get tricked by Lady Luck or a smarter trickster, the rule of the game is not to complain, because the only way to save what's more precious than winning is by taking your loss and coming up grinning. So you better remember what the old folks say about every good dog having his day, because that's the stone-cold truth even though they forgot to say a *word* about bitches!

" 'So now straighten up and stop all this assing around and give some credit to this fine little hound, because thanks to you, this *heah* day is hissen!'

"Then, while the crowd gives him a thunderous hand, Jack pats the hound on the head and takes a bow while Miss Brilliantine hikes her skirt and disappears—and those cameramen keep grinding.

"Then, with a wag of his tail for what Jack said about him doing his natural duty, the hound backs back and kicks real hard, then takes off doing sixty for his own backyard—if he *had* one.

"Because just as nobody had ever seen him before, no one has seen him since, and that's why he's still the subject of great argument in our oldest barbershops, pool halls, and bars—but that's another story. As for now the crowd is delighted with his signifying, self-made part, and while those drunk masked actors discuss the hound's acting skills, the movie men start searching for the hero with that camera.

"And that's exactly when Pulliham's old dog's howling warning takes effect. Because after taking Miss Brilliantine's double-barreled blows to his sobriety, manhood, and self-esteem—and he took it mostly with a smile—the hero was too unstrung to finish with the scene which the drunks had interrupted. And besides, the little leading lady is long, long gone to parts unknown and no one knows where to find her. So after making his polite excuses to one and all, the hero heads for his redheaded Texas woman's house, where he hopes to get his head together and his ashes hauled. That Choc which they made him drink has him pretty groggy, and since the movie men want him rested for his big love scene it's fine with them that he takes off. 'Just take it easy and be ready for tomorrow's shooting,' is what they tell him.

"That was late in the afternoon, but now we come to what happened that evening. Halloween is really popping all up and down the streets, with kids racing around with lighted railroad flares dripping hot sulfur on everybody's feet, throwing firecrackers into crowds, and putting torpedoes and cherry bombs on the streetcar tracks. One bunch went celebrating on the outskirts of town by running through alleys pushing the little outhouses over 'til they landed on the ground. By using teamwork and keeping quiet they'd toppled four in a row when they pushed on one that came alive. They'd just begun to count, a-one, a-two, a-three, and were set to bring it down when they heard a voice from inside yell, 'Wait! Dammit, wait! This ain't no time to clown!' But although some took off running like the ghosts they were pretending to be the others laughed and heaved it over with the doorway facing down. Then with the man cursing and thumping about inside and outraged neighbors firing shotguns in the air they broke all kinds of records as they beat it out of there. And that they considered having fun in those honey-dipper days.

"Another gang stole Mr. McHenry's jackass and pushed him into the parlor of a leading whorehouse, where he spoiled the evening's business by honking and pissing and kicking over chairs. Then a gang of Beaujack's henchmen found an old discarded horse-drawn hearse and pushed it down the street all lit up with flares and with six drunk musicians sitting on top playing '*Oh Didn't He Ramble*' and '*The Bucket's Got a Hole in It*,' all out of time and out of tune. While stretched out inside like a corpse is Mr. Choc Charley, the tailor who's known as the section's best, who's sleeping off a drunk with a red railroad warning lantern glowing on his chest. I tell you, ladies and gentlemen, things had turned primitive and really gone to swinging.

"But now it's dancing time, and the block where the dance hall stood is all lit up and as jammed with folks as the hall three stories up above. In fact, more costumed folks are dancing in the street than could've been packed in the dance hall with a battering ram. But most don't care because they're having such a fine time drinking and carousing that they've forgot all about the movie men while letting BooBoo Beaujack lead them deeper and deeper into what the judge who later fined them called 'a state of extreme and rowdy drunkenness attended by a total and mind-busting disregard for civic peace and universal order.'

"Now about this time Buster and me are up on the hill looking down on the lit-up business block, and from the way folks are dancing and flinging themselves about it's like watching a combination of the chronic heebie-jeebies and the seven-year's itch. Then, way back in the alley, we hear Pulliham's old dog give out with an awful, hair-raising howl. He howls two times and then he takes a deep, deep breath and howls another howl that's so long and eerie that it sounds like it's either turned him inside out or outside in, including his lock, collar, chain, and fence post. This stops us cold, but when he doesn't howl again and we don't hear thunder we decide to wander on down to the action. And when we get there it's easy to see that nobody else had heard him, and no wonder!

"Up in the dance hall, three stories above the street, twelve natural-born musicians are having a ball as they beat out the rhythm with the windows up. While down on the floor the fat young singer and dancing master is urging them on as he cavorts before the crowd in his gleaming golden shoes. The floor had been polished with cornmeal to make it slick, and by now he's led the dancers through every step from the quadrille to the tango, but now they're doing the well-known mess-around, with everybody moving slow and easy to the tune of 'See, See, Rider, Look What You Done Done' which he's singing through his three-foot megaphone. Not that he really needs it except to swing and dip like he's dancing with a partner, because folks down in the street can hear his sweet, sweet tenor ringing like a bell. And above all the noise and rhythm and the muted trumpet's cry he's making those blues laugh, sigh, and signify like Madam Ma Rainey with her love come down and her good man's gone ten thousand miles from Georgia. Talk about some sweet, *sweet* sadness—maaan! Oh, man!

"So now some of you are asking, 'What happened to the moving-picture crew?' Well, the answer is that they were grinding in the street. And not only because there wasn't room for them and that camera up in the hall, but when they tried to get in some men who were out with women other than their girlfriends or their wives wouldn't let them. It didn't matter that everyone was wearing masks, those guys weren't taking any chances of getting caught with the wrong woman wearing the wrong mask, no matter *when* or *wherever* that movie hit the screen. So their spokesman told the movie men, 'Listen here, y'all, and try to understand—we got nothing against what you're doing, and we'd like to help you out, but you have to recognize that if you shoot what a fine time we're having and these local white folks happen to see it they'll get so jealous and raving mad that the next time we have a dance they'll send the Sheriff out here to close us down.' So, being men of the world and far outnumbered, the movie men take their camera and go back to shooting up the action in the street.

"Now on the floor beneath the dance hall ten physicians, all good men and true, are resting back in their swivel chairs with their feet propped up, patting their bellies in time with the music and dreaming sweet dreams about such matters as their shaky rent-houses and their Hippocratic oaths, their be-diamonded women, and their Cadillacs, Auburns, and Pierce-Arrow cars; about cutting and curing and buckets of blood, and about outdoing Doctor Daniel Williams, who dealt cruel Death a blow and earned eternal fame by patching up what could have been a fatal stab wound in a living human heart. So now they're resting back easy in their big desk chairs, and surrounded to a man by grosses of catgut and cotton swabs, bandages and bullet probes, scalpels and hemostats—plus gallons of iodine, ether, and chloroform, gauze, catheters, and surgical needles—in other words, they're waiting for such casualties as gunshot wounds, busted skulls, broken limbs, and switch-blade stabbings to come rolling in. They didn't mind at all that the movie men had mixed up the calendar, because back in those rugged pioneer days folks around here swore by tradition and the tides of the moon that for a real *good* time to be had by all—by which they meant a real rip-snorting, compound-cathartic, knock-down-drag-out celebration—somebody famous had to shed some blood. And as far as anyone could remember it had never failed. They never knew when, and they never knew who, but it *always* happened. And so it did this time.

"Because now, with the festivities really grooving, both in the dance hall and the street, the musicians wailing and the movie men grinding that camera and thinking the leading man is already safe in bed having his loving and his ease—here comes somebody screaming through the street in his B.V.D.'s! And he's running so fast that he's hard to identify, but when folks hear the note he's screaming they know right away that he's shedding blood. Then he comes a little closer, and when they see who it is some begin to scream, some begin to cry, some to moan, and some to stutter, and some react like they'd been hit by laughing gas. In a second it was like the world had up and looped-the-loop and started spinning upside down....

"Yes, it was the hero of the movie they were hoping to be acting in, and when the word spread through the crowd it's like time itself had doubled itself into a knot and they could hear the dreadful grinding of its gears.

"For after all he was very good-looking, tall and strong, and until he'd dropped out of college to help his folks he'd been a first-string quarterback. He was respected as a man among men and a stud among the ladies, a fancy dresser, and a dancer in the class of Tulsa's Tickletoes. He was also good with his dukes and belonged to the local chapter of the N.A.A.C.P., didn't drink liquor, and, being an usher in his church, he was even respected by Miss Janey. So naturally when he got to be the star of the moving picture folks felt he had the world on a string and the key to fame and fortune in his fingers. What's more, to local pride and racial taste nobody in Hollywood movies was any better looking. Then, *wham,* and after acting as a hero just a little while before, he's running through the streets like a broke-back dog from Georgia!

"And it's not the fact that he's jetting blood that gets folks so excited; anybody was liable to bleed on such an occasion. It's his *screaming,* which is so out of character that it hits folks with the kind of chill they get when a heavyweight champion gets knocked on his butt in the first few seconds of an exhibition bout by an unknown fighter. It was enough to make folks rip their clothes and tear their hair—and a heap were doing it. It all happened so sudden, but it wasn't that they hadn't been warned, because not only did Pulliham's old dog let out those horrible howls, many had seen Miss Brilliantine upset the camera crew and put the bad sign on the man. So now, seeing him running bleeding had folks yelling and screaming and foaming at the mouth.

"Given the size of all that mob there's no way in the *world* for everybody to see what's taking place, but the news shoots through the streets like a dose of salts, and pretty soon it's like the story of Chicken Little has come alive, with little kids and sober citizens joining the drunks in yelling that the sky is falling down. Nobody really knows the facts behind the fact of his running, but with everybody busy trying to put what they imagine into words they have the poor man being chased by everything from lions and tigers to *The Hunchback of Notre Dame* and *The Phantom of the Opera*—which were both favorite movies of the time. So by the time the news leaps to the end of the business block and bounces back, little ole ladies are going stiff and passing out, big strong men are chattering like apes and wringing their hands, and tough guys with battle scars and skulls all dented from being hit on the head with brickbats, broken bottles, and big iron taps from the railroad tracks are raving in high falsetto through their Halloween masks.

"I tell you truly, rumors were flying and folks were crying! And when the news hit the red-light district, it turned it upside down and wrongside out. It puts madams in bed, and has the pimps climbing walls over having to turn all those good-paying customers away from what (on the sly) they claimed to be the only fully *integrated* establishments in the whole damn town.

"Now me and Buster were moving through the crowd in our Halloween masks, watching and listening and keeping to the high ground whenever we could. That's when we saw no less than a dozen big-breasted, big-legged, proud-butted ladies of the evening all weeping and wailing without a hint of shame as they called on Jesus in the hero's name. I said one spanking *dozen,* and that's exactly what I mean! And every single one of them beating on her bosom, tearing out her hair, and stirring up the air with her fancy underwear.

"Then one of them who turns out not to even know the hero starts to screaming that she can't go on living without her heart's desire—meaning him—and next thing we know she's climbing up a light pole like the street's caught fire! The crowd couldn't tell if she was clowning or going for broke, but when she gets close to those high-tension wires they start to leaping and grabbing, trying to get her down.

"And naturally, that's when BooBoo Beaujack gets into the act. The fool leaps so high that his head disappears, and when he drops back to the street the woman's up there clinging to that pole wearing nothing but her red silk stockings and some pink lace teddies. Then you talk about somebody having an instant change of mind and a reversal of direction! When she sees her clothes dangling in BooBoo's big cotton-picking hand and folks lamping her southern exposure so bare-face bold, she invents a brand-new technique for sliding down a pole. And when she hits the street she grabs her clothes and tries to hide—which by now was nothing but vanity, because everybody is already after the hero in hot pursuit, and the man is really moving.

"Now the street is massed with upset people and Jack and his henchmen are busy trying to track the man by his screams. Then way up the block where the camera goes on grinding they can tell by the way folks are ducking and dodging from his path that the hero's heading for the building where the dance hall's at. Which they take as a sign that he has his wits about him.

"Because in those days you could find a doctor, a dentist, a lawyer, a tailor, have a prescription filled, get a shave and a haircut and a fine shoe shine, shoot some pool, play a game of tonk, blackjack, stud poker, or the numbers, mail a letter, pay life insurance premiums, buy ice-cream sodas, read library books, or get embalmed—all in the very same building. It was the center of all *kinds* of action, and the place where most of the leading physicians could be found. Everybody knew it, too, so by time the hero hits the entrance to the building the crowd is closing on his heels.

"Oh, but when he shoots up the stairs with his frantic stride he sets off pandemonium in the ground-floor hall where three well-known bootleggers have been doing a thriving rent-free business with folks who wanted to get their gauges high before staggering up to the dancing. Before the hero busted in folks were blocking the entrance and crowding the stairs, ordering liquor by the drink and by the bottle. And with all those crazy-looking folks shaking fists full of money and demanding action those bootleggers were rocking and reeling as they passed out bottles and gathered in that cash. But then, *a-clamity-blam-blam!*—and the hall is like a joint that's being raided.

"False-faced folks are dashing for the backdoor of the hall spraining arms and ankles and ruining hired costumes as silver dollars, greenbacks, and pocket change go flying through the air. Pints, quarts, and jugs of homemade liquor are smashing against the walls and flooding the floor, and three disgusted bootleggers are standing in the middle, cussing their luck and counting the cost as they wonder what the hell has hit them. But the crowd behind the hero has no time for answering questions.

"Now nobody knows for which of the physicians the hero is headed, but as he reaches the second floor and goes sweeping down the hall they give a hopeful sigh. Because there like a sign sent down from heaven above they see, standing in all the doorways cooing like doves, all ten physicians who're rubbing their hands in rubber surgical gloves.

"Oh, they'd responded to the ruckus and are ready to a man for whatever business the holiday has brought them. But hardly before they can go into action it becomes a case of many being called but few being chosen. Because right away their number begins to dwindle.

"When the first doc in line sees what's jetting up the hall he gets so upset he hits the floor and becomes a living doormat for his fellow physicians. And with them buck-dancing on his body, trying to get some traction, in less than a second he's out of the action.

"Then doc Number Two calls for order, yelling, 'This case is an eight-day wonder and a surgeon's dream, but it demands that we act like a proper surgical team!'

" 'He's twelling it like it twiz,' another doc says with a tongue-tied lisp, 'Tho if we going thu get operwaiting we better start cooperwaiting. So let's get coordwinating, like tra-la, la-la, la-la!'

"So, heading for the biggest office, they rush the hero down the hall. Some have him by the arms, some by his feet and legs, and some are snatching and grabbing at anything at all. Then just as they go to make a sharp turn in a very narrow passage, a young doc named Jude damn near makes a wreck of their medical procession.

" 'This case,' he declares with firm conviction, 'looks so outrageous and downright tragic, that maybe instead of our kind of science it calls for *magic!*'

"Which puts his colleagues in such a state of shock that even the drunks could hear Jude's message making echoes in their heads. But then with an unbelievable and unspoken surge of coordination, they start kicking the hell out of Jude as they charge him with speaking rude and being a most unscientific nowhere dude.

"So then eight physicians, all willing and able, squeeze the hero through the doorway and toss him on the table. And naturally there's an awful lot of floundering and skidding about, but old Doc Pugh knows exactly what to do to calm them down. Barking like a sergeant he starts calling for face masks, morphine, and hemostats, and with them ducking and diving like a bunch of white-winged bats it looks like they're finally making progress.

"Oh, but then, out in the hall there's a tremendous pushing and shoving, and sweating and puking—plus a mighty swilling of whiskey, gin, and other brews—not to mention extracts of lemon, vanilla, and Jamaican ginger—which was either guzzled neat, or given a dynamite kick with Sterno canned heat that was strained through a handkerchief and had the poison burned off with matches. And while the crowd is thrashing about waiting to hear the hero's fate they're screaming and scrambling and a-helling and a-damning with a great stepping on of heels and a smashing of tender corns.

"Then this drunk who's got up like a Chinaman, black pajamas, pigtail, and opium pipe, starts to threatening the docs with a rusty three-barreled derringer. And with that the rest of the crowd starts advising him exactly where to stick it before he pulls the trigger. This hurts his drunken feelings and makes him want to cry but he runs into trouble with his narrow false-face eyes. And while the others keep ragging him it's a way of keeping their sagging spirits up as they plunge deeper into despair.

"Because all they can glimpse in the operating room is a rich, thick confusion of an M.D. nature, and nothing that's being done seems to be getting anywhere. They can see seven high-powered physicians bumping heads as they bend over the hero waving needles, gobs of cotton, and reams of catgut thread, but with seven pairs of hands fumbling in his pubic hair the hero's still groaning and writhing in agony. So now the crowd turns downright hostile.

"Then a high-voiced drunk wearing hard-conked hair and a sequin-covered mask and who's big enough to sing 'Ol' Man River' against both George Dewey Washington and Paul Bustill Robeson, expresses his opinion. 'Look, y'all,' he says to the medical men, 'if you don't do something quick for that darlin' man, and I mean *fas'*, I'm gonna start whuppin' some of y'all's *ass!*' And with that the rest join in in spades.

"And as they go spelling out their bills of particulars and battle plans the docs are so busy fumbling with the hero that only one takes time to listen. And that's only because he's short and fat, with arms too short for his heated competition. Being very unhappy over being jockeyed out of what he thinks is his rightful position he announces that for all his good intentions and his doing his level best to serve humanity like the rest, he's been elbowed, stepped on, and crushed in his pride; bled on, cussed at, and shoved aside. So naturally he feels neglected, rejected, and scandalized, *and* the victim of professional discrimination only because of his compact size. Come to think of it, Buster *really* felt sorry for that little doctor.

"So now, to have his revenge, or maybe out of spite, he takes dead aim at a fellow black man-in-white, and rushing at him like a mean little fice in a bulldog fight he goes into action.

> *Oh, with his feelings being hurt*
> *And his nerves being raw,*
> *He fractures his right on his*
> *Colleague's jaw.*
> *Then coming up with as sweet a left jab*
> *As has ever been beheld*
> *He really proceeds*
> *To give him holy hell*
> *Yelling, Here's one for your maw,*
> *One for your paw,*
> *And one for your great-grandmammy*
> *Down in Arkansaw!*

But then, since the doc he hit turns out to be a native of *Little Rock*, his last punch damn near ruins him.

" 'What the hell was that for?' he hears his victim yell and sees him standing blinking after thinking he had fell. And then this iron-jawed Arkansawan proceeds to attack little Doc's snout, break a gold-inlayed bicuspid, straighten his hair, and send him reeling backwards, flopping like a fish and gasping for air.

"Then, as he lies on the floor, little Doc explains with tears streaming from his eyes that he acted in the name of his stepped-on bunion, his aggravated gout, and his deep desire to serve humanity. But while it might have been false, or it might have been true—and even convincing to a colleague or two—in the end it was for conduct unbecoming of a professional that they kicked him out.

"Then, when the crowd sees what's been done to the little champion, they start breaking up furniture and ripping up the rug. Some are even about to risk seven years' bad luck by smashing the mirrors on the walls when the sight of all those false faces glaring back distracts them. So now they're pushing and shoving as they yell, 'Who the hell is you?' and 'Where the hell is *me?*' and keep at it until they hear two physicians feuding over how they'd split the fee. And when all this new who-shot-john interrupts their colleagues' concentration the results is something truly unexpected.

"Halting in the midst of their complex consultation, six physicians swell up in righteous indignation and proceed to give the two the Hippocratic boot for discussing loot and indulging in a crime they denounce as downright *filthy*. And then with the offending twosome looking like egg-sucking dogs caught dead in the act, ole Doc Pugh hits them over the head with a few of those golden, gilt-edge precepts for which he was so famous.

"Pointing at the two with a rubber-gloved finger he really lays it on 'em, saying:

"'Let me give you miserable sinners some good advice on how money relates to saving human life: Never, *never* name a price or discuss a fee, for it can only dull the temper of a surgeon's knife, *and* lead to practicing medicine for charity!

"'This above all, to our profession be true—including all its time-honored tricks, strategies, and improvisations—and you'll never be conned by any patient!

"'Be generous of ear but spare of tongue, short of description, but *long* on prescription. Appear warm but yet cold, be diffident but bold. And when a patient starts to complain about his hungry brats and his weak financial state, just drop him a hint about your own dear loving mate, who has to have her Cadillacs, her diamonds, and her sheets of satin! Then smile at him kindly and hide your aggravation—after which you send the clown a bill all itemized in *Latin!*

"'Dot every *i* and cross every *t,* and for his belated education include only the *rarest* of medical terms for his aching misery so as to impress him with its magnitude and your awesome mystery.

"'Observe these rules of conduct and I'll guarantee that he'll either have a low-grade nervous breakdown trying to save his sanity, or he'll come across, forthwith, with your rightful do-re-me!

"'Bear these few precepts in thy memory and be ye neither discussers of fees nor idle chatterers, and thus not only shall ye prosper in the noble profession which God gaveth thee, but as ye heal the sore ungrateful sick ye shall also instruct and redeem their heathen characters!'

"Like I say, Ole Doc really whacks 'em. And with his younger colleagues left bug-eyed, rededicated, and rebaptized, he stands there smiling and winking his eyes. He's forgotten that the crowd has been out there listening, but they have; and now with the hero moaning and groaning in a minor key they don't like his sermon worth a damn. In fact, the only reason they let it pass is because Doc himself is so old and so generous that most of them owe him money.

"So now, while they grumble and speculate over what they've been hearing, five fine, reinspired physicians, good men and true, dive into the hero's blood and bowels to see what they can do—when, lo and behold, here comes an *undertaker,* wrestling through the crowd with a big long basket!

" 'Gangway! Please step aside,' he shouts, and goes on to explain that he has the sad but solemn duty of transporting the fallen hero basket-wise to where his handsome casket lies. He speaks politely and with professional pride, but the crowd's reaction is most unfriendly. They tell him that he's way, *way* too previous, but out of respect for his swallowtail coat and derby hat, his unctuous manners and weird perfume they let him through. But for all his self-assertion and bold business enterprise he's picked the wrong time, the wrong place, and much too constricted a maneuvering space—not to mention that he sadly underestimates his opposition.

"When he waltzes that basket into where the action is, a big, freckle-faced doc standing six-feet-four in white silk socks looks up in shock, and right away this bold mortician's butt is in great danger. Because when doc does a double-take his freckles begin to dance, his eyes begin to glaze, his hands begin to tremble, and he goes into a rage. Then, as he grabs a firm hold to the first thing handy, we hear him yell, 'I hate what I'm doing but I can't stand a fool,' and he's raining blows on that undertaker's derby with a white iron stool. Then looking down at all that heavy hurt he's laid against the poor man's beat-up head he curls his upper lip and asks him real stern, 'When will you eager-beaver bastards learn to wait your rightful turn?' But right away his own luck goes bad.

"Because just as he turns to help dump the mortician into his own six-foot basket, Doc backs into a syringe-load of pure morphine. And even before his colleagues can ease the needle out he's kicking the gong like Minnie the Moocher and a hie-de-ho.

"So now four determined physicians turn back to the job, calling for jugs of whiskey and cans of chloroform, which Jack BooBoo Beaujack supplies them on the double. But in spite of Jack's eager assistance the dedicated docs are still in trouble. Because when one of them spies a bottle of twenty-five-year-old hundred-proof bonded bourbon he undergoes a sober moment of naked truth. First he looks at the hero, then he looks at the booze, and he knows in his heart that he has to choose. So, taking a swig from the bottle that leaves it either semi-empty or half full, he bows to the crowd and goes on a zoom. For this sad failure of nerve his colleagues complain, but mostly for the benefit of the anxious crowd. Because at last they're down to a comfortable three, a trinity; leaving one to stop the bleeding, one to stop the pain, and one to stitch the hero back together again. But it's then that an unforeseen complication of a very serious nature hits them in the eyes. For when they probe into the hero's machinery they discover that a most important piece is missing. And what's more, it's probably back in the alley lying in that bed of horror where the hero lost his head and started screaming. So now in face of this undeniable natural fact, and the art of surgery being what it was in those pioneer days, three physicians, good men and true, roll up their sleeves to see what they can do.

"But after the star surgeon makes three brave passes with his needle and thread, what's happened to the hero hits him with such bone-rattling shivers that he snatches off his rubber gloves and begins to shake and cry. And even to this day he's famous for wearing metal jockstraps and being scalpel-shy.

"It wasn't his fault that his nerves went bad, but by now folks in the crowd are losing their patience. They're soreheaded as bears and drunk as fish from swigging liquor while breathing chloroform and ether fumes. So now it has them in a rare, disgusted frame of mind. They're cussing and complaining that they're fast losing patience with the weather, with doctors and their medical science. And with them all being products of democracy on the darker side—and mostly from way down South—they're making it known by signifying and *o-rating* on the state of things—and I mean *loud*!

"Pressed against the wall as tight as a tick to a cow's tit there's this drunk who's supposed to be impersonating no less than that famous badman, Stackalee. But not knowing how Stack actually looked he settled for a minstrel man's mask and some blue-lensed horn-rimmed glasses. And he's also wearing some dry-cleaned overalls complete with a jumper that has a gold watch chain dangling from its lapel. He has the collar of his white shirt pinned up high around his neck, but instead of a tie he's sporting a phony diamond stickpin that's flashing like it has a little lightbulb behind it. And to top off his costume he's wearing a beat-up Stetson hat which *he* claims to be exactly like Stackalee's. So now with them pressing him even tighter he upgrades the contention by banging his head against the wall behind him and yelling, 'What's happening here is a dirty 'bomination and a bloody shame! It's a snare and delusion and a damn disgrace! Thass right! And y'all wanna know why? It's 'cause not a single one of these damn M.D.s has what it takes to renovate and save this pruned man's life! So now I'm giving y'all fair warning—and it's based on some unfailing signs which I've seen in the stars and the moon—that if we don't rise up and take command we gonna *lose* that man, and I mean soon! Therefore I say we better use some sense and go get Charlie!'

"To which another drunk juts out his mouth and says, '*Charlie?* Which damn Charlie are you talking about? Three-fourths of the sonsabitches in this here town is named Charlie, so do you mean *Poppa* Charlie?' And this makes the drunk against the wall get fighting mad.

" 'Hell, naw,' he yells, 'I'm not talking about no Papa Charlie—*Choc-drinking* Charlie's the one I mean! Choc Charlie, the Choc-drinking tailor! So I'm repeating what I already said: We better git Charlie or this man is DEAD!'

"But the very idea leaves a nearby drunk outraged.

[CHOCCHOL]

" 'This chump is *insane*,' he yells. 'Let's throw his butt downstairs!'

" 'Yeah! I'm for that,' another drunk yells, 'and then let's get Doc Chisum!'

" 'Now you gon' to talking sense,' another drunk throws in, 'and so the world will know I'm wid you, you can say it again. . . .'

" 'Like hell I will,' the Chisum champion says, 'because I done sang my song and ain't gon' sing no more. But let's git Doc Chisum anyhow.'

" 'Hell, y'all,' a leading blackjack hustler breaks in and says, 'Chisum is chicken, as everybody knows, so for the steel nerves and iron constitution this kinda job requires we can forget that bird!' Then he crows like a bantam rooster trying to wake up the dead—which raises a hue and cry for their favorite physicians.

" 'Get Tanenbaum! Get Davis! Get Haywood Gaylord James! Get Bullard! Git Lampkin, Whitby, Bunn, and Butler! Git Stammler—' were some of the docs they call for. But when someone yells get Fatty-Come-with-Fleas one of them stamps his foot and says, 'Hell, man, Fatty is neither doctor, dentist, or garbageman, so how's *he* gon' cut the mustard?'

" 'Maybe he can't and maybe he can,' the other said, 'but afterwards he'll tell some lies that'll outdo even Lazarus being raised up from the dead.'

"Then a fat man wearing a shark's-head mask breaks in. 'To hell with all that,' he says, 'because the doc we need is young Doc Heminsteen! He's new to the scene but already his way with broken bones, bullet wounds, brain concussions, stabbings, and the bleeding piles makes him the leading expert in his trade!'

" 'Which might be true,' a drunk made up like an Egyptian mummy says, 'but he ain't *nowhere* when it comes to things like razor scrapes, Charleston pistol scalds, and amputations done with axes, 'cause they don't teach such medicine in the place he went to school. And besides, what the hell's he gonna do about that poor man's missing parts?'

" 'At last somebody's talking *sense*,' a woman in a Martha Washington outfit and a red silk turban slaps her hands and says. 'At a time like this we got to think about the fundamentals! And what's more, this case is so serious that it makes even the very *best* we can get only a *little* better than the rest. So after giving it my best consideration I'd say that this man's condition calls for a combination of the Mayo brothers, Doc Fraizer, Doc Harrison, Doc Elwood S. McArdie, *and* that well-known spiritual advisor, Snake Mary!' And she ticked off the names on her white-gloved fingers.

" ' "Snake *Mary*," ' the Chisum champion cries. 'All she'll do is pray over the poor man's hard-earned cash and then work some mumbo-jumbo with some kind of hoo-doo root—which sho in hell ain't the kind he's missing! What he needs is nothing less than some quick'ning resurrecting, and I mean *quick*!!'

" 'Well, how about that ole Native, Love,' the woman in the red silk turban says. 'The one who goes by the State name of New?'

"Then Miss Tommy, who's Miss Brilliantine's twin sister, throws back her head and bellows, 'Ole Love New will never do, because after just one look he'd shoot the poor man in the head like he's no more than a horse with a broken leg!

Are you forgetting that Love looks *down* on folks like us? Hell, if it was up to him that Delilah-minded bitch who ruined this sweet man's life would do the same damn thing to every mother's son of you! So whether he calls himself Love, New, or Nicko-the-dog-assed-demus I say screw him!'

"But then a big pockmarked drunk who's wearing a headpiece of buffalo horns and a necklace of wildcat teeth, and who has his face and chest striped red, white, and blue with war paint, comes alive with a speech complete with gestures.

"Raising his arm in the air like an Indian chief he says, 'How! My brave brothers and beautiful sister squaws, to you I say How!' Which is so unexpected that everybody stares at one another like he's put them in the dozens. Then somebody yells, 'How some hell!' And with that they proceed to give him their undivided attention, yelling things like, 'How who?' 'Who's How?' 'How's your mammy and your mammy's mammy?' 'How, now, if it ain't Chief Hooking Cow!' 'How funky did your armpit smell when it crawled across your nose?'

"Oh, they're really picking on him now and he knows it, but his liquor and that getup he's wearing is casting so strong a spell that he just waves his hand in the air and keeps on going. And in the process he keeps getting his homemade Indian talk mixed up with snatches from the Bible.

" 'Hear me, my powerful braves and beautiful squaws! Hear now my urgent appeal! Let us cease our bickering and palaver together. . . .'

And when Miss Tommy yells, 'Who the hell let this how-minded fool in here?' he comes back with a variation. 'Hear me, my people, hear now my plea that we pay the advice of this brave who stands with his back against the wall some *heed*! To him, I say, let us listen!

" 'A short time ago, as we swayed treetop high in the noon of the night, bad times did smite us hip and thigh—aye! For it was then, in the bright peak of darkness, that a ruthless knife did slash at the vital root of our hero's life! From ambush it struck, it slashed, it mangled, and to a good man did a *terrible* damage. And not only to him, but to ourselves and to all the future members of his tribe. Even to them it did great damage!

" 'So now our ranks are broken and in our despair we wander. We track false trails! We hunt downwind! We zig and zag as we stampede! Like spooked cattle we stampede in circles, and in our panic we caterwaul and bellow! Our hopes grow dim, our vision falters—that's how it is. But wait! Hold on! For if we would but pause and read the signs which our walled-in brave calls to our attention we could get our bearings, close ranks, and help heal our injured hero! So now you ask, what *are* these signs of which I speak, and they are these:

" 'First: The great black dog of Pulliham howled the howl of warning which his wild canine fathers howled, "Aaaarooo, Arrrooooo!" but, alas, he was ignored.

" 'Second: Then high above we heard the sweet-voiced fat boy paint upon the nighttime air that lovely, ideal scene wherein Papa loves Mama and Mama loves

Papa, with everything randy and sweet as can be—ah, yes!—and to which serene domestic scene we said a loud ah-men! Aye, but as we gloried in his sweet glad tidings did we not also hear, but again ignore, the trumpet and trombone as they replied with that vast gut-bucket blast of nasty mockery? We did indeed! And while we ignored their concerted brassy nastiness, that heartless camera took it in and kept on grinding!

" 'And then the night was torn by screams, the air was filled with the stench of panic, and the beat of frantic footsteps made a tom-tom of the street as fresh blood splashed our well-worn trails, our sidewalks, curbs, and gutters. And then, as we knocked the prying camera from our path to track our hero's red-hot trail, his life's blood spills upon the steps and risers of the stairs! *These* are the ignored signs of which I speak! Aye! And the heroic brave who bled and bleeds lies where my pointing finger indicates: He's there, being fumbled and poked upon that blood-soaked table!

" 'First it was that bitch-in-the-manger's malicious blade, and now the fumbling fingers! So here, now, while our frustrated voices snap and snarl and the firewater burns and howls like flaming blackjacks in our bowels, the precious life of our brave brother brave lies swinging in the balance. Aye! In the balance his life lies swinging! So I repeat: It was to this blood-chilling fact that the signs were pointing, and it is in the name of these same sad signs that our drunken brave has spoken. To heel, he cries, to *heel*!

" 'Therefore I say let us heed his warning. To him pay heed, I pray you! For it is through him that these sad signs speak to us as from that wall where once in ancient times fair Minnie Haha tickled the soaring seraphim by rattling the scales of the infidel snake! Therefore let our voices rise up in thunder while as one we read the signs and say, 'Mene, mene take him, we're for him!' And then again as one let us say, 'Whether many take him or don't take him, we're *still* for him! And that as one is what we *all* say!

" 'So take heed! Look with calm cool eyes upon the man who sprawls there on the table. Then look again at our brother brave who stands with his back against the wall and you will see him as *I* first saw him: a brave so loaded up and down with firewater that if that firm wall were to move even the thickness of a skittish jot or ticklish tittle he'd go down like a lamb before the slaughter! Aye, or a raindrop before a flood! But then take a *second* look, and like me you'll see that although our brother brave is stewed to the gills he has been so truly *transformed* by his fierce firewater's inspiring fire that he can't help but speak the *truth*! Aye, and speak it coolly. So hear me, my people! My people hear me now as I interpret our brother brave's most puzzling condition:

" 'Our brave stands pressed against the wall as between a hard place and a rock and he's lit up like the campfire of the white man, that greedy tenderfoot's fire which sears the belly but leaves the backside frosted! Yea, but that very heat and pressure is the secret of his vision! For while the firewater glows in his bowels like coals in the blacksmith's forge, his clear, untainted vision beams like that of Meshack, Shadrack, and their doughty brother—What's-His-Name—cool, steady, and unblurred!

" 'Oh, yes! I know! To the spooked, unseeing eye this brave is *drunk*! You know it and I know it. And from the way he reels and staggers yet stands erect *he* knows it as *we* know it. So behold! my people, against that wall a drunken head with sober eyes! Is it a riddle? Yes! A conundrum? Yes! I must agree, but let that be no mystery. Nay! For as it is written, "In vino veritas!" Which says (and now I translate into the simplest language of ABC) that for seeing truly the nitty in the gritty, being *shicker* is the key!

" 'So now take heart, for as our prophet against the wall has made us see, our mangled brother brave's condition adds up by no means to disaster. Nay, for even though yon wall-pressed brave's most Noah-like condition be one of uncouth sloppy-drunkenness, he's still a fountain of our ancient tribal wisdom. Therefore let us remember that just as in this world the broadest of extremes and roads inevitably meet, just so has our brave brother drunk so deep that now—there on the fair far horizon of his mind—he sees most clearly that which the rest of us have been too shaken and liquored-up to see!

" 'Yea, he has survived! He has weathered the tide! For while the storms of booze have swayed him and the hounds of life have bayed him, still he stands with his wrinkled head unbowed! And though he perfumes these rooms with Choc-laden breath, it is a rare, wise wisdom he distills! So hear me now, my fellow braves and beautiful squaws, as I translate the message he inscribes upon the wall:

" 'For although our wounded brother brave has been counted and weighed and left divided there is still hope if we but aid him. Aye! For as it was with firewater in the old days so be it now in the new days. And while we've grown weary of watching the white man's palefaced medicine grow limp in our shaky M.D.s' trembling hands I have been heeding the words of our drunken Daniel! Yea, and it is to the Great Spirit that I have appealed....'

" 'Hey, man,' a voice calls in from the hall, 'if you gon' talk *religion* I'm wid you, so why don't you cut out all that powwowing and tell us what he said?'

" 'This fine brave has a point,' the Indian orator says as he smiles and lifts his arms into the air, 'for indeed the Great Spirit has confided to me that the words of our drunken brave's firewater falls upon our sad condition as soothing rain upon the seething sun-parched plain! Therefore I can now affirm that although these many docs have tried to cure our injured brother's sad, sad case, they have been counted, weighed, and now stand divided. And this being so it is clear that our brave Charley of the Choctaw beer is now the only man who can complete this terrible task. Therefore, my strong fellow braves and beautiful squaws, I end my palaver with this, my urgent appeal: Let's stop all this assing around and GET...CHOC...CHARLEY!'

" 'Well, thank the Lawd,' a big woman made up like a monarch butterfly exclaims, 'somebody's finally talking sense! And it don't matter that it's a phony Indian! Because if *we* don't do something for that poor man, who else? And what's gonna happen to the moving picture?'

" 'Now that's the stone-cold truth,' somebody calls in from the hall, "cause we *all* have a stake in that poor bleeding man, so where the hell is Charlie?'

"Which was a good question," Cliofus said in his normal high-pitched voice, "because Mister Choc Charlie has been on a blind-staggers drunk for about three days, so it looks like finding him will be a problem. Then somebody remembers seeing him lying in the old horse-drawn hearse with a lantern on his chest, and BooBoo Beaujack knows exactly where to find him. So when Jack pushes him protesting and belching up the stairs the crowd lets out a heartfelt cheer. Choc Charlie doesn't know what it's all about, but when he sees such a solemn crowd he thinks he's in church and sings out, *There is a balm in Gilead that'll heal the sin-sick soul.* But when they get him to the operating table and he sees what's happened to the hero, he wipes his eyes and says, 'How on earth can *any* man rip his britches this doggone bad!'

And with that big Miss Tommy burps and lets out a forlorn moan. Then, while Choc Charlie is peering at what's on the table, some of the crowd come up with a strategy to get him started.

"First they knock the last two physicians out of the way, then slap him on the back and say, 'Lissen Choc, here's a pair of ripped-up britches which need your expert attention. You think you can fix them in time for the picture we been making?' Then Choc-drinking Charlie belches and staggers, steadies himself and sways. Then he leans down and squints at the man's condition out of just one bloodshot eye. Then he calls out loud and clear, 'Somebody gimme a shot of something strong to clear my vision.'

"And while they're fetching a bottle Charlie wavers again and sways, and this causes a proper-talking drunk to sober up and say, 'What the hell are we *doing*? Why, this is obscene! You people have lost your alcoholic minds!'

"But he doesn't faze Choc Charlie. All he does is stagger back a bit to get his man in focus, then he wipes his lips on the back of his hand and says, 'What the hell do you know about it, friend? Yeah, and how good are *you* at whatever the hell you do? And I mean for a *living*! Sho, I have to admit to being maybe a little too high to 'gotiate an invisible patch, but hell, Choc Charlie can *always* stitch a good straight seam! And I admit it, friend, because I'm no goddam amateur! That's right, friend! And you can bet your life on what I say. Because while drinking Choc is my fame, stitching is my living and my game!'

"So now, with folks yelling, 'Tell him about it, Choc,' they pass him a bottle and he takes a swig and shakes his head and shivers. Then he takes up that needle with the catgut thread, and with the last of the physicians guiding him to the target he proceeds. And when he starts to stitching he squints and bats his bloodshot eyes and complains about the curve in the needle and the thickness of the thread. But though lap-legged drunk as he truly is, he stitches steady and he stitches true, and folks swear to this day that by time he's through he's stitched himself a masterpiece.

"Yeah," Cliofus said, "but the sad thing about it was that with Choc making all that medical history, none of it was recorded by that ever-grinding camera. Because while the other cameramen were out there shooting up the street, the guy with all the accents was off somewhere jiving that little leading lady!"

Seeing Cliofus pause to press a huge towel to his perspiring face, Hickman heard the clang of a spoon hitting the floor as the audience waited for the tale to continue. Then, hearing a man strike a table and yell, "I knew damn well that those cats weren't doing all that grinding for nothing," he saw a woman leaping up from a down-front table as she yelled out in triumph, "I told you that he was the one they's have to bleach and watch! I *told* you!" and the room exploded with laughter.

Feeling both uneasy and suddenly exhausted, Hickman joined in as he thought, *So I got what I came to hear and hoped I wouldn't, and if putting it together with what I heard from Love makes sense, that's how it happened.... Lord help that boy—yes, and that boy's boy!* Then, hearing the woman repeat her shrill triumphant cry, he became aware of Cliofus, who sat now leaning forward in the posture of a tired boxer with the towel draping his head as he stared intently in his direction. *Man,* he thought, *like the taxi man said, you are really something!* Then, giving Cliofus a bow of thanks, he waved his clinched hands above his head and left the Wind Cave.

Editors' Note to "McIntyre at Jessie Rockmore's"

"McIntyre at Jessie Rockmore's" appears to be the last portion of the novel that Ellison saved to disk before his death. Given that so much of his attention in the decade of his composition on the computer had been dedicated to revising portions of the novel related to Alonzo Hickman, it is somewhat surprising that this single scene with McIntyre would command his final attention. Nonetheless, Ellison seems to have revised each of the files in the McIntyre sequence in the waning months of 1993.

"McIntyre at Jessie Rockmore's" is a revision of Chapter 13 of Book I, consisting of McIntyre's recollection of his nighttime visit to the scene of a possible crime—the apparent homicide of an elderly black man. McIntyre is struck by several things: It appears that the dead man, Jessie Rockmore, was the owner of the tony townhouse and the museum-quality historical artifacts within. Even more, Rockmore is found dead sitting bolt-upright in a decaying coffin, with both his assistant, Aubrey McMillen, and an aging white prostitute, Cordelia Duval, as witnesses. The entire place reeks of whiskey and defunct goldback currency is strewn across the floor.

Leveraging his contacts with the police, McIntyre insinuates himself into the scene, where he converses with both McMillen and the nearly naked Miss Duval. Through the course of the scene, we come to understand that Rockmore's death was not the result of foul play, but of shock upon the arrival of an unidentified man—whom we may reasonably suspect was Sunraider, though he is never identified by name—who lays claim to the coffin. The episode stops with McIntyre making his way from the townhouse out into the street coincident with the dawning of a new day.

Notably, it appears that Ellison likely conceived this scene as a pivot point in the narrative, marking the confluence of Hickman, Sunraider, and McIntyre and conceivably knotting his various narrative threads. Among the several instances in which he ponders such a connection is the following note: "N.B. Try introducing Hickman and Wilhite immediately after McIntyre leaves the building. And this time it is he who leaves the door open." The Rockmore scene would thus serve both practical and thematic purposes. As Ellison states in another note, included here on page 978, the Rockmore incident was an instance of "trivial chaos... building to some kind of disaster," underscoring the central instance of chaos and disaster brought on by the shooting. Although the precise nature of this scene's connection to the Hickman plot remains unresolved, the fact that it is likely the final episode Ellison revised marks it for special consideration.

McINTYRE AT JESSIE ROCKMORE'S

[MANSION]

THE ADDRESS CITED IN the murder report was that of a four-storied mansion, and seeing detectives and policemen making their way up the walk I gripped my recorder and hurried to join them. But upon reaching the entrance we came to a halt, for although the door was wide open there was no one to receive us. Then came a murmur of voices, and with the Sergeant of detectives leading the way, we entered the thick-carpeted entrance hall and set out to find them.

Straight ahead a grandfather's clock gleamed in a corner, and on our approach it began chiming an hour which was very much later than that on my wristwatch. And then we turned left and encountered a scene which we least expected. For suddenly we were facing a spacious, high-ceilinged vestibule which was crowded with black folk who were dressed in an eye-dazzling assortment of bathrobes, housecoats, and kimonos.

Women and men, they crowded the floor and an elegant staircase which curved to the floor up above, and as I wondered why anyone had need for so many servants they greeted our arrival with expressions which ranged from anxiety and relief to outright hostility. Which in itself was not surprising, for having known at least three of the detectives from on various assignments I was all too aware that some of their tribe were indeed quite prejudiced.

And yet my immediate reaction was one of resentment. For while I took pride in my impartiality on questions of race, the black folk before me appeared to make no distinction between me, a reporter, and the white lawmen for whom as a group they had quite valid reasons, current and historical, for feeling distrustful.

Okay, I thought, *so you don't like the presence of white policemen, but they're here because of a murder. So since you resent others judging you on the basis of color, why not regard me as an individual and make your decision as to my character and competence after*

you've read my report? Who knows, it might prove helpful in bringing the murderer—
whoever it might be—to justice, and even dispel any suspicion of your possible involve-
ment. . . .

But now to the Sergeant's "Where can we find him?" a man on the staircase
pointed to a tall door behind us, and with the Sergeant and his men leading the
way I followed. Then the door was flung upen and I was blinded by a fierce glare
of light, blasted by strong fumes of bourbon, and in a blink of an eye faced a
scene of startling disorder.

[ROCKMORE]

WHAT HAD ONCE BEEN a ballroom was so crammed with furniture, appliances,
and odd works of art that the slightest misstep or unwary gesture could end in
disaster. Worst, I had a feeling that the wild disarray was not accidental but the
product of a conscious, if elusive, design. And struck by the contrast between the
ballroom's disorder and the vestibule's elegance I recalled a designer of interiors
who had scoffed that the American home was fast becoming a cross between a
ragtag museum and a warehouse for gadgets.

Then I moved in with the detectives, and everywhere I looked there were tables and chairs, divans and chaises longues; cabinets, chests, and various utensils;
toys, oil paintings, and miniature sculptures; baskets, crates, and old cardboard
boxes. Through the glass doors of cabinets I saw collections of crystal and
porcelain; antique tables were piled with books, lamps, and musical instruments.
And as I tried to make sense of the mind-teasing chaos I heard a detective exclaim, "Hey, Murphy, what the hell kind of a joint *is* this!"

To which Murphy replied, "Oh, come *on!* Being that it's here in the U.S. of A.,
it could be *any* damn thing! And especially with those boogies out in the hall.
What's more, I'll lay you ten to one that our being here has to do with this booze
we're breathing—isn't that right, McIntyre?"

"It may very well be," I said as I squinted, "but what's bothering me is this
eye-blinding glare."

"So use your shades, McIntyre, use your shades!"

"I could very well use them," I said, "but since it's long after midnight I left
them at home."

"Which is typical of see-all, tell-all reporters," he said with a grin, "so be
careful, old buddy, or next thing you know you'll stumble, and for once in your
life you'll end up writing the truth, the whole truth, and nothing *but* the truth."

"Yes, and then may God help me," I said, "because you'll still insist that your
harebrained preconception of what brought us here is more accurate than my
painstaking efforts to get at the truth. And by the way, since you're so smart and
foresightful, why the hell are you squinting?"

And now, turning away, I realized that one source of the glare was a collection of unshaded lamps. And with the detectives beginning their search for the murdered man's body I stood puzzling as to why the room was so personally disturbing.

Perhaps it was simply the shock of encountering such an incongruous clutter so close to the Capitol, and in a house which was staffed by so many black folk. For while they were as typical of Washington as its historical monuments, this particular household's existence suggested that something was happening in the District of Columbia which had escaped my reporter's awareness. . . .

Whereupon, hearing a thudding behind me, I turned to see a policeman grabbing frantically at a tall stack of books which were tumbling to the floor from a table. And intrigued by the books' leather bindings, I knelt to give him a hand as he stooped to replace them. But not only did the incessant glare render their titles unreadable, the fumes near the floor were so powerful that in the course of standing I staggered. Which increased my suspicion of having blundered onto a scene in which anything could happen.

For now the clash between objects of such disparate styles and places of origin suggested some excess of emotion or confusion of logic that had been doomed from the start to lead ultimately to murder. But now, seeing the officers making their way to a door straight ahead, I began inching my way toward them and decided that once I had the victim's name and his attacker's motive and identity I'd leave the strange house and structure my report in the quiet of my office.

But now I was impatient to have a look at the victim, for suddenly I felt—somewhat irrationally—that although the man responsible for the chaos around me had escaped public notice he had been nevertheless an insidious threat to our center of government. And that even a brief look at his face would assure me that the chaos in which he had chosen to have lived was uniquely his own. And should the detectives discover evidence of crimes other than murder I'd leave that to the Sergeant and the Negroes to deal with. But despite my mounting desire to get the details and take off, my integrity as a reporter demanded that I remain and make note of any facts that were available before structuring my story. . . .

"You know," Murphy exclaimed as he stood sniffing the air, "there has to be a *still* hidden somewhere in this joint."

"Yes, Murphy," the Sergeant replied, "there may very well be, but if so it's evidence and you're not to touch it. Meanwhile, forget it and let's have a look at our stiff."

"If you say so," Murphy said, "but stills are a hell of a lot livelier than stiffs."

"Don't worry," the Sergeant shot back, "because in our line of work *all* stiffs are still."

And with a self-satisfied grin at his banter he pointed to a door behind us and said, "And now to prove it, let's have a look-see."

But when he twisted the knob of the triple-locked door we were startled by the faint sound of moaning.

"Hell, Sergeant," a policeman in uniform said, "whoever's in there is alive!"

"Cool it," the Sergeant said sotto voce. "Do you think I've gone deaf?"

Then, with a twist of the doorknob he shouted, "You in there, open this door!" And receiving no answer he repeated his order.

"Hey, Sarge," Murphy said with a grin, "it would seem that you've turned up a stiff who doubts your authority."

"Dammit, Murph," the Sergeant said with a glare, "that'll be enough out of you!"

And rattling the doorknob he bellowed, "Mr. Rockmore, we're the police, so unlock the door!"

And with the moaning his only reply he turned to a detective and said, "All right, Levine, get it open!"

"Shall I give it my shoulder?" Levine said as he inspected the door frame.

"And scair him to death? Hell no, use your tools."

It was then I annoyed the Sergeant by asking him to explain why a man reported to have been murdered was moaning.

"Not now, McIntyre," he said with a frown, "not now. . . ."

"But do you know the perpetrator's identity?"

"Later, McIntyre, can't you see I'm busy?"

"So am I," I said. "You have your duties and I have mine. So what information do you have? And who reported this case as a murder?"

"Please, McIntyre, step aside and let us get on with our work!" And ignoring my question he turned angrily away.

"And you, Lawson," he barked to one of his men, "go around to the back of this joint and see if there's a door or a window that's open."

Inside the room the moaning continued, and with his companions looking on Levine went to work on the locks, the third of which soon proved so resistant that I moved away and tried making sense of the chaos around me. It was then I saw that a section of the lamp-blazing wall was covered with old lithographs, the subjects of which were deeply interred in my memory. And suddenly I was taken with a disquieting feeling of having been lured to an unnoticed area of Washington by a malicious trickster of historical bent whose motive was to force me to confront certain vague detail from the historical past and make sense of their ties to the present.

And immediately I was drawn to a lithograph in which soldiers in parade uniforms and civilians in black were accompanying a flag-draped coffin which rested on the bed of a horse-drawn camion. The civilians appeared to be men of authority, and with the flag displayed on the coffin I decided that the deceased had been a figure of national importance. Then from the dated dress of the crowd looking on and the long jackets and high domed helmets of the policemen in control of the gathering I realized that the time of the scene was the mid-nineteenth century. Then as I groped for the name of the deceased and the role he had played in the drama of history his funeral cortege seemed to surge and begin moving. Then from somewhere close by gunfire erupted, and with people screaming and scattering the horses took off down the street with a banging of wheels and jangling of harness, the flag was flapping, and the coffin banging the bed of the camion with such thundering force that I had a vision of it landing in the street and sending the deceased sailing through the air like a shot from a cannon. And reeling with vertigo, I was relieved that it was only a vision.

But now the image of Abraham Lincoln loomed in my mind, and with my memory aflap like a book in a whirlwind I thought with relief, *Oh, no—thank God—such a thing didn't happen!*

But at the thought the next lithograph came instantly alive, and I was watching a battlefield scene in which soldiers in blue and in gray were firing rifles and cannons while General Robert E. Lee with saber in hand was galloping northward on his handsome steed Traveller. Whereupon wondering if the scene was of Antietam, Bull Run, or Chancellorsville, I recalled the Battle of Gettysburg and moved to the next lithograph expecting a scene in which General Ulysses S. Grant was finally triumphant.

But instead, surrounded by soldiers with a crowd looking on, John "Osawatomie" Brown was being marched down an old Charlestown street on his way to the gallows. And while most of the crowd are acclaiming his capture, a short distance behind them a slave mother wearing a blue bandana headcloth stands weeping and cuddling her tiny black baby. And seeing the soldiers and prisoner approaching the spot where she's standing she thrust her tiny black child above the crowd's straining heads and beseeches John Brown to give it his blessing.

To which Brown reacts by thrusting out his chin and looking up at the child with an expression in which pride, surprise, and regret are enigmatically mingled. And while the crowd gawks and remains serenely unaware of what's happening above and behind them it's as though Brown were baring his neck for the noose which was ready and waiting at the end of his march.

Then, struck by a blow from the past, I reacted to the slave mother's gesture of hope and respect in the context of the chaos created by the clash between our democratic ideals and our regional self-interests. And with the devastation wrought by the war which erupted soon after sweeping through my mind, I recalled having read that during Brown's raid on the armory at old Harper's Ferry two of his sons had been slain.

And suddenly as I stared at Brown, the crowd, and the weeping slave mother, her symbolic gesture took on a power that wrenched me. For in it tragedy, hope, and sheer hopelessness were so intricately entwined that I moved away in a state of confusion. Then time took a leap, and with a sense of relief my attention was drawn to a thundering contention of fine thoroughbreds.

Mounted by jockeys in eye-dazzling silks, they were rounding the curve past a spectator-filled grandstand, and as I thrilled with excitement any questions raised by Brown and the slave mother's gesture were quickly forgotten. For now time swept me backwards into a mixture of relief and further confusion.

For, while the cheering spectators were white men and women, most of the jockeys—whether black, brown, or high-yellow—were *racially* black men. And in struggling to make sense of that incongruity I noted the unusual postures in which they were riding. For instead of straddling their mounts in the high-perched, short-stirruped, monkey-on-a-stick style of today, they were brandishing their whips in upright positions with their legs extended and feet thrust earthward. And as I watched a black rider maneuvering his mount to the lead of the track-pounding pack a quick glance at the lithograph's legend revealed that his name was Pike Barnes, his horse Proctor Knott, the year 1888, and that the race they were winning the first Futurity. And with the fashionably dressed spectators cheering them on they went galloping past in dream-like bounds as they headed for the finish of a race from which in the very near future jockeys of Barnes' racial identity would be barred from competing. And as though my invisible tormentor was using mute juxtaposition as a means for making me aware of the historical irony, the next lithograph presented a Kentucky scene of Churchill Downs which bore the image of black Isaac Murphy, the celebrated winner of three of its Derbys.

But now time leaped forward and wavered, and down the middle of a Manhattan street a group of smiling black women and men accompanied by a blaring brass band were dancing a high-stepping cakewalk. And while the women were prancing and smiling in a shimmering flurry of pink feather boas, the dashing black beaus, dressed in white ties and tails, were flourishing silk opera hats above their partners' plumed heads. To which, smiling coquettishly, the women were responding by aiming high kicks toward the beaus' gleaming hat brims. And as they swayed and swayed and kicked higher and higher they revealed teasing pink flashes of their ruffled silk lingerie, and their feminine garters were adorned with tiny blue bows. And as I watched them prance to the beat of the blaring brass tune I recalled a snatch of its once popular lyrics, which were echoed years later in a mosaic-like poem by Thomas Stearns Eliot:

> *If you like-a me*
> *Like I*
> *Like-a you . . .*
> *Under the bamboo tree . . .*

Then with a swoop and a flourish the dancers were gone—and I was watching a race between the riverboats *Natchez* and the *Robert E. Lee*. And as they went plowing along with their sidewheels awhirl and their smokestacks billowing a crowd of blacks who were lined on the levee were urging them on with cheers and with laughter.

Which left me wondering at the complex role played in our fractured democracy by the sports and the arts, and struck by the irony of irreverent laughter serving as a balm for the wounds that both bind and divide us . . .

But now, my musing interrupted by the Sergeant's command to one of his men, I turned to see on a table nearby an Edison phonograph, a telegraph key, a Leyden jar, a tintype camera, a collection of antique movie projectors, and a scattered collection of stereoscopic views of early America: Niagara Falls, a spouting Old Faithful, Jamestown, Boston, and Virginia's old Williamsburg. And then I took note of a towering stack of phonographic discs, on the top of which I looked down to see a cracked recording of "The Bear Mash Blues." . . .

Then from behind me the lock expert complained, "Look, Sarge, I could save time by giving this thing a bang with my shoulder."

"And you'd wake up the dead," the Sergeant said, "so stick to that lock 'til you've solved it. That's what you're paid for."

"Okay, but by then whosever's in there could climb out the window."

"Don't worry, the joint's surrounded," the Sergeant said, "so snap to it!"

And with that I continued making notes on the room and its clutter, which was becoming a mind-teasing mixture of weird treasure-house and pack rat's burrow. And in inching my way I grew dizzier and dizzier.

Here was an old Franklin stove supporting a fading framed portrait of Teddy Roosevelt wearing his Rough Rider's uniform. A full-length portrait of Senator Stephen A. Douglas looked down from a wall surrounded by framed collages made of fading handbills that offered rewards in cash for the safe return of runaway slaves. A playbill dated April 14, 1865, announced the final performance of *Our American Cousin*, a drama in which Laura Keene had starred on the stage of Ford's Theater, that site of a deed so fatal that it still finds uneasy echoes in our hesitant memory. And next to that haunting reminder that our country's history possesses elements of tragedy (and no doubt to the delight of my invisible tormenter), I saw a playbill of the same fatal date that proudly announced the presentation of Boucicault's "Great Sensation Drama" *The Octoroon,* and beside it a portrait of young Thomas Jefferson.

And now I moved past a tall weathered totem pole carved with animals, birds, and tribal ancestors—and was brought to a halt by the cast-iron figure of a young blackamoor.

A relic from the days when few cars were available, the figure had once served as a convenient device for tethering horses. But now it stood high on a table with a small palm stretched toward me and a mischievous smile on its shiny black face. And as it stared back with eyes that seemed to look through me, I realized that the object on its head at a debonair angle was the inverted bowl of an old chamber pot, and as I frowned in revulsion it appeared to respond with a gaze of derision—from which unnerving spell I sought to escape by grabbing the offensive utensil and snatching it away.

Whereupon I saw printed on its side in Italian:

Mange Bene,
Cacca Forte,
Vida Longo!

Under which the following comment was written in English:

"But now, alas and alack, Her lovely soft
Thighs shall be bathed
By bright Pearly Tears."

And fearing that the grinning black figure would take off and start dancing a buck dance, I returned the bawdy utensil to its nappy iron head.

But where, I thought as I moved quickly away, are the fumes coming from? Could it be from the fireplace? And could the building actually be, as Murphy suggested, a site for illegal activities? And all the clutter a shield for crimes that had long gone unnoticed? Could the mass of images and objects from the past have been amassed as a façade behind which some violation of law had only now run its course and ended in murder? How did one even *begin* to think about a place in which the weird collection of incongruous objects were evoking a whirl of long surpressed memories? And why were the detectives taking so much time in picking that lock!

Then, inspired by the fumes in the air, I thought, Perhaps there really *is* a still in this building, with its copper coil winding between the walls and the floors and down to the basement, where even now its illegal distillant is being collected.

And making my way to the room's marble fireplace, I examined its opening but found no sign of a still's hidden coil. Instead, in the space usually occupied by andirons, firewood, and ashes, I found an ancient iron safe, on the black door of which I read quotations that were a mix of the Bible and Benjamin Franklin. Painted in red, gold-bordered letters, they offered the following advice to the reader:

REMEMBER THY FATHER IN THE DAYS OF THY YOUTH
FOR A PENNY SAVED IS A PENNY EARNED (!)

Then, hearing the detectives thudding the door to little effect, I moved from the safe to a wall on which I saw a series of photographed portraits of once-famous Indians. Among them Black Hawk and Tecumseh, Sitting Bull and

Chief Joseph, Osceola, Crazy Horse, and Stumickosucks—a name as imposing as its owner's grim image. Here was a ceremonial scene in which white men and Indians were making a treaty, a group of Plains Indians in full regalia posing with impassive dignity for an early daguerreotypist—perhaps no less than the great Mathew Brady.

Then came photographs of President Warren G. Harding. In the first of which, surrounded by cronies, Harding might well have been indulging in the hyper-alliterative oratorical style for which he was famous. Such as his letter "P" accented " . . . palaver on progress without pretense or prejudice or accent upon personal pronouns, and without regard to the perennial pronouncements and unperturbed by people passion-wrought over the loss of promises proposed."

Which phrase I recalled as among the guests who were listening I identified Albert Fall and Harry Daugherty and surmised that the scene might have been snapped about the time Teapot Dome, that nation-shaking scandal of the twenties, was on the point of exploding. And then came photographs of scenes that fairly exulted, "HARDING, HARDING, WARREN GAMALIEL HARDING!"

Harding attired in a suit of white flannel, silk shirt, bow tie, and panama hat while playing croquet on the handsome South Lawn of the White House.

Harding standing on a balcony with a party of ladies with high generous bosoms who displayed fancy wide hats while waving to a mob of small kids who were rolling Easter eggs on the lawn below them.

Harding with hand upraised while taking the oath of his office, his swarthy face somber beneath his white, neatly parted hair.

And Harding in top hat and fur-collared coat smiling suavely as he waved from a limousine to a Fifth Avenue crowd.

And then, just when I was taken with sadness by such poignant reminders of those desperately optimistic days, when this war-weary nation's most popular slogan was "A return to normalcy," I was face-to-face with Jack Johnson, the most notorious of all heavyweight champions, and a man whom certain sports reporters and Sam, my favorite black waiter, regard as an underground hero. Which I confess was an opinion in whose regard I remained strictly neutral. Nevertheless I recognized that Johnson was a figure of national prominence who had indeed been most imposing, skillful, and troublesome. But now, erupting like a ghost from the past, he came jogging toward me like a black Hercules. Broad-shouldered and tall, he's wearing a black-and-white suit of giant houndstooth check, a white turtleneck sweater, and a circular fur cap of Russian design. And gripping a club of a walking cane midway its length he comes jogging toward me with a haughty expression. Then, in Havana, stretched on the canvas, he's shading his eyes from the sun with a nonchalant gesture while Jess Willard, the triumphant "White Hope," waits in a corner while the referee with hand in the air renders his verdict. But was Johnson really defeated—or, as Sam the waiter insisted, simply bowing to the force of white racial prejudice? And thinking, *Damn this room and the questions it raises,* I returned to the present when one of the detectives bumped into a table and a huge music box came alive with a reedy, twangy rendition of "Oh Didn't He Ramble."

Then the Sergeant was cursing and as the tune expired I turned back to see Johnson dressed in a bullfighter's costume while posing with his arms around the shoulders of the Joselito and Belmonte, who like himself were both outstanding athletes. Yes, but unlike our boxing theirs was a sport which was life-risking and tragic.

And now here was Johnson looking sinisterly graceful in his black fighting togs, with his domed, shaven head bobbing and weaving as he taunts and has fun with Jim Jeffries.

Which called to mind an incident from my boyhood in which a little black kid hurled a taunt from the top of a fence in an alley. Sticking out his tongue and thumbing his nose he had yelled,

> *"Hey, whitey! If it hadn't been for*
> *that white referee*
> *Jack Johnson woulda* killed
> *Jim Jefferie!"*

And as I grinned at that forgotten hilarity there came a bang behind me, and I whirled to see the door flying open. And as the Sergeant and his men stepped into the doorway and froze in confusion I rushed to join them, and came face-to-face with a scene for which even the chaotic room had not prepared me.

[RITUAL 1]

HAVING ASSUMED THAT THE victim was white, prostrate, and barely alive, I gasped. For instead, staring toward the door from a throne-like position, an elderly black man sat high in a coffin with his face distorted as though shouting a protest. And as I stared in astonishment I heard Murphy exclaim, "Well, I'll be damned, that guy is a *boogie!*"

And to my dismay certain idealistic notions of democracy to which I still cling were knocked out of kilter by the paradox posed by the mansion, the servants, and the old man's complexion. Yes, and his unusual attire.

For while the lawmen gaped as though their world were collapsing I noted his gray morning coat, blue ascot tie, and pink boutonniere. Then came a glint from his dangling pince-nez and I whispered with mounting amazement, "It's a gag! An outrageous *gag!*"

But now, catching sight of his work-hardened hands, I was struck by what certain French existentialists would have seized as an eloquent symbol of American absurdity:

Sitting with his forearms resting on the closed lower portion of the coffin's curved lid, the old man was gripping a Bible and a half-consumed bottle of Jack Daniel's whiskey. And while I strained to make sense of his odd juxtaposition of coffin, whiskey, and leather-bound Bible, the moaning resumed from somewhere below him and I joined the detectives in search for its source.

Directly below the man in the coffin, a black man dressed in faded blue jeans lay sprawled in a Chippendale chair with his chin on his chest and grasping a glass and a half-empty bottle of the same brand of whiskey. But before there was time for a look at his face the Sergeant exploded.

"What the hell," he yelled, "is *she* doing here!"

And alarmed by the overtones of outrage and panic with which a veteran detective had voiced the word "she," I whirled so abruptly that I took a blow in the crotch from my swinging recorder. And there, back in the shadows to the left of the door, I saw the form of a woman.

Kneeling on the floor, she was grasping the arms of an upholstered chair, and as she struggled to rise I thought, She must be his wife or a grief-stricken relative. . . . But with a step closer that naive assumption was dispelled by her bawdy costume and her scandalous antics.

White, drunk, redheaded, and bloated, she was totally bare but for her high-heeled black shoes and a sly skimp of a skirt that flared from her hips like the pale yellow rays of a surrealist sunburst—from which, now, sensing a stir in the doorway, I looked up to see three men from the vestibule who were staring at the scene with wide-eyed amazement, and heard the Sergeant yell, "Dammit, Morrison, get those Peeping Tom bastards back to the foyer and see that they stay there!"

And with Morrison charging the men like a Hall of Fame tackle, he grabbed hold of the woman and wrestled her up from the floor and into the chair. Then, whirling with a scowl of distaste, he stabbed a finger at a gawking policeman in uniform.

"You," he shouted, "stop staring at the strumpet and get her butt covered!"

"Covered with *what?*" the officer said.

"With anything handy—use your jacket!"

"My *jacket?*"

"Hell, yes! And that's an *order!*"

And now the woman reacted.

Seeing the unhappy policeman approach with his jacket in hand she giggled and blew him a kiss. Then, watching him cover her nudity and step quickly backward, she smiled and lay fingering the cloth of his jacket as though deciding whether to let it lie put or snatch it away. And with that I thought, Whoever she turns out to be, she's by no means a Lady Godiva, and headed back to the Sergeant.

Glaring at the man in the chair, he stood with his back to the coffin, which I now realized was old and quite battered. And in the course of his questioning we learned from the man in the chair that its state of decay had indeed triggered the confusion which followed.

Get this: The man in the coffin had rejected his lifelong faith in religion, fallen into a profound state of frustration, and gone on a Jack Daniel's toot after discovering that time, termites, and an enviable long life had reduced his choice of a last resting place to a worm-eaten shell. Which discovery he denounced as an insult from God, the universe, and the United States Government! Such was the start of the chain of events which led to my being dragged out of bed and into the nightmare in which I now floundered.

Just think of it! A man lives so long that he outlasts his coffin, but instead of prizing his longevity he abandons his faith in religion! Which suggests once again—as others have argued—that some of our black Americans are indeed of a very strange mixture. If so, the man in the chair was a notable example.

Before responding to the Sergeant's questions he had to be reassured that yet another man—and a *white* man at that—was gone from the premises. And then, encouraged by whiskey which the Sergeant had sloshed in his glass, he gulped down a drink, gazed at the man in the coffin with a mournful expression, and nodded. At which, thanks to the pain in my groin, I had the presence of mind to activate my recorder.

Which proved most fortunate, for as it turned out he was either a natural-born mimic with a photographic memory, or a spellbinding trickster whose eye for significant detail and ear for speech rhythms might have served him well as a novelist.

And now with a sigh he gazed at the detectives and said, "Okay, gentlemen, I'll tell you whatever I can."

"Fine," said the Sergeant, "and you can start by giving us your name."

"My name is Aubrey McMillen."

"And his?" the Sergeant said with a nod toward the coffin.

"That's my friend Mister Jessie. . . ."

"Jessie," the Sergeant said, "but what's his first name?"

"That *is* his first name. His last name's Rockmore, just as you called him outside the door. His full name's Jessie Wellington Rockmore."

"Very good," said the Sergeant. And taking the posture of a prosecuting attorney he bent slightly forward.

"And now, Aubrey," he said, "tell us what kind of work do you do."

"I'm a super," McMillen said.

"A super? For whom?"

"For Mister Jessie. I work right here on the premises."

"And what about those servants out in the hall?"

"*Servants?* What servants? Those folks are *tenants!* And what's more, it costs good money to live in this house."

"They're *tenants?*"

"That's right, every man and woman amongst them. And not only that, they all have good jobs and keep up with their taxes."

"I see. And what about you?"

"Me too!"

"Good! And have you other employment?"

"Not anymore. I been working for Mister Jessie for close to ten years. And before that I worked for . . ."

"Never mind," the Sergeant said, "we'll get back to that later. For now just tell us what happened here tonight."

"Well, suh," McMillen said with a sigh and a shake of his head, "it went this-a-way: Early this morning Mister Jessie told me to bring him that coffin up from the cellar. So I got holt of Elroy—that's the young man who gives me a hand now and then—and we brought it up here and sat it there on that table, which is where Mister Jessie told us to put it."

"And why did he want it up here?"

"To tell you the truth, I don't rightly know. Me and Mister Jessie been friends for years and he liked to talk with me about most anything. In fact, he talked to me more than he talked to anybody, but he'd never said a word about having that coffin."

"Does he have relatives, kinfolks?"

"Oh, yes, but Mister Jessie can't stand them. That's why he lives here all by hisself."

"What about his wife, did he have one?"

"Yes suh, but she's been dead for ten years or so."

"And did his relatives ever visit him?"

"Not very often, because with him being so straightlaced and strict they don't get along. And that's how he likes it. Deep down, Mister Jessie doesn't think too highly of what he sees in most folks, whether they be relatives or strangers, black, white, or whatever. So as far as he was concerned his kinfolks were just some more humans and not to be trusted. So rather than arguing with them all the time Mister Jessie chose to sit here day after day reading his Bible. Otherwise he'd be reading books or the *Post* and that paper which Congress puts out. Which was the one he was *always* fussing about over the things they printed. He even tried to give me a subscription so he could argue with me about it. But while I'd argue about the Bible once in a while, that thing Congress puts out just makes me mad. Though no way as mad as it made Mister Jessie."

"And why was that?"

"Because he disagreed with most everything it stands for. And according to him those folks in Congress keep violating the Constitution, the Fifteenth Amendment, the laws of the Bible, and a heap of others which I'm not educated enough to know much about. Not that he'd been to college, but he taught his own self things that even most college folks seem not to know."

"With all the books in this place he was *self-educated*?"

"That's right, along with his magazines he read all kinds of books. He was also well off—as you can see from this building."

"Do you mean that he *owns* it?"

"Oh, yes, he owns it! And what's more, he's proud of it and the rest of his property."

"Which brings us to the point of what happened here tonight. How did it start?"

"Well, it went this-a-way. After me and Elroy get the coffin up here and resting on the table, Mister Jessie looks at it a long time and starts in to mumbling. And right away he seems to forget about Elroy and me. Then he circles his coffin about seven times, and all at once he gives it a thump like he's testing a melon for ripeness. And when a big cloud of dust rises up out of there he bucks his eyes like he's seen him a ghost. Then he goes to mumbling and balls up his fist and comes down on the lid like he's swinging a hammer, and when it explodes with more dust he takes a step back and starts in to coughing. Then he unlatches the lid that's now closed and runs his hand way deep inside and drags out a fancy old suit—a black one—that's falling apart. Then he drags out a pair of those high-button shoes with fancy gray uppers, the kind men who could afford them used to wear years ago. And while he's looking them over he's mumbling and shaking his head. Then his face starts to working up such a storm and that skin under his chin starts to wobbling and shaking like a mad turkey gobbler's. Then his face breaks out with sweat and he starts snatching other stuff out of there like he's looking for something that's really important . . ."

"What kind of stuff?"

"Well, the first was some plates and some bowls and a pitcher. Then some forks and some knives and a statue of a skinny old man who's sitting on a horse that's as skinny as he is. He's some kind of foreigner and thin as a rail, and in one hand he's holding a shield and in the other a long slender sword that's missing its point. Then came a big glass jug with a sailing ship in it, like the kind you see in those movies about Christopher Columbus. And then he pulls out a big box of grits with a picture of a colored man on it. . . ."

"*Grits*," the Sergeant shouted, "what the hell are you telling us?"

"See for yourself," McMillen said, "it's right over there with Uncle Ben on it."

"And what else did he take out of there?"

"Well, then came a box with Aunt Jemima on it, then a Bible and a beat-up pistol—an owlhead, which you can see right over there—and some life-insurance policies that's long past their time. And then he reaches in again, and when he straightens up he's trembling and in his hands he's holding a box that's made out of tin.

"That's when he wipes the sweat from his face and says, 'It's been so doggone long that I damn near forgot it!' And all at once he turns to me and says,

'McMillen, give that there little nappy-chinned helper of yours a dollar and get him the hell out of the house.'

"So instead of a dollar I slips Elroy a couple of bucks and a quarter and he heads for downstairs. . . ."

"Why did *you* pay the boy?"

"That was part of a game Mister Jessie liked to play on me. He'd borrow my money just to see if I had it. Borrow today and pay back tomorrow. Not that he needed it, 'cause not only did he get good rent from those folks out there in the hall, he had plenty cash in the bank and hardly spent any of it except for something to eat and things like underwear and shirts every now and then. Yes, and all those magazines, newspapers, and books. He didn't even smoke or chew tobacco. . . ."

"But judging from that bottle he's holding and the smell of this place he *drank* like a fish, isn't that right?"

To which, grasping his glass, McMillen replied, "Oh, no, he didn't! And if it's that Jack Daniel's you smell that makes you say that I better explain it."

"Then get on with it!"

"Oh, no, gentlemen, Mister Jessie didn't smoke, chew, or drink. Neither did he hang out with women. So he had no need to spend much of his money. What's more, a man from some big museum up there in New York was always coming here and trying to get him to sell him those dishes and things over there in those cabinets. Offered him all kinds of money—way up in the thousands—but Mister Jessie wouldn't sell. And right here in D.C. a Smithsonian man wanted those pictures of Indians and other folks he collected, but Mister Jessie refused him. Told me one time that he'd give some of his pictures to the folks at the college for nothing if only they had enough sense to appreciate them. And when I asked him how come they didn't he said it was because they refuse to learn anything about this country which they don't see right away as being connected directly to them and our people. Said he offered to gift them those pictures of Indians he has in his storeroom—and he has some fine ones—but according to him those folks didn't want them. And that made Mister Jessie *really* disgusted.

" 'McMillen,' he said, 'those fools are supposed to be educated, but the truth of the matter is that they don't even realize that for better or worse the black man has taken the place of the red man, even to getting hog-tied and scalped every time he forgets to sidestep and duck.' Which was too complicated for me, but Mister Jessie used to say some pretty low-rating things about those folks at the college. But as far as *I'm* concerned they seem to be doing a pretty fair job. . . ."

"Never mind what he thought of teachers, get back to my question!"

"Yessuh. So after I pay Elroy his money we go downstairs and I lock the door. And when I get back Mister Jessie's reaching in his coffin and dragging out some of those goldbacks which that lady back yonder is wearing. . . ."

"Do you mean gold certificates?"

"That's right."

"Well, I'll be damned, and she's debasing them! So then what?"

"So then Mister Jessie stacks some of his goldbacks on the lid of his coffin and says, 'McMillen, this stuff's been stashed for so long that it's a crime to even possess it.' And all at once he grabs a bunch of those goldbacks and stares at them, and right away he does something I never heard him do in all the years we been friends—he *cusses*!

" 'Goddamit,' he says, 'it has to slip up on me at a time when by rights I ought to be long dead and buried, but now I'm glad that it's happened. Because for once in my life I broke the damn law!'

"And when I hear that I'm speechless. Because Mister Jessie was as clean-cut a man, black *or* white, as I've ever known. He was what folks who knew him would describe as being an upright citizen and good Christian gentleman. . . ."

To which, with a sly glance at Murphy, a devout but hard-drinking Catholic, the Sergeant smiled.

"All right," he said, "so your friend was some breed of Protestant. Now get on with your story."

"Well, it looks like his cussing causes something to snap in Mister Jessie's poor head. Because after standing there stacking that money and mumbling he stares at it a while like he's mad as hell and getting even madder. And all of a sudden he sweeps it down on the floor like he's truly disgusted.

"And that's when I asked him, 'Mister Jessie, what the hell are you doing, treating your money like that? Sure, it might be old, but it was backed by hard cash. And since you're no criminal or anything like that you can turn it in at the bank and they'll give you full value.'

"Well, suh, why did I say that? Mister Jessie looks like he's about to grab that coffin and wallop me with it.

" 'Full value some hell,' he yells. 'There ain't enough gold in all Fort Knox to repay me for all the trouble that damn stuff has cost me. Back there in the eighties, denying my family most everything they needed. Pulling nickels and dimes out of my own rusty hide and letting that white man use me to beat those poor ignorant white folks out of their family inheritance—all that fine Spode and Chelsea, Sandwich glass and sterling. McMillen,' he says, 'wars, depressions, and thieves in high places have put more dross in our silver and brass in our gold than all the lead in the bullets that got fired in the Battle of Gettysburg. And by now grand theft and bad monetary policies have cut the value of whatever's left over!'

" 'McMillen,' he says, 'when a man reaches my age money turns out to be nothing more than the coldest damn dregs of all his life's labor. Even his sweat is more valuable, because here in this hellhole of Washington it can at least cool him off every once in a while. Hell, I wore out fifteen of those damn straight-life, nickel-today-nickel-when-you-git-it life-insurance policies you see on the floor before I learned I was being drained of my interest on what I thought was a good investment. And that's when I started saving my money in banks. Then next thing I know those damn depressions started eating on me. And twice in my life I get hit by high-placed embezzlers. Once before they set up the Federal Reserve, and again in 1929. And all that time the value of my hard-earned money was going down down down like that elevator out there in the Washington Monument. So don't talk to *me* about the value of money!'

"And then, gentlemen, he *really* starts preaching:

" 'McMillen,' he says, 'for years I've tried to live by a standard that was already depreciating even faster than a strong ooze-out fart can fade in a windstorm. So while I was denying myself the pleasure of good times, women, and whiskey my life was being turned into an outrageous sideshow that outdid anything that even P. T. Barnum ever came up with! That's the truth, and Barnum was the master and still reigning champion of *all* kinds of bullshit. But through all those long years I went about obeying the law and stayed patient and humble. What's more, I prayed and held on to my faith in my old-time religion. That's right, and you know it. As a young man I never went to dances or hung out with whores, and as far as I know I never lied or cheated, even when it caused me to suffer. What's more, I kept gnawing on hope like a dog on a bone, and even during the worst of times I believed that eventually things would get better. Which was a gift of faith from our stubborn ancestors, who learned during slavery that it was better to suffer all kinds of white folk's arrogance, hypocrisy, and foolishness than to lose their faith in God and the future.

" 'McMillen,' he said, 'This was my philosophy: I firmly believed in the perfectibility of all mankind, including black folks like us—even though I recognized that some of us are truly dog-assed and thoroughly disgusting. And most of all, I believed in the progressive improvement of this so-called democracy. Why? Because every once in a while it's been blessed with leaders who have the ability to come up with creative ways of getting things done. Those beliefs were the rock on which I rested my faith. Why? Because when I was just a young boy the good Lord saw fit to free me from slavery. So right then and there I determined to live according to His rules and achieve as much perfectibility as was humanly possible. Mister Lincoln tried to open a way for us to move up in this society, and even had the Constitution amended to help us over the rough spots we'd find in the road. Sure, he got the back of his head blown off for his efforts, but that made me all the more determined to be a patient good citizen and practice manliness so I'd never lose faith and embarrass the sacrifices he'd made for us and the country.'

"And then, gentlemen, Mister Jessie stares at me stern as a judge, and all of a sudden he starts in to laughing. He laughs 'til his cheeks start running with tears, and that gets *me* to laughing from watching *him* laugh. Then he stops for a second and leans back against his coffin, and you could hear something inside of it pop like a firecracker, and that starts him to laughing like he's having a fit.

"Then he says, 'McMillen, for years you've respected my intelligence, but right now I'll have to confess that in so doing you've been sadly mistaken. Because today it turns out that after all my ninety-five years of earthly experience I'm nothing more than a knuckle-headed fool!'

" 'Take it easy, Mister Jessie,' I says, 'and don't you be playing yourself cheap like some broken-down hustler.'

"And he says, 'No, McMillen, you listen to *me*! Like a confounded fool I had everything figured out according to logic. I was born into slavery, you see, so it would take quite a while for me to catch up with the liberty which Jesus Christ and Mister Lincoln had provided. And since there were men at the bottom of society—which is where I started, both in terms of time, of place, and of color—and men at the top such as Abraham Lincoln, Ralph Waldo Emerson' (he was always carrying on about those two), 'Jay Gould, and the Right Reverend Henry Ward Beecher. So there was hope for me, both in the world and this mammy-made nation. And since the Bible teaches that there's heaven above and hell down below, with Satan the master of hell, and the Holy Spirit, God the Father, and his son Christ Jesus sharing the throne of heaven above, then everything in the universe was going along in orderly, metafitical'—no, that's not the word he used—it was *metaphysical,* and the term he used was 'metaphysical progression.'

"Then he went on to say, 'So a man was born and given a chance to help achieve his best possibilities by the way he conducted his living. Then when he died he was buried, and in God's good time he'd be judged and go either to heaven up above or to hell down below. It was a marvelous scheme with a place for everybody and everything in it. And the fact that God up in heaven sent His own only son down here to live as a *human* was enough guarantee that I could at least become a United States citizen with full recognition.

" 'So you see, McMillen,' he says real earnest, like he's pleading for me to believe him, 'I have lived the best way I know how, and was determined to take care of all early matters which I could control, whether they be physical, political, or spiritual. And what's more, I rejected all notions of rebellion—which wasn't easy—and kept playing the game in good faith and with high expectations. So while I was still in the full strength of my manhood I bought that damn casket when it was white and covered with silk. Bought it so when time came for my dying I could be put away in good Christian fashion, and owing no debts outstanding to God, to man, or government. Because I figured that since flesh is weak, and time uncertain, life is a gamble and truly capricious. So I lived in fear of the Lord and clung to my respect for justice and good law and order—such as I found it. That way I kept my faith in the orderly processes of justice, and in the checks and balances of this so-called democracy.

" 'But now look at me and what's around me! Things in Washington have gone to straight hell! Here I'm ninety-five years old and no good to myself or anyone else. I've got enough gadgets in my body to stock anything from a five-and-dime to a hardware store. And except for a few my teeth are all false, I can't read worth a damn without glasses, I keep a miniature radio plugged in my ear in order to hear fairly clearly. So I'm no good for myself and my children don't want me. But even with all that I still don't see any prospect of passing on to my last and long-waited reward . . .' "

"Was he drinking?"

"No suh, just carried away. Because for a man his age he had a good memory and was still pretty spry."

"Then what happened?"

"He keeps on talking, and gentlemen, I'll never forget it.

" 'McMillen,' he says, 'I was in this town when they killed Mister Lincoln, and I watched when they took F.D.R. to his last resting place. And between those sad events I've seen all *kinds* of crooks, thieves, highbinders, and scoundrels come here to Washington and do their nastiness in the name of liberty, economy, and Lord knows what else before they passed from the scene. Different backgrounds and names but the same nasty nastiness. And with few exceptions it's been a matter of highbinders and clipsters, phonies and conmen taking over high places. So instead of times getting better they only get worse.' "

And suddenly, as though alarmed by the trend his recital was taking, McMillen looked at the detectives and said, "Now, gentlemen, please understand that *that* was Mister *Jessie* talking, not me."

"I hope not," the Sergeant said with a dubious frown, "but get on with your story."

"So then Mister Jessie says, 'McMillen, I fought in that war between our country and Spain and left some of my own precious blood on San Juan Hill. Then Teddy Roosevelt gets so much credit for whatever *he* did that you'd have thought he won the war single-handed. And with our people getting little credit for the part they played in winning that fracas I had some crooks in the War Department swindle me out of my pension! I've been a fool, McMillen, a muddle-headed fool! Because all these years I've been so busy worrying about how to die well and not be a burden to my kids and my relatives that I've neglected to *live* well. So instead, day by day, I've been wasting away!'

"Then he says, 'Forty years ago I took some of my savings and bought that coffin. Then I bought a suit shirt and tie, and a pair of Stacy Adams shoes—which were the finest, and something I'd denied myself the pleasure of wearing on earth. But now every damn thing is worn out from waiting. The suit's fallen apart, the shoe leather's gone withered and dry as Adam's first fig leaf, the coffin's full of holes, and now the worms are in there raising hell for me to quit stalling and provide them a banquet.

" 'McMillen,' he says, 'seeing what's happened to this coffin has finally opened my eyes to the true, disgusting nature of our human existence. I've got nothing to live for or look forward to. No *now* or *hereafter.* No justice from my government, and no hope for heaven or escape from hell. Years ago I broke a warm friendship with a fellow for saying that the only reason God made poor Job so downhearted and miserable over all those long years wasn't just a matter of testing the strength of Job's faith, but God's way of having some fun by tricking the Devil. But now look at *me*! Hell, after years of self-sacrifice and right living in hopes for the future, things haven't improved worth a damn! Even my *coffin's* fallen to dust! So with the end drawing nigh it's time I started living for *me*! . . .' "

Suddenly fingering his earlobe, McMillen paused with a sigh and said, "And gentlemen, to my best recollection, that's what happened. . . ."

"Best recollection of *what?*" the Sergeant exploded. "Are you trying to snow us with that talk about Job? You haven't said a *word* about how he came to be sitting up there in that coffin! And that . . . that woman back there, what's she doing in a place like this? What else went on besides a lot of drinking and subversive yakking? Did the two of you rob and kill him before you stuffed his body in there?"

"Now wait," McMillen yelled, "it wasn't *nothing* like that!"

"Then get on and tell us what *happened!*"

"Okay, okay," McMillen said, "but first, can I ask you gentlemen a question?"

"What kind of question?"

"It's whether you gentlemen are Northern or Southern?"

"Northern or Southern! What the hell has *that* got to do with it?"

"Well, you see, Sergeant," McMillen said, "I'm coming to something that's really kinda delicate, and since most *Southern* gentlemen tend to be kinda *touchy* about some of the things I'll be having to say, I don't want them thinking I'm being insulting. . . ."

But before the Sergeant could respond I heard a whoop and a resonant belch and looked around to see the woman reeling in the chair as she stared from the shadows.

"Gen'lmen, gen'lmen," she snickered, "what he wants to know is which side of the line you on. Is it Mason's or Dixon's, or just plain colored—Whoops!"

Snapping suddenly erect the Sergeant bumped into the coffin as he yelled, "That's enough out of you! Just one more word . . ."

"Sure, sure," she said, "but answer Uncle Remus, and then I want you to tell *me* one lil ole thing: How the hell can the poor bastard sit there with a buncha creeps like you and keep confusing you with gen'lmen? Far's *I* can see, he's the only gen'lman among you. Thass right! 'Cause who but a gent would pay me for doing my number in a costume as darling as this!"

And flinging the blue jacket aside, she quivered with laughter.

"Listen, gentlemen," McMillen shouted, "and I want it strictly understood, that lady's being here was no idea of mine—no, suh!"

"Then why the hell is she here?"

"That's what I'm about to tell you, and you can bet your life it's the truth. After Mister Jessie raves some more over his coffin going rotten on him, he just stands there in the middle of the floor with a strange look on his face. He must've been thinking up a storm too, because all at once he's yelling, 'Hell and damnation! Hell and damnation!'

"Then he looks at me and says, 'McMillen, I'd damn near forgot it, but back when I was a youngster and out of a job I portered a while in a whorehouse.'

"Which for him was so unbelievable that I says, 'You did *what?*' 'That's right,' he says, 'I worked there damn near a year and never had a go at the goods!' Then all at once he yells like somebody'd jabbed him in the butt with a pitchfork.

" 'McMillen,' he says, 'here's what I want you to do. I want you to take this money and go get us a case of the best bourbon whiskey you can find . . .'

" 'Now wait, Mister Jessie,' I tells him, 'you don't want no *case* of whiskey.'

" 'You're right,' he says, 'so make it a dozen. And along with the whiskey bring me a woman. And make sure she's a redhead or some kind of blond.' And gentlemen, when he said that he *really* upset me.

"I knew something strange was happening, but I truly couldn't dig it. So I says real quiet, 'Mister Jessie, I know you're upset, but isn't that going too far? First you call for whiskey when you don't even drink. And now you're calling for a woman when you're much too old for that kind of action.'

"And he says, 'Too old? Well, if you're bothered by that, make it a gal who's about reached the age of hanging up her bloomers . . .' "

"Hold it right there," the Sergeant interrupted. "Hang up her bloomers? What the hell does that mean?"

"That's exactly what I asked him, and he says, 'Retire, McMillen, it's a gal who's about to *retire!*' "

[DUVAL]

"So THEN HE SAYS that it was something he heard when he worked in the whorehouse, and explained that whenever a customer asked the madam for a gal who'd retired or got married that's what she told him. Then he imitates the madam and says real proper, 'Why, my dear, haven't you heard? The hooker has hung up her bloomers.'

"So when he comes on like that I asks him real quiet, 'Mister Jessie, could it be that you're *kidding?*' And he says, 'No, McMillen, I'm too damn depressed and disgusted. But I'll take care of that as soon as you leave and come back with a gal and some whiskey.' And from the way he said it I knew he was serious.

"So then I really try talking him out of it, I really did, but Mister Jessie wouldn't hear me. And with us being close friends, what else could I do except what he wanted? So he gives me a big wad of money and I find me a taxi and go to a liquor store to buy him a dozen cases of Jack Daniel's whiskey. Yeah, and right away I run into trouble.

"When I go to pay for the liquor it turns out that some of those beat-up bills he gave me to buy it turn out to be mildewed—and right away the owner of the liquor store gets suspicious. So now I have to wait while a clerk goes to his bank to check if they're stolen or counterfeit. . . ."

"And were they?"

"Oh, no, every one of those bills was for real. So then I takes the whiskey in the taxi and go looking for a fellow I know who works at one of these hit-em-and-skip-em midnight motels. And after calling me a fool and laughing like crazy over a man as old as Mister Jessie wanting a woman, he gives me a drink and that lady's phone number. So right away I get on the phone and I dial her."

"And then what happened?"

"It went this-a-way: First I offers her seventy-five bucks and a tip if Mister Jessie accepts her. But right away she starts in to bargaining and says that on account of there being a big convention in town it'll cost us the top union scale. . . ."

"*Union* scale! What the hell are you saying?"

"That's right, the top union scale—which she claimed is a flat two hundred bucks and a quarter."

"Would you believe it," a detective exclaimed, "two hundred bucks for a woman like that! No wonder this town is inflated!"

"I wouldn't know about that," McMillen said, "but that was her price. So while I'm wanting to please Mister Jessie I'm against riding around town with all that whiskey while I find him a gal whose price was more reasonable. So I drops by the lady's apartment, and right away I'm hit with a new couple of problems.

"First, she's drunk as a coot. Second, she don't look like she's worth anything *near* the money she's asking—but that was my personal opinion. So since my getting him a woman was Mister Jessie's idea and the money was hissen, I tell the lady it's a deal and I pay her."

"And why'd you pay her before he had seen her?"

"Because I'm figgering that if she sees Mister Jessie with his money already on her, she'd think twice before changing her mind and raising a ruckus. And to be frank about it, by now I'm itching to see how Mister Jessie will react when he sees who I got him."

"And how was that?"

"Gimme time, gentlemen, gimme time," McMillen said with a note of anxiety. "Because by now things are getting pretty damn iffey, and I swear I'm not lying.

"So I gives the lady this address and she promises to be here in about thirty minutes. Then I taxis back here and unloads all that whiskey—which brings us to the reason it's bothering some of you gentlemen.

"When I start toting those boxes down to the basement I do it three at a time, and on my last trip I stumble down the steps and end up busting most of the bottles that's in them. Which is why it keeps rising up here through the air ducts. But as much as my wasting all that good bourbon upsets me, by now I'm both curious and worried about poor Mister Jessie. Because after my paying the lady his money I'm afraid that when she sees him she'll up and say to hell with our deal and take off and start making some trouble.

"Anyway, when I get up here to the living room Mister Jessie has shaved and got hisself dressed. That outfit he's wearing is what he wore when he went to his church or met with their big-shot trustees. On work days he could look like a beggar, but always on Sundays he was neat as a pin. So now he really looks sharp, but he's not any calmer than when I took off to buy all that whiskey and find him a woman.

"So, thinking to cheer him a bit I says, 'Mister Jessie, I'm back with all that whiskey you ordered.' But right away he wants to know if I brought him the best. So I says, 'It's the best *I* know about.' So then he says, 'I told you to bring me a gal with the whiskey. Where is she?'

" 'Now don't get excited,' I says, 'she'll be here in about twenty minutes.'

" 'She'd better,' he says, 'or I'll get out of here and find me another! How much did it cost me?'

"So I hands him the rest of his money, and after counting it he says, 'And you talk to me about value? Hell, when I was a boy you could buy a whole barrel of whiskey for fifteen dollars!'

" 'Yessuh, Mister Jessie,' I says, 'and I reckon that's when you should've been drinking. Times have changed, and I told you that you didn't need all that whiskey. You can't even buy a gallon of rot-gut for fifteen dollars. Not today!' And then he looks at me real hard and says, 'So what kind of gal did you get me?' And that's when the lady back there in the corner arrives and he tells me to take off and go let her in.

"And gentlemen, while I'm gone to get her Mister Jessie does something else which was strange as all hell. When I walk back in here with the lady he's nowhere to be seen. So I says to the lady, 'I guess he's either in his bedroom or down in the kitchen. Make yourself comfortable while I go find him.' But before I can move I hear Mister Jessie saying, 'I'm here, McMillen, I'm right over here.'

"And gentlemen, with that Mister Jessie rises up out of that coffin and sits there staring. And with that both me and the lady start to take off. But as luck would have it we're both too excited. Which, looking back, was a piece of bad luck, because if we had, this thing would have ended right then and there. Anyway, with him sitting there looking all stern through his Sunday nose glasses I make up my mind that I've got me some business down in the basement. So I turns to the lady and says, 'Miss, he's the one who sent for you,' and heads for the door.

"I'm figuring that since she's already juiced and him headed straight as a shot for the nuthouse, neither one needed my hanging around. And I just about make it when I hear Mister Jessie saying, 'McMillen, where do you think you're going? We're having a party and you're invited.'

"And that's when the lady staggers back a step with her hands on her hips and speaks her first words.

" 'And for that, Dad,' she says, 'the price will be double.'

"That's right, gentlemen! Never seen Mister Jessie before and right away she's calling him 'Dad'! I'm expecting him to take her head off, right then and there. Because usually when somebody gets sassy with Mister Jessie it's like jumping out of line with Chief Justice Warren. In fact, I'm about to go after her myself when she stares at him with one of those you-can-take-it-or-leave looks on her face and says, 'That's right, Dad, the fee'll be double. And what's the idea of receiving a professional like me in a coffin?'

"Well, with that Mister Jessie frowns and looks at the lady real hard. 'Now miss,' he says, 'you listen to me. You've been paid the price you quoted and I intend for this party to be not only joyful but free of contention. So if you wish to back out of our prior arrangement, just return my money and leave us.' And with that the lady thinks twice and she cools it.

" 'Now, a party is different,' she says, 'But Dad, answer me this: What the hell are you doing sitting up there in that coffin?' And Mister Jessie says, 'I'm resting from waiting so long for you to arrive.'

"So she looks at him all juicy-eyed and says, 'Dad, you must be beat to your socks, and I mean *truly*! But why make it so handy for the damn embalmers? With you in that casket all they'd have to do is shoot you full of formaldehyde and take off for the boneyard. In other words, Dad, you really picked a strange seat for partying.'

" 'Maybe so,' Mister Jessie says, 'but are you objecting?'

" 'Oh, no,' she says, 'but maybe you'll tell me just why it is that every damn time I set out to do business with one of you spooks things turn out to be mad as a hatter? I've never known it to fail, either the joint gets raided, the john comes on like he thinks he's a stud on the prod, or the madam's pet poodle chases a cat under the bed and upsets the party. It never fails. Like the time I'm working interracial in Baltimore when an old Temperance broad busts into the joint and pulls off a black Carrie Nation. That's right, Dad. We were having a ball when here she comes busting in with a bunch of old broads who're singing a hymn and banging like mad on some damn tambourines. And next thing I know she's demanding that everyone swear on her Bible that we'll not only give up our drinking but convert to her style of kinky religion. To which quite a few said okay, and no wonder! Because Dad, instead of a hatchet she's waving a Colt forty-five and threatening to use it! And *now* look what's happening! Here I am in Washington, D.C., and being paid to entertain a spook rigged out in a coffin!'

"And gentlemen, that's when I knew for sure that Mister Jessie was going *see*-nile. Because all he does is to look at the woman real stern. And me? I'm hot as a pistol. After my paying her all that good money in hope that when she gets here and sees how old Mister Jessie is she'd have enough decency to tell him he's acting a fool, she standing here talking some jive and calling us spooks!

"So again I try to take off, but before I can get to the door Mister Jessie says, 'Wait, McMillen,' and asks the lady her name.

" 'It's Cordelia Duval,' she says, 'And yours?' 'I'm Jessie Rockmore,' he says. And pointing to me, he says, 'And that's my friend, Mister Aubrey McMillen. We're both pleased you could join us.' 'Likewise,' she says. 'Good,' he says, 'but before we go further let me ask you a question.' And she says, "Yes, Dad, what is it?' And Mister Jessie says, 'Miss Duval, do you happen to dance?'

" 'Dance?' she says, 'Why, Dad, I was once in the Follies.'

" 'In the Follies,' Mister Jessie says, 'why, I would have thought you were too young for that.'

" 'Oh, no,' she says, 'and what's more, it was no less than Flo Ziegfeld himself who made me a star.'

" 'Now that's very interesting,' Mister Jessie says. 'And have you been practicing your present profession for long?' And she strikes her a high-class pose and says, 'Long enough to match any trick *you* can come up with. And Dad, believe it or not, I once shared the spotlights with stars like Bert Williams and Will Rogers. Most folks didn't know it, but Will was an Indian while that Bert was a Negro. And not only was the spook one hell of a performer, when he took off the blackface makeup he used on the stage he was really so handsome that he looked like a white man. Hell, Dad, I knew them *all*, and every one was so sweet to a young girl like me that at first I couldn't believe it.'

"So then Mister Jessie says, 'That's very interesting, Miss Duval, but why'd you stop dancing?' And she says, 'Dad, it was like this: After reaching stardom I fell in love with a handsome playboy from high society. It was truly a sizzling romance, but once our names hit the headlines the crumb couldn't take it. Too worried about his family background and the money they'd leave him, that kind of thing. So our love affair ended with his breaking my heart, and being young and new to the man-woman game, I was left so disillusioned that right there I said to hell with the stage and the headlines. Dad, do you dig it?'

"And when all Mister Jessie comes up with is something about disappointment being the other side of high expectations I broke in.

" 'Oh, come on, Mister Jessie,' I says, 'you know this woman's lying about being on the stage. And handing you that bull about some society dude putting her down is just her way of playing you for some kinda fool!' But all he does is gimme a frown and say, 'McMillen, watch your language and remember your manners!'

"Then he says, 'That's too bad, Miss Duval, and I'm sorry to hear it. But, like you, I too have known disappointments.' And she says, 'I'm sure of it, Dad, but we're both still in the game and doing our thing. But why're you so interested in my career in the Follies?'

"And Mister Jessie says, 'Because watching you dance would elevate my spirits. Miss Duval, would you do us the honor?'

"And with that the woman jumps salty. 'Dad,' she says, 'what's all this business about dancing? I'm a first-rate professional, so what's wrong with you, don't you find me attractive?'

" 'Of course I do,' Mister Jessie says, 'you're a fine-looking woman, and a proud one at that. Which I appreciate, because until today I've made the mutton-headed mistake of sacrificing my pride on the altar of humility. That's why I'm having this party. I've never had one before, but from what I've been told, among the things a good party requires are wine, women, and song. So unless you're also a singer ours will make do with your dancing, some good talk, and whiskey. It's taken me years to give it a try, but now that I have, would you care to join us, or depart with my blessings?' And with that Miss Duval changes her tune.

"And not just because of what Mister Jessie was saying. Because while he's talking I'm watching her, and when she sees all that money scattered on the floor her eyes bug out of her head like two rubber bulges in a weak inner tube.

" 'Okay, Dad,' she says, 'if that's what you want, that's what you'll get.'

"So Mister Jessie tells me to show her the way to his bedroom and bring up some whiskey and glasses. I'm still worried as hell about his sitting in that coffin and having a woman like that in his house, but now he's beginning to sound pretty sensible."

"Maybe so," the Sergeant said, "but there's not a damn thing sensible about what you're telling us. Quit stalling and get on to what happened!"

"Well, suh," McMillen said, "out in the kitchen I have me a shot of that bourbon. In fact, I have me a double so that woman won't bug me into losing my temper. And by now I figured that if Mister Jessie wanted her here, that was *his* business. So like I said, I have me a drink, and when I get back up here with the whiskey things are going pretty fast and confusing.

"Mister Jessie's leaning with his elbow propped on the lid of his coffin and Miss Duval is sitting back all relaxed in her chair, and they're laughing and talking like long-lost companions. And while she's stopped putting on airs, every now and then I can still see her eyeballing those goldbacks. And right then and there I decide I'll just lay in the bend, start playing it cool, and look out for Mister Jessie's best interests. . . ."

"You mean that you decided to get to his money before she did," the Sergeant said.

"Oh, no," McMillen said, "I could've kept some of what he gave me to pay for that liquor. And while it's true that I drink my whiskey, I'm a hard-working man who respects himself and his folks too much to go around stealing. You might think different, but I'm telling the truth."

"Go on."

"So I decided to lay in the bend and watch out for Mister Jessie and put the freeze on any larceny the woman comes up with. Because after all, I'm an old whiskey drinker while he was just starting. So it wouldn't be long before he'd be needing the benefits of my drinking experience. But although I'm watching like a hawk when he takes his first drink I'm unable to gauge just how hard it's hitting him. Anyway, he's asking Miss Duval if she enjoyed her profession, and she's saying something about her life being rich and full of surprises on account of her enjoying the trade of important gentlemen like congressmen and senators. And . . ."

"What! Are you sure about that," the Sergeant said with alarm, "are you sure?"

"That's right," McMillen said, "that's what she told him."

"You," the Sergeant said to one of the officers, "I want a detailed, A-to-Z rundown on this woman. Check with the F.B.I. And you, boy, get on with it!"

But with that McMillen remained silent as he stared at his glass with a blank expression.

"I said get *on* with it," the Sergeant repeated.

"Oh," McMillen said with a start, "I didn't realize you were speaking to me. . . . But in case you forgot it, my name's Aubrey McMillen. . . . Now, let's see what happens next: By now Mister Jessie is drinking whiskey so fast it's like he's dying of thirst, but I still can't see any change in his manners. He's just sitting there in his coffin looking like a judge while the lady is talking. Then after a while he asks me what kind of whiskey I brought him, and when I tell him to look at the label on the bottle he wants to know why he's not getting some action.

" 'Just give it time, Dad,' Miss Duval tells him, 'because take it from Cordelia, it's truly the finest.'

"Then she downs some more whiskey and takes a slow look around the room and says, 'Dad, this is a fine little pad you have, even though it's a bit overfurnished. What do you do for a living?' And when Mister Jessie says he's retired, she waves her hand in the air and says, 'You wouldn't kid me would you, Dad? I've been around, and while you *might* be retired, a slick spook like you must have been in the rackets. I can tell from this layout. Dad, you probably peddled cocaine, or maybe fenced illegal goods on the side.'

"But instead of telling her to get the hell out of his house, Mister Jessie tells me to pour her a drink and have one myself.

"Then he says, 'Miss Duval, the only way I ever came close to breaking the law was by not telling my telephone customers that the party on this end of the line was a black man. Or when I concealed the fact that my post-office box was rented by a black businessman. Yes, and in failing to advertise the fact that the man who paid for my newspaper and magazine ads wasn't white.' And then he starts telling her all about his real business.

"Gentlemen, remember all that stuff you saw in that big room back there? Well, years ago Mister Jessie started buying stuff like that and selling it. Which was his way of making his living. He'd drive down South to buy it and bring it up here, and after cleaning and fixing whatever needed it, he'd sell it through ads in the magazines and newspapers. Folks down South thought he was working for a white man, and up here he'd only let a few special white folks come here to see him. But with most of them he'd play like he was just looking after things for a white man. That way he didn't have arguments, and if they asked him to come down on his price he'd say he was sorry, but that he had to sell whatever they wanted for the price he'd been told to charge them. . . ."

"In other words," the Sergeant said, "he was a crook and a con man."

"No, but if that's how you see him," McMillen said, "that's how you see him. But to me he was simply a smart businessman. And a very hard worker. When old D.C. houses were being torn down he'd turn up dressed in his overalls and driving his old horse and wagon. Then he'd buy up the marble and wood they had on the fireplaces and the panels they had on the walls. And after he'd scraped off the paint some of them would turn out to be made out of fine kinds of woods, like oak, mahogany, and maple. And he'd grab up fancy old staircases, picture moldings, and all kinds of other old stuff. Sometimes he'd even get it for nothing because the builders were so glad to have him haul it away while charging them nothing.

"Then after he cleaned and restored it he'd take some pictures and send them to folks in the business. Like decorators and folks who put on plays in theaters, and for a while there he had him some of those old-time electric automobiles that steered with a handle. But his specialty was china and crystal. He was really nuts about those.

" 'Miss Duval,' he says, 'you see all that fine porcelain I have in that cabinet behind me? Well, I came in contact with some of the grown-up children of the white folks who owned it, and I know more about its quality than ever they dreamed of. They didn't even value it enough to hold on to it, and yet they thought they were superior to me because I'm black. So they considered me crazy for wanting it. So as a result I was able to buy crates and crates of the fine things which they didn't value. Like fine English shotguns, Italian candelabra, a variety of crystal, and fine pieces of furniture. And after a while it wasn't simply a matter of my making a living, because in time I came to love the meaning of fine craftmanship and set out to perserve it. Which is what those white folks should have done instead of worrying so much about their bloodlines, most of which are riddled with consumption, rickets, and cancer. And the ones who sold me the fine things they were eager to get rid of should have kept them and made sure that their descendants learned to appreciate them. But instead they keep holding on to things that'll fade with their dying.

" 'So you, see, Miss Duval,' he says, 'I tried to preserve what I could to the best of my knowledge. Which meant that I had to learn something of what it was about the things I bought which made them far more valuable than the question of money. And why some were considered superior to other examples of the very same order. So I grew to value the fine craftmanship of beautiful art as I loved the order which God had imposed on the universe. . . .'

"And gentlemen, right there was the point when his liquor ups and knocks the hell out of poor Mister Jessie. He stared at the lady with his eyes all shiny and bulging and he says, 'Miss Duval, it's all a part of God's magnificent design! Consider the silkworm's cocoon and the intricate design of the butterfly's wings. Sunrise and sunset, moonrise and daybreak, the four seasons wheeling through space as they bring forth the flowers and fruit of their foreordained cycles.

" 'Miss Duval,' he says, 'did it ever occur to you that as fragile as they are, snowflakes are as much the flowers of winter as violets and roses are the flowers of spring? Nighttime and daytime, coolness and balminess, hotness and coldness, sweetness and tartness, pepper pods and sugar lumps, wood grain and stone grain, rubber tires and steel rails, bird's-eye maple and flame-grained mahogany, orderly rotation and wild propagation . . .'

"And that's when Miss Duval breaks in and says, 'Wait, Dad, what the hell are you getting at?' And he says, 'The world's unity of opposites, Miss Duval, its sublime unity of opposites . . .'

"And that's when Miss Duval burps with a giggle and says, 'So don't forget fried ham and eggs, Dad. And boys like you and girls like me, which is a fine combination and a sweet little deal.' To which Mister Jessie says, 'Yes, that's true!' Then he starts going on about what he calls the arts of the manly husband and the womanly wife, and mind-sharpening teachers and tender-care nurses. And Miss Duval says, 'And don't leave out us professional gals like lil ole me.'

"And hit by all that liquored-up talk I says, 'Y'all better balance that whiskey with something to eat, otherwise you'll be looping like kites before you know what you're doing.' And Mister Jessie says, 'You're right, McMillen, so bring us some sandwiches and stuff from the kitchen, including some oysters.'

"So I take a good look at the way that money was scattered on the floor and head for the kitchen. . . ."

"Hold it, McMillen," the Sergeant said. "Before you worked as a super what did you do for a living?"

"I worked at racetracks."

"Doing what?"

"Well, in the beginning it was exercising the horses. And along with that I started clocking gaits and their speed on the tracks. Then pretty soon I got so good at it that I started selling hot tips to the gamblers. I guess you could call me a tout for the touts. Because by working for some of the big-time stables I learned all about the bloodlines of horses. Like what stable's stud sired what foal out of what stable's mare, and the fees that it cost the mare's owners for having her foaled. I even remembered most of the colors used by the big stables. . . ."

"How the hell could you remember all that?"

"I had to," McMillen said, "because in the beginning I read very poorly. But then, after putting my mind to reading and writing I found out that my memory was so good that I could tick off the bloodlines of horses like one of our old-time preachers reciting all that begatting and fighting that's found in the Bible."

"You might have that kind of memory, but I doubt it," the Sergeant said, "but go on."

"Take it or leave it," McMillen said, "but sometimes having a memory like mine can be more of a curse than a blessing. Anyway, when I get back with the grub Mister Jessie starts raving again.

"He says, 'Look at me, Miss Duval, years ago by denying the truth of our human condition I bought this coffin and tried to live a life of the spirit. I bought it to guarantee my safe conveyance into the afterlife, but what happens? Hell, it turned out that for years I'd let myself be tricked as to the here-and-now and the there-and-then, and tricked my *own* damned self as to the cloudy hereafter!'

" 'I can see where you're sitting, Dad,' Miss Duval says, 'but what happened?' And Mister Jessie looks down at her and says, 'I'll tell you what happened: When I took a look inside the damn thing and the bugs and worms saw me they damn near cracked up laughing at me. Here, I'll show you.'

"And with that he reaches inside and drops a little ole moth worm on the lid there in front of him. 'Come close, Miss Duval, and you can hear this one laughing.'

" 'No thank you, doll,' Miss Duval says, 'but how does he sound?' And Mister Jessie says, 'Like the sound of a tooth which I cracked on a pickled pig knuckle. And others like ten-penny nails scratching on glass, or an old rusty gate when it swings in the wind.' At which Miss Duval laughs and says, 'Dad, you're better than a three-ring circus.' 'Don't laugh,' he says, 'because these damn little rascals are knocking themselves out from laughing at human futility. No wonder their friends, the damn silverfish, were ruining my books and me unable to find where they were coming from!'

"So then while I'm pouring more drinks Miss Duval says, 'Dad, if you were given your wish on your birthday, what would it be?' And that's when Mister Jessie thinks a bit and runs his eyeglasses up and down on that chain he's wearing and says, 'Miss Duval, I'd get dressed in my best suit of clothes, my best fedora, and my best pair of shoes, and then I'd take my best walking cane and set out for an early morning stroll. And when the President takes off on his early morning ride from the White House I'd be standing at the gate and waiting. And when his chauffeur stops to see if the way is clear I'd step up to his limousine and greet him. "Good morning, Mister President, sir," I'd say, "I'm Mister Jessie

Rockmore, and one of our nation's senior citizens." And then I'd say, "Mister President, I think you should know that I was here in D.C. when your exalted position was held by President Lincoln, and though only a lad I was often nearby when he passed through these gates. Furthermore, I've been living right here while all the presidents who followed, including General Ulysses S. Grant, Warren G. Harding, and Franklin Delano Roosevelt, occupied the White House. And as you can see without asking, I count for very little in the scheme of things political, but I'll tell you something that you might well have missed: If this nation has to have a man in *your* position, it also has to have men in *my* position who've accepted the responsibility of keeping a hopeful eye on your actions. So for years I've devoted a great deal of my time to president-watching, while hoping and praying that things would get better both for the nation, for them, and for me. Therefore I want you to know that I've prayed that like President Lincoln you have been given the strength to meet the demands of your office, and that the cares of the Republic would never prove too much of a burden for the strength of your mind, your temper, and your power of will. And Mister President, as a watchful observer I think you should know how much this country is changing. Because at three-forty-five this morning I reached the ripe old age of ninety-five years, and I want you to know that after all that time of watching and waiting I, Jessie Wellington Rockmore, no longer have faith in this nation's bright promises. So as of now, here at the gate of the White House, I'm relieving you and myself of the burden of my watching and waiting. So sir, I want you to think on this development's significance when you're sitting in that oval office of yours and dealing with the fateful affairs of this nation. Because what *you* think of as *peace* I consider to be nothing more than the late Reconstruction continuing in vacillating words and the endless manipulation of self-interest and prejudice." Then I'd say, "Mister President, take a walk among people like me and you'll get at the roots of your problem." '

"And then Miss Duval cocks her eye on those goldbacks and says, 'Doll, you're wonderful! But after that, what would you do?' And Mister Jessie says, 'Well, by then I'd be surrounded by a pack of reporters, TV cameras, and F.B.I. agents, so I'd bow and I'd say, "Good day, Mister President, gentlemen," and show them the grace of a man from my old hopeful days by tipping my hat as I made my way down the avenue.

" 'That's my birthday wish, Miss Duval,' Mister Jessie says, 'but as big an old fool as these bugs in my coffin have proven me to be I'd never get away with it. Because as frail as I am, they'd probably blast me with bullets for telling the truth. And if not, they'd think I was simply trying to get my name in the papers, so after laughing like hell they'd throw me in jail.'

"Then Mister Jessie takes him a drink and looks at the ceiling a while and says kinda sad, 'Back in Mister Lincoln's time when people wrote and told him their troubles he'd answer them as fast as he could, and in handwritten letters.'

" 'Yes, Dad,' Miss Duval says, 'but today we have TV, so the man in the White

House not only gets to more of us, and quicker than ole Abe, but right into our own beat-up pads.'

" 'True,' Mister Jessie says, 'but with his voice from the platform or his word on a page Mister Lincoln could touch you and make you feel that you counted in the broad scheme of things. Today politicians stand in front of television cameras drinking water and talk more flimflam than the admen. When TV was invented I bought a set just to see what the hell everybody was so excited about, and what do I get? I get that damn Senator Sunraider coming into my living room mouthing insults to me and my people, and all in the name of good government! And him the same devil who's always preaching about science and demanding government ownership of all the TV networks. Next thing we know the bastard will be trying to get a measure passed for the building of government-owned gas ovens!'

"And with that he pounds his coffin with his fist and sends up a big cloud of dust. So I says, 'Mister Jessie, don't be getting all worked up over politics like that. Remember, this is supposed to be a party.' So he looks at me and nods before taking another deep drink of his whiskey. Then he says, 'McMillen, you're right. Besides, what can we do about all the new gimmicks and gadgets, highbinders and clipsters? Folks nowadays don't remember a death in the family longer than it takes to get the body off to the graveyard. Hell, back in his time Mister Lincoln could begin a speech with Four score and seven years ago and have it mean something to everybody. But today if he began it with Four minutes and seven *seconds* ago folks wouldn't remember who the hell or what the hell he was referring to. So let's be like the rest and forget our condition.'

"Then he looks down at the lady and says, 'Miss Duval, won't you help with some dancing?' And when I see her take a quick look at that money I could've kicked my own butt for switching Mister Jessie from politics to partying.

"I could see the lightbulb start blinking over that red head of hers as she gives Mister Jessie a big juicy smile and says, 'Why, of course, Dad, I'd love to dance, but now there's a problem.'

" 'A problem,' Mister Jessie says, 'what kind of problem?' And she looks at me and says, 'Not being told I'd be dancing, I came without a costume.'

"And with that she throws up her hands and gives him another juiced-eyed smile. Me, I want to kill her for mixing me up in her devilment, but before I can speak up Mister Jessie points to that big cedar chest sitting over there and tells her to see if there's anything in it that suits her.

"So she wobbles over and takes her a look. Then she holds up some lace and silk cloth and tells him, 'Dad, this would be lovely but it's much too old-fashioned. But wait,' she says, 'because if there's anything here that's suitable I'll find it.'

"So she starts picking up pieces of cloth and old feather fans and things and tries striking some cover-girl poses. Then she drops them and picks up an old pair of high-heeled, high-topped shoes and starts giggling and says, 'Dad, I'd *really* feel Frenchy in these.' Then she holds up another bundle of cloth and says, 'Now this is lovely, but it'd be a crime to cut it.'

"And that's when Mister Jessie clears his throat and says, 'McMillen, get a taxi and escort Miss Duval home to get her costume, then hurry back so she can get on with her dancing.'

" 'Oh, no, doll,' she says, 'I have a better idea! You remember Josephine Baker?' And Mister Jessie says, 'So, what about her?' And she says, 'Why, doll, she rocketed to stardom wearing little more than a string of bananas! So why not make mine out of newspaper? All I'd need is a needle and thread.'

"So Mister Jessie tells me to get her whatever she needs. And while I know damn well she's out to con him, I can't figure how bananas and newspapers fit in it. So I says, 'Yessuh, Mister Jessie, and I'll better freshen Miss Duval's drink while she's stitching.' And knowing damn well that I'm wasting good whiskey, this time I get a big water glass and fill it to the brim. What else could I do?

"So I bring her some newspaper, some scissors, a needle, and a spool of black thread. And it's only when I see her cutting that newspaper into strips about the size of those goldbacks that I catch on to her game. So I says, 'Mister Jessie, since there's going to be dancing maybe I better straighten up the floor a bit.' To which he stares at me like he's brooding and says, 'McMillen, leave that floor just as it is.' So even though I'm trying to look out for his interests I have to sit there watching her get on with her scam.

"First she starts cutting that newspaper, headlines and all, into strips about the same size of those goldbacks and strings them together on a long piece of thread. And after she's strung two dozen or so she holds them up and says with a frown, 'Dammit, doll, it's a good idea, but this paper keeps tearing!' Then she slams the stuff on the floor and stomps it.

"So with that Mister Jessie says, 'McMillen, go to the library and bring Miss Duval some of my best stationery'—and gentlemen, that's when she leaps in and scores!

" 'Oh, don't go to all that trouble, doll,' she say, 'I see just the thing I need right there on the floor.'

"So, juiced as she is I have to sit there helpless while she grabs a batch of those goldbacks and starts to work with that needle.

"First she makes a strip out of three of those goldbacks by sewing them together end to end, then she takes three more and treats them the same and keeps stitching 'til she has what she needs—which was a heap. But she's as fast with a needle as she is with her scamming, and when she's done she doubles a long piece of thread and runs it through the tops of the goldbacks and stretches it the width of her arms so Mister Jessie can see it.

" 'There, doll,' she says, 'how do you like it?'

"And looking down at his dangling goldbacks, Mister Jessie says, 'Miss Duval, it's good to see the stuff put to some use, so if it suits you I'm happy. Meanwhile I'm waiting to see you perform.'

" 'And you will, doll,' she says, 'and it'll top anything Josephine Baker ever came up with. It's truly a killer, as you'll see as soon as I strip. It'll be even better than my days in the Follies when I performed at a stag which was given in honor of some Wall Street aristocrats. It was at the Astor, and doll, would you believe it, I was hidden in a huge apple pie and marched into the ballroom on the shoulders of four handsome waiters who placed me in the center of a long banquet table. And doll, when the pie was opened did I began to *swing*! And did those bankers and judges sit back in their chairs! Doll, the applause was deafening, and every guest to a man declared I was lovely!

" 'And I had to believe them, because when a woman is lovely she can't help but *know* it. And especially when she's done up in a white ermine jacket, white satin booties, and a lovely white G-string of Oriental pearls. And with the guests all applauding I felt like a *queen*! Then with the orchestra and waiters going into action the party took off like the Fourth of July. Magnums of champagne began exploding like cannon, and with millionaires cheering I began parading the table one step at a time and saluting each of the guests with a smile and a petite bump and grind. And doll, they were so delighted that every Tom, Dick, and Harry among them demanded that I give them the pleasure of toasting my performance by drinking champagne from my darling white booties!'

"And Mister Jessie says, 'Miss Duval, I'm sure you were wonderful, but what about McMillen and me?' And she says, 'Why, of course, doll,' and heads for the bedroom.

"So while she's gone Mister Jessie sips his whiskey and stares at the ceiling. I'm still worried by the way the lady was eyeing his money, but the first time I tried warning him the man wouldn't listen. So I'm about to warn him again when the door comes open. And gentlemen, when I look back and see Miss Duval dressed in nothing but her high-heeled shoes and that skirt she's rigged out of goldbacks my feet start to itch and my brain starts to stagger!

"Never in my life have I seen so *much* of her kind of woman! And it must've been the same for poor Mister Jessie. Because while I'm rocking and reeling he yells, 'Miss Duval, is that *you*?' And she gives him a smile and says, 'Yes, doll, the true one and only!' Then with her hands on her hips she turns in a circle so he can see her and says, 'And isn't my costume a darling?'

"And with that Mister Jessie grabs holt to his coffin and yells, 'Dance, Miss Duval! Get on with your dancing!'

[DANCE]

"So she starts humming a tune and snapping her fingers, and when she starts to dancing it's like watching a big dish of Jell-O that's doing the shimmy. Then with the tips of her fingers she lifts the hem of that skirt she's stitched out of goldbacks and starts to waltzing. But it turns out no better, because being juiced to the gills she stumbles and flubs it. But that doesn't faze her. 'Cause she comes to a halt and throws back her head like she's high on a stage and has just been crowned the new Miss America. And when I look to see how Mister Jessie's taking it he's staring down from his coffin like a judge listening to a cat copping a plea to a crime so outrageous that he can't believe it. And now when I look back Miss Duval has one of her legs stretched out in front and the other behind, and she's sinking to the floor in a gut-busting split. . . ."

"Dammit, McMillen," the Sergeant shouted, "what the hell happened to *Rockmore?*"

"That's what I'm getting to," McMillen said, "only I'm trying to get it together so you and these other gentlemen can *see* it."

"Then get on with it!"

"So just as Miss Duval bumps the floor in doing her split the doorbell rings and I take off to see who it is. But just as I get there the door flies open and there's this white man. . . ."

"A *white* man?"

"Yes, sir, and he's the same one I asked you about when *you* busted in."

"Okay, but who let him in?"

"I don't *know,* but he was *here*—I swear! And when I go to tell him Mister Jessie didn't do business at that time of night he rushes past me. And when Miss Duval hears all the commotion she must've tried to rise out of her split, because when the man gets to her—and I'm right behind him—she has both legs in the air like she's pedaling a bike lying down. And gentlemen, when this white man sees what she's doing it's like somebody's reached down and cool-cracked his head with a baseball bat! He's eyeing her so hard that he's missed Mister Jessie, but when Mister Jessie yells, 'You, sir! What the hell are *you* doing in my establishment!' he turns away from Miss Duval and says, 'I know it's late, but there's something important I must see you about.'

" 'Well, you picked the wrong time,' Mister Jessie yells, 'this is a private affair and I want none of you color-struck Negroes invading my house!'

"And with that the man turns red and yells, 'But I'm *white!*' and Mister Jessie yells, 'You are, are you? Well, even though I'm no segregationist I want no *white* folks stinking up my house!'

"Then for the first time the man realizes that Mister Jessie's sitting there yelling from a coffin and his eyes bug out of his head and he sputters something so strange that I couldn't believe it. . . ."

And now, looking at each of the detectives in turn, McMillen said, "Gentlemen, you have to understand that after Mister Jessie climbed in that coffin things happened pretty fast, and with me drinking pretty heavy just to keep sober my memory is probably a little bit cloudy. But I swear I heard that white man yell, 'Rockmore, what the hell are you doing up there in my coffin?' "

964 · *Three Days Before the Shooting . . .*

"What!"

"I know it sounds crazy," McMillen said, "but that's the *truth*! And when Mister Jessie hears it he stares at the man like he's seeing a ghost. Then he yells, 'Now I know who you are! You're that cutthroat son of a bitch on television,' and yells out a name. And with that the white man spins and staggers like he's been hit by a bullet and heads for the door. Then Mister Jessie yells, 'Grab him, McMillen'— which I'm not even *about* to do—but as the man starts past Miss Duval she rolls over and grabs him by the ankle and yells, 'Wait, good-looking, and have a look at my number.' And next thing I know the man's going hippety-hop for the door and she's skidding on the floor like a kid on a sled. Then with Miss Duval laughing like crazy and the man struggling to get loose Mister Jessie yells, 'Wait 'til I'm finished, you phony highbinder!' And when the man snatches free and heads for the door Mister Jessie tries to climb out of his coffin. And that's when he gets hit by whatever left him looking the way he does now. It must've been some kind of stroke, because nobody touched him. And that goes for me, Miss Duval, and the white man. And gentlemen, believe it or not, that's all I can tell you."

Staring wide-mouthed at McMillen, the Sergeant shouted, "Like hell it is! What was the white man's name?"

"I can't recall it," McMillen said, "because in looking out for Mister Jessie's interests I'd been holding my liquor too long. Then with all hell breaking loose and that white man probably on his way to have us arrested because of Miss Duval's being here entertaining I took another big drink and tried to phone for a doctor. And when that didn't work I did what I could for poor Mister Jessie. I do remember somebody coming in and letting out a scream, but when I looked to see who it was they were gone. So not wanting folks upstairs down here scrambling around in Mister Jessie's apartment I went to the door and locked it. But after that I truly don't know what happened."

Taking a look at Rockmore, the Sergeant turned back to McMillen.

"Aubrey," he said, "I want you to think back and consider this carefully: What kind of name did your friend call the white man?"

"He called him a cutthroat sonofabitch and a jackleg highbinder, just like I said."

"No! I mean his *surname*!"

"I don't *know*, because Mister Jessie was so mad he sounded like he was yelling with his mouth spewing crackers. So all I can tell you about the name is that it sounded familar. But it wasn't what I'd call ordinary."

"Was it Russian or Chinese?"

"Not that I remember."

"How about Italian or Cuban?"

"Not that I remember."

"How do you know, had you heard it before?"

"Now that's what's so puzzling," McMillen said. "I feel that maybe I'd heard it sometime or other on national TV. But if I did, what would a man like that be doing here? And besides, white folks who deal with Mister Jessie know better than to come here at night. And since there's no dope pushers or whores living in the building his being here didn't make sense. At least not to me . . ."

"And what was that . . . that Miss Duval doing after the man left?"

"She was still on the floor struggling to get up."

"Then what did she do?"

"I don't know, I was too busy trying to figure what happened between Mister Jessie and that white man."

Whereupon one of the officers looked up and pointed behind us.

"Sergeant," he said, "you're wanted," and I looked back to see Officer Morrison staring through the door's splintered paneling.

"Sergeant," he called, "could you step out here for a second?"

"Not now," the Sergeant called with annoyance, "I'm busy enough as it is."

"I understand," Morrison said, "but I've a couple of colored fellows out here who say they have a message for McMillen. One says he's a minister but I suspect they're really here after some of that booze I keep smelling."

Suddenly turning in his chair, McMillen called, "Who the hell says I'm a bootlegger?"

"Listen you," the Sergeant said as he reached down and swung McMillen around, "*I'm* asking the question!"

"So go on and ask him," McMillen said. "Yeah, and read me my rights! Because when somebody accuses me of bootlegging I have a right to know who it is."

"What shall I do with him, Sergeant?" Officer Morrison called.

"Hold him," the Sergeant said and added with a glare at McMillen, "I'll get to him as soon as I'm finished with his supplier."

"*Supplier*," McMillen groaned. "Now ain't *this* the shits! After what's happened to Mister Jessie all they can do is signify that I'm a bootlegger!"

And now after listening to the Sergeant resume his questioning to little effect I moved away and had a look at Cordelia Duval.

Sprawled beneath the policeman's jacket she appeared to be sleeping, but after McMillen's account of her unconventional ways I couldn't be sure. And as I gazed at her bare arms and legs I wondered what had led her to choose such an unseemly profession. And from whom had she learned her semi-underworld version of Negro idiom? Was it a really a long-range effect of a failed love affair? And as I stared at her sprawled in the chair my memory whirled with contrasting images:

My mother in her garden clad in a blue denim dress and white floppy hat arranging a bouquet of freshly cut roses. Sara Delano Roosevelt moving along Pennsylvania Avenue in a chauffeur-driven convertible wearing a choker of pearls that gleam in the sun and a luxurious fur that ripples in the breeze of her

966 · *Three Days Before the Shooting...*

passage. A trio of pretty young bridesmaids imitating Gilbert and Sullivan's "three little maids at school are we" with corsages in hand while posing for a photographer who looks on through the unblinking eye of his camera. And the stately, plump Buck Mulligan figure of a young woman descending a staircase wearing a Lillian Russell hat and voluminous dress who delights passing pedestrians with her swaying imitation of a Mae-Westian walk ...

And as I stared I wondered how it would be to have known a woman like Miss Duval; who, apparently, had rejected such bewitching feminine roles to the extent of turning up willingly in Rockmore's chaotic establishment. For now her rowdy condition seemed to imply an utter rejection of everything that respectable women—and especially white women—considered desirable. . . .

So could it be, I thought, that while we fortunate Americans move through our bright blaze of lights unaware an outer darkness constantly explores our most flattering pretensions and makes silent fun of our dreams and our certainties? Cordelia Duval—who was the reality behind that unlikely name? And what would a man like McGowan make of her presence? Was he aware of such women, or did his strongly held views prevent his acknowledging their very existence? And I recalled McGowan's arguing that by unmasking woman's primeval mystery for the eyes of men like Rockmore and McMillen the nude photographs presented by certain girlie magazines were leading to racial imbalance and social disorder. Of course the mystery that concerned him was limited to white women alone, but as she sprawled half-naked in shadows Miss Duval seemed far more mysterious than she could ever have been fully clothed.

Indeed, there was even a mystery in the language she used, as there was in certain details of her past as related by McMillen. And that mystery would remain even if his account proved to be false. She was *shrouded* in mystery, and as she slouched under the blue policeman's jacket I wondered if it were possible that she and McMillen had actually murdered Rockmore and tried to conceal their crime by jamming him into a worm-eaten coffin.

And with that I looked at my watch and realized that I had little time left for filing my story. And hoping to meet my deadline I decided I'd learn whatever I could from Cordelia Duval and get on with it. It was then that she looked up and saw me.

"Listen, doll," she said, "why the hell don't you two-bit gumshoes leave McMillen alone? The poor bastard's told you everything he can tell you, so why don't you go 'n find that stuffed shirt who left Dad sitting up there in a coma?"

"But I'm not a detective," I said, "I'm a newspaper reporter."

"Oh, yeah, so what's the dif? Like the dicks you think McMillen's lying just because he's a spade. Otherwise you'd go find that white dude he told you about. Dammit, just when everything was going fine the bastard barges in and ruins it. I've never known it to fail! Let a spook get near me and *every* damn thing starts coming unraveled!"

"Tell me, Miss Duval," I said, "did you recognize the white man?"

"Hell, no," she said, "but he's probably some drunk who busted in here hoping to find him a spade broad who'd give him a ride and brighten his luck. Or maybe he's hoping to find one who looks like his mother in blackface."

"*What?*"

"What's so strange about that, Mister Reporter? Hell, a heap of you johns go for black magic if it's dressed in a bra and silk panties."

"I don't understand," I said.

"The hell you don't, I know all about you johns and the spook gals. Yes, and even more about spooks who wear britches. You want to hear about one I kept for a while?"

"Not now, Miss Duval," I said, "but do you think you'd recognize the white man if you saw him again?"

"Recognize him? Hell, I want to *forget* the bastard! But you want to hear a secret?"

"All right," I said, "but about this white man . . ."

"Forget him, doll, and learn about life on the dark side: I once lived with a black dude who turned out to be the damndest man who ever kicked off his shoes and punished a gal and a bed. Not that he wasn't good at his business, which he sure as hell was. Doll, he spook-handled *everybody*—johns, house detectives, bellhops, madams, and cops on the beat. And he took care of *me* like a prince. But that's not what I'm getting at, doll. My spook was the type who didn't give a hoot in hell for *any* kind of rules or any kind of law. What's more, he got a kick out of doing any damn thing that folks like you say spooks tend to do because they're naturally inferior. And I mean *any* damn thing!

"Matter of fact, I wish he'd get hold of the bastard who broke up our party. He was a good-looking spook, and after jiving a high-society broad into setting him up with a penthouse apartment—doormen, elevators, stereos, TVs, and everything—the spook made a play for her teenage sister and lost it. And *laughed* about it, doll. That's the truth! Then I gave him cash for a car, and like the prime spook he was he buys a white Cadillac. Then to celebrate he gets dressed in a white suit, white shoes, white hat and gloves, and with his white bitch of a bulldog sitting beside him he drives down South to visit his family. To *Miss-iss-ip-pi,* doll! Can you believe it? And in the month of *July*! That's right! And if his sister hadn't spent years working like a slave for the mayor he'd have got himself lynched and burned to a frazzle! Doll, the spook was so ornery that he'd do *anything*! Once he showed up at a dance wearing everything backwards—shirt, coat, and pants—left shoe on his right foot and right shoe on his left foot. And then he insists that we dance back to back! It got both of us thrown out of the hall but all he did was laugh. And don't mess with the spook when he's high on his liquor!

"One morning after a hard night's hustling I get home limp as a dishrag to find that he's killed my canaries! All sixteen of them, doll! And why did he do it?

Because he couldn't teach them to sing 'The Funky Butt Blues'! Can you imagine a canary singing 'I thought I heard somebody say / funky-butt, funky-butt, take it away?' And then, doll, would you believe it, the spook *baked* the poor little things in a pie and *ate* them! I tell you, doll, that spook was a frigging e-nig-ma!"

"He *ate* your canaries?"

"Yes, doll! And you know something else he did?"

"No, Miss Duval," I said, "but if you'll get back to the white man I'm willing to listen."

"So come closer, doll, and bend down. I won't bite you!"

And seeing me hesitate she pouted like a young girl and said, "What's with you, doll, you never been close to a woman before?"

So with a shrug I bent closer—which was a mistake. For suddenly Cordelia Duval grasped my face in her hands and planted a wet kiss on my lips! And as I tried to escape she thrust the moist tip of her tongue in my right ear and giggled!

"So now, doll," she said, "you've an idea of my spook's kissing style—hey! What's with you, doll? You been spooked by a spook-kiss?"

Shocked by her blatant behavior, I stepped back in anger. But now behind her flushed face quite a different Cordelia Duval seemed to be gauging the effects of her teasing. And torn between laughing and slapping her face I whirled to see the Sergeant pointing a finger at McMillen and Rockmore glaring from the coffin as though shouting a curse at the universe. And with a final look at Cordelia Duval I bumped my way through the warehouse of a ballroom to the vestibule—where among the tenants in nightclothes I saw one of the males calmly viewing scenes of early America through the cloudy lens of a stereoscope. And clutching my recorder I rushed past the grandfather's clock and into the the dim, but most welcome, light of a new day's dawning.

PART III

A Selection of Ellison's Notes

Editors' Note: Ralph Ellison's notes pertaining to his second novel constitute a rich body of work unto themselves. Written over forty years, the hundreds, maybe thousands, of notes track the shifting course of the novel's composition as Ellison grappled with matters of craft and theme. They testify to his sustained commitment to the story of Hickman and Bliss/Sunraider from soon after *Invisible Man*'s publication, in 1952, until shortly before Ellison's death, in 1994. One sees Ellison refining plotting and characterization, as well as offering sometimes startling insights into broader concerns of culture, society, and politics. He kept few notebooks related to the second novel; instead, he most often scribbled on loose scraps of paper. A fair number of the notes are typed (on a manual typewriter, an electric, and finally on the computers he used throughout the 1980s and 1990s), while others are scrawled, sometimes nearly indecipherably, on whatever happened to be close at hand. Most are undated, though it is possible to ascertain an approximate time period for some thanks to Ellison's habit of jotting on the backs of postmarked envelopes.

Read alongside the manuscripts published here, these notes illuminate Ellison's core themes of identity and nationhood, love and sacrifice, kinship and estrangement. A sampling of notes follows that bear upon Ellison's compositional practice, the range of his characters and themes, and the cast of his imagination as he continued to reshape his fiction over the years. Everything below is as Ellison wrote it except for the bracketed editorial notations; the numbers listed at the end of each note correspond to that note's box and folder location in the Ralph Ellison Papers.

On the day of April, 1953 a chartered airplane load of elderly Southern Negroes put down at the . . . (140/4)

WHAT MUST BE DONE // Narrative must be kept moving, and if possible, stepped-up in pace. If we begin with Senator's version of the shooting, we plunge immediately into his consciousness, his past and we are introduced to Hickman at one remove, even while we are wondering about his presence in the Hospital. (139/6)

How to begin before the action? What is the tragic mistake? And who makes it? As things stand we do begin before one tragic mistake, that of the Senator's, when he refuses to see Hickman and company. But if we consider the mistake from the point of Severen then it would require beginning before he acts. 'Two days before the shooting . . . ' begins the first section as it now stands; 'I was there, etc." is how the Second section begins—what is there to prevent our starting the Severen section with 'Several months before the shooting . . . (140/3)

Hickman and the group go to Washington to warn Sunraider that he is in danger but in so doing they lead Severen to him and bring about his death. This is a peripeteia. And, ironically, it is Sunraider's refusal to see them which ruins him. He must recognize this fatal irony. The crucial mistake is, of course, Hickman's. He is the hero and set[s] the plan going out of his love for the little Bliss. // The hospital becomes a sanctuary (and a death room) wherein the sickness of American society comes into conscious focus. Hickman and company, being Christians, turn the other cheek; that is why they come to Washington. But Bliss-Sunraider is pagan. He seeks power and has sought to be formidable and thus above race, human ties and history. // Hickman struggles to understand his "Americanness." (138/4)

Why have they undertaken the trip? To warn him and to see what he has become, this child they all loved in whom they invested such mystical hope. // Why? Out of their fidelity to Hickman. Hickman knows that he is acting obsessively but the circumstances under which he received [the] child are charged with emotion. He lost his brother and mother, his life was endangered by the presence of the white woman and he had taken the child in defiance of the very absurdity of his situation. He feels guilty for having rejected his parents' religion, and feels that had he followed his father's wishes he might have prevented the tragic incident. In other words he has been pushed into an extreme situation and withdrawn from his old free life of jazz. Coupled with this is his acceptance of the religious life and his hope of bringing up the child as a bridge between the old savage relationship which obtained between the races and his vision of a more human society. His vision is a version of the peaceful kingdom, unreal but compelling precisely because it defies the state of things. He undergoes a period of withdraw[al] after the lynching, then emerges a changed man. He fasts, gives up drinking, and although attractive to women abstains from sex. After Bliss runs away he becomes a reader and [he] and his group raise money with which they send young people north to college. // How do they keep in touch with activities of Bliss? // They do so through members of the group who have scattered to the west and north, people who recognize him but whom he fails to see, once he passes and thinks he is secure. Sometimes they are mistaken, but they recognize him as a minstrel man, movie maker, Billy Sunday type preacher, etc. They lose him, only to have him turn up in another part of the country playing a different role. Hickman, realizing the need to keep up with the lives of his people, has persuaded those who leave the state to write him letters, especially those who were Bliss's age. And it's through this that he is able to track the runaway— up to a point, learns also of his triumphs and reversals of expectation in the North and West. (140/1)

Action takes place on the eve of the Rights movement but it forecasts the chaos which would come later. This is a reversal of expectations to consider inasmuch as it reaches beyond the frame of the fiction. This looks forward to the reassertion of the Klan and the terrible, adolescent me-ism of the '70's. (139/5)

One of the main tasks is to dramatize the theories which lead to the unleashing of violence. This should come during an earlier period—but not too early—when the Senator discusses the problem of power with an ambitious white southern politician who sees that he can never become president of the U.S. This frustration increases when he observes another southerner change and become pro-Negro and thus move toward a wider acceptability as possible nominee . . . (140/2)

Make Washington function in Hickman's mind as a place of power and mystery, frustration and possibility. It is historical, it is the past, it is slavery, the Emancipation and a continuation of the betrayal of Reconstruction. He would have to imagine or try to imagine what Bliss knew about the city and its structure of power. He would wonder how, given his early background, Bliss could have gone so far in the gaining and manipulation of power, the juxtapositions of experience and intelligence which allowed him to make his way. (139/4)

If it were a jam session all would start from single incident then proceed to give their own versions. This would allow for extremes of variation while based upon the basic themes, but the 'truth' would remain in the minds of Hickman and Bliss (not Sunraider). // What the white woman gives Hickman is a promise—a descendent of slaves is entrusted with the future and must train the future out of the limitations imposed by his experience. (138/5)

Looking back it seems that three people were involved. A woman, a politician and a preacher. And yet that leaves out many others, and especially the young man who brought down the intricate structure of time and emotion, the joker, the wild card. The unexpected emotional agent of chaos. But even so, this leaves out another woman, long dead, and by her own hand, and the earlier metamorphosis of the man who was responsible and who later paid for his willfulness with his life and who thus was exposed for what he was and for who and what he had been. [Editors' Note: Written on postmarked envelope dated March 24, 1977; Ellison has sketched an American flag in the middle of the note.] (138/2)

Important Note//Hickman and contingent arrive in Washington, attracting attention by their number and dress and the fact that they arrive in a chartered plane and are obviously in a hurry and on a mission of some kind. There would be an advantage in plunging the reader immediately into the mind of Hickman since the issues motivating their arrival could be presented directly and in the fragmented details in which they'd be presented in his mind. Janey's warning letter would play a part in this, as would his memories of Bliss and his regret and bewilderment over what the boy had become. The other advantage would lie in the opportunity to play upon the tension implicit in the unsuccessful quest as it builds from home to frustration through its cycles of purpose, passion, through partial perception to a realignment of purpose leading to other degrees of passion to different orders of perception-frustration. The assumption here is that McIntyre would be eliminated along with the forms of irony his consciousness provides. // What must be considered here is the advantage of approaching the group from outside, which would prepare the reader for the mystery of experience, background and purpose that the group embodies. They must retain their strangeness—So perhaps the best strategy is to proceed as begun but with earlier shift to the dramatic mode centered in Hickman's point of view. Concentrate on scene. (140/2)

Note // Hickman // He is intelligent but untrained in theology. Skilled with words, he reads and mixes his diction as required by his audience. He is also an artist in the deeper sense and [h]as actually been a jazz musician. He has been a ladies' man, but this ceased when he became a preacher. Devout and serious, he is unable to forget his old, profane way of speaking and of thinking of experience. Vernacular term[s] and phrases bloom in his mind even as he corrects them with more pious formulations. In other words he is of mixed culture and frequently formulates the sacred in profane terms—at least within his mind. Orally he checks himself. // He has been a great gambler and although never a drunkard, he has known the uses of alcohol. // Dramatize the matter of culture variations that are possible for one of his background. He is of a unique combination that has gone unaccounted for by sociology. He is without formal training but of keen intelligence, an intelligence which he hides behind his personal and group idiom. He has his own unique way of looking at the U.S. and is much concerned with the <u>meaning</u> of history. There is mysticism involved in his hope for the boy, and an attempt to transcend the hopelessness of racism. After the horrors connected with or coincidental with his coming into possession of the child, he reverts to religion and in his despair begins to grope toward a plan. This involves bringing up the child in love and dedication in the hope that properly raised and trained the child's color and features, his inner substance and his appearance would make it possible for him to enter into the wider affairs of the nation and work toward the betterment of his people and the moral health of the nation. (140/3)

Bliss realizes political and social weakness of Hickman and other Negroes when he's taken from his coffin, and this becomes mixed with his yearning for a mother—whom he now identifies with the red headed woman who tried to snatch him from his coffin. Which was a symbol of resurrection in drama of redemption that Hickman has structured around it. But he goes seeking for life among whites, using the agency of racism to punish Negroes for being weak, and to achieve power of his own. As with many politicians politics is a drama in which he plays a role that doesn't necessarily jibe with his own feelings. Nevertheless he feels humiliated by a fate that threw him among Negroes and deprived him of the satisfaction of knowing whether he is a Negro by blood or only by culture and upbringing. He tells himself that he hates Negroes but can't deny his love for Hickman. Resents this too. // He is a man who sees the weakness in the way societal hierarchy has dealt with race and it is through the chink that he enters white society and exploits it. (140/6)

From 1956 Note Book // Blisses' purpose (immediate) is to get money to carry him further west. Secondarily and psychologically, it is to manipulate possibility and identities of the townspeople and to take revenge upon his own life. And to play! He is the artist as child in this. // So the script, scenario, plot—must: 1) tie in with the larger plot, 2) must present the large writ small and in a variation, 3) it must provide townspeople opportunity to lose old identities for something less good and, 4) it must lead to chaos and to birth of Severen. (141/4)

Bliss Proteus Rhinehart returned to his part very much as a man to his mother or a dog to his vomit, and that's no lie. The thing just happened that way and here he was, flickering before the eye like the film of a cinema camera gone wild. (140/6)

Bliss must sense that Hickman is coming. This is to occur in flashback when he reviews his sensations before the shooting. He hadn't thought of Hickman for some time now, and eliminated him from his consciousness. But now, as his mind was distracted by some of the problems of the day, the figure of the big man strayed across the field of his consciousness, leaving him uneasy. He had contained guilt for a long time, had become disciplined to the task; power required it and it was human even manly to sustain the pain which arose through necessary action. (140/7)

Sunraider is not killed because he abandoned Severen's mother, nor because of his overt political acts, but because he betrayed his past and thus provided Severen the deepest intellectual-emotional motives for murder. He's murdered by way of proving that Severen was free of acceptance of whiteness which was source of Blisses confusion. (139/2)

One way of getting Wilhite more involved is to have him tell Hickman what Hickman knows deep within his own mind but refuses to acknowledge: that the Senator is beyond saving, and that the group knows this. They go along because they love Hickman and because there simply has to be something on which they can pin their earthly hopes. // Consider the idea, if introduced in Hickman's consciousness, should not be presented there in isolated completion; rather, it should be introduced with the voices of others who are central to the plot. It must battle with them, try to convince, anticipate or foreshadow. It should sound with the ideas of the others, and thus it should contain some impression of Wilhite, Bliss become the Senator, Janey, Severen, and certain of the members from the old days. It should also argue with McIntyre—which suggests that he will have come in contact with McIntyre before the shooting. If this is done, then the significant incidents will take on a richer meaning, and will themselves become parts of an intricate dialogue. Rockmore will himself have something significant to say about Hickman's idea—which it refutes. Nor is there any reason why McIntyre's dream sequence should be separate from central dialogue. In fact it is a dialogue which issues from McIntyre's involvement in Hickman's idea-quest. // But Severen remains the problem. Is he as assassin to be left out of it? Impossible. It is he who puts the whole idea to crucial testing. Therefore we must render his consciousness on the brink of the Senate incident. He must be aware of Hickman in Washington and Hickman must be aware that he is somewhere at large. But they will have met earlier. (140/3)

This man McIntyre is a modern reporter who goes around with a compact tape recorder which he uses instead of the regulation sheets of folded paper. He is thus able to come away with the exact dialogue, the exact words of the interviewee. He thus [is] able to report to Vannec in detail and to present McMillen's story in transcription. He is no less confused by what he sees and hears but for once his is accurate. // One must keep to this device; it offers endless opportunities nevertheless, it is no explanation of how McMillen comes by his detailed memory or his ability to recall the action so completely. The answer here, of course, is that he remembers what he remembers, that he is telling the story to a group of white men and thus under psychological pressure to shape the story, to give it form in a way which eliminates that which he finds resistant, that which he fears is too loaded with taboo, and that which was insignificant to his sense of the facts. In short, McMillen is a story-teller and thus an artist. While McIntyre who has wanted to be an artist can only be a reporter because he is dominated by facts—and even then is without the insight which would raise the facts to broader significance. (140/4)

<u>Hickman and Leroy</u> // It seems that Leroy is telling Hickman about an initiation ritual in which the figure in his dark room is conducting. Thus the seven questions—or mistakes—have to do with a riddle. But in the street scene Leroy is putting <u>Hickman</u> through an initiation in which Leroy and his fantasies constitute the riddle. That riddle points to politics and thus to the complex meaning which lies in Hickman's relationship with Sunraider. What is the secret knowledge which underlies all this craziness? (140/2)

Janey could reveal secret out of guilt; or, Oedipus-like, Severen could badger Love until Love tells him directly. Or someone could show Severen a snapshot of his mother and Bliss. This perhaps could be the owner of the movie house who has a collection of photographs taken of entertainers who had performed in theater. But by putting information together Severen learns enough to proceed to Washington. (139/4)

The burning of the Cadillac and Jessie Rockmore's rejection of God are of the same substance. They represent a collapse of walls which kept despair within bounds. And while both are comic they are nevertheless tragic in what they imply for the nation. They should prepare us for the shooting. (140/6)

Rockmore is trying to say that what the president views [as] peace is actually the Civil War continued in the form of words and the manipulation of prejudices. // N.B. Try introducing Hickman and Wilhite immediately after McIntyre leaves the building. And this time it is he who leaves the door open. (RE 51, 9/14/93)

Rereading the Rockmore incident it appears that along with the car burning and the encounter with the senator's secretary et al, trivial chaos is building to some kind of disaster. Each complaint—LeeWillie's, the crossedeyed woman's, Rockmore's—are all concerned with serious matters that are not allowed to be viewed seriously. Lonnie Barnes, like A. B. McDonald is a fool who aspires to play a serious role in government. Sunraider is a trickster who <u>plays</u> a serious role, and perhaps it is he who is behind what's happening. (139/6)

Ellison: Oh for God's sake! I didn't make the statement, Hickman made the statement. He was preaching a sermon about transformation; the recovery—the refusal—to be decimated by slavery. Besides, he was speaking as a Christian minister of the role of his religion in giving unity and a sense of hope to a people that had been deliberately deprived of continuity with their past and its traditions. (139/1)

THINGS TO REMEMBER WHEN PLOTTING // The blue-print of the plot should contain scenes on a rising note of dramatic intensity, leading to the crisis and climax. // No scene within a story has value unless it develops conflict of at least a minor sort.

     A. . . . . .Plot Idea.
     B. . . . . .Sub-plot (stairs)
     C. . . . . .Collateral Material: Characterization,
atmosphere, motivation.

Use one chief character at a time.
Milk the sub-scenes for everything emotional and dramatic that is inherent in them.

Nota Bene: Remember that the sound of your machine, typewriter or computer, helps you work! Start it going, even if at random. (139/4)

Two Early Drafts of the Opening of Book II

Editors' Note: The surviving 4- and 11-page drafts of the opening of Book II are impossible to date precisely. The former opens the 185-page partial draft of Book II from which Ellison in 1959 culled and edited "And Hickman Arrives" for Saul Bellow's journal, *Noble Savage*, published in 1960. Like the prologue to Book I, which became the opening of "And Hickman Arrives," this early draft is spare and dramatic, focused keenly and single-mindedly on the immediate action of the assassination from the perspective of Senator Sunraider, aka Bliss, as he is struck down on the floor of the Senate.

The subsequent 11-page draft is undated. In its expanding themes and focus it lies between the earlier 4-page draft and the longer 24-page draft found in Book II. In it Ellison gives a taste of Sunraider's somewhat florid and ambivalent speech, which is greatly expanded, to mixed effect, in the longest draft of Book II, published on pages 235–249 of the current volume (and also as chapter 2 of *Juneteenth* in 1999).

Considered together with the long opening of Book II published here, these drafts show Ellison's growing purpose and his evolving concern with the Senator's ambiguous political rhetoric.

I

[Circa 1959, the opening of a 185-page partial draft of Book II]

The Senator had no idea what struck him. He had been in the full-throated roar of his rhetoric, had moved beyond the mere meaning of his words onto that plane of verbal exhilaration for which he was notorious and, having placed his audience under the spell of his eloquence, had then decided in the capriciousness of his virtuosity to better the old Senate record for shattering the building's window panes by the sheer resonance of the projected voice. It was then he saw the tall young man rising in the distant visitor's gallery and leaning casually across the rail as though about to point out some detail of a scene to some still seated friend, pausing there in space, the light behind his head. And he thought, *I've lost this one, he's leaving. How can he escape me?* Then as he continued in the full flow of his / suddenly pieces of glass / were bursting from the chandelier above him. *My God!* he thought, *it's the chandelier; I've shattered the chandelier!* hearing the dry, popping sound even before he realized that he had been hit or that the man was shooting at him. *Me,* he thought. *It's come to me at last... with a silencer noise-lessly,* still standing, his arms outflung in rhetorical gesture, as something struck his side with the impact of a solid invisible club; then again, the right side this time, and he staggered backwards then forward, thinking, "*I'm going... I'm...*" and he knew it was important to retreat, to fall backwards, but it was as though he was propped up and held by an invisible cable. Nor could he get his arms down, yet his eyes were recording with the impassive and precise inclusiveness of a motion picture camera thrown suddenly out of phase; the image of the remote man high there in the gallery above firing down at him as calmly as if he were shooting clay pigeons sailing from a trap on a remote shooting range; he could see the others, those on the floor and those around the man above, caught in their atti-tudes of surprise, disbelief or horror, turning slowly with puppet gestures, some rising, some looking at their neighbors, but none moving even now toward the calm man, who seemed as detached from his act and the rise and fall of his pis-tol arm as he was from the Senator. *A silencer,* he thought with awe. *And the others are thrown out of stance. What breed of men are—who's laying me low...? down...? who?* When it was as though someone had dragged a poker at white heat straight down the center of his scalp and at last he felt himself going over backwards, crashing against a chair, thinking, *Down* and feeling something searing hot on the sole of his right foot and his mind spinning out of control even as he heard himself cry out words he knew should not be uttered but which he could no longer control: "Lord, Lawd!" he cried, "Why hast Thou forsaken me?" his voice rising with hys-terical shrillness like that of a Negro preacher who sounded in his practiced fer-vor somewhat like an accomplished actor shouting his lines. And as his words flew up he heard from far away a sound as of shattering glass, and even as he heard his voice begin its echoed return he was filled with a profound sense of self-betrayal as though stripped naked in the Senate. He had the sensation of perspiration bursting from his face like water from a suddenly activated sprin-kler. Still trying to rise now he was gripped by the hot impression that somehow he was trying to fold a huge white circus tent into a packet while a playful wind kept blowing it out of his hands; listening all the time for he was waiting for his voice to ricochet back to him; and now he seemed to hear the words floating calmly down, "For thou had forsaken me..." But no longer his words nor his echoed voice and now he felt, hearing what sounded like singing, a sudden fear, thinking, *No! No!* and trying desperately to sit up, thinking, *Hickman? But how? His voice? Hickman?* Then the very idea that Hickman was there above him raised him up, clutching onto a chair, into a sitting position, trying to see clearly above him as now there came another shot, but this one he did not feel.

He lay now on his back, looking up where the bullet-smashed chandelier swung gently back and forth under the impact of its shattering, creating a watery distortion of crystal light which seemed to settle him in a ring of liquid fire. Beyond the pulsing blaze where the roiling darkness grew he was dimly aware of a burst of action. Now he could hear someone shouting far off. Then someone was shouting quite close to his ear, but he could not bring his mind back into any of its familiar grooves. And he recalled one of his formulas: Be gracious and polite to all in private contacts, regardless of approach in public debate: and tried vainly to respond. For now a darkness was growing, moving close to him and he tried to push it away, to fight it, but it pressed relentlessly upon him.

It hurts here and here and there and there, his mind went on through the rising pain. *Lord, Lord, why—Ha! Turn it, crank it! Who? Ha! Inevitable. Focus in scene. There, Reverend Hickman, you? Donelson! Karp! Get this action—from this angle.*

Rise up on that morning, Bliss. On that great gitting up morning, Bliss? BLISS! NO! ... No! But Bliss be the tie that binds us to ... No! Denied! Rejected!

Then for an instant he felt himself being lifted, as upon a bright red wave of pain. He did not know if it were man or darkness now, nor if he were awake or dreaming. He had entered a region of darks and greys that revolved slowly before his eyes, and yet there was the unyielding darkness which seemed to speak to him and which he wanted to touch but could not manage and whose words he dreaded to hear. *It hurts here*, he thought. *The light comes and goes behind my eyes— in—out—out—in. Shadowless ... If only the throbbing would stop. Who—what—why— Lord, Lord, why hast Thou ... It pains above, Lord, Lord, why?*

Then someone was calling to him from a long way off, "Senator Sunraider, do you hear me?"

And yes he did, very clearly: yet when he tried to answer he seemed to dream, or to remember a dream, to recall to himself a dream.

II

[Undated, likely the 1960s]

Now through the lilt and tear of his soaring voice the Senator became aware of the visitors staring down. Looking up past the chandelier to the gallery he could feel them there *en masse*, seeming suddenly to impose their presence upon his attention as, dressed in the light suits and colorful dresses of spring, they loomed in serried tiers arising above the curving sweep of balcony emblazoned with eagle, flag and seal emblematic of Nationhood. They sat bending slightly forward, caught in the tense attitudes of viewers intrigued by some enigmatic action slowly unfolding on a screen observed from the tortured angle of a theatre peanut gallery. Anonymous from where the Senator stood on the podium, the lectern before him, they seemed for a moment to hover high there in rapt suspension of breath, as though awaiting the fulfillment of revelations already emerging from the now accelerating rhythms, the bounce and boom of words sent flighting across the domed and lucid space from the flex and play of his own throat, tongue and diaphragm.

Pleasurably challenged by their engrossment, the Senator experienced a sudden surge of that gaiety, anguished yet wildly free, which sometimes seized him during a speech, and now as with a smooth shifting of emotional gears he felt himself moving beyond a regard for the mere rhetorical rightness of his words onto that plane of verbal exhilaration for which he was famous and in the gay capriciousness of his virtuosity found himself attempting to equal that feat glorified in senatorial legend whereby through a single flourish of his resonantly projected voice the speaker raises both floor and gallery to fever pitch and shatters the building's window panes... *Do that*, the Senator thought, *and the day is made: so much so that without yelling a single dissenting, "Hell, naw!" the gentlemen from Little Rock will call for changing the name of Arkansaw...*

"I would remind you," the Senator continued, projecting his voice toward the visitor's gallery, "that every hour on the quarter hour, we are interrogated by our conduct and by our lives. By our stated ideals and by those things which we do and do *not* do. Yes, and by the examples of those, humble and illustrious alike, who came upon the scene before us. So note this well: In this our great land, *memory* is *all*! *Memory* is all: touchstone, threat, and guiding star! Where we go is where we have been! Where we have been is where we shall go...."

The Senator paused, his eyes sweeping the anonymous faces above.

"Therefore," he continued, "we must confront forthrightly our national complexity, for great nations live out their own mysteries, evolve in their own most intimate secrets. Thus it is that we must remember so that we may forget—*and* we must forget the past so that we may be free to reassemble its remnants in the glowing design of a more human presence and future. To some this appears too difficult, to others it is too optimistic, but we must not pale before the arduous knowledge which holds that those who reject the lessons of history are doomed to repeat its disasters. For this is true only for those who reject the obligation of bringing forth some finer, some more graceful design, some more generous structure to supplant the inadequate institutions of the past. We become victims of history only if we fail to evolve ways of life that are more free, more transcendent! Only if we fail in the task of creating a way of life which allows each of us to soar, released in human space!

"And this too note well! In this land, to remember is to forget, and to forget is to remember—*creative-ly*!

"For in this land to create is to *destroy*, and to destroy, if we will it so, if we pay our proper respect to remembered things, is to create a more human future! So let us not falter before our complexity, let us not become confused by the double stroke of our national imperatives, nor equivocate before our national ambiguities! Instead, let us forge ahead in faith and in confidence. For it is not our fate to be mere victims of history—Oh, no! Even the wildest black man in a Cadillac knows—bear me out—perhaps this is the secret of his wildness, his defiance before the harsh laws of economics—who knows? But one mystery at a time, I say, so let us remind ourselves that ours is not the role of passive slaves to the past. Ours is the freedom and obligation to be the fearless creators of ourselves, the *re*-constructors of the world! So let the doubters doubt, the faint of heart turn pale. We'll fulfill our nation's need for citizens possessing a multiplicity of creative styles. We'll supply its need for *individuals* possessing the highest quality of personal stamina, daring and grace—

> *'Ho! Build thee more stately mansions,*
> *Oh, my soul'—Yes!*

For *we*," the Senator paused, "are," his arms reaching out in all-embracing gesture, *"A-meri-cans!"*

And it was now, listening to his voice become lost in the explosion of applause accented here and there by rebel yells, the Senator became aware of the rising man....

Up in the front row center of the visitor's gallery the man was pointing across the guardrail now as though about to utter a denunciation, and the Senator thought *Oh, sit down or leave, only spare us futile gestures. I always lose a few, the old, the short-attention-spanned, mamas' boys answering mother nature's call—but use your ears! Most I hold hard, so what can you hope to do...?* Then as he lowered his eyes to the faces of those applauding on the floor below him, the Senator was only dimly aware of the abrupt rise and fall of the man's still pointing arm as a sound of ringing, erupting above, triggered a prismatic turbulence of the light—through which fragments of crystal, fine and fleeting as the first cool-touching flakes of the fall of snow, had begun to shower down upon him, striking sleet-sharp upon the still upturned palms of his gesturing hands.

My god, the Senator thought, *it's the chandelier! I've shattered the chandelier!* Whereupon something smashed into the lectern, driving it against him; and now hearing a dry popping sounding above he felt a vicious stinging in his right shoulder and as he stared through the chaotic refraction of the light toward the gallery he could see the sharp kick of the man's pointing arm and felt a second flare of pain, in his left thigh this time, and was thrown into a state of dream-like lucidity.

Realizing quite clearly that the man was firing toward the floor, he tried desperately to move away, asking himself as he tried to keep the lectern before him,

Is it me? Am I his target? Then something struck his hip with the force of a well-aimed club and he felt the lectern toppling forward as he was spun around to face the gallery. Coughing and staggering backwards now, he felt himself striking against a chair and lurching forward as he marked the sinister *pzap! pzap! pzap!* of the weapon.

I'm going... I'm going... he told himself, knowing lucidly that it was most important to fall backwards, out of the line of fire if possible; but as he struggled to go down it was as though he were being held erect by an invisible cable attached somehow to the gallery from where the man, raising and lowering his arm in measured calm, continued to fire.

The effort to fall brought a burst of sweat streaming from his pores but even now his legs refused to obey, would not collapse. And yet, through the muffled sound of the weapon and the strange ringing of bells, his eyes were recording details of the wildly tossing scene with the impassive and precise inclusiveness of a motion picture camera toppling slowly from its tripod and falling through the unfolding action with the lazy motion of a feather loosed from a bird in soaring flight: panning from the image of the remote gunman in the gallery down to those moving dreamlike on the floor before him, then back to those shooting up behind the men above; all caught in attitudes of surprise, disbelief, horror: some turning slowly with puppet gestures, some still seated, some rising, some looking wildly at their neighbors, some losing control of their flailing arms, their erupting faces, some falling floorward—And up in the balcony now, an erupting of women's frantic forms.

Things had speeded up but, oddly, no one was moving even now toward the gunman—who seemed as detached from the swiftly accelerating action as a marksman popping clay birds on a remote shooting range.

Then it was as though someone had dragged a poker at white heat straight down the center of his scalp following it with a hammering blow; and at last he felt himself going over backwards, crashing against a chair now and hearing it skitter away, thinking mechanically, *Down, down...* and feeling the jolting of his head and elbows striking the floor. Something seared through the sole of his right foot then, and now aware of losing control he struggled to contain himself even as his throat gave cry to words which he knew should not be uttered in this place, whatever the cost of self-containment:

"Lord, LAWD," he heard the words burst forth, "WHY HAST THOU..." smelling the hot presence of blood as the question took off with the hysterical timbre of a Negro preacher who in his disciplined fervor sounded somehow like an accomplished actor shouting the lines.

"Forsaken... forsaken... forsaken," the words went forth, becoming lost in the shattering of glass, the ringing of bells. Writhing on the floor as he struggled to move out of range, the Senator was taken by a profound sense of self-betrayal, as though he had stripped himself naked in the Senate. And now with the full

piercing force of a suddenly activated sprinkler streams of moisture seemed to burst from his face *and somehow he was no longer in that place, but kneeling on the floor of a familiar clearing within a grove of pines, trying desperately to enfold a huge white circus tent into a packet. Here the light was wan and eerie, and as he struggled, trying to force the cloth beneath chest and knee, a damp wind blew down from the tops of the trees, causing the canvas to toss and billow like a live thing beneath him. The wind blew strong and damp through the clearing, causing the tent to flap and billow, and now he felt himself being dragged on his belly steadily toward the edge of the clearing where the light filtered with an unnatural brilliance through the high-flung branches of the pines. And as he struggled to break the forward motion of the tent a cloud of birds took flight, spinning on the wind and into the trees, revealing the low shapes of a group of weed-grown burial mounds arranged beneath the pines. Clusters of tinted bottles had been hung from wooden stakes to mark the row of country graves, and as the tent dragged him steadily closer he could see the glint and sparkle of the glass as the bottles, tossing in the wind, began to ring like a series of crystal bells. He did not like this place and he knew, struggling to brake the motion by digging his toes into the earth, that somewhere beyond the graves and the wall of trees his voice was struggling to return to him.*

But now through the tan and deep-blue ringing of the glass, it was another voice he feared, a voice which threatened to speak from beneath the tent and which it was most important to enfold, to muffle beneath the billowing canvas . . .

Then he was back on the floor again and the forbidden words, now hoarsely transformed, were floating calmly down to him from gallery and dome, then coming on with a rush.

For Thou hath forsaken me, they came—but they were no longer his own words nor was it his own echoing voice. And now, hearing what sounded like a man's voice hoarsely singing, he struggled to bring himself erect, thinking, *No! No! Hickman? But how here? Not here! No time, no place for HICKMAN!*

Then the very idea that Hickman was there somewhere above him raised him up and he was clutching onto a chair, pulling himself into a sitting position, trying to get his head up so as to see clearly above as now there came a final shot which he heard but did not feel . . .

He lay on his back now, looking up through the turbulent space to where the bullet-smashed chandelier, swinging gently beneath the impact of its shattering, created a watery distortion of crystal light which seemed to descend and settle him within a ring of liquid fire. Then beyond the pulsing blaze where a roiling darkness grew he was once more aware of a burst of action.

Now he could hear someone shouting far off. Then a voice was shouting quite close to his ear, but he was unable to bring his mind to it. There were many faces and he was trying to ask them, *Why the hell'd he do it and who else was it?*

I can't understand, can't understand. My rule was graciousness, politeness in all private contacts, but hell, anything goes in public. What? What?

Harry said if it gets too hot hop out the pot. I say if the tit's tough no one asks for milk when the steaks high. *

Lord, lord, but it's hot. HOT! It hurts here and here and there and there, a hell of a clipping. How many rounds?

Lawd . . . Say Lord! Why? Ha! No time to go West but no time to stay East either, so blow the wind westerly, there's grease in the East.

I said, Donelson, crank it, man! Who broke the rhythm of the crowd? Old fat, nasty Poujaque! Don't accuse me: if I could pay them I could teach them! If they could catch me I could raise them up. That's their god-given historical, wood-pile role! Where was Moses, I mean to say? . . . No, let the deal go down. And if the cock crows three, I'm me, ME!

Roll the mammy scratching camera, Karp! On with the lights. Hump it now! Get them over to the right side. It hurts, it was worth something in the right body for the right hand . . .

Then I said, Politics is an art of maneuvering, and to move them you must change home base. Now you tell 'em because Ah stutter, Donelson said. But minds like that will never learn. . . . Hell, I've out-galloped gallup—New Mexico, wasn't it? What happened to body? Well, so long old buddy, I missed touch, lost right hand but didn't forget. How the hell explain?

Karp, you high-minded S.O.B. Will you please *get some light over here? And keep the action going!*

Yes, Yes, Yes! I'm all cud, bud: all chewed up like a dog! Like a dog. It was like shooting fish in a barbell. Fall! Fall! Take a dive! Green persimmons . . .

She said "mother" and screamed and I said mother and it shot out of my throat and something ran like hell up the tent and I doubled back and when I lifted the flap—dark again!

Roll the cameras!

What? What?

Perhaps you're right, but who would have thought what I knew on the back of my neck and ignored was ripening? That was the way it was. Oh, I rose up and she said "Mother," and I doubled back and he looked down upon the babe and said, "Look, boy, you're a son of God! Isn't that enough for you?"

But still I said "mother" and something ran up the tent like a flash and then they came on, grim-faced and glassy-eyed, like the wrath of God in the shape of a leaping, many-headed cat . . . What dreams . . . what dreads . . .

Don't ask me, please. Please don't ask me. I simply can't do it. There are lines and shadows we can't stand to cross or recross. Like walking through the sharp edge of a mirror. All will be well, daddy. Tell them what I said.

ROLL THE CAMERA!

What? What?

Who was? Who did that against me? Who has tuned daddy's fork when he could have preached his bone in all positions and places? I might have been left out of all that—Ask

* In the longest, fullest version of Book II, this phrase is "the steaks are high" (see page 246 of this volume).

Tricky Sam Nanton, there's a preacher hidden in all the troms—Bam! Same tune, only daddy's had a different brand of anguish.

Lawd, Lawd, Why?

What terrible luck! Daddy strutted with some barbecue and the hot sauce on the bread was red and good, good. Yes, but in Austin they chilled the beans.

Mother, she said.

But weren't the greens nice in Birmingham, Sister Lacey said.

And she said Mother, and I came up out of the box and he said "Let there be light"—but he didn't really mean it. And she said cud and that should have been worth the revival. But he wouldn't tell.

Oh Maggie, Jiggs and Aunt Jima! Jadda-dadda—jing-jing! I miss those times sometimes. . . .

This game of politics is fraught with fraud, Ferd said— And a kiyi yippi and a happy nappy! So praise the Lord, and pass the biscuits, pappy! Oh, yes, the A.G. said, Give ole Bill a guitar and the room to holler nigger and he'll forget about trying to pass for an intellectual . . . Hell, it was easy, easy. I was working as the old gentleman's chauffeur and he caught me in bed with his madam. Who are you, anyway, he said. And I thought fast and said, I'm a nigger. So you can forget it, it don't count. What? Yes, I said, or at least I was raised for one. So what are you going to do about it? And he said, do? First I'm going to think about it. Was she satisfied? I don't know, I said, but I've had no complaints. Well, he said, taking that into consideration you might as well continue until she does. Meanwhile I'll think about making you a politician . . . So because she was years younger than the old gentleman I made a classical entry into the house. . . . Yes, but you just wait, he said. The Spades'll learn to play the game and use their power and the old war will be ended. . . .

Oh, no! We'll legislate the hell against them. Sure, they must learn to play the game but power is as power does. Let's not forget what the hell this is all about.

Mister movie man . . .

God is love, I said, but art's the possibility of forms, and shadows are the source of identity. And Donelson said, You tell 'em, buddy, while I go take a physic . . .

Hold the scene, don't fade, don't fade . . . Seven's the number, Senator, I said. Fiscal problems come up seven, remember? Even for Joseph . . . So she said "Mother" and I said me and she said cud was worth all that pain. But he still wouldn't tell.

Back away from me! Cat . . . cat . . . What's the rest?

I simply refused, that was all. Chicken in a casket was a no good—a union like the cloak. Too dark in there. Chick in this town, chick in that town and in the country. Always having to break out of that pink-lined shell.

No, not afraid after a while, but still against it. I was pretty little—little though not pretty, understand. Saw first snow in Kansas. The wind blows cold, but I can't tuck it.

Look, I have to climb out of here immediately, or the wires will flash Cudworth moos for Ma—a hell of a note from now on. And on the other side there's the dark. Daddy Hickman! Hick hic, what day?

To hell with it, I've stood up too long to lie down.

Lawd, Lawd, why?

Inevitable? Well, I suppose so. So focus in the scene. There, there. The right honorable Daddy—Where?

Karp, Karp, pan with the action—See! See! He's riding right out from under the old cardoba. But watch him, Stack wore a magic hat—listen for a bulldog!

Beliss?

No! What do you know about that? I can't hear him bark....

Bliss be eeee thee ti-ee that binds ...

Variants for "Arrival"

Editors' Note: What follows are the multiple variants to "Arrival," the opening computer file in Ellison's "Hickman in Washington, D.C." sequence, which itself is a version of what he wrote in the late 1950s as the prologue to Book I and published in 1960 as the opening to "And Hickman Arrives" in *Noble Savage*. We have reproduced eleven of "Arrival"'s thirteen variants. The two we have not included ("Cap" and "Leaving") pick up in the middle of the file, leaving out the crucial opening paragraphs that Ellison seems to have been intent upon revising. Some of the variants are full versions of "Arrival" and others include only the opening. We have chosen to reproduce just the first few pages of the longer files so as to facilitate comparison across the variants. The eleven files reproduced here were composed, or at least dated, between October 8, 1988, and June 23, 1993. It is important to note that the files dated 1988 could have been composed at any time between Ellison's purchase of an Osborne computer in January 1982 and the transfer of files to his IBM computer in the fall of 1988, which erased the original file dates.

Taken together, these variants capture the character of Ellison's revisions in the last years of his novel's composition. Ellison's tendency is toward tinkering with language as he troubles over how to identify the race of his characters in the opening paragraph. Compare the latest version—"those who at that time were politely identified as Southern 'Negroes'" (Arrival, RE 9, 19)—to this series of variations: "those who at that time were identified as Southern 'Negroes'" (Airport, txt 7), "Southern Negroes" (Arrival, txt 7), "elderly Southern Negroes" (Prologue, txt 8), "passengers—who were known at the time as 'Negroes'" (File 0000), "elderly Afro-Americans" (Attire, RE 9), "passengers . . . marked by the usual mixture of skin shades and features that at the time were conveniently termed 'black,' 'Negro,' or 'Afro-American'" (Plane, RE 9).

In all, these variants attest to the attention Ellison gave to his prose on the level of the sentence as well as on other matters of craft, like transitions and plotting, and also to the fluid, even unstable, condition of African American identity. With few exceptions, nearly all of the computer files in each of the textual sequences published in this volume have variants such as this. Particularly for scholars interested in Ellison's process of composition, these files, now housed in the Library of Congress, offer fruitful material for close study.

AIRPORT (10/8/88, TXT 7)

Two days before the bewildering incident a chartered plane-load of those who at that time were identified as Southern "Negroes" swooped down upon Washington's National Airport and disembarked in a confusion of hand luggage, suitcases, and picnic baskets. Most were quite elderly: old ladies wearing white uniforms and small white lace-trimmed caps tied beneath their chins, and old men in rumpled suits and wide-brimmed hats. Quiet and exceptionally orderly, considering their age and number, they swept through the crowded terminal with such an unmistakable air of agitation that busy airport attendants and travelers alike paused to stare.

They themselves paused only once, when one of the women blocked their outward movement as she looked around with a frown.

"Hold it a second, y'all," she said, "whilst I see if they have one up here like they have down in Atlanta . . ."

"One what?"

"A big bale of cotton with an ole prideless rascal sitting beside it holding on to a dinner bell!"

"Forget him, sister," someone said, "we have other things to worry about."

"I might forgive him," the woman said, "but I won't forget him. Just imagine somebody in this day and age helping to insult his own people!"

"You mean to tell me that he was 'alive,'" one of the men said, "I thought he was a statue!"

Luggage in arm and hand, the group lurched ahead in short-stepping haste to one of the many taxi stands, where a small fleet of taxis was assembled with the aid of the bemused Dispatcher; who then looked on as a huge, towering, dark-brownskinned Negro man saw to it that they arranged themselves beside the machines with a minimum of talk and milling about. This done, the big man— who wore a well-tailored blue suit and vest, a pongee shirt, blue pastel tie, and soft planters style panama—made his way to a public telephone, dialed a number, and carried on a brief conversation. Completing his call, he returned and began seating the group while pausing anxiously from time to time to consult an old-fashion gold watch attached to a thick gold chain which was suspended between the widely-spaced lower pockets of his vast expanse of vest. Communicating mostly by slight nods and gestures his voice seldom arose above a hoarse whisper.

ARRIVAL (10/8/88, TXT 7)

PROLOGUE

Two days before the bewildering incident a chartered plane-load of Southern Negroes swooped down upon the District of Columbia and disembarked at National Airport in a confusion of hand luggage, suitcases and picnic baskets. Most were quite elderly; old ladies dressed in little white lace-trimmed caps and uniforms made of surplus nylon parachute material, the men in neat but old-fashion black suits and wearing wide-brimmed high-crowned hats of black felt or white straw. Quiet and exceptionally orderly for a group of their age and number, they swept through the terminal with such a pronounced air of barely contained agitation that airport attendants and travelers alike paused to stare.

Breathing hard and straining along in the lurching, short-stepping haste of old folk, the group then hurried to one of the several taxi stands; where with the aid of the Dispatcher what amounted to a small fleet of taxis was assembled; beside which, at the direction of a huge, towering, dark-brownskinned man they distributed themselves and luggage with a minimum of talk and milling about. Then the big man, (who, quite unlike his fellows was dressed in a well-tailored blue suit and vest, pongee shirt, blue pastel tie, and soft planters style white panama) made his way to a public telephone, dialed a number, and carried on a brief conversation. His call completed, the big man returned and began assigning the group their seats, pausing anxiously from time to time to consult a gold watch attached to a heavy gold chain suspended between the widely spaced lower pockets of his vast vest. Communicating mostly by nods and gestures of his long well shaped hands his voice seldom arose above a hoarse whisper—Until, just as he climbed in beside the driver of the lead taxi, the Dispatcher asked in a manner that betrayed something more than professional interest their destination.

PROLOGUE (10/8/88, TXT 7)

Two days before the bewildering incident a chartered plane-load of those who at that time were politely identified as Southern "Negroes" swooped down upon Washington's National Airport and disembarked in a confusion of hand luggage, suitcases, and picnic baskets. Most were quite elderly: old ladies wearing white uniforms and small white lace-trimmed caps tied beneath their chins, and old men who wore rumpled ready-made suits and wide-brimmed hats. The single exception being a towering darkbrownskinned man dressed in a well-tailored blue suit with vest, a pongee shirt, blue pastel tie, and soft planters style panama. Quiet and exceptionally orderly, considering their age and number, they swept through the crowded terminal with such an unmistakable air of agitation that busy airport attendants and travelers alike paused to stare.

They themselves paused but briefly, when one of the women came to a sudden stop and looked around the crowded terminal with an indignant frown.

"Hold it a second, y'all," she said, looking high and low, "whilst I see if they have one of them up here like they have down in Atlanta . . ."

"One what, Sister Bea," one of the other women said. "What you talking about?"

"I'm talking about that ole prideless rascal they had sitting in a rocking chair besides that big dirty bale of cotton, and him holding on to a walking cane and a dinner bell!"

"Forget him, Sister Bea," someone said, "we have other things to worry about."

"I might 'forgive' him," the woman said, "but I won't forget him. Just imagine somebody in this day and age helping to insult his own people!"

"You mean to tell me that thing was 'alive,'" one of the men said, "I thought he was a statue!"

"Statue my foot," another man said, "that old grey-headed clown is probably pretending that ole rocking chair's got him just to make enough money to buy him a cotton-picking machine or a Cad'llac!"

"You can laugh if you want to," the big woman said, "but it ain't funny. No, sir, it aint funny worth a dam—And may the Lord forgive me for saying it, because a thing like that is a terrible burden for the rest of us to bear . . ."

Luggage in arm and hand, the group lurched ahead in short-stepping haste to one of the many taxi stands, where with the aid of the Dispatcher a small fleet of taxis was assembled. Then as the Dispatcher stepped aside and looked on in bemusement the towering dark-brownskinned Negro man saw to it that the group arranged themselves beside the machines with a minimum of talk and milling about. This done, the big Negro made his way to a public telephone, dialed a number, and carried on a brief conversation. Completing his call, he started back and stopped short when he noted that the Dispatcher's blue wind-breaker had a pair of dice stenciled on its back. Then, shaking his head he returned and began assigning the group their seats while pausing anxiously from time to time to consult an old-fashion gold watch attached to a thick gold chain suspended between the widely-spaced lower pockets of his vast expanse of vest. Communicating mostly by slight nods and gestures, his voice seldom arose above a hoarse whisper—Until, just as he climbed in beside the driver of the lead taxi, the Dispatcher inquired in a manner that betrayed something more than a professional interest, their destination. . . .

PROLOGUE (10/8/88, TXT 8)

Two days before the bewildering incident a chartered plane-load of elderly Southern Negroes swooped down upon the District of Columbia and disembarked at National Airport in a confusion of hand luggage, suitcases and picnic baskets. Although quiet and exceptionally orderly for a group of such numbers, they swept through the terminal with such a pronounced of barely contained agitation and foreboding that airport attendants and travelers alike paused to stare.

Breathing hard and straining along in the short-stepping haste of old folk, the group then hurried to one of the several taxi stands where with the aid of the Dispatcher what amounted to a small fleet of taxis was assembled, and beside which, under the direction of a huge, towering white-headed, dark-brownskinned man dressed in a well tailored suit, vest and shirt of pongee, blue tie and soft planters style panama hat, they distributed themselves and luggage with a minimum of talk and milling about. Then the big man, their obvious leader, made his way to a public telephone, dialed a number, and carried on a brief conversation. Completing his call, the big man returned and began assigning them their seats as he paused anxiously from time to time to consult a gold watch attached to a huge gold [chain] that was suspended between the widely spaced lower pockets of his vast vest. Communicating mostly by gesture of his well-shaped hands and nods of his head his voice seldom arose above a hoarse whisper—Until, just as he climbed in beside the driver of the lead taxi, the Dispatcher asked, in a voice that betrayed something more than professional interest, their destination. . . .

ARRIVAL (10/30/88, TXT 25)

They arrive in Washington and go to Senator's office.

They are turned away.

They find a hotel.

Hickman and Wilhite go to Senator's hotel suite, but don't get to see him.

That night they go to Jessie Rockmore's house to see McMillen—to no effect.

Next day, Saturday or Sunday, they go to Senator's mansion, hoping to have a look at him, but run into LeeWillie burning his caddy.

They leave and go to the Lincoln Memorial.

ARRIVAL (5/4/89, RE 19)

Two days before the bewildering incident a chartered plane-load of those who at that time were politely identified as Southern "Negroes" swooped down upon

Washington's National Airport and disembarked in a confusion of paper bags, suitcases, and picnic baskets. Most were quite elderly: old ladies wearing white uniforms and small white lace-trimmed caps tied beneath their chins, and old men who wore rumpled ready-made suits and wide-brimmed hats. The single exception being a towering dark brownskinned man dressed in a well-tailored blue suit with vest, a pongee shirt, blue pastel tie, and soft planters-style panama. Quiet and exceptionally orderly, considering their age and number, they swept through the crowded terminal with such an unmistakable air of agitation that busy airport attendants and travelers alike paused to stare.

They themselves paused but briefly, when one of the women came to a sudden stop and looked around the crowded terminal with an indignant frown.

"Hold it a second, y'all," she said, looking high and low, "whilst I see if they have one of them up here like they have down in Atlanta . . ."

"One what, Sister Bea," one of the other women said. "What you talking about?"

"I'm talking about that ole prideless rascal they had sitting in a rocking chair besides that big dirty bale of cotton, and him propped up on a walking cane and holding a dinner bell!"

"Oh, forget him, Sister Bea," someone said, "we have other things to worry about."

"I might *forgive* him," the woman said, "but I won't ever forget him. Just imagine somebody in this day and age helping to insult his own people!"

"You mean to tell me that thing was *alive*," one of the men said, "I thought it was a dummy!"

"Dummy my foot," another man said, "that old grey-headed clown was probably pretending that ole rocking chair got him just after he made enough money to buy him a cotton-picking machine and a Cad'llac! Yeah! And so now he's just taking his ease and watching the world flow by."

"That's right!" another brother said. "And getting paid for jiving the white folks!"

"You can laugh if you want to," the big woman said, "but it ain't funny. No, sir! It aint funny worth a dam—And may the Lord forgive me for saying so, because a thing like that is a terrible burden for the rest of us to bear . . ."

Luggage in arm and hand, the group lurched ahead in short-stepping haste to one of the many taxi stands, where with the aid of the Dispatcher a small fleet of taxis was assembled. Then with the Dispatcher stepping aside and looking on in bemusement the towering dark-brownskinned Negro man saw to it that the group arranged themselves beside the machines with a minimum of talk and milling about. This done, the big Negro made his way to a public telephone, dialed a number, and carried on a brief conversation. Completing his call, he started back and stopped short when he noted that the Dispatcher's blue windbreaker had a pair of dice stenciled on its back. Then, shaking his head he returned and began assigning the group their seats while pausing anxiously from time to time to consult an old-fashion gold watch attached to a thick gold chain suspended between the widely-spaced lower pockets of his vast expanse of vest. Communicating mostly by slight nods and gestures, his voice seldom arose above a hoarse whisper—Until, just as he climbed in beside the driver of the lead taxi, the Dispatcher inquired in a manner that betrayed something more than a professional interest, their destination . . .

PROLOGUE (5/3/91, RE 3)

Two days before the bewildering incident a chartered plane-load of those who at that time were politely identified as Southern "Negroes" swooped down upon Washington's National Airport and disembarked in a confusion of paper bags, suitcases, and picnic baskets. Most were quite elderly: old ladies wearing white uniforms and small white lace-trimmed caps tied beneath their chins, and old men who wore rumpled ready-made suits and wide-brimmed hats. The single exception being a towering dark brownskinned man dressed in a well-tailored blue suit with vest, a pongee shirt, blue pastel tie, and soft planters-style panama. Quiet and exceptionally orderly, considering their age and number, they swept through the crowded terminal with such an unmistakable air of agitation that busy airport attendants and travelers alike paused to stare.

They themselves paused but briefly, when one of the women came to a sudden stop and looked around the crowded terminal with an indignant frown.

"Hold it a second, y'all," she said, looking high and low, "whilst I see if they have one of them up here like they have down in Atlanta . . ."

"One what, Sister Bea," one of the other women said. "What you talking about?"

"I'm talking about that ole prideless rascal they had sitting in a rocking chair besides that big dirty bale of cotton, and him propped up on a walking cane and holding a dinner bell!"

"Oh, forget him, Sister Bea," someone said, "we have other things to worry about."

"I might *forgive* him," the woman said, "but I won't ever forget him. Just imagine somebody in this day and age helping to insult his own people!"

"You mean to tell me that thing was *alive,*" one of the men said, "I thought it was a dummy!"

"Dummy my foot," another man said, "that old grey-headed clown was probably pretending that ole rocking chair got him just after he made enough money to buy him a cotton-picking machine and a Cad'llac! Yeah! And so now he's just taking his ease and watching the world flow by."

"That's right!" another brother said. "And getting paid for jiving the white folks!"

"You can laugh if you want to," the big woman said, "but it ain't funny. No, sir! It aint funny worth a dam—And may the Lord forgive me for saying so, because a thing like that is a terrible burden for the rest of us to bear . . ."

Luggage in arm and hand, the group lurched ahead in short-stepping haste to one of the many taxi stands, where with the aid of the Dispatcher a small fleet of taxis was assembled. Then with the Dispatcher stepping aside and looking on in bemusement the towering dark-brownskinned Negro man saw to it that the group arranged themselves beside the machines with a minimum of talk and milling about. This done, the big Negro made his way to a public telephone, dialed a number, and carried on a brief conversation. Completing his call, he started back and stopped short when he noted that the Dispatcher's blue wind-breaker had a pair of dice stenciled on its back. Then, shaking his head he returned and began assigning the group their seats while pausing anxiously from time to time to consult an old-fashion gold watch attached to a thick gold chain suspended between the widely-spaced lower pockets of his vast expanse of vest. Communicating mostly by slight nods and gestures, his voice seldom arose above a hoarse whisper—Until, just as he climbed in beside the driver of the lead taxi, the Dispatcher inquired in a manner that betrayed something more than a professional interest, their destination.

FILE 0000 (1/27/93, RE 19)

Two days before the bewildering incident a chartered plane swooped down upon Washington where its passengers—who were known at the time as "Negroes"—emerged in a confusion of baskets, suitcases, and brown paper bags. Quite elderly and Southern, the women were uniformly attired in white (including their shoes, stockings and lace-trimmed caps), and most of the men wore dark, ready-made suits and wide-brimmed hats. The single exception was a towering brownskinned man dressed in a blue, well-tailored suit, a pongee shirt, blue pastel tie, and a planters-style panama hat. Quiet and exceptionally orderly, considering their number and ages, they evoked an uneasy sense of the past in the present as they swept through the air terminal's crowd with such an air of controlled agitation that airport attendants and travelers alike paused to stare.

They themselves paused but briefly; when, suddenly, one of the women came to a stop and looked around with a frown on her face.

"Hold it, y'all," she said, "whilst I see if they have one of them up here like they had in Atlanta . . ."

"One *what*, Sister Bea," one of the other women said. "What are you talking about?"

"I'm talking about that ole gray headed rascal the white folks had sitting besides that bale of cotton leaning on a cane and holding a big brass bell in his hand!"

"Oh, forget him, Sister Bea," another woman said, "we're up north now and have other things to worry about."

"I might *forgive* him," Sister Bea said, "but I'll never forget him. Just imagine, in this day and age he's got so little pride in his people that he helps white folks grin and feel superior!"

"Are you telling us that he was *alive*," one of the men said, "why when I read that sign which said 'The Pride of the South' I thought he was some kind of a dummy!"

"Dummy my foot," another man chuckled, "that clown was probably pretending old rocking chair had got him just after he'd bought him a cotton-picking machine and a new Cad'llac! And so now he's signifying by sitting there taking his ease while watching the rest of the world flow by him."

"Right!" another brother said, "and getting paid good money for out-jiving the white folks!"

"You can laugh if you want to," Sister Bea said, "but it ain't funny. No, sir! It aint funny worth a dam—And may the Lord forgive me for saying so. Because a thing like that is just another burden for the rest of us to bear . . ."

Then with luggage in hand, the group lurched ahead in short-stepping haste to a taxi stand, where with the aid of its dispatcher a small fleet of taxis was assembled. And now as the Dispatcher looked on in bemusement the towering Negro in the Panama hat saw to it that the group arranged themselves beside the machines with a minimum of talk and milling about. This done, he made his way to a telephone booth, engaged in a brief conversation. And now returning and noting the pair of white dice stenciled on the dispatcher's jacket he stopped short before signaling the group to enter the taxis. Then with a smile that flickered and faded he glanced at his watch, moved to the lead taxi, and lumbered in beside its driver.

"And now, where are we going," the Dispatcher asked with notebook in hand.

Whereupon, detecting more than a professional interest in the Dispatcher's voice, the big man cleared his throat and boomed in a mellow baritone, "We'd like to be driven to the offices of Senator Sunraider."

The effect was electric. Suddenly the dispatcher's eyes widened, the stiff visor of his cap lifted skyward, and his hands flew to the roof of the taxi.

"Did you say *Sunraider*," he said staring downward.

"That's right," the big man said, "has something happened to him?"

"Why no," the Dispatcher said, "but do you mean *all* of you . . . ?"

"That's right, all of us," the big Negro said. "And, sir," he added as he reached for his wallet, "we'd appreciate it if you'd inform your drivers that it's important that they get us there as quickly as possible. We've been circling the city for over forty-five minutes so now we're about to run out of time . . ."

Then removing two five dollar bills and thrusting them out of the window the big man said, "We'd much appreciate it."

"Oh, that isn't necessary, but thanks," the Dispatcher said as he pocketed the money. "Your problem was caused by a storm somewhere out southwest of here. It's been fouling things up all morning. But don't worry, now that you're down to earth we'll get you there, and fast. And you're lucky because the building you want is only a hop and a skip away."

Then addressing the small lightskinned Negro who had been looking at his passengers with an expression compounded of big-city condescension, disassociation and incredulity, the Dispatcher roared, "You heard the man, so what're you waiting for? Get going!"

"Yeah," the driver said in a crisp Northern voice, "Right on . . ."

Watching impatiently until the last of the taxis was gone, the dispatcher hurried to his station and dialed the number of a leading newspaper and asked for a reporter with whom he had a standing agreement to supply information regarding any unusual incidents that might occur at the airport and carried on a conversation punctuated by intervals of laughter.

"I don't know who they are," he said into the mouthpiece, "but I'm telling you there's quite a bunch of them."

" . . ."

"Why? Now *that* you'll have to tell *me*. You're the reporter. . . ."

" . . ."

"When? Hell, just now! That why I *called* you, McIntyre, they just took off . . ."

" . . ."

"How the hell would I know what for? Maybe they're taking him some candied yams and southern fried chicken. Anyway, they're headed for Sunraider's offices!"

" . . ."

"Yes! That's right, *Sunraider*! The big fellow who seems to be the H.N.I.C. just told me . . ."

" . . ."

"Oh, excuse me, I forgot that you're northern—It means the 'Head Negro in Charge'; in other words, their leader."

" . . ."

"That's all I know, so if you're interested you'd better get over there!"

And now, shaking with laughter, the dispatcher hung up . . .

Arriving at the address of the Senator's office, the big man leaped from his seat and rushed to the next taxi in line to consult with a smaller man seated next to the driver. Nodding his head energetically, the little man got out and hurried back along the line of taxis while the big man looked on, consulting his watch and looking toward the building and then back to where, now, as the smaller man moved past, each of the taxis was swiftly emptied. And now as the drivers placed luggage on the sidewalk in front of the building the owners assembled themselves silently beside their possessions while the big man walked nimbly to the end of the line and started back, looking inside each of the vehicles to see that nothing had been overlooked. Then, after paying the fares and tipping the drivers, he herded the group into the building.

Where, surprised by the sudden influx of Negroes, the uniformed guards in the lobby exchanged quick glances and came to attention. Then as the big man saw two of the guards detaching themselves from the others and starting forward he raised his hand and gestured for the group to halt where they were, a gesture with which they immediately complied while whispering and gazing at the lobby's high pillared ceiling, while he continued forward and asked to be directed to Senator Sunraider's office . . .

ATTIRE (2/26/93, RE 9)

Two days before the shooting a plane loaded with elderly Afro-Americans landed at the National Airport in Washington, where its passengers emerged in a confusion of suitcases, baskets, and brown paper bags. The women wore small white caps and white summer dresses, and except for a towering, brown-skinned old man dressed in a blue, well-tailored suit and a Panama hat, the men wore dark summer suits, white shirts with black ties, and soft felt hats.

Moving from the plane they were quiet and orderly, but upon entering the terminal their manner so old-fashioned and courtly that seasoned white travelers and black skycaps alike stopped and stared as though ghosts from the past were descending among them. But of this the group appeared quite while silently making their way through the crowd with an air of engrossment. And not until they had arrived at the center of the terminal was their silence broken, and this by a tall black woman with the features of an Indian who stopped and looked around with a frown of displeasure.

"Hold it, y'all," she said, "whilst I see if they have one of them up here like they had in Atlanta . . ."

"One of them *what*, Sister Bea," a short woman said, "what are you talking about?"

"I'm talking," the tall woman said, "about that ole gray headed rascal the white folks had sitting besides that big bale of cotton, that's what. You remember the one who was leaning on a cane and holding that big brass bell in his hand!"

"Oh, that," the short woman said with a shrug. "So why let something like that get you upset, Sister Bea? After weathering that storm in the air we have much better things to worry about. So forget him!"

"As a Christian I might *forgive* him, but I'll never forget him," the tall woman said. "Just imagine, here in this day and age he's got so little pride that he sits there giving white folks excuses for laughing and feeling superior!"

PLANE (2/26/93, RE 9)

Two days before the nation was shaken by the incident that it hastily suppressed in its memory a chartered plane arrived at the National Airport in Washington where the ground crew that guided its landing looked on in puzzlement as its elderly passengers poured forth in a chaos of suitcases, baskets, and brown paper bags. And although the passengers were marked by the usual mixture of skin shades and features that at the time were conveniently termed "black," "Negro," or "Afro-American," the main source of the landing crew's puzzlement was the group's attire and their manner.

For while the women's white dresses and small ruffled caps appeared to be uniforms of ceremonial intent, the men's hand-me-down suits and wide brimmed hats were drably informal. And all the more when a towering, brown-skinned old man emerged from the plane wearing a blue tailored suit and a panama hat with a turned down brim.

With luggage in hand the group moved from the plane to the airport, where their appearance and old-fashioned manners were so quaint and at odds with that of those around them that even skycaps, world travelers, and airline pilots stopped and stared as though ghosts from had returned to haunt them. But of this the group appeared unaware as they continued through the crowd with an air of engrossment. Then upon reaching the center of the building a tall, black-skinned woman with Indian features brought the group to a halt by suddenly pausing and looking around with a frown of displeasure.

"Hold it y'all," she said, "whilst I see if they have one of them up here like they had back in Atlanta . . ."

"One of them *what*, Sister Bea," a short woman asked. "What are you talking about?"

"I'm talking about that ole gray headed rascal who was sitting besides that big bale of cotton," the tall woman said. "You remember, he was leaning on a cane and holding that big brass bell in his hand!"

"Oh, that," the short woman said with a shrug. "But why bother with him, Sister Bea? After spending all that time in the air we have better things to worry about. So forget him!"

"As a good Christian I might forgive him," the tall woman said, "but I'll never *forget* him. Just imagine, here in this day and age he's got so little pride that he sits there giving white folks excuses for laughing and feeling superior!"

PROLOGUE (6/23/93, RE 9)

Two days before the bewildering incident a plane chartered in Atlanta landed at the National Airport in Washington, where the crew guiding its landing watched its passengers emerge in a confusion of suitcases, baskets, and brown paper bags. All were elderly and of a range of color and diversity of features which, at the time, were generally classified as "black," "Negro," or "Afro-American." But the focus of the ground crew's attention was their attire and their manners.

And this because the women wore white uniforms and small ruffled caps while the men were dressed in hand-me-down suits and wide brimmed hats. Further, the women displayed a disciplined formality of manners and the men an easy camaraderie that was shared by a towering, brown-skinned old man who wore a blue, well-tailored suit and a panama hat.

Hurrying from the plane with luggage in hand, the group entered the terminal. Where immediately their manner and dress were so at odds with that of the crowd that even skycaps, international pilots, and worldly commuters stopped and stared as though ghosts from the past had swooped down to haunt them. But of this the group appeared unaware as they moved through the crowd with an air of engrossment.

Then upon reaching the center of the airport a tall, black-skinned woman with Indian features brought the group to a halt by suddenly pausing with a frown of displeasure.

"Hold it y'all," she said, "whilst I see if they have one of them up here like they had back in Atlanta . . ."

"One of them *what,* Sister Bea," a short woman asked. "What are you talking about?"

"I'm talking about that ole gray headed heathen who was sitting besides that big bale of cotton," the tall woman said. "You remember, he was leaning on a cane and holding that big brass bell in his hand!"

"So *that's* who you mean," the short woman said with a shrug. "But why bother with him, Sister Bea? After spending all that time in the air we have better things to worry about. So forget him!"

"As a good Christian I might forgive him," the tall woman said, "but I'll never *forget* him. Just imagine, here in this day and age he's got so little pride that he sits there giving white folks excuses for laughing and feeling superior!"

"I declare, Sister Bea," one of the men said as he spun on his toes in feigned surprise, "are you telling us that thing was a *alive?* Why, when I saw him sitting in a rocking chair behind that sign with "THE PRIDE OF THE SOUTH" printed on it I took him for some kind of *statue!*"

"Statue my foot," another man said with a chuckle, "that clown was probably humming *Old Rocking Chair's Got Me* and signifying that the one he was sitting in didn't grab him until after he'd bought him a cotton-picking machine and a new Cad'llac! So now he sits there sipping bourbon out of a Coca Cola can and signifying that he's taking his ease while white folks from up north wonder how it could happen in Georgia."

"Yeah!" another man said, "and deep inside he's probably cracking up over the white folks paying him good money for doing it!"

"Laugh if you want to," Sister Bea said, "but it ain't funny. No, sir! It ain't funny worth a damn—And may the good Lord forgive me for saying it. Because a prideless ole thing like that just adds to the burden the rest of us bear . . ."

"That's true," the short woman said. And while others agreed with a chorus of "amens" the group hurried out of the terminal.

Where, now, in the din of travelers arriving and departing the big man in the panama hat spoke to a white dispatcher who began summoning a small fleet of taxis. And with the drivers assisting the group in loading the dispatcher looked on with a bemused expression. Then after seeing that all were seated the big Negro made his way to a telephone booth where he engaged in a brief conversation and started back with an anxious expression.

But seeing a woman in one of the taxis pointing out of its window with an outraged expression he stopped in his tracks. And looking to where she was pointing he saw a pair of black, white-dotted dice displayed on the dispatcher's white jacket. And in noting that the cast of the dice amounted to seven he suppressed a smile that flickered and faded. Then signaling the woman to ignore it, he hurried to the first taxi in line and took the one vacant seat which was next to its driver.

"Wow!" the dispatcher said as he approached with his clipboard and pencil in hand. "Some lucky hotel is going to be busy, but which will it be?"

"It will if we find one that'll take us," the big Negro said, "but first we must keep an urgent appointment."

"And where will that be?"

"It's the office of Senator Sunraider . . ."

"*Sunraider,*" the dispatcher said with a sudden step backward. "Well I'll be damned!"

"What's wrong," the big Negro said with an anxious stare, "has something happened to the Senator?"

"Why no . . ."

" . . . Thank God for that!"

" . . . but do you mean *all* of you are going . . . ?"

"That's right," the big Negro said, "and sir, we'd appreciate your getting us there as quickly as possible. . . ."

And from his wallet the big Negro removed two five dollar bills and thrust them toward the dispatcher.

"Oh, that wasn't necessary, but thanks," the Dispatcher said as he pocketed his tip. "I understand your concern over being delayed, because our weather is fine, since around about midnight a storm somewhere southeast of here has been fouling things up for the airlines. But don't worry, we'll get you to your appointment!" And bending toward the driver, a light-skinned Negro who'd been listening with a scowl of disdain, the dispatcher struck the roof of the taxi and roared, "You heard the man, so get this rig rolling!"

"That's precisely what I've been waiting to hear," the driver replied in a crisp Northern accent, "and don't go shouting the address, since I already know where they're going."

"You damn well better get them there in a hurry," the dispatcher said.

And with fleet on its way he rushed to telephone a newspaper reporter with whom he had a standing agreement to supply any information regarding unusual arrivals or incidents that occurred at the airport. And in a report punctuated by bursts of uneasy laughter he told him of the group's destination.

EIGHT EXCERPTS PUBLISHED BY ELLISON

Editors' Note: The provenance of the eight excerpts from Ralph Ellison's unfinished novel that appeared in print during his lifetime varies considerably. Two ("It Always Breaks Out" [1963] and "Cadillac Flambé" [1973]) are variants of Chapters 5 and 4 of Book I, found on pages 49–61 and 35–48, respectively, of *Three Days Before the Shooting...*

Book II is the source of four excerpts. Although the first, longest, and most far-reaching, "And Hickman Arrives" (1960), begins with the "Prologue" from Book I (pages 5–9 in *Three Days*), Ellison carefully edited this extensive excerpt to include Senator Sunraider's assassination followed by flashbacks to his boyhood association with Reverend Hickman as the filial young minister in Hickman's black church. For the sake of sharp, centripetal focus, he deleted passages involving later episodes from the Senator's life. "And Hickman Arrives" includes a specially written transitional scene (pages 1008–1013) not found in Ellison's typescripts of Books I or II. The other three excerpts from Book II—"The Roof, the People and the Steeple" (1960), "Juneteenth" (1965), and "Night-Talk" (1969)—are found on pages 283–293, 314–324, and 386–394 in the version of Book II published in this volume.

Ellison's Oklahoma material is represented by "A Song of Innocence" (1970), narrated to McIntyre by Cliofus. A substantially revised version composed two decades later, with Hickman replacing McIntyre as Cliofus's primary audience, is found in the "Hickman in Georgia & Oklahoma" narrative of *Three Days* within the computer file "Words" (pages 871–889).

Finally, there is "Backwacking" (1977), a freestanding offshoot of scenes in Senator Sunraider's office (pages 1097–1101), and a fragment extant in the Ellison Papers.

Singly and together, these excerpts illuminate the eclectic quality and range of Ellison's material as well as his evolving compositional habits and novelistic purpose.

AND HICKMAN ARRIVES

NOBLE SAVAGE 1 (1960): 5–49

Three days before the shooting a chartered planeload of Southern Negroes swooped down upon the District of Columbia and attempted to see the Senator. They were all quite elderly; old ladies dressed in little white caps and white uniforms made of surplus nylon parachute material, and men dressed in neat but old-fashioned black suits, wearing wide-brimmed, deep crowned panama hats which, in the Senator's walnut paneled reception room now, they held with a grave ceremonial air. Solemn, uncommunicative, and quietly insistent, they were led by a huge, distinguished-looking old fellow who on the day of the chaotic event was to prove himself, his age notwithstanding, an extraordinarily powerful man. Tall and broad and of an easy dignity, this was the Reverend A. Z. Hickman—better known, as one of the old ladies proudly informed the Senator's secretary, as "God's Trombone."

This, however, was about all they were willing to explain. Forty-four in number, the women with their fans and satchels and picnic baskets, and the men carrying new blue airline take-on bags, they listened intently while Reverend Hickman did their talking.

"Ma'am," Hickman said, his voice deep and resonant as he nodded toward the door of the Senator's private office, "you just tell the Senator that Hickman has arrived. When he hears who's out here he'll know that it's important and want to see us."

"But I've told you that the Senator isn't available," the secretary said. "Just what is your business? Who are you, anyway? Are you his constituents?"

"Constituents?" Suddenly the old man smiled. "No, miss," he said, "the Senator doesn't even have anybody like us in *his* state. We're from down where we're among the counted but not among the heard."

"Then why are you coming here?" she said. "What is your business?"

"He'll tell you, ma'am," Hickman said. "He'll know who we are; all you have to do is tell him that we have arrived...."

The secretary, a young Mississippian, sighed. Obviously these were Southern Negroes of a type she had known all her life—and old ones; yet, instead of being already in herdlike movement toward the door, they were calmly waiting, as though she hadn't said a word. And now she had a suspicion that, for all their staring eyes, she actually didn't exist for them. They just stood there, now looking oddly like a delegation of Asians who had lost their interpreter along the way, and who were trying to tell her something which she had no interest in hearing, through this old man who himself did not know the language. Suddenly they no longer seemed familiar and a feeling of dreamlike incongruity came over her. They were so many that she could no longer see the large abstract paintings which hung along the paneled wall. Nor the framed facsimiles of State Documents which hung above a bust of Vice-President Calhoun. Some of the old women were calmly plying their palm-leaf fans, as though in serene defiance of the droning air-conditioner. Yet she could see no trace of impertinence in their eyes, nor any of the anger which the Senator usually aroused in members of their group. Instead, they seemed resigned; like people embarked upon a difficult journey who were already far beyond the point of no return. Her uneasiness grew, then she blotted out the others by focusing her eyes narrowly upon their leader. And when she spoke again her voice took on a nervous edge.

"I've told you that the Senator isn't here," she said, "and you must realize that he is a busy man who can only see people by appointment. . . ."

"We know, ma'am," Hickman said, "but . . ."

"You don't just walk in here and expect to see him on a minute's notice."

"We understand that, ma'am," Hickman said, looking mildly into her eyes, his close-cut white head tilted to one side, "but this is something that developed of a sudden. Couldn't you reach him by long distance? We'd pay the charges. And I don't even have to talk, miss; you can do the talking. All you have to say is that we have arrived."

"I'm afraid this is impossible," she said.

The very evenness of the old man's voice made her feel uncomfortably young, and now, deciding that she had exhausted all the tried-and-true techniques her region had worked out (short of violence) for getting quickly rid of Negroes, the secretary lost her patience and telephoned for a guard.

They left as quietly as they had appeared, the old minister waiting behind until the last had stepped into the hall, then he turned, and she saw his full height, framed by the doorway, as the others arranged themselves beyond him in the hall. "You're really making a mistake, miss," he said. "The Senator knows us and . . ."

"*Knows* you," she said indignantly. "I've heard Senator Sunraider state that the only colored he knows is the boy who shines shoes at his golf club."

"Oh?" Hickman shook his head as the others exchanged knowing glances.

"Very well, ma'am," Hickman said. "We're sorry to have caused you this trouble. It's just that it's very important that the Senator know that we're on the scene. So I hope you won't forget to tell him that we have arrived, because soon it might be too late."

There was no threat in it; indeed, his voice echoed the odd sadness which she thought she detected in the faces of the others just before the door blotted them from view.

In the hall they exchanged no words, moving silently behind the guard, who accompanied them down to the lobby. They were about to move into the street, when the security-minded chief guard observed their number, stepped up, and ordered them searched.

They submitted patiently, amused that anyone should consider them capable of harm, and for the first time an emotion broke the immobility of their faces. They chuckled and winked and smiled, fully aware of the comic aspect of the situation. Here they were, quiet, old, and obviously religious black folk who because they had attempted to see the man who was considered the most vehement enemy of their people in either house of Congress, were being energetically searched by uniformed security police, and they knew what the absurd outcome would be. They were found to be armed with nothing more dangerous than pieces of fried chicken and ham sandwiches, chocolate cake and sweet-potato fried pies. Some obeyed the guards' commands with exaggerated sprightliness, the old ladies giving their skirts a whirl as they turned in their flat-heeled shoes. When ordered to remove his wide-brimmed hat, one old man held it for the guard to look inside; then, flipping out the sweatband, he gave the crown a tap, causing something to fall to the floor, then waited with a callused palm extended as the guard bent to retrieve it. Straightening and unfolding the object, the guard saw a worn but neatly creased fifty-dollar bill which he dropped upon the outstretched palm as though it were hot. They watched silently as he looked at the old man and gave a dry, harsh laugh; then as he continued laughing the humor slowly receded behind their eyes. Not until they were allowed to file into the street did they give further voice to their amusement.

"These here folks don't understand nothing," one of the old ladies said. "If we had been the kind to depend on the sword instead of on the Lord, we'd been in our graves long ago—ain't that right Sis' Arter?"

"You said it," Sister Arter said. "In the grave and done long finished mold'ing!"

"Let them worry, our conscience is clear on that...."

"Amen!"

On the sidewalk now, they stood around Reverend Hickman holding a hushed conference, then in a few minutes they had disappeared in a string of taxis and the incident was thought closed.

Shortly afterwards, however, they appeared mysteriously at a hotel where the Senator leased a private suite, and tried to see him. How they knew of this secret suite they would not explain.

Next they appeared at the editorial offices of the newspaper which was most critical of the Senator's methods, but here too they were turned away. They were taken for a protest group, just one more lot of disgruntled Negroes crying for justice as though theirs were the only grievances in the world. Indeed, they received less of a hearing here than elsewhere. They weren't even questioned as to why they wished to see the Senator—which was poor newspaper work, to say the least; a failure of technical alertness, and, as events were soon to prove, a gross violation of press responsibility.

So once more they moved away.

Although the Senator returned to Washington the following day, his secretary failed to report his strange visitors. There were important interviews scheduled and she had understandably classified the old people as just another annoyance. Once the reception room was cleared of their disquieting presence they seemed no more significant than the heavy mail received from white liberals and Negroes, liberal and reactionary alike, whenever the Senator made one of his taunting remarks. She forgot them. Then at about eleven a.m. Reverend Hickman reappeared without the others and started into the building. This time, however, he was not to reach the secretary. One of the guards, the same who had picked up the fifty-dollar bill, recognized him and pushed him bodily from the building.

Indeed, the old man was handled quite roughly, his sheer weight and bulk and the slow rhythm of his normal movements infuriating the guard to that quick, heated fury which springs up in one when dealing with the unexpected recalcitrance of some inanimate object. Say, the huge stone that resists the bulldozer's power or the chest of drawers that refuses to budge from its spot on the floor. Nor did the old man's composure help matters. Nor did his passive resistance hide his distaste at having strange hands placed upon his person. As he was being pushed about, old Hickman looked at the guard with a kind of tolerance, an understanding which seemed to remove his personal emotions to some far, cool place where the guard's strength could never reach them. He even managed to pick up his hat from the sidewalk, where it had been thrown after him, with no great show of breath or hurry, and arose to regard the guard with a serene dignity.

"Son," he said, flicking a spot of dirt from the soft old panama with a white handkerchief, "I'm sorry that this had to happen to you. Here you've worked up a sweat on this hot morning and not a thing has been changed—except that you've interfered with something that doesn't concern you. After all, you're only a guard, you're not a mind-reader. Because if you were, you'd be trying to get me *in* there as fast as you could instead of trying to keep me out. You're probably not even a good guard and I wonder what on earth you'd do if I came here prepared to make some trouble."

Fortunately, there were too many spectators present for the guard to risk giving the old fellow a demonstration and he was compelled to stand silent, his thumbs hooked over his cartridge belt, while old Hickman strolled—or more accurately, *floated* up the walk and disappeared around the corner.

Except for two attempts by telephone, once to the Senator's office and later to his home, the group made no further effort until that afternoon, when Hickman sent a telegram asking Senator Sunraider to phone him at a T Street hotel. A message, which, thanks again to the secretary, the Senator did not see. Following this attempt there was silence.

During the late afternoon the group of closed-mouthed old folk were seen praying quietly within the Lincoln Memorial. An amateur photographer, a high-school boy from the Bronx, was there at the time and it was his chance photograph of the group, standing with bowed heads beneath old Hickman's outspread arms, while facing the great sculpture, that was flashed over the wires following the shooting. Asked why he had photographed that particular group, the boy replied that he had seen them as a "good composition.... I thought their faces would make a good scale of grays between the whiteness of the marble and the blackness of the shadows." And for the rest of the day the group appears to have faded into those same peaceful shadows, to remain there until the next morning—when they materialized shortly before chaos erupted.

Forty-four in all, they were sitting in the Senate's visitors' gallery when Senator Sunraider arose to address the body. They sat in compact rows, their faces marked by that impassive expression which American Negroes often share with Orientals, watching the Senator with a remote concentration of their eyes. Although the debate was not one in which they would normally have been interested (being a question not of civil rights, but of foreign aid) they barely moved while the Senator developed his argument, sitting like a row of dark statuary—until, during an aside, the Senator gave way to his obsession and made a quite gratuitous and mocking reference to their people.

It was then that a tall, elderly woman wearing steel-rimmed glasses arose from her chair and stood shaking with emotion, her eyes flashing. Twice she opened her mouth as though to hurl down some retort upon the head of the man holding forth below; but now the old preacher glimpsed her out of the corner of his eye, and, without turning from the scene below, gravely shook his head. For a second she ignored him, then feeling her still standing, he turned, giving her the full force of his gaze, and she reluctantly took her seat, the muscles ridged out about her dark prognathous jaws as she bent forward, resting her elbows upon her knees, her hands tightly clasped, listening. But although a few whites departed, some angrily shaking their heads over the Senator's remarks, others extending them embarrassed smiles, the rest made no sign. They seemed bound by some secret discipline, their faces remaining composed, their eyes remote as though through some mistake they were listening to a funeral oration for a stranger.

Nevertheless, Reverend Hickman was following the speech with close attention, his gaze playing over the orderly scene below as he tried to identify the men with their importance to the government. So this is where he came to rest, he thought. After all his rambling, this was the goal. Who would have imagined? At first, although he was familiar with his features from the newspapers, he had not recognized the Senator. The remarks, however, were unmistakable. These days, much to the embarrassment of his party and the citizens of his New England state, only Senator Sunraider (certain Southern senators were taken for granted) made such remarks, and Hickman watched him with deep fascination. He's driven to it, Hickman thought, it's so much with him that he probably couldn't stop if he wanted to. He rejected his dedication and his set-asideness, but it's still on him, it's with him night and day.

"Reveren'…" Sister Neal had touched his arm and he leaned toward her, still watching the scene.

"Reveren'," she said, "is that him?"

"Yes, that's him all right," he said.

"Well, he sho don't look much like his pictures."

"It's the distance. Up close though you'd recognize him."

"I guess you right," she said. "All those white folks down there don't make him any more familiar either. It's been so long I don't recognize nothing about him now."

"You will," Hickman whispered. "You just watch—see there…"

"What?"

"The way he's using his right hand. See how he gets his wrist into it?"

"Yeah, yeah!" she said. "And he would have his little white Bible in his other hand. Sure, I remember."

"That's right. See, I told you. Now watch this…."

"Watch what?"

"There, there it goes. I could just see it coming—see the way he's got his head back and tilted to the side?"

"Yeah—why, Reveren', that's *you!* He's still doing you! Oh, my Lord," he heard her moan, "still doing you after all these years and yet he can say all those mean things he says…."

Hearing a catch in her voice, Hickman turned; she was softly crying.

"Don't, Sister Neal," he said. "This is just life; it's not to be cried over, just understood…."

"Yes, I know. But *seeing* him, Reveren'. I forgave him many times for everything, but seeing him *doing you* in front of all these people and humiliating us at the same time—I don't know, it's just too much."

"He probably doesn't know he's doing it," Hickman said. "Anyway, it's just a gesture, something he picked up almost without knowing it. Like the way you can see somebody wearing his hat in a certain way and start to wearing yours the same way."

"Well, he sure knows when he says something about us," she said.

"Yes, I guess he does. But he's not happy in it, he's driven."

"I'd like to drive him the other way a bit," she said. "I could teach him a few things."

Hickman became silent, listening to the Senator develop his argument, thinking, she's partly right, they take what they need and then git. Then they start doing all right for themselves and pride tells them to deny that they ever knew us. That's the way it's been for a long time. Sure, but not Bliss. There's something else, I don't know what it was but it was something different....

"Reveren'." It was Sister Neal again. "What's he talking about? I mean what's back of it all?"

"This is how the laws are made, Sister."

"Why does he want to give away all that money he's talking about?"

"It's politics. He wants to keep those Asian people and the Africans on our side...."

"Then why is he signifying at those other men and going on?"

"That's because he plans to use those Asian folks to divide the men down there who don't like some of the things he's trying to do over here. He's playing divide and rule, Sister Neal. This way he can even put those Asian leaders in his hip pocket. They need the money he's trying to get for foreign aid so bad that naturally they will have to shut up and stop criticizing the way things go over here. Like the way we're treated, for instance...."

"But will they get the money?"

"Oh, yes, they'll get it."

"Does that mean he's really doing some good?"

"It means that he's doing *some* good in order to do *some* bad."

"Oh?"

"Yes," he said, "and some bad in order to do some good. What I mean is, he's complicated. Part of the time he probably doesn't know what he means to do himself. He just does something."

"So what do you think?"

"Well, I think that although it's mixed, all that which he does about scientific research and things like that is on the good side. But that reactionary stuff he's mixed up in, that's bad."

"You mean his playing around with those awful men from down home?"

"That's right, that's part of it."

"Reveren'," she said, "why would he do things like that?"

"I guess he's in the go-long, Sister Neal. He has to play the game so that he can stay and play the game...."

I guess that's the way it is, he thought. Power is as power does—for power. If I knew anything for sure, would I be sitting here?

Silently he listened to the flight of the Senator's voice and searched for echoes of the past. He had never seen the Senate in session before and was mildly surprised that he could follow most of the course of the debate. It's mainly knowing how to manipulate and use words, he thought. And reading the papers. Yes, and knowing the basic issues, because they seldom change. He sure knows how to use the words; he never forgot that. Imagine, going up there to New England and using all that kind of old Southern stuff, our own stuff, which we never get a chance to use on a broad platform—and making it pay off. It's probably the only thing he took with him that he's still proud of, or simply couldn't do without. Sister Neal's right, some of that he's doing is me all right. I could see it and hear it the moment she spotted it. So I guess I have helped to spread some corruption I didn't know about. Just listen to him down there; he's making somebody mighty uncomfortable because he's got them caught between what they profess to believe and what they feel they can't do without. Yes, and he's having himself a fine time doing it. He's almost laughing a devilish laugh in every word. Master, is that from me too? Did he ever hear me doing that?

He leaned toward Sister Neal again.

"Sister, do you follow what's happening?"

"Some, but not quite," she said.

"Well, I'll tell you," he said. "He is going to get this bill passed and pretty soon the money will start to flowing over there and those Indians, those Hindus, and such won't be able to say a thing about their high morals and his low ones. They have a heap of hungry folks to feed and he's making it possible. Let them talk that way then and they'll sound like a man making a speech on the correct way to dress while he's standing on the corner in a suit of dirty drawers...."

"He's got no principles but he's as smart as ever, ain't he?" she said.

Hickman nodded, thinking, yes, he's smart all right. Born with mother wit. He climbed up that high from nowhere, and now look, he's one of the most powerful men on the floor. Lord, what a country this is. Even his name's not his own name. Made himself from the ground up, you might say. But why this mixed-up way and all this sneering at us who never did more than wish him well? Why this craziness which makes it look sometimes like he does everything else, good and bad, clean-cut and crooked, just so he can have more opportunity to scandalize our name? Ah, but the glory of that baby boy. I could never forget it and that's why we had to hurry here. He has to be seen and I'm the one to see him. I don't know how we're going to do it, but soon's this is over we have to find a way to get to him. I hope Janey was wrong, but any time she goes to the trouble of writing a letter herself, she just about knows what she's talking about. So far though we're ahead, but Lord only knows for how long. If only that young woman had told him we were trying to reach him....

He leaned forward, one elbow resting upon a knee, watching the Senator who was now in the full-throated roar of his rhetoric, head thrown back, his arms outspread—when someone crossed his path of vision.

Two rows below a neatly dressed young man had stood up to leave, and, moving slowly toward the aisle as though still engrossed in the speech, had stopped directly in front of him; apparently to remove a handkerchief from his inside jacket pocket. Why doesn't he move on out of the way, Hickman thought, he can blow his nose when he gets outside—when, leaning around so as to see the Senator, he saw that it was not a handkerchief in the young man's hand, but a pistol.

His body seemed to melt. Lord, can this be it? Can this be the one?, he thought, even as he saw the young man coolly bracing himself, his body slightly bent, and heard the dry, muffled popping begin. Unable to move he sat, still bent forward and to one side, seeing glass like stars from a Fourth of July rocket bursting from a huge chandelier which hung directly in the trajectory of the bullets. Lord, no, he thought, no Master, not this, staring at the dreamlike world of rushing confusion below him. Men were throwing themselves to the floor, hiding behind their high-backed chairs, dashing wildly for the exits; while he could see Bliss still standing as when the shooting began, his arms lower now, but still outspread, with a stain blooming on the front of his jacket. Then, as the full meaning of the scene came home to him, he heard Bliss give surprising voice to the old idiomatic cry,

Lord, LAWD, WHY HAST THOU ...?

and staggering backwards and going down, and now he was on his own feet, moving toward the young man.

For all his size Hickman seemed suddenly everywhere at once. First stepping over the back of a bench, his great bulk rising above the paralyzed visitors like a missile, yelling, "No. NO!" to the young man, then lumbering down and reaching for the gun—only to miss it as the young man swerved aside. Then catching sight of the guards rushing, pistols in hand, through the now standing crowd, he whirled, pushing the leader off balance, back into his companion, shouting, "No, don't kill him! Don't kill that Boy! Bliss won't want him killed!" as now some of his old people began to stir. But already now the young man was moving toward the rail, waving a spectator away with his pistol, looking coolly about him as he continued forward; while Hickman, grasping his intention from where he struggled with one of the guards, now trying in beet-faced fury to club him with his pistol, began yelling, "Wait, Wait! Oh, my God, son—WAIT!" holding the guard for all his years like a grandfather quieting a boy throwing a tantrum, "WAIT!" Then calling the strange name, "Severen, wait," and saw the young man throwing him a puzzled, questioning look, then climb over the rail to plunge deliberately head first to the floor below. Pushing the guard from him now, Hickman called a last despairing "Wait" as he stumbled to the rail to stand there crying down as the group of old people quickly surrounded him, the old women pushing and striking at the angry guards with their handbags as they sought to protect him.

For a moment he continued to cry, grasping the rail with his hands and staring down to where the Senator lay twisting upon the dais beside an upturned chair. Then suddenly, in the midst of all the screaming, the shrilling of whistles, and the dry ineffectual banging of the chairman's gavel, he began to sing.

Even his followers were startled. The voice was big and resonant with a grief so striking that the crowd was halted in mid-panic, turning their wide-eyed faces up to where it soared forth to fill the great room with the sound of his astounding anguish. There he stood in the gallery above them, past the swinging chandelier, his white head towering his clustered flock, tears gleaming bright against the darkness of his face, creating with his voice an atmosphere of bafflement and mystery no less outrageous than the shooting which had released it.

"Oh, Lord," he sang, "why hast thou taken our Bliss, Lord? Why now our awful secret son, Lord? ... Snatched down our poor bewildered foundling, Lord? LORD, LORD, Why hast thou ... ?"

Whereupon, seeing the Senator trying to lift himself up and falling heavily back, he called out: "Bliss! You were our last hope, Bliss; now Lord have mercy on this dying land!"

As the great voice died away it was as though all had been stunned by a hammer and there was only the creaking sound made by the serenely swinging chandelier. Then the guards moved, and as the old ladies turned to confront them, Hickman called: "No, it's all right. We'll go. Why would we want to stay here? We'll go wherever they say."

They were rushed to the Department of Justice for questioning, but before this could begin, the Senator, who was found to be still alive upon his arrival at the hospital, began calling for Hickman in his delirium. He was calling for him when he entered the operating room and was still calling for him the moment he emerged from the anesthetic, insisting for all his weakness, that the old man be brought to his room. Against the will of the doctors this was done, the old man arriving mute and with the eyes of one in a trance. Following the Senator's insistence that he be allowed to stay with him through the crisis, he was given a chair beside the bed and sank his great bulk into it without a word, staring listlessly at the Senator, who lay on the bed in one of his frequent spells of unconsciousness. Once he asked a young nurse for a glass of water, but beyond thanking her politely, he made no further comment, offered no explanation for his odd presence in the hospital room.

When the Senator awoke he did not know if it was the shape of a man which he saw beyond him or simply a shadow. Nor did he know if he was awake or dreaming. He seemed to move in a region of grays which revolved slowly before his eyes, ceaselessly transforming shadow and substance, dream and reality. And yet there was still the constant, unyielding darkness which seemed to speak to him silently words which he dreaded to hear. Yet he wished to touch it, but even the idea of movement brought pain and set his mind to wandering. It hurts here, he thought, and here; the light comes and goes behind my eyes. It hurts here and here and there and there. If only the throbbing would cease. Who ... why ... what ... LORD, LORD, LORD WHY HAST THOU ... Then some seemed to call to him from a long way off, *Senator, do you hear me?* Did the Senator hear?

Who? Was the Senator here? And yes, he did, very clearly, yes. And he was. Yes, he was. Then another voice seemed to call, *Bliss?* And he thought is Bliss here? Perhaps. But when he tried to answer he seemed to dream, to remember, to recall to himself an uneasy dream.

It was a bright day and he said, Come on out here, Bliss; I got something to show you. And I went with him through the garden past the apple trees on under the grape arbor to the barn. And there it was, sitting up on two short sawhorses.

Look at that, he said.

It was some kind of long, narrow box. I didn't like it.

I said, What is it?

It's for the service. For the revivals. Remember me and Deacon Wilhite talking about it?

No, sir.

Sho, you remember. It's for you to come up out of. You're going to be resurrected so the sinners can find life ever-lasting. Bliss, a preacher is a man who carries God's load. And that's the whole earth, Bliss boy. The whole earth and all the people. And he smiled.

Oh! I said. I remembered. But before it hadn't meant too much. Since then, Juney had gone away and I had seen one. Juney's was pine painted black, without curves. This was fancy, all carved and covered with white cloth. It seemed to roll and grow beneath my eyes, while he held his belly in his hands, thumbs in trousers top, his great shoes creaking as he walked around it, proudly.

How you like it?

He was examining the lid, swinging it smoothly up and down with his hand. I couldn't see how it was put together. It seemed to be all white cloth bleeding into pink and pink into white again, over the scrolls. Then he let the lid down again and I could see two angels curved in its center. They were blowing long-belled valveless trumpets as they went flying. Behind them, in the egg-shaped space in which they trumpeted and flew, were carved clouds. Their eyes looked down. I said,

Is it for me?

Sho, didn't I tell you? We get it all worked out the way we want it and then, sinners, watch out!

Suddenly I could feel my fingers turn cold at the tips.

But why is it so big, I said. I'm not that tall. In fact, I'm pretty little for my age.

Yeah, but this one has got to last, Bliss. Can't be always buying you one of these like I do when you scuff out your shoes or bust out the seat of your britches.

But my feet won't even touch the end, I said. I hadn't looked inside.

Yeah, but in a few years they will. By time your voice starts to change your feet will be pushing out one end and your head out the other. I don't want even to have to think about another one before then.

But couldn't you get a littler one?

You mean "smaller"—but that's *just* what we don't want, Bliss. If it's too small, they won't notice it or think of it as applying to them. If it's too big, they'll laugh when you come rising up. No, Bliss, it's got to be this size. They have to see it and feel it for what it is, not take it for a toy like one of those little tin wagons or autos. Down there in Mexico one time I saw them selling sugar candy made in this shape, but ain't no use in trying to sugar-coat it. No, sir, Bliss. They have got to see it and know what they're seeing is where they've all got to end up. Bliss, that there sitting right there on those sawhorses is everybody's last clean shirt, as the old saying goes. And they've got to realize that when that sickle starts to cut its swarth, it don't play no favorites. *Everybody* goes when that wagon comes, Bliss; babies and grandmaws too, 'cause there simply ain't no exceptions made. Death is like Justice is *supposed* to be. So you see, Bliss, it's got to be of a certain size. Hop in there and let's see how it fits....

No, please. Please, Daddy Hickman. PLEASE!

It's just for a little while, Bliss. You won't be in the dark long, and you'll be wearing your white dress suit with the satin lapels and the long pants with the satin stripes. You'll like that, won't you, Bliss? Sure you will. In that pretty suit? Course! And you breathe through this here tube we fixed here in the lid. See? It comes through right here—you hear what I'm saying, Bliss? All right then, pay attention. Look here at this tube. All you have to do is lay there and breathe through it. Just breathe in and out like you always do; *only through the tube.* And when you hear me say, Suffer the little children ... you push it up inside the lid, so's they can't see it when Deacon Wilhite goes to open up the lid ...

But then I won't have any air....

Now don't worry about that, there'll be air enough inside the box. Besides, Deacon Wilhite will open it right away....

But suppose something happens and ...

Nothing's *going* to happen, Bliss.

Yes, but suppose he forgets?

He won't forget. How's he going to forget when you're the center of the services?

But I'm scaird. In all that darkness and with that silk cloth around my mouth and eyes.

Silk, he said. He looked down at me steadily. What else you want it lined with, Bliss? Cotton? Would you feel any better about it if it was lined with something most folks have to work all their lives and wear every day—weekdays and Sunday? Something that most of our folks never get away from? You don't want that, do you?

He touched my shoulder with his finger. I said, Do you?

I shook my head, shamed.

He watched me, his head to one side. I'd do it myself, Bliss, but it wouldn't mean as much for the people. It wouldn't touch them in the same way. Besides,

I'm so big most towns wouldn't have men strong enough to carry me. We don't want to have to break anybody's back just to save their souls, do you, Bliss?

I don't guess so, but...

Of course not, he said quickly. And it won't be but a few minutes, Bliss. You can even take Teddy with you—no, I guess you better take your Easter bunny. With your Easter bunny you won't be afraid, will you? Course not. And like I tell you, it will last no longer than it takes for the boys to march you down the aisle. I'll have you some good strong, big fellows, so you don't have to worry about them dropping you. Now, Bliss: you'll hear the music and they'll set it down in front of the pulpit. Then more music and preaching. Then Deacon Wilhite will open the lid. Then I'll say, Suffer the little children, and you sit up, see? I say do you see, Bliss?

Yessuh.

Say *Sir!*

Sir.

Good. Don't talk like I talk; talk like I *say* talk. Words are your business, boy. Not just *the* Word. Words are everything. The key to the Rock, the answer to the Question.

Yes, sir.

Now, when you rise up, you come up slow—don't go bolting up like no jack-in-the-box, understand? You don't want to scair the living daylights out of anybody. You want to come up slow and easy. And be sure you don't mess up your hair. I want the part to be still in it, neat. So don't forget when we close you in—and don't be chewing on no gum or sucking on no sour balls, you hear? Hear me now...

Yes, sir, I said. I couldn't turn away my eyes. His voice rolled on as I wondered which of the two with the trumpets was Gabriel....

...It depends on the size of the church, Bliss. You listening to me?

Yes, sir.

Well, now when you hear me say, *Suffer the little children,* you sit up slow and, like I tell you, things are going to get quiet as the grave. That's the way it'll be.

He stood silently for a moment, one hand on his chin, the other against his hip, one great leg pushed forward, bending at the knee. He wore striped pants.

Bliss, I almost forgot something important: I better have the ladies get us some flowers. Roses would be good. Red ones. Ain't nobody in this town got any lilies—least not anybody we know. I'm glad I thought of it in time.

Now, Bliss. We'll have it sitting near the pulpit so when you rise up you'll be facing to the side and every living soul will see you. But I don't want you to open your eyes right off. Yes, and you better have your Bible in your hands—and leave that rabbit down in there. You won't forget that, will you?

No, sir.

Good. And what are you suppose to say when you rise up?

I ask the Lord how come he has forsaken me.

That's right. That's correct, Bliss. But say it with the true feeling, hear? And in good English. That's right, Bliss; in Good Book English. I guess it's 'bout time I started reading you some Shakespeare and Emerson. Yes, it's about time. Who's Emerson? He was a preacher too, Bliss. Just like you. He wrote a heap of stuff and he was what is called a *philosopher.* Main thing though is that he knew that every tub has to sit on its own bottom. Have you remembered the rest of the sermon I taught you?

Yes, sir; but in the dark I . . .

Never mind the dark—when you come to *Why hast Thou forsaken me,* on the *me,* I want you to open your eyes and let your head go back. And you want to spread out your arms wide—like this, see? Lemme see you try it.

Like this?

That's right. That's pretty good. Only you better look sad, too. You got to look like you feel it, Bliss. You want to feel like everybody has put you down. Then you start with, *I am the resurrection and the life*—say it after me:

I am the resurrection . . .

I am the resurrection . . .

. . . And the life . . .

And the life . . .

That's good, but not too fast now. I am the lily of the valley . . .

I'm the lily of the valley . . .

Uh huh, that's pretty good—I am the bright and morning star. . . .

. . . The bright and morning star.

Thy rod . . .

Thy rod and thy staff.

Good, Bliss. I couldn't trap you. That's enough. You must remember that all of those *I*'s have got to be in it. Don't leave out any of those *I*'s, Bliss; because it takes a heap of *I*'s before they can see the true vision or even hear the true word.

Yes, sir. But can I take Teddy too?

Teddy? Just why you got to have that confounded bear with you all the time, Bliss? Ain't the Easter bunny enough? And your little white leather Bible, your kid-bound Word of God? Ain't that enough for you, Bliss?

But it's dark in there and I feel braver with Teddy. Because you see, Teddy's a bear and bears aren't afraid of the dark.

Never mind all that, Bliss. And don't you start preaching me no sermon; specially none of those you make up yourself. You preach what I been teaching you and there'll be folks enough out there tonight who'll be willing to listen to you. I tell you, Bliss, you're going to make a fine preacher and you're starting at just the right age. You're just a little over six and Jesus Christ himself didn't start until he was twelve. *But you have to go leave that bear alone.* The other day I even heard you preaching to that bear. Bliss, bears don't give a continental about the

Word. Did you ever hear tell of a bear of God? Of course not. There's the Lamb of God, and the Holy Dove, and one of the saints, Jerome, had him a lion. And another had him a bull of some kind—probably an old-fashioned airplane, since he had wings—he said under his breath, and Peter had the keys to the Rock. But no bear, Bliss. So you think about that, you hear?

He looked at me with that gentle, joking look, smiling in his eyes and I felt better.

You think you could eat some ice cream?

Oh, yes, sir.

You do? Well, here; take this four-bits and go get us each a pint. You look today like you could eat just about a pint. What I mean is, you look kind of hot.

He leaned back and squinted down.

I can even see the steam rising out of your collar, Bliss. In fact, I suspect you're on fire, so you better hurry. Make mine strawberry. Without a doubt, ice cream is good for a man's belly, and when he has to sing and preach a lot like I do, it's good for his throat too. Wait a second—where'd I put that money? Here it is. I thought I'd lost it. Ice cream is good if you don't overdo it—but I don't guess I have to recommend it to you though, do I, Bliss? 'Cause you're already sunk chin deep in the ice cream habit. Fact, Bliss, if eating ice cream was a sin you'd sail to hell in a freezer. Ha, ha! I'm sorry, now don't look at me like that. I was only kidding, little boy. Here, take this dime and bring us some of those chocolate marshmallow cookies you love so well. Hurry on now, and watch out for those wagons and autos....

Yes, that was how it began, and that was Hickman.

When he laughed his belly shook like a Santa Claus. A great kettledrum of deep laughter. Huge, tall, slow-moving. Like a carriage of state in ceremonial parade until on the platform, then a man of words evoking action. Black Garrick, Alonzo Zuber, Daddy Hickman.

God's Golden-voiced Hickman
Better known as
GOD'S TROMBONE,

they billed him. Brother A.Z. to Deacon Wilhite, when they were alone. They drank elderberry wine beneath the trees together, discussing the Word; me with a mug of milk and a buttered slice of homemade bread.... That was the beginning and we made every church in the circuit. I learned to rise up slow, the white Bible between my palms, my head thrusting sharp into the frenzied shouting and up, up, into the certainty of his mellow voice soaring isolated and calm like a note of spring water burbling in a glade haunted by the counterrhythms of tumbling, nectar-drunk bumblebees.

I used to lie within, trembling. Breathing through the tube, the hot air and hearing the hypnotic music, the steady moaning beneath the rhythmic clapping of hands, trembling as the boys marched me down a thousand aisles on a thousand nights and days. In the dark, trembling in the dark. Lying in the dark while his words seemed to fall like drops of rain upon the resonant lid. Until each time just as the shapes seemed to close in upon me, Deacon Wilhite would raise the lid and I'd rise up slowly, as he taught me, with the white Bible between my palms, careful not to disturb my hair on the tufted pink lining. Trembling now, with the true hysteria in my cry:

LORD, LORD, WHY HAST THOU...?

Then came the night that changed it all. Yes, Bliss is here, for I can see myself, Bliss, again, dropping down from the back of the platform with the seven black-suited preachers in their high-backed chairs onto the soft earth covered with sawdust, hearing the surge of fevered song rising above me as Daddy Hickman's voice sustained a note without apparent need for breath, rising high above the tent as I moved carefully out into the dark to avoid the ropes and tent stakes, walking softly over the sawdust and heading then across the clearing for the trees where Deacon Wilhite and the big boys were waiting. I moved reluctantly as always, yet hurrying; thinking, he still hasn't breathed. He's still up there, hearing Daddy Hickman soaring above the rest like a great dark bird of light, a sweet yet anguished mellowing cry. Still hearing it hovering there as I began to run to where I can see the shadowy figures standing around where it lies white and threatening upon a table set beneath the pines. Leaning huge against a tree off to the side is the specially built theatrical trunk they carried it in. Then I am approaching the table with dragging feet, hearing one of the boys giggling and saying, What you saying there, Deadman? And I look at it with horror—pink, frog-mouthed, with opened lid. Then looking back without answering, I see with longing the bright warmth of the light beneath the tent and catch the surging movements of the worshippers as they rock in time to the song which now seems to rise up to the still, sustained line of Daddy Hickman's transcendent cry. Then Deacon Wilhite said, Come on little preacher, in you go! Lifting me, his hands firm around my ribs, then my feet beginning to kick as I hear the boys giggling, then going inside and the rest of me slipping past Teddy and Easter bunny, prone now and taking my Bible in my hands and the shivery beginning as the tufted top brings the blackness down.

At Deacon Wilhite's signal they raise me and it is as though the earth has fallen away, leaving me suspended in air. I seem to float in the blackness, the jolting of their measured footsteps guided by Deacon Wilhite's precise instructions, across the contoured ground, all coming to me muted through the pink insulation of the padding which lined the bottom, top, and sides, reaching me at blunt points along my shoulders, buttocks, thighs, heels. A beast with twelve disjointed legs coursing along, and I its inner ear, anxiety; its anxious heart; straining to hear if the voice that sustained its line and me still soared. Because I believed that if he breathed while I was trapped inside, I'd never emerge. And hearing the creaking of a handle near my ear, the thump of Cylee's knuckle against the side to let me know he was out there, giggling squint-eyed at my fear. Through the thick satin-choke of the lining the remote singing seeming miles away and the rhythmical clapping of hands coming to me like sharp, bright flashes of lightning, promising rain. Moving along on the tips of their measured strides like a boat in a slow current as I breathe through the tube in the lid of the hot ejaculatory air, hushed now by the entry and passage among them of that ritual coat of silk and satin, my stiff dark costume made necessary to their absurd and eternal play of death and resurrection. . . .

No, not me but another. Bliss. Resting on his lids, black inside, yet he knew that it was pink, a soft, silky pink blackness around his face, covering even his nostrils. Always the blackness. Inside everything became blackness, even the white Bible and Teddy, even his white suit. It was black even around his ears, deadening the sound except for Reverend Hickman's soaring song; which now, noodling up there high above, had taken on the softness of the piece of black velvet cloth from which Grandma Wilhite had made a nice full-dress overcoat—only better, because it had a wide cape for a collar. *Ayee,* but blackness.

He listened intently, one hand gripping the white Bible, the other frozen to Teddy's paw. Teddy was down there where the top didn't open at all, unafraid, a bold bad bear. He listened to the voice sustaining itself of its lyrics, the words rising out of the Word like Ezekiel's wheels; without breath, straining desperately to keep its throbbing waves coming to him, thinking, If he stops to breathe I'll die. My breath will stop too. Just like Adam's if God had coughed or sneezed.

And yet he knew that he was breathing noisily through the tube set in the lid. Hurry, Daddy Hickman, he thought. Hurry and say the word. Please, let me rise up. Let me come up and out into the light and air. . . .

Bliss?

So they were walking me slowly over the smooth ground and I could feel the slight rocking movement as the box shifted on their shoulders. And I thought, That means we're out in the clearing. Trees back there, voices that-a-way, life and light up there. Hurry! They're moving slow, like an old boat drifting down the big river in the night and me inside looking up into the black sky, no moon or stars and all the folks gone far beyond the levees. And I could feel the shivering creeping up my legs now and squeezed Teddy's paw to force it down. Then the rising rhythm of the clapping hands were coming to me like storming waves heard from a distance; like waves that struck the boat and flew off into the black sky like silver sparks from the shaking of the shimmering tambourines, showering at the zenith like the tails of skyrockets. If I could only open my eyes. It hangs heavy-heavy over my lids. Please hurry! Restore my sight. The night is black and I am far...far...I thought of Easter bunny, he came from the dark inside of a red-and-white striped egg....

And at last they were letting me down, down, down; and I could feel the jar as someone went too fast, as now a woman's shout came to me, seeming to strike the side near my right ear like a flash of lightning streaking jaggedly across a dark night sky.

Jeeeeeeeeeeeeeeeeeeeeee-sus! Have mercy, Jeeeeeee-sus! and the cold quivering flashed up my legs.

Everybody's got to die, sisters and brothers, Daddy Hickman was saying, his voice remote through the dark. That is why each and every one must be redeemed. YOU HAVE GOT TO BE REDEEMED! Yes, even He who was the Son of God and the voice of God to man—even *He* had to die. And what I mean is die as a *man*. So what do you, the lowest of the low, what do you expect you're going to have to do? He had to die in all of man's loneliness and pain because that's the price He had to pay for coming down here and putting on the pitiful, unstable form of man. Have mercy! Even with his godly splendor which could transform the built-in wickedness of man's animal form into an organism that could stretch and strain toward sublime righteousness—Amen! That could show man the highway to progress and toward a more noble way of living—even with all that, even He had to die! Listen to me tell it to you: Even *He* who said, Suffer the little ones to come unto *Me* had to die as a man. And like a man crying from His cross in all of man's pitiful puzzlement at the will of Almighty God!...

It was not yet time. I could hear the waves of Daddy Hickman's voice rolling against the sides, then down and back, now to boom suddenly in my ears as I felt the weight of darkness leave my eyes, my face bursting with sweat as I felt the rush of bright air bringing the odor of flowers. I lay there, blinking up at the lights, the satin corrugations of the slanting lid and the vague outlines of Deacon Wilhite, who now was moving aside, so that it seemed as though he had himself been the darkness. I lay there breathing through my nose, deeply inhaling the flowers as I released Teddy's paw and grasped my white Bible with both hands, feeling the chattering and the real terror beginning and an ache in my bladder. For always it was as though it waited for the moment when I was prepared to answer Daddy Hickman's signal to rise up that it seemed to slide like heavy mud from my face to my thighs and there to hold me like quicksand. Always at the sound of Daddy Hickman's voice I came floating up like a corpse shaken loose from the bottom of a river and the terror rising with me.

We are the children of Him who said, "Suffer..." I heard, and in my mind I could see Deacon Wilhite, moving up to stand beside Daddy Hickman at one of the two lecterns, holding on to the big Bible and looking intently at the page as he repeated, "Suffer..."

And the two men standing side by side, the one large and dark, the other slim and light brown; the other reverends rowed behind them, their faces staring grim with engrossed attention to the reading of the Word; like judges in their carved, high-backed chairs. And the two voices beginning their call and countercall as Daddy Hickman began spelling out the text which Deacon Wilhite read, playing variations on the verses just as he did with his trombone when he really felt like signifying on a tune the choir was singing:

Suffer, meaning in this workaday instance to *surrender,* Daddy Hickman said.

Amen, Deacon Wilhite said, repeating Surrender.

Yes, meaning to surrender with tears and to feel the anguished sense of human loss. Ho, our hearts bowed down!

Suffer the little ones, Deacon Wilhite said.

The little ones—ah yes! *Our* little ones. He was talking to us too, Daddy Hickman said. Our little loved ones. Flesh of our flesh, soul of *our* soul. Our hope for heaven and our charges in this world. Yes! The little lambs. The promise of our fulfillment, the guarantee of our mortal continuance. The little wases-to-bes-Ha!—Amen! The little used-to-bes that we all were to our mammys and pappys, and with whom we are but one with God....

Oh my Lord, just look how the bright word leaps! Daddy Hickman said. First the babe, then the preacher. The babe father to the man, the man father to us all. A kind father calling for the babes in the morning of their earthly day—yes. Then in the twinkling of an eye, Time slams down and He calls us to come on home!

He said to Come, Brother Alonzo.

Ah yes, to Come, meaning to *approach.* To come up and be counted; to go along with Him, Lord Jesus. To move through the narrow gate bristling with spears, up the hill of Calvary, to climb onto the unyielding cross on which even lil' babies are turned into men. Yes, to come upon the proving ground of the human condition. Vanity dropped like soiled underwear. Pride stripped off like a pair of duckings that've been working all week in the mud. Feet dragging with the gravity of the trial ahead. Legs limp as a pair of worn-out galluses. With eyes dim as a flickering lamp-wick! Read to me, Deacon; line me out some more!

He said volumes in just those words. Brother Alonzo, he said, COME UNTO ME, Deacon Wilhite cried.

Yes! Meaning to take up His burden. At first the little baby-sized load that with the first steps we take weighs less than a butter ball; no more than the sugar tit made up for a year-and-a-half-old child. Then, Lord help us, it grows heavier with each step we take along life's way. Until in that moment it weighs upon us like the headstone of the world. Meaning to come bringing it! Come hauling it! Come dragging it! Come even if you have to crawl! Come limping, come lame; come crying in your Jesus' name—but *Come!* Come with your abuses but come with no excuses. Amen! Let me have it again, Rev. Wilhite....

Come unto me, the Master said.

Meaning to help the weak and the downhearted. To stand up to the oppressors. To suffer and hang from the cross for standing up for what you believe. Meaning to undergo His initiation into the life-everlasting. Oh yes, and to Cry, Cry, Cry... Eyeeeee.

I could hear the word rise and spread to become the great soaring trombone note of Daddy Hickman's singing voice now and it seemed somehow to arise there in the box with me, shaking me fiercely as it rose to float with throbbing pain up to him again, who now seemed to stand high above the tent. And trembling I tensed myself and rose slowly from the waist in the controlled manner Daddy Hickman had taught me, feeling the terror gripping my chest like quicksand, feeling the opening of my mouth and the spastic flexing of my diaphragm as the words rushed to my throat to join his resounding cry:

Lord... Lord...

... Why...

... Hast Thou...

Forsaken me... I cried, but now Daddy Hickman was opening up and bearing down:

... More Man than men and yet in that world-destroying-world-creating moment just a little child calling to His Father.... HEAR THE LAMB A-CRYING ON THE TREE!

LORD, LORD, I cried, WHY HAST THOU FORSAKEN ME?

Amen, Daddy Hickman said, Amen!

Then his voice came faster, explosive with gut-toned preacher authority:

The father of no man who yet was Father to all men—the human-son-side of God—Great God A-mighty! Calling out from the agony of the cross! Ho, open up your downcast eyes and see the beauty of the living Word.... All babe, and yet in the mysterious moment, ALL MAN. Him who had taken up the burden of all the little children crying, LORD....

Lord, I cried.

Crying plaintive as a baby sheep...

... Baaaaaaaaa!...

Yes, the little Lamb crying with the tongue of man...

... LORD...

... Crying to the Father...

... Lord, LORD...

... Calling to his pappy...

... Lord, Lord, why hast...

Amen! LORD, WHY...

... Hast Thou...

Forsaken... me...

Aaaaaaaaaaah!

WHY HAST THOU FORSAKEN ME, LORD?

I screamed the words in answer and now I wanted to cry, to be finished, but the sound of Daddy Hickman's voice told me that this was not the time, that the words were taking him where they wanted him to go. I could hear him beginning to walk up and down the platform behind me, pacing in his great black shoes, his voice rising above his heavy tread, his great chest heaving.

Crying—Amen! Crying, Lord, Lord—Amen! On a cross on a hill, His arms spread out like my mammy told me it was the custom to stretch a runaway slave when they gave him the water cure. When they forced water into his mouth until water filled up his bowels and he lay swollen and drowning on the dry land. Drinking water, breathing water, water overflowing his earthbound lungs like a fish drowning of air on the parched dry land.

And nailed NAILED to the cross-arm like a coonskin fixed to the side of a barn, yes, but with the live coon still inside the furry garment! Still in possession, with all nine points of the Roman law a fiery pain to consume the house. Yes, every point of law a spearhead of painful injustice. Ah, yes!

Look! His head is lollying! Green gall is drooling from His lips. Drooling as it had in those long sweet, baby days long gone. AH, BUT NOT TIT SO TOUGH NOR PAP SO BITTER AS TOUCHED THE LIPS OF THE DYING LAMB!

There He is, hanging on; hanging on in spite of knowing the way it would have to be. Yes! Because the body of man does not wish to die! It matters not who's inside the ribs, the heart, the lungs. Because the body of man does not sanction death. That's why suicide is but sulking in the face of hope! Ah, man is *tough*. Man is human! Yes, and by definition man is proud. Even when heaven and hell come slamming together like a twelve-pound sledge on a piece of heavy-gauged railroad steel, man is tough and mannish, and *ish* means like ...

So there He was, stretching from hell-pain to benediction; head in heaven and body in hell—tell me, who said He was weak? Who said He was frail? Because if He was, then we need a new word for *strength*, we need a new word for *courage*. We need a whole new dictionary to capture the truth of that moment.

Ah, but there He is, with the others laughing up at Him, their mouths busted open like melons with rotten seeds—laughing! You know how it was, you've been up there. You've heard that contemptuous sound: IF YOU BE THE KING OF THE JEWS AND THE SON OF GOD, JUMP DOWN! JUMP DOWN, BLACK BASTARD, DIRTY JEW, JUMP DOWN! Scorn burning the wind. Enough halitosis alone to burn up old Moloch and melt him down.

He's bleeding from his side. Hounds baying the weary stag. And yet ... And yet, His the power and the glory locked in the weakness of His human manifestation, bound by His acceptance of His human limitation, His sacrificial humanhood! Ah, yes, for He *willed* to save man by dying as *man* dies, and He was a heap of man in that moment, let me tell you. He was man raised to his most magnificent image, shining like a prism glass with all the shapes and colors of man, and dazzling all who had the vision to see. Man moved beyond mere pain to godly joy.... There He is, with the spikes in His tender flesh. Nailed to the cross. First with it lying flat on the ground, and then being raised in a slow, flesh-rending, bone-scraping arc, one-hundred-and-eighty degrees—Up, up, UP! Aaaaaaaaaaaah! Until He's upright like the ridge-pole of the House of God. Lord, Lord, Why? See Him, Watch Him! Feel Him! His eyes rolling as white as our eyes, looking to His, our Father, the tendons of His neck roped out, straining like the steel cables of a heavenly curving bridge in a storm. His jaw muscles bursting out like kernels of corn on a hot lid. Yea! His mouth trying to refuse the miserable human questioning of His fated words...

Lord, Lord....

Oh, yes, Rev. Bliss. Crying above the laughing ones for whom He left His Father to come down here to save, crying—

Lord, Lord, Why...?

Amen! Crying as no man since—thank you, Jesus—has ever had to cry.

Ah, man, ah, human flesh! This side we all know well. On this weaker, human side we were all up there on the cross, just swarming over Him like microbes. But look at him with me now, look at Him fresh, with the eyes of your most understanding human heart. There He is, hanging on in man-flesh, His face twitching and changing like a field of grain struck by a high wind—hanging puzzled. Bemused and confused. Mystified and teary-eyed, wracked by the realization dawning in the grey matter of His cramped human brain; knowing in the sinews, in the marrow of His human bone, in the living tissue of His most human veins—realizing totally that *man was born to suffer and to die* for other men! There He is, look at Him. Suspended between heaven and hell, hanging on already nineteen centuries of time in one split second of his torment and realizing, I say, realizing in that second of His anguished cry that life in this world is but a zoom between the warm womb and the lonely tomb. Proving for all time, casting the pattern of history forth for all to see in the undeniable concreteness of blood, bone, and human courage before that which has to be borne by every man. Proving, proving that in this lonely, lightning-bug flash of time we call our life on earth we all begin with a slap of a hand across our tender baby bottoms to start us crying the puzzled question with our first drawn breath:

Why was I born?...Aaaaaaaah!

And hardly before we can get it out of our mouths, hardly before we can exhale the first lungful of life's anguished air—even before we can think to ask, Lord, What's my true name? Who, Lord, am I?—here comes the bone-crunching slap of a cold iron spade across our cheeks and it's time to cry, WHY, LORD, WHY WAS I BORN TO DIE?

Why, Rev. Bliss? Because we're men, that's why! The initiation into the lodge is hard! The dues are outrageous and what's more, nobody can refuse to join. Oh, we can wear the uniforms and the red-and-purple caps and capes a while, and we can enjoy the feasting and the marching and strutting and the laughing fellowship—then Dong, Dong! and we're caught between two suspensions of our God-given breath. One to begin and the other to end it, a whoop of joy and a sigh of sadness, the pinch of pain and the tickle of gladness, learning charity if we're lucky, faith if we endure, and hope in sheer downright desperation!

That's why, Reveren' Bliss. But now, thank God, because He passed his test like any mannish man—not like a God, but like any pale, frail, weak man who dared to be his father's son...Amen! Oh, we must dare to be, brothers and sisters.... We must dare, my little children.... We must dare in our own troubled times to be our father's own. Yes, and now we have the comfort and the example to help us through from darkness to lightness, a beacon along the way. Ah, but in that flash of light in which we flower and wither and die, we must find Him so that He can find *us,* ourselves. For it is only a quivering moment—then the complicated tongs of life's old good-bad comes clamping down, grabbing us in our tender places, feeling like a bear's teeth beneath our short-hair. Lord, He taught us how to live, yes! And in the sun-drowning awfulness of that moment, He taught us how to die. There He was on the cross, leading His sheep, showing us how to achieve the heritage of our godliness which He in that most pitiful human moment—with spikes in His hands and through His feet, with the thorny crown of scorn studding His tender brow, with the cruel points of Roman steel piercing His side...Crying...

Lord...

...Lord...

LORD! Amen. Crying from the castrated Roman tree unto his father like an unjustly punished child. And yet, Rev. Bliss, Glory to God, and yet He was guaranteeing with the final expiration of his human breath our everlasting life....

Bliss's throat ached with the building excitement of it all. He could feel the Word working in the crowd now, boiling in the heat of the Word and the weather. Women were shouting and up suddenly to collapse back into their chairs, and far back in the dark he could see someone dressed in white leaping into the air with outflung arms, going up then down—over backwards and up and down again, in a swooning motion which made her seem to float in the air stirred by the agitated movement of women's palm leaf fans. It was long past the time for him to preach St. Mark, but each time he cried Lord, Lord, they shouted and screamed all the louder. Across the platform now he could see Deacon Wilhite lean against the lectern shaking his head, his lips pursed against his great emotion. While behind him, the great preachers in their high-backed chairs thundered out deep staccato Amens, he tried to see to the back of the tent, back where the seams in the ribbed white cloth curved down and were tied in a roll; past where the congregation strained forward or sat rigid in holy transfixation, seeing here and there the hard, bright disks of eyeglasses glittering in the hot, yellow light of lanterns and flares. The faces were rapt and owllike, gleaming with heat and Daddy Hickman's hot interpretation of the Word....

Then suddenly, right down there in front of the coffin he could see an old white-headed man beginning to leap in holy exaltation, bounding high into the air, and sailing down; then up again, higher than his own head, moving like a jumping jack, with bits of sawdust dropping from his white tennis shoes. A brown old man, whose face was a blank mask, set and mysterious like a picture framed on a wall, his lips tight, his eyes starry, like those of a blue-eyed china doll—soaring without effort through the hot shadows of the tent. Sailing as you sailed in dreams just before you fell out of bed. A holy jumper, Brother Pegue....

Bliss turned to look at Daddy Hickman, seeing the curved flash of his upper teeth and the swell of his great chest as with arms outspread he began to sing ... when suddenly from the left of the tent he heard a scream.

It was of a different timbre, and when he turned, he could see the swirling movement of a woman's form; strangely, no one was reaching out to keep her from hurting herself, from jumping out of her underclothes and showing her womanness as some of the ladies sometimes did. Then he could see her coming on, a tall redheaded woman in a purple-red dress; coming screaming through the soprano section of the big choir where the members, wearing their square, flat-topped caps were standing and knocking over chairs to let her through as she dashed among them striking about with her arms.

She's a sinner coming to testify, he thought.... A white? Is she white? hearing the woman scream,

He's mine, MINE! That's Cudworth, my child. My baby. You gipsy niggers stole him, my baby. You robbed him of his birthright!

And he thought, Yes, she's white all right, seeing the wild eyes and the red hair, streaming like a field on fire, coming toward him now at a pace so swift it seemed suddenly dreamlike slow. What's she doing here with us, a white sinner? Moving toward him like the devil in a nightmare, as now a man's voice boomed from far away, Madam, LADY, PLEASE—this here's the House of God!

But even then not realizing that she was clawing and pushing her way toward him. Cudworth, he thought, who's Cudworth? Then suddenly there she was, her hot breath blasting his ear, her pale face shooting down toward him like an image leaping from a toppling mirror, her green eyes wide, her nostrils flaring. Then he felt the bite of her arms locking around him and his head was crushed against her breast, hard into the sharp, sweet woman-smell of her. Me. She means me, he thought, as something strange and painful stirred within him. Then he could no longer breathe. She was crushing his face closer to her, squeezing and shaking him as he felt his Bible slipping from his fingers and tried desperately to hold on. But she screamed again with a sudden movement, her voice bursting hot into the sudden hush. And now he felt his Bible fall irretrievably away in the well-like echo punctuated by the heaving rasp of her breathing as he realized that she was trying to tear him from the coffin.

I'm taking him home to his heritage, he heard. He's mine, you understand, I'm his mother!

It sounded strangely dreamy, like a scene you saw when the big boys told you to open your eyes under the water. Who is she, he thought, where's she taking me? She's strong, but my mother went away, Paradise up high.... Then he was looking around at the old familiar grown folks, seeing their bodies frozen in odd postures, like kids playing a game of statue. And he thought They're scaird; she's scairing them all, as his head was snapped around to where he could see Daddy Hickman leaning over the platform just above, bracing his hands against his thighs, his arms rigid and a wild look of disbelief on his great laughing-happy face, as now he shook his head. Then she moved again and as his head came around the scene broke and splashed like quiet water stirred by a stick.

Now he could see the people standing and leaning forward to see, some standing in chairs holding on to the shoulders of those in front, their eyes and mouths opened wide. Then the scene suddenly crumpled like a funny paper in a fireplace. He saw their mouths uttering the same insistent burst of words so loud and strong that he heard only a blur of loud silence. Yet her breathing came hard and clear. His head came around to her now, and he could see a fringe of freckles shooting across the ridge of the straight thin nose like a covey of quail flushing across a field of snow, the wide-glowing green of her eyes. Stiff copper hair was bursting from the pale white temple, reminding him of the wire bristles of Daddy Hickman's "Electric Hairbrush".... Then the scene changed again with a serene new sound beginning:

JUST DIG MY GRAVE, he heard. JUST DIG MY GRAVE AND READY MY SHROUD, CAUSE THIS HERE AIN'T HAPPENING! OH, NO, IT AIN'T GOING TO HAPPEN. SO JUST DIG-A MY GRAVE!

It was a short, stooped black woman, hardly larger than a little girl, whose shoulders slanted straight down from her neck inside the white collar of her oversized black dress, and from which her deep and vibrant alto voice seemed to issue as from a source other than her mouth. He could see her coming through the crowd, shaking her head and pointing toward the earth, crying, I SAID DIG IT! I SAID GO GET THE DIGGERS!, the words so intense with negation that they sounded serene, the voice rolling with eerie confidence as now she seemed to float in among the white-uniformed deaconesses who stood at the front to his right. And he could see the women turning to stare questioningly at one another, then back to the little woman, who moved between them, grimly shaking her head. And now he could feel the arms tighten around his body, gripping him like a bear and he was being lifted up, out of the coffin; hearing her scream hotly past his ear, DON'T YOU BLUEGUMS TOUCH ME! DON'T YOU DARE!

And again it was as though they had all receded beneath the water to a dimly lit place where nothing would respond as it should. For at the woman's scream he saw the little woman and the deaconesses pause, just as they should have paused in the House of God as well as in the world outside the House of God— then she was lifting him higher and he felt his body come up until only one foot was still caught on the pink lining, and as he looked down he saw the coffin move. It was going over, slowly, like a turtle falling off a log; then it seemed to rise up of its own will, lazily, as one of the sawhorses tilted, causing it to explode. He felt that he was going to be sick in the woman's arms, for glancing down, he could see the coffin still in motion, seeming to rise up of its own will, lazily, indulgently, like Daddy Hickman turning slowly in pleasant sleep—only it seemed to laugh at him with its pink frog-mouth. Then as she moved him again, one of the sawhorses shifted violently, and he could see the coffin tilt at an angle and heave, vomiting Teddy and Easter bunny and his glass pistol with its colored candy bee-bee bullets, like prizes from a paper horn-of-plenty. Even his white leather Bible was spurted out, its pages fluttering open for everyone to see.

He thought, He'll be mad about my Bible and my bear, feeling a scream start up from where the woman was squeezing his stomach, as now she swung him swiftly around, causing the church tent, the flares, and the people to spin before his eyes like a great tin humming top. Then he felt his head snap forward and back, rattling his teeth—and in the sudden break of movement he saw the deaconesses springing forward even as the spilled images from the toppling coffin quivered vividly before his eyes then fading like a splash of water in bright sunlight—just as a tall woman with short, gleaming hair and steel-rimmed glasses shot from among the deaconesses and as her lenses glittered harshly he saw her mouth come open, causing the other women to freeze and a great silence to explore beneath the upward curve of his own shrill scream. Then he saw her head go back with an angry toss and he felt the sound slap hard against him.

What? Y'all mean to tell *me*? Here in the House-a-God? She's coming in *here*—who? WHOOOO! JUST TELL ME WHO BORN OF MAN'S HOT CONJUNCTION WITH A WOMAN'S SINFUL BOWELS?

And like an eerie echo now, the larger voice of the smaller woman floated up from the sawdust-covered earth, JUST DIG MY GRAVE! I SAY JUST READY MY SHROUD! JUST ... and the voices booming and echoing beneath the tent like a duet of angry ghosts. Then it was as though something heavy had plunged from a great height into the water, throwing the images into furious motion and he could see the frozen women leap forward.

They came like shadows flying before a torch tossed into the dark, their weight seeming to strike the white woman who held him out of one single, slow, long-floating, space-defying leap, sending her staggering backward and causing her arms to squash the air from his lungs—Aaaaaaaah! Their faces, wet with wrath, loomed before him, seeming to enter where his breath had been, their dark, widespread hands beginning to tear at his body like the claws of great cats with human heads; lifting him screaming clear of earth and coffin and suspending him there between the redheaded woman who now held his head and the others who had seized possession of his legs, arms, and body. And again he felt, but could not hear, his own throat's *Aaaaaaaaaaaayee!*

·   ·   ·

The Senator was first aware of the voice, then the dry taste of fever filled his mouth and he had the odd sensation that he had been listening to a foreign language that he knew but had neglected, so that now it was necessary to concentrate upon each word in order to translate its meaning. The very effort seemed to reopen his wounds and now his fingers felt for the button to summon the nurse but the voice was still moving around him, mellow and evocative. He recognized it now, allowing the button to fall as he opened his eyes. Yes, it was Hickman's, still there. And now it was as though he had been listening all along, for Hickman did not pause, his voice flowed on with an urgency which compelled him to listen, to make the connections.

"Well, sir, Bliss," Hickman said, "here comes this white woman pushing over everybody and loping up to the box and it's like hell had erupted at a side show. She rushed up to the box and..."

"*Box?*" the Senator said. "You mean coffin, don't you?"

He saw Hickman look up, frowning judiciously. "No, Bliss, I mean 'box'; it ain't actually a coffin till it holds a dead man.... So, as I was saying, she rushed up and grabs you in the box and the deaconesses leaped out of their chairs and folks started screaming, and I looked out there for some white folks to come and get her, but couldn't see a single one. So there I was. I could have cried like a baby, because I knew that one miserable woman could bring the whole state down on us. Still there she is, floating up out of nowhere like a puff of poison gas to land right smack in the middle of our meeting. Bliss, it was like God had started playing practical jokes.

"Next thing I know she's got you by the head and Sister Susie Trumball's got one leg and another sister's got the other, and others are snatching you by the arms—talking about King Solomon, he didn't have but *two* women to deal with, I had seven. And one convinced that she's a different breed of cat from the rest. Yes, and the others chock-full of disagreement and out to prove it. I tell you, Bliss, when it comes to chillen, women just ain't gentlemen.

"For a minute there it looked like they were going to snatch you limb from limb and dart off in seven different directions. *And* the folks were getting outraged a mile a minute. Because although you might have forgot it, nothing makes our people madder and will bring them to make a killing-floor stand quicker than to have white folks come bringing their craziness into the church. We just can't stand to have our one place of peace broken up, and nothing'll upset us worse—*unless* it's messing with one of our babies. You could just see it coming on, Bliss. I turned and yelled at them to regard the House of God— when here comes another woman, one of the deaconesses, Sister Bearmasher. She's a six-foot city woman from Birmingham, wearing eyeglasses and who ordinarily was the kindest woman you'd want to see. Soft-spoken and easy going the way some big women get to be because most of the attention goes to the little cute ones. Well, Bliss, she broke it up.

"I saw her coming down the aisle from the rear of the tent and reaching over the heads of the others, and before I could move she's in that woman's head of long red hair like a wild cat in a weaving mill. I couldn't figure what she was up to in all that pushing and tugging, but when they kind of rumbled around and squatted down low like they were trying to grab better holts I could see somebody's shoe and a big comb come sailing out, then they squatted again a couple of times—real fast, and when they come up, she's got all four feet or so of that woman's red hair wrapped around her arm like an ell of copper-colored cloth. And Bliss, she's talking calm and slapping the others away with her free hand like they were babies. Saying, 'Y'all just leave her to *me* now, sisters. Everything's going to be all right. She ain't no trouble, darlings; not now. Get on away now, Sis' Trumball. Let her go now. You got rumatism in you shoulder anyway. Y'all let her loose, now. Coming here into the House of God talking about this is *her* child. Since when? I want to know, since *when?* HOLD STILL DARLING!' she tells the white woman. 'NOBODY WANTS TO HURT YOU, BUT YOU MUST UNDERSTAND THAT YOU HAVE GONE TOO FAR!'

"And that white woman is holding on to you for dear life, Bliss; with her head snubbed back, way back, like a net full of red snappers and flounders being wound up on a ship's winch. And this big amazon of a woman, who could've easily set horses with a Missouri mule, starts then to preaching her own sermon. Saying, 'If this Revern-Bliss-the-Preacher is her child then all the yellow bastards in the nation has got to be hers. So when, I say, so when's she going to testify to all that? You sisters let her go now; just let me have her. Y'all just take that child. Take that child, I say. I love that child cause he's God's child and y'all love that child. So I say take that child out of this foolish woman's sacrilegious hands. TAKE HIM, I SAY! And if this be the time then this is the time. If it's the time to die, then I'm dead. If it's the time to bleed, then I'm bleeding—but take that child. 'Cause whatever time it is, this is one kind of foolishness that's got to be stopped before it gets any further under way!'

"Well, sir, there you were, Bliss, with the white woman still got holt of you but with her head snubbed back now and her head bucking like a frightened mare's, screaming, 'He's mine, he's mine.' *Claiming* you, boy, claiming you right out of our hands. At least out of those women's hands. Because us men were petrified, thrown out of action by that white woman's nerve. And that big, strong Bearmasher woman threatening to snatch her scalp clean from her head.

"And all the time Sister Bearmasher is preaching her sermon. Saying, 'If he was just learning his abc's like the average child instead of being a true, full-fledged preacher of the Gospel you wouldn't want him and you'd yell down destruction on anybody who even signified he was yours—WHERE'S HIS DADDY? YOU AIN'T THE VIRGIN MARY, SO YOU SHO MUST'VE PICKED OUT HIS DADDY. WHO'S THE BLACK MAN YOU PICKED TO DIE?'

"And then, Bliss, women all over the place started to taking it up: 'YES! That's right, who's the man? Amen! Just tell us!' and all like that.... Bliss, I'm a man with great puzzlement about life and I enjoy the wonderment of how things can happen and how folks can act, so I guess I must have been just standing there with my mouth open and taking it all in. But when those women started to making a chorus and working themselves up to do something outrageous, I broke loose. I reached down and grabbed my old trombone and started to blow. But instead of playing something calming, I was so excited that I broke into the 'St. Louis Blues,' like we used to when I was a young hellion and a fight would break out at a dance. Just automatically, you know; and I caught myself on about the seventh note and smeared into 'Listen to the Lambs,' but my lip was set wrong and there I was half laughing at how my sinful days had tripped me up—so that it came out 'Let Us Break Bread Together,' and by that time Deacon Wilhite had come to life and started singing and some of the men joined in—in fact, it was a men's chorus, because those women were still all up in arms. I blew me a few bars then put down that horn and climbed down to the floor to see if I could untangle that mess.

"I didn't want to touch that woman, so I yelled for somebody who knew her to come forward and get her out of there. Because even after I had calmed them a bit, she kept her death grip on you and was screaming, and Sister Bearmasher still had all that red hair wound round her arm and wouldn't let go. Finally a woman named Lula Strothers came through and started to talk to her like you'd talk to a baby and she gave you up. I'm expecting the police or some of her folks by now, but luckily none of them had come out to laugh at us that night. So Bliss, I got you into some of the women's hands and me and Sister Bearmasher got into the woman's rubber-tired buggy and rode off into town. She had two snow-white horses hitched to it, and luckily I had handled horses as a boy, because they were almost wild. And she was screaming and they reared and pitched until I could switch them around; then they hit that midnight road for a fare-thee-well.

"The woman is yelling, trying to make them smash us up, and cursing like a trooper and calling for you—though by the name of Cudworth—while Sister Bearmasher is still got her bound up by the hair. It was dark of the moon, Bliss, and a country road, and we took every curve on two wheels. Yes, and when we crossed a little wooden bridge it sounded like a burst of rifle fire. It seemed like those horses were rushing me to trouble so fast that I'd already be there before I could think of what I was going to say. How on earth was I going to explain what had happened, with that woman there to tell the sheriff something different—with her just *being* with us more important than the truth? I thought about Sister Bearmasher's question about who the man was that had been picked to die, and I tell you, Bliss, I thought that man was me. There I was, hunched over and holding on to those reins for dear life, and those mad animals frothing and foaming in the dark so that the spray from their bits was about to give us a bath and just charging us into trouble. I could have taken a turn away from town, but that would've only made it worse, putting the whole church in danger. So I was bound to go ahead since I was the minister responsible for their bodies as well as their souls. Sister Bearmasher was the only calm one in that carriage. She's talking to that woman as polite as if she was waiting on table or massaging her feet or something. And all the time she's still wound up in the woman's hair.

"But the woman wouldn't stop screaming, Bliss; and she's cussing some of the worst oaths that ever fell from the lips of man. And at a time when we're flying through the dark and I can see the eyes of wild things shining out at us, at first up ahead, then disappearing. And the sound of the galloping those horses made! They were hitting a lick on that road like they were in a battle charge.

" 'Revern'?' Sister Bearmasher yelled over to me.

" 'Yes, Sister?' I called back over to her.

" 'I say, are you praying?'

" 'Praying,' I yelled. 'Sister, my whole body and soul is crying out to God, but it's about as much as I can do to hold on to these devilish reins. You just keep that woman's hands from scratching at my face.'

"Well, Bliss, about that time we hit a straightaway, rolling past some fields, and way off to one side I looked and saw somebody's barn on fire. It was like a dream, Bliss. There we was making better time than the Hamiltonian, with foam flying, the woman screeching, leather straining, hooves pounding and Sister Bearmasher no longer talking to the woman but moaning a prayer like she's bending over a washtub somewhere on a peaceful sunny morning. And managing to sound so through all that rushing air. And then, there it was, way off yonder across the dark fields, that big barn filling the night with silent flames. It was too far to see if anyone was there to know about it, and it was too big for anybody except us not to see it; and as we raced on there seemed no possible way to miss it burning across the night. We seemed to wheel around it, the earth was so flat and the road so long and winding. Lonesome, Bliss; that sight was lonesome. Way yonder, isolated and lighting up the sky like a solitary torch. And then as we swung around a curve where the road swept into a lane of trees, I looked through the flickering of the trees and saw it give way and collapse. Then all at once the flames sent a big cloud of sparks to sweep the sky. Poor man, I thought, poor man, as that buggy hit a rough stretch of road. Then I was praying. Boy, I was really praying. I said, 'Lord, bless these bits, these bridles and these reins. Lord, please keep these thin wheels and rubber tires hugging firm to your solid ground, and Lord, bless these hames, these cruppers, and this carriage tongue. Bless the breast-straps, Lord and these straining leather belly-bands.' And Bliss, I listened to those pounding hoofbeats and felt those horses trying to snatch my arms clear out of their sockets and I said, 'Yea, Lord, and bless this wiffle tree.' Then I thought about that fire and looked over at the white woman and finally I prayed, 'Lord, please bless this wild redheaded woman and that man back there with that burning barn. And Lord, since you know all about Sister Bearmasher and me, all we ask is that you please just keep us steady in your sight.'

"Those horses moved, Bliss. Zip, and we're through the land and passing through a damp place like a swamp, then up a hill through a burst of heat. And all the time, Bliss..."

The voice had ceased. Then the Senator heard, "Bliss, are you there, boy?"

"Still here," the Senator said from far away. "Don't stop. I hear."

Then through his blurring eyes he saw the dark shape come closer, and now the voice sounded small as though Hickman stood on a hill somewhere inside his head.

"I say, Bliss, that all the time I should have been praying for you, back there all torn up inside by those women's hands. Because, after all, a lot of prayer and sweat and dedication had gone into that buggy along with the money-greed and show-off pride. Because it held together through all that rough ride even though its wheels were humming like guitar strings, and it took me and Sister Bear-masher to jail and a pretty hot time before they let us go. So there between a baby, a buggy, and a burning barn I prayed the wrong prayer. I left you out Bliss, and I guess right then and there you started to wander...."

Hickman leaned closer now, gazing into the quiet face.

The Senator slept.

THE ROOF, THE STEEPLE AND THE PEOPLE

QUARTERLY REVIEW OF LITERATURE 10 (1960): 115–28

Bliss, Daddy Hickman said, you keep asking me to take you even though I keep telling you that folks dont like to see preachers hanging around a place they think of as one of the Devil's hangouts. All right, so now I'm going to take you so you can see for yourself, and you'll see that its just like the world—full of sinners and with a few believers, a few good folks and a heap of mixed-up and bad ones. Yes, and beyond the fun of sitting there looking at the marvelous happenings in the dark, there's all the same old snares and delusions we have to side-step everyday right out here in the bright sunlight. Because you see, Bliss, it's not so much a matter of where you *are* as what you *see*....

Yes, sir, I said.

No, dont agree too quick, Bliss; wait until you understand. But like old Luke says, "The light of the body is the eye," so you want to be careful that the light that your eye lets into you isn't the light of darkness. I mean you always have to be sure that you *see* what you're looking at.

I nodded my head, watching his eyes. I could see him studying the Word as he talked.

That's right, he said, many times you will have to preach goodness out of badness, little boy. Yes, and hope out of hopelessness. God made the world and gave it a chance, and when it's bad we have to remember that it's still his plan for it to be redeemed through the striving of a few good women and men. So come on, we're going to walk down there and take us a good look. We're going to do it in style too, with some popcorn and peanuts and some crackerjacks and candy bars. You might as well get some idea of what you will have to fight against, because I dont believe you can really lead folks if you never have to face up to any of the temptations they face. Christ had to put on the flesh, Bliss; you understand?

Yes, sir.

But wait here a second, Bliss—

He looked deep into me and I felt a tremor. Sir? I said.

His eyes became sad as he hesitated, then:

Now dont think this is going to become a habit, Bliss. I know you're going to like being in there looking in the dark, even though you have to climb up those filthy pissy stairs to get there. Oh yes, you're going to enjoy looking at the pictures just about like I used to enjoy being up there on the bandstand playing music for folks to enjoy themselves back there in my olden days. Yes, you're going to like looking at the pictures, most likely you're going to be bugeyed with the excitement; but I'm telling you right now that it's one of those pleasures we preachers have to leave to other folks. And I'll tell you why, little preacher: too much looking at those pictures is going to have a lot of folks raising a crop of confusion. The show hasn't been here but a short while but I can see it coming already. Because folks are getting themselves mixed up with those shadows spread out against the wall, with people that are no more than some smoke drifting up from hell or pouring out of a bottle. So they lose touch with who they're supposed to be, Bliss. They forget to be what the Book tells them they were meant to be—and that's in God's *own* image. The preacher's job, his main job, Bliss, is to help folks find themselves and to keep reminding them to remember who they are. So you see, those pictures can go against our purpose. If they look at those shows too often they'll get all mixed up with so many of those shadows that they'll lose their way. They wont know who they *are* is what I mean. So you see, if we start going to the picture-show all the time, folks will think we're going to the devil and backsliding from what we preach. We have to set them an example, Bliss; so we're going in there for the first and last time—

Now dont look at me like that; I know it seems like everytime a preacher turns around he has to give up something else. But, Bliss, there's a benefit in it too; because pretty soon he develops control over himself. *Self-control*'s the word. That's right, you develop discipline, and you live so you can feel the grain of things and you learn to taste the sweet that's in the bitter and you live more deeply and earnestly. A man doesn't live just one life, Bliss, he lives more lives than a cat—only he doesn't like to face it because the bitter is there nine times nine, right along with the sweet he wants all the time. So he forgets.

You too, Daddy Hickman? I said, Do you have more than one life?

He smiled down at me,

Me too, Bliss, he said. Me too.

But how? How can they have nine lives and not know it?

They forget and wander on, Bliss. But let's us leave this now and go face up to those shadows. Maybe the Master meant for them to show us some of the many sides of the old good-bad. I know, Bliss, you dont understand that, but you will, boy, you will....

Ah, but by then Body had brought the news:

We were sitting on the porch-edge eating peanuts, gooberpeas, as Deacon Wilhite called them. Discarded hulls littered the ground below the contented dangling of our feet. We were barefoot, I was allowed to be that day, and in overalls. A flock of sparrows rested on the strands of electric wire across the unpaved road, darting down from time to time and sending up little clouds of dust. Body was humming as he chewed. Except in church we were always together, he was my right hand. Body said,

Bliss, you see that thing they all talking about?

Who, I said.

All the kids. You see it yet?

Seen what, Body. Why do you always start preaching before you state your text?

You the preacher, aint you? Look like to me a preacher'd *know* what a man is talking about.

I looked at him hard and he grinned, trying to keep his face straight.

You ought to know where all the words come from, even before anybody starts to talk. Preachers is suppose to see visions and things, aint they?

Now don't start playing around with God's work, I warned him. Like Daddy Hickman says, Everybody has to die and pay their bills—Have I seen what?

That thing Sammy Leaderman's got to play with. It makes pictures.

No, I haven't. You mean a kodak? I've seen one of those. Daddy Hickman has him a big one. Made like a box with little pearly glass windows in it and one round one, like an eye.

He shook his head. I put down the peanuts and fitted my fingers together. I said,

> *Here's the roof,*
> *Here's the steeple,*
> *Open it up and see*
> *the people.*

Body sneered. That steeple's got dirt under the finger nails, why dont you wash your hands? You think I'm a baby? Lots of folks have those kodaks, this here is something different.

Well, what is it then?

I dont rightly know, he said. I just heard some guys talking about it down at the liberty stable. But they was white and I didn't want to ask them any questions. I rather be ignorant than ask them anything.

So why didn't you ask Sammy, he aint white.

Naw, he a Jew; but he looks white, and sometimes he acts white too. Specially when he's with some of those white guys.

He always talks to me, I said, calls me *rabbi*.

The doubt came into Body's eyes like a thin cloud. He frowned. He was my right hand and I could feel his doubt.

You look white too, Rev. Why you let him call you 'rabbit'?

I looked away, toward the dusting birds.

Body, can't you hear? I said he calls me *rabbi*.

Oh, it sounds like my little brother trying to spell rabbit. Re-abbi-tee, *rabbit*, he say. He a fool, man.

He sure is, he's your brother, aint he?

Dont start that now, you a preacher, remember? How come you let Sammy play the Dozens with you, you want to be white?

No! And Sammy aint white and that's not playing the Dozens, it means preacher in Jewish talk. Quit acting a fool. What kind of toy is this you heard them talking about?

His lids came down low and his eyes hid when I tried to look for the truth in them.

All I know is that it makes pictures, Body said.

It makes pictures and not a kodak?

That's right, Rev.

I chewed a while and thought of all I had heard about, airplanes and Stutz Bearcats and Stanley Steamers. Then I thought I had it:

It makes pictures but not a kodak? So maybe he's got hold to one of those big ones like they use to take your picture at the circus. You know, the kind they take you out of wet and you have to wait around until you dry.

Body shook his head, No, Rev, this here is something different. This is something they say you have to be in the dark to see. These folks come out already dry.

You mean a nickleodeon? I heard them talking about one of those when we were out there preaching in Denver.

I dont think so, Rev, but maybe that's what they meant. But, man, how's Sammy going to get something like that just to play with. A thing like that must cost about a zillion dollars.

I dont know, I said. But remember, his pappa has that grocery store. Besides, Sammy's so smart he might've made him one, man.

That's right, he a Jew, aint he? He talk much of that Jew Talk to you, Bliss?

No, how could he when I can't talk back? I wish I could, though, cause they're real nice to you, man.

How you know if you caint talk it?

Because once when Daddy Hickman took me with him to preach out there in Tulsa and we got broke he ran into one of his Pullman porter friends from Kansas City and told him about it, and this porter took us to one of those big stores run by some Jews—a real fancy one, man—and the minute we stepped through the door those Jews left everything and came gathering round Daddy Hickman's friend to hear him talk some Jewish...

He was colored and could talk their talk?

That's right, man...

Body doubted me. How'd he learn to do that, he go to Jew School?

He was raised with them, Daddy Hickman said. And he used to work for some up there in Kansas City. Daddy Hickman said they used to let him run the store on Saturday. He was the boss then, man; with all the other folks working under him. Imagine that, Body, being the *boss*.

Yeah, but what happened on Monday?

He went back to being just the porter.

So why'd he do it? That dont make much sense.

I know but Daddy Hickman said he went to running on the road because he couldn't stand pushing that broom on Monday after handling all that cash on Saturday.

I dont blame him, cause that musta been like a man being made monitor of the class in the morning, he can bet a fat man against a biscuit that one of those big guys will knock a hicky on his head after school is out—So what happened?

Well, Daddy Hickman's friend laughed and talked with those Jews and they liked him so well that when he told him that we needed some money to get back home with, they took up a collection for us. We walked out of there with fifty dollars, man. And they even gave me a couple of new bow ties to preach in.

Honest, Bliss?

Honest, man. Those Jews was crazy about that porter. You'd have thought he was the prodigal son. Here, eat some of these goobers.

Wonder what he said to talk them out of all that money, Body said. He know something bad on them?

There you go thinking evil, I said. They were happy to be talking with some-body different, I guess.

Body shook his head. That porter sure was smart, talking those Jews out of that money. I like to learn how to do that, I *never* be out of candy change.

Those Jews were helping out with the Lord's work, fool. I wish you would re-member some more about that box. It's probably just a magic lantern—except in those the pictures dont move.

I hulled seven peanuts and chewed them, trying to imagine what Body had heard while his voice flowed on about the Jews. Somehow I seemed to remem-ber Daddy Hickman describing something similar but it kept sliding away from me, like when you bob for apples floating in a tub.

Say, Rev, Body said.

Can't you hear? I said do you remember in the Bible where it tells about Samson and it says he had him a boy to lead him up to the wall so he could shake the building down?

That's right, I said.

Well answer me this, you think that little boy got killed?

Killed, I said; who killed him?

What I mean is, do you think old Samson forgot to tell that boy what he was fixing to do?

I cut my eyes over at Body. I didn't like the idea. Once Daddy Hickman had said: Bliss, you must be a hero just like that little lad who led blind Samson to the wall, because a great many grown folks are blind and have to be led toward the light.... The question worried me and I pushed it away.

Look, Body, I said, I truly dont feel like working today. Because, you see, while you're out playing cowboy and acting the fool and going on cotton picks and chunking rocks at the other guys and things like that, *I* have to always be preaching and praying and studying my Bible....

What's all that got to do with what I asked you? You want somebody to cry for you?

No, but right now it looks to you like we just eating these here good goobers and talking together and watching those sparrows out there beating up dust in the road—*I'm* really resting from my pastorial duties, understand? So now I just want to think some more about this box that Sammy Leaderman's supposed to have. How did those white guys say it looked?

Man, Body said, you just like a bulldog with a bone when you start in to thinking about something. I done told you, they say Sammy got him a machine that has people in it...

People in it? Watch out there, Body...

Sho, Rev—folks. They say he points it at the wall and stands back in the dark cranking on a handle and they come out and move around. Just like a gang of ghosts, man.

Seeing me shake my head, his face lit up, his eyes shining.

Body, you expect me to believe that?

Now listen here, Bliss; I had done left that box because I wanted to talk about Samson and you didn't want to. So dont come trying to call me no lie...

Forget about Samson, man. Where does he have this thing?

In his daddy's basement under the grocery store. You got a nickle?

I looked far down the street, past the chinaberry trees. Some little kids were pushing a big one on a racer made out of a board and some baby buggy wheels. He was guiding it with a rope like a team of horses, with them drawn all up in a knot, pushing him. I said:

Man, we ought to go somewhere and roast these gooberpeas. That would make them even better. Maybe Sister Judson would do it for us. She makes some fine fried pies too and she just might be baking today. I have to remember to pray for her tonight, she's a nice lady. What's a nickle got to do with it?

Cause Sammy charges you two cents to see them come out and move.

I looked at him. Body had a round face with laughing eyes and was smooth black, a head taller than me and very strong. He saw me doubting and grinned.

They *move,* man. I swear on my grandmother that they move. And that aint all: they walk and talk—only you cant hear what they say—and they dance and fist-fight and shoot and stab one another; and sometimes they even kiss, but not too much. And they drink liquor, man, and go staggering all around.

They sound like folks, all right, I said.

Sho, and they ride hosses and fight some Indians and all stuff like that. It's real nice, Bliss. They say it's really keen.

I willed to believe him. I said: And they all come out of this box?

That's right, Rev.

How big are the people he has in there, they midgets?

Well, it's a box about this size . . .

Now I *know* you're lying. . . . I said, Body?

What?

You know lying is a sin, dont you? You surely ought to by now, because I've told you often enough.

He looked at me then cut his eyes away, scowling. Listen, Bliss, a little while ago you wouldn't tell me whether that boy who led Samson got killed or not, so now dont come preaching me no sermon. Cause you know I can kick your butt. I dont have to take no stuff off you. This here aint no Sunday, no how. Cant no-body make me go to church on no Friday, cause on a Friday I'm liable to boot a preacher's behind until his nose bleeds.

I rebuked him with my face but now he was out to tease me.

That's the truth, Rev, and you know the truth is what the Lord loves. I'll give a doggone preacher *hell* on a Friday. Let him catch me on Sunday if he wants to, that's all right providing he aint too long-winded. And even on Wednesday aint so bad, but please, *please,* dont let him fool with me on no Friday.

I flipped a goober at his boasting head. He didn't dodge and tried to stare me down. Then we dueled with our faces, our eyes, but I won when his lips quivered and he laughed.

Rev, he said, shaking his head, I swear you're my ace buddy, preacher or no—but why do preachers always have to be so serious? Look at that face! Let's see how you look when you see one of those outrageous sinners. One of those mid-night rambling, whiskey drinking gamblers. . . .

I rebuked him with my eyes, but he kept on laughing. Come on, Rev, let's see you . . .

I've told you now, Body . . .

Man, you too serious. But I'm not lying about that box though, honest. It's suppose to be about this size, but when they come out on the wall they git as big as grown folks—Hecks, *bigger.* It's magic, man.

It must be, I said. What kind of folks has he got in that box? You might as well tell a really big lie.

White folks, man. What you think—Well, he *has* got a few Indians in there. That is if any of them are left after they're supposed to have been killed.

No colored?

Naw, just white. You know they gon' keep all the new things for theyselves. They put us in there about the time it's fixing to wear out.

We giggled, holding one hand across our mouths and slapping our thighs with the other as grown men did when a joke was outrageously simpleminded and yet somehow true.

Then that's got to be magic, I said. Because that's the only way they can get rid of the colored. But really, Body, dont you ever tell the truth?

Sure I do, all the time. I know you think I'm lying, Rev, but I'm telling you the Lord's truth. Sammy got them folks in that machine like lightning bugs in a jug.

And about how many you think he's got in there?

He held his head to one side and squinted,

About two hundred, man; maybe more.

And you think I'm going to believe that too?

It's true, man. He got them jugged in there and for four cents me and you can go see him let 'em come out and move. You can see for yourself. You got four cents?

Sure, but I'm saving 'em. You have to tell a better lie than that to get my money; a preacher's money comes hard.

Shucks, that's what you say. All y'all do is hoop and holler a while, then you pass the plate. But that's all right, you can keep your old money if you want to be so stingy, because I seen it a coupla times all ready.

You saw it? So why're you just now telling me?

I felt betrayed, Body was of my right hand. I saw him skeet through the liar's gap in his front teeth and roll his eyes.

Shoots, you dont believe nothing I say no how. I get tired of you 'sputing my word. But just the same I'm telling the truth; they come out and move and they move fast. Not like ordinary folks. And last time I was down there Sammy made them folks come out big, man. They was twice as big as grown folks, and they had a whole train with them...

A whole train?

Sho, a real train running over a trestle just like the Southern does. And some cowboys was chasing it on they hosses.

Body, I'm going to pray for you, hear? Fact is, I'm going to have Daddy Hickman have the whole church pray for you.

Dont you think you're so good, Bliss. You better ask him to pray for yourself while you doing it, cause you believe nothing anybody says. Shucks, I'm going home.

Now dont get mad—hey, wait a minute, Body. Come back here, where you going? Come on back. *Please.* Body. Caint you hear me say "please." But now the dust was spurting behind his running feet. I was sad, he was of my right hand.

So now I wanted to say, No, Daddy Hickman; if that's the way it has to be, let's not go. Because it was one more thing I'd have to deny myself because of being a preacher, and I didn't want the added yearning. Better to listen to the others telling the stories, as I had for some time now, since Body had brought the news and the movies had come to town. Better to listen while sitting on the curb stones in the evening, or watching them acting out the parts during recess and lunchtime on the school grounds. Any noontime I could watch them reliving the stories and the magic gestures and see the flickery scenes unreeling inside my eye just as Daddy Hickman could make people relive the action of the Word. And seeing them, I could feel myself drawn into the world they shared so intensely that I felt that I had actually taken part not only in the seeing, but in the actions unfolding in the depths of the wall I'd never seen; experiencing with the excruciating intensity a camel would feel if drawn through the eye of a needle a whole world uncoiling through an eye of glass.

So Daddy Hickman was too late, already the landscape of my mind had been trampled by the great droves of galloping horses and charging redskins and the yelling charges of cowboys and cavalrymen, and I had reeled before exploding faces that imprinted themselves upon one's eyeball with the impact of a water-soaked snowball bursting against the tender membrane to leave a felt-image of blue-white pain throbbing with every pulse of blood propelled toward vision. And I had sat dizzy with the vastness of the action and the scale of the characters and the dimensions of the emotions and responses; had seen laughs so large and villainous with such rotting, tombstone teeth in mouths so cavernous that they seemed to yawn wall-wide and threaten to gulp the whole audience into their traps of hilarious maliciousness. And meanness transcendent, yawning in one overwhelming face; and heroic goodness expressed in actions as cleanly violent as a cyclone seen from a distance, rising ever above the devilish tricks of the badguys, and the women's eyes looking ever wider with horror or welling ever limpid with love, shocked with surprise over some bashful movement of the hero's lips, his ocean waves of hair, his heaving chest and anguished eyes. Or determined with womanly virtue to escape the badguy and escaping in the panting end with the goodguy's shy help; escaping even the Indian chief's dark clutches even as I cowered in my seat beneath his pony's flying hooves, surviving to see her looking with wall-wide head and yard-wide smiling mouth melting with the hero's to fade into the darkness sibilant with women's and young girls' sighs.

Or the trains running wild and threatening to jump the track and crash into the white sections below, with smoke and steam threatening to scald the air and bring hell fire to those trapped there in their favored seats—screaming as fireman and engineer battled to the death with the Devil now become a Dalton boy or a James or a Younger, and whose horses of devil flesh outran again and again the iron horses of the trains, upgrade and down, and with their bullets flying to burst ever against the sacred sanctuary of Uncle Sam's mail cars, where the gold was stored and the hero waited; killing multitudes of clerks and passengers, armed and unarmed alike, in joy and in anger, in fear and in fun. And bushwhacking the Sheriff and his deputies again and again, dropping them over cliffs and into cascading waterfalls, until like the sun the Hero loomed and doomed the arch-villain to join his victims, tossed too from a cliff, shot in the belly with the blood flowing dark; or hung blackhooded with his men, three in a row, to drop from a common scaffold to swing like sawdust filled dolls in lonely winds.

All whirled through my mind as filtered through Body's and the other's eyes and made concrete in their shouting pantomime of conflict, their accurately aimed pistol and rifle blasts, their dying falls with faces fixed in death's most dramatic agony as their imaginary sixshooters blazed one last poetic bullet of banging justice to bring their murderers down down down to hell, now heaving heaven high in wonder beneath our feet....

So I wanted to leave the place unentered, even if it had a steeple higher than any church in the world, leave it, pass it ever by, rather than see it once, then never to enter it again—with all the countless unseen episodes to remain a mystery and like my mother flown forever.

But I could not say it, nor could I refuse; for no language existed between child and man. So I, Bliss the preacher, ascended, climbed, holding reluctantly Daddy Hickman's huge hand, climbed up the steep, narrow stairs crackling with peanut hulls and discarded candy wrappers—up into the hot, breathing darkness, up, until the roof seemed to rest upon the crowns of old heads.... And as we come into the pink-tinted light with its tiered, hierarchical order of seats, I pull back upon his hand, frightened by what I do not know. And he says, Come along, Bliss boy—deep and comforting in the dark. It's all right, he says, I'm going with you. You just hold my hand.

And I ascended, holding on.

IT ALWAYS BREAKS OUT

PARTISAN REVIEW 30 (SPRING 1963): 13–28

What a country, what a world! I don't know which was the more outrageous, the more scandalous—the burning of the Cadillac on the senator's beautiful lawn, the wild speech made by the arsonist while the beautiful machine smoked and glowed in flames, or the crowd's hysterical reaction to the weird, flamboyant sacrifice. I know only that I have neither the power nor the will to convey the incident to Monsieur Vannec. How can I, when I've been unable to frame it for myself? To hell with the inquisitive Frenchman, there is simply too much unexpected chaos involved, too many unsettling contradictions have appeared. Besides, I refuse to reveal to him that I'm so much without presence before a phenomenon of my own country. It is a matter of pride: personal, intellectual, national. And especially is this true when I consider Vannec's passionate need to define all phenomena—whether social, political or cultural—and codify them and reduce them to formulae—intricate ones—that can be displayed in the hard sparkling center of a crystal paperweight.

And speaking of paper, how should I explain the manner in which the car burning was handled by the press? How the newspapers reduced the event to a small item which stated simply that a deranged jazz musician had set fire to his flashy automobile on the senator's lawn—with all references to his wild speech and the crowd's reaction omitted? And here is the shameful part requiring an unwilling confession: I would have to tell Vannec that we, the newspapermen, members of the working press, champions of the reported fact who insist upon the absolute accessibility of the news, that we ourselves suppressed it, reduced it to insignificance by reflex and with no editorial urging whatsoever!

Or at least we tried; but despite what we did the event has had, is having, its effect. It spreads by word of mouth, it imposes itself like a bad smell carried by the wind into private homes and into private conversations. Yes, and into our private thoughts. It balloons, it changes its shape, it grows. Worse, it seeps back into consciousness despite all we do to forget it. And we, remember, are tough-minded newspapermen.

Get this: a group of us met that evening to eat and drink and chat—just as we've done once a week for quite some time. Sometimes we exchange information and discuss that part of the news which, for one reason or another, is considered untimely or unfit to print. Often, as on this occasion, we enjoy our private jokes at the expense of some public figure or incident which, in reporting, we find expedient to treat with formal propriety. But tonight our mood was light, almost gay. Or at least it seemed so at the beginning. We were delighted that at last one of the senator's butts had succeeded in answering him, if only briefly and at outrageous expense. But beneath our banter we were somewhat uneasy. The wildman Negro jazzman had made us so. Certainly there was no other reason for it—unless it was the intimate knowledge which each of us possessed of our filed accounts. Otherwise why the uneasy undertone as we relaxed there in the brightly lighted dining room with its sparkle of silver and crystal, its sheen of rich woods, its tinkle of iced glasses and buzz of friendly talk? The very paintings on the wall, scenes of early life on the then remote frontier, moody, misty scenes of peaceful life in great forest clearings, formal portraits of the nineteenth-century founders of the club—all made for a sense of security. Even Sam, our inscrutable but familiar Negro waiter, was part of a ritual. And while I don't mean to imply that the club is a great place, it is a good place indeed, and its food and drink are excellent; its atmosphere, resonant with historical associations and warmly civilized values, most relaxing.

But tonight, as I say, something was working within each of us and it was just after Sam's dark hands had served the second round of after-dinner drinks, placed clean ashtrays before us and withdrawn, that Wiggins, the economics expert, released it.

"What," he said, "do you think of the new style in conspicuous consumption?"

And there it was, right out in the open, wearing a comic disguise. We laughed explosively, not so much at his remark but at ourselves, at the quick summoning up of what lay beneath our calm.

"It was a lulu," Thompson said, "a real lulu."

"Where on earth did that fellow come from?" Wilson said.

"From Chattanooga. He rose up like a wave of heat from the Jeff Davis highway," Wilkins said. "Didn't you hear him say it?"

"I wasn't there," Wiggins said, "but when I heard of it I thought, *Thorstein Veblen, your theory has been carried to the tenth power!*"

"And in horse power," I said. "Wiggins, you always said that Veblen was the comedian of economics. Now I'm beginning to understand."

"That's right, he was an ironist, a humorist of economic theory," Wiggins said, "and all he needed to make that clear was to have had that black boy illustrate his books."

"The learned doctor would have flipped," Larkin said.

"Did you ever see anything like it, a man burning his own car before an audience?"

"He's as wild as those rich Oklahoma Indians who preferred to travel in hook-and-ladder fire trucks or brand new hearses instead of limousines," Wiggins said.

"Yes," I said, "but that was a cultural preference. The Indians were really living in a different world, but this fellow today must have been mad. Off his rocker."

"Just leave it to the senator," Wilson said. "If there's something outrageous to be brought out in people he's the man to do it."

"It'll be interesting to see what this will bring out of the insurance people," Larkin said.

"They'll be wild."

"Man, they're already rewriting their policies!"

"Well, I'll bet no one is as wild as the senator," Thompson said. "He's probably searching for laws to rewrite."

"Can you blame him, that boy tried to tie a knot in his tail."

"Yeah," McGowan said, "ole senator was up there cooking up a barbecue for his v.i.p. guests and here comes a Nigra straight out of nowhere to prepare the hot sauce!"

"I wouldn't be too sure about how the senator is taking it," I said. "I wouldn't be surprised if he isn't sitting in his study right this minute laughing his head off."

"He's baited those people so often that he shouldn't mind when one answers back."

"The senator is an actor," I said, "nothing seems to touch him."

"He's a thick-skinned scoundrel," said Larkin, "a thick-skinned, brilliant scoundrel and a joker."

"Well, that colored fellow really tried to cap his joke. What is this country coming to? A United States senator stands on the floor of the senate and allows himself the license of saying that so many Negro citizens are driving Cadillac cars that he suggests that the name, the trade mark, be changed to the *Coon Cage Eight*—imagine! And as though that weren't scandalous enough, hardly before the news is on the air, a Negro drives an expensive Cadillac onto the senator's grounds and in rebuttal sets it afire! What on earth are we coming to?"

"The senator's a joker, the Negro is a joker, this is a nation of jokers. We aren't coming, we've arrived. Welcome to the United States of Jokeocracy."

"Hell, that was no joke, not the car. That fellow was dead serious."

"The point that interests me," Wilson said, "is that a fellow like that was willing to pay for it. He probably decided that he'd do anything to get back at the senator and this was the damndest way he could find. If I were the senator I'd reflect on that."

"What do you mean?"

"I mean that it's possible that someone else might decide to call him, and in a more personal way. In fact, I'm surprised that he hasn't provoked someone long before today..."

Wilson's voice faded into his thinking and then just as the swift, barely-formed idea flashed into my own mind, Wilson looked around the table, frowning.

"Say," he said, "have we ever had a Negro assassin?"

I looked at him, open-mouthed. It was as though the words had been transferred from my mind to his. I held my breath. Past Wilson's shoulder and far across the room I could see Sam, standing with folded arms. Several pitchers of iced water and a large white crock piled high with iced squares of butter rested on the stand beside him while he glanced casually down the long sweep of the room to where a girl moved gracefully through the door. Her red hair flowed in waves to the shoulders of her white suit and she carried a large blue bag and I thought, *Hail Columbia, long may she wave....* Then I heard Thompson saying,

"You mean in the *United States?*"

"That's right," Wilson said, "have we?"

"Now why on earth would you think of that," I said.

"It just struck me. I don't know. But after today maybe it's time we started thinking about such possibilities..."

McGowan made a cage of his fat fingers and lowered them around his drink. "What Wilson means, gentlemen, is that a Nigra who'd burn a Cadillac car would do just about anything. He means that a Nigra like that'll burn good United States currency."

We smiled. McGowan could be amusing about Negroes but we would have liked it better had he not been a Southerner. Somehow they obsessed him and he was constantly sounding off over something they did to disturb his notion of a well-ordered society. And now that I could feel him working up a disquisition on the nature and foibles of the Negro I was glad that Sam was far across the room. McGowan took a drink, sighed and smiled.

"Well, Wilson, I have to agree: that was *quite* a Nigra. But you all don't have to go into any brainstorm to analyze what that Nigra was doing. I'm here to tell you that what the Nigra was doing was running a-muck! His brain snapped, that's what happened; and far as he was concerned he was back up a tree throwing coconuts."

Across from me Wilson was still frowning, looking like a man remembering a bad dream. McGowan's humor wasn't reaching me either.

"I'm serious," Wilson said. "Has there ever been one?"

"I've been thinking about it," Larkin said. "There were McKinley, Roosevelt—Cermac that is, Huey Long—but none of the assassins were colored."

"A Nigra *assassin*," McGowan said. "Are y'all getting drunk already?"

"There might have been a few local killings with a political motive," Thompson said. "Here and there over the years some small town Southern politician might have been shot or knifed. Like that fellow down in Louisiana who made the mistake of getting into a colored man's bed and allowed himself to get caught. But you wouldn't call that political. That was sheer bad judgment and I'd have shot the bastard myself…"

"I say, are y'all getting drunk?" McGowan said.

"Come to think about it though," Thompson went on, "how can you tell when those people are doing something politically significant? Down home not enough of them vote and here in the North so few take a part in civic affairs that it's hard to tell what they're up to. We just don't know enough about them for all the statistics we have. We don't have, or *they* don't have, enough social forms through which we can see them with any clarity."

"*Forms?*" McGowan said, "What forms? We don't need any cotton-picking forms! Don't you Yankees recognize that everything the Nigra *does* is political? Thompson, you amaze me. You are Southern born and bred and there are three things we Southerners are supposed to know about and they're history, politics—and Nigras. And especially do we know about the political significance of the Nigra."

"Oh drop it, McGowan," Thompson said, "I'm being serious."

"No sir, I beg to differ," McGowan said, "*I'm* being serious; *you're* being Yankee frivolous. Gentlemen, will y'all grant me a few minutes?"

"Grant you?" Wilkins said. "Hell, you can't talk without making a filibuster. So go on, get it over with."

"Thank you kindly. Gentlemen, I'm going to tell you once and for all, I'm going to impress upon you once and for all, the fact that everything the Nigra does is political. I don't like to take up so sobering a matter so early in the evening but some of us here are getting too drunk too soon..."

"Do you mean 'everything' literally?" Wiggins said.

"I mean *everything*," McGowan said. "And especially things which you Yankees would pass over as insignificant. We can start at random. Listen: If you catch a Nigra in the wrong section of town after dark—he's being political because he knows he's got no business being there. If he brushes against a white man on the street or on a stairway, that's very political. Because every once in a while the Nigras get together and organize these 'bumping campaigns' against the white folks. They'll try to knock you off the sidewalk and break your ribs and then they'll beg your pardon as though it was an accident, when we know damn well that it was politics.

"So watch the Nigra's face. If a Nigra rolls his eyes and pokes out his mouth at you—that's downright subversive. If he puts on aristocratic airs—watch him! If he talks about moving up North, he's being political again. Because we know for a fact that the Nigras are moving North in keeping with a long-range plan to seize control of the American government. If he talks too loud on the street or talks about sending his kids up North to college in your presence, or if he buys a tractor—all this is political. Be especially wary of the Nigra who tries to buy himself a bulldozer so he can compete against white men because that is one of the most dangerous political acts of all. A Nigra like that is out to knock down Southern tradition and bury it, lock stock and barrel. He's worse than a whole herd of carpetbaggers or seven lean years of bollweevils. Waiter," he called to Sam, "bring us another round!" and then to us, "There's absolutely nothing to dry a man out like trying to educate a bunch of Yankees."

As I watched Sam approach, I became uneasy that McGowan in his excitement would offend him. After all, I had learned during the Thirties to respect the sensibilities of his people and to avoid all anti-minority stereotypes and clichés. One simply didn't laugh at unfortunates—within their hearing. But if Sam was aware of our conversation his face revealed nothing.

"Hy ya, Sam," McGowan said.

"Fine, Mr. McGowan," Sam said, and looking around the table, "Gentlemen?"

And we ordered, after which Sam slipped away.

"Let me tell y'all something else," McGowan went on. "If you catch a Nigra buying his food and clothing from the wrong dealer—or worse, if he goes to another town to trade, that's Nigra politics *pretending* to be Nigra economics. That's something for you to think about, Wiggins. If a Nigra owns more than one shotgun, rifle, or pistol, it's political. If he forgets to say 'sir' to a white man or tries to talk Yankee talk or if he drives too doggone slow or too doggone fast, or if he comes up with one of these little bug-eyed foreign cars—all these things are political and don't you forget it!"

McGowan paused. Sam was crossing the floor with a tray of drinks, which he placed before us and left.

"Come on, educate us some more," Thompson said. "Then we can talk seriously."

McGowan's eyes twinkled. "I'd be glad to. But if you think this isn't serious, study history. For instance, if a Nigra buys his woman a washing machine— watch him, he's dangerous! And if he gets her a clothes dryer and a dishwasher— put that Nigra under the jail for trying to undercut our American way of life. You all can smile if you want to but things like that are most political. In fact, there are few things in this world as political as a black Nigra woman owning her own washing machine.

"Now don't laugh about it. You Yankees must remember that the Industrial Revolution was *revolutionary*, because if y'all don't the Nigra does, and he never stops scheming to make it more so. So verily verily I say unto you Yankees: Watch the Nigra who owns more than one T.V. because he's getting too ambitious and that's bound to lead him into politics. What's more, if you allow the Nigra to see Indians killing white folks week after week—which is another Yankee mistake—he's apt to go bad and the next thing you know he's learning about that Nehru, Nasser, and those Mau-Maus and that's most politically unwise. It doesn't matter that the Indians are always defeated because the Nigra has the feeling deep down that *he* can win. After all, Nigras are Southern too.

"And I'll tell you something else: If his woman or his gal chillun come up wearing blonde wigs, or if they dye their kinky Nigra hair red, you might think it amusing but I know that those Nigra women are being defiantly political. On the other hand, if they *stop* straightening their hair in the old Southern darky tradition and start wearing it short and natural like those African Nigras—right there you have you a bunch of homegrown Nigras who're on the way to being hopelessly contaminated. Those Nigras are sweating and breathing politics. Call Edgar Hoover!

"Watch the papers the Nigra reads, especially if you see him subscribing to the *Wall Street Journal* or the *New York Times*. Watch him closely if he gets interested in the stock market. Because such a Nigra is power hungry and the next thing you know he'll want to vote and run for public office...."

"There," Wiggins said, "that's what really worries you, isn't it?"

McGowan shook his head.

"I wouldn't say that. Although I'll admit that between a Nigra making big money and getting the vote, money is the lesser evil. A Nigra millionaire—once you can stomach the idea—is a pretty safe Nigra. Because if the old saying is still true that there's nothing more timid than a million bucks, then a million *Nigra* bucks are bound to be ten times as afraid. So don't worry about the Nigra millionaire; he's just a Nigra with more money than he knows how to spend. Ever hear of one endowing a college or building a library, setting up a scientific laboratory? Hell no!"

"I'm glad to learn that there's at least *something* about the Negro which isn't political," Thompson said.

"There is, but not too much," McGowan said. "Because the Nigra is a *political* animal. He came out of Africa that way. He makes politics the same way a dirt dauber makes mud houses or a beaver builds dams. So watch his environment. If you see his woman putting up pictures on the wall—regard her with suspicion because she's liable to break out in a *rash* of politics.

"If a Nigra joins the Book-of-the-Month Club or the Great Books program—investigate him. Because when a Nigra gets hold to such deals they become more political than *Das Kapital* and the Communist Manifesto put together. There was a time when everybody thought that the Bible was the only book that a Nigra should be allowed to read, but now I be damned if he hasn't even made the Good Book political.

"So I counsel you to watch your educated Nigra. If he reads Bill Shakespeare, that's all right because no Nigra who ever lived would know how to apply the Bard—not even that big, stupid buck Nigra, Othello, who was so dumb that when his poor, dear, sweet little wife, Desdemona, dropped her kotex in the wrong place and he heard about it, right away he thinks in his ignorant Nigra fashion that she's allowed somebody to tamper with her and he lets that nasty Italian bastard—what's his name—confuse him and agitate him into taking her life. Poor little thing. No sir, no Nigra born has ever been up to dealing with Bill Shakespeare. But if you catch you a Nigra reading that lowdown, Nigra-loving Bill Faulkner and *liking* him, there you have you a politically dangerous, integrationist Nigra!"

"Why do you specify his *liking* what he reads?" Thompson said.

"That's the kind of question for a Yankee to ask, not you; because you're suppose to know that any sensible Nigra would get scaird spitless reading what that fellow Faulkner writes. He's more dangerous to our tradition than a bulldozer.

"But now let's look into another area. You want to watch what the Nigra eats because it has been established that some Nigra foods are political while others are not. And it's a proven fact that the moment the Nigra changes his diet he gets dissatisfied and restless. So watch what he eats. Fat meat, cornbread, lima beans, ham hocks, chitterlings, watermelon, blackeyed peas, molasses, collard greens, buttermilk and clabber, neckbones and red beans and rice, hominy, both grit and lye hominy—these are traditional foods and healthy for the Nigra and *usually*— and I stress the *usually*—not political..."

"What about chicken," Larkin said, "you overlooked chicken."

"Chicken is no problem," McGowan said. "It's traditional and harmless in the political sense—unless, of course, a wrong-headed political Nigra is caught stealing one. And even so, there's nothing necessarily political about a Nigra stealing a chicken. In fact, down South we agree that a Nigra's suppose to steal him a chicken every now and then and the only crime involved is in his getting caught.

"But," McGowan said, holding up his hand and allowing it to slap the table, *Pow!* "*lobster* is out!"

Wiggins sputtered over his drink. "Oh Lord," he said. "Oh Lord protect us!"

"Gentlemen, I tell you truly; lobster on a Nigra's table is political as hell. Lobster gives him false courage. It puts rocks in his Nigra jaws and wild ideas in his Nigra brain. In short, lobster, any kind of lobster, broiled, boiled, fried, fradiavalloed—serve it anyway you damn please—lobster simply messes a Nigra *up*. If the price of lobster ever hits bottom this country will have bad trouble.

"And watch the rascal if he develops a taste for T-bone steaks, cornish hens, sweetbreads, calves liver (although pig liver is traditional and O.K.), parsnips, artichokes, venison, or quiche lorraine—he's been under bad influences and getting political again. Therefore it's a good idea to watch what he does with traditional foods. For instance, if he starts to baking his pigs feet in cheese cloth instead of boiling them naked in the Southern Nigra fashion—right there you have a potentially bad Nigra on your hands.

"And don't overlook the political implications of a Nigra eating too much Chinese, Japanese or Jewish food. Call the F.B.I. if you catch him buying French wines, German beer or drinks like Aquavit or Pernod. One time down in New Orleans a Nigra drank a glass of that Pernod and went straight down to the courthouse and cussed out the judge, a distinguished Cayjun, in French! Nigras who drink such liquors have jumped the reservation and are out to ruin this nation.

"Scotch whiskey is just as bad. A Nigra doesn't even have to have heard about Bonny Prince Charlie, but let him start drinking Scotch whiskey and he swears he's George Washington's great-great-grandson and the rightful head of the United States Government. And not only that, a Nigra who switches to Scotch after being brought up on good corn and bourbon is putting on airs, has forgotten his place and is in implicit rebellion. Besides, have you ever considered what would happen to our liquor industry if all the Nigras switched to drinking Scotch? A calamity! a catastrophe!"

McGowan leaned forward, lowering his voice confidentially, his eyes intense.

"At this point I want to get on to other aspects of the subject but before I do let me remark on one of the meanest, lowdownest forms of Nigra politics I have observed, and one which I mention among a bunch of gentlemen only with the greatest reluctance. That's when a sneaky, ornery, smart-alecky Nigra stands up in a crowd of peaceful, well-meaning white folks, who've gathered together in a public place to see Justice done, and that Nigra ups and breaks wind!

"I was attending a murder trial once and just as the judge was charging the jury, some politically subversive Nigra standing way back in the rear of the courtroom—because that's *exactly* where it came from—he let loose, and gentlemen, all at once the courthouse is in an uproar. Folks are standing up protesting and complaining, ladies are fanning themselves and fainting and the flabber-gasted judge is fairly beating his gavel to a frazzle ordering the windows thrown open and the courtroom cleared. It was simply what you call a *mess.* And in all that disruptive atmosphere the poor jury gets so confused that not only is the case thrown out of court but the guilty Nigra standing trial goes scot free! And would you believe it, that nasty rascal didn't even have himself a lawyer!"

"The hell you say!" Wiggins roared.

"It's sad, gentlemen," McGowan said as we sputtered for breath, "but it's true. You simply have to be constantly alert and vigilant against Nigra politics be-cause it can break out in a thousand forms. For instance, when you find a Nigra boy looking at these so-called 'girlie' magazines that flagrantly display naked white womanhood—which is something else you Yankees are responsible for—whip his head. Because when a Nigra starts looking at that type magazine he's long gone along the road laid down by those Japs who broke the white man's power in Asia by ordering their soldiers to sleep with every white trash whore gal they could lay their filthy yalla hands on. In the eyes of a Nigra boy all such photographs and cartoons become insidiously political ..."

"Oh come now," someone said.

"You wonder why?" McGowan thrust forth his jaw, his eyes burning. "Because they undermine the white man's mastery, and over-expose the white woman's mystery; that's why. They show the buck Nigra everything we've been working three hundred years to keep concealed. You have to remember that those renais-sance fellows had nothing on the American Nigra except power! With him even *poon* tang is a political instrument! So you think about it.

"Now Thompson here was talking about our not having any 'forms' through which we can see what the Nigra is up to politically and I've been demonstrat-ing that he's mistaken. But he's right to the extent that the Nigra hasn't devel-oped any forms of his own. He's just copied the white man and twisted what he copied to fit the Nigra taste. But he does have his own Nigra church, and his own Nigra religion, and the point I want to make is that he gets *political* according to his religion. Did you ever hear that explained before?"

"*I* haven't," I said.

"I know it. None of you have; so I'll go on and tell you. Baptist Nigras and Methodist Nigras and Holy Roller Nigras are O.K. Even Seven Day Adventist Nigras are all right—even though they're a bit strange even to other Nigras. All these Nigra religions are O.K. But you have got to watch the Nigra who changes *from* Baptist *to* Episcopalian *or* Catholic. Because that is a Nigra who has gone ambitious and turned his back on the South. And make no mistake, that Nigra isn't searching for God, no siree; he's looking for a political scantling to head-whip you with.

"And watch the young Nigra who joins up with Father Divine. It's not the same as when a pore old-fashioned Nigra who's lost in the North gets homesick for the South and joins up; the young one is out to undermine society and is probably staying up nights scheming and praying and trying to get God on the Nigra side. Same thing when a Nigra becomes a Jew—who the hell ever heard of one of our *good* Nigras joining up with the Jews? When a Nigra does that he's political, subversive, unruly and probably over-sexed—even for a Nigra!

"Now what are some of the political aspects of the Nigra here in D.C.? Well, around here things are so out of hand, mongrelized and confused that I don't know where to begin, but here are a few manifestations: Nigras visiting white folks; walking or riding along the streets with white women; visiting the Congress; hanging around Abe Lincoln's monument; visiting white churches; carrying picket signs; sending delegations to see the President; carrying briefcases with real papers in them; Nigras wearing homburg hats and Chesterfield overcoats; hiring uniformed chauffeurs, especially if the chauffeur is white. All these things are political, because the Nigra who does them is dying to become a diplomat so that he can get assigned abroad from where he aims to monkey with our sovereign states rights.

"To these add those Nigras from Georgia and Mississippi who turn up wearing those African robes and turbans in an effort to break into white society and get closer to white folks. Gentlemen, there's nothing worse or more political than a Nigra who denies the United States of America because that is a Nigra who has not only turned his back on his mammy and pappy but has denied the South!

"Here are some other forms of Nigra politics which y'all have over-looked: these young buck Nigras going around wearing berets, beards and tennis shoes in the wintertime and whose britches are so doggone tight that they look like they're 'bout to bust out of them. They're not the same as the white boys who dress that way, they're politically dangerous and it's worse, in the long run, than letting a bunch of Nigras run around the Capital carrying loaded pistols. A law ought to be passed before something serious occurs.

"And be on watch for your quiet Nigra. Be very careful of the Nigra who's too quiet when other loud-mouthed Nigras—who are safe Nigras—are out sassing white folks on the street corners and in the Yankee press and over the Yankee radio and T.V. Never mind the loudmouths, they're like the little fyce dogs that bark at you when you approach the big gate and then, when you walk into the yard they run to lick your hand. Throw them a bone. But keep your eye on the quiet Nigra who watches every move the white man makes and studies it, because he's probably trying to think up a theory and a strategy and tactic to subvert something...."

"But go back to the automobile," Wiggins said. "My father-in-law is a dealer and I think he needs instruction."

"I'm glad you reminded me," McGowan said. "Now I've told you about those little foreign cars but there's more to the political significance of Nigras and autos. Cadillacs *used* to be O.K. but after what that Nigra did today on Senator Sunraider's lawn, I'm not so positive. That doggone Nigra was trying to politicalize the Cadillac! Which proves again what I say about everything the Nigra does being potentially political. But once you grasp this fact you also have to watch the Nigra who doesn't want a Cadillac, because he can stand a heap of political analysis.

"And pay close attention to the Nigra who has the money to buy one but picks an Imperial instead. Likewise the Nigras who love English autos. Watch all Nigras who pick Jaguars, Humbers, and if you ever hear of one, Rolls Royces. Likewise those who go around bragging about the Nigra vote electing the president of the United States. Such Nigras are playing dirty politics even though they might not be able to vote themselves. Yes, and watch the Nigra who comes telling a white man about the Nigra's 'gross yearly income,' because there you have an arrogant, biggety Nigra who is right up in your face talking open politics and who thinks you don't recognize it. Unless of course, you're convinced that the Nigra is really trying to tell you that he knows how you and him can make some quick money. In such a case the Nigra is just trying to make a little hustle for himself, so make a deal with him and don't worry about it because that Nigra doesn't give a damn about anybody or anything except himself—while the other type is trying to intimidate you.

"Then there's the Nigra who reads the Constitution and the law books and *broods* over them. That's one of the most political types there is. And like unto him is the Nigra who scratches his behind when he talks to a white man instead of scratching his head in the traditional Southern Nigra manner—because even where the Nigra *scratches* is political!

"But gentlemen, let me hasten to say after this very brief and inadequate catalogue of Nigra political deviousness, that to my considerable knowledge no Nigra has ever even *thought* about assassinating anybody. And I'll tell y'all why: It was bred out of him years ago!"

Even as I laughed I watched the conflicting expressions moving back and forth across McGowan's broad face. It looked as though he wanted desperately to grin but like a postage stamp which had become too wet, the grin kept sliding in and out of position. And I in turn became agitated. My laughter—it was really hysteria—was painful. For I realized that McGowan was obsessed by history to the point of nightmare. He had the dark man confined in a package and this was the way he carried him everywhere, saw him in everything. But now, laughing, I realized that I envied McGowan and admitted to myself with a twinge of embarrassment, that some of the things he said were not only amusing but true. And perhaps the truth lay precisely in their being seen humorously. For McGowan said things about Negroes with absolute conviction which I dared not even think. Could it be that he was more honest than I, that his free expression of his feelings, his prejudices, made him freer than I? Could it be that his freedom to say what he felt about all that Sam the waiter symbolized actually made him freer than I? Suddenly I despised his power to make me feel buried fears and possibilities, his power to define so much of the reality in which I lived and which I seldom bothered to think about.

And was it possible that the main object of McGowan's passion was really an idea, the idea of a non-existent past rather than a living people?

"Yes, gentlemen," McGowan was saying. "The only way to protect yourself from the Nigra is to master politics and that you Yankees have never done because y'all have never studied the Nigra."

Across the room I watched Sam, his hands held behind him, smiling as he chatted pleasantly with a white-haired old gentleman. Were there Negroes like McGowan, I wondered. And what would they say about me? How completely did I, a liberal, ex-radical, northerner, dominate Sam's sense of life, his idea of politics? Absolutely, or not at all? Was he, Sam, prevented by some piety from confronting me in a humorous manner, as my habit of mind, formed during the radical Thirties, prevented me from confronting him; or did he, as some of my friends suspected, regard all whites through the streaming eyes and aching muscles of one continuous, though imperceptible and inaudible, belly laugh? *What the hell,* I thought, *is Sam's last name?*

JUNETEENTH

QUARTERLY REVIEW OF LITERATURE 4 (1965): 262–76

No, the wounded man thought, Oh no! Get back to that; back to a bunch of old-fashioned Negroes celebrating an illusion of emancipation, and getting it mixed up with the Resurrection, minstrel shows and vaudeville routines? Back to that tent in the clearing surrounded by trees, that bowl-shaped impression in the earth beneath the pines?... Lord, it hurts. Lordless and without loyalty, it hurts. Wordless, it hurts. Here and especially here. Still I see it after all the roving years and flickering scenes: Twin lecterns on opposite ends of the platform, behind one of which I stood on a wide box, leaning forward to grasp the lectern's edge. Back. Daddy Hickman at the other. Back to the first day of that week of celebration. Juneteenth. Hot, dusty. Hot with faces shining with sweat and the hair of the young dudes metallic with grease and straightening irons. Back to that? He was not so heavy then, but big with the quick energy of a fighting bull and still kept the battered silver trombone on top of the piano, where at the climax of a sermon he could reach for it and stand blowing tones that sounded like his own voice amplified; persuading, denouncing, rejoicing—moving beyond words back to the undifferentiated cry. In strange towns and cities the jazz musicians were always around him. Jazz. What was jazz and what religion back there? Ah yes, yes, I loved him. Everyone did, deep down. Like a great, kindly, daddy bear along the streets, my hand lost in his huge paw. Carrying me on his shoulder so that I could touch the leaves of the trees as we passed. The true father, but black, black. Was he a charlatan—am I—or simply as resourceful in my fashion. Did he know himself, or care? Back to the problem of all that. Must I go back to the beginning when only he knows the start...?

Juneteenth and him leaning across the lectern, resting there looking into their faces with a great smile, and then looking over to me to make sure that I had not forgotten my part, winking his big red-rimmed eye at me. And the women looking back and forth from him to me with that bright, bird-like adoration in their faces; their heads cocked to one side. And him beginning:

On this God-given day, brothers and sisters, when we have come together to praise God and celebrate our oneness, our slipping off the chains, let's us begin this week of worship by taking a look at the ledger. Let us, on this day of deliverance, take a look at the figures writ on our bodies and on the living tablet of our heart. The Hebrew children have their Passover so that they can keep their history alive in their memories—so let us take one more page from their book and, on this great day of deliverance, on this day of emancipation, let's us tell ourselves our story....

Pausing, grinning down.... Nobody else is interested in it anyway, so let us enjoy it ourselves, yes, and learn from it.

And thank God for it. Now let's not be too solemn about it either, because this here's a happy occasion. Rev. Bliss over there is going to take the part of the younger generation, and I'll try to tell it as it's been told to me. Just look at him over there, he's ready and raring to go—because he knows that a true preacher is a kind of educator, and that we have got to know our story before we can truly understand God's blessings and how far we have still got to go. Now you've heard him, so you know that he can preach.

Amen! They all responded and I looked preacher-faced into their shining eyes, preparing my piccolo voice to support his baritone sound.

Amen is right, he said. So here we are, five thousand strong, come together on this day of celebration. Why? We just didn't happen. We're here and that is an undeniable fact—but how come we're here? How and why here in these woods that used to be such a long way from town? What about it, Rev. Bliss, is that a suitable question on which to start?

God, bless you, Rev. Hickman, I think that's just the place we have to start. We of the younger generation are still ignorant about these things. So please, sir, tell us just how we came to be here in our present condition and in this land....

Not back to that me, not to that six-seven year old ventriloquist's dummy dressed in a white evening suit. Not to that charlatan born—must I have no charity for me?....

Was it an act of God, Rev. Hickman, or an act of man.... Not to that puppet with a memory like a piece of flypaper....

We came, amen, Rev. Bliss, sisters and brothers, as an act of God, but through—I said through, an act of cruel, ungodly man.

An act of almighty God, *my treble echo sounded,* but through the hands of cruel man.

Amen, Rev. Bliss, that's how it happened. It was, as I understand it, a cruel calamity laced up with a blessing—or maybe a blessing laced up with a calamity....

Laced up with a blessing, Rev. Hickman? We understand you partially because you have taught us that God's sword is a two-edged sword. But would you please tell us of the younger generation just why it was a blessing?

It was a blessing, brothers and sisters, because out of all the pain and the suffering, out of the night of storm, we found the Word of God.

So here we found the Word. Amen, so now we are here. But where did we come from, Daddy Hickman?

We come here out of Africa, son; out of Africa.

Africa? Way over across the ocean? The black land? Where the elephants and monkeys and the lions and tigers are?

Yes, Rev. Bliss, the jungle land. Some of us have fair skins like you, but out of Africa too.

Out of Africa truly, sir?

Out of the ravaged mama of the black man, son.

Lord, thou hast taken us out of Africa...

Amen, out of our familar darkness. Africa. They brought us here from all over Africa, Rev. Bliss. And some were the sons and daughters of heathen kings...

Some were kings, Daddy Hickman? Have we of the younger generation heard you correctly? Some were kin to kings? Real kings?

Amen! I'm told that some were the sons and the daughters of kings...

...Of Kings!...

And some were the sons and daughters of warriors...

...Of warriors...

Of fierce warriors. And some were the sons and the daughters of farmers...

Of African farmers...

...And some of musicians...

...Musicians...

And some were the sons and daughters of weapon makers and of smelters of brass and iron...

But didn't they have judges, Rev. Hickman? And weren't there any preachers of the word of God?

Some were judges but none were preachers of the word of God, Rev. Bliss. For we come out of heathen Africa...

Heathen Africa?

Out of heathen Africa. Let's tell this thing true; because the truth is the light. And they brought us here in chains...

In chains, son; in iron chains...

From half-a-world away, they brought us...

In chains and in boats that the history tells us weren't fit for pigs—because pigs cost too much money to be allowed to waste and die as we did. But they stole us and brought us in boats which I'm told could move like the swiftest birds of prey, and which filled the great trade winds with the stench of our dying and their crime...

What a crime! Tell us why, Rev. Hickman...

It was a crime, Rev. Bliss, brothers and sisters, like the fall of proud Lucifer from Paradise.

But why, Daddy Hickman? You have taught us of the progressive younger generation to ask why. So we want to know how come it was a crime?

Because, Rev. Bliss, this was a country dedicated to the principles of almighty God. That Mayflower boat that you hear so much about Thanksgiving Day was a *Christian* ship—Amen! Yes, and those many-named floating coffins we came here in were Christian too. They had turned traitor to the God who set them free from Europe's tyrant kings. Because, God have mercy on them, no sooner than they got free enough to breathe themselves, they set out to bow us down...

They made our Lord shed tears!

Amen! Rev. Bliss, amen. God must have wept like Jesus. Poor Jonah went down into the belly of the whale, but compared to our journey his was like a trip to paradise on a silvery cloud.

Worse than old Jonah, Rev. Hickman?

Worse than Jonah slicked all over with whale puke and gasping on the shore. We went down into hell on those floating coffins and don't you youngsters forget it! Mothers and babies, men and women, the living and the dead and the dying—all chained together. And yet, praise God, most of us arrived here in this land. The strongest came through. Thank God, and we arrived and that's why we're here today. Does that answer the question, Rev. Bliss?

Amen, Daddy Hickman, amen. But now the younger generation would like to know what they did to us when they got us here. What happened then?

They brought us up onto this land in chains...

...In chains...

...And they marched us into the swamps...

...Into the fever swamps, they marched us...

And they set us to work draining the swampland and toiling in the sun...

...They set us to toiling...

They took the white fleece of the cotton and the sweetness of the sugar cane and made them bitter and bloody with our toil...And they treated us like one great unhuman animal without any face...

Without a *face,* Rev. Hickman?

Without personality, without names, Rev. Bliss, we were made into nobody and not even *mister* nobody either, just nobody. They left us without names. Without choice. Without the right to do or not to do, to be or not to be...

You mean without faces and without eyes? We were eyeless like Samson in Gaza? Is that the way, Rev. Hickman?

Amen, Rev. Bliss, like baldheaded Samson before that nameless little lad like you came as the Good Book tells us and led him to the pillars whereupon the big house stood—Oh, you little black boys, and oh, you little brown girls, you're going to shake the building down! And then, Oh, how you will build in the name of the Lord!

Yes Reverend Bliss, we were eyeless like unhappy Samson among the Philistines—and worse...

And WORSE?

Worse, Rev. Bliss, because they chopped us up into little bitty pieces like a farmer when he cuts up a potato. And they scattered us around the land. All the way from Kentucky to Florida; from Louisiana to Texas; from Missouri all the way down the great Mississippi to the Gulf. They scattered us around this land.

How now, Daddy Hickman? You speak in parables which we of the younger generation don't clearly understand. How do you mean, they scattered us?

Like seed, Rev. Bliss; they scattered us just like a dope-fiend farmer planting a field with dragon teeth!

Tell us about it, Daddy Hickman.

They cut out our tongues...

... They left us speechless...

... They cut out our tongues...

... Lord, they left us without words...

... Amen! They scattered our tongues in this land like seed...

... And left us without language...

... They took away our talking drums...

... Drums that talked, Daddy Hickman? Tell us about those talking drums...

Drums that talked like a telegraph. Drums that could reach across the country like a church bell sound. Drums that told the news almost before it happened! Drums that spoke with big voices like big men! Drums like a conscience and a deep heart-beat that knew right from wrong. Drums that told glad tidings! Drums that sent the news of trouble speeding home! Drums that told us *our* time and told us where we were...

Those were some drums, Rev. Hickman...

... Yes and they took those drums away...

Away, Amen! Away! And they took away our heathen dances...

... They left us drumless and they left us danceless...

Ah yes, they burnt up our talking drums and our dancing drums...

... Drums...

... And they scattered the ashes...

... Ah, Aaaaaah! Eyeless, tongueless, drumless, danceless, ashes...

And a worst devastation was yet to come, Lord God!

Tell us, Reveren Hickman. Blow on your righteous horn!

Ah, but Rev. Bliss, in those days we didn't have any horns...

No *horns?* Hear him!

And we had no songs...

...No songs...

...And we had no...

...Count it on your fingers, see what cruel man has done...

Amen, Rev. Bliss, lead them...

We were eyeless, tongueless, drumless, danceless, hornless, songless!

All true, Rev. Bliss. No eyes to see. No tongue to speak or taste. No drums to raise the spirits and wake up our memories. No dance to stir the rhythm that makes life move. No songs to give praise and prayers to God!

We were truly in the dark, my young brothern and sisteren. Eyeless, earless, tongueless, drumless, danceless, songless, hornless, soundless...

And worse to come!

...And worse to come...

Tell us, Rev. Hickman. But not too fast so that we of the younger generation can gather up our strength to face it. So that we may listen and not become discouraged!

I said, Rev. Bliss, brothers and sisters, that they snatched us out of the loins of Africa. I said that they took us from our mammys and pappys and from our sisters and brothers. I said that they scattered us around this land...

...And we, let's count it again, brothers and sisters; let's add it up. Eyeless, tongueless, drumless, danceless, songless, hornless, soundless, sightless, dayless, nightless, wrongless, rightless, motherless, fatherless—scattered.

Yes, Rev. Bliss, they scattered us around like seed...

...Like seed...

...Like seed, that's been flung broadcast on unplowed ground...

Ho, chant it with me, my young brothers and sisters! Eyeless, tongueless, drumless, danceless, songless, hornless, soundless, sightless, wrongless, rightless, motherless, fatherless, brotherless, sisterless, powerless...

Amen! But though they took us like a great black giant that had been chopped up into little pieces and the pieces buried; though they deprived us of our heritage among strange scenes in strange weather; divided and divided and divided us again like a gambler shuffling and cutting a deck of cards. Although we were ground down, smashed into little pieces; spat upon, stamped upon, cursed and buried, and our memory of Africa ground down into powder and blown on the winds of foggy forgetfulness...

...Amen, Daddy Hickman! Abused and without shoes, pounded down and ground like grains of sand on the shores of the sea...

...Amen! And God—Count it, Rev. Bliss...

...Left eyeless, earless, noseless, throatless, teethless, tongueless, handless, feetless, armless, wrongless, rightless, harmless, drumless, danceless, songless, hornless, soundless, sightless, wrongless, rightless, motherless, fatherless, sisterless, brotherless, plowless, muleless, foodless, mindless—and Godless, Rev. Hickman, did you say Godless?

...At first, Rev. Bliss, he said, his trombone entering his voice, broad, somber and noble. At first. Ah, but though divided and scattered, ground down and battered into the earth like a spike being pounded by a ten pound sledge, we were on the ground and in the earth and the earth was red and black like the earth of Africa. And as we moldered underground we were mixed with this land. We liked it. It fitted us fine. It was in us and we were in it. And then—praise God— deep in the ground, deep in the womb of this land, we began to stir!

Praise God!

At last, Lord, at last.

Amen!

Oh the truth, Lord, it tastes so sweet!

What was it like then, Rev. Bliss? You read the scriptures, so tell us. Give us a word.

WE WERE LIKE THE VALLEY OF DRY BONES!

Amen. Like the Valley of Dry Bones in Ezekiel's dream. Hoooh! We lay scattered in the ground for a long dry season. And the winds blew and the sun blazed down and the rains came and went and we were dead. Lord, we were dead! Except...Except...

...Except what, Rev. Hickman?

Except for one nerve left from our ear...

Listen to him!

And one nerve in the soles of our feet...

...Just watch me point it out, brothers and sisters...

Amen, Bliss, you point it out...and one nerve left from the throat...

...From our throat—right *here*!

...Teeth...

...From our teeth, one from all thirty-two of them...

...Tongue...

...Tongueless...

...And another nerve left from our heart...

...Yes, from our heart...

...And another left from our eyes and one from our hands and arms and legs and another from our stones...

Amen, Hold it right there, Rev. Bliss...

...All stirring in the ground...

...Amen, stirring, and right there in the midst of all our death and buriedness, the voice of God spoke down the Word...

...Crying Do! I said, Do! Crying Doooo—

These dry bones live?

He said, Son of Man . . . under the ground, Ha! Heatless beneath the roots of plants and trees . . . Son of man, do . . .

I said, Do . . .

. . . I said Do, Son of Man, Doooooo!—

These dry bones live?

Amen! And we heard and rose up. Because in all their blasting they could not blast away one solitary vibration of God's true word . . . We heard it down among the roots and among the rocks. We heard it in the sand and in the clay. We heard it in the falling rain and in the rising sun. On the high ground and in the gullies. We heard it lying moldering and corrupted in the earth. We heard it sounding like a bugle call to wake up the dead. Crying, Dooooo! Ay, do these dry bones live!

And did our dry bones live, Daddy Hickman?

Ah, we sprang together and walked around. All clacking together and clicking into place. All moving in time! Do! I said, Dooooo—these dry bones live!

And now strutting in my white tails, across the platform, filled with the power almost to dancing.

Shouting, Amen, Daddy Hickman, is this the way we walked?

Oh we walked through Jerusalem, just like John—That's it, Rev. Bliss, walk! Show them how we walked!

Was this the way?

That's the way. Now walk on back. Lift your knees! Swing your arms! Make your coat tails fly! Walk! And him strutting me three times around the pulpit across the platform and back. Ah, yes! And then his voice deep and exultant: And if they ask you in the city why we praise the Lord with bass drums and brass trombones tell them we were rebirthed dancing, we were rebirthed crying affirmation of the Word, quickening our transcended flesh.

Amen!

Oh, Rev. Bliss, we stamped our feet at the trumpet's sound and we clapped our hands, ah, in joy! And we moved, yes, together in a dance, amen! Because we had received a new song in a new land and been resurrected by the Word and Will of God!

Amen! . . .

. . . —We were rebirthed from the earth of this land and revivified by the Word. So now we had a new language and a brand new song to put flesh on our bones . . .

New teeth, new tongue, new word, new song!

We had a new name and a new blood, and we had a new task . . .

Tell us about it, Reveren Hickman . . .

We had to take the Word for bread and meat. We had to take the Word for food and shelter. We had to use the Word as a rock to build up a whole new nation, cause to tell it true, we were born again in chains of steel. Yes, and chains of ignorance. And all we knew was the spirit of the word. We had no schools. We owned no tools; no cabins, no churches, not even our own bodies.

We were chained, young brothers, in steel. We were chained, young sisters, in ignorance. We were school-less, tool-less, cabinless—owned ...

Amen, Reveren Bliss. We were owned and faced with the awe-inspiring labor of transforming God's word into a lantern so that in the darkness we'd know where we were. Oh God hasn't been easy with us because He always plans for the loooong haul. He's looking far ahead and this time He wants a well-tested people to work his will. He wants some sharp-eyed, quick-minded, generous-hearted people to give names to the things of this world and to its values. He's tired of untempered tools and half-blind masons! Therefore, He's going to keep on testing us against the rocks and in the fires. He's going to heat us till we almost melt and then He's going to plunge us into the ice-cold water. And each time we come out we'll be blue and as tough as cold-blue steel! Ah yes! He means for us to be a new kind of human. Maybe we won't be that people but we'll be a part of that people, we'll be an element in them, Amen! He wants us limber as willow switches and he wants us tough as whit leather, so that when we have to bend, we can bend and snap back into place. He's going to throw bolts of lightning to blast us so that we'll have good foot work and lightning-fast minds. He'll drive us hither and yon around this land and make us run the gauntlet of hard times and tribulations, misunderstanding and abuse. And some will pity you and some will despise you. And some will try to use you and change you. And some will deny you and try to deal you out of the game. And sometimes you'll feel so bad that you'll wish you could die. But it's all the pressure of God. He's giving you a will and He wants you to use it. He's giving you brains and he wants you to train them lean and hard so that you can overcome all the obstacles. Educate your minds! Make do with what you have so as to get what you need! Learn to look at what *you* see and not what somebody tells you is true. Pay lip-service to Caesar if you have to, but put your trust in God. Because nobody has a patent on truth or a copyright on the best way to live and serve almighty God. Learn from what we've lived. Remember that when the labor's back-breaking and the boss man's mean our singing can lift us up. That it can strengthen us and make his meanness but the flyspeck irritation of an empty man. Roll with the blow like ole Jack Johnson. Dance on out of his way like Williams and Walker. Keep to the rhythm and you'll keep to life. God's time is long; and all short-haul horses shall be like horses on a merry-go-round. Keep, keep, keep to the rhythm and you won't get weary. Keep to the rhythm and you won't get lost. We're handicapped, amen! Because the Lord wants us strong! We started out with nothing but the Word—just like the others but they've forgot it ... We worked and stood up under hard times and tribulations. We learned patience and to understand Job. Of all the animals, man's the only one not born knowing almost everything he'll ever know. It takes him longer than an elephant to grow up because God didn't mean him to leap to any conclusions, for God himself is in the very process of things. We learned that all blessings come mixed with sorrow and all hardships have a streak of laughter. Life is a streak-a-lean—a—streak-a-fat. Ha, yes! We learned to bounce back and to disregard the prizes of fools. And we must keep on learning. Let them have their fun. Even let them eat humming bird's wings and tell you it's too good for you.—Grits and greens don't turn to ashes in anybody's mouth—How about it, Rev. Eatmore? Amen? Amen! Let everybody say amen. Grits and greens are humble but they make you strong and when the right folks get together to share them they can taste like ambrosia. So draw, so let us draw on our own wells of strength.

Ah yes, so we were reborn, Rev. Bliss. They still had us harnessed, we were still laboring in the fields, but we had a secret and we had a new rhythm...

So tell us about this rhythm, Reveren Hickman.

They had us bound but we had our kind of time, Rev. Bliss. They were on a merry-go-round that they couldn't control but we learned to beat time from the seasons. We learned to make this land and this light and darkness and this weather and their labor fit us like a suit of new underwear. With our new rhythm, amen, but we weren't free and they still kept dividing us. There's many a thousand gone down the river. Mama sold from papa and chillun sold from both. Beaten and abused and without shoes. But we had the Word, now, Rev. Bliss, along with the rhythm. They couldn't divide us now. Because anywhere they dragged us we throbbed in time together. If we got a chance to sing, we sang the same song. If we got a chance to dance, we beat back hard times and tribulations with a clap of our hands and the beat of our feet, and it was the same dance. Oh they come out here sometimes to laugh at our way of praising God. They can laugh but they can't deny us. They can curse and kill us but they can't destroy us all. This land is ours because we come out of it, we bled in it, our tears watered it, we fertilized it with our dead. So the more of us they destroy the more it becomes filled with the spirit of our redemption. They laugh but we know who we are and where we are, but they keep on coming in their millions and they don't know and can't get together.

But tell us, how do we know who we are, Daddy Hickman?

We know where we are by the way we walk. We know where we are by the way we talk. We know where we are by the way we sing. We know where we are by the way we dance. We know where we are by the way we praise the Lord on high. We know where we are because we hear a different tune in our minds and in our hearts. We know who we are because when we make the beat of our rhythm to shape our day the whole land says, Amen! It smiles, Rev. Bliss, and it moves to our time! Don't be ashamed, my brothern! Don't be cowed. Don't throw what you have away! Continue! Remember! Believe! Trust the inner beat that tells us who we are. Trust God and trust life and trust this land that is you! Never mind the laughers, the scoffers, they come around because they can't help themselves. They can deny you but not your sense of life. They hate you because whenever they look into a mirror they fill up with bitter gall. So forget them and most of all don't deny yourselves. They're tied by the short hair to a run-away merry-go-round. They make life a business of struggle and fret, fret and struggle. See who you can hate; see what you can get. But you just keep on inching along like an old inchworm. If you put one and one and one together soon they'll make a million too. There's been a heap of Juneteenths before this one and I tell you there'll be a heap more before we're truly free! Yes! But keep to the rhythm, just keep to the rhythm and keep to the way. Man's plans are but a joke to God. Let those who will despise you, but remember deep down inside yourself that the life we have to lead is but a preparation for other things, it's a discipline, Reveren Bliss, Sisters and Brothers; a discipline through which we may see that which the others are too self-blinded to see. Time will come round when we'll have to be their eyes; time will swing and turn back around. I tell you, time shall swing and spiral back around...

NIGHT-TALK

QUARTERLY REVIEW OF LITERATURE 16 (1969): 317–29

This excerpt from a novel-in-progress (very long in progress) is set in a hospital room located in Washington, D.C., circa 1955, the year the novel was conceived. In it the Senator is passing through alternate periods of lucidity and delirium attending wounds resulting from a gunman's attempt on his life. Hickman, in turn, is weary from the long hours of sleeplessness and emotional strain which have accumulated while he has sought to see the Senator through his ordeal. The men have been separated for many years, and time, conflicts of value, the desire of one to remember nothing and the tendency of the other to remember too much, have rendered communication between them difficult.

Sometimes they actually converse, sometimes the dialogue is illusory and occurs in the isolation of their individual minds, but through it all it is antiphonal in form and an anguished attempt to arrive at the true shape and substance of a sundered past and its meaning.

    R.E.

"...Oh, yes," Hickman said, fanning the Senator's perspiring face, "you were giving us a natural fit! All of a sudden you were playing hooky from the services and hiding from everybody—including me. Why, one time you took off and we had about three hundred folks out looking for you. We searched the streets and the alleys and the playgrounds, the candy stores and the parks and we questioned all the children in the neighborhood—but no Bliss. We even searched the steeple of the church where the revival was being held but that only upset the pigeons and caused even more confusion when somebody knocked against the bell and set it ringing as though there had been a fire or the river was flooding.

"So then we spread out and really started hunting. I had begun to think about going to the police—which we hated to do, considering that they'd probably have made things worse—because, you see, I thought that she—that is, I thought that you might have been kidnapped. In fact, we were already headed along a downtown street when, lo and behold, we look up and see you coming out of a picture house where it was against the law for us to go! Yes, sir, there you were, coming out of there with all those people, blinking your eyes and with your face all screwed up with crying. But thank God you were all right. I was so relieved that I couldn't say a word, and while we stood at the curb watching to see what you would do, Deacon Wilhite turned to me and said, 'Well, 'Lonzo—A.Z.—it looks like Rev. Bliss has gone and made himself an outlaw, but at least we can be thankful that he wasn't stolen into Egypt.'... And that's when you looked up and saw us and tried to run again. I tell you, Bliss, you were giving us quite a time. *Quite* a time...."

Suddenly Hickman's head fell forward, his voice breaking off; and as he slumped in his chair the Senator stirred behind his eyelids, saying, "What? What?" But except for the soft burr of Hickman's breathing it was as though a line had gone dead in the course of an important call.

"What? What?" the Senator said, his face straining toward the huge, shadowy form in the bedside chair. Then came a sudden gasp and Hickman's voice was back again, soft but moving as though there had been no interruption.

"And so," Hickman was saying, "when you started asking me that, I said, Bliss, thy likeness is in the likeness of God, the Father. Because, Reverend Bliss, God's likeness is that of *all* babes. Now for some folks this fact is like a dose of castor oil as bitter as the world, but it's the truth. It's hard and bitter and a compound cathartic to man's pride—which is as big and violent as the whole wide world. Still it gives the faint of heart a pattern and a faith to grow by...."

"And when they ask me, 'Where shall man look for God, the Father?' I say, let him who seeks look into his own *bed*. I say let him look into his own *heart*. I say, let him search his own *loins*. And I say that each man's bedmate is likely to be a mary—No, don't ask me that—is most likely a mary even though she be a magdalene. That's another form of the mystery, Bliss, and it challenges our ability to think. There's always the mystery of the one in the many and the many in one, the you in them and the them in you—Ha! And it mocks your pride, mocks it to the billionth, trillionth power. Yes, Bliss, but it's always present and it's a rebuke to the universe of man's terrible pride and it's the shape and substance of all human truth...."

... Listen, listen! Go back, the Senator tried desperately to say. It was Atlanta! On the side of a passing streetcar, in which smiling, sharp-nosed women in summer dresses talked sedately behind the open grillwork and looked out on the passing scene I saw

her picture moving past, all serene and soulful in the sunlight, and I was swept along beside the moving car until she got away. Soon I was out of breath, but then I followed the gleaming rails, hurrying through crowded streets, past ice cream and melon vendors crying their wares above the backs of ambling horses and past kids on lawns selling lemonade two cents a glass from frosted pitchers, and on until the lawns and houses gave way to buildings in which fancy dicty dummies dressed in fine new clothes showed behind wide panes of shopwindow glass. Then I was in a crowded Saturday afternoon street sweet with the smell of freshly cooked candy and the odor of perfume drifting from the revolving doors of department stores and fruit stands with piles of yellow delicious apples, bananas, coconuts and sweet white seedless grapes—and there, in the middle of a block, I saw her once again. The place was all white and pink and gold, trimmed with rows of blinking lights red, white and blue in the shade; and colored photographs in great metal frames were arranged to either side of a ticket booth with thin square golden bars and all set beneath a canopy encrusted with glowing lights. The fare was a quarter and I felt in my pocket for a dollar bill, moist to my touch as I pulled it out, but I was too afraid to try. Instead I simply looked on a while as boys and girls arrived and reached up to buy their tickets then disappeared inside. I yearned to enter but was afraid. I wasn't ready. I hadn't the nerve. So I moved on past in the crowd. For a while I walked beside a strolling white couple pretending that I was their little boy and that they were taking me to have ice cream before they took me in to see the pictures. They sounded happy and I was enjoying their talk when they turned off and went into a restaurant. It was a large restaurant and through the glass I could see a jolly fat black man cutting slices from a juicy ham. He wore a white chef's cap and jacket with a cloth around his neck and when he saw me he winked as though he knew me and I turned and ran dodging through the sauntering crowd, then slowed to a walk, going back to where she smiled from her metal frame. This time I followed behind a big boy pushing a red and white striped bicycle. A small Confederate flag fluttered from each end of the handlebars on which two rear-view mirrors showed reflecting my face in the crowd, and two shining horns with red rubber bulbs and a row of red glass reflectors ridged along the curve of the rear fender, throwing a dazzled red diamond light, and the racing seat was hung with dangling coon tails. It was keen and I ran around in front and walked backwards a while, watching him roll it. He looked at me and I looked at him but mainly at his bike. A shiny bull with lowered horns gleamed from the end of the front fender, followed by a screaming eagle with outstretched wings and a toy policeman with big flat hands which turned and whirled its arms in the breeze as he guided it by holding one hand on the handlebar and the other on the seat. And on the fork which held the front wheel there was a siren which let out a low howl whenever he pulled the chain to warn the people he was coming. And as it moved the spokes sparkled bright and handsome in the sun. It was keen. I followed him back up the street until we reached the picture show where I stopped and watched him go on. Then I understood why he didn't ride: his rear tire had a flat in it. But I was still afraid so I walked up to the drugstore on the corner and listened a while to some Eskimo pie men in white pants and shoes telling lies about us and the Yankees as they leaned on the handlebars of their wag-

ons, before going back to give it another try. This time I made myself go up to the booth and looked up through the golden bars where the blue eyes looked mildly down at me from beneath white cotton candy bangs. I....

"Bliss?"

Was it Mary? No, here to forget is best. They criticize me, me a senator now, especially Karp who's still out there beating hollow wood to bully rhythms all smug and still making ranks of dead men flee the reality of the shadow upon them, then Who? What cast it? stepping with the fetch to the bank and Geneva with tithes for Israel while ole man Muggin has to keep on bugging his eyes and rolling those bales so tired of living but they refuse to let him die. Who's Karp kidding? Who's kidding Karp? making a fortune in bleaching cream, hair straightener and elevator shoes, buying futures in soy beans, corn and porkers and praising his God but still making step fetch it for the glory of getting but keeping his hands clean, he says. And how do they feel, still detroiting my mother who called me Goodrich Hugh Cuddyear in the light of tent flares then running away and them making black bucks into millejungs and fraud pieces in spectacularmythics on assembly lines? Who'll speak the complicated truth? With them going from pondering to pandering the nation's secret to pandering their pondering? So cast the stone if you must and if you see a ghost rise up, make him bleed. Hell, yes, primitives were right—mirrors do steal souls. So Odysseus plunged that matchstick into Polyphemus' crystal! Here in this country it's change the reel and change the man. Don't look! Don't listen! Don't say and the living is easy! O.K., so they can go fighting the war but soon the down will rise up and break the niggonography and those ghosts who created themselves in the old image won't know why they are what they are and then comes a screaming black bable and white connednation! Who, who, who, boo, are we? Daddy, I say where in the dead place between the shadow there does mothermatermammy—mover so moving on? Where in all the world pile hides?

...but instead of chasing me away this kindly blueyed cotton-headed Georgiagrinder smiled down and said, What is it, little boy? Would you like a ticket? We have some fine features today.

And trembling, I hid behind my face, hoping desperately that the epiderm would hide the corium and corium rind the natural man. Stood there wishing for a red neck and linty head, a certain expression of the eyes. Then she smiled, saying, Why of course you do. And you're lucky today because it's only a quarter and some very very fine *pictures and cartoons....*

I watched her eyes, large and lucid behind the lenses, then tip-toed and reached, placing my dollar bill through the golden bars of the ticket booth.

My, my! but we're rich today. Aren't we now, she said.

No, mam, I said, 'cause it's only a dollar.

And she said, That's true and a dollar doesn't go very far these days. But I'm sure you'll get plenty more because you're learning about such things so early. So live while you may, I say, and let the rosebuds bloom tomorrow—ha! ha! She pushed the pink ticket through the bars so I could reach it.

Now wait for your change, she said. Two whole quarters, two dimes and a nickle—which still leaves you pretty rich for a man of your years, I'd say.

Yes, mam. Thank you, mam, I said.

She shook her blonde head and smiled. We have some nice fresh buttered popcorn just inside, she said, you might want to try some. It's very good.

Yes, mam, thank you mam, I said, knotting the change in the corner of my handkerchief and hurrying behind the red velvet barrier-rope. Then I was stepping over two blue naked men with widespread wings who were flying on the white tiled lobby floor, only the smaller one was falling into the white tile water, and approached the tall man who took the tickets. He wore a jaunty, square-visored cap and a blue uniform with spats and I saw him look down at me and look away disgusted, making me afraid. He stood stiff like a soldier and something was wrong with his eyes. I crossed my fingers. I didn't have a hat to spit in. Then suddenly he looked down again and smirked and though afraid I read him true. You're not a man, I thought, only a big boy. You're just a big old freckly face....

> *Peckerwood, peckerwood,*
> *You can't see me!*
> *You're just a red head gingerbread*
> *Five cents a cabbage head—*

Alright, kid, he said, where's your maw?

Sir?

You heard me, Ezra. I'm not supposed to let you little snots in here without your folks. So come on now, Clyde, where's ya' maw?

Watching his face, I pointed into the dark, thinking I ain't your Clyde and I ain't your Ezra, I'm Bliss... She's in there, I said. She's waiting for me.

She's in dere, he mimicked me, his eyes crossing upon my face and then quickly away. You wouldn't kid me would you, Ezra, he said.

Oh, no, sir, I said, she's really and truly in there like I said.

Then in the dark I could hear the soaring of horns and laughter.

Oh, yeah—he began and broke off, holding down his white-gloved hand for silence. Out on the walk some girls in white silk stockings and pastel dresses came to a giggling halt before the billboards, looking at the faces and going 'Oooh! AAAh!'

Well did Ah evuh wet dream of Jeannie and her cawn sulk hair, he said, snapping his black bow tie hard against his stiff white collar. He stood back in his knees, like Deacon Wilhite, and then drummed his fingers on the edge of the ticket hopper and grinned. Inside the music surged and flared.

Hold it a minit, Clyde, he said, Hold it! looking out at the giggling girls.

Sir? I said, Sir?

Hush, son, he said and pray you'll understand it better bye'n bye, cause right now I got me some other fish to fry. You'all come on in, gals, he said in a low, signifying voice. Come on in, you sweet misstreaters, you fluffy teasers. I got me a special show for ever one of you lily-white dewy-delled mama's gals. Yes, sir! You chickens come to pappa, cause I got the cawn right here on the evuh-lovin' cob!

Here mister, I said . . .

He rubbed his white gloves together, watching the girls. What's that you say, kid?

I say my mamma's in there waiting for me, I said.

He waved his hand at me. Quiet, son, quiet! he said.

Then the girls moved again. Oh, hell, he said, watching them as they turned on their toes, their skirts swirling as they flounced away, laughing and tossing their hair.

Then he was looking down again.

Clyde, he said, what's your mama's name?

Her name's 'Mamma'—I mean Miz Pickford, I said.

Suddenly his mouth came open and I could see the freckles bunch together across his nose.

Lissen, kid—you trying to kid me?

Oh, no sir, I said. That's the honest truth.

Well, I'll be dam!

He shook his head.

Honest, mister. She's waiting in there just like I said . . . I held out my ticket.

He pulled hard on the top of his glove, watching me.

Honest, I said.

Dammit, Clyde, he said, if that's the truth your daddy shore must have his hands full, considering all the folks who are just dying to help him out. I guess you better hurry on in there and hold on to her tight. Protect his interest, Ezra. Because with a name like that some-body big and black might get holt to her first.—Yas, suh! An' mah mammy call me Tee-bone!

Smirking, he took the ticket, tearing it in half and holding out the stub.

Here, Mister Bones, Mister Tambo, he said, take this and don't lose it. And you be quiet, you hear? I ain't here for long but don't let me come in there and find you'all down front mak-ing noise along with those other snotty-shitty little bastards. You hear?

Yes, sir, I said, starting away.

Hey, wait a minit! Hold it right there, Clyde!

Sir?

Lissen here, you lying little peckerwood—why aren't you in school today?

I looked at him hard. Because it's Saturday, *mister, I said, and because my mamma is in there* waiting *for me.*

He grinned down at me. O.K., Ezra, he said, you can scoot—and watch the hay. But mamma or no mamma, you be quiet, you hear? This is way down south and de lan' uv cot-ton, as the boys say, but y'all be quiet, y'all heah-uh? An' Rastus, Ah mean it!

I hesitated, watching him and wondering whether he had found me out.

Well, go on! he barked, And I obeyed.

Then I was moving through the sloping darkness and finding my way by the dim lights which marked the narrow seatrows, going slowly until the lights came up and then there were red velvet drapes emerging and eager faces making a murmuring of voices, and golden cherubim, trumpets and Irish harps flowing out in space above the high proscenium arch, while in the hidden pit the orchestra played sweet, soothing airs. Then in the dimming of the lights I found a seat and horses and wagons flowed into horses and wagons and wagons sur-

rounded by cowboys and Indians and keystone cops and bathing beauties and flying pies and collapsing flivvers and running hoboes and did ever so many see themselves humorously in quite so few? And ads on the backdrop asking Will The Ladies Please Remove Their Masks and Reveal Their True ... and everyone and everything moving too swiftly, vertigoing past, so that I couldn't go in, couldn't enter even when they came close and their faces were not her face. So in the dark I squirmed and waited for her to come to me but there were only the others, big-eyed and pretty in their headbands and bathing suits and beaded gowns but bland with soft-looking breasts like Sister Georgia's only unsanctified and with no red fire in green eyes. She called me Goodhugh Gudworthy and I couldn't go in to search and see....

On the hill the cattle tinkled their bells and she said, Mister Movie man, I have to live here, you know. Will you be nice to me and the blossoms were falling where the hill hung below the afternoon and we sprawled embraced and out of time that never entered into future time except as one nerve cell, tooth, hair and tongue and drop of heart's blood into the bucket. Oh, if only I could have controlled me my she I and the search and have accepted you as the dark daddy of flesh and Word—Hickman? Hickman, you after all. Later I thought many times that I should have faced them down—faced me down and said, Look, this is where I'll make my standing place and with her in all her grace and sweet wonder. But how make a rhyme of a mystery? If I had only known then what I came to know about the shape of honor and the smell of pride—I say, HOW THE HELL DO YOU GET LOVE INTO POLITICS OR COMPASSION INTO HISTORY? And if you can't get here from there, that too is truth. If he can't drag the hill on his shoulders must a man wither beneath the stone? Yes, the whole hill moved, the cattle lowed, birds sang and blossoms fell, fell gently but I was ... I was going in but couldn't go in and then it ended and the lights came on. But still I waited, hoping she'd appear in the next run, so I sat low in my seat, hiding from the ticket man as they moved in and out around me. Then it was dark again and I knew I should leave but was afraid lest she appear larger than life and I would go in—why couldn't you say, Daddy Hickman: Man is born of woman but then there's history and towns and states and between the passion and the act there are mysteries. Always. Appointive and elective mysteries so I told myself: man and woman are a baby's device for achieving governments—ergo ego I'm a politician. Or again, shadows that move on screens and words that dance on pages are a stud's device for mounting the nightmare that gallops by day. And I told myself years ago, Let Hickman wear black, I, Bliss, will wear a suit of sable. Being born under a circus tent in the womb of wild women's arms I reject circumstance, live illusion. Then I told myself, speed up the process, make them dance. Extend their vision until they disgust themselves, until they gag. Stretch out their nerves, amplify their voices, extend their grasp until history is rolled into a pall. The past is in your skins, I cried, face fortune and be filled. No, there's never a gesture I've made since I've been here that hasn't tried to say, Look, this is me, me Can't you hear? Change the rules! Strike back hard in angry collaboration and you're free but I couldn't go in I have to live here, mister movie man, she said and I found a resistance of buttons and bows. Imagine, there and in those times, a flurry of fluffy things, an intricacy of Lord knows what garment styles, there beneath the hill....

"Bliss, are you there?"

So I waited, hoping I could get into it during the next show and she would be there and I waited yearning for one more sight word goodhugh even if seventy outraged deaconesses tore through the screen to tear down the house around us. But couldn't go in and sat wet and lonely and ashamed and wet down my leg and outside all that racing life swirling before me but once more the scenes came and tore past, sweeping me deeper into anguish yet when I came out of all that intensified time into the sun the world had grown larger for my having entered that forbidden place and yet smaller for now I knew that I could enter in if I entered there alone... I ran—Bliss ran.

... Where are we? Open the damper, daddy: it heats hard. So I told myself that I shall think sometime about time. It was all a matter of time; just a little time. I shall think too of the camera and the swarth it cut through the country of my travels, and how after the agony I had merely stepped into a different dimension of time. Between the frames in blackness I left and in time discovered that it was no mere matter of place which made the difference but time. And not chronology either, only time. Because I was no older and although I discovered early that in different places I became a different me. What did it all mean? How did she who called Cud forth become shadow and then turn flesh? She broke the structure of ritual and the world erupted. A blast of time flooded in upon me, knocking me out of the coffin into a different time.

... My grandpap said the colored don't need rights, Donelson said: they only need rites. You get it? Just give niggers a baptism or a parade or a dance and they're happy. And that, Karp said, is pappy-crap... And I was stunned.

So now when I changed places I changed me, and when I entered a place that place changed imperceptibly. The mystery went with me, entered with me, realigning time and place and personality. When I entered all was changed, as by an odorless gas. So the mystery pursued me, shifting and changing faces. Understand?

And later whenever instead of taking in a scene the camera seemed to focus forth my own point of view I felt murderous, felt that justifiable murder was being committed and my images a blasting of the world. I felt sometimes that a duplicity was being commissioned, an ambuscado trained upon those who thought they knew themselves and me. And yet I felt that I was myself a dupe because there was always the question aroused by my ability to see into events and the awareness of the joke implicit my being me. Who? So I said, What is the meaning of this arrangement of time place and circumstance that flames and dampens murder in my heart? And what is this desire to identify with others, this need to extend myself and test my most far-fetched possibilities with only the agency of shadows? Merely shadows. All shadowy they promised me my mother and denied me solid life. Oh, yes, mirrors do steal souls. So indeed Narcissus was weird....

"Rev. Bliss," Hickman was saying, "in the dark of night, alone in the desert of my own loneliness I have thought long upon this. I have thought upon you and me and all the old scriptural stories of Isaac and Joseph and upon our slave forefathers who killed their babes rather than have them lost in bondage, and upon my life here and the trials and tribulations and the jokes and laughter and all the endless turns-about that mark man's life in this world—And each time I return, each time my mind returns and makes its painful way back to the mystery of you and the mystery of birth and resurrection and hope which now seems endless in its complication. Yes, and I think upon the mystery of my involvement in it— Me, a black preacher's wilful son, a gambler-musician who rejoiced in the sounds of our triumph in this world of deceitful triumphs. Me, given you and your gifts, your possibilities in this whirlwind of circumstance. How and why did it happen? Why was I, the weakest of vessels, chosen to give so much and to have to try to understand so much which hardly seems understandable? Why did he give me this mysterious burden and then seem to mock me and challenge me and let men revile and despise me and wipe my heart upon the floor of this world after I had suffered and offered it up in sacrifice because in the coming together of hate and love and life and death, that marked the beginning, I looked upon those I love and upon them who caused their death and was unable to accept it except as I'd already accepted the blues, the clap, the loss of love, as the fate of man...I bared my breast, I lowered my head into the ashes where they had burned my own, my loved ones and accepted Thy will. Why didst Thou choose me, single me out for further humiliation who had been designated to humiliation by men unworthy, by men most unworthy, Lord. Why? Why me? me who had accepted my blackness as my fate, in the dark and shadowy complication of Thy will? And yet, down there in the craziness of the southland, in the madhouse of down home, the old motherland where I in all my ignorance and desperation was taught to deal with the complications of Thy plan, yes, and at a time when I was learning to live and to glean some sense of how Thy voice could sing through the blues and even speak through the dirty dozens if only the players were rich-spirited and resourceful enough, comical enough, vital enough and enough aware of the disciplines of life. In the zest and richness Thou were there, yes! But still, still, still, my question Lord! Though I say, quiet, quiet, my tongue. So teach me, Lord, to move on and yet be still; to question and not cry out, Lord, Lord, WHY?. Why?." And Hickman slept.

A SONG OF INNOCENCE

IOWA REVIEW 1 (SPRING 1970): 30–40

Mr. McIntyre was standing there and I didn't recognize him, and then it started happening. I thought one of my bad spells was coming on, the words were coming out of me so fast that while I could hear them inside me I couldn't connect up with them. It was like in the night when you're in bed and somebody walking along in the middle of the street in the dark lets out one of those ole long, slow-winding whoops that's neither a word or a song—you know.... And you hear it come sailing over the houses and the trees and on until it's starting to die away like a train's whistle when it's moving way yonder, out in the west, and then somebody else hears it falling away in a far street and he lets out a whoop because he can't help but keep it going and you hear it floating back out of the shadows and the dark while you lie there listening to both of them walking and listening and whooping and whooping and walking and listening with neither one knowing what those whoops are saying or who they're saying it to. But you know that they've got to be saying *something* because all that lonesome rising and falling of sound like singing has you by the short hair and dragging you out *into the ole calcified night of loneliness toward the unsayable meaning of mankind's outrageous condition in this world* (See, there they go again! Pay them no mind, Mr. McIntyre, they on their own. I try, I try awfully hard but they won't behave)....

So I roll over on the pallet and listen to those whoops rising and falling and dying and you try to understand what they're saying and even though you will never in this world quite make it before sleep comes down, you know just the same that it means beyond anything the straight words could ever say. You're here and they're there and there and you're still here and they're moving on and the sound and the meaning's passing out there back and forth in the night. So you fall asleep and the sound falls off the soft edge of your mind into the depths of all you can't hold or understand, or see or be, and they keep walking and whooping as though you'd never been born or had no ears to hear. Have some lemonade, Mr. McIntyre.

Listen. So when he had walked in here I couldn't do anything about it. I couldn't control those words and he was standing on the steps by now so that I couldn't get up and struggle down to where I could hear the freight trains making up down in the yards. I get up in the night sometimes and watch them just like I used to do when he was living here and was always with me in case I had a spell and fell and hurt myself, and I stand there on the hill back of the house and look down through the dark at the light and smell the good clean smell of the steam as it comes purling from the engine and there's red coals glowing in its grate and it's standing there huge in the dark, looking just like it's breathing and waiting to take off to all those places I always wanted to see but never could, and I can feel the words moiling up inside me and I want to go along with it. Sometimes I come to the very edge of a spell too, but never over it when I'm standing there looking. So, yes indeed, I want to go, with it big and black and full of fire and steam and just rolling all over the land through the daylight and the dark on those shining rails. It's a dream without rhyme or reason, but just the same, I could go along sitting right up there behind that smokestack where I could look all around and see over the hills and through the towns like it was the daddy and I was the baby riding high on his shoulders. Sure, this said so my soul sighs and what's your silly dream, Mr. McIntyre? A one-eyed man in this town stole an elephant once when Severen was a boy, and hid him in a patch of trees and was trying to feed him on yard grass, and he's one my words didn't make up.

Anyway, Severen knew though I was sitting here ignorant of his coming. He knew all about me and the trains even way back there, and once he drew me a tablet full of engines and colored them with crayons, because he knew how the trains eased me. In fact he was the first to understand what they did for me. He used to go with me to watch the trains and after he went away Miss Janey took me to watch whenever she had the time. She used to say, "Cliofus, you really must have been born with a truly aching heart to need a whole big engine and line of cars to soothe your agitation."

Miss Janey's right, though; those trains ease me. —Eeeeease me! What I mean is, they ease my aching mind. When I watch those engines and boxcars and gondolas I start to moving up and down in my body's joy and when I see those drivers start to roll, all those words go jumping out to them like the swine in the Bible that leaped off the cliff into the sea—only they hop on the Katy, the Rock Island and the Santa Fe.... Space, time and distance, like they say, I'm a yearning man who has to sit still. Maybe those trains need those words to help them find their way across this here wide land in the dark, I don't know. But for me it's like casting bread on the water because not only am I eased in my restless mind, but once in a while, deep in the night, when everything is quiet and all those voices and words are resting and all those things that I've been tumbling and running and bouncing through my mind all day have got quiet as a ship in a bottle on a shelf, then I can hear those train whistles talking to me, just to me, and in those times I know I have all in this world I'll ever need—mama and papa and jelly-roll....

So there Severen was and I couldn't do anything about those words—which is what makes me *me*. They say that folks misuse words, but I see it the other way around, words misuse people. Usually when you think you're saying what you mean you're really saying what the words want you to say. It's just like a drunk piano player I know who says that when he's drinking he plays where his fingers take him. Well, once upon a time they took him straight into the biggest church in town and got him thrown into jail for playing "Funky Butt" on the godbox, which is Mr. Fats Waller's name for the pipe organ. One never knows, *do* one, as he used to say, *Vox Humana, vox excelsis....* Mr. McIntyre. But words are tricky, they keep a thumb stuck in their noses and wave their fingers at you all the time, because they know that a sign or a gesture is the only thing you can control because no matter what you try to do, words can never mean meaning. Now you just wave your hand at somebody and it means bye-bye. Throw a kiss or hold out your arms and even a baby can understand you. But just try to say it in words and you raise up Babel and the grapes of wrath. If you nod your head and smile even folks who don't speak your language will get the idea, but you just whisper *peace* somebody will claim you declared war and will insist on trying to kill you. No wonder we have war! No wonder history is a bitch on wheels with wings traveling inside a submarine. Words are behind it all.

And with me it's even worse because since I can't always control my body even my gestures make me out a fool. Like the time the teacher said, *Cliofus, who was the father of our country?*

This was the first grade, even though the desk was already so small my knees stuck out in the aisles and my head was high enough to make the best target in the class.

Who was the daddy of our country? she said.

I don't know, mam, I told her.

You don't know? Then think a bit, she said.

So I thought a while with all the others watching and then I tried to guess. I said, Is it Him who art in heaven?

She grinned then, then she tried to hide it, but those outlaws like Buster, and Leroy, and Tommy Dee started to laughing and banging on their desks and jeering at me, saying.

Cliofus is a dummy! Cliofus is a *pure* fool! And the teacher looked at me real disgusted.

Quiet, she said, Quiet! And she started to frowning so hard it confused me. I wasn't very sociable in those days even though Miss Janey had tried to teach me my manners long before they decided to let me go to school.

Cliofus, the teacher said. You must know history, she said. Just like that.

And I said, Yes, mam . . .

But because I thought she was talking about *Mister* History, who was the father of our country I told her, "I be pleased to meet him, mam" . . . and I knew even before the words got out that I was wrong because Buster was already saying,

Listen to ole Seeofus, y'all. He a *bad* granny-dodger this morning!

I heard him plain as day, but I was losing ground to those words so fast I was already saying,

but do you think Mr. History would have time to be bothered with somebody like me, mam?—Not because I was sassy, you understand, but because I already felt despised and so unnecessary. Folks were already calling me a fool and in those days I didn't know whether I was or wasn't or even just what kind of a fool I was. I just figured I was pretty lucky that they let me go to school even though they waited so long to do it. So you see, the words had betrayed me twice over, and those fiends were really laughing at me now. It was like it was springtime recess near the last day of school and they'd already broken out most of the window-lights. So when the teacher slammed a book on the desk and said,

Boy, what do you mean, all I could do was stutter and shake, because I didn't know what the words would do next. Then the pains burst in the back of my head and everything around me started rushing away like a fast freight leaving a tramp and right in the middle of it I heard a voice just like mine saying, *Why shucks, Miss Kindly, I'm plumb full of history; even the dogs know that.*

And for a second there I thought it was the words playing a mean new trick on me, but it was Jack. He was throwing his voice from the back of the room and that set those howling heathens off again. Buster jumped out into the aisle and did a buck dance, singing,

> *Well, if at first you don't succeed*
> *Well a-keep on a-sucking*
> *Till you do sucka seed*

and the rest joined in yelling:

> *Cliofus ripped it, he ripped it, he ripped it, he*
> *really ripped it*
> *like a fool!*

And before the teacher could say a word, Tyree jumped on top of his desk and spread out his arms like a Calhoun or a Cicero and yelled,

> *Friends, Romans and Country women, Cliofus*
> *is an ape-sweat with too much mustard on his*
> *bun!*

And he frowned and slammed his fist down hard on his desk (Bang!) and shook his cheeks like a bad bull dog.

That really started them to yelling and holding their noses and saying *Phew!* and *He aint on my mama's table* and things like that even though an ape-sweat was what they used to call a hamburger when they didn't want anybody to beg for a bite.

Tell us some more, they said, and ole Tyree flapped his arms like a rooster and strutted around in a circle pecking with his head and said, Brothers and sisters and grand-mammy-dodgers, Cliofus is a soft horse-apple and a ripe goose egg!

That started them off again, yelling, Yaaaay! *He ripped it, he ripped it, he ripped it!* Cliofus really ripped it like a fool! Then somebody hit the blackboard with a biscuit soaked in molasses and a baked yam sailed past my head and squashed all over the big map of the United States that hung up front on a stand. But Miss Kindly was looking straight at me. The woman didn't even dodge!

Young man, you march right up here and apologize to me and to the rest of the class, she said.

But before I could move Jack spoke up in his natural voice, which he had already made as rough and deep as Mister Louis Armstrong's.

Said: Why, Miss Kindly, what do you mean apologize? All Cliofus means is that he's fulla brown and that's a natural fact. You don't believe him, sniff him. . . .

They exploded then and even those good little girls, whose mama wrapped their braids in gingham rags, joined in. Started shooting off cap pistols, rolling in the aisles and throwing erasers at my head.

You a good boy but you got no brakes or steering wheel, have you Cli, Jack said, and I felt something slimy hit the back of my head and run down my neck. And when I turned to look, a bunch of grapes hit me square in the face. They really had my range that morning. Jack had swiped a whole crate of overripe grapes from the produce house and passed them around to the other outlaws. When I tried to stand everybody seemed to be hitting me with those grapes. You could just see my white sweater turning purple beneath your eyes, just like somebody was stirring it in a tub of Concords and that started me to getting sick. I dearly loved that sweater because Miss Janey knitted it for me and I could feel a spell coming down and Miss Kindly's banging on her desk didn't help me fight it off. I would rather have died than have a spell hit me in front of those fools but when I held up my hand to be excused my doggone fingers wouldn't open. It looked like I was shaking my fist at the world and Miss Kindly turned a gallish green and her eyes started to pop and it was getting dark and I could feel myself falling. Then I was in the aisle and it was turning from black to red in my eyes and all I could hear, back there in the fire and gas where I had gone was Miss Kindly yelling ORDER!

Which she didn't get because by the time Miss Janey drove the mule and the wagon over to get me they had poured ink in my ear and painted my face white with eraser chalk. Miss Janey gave them hell—

But I was telling about Severen and it was almost the same. After all that time, he came through the gate and on up here on the porch with me rocking slow and watching him and batting at the flies round my rocking chair while I was thinking on the New Jerusalem, which is what Miss Janey likes to call this State—You know:

> *Give me my Bow of burning gold*
> *Give me my Arrows of desire*
> *Give me my Spear: O clouds unfold*
> *Bring me my chariot of fire....*

which was dancing in my mind like gnats around the eyes of a sleeping dog, and Severen came on not saying a word and stopped right there beside that post and was looking at me when the *words* started to talk to him. It was as though he'd asked a question and they were out to answer before I had a chance to stop them. They didn't need me anyway, they were in there waiting to get out and didn't even care how they got started. Because they had recognized him long before I did, smelled him or heard him coming from a long way off like dogs do. And I don't know who he is even after they get started, although I might have, just by his standing there looking pokerfaced and listening. Which should've told me that he was somebody who knew something about me because no stranger would look at me, sitting here weighing over 300 and talking break-neck as I have to talk. Oh I see me. Mr. McIntyre, do you see you? Because all things considered I got a built-in feed-back, if you know what I mean. The words take over but I listen and remember. Anyway, a stranger would've listened a minute and then backed down those steps and cut out. Wouldn't even'av said goodbye.

But he was just standing there, a young man in those fine clothes and definitely not an insurance collector or a Jehovah's Witness, because he's empty-handed and his eyes are asking instead of telling or demanding or working out a strategy to take advantage of a fool. Or trying to scare somebody to save his soul. In fact, he's looking at me like I'm normal even though those words were working up such a head of steam that I'm already stuttering—which should have warned me because from the very beginning until he went away he always treated me like I was just like anybody else. But I swear that apart from those words I didn't know him from Adam—or Lazarus, which is more like it, since Adam only had one time to die and Lazarus had him at least two. And as long as Severen had been gone from this town he might just as well been dead. The words knew though, and were going at him like a bunch of fools bursting out of a barbershop to watch a dogfight or to see the wind blowing a woman's skirt up over her head.

So when I hear them saying, *There was the big one in the union suit,* I just wanted to forget it and get up right then and there and go watch me some trains.

But he just looked at me with a funny light in his blue eyes and that blue tie he was wearing gave them a deeper color than my own eyes could have remembered even if I'd recognized him and he just stood there in his white suit looking at me and listening to the words come crowding out:

That's right, they said, *Jack who one time cried, Hey Lawdy Mama, in the moving picture show and almost caused a panic. Remember? As clear and present a danger as you ever could see. Beyond the faintest shadow of a shadow of a shadow of a doubt.*

He frowned then and I could see that he was thinking.

Jack, Beau Jack, the words said, *Boo Boo. You remember him. The big one. The burly one. The one they used to call ole Sacka Fat, ole Funky London, Mister Loud-fart-in-a-cyclone-with-a-derby-on. Ole Doggy Poppa? Boo-Boo Beau Jack, Weinstein's Bear? Talk about a bull in a china shop, Weinstein, who was supposed to be so smart, had him a bear working in his jewelry store but had to fire him. Jack wouldn't keep all those clocks running on time and then he brought a batch of cheap rings from the Five and Ten and gave them to some girls telling them he stole them from Weinstein's best stock. Had more green fingers feeling and fumbling around this town than there's Okies in California before they caught on...Dam' near ruined Weinstein for the high school graduation trade.*

So he looked at me and laughed at this and he said his first words:

I can't place him.... Where did Jack live?

Out in the heights, we said, and a very famous character in those times. The same one who threw his voice and worked the class. Had a sweet tenor voice and could sing like a bird when he wanted to but preferred to sound like Satchel mouth with a bad cold. Once he took your marbles. Came storming across the schoolground yelling 'Snatch-grabs' and kicking up dust and unholy terror among the little kids, knocking people down and laughing at 'em fall. Made you so mad you just lay on the ground and howled. Jack Boo-Boo Beau Jack, he was stealing the Communion grape juice from seven churches and was drinking it with his henchmen for three straight years before they caught the fool. Said he was teaching 'em what wine was really for. Those were the olden days, before they hired those colored cops and brought some civilization to this town. You still can't place him?

Severen shook his head then and I said

Something must have happened to your memory.

It's been a long time, he said, but yours seems O.K. Go on.

And I said, it's not my recollection that counts, it's what I can't help but say.

Do you mean that you always tell the truth?

And I told him No, but the truth gets into it.

Then the words said, *Look: Remember the little childrun sitting in rows, stinking and snorting and sniggling and snotting, knotty-headed and hockey-pants and stealing bites out of their bags of lunch whenever the old-maid teacher's back went around or she dropped her weary eye? All small, all of y'all but Jack and me the biggest in the class. Miss Mable Kindly was her name. She used to talk real proper, rolling her rr's and her eyes and wore her hair done up in three big buns with the rats always peeping out the skimpy back. And as flat-chested as Miss Janey's best ironing board. Straight as a ram rod, man. Her corset stays stuck out round her narrow hips like umbrella spines in a strong mean April wind, and her powdered face was as grey as the blackboard behind her head. Swore all the kids were hea-thens and the cross she had to bear and Jack did all he could to prove she wasn't lying. Used to see her walking sedately down the street as though she was carrying a thin-shelled egg be-tween her knees and he'd yell out 'Cherries are ripe! Cherries are ripe!' then whistle like a crazy robin red breast. Poor woman'd start pulling down on her dress and patting herself on the chest and back of the neck and marching in double-quick time, and dark as she was her face'd turn cherry red.*

You remember I said, Dust-Mop Mable, these big bad gals used to call her while they shagged their hot young nasties up and down the hall between classes, singing,

> *Oh Dust Mop Mable*
> *She swears she would if she could*
> *But she a-just aint able—Mable!*

And there she was teaching arithmetic.

"What's the difference between a multiplier and a multiplican?" her question was.

And shame on her! We were sitting there innocent and bland behind our second grade desks when Jack, who was facing the class in a chair for punishment, fell back on his shoulders and slouched way forward like he was throwing a faint and flipped a big hickey-headed sour pickle from his fly and shook confusion into her very soul. Her eyes got big as if she'd seen the devil come straight from hell and then Jack threw the pickle at the electric light and it hit the fixture and skidded across the ceiling and she rocked around and started to sway then caught herself and hit that hall screaming rape and resurrection—No now, don't come asking me why, but 'rape and resurrection' just the same.

So then ole Jack fell off his chair from laughing and rolled on the floor like he was about to die, and here comes the principal. Dr. Peter Osgood Eliot, who usually looked no more human than a granite general astride a concrete horse but now his iron grey hair is standing up on end, his bowels are in a fair uproar, and his false teeth are rattling like a mixed-up telegraph. He started pointing at us all like his arm was a sabre and put the whole class under quarantine, accusing us all of flipping the pickle, singing "The Boy in The Boat," writing nasty language on the schoolhouse walls and saying "spit" that dirty word. Then he hurried out to call the law.

And right away in leaps Blue Goose with his well-stropped head dragging half a tree limb behind him got to whipping Jack's behind and all the boys in the first five rows—And most of us not even knowing what it was all about or even able to believe what our own dear eyes had seen. I tell you, Justice was deaf, dumb, blind and ball-headed that day, my weed.

Blue Goose is a name I remember, Severen said. And I stopped him right there.

Now you're highballing, I said. And I knew then that I had to get closer to what those words were digging up and stretching out but I didn't let on to him...

I said, Of course you remember. He used to knock on the classroom doors saying, Miss So-and-So, you have any boys you want me to beat—and wouldn't take no for an answer. Just started to choosing us like picking sides to play a game: You and you and you over yonder on the aisle—Get on your devilish feet and march! And he'd stand there trembling in his striped tan suit and his yellow shoes, his dusty brown derby and glaring at us all out of his snuff-colored eyes.

Yes! And if the teacher said, "But not him Reveren Samson, he's a good boy who makes all A's," Blue Goose would tell her, Is that right? Well I aim to keep him good and a little beating won't hurt his A's or B's one single bit! I don't aim to touch 'em.

So for no good reason we all marched down into the basement among the pipes and pisserines where went the snows of then, and lined up bottoms-up with lowered pants while Blue Goose laid on the strap—Strap hell! It was the thick solid rubber tire from the big wheel of a large tricycle that raised a welt like alligator hide! Dam' his soul, dam' his ball-headed soul to hell. Blue Goose, your nickname was our small revenge. Those fast, fleet-footed runners used to yell at him from under the viaduct when he rode his bicycle over and they'd honk at him, Blue Goose, from under the windows when he was preaching in his church but I could never move with enough control to even try it.

He whipped China Jackson that time and China ran down the tracks home and came racing back with his daddy's forty-four and shot at Blue Goose six straight times, raising up steady and leveling down slow and busting those caps like Jesse James—Wham! wham-wham-wham-Wham!—and missed the snuff-dipping bastard every time.

Because, you see, poor China was pulling the trigger when the barrel was pointing at twelve o'clock instead of three on account of seeing too many of those shoot-em-up cowboy movies. One o'clock would have drilled him another eye; four would have hit his spareribs or his chitterlings; nine o'clock or three would have called for his last clean shirt right then and there. But it wasn't in the cards, he choked on a fishbone one Fourth of July.

Just the same, when Blue Goose heard all that gunfire he took off honking bloody murder. In fact, he ripped his pants and swallowed his lipful of Garret's Snuff and busted the soles loose from his brogan shoes. And when he stopped running and found he was all in one piece he preached the Book of Revelations down on poor China's soul. What I mean is, Blue Goose put the badmouth on him.

Ah, but China boy, you're gone but your aim is there on the ceiling to mark your glory. Little snotnose kid up the street told me the other day that the Indians put all those bullet holes up there in the ceiling. I said if they did one had to be named Chief China Lee Jackson. I said to Severen, You remember things like that, because these young ones try to make up history as they go along. Or else they think all the lessons are in the book; all the lessons are about the times *they* been taught...

And Severen said, But what about the one in the union suit?

I said in the union station, you mean. Well, that was the time Miss Kindly marched the whole class over to the Santa Fe Crossing holding hands to see the whale. Remember, you held my hand and your mittens were pinned to your sleeves with safety pins and we passed under Case's golden eagle sitting on top of the world like he owned it and went past the ice cream factory and all those machine shops and through the smell of roasting coffee and baking bread and down there, in the bowels of town, surrounded by boxcars and factories we found the whale. It was laying up there on that long flatcar on planks and canvas painted blue and white to look like ocean waves, and him as big as three locomotives hooked end to end, as far from home as he ever could be and smelling sick-to-the-stomach sweetish like a whole ocean of embalming fluid. Miss Kindly made us gather round like we were about to sing *Praise God From Whom All Blessings Flow,* while she strutted back and forth with her head cocked to one side, her finger pressed to her cheek and her eyes lit up and far away like Singapore.

See the great whale, chill-dreen, Miss Kindly said.

And we stood there straining our necks as though he was two miles in the air and flying like a bird.

See the Great whale, chill-dreen, Miss Kindly said. And we said,

Yes, mam, we sees him, mam, and stood there bugging out our eyes.

Remember he was roped all over with electricity wires and had two red light bulbs sticking where his eyes were supposed to be, one on one side and the other way, way around on the other side, and with those harpoons trembling in his hump whenever a truck rolled past it looked like somebody had been sticking needles and thread into a black rubber mountain—But great God-a-mighty, wasn't that a fish! I mean wasn't that a *fish!*

Well, Miss Kindly looked at the whale and got real frisky.

See, chill-dreen, how the great whale is made of blubber, Miss Kindly said.

Yes, mam, we said. *Us sees all that blubber.*

And she arched her eyebrows and her hand fell over backwards in a limp-wristed curve then her lips puckered up like she was sucking a lemon or pulling tight the string on a tobacco sack.

The whale, chill-dreen, Miss Kindly said, *is an ani-mule. Do you understand?* (Miss Kindly was a fool for natural science, teacups and fancy manners especially for girls).

Yes, mam, Miss Kindly, we said all at once. *Whales is chilldreen is ani-mules is— mam? Ma-aam!*

Thus, chill-dreen, Miss Kindly said, *whale babies drink good rich milk. Isn't that truly wonderful,* Miss Kindly said.

Yes, mam! we said. *Good rich fish milk is good for you. Yes, mam.*

And now chill-dreen, Miss Kindly said, *would you like to ask any questions about the great big beautiful whale?*

So while we looked dumb and tried to think up some questions Miss Kindly made big eyes at the whale and turned around and sah-shayed back and forth with her eyebrows arched and walking as proper as the queen of Spain then all of a sudden she dropped her handkerchief on the cinders right in front of us and when a little girl dressed in apple green started to pick it up, Miss Kindly stamped her foot and her voice got high as a flute saying, "Nu nu nu nu nu!" and she stamped her foot again and froze that little girl like she'd been struck by the frost and a great big worm. Then she pointed at me, looking very grand, and said, Let *heeeem* pick it up. You are uh lay-di! And I stooped down to try it and fell flat on my face in the cinders and the heathens all snickered, but Miss Kindly was back picking on the poor whale again, talking about, *Well, I'm still waiting for your questions, chill-dreen. Use your imaginations.*

And that's when a little bowlegged, knock-kneed, pigeon-toed, mariney son-of-a-gun named Bernard said, Yes, mam, Miss Kindly I've got one.

And Miss Kindly said, Now that's very good, Bernard. That's how we learn chill-dreen, by asking questions. I'm surprised that with this great big wonderful whale brought all the way from the ocean for you to see you have so little to ask about this wonder of nature. Now you just listen to Bernard and learn from him. Bernard is *highly* intelligent. What is your question, Bernard?

And old Bernard asked it. He said, Miss Kindly, if that there whale is an ani-mule, what gives rich milk, where do she carry her tits?

Miss Kindly lit up and turned a boxcar red, and lucky for old Bernard, that was when the door to the little house with the tall smokestack where the man who watched the crossing used to sit came open and out comes a little red-headed man smoking a crooked pipe and hobbling on an ole beat-up wooden leg—who right away charged us all a nickel a piece just to listen to him lie. Said he caught that whale as easy as falling off a log or digging a crawdad out of a hole. Then he turned right around and swore that the whale bit off his leg. And Miss Kindly didn't say a word. So we watched him hobbling along lying a mile a minute from that whale's head to his tail and around and back again, telling us all about Jonah, whale oil, corset stays and bone hairpins. And then he showed us that big cud of ambergris that looked like something he'd fetched from the profoundest depth of the sea but which smelled like he should've left it right where it was.

That's when ole hoarse-voiced Tyree looked it over real close and wrinkled up his nose and whispered so everybody in half-a block could hear:

Lissen here, y'all, that *there* is whale hockey; I don't care *what* that white man says!

And here the man had just been telling us that the stuff was worth ten times its weight in gold and made the very best perfume.

Now isn't that amazing, child-reen, Miss Kindly said.

Yes, mam, we all said. We 'mazed. And the great big high-headed whale just lay there winking his bloodshot light-bulb eyes.

Now isn't that wonderful, Chill-reen, Miss Kindly said. See the great whale blinking his eyes. That proves he's an animule.

Yes mam, Miss Kindly, we all chimed in, *we see him winking his animules.*

He's animule.

He's a mule.

He's fish eyes.

He's an animaleyed fish, that's what he is.

And that's when the little man took him a chew of tobacco and ducked down under the flatcar and turned the valve. And the next thing we knew, a spout of water was shooting from the top of the great whale's head. And the little man yelled, "Thar she blows," and the whole class broke and ran for cover, but be-cause of me you got all wet.

You remember that, I said, and Severen was laughing a real down home laugh. He took out a pack of cigarettes then and said, Cliofus, do you smoke? And I told him no and he took one out and lit it and took a puff then laughed some more. And then he was kind of crying and I asked him why. And he said, "For the whale; for the poor old whale."

CADILLAC FLAMBÉ

AMERICAN REVIEW 16 (FEBRUARY 1973): 249–69

It had been a fine spring day made even pleasanter by the lingering of the cherry blossoms and I had gone out before dawn with some married friends and their children on a bird-watching expedition. Afterwards we had sharpened our appetites for brunch with rounds of bloody marys and bullshots. And after the beef bouillon ran out, our host, an ingenious man, had improvised a drink from chicken broth and vodka which he proclaimed the "chicken-shot." This was all very pleasant and after a few drinks my spirits were soaring. I was pleased with my friends, the brunch was excellent and varied—chili con carne, cornbread, and oysters Rockefeller, etc.—and I was pleased with my tally of birds. I had seen a bluebird, five rose-breasted grosbeaks, three painted buntings, seven goldfinches, and a rousing consort of mockingbirds. In fact, I had hated to leave.

Thus it was well into the afternoon when I found myself walking past the Senator's estate. I still had my binoculars around my neck, and my tape recorder—which I had along to record bird songs—was slung over my shoulder. As I approached, the boulevard below the Senator's estate was heavy with cars, with promenading lovers, dogs on leash, old men on canes, and laughing children, all enjoying the fine weather. I had paused to notice how the Senator's lawn rises from the street level with a gradual and imperceptible elevation that makes the mansion, set far at the top, seem to float like a dream castle; an illusion intensified by the chicken-shots, but which the art editor of my paper informs me is the result of a trick copied from the landscape architects who designed the gardens of the Bellevedere Palace in Vienna. But be that as it may, I was about to pass on when a young couple blocked my path, and when I saw the young fellow point up the hill and say to his young blonde of a girl, "I bet you don't know who that is up there," I brought my binoculars into play, and there, on the right-hand terrace of the mansion, I saw the Senator.

Dressed in a chef's cap, apron, and huge asbestos gloves, he was armed with a long-tined fork which he flourished broadly as he entertained the notables for whom he was preparing a barbecue. These gentlemen and ladies were lounging in their chairs or standing about in groups sipping the tall iced drinks which two white-jacketed Filipino boys were serving. The Senator was dividing his attention between the spareribs cooking in a large chrome grill-cart and displaying his great talent for mimicking his colleagues with such huge success that no one at the party was aware of what was swiftly approaching. And, in fact, neither was I.

I was about to pass on when a gleaming white Cadillac convertible, which had been moving slowly in the heavy traffic from the east, rolled abreast of me and suddenly blocked the path by climbing the curb and then continuing across the walk and onto the Senator's lawn. The top was back and the driver, smiling as though in a parade, was a well-dressed Negro man of about thirty-five, who sported the gleaming hair affected by their jazz musicians and prize-fighters, and who sat behind the wheel with that engrossed, yet relaxed, almost ceremonial attention to form that was once to be observed only among the finest horsemen. So closely did the car brush past that I could have reached out with no effort and touched the rich ivory leather upholstery. A bull fiddle rested in the back of the car. I watched the man drive smoothly up the lawn until he was some seventy-five yards below the mansion, where he braked the machine and stepped out to stand waving toward the terrace, a gallant salutation grandly given.

At first, in my innocence, I placed the man as a musician, for there was, after all, the bull fiddle; then in swift succession I thought him a chauffeur for one of the guests, a driver for a news or fashion magazine or an advertising agency or television network. For I quickly realized that a musician wouldn't have been asked to perform at the spot where the car was stopped, and that since he was alone, it was unlikely that anyone, not even the Senator, would have hired a musician to play serenades on a bull fiddle. So next I decided that the man had either been sent with equipment to be used in covering the festivities taking place on the terrace, or that he had driven the car over to be photographed against the luxurious background. The waving I interpreted as the expression of simpleminded high spirits aroused by the driver's pleasure in piloting such a luxurious automobile, the simple exuberance of a Negro allowed a role in what he considered an important public spectacle. At any rate, by now a small crowd had gathered and had begun to watch bemusedly.

Since it was widely known that the Senator is a master of the new political technology, who ignores no medium and wastes no opportunity for keeping his image ever in the public's eye, I wasn't disturbed when I saw the driver walk to the trunk and begin to remove several red objects of a certain size and place them on the grass. I wasn't using my binoculars now and thought these were small equipment cases. Unfortunately, I was mistaken.

For now, having finished unpacking, the driver stepped back behind the wheel, and suddenly I could see the top rising from its place of concealment to soar into place like the wing of some great, slow, graceful bird. Stepping out again, he picked up one of the cases—now suddenly transformed into the type of can which during the war was sometimes used to transport high-octane gasoline in Liberty ships (a highly dangerous cargo for those round bottoms and the men who shipped in them)—and, leaning carefully forward, began emptying its contents upon the shining chariot.

And thus, I thought, *is gilded an eight-valved, three-hundred-and-fifty-horsepowered air-conditioned lily!*

For so accustomed have we Americans become to the tricks, the shenanigans, and frauds of advertising, so adjusted to the contrived fantasies of commerce—

indeed, to pseudo-events of all kinds—that I thought that the car was being drenched with a special liquid which would make it more alluring for a series of commercial photographs.

Indeed, I looked up the crowded boulevard behind me, listening for the horn of a second car or station wagon which would bring the familiar load of pretty models, harassed editors, nervous wardrobe mistresses, and elegant fashion photographers who would convert the car, the clothes, and the Senator's elegant home, into a photographic rite of spring.

And with the driver there to remind me, I even expected a few ragged colored street urchins to be brought along to form a poignant but realistic contrast to the luxurious costumes and high-fashion surroundings: an echo of the somber iconography in which the crucified Christ is flanked by a repentant and an unrepentant thief, or that in which the three Wise Eastern Kings bear their rich gifts before the humble stable of Bethlehem.

But now reality was moving too fast for the completion of this foray into the metamorphosis of religious symbolism. Using my binoculars for a closer view, I could see the driver take a small spherical object from the trunk of the car and a fuzzy tennis ball popped into focus against the dark smoothness of his fingers. This was joined by a long wooden object which he held like a conductor's baton and began forcing against the ball until it was pierced. This provided the ball with a slender handle which he tested delicately for balance, drenched with liquid, and placed carefully behind the left fin of the car.

Reaching into the back seat now, he came up with a bass fiddle bow upon which he accidently spilled the liquid, and I could see drops of fluid roping from the horsehairs and falling with an iridescent spray into the sunlight. Facing us now, he proceeded to tighten the horsehairs, working methodically, very slowly, with his head gleaming in the sunlight and beads of sweat standing over his brow.

As I watched, I became aware of the swift gathering of a crowd around me, people asking puzzled questions, and a certain tension, as during the start of a concert, was building. And I had just thought, *And now he'll bring out the fiddle,* when he opened the door and hauled it out, carrying it, with the dripping bow swinging from his right hand, up the hill some thirty feet above the car, and placed it lovingly on the grass. A gentle wind started to blow now, and I swept my glasses past his gleaming head to the mansion, and as I screwed the focus to infinity, I could see several figures spring suddenly from the shadows on the shaded terrace of the mansion's far wing. They were looking on like the spectators of a minor disturbance at a dull baseball game. Then a large woman grasped that something was out of order and I could see her mouth come open and her eyes blaze as she called out soundlessly, "Hey, you down there!" Then the driver's head cut into my field of vision and I took down the glasses and watched him moving, broad-shouldered and jaunty, up the hill to where he'd left the fiddle. For a moment he stood with his head back, his white jacket taut across his shoulders, looking toward the terrace. He waved then, and shouted words that escaped me. Then, facing the machine, he took something from his pocket and I saw him touch the flame of a cigarette lighter to the tennis ball and begin blowing gently upon it; then, waving it about like a child twirling a Fourth of July sparkler, he watched it sputter into a small blue ball of flame.

I tried, indeed I anticipated what was coming next, but I simply could not accept it! The Negro was twirling the ball on that long, black-tipped wooden needle—the kind used for knitting heavy sweaters—holding it between his thumb and fingers in the manner of a fire-eater at a circus, and I couldn't have been more surprised if he had thrown back his head and plunged the flame down his throat than by what came next. Through the glasses now I could see sweat beading out beneath his scalp line and on the flesh above the stiff hairs of his moustache as he grinned broadly and took up the fiddle bow, and before I could move he had shot his improvised, flame-tipped arrow onto the cloth top of the convertible.

"Why that black son of the devil!" someone shouted, and I had the impression of a wall of heat springing up from the grass before me. Then the flames erupted with a stunning blue roar that sent the spectators scattering. People were shouting now, and through the blue flames before me I could see the Senator and his guests running from the terrace to halt at the top of the lawn, looking down, while behind me there were screams, the grinding of brakes, the thunder of footfalls as the promenaders broke in a great spontaneous wave up the grassy slope, then sensing the danger of exploding gasoline, receded hurriedly to a safer distance below, their screams and curses ringing above the roar of the flames.

How, oh, how, I wished for a cinema camera to synchronize with my tape recorder!—which automatically I now brought into play as heavy fumes of alcohol and gasoline, those defining spirits of our age, filled the air. There before me unfolding in *tableau vivant* was surely the most unexpected picture in the year: in the foreground at the bottom of the slope, a rough semicircle of outraged faces; in the mid-foreground, up the gentle rise of the lawn, the white convertible shooting into the springtime air a radiance of intense blue flame, a flame like that of a welder's torch or perhaps of a huge fowl being flambéed in choice cognac; then on the rise above, distorted by heat and flame, the dark-skinned, white-suited driver, standing with his gleaming face expressive of high excitement as he watched the effect of his deed. Then, rising high in the background atop the grassy hill, the white-capped Senator surrounded by his notable guests—all caught in postures eloquent of surprise, shock, or indignation.

The air was filled with an overpowering smell of wood alcohol, which, as the leaping red and blue flames took firm hold, mingled with the odor of burning paint and leather. I became aware of the fact that the screaming had suddenly faded now, and I could hear the swoosh-pop-crackle-and-hiss of the fire. And with the gaily dressed crowd become silent, it was as though I were alone, isolated, observing a conflagration produced by a stroke of lightning flashed out of a clear blue springtime sky. We watched with that sense of awe similar to that with which medieval crowds must have observed the burning of a great cathedral. We were stunned by the sacrificial act and, indeed, it was as though we had become the unwilling participants in a primitive ceremony requiring the sacrifice of a beautiful object in appeasement of some terrifying and long-dormant spirit, which the black man in the white suit was summoning from a long, black sleep. And as we watched, our faces strained as though in anticipation of the spirit's materialization from the fiery metamorphosis of the white machine, a spirit that I was afraid, whatever the form in which it appeared, would be powerfully good or powerfully evil, and absolutely out of place here and now in Washington. It was, as I say, uncanny. The whole afternoon seemed to float, and when I looked again to the top of the hill the people there appeared to move in slow motion through watery waves of heat. Then I saw the Senator, with chef cap awry, raising his asbestos gloves above his head and beginning to shout. And it was then that the driver, the firebrand, went into action.

Till now, looking like the chief celebrant of an outlandish rite, he had held firmly to his middle-ground; too dangerously near the flaming convertible for anyone not protected by asbestos suiting to risk laying hands upon him, yet far enough away to highlight his human vulnerability to fire. But now as I watched him move to the left of the flames to a point allowing him an uncluttered view of the crowd, his white suit reflecting the flames, he was briefly obscured by a sudden swirl of smoke, and it was during this brief interval that I heard the voice.

Strong and hoarse and typically Negro in quality, it seemed to issue with eerie clarity from the fire itself. Then I was struggling within myself for the reporter's dedicated objectivity and holding my microphone forward as he raised both arms above his head, his long, limber fingers wide-spread as he waved toward us.

"Ladies and gentlemen," he said, "please don't be disturbed! I don't mean you any harm, and if you'll just cool it a minute I'll tell you what this is all about..."

He paused and the Senator's voice could be heard angrily in the background.

"Never mind that joker up there on top of the hill," the driver said. "You can listen to him when I get through. He's had too much free speech anyway. Now it's *my* turn."

And at this a man at the other end of the crowd shouted angrily and tried to break up the hill. He was grabbed by two men and an hysterical, dark-haired woman wearing a well-filled chemise-style dress, who slipped to the ground holding a leg, shouting, "No, Fleetwood. No! That crazy nigger will kill you!"

The arsonist watched with blank-faced calm as the man was dragged protesting back into the crowd. Then a shift in the breeze whipped smoke down upon us and gave rise to a flurry of coughing.

"Now believe me," the arsonist continued, "I know that it's very, very hard for you folks to look at what I'm doing and not be disturbed, because for you it's a crime and a sin."

He laughed, swinging his fiddle bow in a shining arc as the crowd watched him fixedly.

"That's because you know that most folks can't afford to own one of these Caddies. Not even good, hard-working folks, no matter what the pictures in the papers and magazines say. So deep down it makes you feel some larceny. You feel that it's unfair that everybody who's willing to work hard can't have one for himself. That's right! And you feel that in order to get one it's OK for a man to lie and cheat and steal—yeah, even swindle his own mother *if* she's got the cash. That's the difference between what you *say* you believe and the way you *act* if you get the chance. Oh yes, because words is words, but life is hard and earnest and these here Caddies is way, way out of this world!"

Pausing, he loosened the knot in his blue and white tie so that it hung down the front of his jacket in a large loop, then wiped his brow with a blue silk handkerchief.

"I don't mean to insult you," he said, bending toward us now, the fiddle bow resting across his knee, "I'm just reminding you of the facts. Because I can see in your eyes that it's going to cost me more to get *rid* of this Caddy the way I have to do it than it cost me to get it. I don't rightly know what the price will be, but I know that when you people get scaird and shook up, you get violent. —No, wait a minute…" He shook his head. "That's not how I meant to say it. I'm sorry. I apologize.

"Listen, here it is: This *morning*," he shouted now, stabbing his bow toward the mansion with angry emphasis. "This morning that fellow Senator *Sunraider* up there, *he* started it when he shot off his mouth over the *radio*. That's what this is all about! I realized that things had gotten out of *control*. I realized all of a sudden that the man was *messing*… with… my *Cadillac*, and ladies and gentlemen, that's serious as all *hell*…

"Listen to me, y'all: A little while ago I was romping past *Richmond*, feeling fine. I had played myself three hundred and seventy-five dollars and thirty-three cents worth of gigs down in Chattanooga, and I was headed home to *Harlem* as straight as I could go. I wasn't bothering any*body*. I didn't even mean to stop by here, because this town has a way of making a man feel like he's living in a fool's *paradise*. When I'm *here* I never stop thinking about the difference between what it *is* and what it's *supposed* to be. In fact, I have the feeling that somebody put the *Indian* sign on this town a long, long time ago, and I don't want to be around when it takes effect. So, like I say, I wasn't even thinking about this town. I was rolling past Richmond and those whitewalls were slapping those concrete slabs and I was rolling and the wind was feeling fine on my face—and that's when I made my sad mistake. Ladies and gentlemen, I turned on the radio. I had nothing against anybody. I was just hoping to hear some Dinah, or Duke, or Hawk so that I could study their phrasing and improve my style and enjoy myself. —But what do I get? I'll tell you what I got—"

He dropped his shoulders with a sudden violent twist as his index finger jabbed toward the terrace behind him, bellowing, "I GOT THAT NO GOOD,

NOWHERE SENATOR SUNRAIDER! THAT'S WHAT I GOT! AND WHAT WAS HE DOING? HE WAS TRYING TO GET THE UNITED STATES GOVERNMENT TO MESS WITH MY CADILLAC! AND WHAT'S MORE, HE WAS CALLING MY CADDY A 'COON CAGE.'

"Ladies and gentlemen, I couldn't believe my *ears*. I don't know that Senator and I know he doesn't know me from old *Bodiddly*. But just the same, there he is, talking straight to me and there was no use of my trying to dodge. Because I do live in Harlem and I lo-mo-sho do drive a Cadillac. So I had to sit there and take it like a little man. There he was, a United States SENATOR, coming through my own radio telling me what I ought to be driving, and recommending to the United States Senate and the whole country that the name of my car be changed simply because *I*, me, LeeWillie Minifees, was driving it!

"It made me feel faint. It upset my mind like a midnight telegram!

"I said to myself, 'LeeWillie, what on earth is this man *talking* about? Here you been thinking you had it *made*. You been thinking you were as free as a bird—even though a black bird. That good-rolling Jersey Turnpike is up ahead to get you home. —And now here comes this Senator putting you in a cage! What in the world is going on?'

"I got so nervous that all at once my foot weighed ninety-nine pounds, and before I knew it I was doing *seventy-five*. I was breaking the law! I guess I was really trying to get away from that voice and what the man had said. But I was rolling and I was listening. I couldn't *help* myself. What I was hearing was going against my whole heart and soul, but I was listening *anyway*. And what I heard was beginning to make me see things in a new light. Yes, and that new light was making my eyeballs ache. And all the time Senator Sunraider up in the Senate was calling my car a 'coon cage.'

"So I looked around and I saw all that fine ivory leather there. I looked at the steel and at the chrome. I looked through the windshield and saw the road unfolding and the houses and the trees was flashing by. I looked up at the top and I touched the button and let it go back to see if that awful feeling would leave me. But it wouldn't leave. The *air* was hitting my face and the *sun* was on my head and I was feeling that good old familiar feeling of *flying*—but ladies and gentlemen, it was no longer the same! Oh, no—because I could still hear that Senator playing the *dozens* with my Cadillac!

"And just then, ladies and gentlemen, I found myself rolling toward an old man who reminded me of my granddaddy by the way he was walking beside the highway behind a plow hitched to an old, white-muzzled Missouri mule. And when that old man looked up and saw me he waved. And I looked back through the mirror as I shot past him and I could see him open his mouth and say something like, 'Go on, fool!' Then him and that mule was gone even from the mirror and I was rolling on.

"And then, ladies and gentlemen, in a twinkling of an eye it struck me. A voice said to me, 'LeeWillie, that old man is right: you are a fool. And that doggone Senator Sunraider is right, LeeWillie, you are a fool in a coon cage!'

"I tell you, ladies and gentlemen, that old man and his mule both were talking to me. I said, 'What do you mean about his being right?' And they said, 'LeeWillie, look who he *is*,' and I said, 'I *know* who he is,' and they said, 'Well, LeeWillie, if a man like that, in the position he's in, can think the way he doin, then LeeWillie, you have GOT to be wrong!'

"So I said, 'Thinking like that is why you've still got that mule in your lap,' man. 'I worked hard to get the money to buy this Caddy,' and he said, '*Money?* LeeWillie, can't you see that it ain't no longer a matter of money? Can't you see it's done gone way past the question of money? Now it's a question of whether you can afford it in terms *other than money.*'

"And I said, 'Man, what are you talking about, "terms other than money." ' and he said, 'LeeWillie, even this damn mule knows that if a man like that feels the way he's talking and can say it right out over the radio and the T.V., and from the place where he's saying it—there's got to be something drastically wrong with you for even wanting one. Son, the man's done made it mean something different. All you wanted was to have a pretty automobile, but fool, he done changed the Rules on you!'

"So against myself, ladies and gentlemen, I was forced to *agree* with the old man and the mule. That Senator up there wasn't simply degrading my Caddy. That wasn't the *point.* It's that he would low-rate a thing so truly fine as a *Cadillac* just in order to degrade *me* and my *people.* He was accusing *me* of lowering the value of the auto, when all I ever wanted was the very best!

"Oh, it hurt me to the quick, and right then and there I had me a rolling revelation. The *scales* dropped from my eyes. I had been BLIND, but the Senator up there on that hill was making me SEE. He was making me see some things I didn't *want* to see! I'd thought I was dressed real FINE, but I was as naked as a jaybird sitting on a limb in the drifting snow. I THOUGHT I was rolling past *Richmond,* but I was really trapped in a COON CAGE, running on one of those little TREADMILLS like a SQUIRREL or a HAMSTER. So now my EYEBALLS were aching. My head was in such a whirl that I shot the car up to ninety, and all I could see up ahead was the road getting NARROW. It was getting as narrow as the eye of a NEEDLE, and that needle looked like the Washington MONUMENT lying down. Yes, and I was trying to thread that Caddy straight through that eye and I didn't care if I made it or not. But while I managed to get that Caddy through I just couldn't thread that COON CAGE because it was like a two-ton knot tied in a piece of fine silk thread. The sweat was pouring off me now, ladies and gentlemen, and my brain was on fire, so I pulled off the highway and asked myself some questions, and I got myself some answers. It went this way:

" 'LeeWillie, who put you in this cage?'

" 'You put your own self in there,' a voice inside me said.

" 'But I paid for it, it's mine. I own it…' I said.

" 'Oh, no, LeeWillie,' the voice said, 'what you mean is that it owns *you,* that's why you're *in* the cage. *Admit* it, daddy; you have been NAMED. Senator Sunraider has put the badmouth, the NASTY mouth on you and now your Cadillac ain't no Caddy anymore! Let's face it, LeeWillie, from now on everytime you sit behind this wheel you're going to feel those RINGS shooting round and round your TAIL and one of those little black COON'S masks is going to settle down over your FACE, and folks standing on the streets and hanging out the windows will sing out, "HEY! THERE GOES MISTER COON AND HIS COON CAGE!" That's right, LeeWillie! And all those little husky-voiced colored CHILDREN playing in the gutters will point at you and say, "THERE GOES MISTAH GOON AND HIS GOON GAGE"—and that will be right in Harlem!'

"And that did it, ladies and gentlemen; that was the capper, and THAT'S why I'm here!

"Right then and there, beside the *highway*, I made my decision. I rolled that Caddy, I made a U-turn and I stopped only long enough to get me some of that good white wood *alcohol* and good *white* gasoline, and then I headed straight here. So while some of you are upset, you can see that you don't have to be afraid because LeeWillie means nobody any harm.

"I am here, ladies and gentlemen, to make the Senator a present. Yes, sir and yes, mam, and it's Sunday and I'm told that *confession* is good for the *soul*. —So Mister Senator," he said, turning toward the terrace above, "this is my public testimony to my coming over to your way of thinking. This is my surrender of the Coon Cage Eight! You have unconverted me from the convertible. In fact, I'm giving it to you, Senator Sunraider, and it is truly mine to give. I hope all my people will do likewise. Because after your speech they ought to run whenever they even *look* at one of these. They ought to make for the bomb shelters whenever one comes close to the curb. So I, me, LeeWillie Minifees, am setting an example and here it is. You can HAVE it, Mister Senator. I don't WANT it. Thank you KINDLY and MUCH obliged..."

He paused, looking toward the terrace, and at this point I saw a great burst of flame which sent the crowd scurrying backward down the hill, and the white-suited firebrand went into an ecstatic chant, waving his violin bow, shaking his gleaming head and stamping his foot:

"Listen to me, Senator: I don't want no JET! (stamp!) But thank you kindly.

"I don't want no FORD! (stamp!)

"Neither do I want a RAMBLER! (stamp!)

"I don't want no NINETY-EIGHT! (stamp!)

"Ditto the THUNDERBIRD! (stamp-stamp!)

"Yes, and keep those CHEVYS and CHRYSLERS away from me—do you (stamp!) *hear* me, Senator?

"YOU HAVE TAKEN THE BEST," he boomed, "SO, DAMMIT, TAKE ALL THE REST! Take ALL the rest!

"In fact, now I don't want anything you think is too good for me and my people. Because, just as that old man and the mule said, if a man in your position is against our having them, then there must be something WRONG in our *want-*

ing them. So to keep you happy, I, me, LeeWillie Minifees, am prepared to WALK. I'm ordering me some club-footed, pigeon-toed SPACE SHOES. I'd rather crawl or FLY. I'd rather save my money and wait until the A-RABS make a car. The Zulus even. Even the ESKIMOS! Oh, I'll walk and wait. I'll grab me a GREYHOUND or a FREIGHT! So you can have my coon cage, fare thee well!

"Take the TAIL FINS and the WHITEWALLS. Help yourself to the poor raped RADIO. ENJOY the automatic dimmer and the power brakes. ROLL, Mister Senator, with that fluid DRIVE. Breathe that air-conditioned AIR. There's never been a Caddy like this one and I want you to HAVE IT. Take my scientific dreamboat and enjoy that good ole GRACIOUS LIVING! The key's in the ignition and the REGISTRATION'S in the GLOVE compartment! And thank you KINDLY for freeing me from the Coon Cage. Because before I'd be in a CAGE, I'll be buried in my GRAVE—Oh! Oh!"

He broke off, listening; and I became aware of the shrilling of approaching sirens. Then he was addressing the crowd again.

"I knew," he called down with a grin, "that THOSE would be coming soon. Because they ALWAYS come when you don't NEED them. Therefore, I only hope that the Senator will beat it on down here and accept his gift before they arrive. And in the meantime, I want ALL you ladies and gentlemen to join LeeWillie in singing 'God Bless America' so that all this won't be in vain.

"I want you to understand that that was a damned GOOD Caddy and I loved her DEARLY. That's why you don't have to worry about me. I'm doing fine. Everything is copacetic. Because, remember, nothing makes a man feel better than giving AWAY something, than SACRIFICING something, that he dearly LOVES!"

And then, most outrageous of all, he threw back his head and actually sang a few bars before the noise of the short-circuited horn set the flaming car to wailing like some great prehistoric animal heard in the throes of its dying.

Behind him now, high on the terrace, the Senator and his guests were shouting, but on the arsonist sang, and the effect on the crowd was maddening. Perhaps because from the pleasurable anticipation of watching the beginning of a clever advertising stunt, they had been thrown into a panic by the deliberate burning, the bizarre immolation of the automobile. And now with a dawning of awareness they perceived that they had been forced to witness (and who could turn away?) a crude and most portentous political gesture.

So suddenly they broke past me, dashing up the hill in moblike fury, and it was most fortunate for Minifees that his duet with the expiring Cadillac was interrupted by members of the police and fire departments, who, arriving at this moment, threw a flying wedge between the flaming machine and the mob. Through the noisy action I could see him there, looming prominently in his white suit, a mocking smile flickering on his sweaty face, as the action whirled toward where he imperturbably stood his ground, still singing against the doleful wailing of the car.

He was still singing, his wrists coolly extended now in anticipation of handcuffs—when struck by a veritable football squad of asbestos-garbed policemen and swept, tumbling, in a wild tangle of arms and legs, down the slope to where I stood. It was then I noted that he wore expensive black alligator shoes.

And now, while the crowd roared its approval, I watched as LeeWillie Minifees was pinned down, lashed into a straitjacket and led toward a police car. Up the hill two policemen were running laboredly toward where the Senator stood, silently observing. About me there was much shouting and shoving as some of the crowd attempted to follow the trussed-up and still grinning arsonist but were beaten back by the police.

It was unbelievably wild. Some continued to shout threats in their outrage and frustration, while others, both men and women, filled the air with a strangely brokenhearted and forlorn sound of weeping, and the officers found it difficult to disperse them. In fact, they continued to mill angrily about even as firemen in asbestos suits broke through, dragging hoses from a roaring pumper truck and sprayed the flaming car with a foamy chemical, which left it looking like the offspring of some strange animal brought so traumatically and precipitantly to life that it wailed and sputtered in protest, both against the circumstance of its debut into the world and the foaming presence of its still-clinging afterbirth...

And what had triggered it? How had the Senator sparked this weird conflagration? Why, with a joke! The day before, while demanding larger appropriations for certain scientific research projects that would be of great benefit to our electronics and communications industries, and of great importance to the nation as a whole, the Senator had aroused the opposition of a liberal Senator from New York who had complained, in passing, of what he termed the extreme vapidness of our recent automobile designs, their lack of adequate safety devices, and of the slackness of our quality-control standards and procedures. Well, it was in defending the automobile industry that the Senator passed the remark that triggered LeeWillie Minifees's bizarre reply.

In his rebuttal—the committee session was televised and aired over radio networks—the Senator insisted that not only were our cars the best in the world, the most beautiful and efficiently designed, but that, in fact, his opponent's remarks were a gratuitous slander. Because, he asserted, the only ground which he could see for complaint lay in the circumstance that a certain make of luxury automobile had become so outrageously popular in the nation's Harlems—the archetype of which is included in his opponent's district—that he found it embarrassing to own one. And then with a face most serious in its composure he went on to state:

"We have reached a sad state of affairs, gentlemen, wherein this fine product of American skill and initiative has become so common in Harlem that much of its initial value has been sorely compromised. Indeed, I am led to suggest, and quite seriously, that legislation be drawn up to rename it the 'Coon Cage Eight.' And not at all because of its eight, super-efficient cylinders, nor because of the lean, springing strength and beauty of its general outlines. Not at all, but because it has now become such a common sight to see eight or more of our darker brethren crowded together enjoying its power, its beauty, its neo-pagan comfort, while weaving recklessly through the streets of our great cities and along our super-highways. In fact, gentlemen, I was run off the road, forced into a ditch by such a power-drunk group just the other day. It is enough to make a citizen feel alienated from his own times, from the abiding values and recent developments within his own beloved nation.

"And yet, we continue to hear complaints to the effect that these constituents of our worthy colleague are ill-housed, ill-clothed, ill-equipped and under-*treaded!* But, gentlemen, I say to you in all sincerity: Look into the streets! Look at the statistics for automobile sales! And I don't mean the economy cars, but our most expensive luxury machines. Look and see who is purchasing them! Give your attention to who it is that is creating the scarcity and removing these superb machines from the reach of those for whom they were intended! With so many of these good things, what, pray, do those people desire—is it a jet plane on every Harlem rooftop?"

Now for Senator Sunraider this had been mild and far short of his usual maliciousness. And while it aroused some slight amusement and brought replies of false indignation from some of his opponents, it was edited out, as is frequently the case, when the speech appeared in the Congressional Record and in the press. But who could have predicted that Senator Sunraider would have brought on LeeWillie Minifees's wild gesture? Perhaps he had been putting on an act, creating a happening, as they say, though I doubted it. There was something more personal behind it. Without question, the Senator's remarks were in extremely bad taste, but to cap the joke by burning an expensive car seemed so extreme a reply as to be almost metaphysical.

And yet, I reminded myself, it might simply be a case of overreacting expressed in true Negro abandon, an extreme gesture springing from the frustration of having no adequate means of replying, or making himself heard above the majestic roar of a Senator. There was, of course, the recent incident involving a black man suffering from an impacted wisdom tooth who had been so maddened by the blaring of a moisture-shorted automobile horn which had blasted his sleep about three o'clock of an icy morning, that he ran out into the street clothed only in an old-fashioned nightshirt and blasted the hood of the offending automobile with both barrels of a twelve-gauge over-and-under shotgun.

But while toothaches often lead to such extreme acts—and once in a while to suicide—LeeWillie Minifees had apparently been in no pain—or at least not in *physical* pain. And on the surface at least his speech had been projected clearly enough (allowing for the necessity to shout) and he had been smiling when they led him away. What would be his fate? I wondered; and where had they taken him? I would have to find him and question him, for his action had begun to sound in my mind with disturbing overtones which had hardly been meaningful. Rather they had been like the brief interruption one sometimes hears while listening to an F.M. broadcast of the musical *Oklahoma!*, say, with original cast, when the signal fades and a program of quite different mood from a different wavelength breaks through. It had happened but then a blast of laughter had restored us automatically to our chosen frequency.

BACKWACKING, A PLEA TO THE SENATOR

MASSACHUSETTS REVIEW 18 (AUTUMN 1977): 411–16

Braxas, Alabama
April 4th, 1953

To the Right Honorable
Senator Sunraider
Washington, D.C.

Dear Senator Sunraider:

    This evening I take my pen in hand to write you our deep appreciation for all the good things you have been doing for this pore beat down country of ours. That Cadillac speech you gave us was straight forward and to the point and much needed saying. So I thank you and my wife Marthy wants to thank you. In fact we both thank you for looking out for folks like us who firmly believe that all this WELFARE *the Guv. is shoveling out to the lazy nogooders and freeloaders is something that stinks in the nostril of Heaven worse than a batch of rotten catfish that some unGodly thief has stole and scattered all over Courthouse Square at high noon on the 4th day of July. We are with you Senator because you are a good man. You have done great things for the God-fearing folks of this country and we respect you for it. And as you are one of the very <u>few</u> men in Guv. who we can depend on when the going gets real* TOUGH *I now take the liberty of calling something to your kind attention that is taking place down here in these parts.*

    *I refer to this new type of sinful activity that has cropped up amongst the niggers. It is known as "*BACKWACKING," *which I am prepared to say under oath is probably one of the most* UNGODLY *and also* UNNATURAL *activity that anybody has ever yet invented! Senator, it is no less than* RADICAL! *And so naturally the nigger has been going at it so* HARD *that he is fast getting out of hand and out of control. Here is what he is doing.* HE *and his woman have taken to getting undressed and standing back to back and heel to heel, shoulderblade to shoulderblade, and tale to tale with his against her's and her's against his, and then after they have horsed around and manuvered like cats in heat and worked as tight together as a tick to a cow's tit,* HE *ups and starts in to* HAVING AFTER HER BACKWARDS!

Now I know, Senator, that this sounds like he is taking a very roundabout and also mullet-headed path to Robin Hood's barn, but I have it on the most reliable authority that this is exactly how he is going about it. Yessir! The facts have been well established even though I have to admit that on account of he is not only defying common decency but also NATURE, I cannot explain in full detail just _how_ the nigger is proceeding in this tradition busting business. Because naturally he thinks that he has him a good thing going and is trying to keep the WHITE MAN in the DARK. Even so, I want you to know that ever since it was brought to my attention I been putting a great deal of effort into trying to untangle what he is doing. I have figgered HARD and I have figgered LONG but to date nothing I have come up with seems to fit WHAT he is doing with HOW he is going about it. Neither, I am sad to report, has anybody else. So it appears that once again and after all the trouble we have seen we are being VICTIMIZED by yet another so-called "nigger mystery." It is a crying sin and a dirty shame but once again the nigger has tossed the responsible citizenry of these parts a terrible tough nut to crack. Once again it appears that like the time he came back from Cuba at the end of the Spanish American War and then again when he came back from Paris France after World War I, he is HELLBENT on taking advantage of our good nature. But be that as it may, I hasten to assure you that we down here are not taking it laying down. We are going after him not only with might and main but with foresight and hindsight. And as for me personal, I am doing my level best to bring him to heel and can be counted on to KEEP ON doing it! Senator, you have my word on that. I have known niggers all my life and am well acquainted with smart ones as well as dumb ones, but while heretofore this has been an advantage in many a tight place in my dealings with him, in this particular situation I am forced to admit that I have yet to come across any as backwards-acting as my most reliable information makes these here out to be. Evidently these are of a different breed, because considering that I am a GODFEARING white man in my 80th year if _I_ have not heard of this "BACKWACKING" until now it has got to be something NEW! So in my considered opinion it is something that some black rascal has brought in here from somewheres else, probably from up NORTH.

But Senator, wherever this "BACKWACKING" comes from it calls for some ruthless INVESTIGATING and drastic CONTROL! Because not only is the nigger conducting himself in this UNGODLY jiggsawing fashion I have described to you, but there is OVERPOWERING evidence that he is doing it too much for his own or anybody elses good, and I say so for the following reasons. I am informed that when he and his woman reach the climax of this radical new way of sinning they get blasted by one of the _darndest_ feelings that has ever been known to hit the likes of Man! My friend says it is like watching somebody being struck down by greased lightening, and he says that when it hits the nigger it is like seeing somebody being knocked down and dragged by an L & N freight train that has been doing a high-ball on a down-hill grade with its brakeshoes busted and with no red light ahead! Yes, sir! It is a mind graveler and a viscious back breaker. He says that watching it work on the black rascal is like seeing somebody get blasted to as close to dying as any normal human being can possibly come and still not die. Like he says this "BACKWACKING" is a real humdinging ripsnorter and a danger to life, limb and social order—only you wouldn't think so if you could see how some who are practicing it are around here strutting and grinning.

Yes, sir, Senator, they are out trying to make some slick nigger propaganda to the point that they had all at once jumped way ahead of the WHITE man! But of course and as we both well know, they are badly mistaken in this regard. Because if the truth be known, all they are doing is setting back their own RACE. There is no doubt about it, because it is a "well established fact" and as I have always held No race can pull itself up by their bootstraps and bring home the bacon that dedicates itself to indulging in such UNNATURAL activity as the one these here are messing with. But yet and still and as niggers will, they are going at it like old fashioned common sense has gone plum out of style! Senator, the situation he is creating is no less than critical! And it is right here that we come face to face with the most confounding detail of this "BACKWACKING."

Now you would expect that all this powerful feeling he generates would knock the nigger out, and as I have stated it trully staggers him. It knocks the rascal as limber as a bacon rine that has been boiled in a mess of collards and turns his bones to rubber. Yes, sir! But then an absolutely CONFUSING thing takes place. Like I say, when this feeling strikes the nigger it blasts him so hard that it seems that it has knocked all such nasty notions out of his ignorant head. He goes out like a lantern in a wind storm and you would swear that he was already at the gates of hell, which is shorely where he is headed, yessir! But then it jacks him up, and the next thing you know he comes up with a quick second wind! That is the unGodly truth, Senator, and I'll swear to it. Instead of keeling over and breathing his last or at least taking him a nap, the nigger just lets out a big ole hoop-and-a-holler and leaps back to his position and commences to practicing this "BACKWACKING" again! So when you think about that and all the raw naked POWER he lets loose it is my firm opinion that this "BACKWACKING" must do no less than throw him into some new kind of TRANCE. Something about this new way of sinning he is practicing simply takes the rascal OVER. Otherwise I ask you how is it that as soon as he uses up his second-wind—which takes him a full five minutes longer by a good stop-watch—according to my friend he right away "BACKWACKS" his way into a third and then into a fourth and *fifth* wind? So it stands to reason that nothing less than a TRANCE can explain it, therefore I must stand on that. It simply has to be what happens, especially since he has been known to keep on going in this fashion until he is vibrating like a sheet-tin roof in a wind storm and his petered-out woman is wore plumb down to a slam-banging *frazzle!*

Senator, after observing this disgraceful business on several occasions, my friend holds that it is a crying pity and a down-right shame that it don't just knock the nigger out of commission the first shot out of the box, and I whole-heartedly agree. Because if this "BACKWACKING" was to kill off a few of the ornery ones who is practicing it this thing would be brought to a quick and abrupt conclusion. After that the rest of the niggers would sober up to the firmly grounded truth of the proposition which states that "No Race can prosper or long endure" that devotes itself to going against NATURE *like these down here have been doing. Therefore they would go back and devote themselves to conducting their business in the old fashion way they was taught by the* WHITE *man back there in slavery.*

Now mind you Senator, I say that that is the proposition the nigger OUGHT *to be living by, but this being a new day and age, and one in which he has lost all sense of direction, he is* NOT. *Instead he is coming up daily with all* KINDS *of new minds and new notions, most of them nasty, radical and* UNGODLY. *So with the nigger continuing on his "BACKWACKING" rampage it is most unfortunate that some of the most responsible citizens in these parts are dying off while some of the rest have given up the struggle and grown discouraged. Some are even thinking about migrating to Australia! And only the other day a friend of mine was even talking about moving to South Africa, just to get away from some of the outrages taking place down here. He's ready to cut bait and run! "Let the nigger take over, and get out while the getting is good," he says. "That's what I'm thinking. Just let him have it, lock, stock, barrel and gatepost, because that's exactly what he's out to do. One way or another, either by hook, or by crook or sinning, he means to seize control. So I'm going somewhere a* WHITE *man still has a chance to live in peace." That is what he says and he's from one of the finest old families in these parts. Yessir, that's just how pessimistic some folks have come to feel. But fortunately folks like my friend are in the minority and I hasten to assure you Senator that all is not lost, no, sir! Not by a long shot. Because while a few have let themselves become discouraged and intimidated by this recent rash of nigger outrages a determined* VANGUARD *remains on the firing line and is putting up a firm resistance. And for this I say "Praise the* LORD!" *as there is a growing concern that if the nigger ain't soon checked and returned to his proper balance—and I mean by any means* NECESSARY—*or if he don't just naturally run out of gas on his own accord, he will keep on plunging down this unnatural path he is on until he is out on the street grabbing and "BACKWACKING" each and every female woman he can lay his corrupted eyes on. Such is the terrible prospect we face in a nutshell.*

So it is my considered opinion that we are confronted by a crisis the likes of which we haven't had to face since back in 1918 when the nigger come home trying to talk and act like French men. Therefore I have tried to the best of my ability to give you a clear and accurate picture of our situation. What we actually have down here is not only a serious threat to our orderly society but we are in the middle of something that can best be described as a "clear and present danger"! I insist on that, Senator, and it is a danger that threatens <u>everybody</u>, including the nigger, who seems bent on no less than downright self-annihilation! And what makes our predicament so untenable is the fact that the nigger is so sly and <u>devious</u>. He knows we're watching him so he's coming up with all kinds of "diversionary tactics." But while we have yet to discover what he is sneaking around eating and drinking in order to do what he is doing and while he is keeping his hand well hid, down here in Alabama his offenses to common decency is causing a terrible stir. Senator, our backs are against the wall and our nerves are on edge and our patience is running thin. And it is doing it so <u>fast</u> that I tell you confidential that all this "BACKWACK-ING" he is doing has got our STORM WARNINGS up. By which I mean to say that this latest of many aggravating "nigger mysteries," grievous offenses, and attacks on moral integrity and clean living has got folks so flustered and upset that they are beginning to cry out loud for some RELIEF! So Senator it is in their name as well as my own that I am calling upon you to hurry down here with a committee of your best people and INVESTIGATE! We are calling upon you because from your Cadillac speech the other day we are firmly convinced that you are the ONE for the role. You have the "intestinal fortitude" to do what needs to be done and you have the authority to SEE that it is done. So please heed our plea. Because even if what the nigger is up to wasn't against NATURE, which it simply has to be, there is no question but that he is going both against the BIBLE and against our most hallowed tradition and therefore what he is doing calls for the firm and unyielding hand of the LAW!

Senator, the above constitutes our unhappy bill of particulars, and as I appreciate that you are a busy man I beg pardon for taking up so much of your precious time. But please understand that our situation is DESPERATE and we call upon your aid because you are one of the few that trully stands for LAW AND ORDER and really looks out for the welfare of the good WHITE people, who as I have tried to make crystal clear, are once again being sorely tried and tested. So in closing both me and Marthy thank you in advance for your kind consideration and look forward to the time when we will once again be safe and at peace with our fine and honorable tradition and our straightforward way of doing things. We wish you a long life and the best of everything, and we hope and pray that you will soon find time to lay the firm hand of the law on this "BACKWACKING" and bring it to a teeth-rattling HALT! Just look into the nigger is all we ask, and GOD BLESS.

Respectfully Yrs.

Norm A. Mauler

A CONCERN CITIZEN